NOBLE HOUSE

Volume 1

NOBLE HOUSE
is the fourth novel in the Asian Saga
that so far consists of:

James Clavell

NOBLE HOUSE

A Novel of Contemporary Hong Kong

Volume 1

DELACORTE PRESS/NEW YORK

I would like to offer this
work as a tribute to
Her Britannic Majesty,
Elizabeth II, to the people
of Her Crown Colony of
Hong Kong—*and perdition
to their enemies.*

Of course this is a novel. It is peopled
with imaginary persons and companies
and no reference to any person or
company that was, or is, part of
Hong Kong or Asia is intended.

I would also like to apologize at
once to all Hong Kong *yan*—all
Hong Kong *persons*—for rearranging
their beautiful city, for taking incidents
out of context, for inventing people
and places and streets and companies
and incidents that, hopefully, may
appear to have existed but have never
existed, for this, truly, is a story. . . .

June 8, 1960

PROLOGUE

His name was Ian Dunross and in the torrential rain he drove his old MG sports car cautiously around the corner into Dirk's Street that skirted the Struan Building on the waterfront of Hong Kong. The night was dark and foul. Throughout the Colony—here on Hong Kong Island, across the harbor in Kowloon and the New Territories that were part of the China Mainland—streets were almost totally deserted, everyone and everything battened down, waiting for Typhoon Mary. The number nine storm warning had been hoisted at dusk and already eighty- to a hundred-knot gusts came out of the tempest that stretched a thousand miles southward to send the rain horizontal against the roofs and hillsides where tens of thousands of squatters huddled defenseless in their shantytowns of make-shift hovels.

Dunross slowed, blinded, the wipers unable to cope with the quantity of rain, the wind tearing at the canvas roof and side screens. Then the windshield cleared momentarily. At the end of Dirk's Street, directly ahead, was Connaught Road and the praya, then sea walls and the squat bulk of the Golden Ferry Terminal. Beyond in the vast, well-protected harbor, half a thousand ships were snug with all anchors out.

Ahead on the praya, he saw an abandoned street stall ripped bodily off the ground by a gust and hurled at a parked car, wrecking it. Then the car and the stall were sent skittering out of sight. His wrists were very strong and he held the wheel against the eddies that trembled his car violently. The car was old but well kept, the souped-up engine and brakes perfect. He waited, his heart beating nicely, loving storm, then eased up onto the sidewalk to park in the lee, well against the building, and got out.

He was fair-haired with blue eyes, in his early forties, lean and trim and he wore an old raincoat and cap. Rain drenched him as he hurried along the side street then ducked around the corner to hurry for the main en-trance of the twenty-two-story building. Over the huge doorway was the Struan crest—the Red Lion of Scotland entwined with the Green Dragon of China. Gathering himself he strode up the broad steps and went in.

"Evening, Mr. Dunross," the Chinese concierge said.

"The tai-pan sent for me."

"Yes sir." The man pressed the elevator button for him.

When the elevator stopped, Dunross walked across the small hall, knocked and went into the penthouse living room. "Evening, tai-pan," he said with cold formality.

Alastair Struan was leaning against the fine fireplace. He was a big, ruddy, well-kept Scotsman with a slight paunch and white hair, in his sixties, and he had ruled Struan's for eleven years. "Drink?" He waved a hand at the Dom Pérignon in the silver bucket.

"Thank you." Dunross had never been in the tai-pan's private quarters before. The room was spacious and well furnished, with Chinese lacquer and good carpets, old oils of their early clipper ships and steamers on the walls. The big picture windows that would normally overlook all Hong Kong, the harbor and Kowloon across the harbor were now black and rain streaked.

He poured. "Health," he said formally.

Alastair Struan nodded and, equally coldly, raised his glass in return. "You're early."

"Five minutes early is on time, tai-pan. Isn't that what Father hammered into me? Is it important that we meet at midnight?"

"Yes. It's part of our custom. Dirk's custom."

Dunross sipped his wine, waiting in silence. The antique ship's clock ticked loudly. His excitement increased, not knowing what to expect. Over the fireplace was a marriage portrait of a young girl. This was Tess Struan who had married Culum, second tai-pan and son of their founder Dirk Struan, when she was sixteen.

Dunross studied it. A squall dashed the windows. "Filthy night," he said.

The older man just looked at him, hating him. The silence grew. Then the old clock chimed eight bells, midnight.

There was a knock on the door.

"Come in," Alastair Struan said with relief, glad that now they could begin.

The door was opened by Lim Chu, the tai-pan's personal servant. He stepped aside to admit Phillip Chen, compradore of Struan's, then closed the door after him.

"Ah, Phillip, you're on time as usual," Alastair Struan said, trying to sound jovial. "Champagne?"

"Thank you, tai-pan. Yes, thank you. Good evening, Ian Struan Dunross," Phillip Chen said to the younger man with unusual formality, his English very upper-class British. He was Eurasian, in his late sixties, spare, rather more Chinese than European, a very handsome man with gray hair and high cheekbones, fair skin, and dark, very dark Chinese eyes. "Dreadful night, what?"

"Yes, it is indeed, Uncle Chen," Dunross replied, using the polite Chinese form of address for Phillip, liking him and respecting him as much as he despised his cousin Alastair.

"They say this typhoon's going to be a bastard." Alastair Struan was pouring the champagne into fine glasses. He handed Phillip Chen a glass first, then Dunross. "Health!"

They drank. A rain squall rattled the windows. "Glad I'm not afloat tonight," Alastair Struan said thoughtfully. "So, Phillip, here you are again."

"Yes, tai-pan. I'm honored. Yes, very honored." He sensed the violence between the two men but dismissed it. Violence is a pattern, he thought, when a tai-pan of the Noble House hands over power.

Alastair Struan sipped again, enjoying the wine. At length he said, "Ian, it's our custom that there be a witness to a handing over from tai-pan to tai-pan. It's always—and only—our current compradore. Phillip, how many times does this make?"

"I've been witness four times, tai-pan."

"Phillip has known almost all of us. He knows too many of our secrets. Eh, old friend?" Phillip Chen just smiled. "Trust him, Ian. His counsel's wise. You can trust him."

As much as any tai-pan should trust anyone, Dunross thought grimly. "Yes sir."

Alastair Struan set down his glass. "First: Ian Struan Dunross, I ask you formally, do you want to be tai-pan of Struan's?"

"Yes sir."

"You swear by God that all of these proceedings will be kept secret by you and not divulged to anyone but your successor?"

"Yes sir."

"Swear it formally."

"I swear by God these proceedings will be secret and never divulged to anyone but my successor."

"Here." The tai-pan handed him a parchment, yellow with age. "Read it aloud."

Dunross took it. The writing was spidery, but perfectly legible. He glanced at the date—August 30, 1841—his excitement soaring. "Is this Dirk Struan's writing?"

"Aye. Most of it—part was added by his son, Culum Struan. Of course we've photocopies in case of damage. Read it!"

" 'My Legacy shall bind every tai-pan that succeedeth me and he shall read it aloud and shall swear before God in front of witnesses in the manner set forth by me, Dirk Struan, founder of Struan and Company, to accept them, and to ever keep them secret, prior to taking to himself my mantle. I require this to ensure a pleasing continuity and in anticipation of difficulties which will, in the following years, beset my successors because of the blood I have spilled, because of my debts of honor, and because of the vagaries of the ways of China to which we are wedded, which are without doubt unique on this earth. This is my Legacy:

"'First: There shall be only one tai-pan at one time and he hath total, absolute authority over the Company, power to employ or remove from employment all others, authority over all our captains and our ships and companies wherever they may be. The tai-pan is always alone, that being the joy and the hurt of it. His privacy must be guarded by all and his back protected by all. Whatsoever he orders, it shall be obeyed, and no committees or courts or inner circles shall ever be formed or allowed in the Company to curb this absolute power.

"'Second: When the tai-pan stands on the quarterdeck of any of our ships he takes precedence over the captain thereof, and his battle orders or sailing orders are law. All captains will be so sworn before God, before appointment to any of our ships.

"'Third: The tai-pan alone chooses his successor who shall be selected only from an Inner Court of six men. Of these, one shall be our compradore who shall, in perpetuity, be from the House of Chen. The other five shall be worthy to be tai-pan, shall be good men and true with at least five whole years of service in the Company as China Traders, and shall be wholesome in spirit. They must be Christian and must be kinsmen to the clan Struan by birth or marriage—my line and my brother Robb's line not taking precedence, unless by fortitude or qualities over and above all others. This Inner Court may be advisors to the tai-pan if he so desires, but let it be said again, the vote of the tai-pan shall weight seven against one for each of them.

"'Fourth: If the tai-pan be lost at sea, or killed in battle, or vanished for six lunar months, before he hath his successor chosen, then the Inner Court shall elect one of their members to succeed, each having one vote, except the vote of the compradore shall count four. The tai-pan shall then be sworn in the same manner set forth before his fellows—those who voted against his election in open ballot being expelled at once, without remuneration, from the Company forever.

"'Fifth: Election to the Inner Court, or removal therefrom, shall be solely at the tai-pan's pleasure and, on his retirement which shall be at a time when it pleasures him, he shall take no more than ten parts of every hundred of all value for himself, except that all our ships shall always be excluded from any valuation . . . our ships, their captains and their crews being our lifeblood and our lifeline into future times.

"'Sixth: Each tai-pan shall approve the election of the compradore. The compradore shall acknowledge in writing prior to his election that he may be removed at any time, without need for explanations, that he will step aside should the tai-pan wish it.

"'Last: The tai-pan shall swear his successor, whom he alone chooses, in the presence of the compradore using the words set down under my hand in our family Bible, here in Hong Kong, this thirtieth day of August in the year of our Lord 1841.'"

Dunross exhaled. "It's signed by Dirk Struan and witnessed by— I can't read the chop characters, sir, they're archaic."

Alastair glanced at Phillip Chen who said, "The first witness is my grandfather's foster father, Chen Sheng Arn, our first compradore. The second, my great-aunt, T'Chung Jin May-may."

"Then the legend's true!" Dunross said.

"Some of it. Yes, some of it." Phillip Chen added, "Talk to my auntie Sarah. Now that you're to be tai-pan she'll tell you lots of secrets. She's eighty-four this year. She remembers my grandfather, Sir Gordon Chen, very well, and Duncan and Kate T'Chung, May-may's children by Dirk Struan. Yes. She remembers many things. . . ."

Alastair Struan went over to the lacquered bureau and very carefully picked out the heavy threadbare Bible. He put on his spectacles and Dunross felt the hackles on his neck rise. "Repeat after me: I, Ian Struan Dunross, kinsman to the Struans, Christian, sweareth before God in the presence of Alastair McKenzie Duncan Struan, eleventh tai-pan, and Phillip T'Chung Sheng Chen, fourth compradore, that I shall obey all the Legacy read out by me in their presence here in Hong Kong, that I shall further bind the Company to Hong Kong and to the China trade, that I shall maintain my main place of business here in Hong Kong while tai-pan, that, before God, I assume the promises, responsibility and the gentleman's word of honor of Dirk Struan to his eternal friend Chen-tse Jin Arn, also known as Jin-qua, or to his successors; further, that I w—"

"What promises?"

"You swear before God, blind, like all the tai-pans did before you! You'll learn soon enough what you inherit."

"And if I won't?"

"You know the answer to that!"

The rain was battering the windows and its violence seemed to Dunross to equal the thumping in his chest as he weighed the insanity of such an open-ended commitment. But he knew he could not be tai-pan unless he did, and so he said the words and made the commitment before God, and continued to say the words read out to him.

". . . further that I will use all powers, and any means, to keep the Company steadfast as the First House, the Noble House of Asia, that I swear before God to commit any deed necessary to vanquish, destroy and cast out from Asia the company called Brock and Sons and particularly my enemy, the founder, Tyler Brock, his son Morgan, their heirs or any of their line excepting only Tess Brock and her issue, the wife of my son Culum, from the face of Asia. . . ." Dunross stopped again.

"When you've finished you can ask any questions you want," Alastair Struan said. "Finish it!"

"Very well. Lastly: I swear before God that my successor as tai-pan will also be sworn, before God, to all of this Legacy, so help me God!"

Now the silence was broken only by the rain slashing the windows. Dunross could feel the sweat on his back.

Alastair Struan put down the Bible and took off his spectacles. "There, it's done." Tautly he put out his hand. "I'd like to be the first to wish you well, tai-pan. Anything I can do to help, you have."

"And I'm honored to be second, tai-pan," Phillip Chen said with a slight bow, equally formally.

"Thank you." Dunross's tension was great.

"I think we all need a drink," Alastair Struan said. "With your permission, I'll pour," he added to Dunross with untoward formality. "Phillip?"

"Yes, tai-pan. I—"

"No. Ian's tai-pan now." Alastair Struan poured the champagne and gave the first glass to Dunross.

"Thank you," Dunross said, savoring the compliment, knowing nothing had changed. "Here's to the Noble House," he said, raising his glass.

The three men drank, then Alastair Struan took out an envelope. "This is my resignation from the sixty-odd chairmanships, managing directorships and directorships that automatically go with the tai-pan position. Your appointment in my stead is equally automatic. By custom I become chairman of our London subsidiary—but you can terminate that anytime you wish."

"It's terminated," Dunross said at once.

"Whatever you say," the old man muttered, but his neck was purple.

"I think you'd be more useful to Struan's as deputy chairman of the First Central Bank of Edinburgh."

Struan looked up sharply. "What?"

"That's one of our appointments, isn't it?"

"Yes," Alastair Struan said. "Why that?"

"I'm going to need help. Struan's goes public next year."

Both men stared at him, astounded. "What!"

"We're going publ—"

"We've been a private company for 132 years!" the old man roared. "Jesus bloody Christ I've told you a hundred times that's our strength, with no god-cursed stockholders or outsiders prying into our private affairs!" His face was flushed and he fought to control his anger. "Don't you ever listen?"

"All the time. Very carefully," Dunross said in an unemotional voice. "The only way we can survive is to go public . . . that's the only way we can get the capital we need."

"Talk to him, Phillip—get some sense into him."

Nervously the compradore said, "How will this affect the House of Chen?"

"Our formal compradore system is ended from tonight." He saw Phillip

Chen's face go white but he continued, "I have a plan for you—in writing. It changes nothing, and everything. Officially you'll still be compradore, unofficially we'll operate differently. The major change is that instead of making about a million a year, in ten years your share will bring you 20, in fifteen years about 30."

"Impossible!" Alastair Struan burst out.

"Our net worth today's about 20 million U.S. In ten years it'll be 200 million and in fifteen, with joss, it'll be 400 million—and our yearly turnover approaching a billion."

"You've gone mad," Struan said.

"No. The Noble House is going international—the days of being solely a Hong Kong trading company are gone forever."

"Remember your oath, by God! We're Hong Kong based!"

"I won't forget. Next: What responsibility do I inherit from Dirk Struan?"

"It's all in the safe. Written down in a sealed envelope marked 'The Legacy.' Also the Hag's 'Instructions to future tai-pans.'"

"Where's the safe?"

"Behind the painting in the Great House. In the study." Sourly Alastair Struan pointed to an envelope beside the clock on the mantelpiece. "That contains the special key—and the present combination. You will of course change it. Put the figures into one of the tai-pan's private safety deposit boxes at the bank, in case of accidents. Give Phillip one of the two keys."

Phillip Chen said, "By our rules, while you're alive, the bank is obliged to refuse me permission to open it."

"Next: Tyler Brock and his sons—those bastards were obliterated almost a hundred years ago."

"Aye, the legitimate male line was. But Dirk Struan was vindictive and his vengeance reaches out from his grave. There's an up-to-date list of Tyler Brock's descendents, also in the safe. It makes interesting reading, eh Phillip?"

"Yes, yes it does."

"The Rothwells and the Tomms, Yadegar and his brood, you know about. But Tusker's on the list though he doesn't know it, Jason Plumm, Lord Depford-Smyth and, most of all, Quillan Gornt."

"Impossible!"

"Not only is Gornt tai-pan of Rothwell-Gornt, our main enemy, but he's also a secret, direct male descendent of Morgan Brock—direct though illegitimate. He's the last of the Brocks."

"But he's always claimed his great-grandfather was Edward Gornt, the American China Trader."

"He comes from Edward Gornt all right. But Sir Morgan Brock was really Edward's father and Kristian Gornt his mother. She was an American from Virginia. Of course it was kept secret—society wasn't any more forgiving then than now. When Sir Morgan became tai-pan of Brock's in

1859, he fetched this illegitimate son of his out of Virginia, bought him a partnership in the old American trading firm of Rothwell and Company in Shanghai, and then he and Edward bided their time to destroy us. They almost did—certainly they caused the death of Culum Struan. But then Lochlin and Hag Struan broke Sir Morgan and smashed Brock and Sons. Edward Gornt never forgave us, his descendents never will either— I'd wager they too have a pact with their founder."

"Does he know we know?"

"I don't know. But he's enemy. His genealogy's in the safe, with all the others. My grandfather was the one who discovered it, quite by chance, during the Boxer Rebellion in '99. The list is interesting, Ian, very. One particular person for you. The head of—"

A sudden violent gust shook the building. One of the ivory bric-a-brac on the marble table toppled over. Nervously Phillip Chen stood it up. They all stared at the windows, watching their reflections twist nauseatingly as the gusts stretched the huge panes of glass.

"*Tai-fun!*" Phillip muttered, sweat beading him.

"Yes." They waited breathlessly for the "Devil Wind" to cease. These sudden squalls came haphazardly from all points of the compass, sometimes gusting to a hundred and fifty knots. In their wake was always devastation.

The violence passed. Dunross went over to the barometer, checked it and tapped it. 980.3.

"Still falling," he said.

"Christ!"

Dunross squinted at the windows. Now the rain streaks were almost horizontal. "*Lasting Cloud* is due to dock tomorrow night."

"Yes, but now she'll be hove to somewhere off the Philippines. Captain Moffatt's too canny to get caught," Struan said.

"I don't agree. Moffatt likes hitting schedules. This typhoon's unscheduled. You . . . he should have been ordered." Dunross sipped his wine thoughtfully. "*Lasting Cloud* better not get caught."

Phillip Chen heard the undercurrent of fury. "Why?"

"We've our new computer aboard and two million pounds' worth of jet engines. Uninsured—at least the engines are." Dunross glanced at Alastair Struan.

Defensively the old man said, "It was that or lose the contract. The engines are consigned to Canton. You know we can't insure them, Phillip, since they're going to Red China." Then he added irritably, "They're, er, they're South American owned and there're no export restrictions from South America to China. Even so, no one's willing to insure them."

After a pause Phillip Chen said, "I thought the new computer was coming in March."

"It was but I managed to jump it forward," Alastair said.

"Who's carrying the paper on the engines?" Phillip Chen asked.

"We are."

"That's a lot of risk." Phillip Chen was very uneasy. "Don't you agree, Ian?"

Dunross said nothing.

"It was that or lose the contract," Alastair Struan said, even more irritably. "We stand to double our money, Phillip. We need the money. But more than that the Chinese need the engines, they made that more than clear when I was in Canton last month. And we need China—they made that clear too."

"Yes, but 12 million, that's . . . a lot of risk in one ship," Phillip Chen insisted.

Dunross said, "Anything we can do to take business away from the Soviets is to our advantage. Besides, it's done. You were saying, Alastair, there's someone on the list I should know about? The head of?"

"Marlborough Motors."

"Ah," Dunross said with sudden grim delight. "I've detested those sods for years. Father and son."

"I know."

"So the Nikklins're descendents of Tyler Brock? Well it won't be long before we can wipe them off the list. Good, very good. Do they know they're on Dirk Struan's oblit list?"

"I don't think so."

"That's even better."

"I don't agree! You hate young Nikklin because he beat you." Angrily Alastair Struan stabbed a finger at Dunross. "It's time you gave up car racing. Leave all the hill climbs and Macao Grand Prix to the semiprofessionals. The Nikklins have more time to spend on their cars, it's their life, and now you've other races to run, more important ones."

"Macao's amateur and those bastards cheated last year."

"That was never proved—your engine blew up. A lot of engines blow up, Ian. That was just joss!"

"My car was tampered with."

"And that was never proved either! For Christ's sake, you talk about bad blood? You're as stupid about some things as Devil Struan himself!"

"Oh?"

"Yes, and—"

Phillip Chen interrupted quickly, wanting an end to the violence in the room. "If it's so important, please let me see if I can find out the truth. I've sources not available to either of you. My Chinese friends will know, should know, if either Tom or young Donald Nikklin were involved. Of course," he added delicately, "if the tai-pan wishes to race, then that's up to the tai-pan. Isn't it, Alastair?"

The older man controlled his rage though his neck was still choleric. "Yes, yes you're right. Still, Ian, my advice is you cease. They'll be after you even more because they detest you equally."

"Are there others I should know about—on the list?"

After a pause, Struan said, "No, not now." He opened the second bottle and poured as he talked. "Well, now it's all yours—all the fun and all the sweat. I'm glad to pass everything over to you. After you've been through the safe you'll know the best, and the worst." He gave them each a glass and sipped his. "By the Lord Jesus, that's as fine a wine as ever came out of France."

"Yes," Phillip Chen said.

Dunross thought Dom Pérignon overpriced and overrated and knew the year, '54, was not a particularly good one. But he held his peace.

Struan went over to the barometer. It read 979.2. "We're in for a bad one. Well, never mind that. Ian, Claudia Chen has a file for you on important matters, and a complete list of our stockholdings—with names of the nominees. Any questions, have them for me before the day after tomorrow—I'm booked for London then. You'll keep Claudia on, of course."

"Of course." Claudia Chen was the second link from tai-pan to tai-pan after Phillip Chen. She was executive secretary to the tai-pan, a distant cousin to Phillip Chen.

"What about our bank—the Victoria Bank of Hong Kong and China?" Dunross asked, savoring the question. "I don't know our exact holdings."

"That's always been tai-pan knowledge only."

Dunross turned to Phillip Chen. "What's your holding, openly or through nominees?"

The compradore hesitated, shocked.

"In future I'm going to vote your holdings as a block with ours." Dunross kept his eyes on the compradore's. "I want to know now and I'll expect a formal transfer of perpetual voting power, in writing, to me and following tai-pans, tomorrow by noon, and first refusal on the shares should you ever decide to sell."

The silence grew.

"Ian," Phillip Chen began, "those shares . . ." But his resolve wavered under the power of Dunross's will. "6 percent . . . a little over 6 percent. I . . . you'll have it as you wish."

"You won't regret it." Dunross put his attention on Alastair Struan and the older man's heart missed a beat. "How much stock have we? How much's held by nominees?"

Alastair hesitated. "That's tai-pan knowledge only."

"Of course. But our compradore is to be trusted, absolutely," Dunross said, giving the old man face, knowing how much it had hurt to be dominated in front of Alastair Struan. "How much?"

Struan said, "15 percent."

Dunross gasped and so did Phillip Chen and he wanted to shout, Jesus bloody Christ, we have 15 percent and Phillip another 6 percent and you haven't had the sodding intelligence to use what's got to be a major interest to get us major funding when we're almost bankrupt?

But instead he reached forward and poured the remains of the bottle into the three glasses and this gave him time to stop the pounding of his heart.

"Good," he said with his flat unemotional voice. "I was hoping together we'd make it better than ever." He sipped his wine. "I'm bringing forward the Special Meeting. To next week."

Both men looked up sharply. Since 1880, the tai-pans of Struan's, Rothwell-Gornt and the Victoria Bank had, despite their rivalry, met annually in secret to discuss matters that affected the future of Hong Kong and Asia.

"They may not agree to bring the meeting forward," Alastair said.

"I phoned everyone this morning. It's set for Monday next at 9 A.M. here."

"Who's coming from the bank?"

"Deputy Chief Manager Havergill—the old man's in Japan then England on leave." Dunross's face hardened. "I'll have to make do."

"Paul's all right," Alastair said. "He'll be the next chief."

"Not if I can help it," Dunross said.

"You've never liked Paul Havergill, have you, Ian?" Phillip Chen said.

"No. He's too insular, too Hong Kong, too out of date, and too pompous."

"And he supported your father against you."

"Yes. But that's not the reason he should go, Phillip. He should go because he's in the way of the Noble House. He's too conservative, far too generous to Asian Properties and I think he's a secret ally of Rothwell-Gornt."

"I don't agree," Alastair said.

"I know. But we need money to expand and I intend to get the money. So I intend to use *my* 21 percent very seriously."

The storm outside had intensified but they did not seem to notice.

"I don't advise you to set your cap against the Victoria," Phillip Chen said gravely.

"I agree," Alastair Struan said.

"I won't. Provided *my* bank cooperates." Dunross watched the rain streaks for a moment. "By the way, I've also invited Jason Plumm to the meeting."

"What the hell for?" Struan asked, his neck reddening again.

"Between us and his Asian Properties we—"

"Plumm's on Dirk Struan's oblit list, as you call it, and absolutely opposed to us."

"Between the four of us we have a majority say in Hong Kong—" Dunross broke off as the phone rang loudly. They all looked at it.

Alastair Struan said sourly, "It's your phone now, not mine."

Dunross picked it up. "Dunross!" He listened for a moment then said, "No, Mr. Alastair Struan has retired, I'm tai-pan of Struan's now. Yes. Ian Dunross. What's the telex say?" Again he listened. "Yes, thank you."

He put down the phone. At length he broke the silence. "It was from our office in Taipei. *Lasting Cloud* has foundered off the north coast of Formosa. They think she's gone down with all hands. . . ."

SUNDAY,
August 18, 1963

1

8:45 P.M.:

The police officer was leaning against one corner of the information counter watching the tall Eurasian without watching him. He wore a light tropical suit and a police tie and white shirt, and it was hot within the brightly lit terminal building, the air humid and smell laden, milling noisy Chinese as always. Men, women, children, babes. An abundance of Cantonese, some Asians, a few Europeans.

"Superintendent?"

One of the information girls was offering him a phone. "It's for you, sir," she said and smiled prettily, white teeth, dark hair, dark sloe eyes, lovely golden skin.

"Thanks," he said, noticing that she was Cantonese and new, and did not mind that the reality of her smile was empty, with nothing behind it but a Cantonese obscenity. "Yes?" he said into the phone.

"Superintendent Armstrong? This is the tower—*Yankee* 2's just landed. On time."

"Still Gate 16?"

"Yes. She'll be there in six minutes."

"Thanks." Robert Armstrong was a big man and he leaned across the counter and replaced the phone. He noticed her long legs and the curve of her rump in the sleek, just too tight, uniformed *chong-sam* and he wondered briefly what she would be like in bed. "What's your name?" he asked, knowing that any Chinese hated to be named to any policeman, let alone a European.

"Mona Leung, sir."

"Thank you, Mona Leung." He nodded to her, kept his pale blue eyes on her and saw a slight shiver of apprehension go through her. This pleased him. Up yours too, he thought, then turned his attention back to his prey.

The Eurasian, John Chen, was standing beside one of the exits, alone, and this surprised him. Also that he was nervous. Usually John Chen was unperturbable, but now every few moments he would glance at his watch, then up at the arrivals board, then back to his watch again.

Another minute and then we'll begin, Armstrong thought.

He began to reach into his pocket for a cigarette, then remembered that he had given up smoking two weeks ago as a birthday present to his wife, so he cursed briefly and stuck his hands deeper into his pockets.

Around the information counter harassed passengers and meeters-of-passengers rushed up and pushed and went away and came back again, loudly asking the where and when and how and why and where once more in myriad dialects. Cantonese he understood well. Shanghainese and Mandarin a little. A few Chu Chow expressions and most of their swear words. A little Taiwanese.

He left the counter now, a head taller than most of the crowd, a big, broad-shouldered man with an easy, athletic stride, seventeen years in the Hong Kong Police Force, now head of CID—Criminal Investigation Department—of Kowloon.

"Evening, John," he said. "How're things?"

"Oh hi, Robert," John Chen said, instantly on guard, his English American-accented. "Everything's great, thanks. You?"

"Fine. Your airport contact mentioned to Immigration that you were meeting a special plane. A charter—*Yankee* 2."

"Yes—but it's not a charter. It's privately owned. By Lincoln Bartlett—the American millionaire."

"He's aboard?" Armstrong asked, knowing he was.

"Yes."

"With an entourage?"

"Just his Executive VP—and hatchet man."

"Mr. Bartlett's a friend?" he asked, knowing he was not.

"A guest. We hope to do business with him."

"Oh? Well, his plane's just landed. Why don't you come with me? We'll bypass all the red tape for you. It's the least we can do for the Noble House, isn't it?"

"Thanks for your trouble."

"No trouble." Armstrong led the way through a side door in the Customs barrier. Uniformed police looked up, saluting him instantly and watched John Chen thoughtfully, recognizing him at once.

"This Lincoln Bartlett," Armstrong continued with pretended geniality, "doesn't mean anything to me. Should it?"

"Not unless you were in business," John Chen said, then rushed on nervously, "He's nicknamed 'Raider'—because of his successful raids and takeovers of other companies, most times much bigger than himself. Interesting man, I met him in New York last year. His conglomerate grosses almost half a billion dollars a year. He says he started in '45 with two thousand borrowed dollars. Now he's into petrochemicals, heavy engineering, electronics, missiles—lots of U.S. Government work—foam, polyurethane foam products, fertilizers—he even has one company that makes and sells skis, sports goods. His group's Par-Con Industries. You name it, he has it."

"I thought your company owned everything already."

John Chen smiled politely. "Not in America," he said, "and it is not my company. I'm just a minor stockholder of Struan's, an employee."

"But you're a director and you're the eldest son of Noble House Chen so you'll be next compradore." By historic custom the compradore was a Chinese or Eurasian businessman who acted as the exclusive intermediary between the European trading house and the Chinese. All business went through his hands and a little of everything stuck there.

So much wealth and so much power, Armstrong thought, yet with a little luck, we can bring you down like Humpty-Dumpty and Struan's with you. Jesus Christ, he told himself, the anticipation sickly sweet, if that happens the scandal's going to blow Hong Kong apart. "You'll be compradore, like your father and grandfather and great-grandfather before you. Your great-grandfather was the first, wasn't he? Sir Gordon Chen, compradore to the great Dirk Struan who founded the Noble House and damn nearly founded Hong Kong."

"No. Dirk's compradore was a man called Chen Sheng. Sir Gordon Chen was compradore to Dirk's son, Culum Struan."

"They were half-brothers weren't they?"

"So the legend goes."

"Ah yes, legends—the stuff we feed on. Culum Struan, another legend of Hong Kong. But Sir Gordon, he's a legend too—you're lucky."

Lucky? John Chen asked himself bitterly. To be descended from an illegitimate son of a Scots pirate—an opium runner, a whoring evil genius and murderer if some of the stories are true—and a Cantonese singsong girl bought out of a filthy little cathouse that still exists in a filthy little Macao alley? To have almost everyone in Hong Kong know your lineage and to be despised for it by both races? "Not lucky," he said, trying to be outwardly calm. His hair was gray-flecked and dark, his face Anglo-Saxon and handsome, though a little slack at the jowls, and his dark eyes only slightly Asian. He was forty-two and wore tropicals, impeccably cut as always, with Hermès shoes and Rolex watch.

"I don't agree," Armstrong said, meaning it. "To be compradore to Struan's, the Noble House of Asia . . . that's something. Something special."

"Yes, that's special." John Chen said it flat. Ever since he could think, he had been bedeviled by his heritage. He could feel eyes watching him—him, the eldest son, the next in line—he could feel the everlasting greed and the envy. It had terrified him continuously, however much he tried to conquer the terror. He had never wanted any of the power or any of the responsibility. Only yesterday he had had another grinding row with his father, worse than ever before. "I don't want any part of Struan's!" he had shouted. "For the hundredth time I want to get the hell out of Hong Kong, I want to go back to the States, I want to lead my own life, as I want, where I want, and how I want!"

"For the thousandth time, you'll listen to me. I sent you to Am—"

"Let me run our American interests, Father. Please. There's more than enough to do! You could let me have a couple of mill—"

"*Ayeeyah* you will listen to me! It's here, here in Hong Kong and Asia we make our money! I sent you to school in America to prepare the family for the modern world. You are prepared, it's your duty to the fam—"

"There's Richard, Father, and young Kevin—Richard's ten times the businessman I am and chomping at the bit. What about Uncle Jam—"

"You'll do as I say! Good God, you know this American Bartlett is vital to us. We need your knowl—"

"—Uncle James or Uncle Thomas. Uncle James'd be the best for you; best for the family and the bes—"

"You're my eldest son. You're the next head of the family and the next compradore!"

"I won't be by God!"

"Then you won't get another copper cash!"

"And that won't be much of a change! We're all kept on a pittance, whatever outsiders think! What are you worth? How many millions? Fifty? Seventy? A hun—"

"Unless you apologize at once and finish with all this nonsense, finish with it once and for all, I'll cut you off right now! Right now!"

"I apologize for making you angry but I'll never change! Never!"

"I'll give you until my birthday. Eight days. Eight days to become a dutiful son. That's my last word. Unless you become obedient by my birthday I'll chop you and your line off our tree forever! Now get out!"

John Chen's stomach twisted uneasily. He hated the interminable quarreling, his father apoplectic with rage, his wife in tears, his children petrified, his stepmother and brothers and cousins all gloating, wanting him gone, all of his sisters, most of his uncles, all their wives. Envy, greed. The hell with it and them, he thought. But Father's right about Bartlett, though not the way he thinks. No. This one is for me. This deal. Just this one then I'll be free forever.

They were almost through the long, brightly lit Customs Hall now.

"You going racing Saturday?" John Chen asked.

"Who isn't!" The week before, to the ecstasy of all, the immensely powerful Turf Club with its exclusive monopoly on horse racing—the only legal form of gambling allowed in the Colony—had put out a special bulletin: "Though our formal season does not start this year until October 5, with the kind permission of our illustrious Governor, Sir Geoffrey Allison, the Stewards have decided to declare Saturday, August 24 a Very Special Race Day for the enjoyment of all and as a salute to our hardworking population who are bearing the heavy weight of the second worst drought in our history with fortitude. . . ."

"I hear you've got Golden Lady running in the fifth," Armstrong said.

"The trainer says she's got a chance. Please come by Father's box and have a drink with us. I could use some of your tips. You're a great punter."

"Just lucky. But my ten dollars each way hardly compares with your ten thousand."

"But that's only when we've one of our horses running. Last season was a disaster. . . . I could use a winner."

"So could I." Oh Christ how I need a winner, Armstrong thought. But you, Johnny Chen, it doesn't matter a twopenny tick in hell if you win or lose ten thousand or a hundred thousand. He tried to curb his soaring jealousy. Calm down, he told himself. Crooks're a fact and it's your job to catch them if you can—however rich, however powerful—and to be content with your rotten pay when every street corner's groaning with free silver. Why envy this bastard—he's for the chopper one way or another. "Oh by the way, I sent a constable to your car to take it through the gate. It'll be waiting at the gangway for you and your guests."

"Oh, that's great, thanks. Sorry for the trouble."

"No trouble. It's a matter of face. Isn't it. I thought it must be pretty special for you to come yourself." Armstrong could not resist another barb. "As I said, nothing's too much trouble for the Noble House."

John Chen kept his polite smile but screw you, he thought. We tolerate you because of what you are, a very important cop, filled with envy, heavily in debt, surely corrupt and you know nothing about horses. Screw you in spades. *Dew neh loh moh* on all your generations, John Chen thought, but he kept the obscenity hidden carefully, for though Armstrong was roundly hated by all Hong Kong *yan*, John Chen knew from long experience that Armstrong's ruthless, vengeful cunning was worthy of a filthy Manchu. He reached up to the half-coin he wore on a thin leather thong around his neck. His fingers trembled as they touched the metal through his shirt. He shivered involuntarily.

"What's the matter?" Armstrong asked.

"Nothing. Nothing at all." Get hold of yourself, John Chen thought.

Now they were through the Customs Hall and into the Immigration area, the night dark outside. Lines of anxious, unsettled, tired people waited in front of the neat, small desks of the cold-faced, uniformed Immigration officers. These men saluted Armstrong. John Chen felt their searching eyes.

As always, his stomach turned queasy under their scrutiny even though he was safe from their probing questions. He held a proper British passport, not just a second-class Hong Kong passport, also an American Green Card—the Alien Card—that most priceless of possessions that gave him free access to work and play and live in the U.S.A., all the privileges of a born American except the right to vote. Who needs to vote, he thought, and stared back at one of the men, trying to feel brave, but still feeling naked under the man's gaze.

"Superintendent?" One of the officers was holding up a phone. "It's for you, sir."

He watched Armstrong walk back to take the call and he wondered what it would be like to be a policeman with so much opportunity for so much graft, and, for the millionth time, what it would be like to be all British or all Chinese, and not a Eurasian despised by both.

He watched Armstrong listening intently, then heard him say above the hubbub, "No, just stall. I'll deal with it personally. Thanks, Tom."

Armstrong came back. "Sorry," he said, then headed past the Immigration cordon, up a small corridor and into the VIP Lounge. It was neat and expansive, with bar facilities and a good view of the airport and the city and the bay. The lounge was empty except for two Immigration and Customs officers and one of Armstrong's men waiting beside Gate 16—a glass door that let out onto the floodlit tarmac. They could see the 707 coming onto her parking marks.

"Evening, Sergeant Lee," Armstrong said. "All set?"

"Yes sir. *Yankee 2*'s just shutting down her engines." Sergeant Lee saluted again and opened the gate for them.

Armstrong glanced at John Chen, knowing the neck of the trap was almost closed. "After you."

"Thanks." John Chen walked out onto the tarmac.

Yankee 2 towered over them, its dying jets now a muted growl. A ground crew was easing the tall, motor-driven gangway into place. Through the small cockpit windows they could see the dimly lit pilots. To one side, in the shadows, was John Chen's dark blue Silver Cloud Rolls, the uniformed Chinese chauffeur standing beside the door, a policeman nearby.

The main cabin door of the aircraft swung open and a uniformed steward came out to greet the two airport officials who were waiting on the platform. He handed one of the officials a pouch with the airplane's documents and arrival manifests, and they began to chat affably. Then they all stopped. Deferentially. And saluted politely.

The girl was tall, smart, exquisite and American.

Armstrong whistled quietly. *"Ayeeyah!"*

"Bartlett's got taste," John Chen muttered, his heart quickening.

They watched her come down the stairs, both men lost in masculine musings.

"You think she's a model?"

"She moves like one. A movie star, maybe?"

John Chen walked forward. "Good evening. I'm John Chen of Struan's. I'm meeting Mr. Bartlett and Mr. Tchuluck."

"Oh yes of course, Mr. Chen. This's very kind of you, sir, particularly on a Sunday. I'm pleased to meet you. I'm K.C. Tcholok. Linc says if you . . ."

"Casey Tchuluck?" John Chen gaped at her. "Eh?"

"Yes," she said, her smile nice, patiently passing over the mispronunciation. "You see my initials are *K.C.*, Mr. Chen, so *Casey* became my nickname." She turned her eyes on Armstrong. "Evening. You're also from Struan's?" Her voice was melodious.

"Oh, er, excuse me, this, this is Superintendent Armstrong," John Chen stuttered, still trying to recover.

"Evening," Armstrong said, noticing that she was even more attractive close up. "Welcome to Hong Kong."

"Thank you. Superintendent? That's police?" Then the name clicked into place. "Ah, Armstrong. Robert Armstrong? Chief of CID Kowloon?"

He covered his surprise. "You're very well informed, Miss Tcholok."

She laughed. "Just part of my routine. When I go to a new place, particularly one like Hong Kong, it's my job to be prepared . . . so I just sent for your current listings."

"We don't have published listings."

"I know. But the Hong Kong Government puts out a government phone book which anyone can buy for a few pennies. I just sent for one of those. All police departments are listed—heads of departments, most with their home numbers—along with every other government office. I got one through your Hong Kong PR office in New York."

"Who's head of Special Branch?" he asked, testing her.

"I don't know. I don't think that department was listed. Is it?"

"Sometimes."

A slight frown stood in her eyes. "You greet all private airplanes, Superintendent?"

"Only those I wish to." He smiled at her. "Only those with pretty, well-informed ladies aboard."

"Something's wrong? There's trouble?"

"Oh no, just routine. Kai Tak's part of my responsibility," Armstrong said easily. "May I see your passport please?"

"Of course." Her frown deepened as she opened her handbag and handed her U.S. passport over.

Years of experience made his inspection very detailed indeed. "Born Providence, Rhode Island, November 25, 1936, height 5 feet 8 inches, hair blond, eyes hazel." Passport's valid with two years left to run. Twenty-six, eh? I'd've guessed younger, though there's a strangeness to her eyes if you look closely.

With apparent haphazardness he flipped carelessly through the pages. Her three-month Hong Kong visa was current and in order. A dozen immigration visa stamps, all England, France, Italy or South American. Except one. USSR, dated July this year. A seven-day visit. He recognized the Moscow frank. "Sergeant Lee!"

"Yes sir?"

"Get it stamped for her," he said casually, and smiled down at her. "You're all cleared. You may stay more or less as long as you like. Towards the end of three months just go to the nearest police station and we'll extend your visa for you."

"Thanks very much."

"You'll be with us for a while?"

"That depends on our business deal," Casey said after a pause. She smiled at John Chen. "We hope to be in business for a long time."

John Chen said, "Yes. Er, we hope so too." He was still nonplussed, his mind churning. It's surely not possible for Casey Tcholok to be a woman, he thought.

Behind them the steward, Sven Svensen, came bouncing down the stairs, carrying two air suitcases. "Here you are, Casey. You're sure this's enough for tonight?"

"Yes. Sure. Thanks, Sven."

"Linc said for you to go on. You need a hand through Customs?"

"No thanks. Mr. John Chen kindly met us. Also, Superintendent Armstrong, head of Kowloon CID."

"Okay." Sven studied the policeman thoughtfully for a moment. "I'd better get back."

"Everything all right?" she asked.

"I think so." Sven Svensen grinned. "Customs're just checking our stocks of booze and cigarettes." Only four things were subject to any import license or customs duty in the Colony—gold, liquor, tobacco and gasoline—and only one contraband—apart from narcotics—and totally forbidden: all forms of firearms and ammunition.

Casey smiled up at Armstrong. "We've no rice aboard, Superintendent. Linc doesn't eat it."

"Then he's in for a bad time here."

She laughed then turned back to Svensen. "See you tomorrow. Thanks."

"9 A.M. on the dot!" Svensen went back to the airplane and Casey turned to John Chen.

"Linc said for us not to wait for him. Hope that's all right," she said.

"Eh?"

"Shall we go? We're booked into the Victoria and Albert Hotel, Kowloon." She began to pick up her bags but a porter materialized out of the darkness and took them from her. "Linc'll come later . . . or tomorrow."

John Chen gawked at her. "Mr. Bartlett's not coming?"

"No. He's going to stay in the airplane overnight if he can get permission. If not, he'll follow us by cab. In any event he'll join us tomorrow for lunch as arranged. Lunch is still on, isn't it?"

"Oh yes, but . . ." John Chen was trying to get his mind working. "Then you'll want to cancel the 10 A.M. meeting?"

"Oh no. I'll attend that as arranged. Linc wasn't expected at that meeting. That's just financing—not policy. I'm sure you understand. Linc's very tired, Mr. Chen," she said. "He just got back yesterday from Europe." She looked back at Armstrong. "The captain asked the tower if Linc could sleep in, Superintendent. They checked with Immigration who said they'd get back to us but I presume our request'll come through channels to you. We'd certainly appreciate it if you'd approve. He's really been on the jet lag trail for too long."

Armstrong found himself saying, "I'll chat with him about it."

"Oh thanks. Thanks very much," she said, and then to John Chen, "Sorry for all this trouble, Mr. Chen. Shall we go?" She began to head for Gate 16, the porter following, but John Chen pointed to his Rolls. "No, this way, Miss Tchu—er, Casey."

Her eyes widened. "No Customs?"

"Not tonight," Armstrong said, liking her. "A present from Her Majesty's Government."

"I feel like visiting royalty."

"All part of the service."

She got into the car. Lovely smell of leather. And luxury. Then she saw the porter hurrying through the gate into the terminal building. "But what about my bags?"

"No need to worry about those," John Chen said irritably. "They'll be in your suite before you are."

Armstrong held on to the door for a moment. "John came with two cars. One for you and Mr. Bartlett—the other for luggage."

"Two cars?"

"Of course. Don't forget you're in Hong Kong now."

He watched the car drive off. Linc Bartlett's a lucky man, he thought, and wondered absently why Special Intelligence was interested in her.

"Just meet the airplane and go through her passport personally," the director of SI had told him this morning. "And Mr. Lincoln Bartlett's."

"May I ask why, sir?"

"No, Robert, you may not ask why. You're no longer in this branch—you're in a nice cushy job at Kowloon. A positive sinecure, what?"

"Yes sir."

"And Robert, kindly don't balls up this operation tonight—there may be a lot of very big names involved. We go to a great deal of trouble to keep you fellows abreast of what the nasties are doing."

"Yes sir."

Armstrong sighed as he walked up the gangway followed by Sergeant Lee. *Dew neh loh moh* on all senior officers, particularly the director of SI.

One of the Customs officials was waiting at the top of the gangway with Svensen. "Evening, sir," he said. "Everything's shipshape aboard. There's a .38 with a box of a hundred shells unopened as part of ship's stores. A Verey Light pistol. Also three hunting rifles and a twelve-bore with ammo belonging to Mr. Bartlett. They're all listed on the manifest and I inspected them. There's a locked gun cabinet in the main cabin. Captain has the key."

"Good."

"You need me anymore, sir?"

"No, thanks." Armstrong took the airplane's manifest and began to check it. Lots of wine, cigarettes, tobacco, beer and spirits. Ten cases of Dom Pérignon '59, fifteen Puligny Montrachet '53, nine Château Haut Brion '53. "No Lafite Rothschild 1916, Mr. Svensen?" he said with a small smile.

"No sir." Svensen grinned. "'16 was a very bad year. But there's half a case of the 1923. It's on the next page."

Armstrong flipped the page. More wines and the cigars were listed. "Good," he said. "Of course all this is in bond while you're on the ground."

"Yes sir. I'd already locked it—your man's tagged it. He said it was okay to leave a twelve-pack of beer in the cooler."

"If the owner wants to import any of the wines, just let me know. There's no fuss and just a modest contribution to Her Majesty's bottom drawer."

"Sir?" Svensen was perplexed.

"Eh? Oh, just an English pun. Refers to a lady's bottom drawer in a chest of drawers—where she puts away the things she needs in the future. Sorry. Your passport please." Svensen's passport was Canadian. "Thanks."

"May I introduce you to Mr. Bartlett? He's waiting for you."

Svensen led the way into the airplane. The interior was elegant and simple. Right off the small hallway was a sitting area with half a dozen deep leather chairs and a sofa. A central door closed off the rest of the airplane, aft. In one of the chairs a stewardess was half asleep, her travel bags beside her. Left was the cockpit door. It was open.

The captain and first officer/copilot were in their seats, still going through their paper work.

"Excuse me, Captain. This is Superintendent Armstrong," Svensen said, and stepped aside.

"Evening, Superintendent," the captain said. "I'm Captain Jannelli and this's my copilot, Bill O'Rourke."

"Evening. May I see your passports please?"

Both pilots had massed international visas and immigration stamps. No Iron Curtain countries. Armstrong handed them to Sergeant Lee for stamping. "Thank you, Captain. Is this your first visit to Hong Kong?"

"No sir. I was here a couple of times R and R during Korea. And I had a six-month tour with Far Eastern as first officer on their round-the-world route in '56, during the riots."

"What riots?" O'Rourke asked.

"The whole of Kowloon blew apart. Couple hundred thousand Chinese went on a sudden rampage, rioting, burning. The cops—sorry, the police tried to settle it with patience, then the mobs started killing so the cops, police, they got out a couple of Sten guns and killed half a dozen jokers and everything calmed down very fast. Only police have guns here which is a great idea." To Armstrong he said, "I think your guys did a hell of a job."

"Thank you, Captain Jannelli. Where did this flight emanate?"

"L.A.—Los Angeles. Linc's—Mr. Bartlett's head office's there."

"Your route was Honolulu, Tokyo, Hong Kong?"

"Yes sir."

"How long did you stop in Tokyo?"

Bill O'Rourke turned up the flight log at once. "Two hours and seventeen minutes. Just a refueling stop, sir."

"Just enough time to stretch your legs?"

Jannelli said, "I was the only one who got out. I always check my gear, the landing gear, and do an exterior inspection whenever we land."

"That's a good habit," the policeman said politely. "How long are you staying?"

"Don't know, that's up to Linc. Certainly overnight. We couldn't leave before 1400. Our orders're just to be ready to go anywhere at any time."

"You've a fine aircraft, Captain. You're approved to stay here till 1400. If you want an extension, call Ground Control before that time. When you're ready, just clear Customs through that gate. And would you clear all your crew together, please."

"Sure. Soon as we're refueled."

"You and all your crew know the importing of any firearms into the Colony is absolutely forbidden? We're very nervous about firearms in Hong Kong."

"So am I, Superintendent—anywhere. That's why I've the only key to the gun cabinet."

"Good. Any problems, please check with my office." Armstrong left and went into the anteroom, Svensen just ahead.

Jannelli watched him inspect the air hostess's passport. She was pretty, Jenny Pollard. "Son of a bitch," he muttered, then added quietly, "Something stinks around here."

"Huh?"

"Since when does CID brass check goddamn passports for chrissake? You sure we're not carrying anything curious?"

"Hell no. I always check everything. Including Sven's stores. Of course I don't go through Linc's stuff—or Casey's—but they wouldn't do anything stupid."

"I've flown him for four years and never once . . . Even so, something sure as hell stinks." Jannelli wearily twisted and settled himself in his pilot's seat more comfortably. "Jesus, I could use a massage and a week off."

In the anteroom Armstrong was handing the passport to Sergeant Lee who stamped it. "Thank you, Miss Pollard."

"Thank you."

"That's all the crew, sir," Svensen said. "Now Mr. Bartlett."

"Yes, please."

Svensen knocked on the central door and opened it without waiting. "Linc, this's Superintendent Armstrong," he said with easy informality.

"Hi," Linc Bartlett said, getting up from his desk. He put out his hand. "May I offer you a drink? Beer?"

"No thanks. Perhaps a cup of coffee."

Svensen turned for the galley at once. "Coming up," he said.

"Make yourself at home. Here's my passport," Bartlett said. "Won't be a moment." He went back to the typewriter and continued tapping the keys with two fingers.

Armstrong studied him leisurely. Bartlett was sandy haired with gray-flecked blue eyes, a strong good-looking face. Trim. Sports shirt and jeans. He checked the passport. Born Los Angeles, October 1, 1922. He looks young for forty, he thought. Moscow franking, same as Casey Tcholok, no other Iron Curtain visits.

His eyes wandered the room. It was spacious, the whole width of the airplane. There was a short central corridor aft with two cabins off it and two toilets. And at the end a final door which he presumed was the master suite.

The cabin was fitted as if it were a communications center. Teletype, international telephone capability, built-in typewriters. An illuminated world time clock on a bulkhead. Filing cabinets, duplicator and a built-in leather-topped desk strewn with papers. Shelves of books. Tax books. A few paperbacks. The rest were war books and books on generals or by generals. Dozens of them. Wellington and Napoleon and Patton, Eisenhower's *Crusade in Europe*, Sun Tzu's *The Art of War* . . .

"Here you are, sir," broke into Armstrong's inspection.

"Oh, thank you, Svensen." He took the coffee cup and added a little cream.

Svensen put a fresh, opened can of chilled beer beside Bartlett, picked up the empty, then went back to the galley, closing the door after him. Bartlett sipped the beer from the can, rereading what he had written, then pressed a buzzer. Svensen came at once. "Tell Jannelli to ask the tower to send this off." Svensen nodded and left. Bartlett eased his shoulders and swung around in the swivel chair. "Sorry—I had to get that right off."

"That's all right, Mr. Bartlett. Your request to stay overnight is approved."

"Thanks—thanks very much. Could Svensen stay as well?" Bartlett grinned. "I'm not much of a housekeeper."

"Very well. How long will your aircraft be here?"

"Depends on our meeting tomorrow, Superintendent. We hope to go into business with Struan's. A week, ten days."

"Then you'll need an alternate parking place tomorrow. We've another VIP flight coming in at 1600 hours. I told Captain Jannelli to phone Ground Control before 1400 hours."

"Thanks. Does the head of CID Kowloon usually deal with parking around here?"

Armstrong smiled. "I like to know what's going on in my division. It's a tedious habit but ingrained. We don't often have private aircraft visiting us—or Mr. Chen meeting someone personally. We like to be accommodating if we can. Struan's owns most of the airport and John's a personal friend. He's an old friend of yours?"

"I spent time with him in New York and L.A. and liked him a lot. Say, Superintendent, this airplane's my comm—" One of the phones rang. Bartlett picked it up. "Oh hello Charlie, what's happening in New York? . . . Jesus, that's great. How much? . . . Okay Charlie, buy the whole block. . . . Yes, the whole 200,000 shares. . . . Sure, first thing Monday morning, soon as the market opens. Send me a confirm by telex. . . ." Bartlett put the phone down and turned to Armstrong. "Sorry. Say, Superintendent, this's my communications center and I'll be lost without it. If we park for a week is it okay to come back and forth?"

"I'm afraid that might be dicey, Mr. Bartlett."

"Is that yes or no or maybe?"

"Oh that's slang for difficult. Sorry, but our security at Kai Tak's very particular."

"If you have to put on extra men, I'd be glad to pay."

"It's a matter of security, Mr. Bartlett, not money. You'll find Hong Kong's phone system first class." Also it will be far easier for Special Intelligence to monitor your calls, he thought.

"Well, if you can I'd appreciate it."

Armstrong sipped the coffee. "This's your first visit to Hong Kong?"

"Yes sir. My first time in Asia. Farthest I've gotten was Guadalcanal, in '43."

"Army?"

"Sergeant, Engineers. Construction—we used to build anything: hangars, bridges, camps, anything. A great experience." Bartlett sipped from the can. "Sure I can't give you a drink?"

"No thanks." Armstrong finished his cup, began to get up. "Thanks for the coffee."

"Now may I ask you a question?"

"Of course."

"What's Dunross like? Ian Dunross. The head of Struan's?"

"*The* tai-pan?" Armstrong laughed outright. "That depends whom you ask, Mr. Bartlett. You've never met him?"

"No, not yet. I do tomorrow. At lunch. Why do you call him *the tai-pan?*"

"*Tai-pan* means 'supreme leader' in Cantonese—the person with the ultimate power. The European heads of all the old trading companies are all tai-pans to the Chinese. But even among tai-pans there's always the greatest. *The* tai-pan. Struan's is nicknamed the 'Noble House' or 'Noble Hong,' *hong* meaning 'company.' It goes back to the beginning of the China trade and the early days of Hong Kong. Hong Kong was founded in 1841, January 26, actually. The founder of Struan and Company was a legend, still is in some ways—Dirk Struan. Some say he was a pirate, some a prince. In any event he made a fortune smuggling Indian opium into China, then converting that silver into China teas which he shipped to England in a fleet of China clippers. He became a merchant prince, earned the title of *the* tai-pan, and ever since, Struan's has always tried to be first in everything."

"Are they?"

"Oh a couple of companies dog their heels, Rothwell-Gornt particularly, but yes, I'd say they were first. Certainly not a thing comes into Hong Kong or goes out, is eaten or buried or made without Struan's, Rothwell-Gornt, Asian Properties, Blacs—the Bank of London and China—or the Victoria Bank having a finger in the stew somewhere."

"And Dunross himself? What's he like?"

Armstrong thought a moment, then said lightly, "Again it depends very much whom you ask, Mr. Bartlett. I know him just a little, socially—we meet from time to time at the races. I've had two official meetings with him. He's charming, very good at his job. . . . I suppose *brilliant* might sum him up."

"He and his family own a lot of Struan's?"

"I don't know that for certain. I doubt if anyone does, outside of the family. But his stockholdings aren't the key to the tai-pan's desk. Oh no. Not of Struan's. Of that I'm very certain." Armstrong locked his eyes on Bartlett's. "Some say Dunross is ruthless and ready to kill. I know I wouldn't like him as an enemy."

Bartlett sipped his beer and the little lines beside his eyes crinkled with a curious smile. "Sometimes an enemy's more valuable than a friend."

"Sometimes. I hope you have a profitable stay."

At once Bartlett got up. "Thanks. I'll see you out." He opened the door and ushered Armstrong and Sergeant Lee through it, then followed them out of the main cabin door onto the landing steps. He took a deep breath of air. Once again he caught a strangeness on the wind, neither pleasant nor unpleasant, neither odor nor perfume—just strange, and curiously exciting. "Superintendent, what's that smell? Casey noticed it too, the moment Sven opened the door."

Armstrong hesitated. Then he smiled. "That's Hong Kong's very own, Mr. Bartlett. It's money."

2

"All gods bear witness to the foul luck I'm having tonight," Four Finger Wu said and spat on the deck. He was aft, on the high poop of his ocean-going junk that was moored to one of the great clusters of boats that sprawled over Aberdeen harbor on the south coast of Hong Kong Island. The night was hot and humid and he was playing mah-jong with three of his friends. They were old and weatherbeaten like himself, all captains of junks that they owned. Even so, they sailed in his fleet and took orders from him. His formal name was Wu Sang Fang. He was a short, illiterate fisherman, with few teeth and no thumb on his left hand. His junk was old, battered and filthy. He was head of the seaborne Wu, captain of the fleets, and his flag, the Silver Lotus, flew on all the four seas.

When it was his turn again, he picked up another of the ivory tiles. He glanced at it and as it did not improve his hand, discarded it noisily and spat again. The spittle glistened on the deck. He wore a ragged old undershirt and black coolie pants, like his friends, and he had ten thousand dollars riding on this single game.

"*Ayeeyah,*" Pockmark Tang said, pretending disgust though the tile he had just picked up made him only one short of a winning combination—the game somewhat like gin rummy. "Fornicate all mothers except ours if I don't win!" He discarded a tile with a flourish.

"Fornicate yours if you win and I don't!" another said and they all laughed.

"And fornicate those foreign devils from the Golden Mountain if they don't arrive tonight," Goodweather Poon said.

"They'll arrive," Four Finger Wu told him confidently. "Foreign devils are glued to schedules. Even so, I sent Seventh Son to the airport to make sure." He began to pick up a tile but stopped and looked over his shoulder and watched critically as a fishing junk eased past, chugging quietly, heading up the twisting, narrow access channel between the banks of boats toward the neck of the harbor. She had only riding lights, port and star-board. Ostensibly she was just going fishing but this junk was one of his and she was out to intercept a Thai trawler with a cargo of opium. When she was safely passed, he concentrated on the game once more. It was low tide now, but there was deep water around most of the boat islands. From the shore and flats came the stench of rotting seaweed, shellfish and human waste.

Most of the sampans and junks were dark now, their multitudes sleep-ing. There were a few oil lamps here and there. Boats of all sizes were moored precariously to each other, seemingly without order, with tiny sea alleys between the floating villages. These were the homes of the Tanka and Haklo people—the boat dwellers—who lived their lives afloat, were born afloat and died afloat. Many of these boats never moved from these moorings but stayed locked together until they sank or fell apart, or went down in a typhoon or were burnt in one of the spectacular conflagrations that frequently swept the clusters when a careless foot or hand knocked over a lamp or dropped something inflammable into the inevitable open fires.

"Grandfather!" the youthful lookout called.

"What is it?" Wu asked.

"On the jetty, look! Seventh Son!" The boy, barely twelve, was pointing to the shore.

Wu and the others got up and peered shorewards. The young Chinese was paying off a taxi. He wore jeans and a neat T-shirt and sneakers. The taxi had stopped near the gangway of one of the huge floating restaurants that were moored to the modern jetties, a hundred yards away. There were four of these gaudy floating palaces—three, four or five stories tall—ablaze with lights, splendiferous in scarlet and green and gold with fluted Chinese roofs and gods, gargoyles and dragons.

"You've good eyes, Number Three Grandson. Good. Go and meet Sev-enth Son." Instantly the child scurried off, sure-footed across the rickety planks that joined this junk to others. Four Fingers watched his seventh son head for one of the jetties where ferry sampans that serviced the harbor were clustered. When he saw that the boatman he had sent had inter-cepted him, he turned his back on the shore and sat down again. "Come on, let's finish the game," he said grimly. "This's my last fornicating hand. I've got to go ashore tonight."

They played for a moment, picking up tiles and discarding them.

"*Ayeeyah!*" Pockmark Tang said with a shout as he saw the face of the tile that he had just picked up. He slammed it onto the table face upwards with a flourish and laid down his other thirteen hidden tiles that made up his winning hand. "Look, by all the gods!"

Wu and the others gawked at the hand. "Pisss!" he said and hawked loudly. "Piss on all your generations, Pockmark Tang! What luck!"

"One more game? Twenty thousand, Four Finger Wu?" Tang said

gleefully, convinced that tonight old devil, Chi Kung, the god of gamblers, was sitting on his shoulder.

Wu began to shake his head, but at that moment a seabird flew overhead and called plaintively. "Forty," he said immediately, changing his mind, interpreting the call as a sign from heaven that his luck had changed. "Forty thousand or nothing! But it'll have to be dice because I've no time now."

"I haven't got forty cash by all gods, but with the twenty you owe me, I'll borrow against my junk tomorrow when the bank opens and give you all my fornicating profit on our next gold or opium shipment until you're paid, *heya?*"

Goodweather Poon said sourly, "That's too much on one game. You two fornicators've lost your minds!"

"Highest score, one throw?" Wu asked.

"*Ayeeyah,* you've gone mad, both of you," Poon said. Nonetheless, he was as excited as the others. "Where are the dice?"

Wu produced them. There were three. "Throw for your fornicating future, Pockmark Tang!"

Pockmark Tang spat on his hands, said a silent prayer, then threw them with a shout.

"Oh oh oh," he cried out in anguish. A four, a three and another four. "Eleven!" The other men were hardly breathing.

Wu spat on the dice, cursed them, blessed them and threw. A six, a two and a three. "Eleven! Oh all gods great and small! Again—throw again!"

Excitement gathered on the deck. Pockmark Tang threw. "Fourteen!"

Wu concentrated, the tension intoxicating, then threw the dice. "*Ayeeyah!*" he exploded, and they all exploded. A six, a four and a two.

"Eeeee," was all Pockmark Tang could say, holding his belly, laughing with glee as the others congratulated him and commiserated with the loser.

Wu shrugged, his heart still pounding in his chest. "Curse all seabirds that fly over my head at a time like that!"

"Ah, is that why you changed your mind, Four Finger Wu?"

"Yes—it was like a sign. How many seabirds call as they fly overhead at night?"

"That's right. I would have done the same."

"Joss!" Then Wu beamed. "Eeeee, but the gambling feeling's better than the Clouds and the Rain, *heya?*"

"Not at my age!"

"How old are you, Pockmark Tang?"

"Sixty—perhaps seventy. Almost as old as you are." Haklos did not have permanent records of births like all village land dwellers. "I don't feel more than thirty."

"Have you heard the Lucky Medicine Shop at Aberdeen Market's got a new shipment of Korean ginseng, some of it a hundred years old! That'll stick fire in your stalk!"

"His stalk's all right, Goodweather Poon! His third wife's with child again!" Wu grinned toothlessly and pulled out a big roll of 500-dollar notes. He began counting, his fingers nimble even though his left thumb was missing. Years ago it had been hacked off during a fight with river pirates during a smuggling expedition. He stopped momentarily as his number seven son came on deck. The young man was tall for a Chinese, twenty-six. He walked across the deck awkwardly. An incoming jet began to whine past overhead.

"Did they arrive, Seventh Son?"

"Yes, Father, yes they did."

Four Fingers pounded the upturned keg with glee. "Very good. Now we can begin!"

"Hey, Four Fingers," Pockmark Tang said thoughtfully, motioning at the dice. "A six, a four and a two—that's twelve, which's also three, the magic three."

"Yes, yes I saw."

Pockmark Tang beamed and pointed northwards and a little east to where Kai Tak airport would be—behind the Aberdeen mountains, across the harbor in Kowloon, six miles away. "Perhaps your luck has changed, *heya?*"

MONDAY

3

At half-dawn a jeep with two overalled mechanics aboard came around Gate 16 at the eastern end of the terminal and stopped close beside the main landing gear of *Yankee* 2. The gangway was still in place and the main door slightly ajar. The mechanics, both Chinese, got out and one began to inspect the eight-wheeled main gear while the other, equally carefully, scrutinized the nose gear. Methodically, they checked the tires and wheels and then the hydraulic couplings of the brakes, then peered into the landing bays. Both used flashlights. The mechanic at the main landing gear took out a spanner and stood on one of the wheels for a closer inspection, his head and shoulder now well into the belly of the airplane. After a moment he called out softly in Cantonese, "*Ayeeyah!* Hey, Lim, take a look at this."

The other man strolled back and peered up, sweat staining his white overalls. "Are they there or not, I can't see from down here."

"Brother, put your male stalk into your mouth and flush yourself down a sewer. Of course they're here. We're rich. We'll eat rice forever! But be quiet or you'll wake the dung-stained foreign devils above! Here . . ." The man handed down a long, canvas-wrapped package which Lim took and stowed quietly and quickly in the jeep. Then another and another small one, both men sweating and very nervous, working fast but quietly.

Another package. And another . . .

And then Lim saw the police jeep whirl around the corner and simultaneously other uniformed men come pouring out of Gate 16, among them Europeans. "We're betrayed," he gasped as he fled in a hopeless dash for freedom. The jeep intercepted him easily and he stopped, shivering with pent-up terror. Then he spat and cursed the gods and withdrew into himself.

The other man had jumped down at once and leaped into the driving seat. Before he could turn on the ignition he was swamped and handcuffed.

"So, little oily mouth," Sergeant Lee hissed, "where do you think you're going?"

"Nowhere, Officer, it was him, him there, that bastard son of a whore, Officer, he swore he'd cut my throat if I didn't help him. I don't know anything on my mother's grave!"

"You lying bastard, you never had a mother. You're going to go to jail for fifty years if you don't talk!"

"I swear, Officer, by all the gods th—"

"Piss on your lies, dungface. Who's paying you to do this job?"

Armstrong was walking slowly across the tarmac, the sick sweet taste of the kill in his mouth. "So," he said in English, "what have we here, Sergeant?" It had been a long night's vigil and he was tired and unshaven and in no mood for the mechanic's whining protestations of innocence, so he said softly in perfect gutter Cantonese, "One more tiny, insignificant word out of you, purveyor of leper dung, and I'll have my men jump on your Secret Sack."

The man froze.

"Good. What's your name?"

"Tan Shu Ta, lord."

"Liar! What's your friend's name?"

"Lim Ta-cheung, but he's not my friend, lord, I never met him before this morning."

"Liar! Who paid you to do this?"

"I don't know who paid him, lord. You see he swore he'd cut—"

"Liar! Your mouth's so full of dung you must be the god of dung himself. What's in those packages?"

"I don't know. I swear on my ancestor's gr—"

"Liar!" Armstrong said it automatically, knowing that the lies were inevitable.

"John *China*man's not the same as us," his first police teacher, an old China hand, had told him. "Oh I don't mean cut on the cross or anything like that—he's just different. He lies through his teeth all the time to a copper and when you nab a villain fair and square he'll still lie and be as slippery as a greased pole in a pile of shit. He's different. Take their names. All Chinese have four different names, one when he's born, one at puberty, one when he's an adult and one he chooses for himself, and they forget one or add another at the drop of a titfer. And their names—God stone the crows! Chinese call themselves *lao-tsi-sing*—the Ancient One Hundred Names. They've only got a basic hundred surnames in all China and of those there're twenty Yus, eight Yens, ten Wus and God knows how many Pings, Lis, Lees, Chens, Chins, Chings, Wongs and Fus and each one of them you pronounce five different ways so God knows who's who!"

"Then it's going to be difficult to identify a suspect, sir?"

"Full marks, young Armstrong! Full marks, lad. You can have fifty Lis, fifty Changs and four hundred Wongs and not one related to the other. God stone the crows! That's the problem here in Hong Kong."

Armstrong sighed. After eighteen years Chinese names were still as confusing as ever. And on top of that everyone seemed to have a nickname by which they were generally known.

"What's your name?" he asked again and didn't bother to listen to the answer. "Liar! Sergeant! Unwrap one of those! Let's see what we've got."

Sergeant Lee eased aside the last covering. Inside was an M14, an automatic rifle, U.S. Army. New and well greased.

"For this, you evil son of a whore's left tit," Armstrong grated, "you'll howl for fifty years!"

The man was staring at the gun stupidly, aghast. Then a low moan came from him. "Fornicate all gods I never knew they were guns."

"Ah, but you did know!" Armstrong said. "Sergeant, put this piece of dung in the wagon and book him for smuggling guns."

The man was dragged away roughly. One of the young Chinese policemen was unwrapping another package. It was small and square. "Hold it!" Armstrong ordered in English. The policeman and everyone in hearing distance froze. "One of them may be booby-trapped. Everyone get away from the jeep!" Sweating, the man did as he was ordered. "Sergeant, get our bomb disposal wallahs. There's no hurry now."

"Yes sir." Sergeant Lee hurried to the intercom in the police wagon.

Armstrong went under the airplane and peered into the main gear bay. He could see nothing untoward. Then he stood on one of the wheels. "Christ!" he gasped. Five snug racks were neatly bolted to each side of the inner bulkhead. One was almost empty, the others still full. From the size and shape of the packages he judged them to be more M14's and boxes of ammo—or grenades.

"Anything up there, sir?" Inspector Thomas asked. He was a young Englishman, three years in the force.

"Take a look! But don't touch anything."

"Christ! There's enough for a couple of riot squads!"

"Yes. But who?"

"Commies?"

"Or Nationalists—or villains. These'd—"

"What the hell's going on down there?"

Armstrong recognized Linc Bartlett's voice. His face closed and he jumped down, Thomas following him. He went to the foot of the gangway. "I'd like to know that too, Mr. Bartlett," he called up curtly.

Bartlett was standing at the main door of the airplane, Svensen beside him. Both men wore pajamas and robes and were sleep tousled.

"I'd like you to take a look at this." Armstrong pointed to the rifle that was now half hidden in the jeep.

At once Bartlett came down the gangway, Svensen following. "What?"

"Perhaps you'd be kind enough to wait in the airplane, Mr. Svensen."

Svensen started to reply, stopped. Then he glanced at Bartlett who nodded. "Fix some coffee, Sven, huh?"

"Sure, Linc."

"Now what's this all about, Superintendent?"

"That!" Armstrong pointed.

"That's an M14." Bartlett's eyes narrowed. "So?"

"So it seems your aircraft is bringing in guns."

"That's not possible."

"We've just caught two men unloading. There's one of the buggers"—Armstrong stabbed a finger at the handcuffed mechanic waiting sullenly beside the jeep—"and the other's in the wagon. Perhaps you'd be kind enough to look up in the main gear bay, sir."

"Sure. Where?"

"You'll have to stand on a wheel."

Bartlett did as he was told. Armstrong and Inspector Thomas watched exactly where he put his hands for fingerprint identification. Bartlett stared blankly at the racks. "I'll be goddamned! If these're more of the same, it's a goddamn arsenal!"

"Yes. Please don't touch them."

Bartlett studied the racks, then climbed down, wide awake now. "This isn't a simple smuggling job. Those racks are custom made."

"Yes. You've no objection if the aircraft's searched?"

"No. Of course not."

"Go ahead, Inspector," Armstrong said at once. "And do it very carefully indeed. Now, Mr. Bartlett, perhaps you'd be kind enough to explain."

"I don't run guns, Superintendent. I don't believe my captain would—or Bill O'Rourke. Or Svensen."

"What about Miss Tcholok?"

"Oh for chrissake!"

Armstrong said icily, "This is a very serious matter, Mr. Bartlett. Your aircraft is impounded and without police approval until further notice neither you nor any of your crew may leave the Colony pending our inquiries. Now, what about Miss Tcholok?"

"It's impossible, it's totally impossible that Casey is involved in any way with guns, gun smuggling or any kind of smuggling. Impossible." Bartlett was apologetic but quite unafraid. "Nor would any of the rest of us." His voice sharpened. "You were tipped off, weren't you?"

"How long did you stop at Honolulu?"

"An hour or two, just to refuel, I don't remember exactly." Bartlett thought for a moment. "Jannelli got off but he always does. Those racks couldn't've been loaded in an hour or so."

"Are you sure?"

"No, but I'd still bet it was done before we left the States. Though when and where and why and who I've no idea. Have you?"

"Not yet." Armstrong was watching him keenly. "Perhaps you'd like to go back to your office, Mr. Bartlett. We could take your statement there."

"Sure." Bartlett glanced at his watch. It was 5:43 A.M. "Let's do that now, then I can make a few calls. We're not wired into your system yet. There's a local phone there?" He pointed to the terminal.

"Yes. Of course we'd prefer to question Captain Jannelli and Mr. O'Rourke before you do—if you don't mind. Where are they staying?"

"At the Victoria and Albert."

"Sergeant Lee!"

"Yes sir."

"Get on to HQ."

"Yes sir."

"We'd also like to talk to Miss Tcholok first. Again if you don't mind."

Bartlett walked up the steps, Armstrong beside him. At length he said, "All right. Provided you do that personally, and not before 7:45. She's been working overtime and she's got a heavy day today and I don't want her disturbed unnecessarily."

They went into the airplane. Sven was waiting by the galley, dressed now and very perturbed. Uniformed and plainclothes police were everywhere, searching diligently.

"Sven, how about that coffee?" Bartlett led the way through the anteroom into his office-study. The central door, aft, at the end of the corridor, was open. Armstrong could see part of the master suite with its king-size bed. Inspector Thomas was going through some drawers.

"Shit!" Bartlett muttered.

"Sorry," Armstrong said, "but this is necessary."

"That doesn't mean I have to like it, Superintendent. Never did like strangers peeking into my private life."

"Yes. I agree." The superintendent beckoned one of the plainclothes officers. "Sung!"

"Yes sir."

"Take this down will you please."

"Just a minute, let's save some time," Bartlett said. He turned to a bank of electronic gear and pressed two switches. A twin cassette tape deck clicked into operation. He plugged in a microphone and set it on the desk. "There'll be two tapes, one for you, one for me. After your man's typed it up—if you want a signature I'm here."

"Thank you."

"Okay, let's begin."

Armstrong was suddenly uneasy. "Would you please tell me what you know about the illegal cargo found in the main gear bay of your aircraft, Mr. Bartlett."

Bartlett repeated his denial of any knowledge. "I don't believe any of my crew or any of my people are involved in any way. None of them has ever been involved with the law as far as I know. And I would know."

"How long has Captain Jannelli been with you?"

"Four years. O'Rourke two. Svensen since I got the airplane in '58."

"And Miss Tcholok?"

After a pause Bartlett said, "Six—almost seven years."

"She's a senior executive in your company?"

"Yes. Very senior."

"That's unusual, isn't it, Mr. Bartlett?"

"Yes. But that has nothing to do with this problem."

"You're the owner of this aircraft?"

"My company is. Par-Con Industries Incorporated."

"Do you have any enemies—anyone who'd want to embarrass you seriously?"

Bartlett laughed. "Does a dog have fleas? You don't get to head a half-billion-dollar company by making friendships."

"No enemy in particular?"

"You tell me. Running guns is a special operation—this has to have been done by a professional."

"Who knew about your flight plan to Hong Kong?"

"The visit's been scheduled for a couple of months. My board knew. And my planning staff." Bartlett frowned. "It was no real secret. No reason to be." Then he added, "Of course Struan's knew—exactly. For at least two weeks. In fact we confirmed the date on the 12th by telex, exact ETD and ETA. I wanted it sooner but Dunross said Monday the 19th'd suit him better, which is today. Maybe you should ask him."

"I will, Mr. Bartlett. Thank you, sir. That will do for the moment."

"I've got some questions, Superintendent, if you don't mind. What's the penalty for smuggling guns?"

"Ten years without parole."

"What's the value of this cargo?"

"Priceless, to the right buyer, because no guns—absolutely none—are available to anyone."

"Who's the right buyer?"

"Anyone who wants to start a riot, insurrection, or commit mass murder, bank robbery, or some crime of whatever magnitude."

"Communists?"

Armstrong smiled and shook his head. "They don't have to shoot at us to take over the Colony, or smuggle M14's—they've got guns a-plenty of their own."

"Nationalists? Chiang Kai-shek's men?"

"They're more than well supplied with all sorts of armaments by the U.S. Government, Mr. Bartlett. Aren't they? So they don't need to smuggle this way either."

"A gang war maybe?"

"Good God, Mr. Bartlett, our gangs don't shoot each other. Our gangs—triads as we call them—our triads settle their differences in sensible, civilized Chinese fashion, with knives and axes and fighting irons and anonymous calls to the police."

"I'll bet it was someone in Struan's. That's where you'll find the answer to the riddle."

"Perhaps." Armstrong laughed strangely, then said again, "Perhaps. Now if you'll excuse me . . ."

"Of course." Bartlett turned off the recorder, took out the two cassettes and handed one over.

"Thank you, Mr. Bartlett."

"How long will this search go on?"

"That depends. Perhaps an hour. We may wish to bring in some experts. We'll try to make it as easy as possible. You'll be off the plane before lunch?"

"Yes."

"If you want access please check with my office. The number's 88-77-33. There'll be a permanent police guard here for the time being. You'll be staying at the Vic?"

"Yes. Am I free to go into town now, do what I like?"

"Yes sir, provided you don't leave the Colony, pending our inquiries."

Bartlett grinned. "I've got that message already, loud and clear."

Armstrong left. Bartlett showered and dressed and waited until all the police went away except the one who was guarding the gangway. Then he went back into his office suite and closed the door. Quite alone now he checked his watch. It was 7:37. He went over to his communications center and clicked on two micro switches and pressed the sending button.

In a moment there was a crackle of static and Casey's sleepy voice. "Yes, Linc?"

"*Geronimo,*" he said clearly, into the mike.

There was a long pause. "Got it," she said. The loudspeaker went dead.

4

The Rolls came off the car ferry that linked Kowloon to Hong Kong Island and turned east along Connaught Road, joining the heavy traffic. The morning was very warm, humid and cloudless under a nice sun. Casey settled deeper into the back cushions. She glanced at her watch, her excitement growing.

"Plenty time, Missee," the sharp-eyed chauffeur said. "Noble House down street, tall building, ten, fifteen minutes never mind."

"Good."

This is the life, she told herself. One day I'll have a Rolls of my very own and a neat, polite, quiet Chinese chauffeur and I'll not have to worry about the price of gas. Not ever. Maybe—at long last—this is where I'm going to get my *drop dead* money. She smiled to herself. Linc was the first one who had explained about drop dead money. He had called it *screw you* money. Enough to say screw you to anybody or anything. "Screw you money's the most valuable in the world . . . but the most expensive," he had said. "If you work for me—with me but for me—I'll help you get your screw you money. But Casey, I don't know if you'll want to pay the cost."

"What's the cost?"

"I don't know. I only know it varies, person to person—and always costs you more than you're prepared to pay."

"Has yours?"

"Oh yes."

Well, she thought, the price hasn't been too high yet. I make $52,000 a year, my expense account is good and my job stretches my brain. But the government takes too much and there's not enough left to be drop dead money. "Drop dead money comes from a killing," Linc had said. "Not from cash flow."

How much do I need?

She had never asked herself the question before.

$500,000? At 7 percent that'll bring $35,000 a year forever but that's taxable. What about the Mexican Government guarantee of 11 percent, less 1 for them for their trouble? Still taxable. In tax free bonds at 4 percent it's $20,000 but bonds are dangerous and you don't gamble your drop dead money.

"That's the first rule, Casey," Linc had said. "You never risk it. Never." Then he had laughed that lovely laugh of his which disarmed her as always. "You never risk your screw you money except the once or twice you decide to."

A million? Two? Three?

Get your mind on the meeting and don't dream, she told herself. I won't but my price is 2 million cash in the bank. Tax free. That's what I want. 2 million at 5¼ percent tax free will bring $105,000 a year. And that will give me and the family everything I want with enough to spare forever. And I could better 5¼ percent on my money.

But how to get 2 million tax free?

I don't know. But somehow I know this's the place.

The Rolls stopped suddenly as a mass of pedestrians dodged through the tightly packed lines of cars and double-decker buses and taxis and trucks and carts and lorries and bicycles and handcarts and some rickshaws. Thousands of people scurried this way and that, pouring out of or into the alleys and side roads, spilling off the pavements onto the roadway in the morning rush hour. Rivers of human ants.

Casey had researched Hong Kong well, but she was still not prepared for the impact that the incredible overcrowding had made upon her.

"I never saw anything like it, Linc," she had said this morning when he had arrived at the hotel just before she left for the meeting. "It was after ten when we drove here from the airport, but there were thousands of people out—including kids—and everything—restaurants, markets, shops— were still open."

"People mean profit—why else're we here?"

"We're here to usurp the Noble House of Asia with the secret help and collusion of a Judas Iscariot, John Chen."

Linc had laughed with her. "Correction. We're here to make a deal with Struan's, and to look around."

"Then the plan's changed?"

"Tactically yes. The strategy's the same."

"Why the change, Linc?"

"Charlie called last night. We bought another 200,000 shares of Rothwell-Gornt."

"Then the bid for Struan's is just a blind and our real target's Rothwell-Gornt?"

"We still have three targets: Struan's, Rothwell-Gornt and Asian Properties. We look around and we wait. If things look good we attack. If not, we can make 5, maybe 8 million this year on our straight deal with Struan's. That's cream."

"You're not here for 5 or 8 million. What's the real reason?"

"Pleasure."

The Rolls gained a few yards then stopped again, the traffic heavier now as they approached Central District. Ah Linc, she thought, your pleasure covers a multitude of piracies.

"This first visit to Hong Kong, Missee?" broke into her thoughts.

"Yes, yes it is. I arrived last night," she said.

"Ah very good. Weather very bad never mind. Very smelly, very humid. Always humid in summer. First day very pretty, *heya?*"

First day had started with the sharp buzz of her citizens band transceiver jerking her out of sleep. And "*Geronimo.*"

It was their code word for danger—beware. She had showered and dressed quickly, not knowing where the danger was coming from. She had just put in her contact lenses when the phone rang. "This is Superintendent Armstrong. Sorry to bother you so early, Miss Tcholok, but could I see you for a moment?"

"Certainly, Superintendent." She had hesitated. "Give me five minutes —I'll meet you in the restaurant?"

They had met and he had questioned her, telling her only that contraband had been found aboard the airplane.

"How long have you worked for Mr. Bartlett?"

"Directly, six years."

"Have there ever been any police problems before? Of any sort?"

"You mean with him—or with me?"

"With him. Or with you."

"None. What's been found aboard, Superintendent?"

"You don't seem unduly worried, Miss Tcholok."

"Why should I be? I've done nothing illegal, neither has Linc. As to the crew, they're carefully picked professionals, so I'd doubt they have anything to do with smuggling. It's drugs, isn't it? What sort of drugs?"

"Why should it be drugs?"

"Isn't that what people smuggle in here?"

"It was a very large shipment of guns."

"*What?*"

There had been more questions, most of which she had answered, and then Armstrong was gone. She had finished her coffee and refused, for the fourth time, the home-baked, warm hard French rolls offered by a starched and smiling boy-waiter. They reminded her of those she had had in the south of France three years ago.

Ah, Nice and Cap D'Ail and the vin de Provence. And dear Linc, she had thought, going back to the suite to wait for him to phone.

"Casey? Listen, th—"

"Ah Linc, I'm glad you called," she had said at once, deliberately inter-

rupting him. "Superintendent Armstrong was here a few minutes ago—
and I forgot to remind you last night to call Martin about the shares."
Martin was also a code word, meaning, "I think this conversation's being
overheard."

"I'd thought about him too. That's not important now. Tell me exactly
what happened."

So she told him. He related briefly what had occurred. "I'll fill in the
rest when I get there. I'm heading for the hotel right now. How's the
suite?"

"Fantastic! Yours's called Fragrant Spring, my room's adjoining, guess
it's normally part of it. Seems like there are ten houseboys per suite. I
called room service for coffee and it arrived on a silver tray before I'd put
the phone down. The bathrooms're big enough for a cocktail party for
twenty with a three-piece combo."

"Good. Wait for me."

She sat in one of the deep leather sofas in the luxurious sitting room
and began to wait, enjoying the quality that surrounded her. Beautiful
Chinese lacquered chests, a well-stocked bar in a mirrored alcove, discreet
flower arrangements and a bottle of monogrammed Scotch—Lincoln Bartlett—with the compliments of the chief manager. Her bedroom suite
through an interlocking door was one side, his, the master suite, the other.
Both were the biggest she had ever seen, with king-size beds.

Why were guns put on our airplane and by whom?

Lost in thought she glanced out of the wall-to-wall window and faced
Hong Kong Island and the dominating Peak, the tallest mountain on the
island. The city, called Victoria after Queen Victoria, began at the shore-
line, then rose, tier on tier, on the skirts of the sharply rising mountain,
lessening as the slopes soared, but there were apartment buildings near the
crest. She could see one just above the terminal of the Peak's funicular.
The view from there must be fantastic, she thought absently.

The blue water was sparkling nicely, the harbor as traffic-bound as the
streets of Kowloon below. Liners and freighters were anchored or tied up
alongside the wharves of Kowloon or steaming out or in, their sirens
sounding merrily. Over at the dockyard Hong Kong side was a Royal
Navy destroyer and, nearby at anchor, a dark-gray U.S. Navy frigate.
There were hundreds of junks of every size and age—fishing vessels mostly
—some powered, some ponderously sailing this way and that. Crammed
double-decker ferries darted in and out of the traffic like so many drag-
onflies, and everywhere tiny sampans, oared or powered, scurried unafraid across the ordered sea-lanes.

Where do all these people live? she asked herself, appalled. And how do
they support themselves?

A room boy opened the door with his passkey, without knocking, and
Linc Bartlett strode in. "You look great, Casey," he said, shutting the door
behind him.

"So do you. This gun thing's bad, isn't it?"

"Anyone here? Any maids in the rooms?"

"We're alone, but the houseboys seem to come in and out as they please."

"This one had his key out before I reached the door." Linc told her what had happened at the airport. Then he dropped his voice. "What about John Chen?"

"Nothing. He just made nervous, light conversation. He didn't want to talk shop. I don't think he'd recovered from the fact that I'd turned out to be a woman. He dropped me at the hotel and said they'd send a car at 9:15."

"So the plan worked fine?"

"Very fine."

"Good. Did you get it?"

"No. I said I was authorized by you to take delivery and offered the initial sight draft. But he pretended to be surprised and said he'd talk to you privately when he drives you back after the lunch. He seemed very nervous."

"Doesn't matter. Your car'll be here in a few minutes. I'll see you at lunch."

"Should I mention the guns to Struan's? To Dunross?"

"No. Let's wait and see who brings it up."

"You think it might be them?"

"Easily. They knew our flight plan, and they've a motive."

"What?"

"To discredit us."

"But why?"

"Maybe they think they know our battle plan."

"But then wouldn't it have been much wiser for them not to do anything—to sucker us in."

"Maybe. But this way they've made the opening move. Day One: Knight to King Bishop 3. The attack's launched on us."

"Yes. But by whom—and are we playing White or Black?"

His eyes hardened and lost their friendliness. "I don't care, Casey, as long as we win." He left.

Something's up, she told herself. Something dangerous he's not telling me about.

"Secrecy's vital, Casey," he had said back in the early days. "Napoleon, Caesar, Patton—any of the great generals—often hid their *real* plan from their staff. Just to keep them—and therefore enemy spies—off balance. If I withhold from you it's not mistrust, Casey. But you must never withhold from me."

"That's not fair."

"Life's not fair. Death's not fair. War's not fair. Big business is war. I'm playing it like it was war and that's why I'm going to win."

"Win what?"

"I want Par-Con Industries bigger than General Motors and Exxon combined."

"Why?"

"For my goddamn pleasure."

"Now tell me the real reason."

"Ah, Casey, that's why I love you. You listen and you know."

"Ah, Raider, I love you too."

Then they had both laughed together for they knew they did not love the other, not in the ordinary sense of that word. They had agreed, way back in the beginning, to put aside the ordinary for the extraordinary. For seven years.

Casey looked out of the window at the harbor and the ships in the harbor.

Crush, destroy, and win. Big Business, the most exciting Monopoly game in the world. And my leader's Raider Bartlett, Mastercraftsman. But time's running out on us, Linc. This year, the seventh year, the last year ends on my birthday, November 25, my twenty-seventh birthday. . . .

Her ears heard the half knock and the passkey in the lock and she turned to say come in but the starched houseboy was already in.

"Morning Missee I'm Number One Houseboy Daytime Chang." Chang was gray haired and solicitous. He beamed. "Tidy room plees?"

"Don't any of you ever wait for someone to say come in?" she asked sharply.

Chang stared at her blankly. "Missee?"

"Oh never mind," she said wearily.

"Pretty day, *heya*? Which first, Master's room or Missee's?"

"Mine. Mr. Bartlett hasn't used his yet."

Chang grinned toothily. *Ayeeyah*, did you and Master tumble together in yours, Missee, before he went out? But there were only fourteen minutes between Master's arrival and leaving and certainly he did not look flushed when he went away.

Ayeeyah, first it's supposed to be two men foreign devils sharing my suite and then one's a she—confirmed by Nighttime Ng, who of course went through her luggage and found serious proof that she was a true she —proof reconfirmed this morning with great gusto by Third Toiletmaid Fung.

Golden pubics! How vile!

And Golden Pubics is not only *not* the Master's chief wife—she is not even a second wife, and oh ko, worst of all she did not have the good manners to pretend she was so the hotel rules could be honored and everyone save face.

Chang chortled, for this hotel had always had astounding rules about ladies in men's rooms—oh gods what else is a bed for?—and now a female was living openly in barbarian sin! Oh how tempers had soared last night.

Barbarians! *Dew neh loh moh* on all barbarians! But this one is surely a dragon because she stared down the Eurasian assistant manager, and the Eurasian night manager, and even old mealy-mouth, Chief Manager Big Wind himself.

"No no no," he had wailed, so Chang had been told.

"Yes yes yes," she had replied, insisting that she have the adjoining half of the Fragrant Spring suite.

It was then that Honorable Mong, chief porter and chief triad and therefore leader of the hotel, solved the unsolvable. "The Fragrant Spring suite has three doors, *heya?*" he had said. "One for each bedroom, one for the main room. Let her be shown into Fragrant Spring B which is the inferior room anyway, through its own door. But the inner door to the main sitting room and thence to the Master's quarters shall be tight locked. But let a key be left nearby. If the mealy-mouthed whore unlocks the door herself . . . what can one do? And then, if there happens to be a mix-up in bookings tomorrow or the next day and our honorable chief manager has to ask the billionaire and his strumpet from the Land of the Golden Mountain to leave, well so sorry never mind, we have bookings enough and to spare and our face to protect."

And so it was done.

The outer door to B was unlocked and Golden Pubics invited in. That she took up the key and at once unlocked the inner door—who is to say? That the door is open now, well, certainly I would never tell any outsider, my lips are sealed. As always.

Ayeeyah, but though outer doors may be locked and be prudish, the inner ones may be flung wide and be luscious. Like her Jade Gate, he thought pensively. *Dew neh loh moh* I wonder what it would be like to storm a Jade Gate the size of hers? "Make bed, Missee?" he asked sweetly in English.

"Go right ahead."

Oh how truly awful the sound of their barbarian tongue is. Ugh!

Daytime Chang would have hawked and cleared the spit god from his mouth, but that was against hotel rules.

"*Heya*, Daytime Chang," Third Toiletmaid Fung said brightly as she came into the bedroom after knocking half-heartedly on the suite door long after she had opened it. "Yes, Missee, so sorry, Missee," in English, then again to Chang in Cantonese, "Haven't you finished yet? Is her dung so sweet you want to dawdle in her drawers?"

"*Dew neh loh moh* in yours, Sister. Watch your tongue or your old father may give you a good drubbing."

"The only drubbing your old mother wants, you can't help me with! Come on, let me help you make her bed quickly. There's a mah-jong game beginning in half an hour. Honorable Mong sent me for you."

"Oh, thank you, Sister. *Heya*, did you really see her pubics?"

"Haven't I told you already? Am I a liar? They're pure golden, lighter than her head hair. She was in the bath and I was as close as we are now. And, oh yes, her nipples're pinkish, not brown."

"Eeee! Imagine!"

"Just like a sow's."

"How awful!"

"Yes. Did you read today's *Commercial Daily?*"

"No, Sister, not yet. Why?"

"Well their astrologer says this is a very good week for me and today the financial editor says it looks as though there's a new boom beginning."

"*Dew neh loh moh* you don't say!"

"So I told my broker this morning to buy a thousand more Noble House, the same Golden Ferry, 40 of Second Great House and 50 Good Luck Properties. My bankers are generous but now I haven't a single brass cash left in Hong Kong I can beg or borrow!"

"Eeeee, you're plunging, Sister. I'm stretched out myself. Last week I borrowed from the bank on my shares and bought another 600 Noble House. That was Tuesday. I bought in at 25.23!"

"*Ayeeyah*, Honorable Chang, they were 29.14 at close last night." Third Toiletmaid Fung made an automatic calculation. "You're already 2,348 Hong Kong ahead! And they say Noble House's going to bid for Good Luck Properties. If they try, it will send their enemies' rage to boiling point. Ha! The tai-pan of Second Great House will fart dust!"

"Oh oh oh but meanwhile the shares will skyrocket! Of all three companies! Ha! *Dew neh loh moh*, where can I get more cash?"

"The races, Daytime Chang! Borrow 500 against your present winnings and put it on the daily double on Saturday or the double quinella. 4 and 5 are my lucky numbers. . . ."

They both looked up as Casey came into the bedroom. Chang switched to English. "Yes Missee?"

"There's some laundry in the bathroom. Can you have it picked up, please?"

"Oh yes I fix. Today six o'clock come by okay never mind." These foreign devils are so stupid, Chang thought contemptuously. What am I, an empty-headed dung heap? Of course I'll take care of the laundry if there's laundry.

"Thank you."

They both watched fascinated as she checked her makeup in the bedroom mirror, preparing to leave.

"Her tits don't droop at all, do they, Sister?" Chang said. "Pink nipples *heya?* Extraordinary!"

"Just like a sow's, I told you. Are your ears merely pots to piss in?"

"In your ear, Third Toiletmaid Fung."

"Has she tipped you yet?"

"No. The Master gave too much and she nothing. Disgusting *heya?*"

"Yes. What can you do? People from the Golden Mountain are really very uncivilized, aren't they, Daytime Chang?"

5

The tai-pan came over the rise and barreled down the Peak Road in his E-Type Jaguar, going east toward Magazine Gap. On the winding road there was but a single lane each side with few places to pass and precipitous on most corners. Today the surface was dry and, knowing the way so well, Ian Dunross rode the bends fast and sweetly, hugging the mountainside, his scarlet convertible tight to the inside curve. He did a racing shift down and braked hard as he swooped a bend and came up to an ancient, slow-moving truck. He waited patiently, then, at the perfect moment, swung out onto the wrong side and was past safely before the oncoming car had rounded the blind corner ahead.

Now Dunross was clear for a short stretch and could see that the snaking road ahead was empty. He jammed his foot down and slid some corners, usurping the whole of the road, taking the straightest line, using hand and eye and foot and brake and gearshift in unison, feeling the vast power of the engine and the wheels in all of him. Ahead, suddenly, was an oncoming truck from the far corner and his freedom vanished. He geared down and braked in split-second time, hugging his side, regretting the loss of freedom, then accelerated and was away again into more treacherous bends. Now another truck, this time ladened with passengers, and he waited a few yards behind, knowing there was no place to pass for a while. Then one of the passengers noticed his number plate, 1-1010, and she pointed and they all looked, chattering excitedly one to another, and one of them banged on the cabin of the truck. The driver obligingly squeezed off the road onto the tiny shoulder and flagged him on. Dunross made sure he was safe then passed, waving to them with a grin.

More corners, the speed and the waiting-to-pass and the passing and the danger pleasing him. Then he cut left into Magazine Gap Road, down the hill, the bends trickier, the traffic building up now and slower. He overtook a taxi and jumped three cars very fast and was back in line

though still over the speed limit when he saw the traffic motorcycle policemen waiting ahead. He changed down and passed them going the regulation 30 mph. He waved good-naturedly. They waved back.

"You really must slow down, Ian," his friend, Henry Foxwell, Senior
Superintendent of Traffic, had said recently. "You really should."

"I've never had an accident—yet. Or a ticket."

"Good God, Ian, there's not a traffic copper on the island who'd dare
give you one! You, *the* tai-pan? Perish the thought. I meant for your own
good. Keep that speed devil of yours bottled for Monaco, or your Macao
Road Race."

"Monaco's professional. I don't take chances, and I don't drive that fast
anyway."

"67 mph over Wongniechong isn't exactly slow, old chap. Admittedly it
was 4:23 A.M. on an almost empty road. But it is a 30 mph zone."

"There're lots of E-Types in Hong Kong."

"Yes, I agree. Seven. Scarlet convertibles with a special number plate?
With a black canvas roof, racing wheels and tires, that goes like the
clappers of hell? It was last Thursday, old chap. Radar and all that. You'd
been to . . . to visit friends. In Sinclair Road I believe."

Dunross had contained his sudden rage. "Oh?" he said, the surface of
his face smiling. "Thursday? I seem to remember I had dinner with John
Chen then. At his apartment in Sinclair Towers. But I thought I was
home long before 4:23."

"Oh I'm sure you were. I'm sure the constable got the number plate
and color and everything all wrong." Foxwell clapped him on the back in
friendly style. "Even so, slow down a little will you? It'd be so boring if
you killed yourself during my term. Wait till I'm transferred back to Special Branch—or the police college, eh? Yes, I'm sure he made a mistake."

But there was no mistake, Dunross had said to himself. You know it, I
know it, and John Chen would know it and so would Wei-wei.

So you fellows know about Wei-wei! That's interesting.

"Are you fellows watching me?" he had asked bluntly.

"Good God no!" Foxwell had been shocked. "Special Intelligence was
watching a villain who's got a flat at Sinclair Towers. You happened to be
seen. You're very important here, you know that. I happened to pick it up
through channels. You know how it is."

"No, I don't."

"They say one word to the wise is sufficient, old chap."

"Yes they do. So perhaps you'd better tell your Intelligence fellows to
be more intelligent in future."

"Fortunately they're very discreet."

"Even so I wouldn't like my movements a matter of record."

"I'm sure they're not. Not a matter of record."

"Good. What villain in Sinclair Towers?"

"One of our important capitalist dogs but suspected secret Commie fellows. Very boring but SI have to earn their daily bread, don't they?"

"Do I know him?"

"I imagine you know everyone."

"Shanghainese or Cantonese?"

"What makes you think he's either?"

"Ah, then he's European?"

"He's just a villain, Ian. Sorry, it's all very hush-hush at the moment."

"Come on, we own that block. Who? I won't tell anyone."

"I know. Sorry old boy, but I can't. However, I've another hypothetical idea for you. Say a hypothetical married VIP had a lady friend whose uncle happened to be the undercover deputy chief of the illegal Kuomintang Secret Police for Hong Kong. Say, hypothetically, the Kuomintang wanted this VIP on their side. Certainly he could be pressured by such a lady. Couldn't he?"

"Yes," Dunross had said easily. "If he was stupid." He already knew about Wei-wei Jen's uncle and had met him at a number of private parties several times in Taipei. And liked him. No problem there, he had thought, because she's not my mistress or even a lady friend, however beautiful and desirable. And tempting.

He smiled to himself as he drove in the stream of traffic down Magazine Gap Road then waited in line to circle the roundabout and head down Garden Road toward Central, half a mile below, and to the sea.

Now he could see the soaring modern office block that was Struan's. It was twenty-two stories high and fronted Connaught Road and the sea, almost opposite the Terminal of the Golden Ferries that plied between Hong Kong and Kowloon. As always, the sight pleased him.

He weaved in and out of heavy traffic where he could, crawled past the Hilton Hotel and the Cricket Ground on his left, then turned into Connaught Road, the sidewalks jammed with pedestrians. He stopped outside his front entrance.

This's the big day, he thought. The Americans have arrived.

And, with joss, Bartlett's the noose that'll strangle Quillan Gornt once and for all time. Christ, if we can pull this off!

"Morning, sir." The uniformed doorman saluted crisply.

"Morning, Tom." Dunross eased himself out of the low-slung car and ran up the marble steps, two at a time, toward the huge glass entrance. Another doorman drove the car off to its underground parking and still another opened the glass door for him. He caught the reflection of the Rolls drawing up. Recognizing it, he glanced back. Casey got out and he whistled involuntarily. She carried a briefcase. Her sea-green silk suit was tailored and very conservative, but even so, it hid none of the trim of her figure or the dance to her stride and the sea green enhanced the tawny gold of her hair.

She looked around, feeling his eyes. Her recognition was immediate and she measured him as he measured her and though the instant was short it seemed long to both of them. Long and leisurely.

She moved first and walked toward him. He met her halfway.

"Hello, Mr. Dunross."

"Hello. We've never met, have we?"

"No. But you're easy to recognize from your photos. I didn't expect to have the pleasure of meeting you till later. I'm Cas—"

"Yes," he said and grinned. "I had a deranged call from John Chen last night. Welcome to Hong Kong, Miss Tcholok. It is Miss, isn't it?"

"Yes. I hope my being a woman won't upset things too much."

"Oh yes it will, very much. But we'll try to accommodate the problem. Would you and Mr. Bartlett care to be my guests at the races on Saturday? Lunch and all that?"

"I think that would be lovely. But I have to check with Linc—may I confirm this afternoon?"

"Of course." He looked down at her. She looked back. The doorman still held the door open.

"Well, come along, Miss Tcholok, and let battle commence."

She glanced at him quickly. "Why should we battle? We're here to do business."

"Oh yes, of course. Sorry, it's just a Sam Ackroyd saying. I'll explain another time." He ushered her in and headed for the bank of elevators. The many people already lined up and waiting immediately moved aside for them to get into the first elevator, to Casey's embarrassment.

"Thanks," Dunross said, not noticing anything out of the ordinary. He guided her in, pressed 20, the top button, noticing absently that she wore no perfume or jewelry, just a thin gold chain around her neck.

"Why's the front door at an angle?" she asked.

"Sorry?"

"The front entrance seems to be on a slight tilt—it's not quite straight—I was wondering why."

"You're very observant. The answer is *fung sui*. When the building was put up four years ago, somehow or other we forgot to consult our house *fung sui* man. He's like an astrologer, a man who specializes in heaven, earth, water currents, and devils, that sort of thing, and makes sure you're building on the Earth Dragon's back and not on his head."

"What?"

"Oh yes. You see every building in the whole of China's on some part of the Earth Dragon. To be on his back's perfect, but if you're on his head it's very bad, and terrible if you're on his eyeball. Anyway, when we did get around to asking, our *fung sui* man said we were on the Dragon's back —thank God, otherwise we'd've had to move—but that devils were getting in the door and this was what was causing all the trouble. He advised me to reposition the door, and so, under his direction we changed the angle and now the devils are all deflected."

She laughed. "Now tell me the real reason."

"*Fung sui*. We had very bad joss here—bad luck—rotten in fact until the door was changed." His face hardened momentarily then the shadow passed. "The moment we changed the angle, everything became good again."

"You're telling me you really believe that? Devils and dragons?"

"I believe none of it. But you learn the hard way when you're in China that it's best to act a little Chinese. Never forget that though Hong Kong's British it's still China."

"Did you learn th—"

The elevator stopped and opened on a paneled hallway and a desk and a neat, efficient Chinese receptionist. Her eyes priced Casey's clothes and jewelry instantly.

Cow, Casey thought, reading her loud and clear, and smiled back as sweetly.

"Morning, tai-pan," the receptionist said smoothly.

"Mary, this is Miss K. C. Tcholok. Please show her into Mr. Struan's office."

"Oh but—" Mary Li tried to cover her shock. "They're, they're waiting for a . . ." She picked up the phone but he stopped her. "Just show her in. Now. No need to announce her." He turned back to Casey and smiled. "You're launched. I'll see you shortly."

"Yes, thanks. See you."

"Please follow me, Miss Tchuluck," Mary Li said and started down the hall, her *chong-sam* tight and slit high on her thighs, long silk-stockinged legs and saucy walk. Casey watched her for a moment. It must be the cut that makes their walk so blatantly sexual, she thought, amused by such obviousness. She glanced at Dunross and raised an eyebrow.

He grinned. "See you later, Miss Tcholok."

"Please call me Casey."

"Perhaps I'd prefer Kamalian Ciranoush."

She gaped at him. "How do you know my names? I doubt if even Linc remembers."

"Ah, it pays to have friends in high places, doesn't it?" he said with a smile. "*À bientôt.*"

"*Oui, merci*," she replied automatically.

He strode for the elevator opposite and pressed the button. The doors opened instantly and closed after him.

Thoughtfully Casey walked after Mary Li who was waiting, ears still tuned for every nuance.

Inside the elevator Dunross took out a key and inserted it into the lock and twisted it. Now the elevator was activated. It serviced the top two floors only. He pressed the lower button. Only three other persons had similar keys: Claudia Chen, his executive secretary; his personal secretary, Sandra Yi; and his Number One Houseboy, Lim Chu.

The twenty-first floor contained his private offices, and the Inner Court boardroom. The twenty-second, the penthouse, was the tai-pan's personal suite. And he alone had the key to the last private elevator that connected the basement garage directly with the penthouse.

"Ian," his predecessor tai-pan, Alastair Struan, had said when he handed over the keys after Phillip Chen had left them, "your privacy's the most valuable thing you have. That too Dirk Struan laid down in his legacy and how wise he was! Never forget, the private lifts aren't for luxury or ostentation, any more than the tai-pan's suite is. They're there just to give you the measure of secrecy you'll need, perhaps even a place to hide yourself. You'll understand better after you've read the legacy and been through the tai-pan's safe. Guard that safe with all you've got. You can't be too careful, there's lots of secrets there—too many I think sometimes— and some are not so pretty."

"I hope I won't fail," he had said politely, detesting his cousin, his excitement huge that at long last he had the prize he had worked so hard to achieve and gambled so much for.

"You won't. Not you," the old man had said tautly. "You've been tested, and you've wanted the job ever since you could think. Eh?"

"Yes," Dunross had said. "I've tried to train for it. Yes. I'm only surprised you've given it to me."

"You're being given the ultimate in Struan's not because of your birthright—that only made you eligible for the Inner Court—but because I think you're the best we've got to follow me, and you've been conniving and pushing and shoving for years. That's the truth, isn't it?"

"Struan's needs changing. Let's have more truth: The Noble House is in a mess. It's not all your fault, there was the war, then Korea, then Suez —you've had bad joss for several years. It'll take years to make us safe. If Quillan Gornt—or any one of twenty enemies—knew half the truth, knew how far we're overextended, we'd be drowned in our own useless paper within the week."

"Our paper's good—it's not useless! You're exaggerating—as usual!"

"It's worth twenty cents on the dollar because we've insufficient capital, not enough cash flow and we're absolutely in mortal danger."

"Rubbish!"

"Is it?" Dunross's voice had sharpened for the first time. "Rothwell-Gornt could swallow us in a month if they knew the value of our present accounts receivable, against our pressing liabilities."

The old man had just stared at him without answering. Then he said, "It's a temporary condition. Seasonable and temporary."

"Rubbish! You know very well you're giving me the job because I'm the only man who can clean up the mess you leave, you, my father, and your brother."

"Aye, I'm gambling you can. That's true enough," Alastair had flared at him. "Aye. You've surely got the right amount of Devil Struan in your blood to serve that master if you've a mind."

"Thank you. I admit I'll let nothing stand in my way. And since this is a night for truth, I can tell you why you've always hated me, why my own father has also hated me."

"Can you now?"

"Yes. It's because I survived the war and your son didn't and your nephew, Linbar, the last of your branch of the Struan's, is a nice lad but useless. Yes, I survived but my poor brothers didn't, and that's still sending my father around the bend. It's the truth, isn't it?"

"Yes," Alastair Struan had said. "Aye, I'm afraid it is."

"I'm not afraid it is. I'm not afraid of anything. Granny Dunross saw to that."

"*Heya*, tai-pan," Claudia Chen said brightly as the elevator door opened. She was a jolly, gray-haired Eurasian woman in her mid-sixties, and she sat behind a huge desk that dominated the twenty-first-floor foyer. She had served the Noble House for forty-two years and succeeding tai-pans, exclusively, for twenty-five of them. "*Neh hoh mah?*" How're you?

"*Ho ho,*" he replied absently. Good. Then in English, "Did Bartlett call?"

"No." She frowned. "He's not expected until lunch. Do you want me to try to reach him?"

"No, never mind. What about my call to Foster in Sydney?"

"That's not through either. Or your call to Mr. MacStruan in Edinburgh. Something's troubling you?" she asked, having instantly sensed his mood.

"What? Oh, no, nothing." He threw off his tension and walked past her desk into his office that overlooked the harbor and sat in an easy chair beside the phone. She closed the door and sat down nearby, her notepad ready.

"I was just remembering my D Day," he said. "The day I took over."

"Oh. Joss, tai-pan."

"Yes."

"Joss," she repeated, "and a long time ago."

He laughed. "Long time? It's forty lifetimes. It's barely three years but the whole world's changed and it's going so fast. What's the next couple of years going to be like?"

"More of the same, tai-pan. I hear you met Miss Casey Tcholok at our front door."

"Eh, who told you that?" he asked sharply.

"Great good God, tai-pan, I can't reveal my sources. But I heard you stared at her and she stared at you. *Heya?*"

"Nonsense! Who told you about her?"

"Last night I called the hotel to see that everything was all right. The manager told me. Do you know that silly man was going to be 'over-booked'? Huh, if they share a suite or a bed or don't, never mind I told him. This is 1963 and the modern age with lots of liberations, and anyway it's a fine suite with two entrances and separate rooms and most important they're our guests." She chortled. "I pulled a little rank. . . . *Ayeeyah*, power is a pretty toy."

"Did you tell young Linbar or the others, about K. C. being female?"

"No. No one. I knew you knew. Barbara Chen told me Master John had already phoned you about Casey Tcholok. What's she like?"

"*Beddable* would be one word," he said and grinned.

"Yes—but what else?"

Dunross thought a moment. "She's very attractive, very well dressed—though subdued today, for our benefit I imagine. Very confident and very observant—she noticed the front door was out of whack and asked about it." He picked up an ivory paper knife and toyed with it. "John didn't like her at all. He said he'd bet she was one of those pathetic American women who're like California fruit: great to look at, with plenty of body, but no taste whatsoever!"

"Poor Master John, much as he likes America, he does prefer certain, er, aspects of Asia!"

Dunross laughed. "How clever a negotiator she is we'll soon find out." He smiled. "I sent her in unannounced."

"I'll wager 50 HK at least one of them knew in advance she was a she."

"Phillip Chen of course—but that old fox wouldn't tell the others. A hundred says neither Linbar, Jacques or Andrew Gavallan knew."

"Done," Claudia said happily. "You can pay me now, tai-pan. I checked very discreetly, this morning."

"Take it out of petty cash," he told her sourly.

"So sorry." She held out her hand. "A bet is a bet, tai-pan."

Reluctantly he gave her the red one-hundred-dollar note.

"Thank you. Now, a hundred says Casey Tcholok will walk all over Master Linbar, Master Jacques and Andrew Gavallan."

"What do you know?" he asked her suspiciously. "Eh?"

"A hundred?"

"All right."

"Excellent!" she said briskly, changing the subject. "What about the dinners for Mr. Bartlett? The golf match and the trip to Taipei? Of course, you can't take a woman along on those. Shall I cancel them?"

"No. I'll talk to Bartlett—he'll understand. I did invite her to Saturday's races though, with him."

"Oh, that's two too many. I'll cancel the Pangs, they won't mind. Do you want to sit them together at your table?"

Dunross frowned. "She should be at my table, guest of honor, and sit him next to Penelope, guest of honor."

"Very well. I'll call Mrs. Dunross and tell her. Oh and Barbara—Master John's wife—wants to talk with you." Claudia sighed and smoothed a crease in her neat dark blue *chong-sam*. "Master John didn't come back last night—not that that's anything out of the ordinary. But it's 10:10 now and I can't find him either. It seems he wasn't at Morning Prayers."

"Yes, I know. Since he dealt with Bartlett last night I told him to skip them." Morning Prayers was the jocular way that insiders in Struan's referred to the daily obligatory 8:00 A.M. meeting with the tai-pan of all managing directors of all Struan's subsidiaries. "No need for him to come today, there's nothing for him to do until lunch." Dunross pointed out of the window at the harbor. "He's probably on his boat. It's a great day for a sail."

"Her temperature's very high, tai-pan, even for her."

"Her temperature's always high, poor bugger! John's on his boat—or at Ming-li's flat. Did you try her flat?"

She sniffed. "Your father used to say a closed mouth catches no wee beasties. Even so, I suppose I can tell you now, Ming-li's been Number Two Girl Friend for almost two months. The new favorite calls herself Fragrant Flower, and she occupies one of his 'private flats' off Aberdeen Main Road."

"Ah, conveniently near his mooring!"

"Oh very yes. She's a flower all right, a Fallen Flower from the Good Luck Dragon Dance Hall in Wanchai. But she doesn't know where Master John is either. He didn't visit either of them though he had a date with Miss Fallen Flower, so she says, at midnight."

"How did you find out all this?" he asked, filled with admiration.

"Power, tai-pan—and a network of relations built up over five generations. How else do we survive, *heya?*" She chuckled. "Of course if you want a little real scandal, John Chen doesn't know she wasn't the virgin she and the broker claimed she was when he first pillowed her."

"Eh?"

"No. He paid the broker . . ." One of the phones rang and she picked it up and said "Please hold one moment," clicked on the hold button and continued happily in the same breath, ". . . 500 cash, U.S. dollars, but all her tears and all the, er, evidence, was a pretend. Poor fellow, but it serves him right, eh, tai-pan? What should a man like him at his age want virginity to nourish the yang for—he's only forty-two, *heya?*" She pressed the *on* connection. "Tai-pan's office, good morning," she said attentively.

He watched her. He was amused and bemused, astounded as always at her sources of information, pithy and otherwise, and her delight in knowing secrets. And passing them on. But only to clan members and special insiders.

"Just one moment please." She clicked the hold button. "Superintendent Armstrong would like to see you. He's downstairs with Superintendent Kwok. He's sorry to come without an appointment but could you spare them a moment?"

"Ah, the guns. Our police're getting more efficient every day," he said with a grim smile. "I didn't expect them till after lunch."

At seven this morning he had had a detailed report from Phillip Chen who had been called by one of the police sergeants who made the raid and was a relation of the Chens.

"You'd better put all our private sources on finding out the who and the why, Phillip," he had said, very concerned.

"I already have. It's too much of a coincidence that guns should be on Bartlett's plane."

"It could be highly embarrassing if we're found to be connected with it in any way."

"Yes."

He saw Claudia waiting patiently. "Ask Armstrong to give me ten minutes. Bring them up then."

She dealt with that, then said, "If Superintendent Kwok's been brought in so soon, it must be more serious than we thought, *heya*, tai-pan?"

"Special Branch or Special Intelligence has to be involved at once. I'll bet the FBI and CIA have already been contacted. Brian Kwok's logical because he's an old mate of Armstrong's—and one of the best they've got."

"Yes," Claudia agreed proudly. "Eeeee what a lovely husband he'd make for someone."

"Provided she's a Chen—all that extra power, *heya*?" It was common knowledge that Brian Kwok was being groomed to be the first Chinese assistant commissioner.

"Of course such power has to be kept in the family." The phone rang. She answered it. "Yes, I'll tell him, thank you." She replaced the phone huffily. "The governor's equerry—he called to remind you about cocktails at 6:00 P.M.—huh, as if I'd forget!"

Dunross picked up one of the phones and dialed.

"*Weyyyy?*" came the coarse voice of the *amah*, the Chinese servant. Hello?

"Chen *tai-tai*," he said into the phone, his Cantonese perfect. "Mrs. Chen please, this is Mr. Dunross."

He waited. "Ah, Barbara, good morning."

"Oh hello, Ian. Have you heard from John yet? Sorry to bother you," she said.

"No bother. No, not yet. But the moment I do I'll get him to call you. He might have gone down to the track early to watch Golden Lady work out. Have you tried the Turf Club?"

"Yes, but they don't remember him breakfasting there, and the workout's between 5:00 and 6:00. Damn him! He's so inconsiderate. *Ayeeyah*, men!"

"He's probably out on his boat. He's got nothing here until lunch and it's a great day for a sail. You know how he is—have you checked the mooring?"

"I can't, Ian, not without going there, there's no phone. I have a hairdressing appointment which I simply can't break—all Hong Kong will be at your party tonight—I simply can't go rushing off to Aberdeen."

"Send one of your chauffeurs," Dunross said dryly.

"Tang's off today and I need Wu-chat to drive me around, Ian. I simply can't send him over to Aberdeen—that could take an hour and I've a mah-jong game from two till four."

"I'll get John to call you. It'll be around lunch."

"I won't be back till five at the earliest. When I catch up with him he's going to get what for never mind. Oh well, thanks, sorry to bother you. 'Bye."

"'Bye." Dunross put the phone down and sighed. "I feel like a bloody nursemaid."

"Talk to John's father, tai-pan," Claudia Chen said.

"I have. Once. And that's enough. It's not all John's fault. That lady's enough to drive anyone bonkers." He grinned. "But I agree her temperature's gone to the moon—this time it's going to cost John an emerald ring or at least a mink coat."

The phone rang again. Claudia picked it up. "Hello, the tai-pan's office! Yes? Oh!" Her happiness vanished and she hardened. "Just a moment, please." She punched the hold button. "It's a person to person from Hiro Toda in Yokohama."

Dunross knew how she felt about him, knew she hated the Japanese and loathed the Noble House's connection with them. He could never forgive the Japanese either for what they had done to Asia during the war. To those they had conquered. To the defenseless. Men, women and children. The prison camps and unnecessary deaths. Soldier to soldier he had no quarrel with them. None. War was war.

His own war had been against the Germans. But Claudia's war had been here in Hong Kong. During the Japanese Occupation, because she was Eurasian, she had not been put into Stanley Prison with all European civilians. She and her sister and brother had tried to help the POWs with food and drugs and money, smuggling it into the camp. The Kampeitai, the Japanese military police, had caught her. Now she could have no children.

"Shall I say you're out?" she asked.

"No." Two years before Dunross had committed an enormous amount of capital to Toda Shipping Industries of Yokohama for two giant bulk ships to build up the Struan fleet that had been decimated in the war. He had chosen this Japanese shipyard because their product was the finest, their terms the best, they guaranteed delivery and all the things the British shipyards would not, and because he knew it was time to forget.

"Hello, Hiro," he said, liking the man personally. "Nice to hear from you. How's Japan?"

"Please excuse me for interrupting you, tai-pan. Japan's fine though hot and humid. No change."

"How're my ships coming along?"

"Perfectly, tai-pan. Everything is as we arranged. I just wanted to advise you that I will be coming to Hong Kong on Saturday morning for a business trip. I will be staying for the weekend, then on to Singapore and Sydney, back in time for our closing in Hong Kong. You'll still be coming to Yokohama for both launchings?"

"Oh yes. Yes, absolutely. What time do you arrive Saturday?"

"At 11:10, Japan Air Lines."

"I'll send a car to meet you. What about coming directly to Happy Valley to the races? You could join us for lunch, then my car will take you to the hotel. You're staying at the Victoria and Albert?"

"This time at the Hilton, Hong Kong side. Tai-pan, please excuse me, I do not wish to put you to any trouble, so sorry."

"It's nothing. I'll have one of my people meet you. Probably Andrew Gavallan."

"Ah, very good. Then thank you, tai-pan. I look forward to seeing you, so sorry to inconvenience you."

Dunross put the phone down. I wonder why he called, the real reason? he asked himself. Hiro Toda, managing director of the most go-ahead shipbuilding complex in Japan, never does anything suddenly or unpremeditated.

Dunross thought about the closing of their ship deal and the three payments of 2 million each that were due imminently on September 1, 11 and 15, the balance in ninety days. $12 million U.S. in all that he didn't have at the moment. Or the charterer's signed contract that was necessary to support the bank loan that he did not have, yet. "Never mind," he said easily, "everything's going to be fine."

"For them, yes," Claudia said. "You know I don't trust them, tai-pan. Any of them."

"You can't fault them, Claudia. They're only trying to do economically what they failed to do militarily."

"By pricing everyone out of the world markets."

"They're working hard, they're making profits and they'll bury us, if we let them." His eyes hardened too. "But after all, Claudia, scratch an Englishman—or a Scot—and find a pirate. If we're such bloody fools to allow it we deserve to go under—isn't that what Hong Kong's all about?"

"Why help the enemy?"

"They were the enemy," he said kindly. "But that was only for twenty-odd years and our connections there go back a hundred. Weren't we the first traders into Japan? Didn't Hag Struan buy us the first plot offered for sale in Yokohama in 1860? Didn't she order that it be a cornerstone of Struan's policy to have the China-Japan-Hong Kong triangle?"

"Yes, tai-pan, but don't you thi—"

"No, Claudia, we've dealt with the Todas, the Kasigis, the Toranagas for a hundred years, and right now Toda Shipping's very important to us."

The phone rang again. She answered it. "Yes, I'll phone him back." Then to Dunross. "It's the caterers—about your party tonight."

"What's the problem?"

"None, tai-pan—they're moaning. After all, it's *the* tai-pan's twentieth wedding anniversary. All Hong Kong will be there and all Hong Kong better be impressed." Again the phone rang. She picked it up. "Ahh good! Put him through. . . . It's Bill Foster from Sydney."

Dunross took the phone. "Bill . . . no, you were top of the list. Have you closed on the Woolara Properties deal yet? . . . What's the hold-up? . . . I don't care about that." He glanced at his watch. "It's just past noon your time. Call them right now and offer then fifty cents Australian more a share, the offer good till the close of business today. Get on to the bank in Sydney at once and tell them to demand full repayment of all their loans at the close of business today. . . . I couldn't care less, they're thirty days overdue already. I want control of that company now. Without it our new bulk-carrier charter deal will fall apart and we'll have to begin all over again. And catch the Qantas Flight 543 on Thursday. I'd like you here for a conference." He put the phone down. "Get Linbar up here as soon as the Tcholok meeting's over. Book him on Qantas 716 for Sydney on Friday morning."

"Yes, tai-pan." She made a note and handed him a list. "Here're your appointments for today."

He glanced at it. Four board meetings of some subsidiary companies this morning: Golden Ferry at 10:30, Struan's Motor Imports of Hong Kong at 11:00, Chong-Li Foods at 11:15 and Kowloon Investments at 11:30. Lunch with Lincoln Bartlett and Miss Casey Tcholok 12:40 to 2:00 P.M. More board meetings this afternoon, Peter Marlowe at 4:00 P.M., Phillip Chen at 4:20, cocktails at 6:00 with the governor, his anniversary party beginning at 8:00, a reminder to call Alastair Struan in Scotland at 11:00, and at least fifteen other people to phone throughout Asia during the day.

"Marlowe?" he asked.

"He's a writer, staying at the Vic—remember, he wrote for an appointment a week ago. He's researching a book on Hong Kong."

"Oh yes—the ex-RAF type."

"Yes. Would you like him put off?"

"No. Keep everything as arranged, Claudia." He took out a thin black leather memo-card case from his back pocket and gave her a dozen cards covered with his shorthand. "Here're some cables and telexes to send off at once and notes for the various board meetings. Get me Jen in Taipei, then Havergill at the bank, then run down the list."

"Yes, tai-pan. I hear Havergill's going to retire."

"Marvelous. Who's taking over?"

"No one knows yet."

"Let's hope it's Johnjohn. Put your spies to work. A hundred says I find out before you do!"

"Done!"

"Good." Dunross held out his hand and said sweetly, "You can pay me now. It's Johnjohn."

"Eh?" She stared at him.

"We decided it last night—all the directors. I asked them to tell no one until eleven today."

Reluctantly she took out the hundred-dollar note and offered it. "*Ayeeyah*, I was particularly attached to this note."

"Thank you," Dunross said and pocketed it. "I'm particularly attached to that one myself."

There was a knock on the door. "Yes?" he said.

The door was opened by Sandra Yi, his private secretary. "Excuse me, tai-pan, but the market's up two points and Holdbrook's on line two." Alan Holdbrook was head of their in-house stockbroking company.

Dunross punched the line two button. "Claudia, soon as I'm through bring in Armstrong." She left with Sandra Yi.

"Yes, Alan?"

"Morning, tai-pan. First: There's a heavy rumor that we're going to make a bid for control of Asian Properties."

"That's probably put out by Jason Plumm to boost his shares before their annual meeting. You know what a canny bastard he is."

"Our stock's gone up ten cents, perhaps on the strength of it."

"Good. Buy me 20,000 at once."

"On margin?"

"Of course on margin."

"All right. Second rumor: We've closed a multimillion-dollar deal with Par-Con Industries—huge expansion."

"Pipe dreams," Dunross said easily, wondering furiously where the leaks were. Only Phillip Chen—and in Edinburgh, Alastair Struan and old Sean MacStruan—was supposed to know about the ploy to smash Asian Properties. And the Par-Con deal was top secret to the Inner Court only.

"Third: Someone's buying large parcels of our stock."

"Who?"

"I don't know. But there's something smelly going on, tai-pan. The way our stock's been creeping up the last month . . . There's no reason that I know of, except a buyer, or buyers. Same with Rothwell-Gornt. I heard a block of 200,000 was bought offshore."

"Find out who."

"Christ, I wish I knew how. The market's jittery, and very nervous. A lot of Chinese money's floating around. Lots of little deals going on . . . a few shares here, a few there, but multiplied by a hundred thousand or so . . . the market might start to fall apart . . . or to soar."

"Good. Then we'll all make a killing. Give me a call before the market closes. Thanks, Alan." He put the phone down, feeling the sweat on his back. "Shit," he said aloud. "What the hell's going on?"

In the outer office Claudia Chen was going over some papers with Sandra Yi who was her niece on her mother's side—and smart, very good to look at, twenty-seven with a mind like an abacus. Then she glanced at her watch and said in Cantonese, "Superintendent Brian Kwok's downstairs, Little Sister, why don't you fetch him up—in six minutes."

"*Ayeeyah*, yes, Elder Sister!" Sandra Yi hastily checked her makeup and swished away. Claudia smiled after her and thought Sandra Yi would be perfect—a perfect choice for Brian Kwok. Happily she sat behind her desk and began to type the telexes. Everything's done that should be done, she told herself. No, something the tai-pan said . . . what was it? Ah yes! She dialed her home number.

"*Weyyyyy?*" said her *amah*, Ah Sam.

"Listen, Ah Sam," she said in Cantonese, "isn't Third Toiletmaid Fung at the Vic your cousin three times removed?"

"Oh yes, Mother," Ah Sam replied, using the Chinese politeness of servant to mistress. "But she's four times removed, and from the Fung-tats, not the Fung-sams which is my branch."

"Never mind that, Ah Sam. You call her and find out all you can about two foreign devils from the Golden Mountain. They're in Fragrant Spring suite." Patiently she spelled their names, then added delicately, "I hear they have peculiar pillow habits."

"*Ayeeyah*, if anyone can find out, Third Toiletmaid Fung can. Ha! What peculiars?"

"Strange peculiars, Ah Sam. You get on with it, little oily mouth." She beamed and hung up.

The elevator doors opened and Sandra Yi ushered the two police officers in, then left reluctantly. Brian Kwok watched her go. He was thirty-nine, tall for a Chinese, just over six foot, very handsome, with blue-black hair. Both men wore civilian clothes. Claudia chatted with them politely, but the moment she saw the light on line two go out she ushered them in and closed the door.

"Sorry to come without an appointment," Armstrong said.

"No sweat, Robert. You look tired."

"A heavy night. It's all the villainy that goes on in Hong Kong," Armstrong said easily. "Nasties abound and saints get crucified."

Dunross smiled, then glanced across at Kwok. "How's life treating you, Brian?"

Brian Kwok smiled back. "Very good, thanks, Ian. Stock market's up—I've a few dollars in the bank, my Porsche hasn't fallen apart yet, and ladies will be ladies."

"Thank God for that! Are you doing the hill climb on Sunday?"

"If I can get Lulu in shape. She's missing an offside hydraulic coupling."

"Have you tried our shop?"

"Yes. No joy, tai-pan. Are you going?"

"Depends. I've got to go to Taipei Sunday afternoon—I will if I've got time. I entered anyway. How's SI?"

Brian Kwok grinned. "It beats working for a living." Special Intelligence was a completely independent department within the elite, semi-secret Special Branch responsible for preventing and detecting subversive activities in the Colony. It had its own secret ways, secret funding and overriding powers. And it was responsible to the governor alone.

Dunross leaned back in the chair. "What's up?"

Armstrong said, "I'm sure you already know. It's about the guns on Bartlett's plane."

"Oh yes, I heard this morning," he said. "How can I help? Have you any idea why and where they were destined? And by whom? You caught two men?"

Armstrong sighed. "Yes. They were genuine mechanics all right—both ex-Nationalist Air Force trained. No previous record, though they're suspected of being members of secret triads. Both have been here since the exodus of '49. By the way, can we keep this all confidential, between the three of us?"

"What about your superiors?"

"I'd like to include them in—but keep it just for your ears only."

"Why?"

"We have reason to believe the guns were destined for someone in Struan's."

"Who?" Dunross asked sharply.

"Confidential?"

"Yes. Who?"

"How much do you know about Lincoln Bartlett and Casey Tcholok?"

"We've a detailed dossier on him—not on her. Would you like it? I can give you a copy, providing it too is kept confidential."

"Of course. That would be very helpful."

Dunross pressed the intercom.

"Yes sir?" Claudia asked.

"Make a copy of the Bartlett dossier and give it to Superintendent Armstrong on his way out." Dunross clicked the intercom off.

"We won't take much more of your time," Armstrong said. "Do you always dossier potential clients?"

"No. But we like to know who we're dealing with. If the Bartlett deal goes through it could mean millions to us, to him, a thousand new jobs to Hong Kong—factories here, warehouses, a very big expansion—along with equally big risks to us. Everyone in business does a confidential financial statement—perhaps we're a bit more thorough. I'll bet you fifty dollars to a broken hatpin he's done one on me."

"No criminal connections mentioned?"

Dunross was startled. "Mafia? That sort of thing? Good God no, nothing. Besides, if the Mafia were trying to come in here they wouldn't send a mere ten M14 rifles and two thousand rounds and a box of grenades."

"Your information's damn good," Brian Kwok interrupted. "Too damn good. We only unpacked the stuff an hour ago. Who's your informant?"

"You know there're no secrets in Hong Kong."

"Can't even trust your own coppers these days."

"The Mafia would surely send in a shipment twenty times that and they'd be handguns, American style. But the Mafia would be bound to fail here, whatever they did. They could never displace our triads. No, it can't be Mafia—only someone local. Who tipped you about the shipment, Brian?"

"Tokyo Airport Police," Kwok said. "One of their mechanics was doing a routine inspection—you know how thorough they are. He reported it to his superior, their police phoned us and we said to let it through."

"In that case get hold of the FBI and the CIA—get them to check back to Honolulu—or Los Angeles."

"You went through the flight plan too?"

"Of course. That's obvious. Why someone in Struan's?"

"Both of the villains said . . ." Armstrong took out his pad and referred to it. "Our question was, 'Where were you to take the packages?' Both answered using different words: 'To 15 go-down, we were to put the packages in Bay 7 at the back.'" He looked up at Dunross.

"That proves nothing. We've the biggest warehouse operation at Kai Tak—just because they take it to one of our go-downs proves nothing—other than they're smart. We've got so much merchandise going through, it'd be easy to send in an alien truck." Dunross thought a moment. "15's right at the exit—perfect placing." He reached for the phone. "I'll put my security folk on it right n—"

"Would you not, please, just for the moment."

"Why?"

"Our next question," Armstrong continued, "was, 'Who employed you?' Of course they gave fictitious names and descriptions and denied everything but they'll be more helpful soon." He smiled grimly. "One of them did say, however, when one of my sergeants was twisting his ear a little, figuratively speaking of course"—he read from the pad—"'You leave me alone, I've got very important friends!' 'You've no friends in the world,' the sergeant said. 'Maybe, but the Honorable Tsu-yan has and Noble House Chen has.'"

The silence became long and heavy. They waited.

Those God-cursed guns, Dunross thought furiously. But he held his face calm and his wits sharpened. "We've a hundred and more Chens working for us, related, unrelated—Chen's as common a name as Smith."

"And Tsu-yan?" Brian Kwok asked.

Dunross shrugged. "He's a director of Struan's—but he's also a director of Blacs, the Victoria Bank and forty other companies, one of the richest men in Hong Kong and a name anyone in Asia could pull out of a hat. Like Noble House Chen."

"Do you know he's suspected of being very high up in the triad hierarchy—specifically in the Green Pang?" Brian Kwok asked.

"Every important Shanghainese's equally suspect. Jesus Christ, Brian, you know Chiang Kai-shek was supposed to have given Shanghai to the Green Pang years ago as their exclusive bailiwick if they'd support his northern campaign against the warlords. Isn't the Green Pang still, more or less, an official Nationalist secret society?"

Brian Kwok said, "Where'd Tsu-yan make his money, Ian? His first fortune?"

"I don't know. You tell me, Brian."

"He made it during the Korean War smuggling penicillin, drugs and petrol—mostly penicillin—across the border to the Communists. Before Korea all he owned was a loincloth and a broken-down rickshaw."

"That's all hearsay, Brian."

"Struan's made a fortune too."

"Yes. But it would really be very unwise to imply we did it smuggling—publicly or privately," Dunross said mildly. "Very unwise indeed."

"Didn't you?"

"Struan's began with a little smuggling 120-odd years ago, so rumor has it, but it was an honorable profession and never against British law. We're law-abiding capitalists and China Traders and have been for years."

Brian Kwok did not smile. "More hearsay's that a lot of his penicillin was bad. Very bad."

"If it was, if that's the truth, then please go get him, Brian," Dunross said coldly. "Personally I think that's another rumor spread by jealous competitors. If it was true he'd be floating in the bay with the others who tried, or he'd be punished like Bad Powder Wong." He was referring to a Hong Kong smuggler who had sold a vast quantity of adulterated penicillin over the border during the Korean War and invested his fortune in stocks and land in Hong Kong. Within seven years he was very very rich. Then certain triads of Hong Kong were ordered to balance the books. Every week one member of his family vanished, or died. By drowning, car accident, strangulation, poison or knife. No assailant was ever caught. The killing went on for seventeen months and three weeks and then stopped. Only he and one semi-imbecile infant grandson remained alive. They lived today, still holed up in the same vast, once luxurious penthouse apartment with one servant and one cook, in terror, guarded night and day, never going out—knowing that no guards or any amount of money could ever prevent the inexorability of his sentence published in a tiny box in a local Chinese newspaper: Bad Powder Wong will be punished, he and all his generations.

Brian Kwok said, "We interviewed that sod once, Robert and I."

"Oh?"

"Yes. Scary. Every door's double locked and chained, every window nailed up and boarded over with planks—just spy holes here and there. He hasn't been out since the killing started. The place stank, my God did it stink! All he does is play Chinese checkers with his grandson and watch television."

"And wait," Armstrong said. "One day they'll come for both of them. His grandson must be six or seven now."

Dunross said, "I think you prove my point. Tsu-yan's not like him and never was. And what possible use could Tsu-yan have for a few M14's? If he wanted to, I imagine he could muster half the Nationalist army along with a battalion of tanks."

"In Taiwan but not in Hong Kong."

"Has Tsu-yan ever been involved with Bartlett?" Armstrong asked. "In your negotiations?"

"Yes. He was in New York once and in Los Angeles on our behalf. Both times with John Chen. They initialed the agreement between Struan's and Par-Con Industries which is to be finalized—or abandoned—here this month, and they formally invited Bartlett to Hong Kong on my behalf."

Armstrong glanced at his Chinese partner. Then he said, "When was this?"

"Four months ago. It's taken that time for both sides to prepare all the details."

"John Chen, eh?" Armstrong said. "He certainly could be Noble House Chen."

"You know John's not the type," Dunross said. "There's no reason why he should be mixed up in such a ploy. It must be just coincidence."

"There's another curious coincidence," Brian Kwok said. "Tsu-yan and John Chen both know an American called Banastasio, at least both have been seen in his company. Does that name mean anything?"

"No. Who's he?"

"A big-time gambler and suspected racketeer. He's also supposed to be closely connected with one of the Cosa Nostra families. Vincenzo Banastasio."

Dunross's eyes narrowed. "You said, 'seen in his company.' Who did the seeing?"

"The FBI."

The silence thickened a little.

Armstrong reached into his pocket for a cigarette.

Dunross pushed across the silver cigarette box. "Here."

"Oh, thanks. No, I won't—I wasn't thinking. I've stopped for the last couple of weeks. It's a killer." Then he added, trying to curb the desire, "The FBI passed the info on to us because Tsu-yan and Mr. John Chen are so prominent here. They asked us to keep an eye on them."

Then Dunross suddenly remembered Foxwell's remark about a prominent capitalist who was a secret Communist that they were watching in Sinclair Towers. Christ, he thought, Tsu-yan's got a flat there, and so has John Chen. Surely it's impossible either'd be mixed up with Communists.

"Of course heroin's big business," Armstrong was saying, his voice very hard.

"What does that mean, Robert?"

"The drug racket requires huge amounts of money to finance it. That kind of money can only come from banks or bankers, covertly of course. Tsu-yan's on the board of a number of banks—so's Mr. Chen."

"Robert, you'd better go very slow on that sort of remark," Dunross grated. "You are drawing very dangerous conclusions without any proof whatsoever. That's actionable I'd imagine and I won't have it."

"You're right, sorry. I withdraw the coincidence. Even so, the drug trade's big business, and it's here in Hong Kong in abundance, mostly for ultimate U.S. consumption. Somehow I'm going to find out who our nasties are."

"That's commendable. And you'll have all the help you want from Struan's and me. I hate the traffic too."

"Oh I don't hate it, tai-pan, or the traffickers. It's a fact of life. It's just another business—illegal certainly but still a business. I've been given the job of finding out who the tai-pans are. It's a matter of personal satisfaction, that's all."

"If you want help, just ask."

"Thank you." Armstrong got up wearily. "Before we go there're a couple more coincidences for you. When Tsu-yan and Noble House Chen were named this morning we thought we'd like to chat with them right away, but shortly after we ambushed the guns Tsu-yan caught the early flight to Taipei. Curious, eh?"

"He's back and forth all the time," Dunross said, his disquiet soaring. Tsu-yan was expected at his party this evening. It would be extraordinary if he did not appear.

Armstrong nodded. "It seems it was a last-minute decision—no reservation, no ticket, no luggage, just a few extra dollars under the counter and someone was bounced off and him on. He was carrying only a briefcase. Strange, eh?"

Brian Kwok said, "We haven't a hope in hell of extraditing him from Taiwan."

Dunross studied him then looked back at Armstrong, his eyes steady and the color of sea ice. "You said there were a couple of coincidences. What's the other?"

"We can't find John Chen."

"What're you talking about?"

"He's not at home, or at his lady friend's, or at any of his usual haunts. We've been watching him and Tsu-yan off and on for months, ever since the FBI tipped us."

The silence gathered. "You've checked his boat?" Dunross asked, sure that they had.

"She's at her moorings, hasn't been out since yesterday. His boat-boy hasn't seen him either."

"Golf course?"

"No, he's not there," Armstrong said. "Nor at the racetrack. He wasn't at the workout, though he was expected, his trainer said. He's gone, vanished, scarpered."

6

There was a stunned silence in the boardroom.

"What's wrong?" Casey asked. "The figures speak for themselves."

The four men around the table looked at her. Andrew Gavallan, Linbar Struan, Jacques deVille and Phillip Chen, all members of the Inner Court.

Andrew Gavallan was tall and thin and forty-seven. He glanced at the sheaf of papers in front of him. *Dew neh loh moh* on all women in business, he thought irritably. "Perhaps we should check with Mr. Bartlett," he said uneasily, still very unsettled that they were expected to deal with a woman.

"I've already told you I have authority in all these areas," she said, trying to be patient. "I'm treasurer and executive vice-president of Par-Con Industries and empowered to negotiate with you. We confirmed that in writing last month." Casey held her temper. The meeting had been very heavy going. From their initial shock that she was a woman to their inevitable, overpolite awkwardness, waiting for her to sit, waiting for her to talk, then not sitting until she had asked them to, making small talk, not wanting to get down to business, not wishing to negotiate with her as a person, a business person, at all, saying instead that their wives would be delighted to take her shopping, then gaping because she knew all the intimate details of their projected deal. It was all part of a pattern that, normally, she could deal with. But not today. Jesus, she thought, I've got to succeed. I've got to get through to them.

"It's really quite easy," she had said initially, trying to clear their awkwardness away, using her standard opening. "Forget that I'm a woman—judge me on my ability. Now, there are three subjects on our agenda: the polyurethane factories, our computer-leasing representation and last, general representation of our petrochemical products, fertilizers, pharmaceutical and sports goods throughout Asia. First let's sort out the polyurethane factories, the chemical mix supplies and a projected time schedule for the financing." At once she gave them graphics and prepared documentation, verbally synopsized all the facts, figures and percentages, bank charges and interest charges, simply and very quickly, so that even the slowest brain could grasp the project. And now they were staring at her.

Andrew Gavallan broke the silence. "That's . . . that's very impressive, my dear."

"Actually I'm not your 'dear,'" she said with a laugh. "I'm very hard-nosed for my corporation."

"But mademoiselle," Jacques deVille said with a suave Gallic charm, "your nose is perfect and not hard at all."

"*Merci, monsieur,*" she replied at once, and added lightly in passable French, "but please may we leave the shape of my nose for the moment and discuss the shape of this deal. It's better not to mix the two, don't you think?"

Another silence.

Linbar Struan said, "Would you like some coffee?"

"No thanks, Mr. Struan," Casey said, being careful to conform to their customs and not to call them by their Christian names too early. "May we zero in on this proposal? It's the one we sent you last month. . . . I've tried to cover your problems as well as ours."

There was another silence. Linbar Struan, thirty-four, very good-looking with sandy hair and blue eyes with a devil-may-care glint to them, persisted, "Are you sure you wouldn't like coffee? Tea perhaps?"

"No thanks. Then you accept our proposal as it stands?"

Phillip Chen coughed and said, "In principle we agree to want to be in business with Par-Con in several areas. The Heads of Agreement indicate that. As to the polyurethane factories . . ."

She listened to his generalizations, then once more tried to get to the specifics—the whole reason for this meeting. But the going was very hard and she could feel them squirming. This's the worst it's ever been. Perhaps it's because they're English, and I've never dealt with the English before.

"Is there anything specific that needs clarifying?" she asked. "If there's anything you don't understand . . ."

Gavallan said, "We understand very well. You present us with figures which are lopsided. We're financing the building of the factories. You provide the machines but their cost is amortized over three years which'll mess up any cash flow and mean no profits for five years at least."

"I'm told it is your custom in Hong Kong to amortize the full cost of a building over a three-year period," she replied equally sharply, glad to be challenged. "We're just proposing to follow your custom. If you want five —or ten years—you may have them, provided the same applies to the building."

"You're not paying for the machines—they're on a lease basis and the monthly charge to the joint venture is high."

"What's your bank prime rate today, Mr. Gavallan?"

They consulted, then told her. She used her pocket slide rule for a few seconds. "At today's rate you'd save 17,000 HK a week per machine if you take our deal which, over the period we're talking . . ." Another quick calculation. ". . . would jump your end of the profits 32 percent over the best you could do—and we're talking in millions of dollars."

They stared at her in silence.

Andrew Gavallan cross-questioned her about the figures but she never faltered. Their dislike for her increased.

Silence.

She was sure they were fogged by her figures. What else can I say to convince them? she thought, her anxiety growing. Struan's will make a bundle if they get off their asses, we'll make a fortune and I'll get my drop dead money at long last. The foam part of the deal alone will make Struan's rich and Par-Con nearly $80,000 net a month over the next ten years and Linc said I could have a piece.

"How much do you want?" he had asked her, just before they had left the States.

"51 percent," she had replied with a laugh, "since you're asking."

"3 percent."

"Come on, Linc, I need my drop dead money."

"Pull off the whole package and you've got a stock option of 100,000 Par-Con at four dollars below market."

"You're on. But I want the foam company too," she had said, holding her breath. "I started it and I want that. 51 percent. For me."

"In return for what?"

"Struan's."

"Done."

Casey waited outwardly calm. When she judged the moment correct she said innocently, "Are we agreed then, that our proposal stands as is? We're fifty-fifty with you, what could be better than that?"

"I still say you're not providing 50 percent of the financing of the joint venture," Andrew Gavallan replied sharply. "You're providing the machines and materials on a lease carry-back so your risk's not equivalent to ours."

"But that's for our tax purposes and to lessen the amount of cash outlay, gentlemen. We're financing from cash flow. The figures add up the same. The fact that we get a depreciation allowance and various rebates is neither here nor there." Even more innocently, baiting the trap, she added, "We finance in the States, where we've the expertise. You finance in Hong Kong where you're the experts."

* * *

Quillan Gornt turned back from his office window. "I repeat, we can better any arrangement you can make with Struan's, Mr. Bartlett. Any arrangement."

"You'd go dollar for dollar?"

"Dollar for dollar." The Englishman strolled back and sat behind his paperless desk and faced Bartlett again. They were on the top floor of the Rothwell-Gornt Building also fronting Connaught Road and the waterfront. Gornt was a thickset, hard-faced, bearded man, just under six feet, with graying black hair and graying bushy eyebrows and brown eyes. "It's no secret our companies are very serious rivals, but I assure you we can outbid them and outmatch them, and I'd arrange our side of the financing within the week. We could have a profitable partnership, you and I. I'd suggest we set up a joint company under Hong Kong law—the taxes here're really quite reasonable—15 percent of everything earned in Hong Kong, with the rest of the world free of all taxes." Gornt smiled. "Better than the U.S.A."

"Much better," Bartlett said. He was sitting in a high-backed leather chair. "Very much better."

"Is that why you're interested in Hong Kong?"

"One reason."

"What're the others?"

"There's no American outfit as big as mine here in strength yet, and there should be. This is the age of the Pacific. But you could benefit from our coming. We've a lot of expertise you don't have and a major say in areas of the U.S. market. On the other hand, Rothwell-Gornt—and Struan's—have the expertise we lack and a major say in the Asian markets."

"How can we cement a relationship?"

"First I have to find out what Struan's are after. I started negotiating with them, and I don't like changing airplanes in mid-ocean."

"I can tell you at once what they're after: profit for them and the hell with anyone else." Gornt's smile was hard.

"The deal we've discussed seems very fair."

"They're past masters at appearing to be very fair and putting up a half share, then selling out at their own choosing to skim the profit and yet retain control."

"That wouldn't be possible with us."

"They've been at it for almost a century and a half. They've learned a few tricks by now."

"So've you."

"Of course. But Struan's is very different from us. We own things and companies—they're percentagers. They've little more than a 5 percent holding in most of their subsidiaries yet they still exercise absolute control by special voting shares, or by making it mandatory in the Articles of Association that their tai-pan's also tai-pan of the subsidiary with overriding say."

"That sounds smart."

"It is. And they are. But we're better and straighter—and our contacts and influence in China and throughout the Pacific Rim, except for the U.S. and Canada, are stronger than theirs and growing stronger every day."

"Why?"

"Because our company operations originated in Shanghai—the greatest city in Asia—where we were dominant. Struan's has always concentrated on Hong Kong which, until recently, was almost a provincial backwater."

"But Shanghai's a dead issue and has been since the Commies closed off the Mainland in '49. There's no foreign trade going through Shanghai today—it's all through Canton."

"Yes. But it's the Shanghainese who left China and came south with money, brains and guts, who made Hong Kong what it is today and what it'll be tomorrow: the now and future metropolis of the whole Pacific."

"Better than Singapore?"

"Absolutely."

"Manila?"

"Absolutely."

"Tokyo?"

"That will ever only be for Japanese." Gornt's eyes sparkled, the lines on his face crinkled. "Hong Kong is the greatest city in Asia, Mr. Bartlett. Whoever masters it will eventually master Asia. . . . Of course I'm talking about trade, financing, shipping and big business."

"What about Red China?"

"We think Hong Kong benefits the PRC—as we call the People's Republic of China. We're the controlled 'open door' for them. Hong Kong and Rothwell-Gornt represent the future."

"Why?"

"Because since Shanghai was the business and industrial center of China, the pacesetter, Shanghainese are the go-getters of China, always have been and always will be. And now the best are with us here. You'll soon see the difference between Cantonese and Shanghainese. Shanghainese're the entrepreneurs, the industrialists, promoters and internationalists. There's not a great textile or shipping magnate or industrialist who isn't Shanghainese. Cantonese-run family businesses, Mr. Bartlett, they're loners, but Shanghainese understand partnerships, corporate situations and above all, banking and financing." Gornt lit another cigarette. "That's where our strength is, why we're better than Struan's—why we'll be number one eventually."

Linc Bartlett studied the man opposite him. From the dossier that Casey had prepared he knew that Gornt had been born in Shanghai of British parents, was forty-eight, a widower with two grown children, and that he had served as a captain in the Australian infantry '42–'45 in the Pacific. He knew too that he ruled Rothwell-Gornt very successfully as a private fief and had done so for eight years since he took over from his father.

Bartlett shifted in the deep leather chair. "If you've got this rivalry with Struan's and you're so sure you'll be number one eventually, why wait? Why not take them now?"

Gornt was watching him, his craggy face set. "There's nothing in the world that I'd like to do more. But I can't, not yet. I nearly did three years ago—they'd overreached themselves, the previous tai-pan's joss had run out."

"Joss?"

"It's a Chinese word meaning luck, fate, but a bit more." Gornt watched him thoughtfully. "We're very superstitious out here. Joss is very important, like timing. Alastair Struan's joss ran out, or changed. He had a disastrous last year, and then, in desperation, handed over to Ian Dunross. They almost went under that time. A run had started on their stock. I went after them, but Dunross squeezed out of the run and stabilized the market."

"How?"

"Let's say he exercised an undue amount of influence in certain banking circles." Gornt remembered with cold fury how Havergill at the bank had suddenly, against all their private, secret agreements, not opposed Struan's request for a temporary, enormous line of credit that had given Dunross the time to recover.

Gornt remembered his blinding rage when he had called Havergill. "What the hell did you do that for?" he had asked him. "A hundred million as an Extraordinary Credit? You've saved their necks for chrissake! We had them. Why?" Havergill had told him that Dunross had mustered enough votes on the board and put an extreme amount of personal pressure on him. "There was nothing I could do. . . ."

Yes, Gornt thought, looking at the American. I lost that time but I think you're the twenty-four-carat explosive key that will trigger the bomb to blow Struan's to hell out of Asia forever. "Dunross went to the edge that time, Mr. Bartlett. He made some implacable enemies. But now we're equally strong. It's what you'd call a standoff. They can't take us and we can't take them."

"Unless they make a mistake."

"Or we make a mistake." The older man blew a smoke ring and studied it. At length he glanced back at Bartlett. "We'll win eventually. Time in Asia's a little different from time in the U.S.A."

"That's what people tell me."

"You don't believe it?"

"I know the same rules of survival apply here, there or where the hell ever. Only the degree changes."

Gornt watched the smoke from his cigarette curling to the ceiling. His office was large with well-used old leather chairs and excellent oils on the walls and it was filled with the smell of polished leather and good cigars. Gornt's high-backed chair, old oak and carved, with red plush fitted seat and back looked hard, functional and solid, Bartlett thought, like the man.

"We can outbid Struan's and we've time on our side, here, there, where the hell ever," Gornt said.

Bartlett laughed.

Gornt smiled too but Bartlett noticed his eyes weren't smiling. "Look around Hong Kong, Mr. Bartlett. Ask about us, and about them. Then make up your mind."

"Yes, I'll do that."

"I hear your aircraft's impounded."

"Yes. Yes it is. The airport cops found some guns aboard."

"I heard. Curious. Well, if you need any help to unimpound it, perhaps I can be of service."

"You could help right now by telling me why and who."

"I've no idea—but I'll wager someone in Struan's knows."

"Why?"

"They knew your exact movements."

"So did you."

"Yes. But it was nothing to do with us."

"Who knew we were to have this meeting, Mr. Gornt?"

"You and I. As we agreed. There was no leak from here, Mr. Bartlett. After our private meeting in New York last year, everything's been by telephone—not even a confirming telex. I subscribe to your wisdom of caution, secrecy and dealing face to face. In private. But who on your side knows of our . . . our continuing interest?"

"No one but me."

"Not even your lady treasurer executive vice-president?" Gornt asked with open surprise.

"No sir. When did you learn Casey was a she?"

"In New York. Come now, Mr. Bartlett, it's hardly likely we'd contemplate an association without ascertaining your credentials and those of your chief executives."

"Good. That will save time."

"Curious to have a woman in such a key position."

"She's my right and left arm and the best executive I've got."

"Then why wasn't she told of our meeting today?"

"One of the first rules of survival is to keep your options open."

"Meaning?"

"Meaning I don't run my business by committee. Besides, I like to play off the cuff, to keep certain operations secret." Bartlett thought a moment then added, "It's not lack of trust. Actually, I'm making it easier for her. If anyone at Struan's finds out and asks her why I'm meeting with you now, her surprise will be genuine."

After a pause Gornt said, "It's rare to find anyone really trustworthy. Very rare."

"Why would someone want M14's and grenades in Hong Kong and why would they use my plane?"

"I don't know but I'll make it my business to find out." Gornt stubbed out his cigarette. The ashtray was porcelain—Sung dynasty. "Do you know Tsu-yan?"

"I've met him a couple of times. Why?"

"He's a very good fellow, even though he's a director of Struan's."

"He's Shanghainese?"

"Yes. One of the best." Gornt looked up, his eyes very hard. "It's possible there could be peripheral benefit to dealing with us, Mr. Bartlett. I hear Struan's is quite extended just now—Dunross's gambling heavily on his fleet, particularly on the two super bulk cargo carriers he has on order from Japan. The first's due to be paid for substantially in a week or so. Then, too, there's a strong rumor he's going to make a bid for Asian Properties. You've heard of them?"

"A big land operation, real estate, all over Hong Kong."

"Yes. They're the biggest—even bigger than his own K.I."

"Kowloon Investments is part of Struan's? I thought they were a separate company."

"They are, outwardly. But Dunross is tai-pan of K.I.—they always have the same tai-pan."

"Always?"

"Always. It's in their Heads of Agreement. But Ian's overriding himself. The Noble House may soon become ignoble. He's very cash light at the moment."

Bartlett thought a moment, then he asked, "Why don't you join with another company, maybe Asian Properties, and take Struan's? That's what I'd do in the States if I wanted a company I couldn't take alone."

"Is that what you want to do here, Mr. Bartlett?" Gornt asked at once, pretending shock. "To 'take' Struan's?"

"Is it possible?"

Gornt looked at the ceiling carefully before answering. "Yes—but you'd have to have a partner. Perhaps you could do it with Asian Properties but I doubt it. Jason Plumm, the tai-pan, hasn't the balls. You'd need us. Only we have the perspicacity, the drive, the knowledge and the desire. Nevertheless, you'd have to risk a very great deal of money. Cash."

"How much?"

Gornt laughed outright. "I'll consider that. First you'll have to tell me how serious you are."

"And if I am, would you want in?"

Gornt stared back, his eyes equally level. "First I would have to be sure, very sure, how serious you are. It's no secret I detest Struan's generally and Ian Dunross personally, would want them obliterated. So you already know my long-term posture. I don't know yours. Yet."

"If we could take over Struan's—would it be worth it?"

"Oh yes, Mr. Bartlett. Oh yes—yes it'd be worth it," Gornt said jovially, then once more his voice iced. "But I still need to know how serious you are."

"I'll tell you when I've seen Dunross."

"Are you going to suggest the same thought to him—that together you can swallow Rothwell-Gornt?"

"My purpose here is to make Par-Con international, Mr. Gornt. Maybe up to a $30 million investment to cover a whole range of merchandising, factories and warehousing. Up to a short time ago I'd never heard of Struan's—or Rothwell-Gornt. Or your rivalry."

"Very well, Mr. Bartlett, we'll leave it at that. Whatever you do will be interesting. Yes. It will be interesting to see if you can hold a knife."

Bartlett stared at him, not understanding.

"That's an old Chinese cooking term, Mr. Bartlett. Do you cook?"

"No."

"It's a hobby of mine. The Chinese say it's important to know how to hold a knife, that you can't use one until you can hold it correctly. Otherwise you'll cut yourself and be off to a very bad start indeed. Won't you?"

Bartlett grinned. "Hold a knife, is it? I'll remember that. No, I can't cook. Never got around to learning—Casey can't cook worth a damn either."

"The Chinese say there're three arts in which no other civilization can compare to theirs—literature, brush painting and cooking. I'm inclined to agree. Do you like good food?"

"The best meal I ever had was in a restaurant just outside Rome on the Via Flaminia, the Casale."

"Then we've at least that in common, Mr. Bartlett. The Casale's one of my favorites too."

"Casey took me there once—*spaghetti alla matriciana al dente* and *buscetti* with an ice-cold bottle of beer followed by the *piccata* and more beer. I'll never forget it."

Gornt smiled. "Perhaps you'll have dinner with me while you're here. I can offer you *alla matriciana* too—actually it'll compare favorably, it's the very same recipe."

"I'd like that."

"And a bottle of Valpolicella, or a great Tuscany wine."

"Personally, I like beer with pasta. Iced American beer out of the can."

After a pause Gornt asked, "How long are you staying in Hong Kong?"

"As long as it takes," Bartlett said without hesitation.

"Good. Then dinner one day next week? Tuesday or Wednesday?"

"Tuesday'd be fine, thanks. May I bring Casey?"

"Of course." Then Gornt added, his voice flatter, "By that time perhaps you'll be more sure of what you want to do."

Bartlett laughed. "And by that time you'll find out if I can hold a knife."

"Perhaps. But just remember one thing, Mr. Bartlett. If we ever join forces to attack Struan's, once the battle is joined, there will be almost no way to withdraw without getting severely mauled. Very severely mauled indeed. I'd have to be very sure. After all, you can always retire hurt to the U.S.A. to fight another day. We stay—so the risks are unequal."

"But the spoils are unequal too. You'd gain something priceless which doesn't mean ten cents to me. You'd become the Noble House."

"Yes," Gornt said, his eyes lidding. He leaned forward to select another cigarette and his left foot moved behind the desk to press a hidden floor switch. "Let's leave everything until Tues—"

The intercom clicked on. "Excuse me, Mr. Gornt, would you like me to postpone the board meeting?" his secretary asked.

"No," Gornt said. "They can wait."

"Yes sir. Miss Ramos is here. Could you spare her a few minutes?"

Gornt pretended to be surprised. "Just a moment." He looked up at Bartlett. "Have we concluded?"

"Yes." Bartlett got up at once. "Tuesday's firm. Let's keep everything cooking till then." He turned to go but Gornt stopped him. "Just a moment, Mr. Bartlett," he said, then into the intercom, "ask her to come in." He clicked off the switch and stood up. "I'm glad to have had the meeting."

The door opened and the girl came in. She was twenty-five and stunning with short black hair and sloe eyes, clearly Eurasian, casually dressed in tight, American washed jeans and a shirt. "Hello, Quillan," she said with a smile that warmed the room, her English slightly American accented. "Sorry to interrupt but I've just got back from Bangkok and wanted to say hello."

"Glad you did, Orlanda." Gornt smiled at Bartlett who was staring at her. "This is Linc Bartlett, from America. Orlanda Ramos."

"Hello," Bartlett said.

"Hi . . . oh, Linc Bartlett? The American millionaire gun-runner?" she said and laughed.

"What?"

"Oh don't look so shocked, Mr. Bartlett. Everyone in Hong Kong knows—Hong Kong's just a village."

"Seriously—how did you know?"

"I read it in my morning paper."

"Impossible! It only happened at 5:30 this morning."

"It was in the *Fai Pao*—the *Express*—in the Stop Press column at nine o'clock. It's a Chinese paper and the Chinese know everything that's going on here. Don't worry, the English papers won't pick it up till the afternoon editions, but you can expect the press on your doorstep around the happy hour."

"Thanks." The last thing I want's the goddamn press after me, Bartlett thought sourly.

"Don't worry, Mr. Bartlett, I won't ask you for an interview, even though I am a free-lance reporter for the Chinese press. I'm really very discreet," she said. "Am I not, Quillan?"

"Absolutely. I'll vouch for that," Gornt said. "Orlanda's absolutely trustworthy."

"Of course if you want to *offer* an interview—I'll accept. Tomorrow."

"I'll consider it."

"I'll guarantee to make you look marvelous!"

"The Chinese really know everything here?"

"Of course," she said at once. "But *quai loh*—foreigners—don't read the Chinese papers, except for a handful of old China hands—like Quillan."

"And the whole of Special Intelligence, Special Branch and the police in general," Gornt said.

"And Ian Dunross," she added, the tip of her tongue touching her teeth.

"He's that sharp?" Bartlett asked.

"Oh yes. He's got Devil Struan's blood in him."

"I don't understand."

"You will, if you stay here long enough."

Bartlett thought about that, then frowned. "You knew about the guns too, Mr. Gornt?"

"Only that the police had intercepted contraband arms aboard 'the millionaire American's private jet which arrived last night.' It was in my Chinese paper this morning too. The *Sing Pao*." Gornt's smile was sardonic. "That's *The Times* in Cantonese. It was in their Stop Press column too. But, unlike Orlanda, I am surprised you haven't been intercepted by members of our English press already. They're very diligent here in Hong Kong. More diligent than Orlanda gives them credit for being."

Bartlett caught her perfume but persisted. "I'm surprised you didn't mention it, Mr. Gornt."

"Why should I? What do guns have to do with our possible future association?" Gornt chuckled. "If worst comes to worst we'll visit you in jail, Orlanda and I."

She laughed. "Yes indeed."

"Thanks a lot!" Again her perfume. Bartlett put aside the guns and concentrated on her. "Ramos—that's Spanish?"

"Portuguese. From Macao. My father worked for Rothwell-Gornt in Shanghai—my mother's Shanghainese. I was brought up in Shanghai until '49, then went to the States for a few years, to high school in San Francisco."

"Did you? L.A.'s my hometown—I went to high school in the Valley."

"I love California," she said. "How d'you like Hong Kong?"

"I've just arrived." Bartlett grinned. "Seems I made an explosive entrance."

She laughed. Lovely white teeth. "Hong Kong's all right—provided you can leave every month or so. You should visit Macao for a weekend—it's old worldly, very pretty, only forty miles away with good ferries. It's very different from Hong Kong." She turned back to Gornt. "Again, I'm sorry to interrupt, Quillan, just wanted to say hello. . . ." She started to leave.

"No, we're through—I was just going," Bartlett said, interrupting her. "Thanks again, Mr. Gornt. See you Tuesday if not before. . . . Hope to see you again, Miss Ramos."

"Yes, that would be nice. Here's my card—if you'll grant the interview I guarantee a good press." She held out her hand and he touched it and felt her warmth.

Gornt saw him to the door and then closed it and came back to his desk and took a cigarette. She lit the match for him and blew out the flame, then sat in the chair Bartlett had used.

"Nice-looking man," she said.

"Yes. But he's American, naive, and a very cocky bastard who may need taking down a peg."

"That's what you want me to do?"

"Perhaps. Did you read his dossier?"

"Oh yes. Very interesting." Orlanda smiled.

"You're not to ask him for money," Gornt said sharply.

"*Ayeeyah*, Quillan, am I that dumb?" she said as abrasively, her eyes flashing.

"Good."

"Why would he smuggle guns into Hong Kong?"

"Why indeed, my dear? Perhaps someone was just using him."

"That must be the answer. If I had all his money I wouldn't try something as stupid as that."

"No," Gornt said.

"Oh, did you like that bit about my being a free-lance reporter? I thought I did that very well."

"Yes, but don't underestimate him. He's no fool. He's very sharp. Very." He told her about the Casale. "That's too much of a coincidence. He must have a dossier on me too, a detailed one. Not many know of my liking for that place."

"Maybe I'm in it too."

"Perhaps. Don't let him catch you out. About the free lancing."

"Oh, come on, Quillan, who of the tai-pans except you and Dunross read the Chinese papers—and even then you can't read all of them. I've already done a column or two . . . 'by a Special Correspondent.' If he grants me an interview I can write it. Don't worry." She moved the ash-tray closer for him. "It went all right, didn't it? With Bartlett?"

"Perfectly. You're wasted. You should be in the movies."

"Then talk to your friend about me, please, please, Quillan dear. Charlie Wang's the biggest producer in Hong Kong and owes you lots of favors. Charlie Wang has so many movies going that . . . just one chance is all I need. . . . I could become a star! Please?"

"Why not?" he asked dryly. "But I don't think you're his type."

"I can adapt. Didn't I act exactly as you wanted with Bartlett? Am I not dressed perfectly, American style?"

"Yes, yes you are." Gornt looked at her, then said delicately, "You could be perfect for him. I was thinking you could perhaps have something more permanent than an affair. . . ."

All her attention concentrated. "What?"

"You and he could fit together like a perfect Chinese puzzle. You're good-humored, the right age, beautiful, clever, educated, marvelous at the pillow, very smart in the head, with enough of an American patina to put him at ease." Gornt exhaled smoke and added, "And of all the ladies I know, you could really spend his money. Yes, you two could fit perfectly . . . he'd be very good for you and you'd brighten his life considerably. Wouldn't you?"

"Oh yes," she said at once. "Oh yes I would." She smiled then frowned. "But what about the woman he has with him? They're sharing a suite at the Vic. I heard she's gorgeous. What about her, Quillan?"

Gornt smiled thinly. "My spies say they don't sleep together though they're better than friends."

Her face fell. "He's not queer, is he?"

Gornt laughed. It was a good rich laugh. "I wouldn't do that to you, Orlanda! No, I'm sure he's not. He's just got a strange arrangement with Casey."

"What is it?"

Gornt shrugged.

After a moment she said, "What do I do about her?"

"If Casey Tcholok's in your way, remove her. You've got claws."

"You're . . . Sometimes I don't like you at all."

"We're both realists, you and I. Aren't we." He said it very flat.

She recognized the undercurrent of violence. At once she got up and leaned across the desk and kissed him lightly. "You're a devil," she said, placating him. "That's for old times."

His hand strayed to her breast and he sighed, remembering, enjoying the warmth that came through the thin material. "Ayeeyah, Orlanda, we had some good times, didn't we?"

She had been his mistress when she was seventeen. He was her first and he had kept her for almost five years and would have continued but she went with a youth to Macao when he was away and he had been told about it. And so he had stopped. At once. Even though they had a daughter then, he and she, one year old.

"Orlanda," he had told her as she had begged for forgiveness, "there's nothing to forgive. I've told you a dozen times that youth needs youth, and there'd come a day. . . . Dry your tears, marry the lad—I'll give you a dowry and my blessing. . . ." And throughout all her weepings he had remained firm. "We'll be friends," he had assured her, "and I'll take care of you when you need it. . . ."

The next day he had turned the heat of his covert fury on the youth, an Englishman, a minor executive in Asian Properties and, within the month, he had broken him.

"It's a matter of face," he had told her calmly.

"Oh I know, I understand but . . . what shall I do now?" she had wailed. "He's leaving tomorrow for England and he wants me to go with him and marry him but I can't marry now, he's got no money or future or job or money. . . ."

"Dry your tears, then go shopping."

"What?"

"Yes. Here's a present." He had given her a first-class, return ticket to London on the same airplane that the youth was traveling tourist. And a thousand pounds in crisp, new ten-pound notes. "Buy lots of pretty clothes, and go to the theater. You're booked into the Connaught for eleven days—just sign the bill—and your return's confirmed, so have a happy time and come back fresh and without problems!"

"Oh thank you, Quillan darling, oh thank you. . . . I'm so sorry. You forgive me?"

"There's nothing to forgive. But if you ever talk to him again, or see him privately . . . I won't be friendly to you or your family ever again."

She had thanked him profusely through her tears, cursing herself for her stupidity, begging for the wrath of heaven to descend upon whoever had betrayed her. The next day the youth had tried to speak to her at the airport and on the plane and in London but she just cursed him away. She knew where her rice bowl rested. The day she left London he committed suicide.

When Gornt heard about it, he lit a fine cigar and took her out to a dinner atop the Victoria and Albert with candelabra and fine linen and fine silver, and then, after he had had his Napoleon brandy and she her crème de menthe, he had sent her home, alone, to the apartment he still paid for. He had ordered another brandy and stayed, watching the lights of the harbor, and the Peak, feeling the glory of vengeance, the majesty of life, his face regained.

"*Ayeeyah*, we had some good times," Gornt said again now, still desiring her, though he had not pillowed with her from the time he had heard about Macao.

"Quillan . . ." she began, his hand warming her too.

"No."

Her eyes strayed to the inner door. "Please. It's three years, there's never been anyone . . ."

"Thank you but no." He held her away from him, his hands now firm on her arms but gentle. "We've already had the best," he said as a connoisseur would. "I don't like second best."

She sat back on the edge of the desk, watching him sullenly. "You always win, don't you."

"The day you become lovers with Bartlett I'll give you a present," he said calmly. "If he takes you to Macao and you stay openly with him for three days I'll give you a new Jag. If he asks you to marry him you get the apartment and everything in it, and a house in California as a wedding present."

She gasped, then smiled gloriously. "An XK-E, a black one, Quillan, oh that would be perfect!" Then her happiness evaporated. "What's so important about him? Why is he so important to you?"

He just stared at her.

"Sorry," she said, "sorry, I shouldn't have asked." Thoughtfully she reached for a cigarette and lit it and leaned over and gave it to him.

"Thanks," he said, seeing the curve of her breast, enjoying it, yet a little saddened that such beauty was so transient. "Oh, by the way, I wouldn't like Bartlett to know of our arrangement."

"Nor would I." She sighed and forced a smile. Then she got up and shrugged. *"Ayeeyah,* it would never have lasted with us anyway. Macao or not Macao. You would have changed—you'd have become bored, men always do."

She checked her makeup and her shirt and blew him a kiss and left him. He stared at the closed door then smiled and stubbed out the cigarette she had given him, never having puffed on it, not wanting the taint of her lips. He lit a fresh one and hummed a little tune.

Excellent, he thought happily. Now we'll see, Mr. Bloody Cocky Confident Yankee Bartlett, now we'll see how you handle that knife. Pasta with beer indeed!

Then Gornt caught a lingering whiff of her perfume and he was swept back momentarily into memories of their pillowing. When she was young, he reminded himself. Thank God there's no premium on youth or beauty out here, and a substitution's as close as a phone call or a hundred-dollar note.

He reached for the phone and dialed a special private number, glad that Orlanda was more Chinese than European. Chinese are such practical people.

The dial tone stopped and he heard Paul Havergill's crisp voice. "Yes?"

"Paul, Quillan. How're things?"

"Hello, Quillan—of course you know Johnjohn's taking over the bank in November?"

"Yes. Sorry about that."

"Damnable. I thought I was going to be confirmed but instead the board chose Johnjohn. It was official last night. It's Dunross again, his clique, and the damned stock they have. How did your meeting go?"

"Our American's chomping at the bit, just as I told you he would be." Gornt took a deep drag of his cigarette and tried to keep the excitement out of his voice. "How would you like a little special action before you retire?"

"What had you in mind?"

"You're leaving end of November?"

"Yes. After twenty-three years. In some ways I won't be sorry."

Nor will I, Gornt thought contentedly. You're out of date and too bloody conservative. The only thing in your favor is that you hate Dunross. "That's almost four months. That'd give us plenty of time. You, me and our American friend."

"What do you have in mind?"

"You remember one of my hypothetical game plans, the one I called 'Competition'?"

Havergill thought a moment. "That was how to take over or eliminate an opposition bank, wasn't it? Why?"

"Say someone dusted off the plan and made a few changes and pushed the *go* button . . . two days ago. Say someone knew Dunross and the others would vote you out and wanted some revenge. Competition would work perfectly."

"I don't see why. What's the point of attacking Blacs?" The Bank of London, Canton and Shanghai was the Victoria's main opposition. "Doesn't make sense."

"Ah, but say someone changed the target, Paul."

"To whom?"

"I'll come by at three and explain."

"To whom?"

"Richard." Richard Kwang controlled the Ho-Pak Bank—one of the largest of all the many Chinese banks in Hong Kong.

"Good God! But that's . . ." There was a long pause. "Quillan, you've really begun Competition . . . to put it into effect?"

"Yes, and no one knows about it except you and me."

"But how is that going to work against Dunross?"

"I'll explain later. Can Ian meet his commitments on his ships?"

There was a pause which Gornt noted. "Yes," he heard Havergill say. "Yes, but what?"

"But I'm sure he'll be all right."

"What other problems has Dunross got?"

"Sorry, but that wouldn't be ethical."

"Of course." Gornt added thinly, "Let me put it another way: Say their boat was a little rocked. Eh?"

There was a longer pause. "At the right moment, a smallish wave could scuttle them, or any company. Even you."

"But not the Victoria Bank."

"Oh no."

"Good. See you at three." Gornt hung up and mopped his brow again, his excitement vast. He stubbed out his cigarette, made a quick calculation, lit another cigarette, then dialed. "Charles, Quillan. Are you busy?"

"No. What can I do for you?"

"I want a balance sheet." A balance sheet was a private signal for the attorney to telephone eight nominees who would buy or sell on the stock market on Gornt's behalf, secretly, to avoid the trading being traced back to him. All shares and all monies would pass solely through the attorney's hands so that neither the nominees nor the brokers would know for whom the transactions were being made.

"A balance sheet it will be. What sort, Quillan?"

"I want to sell short." To sell short meant he sold shares he did not own on the presumption their value would go down. Then, before he had to buy them back—he had a maximum margin of two weeks in Hong Kong—if the stock had indeed gone down, he would pocket the difference. Of course if he gambled wrong and the stock had gone up, he would have to pay the difference.

"What shares and what numbers?"

"A hundred thousand shares of Ho-Pak . . ."

"Holy Christ . . ."

". . . the same, as soon as the market opens tomorrow, and another 200 during the day. I'll give you further instructions then."

There was a stunned silence. "You did say Ho-Pak?"

"Yes."

"It'll take time to borrow all those shares. Good God, Quillan, four hundred thousand?"

"While you're about it, get another hundred. A round half a million."

"But . . . but Ho-Pak's as blue a blue chip as we've got. It hasn't gone down in years."

"Yes."

"What've you heard?"

"Rumors," Gornt said gravely and chuckled to himself. "Would you like an early lunch, eat at the club?"

"I'll be there."

Gornt hung up, then dialed another private number.

"Yes?"

"It's me," Gornt said cautiously. "Are you alone?"

"Yes. And?"

"At our meeting, the Yankee suggested a raid."

"*Ayeeyah!* And?"

"And Paul's in," he said, the exaggeration coming easily. "Absolutely secretly, of course. I've just talked to him."

"Then I'm in. Provided I get control of Struan's ships, their Hong Kong property operation and 40 percent of their landholdings in Thailand and Singapore."

"You must be joking!"

"Nothing's too much to smash them. Is it, old boy?"

Gornt heard the well-bred, mocking laugh and hated Jason Plumm for it. "You despise him just as much as I do," Gornt said.

"Ah, but you'll need me and my special friends. Even with Paul on or off the fence, you and the Yankee can't pull it off, not without me and mine."

"Why else am I talking to you?"

"Listen, don't forget I'm not asking for any piece of the American's pie."

Gornt kept his voice calm. "What's that got to do with anything?"

"I know you. Oh yes. I know you, old boy."

"Do you now?"

"Yes. You won't be satisfied just with destructing our 'friend,' you'll want the whole pie."

"Will I now?"

"Yes. You've wanted a stake in the U.S. market too long."

"And you."

"No. We know where our toast's toasted. We're content to trail along behind. We're content with Asia. We don't want to be a noble anything."

"Oh?"

"No. Then it's a deal?"

"No," Gornt said.

"I'll drop the shipping totally. Instead I'll take Ian's Kowloon Investments, the Kai Tak operation, and 40 percent of the landholdings in Thailand and Singapore, and I'll accept 25 percent of Par-Con and three places on the board."

"Get stuffed!"

"The offer's good till Monday."

"Which Monday?"

"Next Monday."

"*Dew neh loh moh* on all your Mondays!"

"And yours! I'll make you a last offer. Kowloon Investments and their Kai Tak operation totally, 35 percent of all their landholdings in Thailand and Singapore, and 10 percent of the Yankee pie with three seats on the board."

"Is that all?"

"Yes. Again, the offer's good till next Monday. And don't think you can gobble us in the process."

"Have you gone mad?"

"I told you—I know you. Is it a deal?"

"No."

Again the soft, malevolent laugh. "Till Monday—next Monday. That's time enough for you to make up your mind."

"Will I see you at Ian's party tonight?" Gornt asked thinly.

"Have you gone bonkers! I wouldn't go if . . . Good God, Quillan, are you really going to accept? *In person?*"

"I wasn't going to—but now I think I will. I wouldn't want to miss perhaps the last great party of the Struans' last tai-pan. . . ."

7

In the boardroom it was still rough going for Casey. They would take none of the baits she offered. Her anxiety had increased and now as she waited she felt a wave of untoward fear go through her.

Phillip Chen was doodling, Linbar fiddling with his papers, Jacques deVille watching her thoughtfully. Then Andrew Gavallan stopped writing the latest percentages she had quoted. He sighed and looked up at her. "Clearly this should be a co-financing operation," he said, his voice sharp. Electricity in the room soared and Casey had difficulty suppressing a cheer as he added, "How much would Par-Con be prepared to put up, joint financing, for the whole deal?"

"18 million U.S. this year should cover it," she answered immediately, noting happily that they all covered a gasp.

The published net worth of Struan's last year was almost 28 million, and she and Bartlett had gauged their offer on this figure.

"Make the first offer 20 million," Linc had told her. "You should hook 'em at 25 which'd be great. It's essential we co-finance, but the suggestion's got to come from them."

"But look at their balance sheet, Linc. You can't tell for sure what their real net worth is. It could be 10 million either way, maybe more. We don't know how strong they really are . . . or how weak. Look at this item: '14.7 million retained in subsidiaries.' What subsidiaries, where and what for? Here's another one: '7.4 million transferred to—'"

"So what, Casey? So it's 30 million instead of 25. Our projection's still valid."

"Yes—but their accounting procedures . . . My God, Linc, if we did one percent of this in the States the SEC'd have our asses in a sling and we'd end up in jail for fifty years."

"Yes. But it's not against *their* law, which is a major reason for going to Hong Kong."

"20 is too much for openers."

"I'll leave it to you, Casey. Just remember in Hong Kong we play Hong Kong rules—whatever's legal. I want in their game."

"Why? And don't say 'for my goddamn pleasure.'"

Linc had laughed. "Okay—then for *your* goddamn pleasure. Just make the Struan deal!"

The humidity in the boardroom had increased. She would have liked to reach for a tissue but she kept still, willing them onward, pretending calm.

Gavallan broke the silence. "When would Mr. Bartlett confirm the offer of 18 million . . . if we accepted?"

"It's confirmed," she said sweetly, passing over the insult. "I have clearance to commit up to 20 million on this deal without consulting Linc or his board," she said, deliberately giving them room to maneuver. Then she added innocently, "Then it's all settled? Good." She began to sort out her papers. "Next: I'd—"

"Just a moment," Gavallan said, off balance. "I, er, 18 is . . . In any event we have to present the package to the tai-pan."

"Oh," she said, pretending surprise. "I thought we were negotiating as equals, that you four gentlemen had powers equal to mine. Perhaps I'd better talk to Mr. Dunross directly in the future."

Andrew Gavallan flushed. "The tai-pan has final say. In everything."

"I'm very glad to know it, Mr. Gavallan. I only have final say up to 20 million." She beamed at them. "Very well, put it to your tai-pan. Meanwhile, shall we set a time limit on the consideration period?"

Another silence.

"What do you suggest?" Gavallan said, feeling trapped.

"Whatever the minimum is. I don't know how fast you like to work," Casey said.

Phillip Chen said, "Why not table that answer until after lunch, Andrew?"

"Yes—good idea."

"That's fine with me," Casey said. I've done my job, she thought. I'll settle for 20 million when it could've been 30 and they're men and expert, and over twenty-one and they think I'm a sucker. But now I get my drop dead money. Dear God in heaven let this deal go through because then I'm free forever.

Free to do what?

Never mind, she told herself. I'll think about that later.

She heard herself continue the pattern: "Shall we go through the details of how you'd like the 18 million and . . ."

"18 is hardly adequate," Phillip Chen interrupted, the lie coming very easily. "There are all sorts of added costs. . . ."

In perfect negotiating style Casey argued and allowed them to push her to 20 million and then, with apparent reluctance, she said, "You gentlemen are exceptional businessmen. Very well, 20 million." She saw their hidden smiles and laughed to herself.

"Good," Gavallan said, very satisfied.

"Now," she said, wanting to keep the pressure on, "how do you want our joint venture corporate structure to be? Of course subject to your tai-pan—sorry, subject to *the* tai-pan's approval," she said, correcting herself with just the right amount of humility.

Gavallan was watching her, irritably wishing she were a man. Then I could say, up yours, or go shit in your hat, and we'd laugh together because you know and I know you always have to check with the tai-pan in some way or another—whether it's Dunross or Bartlett or a board or your wife. Yes, and if you were a man we wouldn't have this bloody sexuality in the boardroom which doesn't belong here in the first place. Christ, if you were an old bag maybe that'd make a difference but, shit, a bird like you?

What the hell gets into American women? Why in the name of Christ don't they stay where they belong and be content with what they're great at? Stupid!

And stupid to concede financing so quickly, and even more stupid to give us an extra two million when ten would probably have been acceptable in the first place. For God's sake, you should have been more patient and you would have made a much better deal! That's the trouble with you Americans, you've—no finesse and no patience and no style and you don't understand the art of negotiation, and you, dear lady, you're much too impatient to prove yourself. So now I know how to play you.

He glanced at Linbar Struan who was watching Casey covertly, waiting for him or Phillip or Jacques to continue. When I'm tai-pan, Gavallan thought grimly, I'm going to break you, young Linbar, break you or make you. You need shoving out into the world on your own, to make you think for yourself, to rely on yourself, not on your name and your heritage. Yes, with a lot more hard work to take some of the heat out of your yang—the sooner you remarry the better.

His eyes switched to Jacques deVille who smiled back at him. Ah Jacques, he thought without rancor, you're my main opposition. You're doing what you usually do: saying little, watching everything, thinking a lot—rough, tough and mean if necessary. But what's in your mind about this deal? Have I missed something? What does your canny legal Parisian mind forecast? Ah but she stopped you in your tracks with her joke about your joke about her nose, eh?

I'd like to bed her too, he thought absently, knowing Linbar and Jacques had already decided the same. Of course—who wouldn't?

What about you, Phillip Chen?

Oh no. Not you. You like them very much younger and have it done to you, strangely, if there's any truth to the rumors, *heya*?

He looked back at Casey. He could read her impatience. You don't look lesbian, he thought and groaned inwardly. Is that your other weakness? Christ, that'd be a terrible waste!

"The joint venture should be set up under Hong Kong law," he said.
"Yes of course. There's—"

"Sims, Dawson and Dick can advise us how. I'll arrange an appointment
for tomorrow or the day after."

"No need for that, Mr. Gavallan. I already got their tentative proposals,
hypothetical and confidential, of course, just in case we decided to conclude."

"What?" They gaped at her as she took out five copies of a short form,
legal contract and handed one to each of them.

"I found out they were your attorneys," she said brightly. "I had our
people check them out and I was advised they're the best so they were
fine with us. I asked them to consider our joint hypothetical needs—yours
as well as ours. Is anything the matter?"

"No," Gavallan said, suddenly furious that their own firm had not told
them of Par-Con's inquiries. He began to scan the letter.

Dew neh loh moh on Casey bloody whatever her names are, Phillip
Chen was thinking, enraged at the loss of face. May your golden gully
wither and be ever dry and dust-filled for your foul manners and your
fresh, filthy, unfeminine habits!

God protect us from American women!

Ayeeyah, it is going to cost Lincoln Bartlett a pretty penny for daring to
stick this . . . this creature upon us, he promised himself. How dare he!

Nevertheless, his mind was estimating the staggering value of the deal
they were being offered. It has to be at least 100 million U.S., potentially,
over the next few years, he told himself, his head reeling. This will give
the Noble House the stability it needs.

Oh happy day, he gloated. And co-financing dollar for dollar! Unbelievable! Stupid to give us that so quickly without even a tiny concession
in return. Stupid, but what can you expect from a stupid woman?
Ayeeyah, the Pacific Rim will gorge on all the polyurethane foam products we can make—for packaging, building, bedding and insulating. One
factory here, one in Taiwan, one in Singapore, one in Kuala Lumpur and
a last, initially, in Jakarta. We'll make millions, tens of millions. And as to
the computer-leasing agency, why at the rental these fools are offering us,
10 percent less than IBM's list price, less our 7½ percent commission—
with just a little haggling we would have been delighted to agree to 5 percent—by next weekend I can sell three in Singapore, one here, one in
Kuala Lumpur and one to that shipping pirate in Indonesia for a clear
profit of $67,500 each, or $405,000 for six phone calls. And as to
China . . .

And as to China . . .

Oh all gods great and small and very small, help this deal to go through
and I will endow a new temple, a cathedral, in Tai-ping Shan, he promised, consumed with fervor. If China will drop some controls, or even
ease them just a fraction, we can fertilize the paddy fields of Kwantung

Province and then of all China and over the next twelve years this deal will mean tens of hundreds of millions of dollars, U.S. dollars not Hong Kong dollars!

The thought of all this profit mollified his rage considerably. "I think this proposal can form the basis for further discussion," he said, finishing reading. "Don't you, Andrew?"

"Yes." Gavallan put the letter down. "I'll call them after lunch. When would it be convenient for Mr. Bartlett . . . and you of course . . . to meet?"

"This afternoon—the sooner the better—or anytime tomorrow but Linc won't come. I handle all the details, that's my job," Casey said crisply. "He sets policy—and will formally sign the final documents—after I've approved them. That's the function of the commander-in-chief, isn't it?" She beamed at them.

"I'll make an appointment and leave a message at your hotel," Gavallan was saying.

"Perhaps we could set it up now—then that's out of the way?"

Sourly Gavallan glanced at his watch. Almost lunch, thank God. "Jacques—how're you fixed tomorrow?"

"Morning's better than the afternoon."

"And for John too," Phillip Chen said.

Gavallan picked up the phone and dialed. "Mary? Call Dawson and make an appointment for eleven tomorrow to include Mr. deVille and Mr. John Chen and Miss Casey. At their offices." He put the phone down. "Jacques and John Chen handle all our corporate matters. John's sophisticated on American problems and Dawson's the expert. I'll send the car for you at 10:30."

"Thanks, but there's no need for you to trouble."

"Just as you wish," he said politely. "Perhaps this is a good time to break for lunch."

Casey said, "We've a quarter of an hour yet. Shall we start on how you'd like our financing? Or if you wish we can send out for a sandwich and work on through."

They stared at her, appalled. "Work through lunch?"

"Why not? It's an old American custom."

"Thank God it's not a custom here," Gavallan said.

"Yes," Phillip Chen snapped.

She felt their disapproval descend like a pall but she did not care. Shit on all of you, she thought irritably, then forced herself to put that attitude away. Listen, idiot, don't let these sons of bitches get you! She smiled sweetly. "If you want to stop now for lunch, that's fine with me."

"Good," Gavallan said at once and the others breathed a sigh of relief. "We begin lunch at 12:40. You'll probably want to powder your nose first."

"Yes, thank you," she said, knowing they wanted her gone so they could discuss her—and then the deal. It should be the other way around, she thought, but it won't be. No. It'll be the same as always: they'll lay bets as to who'll be the first to score. But it'll be none of them, because *I* don't want any of *them* at the moment, however attractive they are in their way. These men are like all the others I've met: they don't want love, they just want sex.

Except Linc.

Don't think about Linc and how much you love him and how rotten these years have been. Rotten and wonderful.

Remember your promise.

I won't think about Linc and love.

Not until my birthday which is ninety-eight days from now. The ninety-eighth day ends the seventh year and because of my darling by then I'll have my drop dead money and really be equal, and, God willing, we'll have the Noble House. Will that be my wedding present to him? Or his to me?

Or a good-bye present.

"Where's the ladies' room?" she asked, getting up, and they all stood and towered over her, except Phillip Chen whom she topped by an inch, and Gavallan directed her.

Linbar Struan opened the door for her and closed it behind her. Then he grinned. "A thousand says you'll never make it, Jacques."

"Another thousand," Gavallan said. "And ten that you won't, Linbar."

"You're on," Linbar replied, "provided she's here a month."

"You're slowing up, aren't you, old chap?" Gavallan said, then to Jacques, "Well?"

The Frenchman smiled. "Twenty that you, Andrew, will never charm such a lady into bed—and as to you, poor young Linbar. Fifty against your racehorse says the same."

"I like my filly for God's sake. Noble Star's got a great chance of being a winner. She's the best in our stable."

"Fifty."

"A hundred and I'll consider it."

"I don't want any horse that much." Jacques smiled at Phillip Chen. "What do you think, Phillip?"

Phillip Chen got up. "I think I'll go home to lunch and leave you stallions to your dreams. It's curious though that you're all betting the others won't—not that any of you could." Again they laughed.

"Stupid to give us the extra, eh?" Gavallan said.

"The deal's fantastic," Linbar Struan said. "Christ, Uncle Phillip, fantastic!"

"Like her *derrière*," deVille said as a connoisseur would. "Eh, Phillip?"

Good-naturedly Phillip Chen nodded and walked out, but as he saw Casey disappearing into the ladies' room, he thought, *Ayeeyah*, who'd want the big lump anyway?

Inside the ladies' room, Casey looked around, appalled. It was clean but smelled of old drains and there were pails piled one on top of another and some were filled with water. The floor was tiled but water-spotted and messy. I've heard the English are not very hygienic, she thought disgustedly, but here in the Noble House? Ugh! Astonishing!

She went into one of the cubicles, its floor wet and slippery, and after she had finished she pulled the handle and nothing happened. She tried it again, and again, and still nothing happened so she cursed and lifted off the top of the cistern. The cistern was dry and rusty. Irritably she unbolted the door and went to the basin and turned on the water but none came out.

What's the matter with this place? I'll bet those bastards sent me here deliberately!

There were clean hand towels so she poured a pail of water into the basin awkwardly, spilling some, washed her hands, then dried them, furious that her shoes had got splashed. At a sudden thought, she took another pail and flushed the toilet, then used still another bucket to clean her hands again. When she left, she felt very soiled.

I suppose the goddamn pipe's broken somewhere and the plumber won't come until tomorrow. Goddamn all water systems!

Calm down, she told herself. You'll start making mistakes.

The corridor was covered with fine Chinese silk carpet, and the walls were lined with oil paintings of clipper ships and Chinese landscapes. As she approached she could hear the muted voices from the boardroom and a laugh—the kind of laugh that comes from a ribald joke or a smutty remark. She knew the moment she opened the door, the good humor and comradeship would vanish and the awkward silence would return.

She opened the door and they all got up.

"Are you having trouble with your water mains?" she asked, holding her anger down.

"No, I don't think so," Gavallan said, startled.

"Well, there's no water. Didn't you know?"

"Of course there's no— Oh!" He stopped. "You're staying at the V and A so . . . Didn't anyone tell you about the water shortage?"

They all began talking at once but Gavallan dominated them. "The V and A has its own water supply—so do a couple of other hotels—but the rest of us're on four hours of water every fourth day, so you've got to use a pail. Never occurred to me you didn't know. Sorry."

"How do you manage? *Every fourth day?*"

"Yes. For four hours, 6:00 A.M. till 8:00 A.M., then 5:00 till 7:00 in the evening. It's a frightful bore because of course it means we've got to store four days' supply. Pails, or the bath, whatever you can. We're short of pails—it's our water day tomorrow. Oh my God, there was water for you, wasn't there?"

"Yes, but . . . You mean the water mains are turned off? Everywhere?" ske asked incredulously.

"Yes," Gavallan said patiently. "Except for those four hours every fourth day. But you're all right at the V and A. As they're right on the waterfront they can refill their tanks daily from lighters—of course, they have to buy it."

"You can't shower or bathe?"

Linbar Struan laughed. "Everyone gets pretty grotty after three days in this heat but at least we're all in the same sewer. Still it's survival training to make sure there's a full pail before you go."

"I had no idea," she said, aghast that she had used *three* pails.

"Our reservoirs are empty," Gavallan explained. "We've had almost no rain this year and last year was dry too. Bloody nuisance but there you are. Just one of those things. Joss."

"Then where does your water come from?"

They stared at her blankly. "From China of course. By pipes over the border into the New Territories, or by tanker from the Pearl River. The government's just chartered a fleet of ten tankers that go up the Pearl River, by agreement with Peking. They bring us about 10 million gallons a day. It'll cost the government upwards of 25 million for this year's charter. Saturday's paper said our consumption's down to 30 million gallons a day for our 3½ million population—that includes industry. In your country, one person uses 150 gallons a day, so they say."

"It's the same for everyone? Four hours every fourth day?"

"Even at the Great House you use a pail." Gavallan shrugged again. "But the tai-pan's got a place at Shek-O that has its own well. We all pile over there when we're invited, to get the slime off."

She thought again of the three pails of water she had used. Jesus, she thought, did I use it all? I don't recall if there's any left.

"I guess I've a lot to learn," she said.

Yes, they all thought. Yes, you bloody have.

"Tai-pan?"

"Yes, Claudia?" Dunross said into the intercom.

"The meeting with Casey's just broken for lunch. Master Andrew is on line four. Master Linbar's on his way up."

"Cancel him till after lunch. Any luck on Tsu-yan?"

"No sir. The plane landed on time at 8:40. He's not at his office in Taipei. Or his flat. I'll keep trying, of course. Another thing, I've just had an interesting call, tai-pan. It seems that Mr. Bartlett went to Rothwell-Gornt this morning and had a private meeting with Mr. Gornt."

"Are you sure?" he asked, ice in his stomach suddenly.

"Yes, oh very yes."

Bastard, Dunross thought. Does Bartlett mean me to find out? "Thanks," he said, putting the question aside for the moment, but very glad to know. "You've got a thousand dollars on any horse on Saturday."

"Oh thank you, tai-pan."

"Back to work, Claudia!" He punched the number four button. "Yes, Andrew? What's the deal?"

Gavallan told him the important part.

"20 million in cash?" he asked with disbelief.

"In marvelous, beautiful U.S. cash!" Dunross could feel his beam down the phone. "And when I asked when Bartlett would confirm the deal the little scrubber had the bloody cheek to say, 'Oh it's confirmed now—I can commit up to 20 million on this deal without consulting him or anyone.' Do you think that's possible?"

"I don't know." Dunross felt a little weak in the knees. "Bartlett's due any moment. I'll ask."

"Hey, tai-pan, if this goes through . . ."

But Dunross was hardly listening as Gavallan ran on ecstatically. It's an unbelievable offer, he was telling himself.

It's too good. Where's the flaw?

Where's the flaw?

Ever since he had become tai-pan he had had to maneuver, lie, cajole and even threaten—Havergill of the bank for one—far more than ever he had expected, to stay ahead of the disasters he had inherited, and the natural and political ones that seemed to be besetting the world. Even going public had not given him the capital and time he had expected because a worldwide slump had ripped the markets to pieces. And last year in August, Typhoon Wanda had struck, leaving havoc in her wake, hundreds dead, a hundred thousand homeless, half a thousand fishing boats sunk, twenty ships sunk, one of their three thousand tonners flung ashore, their giant half-completed wharf wrecked and their entire building program smashed for six months. In the fall the Cuban crisis and more slump. This spring de Gaulle had vetoed Britain's entry into the Common Market and more slump. China and Russia quarreling and more slump. . . .

And now I've almost got 20 million U.S. but I think we're somehow involved in gun-running, Tsu-yan's apparently on the run and John Chen's God knows where!

"Christ all sodding mighty!" he said angrily.

"What?" Gavallan stopped, aghast, in midflow. "What's up?"

"Oh nothing—nothing, Andrew," he said. "Nothing to do with you. Tell me about her. What's she like?"

"Good at figures, fast and confident, but impatient. And she's the best-looking bird I've seen in years, with potentially the best pair of knockers in town." Gavallan told him about the bets. "I think Linbar's got the inside track."

"I'm going to fire Foster and send Linbar down to Sydney for six months, get him to sort everything out there."

"Good idea." Gavallan laughed. "That'll stop his farting in church—though they say the ladies Down Under are very accommodating."

"You think this deal will go through?"

"Yes. Phillip was ecstatic about it. But it's shitty dealing through a woman and that's the truth. Do you think we could bypass her and deal with Bartlett direct?"

"No. He was quite clear in his correspondence that K. C. Tcholok was his chief negotiator."

"Oh well . . . into the breach and all that! What we do for the Noble House!"

"Have you found her weak spot?"

"Impatience. She wants to 'belong'—to be one of the boys. I'd say her Achilles' heel is that she desperately wants acceptance in a man's world."

"No harm in wanting that—like the Holy Grail. The meeting with Dawson's set for eleven tomorrow?"

"Yes."

"Get Dawson to cancel it, but not until nine tomorrow morning. Tell him to make an excuse and reset it for Wednesday at noon."

"Good idea, keep her off balance, what?"

"Tell Jacques I'll take that meeting myself."

"Yes, tai-pan. What about John Chen? You'll want him there?"

After a pause Dunross said, "Yes. Have you seen him yet?"

"No. He's expected for lunch—you want me to chase him?"

"No. Where's Phillip?"

"He went home. He's coming back at 2:30."

Good, Dunross thought, and tabled John Chen until that time. "Listen . . ." The intercom buzzed. "Just a minute, Andrew." He punched the hold. "Yes, Claudia?"

"Sorry to interrupt, tai-pan, but I've got your call to Mr. Jen in Taipei on line two and Mr. Bartlett's just arrived downstairs."

"Bring him in as soon as I'm through with Jen." He stabbed line four again. "Andrew, I may be a couple of minutes late. Host drinks and that sort of thing for me. I'll bring Bartlett up myself."

"Okay."

Dunross stabbed line two. "Tsaw an," he said in Mandarin dialect—How are you?—glad to talk to Wei-wei's uncle, General Jen Tang-wa, deputy chief of the illegal Kuomintang secret police for Hong Kong.

"Shey-shey," then in English, "What's up, tai-pan?"

"I thought you should know . . ." Dunross told him briefly about the guns and Bartlett, that the police were involved, but not about Tsu-yan or John Chen.

"Ayeeyah! That's very curious indeed."

"Yes. I thought so too. Very curious."

"You're convinced it's not Bartlett?"

"Yes. There appears to be no reason. None at all. It'd be stupid to use

your own plane. Bartlett's not stupid," Dunross said. "Who'd need that
sort of armament here?"

There was a pause. "Criminal elements."

"Triads?"

"Not all triads are criminals."

"No," Dunross said.

"I'll see what I can find out. I'm sure it's nothing to do with us, Ian.
Are you still coming Sunday?"

"Yes."

"Good. I'll see what I can find out. Drinks at 6:00 P.M.?"

"How about eight o'clock? Have you seen Tsu-yan yet?"

"I thought he wasn't due until the weekend. Isn't he making up our
foursome on Monday with the American?"

"Yes. I heard he caught an early flight today." Dunross kept his voice
matter-of-fact.

"He's sure to call—do you want him to phone?"

"Yes. Anytime. It's nothing important. See you Sunday at eight."

"Yes, and thanks for the information. If I get anything I'll phone at
once. 'Bye."

Dunross put the phone down. He had been listening very carefully to
the tone of Jen's voice but he had heard nothing untoward. Where the
hell's Tsu-yan?

A knock.

"Come in." He got up and went to meet Bartlett. "Hello." He smiled
and held out his hand. "I'm Ian Dunross."

"Linc Bartlett." They shook hands firmly. "Am I too early?"

"You're dead on time. You must know I like punctuality." Dunross
laughed. "I heard the meeting went well."

"Good," Bartlett replied, wondering if Dunross meant the Gornt meeting. "Casey knows her facts and figures."

"My fellows were most impressed—she said she could finalize things
herself. Can she, Mr. Bartlett?"

"She can negotiate and settle up to 20 million. Why?"

"Nothing. Just wanted to find out your form. Please sit down—we've a
few minutes yet. Lunch won't begin till 12:40. It sounds as though we
may have a profitable enterprise in front of us."

"I hope so. As soon as I've checked with Casey, perhaps you and I can
get together?"

Dunross looked at his calendar. "Tomorrow at ten. Here?"

"You're on."

"Smoke?"

"No thanks. I quit a few years back."

"So did I—still want a cigarette though." Dunross leaned back in his
chair. "Before we go to lunch, Mr. Bartlett, there're a couple of minor
points. I'm going to Taipei on Sunday afternoon, will be back Tuesday in

time for dinner, and I'd like you to come along. There're a couple of people I'd like you to meet, a golf match you might enjoy. We could chat leisurely, you could see the potential plant sites. It could be important. I've made all the arrangements, but it's not possible to take Miss Tcholok."

Bartlett frowned, wondering if Tuesday was just a coincidence. "According to Superintendent Armstrong I can't leave Hong Kong."

"I'm sure that could be changed."

"Then you know about the guns too?" Bartlett said and cursed himself for the slip. He managed to keep his eyes steady.

"Oh yes. Someone else's been bothering you about them?" Dunross asked, watching him.

"The police even chased Casey! Jesus! My airplane's seized, we're all suspect, and I don't know a goddamn thing about any guns."

"Well, there's no need to worry, Mr. Bartlett. Our police are very good."

"I'm not worried, just teed off."

"That's understandable," Dunross said, glad the Armstrong meeting was confidential. Very glad.

Christ, he thought queasily, if John Chen and Tsu-yan are involved somehow, Bartlett's going to be very teed off indeed, and we'll lose the deal and he'll throw in with Gornt and then . . .

"How did you hear about the guns?"

"We were informed by our office at Kai Tak this morning."

"Nothing like this ever happened before?"

"Yes." Dunross added lightly, "But there's no harm in smuggling or even a little gun-running—actually they're both very honorable professions —of course we do them elsewhere."

"Where?"

"Wherever Her Majesty's Government desires." Dunross laughed. "We're all pirates here, Mr. Bartlett, at least we are to outsiders." He paused. "Presuming I can make arrangements with the police, you're on for Taipei?"

Bartlett said, "Casey's very close-mouthed."

"I'm not suggesting she's not to be trusted."

"She's just not invited?"

"Certain of our customs here are a little different from yours, Mr. Bartlett. Most times she'll be welcome—but sometimes, well, it would save a lot of embarrassment if she were excluded."

"Casey doesn't embarrass easily."

"I wasn't thinking of her embarrassment. Sorry to be blunt but perhaps it's wiser in the long run."

"And if I can't 'conform'?"

"It will probably mean you cannot take advantage of a unique opportunity, which would be a very great pity—particularly if you intend a longterm association with Asia."

"I'll think about that."

"Sorry, but I have to have a yes or no now."

"You do?"

"Yes."

"Then go screw!"

Dunross grinned. "I won't. Meanwhile, finally: yes or no."

Bartlett broke out laughing. "Since you put it that way, I'm on for Taipei."

"Good. Of course I'll have my wife look after Miss Tcholok while we're away. There'll be no loss of face for her."

"Thank you. But you needn't worry about Casey. How are you going to fix Armstrong?"

"I'm not going to *fix* him, just ask the assistant commissioner to let me be responsible for you, there and back."

"Parole me in your custody?"

"Yes."

"How do you know I won't just leave town? Maybe I was gun-running."

Dunross watched him. "Maybe you are. Maybe you'll try—but I can deliver you back dead or alive, as they say in the movies. Hong Kong and Taipei are within my fief."

"Dead or alive, eh?"

"Hypothetically, of course."

"How many men have you killed in your lifetime?"

The mood in the room changed and both men felt the change deeply.

It's not dangerous yet between him and me, Dunross thought, not yet.

"Twelve," he replied, his senses poised, though the question had surprised him. "Twelve that I'm sure of. I was a fighter pilot during the war. Spitfires. I got two single-seat fighters, a Stuka, and two bombers—they were Dornier 17s and they'd have a crew of four each. All the planes burned as they went down. Twelve that I'm sure of, Mr. Bartlett. Of course we shot up a lot of trains, convoys, troop concentrations. Why?"

"I'd heard you were a flier. I don't think I've killed anyone. I was building camps, bases in the Pacific, that sort of thing. Never shot a gun in anger."

"But you like hunting?"

"Yes. I went on a safari in '59 in Kenya. Got an elephant and a great kudu bull and lots of game for the pot."

Dunross said after a pause, "I think I prefer to kill planes and trains and boats. Men, in war, are incidental. Aren't they?"

"Once the general's been put into the field by the ruler, sure. That's a fact of war."

"Have you read Sun Tzu's *The Art of War*?"

"The best book on war I've ever read," Bartlett said enthusiastically.

"Better'n Clausewitz or Liddell Hart, even though it was written in 500 B.C."

"Oh?" Dunross leaned back, glad to get away from the killings. I haven't remembered the killing for years, he thought. That's not fair to those men, is it?

"Did you know Sun Tzu's book was published in French in 1782? I've a theory Napoleon had a copy."

"It's certainly in Russian—and Mao always carried a copy that was dog-eared with use," Dunross said.

"You've read it?"

"My father beat it into me. I had to read the original in characters—in Chinese. And then he'd question me on it, very seriously."

A fly began to batter itself irritatingly against the windowpane. "Your dad wanted you to be a soldier?"

"No. Sun Tzu, like Machiavelli, wrote about life more than death—and about survival more than war. . . ." Dunross glanced at the window then got up and went over to it and obliterated the fly with a controlled savagery that sent warning signals through Bartlett.

Dunross returned to his desk. "My father thought I should know about survival and how to handle large bodies of men. He wanted me to be worthy to become tai-pan one day, though he never thought I'd amount to much." He smiled.

"He was tai-pan too?"

"Yes. He was very good. At first."

"What happened?"

Dunross laughed sardonically. "Ah, skeletons so early, Mr. Bartlett? Well, briefly, we had a rather tedious, long-drawn-out difference of opinion. Eventually he handed over to Alastair Struan, my predecessor."

"He's still alive?"

"Yes."

"Does your British understatement mean you went to war with him?"

"Sun Tzu's very specific about going to war, Mr. Bartlett. Very bad to go to war he says, unless you need to. Quote: 'Supreme excellence of generalship consists in breaking the enemy's resistance without fighting.'"

"You broke him?"

"He removed himself from the field, Mr. Bartlett, like the wise man he was."

Dunross's face had hardened. Bartlett studied him. Both men knew they were drawing battle lines in spite of themselves.

"I'm glad I came to Hong Kong," the American said. "I'm glad to meet you."

"Thank you. Perhaps one day you won't be."

Bartlett shrugged. "Maybe. Meanwhile we've got a deal cooking—good for you, good for us." He grinned abruptly, thinking about Gornt and the cooking knife. "Yes. I'm glad I came to Hong Kong."

"Would you and Casey care to be my guests this evening? I'm having a modest bash, a party, at 8:30 odd."

"Formal?"

"Just dinner jacket—is that all right?"

"Fine. Casey said you like the tux and black tie bit." Then Bartlett noticed the painting on the wall: an old oil of a pretty Chinese boat girl carrying a little English boy, his fair hair tied in a queue. "That a Quance? An Aristotle Quance?"

"Yes, yes it is," Dunross said, barely covering his surprise.

Bartlett walked over and looked at it. "This the original?"

"Yes. You know much about art?"

"No, but Casey told me about Quance as we were coming out here. She said he's almost like a photographer, really a historian of the early times."

"Yes, yes he is."

"If I remember this one's supposed to be a portrait of a girl called Maymay, May-may T'Chung, and the child is one of Dirk Struan's by her?"

Dunross said nothing, just watched Bartlett's back.

Bartlett peered a little closer. "Difficult to see the eyes. So the boy is Gordon Chen, Sir Gordon Chen to be?" He turned and looked at Dunross.

"I don't know for certain, Mr. Bartlett. That's one story."

Bartlett watched him for a moment. The two men were well matched, Dunross slightly taller but Bartlett wider in the shoulders. Both had blue eyes, Dunross's slightly more greenish, both wideset in lived-in faces.

"You enjoy being tai-pan of the Noble House?" Bartlett asked.

"Yes."

"I don't know for a fact what a tai-pan's powers are, but in Par-Con I can hire and fire anyone, and can close it down if I want."

"Then you're a tai-pan."

"Then I enjoy being a tai-pan too. I want in in Asia—you need an in in the States. Together we could sew up the whole Pacific Rim into a tote bag for both of us."

Or a shroud for one of us, Dunross thought, liking Bartlett despite the fact that he knew it was dangerous to like him.

"I've got what you lack, you've got what I lack."

"Yes," Dunross said. "And now what we both lack is lunch."

They turned for the door. Bartlett was there first. But he did not open it at once. "I know it's not your custom but since I'm going with you to Taipei, could you call me Linc and I call you Ian and we begin to figure out how much we're gonna bet on the golf match? I'm sure you know my handicap's thirteen, officially, and I know yours's ten, officially, which probably means at least one stroke off both of us for safety."

"Why not?" Dunross said at once. "But here we don't normally bet money, just balls."

"I'm goddamned if I'm betting mine on a golf match."

Dunross laughed. "Maybe you will, one day. We usually bet half a dozen golf balls here—something like that."

"It's a bad British custom to bet money, Ian?"

"No. How about five hundred a side, winning team take all?"

"U.S. or Hong Kong?"

"Hong Kong. Among friends it should be Hong Kong. Initially."

Lunch was served in the directors' private dining room on the nineteenth floor. It was an L-shaped corner room, with a high ceiling and blue drapes, mottled blue Chinese carpets and large windows from which they could see Kowloon and the airplanes taking off and landing at Kai Tak and as far west as Stonecutters Island and Tsing Yi Island, and, beyond, part of the New Territories. The great, antique oak dining table which could seat twenty easily was laid with placemats and fine silver, and Waterford's best crystal. For the six of them, there were four silent, very well-trained waiters in black trousers and white tunics embroidered with the Struan emblem.

Cocktails had been started before Bartlett and Dunross arrived. Casey was having a dry vodka martini with the others—except for Gavallan who had a double pink gin. Bartlett, without being asked, was served an ice-cold can of Anweiser, on a Georgian silver tray.

"Who told you?" Bartlett said, delighted.

"Compliments of Struan and Company," Dunross said. "We heard that's the way you like it." He introduced him to Gavallan, deVille and Linbar Struan, and accepted a glass of iced Chablis, then smiled at Casey. "How are you?"

"Fine, thanks."

"Excuse me," Bartlett said to the others, "but I have to give Casey a message before I forget. Casey, will you call Johnston in Washington tomorrow—find out who our best contact'd be at the consulate here."

"Certainly. If I can't get him I'll ask Tim Diller."

Anything to do with Johnston was code for: how's the deal progressing? In answer: Diller meant good, Tim Diller very good, Jones bad, George Jones very bad.

"Good idea," Bartlett said and smiled back, then to Dunross, "This is a beautiful room."

"It's adequate," Dunross said.

Casey laughed, getting the underplay. "The meeting went very well, Mr. Dunross," she said. "We came up with a proposal for your consideration."

How American to come out with it like that—no finesse! Doesn't she know business is for after lunch, not before. "Yes. Andrew gave me the outline," Dunross replied. "Would you care for another drink?"

"No thanks. I think the proposal covers everything, sir. Are there any points you'd like me to clarify?"

"I'm sure there will be, in due course," Dunross said, privately amused, as always, by the *sir* that many American women used conversationally, and often, incongruously, to waiters. "As soon as I've studied it I'll get back to you. A beer for Mr. Bartlett," he added, once more trying to divert business until later. Then to Jacques, "*Ça va?*"

"*Oui merci. A rien.*" Nothing yet.

"Not to worry," Dunross said. Yesterday Jacques's adored daughter and her husband had had a bad car accident while on holiday in France—how bad he was still waiting to hear. "Not to worry."

"No." Again the Gallic shrug, hiding the vastness of his concern.

Jacques was Dunross's first cousin and he had joined Struan's in '45. His war had been rotten. In 1940 he had sent his wife and two infants to England and had stayed in France. For the duration. Maquis and prison and condemned and escaped and Maquis again. Now he was fifty-four, a strong, quiet man but vicious when provoked, with a heavy chest and brown eyes and rough hands and many scars.

"In principle does the deal sound okay?" Casey asked.

Dunross sighed inwardly and put his full concentration on her. "I may have a counterproposal on a couple of minor points. Meanwhile," he added decisively, "you can proceed on the assumption that, in general terms, it's acceptable."

"Oh fine," Casey said happily.

"Great," Bartlett said, equally pleased, and raised his can of beer. "Here's to a successful conclusion and big profits—for you and for us."

They drank the toast, the others reading the danger signs in Dunross, wondering what the tai-pan's counterproposal would be.

"Will it take you long to finalize, Ian?" Bartlett asked, and all of them heard the *Ian.* Linbar Struan winced openly.

To their astonishment, Dunross just said, "No," as though the familiarity was quite ordinary, adding, "I doubt if the solicitors will come up with anything insurmountable."

"We're seeing them tomorrow at eleven o'clock," Casey said. "Mr. de-Ville, John Chen and I. We've already gotten their advance go-through . . . no problems there."

"Dawson's very good—particularly on U.S. tax law."

"Casey, maybe we should bring out our tax guy from New York," Bartlett said.

"Sure, Linc, soon as we're set. And Forrester." To Dunross she said, "He's head of our foam division."

"Good. And that's enough shoptalk before lunch," Dunross said. "House rules, Miss Casey: no shop with food, it's very bad for the digestion." He beckoned Lim. "We won't wait for Master John."

Instantly waiters materialized and chairs were held out and there were typed place names in silver holders and the soup was ladled.

The menu said sherry with the soup, Chablis with the fish—or claret with the roast beef and Yorkshire pudding if you preferred it—boiled string beans and boiled potatoes and boiled carrots. Sherry trifle as dessert. Port with the cheese tray.

"How long will you be staying, Mr. Bartlett?" Gavallan asked.

"As long as it takes. But Mr. Gavallan, since it looks as though we're going to be in business together a long time, how about you dropping the 'Mr.' Bartlett and the 'Miss' Casey and calling us Linc and Casey."

Gavallan kept his eyes on Bartlett. He would have liked to have said, Well Mr. Bartlett, we prefer to work up to these things around here—it's one of the few ways you tell your friends from your acquaintances. For us first names are a private thing. But as the tai-pan hasn't objected to the astonishing "Ian" there's not a thing I can do. "Why not, Mr. Bartlett?" he said blandly. "No need to stand on ceremony. Is there?"

Jacques deVille and Struan and Dunross chuckled inside at the "Mr. Bartlett," and the way Gavallan had neatly turned the unwanted acceptance into a put-down and a loss of face that neither of the Americans would ever understand.

"Thanks, Andrew," Bartlett said. Then he added, "Ian, may I bend the rules and ask one more question before lunch: Can you finalize by next Tuesday, one way or another?"

Instantly the currents in the room reversed. Lim and the other servants hesitated, shocked. All eyes went to Dunross. Bartlett thought he had gone too far and Casey was sure of it. She had been watching Dunross. His expression had not changed but his eyes had. Everyone in the room knew that the tai-pan had been called as a man will call another in a poker game. Put up or shut up. By next Tuesday.

They waited. The silence seemed to hang. And hang.

Then Dunross broke it. "I'll let you know tomorrow," he said, his voice calm, and the moment passed and everyone sighed inwardly and the waiters continued and everyone relaxed. Except Linbar. He could still feel the sweat on his hands because he alone of them knew the thread that went through all of the descendents of Dirk Struan—a strange, almost primeval, sudden urge to violence—and he had seen it almost surface then, almost but not quite. This time it had gone away. But the knowledge of it and its closeness terrified him.

His own line was descended from Robb Struan, Dirk Struan's half-brother and partner, so he had none of Dirk Struan's blood in his veins. He bitterly regretted it and loathed Dunross even more for making him sick with envy.

Hag Struan on you, Ian bloody Dunross, and all your generations, he thought, and shuddered involuntarily at the thought of her.

"What's up, Linbar?" Dunross asked.

"Oh nothing, tai-pan," he said, almost jumping out of his skin. "Nothing—just a sudden thought. Sorry."

"What thought?"

"I was just thinking about Hag Struan."

Dunross's spoon hesitated in midair and the others stared at him. "That's not exactly good for your digestion."

"No sir."

Bartlett glanced at Linbar, then at Dunross. "Who's Hag Struan?"

"A skeleton," Dunross said with a dry laugh. "We've lots of skeletons in our family."

"Who hasn't?" Casey said.

"Hag Struan was our eternal bogeyman—still is."

"Not now, tai-pan, surely," Gavallan said. "She's been dead for almost fifty years."

"Maybe she'll die out with us, with Linbar, Kathy and me, with our generation, but I doubt it." Dunross looked at Linbar strangely. "Will Hag Struan get out of her coffin tonight and gobble us up?"

"I swear to God I don't like even joking about her like that, tai-pan."

"The pox on Hag Struan," Dunross said. "If she was alive I'd say it to her face."

"I think you would. Yes," Gavallan laughed suddenly. "That I'd like to have seen."

"So would I." Dunross laughed with him, then he saw Casey's expression. "Ah, just bravado, Casey. Hag Struan was a fiend from hell if you believe half the legends. She was Culum Struan's wife—he was Dirk Struan's son—our founder's son. Her maiden name was Tess, Tess Brock and she was the daughter of Dirk's hated enemy, Tyler Brock. Culum and Tess eloped in 1841, so the story goes. She was sweet sixteen and a beauty, and he heir to the Noble House. It was rather like Romeo and Juliet—except they lived and it made no difference whatsoever to the blood feud of Dirk against Tyler or the Struans versus the Brocks, it just heightened and complicated it. She was born Tess Brock in 1825 and died Hag Struan in 1917, aged ninety-two, toothless, hairless, besotten, vicious and dreadful to her very last day. Life's strange, *heya?*"

"Yes. Unbelievable sometimes," Casey said thoughtfully. "Why is it people change so much growing old—get so sour and bitter? Particularly women?"

Fashion, Dunross could have answered at once, and because men and women age differently. It's unfair—but an immortal fact. A woman sees the lines beginning and the sagging beginning and the skin no longer so fresh and firm but her man's still fine and sought after and then she sees the young dolly birds and she's petrified she'll lose him to them and eventually she will because he'll become bored with her carping and the self-fed agony of the self-mutilation—and too, because of his built-in uncontrollable urge toward youth. . . .

"*Ayeeyah*, there's no aphrodisiac in the world like youth," old Chen-Chen—Phillip Chen's father—Ian's mentor would always say. "None, young Ian, there's none. None none none. Listen to me. The yang needs the yin juices, but young juices, oh yes they should be young, the juices young to extend your life and nourish the yang—oh oh oh! Remember, the older your Male Stalk becomes the more it needs youth and change and young enthusiasm to perform exuberantly, and the more the merrier! But also remember that the Beauteous Box that nests between all their thighs, peerless though it is, delectable, delicious, unearthly, oh so sweet and oh so satisfying as it also is, beware! Ha! It's also a trap, ambush, torture chamber and your coffin!" Then the old, old man would chuckle and his belly would jump up and down and the tears would run down his face. "Oh the gods are marvelous, are they not? They grant us heaven on earth but it's living hell when you can't get your one-eyed monk to raise his head to enter paradise. Joss, my child! That's our joss—to crave the Greedy Gully until she eats you up, but oh oh oh . . ."

It must be very difficult for women, particularly Americans, Dunross thought, this trauma of growing old, the inevitability of it happening so early, too early—worse in America than anywhere else on earth.

Why should I tell you a truth you must already know in your bones, Dunross asked himself. Or say further that American fashion demands you try to grasp an eternal youth neither God nor devil nor surgeon can give you. You can't be twenty-five when you're thirty-five nor have a thirty-five-year-old youthfulness when you're forty-five, or forty-five when you're fifty-five. Sorry, I know it's unfair but it's a fact.

Ayeeyah, he thought fervently, thank God—if there is a God—thank all gods great and small I'm a man and not a woman. I pity you, American lady with the beautiful names.

But Dunross answered simply, "I suppose that's because life's no bed of roses and we're fed stupid pap and bad values growing up—not like the Chinese who're so sensible—Christ, how unbelievably sensible they are! In Hag Struan's case perhaps it was her rotten Brock blood. I think it was her joss—her fate or luck or unluck. She and Culum had seven children, four sons and three daughters. All her sons died violently, two of the 'flux' —probably plague—here in Hong Kong, one was murdered, knifed in Shanghai, and the last was drowned off Ayr in Scotland, where our family lands are. That'd be enough to send any mother around the bend, that and the hatred and envy that surrounded Culum and her all their lives. But when you add this to all the problems of living in Asia, the passing over of the Noble House to other people's sons . . . well, you can understand." Dunross thought a moment, then added, "Legend has it she ruled Culum Struan all his life and tyrannized the Noble House till the day she died—and all tai-pans, all daughters-in-law, all sons-in-law and all the children as well. Even after she died. I can remember one English nanny I had, may she burn in hell forever, saying to me, 'You better behave,

Master Ian, or I'll conjure up Hag Struan and she'll gobble you up. . . .'
I can't have been more than five or six."

"How terrible," Casey said.

Dunross shrugged. "Nannies do that to children."

"Not all of them, thank God," Gavallan said.

"I never had one who was any good at all. Or a *gan sun* who was ever bad."

"What's a *gan sun?*" Casey asked.

"It means 'near body,' it's the correct name for an *amah*. In China pre-'49, children of well-to-do families and most of the old European and Eurasian families out here always had their own 'near body' to look after them —in many cases they kept them all their lives. Most *gan sun* take a vow of celibacy. You can always recognize them by the long queue they wear down their back. My *gan sun*'s called Ah Tat. She's a great old bird. She's still with us," Dunross said.

Gavallan said, "Mine was more like a mother to me than my real mother."

"So Hag Struan's your great-grandmother?" Casey said to Linbar.

"Christ no! No, I'm—I'm not from Dirk Struan's line," he replied and she saw sweat on his forehead that she did not understand. "My line comes from his half-brother, Robb Struan. Robb Struan was Dirk's partner. The tai-pan's descended directly from Dirk, but even so . . . none of us're descended from the Hag."

"You're all related?" Casey asked, feeling curious tensions in the room. She saw Linbar hesitate and glance at Dunross as she looked at him.

"Yes," he said. "Andrew's married to my sister, Kathy. Jacques is a cousin, and Linbar . . . Linbar carries our name." Dunross laughed. "There're still lots of people in Hong Kong who remember the Hag, Casey. She always wore a long black dress with a big bustle and a funny hat with a huge moth-eaten feather, everything totally out of fashion, and she'd have a black stick with a silver handle on it with her. Most times she was carried in a sort of palanquin by four bearers up and down the streets. She wasn't much more than five foot but round and tough as a coolie's foot. The Chinese were equally petrified of her. Her nickname was 'Honorable Old Foreign Devil Mother with the Evil Eye and Dragon's Teeth.'"

"That's right," Gavallan said with a short laugh. "My father and grandmother knew her. They had their own trading company here and in Shanghai, Casey, but got more or less wiped out in the Great War and joined up with Struan's in '19. My old man told me that when he was a boy he and his friends used to follow the Hag around the streets and when she got particularly angry she'd take out her false teeth and chomp them at them." They all laughed with him as he parodied her. "My old man swore the teeth were two feet tall and on some form of spring and they'd go, crunch crunch crunch!"

"Hey Andrew, I'd forgotten that," Linbar broke in with a grin. "My *gan sun,* old Ah Fu, knew Hag Struan well and every time you'd mention her, Ah Fu's eyes'd turn up and she'd petition the gods to protect her from the evil eye and magic teeth. My brother Kyle and I . . ." He stopped, then began again in a different voice. "We used to tease Ah Fu about her."

Dunross said to Casey, "There's a portrait of her up at the Great House —two in fact. If you're interested, I'll show them to you one day."

"Oh thanks—I'd like that. Is there one of Dirk Struan?"

"Several. And one of Robb, his half-brother."

"I'd love to see them."

"Me too," Bartlett said. "Hell, I've never even seen a photo of my grandparents, let alone a portrait of my great-great-grandfather. I've always wanted to know about my forebears, what they were like, where they came from. I know nothing about them except my grandpa was supposed to have run a freight company in the Old West in a place called Jerrico. Must be great to know where you're from. You're lucky." He had been sitting back listening to the undercurrents, fascinated by them, seeking clues against the time he'd have to decide: Dunross or Gornt. If it's Dunross, Andrew Gavallan's an enemy and will have to go, he told himself. Young Struan hates Dunross, the Frenchman's an enigma and Dunross himself is nitroglycerine and just as dangerous. "Your Hag Struan sounds fantastic," he said. "And Dirk Struan too must have been quite a character."

"Now that's a masterpiece of understatement!" Jacques deVille said, his dark eyes sparkling. "He was the greatest pirate in Asia! You wait—you look at Dirk's portrait and you'll see the family resemblance! Our tai-pan's the spitting image, and *ma foi,* he's inherited all the worst parts."

"Drop dead, Jacques," Dunross said good-naturedly. Then to Casey, "It's not true. Jacques is always ribbing me. I'm nothing like him at all."

"But you're descended from him."

"Yes. My great-grandmother was Winifred, Dirk's only legitimate daughter. She married Lechie Struan Dunross, a clansman. They had one son who was my grandfather—he was tai-pan after Culum. My family— the Dunrosses are Dirk Struan's only direct descendents, as far as we know."

"You, you said legitimate?"

Dunross smiled. "Dirk had other sons and daughters. One son, Gordon Chen, was from a lady called Shen actually, that you know of. That's the Chen line today. There's also the T'Chung line—from Duncan T'Chung and Kate T'Chung, his son and daughter by the famous May-may T'Chung. Anyway that's the legend, they're accepted legends here though no one can prove or disprove them." Dunross hesitated and his eyes crinkled with the depth of his smile. "In Hong Kong and Shanghai our predecessors were, well, friendly, and the Chinese ladies beautiful, then as now. But they married their ladies rarely and the pill's only a very recent invention—so you don't always know who you might be related to. We, ah, we don't discuss this sort of thing publicly—in true British fashion we pretend it doesn't exist though we all know it does, then no one loses face. Eurasian families of Hong Kong usually took the name of their mothers, in Shanghai their fathers. We all seem to have accommodated the problem."

"It's all very friendly," Gavallan said.

"Sometimes," Dunross said.

"Then John Chen's related to you?" Casey asked.

"If you go back to the garden of Eden everyone's related to everyone I suppose." Dunross was looking at the empty place. Not like John to run off, he thought uneasily, and he's not the sort to get involved in gun smuggling, for any reason. Or be so stupid as to get caught. Tsu-yan? Well he's Shanghainese and he could easily be panicked—if he's mixed up in this. John's too easily recognized not to have been seen getting on a plane this morning so it's not that way. It has to be by boat—if he has run off. A boat where? Macao—no, that's a dead end. Ship? Too easy, he thought, if it was planned or even not planned and arranged at an hour's notice. Any day of the year there'd be thirty or forty scheduled sailings to all parts of the world, big ships and little ships, let alone a thousand junks nonscheduled, and even if on the run, a few dollars here and there and too easy to smuggle out—out or in. Men, women, children. Drugs. Anything. But no reason to smuggle inward except humans and drugs and guns and liquor and cigarettes and petrol—everything else is duty free and unrestricted.

Except gold.

Dunross smiled to himself. You import gold legally under license at thirty-five dollars an ounce for transit to Macao and what happens then is nobody's business but immensely profitable. Yes, he thought, and our Nelson Trading board meeting's this afternoon. Good. That's one business venture that never fails.

As he took some of the fish from the proffered silver tray he noticed Casey staring at him. "Yes, Casey?"

"Oh I was just wondering how you knew my names." She turned to Bartlett. "The tai-pan surprised me, Linc. Before we were even introduced he called me Kamalian Ciranoush as though it were Mary Jane."

"That's Persian?" Gavallan asked at once.

"Armenian originally."

"Kamahly-arn Cirrrannoooossssh," Jacques said, liking the sibilance of the names. "*Très jolie, mademoiselle. Ils ne sont pas difficile sauf pour les cretins.*"

"*Ou les* English," Dunross said and they all laughed.

"How did you know, tai-pan?" Casey asked him, feeling more at home with *tai-pan* than with Ian. *Ian doesn't belong, yet,* she thought, swept by his past and Hag Struan and the shadows that seemed to be surrounding him.

"I asked your attorney."

"What do you mean?"

"John Chen called me last night around midnight. You hadn't told him what K.C. stood for and I wanted to know. It was too early to talk to your office in Los Angeles—just 8 A.M., L.A. time—so I called your attorney in New York. My father used to say, when in doubt ask."

"You got Seymour Steigler III on a Saturday?" Bartlett asked, amazed.

"Yes. At his home in White Plains."

"But his home number's not in the book."

"I know. I called a Chinese friend of mine in the UN. He tracked him down for me. I told Mr. Steigler I wanted to know because of invitations—which is, of course, the truth. One should be accurate, shouldn't one?"

"Yes," Casey said, admiring him greatly. "Yes one should."

"You knew Casey was . . . Casey was a woman, last night?" Gavallan asked.

"Yes. Actually I knew several months ago, though not what K.C. stood for. Why?"

"Nothing, tai-pan. Casey, you were saying about Armenia. Your family immigrated to the States after the war?"

"After the First World War in 1918," Casey said, beginning the oft-told story. "Originally our surname was Tcholokian. When my grandparents arrived in New York they dropped the *ian* for simplicity, to help Americans. I still got Kamalian Ciranoush though. As you know, Armenia is the southern part of Caucasus—just north of Iran and Turkey and south of Russian Georgia. It used to be a free sovereign nation but now it's all absorbed by Soviet Russia or Turkey. My grandmother was Georgian—there was lots of intermarriage in the old days. My people were spread all over the Ottoman Empire, about two million, but the massacres, particularly in 1915 and '16 . . ." Casey shivered. "It was genocide really. There're barely 500,000 of us left and now we're scattered throughout the world. Armenians were traders, artists, painters and jewelry makers, writers, warriors too. There were nearly 50,000 Armenians in the Turkish Army before they were disarmed, outcast and shot by the Turks during World War One—generals, officers and soldiers. They were an elite minority and had been for centuries."

"Is that why the Turks hated them?" deVille asked.

"They were hardworking and clannish and very good traders and businessmen for sure—they controlled lots of business and trade. My granddad said trading's in our blood. But perhaps the main reason is that Armenians are Christian—they were the first Christian state in history under the Romans—and of course the Turks are Mohammedan. The Turks conquered Armenia in the sixteenth century and there was always a border war going on between Christian Tsarist Russia and the 'Infidel' Turks.

Up to 1917 Tsarist Russia was our real protector. . . . The Ottoman Turks were always a strange people, very cruel, very strange."

"Your family got out before the trouble?"

"No. My grandparents were quite rich, and like a lot of people thought nothing could happen to them. They escaped just ahead of the soldiers, took two sons and a daughter out the back door with just what they could grab in their dash for freedom. The rest of the family never made it. My grandfather bribed his way out of Istanbul onto a fishing boat that smuggled him and my grandmother to Cyprus where, somehow, they got visas to the States. They had a little money and some jewelry—and lots of talent. Granny's still alive . . . she can still haggle with the best of them."

"Your grandfather was a trader?" Dunross asked. "Is that how you first got interested in business?"

"We certainly had it drummed into us as soon as we could think about being self-sufficient," Casey said. "My granddad started an optical company in Providence, making lenses and microscopes and an import-export company dealing mostly in carpets and perfumes, with a little gold and precious stones trading on the side. My dad designed and made jewelry. He's dead now but he had a small store of his own in Providence, and his brother, my uncle Bghos, worked with Granddad. Now, since Granddad died, my uncle runs the import-export company. It's small but stable. We grew up, my sister and I, around haggling, negotiating and the problem of profit. It was a great game and we were all equals."

"Where . . . oh, more trifle, Casey?"

"No thanks, I'm fine."

"Where did you take your business degree?"

"I suppose all over," she said. "After I got out of high school, I put myself through a two-year business course at Katharine Gibbs in Providence: shorthand, typing, simple accounting, filing, plus a few business fundamentals. But ever since I could count I worked nights and holidays and weekends with Granddad in his businesses. I was taught to think and plan and put the plan into effect, so most of my training's been in the field. Of course since I've gotten out of school I've kept up with specialized courses that I wanted to take—at night school mostly." Casey laughed. "Last year I even took one at the Harvard Business School which went down like an H-bomb with some members of the faculty, though it's getting a little easier now for a woman."

"How did you manage to become hatchetman—hatchetlady to Par-Con Industries?" Dunross said.

"Perspicacity," she said and they laughed with her.

Bartlett said, "Casey's a devil for work, Ian. Her speed reading's fantastic so she can cover more ground than two normal execs. She's got a great nose for danger, she's not afraid of a decision, she's more of a deal maker than a deal breaker, and she doesn't blush easily."

"That's my best point," Casey said. "Thanks, Linc."

"But isn't it very hard on you, Casey?" Gavallan asked. "Don't you have to concede a hell of a lot as a woman to keep up? It can't be easy for you to do a man's job."

"I don't consider my job a man's job, Andrew," she replied at once. "Women have just as good brains and work capacity as men."

There was an immediate hoot of friendly derision from Linbar and Gavallan and Dunross overrode them and said, "I think we'll table that one for later. But again, Casey, how did you get where you are at Par-Con?"

Shall I tell you the real story, Ian lookalike to Dirk Struan, the greatest pirate in Asia, or shall I tell you the one that's become legend, she asked herself.

Then she heard Bartlett begin and she knew she could safely drift for she had heard his version a hundred times before and it was part true, part false and part what he wanted to believe had happened. How many of *your* legends are true—Hag Struan and Dirk Struan and what's your real story and how did you become tai-pan? She sipped her port, enjoying the smooth sweetness, letting her mind wander.

There's something wrong here, she was thinking now. I can feel it strongly. Something's wrong with Dunross.

What?

"I first met Casey in Los Angeles, California—about seven years ago," Bartlett had begun. "I'd gotten a letter from a Casey Tcholok, president of Hed-Opticals of Providence, who wanted to discuss a merger. At that time I was in construction all over the L.A. area—residential, supermarkets, a couple of good-sized office buildings, industrial, shopping centers—you name it, I'd build it. We had a turnover of 3.2 million and I'd just gone public—but I was still a million miles away from the Big Board. I'd—"

"You mean the New York Stock Exchange?"

"Yes. Anyway, Casey comes in bright as a new penny and says she wants me to merge with Hed-Opticals which she says grossed $277,600 last year, and then together, we'd go after Randolf Opticals, the grand-daddy of them all—53 million in sales, quoted on the Big Board, a huge slice of the lens market and lots of cash in the bank—and I said you're crazy but why Randolf? She said because first she was a stockholder in Bartlett Constructions—she'd bought ten one-dollar shares—I'd capitalized at a million shares and sold 500,000 at par—and she figured it'd be dandy for Bartlett Construction to own Randolf, and second, 'because this son of a bitch George Toffer who runs Randolf Opticals is a liar, a cheat, a thief, and he's trying to put me out of business.'"

Bartlett grinned and paused for breath and Dunross broke in with a laugh. "This's true, Casey?"

Casey came back quickly. "Oh yes, I said that George Toffer was a liar, a cheat, thief and son of a bitch. He still is." Casey smiled without humor. "And he was certainly trying to put me out of business."

"Why?"

"Because I had told him to go—to drop dead."

"Why'd you do that?"

"I'd just taken over Hed-Opticals. My granddad had died the previous year and we'd flipped a coin, my uncle Bghos and I, who'd get which business. . . . I'd won Hed-Opticals. We'd had an offer from Randolf to buy us out a year or so back but we'd turned it down—we had a nice, small operation, a good work force, good technicians—a number of them Armenians—a little slice of the market. But no capital and no room to maneuver but we got by and the quality of Hed-Opticals was optimum. Just after I took over, George Toffer 'happened to drop by.' He fancied himself, my God how he fancied himself. He claimed he was a U.S. Army war hero but I found out he wasn't—he was that sort of guy. Anyway, he made me another ridiculous offer to take Hed-Opticals off my hands . . . the poor little girl who should be in the kitchen bit, along with the 'let's have dinner tonight in my suite and why don't we have a little fun because I'm here alone for a few days. . . .' I said no thanks and he was very put out. Very. But he said okay and went back to business and suggested that instead of a buy-out we subcontract some of his contracts. He made me a good offer and after haggling a bit we agreed on terms. If I performed on this one he said he'd double the deal. Over the next month we did the work better and cheaper than he could ever have done it—I delivered according to contract and he made a fantastic profit. But then he reneged on a verbal clause and deducted—stole—$20,378, and the next day five of my best customers left us for Randolf, and the next week another seven—they'd all been offered deals at less than cost. He let me sweat for a week or two then he phoned. 'Hi, baby,' he said, happy as a toad in a pail of mud, 'I'm spending the weekend alone at Martha's Vineyard.' That's a little island off the East Coast. Then he added, 'Why don't you come over and we'll have some fun and discuss the future and doubling our orders.' I asked for my money, and he laughed at me and told me to grow up and suggested I better reconsider his offer because at the rate I was going soon there'd be no Hed-Opticals.

"I cursed him," Casey said. "I can curse pretty good when I get mad and I told him what to do with himself in three languages. Within four more weeks I'd no customers left. Another month and the work force had to get other jobs. About that time I thought I'd try California. I didn't want to stay in the East." She smiled wryly. "It was a matter of face—if I'd known about face then. I thought I'd take a couple of weeks off to figure out what to do. Then one day I was wandering aimlessly around a state fair in Sacramento and Linc was there. He was selling shares in Bartlett Construction in a booth and I bought—"

"He what?" Dunross asked.

"Sure," Bartlett said. "I sold upwards of 20,000 shares that way. I covered state fairs, mail orders, supermarkets, stockbrokers, shopping centers—along with investment banks. Sure. Go on, Casey!"

"So I read his prospectus and watched him awhile and thought he had a lot of get up and go. His figures and balance sheet and expansion rate were exceptional and I thought anyone who'd pitch his own stock has got to have a future. So I bought ten shares, wrote him and went to see him. End of story."

"The hell it is, Casey," Gavallan said.

"You tell it, Linc," she said.

"Okay. Well, then—"

"Some port, Mr.—sorry, Linc?"

"Thanks Andrew, but, er, may I have another beer?" It arrived instantly. "So Casey'd come to see me. After she'd told it, almost like she's told it now, I said, 'One thing, Casey, Hed-Opticals grossed less than 300,000-odd last year. What's it going to do this year?'

"'Zero,' she said with that smile of hers. 'I'm Hed-Opticals' total asset. In fact, I'm all there is.'

"'Then what's the use of my merging with zero—I've got enough problems of my own.'

"'I know how to take Randolf Opticals to the cleaners.'

"'How?'

"'22 percent of Randolf's is owned by three men—all of whom despise Toffer. With 22 percent you could get control. I know how you could get their proxies, and most of all, I know the weakness of Toffer.'

"'What's that?'

"'Vanity, and he's a megalomaniac, but most of all he's stupid.'

"'He can't be stupid and run that company.'

"'Perhaps he wasn't once, but now he is. He's ready to be taken.'

"'And what do you want out of this, Casey?'

"'Toffer's head—I want to do the firing.'

"'What else?'

"'If I succeed in showing you how . . . if we succeed in taking over Randolf Opticals, say within six months, I'd like . . . I'd like a one-year deal with you, to be extended to seven, at a salary you think is commensurate with my ability, as your executive vice-president in charge of acquisitions. But I'd want it as a person, not as a woman, just as an equal person to you. You're the boss of course, but I'm to be equal as a man would be equal, as an individual . . . if I deliver.'"

Bartlett grinned and sipped his beer. "I said, okay you've got a deal. I thought, what've I got to lose—me with my lousy three-quarter million and her with her nothing zero balance for Randolf Opticals in six months, now that's one helluva steal. So we shook, man to woman." Bartlett laughed. "First time I'd ever made a deal with a woman, just like that—and I've never regretted it."

"Thanks, Linc," Casey said softly, and every one of them was envious.

And what happened after you fired Toffer, Dunross was thinking with all the others. Is that when you two began?

"The takeover," he said to Bartlett. "It was smooth?"

"Messy, but we got blooded and the lessons I learned, we learned, paid off a thousand percent. In five months we'd control. Casey and I had conquered a company 53½ times our size. At D-hour minus one I was down to minus 4 million dollars in the bank and goddamn near in jail, but the next hour I'd control. Man, that was a battle and a half. In a month and a half we'd reorganized it and now Par-Con's Randolf Division grosses $150 millions yearly and the stock's way up. It was a classic blitzkrieg and set the pattern for Par-Con Industries."

"And this George Toffer, Casey? How did you fire him?"

Casey took her tawny eyes off Linc and turned them on Dunross and he thought, Christ I'd like to possess you.

Casey said, "The hour we got control I—" She stopped as the single phone rang and there was a sudden tension in the room. Everyone, even the waiters, immediately switched their total attention to the phone—except Bartlett. The color had drained out of Gavallan's face and deVille's. "What's the matter?" Casey asked.

Dunross broke the silence. "It's one of our house rules. No phone calls are put through during lunch unless it's an emergency—a personal emergency—for one of us."

They watched Lim put down the coffee tray. It seemed to take him forever to walk across the room and pick up the phone. They all had wives and children and families and they all wondered what death or what disaster and please God, let the call be for someone else, remembering the last time the phone had rung, two days ago. For Jacques. Then another time last month, for Gavallan, his mother was dying. They had all had calls, over the years. All bad.

Andrew Gavallan was sure the call was for him. His wife, Kathren, Dunross's sister, was at the hospital for the results of exhaustive tests—she had been sick for weeks for no apparent reason. Jesus Christ, he thought, get hold of yourself, conscious of others watching him.

"*Weyyyy?*" Lim listened a moment. He turned and offered the phone. "It's for you, tai-pan."

The others breathed again and watched Dunross. His walk was tall. "Hello? . . . Oh hel— What? . . . . No . . . no, I'll be right there. . . . No, don't do anything, I'll be right there." They saw his shock as he replaced the phone in the dead silence. After a pause he said, "Andrew, tell Claudia to postpone my afternoon board meetings. You and Jacques continue with Casey. That was Phillip. I'm afraid poor John Chen's been kidnapped." He left.

8

Dunross got out of his car and hurried through the open door of the vast, Chinese-style mansion that was set high on the mountain crest called Struan's Lookout. He passed a glazed servant who closed the door after him, and went into the living room. The living room was Victorian and gaudy and overstuffed with bric-a-brac and ill-matched furniture.

"Hello, Phillip," he said. "I'm so sorry. Poor John! Where's the letter?"

"Here." Phillip picked it up from the sofa as he got up. "But first look at that." He pointed at a crumpled cardboard shoebox on a marble table beside the fireplace.

As Dunross crossed the room he noticed Dianne, Phillip Chen's wife, sitting in a high-backed chair in a far corner. "Oh, hello, Dianne, sorry about this," he said again.

She shrugged impassively. "Joss, tai-pan." She was fifty-two, Eurasian, Phillip Chen's second wife, an attractive, bejeweled matron who wore a dark brown *chong-sam,* a priceless jade bead necklace and a four-carat diamond ring—amid many other rings. "Yes, joss," she repeated.

Dunross nodded, disliking her a little more than usual. He peered down at the contents of the box without touching them. Among loose, crumpled newspaper he saw a fountain pen that he recognized as John Chen's, a driving license, some keys on a key ring, a letter addressed to John Chen, 14A Sinclair Towers, and a small plastic bag with a piece of cloth half-stuffed into it. With a pen that he took out of his pocket he flipped open the cover of the driving license. John Chen.

"Open the plastic bag," Phillip said.

"No. I might mess up any fingerprints that're on it," Dunross said, feeling stupid but saying it anyway.

"Oh—I'd forgotten about that. Damn. Of course, fingerprints! Mine are . . . I opened it of course. Mine must be all over it—all over everything."

"What's in it?"

"It's—" Phillip Chen came over and before Dunross could stop him pulled the cloth out of the plastic, without touching the plastic again. "You can't have fingerprints on cloth, can you? Look!" The cloth contained most of a severed human ear, the cut clean and sharp and not jagged.

Dunross cursed softly. "How did the box arrive?" he asked.

"It was hand delivered." Phillip Chen shakily rewrapped the ear and put it back in the box. "I just . . . I just opened the parcel as anyone would. It was hand delivered half an hour or so ago."

"By whom?"

"We don't know. He was just a youth, the servant said. A youth on a motor scooter. She didn't recognize him or take any number. We get lots of parcels delivered. It was nothing out of the ordinary—except the 'Mr. Phillip Chen, a matter of great importance, to open personally,' on the outside of the package, which she didn't notice at once. By the time I'd opened it and read the letter . . . it was just a youth who said, 'Parcel for Mr. Phillip Chen,' and went away."

"Have you called the police?"

"No, tai-pan, you said to do nothing."

Dunross went to the phone. "Have you got hold of John's wife yet?"

Dianne said at once, "Why should Phillip bear bad tidings to her? She'll throw a temperament that will raise the roof tiles never mind. Call Barbara? Oh dear no, tai-pan, not . . . not until we've informed the police. They should tell her. They know how to do these things."

Dunross's disgust increased. "You'd better get her here quickly." He dialed police headquarters and asked for Armstrong. He was not available. Dunross left his name then asked for Brian Kwok.

"Yes tai-pan?"

"Brian, can you come over here right away? I'm at Phillip Chen's house up on Struan's Lookout. John Chen's been kidnapped." He told him about the contents of the box.

There was a shocked silence, then Brian Kwok said, "I'll be there right away. Don't touch anything and don't let him talk to anyone."

"All right."

Dunross put the phone down. "Now give me the letter, Phillip." He handled it carefully, holding it by the edges. The Chinese characters were clearly written but not by a well-educated person. He read it slowly, knowing most of the characters:

Mr. Phillip Chen, I beg to inform you that I am badly in need of 500,000 Hong Kong currency and I hereby consult you about it. You are so wealthy that this is like plucking one hair from nine oxen. Being afraid that you might refuse I therefore have no alternative but to hold your son hostage. By doing so there is not a fear of your refusal. I hope you will think it over carefully thrice and take it into serious consideration. It is up to you whether you report to the police or not. I send herewith some articles which your son uses every day as proof of the situation your son is in. Also sent is a little bit of your son's ear. You should realize the mercilessness and cruelty of my actions. If you smoothly pay the money the safety of your son will be ensured. Written by the Werewolf.

Dunross motioned at the box. "Sorry, but do you recognize the, er . . . that?"

Phillip Chen laughed nervously and so did his wife. "Do you, Ian? You've known John all your life. That's . . . how does one recognize something like that, *heya?*"

"Does anyone else know about this?"

"No, except the servants of course, and Shitee T'Chung and some friends who were lunching with me here. They . . . they were here when the parcel arrived. They, yes, they were here. They left just before you arrived."

Dianne Chen shifted in her chair and said what Dunross was thinking. "So of course it will be all over Hong Kong by evening!"

"Yes. And banner headlines by dawn." Dunross tried to collate the multitude of questions and answers flooding his mind. "The press'll pick up about the, er, ear and the 'Werewolf' and make it a field day."

"Yes. Yes they will." Phillip Chen remembered what Shitee T'Chung had said the moment they had all read the letter. "Don't pay the ransom for at least a week, Phillip old friend, and you'll be world famous! *Ayeeyah,* fancy, a piece of his ear and Werewolf! Eeeee, you'll be world famous!"

"Perhaps it's not his ear at all and a trick," Phillip Chen said hopefully.

"Yes." If it is John's ear, Dunross thought, greatly perturbed, and if they've sent it on the first day before any negotiation or anything, I'll bet the poor sod's already dead. "No point in hurting him like that," he said. "Of course you'll pay."

"Of course. It's lucky we're not in Singapore, isn't it?"

"Yes." By law in Singapore now, the moment anyone was kidnapped all bank accounts of the family were frozen to prevent payment to the kidnappers. Kidnapping had become endemic there with almost no arrests, Chinese preferring to pay quickly and quietly and say nothing to the police. "What a bastard! Poor old John."

Phillip said, "Would you like some tea—or a drink? Are you hungry?"

"No thanks. I'll wait until Brian Kwok gets here then I'll be off." Dunross looked at the box and at the keys. He had seen the key ring many times. "The safety deposit key's missing," he said.

"What key?" Dianne Chen asked.

"John always had a deposit box key on his ring."

She did not move from her chair. "And it's not there now?"

"No."

"Perhaps you're mistaken. That he always had it on the ring."

Dunross looked at her and then at Phillip Chen. They both stared back at him. Well, he thought, if the crooks didn't take it, now Phillip or Dianne have, and if I were them I'd do the same. God knows what might be in such a box. "Perhaps I'm mistaken," he said levelly.

"Tea, tai-pan?" Dianne asked, and he saw the shadow of a smile in the back of her eyes.

"Yes, I think I will," he said, knowing they had taken the key.

She got up and ordered tea loudly and sat down again. "Eeee, I wish they'd hurry up . . . the police."

Phillip was looking out of the window at the parched garden. "I wish it would rain."

"I wonder how much it'll cost to get John back," she muttered.

After a pause, Dunross said, "Does it matter?"

"Of course it matters," Dianne said at once. "Really, tai-pan!"

"Oh yes," Phillip Chen echoed. "$500,000! Ayeeyah, $500,000—that's a fortune. Damn triads! Well, if they ask five I can settle for $150,000. Thank God they didn't ask a million!" His eyebrows soared and his face became more ashen. "Dew neh loh moh on all kidnappers. They should get the chop—all of them."

"Yes," Dianne said. "Filthy triads. The police should be more clever! More sharp and more clever and protect us better."

"Now that's not fair," Dunross said sharply. "There hasn't been a major kidnapping in Hong Kong for years and it happens every month in Singapore! Crime's fantastically low here—our police do a grand job—grand."

"Huh," Dianne sniffed. "They're all corrupt. Why else be a policeman if it's not to get rich? I don't trust any of them. . . . We know, oh yes we know. As to kidnapping, huh, the last one was six years ago. It was my third cousin, Fu San Sung—the family had to pay $600,000 to get him back safely. . . . It nearly bankrupted them."

"Ha!" Phillip Chen scoffed. "Bankrupt Hummingbird Sung? Impossible!" Hummingbird Sung was a very wealthy Shanghainese shipowner in his fifties with a sharp nose—long for a Chinese. He was nicknamed Hummingbird Sung because he was always darting from dance hall to dance hall, from flower to flower, in Singapore, Bangkok and Taipei, Hong Kong, dipping his manhood into a myriad of ladies' honey pots, the rumor being it wasn't his manhood because he enjoyed mutual cunnilingus.

"The police got most of the money back if I remember rightly, and sent the criminals to jail for twenty years."

"Yes, tai-pan, they did. But it took them months and months. And I wouldn't mind betting one or two of the police knew more than they said."

"Absolute nonsense!" Dunross said. "You've no cause to believe anything like that! None."

"Quite right!" Phillip Chen said irritably. "They caught them, Dianne." She looked at him. At once he changed his tone. "Of course, dear, some police may be corrupt but we're very lucky here, very lucky. I suppose I wouldn't mind so much about, about John—it's only a matter of ransom and as a family we've been very lucky so far—I wouldn't mind except for . . . for that." He motioned at the box disgustedly. "Terrible! And totally uncivilized."

"Yes," Dunross said, and wondered if it wasn't John Chen's ear, whose was it—where do you get an ear from? He almost laughed at the ridiculousness of his questions. Then he put his mind back to pondering if the kidnapping was somehow tied in with Tsu-yan and the guns and Bartlett. It's not like a Chinese to mutilate a victim. No, and certainly not so soon. Kidnapping's an ancient Chinese art and the rules have always been clear: pay and keep silent and no problem, delay and talk and many problems.

He stared out of the window at the gardens and at the vast northern panorama of city and seascape below. Ships and junks and sampans dotted the azure sea. There was a fine sky above and no promise of rain weather, the summer monsoon steady from the southwest and he wondered absently what the clippers had looked like as they sailed before the wind or beat up against the winds in his ancestors' time. Dirk Struan had always had a secret lookout atop the mountain above. There the man could see south and east and west and the great Sheung Sz Mun Channel which approached Hong Kong from the south—the only path inward bound for ships from home, from England. From Struan's Lookout, the man could secretly spot the incoming mail ship and secretly signal below. Then the tai-pan would dispatch a fast cutter to get the mails first, to have a few hours leeway over his rivals, the few hours perhaps meaning the trading difference between fortune and bankruptcy—so vast the time from home. Not like today with instant communication, Dunross thought. We're lucky—we don't have to wait almost two years for a reply like Dirk did. Christ, what a man he must have been.

I must not fail with Bartlett. I must have those 20 million.

"The deal looks very good, tai-pan," Phillip Chen said as though reading his mind.

"Yes. Yes it is."

"If they really put up cash we'll all make a fortune and it'll be *h'eung yau* for the Noble House," he added with a beam.

Dunross's smile was again sardonic. *H'eung yau* meant "fragrant grease" and normally referred to the money, the payoff, the squeeze, that was paid by all Chinese restaurants, most businesses, all gambling games, all dance halls, all ladies of easy virtue, to triads, some form of triad, throughout the world.

"I still find it staggering that *h'eung yau's* paid wherever a Chinese is in business."

"Really, tai-pan," Dianne said as though he were a child. "How can any business exist without protection? You expect to pay, naturally, so you pay never mind. Everyone gives *h'eung yau*—some form of *h'eung yau*." Her jade beads clicked as she shifted in her chair, her eyes dark in the whiteness of her face—so highly prized among Chinese. "But the Bartlett deal, tai-pan, do you think the Bartlett deal will go through?"

Dunross watched her. Ah Dianne, he told himself, you know every important detail that Phillip knows about his business and my business, and a lot Phillip would weep with fury if he knew you knew. So you know Struan's could be in very great trouble if there's no Bartlett deal, but if the deal is consummated then our stock will skyrocket and we'll be rich again —and so will you be, if you can get in early enough, to buy early enough. Yes.

And I know you Hong Kong Chinese ladies like poor Phillip doesn't, because I'm not even a little part Chinese. I know you Hong Kong Chinese ladies are the roughest women on earth when it comes to money—or perhaps the most practical. And you, Dianne, I also know you are ecstatic now, however much you'll pretend otherwise. Because John Chen's not your son. With him eliminated, your own two sons will be direct in line and your eldest, Kevin, heir apparent. So you'll pray like you've never prayed before that John's gone forever. You're delighted. John's kidnapped and probably murdered but what about the Bartlett deal?

"Ladies are so practical," he said.

"How so, tai-pan?" she asked, her eyes narrowing.

"They keep things in perspective."

"Sometimes I don't understand you at all, tai-pan," she replied, an edge to her voice. "What more can we do now about John Chen? Nothing. We've done everything we can. When the ransom note arrives we negotiate and we pay and everything's as it was. But the Bartlett deal is important, very important, very very important whatever happens, *heya? Moh ching, moh meng.*" No money, no life.

"Quite. It is very important, tai-pan." Phillip caught sight of the box and shuddered. "I think under the circumstances, tai-pan, if you'll excuse us this evening . . . I don't th—"

"No, Phillip," his wife said firmly. "No. We must go. It's a matter of face for the whole House. We'll go as planned. As difficult as it will be for us—we will go as planned."

"Well, if you say so."

"Yes." Oh very yes she was thinking, replanning her whole ensemble to enhance the dramatic effect of their entrance. We'll go tonight and we'll be the talk of Hong Kong. We'll take Kevin of course. Perhaps he's heir now. *Ayeeyah!* Who should my son marry? I've got to think of the future now. Twenty-two's a perfect age and I have to think of his new future. Yes, a wife. Who? I'd better choose the right girl at once and quickly if he's heir, before some young filly with a fire between her legs and a rapacious mother does it for me. *Ayeeyah,* she thought, her temperature rising, gods forbid such a thing! "Yes," she said, and touched her eyes with her handkerchief as though a tear were there, "there's nothing more to be done for poor John but wait—and continue to work and plan and maneuver for the good of the Noble House." She looked up at Dunross, her eyes glittering. "The Bartlett deal would solve everything, wouldn't it?"

"Yes." And you're both right, Dunross thought. There's nothing more to be done at the moment. Chinese are very wise and very practical.

So put your mind on important things—he told himself. Important things—like do you gamble? Think. What better place or time than here and now could you find to begin the plan you've been toying with ever since you met Bartlett?

None.

"Listen," he said, deciding irrevocably, then looked around at the door that led to the servants' quarters, making sure that they were alone. He lowered his voice to a conspiratorial whisper and Phillip and his wife leaned forward to hear better. "I had a private meeting with Bartlett before lunch. We've made the deal. I'll need some minor changes, but we close the contract formally on Tuesday of next week. The 20 million's guaranteed and a further 20 million next year."

Phillip Chen's beam was huge. "Congratulations."

"Not so loud, Phillip," his wife hissed, equally pleased. "Those turtle mouth slaves in the kitchen have ears that can reach to Java. Oh but that's tremendous news, tai-pan."

"We'll keep this in the family," Dunross said softly. "This afternoon I'm instructing our brokers to start buying Struan's stock secretly—every spare penny we've got. You do the same, in small lots and spread the orders over different brokers and nominees—the usual."

"Yes. Oh yes."

"I bought 40 thousand this morning personally."

"How much will the stock go up?" Dianne Chen asked.

"Double!"

"How soon?"

"Thirty days."

"Eeeee," she chortled. "Think of that."

"Yes," Dunross said agreeably. "Think of that! Yes. And you two will only tell your very close relations, of which there are many, and they will only tell their very close relations, of which there are a multitude, and you'll all buy and buy because this is an inside-inside, gilt-edged tip and hardly any gamble at all which will further fuel the stock rise. The fact that it's only family will surely leak and more will jump in, then more, and then the formal announcement of the Par-Con deal will add fire and then, next week, I'll announce the takeover bid for Asian Properties and then all Hong Kong will buy. Our stock will skyrocket. Then, at the right moment, I dump Asian Properties and go after the real target."

"How many shares, tai-pan?" Phillip Chen asked—his mind swamped by his own calculations of the possible profits.

"Maximum. But it has to be family only. Our stocks'll lead the boom."

Dianne gasped. "There's going to be a boom?"

"Yes. We'll lead it. The time's ripe, everyone in Hong Kong's ready. We'll supply the means, we'll be the leader, and with a judicious shove here and there, there'll be a stampede."

There was a great silence. Dunross watched the avarice on her face.

Her fingers clicked the jade beads. He saw Phillip staring into the distance and he knew that part of his compradore's mind was on the various notes that he, Phillip, had countersigned for Struan's that were due in thirteen to thirty days: $12 million U.S. to Toda Shipping Industries of Yokohama for the two super bulk cargo freighters, $6,800,000 to the Orlin International Merchant Bank, and $750,000 to Tsu-yan, who had covered another problem for him. But most of Phillip's mind would be on Bartlett's 20 million and the stock rise—the doubling that he had arbitrarily forecast.

Double?

No way—no not at all, not a chance in hell . . .

Unless there's a boom. Unless there's a boom!

Dunross felt his heart quicken. "If there's a boom . . . Christ, Phillip, we can do it!"

"Yes—yes, I agree, Hong Kong's ripe. Ah yes." Phillip Chen's eyes sparkled and his fingers drummed. "How many shares, tai-pan?"

"Every bl—"

Excitedly Dianne overrode Dunross, "Phillip, last week my astrologer said this was going to be an important month for us! A boom! That's what he must have meant."

"That's right, I remember you telling me, Dianne. Oh oh oh! How many shares, tai-pan?" he asked again.

"Every bloody penny! We'll make this the big one. But family only until Friday. Absolutely until Friday. Then, after the market closes I'll leak the Bartlett deal. . . ."

"Eeeeee," Dianne hissed.

"Yes. Over the weekend I'll say 'no comment'—you make sure you're not available, Phillip—and come Monday morning, everyone'll be chomping at the bit. I'll still say 'no comment,' but Monday we buy openly. Then, just after close of business Monday, I'll announce the whole deal's confirmed. Then, come Tuesday . . ."

"The boom's on!"

"Yes."

"Oh happy day," Dianne croaked delightedly. "And every *amah*, houseboy, coolie, businessman, will decide their joss is perfect and out will come their savings and everything gets fed, all stocks will rocket. What a pity there won't be an editorial tomorrow . . . even better, an astrologer in one of the papers . . . say Hundred Year Fong . . . or . . ." Her eyes almost crossed with excitement. "What about *the* astrologer, Phillip?"

He stared at her, shocked. "Old Blind Tung?"

"Why not? Some *h'eung yau* in his palm . . . or the promise of a few shares of whatever stock you name. *Heya?*"

"Well, I—"

"Leave that one to me. Old Blind Tung owes me a favor or two, I've sent him enough clients! Yes. And he won't be far wrong announcing heavenly portents that herald the greatest boom in Hong Kong's history, will he?"

9

The police pathologist, Dr. Meng, adjusted the focus of the microscope and studied the sliver of flesh that he had cut from the ear. Brian Kwok watched him impatiently. The doctor was a small pedantic little Cantonese with thick-lensed glasses perched on his forehead. At length he looked up and his glasses fell conveniently onto his nose. "Well, Brian, it could have been sliced from a living person and not a corpse . . . possibly. Possibly within the last eight or ten hours. The bruising . . . here, look at the back"—Dr. Meng motioned delicately at the discoloration at the back and at the top—". . . that certainly indicates to me that the person was alive at the time."

"Why bruising, Dr. Meng? What caused it? The slash?"

"It could have been caused by someone holding the specimen tightly," Dr. Meng said cautiously, "while it was being removed."

"By what—knife, razor, zip knife, or Chinese chopper—cooking chopper?"

"By a sharp instrument."

Brian Kwok sighed. "Would that kill someone? The shock? Someone like John Chen?"

Dr. Meng steepled his fingers. "It could, possibly. Possibly not. Does he have a history of a weak heart?"

"His father said he hadn't—I haven't checked with his own doctor yet— the bugger's on holiday but John's never given any indication of being anything but healthy."

"This mutilation probably shouldn't kill a healthy man but he'd be very uncomfortable for a week or two." The doctor beamed. "Very uncomfortable indeed."

"Jesus!" Brian said. "Isn't there anything you can give me that'll help?"

"I'm a forensic pathologist, Brian, not a seer."

"Can you tell if the ear's Eurasian—or pure Chinese?"

"No. No, with this specimen that'd be almost impossible. But it's certainly not Anglo-Saxon, or Indian or Negroid." Dr. Meng took off his glasses and stared myopically up at the tall superintendent. "This could possibly cause quite a ripple in the House of Chen, *heya?*"

"Yes. And the Noble House." Brian Kwok thought a moment. "In your opinion, this Werewolf, this maniac, would you say he's Chinese?"

"The writing could have been a civilized person's, yes—equally it could have been done by a *quai loh* pretending to be a civilized person. But if he or she was a civilized person that doesn't necessarily mean that the same person who did the act wrote the letter."

"I know that. What are the odds that John Chen's dead?"

"From the mutilation?"

"From the fact that the Werewolf, or more probably Werewolves, sent the ear even before starting negotiations."

The little man smiled and said dryly, "You mean old Sun Tzu's 'kill one to terrorize ten thousand'? I don't know. I don't speculate on such imponderables. I only estimate odds on horses, Brian, or the stock market. What about John Chen's Golden Lady on Saturday?"

"She's got a great chance. Definitely. And Struan's Noble Star—Gornt's Pilot Fish and even more, Richard Kwang's Butterscotch Lass. She'll be the favorite I'll bet. But Golden Lady's a real goer. She'll start about three to one. She's a flier and the going'll be good for her. Dry. She's useless in the wet."

"Ah, any sign of rain?"

"Possible. They say there's a storm coming. Even a sprinkle could make all the difference."

"Then it better not rain till Sunday, *heya?*"

"It won't rain this month—not unless we're enormously lucky."

"Well if it rains it rains and if it doesn't it doesn't never mind! Winter's coming—then this cursed humidity will go away." Dr. Meng glanced at the wall clock. It was 5:35 P.M. "How about a quick one before we go home?"

"No thanks. I've still got a few things to do. Bloody nuisance this."

"Tomorrow I'll see what clues I can come up with from the cloth, or the wrapping paper or the other things. Perhaps fingerprinting will help you," the doctor added.

"I wouldn't bet on that. This whole operation is very smelly. Very smelly indeed."

Dr. Meng nodded and his voice lost its gentleness. "Anything to do with the Noble House and their puppet House of Chen's smelly. Isn't it?"

Brian Kwok switched to *sei yap*, one of the main dialects of the Kwantung Province, spoken by many Hong Kong Cantonese. "Eh, Brother, don't you mean any and all capitalist running dogs are smelly, of which the Noble House and the House of Chen are chief and dung heavy?" he said banteringly.

"Ah, Brother, don't you know yet, deep in your head, that the winds of change are whirling throughout the world? And China under the immortal guidance of Chairman Mao, and Mao Thought, is the lead—"

"Keep your proselytizing to yourself," Brian Kwok said coldly, switching back to English. "Most of the thoughts of Mao are out of the writings of Sun Tzu, Confucius, Marx, Lao Tsu and others. I know he's a poet—a great one—but he's usurped China and there's no freedom there now. None."

"Freedom?" the little man said defiantly. "What's freedom for a few years when, under the guidance of Chairman Mao, China's once more China and has taken back her rightful place in the world. Now China is feared by all filthy capitalists! Even by revisionist Russia."

"Yes. I agree. For that I thank him. Meanwhile if you don't like it here go home to Canton and sweat your balls off in your Communist paradise and *dew neh loh moh* on all Communists—and their fellow travelers!"

"You should go there, see for yourself. It's propaganda that communism's bad for China. Don't you read the newspapers? No one's starving now."

"What about the twenty-odd million who were murdered after the take-over? What about all the brainwashing?"

"More propaganda! Just because you've been to English and Canadian public schools and talk like a capitalist swine doesn't mean you're one of them. Remember your heritage."

"I do. I remember it very well."

"Your father was mistaken to send you away!" It was common knowledge that Brian Kwok had been born in Canton and, at the age of six, sent to school in Hong Kong. He was such a good student that in '37, when he was twelve, he had won a scholarship to a fine public school in England and had gone there, and then in '39, with the beginning of World War II, the whole school was evacuated to Canada. In '42, at eighteen, he had graduated top of his class, senior prefect, and had joined the Royal Canadian Mounted Police in their plainclothes branch in Vancouver's huge Chinatown. He spoke Cantonese, Mandarin, *sei yap*, and had served with distinction. In '45 he had requested a transfer to the Royal Hong Kong Police. With the reluctant approval of the RCMP, who had wanted him to stay on, he had returned. "You're wasted working for them, Brian," Dr. Meng continued. "You should serve the masses and work for the Party!"

"The Party murdered my father and my mother and most of my family in '43!"

"There was never proof of that! Never. It was hearsay. Perhaps the Kuomintang devils did it—there was chaos then in Canton. I was there, I know! Perhaps the Japanese swine were responsible—or triads—who knows? How can you be certain?"

"I'm certain, by God."

"Was there a witness? No! You told me that yourself!" Meng's voice rasped and he peered up at him myopically. "*Ayeeyah*, you're Chinese, use your education for China, for the masses, not for the capitalist overlord."

"Up yours!"

Dr. Meng laughed and his glasses fell on to the top of his nose. "You wait, Superintendent Kar-shun Kwok. One day your eyes will open. One day you will see the beauty of it all."

"Meanwhile get me some bloody answers!" Brian Kwok strode out of the laboratory and went up the corridor to the elevator, his shirt sticking to his back. I wish it would rain, he thought.

He got into the elevator. Other policemen greeted him and he them. At the third floor he got out and walked along the corridor to his office. Armstrong was waiting for him, idly reading a Chinese newspaper. "Hi, Robert," he said, pleased to see him. "What's new?"

"Nothing. How about you?"

Brian Kwok told him what Dr. Meng had said.

"That little bugger and his 'could possiblys'! The only thing he's ever emphatic about's a corpse—and even then he'll have to check a couple of times."

"Yes—or about Chairman Mao."

"Oh, he was on that broken record again?"

"Yes." Brian Kwok grinned. "I told him to go back to China."

"He'll never leave."

"I know." Brian stared at the pile of papers in his in tray and sighed. Then he said, "It's not like a local to cut off an ear so soon."

"No, not if it's a proper kidnapping."

"What?"

"It could be a grudge and the kidnapping a cover," Armstrong said, his well-used face hardening. "I agree with you and Dunross. I think they did him in."

"But why?"

"Perhaps John was trying to escape, started a fight, and they or he panicked and before they or he knew what was happening, they or he'd knifed him, or bonked him with a blunt instrument." Armstrong sighed and stretched to ease the knot in his shoulders. "In any event, old chap, our Great White Father wants this solved quickly. He honored me with a call to say the governor had phoned personally to express his concern."

Brian Kwok cursed softly. "Foul news travels quickly! Nothing in the press yet?"

"No, but it's all over Hong Kong and we'll have a red hot wind fanning our tails by morning. Mr. Bloody Werewolf Esquire—assisted by the pox-ridden, black-hearted, uncooperative Hong Kong press—will, I fear, cause us nothing but grief until we catch the bastard, or bastards."

"But catch him we will, oh yes, catch him we will!"

"Yes. How about a beer—or better, a very large gin and tonic? I could use one."

"Good idea. Your stomach off again?"

"Yes. Mary says it's all the good thoughts I keep bottled up." They laughed together and headed for the door and were in the corridor when the phone rang.

"Leave the bloody thing, don't answer it, it's only trouble," Armstrong said, knowing neither he nor Brian would ever leave it.

Brian Kwok picked up the phone and froze.

It was Roger Crosse, senior superintendent, director of Special Intelligence. "Yes sir?"

"Brian, would you please come up right away."

"Yes sir."

"Is Armstrong with you?"

"Yes sir."

"Bring him too." The phone clicked off.

"Yes sir." He replaced the receiver and felt the sweat on his back. "God wants us, on the double."

Armstrong's heart jumped a beat. "Eh? Me?" He caught up with Brian who was heading for the elevator. "What the hell does he want me for? I'm not in SI now."

"Ours not to reason why, ours just to shit when he murmurs." Brian Kwok pressed the *up* button. "What's up?"

"Got to be important. The Mainland perhaps?"

"Chou En-lai's ousted Mao and the moderates're in power?"

"Dreamer! Mao'll die in office—the Godhead of China."

"The only good thing you can say about Mao is that he's Chinese first and Commie second. God-cursed Commies!"

"Hey, Brian, maybe the Soviets are hotting up the border again. Another incident?"

"Could be. Yes. War's coming—yes, war's coming between Russia and China. Mao's right in that too."

"The Soviets aren't that stupid."

"Don't bet on it, old chum. I've said it before and I've said it again, the Soviets are the world enemy. There'll be war—you'll soon owe me a thousand dollars, Robert."

"I don't think I want to pay that bet. The killing'll be hideous."

"Yes. But it'll still happen. Again Mao's right in that. It'll be hideous all right—but not catastrophic." Irritably Brian Kwok punched the elevator button again. He looked up suddenly. "You don't think the invasion from Taiwan's launched at long last?"

"That old chestnut? That old pipe dream? Come off it, Brian! Chiang Kai-shek'll never get off Taiwan."

"If he doesn't the whole world's in the manure pile. If Mao gets thirty years to consolidate . . . Christ, you've no idea. A billion automatons?

Chiang was so right to go after the Commie bastards—they're the real enemy of China. They're the plague of China. Christ, if they get time to Pavlov all the kids."

Armstrong said mildly, "Anyone'd think you're a running dog Nationalist. Simmer down, lad, everything's lousy in the world which is now and ever shall be normal—but you, capitalist dog, you can go racing Saturday, hill climbing Sunday and there're lots of birds ready to be plucked. Eh?"

"Sorry." They got into the elevator. "That little bastard Meng caught me off balance," Brian said, stabbing the top-floor button.

Armstrong switched to Cantonese. *"Thy mother on your sorry, Brother."*

"And thine was stuffed by a vagrant monkey with one testicle in a pail of pig's nightsoil."

Armstrong beamed. "That's not bad, Brian," he said in English. "Not bad at all."

The elevator stopped. They walked along the drab corridor. At the door they prepared themselves. Brian knocked gently.

"Come in."

Roger Crosse was in his fifties, a thin tall man with pale blue eyes and fair thinning hair and small, long-fingered hands. His desk was meticulous, like his civilian clothes—his office spartan. He motioned to chairs. They sat. He continued to read a file. At length he closed it carefully and set it in front of him. The cover was drab, interoffice and ordinary. "An American millionaire arrives with smuggled guns, an ex-drug peddling, very suspect Shanghainese millionaire flees to Taiwan, and now a VIP kidnapping with, God help us, Werewolves and a mutilated ear. All in nineteen-odd hours. Where's the connection?"

Armstrong broke the silence. "Should there be one, sir?"

"Shouldn't there?"

"Sorry sir, I don't know. Yet."

"That's very boring, Robert, very boring indeed."

"Yes sir."

"Tedious in fact, particularly as the powers that be have already begun to breathe heavily down my neck. And when that happens . . ." He smiled at them and both suppressed a shudder. "Of course Robert, I did warn you yesterday that important names might be involved."

"Yes sir."

"Now Brian, we're grooming you for high office. Don't you think you could take your mind off horse racing, car racing and almost anything in skirts and apply some of your undoubted talents to solving this modest conundrum."

"Yes sir."

"Please do. Very quickly. You're assigned to the case with Robert because it might require your expertise—for the next few days. I want this out of the way very very quickly indeed because we've a slight problem.

One of our American friends in the consulate called me last night. Privately." He motioned at the file. "This is the result. With his tip we intercepted the original in the bleak hours—of course this's a copy, the original was naturally returned and the . . ." He hesitated, choosing the correct word, ". . . the courier, an amateur by the way, left undisturbed. It's a report, a sort of newsletter with different headings. They're all rather interesting. Yes. One's headed, 'The KGB in Asia.' It claims that they've a deep-cover spy ring I've never even heard of before, code name 'Sevrin,' with high-level hostiles in key positions in government, police, business— at the tai-pan level—throughout Southeast Asia, *particularly here in Hong Kong*."

The air hissed out of Brian Kwok's mouth.

"Quite," Crosse said agreeably. "If it's true."

"You think it is, sir?" Armstrong said.

"Really, Robert, perhaps you're in need of early retirement on medical grounds: softening of the brain. If I wasn't perturbed do you think I'd endure the unhappy pleasure of having to petition the assistance of the CID Kowloon?"

"No sir, sorry sir."

Crosse turned the file to face them and opened it to the title page. Both men gasped. It read, "*Confidential to Ian Dunross only. By hand, report 3/1963. One copy only.*"

"Yes," he continued. "Yes. This's the first time we've actual proof Struan's have their own intelligence system." He smiled at them and their flesh crawled. "I'd certainly like to know how tradesmen manage to be privy to all sorts of very intimate information we're supposed to know ages before them."

"Yes sir."

"The report's obviously one of a series. Oh yes, and this one's signed on behalf of Struan's Research Committee 16, by a certain A. M. Grant— dated in London three days ago."

Brian Kwok gasped again. "Grant? Would that be the Alan Medford Grant, the associate of the Institute for Strategic Planning in London?"

"Full marks, Brian, ten out of ten. Yes. Mr. AMG himself. Mr. VIP, Mr. Advisor to Her Majesty's Government for undercover affairs who really knows onions from leeks. You know him, Brian?"

Brian Kwok said, "I met him a couple of times in England last year, sir, when I was on the Senior Officers Course at the General Staff College. He gave a paper on advanced strategic considerations for the Far East. Brilliant. Quite brilliant."

"Fortunately he's English and on our side. Even so . . ." Crosse sighed again. "I certainly hope he's mistaken this time or we're in the mire deeper than even I imagined. It seems few of our secrets are secrets anymore. Tiring. Very. And as to this," he touched the file again, "I'm really quite shocked."

"Has the original been delivered, sir?" Armstrong asked.

"Yes. To Dunross personally at 4:18 this afternoon." His voice became even more silky. "Fortunately, thank God, my relations with our cousins across the water are first class. Like yours, Robert—unlike yours, Brian. You never did like America, did you, Brian?"

"No sir."

"Why, may I ask?"

"They talk too much, sir, you can't trust them with any secrets—they're loud, and I find them stupid."

Crosse smiled with his mouth. "That's no reason not to have good relations with them, Brian. Perhaps you're the stupid one."

"Yes sir."

"They're not all stupid, oh dear no." The director closed the file but left it facing them. Both men stared at it, mesmerized.

"Did the Americans say how they found out about the file, sir?" Armstrong asked without thinking.

"Robert, I really do believe your sinecure in Kowloon has addled your brain. Shall I recommend you for a medical retirement?"

The big man winced. "No sir, thank you sir."

"Would we reveal our sources to them?"

"No sir."

"Would they have told me if I'd been so crass as to ask them?"

"No sir."

"This whole business is very tedious and filled with loss of face. Mine. Don't you agree, Robert?"

"Yes sir."

"Good, that's something." Crosse leaned back in his chair, rocking it. His eyes ground into them. Both men were wondering who the tipster was, and why.

Can't be the CIA, Brian Kwok was thinking. They'd have done the intercept themselves, they don't need SI to do their dirty work for them. Those crazy bastards'll do anything, tread on any toes, he thought disgustedly. If not them, who?

Who?

Must be someone who's in Intelligence but who can't, or couldn't do the intercept, who's on good terms, safe terms with Crosse. A consular official? Possible. Johnny Mishauer, Naval Intelligence? Out of his channel. Who? There's not many . . . Ah, the FBI man, Crosse's protégé! Ed Langan. Now, how would Langan know about this file? Information from London? Possible, but the FBI doesn't have an office there. If the tip came from London, probably MI-5 or 6 would know it first and they'd've arranged to get the material at the source and would have telexed it to us, and given us hell for being inept in our own backyard. Did the courier's aircraft land at Lebanon? There's an FBI man there I seem to recall. If not from London or Lebanon, the information must have come from the aircraft itself. Ah, an accompanying friendly informer who saw the file, or the cover? Crew? *Ayeeyah!* Was the aircraft TWA or Pan Am? The FBI has all sorts of links, close links—with all sorts of ordinary businesses, rightly so. Oh yes. Is there a Sunday flight? Yes. Pan Am, ETA 2030. Too late for a night delivery by the time you've got to the hotel. Perfect.

"Strange that the courier came Pan Am and not BOAC—it's a much better flight," he said, pleased with the oblique way his mind worked.

"Yes. I thought the same," Crosse said as evenly. "Terribly un-British of him. Of course, Pan Am does land on time whereas you never know with poor old BOAC these days—" He nodded at Brian agreeably. "Full marks again. Go to the head of the class."

"Thank you sir."

"What else do you deduce?"

After a pause Brian Kwok said, "In return for the tip, you agreed to provide Langan with an exact copy of the file."

"And?"

"And you regret having honored that."

Crosse sighed. "Why?"

"I'll know only after I've read the file."

"Brian, you really are surpassing yourself this afternoon. Good." Absently the director fingered the file and both men knew he was titillating them, deliberately, but neither knew why. "There are one or two very curious coincidences in other sections of this. Names like Vincenzo Banastasio . . . meeting places like Sinclair Towers . . . Does Nelson Trading mean anything to either of you?"

They both shook their heads.

"All very curious. Commies to the right of us, commies to the left . . ." His eyes became even stonier. "It seems we even have a nasty in our own ranks, possibly at superintendent level."

"Impossible!" Armstrong said involuntarily.

"How long were you with us in SI, dear boy?"

Armstrong almost flinched. "Two tours, almost five years sir."

"The spy Sorge was impossible—Kim Philby was impossible—dear God Philby!" The sudden defection to Soviet Russia in January this year by this Englishman, this onetime top agent of MI-6—British military intelligence for overseas espionage and counterespionage—had sent shock waves throughout the Western world, particularly as, until recently, Philby had been first secretary at the British Embassy in Washington, responsible for liaison with U.S. Defense, State, and the CIA on all security matters at the highest level. "How in the name of all that's holy he could have been a Soviet agent for all those years and remain undetected is impossible, isn't it, Robert?"

"Yes sir."

"And yet he was, and privy to our innermost secrets for years. Certainly from '42 to '58. And where did he start spying? God save us, at Cambridge in 1931. Recruited into the Party by the other arch-traitor, Burgess, also of Cambridge, and his friend Maclean, may they both toast in hell for all eternity." Some years ago these two highly placed Foreign Office diplomats —both of whom had also been in Intelligence during the war—had abruptly fled to Russia only seconds ahead of British counterespionage agents and the ensuing scandal had rocked Britain and the whole of NATO. "Who else did they recruit?"

"I don't know, sir," Armstrong said carefully. "But you can bet that now they're all VIP's in government, the Foreign Office, education, the press, particularly the press—and, like Philby, all burrowed very bloody deep."

"With people nothing's impossible. Nothing. People are really very dreadful." Crosse sighed and straightened the file slightly. "Yes. But it's a privilege to be in SI, isn't it, Robert?"

"Yes sir."

"You have to be invited in, don't you? You can't volunteer, can you?"

"No sir."

"I never did ask why you didn't stay with us, did I?"

"No sir."

"Well?"

Armstrong groaned inwardly and took a deep breath. "It's because I like being a policeman, sir, not a cloak-and-dagger man. I like being in CID. I like pitting your wits against the villain, the chase and the capture and then the proving it in court, according to rules—to the law, sir."

"Ah but in SI we don't, eh? We're not concerned with courts or laws or anything, only results?"

"SI and SB have different rules, sir," Armstrong said carefully. "Without them the Colony'd be up the creek without a paddle."

"Yes. Yes it would. People are dreadful and fanatics multiply like maggots in a corpse. You were a good undercover man. Now it seems to me it's time to repay all the hours and months of careful training you've had at Her Majesty's expense."

Armstrong's heart missed twice but he said nothing, just held his breath and thanked God that even Crosse couldn't transfer him out of CID against his will. He had hated his tours in SI—in the beginning it had been exciting and to be chosen was a great vote of confidence, but quickly it had palled—the sudden swoop on the villain in the dark hours, hearings *in camera*, no worry about exact proof, just results and a quick, secret deportation order signed by the governor, then off to the border at once, or onto a junk to Taiwan, with no appeal and no return. Ever.

"It's not the British way, Brian," he had always said to his friend. "I'm for a fair, open trial."

"What's it matter? Be practical, Robert. You know the bastards're all guilty—that they're the enemy, Commie enemy agents who twist our rules to stay here, to destroy us and our society—aided and abetted by a few bastard lawyers who'd do anything for thirty pieces of silver, or less. The same in Canada. Christ, we had the hell of a time in the RCMP, our own lawyers and politicians were the enemy—and recent Canadians—curiously always British—all socialist trades unionists who were always in the forefront of any agitation. What does it matter so long as you get rid of the parasites?"

"It matters, that's what I think. And they're not all Commie villains here. There's a lot of Nationalist villains who want to—"

"The Nationalists want Commies out of Hong Kong, that's all."

"Balls! Chiang Kai-shek wanted to grab the Colony after the war. It was only the British navy that stopped him after the Americans gave us away. He still wants sovereignty over us. In that he's no different from Mao Tse-tung!"

"If SI doesn't have the same freedom as the enemy how are we going to keep us out of the creek?"

"Brian, lad, I just said *I* don't like being in SI. You're going to enjoy it. I just want to be a copper, not a bloody Bond!"

Yes, Armstrong thought grimly, just a copper, in CID until I retire to good old England. Christ, I've enough trouble now with the god-cursed Werewolves. He looked back at Crosse and kept his face carefully noncommittal and waited.

Crosse watched him then tapped the file. "According to this we're very much deeper in the mire than even I imagined. Very distressing. Yes." He looked up. "This report refers to previous ones sent to Dunross. I'd certainly like to see them as soon as possible. Quickly and quietly."

Armstrong glanced at Brian Kwok. "How about Claudia Chen?"

"No. No chance. None."

"Then what do you suggest, Brian?" Crosse asked. "I imagine my American friend will have the same idea . . . and if he's been misguided enough to pass on the file, a copy of the file, to the director of the CIA here . . . I really would be very depressed if they were there first again."

Brian Kwok thought a moment. "We could send a specialized team into the tai-pan's executive offices and his penthouse, but it'd take time—we just don't know where to look—and it would have to be at night. That one could be hairy, sir. The other reports—if they exist—might be in a safe up at the Great House, or at his place at Shek-O—even at his, er, at his private flat at Sinclair Towers or another one we don't even know about."

"Distressing," Crosse agreed. "Our intelligence is getting appallingly lax even in our own bailiwick. Pity. If we were Chinese we'd know everything, wouldn't we, Brian?"

"No sir, sorry sir."

"Well, if you don't know where to look you'll have to ask."

"Sir?"

"Ask. Dunross's always seemed to be cooperative in the past. After all he is a friend of yours. Ask to see them."

"And if he says no, or that they were destroyed?"

"You use your talented head. You cajole him a little, you use a little art, you warm to him, Brian. And you barter."

"Do we have something current to barter with, sir?"

"Nelson Trading."

"Sir?"

"Part's in the report. Plus a modest little piece of information I'll be delighted to give you later."

"Yes sir, thank you sir."

"Robert, what have you done to find John Chen and the Werewolf or Werewolves?"

"The whole of CID's been alerted, sir. We got the number of his car at once and that's on a 1098. We've interviewed his wife Mrs. Barbara Chen, among others—she was in hysterics most of the time, but lucid, very lucid under the flood."

"Oh?"

"Yes sir. She's . . . Well, you understand."

"Yes."

"She said it wasn't unusual for her husband to stay out late—she said he had many late business conferences and sometimes he'd go early to the track or to his boat. I'm fairly certain she knew he was a man about town. Retracing his movements last night's been fairly easy up to 2:00 A.M. He dropped Casey Tcholok at the Old Vic at about 10:30—"

"Did he see Bartlett last night?"

"No sir, Bartlett was in his aircraft at Kai Tak all the time."

"Did John Chen talk to him?"

"Not unless there's some way for the airplane to link up with our phone system. We had it under surveillance until the pickup this morning."

"Go on."

"After dropping Miss Tcholok—I discovered it was his father's Rolls by the way—he took the car ferry to the Hong Kong side where he went to a private Chinese club off Queen's Road and dismissed the car and chauffeur. . . ." Armstrong took out his pad and referred to it. ". . . It was the Tong Lau Club. There he met a friend and business colleague, Wo Sang Chi, and they began to play mah-jong. About midnight the game broke up. Then, with Wo Sang Chi and the two other players, both friends, Ta Pan Fat, a journalist, and Po Cha Sik, a stockbroker, they caught a taxi."

Robert Armstrong heard himself reporting the facts, falling into the familiar police pattern and this pleased him and took his mind off the file and all the secret knowledge he possessed, and the problem of the money that he needed so quickly. I wish to God I could just be a policeman, he thought, detesting Special Intelligence and the need for it. "Ta Pan Fat left the taxi first at his home on Queen's Road, then Wo Sang Chi left on the same road shortly afterwards. John Chen and Po Cha Sik—we think he's got triad connections, he's being checked out now very carefully— went to the Ting Ma Garage on Sunning Road, Causeway Bay, to collect John Chen's car, a 1960 Jaguar." Again he referred to his notebook, wanting to be accurate, finding the Chinese names confusing as always, even after so many years. "A garage apprentice, Tong Ta Wey, confirms this. Then John Chen drove his friend Po Cha Sik to his home at 17 Village Street in Happy Valley where the latter left the car. Meanwhile Wo Sang Chi, John Chen's business colleague, who, curiously, heads Struan's haulage company which has the monopoly of cartage to and from Kai Tak, had gone to the Sap Wah Restaurant on Fleming Road. He states that after being there for thirty minutes, John Chen joined him and they left the restaurant in Chen's car, intending to pick up some dancing girls in the street and take them to supper—"

"He wouldn't even go to the dance hall and buy the girls out?" Crosse asked thoughtfully. "What's the going rate, Brian?"

"Sixty dollars Hong Kong, sir, at that time of night."

"I know Phillip Chen's got the reputation of being a miser, but is John Chen the same?"

"At that time of night, sir," Brian Kwok said helpfully, "lots of girls start leaving the clubs if they haven't arranged a partner yet—most of the clubs close around 1:00 A.M.—Sunday's not a good pay night, sir. It's quite usual to cruise, there's certainly no point in wasting sixty, perhaps two or three times sixty dollars, because the decent girls are in twos or threes and you usually take two or three to dinner first. No point wasting all that money is there, sir?"

"Do you cruise, Brian?"

"No sir. No need—no sir."

Crosse sighed and turned back to Armstrong. "Go on, Robert."

"Well sir, they failed to pick up any girls and went to the Copacabana Night Club in the Sap Chuk Hotel in Gloucester Road for supper, getting there about one o'clock. About 1:45 A.M. they left and Wo Sang Chi said he saw John Chen get into his car, but he did not see him drive off—then he walked home, as he lived nearby. He said John Chen was not drunk or bad-tempered, anything like that, but seemed in good spirits, though earlier at the club, the Tong Lau Club, he'd appeared irritable and cut the mah-jong game short. There it ends. John Chen's not known to have been seen again by any of his friends—or family."

"Did he tell Wo Sang Chi where he was going?"

"No. Wo Sang Chi told us he presumed he was going home—but then he said, 'He might have gone to visit his girl friend.' We asked him who, but he said he didn't know. After pressing him he said he seemed to remember a name, Fragrant Flower, but no address or phone number— that's all."

"Fragrant Flower? That could cover a multitude of ladies of the night."

"Yes sir."

Crosse was lost in thought for a moment. "Why would Dunross want John Chen eliminated?"

The two police officers gaped at their superior.

"Put that in your abacus brain, Brian."

"Yes sir, but there's no reason. John Chen's no threat to Dunross, wouldn't possibly be—even if he became compradore. In the Noble House the tai-pan holds all the power."

"Does he?"

"Yes. By definition." Brian Kwok hesitated, thrown off balance again. "Well yes sir—I . . . in the Noble House, yes."

Crosse turned his attention to Armstrong. "Well?"

"No reason I can think of, sir. Yet."

"Well think about it."

Crosse lit a cigarette and Armstrong felt the smoke hunger pangs heavily. I'll never keep my vow, he thought. Bloody bastard Crosse-that-we-all-have-to-carry! What the hell's in his mind? He saw Crosse offer him a packet of Senior Service, the brand he always used to smoke—don't fool yourself, he thought, the brand you still smoke. "No thank you sir," he heard himself say, shafts of pain in his stomach and through all of him.

"You're not smoking, Robert?"

"No sir, I've stopped . . . I'm just trying to stop."

"Admirable! Why should Bartlett want John Chen eliminated?"

Again both police officers gawked at him. Then Armstrong said throatily, "Do you know why, sir?"

"If I knew, why should I ask you? That's for you to find out. There's a connection somewhere. Too many coincidences, too neat, too pat—and too smelly. Yes it smells of KGB involvement to me, and when that happens in my domain I must confess I get irritable."

"Yes sir."

"Well, so far so good. Put surveillance on Mrs. Phillip Chen—she could easily be implicated somewhere. The stakes for her are certainly high enough. Tail Phillip Chen for a day or two as well."

"That's already done, sir. Both of them. On Phillip Chen, not that I suspect him but just because I think they'll both do the usual—be uncooperative, keep mum, negotiate secretly, pay off secretly and breathe a sigh of relief once it's over."

"Quite. Why is it these fellows—however well educated—think they're so much smarter than we are and won't help us do the work we're paid to do?"

Brian Kwok felt the steely eyes grinding into him and the sweat trickled down his back. Control yourself, he thought. This bastard's only a foreign devil, an uncivilized, manure-eating, dung-ladened, motherless, *dew neh loh moh* saturated, monkey-descended foreign devil. "It's an old Chinese custom which I'm sure you know, sir," he said politely, "to distrust all police, all government officials—they've four thousand years of experience, sir."

"I agree with the hypothesis, but with one exception. The British. We have proved beyond all doubt we're to be trusted, we can govern, and, by and large, our bureaucracy's incorruptible."

"Yes sir."

Crosse watched him for a moment, puffing his cigarette. Then he said, "Robert, do you know what John Chen and Miss Tcholok said or talked about?"

"No sir. We haven't been able to interview her yet—she's been at Struan's all day. Could it be important?"

"Are you going to Dunross's party tonight?"

"No sir."

"Brian?"

"Yes sir."

"Good. Robert, I'm sure Dunross won't mind if I bring you with me, call for me at 8:00 P.M. All Hong Kong that counts will be there—you can keep your ears to the grindstone and your nose everywhere." He smiled at his own joke and did not mind that neither smiled with him. "Read the report now. I'll be back shortly. And Brian, please don't fail tonight. It really would be very boring."

"Yes sir."

Crosse left.

When they were alone Brian Kwok mopped his brow. "That bugger petrifies me."

"Yes. Same for me, old chum, always has."

"Would he really order a team into Struan's?" Brian Kwok asked incredulously. "Into the inner kernel of the Noble House?"

"Of course. He'd even lead it himself. This's your first tour with SI, old lad, so you don't know him like I do. That bugger'd lead a team of assassins into hell if he thought it important enough. Bet you he got the file himself. Christ, he's been over the border twice that I know of to chat to a friendly agent. He went alone, imagine that!"

Brian gasped. "Does the governor know?"

"I wouldn't think so. He'd have a hemorrhage, and if MI-6 ever heard, he'd be roasted and Crosse'd get sent to the Tower of London. He knows too many secrets to take that chance—but he's Crosse and not a thing you can do about it."

"Who was the agent?"

"Our guy in Canton."

"Wu Fong Fong?"

"No, a new one—at least he was new in my time. In the army."

"Captain Ta Quo Sa?"

Armstrong shrugged. "I forget."

Kwok smiled. "Quite right."

"Crosse still went over the border. He's a law unto himself."

"Christ, you can't even go to Macao because you were in SI a couple of years ago and he goes over the border. He's bonkers to take that risk."

"Yes." Armstrong began to mimic Crosse. "And how is it tradesmen know things before we do, dear boy? Bloody simple," he said, answering himself, and his voice lost its banter. "They spend money. They spend lots of bloody money, whereas we've sweet f.a. to spend. He knows it and I know it and the whole world knows it. Christ, how does the FBI, CIA, KGB or Korean CIA work? They spend money! Christ, it's too easy to get Alan Medford Grant on your team—Dunross hired him. Ten thousand pounds retainer, that'd buy lots of reports, that's more than enough, perhaps it was less. How much are we paid? Two thousand quid a year for three hundred and sixty-six, twenty-five hour days and a copper on the beat gets four hundred quid. Look at the red tape we'd have to go through to get a secret ten thousand quid to pay to one man to buy info. Where'd the FBI, CIA and god-cursed KGB be without unlimited funds? Christ," he added sourly, "it'd take us six months to get the money, if we could get it, whereas Dunross and fifty others can take it out of petty cash." The big man sat in his chair slouched and loose-limbed, dark shadows under his eyes that were red rimmed, his cheekbones etched by the overhead light. He glanced at the file on the desk in front of him but did not touch it yet, just wondered at the evil news it must contain. "It's easy for the Dunrosses of the world," he said.

Brian Kwok nodded and wiped his hands and put his kerchief away. "They say Dunross's got a secret fund—the tai-pan's fund—started by Dirk Struan in the beginning with the loot he got when he burned and sacked Foochow, a fund that only the current tai-pan can use for just this sort of thing, for _h'eung yau_ and payoffs, anything—maybe even a little murder. They say it runs into millions."

"I'd heard that rumor too. Yes. I wish to Christ . . . oh well." Armstrong reached for the file, hesitated, then got up and went for the phone. "First things first," he told his Chinese friend with a sardonic smile. "First we'd better breathe on a few VIPs." He dialed Police HQ in Kowloon. "Armstrong—give me Divisional Staff Sergeant Tang-po please."

"Good evening, sir. Yes sir?" Divisional Staff Sergeant Tang-po's voice was warm and friendly.

"Evening, 'Major," he said sweetly using the contraction of Sergeant Major as was customary. "I need information. I need information on who the guns were destined for. I need information on who the kidnappers of John Chen are. I want John Chen—or his body—back in three days. And I want this Werewolf—or Werewolves, in the dock very quickly."

There was a slight pause. "Yes sir."

"Please spread the word. The Great White Father is very angry indeed. And when he gets even just a little angry superintendents get posted to other commands, and so do inspectors—even sergeants, even divisional

staff sergeants class one. Some even get demoted to police constable and
sent to the border. Some might even get discharged or deported or go to
prison. Eh?"

There was an even longer pause. "Yes sir."

"And when he's very angry indeed wise men flee, if they can, before
anticorruption falls on the guilty—and even on innocents."

Another pause. "Yes sir. I'll spread the word, sir, at once. Yes, at once."

"Thank you, 'Major. The Great White Father is really very angry indeed. And oh, yes." His voice became even thinner. "Perhaps you'd ask
your brother sergeants to help. They'll surely understand, too, my modest
problem is theirs as well." He switched to Cantonese. *"When the Dragons
belch, all Hong Kong defecates. Heya?"*

A longer pause. "I'll take care of it, sir."

"Thank you." Armstrong replaced the receiver.

Brian Kwok grinned. "That's going to cause a few sphincter muscles to
oscillate."

The Englishman nodded and sat down again but his face did not lose
its hardness. "I don't like to pull that too often—actually that's only the
second time I've ever done it—but I've no option. He made that clear, so
did the Old Man. You better do the same with your sources."

"Of course. 'When the Dragons belch . . .' You were punning on the
legendary Five Dragons?"

"Yes."

Now Brian Kwok's handsome face settled into a mold—cold black eyes
in his golden skin, his square chin almost beardless. "Tang-po's one of
them?"

"I don't know, not for certain. I've always thought he was, though I've
nothing to go on. No, I'm not certain, Brian. Is he?"

"I don't know."

"Well, it doesn't matter if he is or isn't. The word'll get to one of them,
which is all I'm concerned about. Personally I'm pretty certain the Five
Dragons exist, that they're five Chinese divisional sergeants, perhaps even
station sergeants, who run all the illegal street gambling of Hong Kong—
and probably, possibly, some protection rackets, a few dance halls and girls
—five out of eleven. Five senior sergeants out of eleven possibilities. Eh?"

"I'd say the Five Dragons're real, Robert—perhaps there are more, perhaps less, but all street gambling's run by police."

"*Probably* run by Chinese members of our Royal Police Force, lad,"
Armstrong said, correcting him. "We've still no proof, none—and we've
been chasing that will o' the wisp for years. I doubt if we'll ever be able to
prove it." He grinned. "Maybe you will when you're made assistant commissioner."

"Come off it, for God's sake, Robert."

"Christ, you're only thirty-nine, you've done the special bigwig Staff

College course and you're a super already. A hundred to ten says you'll end up with that rank."

"Done."

"I should have made it a hundred thousand," Armstrong said, pretending sourness. "Then you wouldn't have taken it."

"Try me."

"I won't. I can't afford to lose that amount of tootie—you might get killed or something, this year or next, or resign—but if you don't you're in for the big slot before you retire, presuming you want to go the distance."

"Both of us."

"Not me—I'm too mad dog English." Armstrong clapped him on the back happily. "That'll be a great day. But you won't close down the Dragons either—even if you'll be able to prove it, which I doubt."

"No?"

"No. I don't care about the gambling. All Chinese want to gamble and if some Chinese police sergeants run illegal street gambling it'll be mostly clean and mostly fair though bloody illegal. If they don't run it, triads will, and then the splinter groups of rotten little bastards we so carefully keep apart will join together again into one big *tong* and then we'll really have a real problem. You know me, lad, I'm not one to rock any boats, that's why I won't make assistant commissioner. I like the status quo. The Dragons run the gambling so we keep the triads splintered—and just so long as the police always stick together and are absolutely the strongest triad in Hong Kong, we'll always have peace in the streets, a well-ordered population and almost no crime, violent crime."

Brian Kwok studied him. "You really believe that, don't you?"

"Yes. In a funny sort of a way, right now the Dragons are one of our strongest supports. Let's face it, Brian, only Chinese can govern Chinese. The status quo's good for them too—violent crime's bad for them. So we get help when we need it—sometimes, probably—help that we foreign devils couldn't get any other way. I'm not in favor of their corruption or of breaking the law, not at all—or bribery or all the other shitty things we have to do, or informers, but what police force in the world could operate without dirty hands sometimes and snotty little bastard informers? So the evil the Dragons represent fills a need here, I think. Hong Kong's China and China's a special case. Just so long as it's just illegal gambling I don't care never mind. Me, if it was left up to me I'd make gambling legal tonight but I'd break anyone for any protection racket, any dance hall protection or girls or whatever. I can't stand pimps as you know. Gambling's different. How can you stop a Chinese gambling? You can't. So make it legal and everyone's happy. How many years have the Hong Kong police been advising that and every year we're turned down. Twenty that I know of. But oh no and why? Macao! Simple as that. Dear old Portuguese Macao feeds off illegal gambling and gold smuggling and that's what keeps them alive and we can't afford, we, the UK, we can't afford to have our old ally go down the spout."

"Robert Armstrong for prime minister!"

"Up yours! But it's true. The take on illegal gambling's our only slush fund—a lot of it goes to pay our ring of informers. Where else can we get quick money? From our grateful government? Don't make me laugh! From a few extra tax dollars from the grateful population we protect? Ha!"

"Perhaps. Perhaps not, Robert. But it's certainly going to backfire one day. The payoffs—the loose and uncounted money that 'happens' to be in a station drawer? Isn't it?"

"Yes, but not on me 'cause I'm not in on it, or a taker, and the vast majority aren't either. British *or Chinese*. Meanwhile how do we three hundred and twenty-seven poor foreign devil police officers control eight odd thousand civilized junior officers and coppers, and another three and a half million civilized little bastards who hate our guts never mind."

Brian Kwok laughed. It was an infectious laugh and Armstrong laughed with him and added, "Up yours again for getting me going."

"Likewise. Meanwhile are you going to read that first or am I?"

Armstrong looked down at the file he held in his hand. It was thin and contained twelve closely typewritten pages and seemed to be more of a newsletter with topics under different headings. The contents page read: Part One: The Political and Business Forecast of the United Kingdom. Part Two: The KGB in Asia. Part Three: Gold. Part Four: Recent CIA Developments.

Wearily Armstrong put his feet on the desk and eased himself more comfortably in his chair. Then he changed his mind and passed the file over. "Here, you can read it. You read faster than I do anyway. I'm tired of reading about disaster."

Brian Kwok took it, his impatience barely contained, his heart thumping heavily. He opened it and began to read.

Armstrong watched him. He saw his friend's face change immediately and lose color. That troubled him greatly. Brian Kwok was not easily shocked. He saw him read through to the end without comment, then flick back to check a paragraph here and there. He closed the file slowly.

"It's that bad," Armstrong said.

"It's worse. Some of it—well, if it wasn't signed by A. Medford Grant, I'd say he was off his rocker. He claims the CIA have a serious connection with the Mafia, that they're plotting and have plotted to knock off Castro, they're into Vietnam in strength, into drugs and Christ knows what else— here—read it for yourself."

"What about the mole?"

"We've a mole all right." Brian reopened the file and found the paragraph. "Listen: 'There's no doubt that presently there is a high-level Communist agent in the Hong Kong police. Top-secret documents brought to our side by General Hans Richter—second-in-command of the East German Department of Internal Security—when he defected to us in March of this year clearly state the agent's code name is "Our Friend," that he has been in situ for at least ten, probably fifteen years. His contact is probably a KGB officer in Hong Kong posing as a visiting friendly businessman from the Iron Curtain countries, possibly as a banker or journalist, or posing as a seaman off one of the Soviet freighters visiting or being repaired in Hong Kong. Among other documented information we now know "Our Friend" has provided the enemy with are: All restricted radio channels, all restricted private phone numbers of the governor, chief of police and top echelon of the Hong Kong Government, along with very private dossiers on most of them . . .'"

"Dossiers?" Armstrong interrupted. "Are they included?"

"No."

"Shit! Go on, Brian."

"'. . . most of them; the classified police battle plans against a Communist-provoked insurrection, or a recurrence of the Kowloon riots; copies of all private dossiers of all police officers above the rank of inspector; the names of the chief six Nationalist undercover agents of the Kuomintang operating in Hong Kong under the present authority of General Jen Tang-wa (Appendix A); a detailed list of Hong Kong's Special Intelligence agents in Kwantung under the general authority of Senior Agent Wu Fong Fong (Appendix B).'"

"Jesus!" Armstrong gasped. "We'd better get old Fong Fong and his lads out right smartly."

"Yes."

"Is Wu Tat-sing on the list?"

Kwok checked the appendix. "Yes. Listen, this section ends: '. . . It is the conclusion of your committee that until this traitor is eliminated, the internal security of Hong Kong is hazardous. Why this information has not yet been passed on to the police themselves we do not yet know. We presume this ties in with the current political Soviet infiltration of UK administration on all levels which enables the Philbys to exist, and permits such information as this to be buried, or toned down, or misrepresented (which was the material for Study 4/1962). We would suggest this report —or portions of it, should be leaked at once to the governor or the commissioner of police, Hong Kong, *if you consider them trustworthy*.'" Brian Kwok looked up, his mind rocking. "There's a couple of other pieces here, Christ, the political situation in the UK and then there's Sevrin. . . . Read it." He shook his head helplessly. "Christ, if this's true . . . we're in it up to our necks. God in Heaven!"

Armstrong swore softly. "Who? Who could the spy be? Got to be high up. Who?"

After a great silence, Brian said, "The only one . . . the only one who could know all of this's Crosse himself."

"Oh come on for chrissake!"

"Think about it, Robert. He knew Philby. Didn't he go to Cambridge also? Both have similar backgrounds, they're the same age group, both were in Intelligence during the war—like Burgess and Maclean. If Philby could get away with it for all those years, why not Crosse?"

"Impossible!"

"Who else but him? Hasn't he been in MI-6 all his life? Didn't he do a tour here in the early fifties and wasn't he brought back here to set up our SI as a separate branch of SB five years ago? Hasn't he been director ever since?"

"That proves nothing."

"Oh?"

There was a long silence. Armstrong was watching his friend closely. He knew him too well not to know when he was serious. "What've you got?" he asked uneasily.

"Say Crosse is homosexual."

"You're plain bonkers," Armstrong exploded. "He's married and . . . and he may be an evil son of a bitch but there's never been a smell of anything like that, never."

"Yes, but he's got no children, his wife's almost permanently in England and when she's here they have separate rooms."

"How do you know?"

"The *amah* would know so if I wanted to know it'd be easy to find out."

"That proves nothing. Lots of people have separate rooms. You're wrong about Crosse."

"Say I could give you proof?"

"What proof?"

"Where does he always go for part of his leave? The Cameron Highlands in Malaya. Say he had a friend there, a young Malayan, a known deviate."

"I'd need photos and we both know photos can be easily doctored," Armstrong said harshly. "I'd need tape recordings and we both know those can be doctored too. The youth himself? That proves nothing—it's the oldest trick in the book to produce false testimony and false witnesses. There's never been a hint . . . and even if he's AC-DC, that proves nothing—not all deviates are traitors."

"No. But all deviates lay themselves open to blackmail. And if he is, he'd be highly suspect. Highly suspect. Right?"

Armstrong looked around uneasily. "I don't even like talking about it here, he could have this place tapped."

"And if he has?"

"If he has and if it's true he can fry us so quickly your head would spin. He can fry us anyway."

"Perhaps—but if he is the one then he'll know we're on to him and if he's not he'll laugh at us and I'm out of SI. In any event, Robert, he can't fry every Chinese in the force."

Armstrong stared at him. "What's that supposed to mean?"

"Perhaps there's a file on him. Perhaps every Chinese above the rank of corporal's read it."

"What?"

"Come on, Robert, you know Chinese are great joiners. Perhaps there's a file, per—"

"You mean you're all organized into a brotherhood? A *tong*, a secret society? A triad within the force?"

"I said perhaps. This is all surmise, Robert. I said perhaps and maybe."

"Who's the High Dragon? You?"

"I never said there was such a grouping. I said perhaps."

"Are there other files? On me, for instance?"

"Perhaps."

"And?"

"And if there was, Robert," Brian Kwok said gently, "it'd say you were a fine policeman, uncorrupted, that you had gambled heavily on the stock market and gambled wrong and needed twenty-odd thousand to clean up some pressing debts—and a few other things."

"What other things?"

"This is China, old chum. We know almost everything that goes on with *quai loh* here. We have to, to survive, don't we?"

Armstrong looked at him strangely. "Why didn't you tell me before?"

"I haven't told you anything now. Nothing. I said perhaps and I repeat perhaps. But if this's all true . . ." He passed over the file and wiped the sweat off his upper lip. "Read it yourself. If it's true we're up the creek without a paddle and we'll need to work very quickly. What I said was all surmise. But not about Crosse. Listen Robert, I'll bet you a thousand . . . a thousand to one, he's the mole."

10

Dunross finished reading the blue-covered file for the third time. He had read it as soon as it had arrived—as always—then again on the way to the Governor's Palace. He closed the blue cover and set it onto his lap for a moment, his mind possessed. Now he was in his study on the second floor of the Great House that sat on a knoll on the upper levels of the Peak, the leaded bay windows overlooking floodlit gardens, and then far below, the city and the immensity of the harbor.

The ancient grandfather clock chimed a quarter to eight.

Fifteen minutes to go, he thought. Then our guests arrive and the party begins and we all take part in a new charade. Or perhaps we just continue the same one.

The room had high ceilings and old oak paneling, dark green velvet curtains and Chinese silk rugs. It was a man's room, comfortable, old, a little worn and very cherished. He heard the muted voices of the servants below. A car came up the hill and passed by.

The phone rang. "Yes? Oh hello, Claudia."

"I haven't reached Tsu-yan yet, tai-pan. He wasn't in his office. Has he called?"

"No. No not yet. You keep trying."

"Yes. See you in a little while. 'Bye."

He was sitting in a deep, high-winged chair and wore a dinner jacket, his tie not yet tied. Absently he stared out of the windows, the view ever pleasing. But tonight he was filled with foreboding, thinking about Sevrin and the traitor and all the other evil things the report had foretold.

What to do?

"Laugh," he said out loud. "And fight."

He got up and went with his easy stride to the oil painting of Dirk Struan that was on the wall over the mantelpiece. Its frame was heavy and carved gilt and old, the gilt chipped off here and there, and it was secretly hinged on one side. He moved it away from the wall and opened the safe the painting covered. In the safe were many papers, some neatly tied with scarlet ribbons, some ancient, some new, a few small boxes, a neat, well-oiled, loaded Mauser in a clip attached to one of the sides, a box of ammunition, a vast old Bible with the Struan arms etched into the fine old leather and seven blue-covered files similar to the one he had in his hand.

Thoughtfully he slid the file alongside the others in sequence. He stared at them a moment, began to close the safe but changed his mind as his eyes fell on the ancient Bible. His fingers caressed it, then he lifted it out and opened it. Affixed to the thick flyleaf with old sealing wax were halves of two old Chinese bronze coins, crudely broken. Clearly, once upon a time, there had been four such half-coins for there was still the imprint of the missing two and the remains of the same red sealing wax attached to the ancient paper. The handwriting heading the page was beautiful copperplate: "I swear by the Lord God that whomsoever produces the other half of any of these coins, I will grant him whatsoever he asks." It was signed Dirk Struan, June 10, 1841, and below his signature was Culum Struan's and all the other tai-pans and the last name was Ian Dunross.

Alongside the first space where once a coin had been was written: "Wu Fang Choi, paid in part, August 16, Year of our Lord 1841," and signed again by Dirk Struan and cosigned below by Culum Struan and dated 18 June 1845 "paid in full." Alongside the second: "Sun Chen-yat, paid in full, October 10, 1911," and signed boldly, Hag Struan.

Ah, Dunross told himself, bemused, what lovely arrogance—to be so secure to be able to sign the book thus and not Tess Struan, for future generations to see.

How many more generations? he asked himself. How many more tai-pans will have to sign blindly and swear the Holy Oath to do the bidding of a man dead almost a century and a half?

Thoughtfully he ran his finger over the jagged edges of the two remaining half-coins. After a moment he closed the Bible firmly, put it into its place again, touched it once for luck and locked the safe. He swung the painting back into its place and stared up at the portrait, standing now with his hands deep in his pockets in front of the mantelpiece, the heavy old oak carved with the Struan arms, chipped and broken here and there, an old Chinese fire screen in front of the huge fireplace.

This oil of Dirk Struan was his favorite and he had taken it out of the long gallery when he became tai-pan and had hung it here in the place of honor—instead of the portrait of Hag Struan that had been over the mantelpiece in the tai-pan's study ever since there was a Great House. Both had been painted by Aristotle Quance. In this one, Dirk Struan was standing in front of a crimson curtain, broad-shouldered and arrogant, his high-cut coat black and his waistcoat and cravat and ruffled shirt white and high-cut. Heavy eyebrows and strong nose and clean-shaven, with reddish hair and muttonchop sideburns, lips curled and sensual and you could feel the eyes boring into you, their green enhanced by the black and white and crimson.

Dunross half-smiled, not afraid, not envious, more calmed than anything by his ancestor's gaze—knowing he was possessed, partially possessed by him. He raised his glass of champagne to the painting in half-mocking jest as he had done many times before: "Health!"

The eyes stared back at him.

What would you do, Dirk—Dirk o' the will o' the wisp, he thought.

"You'd probably say just find the traitors and kill them," he mused aloud, "and you'd probably be right."

The problem of the traitor in the police did not shatter him as much as the information about the Sevrin spy ring, its U.S. connections and the astonishing, secret gains made by the Communists in Britain. Where the hell does Grant get all his info? he asked himself for the hundredth time.

He remembered their first meeting. Alan Medford Grant was a short, elflike, balding man with large eyes and large teeth, in his neat pin-striped suit and bowler hat and he liked him immediately.

"Don't you worry, Mr. Dunross," Grant had said when Dunross had hired him in 1960, the moment he became tai-pan. "I assure you there'll be no conflict of interest with Her Majesty's Government if I chair your research committee on the nonexclusive basis we've discussed. I've already cleared it with them in fact. I'll only give you—confidentially of course, for you personally of course, and absolutely not for publication—I'll only give you classified material that does not, in my opinion, jeopardize the national interest. After all, our interests are the same there, aren't they?"

"I think so."

"May I ask how you heard of me?"

"We have friends in high places, Mr. Grant. In certain circles your name is quite famous. Perhaps even a foreign secretary would recommend you," he had added delicately.

"Ah yes."

"Our arrangement is satisfactory?"

"Yes—one year initially, extended to five if everything goes well. After five?"

"Another five," Dunross said. "If we achieve the results I want, your retainer will be doubled."

"Ah. That's very generous. But may I ask why you're being so generous —perhaps *extravagant* would be the word—with me and this projected committee?"

"Sun Tzu said: 'What enables a wise sovereign or good general to strike and to conquer and to achieve things beyond the reach of normal men is foreknowledge. Foreknowledge comes only through spies. Nothing is of more importance to the state than the quality of its spies. *It is ten thou-*

sand times cheaper to pay the best spies lavishly than even a tiny army poorly.'"

Alan Medford Grant beamed. "Quite right! My 8,500 pounds a year is lavish indeed, Mr. Dunross. Oh yes. Yes indeed."

"Can you think of a better investment for me?"

"Not if I perform correctly, if I and the ones I choose are the best to be had. Even so, 30-odd thousand pounds a year in salaries—a fund of up to 100,000 pounds to draw on for . . . for informants and information, all secret monies . . . well, I hope you will be satisfied with your investment."

"If you're the best I'll recoup a thousandfold. I expect to recoup a thousandfold," he had said, meaning it.

"I'll do everything in my power of course. Now, specifically what sort of information do you want?"

"Anything and everything, commercial, political, that'd help Struan's plan ahead, with accent on the Pacific Rim, on Russian, American and Japanese thinking. We'd probably know more about Chinese attitudes ourselves. Please give me more rather than less. Actually anything could be valuable because I want to take Struan's out of the China trade—more specifically I want the company international and want to diversify out of our present dependence on China trade."

"Very well. First: I would not like to trust our reports to the mails."

"I'll arrange a personal courier."

"Thank you. Second: I must have free range to select, appoint and remove the other members of the committee—and spend the money as I see fit?"

"Agreed."

"Five members will be sufficient."

"How much do you want to pay them?"

"5,000 pounds a year for a nonexclusive retainer each would be excellent. I can get top men for that. Yes. I'll appoint associate members for special studies as I need them. As, er, as most of our contacts will be abroad, many in Switzerland, could funds be available there?"

"Say I deposit the full amount we've agreed quarterly in a numbered Swiss account. You can draw funds as you need them—your signature or mine only. You account to me solely, quarterly in arrears. If you want to erect a code that's fine with me."

"Excellent. I won't be able to name anyone—I can't account to whom I give money."

After a pause Dunross had said, "All right."

"Thank you. We understand one another, I think. Can you give me an example of what you want?"

"For example, I don't want to get caught like my predecessor was over Suez."

"Oh! You mean the 1956 fiasco when Eisenhower betrayed us again and caused the failure of the British-French-Israeli attack on Egypt—because Nasser had nationalized the canal?"

"Yes. That cost us a fortune—it wrecked our Middle East interests, almost ruined us. If the previous tai-pan'd known about a possible closure of Suez we could have made a fortune booking cargo space—increasing our fleet . . . or if we'd had an advanced insight into American thinking, particularly that Eisenhower would side again with Soviet Russia against us, we could certainly have cut our losses."

The little man had said sadly, "You know he threatened to freeze all British, French and Israeli assets in the States instantly if we did not at once withdraw from Egypt when we were a few hours from victory? I think all our present problems in the Middle East stem from that U.S. decision. Yes. Inadvertently the U.S. approved international piracy for the first time and set a pattern for future piracies. Nationalization. What a joke! *Theft* is a better word—or piracy. Yes. Eisenhower was ill-advised. And very ill-advised to go along with the fatuous political Yalta agreement of an ailing Roosevelt, the incompetent Attlee to allow Stalin to gorge most of Europe, when it was militarily clear to even the most stupid politician or hidebound general that *it was contrary to our absolute national interest, ours and the United States to hold back.* I think Roosevelt hated us really, and our British Empire."

The little man steepled his fingers and beamed. "I'm afraid there's one big disadvantage in employing me, Mr. Dunross. I'm entirely pro-British, anti-Communist, and particularly anti-KGB which is the main instrument of Soviet foreign policy, which is openly and forever committed to our destruction, so some of my more peppery forecasts you can discount, if you wish. I'm entirely against a left-wing dominated Labour Party and I will constantly remind anyone who will listen that the anthem of the Labour Party's 'The Red Flag.'" Alan Medford Grant smiled in his pixy way. "It's best you know where you stand in the beginning. I'm royalist, loyalist and believe in the British parliamentary way. I'll never knowingly give you false information though my evaluations will be slanted. May I ask what your politics are?"

"We have none in Hong Kong, Mr. Grant. We don't vote, there are no elections—we're a colony, particularly a free-port colony, not a democracy. The Crown rules—actually the governor rules despotically for the Crown. He has a legislative council but it's a rubber-stamp council and the historic policy is *laissez-faire*. Wisely he leaves things alone. He listens to the business community, makes social changes very cautiously and leaves everyone to make money or not make money, to build, expand, go broke, to go or to come, to dream or to stay awake, to live or to die as best you can. And the maximum tax is 15 percent but only on money earned in Hong Kong. We don't have politics here, don't want politics here—neither does China want us to have any here. They're for the status quo too. My personal politics? I'm royalist, I'm for freedom, for freebooting and free trade. I'm a Scotsman, I'm for Struan's, I'm for *laissez-faire* in Hong Kong and freedom throughout the world."

"I think we understand one another. Good. I've never worked for an individual before—only the government. This will be a new experience for me. I hope I will satisfy you." Grant paused and thought a moment. "Like Suez in '56?" The lines beside the little man's eyes crinkled. "Very well, plan that the Panama Canal will be lost to America."

"That's ridiculous!"

"Oh don't look so shocked, Mr. Dunross! It's too easy. Give it ten or fifteen years of enemy spadework and lots of liberal talk in America, ably assisted by do-gooders who believe in the benevolence of human nature, add to all this a modest amount of calculated Panamanian agitation, students and so on—preferably, ah, always students—artfully and secretly assisted by a few highly trained, patient, professional agitators and oh so secret KGB expertise, finance and a long-range plan—ergo, in due course the canal could be out of U.S. hands into the enemy's."

"They'd never stand for it."

"You're right, Mr. Dunross, but they will sit for it. What could be a better garrotte in time of hostilities, or even crisis, against your main, openly stated capitalistic enemy than to be able to inhibit the Panama Canal or rock it a little? One ship sunk in any one of a hundred spots, or a lock wrecked, could dam up the canal for years."

Dunross remembered how he had poured two more drinks before answering, and then he had said, "You're seriously suggesting we should make contingency plans against that."

"Yes," the little man said with his extraordinary innocence. "I'm very serious about my job, Mr. Dunross. My job, the one I've chosen for me, is to seek out, to uncover and evaluate enemy moves. I'm not anti-Russian or anti-Chinese or anti-East German or anti any of that bloc—on the absolute contrary I want desperately to help them. I'm convinced that we're in a state of war, that the enemy of all the people is the Communist Party member, whether British, Soviet, Chinese, Hungarian, American, Irish . . . even Martian . . . and all are linked in one way or another; that the KGB, like it or not, is in the center of their web." He sipped the drink Dunross had just refilled for him. "This is marvelous whiskey, Mr. Dunross."

"It's Loch Vey—it comes from a small distillery near our homelands in Ayr. It's a Struan company."

"Marvelous!" Another appreciative sip of the whiskey and Dunross reminded himself to send Alan Medford Grant a case for Christmas—if the initial reports proved interesting.

"I'm not a fanatic, Mr. Dunross, nor a rabble-rouser. Just a sort of reporter and forecaster. Some people collect stamps, I collect secrets. . . ."

The lights of a car rounding the half-hidden curve of the road below distracted Dunross momentarily. He wandered over to the window and watched the car until it had gone, enjoying the sound of the highly tuned engine. Then he sat in a high-winged chair and let his mind drift again. Yes, Mr. Grant, you certainly collect secrets, he thought, staggered as usual by the scope of the little man's knowledge.

Sevrin—Christ almighty! If that's true . . .

How accurate are you this time? How far do I trust you this time—how far do I gamble?

In previous reports Grant had given two projections that, so far, could be proved. A year in advance, Grant had predicted that de Gaulle would veto Britain's effort to join the EEC, that the French general's posture would be increasingly anti-British, anti-American and pro-Soviet, and that de Gaulle would, prompted by outside influences and encouraged by one of his closest advisors—an immensely secret, covert KGB mole—mount a long-term attack on the U.S. economy by speculation in gold. Dunross had dismissed this as farfetched and so had lost a potential fortune.

Recently, six months in advance, Grant had forecast the missile crisis in Cuba, that Kennedy would slam down the gauntlet, blockade Cuba and exert the necessary pressure and not buckle under the strain of brinkmanship, that Khrushchev would back off under pressure. Gambling that Grant was correct this time—though a Cuban missile crisis had seemed highly unlikely at the time forecast—Dunross had made Struan's half a million pounds by buying Hawaiian sugar futures, another 600,000 on the stock market, plus 600,000 for the tai-pan's secret fund—and cemented a long-range plan to invest in Hawaiian sugar plantations as soon as he could find the financial tool. And you've got it now, he told himself gleefully. Par-Con.

"You've almost got it," he muttered, correcting himself.

How far do I trust this report? Thus far AMG's committee's been a gigantic investment for all his meanderings, he thought. Yes. But it's almost like having your own astrologer. A few accurate forecasts don't mean they'll all be. Hitler had his own forecaster. So did Julius Caesar. Be wise, be cautious, he reminded himself.

What to do? It's now or never.

Sevrin. Alan Medford Grant had written: "Documents brought to us and substantiated by the French spy Marie d'Orleans caught by the Sûreté June 16 indicate that the KGB Department V (Disinformation—FAR EAST) have in situ a hitherto unknown, deep-cover espionage network throughout the Far East, code name *Sevrin*. The purpose of Sevrin is clearly stated in the stolen Head Document:

"Aim: To cripple revisionist China—formally acknowledged by the Central Committee of the USSR as the main enemy, second only to capitalist U.S.A.

"Procedure: The permanent obliteration of Hong Kong as the bastion of capitalism in the Far East and China's preeminent source of all foreign currency, foreign assistance and all technical and manufactured assistance of every kind.

"Method: Long-term infiltration of the press and media, the government, police, business and education with friendly aliens controlled by Center—but only in accordance with most special procedures throughout Asia.

"Initiation date: Immediate.

"Duration of operation: Provisionally thirty years.

"Target date: 1980–83.

"Classification: *Red One.*

"Funding: Maximum.

"Approval: L.B. March 14, 1950.

"It's interesting to note," Grant had continued, "that the document is signed in 1950 by L.B.—presumed to be Lavrenti Beria—when Soviet Russia was openly allied with Communist China, and that, even in those days, China was secretly considered their Number Two enemy. (Our previous report 3/1962, Russia versus China refers.)

"China, historically, is the great prize that always was—and ever will be —sought by imperialistic and hegemonic Russia. Possession of China, or its mutilation into balkanized subject states, is the perpetual keystone of Russian foreign policy. First is, of course, the obliteration of Western Europe, for then, Russia believes, China can be swallowed at will.

"The documents reveal that the Hong Kong cell of Sevrin consists of a resident controller, code name Arthur, and six agents. We know nothing about Arthur, other than that he has been a KGB agent since recruitment in England in the thirties (it's not known if he was born in England, or if his parents are English, but he would be in his late forties or early fifties). His mission is, of course, a long-term, deep-cover operation.

"Supporting top-secret intelligence documents stolen from the Czechoslovak STB (State Secret Security) dated April 6, 1959, translate in part, '. . . between 1946 and 1959 six key, deep-cover agents have been recruited through information supplied by the controller, Arthur: one each in the Hong Kong Colonial Office (code name Charles), Treasury (code name Mason), Naval Base (John), the Bank of London and China (Vincent), the Hong Kong Telephone Company (William), and Struan and Company (Frederick). According to normal procedures only the controller knows the true identity of the others. Seven safe houses have been established. Among them are Sinclair Towers on Hong Kong Island and the Nine Dragons Hotel in Kowloon. Sevrin's New York contact, has the code name Guillio. He is very important to us because of his Mafia and CIA connections.'"

Grant had continued, "Guillio is believed to be Vincenzo Banastasio, a substantial racketeer and the present don of the Sallapione family. This is being checked through our U.S. sources. We don't know if the deep-cover enemy agent in the police (covered in detail in another section) is part of Sevrin or not but presume he is.

"In our opinion, China will be forced to seek ever-increasing amounts of trade with the West to counterbalance imperialist Soviet hegemony and to fill the void and chaos created by the sudden withdrawal in 1960 of all Soviet funding and technicians. China's armed forces badly need modernizing. Harvests have been bad. Therefore all forms of strategic materials and military hardware will find a ready market for many years to come, and food, basic foodstuffs. The long-range purchase of American rice futures is recommended.

"I have the honor to be, sir, your obedient servant, AMG, London, August 15, 1963."

Jets and tanks and nuts and bolts and rockets and engines and trucks and petrol and tires and electronics and food, Dunross thought, his mind soaring. A limitless spectrum of trade goods, easy to obtain, easy to ship, and nothing on earth like a war for profit if you can trade. But China's not buying now, whatever they need, whatever Grant says.

Who could Arthur be?

Who in Struan's? Jesus Christ! John Chen and Tsu-yan and smuggled guns and now a KGB agent within. Who? What about . . .

There was a gentle knock on the door.

"Come in," he said, recognizing his wife's knock.

"Ian, it's almost eight," Penelope, his wife, said, "I thought I'd better tell you. You know how you are."

"Yes."

"How did it go today? Awful about John Chen, isn't it? I suppose you read the papers? Are you coming down?"

"Yes. Champagne?"

"Thanks."

He poured for her and replenished his glass. "Oh by the way, Penn, I invited a fellow I met this afternoon, an ex-RAF type. He seemed a decent fellow—Peter Marlowe."

"Fighters?"

"Yes. But Hurricanes—not Spits. Is that a new dress?"

"Yes."

"You look pretty," he said.

"Thank you but I'm not. I feel so old, but thank you." She sat in the other winged chair, her perfume as delicate as her features. "Peter Marlowe, you said?"

"Yes. Poor bugger got caught in Java in '42. He was a POW for three and a half years."

"Oh, poor man. He was shot down?"

"No, the Japanese plastered the 'drome before he could scramble. Perhaps he was lucky. The Zeros got two on the ground and the last two just after they were airborne—the pilots flamed in. Seems those four Hurricanes were the last of the Few—the last of the whole air defense of the Far East. What a balls-up that was!"

"Terrible."

"Yes. Thank God our war was in Europe." Dunross watched her. "He said he was a year in Java, then the Japanese sent him to Singapore on a work party."

"To Changi?" she asked, her voice different.

"Yes."

"Oh!"

"He was there for two and a half years." Changi in Malay meant "clinging vine," and Changi was the name of the jail in Singapore that was used by the Japanese in World War II for one of their infamous prisoner-of-war camps.

She thought a moment, then smiled a little nervously. "Did he know Robin there?" Robin Grey was her brother, her only living relative: her parents had been killed in an air raid in London in 1943, just before she and Dunross were married.

"Marlowe said yes, he seemed to remember him, but clearly he didn't want to talk about those days so I let it drop."

"I can imagine. Did you tell him Robin was my brother?"

"No."

"When's Robin due back here?"

"I don't know exactly. In a few days. This afternoon the governor told me the delegation's in Peking now." A British Parliamentary Trade Delegation drawn from MPs of the three parties—Conservative, Liberal and Labour—had been invited out from London by Peking to discuss all manner of trade. The delegation had arrived in Hong Kong two weeks ago and had gone directly on to Canton where all trade negotiations were conducted. It was very rare for anyone to get an invitation, let alone a parliamentary delegation—and even rarer to be invited on to Peking. Robin Grey was one of the members—representative of the Labour Party. "Penn darling, don't you think we should acknowledge Robin, give a reception for him? After all, we haven't seen him for years, this's the first time he's been to Asia—isn't it time you buried the hatchet and made peace?"

"He's not invited to my house. Any of my houses."

"Isn't it time you relaxed a little, let bygones be bygones?"

"No, I know him, you don't. Robin has his life and we have ours, that's what he and I agreed years ago. No, I've no wish to see him ever again. He's awful, dangerous, foul-mouthed and a bloody bore."

Dunross laughed. "I agree he's obnoxious and I detest his politics—but he's only one of a half dozen MPs. This delegation's important. I should do something to entertain them, Penn."

"Please do, Ian. But preferably not here—or else tell me in good time so I can have the vapors and see that the children do the same. It's a matter of face and that's the end of it." Penelope tossed her head and shook off her mood. "God! Let's not let him spoil this evening! What's this Marlowe doing in Hong Kong?"

"He's a writer. Wants to do a book on Hong Kong, he said. He lives in America now. His wife's coming too. Oh, by the way, I also invited the Americans, Linc Bartlett and Casey Tcholok."

"Oh!" Penelope Dunross laughed. "Oh well, four or forty extra won't make any difference at all—I won't know most of them anyway, and Claudia's organized everything with her usual efficiency." She arched an eyebrow. "So! A gun-runner amongst the pirates! That won't even cause a ripple."

"Is he?"

"Everyone says so. Did you see the piece in this afternoon's *Mirror*, Ian? Ah Tat's convinced the American is bad joss—she informed the whole staff, the children and me—so that makes it official. Ah Tat told Adryon that her astrologer insisted she tell you to watch out for bad influence from the East. Ah Tat's sure that means the Yanks. Hasn't she bent your ear yet?"

"Not yet."

"God, I wish I could chatter Cantonese like you and the children. I'd tell that old harpy to keep her superstitions and opinions to herself—she's a bad influence."

"She'd give her life for the children."

"I know she's your *gan sun* and almost brought you up and thinks she's God's gift to the Dunross clan. But as far as I'm concerned she's a cantankerous, loathsome old bitch and I hate her." Penelope smiled sweetly. "I hear the American girl's pretty."

"Attractive—not pretty. She's giving Andrew a bad time."

"I can imagine. A lady talking business! What are we coming to in this great world of ours? Is she any good?"

"Too soon to tell. But she's very smart. She's—she'll make things awkward certainly."

"Have you seen Adryon tonight?"

"No—what's up?" he asked, instantly recognizing the tone of voice.

"She's been into my wardrobe again—half my best nylons are gone, the rest are scattered, my scarves are all jumbled up, my new blouse's missing and my new belt's disappeared. She's even whipped my best Hermès . . . that child's the end!"

"Nineteen's hardly a child," he said wearily.

"She's the end! The number of times I've told her!"

"I'll talk to her again."

"That won't do a bit of good."

"I know."

She laughed with him. "She's such a pill."

"Here." He handed her a slim box. "Happy twentieth!"

"Oh thank you, Ian. Yours is downstairs. You'll . . ." She stopped and opened the box. It contained a carved jade bracelet, the jade inset into silver filigree, very fine, very old—a collector's piece. "Oh how lovely, thank you, Ian." She put it on her wrist over the thin gold chain she was wearing and he heard neither real pleasure nor real disappointment under her voice, his ears tuned to her. "It's beautiful," she said and leaned forward and brushed her lips against his cheek. "Thank you, darling. Where did you get it? Taiwan?"

"No, here on Cat Street. At Wong Chun Kit's, he ga—"

The door flew open and a girl barreled in. She was tall and slim and oh so fair and she said in a breathless rush, "I hope it's all right I invited a date tonight and I just had the call that he's coming and he'll be late but I thought it'd be okay. He's cool. And very trick."

"For the love of God, Adryon," Dunross said mildly, "how many times do I have to ask you to knock before you charge in here and would you kindly talk English? What the hell's *trick?*"

"Good, great, cool, trick. Sorry, Father, but you really are rather square because cool and trick are very in, even in Hong Kong. See you soon, have to dash, after the party I'm going out—I'll be late so don't—"

"Wait a min—"

"That's my blouse, my new blouse," Penelope burst out. "Adryon, you take it off this minute! I've told you fifty times to stay the hell out of my wardrobe."

"Oh, Mother," Adryon said as sharply, "you don't need it, can't I borrow it for this evening?" Her tone changed. "Please? Pretty please? Father, talk to her." She switched to perfect *amah* Cantonese, "Honorable Father . . . please help your Number One Daughter to achieve the unachievable or I shall weep weep weep *oh ko* . . ." Then back into English in the same breath, "Mother . . . you don't need it and I'll look after it, truly. Please?"

"No."

"Come on, pretty please, I'll look after it, I promise."

"No."

"Mother!"

"Well if you pr—"

"Oh thanks." The girl beamed and turned and rushed out and the door slammed behind her.

"Jesus bloody Christ," Dunross said sourly, "why the hell does a door always happen to slam behind her!"

"Well at least it's not deliberate now." Penelope sighed. "I don't think I could go through that siege again."

"Nor me. Thank God Glenna's reasonable."

"It's purely temporary, Ian. She takes after her father, that one, like Adryon."

"Huh! I don't have a filthy temper," he said sharply. "And since we're on the subject I hope to God Adryon has found someone decent to date instead of the usual shower! Who is this she's bringing?"

"I don't know, Ian. This is the first I've heard of it too."

"They're always bloody awful! Her taste in men's appalling. . . . Remember that melon-headed berk with the neolithic arms that she was 'madly in love with'? Christ Jesus, she was barely fifteen an—"

"She was almost sixteen."

"What was his name? Ah yes, Byron. Byron for chrissake!"

"You really shouldn't have threatened to blow his head off, Ian. It was just puppy love."

"It was gorilla bloody love, by God," Dunross said even more sourly. "He was a bloody gorilla. . . . You remember that other one, the one before bloody Byron—the psychiatric bastard . . . what was his name?"

"Victor. Yes, Victor Hopper. He was the one . . . oh yes, I remember, he was the one who asked if it was all right if he slept with Adryon."

"He what?"

"Oh yes." She smiled up at him so innocently. "I didn't tell you at the time . . . thought I'd better not."

"He *what?*"

"Don't get yourself all worked up, Ian. That's at least four years ago. I told him no, not at the moment, Adryon's only fourteen, but yes, certainly, when she was twenty-one. That was another that died on the vine."

"Jesus Christ! *He asked* you if he co—"

"At least he asked, Ian! That was something. It's all so very ordinary." She got up and poured more champagne into his glass, and some for herself. "You've only got another ten years or so of purgatory, then there'll be the grandchildren. Happy anniversary and the best of British to you!" She laughed and touched his glass and drank and smiled at him.

"You're right again," he said and smiled back, liking her very much. So many years, good years. I've been lucky, he thought. Yes. I was blessed that first day. It was at his RAF station at Biggin Hill, a warm, sunny August morning in 1940 during the Battle of Britain and she was a WAAF and newly posted there. It was his eighth day at war, his third mission that day and first kill. His Spitfire was latticed with bullet holes, parts of his wing gone, his tail section tattooed. By all the rules of joss, he should be dead but he wasn't and the Messerschmitt was and her pilot was and he was home and safe and blood raging, drunk with fear and shame and relief that he had come back and the youth he had seen in the other cockpit, the enemy, had burned screaming as he spiraled.

"Hello, sir," Penelope Grey had said. "Welcome home sir. Here." She had given him a cup of hot sweet tea and she had said nothing else though she should have begun debriefing him at once—she was in Signals. She said nothing but smiled and gave him time to come out of the skies of death into life again. He had not thanked her, just drank the tea and it was the best he had ever had.

"I got a Messerschmitt," he had said when he could talk, his voice trembling like his knees. He could not remember unsnapping his harness or getting out of his cockpit or climbing into the truck with the other survivors. "It was a 109."

"Yes sir, Squadron Leader Miller has already confirmed the kill and he says to please get ready, you're to scramble any minute again. You're to take Poppa Mike Kilo this time. Thank you for the kill, sir, that's one less of those devils . . . oh how I wish I could go up with you to help you all kill those monsters. . . ."

But they weren't monsters, he thought, at least the first pilot and first plane that he had killed had not been—just a youth like himself, perhaps the same age, who had burned screaming, died screaming, a flaming falling leaf, and this afternoon or tomorrow or soon it would be his turn—too many of them, the enemy, too few of us.

"Did Tommy get back, Tom Lane?"

"No sir, sorry sir. He . . . the squadron leader said Flight Lieutenant Lane was jumped over Dover."

"I'm petrified of burning, going down," he had said.

"Oh you won't, sir, not you. They won't shoot you down. *I know.* You won't, sir, no, not you. They'll never get you, never never never," she had said, pale blue eyes, fair hair and fair of face, not quite eighteen but strong, very strong and very confident.

He had believed her and her faith had carried him through four more months of missions—sometimes five missions each day—and more kills and though she was wrong and later he was blown out of the sky, he lived and burned only a little. And then, when he came out of the hospital, grounded forever, they had married.

"Doesn't seem like twenty years," he said, holding in his happiness.

"Plus two before," she said, holding in her happiness.

"Plus two be—"

The door opened. Penelope sighed as Ah Tat stalked into the room, talking Cantonese fifty to the dozen, "*Ayeeyah,* my Son, but aren't you ready yet, our honored guests will be here any moment and your tie's not tied and that motherless foreigner from North Kwantung brought unnecessarily into our house to cook tonight . . . that smelly offspring of a one-dollar strumpet from North Kwantung where all the best thieves and worst whores come from who fancies himself a cook . . . ha! . . . This man and his equally despicable foreign staff is befouling our kitchen and stealing our peace. *Oh ko,*" the tiny wizened old woman continued without a breath as her clawlike fingers reached up automatically and deftly tied his tie, "and that's not all! Number Two Daughter . . . Number Two Daughter just won't put on the dress that Honorable First Wife has chosen for her and her rage is flying to Java! Eeeee, this family! Here, my Son," she took the telex envelope out of her pocket and handed it to Dunross, "here's another barbarian message bringing more congratulations for this happy day that your poor old Mother had to carry up the stairs herself on her poor old legs because the other good-for-nothing servants are good for nothing and bone idle. . . ." She paused momentarily for breath.

"Thank you, Mother," he said politely.

"In your Honorable Father's day, the servants worked and knew what to do and your old Mother didn't have to endure dirty strangers in our Great House!" She walked out muttering more curses on the caterers. "Now don't you be late, my Son, otherwise . . ." She was still talking after she'd closed the door.

"What's up with *her?*" Penelope asked wearily.

"She's rattling on about the caterers, doesn't like strangers—you know what she's like." He opened the envelope. In it was the folded telex.

"What was she saying about Glenna?" his wife asked, having recognized *yee-chat*, Second Daughter, though her Cantonese was minimal.

"Just that she was having a fit about the dress you picked for her."

"What's wrong with it?"

"Ah Tat didn't say. Look, Penn, perhaps Glenna should just go to bed —it's almost past her bedtime now and sh—"

"Dreamer! No chance till hell freezes over. Even Hag Struan wouldn't keep Glenna from her first grown-up as she calls it! You did agree Ian, *you* agreed, I didn't, you did!"

"Yes, but don't you th—"

"No. She's quite old enough. After all she's thirteen going on thirty." Penelope calmly finished her champagne. "Even so I shall now deal with that young lady never mind." She got up. Then she saw his face. He was staring at the telex.

"What's the matter?"

"One of our people's been killed. In London. Grant. Alan Medford Grant."

"Oh. I don't know him, do I?"

"I think you met him once in Ayrshire. He was a small, pixyish man. He was at one of our parties at Castle Avisyard—it was on our last leave."

She frowned. "Don't remember." She took the offered telex. It read: "Regret to inform you A. M. Grant was killed in motorcycle accident this morning. Details will follow when I have them. Sorry. Regards, Kiernan."

"Who's Kiernan?"

"His assistant."

"Grant's . . . he was a friend?"

"In a way."

"He's important to you?"

"Yes."

"Oh, sorry."

Dunross forced himself to shrug and keep his voice level. But in his mind he was cursing obscenely. "Just one of those things. Joss."

She wanted to commiserate with him, recognizing at once the depth of his shock. She knew he was greatly perturbed, trying to hide it—and she wanted to know immediately the who and the why of this unknown man. But she held her peace.

That's my job, she reminded herself. Not to ask questions, to be calm and to be there—to pick up the pieces, but only when I'm allowed to. "Are you coming down?"

"In a moment."

"Don't be long, Ian."

"Yes."

"Thanks again for my bracelet," she said, liking it very much and he said, "It's nothing," but she knew he had not really heard her. He was already at the phone asking for long distance. She walked out and closed the door quietly and stood miserably in the long corridor that led to the east and west wings, her heart thumping. Curse all telexes and all telephones and curse Struan's and curse Hong Kong and curse all parties and all hangers-on and oh how I wish we could leave forever and forget Hong Kong and forget work and the Noble House and Big Business and the Pacific Rim and the stock market and all curs—

"Motherrrrr!"

She heard Glenna's voice screeching from the depths of her room around the far corner in the east wing and at once all her senses concentrated. There was frustrated rage in Glenna's voice, but no danger, so she did not hurry, just called back, "I'm coming . . . what is it, Glenna?"

"Where are youuuuu?"

"I'm coming, darling," she called out, her mind now on important things. Glenna will look pretty in that dress, she thought. Oh I know, she told herself happily, I'll lend her my little rope of pearls. That'll make it perfect.

Her pace quickened.

Across the harbor in Kowloon, Divisional Staff Sergeant Tang-po, CID, the High Dragon, climbed the rickety stairs and went into the room. The inner core of his secret triad was already there. "Get this through that bone some of you carry between your ears: the Dragons want Noble House Chen found and these pox-dripping, dung-eating Werewolves caught so fast even gods will blink!"

"Yes, Lord," his underlings chorused, shocked at the quality of his voice.

They were in Tang-po's safe house, a small, drab, three-room apartment behind a drab front door on the fifth floor of an equally drab apartment building over very modest shops in a dirty alley just three blocks from their police headquarters of Tsim Sha Tsui District that faced the harbor and the Peak on the tip of Kowloon Peninsula. There were nine of them:

one sergeant, two corporals, the rest constables—all plainclothes detectives of the CID, all Cantonese, all handpicked and sworn with blood oaths to loyalty and secrecy. They were Tang-po's secret *tong* or Brotherhood, which protected all street gambling in Tsim Sha Tsui District.

"Look everywhere, talk to everyone. We have three days," Tang-po said. He was a strongly built man of fifty-five with slightly graying hair and heavy eyebrows and his rank was the highest he could have and not be an officer. "This is the order of me—all my Brother Dragons—and the High One himself. Apart from that," he added sourly, "Big Mountain of Dung has promised to demote and post us to the border or other places, all of us, if we fail, and that's the first time he's ever threatened that. All gods piss from a great height on all foreign devils, particularly those motherless fornicators who won't accept their rightful squeeze and behave like civilized persons!"

"Amen!" Sergeant Lee said with great fervor. He was a sometimes Catholic because in his youth he had gone to a Catholic school.

"Big Mountain of Dung made it quite clear this afternoon: results, or off to the border where there's not a pot to piss in and no squeeze within twenty miles. *Ayeeyah*, all gods protect us from failure!"

"Yes," Corporal Ho said for all of them, making a note in his book. He was a sharp-featured man who was studying at night school to become an accountant, and it was he who kept the Brotherhood's books and minutes of their meetings.

"Elder Brother," Sergeant Lee began politely, "is there a fixed reward we can offer our informers? Is there a minimum or a maximum?"

"Yes," Tang-po told them, then added carefully, "The High Dragon has said 100,000 HK if within three days . . ." The room was suddenly silent at the vastness of the reward. ". . . half for finding Noble House Chen, half for finding the kidnappers. And a bonus of 10,000 to the Brother whose informer produces either—and promotion."

"One 10,000 for Chen and one ten for the kidnappers?" the corporal asked. O gods grant me the prize, he prayed, as they all were praying. "Is that right, Elder Brother?"

"*Dew neh loh moh* that's what I said," Tang-po replied sharply, puffing his cigarette. "Are your ears filled with pus?"

"Oh no, sorry Honorable Sir. Please excuse me."

All their minds were on the prize. Sergeant Lee was thinking, Eeee, 10,000 and—and promotion if in three days! Ah, if within three days then it will be in time for Race Day and then . . . O all gods great and small bless me this once and a second time on Saturday's double quinella.

Tang-po was referring to his notes. "Now to other business. Through the cooperation of Daytime Chang and the Honorable Song, the Brotherhood can use their showers daily at the V and A between 8:00 A.M. and 9:00 A.M., not 7:00 A.M. to 8:00 A.M. as before. Wives and concubines on a roster basis. Corporal Ho, you rearrange the roster."

"Hey, Honored Lord," one of the young detectives called out, "did you hear about Golden Pubics?"

"Eh?"

The youth related what Daytime Chang had told him this morning when he went to the hotel kitchens for breakfast. They all guffawed.

"*Ayeeyah*, imagine that! Like gold, *heya*?"

"Have you ever pillowed a foreign devil, Honorable Lord?"

"No never. No. *Ayeeyah*, the very thought . . . ugh!"

"I'd like one," Lee said with a laugh, "just to see what was what!"

They laughed with him and one called out, "A Jade Gate's a Jade Gate but they say some foreign devils are lopsided!"

"I heard they were cleft sideways!"

"Honored Sir, there was another thing," the young detective said when the laughter had died down. "Daytime Chang told me to tell you Golden Pubics has a miniature transmitter-receiver—best he'd ever seen, better than anything we've got, even in Special Branch. She carries it around with her."

Tang-po stared at him. "That's curious. Now why should a foreign devil woman want a thing like that?"

Lee said, "Something to do with the guns?"

"I don't know, Younger Brother. Women with transceivers? Interesting. It wasn't in her luggage when our people went through it last night, so it must've been in her handbag. Good, very good. Corporal Ho, after our meeting leave a gift for Daytime Chang—a couple of reds." A red note was 100 HK. "I'd certainly like to know who those guns were for," he added thoughtfully. "Make sure all our informers know I'm very interested in that too."

"Is Noble House Chen tied into the guns and these two foreign devils?" Lee asked.

"I think so, Younger Brother. I think so. Yes. Another curiosity—to send an ear is not civilized—not so soon. Not civilized at all."

"Ah, then you think the Werewolves're foreign devils? Or fornicating half-persons? Or Portuguese?"

"I don't know," Tang-po said sourly. "But it happened in our district, so it's a matter of face for all of us. Big Mountain of Dung is very enraged. His face is in the mangle too."

"Eeee," Lee said, "that fornicator has such a very filthy temper."

"Yes. Perhaps the information about the transceiver will appease him. I think I'll ask all my Brothers to put surveillance on Golden Pubics and her gun-running friend just in case. Now, there was something else. . . ." Again Tang-po referred to his notes. "Ah yes, why is our contribution from the Happy Hostess Night Club down 30 percent?"

"A new ownership's just taken over, Honored Sir," Sergeant Lee, in whose area the dance hall was, said. "One Eye Pok sold out to a Shanghainese fornicator called Wang—Happy Wang. Happy Wang says the Fragrant Grease's too high, business is bad, very bad."

"*Dew neh loh moh* on all Shanghainese. Is it?"

"It's down, but not much."

"That's right, Honored Sir," Corporal Ho said. "I was there at midnight to collect the fornicating week's advance—the stink fornicating place was about half full."

"Any foreign devils there?"

"Two or three, Honored Lord. No one of importance."

"Give Honorable Happy Wang a message from me: He has three weeks to improve his business. Then we'll reconsider. Corporal Ho, tell some of the girls at the Great New Oriental to recommend the Happy Hostess for a month or so—they've plenty of foreign devil customers . . . and tell Wang that there's a nuclear aircraft carrier—the *Corregidor*—coming in the day after tomorrow for R and R . . ." He used the English letters, everyone understanding rest and recreation from the Korean War days. "I'll ask my Brother Dragon in Wanchai and the dock area if Happy Wang can send some visiting cards over there. A thousand or so Golden Country barbarians will certainly be a help! They're here for eight days."

"Honored Sir, I'll do that tonight," Corporal Ho promised.

"My friend in marine police told me that there are going to be lots of visiting warships soon—the American Seventh Fleet is being increased." Tang-po frowned. "Doubled, so he says. The talk from the Mainland is that American soldiers are going to go into Vietnam in strength—they already run an airline there—at least," he added, "their triad CIA does."

"Eeee, that's good for business! We'll have to repair their ships. And entertain their men. Good! Very good for us."

"Yes. Very good. But very stupid for them. Honorable Chou En-lai's sent them warnings, politely, for months that China doesn't want them there! Why won't they listen? Vietnam's our outer barbarian sphere! Stupid to pick that foul jungle and those detestable barbarians to fight against. If China couldn't subdue those outer barbarians for centuries, how can they?" Tang-po laughed and lit another cigarette. "Where's old One Eye Pok gone?"

"That old fox's permanent visa came through and he was off on the next airplane to San Francisco—him, his wife and eight kids."

Tang-po turned to his accountant. "Did he owe us any money?"

"Oh no Honored Sir. He was fully paid up-to-date, Sergeant Lee saw to that."

"How much did it cost that old fornicator? To get the visa?"

"His exit was smoothed by a gift of 3,000 HK to Corporal Sek Pun So in Immigration on our recommendation—our percentage was paid—we also assisted him to find the right diamond merchant to convert his wealth into the best blue whites available." Ho referred to his books. "Our 2 percent commission came to 8,960 HK."

"Good old One Eye!" Tang-po said, pleased for him. "He's done very well for himself. What was his 'unique services' job for his visa?"

Sergeant Lee said, "A cook in a restaurant in Chinatown—the Good Eating Place it's called. *Oh ko,* I've tasted his home cooking and old One Eye is very bad indeed."

"He'll hire another to take his place while he goes into real estate, or gambling and a nightclub," someone said. "Eeee, what joss!"

"But what did his U.S. visa cost him?"

"Ah, the golden gift to Paradise!" Ho sighed. "I heard he paid 5,000 U.S. to jump to the head of the list."

"*Ayeeyah,* that's more than usual! Why?"

"It seems there's also a promise of a U.S. passport as soon as the five years are up and not too much harassment about his English—old One Eye doesn't talk English as you know. . . ."

"Those fornicators from the Golden Country—they squeeze but they aren't organized. They've no style, none at all," Tang-po said scornfully. "One or two visas here and there—when everyone here knows you can buy one if you're at the right time with the right squeeze. So why don't they do it properly in a civilized way? Twenty visas a week—even forty— they're all mad these foreign devils!"

"*Dew neh loh moh* but you're right," Sergeant Lee said, his mind boggled at the potential amount of squeeze he could make if he were a vice-consul in the U.S. Consulate of Hong Kong in the Visa Department. "Eeeeee!"

"We should have a civilized person in that position, then we'd soon be set up like Mandarins and policing San Francisco!" Tang-po said, and they all guffawed with him. Then he added disgustedly, "At least they should have a man there, not one who likes a Steaming Stalk in his Ghastly Gulley, or his in another's!"

They laughed even more. "Hey," one of them called out, "I heard his partner's young Foreign Devil Stinknose Pork Belly in the Public Works— you know, the one who's selling building permits that shouldn't be!"

"That's old news, Chan, very old. They've both moved on to unwiser pastures. The latest rumor is our vice-consul devil's connected with a youth. . . ." Tang-po added delicately, "Son of a prominent accountant who's also a prominent Communist."

"Eeeee, that's not good," Sergeant Lee said, knowing at once who the man was.

"No," Tang-po agreed. "Particularly as I heard yesterday the youth has a secret flat around the corner. In my district! And my district has the least crime of any."

"That's right," they all said proudly.

"Should he be spoken to, Elder Brother?" Lee asked.

"No, just put under special surveillance. I want to know all about these two. Everything. Even if they belch." Tang-po sighed. He gave Sergeant

Lee the address and made the work assignments. "Since you're all here, I've decided to bring payday forward from tomorrow." He opened the large bag that contained bank notes. Each man received the equivalent of his police pay plus authorized expenses.

300 HK a month salary with no expenses was not enough for a constable to feed even a small family and have a small flat, not even a two-room apartment with one tap and no sanitation, and to send one child to school; or enough to be able to send a little back to the home village in the Kwantung to needy fathers and grandmothers and mothers and uncles and grandfathers, many of whom, years upon years ago, had given their life's saving to help launch him on the broken road to Hong Kong.

Tang-po had been one of these. He was very proud that he had survived the journey as a six-year-old, alone, and had found his relations and then, when he was eighteen, had joined the police—thirty-six years ago. He had served the Queen well, the police force impeccably, the Japanese enemy during their occupation not at all and now was in charge of a key division in the Colony of Hong Kong. Respected, rich, with one son in college in San Francisco, another owning half a restaurant in Vancouver, Canada, his family in Kwantung supported—and, most important, his Division of Tsim Sha Tsui with less unsolved robberies, less unsolved woundings and maimings and triad wars than any other district—and only three murders in four years and all solved and the culprits caught and sentenced, and one of those a foreign devil seaman who'd killed another over a dance-hall girl. And almost no petty theft and never a tourist foreign devil harassed by beggars or sneak thieves and this the largest tourist area with upward of also 300,000 civilized persons to police and protect from evildoers and from themselves.

Ayeeyah, yes, Tang-po told himself. If it wasn't for us those bone-headed fornicating peasants'd be at each other's throats, raging, looting, killing, and then the inevitable mob cry would go up: Kill the foreign devils! And they would try and then we would be back in the riots again. Fornicate disgustingly all wrongdoers and unpeaceful persons!

"Now," he said affably, "we'll meet in three days. I've ordered a ten-course feast from Great Food Chang's. Until then, let everyone put an eye to the orifice of the gods and get me the answers. I want the Werewolves —and I want John Chen back. Sergeant Lee, you stay a moment. Corporal Ho, write up the minutes and let me have the accounts tomorrow at five."

"Yes, Honored Lord."

They all trooped out. Tang-po lit another cigarette. So did Sergeant Lee. Tang-po coughed.

"You should quit smoking, Elder Brother."

"So should you!" Tang-po shrugged. "Joss! If I'm to go, I'm to go. Joss. Even so, for peace I've told my Chief Wife I've stopped. She nags and nags and nags."

"Show me one that doesn't and she'll turn out to be a he with a ghastly gulley."

They laughed together.

"That's the truth. *Heya*, last week she insisted I see a doctor and you know what that motherless fornicator said? He said, you'd better give up smoking, old friend, or you'll be nothing but a few cinders in a burial jar before you're twenty moons older and then I guarantee your Chief Wife'll be spending all your money on loose boys and your concubine'll be tasting another's fruits!"

"The swine! Oh the swine!"

"Yes. He really frightened me—I felt his words right down in my secret sack! But maybe he was speaking the truth."

He took out a handkerchief, blew his nose, his breath wheezing, cleared his throat noisily and spat into the spittoon. "Listen, Younger Brother, our High Dragon says the time has come to organize Smuggler Yuen, White Powder Lee, and his cousin Four Finger Wu."

Sergeant Lee stared at him in shock. These three men were believed to be the High Tigers of the opium trade in Hong Kong. Importers and exporters. For local use and also, rumor had it, for export to the Golden Country where the great money was. Opium brought in secretly and converted into morphine and then into heroin. "Bad, very bad. We've never touched that trade before."

"Yes," Tang-po said delicately.

"That'd be very dangerous. Narcotics Branch are very serious against it. Big Mountain of Dung himself is very seriously interested in catching those three—very fornicating serious."

Tang-po stared at the ceiling. Then he said, "The High Dragon explained it this way: A ton of opium in the Golden Triangle costs 67,000 U.S. Changed into fornicating morphine and then into fornicating heroin and the pure heroin diluted to 5 percent, the usual strength on the streets of the Golden Country, delivered there you have almost 680 million worth in American dollars. From one ton of opium." Tang-po coughed and lit another cigarette.

The sweat began on Lee's back. "How many tons could go through those three fornicators?"

"We don't know. But he's been told about 380 tons a year are grown in the whole Golden Triangle—Yunnan, Burma, Laos and Thailand. Much of it comes here. They'd handle 50 tons, he said. He's certain of 50 tons."

"*Oh ko!*"

"Yes." Tang-po was sweating too. "Our High Dragon says we should invest in the trade now. It's going to grow and grow. He has a plan to get Marine with us. . . ."

"*Dew neh loh moh*, you can't trust those seagoing bastards."

"That's what I said, but he said we need the seagoing bastards and we can trust a selected few, who else can snatch and intercept a token 20 percent—even 50 percent to appease Mountain of Dung himself at prear-ranged moments?" Tang-po spat deftly again. "If we could get Marine, Narcotics Branch, and the Gang of Three, our present *h'eung yau* would be like an infant's piddle in the harbor."

There was a serious silence in the room.

"We would have to recruit new members and that's always dangerous."

"Yes."

Lee helped himself to the teapot and poured some jasmine tea, sweat running down his back now, the smoke-ladened air sultry and over-bearing. He waited.

"What do you think, Younger Brother?"

These two men were not related but used the Chinese politeness be-tween themselves because they had trusted each other for more than fifteen years. Lee had saved his superior's life in the riots of 1956. He was thirty-five now and his heroism in the riots had earned him a police medal. He was married and had three children. He had served sixteen years in the force and his whole pay was 843 HK a month. He took the tram to work. Without supplementing his income through the Brotherhood, like all of them, he would have had to walk or bicycle, most days. The tram took two hours.

"I think the idea is very bad," he said. "Drugs, any drugs, that's for-nicating bad—yes, very bad. Opium, that's bad though it's good for old people—the white powder, cocaine, that's bad, but not as bad as the death squirts. It'd be bad joss to deal in the death squirts."

"I told him the same."

"Are you going to obey him?"

"What's good for one Brother should be good for all," Tang-po said thoughtfully, avoiding an answer.

Again Lee waited. He did not know how a Dragon was elected, or ex-actly how many there were, or who the High Dragon was. He only knew that his Dragon was Tang-po who was a wise and cautious man who had their interests at heart.

"He also said one or two of our foreign devil superiors are getting itchy piles about their fornicating slice of the gambling money."

Lee spat disgustedly. "What do those fornicators do for their share? Nothing. Just close their fornicating eyes. Except the Snake." This was the nickname of Chief Inspector Donald C. C. Smyth who openly organ-ized his district of East Aberdeen and sold favors and protection on all levels, in front of his Chinese underlings.

"Ah him! He should be stuffed down the sewer, that fornicator. Soon those who he pays off above him won't be able to hide his stink anymore. And his stench'll spread over all of us."

"He's due to retire in a couple of years," Lee said darkly. "Perhaps he'll finger his rear to all those high-ups until he leaves and there won't be a thing they can do. His friends are very high, so they say."

"Meanwhile?" Tang-po asked.

Lee sighed. "My advice, Elder Brother, is to be cautious, not to do it if you can avoid it. If you can't . . ." he shrugged. "Joss. Is it decided?"

"No, not yet. It was mentioned at our weekly meeting. For consideration."

"Has an approach been made to the Gang of Three?"

"I understand White Powder Lee made the approach, Younger Brother. It seems the three are going to join together."

Lee gasped. "With blood oaths?"

"It seems so."

"They're going to work together? Those devils?"

"So they said. I'll bet old Four Finger Wu will be the Highest Tiger."

"*Ayeeyah*, that one? They say he's murdered fifty men himself," Lee said darkly. He shivered at the danger. "They must have three hundred fighters in their pay. It'd be better for all of us if those three were dead—or behind bars."

"Yes. But meanwhile White Powder Lee says they're ready to expand, and for a little cooperation from us they can *guarantee* a giant return." Tang-po mopped his brow and coughed and lit another cigarette. "Listen, Little Brother," he said softly. "He swears they've been offered a very large source of American money, cash money and bank money, and a very large retail outlet for their goods there, based in this place called Manhattan."

Lee felt the sweat on his forehead. "A retail outlet there . . . *ayeeyah*, that means millions. They will guarantee?"

"Yes. With very little for us to do. Except close our eyes and make sure Marine and Narcotics Branch seize only the correct shipments and close their eyes when they're supposed to. Isn't it written in the Ancient Books: If you don't squeeze, lightning will strike you?"

Again a silence. "When does the decision . . . when's it going to be decided?"

"Next week. If it's decided yes, well, the flow of trade will take months to organize, perhaps a year." Tang-po glanced at the clock and got up. "Time for our shower. Nighttime Song has arranged dinner for us afterwards."

"Eeeee, very good." Uneasily Lee turned out the single overhead light. "And if the decision is no?"

Tang-po stubbed out his cigarette and coughed. "If no . . ." He shrugged. "We only have one life, gods notwithstanding, so it is our duty to think of our families. One of my relations is a captain with Four Finger Wu. . . ."

11

"Hello, Brian," Dunross said. "Welcome."

"Evening, tai-pan—congratulations—great night for a party," Brian Kwok said. A liveried waiter appeared out of nowhere and he accepted a glass of champagne in fine crystal. "Thanks for inviting me."

"You're very welcome." Dunross was standing beside the door of the ballroom in the Great House, tall and debonair, Penelope a few paces away greeting other guests. The half-full ballroom was open to crowded floodlit terraces and gardens where the majority of brightly dressed ladies and dinner-jacketed men stood in groups or sat at round tables. A cool breeze had come with nightfall.

"Penelope darling," Dunross called out, "you remember Superintendent Brian Kwok."

"Oh of course," she said, threading her way over to them with her happy smile, not remembering at all. "How're you?"

"Fine thanks—congratulations!"

"Thank you—make yourself at home. Dinner's at nine fifteen, Claudia has the seating lists if you've lost your card. Oh excuse me a moment. . . ." She turned away to intercept some other guests, her eyes trying to watch everywhere to see that everything was going well and that no one stood alone—knowing in her secret heart that if there was a disaster there was nothing for her to do, that others would make everything well again.

"You're very lucky, Ian," Brian Kwok said. "She gets younger every year."

"Yes."

"So. Here's to twenty more years! Health!" They touched glasses. They had been friends since the early fifties when they had met at the first racing hill climb and had been friendly rivals ever since—and founding members of the Hong Kong Sports Car and Rally Club.

"But you, Brian, no special girl friend? You arrive alone?"

"I'm playing the field." Brian Kwok dropped his voice. "Actually I'm staying single permanently."

"Dreamer! This's your year—you're the catch of Hong Kong. Even Claudia's got her eyes on you. You're a dead duck, old chap."

"Oh Christ!" Brian dropped the banter for a moment. "Say, tai-pan, could I have a couple of private minutes this evening?"

"John Chen?" Dunross asked at once.

"No. We've got every man looking, but nothing yet. It's something else."

"Business?"

"Yes."

"How private?"

"Private."

"All right," Dunross said, "I'll find you after dinner. What ab—"

A burst of laughter caused them to look around. Casey was standing in the center of an admiring group of men—Linbar Struan and Andrew Gavallan and Jacques deVille among them—just outside one of the tall French doors that led to the terrace.

"Eeeee," Brian Kwok muttered.

"Quite," Dunross said and grinned.

She was dressed in a floor-length sheath of emerald silk, molded just enough and sheer just enough.

"Christ, is she or isn't she?"

"What?"

"Wearing anything underneath?"

"Seek and ye shall find."

"I'd like to. She's stunning."

"I thought so too," Dunross said agreeably, "though I'd say 100 percent of the other ladies don't."

"Her breasts are perfect, you can see that."

"Actually you can't. Just. It's all in your mind."

"I'll bet there isn't a pair in Hong Kong to touch them."

"Fifty dollars to a copper cash says you're wrong—provided we include Eurasians."

"How can we prove who wins?"

"We can't. Actually I'm an ankle man myself."

"What?"

"Old Uncle Chen-Chen used to say, 'First look at the ankles, my son, then you tell her breeding, how she'll behave, how she'll ride, how she'll . . . like any filly. But remember, all crows under heaven are black!'"

Brian Kwok grinned with him then waved at someone in friendly style. Across the room a tall man with a lived-in face was waving back. Beside him was an extraordinarily beautiful woman, tall, fair, with gray eyes. She waved happily too.

"Now there's an English beauty at her best!"

"Who? Oh, Fleur Marlowe? Yes, yes she is. I didn't know you knew the Marlowes, tai-pan."

"Likewise! I met him this afternoon, Brian. You've known him long?"

"Oh a couple of months-odd. He's persona grata with us."

"Oh?"

"Yes. We're showing him the ropes."

"Oh? Why?"

"Some months ago he wrote to the commissioner, said he was coming to Hong Kong to research a novel and asked for our cooperation. Seems the Old Man happened to have read his first novel and had seen some of his films. Of course we checked him out and he appears all right." Brian Kwok's eyes went back to Casey. "The Old Man thought we could do with an improved image so he sent word down that, within limits, Peter was approved and to show him around." He glanced back at Dunross and smiled thinly. "Ours not to reason why!"

"What was his book?"

"Called *Changi*, about his POW days. The Old Man's brother died there, so I suppose it hit home."

"Have you read it?"

"Not me—I've too many mountains to climb! I did skim a few pages. Peter says it's fiction but I don't believe him." Brian Kwok laughed. "He can drink beer though. Robert had him on a couple of his Hundred Pinters and he held his end up." A Hundred Pinter was a police stag party to which the officers contributed a barrel of a hundred pints of beer. When the beer was gone, the party ended.

Brian Kwok's eyes were feasting on Casey, and Dunross wondered for the millionth time why Asians favored Anglo-Saxons and Anglo-Saxons favored Asians.

"Why the smile, tai-pan?"

"No reason. But Casey's not bad at all, is she?"

"Fifty dollars says she's *bat jam gai, heya?*"

Dunross thought a moment, weighing the bet carefully. *Bat jam gai* meant, literally, white chicken meat. This was the way Cantonese referred to ladies who shaved off their pubic hair. "Taken! You're wrong, Brian, she's *see yau gai*," which meant soya chicken, "or in her case red, tender and nicely spicy. I have it on the highest authority!"

Brian laughed. "Introduce me."

"Introduce yourself. You're over twenty-one."

"I'll let you win the hill climb on Sunday!"

"Dreamer! Off you go and a thousand says you won't."

"What odds'll you give me?"

"You must be joking!"

"No harm in asking. Christ, I'd like to carry the book on that one. Where's the lucky Mr. Bartlett?"

"I think he's in the garden—I told Adryon to chaperone him. Excuse me a moment. . . ." Dunross turned away to greet someone Brian Kwok did not recognize.

Upward of 150 guests had already arrived and been greeted personally. Dinner was for 217, each carefully seated according to face and custom at round tables that were already set and candlelit on the lawns. Candles and candelabra in the halls, liveried waiters offering champagne in cut glass crystal, or smoked salmon and caviar from silver trays and tureens.

A small band was playing on the dais and Brian Kwok saw a few uniforms among the dinner jackets, American and British, army, navy and air force. It was no surprise that Europeans were dominant. This party was strictly for the British inner circle that ruled Central District and were the power block of the Colony, their Caucasian friends, and a few very special Eurasians, Chinese and Indians. Brian Kwok recognized most of the guests: Paul Havergill of the Victoria Bank of Hong Kong, old Sir Samuel Samuels, multimillionaire, tai-pan of twenty real estate, banking, ferry and stockbroking companies; Christian Toxe, editor of the *China Guardian*, talking to Richard Kwang, chairman of the Ho-Pak Bank; multimillionaire shipowner V. K. Lam talking to Phillip and Dianne Chen, their son Kevin with them; the American Zeb Cooper, inheritor of the oldest American trading company, Cooper-Tillman, having his ear bent by Sir Dunstan Barre, tai-pan of Hong Kong and Lan Tao Farms. He noticed Ed Langan, the FBI man, among the guests and this surprised him. He had not known that Langan or the man he was talking to, Stanley Rosemont, a deputy director of the China-watching CIA contingent, were friends of Dunross. He let his eyes drift over the chattering group of men, and the mostly separate groups of their wives.

They're all here, he thought, all the tai-pans except Gornt and Plumm, all the pirates, all here in incestuous hatred to pay homage to *the* tai-pan.

Which one is the spy, the traitor, controller of Sevrin, *Arthur*?

He's got to be European.

I'll bet he's here. And I'll catch him. Yes. I'll catch him, soon, now that I know about him. We'll catch him and catch them all, he thought grimly. And we'll catch these crooks with their hands in their tills, we'll stamp out their piracies for the common good.

"Champagne, Honored Sir," the waiter asked in Cantonese with a toothy smile.

Brian accepted a full glass. "Thank you."

The waiter bowed to hide his lips. "The tai-pan had a blue-covered file among his papers when he came in tonight," he whispered quickly.

"Is there a safe, a secret hiding place here?" Brian asked equally cautiously in the same dialect.

"The servants say in his office on the next floor," the man said. His name was Wine Waiter Feng, and he was one of SI's undercover network of intelligence agents. His cover as a waiter for the company that catered all Hong Kong's best and most exclusive parties gave him great value.

"Perhaps it's behind the painting, I heard. . . ." He stopped suddenly and switched to pidgin English. "Champ-igy-nee Missee?" he asked tooth-ily, offering the tray to the tiny old Eurasian lady who was coming up to them. "Wery wery first class."

"Don't you Missee me, you impertinent young puppy," she rapped haughtily in Cantonese.

"Yes, Honored Great-Aunt, sorry, Honored Great-Aunt." He beamed and fled.

"So, young Brian Kwok," the old lady said, peering up at him. She was eighty-eight, Sarah Chen, Phillip Chen's aunt, a tiny birdlike person with pale white skin and Asian eyes that darted this way and that. And though she appeared frail her back was upright and her spirit very strong. "I'm glad to see you. Where's John Chen? Where's my poor grand-nephew?"

"I don't know, Great Lady," he said politely.

"When are you going to get my Number One Grand-nephew back?"

"Soon. We're doing everything we can."

"Good. And don't you interfere with young Phillip if he wants to pay John's ransom privately. You see to it."

"Yes. I'll do what I can. Is John's wife here?"

"Eh? Who? Speak up, boy!"

"Is Barbara Chen here?"

"No. She came earlier but as soon as *that* woman arrived she 'got a headache' and left. Huh, I don't blame her at all!" Her old rheumy eyes were watching Dianne Chen across the room. "Huh, that woman! Did you see her entrance?"

"No, Great Lady."

"Huh, like Dame Nellie Melba herself. She swept in, handkerchief to her eyes, her eldest son Kevin in tow—I don't like that boy—and my poor nephew Phillip like a second-class cook boy in the rear. Huh! The only time Dianne Chen ever wept was in the crash of '56 when her stocks went down and she lost a fortune and wet her drawers. Ha! Look at her now, preening herself! Pretending to be upset when everyone knows she's act-ing as though she's already Dowager Empress! I could pinch her cheeks! Disgusting!" She looked back at Brian Kwok. "You find my grand-nephew John—I don't want that woman or her brat *loh-pan* of our house."

"But he can be *tai-pan?*"

They laughed together. Very few Europeans knew that though *tai-pan* meant great leader, in the old days in China a *tai-pan* was the colloquial title of a man in charge of a whorehouse or public toilet. So no Chinese would ever call himself *tai-pan*, only *loh-pan*—which also meant great leader or head leader. Chinese and Eurasians were greatly amused that Europeans enjoyed calling themselves *tai-pan*, stupidly passing over the correct title.

"Yes. If he's the right *pan*," the old woman said and they chuckled. "You find my John Chen, young Brian Kwok!"

"Yes. Yes we'll find him."

"Good. Now, what do you think of Golden Lady's chances on Saturday?"

"Good, if the going's dry. At three to one she's worth a bundle. Watch Noble Star—she's got a chance too."

"Good. After dinner come and find me. I want to talk to you."

"Yes, Great Lady." He smiled and watched her go off and knew that all she wanted was to try to act the marriage broker for some great-niece. *Ayeeyah*, I'll have to do something about that soon, he thought.

His eyes strayed back to Casey. He was delighted by the disapproving looks from all the women—and the cautious covert admiration from all their escorts. Then Casey glanced up and saw him watching her across the room and she stared back at him briefly with equal frank appraisal.

Dew neh loh moh, he thought uneasily, feeling somehow undressed. I'd like to possess that one. Then he noticed Roger Crosse with Armstrong beside him. He put his mind together and headed for them.

"Evening, sir."

"Evening, Brian. You're looking very distinguished."

"Thank you, sir." He knew better than to volunteer anything pleasant in return. "I'm seeing the tai-pan after dinner."

"Good. As soon as you've seen him, find me."

"Yes sir."

"So you think the American girl stunning?"

"Yes sir." Brian sighed inwardly. He had forgotten that Crosse could lip-read English, French and some Arabic—he spoke no Chinese dailects—and that his eyesight was exceptional.

"Actually she's rather obvious," Crosse said.

"Yes sir." He saw Crosse concentrating on her lips and knew that he was overhearing her conversation from across the room and he was furious with himself that he had not developed the talent.

"She seems to have a passion for computers." Crosse turned his eyes back on them. "Curious, what?"

"Yes sir."

"What did Wine Waiter Feng say?"

Brian told him.

"Good. I'll see Feng gets a bonus. I didn't expect to see Langan and Rosemont here."

"It could be a coincidence, sir," Brian Kwok volunteered. "They're both keen punters. They've both been to the tai-pan's box."

"I don't trust coincidences," Crosse said. "As far as Langan's concerned, of course you know nothing, either of you."

"Yes sir."

"Good. Perhaps you'd both better be about our business."

"Yes sir." Thankfully the two men turned to leave but stopped as there was a sudden hush. All eyes went to the doorway. Quillan Gornt stood there, black-browed, black-bearded, conscious that he had been noticed. The other guests hastily picked up their conversations and kept their eyes averted but their ears concentrated.

Crosse whistled softly. "Now why is he here?"

"Fifty to one says he's up to no good," Brian Kwok said, equally astounded.

They watched Gornt come into the ballroom and put out his hand to Dunross and Penelope beside him. Claudia Chen who was nearby was in shock, wondering how she could reorganize Dunross's table at such short notice because of course Gornt would have to be seated there.

"I hope you don't mind my changing my mind at the last moment," Gornt was saying, his mouth smiling.

"Not at all," Dunross replied, his mouth smiling.

"Good evening, Penelope. I felt I had to give you my congratulations personally."

"Oh, thank you," she said. Her smile was intact but her heart was beating very fast now. "I, I was sorry to hear about your wife."

"Thank you." Emelda Gornt had been arthritic and confined to a wheelchair for some years. Early in the year she had caught pneumonia and had died. "She was very unlucky," Gornt said. He looked at Dunross. "Bad joss about John Chen too."

"Very."

"I suppose you read the afternoon *Gazette?*"

Dunross nodded and Penelope said, "Enough to frighten everyone out of their wits." All the afternoon papers had had huge headlines and dwelt at length on the mutilated ear and the Werewolves. There was a slight pause. She rushed to fill it. "Your children are well?"

"Yes. Annagrey's going to the University of California in September— Michael is here on his summer holiday. They're all in very good shape I'm glad to say. And yours?"

"They're fine. I do wish Adryon would go to university though. Dear me, children are very difficult these days, aren't they?"

"I think they always were." Gornt smiled thinly. "My father was always pointing out how difficult I was." He looked at Dunross again.

"Yes. How is your father?"

"Hale and hearty I'm glad to say. The English climate suits him, he says. He's coming out for Christmas." Gornt accepted a proffered glass of champagne. The waiter quailed under his look, and fled. He raised his glass. "A happy life and many congratulations."

Dunross toasted him in return, still astonished that Gornt had arrived. It was only for politeness and for face that Gornt and other enemies had been sent formal invitations. A polite refusal was all that was expected— and Gornt had already refused.

Why's he here?

He's come to gloat, Dunross thought. Like his bloody father. That must be the reason. But why? What devilment has he done to us? Bartlett? Is it through Bartlett?

"This's a lovely room, beautiful proportions," Gornt was saying. "And a lovely house. I've always envied you this house."

Yes, you bastard, I know, Dunross thought furiously, remembering the last time any of the Gornts had been in the Great House. Ten years ago, in 1953, when Ian's father, Colin Dunross, was still *the* tai-pan. It was during Struan's Christmas party, traditionally the biggest of the season, and Quillan Gornt had arrived with his father, William, then tai-pan of Rothwell-Gornt, again unexpectedly. After dinner there had been a bitter, public clash between the two tai-pans in the billiard room where a dozen or so of the men had gathered for a game. That was when Struan's had just been blocked by the Gornts and their Shanghainese friends in their attempt to take over South Orient Airways, which, because of the Communist conquest of the Mainland, had just become available. This feeder airline monopolized all air traffic in and out of Shanghai from Hong Kong, Singapore, Taipei, Tokyo and Bangkok, and if merged with Air Struan, their fledgling airline, Struan's would have virtual feeder monopoly in the Far East based out of Hong Kong. Both men had accused the other of underhand practices—both accusations were true.

Yes, Ian Dunross told himself, both men went to the brink that time. William Gornt had tried every way to become established in Hong Kong after Rothwell-Gornt's huge losses in Shanghai. And when Colin Dunross knew Struan's could not prevail, he had snatched South Orient out of William Gornt's grasp by throwing his weight to a safe Cantonese group.

"And so you did, Colin Dunross, so you did. You fell into the trap and you'll never stop us now," William Gornt had gloated. "We're here to stay. We'll hound you out of Asia, you and your god-cursed Noble House. South Orient's just the beginning. We've won!"

"The hell you have! The Yan-Wong-Sun group's associated with us. We have a contract."

"It's hereby canceled." William Gornt had motioned to Quillan, his eldest son and heir apparent, who took out the copy of an agreement. "This contract's between the Yan-Wong-Sun group who're nominees of the Tso-Wa-Feng group," he said happily, "who're nominees of Ta-Weng-Sap who sells control of South Orient to Rothwell-Gornt for one dollar more than the original cost!" Quillan Gornt had laid it on the billiard table with a flourish. "South Orient's ours!"

"I don't believe it!"

"You can. Happy Christmas!" William Gornt had given a great, scorn-filled laugh, and walked out. Quillan had replaced his billiard cue, laughing too. Ian Dunross had been near the door.

"One day I'll own this house," Quillan Gornt had hissed at him, then turned and called out to the others, "If any of you want jobs, come to us. Soon you'll all be out of work. Your Noble House won't be noble much longer." Andrew Gavallan had been there, Jacques deVille, Alastair Struan, Lechie and David MacStruan, Phillip Chen, even John Chen.

Dunross remembered how his father had raged that night, and blamed treachery and nominees and bad joss, knowing all the time that he himself had warned him, many times, and that his warnings had been shoved aside. Christ, how we lost face! All Hong Kong laughed at us that time— the Noble House peed on from a great height by the Gornts and their Shanghainese interlopers.

Yes. But that night finalized Colin Dunross's downfall. That was the night I decided that he had to go before the Noble House was lost forever. I used Alastair Struan. I helped him to shove my father aside. Alastair Struan had to become tai-pan. Until I was wise enough and strong enough to shove him aside.

Am I wise enough now?

I don't know, Dunross thought, concentrating on Quillan Gornt now, listening to his pleasantries, hearing himself react with equal charm, while his mind said, I haven't forgotten South Orient, or that we had to merge our airline with yours at a fire-sale price and lose control of the new line renamed All Asia Airways. Nothing's forgotten. We lost that time but this time we'll win. We'll win everything, by God.

Casey was watching both men with fascination. She had noticed Quillan Gornt from the first moment, recognizing him from the photographs of the dossier. She had sensed his strength and masculinity even from across the room and had been uneasily excited by him. As she watched, she could almost touch the tension between the two men squaring off—two bulls in challenge.

Andrew Gavallan had told her at once who Gornt was. She had volunteered nothing, just asked Gavallan and Linbar Struan why they were so shocked at Gornt's arrival. And then, as they were alone now, the four of them—Casey, Gavallan, deVille and Linbar Struan—they told her about the "Happy Christmas" and "One day I'll own this house."

"What did the tai-pan . . . what did Ian do?" she asked.

Gavallan said, "He just looked at Gornt. You knew if he had a gun or a knife or a cudgel he'd've used it, you just knew it, and as he hadn't a weapon you knew any moment he was going to use his hands or teeth. . . . He just stood rock still and looked at Gornt and Gornt went back a pace, out of range—literally. But that bugger Gornt's got *cojones*. He sort of gathered himself together and stared back at Ian for a moment. Then, without saying a word he went around him slowly, very cautiously, his eyes never leaving Ian, and he left."

"What's that bastard doing here tonight?" Linbar muttered.

Gavallan said, "It's got to be important."

"Which one?" Linbar asked. "Which important?"

Casey looked at him and at the edge of her peripheral vision she saw Jacques deVille shake his head warningly and at once the shades came down on Linbar and on Gavallan. Even so she asked, "What *is* Gornt doing here?"

"I don't know," Gavallan told her, and she believed him.

"Have they met since that Christmas?"

"Oh yes, many times, all the time," Gavallan told her. "Socially of course. Then, too, they're on the boards of companies, committees, councils together." Uneasily he added, "But . . . well I'm sure they're both just waiting."

She saw their eyes wander back to the two enemies and her eyes followed. Her heart was beating strongly. They saw Penelope move away to talk to Claudia Chen. In a moment, Dunross glanced across at them. She knew he was signaling Gavallan in some way. Then his eyes were on her. Gornt followed his glance. Now both men were looking at her. She felt their magnetism. It intoxicated her. A devil in her pushed her feet toward them. She was glad now that she had dressed as she had, more provocatively than she had planned, but Linc had told her this was a night to be less businesslike.

As she walked she felt the brush of the silk, and her nipples hardened. She felt their eyes flow over her, undressing her, and this time, strangely, she did not mind. Her walk became imperceptibly more feline.

"Hello, tai-pan," she said with pretended innocence. "You wanted me to join you?"

"Yes," he replied at once. "I believe you two know each other."

She shook her head and smiled at both of them, not noticing the trap. "No. We've never met. But of course I know who Mr. Gornt is. Andrew told me."

"Ah, then let me introduce you formally. Mr. Quillan Gornt, tai-pan of Rothwell-Gornt. Miss Tcholok—Ciranoush Tcholok—from America."

She held out her hand, knowing the danger of getting between the two men, half her mind warmed by the danger the other half shouting, Jesus, what're you doing here.

"I've heard a lot about you, Mr. Gornt," she said, pleased that her voice was controlled, pleased by the touch of his hand—different from Dunross's, rougher and not as strong. "I believe the rivalry of your firms goes back generations?"

"Only three. It was my grandfather who first felt the not so tender mercies of the Struans," Gornt said easily. "One day I'd enjoy telling you our side of the legends."

"Perhaps you two should smoke a pipe of peace," she said. "Surely Asia's wide enough for both of you."

"The whole world isn't," Dunross said affably.

"No," Gornt agreed, and if she had not heard the real story she would have presumed from their tone and manner they were just friendly rivals.

"In the States we've many huge companies—and they live together peacefully. In competition."

"This isn't America," Gornt said calmly. "How long will you be here, Miss Tcholok?"

"That depends on Linc—Linc Bartlett—I'm with Par-Con Industries."

"Yes, yes I know. Didn't he tell you we're having dinner on Tuesday?"

The danger signals poured through her. "Tuesday?"

"Yes. We arranged it this morning. At our meeting. Didn't he mention it?"

"No," she said, momentarily in shock. Both men were watching her intently and she wished she could back off and come back in five minutes when she had thought this through. Jesus, she thought and fought to retain her poise as all the implications swamped her. "No," she said again, "Linc didn't mention any meeting. What did you arrange?"

Gornt glanced at Dunross who still listened expressionlessly. "Just to have dinner next Tuesday. Mr. Bartlett and yourself—if you're free."

"That would be nice—thank you."

"Where's your Mr. Bartlett now?" he asked.

"In—in the garden, I think."

Dunross said, "Last time I saw him he was on the terrace. Adryon was with him. Why?"

Gornt took out a gold cigarette case and offered it to her.

"No thank you," she said. "I don't smoke."

"Does it bother you if I do?"

She shook her head.

Gornt lit a cigarette and looked at Dunross. "I'd just like to say hello to him, before I leave," he said pleasantly. "I hope you don't mind me coming for just a few minutes—if you'll excuse me I won't stay for dinner. I have some pressing business to attend to . . . you understand."

"Of course." Dunross added, "Sorry you can't stay."

Neither man showed anything in his face. Except the eyes. It was in their eyes. Hatred. Fury. The depth shocked her. "Ask Ian Dunross to show you the Long Gallery," Gornt was saying to her. "I hear there're some fine portraits there. I've never been in the Long Gallery—only the billiard room." A chill went down her spine as he looked again at Dunross who watched him back.

"This meeting this morning," Casey said, thinking clearly now, judging it wise to bring everything out in front of Dunross at once. "When was it arranged?"

"About three weeks ago," Gornt said. "I thought you were his chief executive, I'm surprised he didn't mention it to you."

"Linc's our tai-pan, Mr. Gornt. I work for him. He doesn't have to tell me everything," she said, calmer now. "Should he have told me, Mr. Gornt? I mean, was it important?"

"It could be. Yes. I confirmed, formally, that we can better any offer

Struan's can make. Any offer." Gornt glanced back at the tai-pan. His voice hardened a fraction. "Ian, I wanted to tell you, personally, that we're in the same marketplace."

"Is that why you came?"

"One reason."

"The other?"

"Pleasure."

"How long have you known Mr. Bartlett?"

"Six months or so. Why?"

Dunross shrugged, then looked at Casey and she could read nothing from his voice or face or manner other than friendliness. "You didn't know of any Rothwell-Gornt negotiations?"

Truthfully she shook her head, awed by Bartlett's skillful long-range planning. "No. Are negotiations in progress, Mr. Gornt?"

"I would say yes." Gornt smiled.

"Then we shall see, won't we," Dunross said. "We shall see who makes the best deal. Thank you for telling me personally, though there was no need. I knew, of course, that you'd be interested too. There's no need to belabor that."

"Actually there's a very good reason," Gornt said sharply. "Neither Mr. Bartlett nor this lady may realize how vital Par-Con is to you. I felt obliged to make the point personally to them. And to you. And of course to offer my congratulations."

"Why vital, Mr. Gornt?" Casey asked, committed now.

"Without your Par-Con deal and the cash flow it will generate, Struan's will go under, could easily go under in a few months."

Dunross laughed and those few who listened covertly shuddered and moved their own conversations up a decibel, aghast at the thought of Struan's failing, at the same time thinking, What deal? Par-Con? Should we sell or buy? Struan's or Rothwell-Gornt?

"No chance of that," Dunross said. "Not a chance in hell!"

"I think there's a very good chance." Gornt's tone changed. "In any event, as you say, we shall see."

"Yes, we will—meanwhile . . ." Dunross stopped as he saw Claudia approaching uneasily.

"Excuse me, tai-pan," she said, "your personal call to London's on the line."

"Oh thank you." Dunross turned and beckoned Penelope. She came over at once. "Penelope, would you entertain Quillan and Miss Tcholok for a moment. I've got a phone call—Quillan's not staying for dinner—he has pressing business." He waved cheerily and left them. Casey noticed the animal grace to his walk.

"You're not staying for dinner?" Penelope was saying, her relief evident though she tried to cover it.

"No. I'm sorry to inconvenience you—arriving so abruptly, after declining your kind invitation. Unfortunately I can't stay."

"Oh. Then . . . would you excuse me a moment, I'll be back in a second."

"There's no need to worry about us," Gornt said gently. "We can look after ourselves. Again, sorry to be a nuisance—you're looking marvelous, Penelope. You never change." She thanked him and he willed her away. Gratefully she went over to Claudia Chen who was waiting nearby.

"You're a curious man," Casey said. "One moment war, the next great charm."

"We have rules, we English, in peace and war. Just because you loathe someone, that's no reason to curse him, spit in his eye or abuse his lady." Gornt smiled down at her. "Shall we find your Mr. Bartlett? Then I really should go."

"Why did you do that? To the tai-pan? The battle challenge—the 'vital' bit. That was the formal gauntlet, wasn't it? In public."

"Life's a game," he said. "All life's a game and we English play it with different rules from you Americans. Yes. And life's to be enjoyed. Ciranoush—what a lovely name you have. May I use it?"

"Yes," she said after a pause. "But why the challenge now?"

"Now was the time. I didn't exaggerate about your importance to Struan's. Shall we go and find your Mr. Bartlett?"

That's the third time he's said *your* Mr. Bartlett, she thought. Is that to probe, or to needle? "Sure, why not?" She turned for the garden, conscious of the looks, overt and covert, of the other guests, feeling the danger pleasantly. "Do you always make dramatic entrances like this?"

Gornt laughed. "No. Sorry if I was abrupt, Ciranoush—if I distressed you."

"You mean about your private meeting with Linc? You didn't. It was very shrewd of Linc to approach the opposition without my knowledge. That gave me a freedom of action that otherwise I'd not have had this morning."

"Ah, then you're not irritated that he didn't trust you in this?"

"It has nothing to do with trust. I often withhold information from Linc, until the time's ripe, to protect him. He was obviously doing the same for me. Linc and I understand one another. At least I think I understand him."

"Then tell me how to finalize a deal."

"First I have to know what you want. Apart from Dunross's head."

"I don't want his head, or death or anything like that—just an early demise of their Noble House. Once Struan's is obliterated we become the Noble House." His face hardened. "Then all sorts of ghosts can sleep."

"Tell me about them."

"Now's not the time, Ciranoush, oh no. Too many hostile ears. That'd be for your ears only." They were out in the garden now, the gentle breeze grand, a fine night sky overhead, star filled. Linc Bartlett was not on this terrace so they went down the wide stone steps through other guests to the lower one, toward the paths that threaded the lawns. Then they were intercepted.

"Hello, Quillan, this's a pleasant surprise."

"Hello, Paul. Miss Tcholok, may I introduce you to Paul Havergill? Paul's presently in charge of the Victoria Bank."

"I'm afraid that's very temporary, Miss Tcholok, and only because our chief manager's on sick leave. I'm retiring in a few months."

"To our regret," Gornt said, then introduced Casey to the rest of this group: Lady Joanna Temple-Smith, a tall, stretched-faced woman in her fifties, and Richard Kwang and his wife Mai-ling. "Richard Kwang's chairman of the Ho-Pak, one of our finest Chinese banks."

"In banking we're all friendly competitors, Miss, er, Miss, except of course for Blacs," Havergill said.

"Sir?" Casey said.

"Blacs? Oh that's a nickname for the Bank of London, Canton and Shanghai. They may be bigger than we are, a month or so older, but we're the best bank here, Miss, er . . ."

"Blacs're my bankers," Gornt said to Casey. "They do me very well. They're first-class bankers."

"Second-class, Quillan."

Gornt turned back to Casey. "We've a saying here that Blacs consists of gentlemen trying to be bankers, and those at the Victoria are bankers trying to be gentlemen."

Casey laughed. The others smiled politely.

"You're all just friendly competition, Mr. Kwang?" she asked.

"Oh yes. We wouldn't dare oppose Blacs or the Victoria," Richard Kwang said amiably. He was short and stocky and middle-aged with gray-flecked black hair and an easy smile, his English perfect. "I hear Par-Con's going to invest in Hong Kong, Miss Tchelek."

"We're here to look around, Mr. Kwang. Nothing's firm yet." She passed over his mispronunciation.

Gornt lowered his voice. "Just between ourselves, I've formally told both Bartlett and Miss Tcholok that I will better any offer Struan's might make. Blacs are supporting me one hundred percent. And I've friendly bankers elsewhere. I'm hoping Par-Con will consider all possibilities before making any commitment."

"I imagine that would be very wise," Havergill said. "Of course Struan's does have the inside track."

"Blacs and most of Hong Kong would hardly agree with you," Gornt said.

"I hope it won't come to a clash, Quillan," Havergill said. "Struan's is our major customer."

Richard Kwang said, "Either way, Miss Tchelek, it would be good to have such a great American company as Par-Con here. Good for you, good for us. Let's hope that a deal can be found that suits Par-Con. If Mr. Bartlett would like any assistance . . ." The banker produced his business card. She took it, opened her silk handbag and offered hers with equal dexterity, having come prepared for the immediate card exchanging that is good manners and obligatory in Asia. The Chinese banker glanced at it then his eyes narrowed.

"Sorry I haven't had it translated into characters yet," she said. "Our bankers in the States are First Central New York and the California Merchant Bank and Trust Company." Casey mentioned them proudly, sure the combined assets of these banking giants were in excess of 6 billions. "I'd be gl—" She stopped, startled at the sudden chill surrounding her. "Is something wrong?"

"Yes and no," Gornt said after a moment. "It's just that the First Central New York Bank's not at all popular here."

"Why?"

Havergill said disdainfully, "They turned out to be a shower—that's, er, English for a bad lot, Miss, er, Miss. The First Central New York did some business here before the war, then expanded in the mid-forties while we at the Victoria and other British institutions were picking ourselves off the floor. In '49 when Chairman Mao threw Chiang Kai-shek off the Mainland to Taiwan, Mao's troops were massed on our border just a few miles north in the New Territories. It was touch and go whether or not the hordes would spill over and overrun the Colony. A lot of people cut and ran, none of us of course, but all the Chinese who could got out. Without any warning, the First Central New York called in all their loans, paid off their depositors, closed their doors and fled—all in the space of one week."

"I didn't know," Casey said, aghast.

"They were a bunch of yellow bastards, my dear, if you'll excuse the expression," Lady Joanna said with open contempt. "Of course, they were the *only* bank that scarpered—ran away. But then they were . . . well, what can you expect, my dear?"

"Probably better, Lady Joanna," Casey said, furious with the VP in charge of their account for not warning them. "Perhaps there were mitigating circumstances. Mr. Havergill, were the loans substantial?"

"At that time, very, I'm afraid. Yes. That bank ruined quite a lot of important businesses and people, caused an enormous amount of grief and loss of face. Still," he said with a smile, "we all benefited by their leaving. A couple of years ago they had the effrontery to apply to the financial secretary for a new charter!"

Richard Kwang added jovially, "That's one charter that'll never be renewed! You see, Miss Tchelek, all foreign banks operate on a renewable yearly charter. Certainly we can do very well without that one, or for that matter any other American bank. They're such . . . well, you'll find the

Victoria, Blacs or the Ho-Pak, perhaps all three Miss K.C., can fulfill all Par-Con's needs perfectly. If you and Mr. Bartlett would like to chat . . ."

"I'd be glad to visit with you, Mr. Kwang. Say tomorrow? Initially I handle most of our banking needs. Maybe sometime in the morning?"

"Yes, yes of course. You'll find us competitive," Richard Kwang said without a flicker. "At ten?"

"Great. We're at the V and A, Kowloon. If ten's not good for you just let me know," she said. "I'm pleased to meet you personally too, Mr. Havergill. I presume our appointment for tomorrow is still in order?"

"Of course. At four, isn't it? I look forward to chatting at length with Mr. Bartlett . . . and you, of course, my dear." He was a tall, lean man and she noticed his eyes rise from her cleavage. She dismissed her immediate dislike. I may need him, she thought, and his bank.

"Thank you," she said with the right amount of deference and turned her charm on Lady Joanna. "What a pretty dress, Lady Joanna," she said, loathing it and the row of small pearls that circled the woman's scrawny neck.

"Oh, thank you, my dear. Is yours from Paris too?"

"Indirectly. It's a Balmain but I got it in New York." She smiled down at Richard Kwang's wife, a solid, well-preserved Cantonese lady with an elaborate coiffure, very pale skin and narrow eyes. She was wearing an immense imperial jade pendant and a seven-carat diamond ring. "Pleased to meet you, Mrs. Kwang," she said, awed by the wealth that the jewelry represented. "We were looking for Linc Bartlett. Have you seen him?"

"Not for a while," Havergill volunteered. "I think he went into the east wing. Believe there's a bar there. He was with Adryon—Dunross's daughter."

"Adryon's turned out to be such a pretty girl," Lady Joanna said. "They make such a nice couple together. Charming man, Mr. Bartlett. He's not married, is he, dear?"

"No," Casey said, equally pleasantly, adding Lady Joanna Temple-Smith to her private list of loathsome people. "Linc's not married."

"He'll be gobbled up soon, mark my words. I really believe Adryon's quite smitten. Perhaps you'd like to come to tea on Thursday, my dear? I'd love you to meet some of the girls. That's the day of our Over Thirty Club."

"Thank you," Casey said. "I don't qualify—but I'd love to come anyway."

"Oh I'm sorry, dear! I'd presumed . . . I'll send a car for you. Quillan, are you staying for dinner?"

"No, can't. Got pressing business."

"Pity." Lady Joanna smiled and showed her bad teeth.

"If you'll excuse us—just want to find Bartlett and then I have to leave. See you Saturday." Gornt took Casey's arm and guided her away.

They watched them leave. "She's quite attractive in a common sort of way, isn't she?" Lady Joanna said. "Chuluk. That's Middle European, isn't it?"

"Possibly. It could be Mideastern, Joanna, you know, Turkish, something like that, possibly the Balkans. . . ." Havergill stopped. "Oh, I see what you mean. No, I don't think so. She certainly doesn't look Jewish."

"One really can't tell these days, can one? She might have had her nose fixed—they do marvelous things these days, don't they?"

"Never occurred to me to look. Hum! Do you think so?"

Richard Kwang passed Casey's card over to his wife who read it instantly and got the same message instantly. "Paul, her card says treasurer and executive VP of the holding company . . . that's quite impressive, isn't it? Par-Con's a big company."

"Oh my dear fellow, but they're American. They do extraordinary things in America. Surely it's just a title—that's all."

"Giving his mistress face?" Joanna asked.

12

The billiard cue struck the white ball and it shot across the green table and slashed the red into a far pocket and stopped perfectly behind another red.

Adryon clapped gleefully. "Oh Linc, that was super! I was sure you were just boasting. Oh do it again!"

Linc Bartlett grinned. "For one dollar that red around the table and into that pocket and the white here." He marked the spot with a flick of chalk.

"Done!"

He leaned over the table and sighted and the white stopped within a millimeter of his mark, the red sunk with marvelous inevitability.

"*Ayeeyah!* I haven't got a dollar with me. Damn! Can I owe it to you?"

"A lady—however beautiful—has to pay her gambling debts at once."

"I know. Father says the same. Can I pay you tomorrow?"

He watched her, enjoying her, pleased that his skill pleased her. She was wearing a knee-length black skirt and the lovely silk blouse. Her legs were long, very long, and perfect. "Nope!" He pretended ill humor and then they laughed together in the huge room, the vast lights low over the full-size billiard table, the rest of the room dark and intimate but for the shaft of light from the open door.

"You play incredibly well," she said.

"Don't tell anyone but I made my living in the Army playing pool."

"In Europe?"

"No. Pacific."

"My father was a fighter pilot. He got six planes before he was shot down and grounded."

"I guess that made him an ace, didn't it?"

"Were you part of those awful landings against the Japs?"

"No. I was in construction. We came in when everything was secured."

"Oh."

"We built bases, airfields in Guadalcanal, and islands all over the Pacific. My war was easy—nothing like your dad's." As he went over to the cue rack, he was sorry for the first time that he had not been in the Marines. Her expression when he had said construction made him feel unmanned. "We should go look for your boyfriend. Maybe he's here by now."

"Oh he's not important! He's not a real boyfriend, I just met him a week or so ago at a friend's party. Martin's a journalist on the *China Guardian*. He's not a lover."

"Are all young English ladies so open about their lovers?"

"It's the pill. It's released us from masculine servitude forever. Now we're equal."

"Are you?"

"I am."

"Then you're lucky."

"Yes I know I'm very lucky." She watched him. "How old are you, Linc?"

"Old." He snapped the cue into its rack. It was the first time in his life that he had not wanted to tell his age. Goddamn, he thought, curiously unsettled. What's your problem?

None. There's no problem. Is there?

"I'm nineteen," she was saying.

"When's your birthday?"

"October 27—I'm a Scorpio. When's yours?"

"October 1."

"Oh it's not! Tell me honestly!"

"Cross my heart and hope to die."

She clapped her hands with delight. "Oh that's marvelous! Father's the tenth. That's marvelous—a good omen."

"Why?"

"You'll see." Happily she opened her handbag and found a crumpled cigarette package and a battered gold lighter. He took the lighter and flicked it for her but it did not light. A second and a third time but nothing.

"Bloody thing," she said. "Bloody thing's never worked properly but Father gave it to me. I love it. Of course I dropped it a couple of times."

He peered at it, blew the wick and fiddled a moment. "You shouldn't smoke anyway."

"That's what Father always says."

"He's right."

"Yes. But I like smoking for the time being. How old are you, Linc?"

"Forty."

"Oh!" He saw the surprise. "Then you're the same age as Father! Well, almost. He's forty-one."

"Both were great years," Linc said dryly, and he thought, Whichever way you figure it, Adryon, I really am old enough to be your father.

Another frown creased her brow. "It's funny, you don't seem the same age at all." Then she added in a rush, "In two years I'll be twenty-one and that's practically over the hill, I just can't imagine being twenty-five let alone thirty and as to forty . . . God, I think I'd rather be pushing up daisies."

"Twenty-one's old—yes ma'am, mighty old," he said. And he thought, It's a long time since you spent time with such a young one. Watch yourself. This one's dynamite. He flicked the lighter and it lit. "What d'you know!"

"Thanks," she said and puffed her cigarette alight. "You don't smoke?" she asked.

"No, not now. Used to but Casey sent me illustrated pamphlets on cancer and smoking every hour on the hour until I got the message. Didn't phase me a bit to stop—once I'd decided. It sure as hell improved my golf and tennis and . . ." He smiled. "And all forms of sports."

"Casey is gorgeous. Is she really your executive vice-president?"

"Yes."

"She's going to . . . it'll be very difficult for her here. The men won't like dealing with her at all."

"Same in the States. But they're getting used to it. We built Par-Con in six years. Casey can work with the best of them. She's a winner."

"Is she your mistress?"

He sipped his beer. "Are all young English ladies so blunt?"

"No." She laughed. "I was just curious. Everyone says . . . everyone presumes she is."

"That a fact?"

"Yes. You're the talk of Hong Kong society, and tonight will cap everything. You both made rather a grand entrance, what with your private jet, the smuggled guns and Casey being the last European to see John Chen, so the papers said. I liked your interview."

"Eh, those bas—those press guys were waiting on the doorstep this afternoon. I tried to keep it short and sharp."

"Par-Con's really worth half a billion dollars?"

"No. About 300 million—but it'll be a billion-dollar company soon. Yes, it'll be soon now."

He saw her looking at him with those frank, gray-green eyes of hers, so adult yet so young. "You're a very interesting man, Mr. Linc Bartlett. I like talking to you. I like you too. Didn't at first. I screamed bloody murder when Father told me I had to chaperone you, introduce you around for a while. I haven't done a very good job, have I?"

"It's been *super*."

"Oh come on." She grinned too. "I've totally monopolized you."

"Not true. I met Christian Toxe the editor, Richard Kwang and those two Americans from the consulate. Lannan wasn't it?"

"Langan, Edward Langan. He's nice. I didn't catch the other one's name—I don't know them really, they've just been racing with us. Christian's nice and his wife's super. She's Chinese so she's not here tonight."

Bartlett frowned. "Because she's Chinese?"

"Oh, she was invited but she wouldn't come. It's face. To save her husband's face. The nobs don't approve of mixed marriages."

"Marrying the natives?"

"Something like that." She shrugged. "You'll see. I'd better introduce you to some more guests or I'll get hell!"

"How about to Havergill the banker? What about him?"

"Father thinks Havergill's a berk."

"Then by God he's a twenty-two-carat berk from here on in!"

"Good," she said and they laughed together.

"Linc?"

They looked around at the two figures silhouetted in the shaft of light from the doorway. He recognized Casey's voice and shape at once but not the man. It was not possible from where they were to see against the light.

"Hi, Casey! How's it going?"

He took Adryon's arm casually and propelled her toward the silhouette. "I've been teaching Adryon the finer points of pool."

Adryon laughed. "That's the understatement of the year, Casey. He's super at it, isn't he?"

"Yes. Oh Linc, Quillan Gornt wanted to say hi before he left."

Abruptly Adryon jerked to a stop and the color left her face. Linc stopped, startled. "What's wrong?" he asked her.

"Evening, Mr. Bartlett," Gornt said, moving toward them into the light. "Hello, Adryon."

"What're you doing here?" she said in a tiny voice.

"I just came for a few minutes," Gornt said.

"Have you seen Father?"

"Yes."

"Then get out. Get out and leave this house alone." Adryon said it in the same small voice.

Bartlett stared at her. "What the hell's up?"

Gornt said calmly, "It's a long story. It can wait until tomorrow—or next week. I just wanted to confirm our dinner on Tuesday—and if you're free over the weekend, perhaps you two would like to come out on my boat for the day. Sunday if the weather's good."

"Thanks, I think so, but may we confirm tomorrow?" Bartlett asked, still nonplussed by Adryon.

"Adryon," Gornt said gently, "Annagrey's leaving next week, she asked me to ask you to give her a call." Adryon did not answer, just stared at him, and Gornt added to the other two, "Annagrey's my daughter.

They're good friends—they've both gone to the same schools most of their lives. She's off to university in California."

"Oh—then if there's anything we could do for her . . ." Casey said.

"That's very kind of you," he said. "You'll meet her Tuesday. Perhaps we can talk about it then. I'll say g—"

The door at the far end of the billiard room swung open and Dunross stood there.

Gornt smiled and turned his attention back to them. "Good night, Mr. Bartlett—Ciranoush. See you both on Tuesday. Good night, Adryon." He bowed slightly to them and walked the length of the room and stopped. "Good night, Ian," he said politely. "Thank you for your hospitality."

"'Night," Dunross said, as politely, and stood aside, a slight smile twisting his lips.

He watched Gornt walk out of the front door and then turned his attention back to the billiard room. "Almost time for dinner," he said, his voice calm. And warm. "You must all be starving. I am."

"What . . . what did he want?" Adryon said shakily.

Dunross came up to her with a smile, gentling her. "Nothing. Nothing important, my pet. Quillan's mellowing in his old age."

"You're sure?"

"Sure." He put his arm around her and gave her a little hug. "No need to worry your pretty head."

"Has he gone?"

"Yes."

Bartlett started to say something but stopped instantly as he caught Dunross's eye over Adryon's head.

"Yes. Everything's grand, my darling," Dunross was saying as he gave her another little hug, and Bartlett saw Adryon gather herself within the warmth. "Nothing to worry about."

"Linc was showing me how he played pool and then . . . It was just so sudden. He was like an apparition."

"You could have knocked me down with a feather too when he appeared like the Bad Fairy." Dunross laughed, then added to Bartlett and Casey, "Quillan goes in for dramatics." Then to Bartlett alone, "We'll chat about that after dinner, you and I."

"Sure," Bartlett said, noticing the eyes weren't smiling.

The dinner gong sounded. "Ah, thank God!" Dunross said. "Come along, everyone, food at long last. Casey, you're at my table." He kept his arm around Adryon, loving her, and guided her out into the light.

Casey and Bartlett followed.

Gornt got into the driver's seat of the black Silver Cloud Rolls that he had parked just outside the Great House. The night was good, though the humidity had increased again. He was very pleased with himself. And now for dinner and Jason Plumm, he thought. Once that bugger's committed, Ian Dunross's as good as finished and I own this house and Struan's and the whole kit and caboodle!

It couldn't have been better: first Casey and Ian almost at once, and everything laid out in front of him and in front of her. Then Havergill and Richard Kwang together. Then Bartlett in the billiard room and then Ian himself again.

Perfect!

Now Ian's called, Bartlett's called, Casey, Havergill, Richard Kwang and so's Plumm. Ha! If they only knew.

Everything's perfect. Except for Adryon. Pity about her, pity that children have to inherit the feuds of the fathers. But that's life. Joss. Pity she won't go out into the world and leave Hong Kong, like Annagrey—at least until Ian Dunross and I have settled our differences, finally. Better she's not here to see him smashed—nor Penelope too. Joss if they're here, joss if they're not. I'd like him here when I take possession of his box at the races, the permanent seat on all boards, all the sinecures, the legislature—oh yes. Soon they'll all be mine. Along with the envy of all Asia.

He laughed. Yes. And about time. Then all the ghosts will sleep. God curse all ghosts!

He switched on the ignition and started the engine, enjoying the luxury of real leather and fine wood, the smell rich and exclusive. Then he put the car into gear and swung down the driveway, past the carpark where all the other cars were, down to the huge wrought-iron main gates with the Struan arms entwined. He stopped for passing traffic and caught sight of the Great House in his rear mirror. Tall, vast, the windows ablaze, welcoming.

Soon I really will own you, he thought. I'll throw parties there that Asia's never seen before and never will again. I suppose I should have a hostess.

What about the American girl?

He chuckled. "Ah, Ciranoush, what a lovely name," he said out loud with the same, perfect amount of husky charm that he had used previously. That one's a pushover, he told himself confidently. You just use old world charm and great wine, light but excellent food and patience—along with the very best of upper-class English, masculine sophistication and no swear words and she'll fall where and when you want her to. And then, if you choose the correct moment, you can use gutter English and a little judicious roughness, and you'll unlock all her pent-up passion like no man ever has done.

If I read her correctly she needs an expert pillowing rather badly. So either Bartlett's inadequate or they're really not lovers as the confidential report suggested. Interesting.

But do you want her? As a toy—perhaps. As a tool—of course. As a hostess no, much too pushy.

Now the road was clear so he pulled out and went down to the junction and turned left and soon he was on Peak Road going downhill toward Magazine Gap where Plumm's penthouse apartment was. After dinner with him he was going to a meeting, then to Wanchai, to one of his private apartments and the welcoming embrace of Mona Leung. His pulse quickened at the thought of her violent lovemaking, her barely hidden hatred for him and all *quai loh* that was ever in perpetual conflict with her love of luxury, the apartment that was on loan to her and the modest amount of money he gave her monthly.

"Never give 'em enough money," his father William had told him early on. "Clothes, jewelry, holidays—that's fine. But not too much money. Control them with dollar bills. And never think they love you for you. They don't. It's only your money, only your money and always will be. Just under the surface they'll despise you, always will. That's fair enough if you think about it—we're not Chinese and never will be."

"There's never an exception?"

"I don't think so. Not for a *quai loh*, my son. I don't think so. Never has been with me and I've known a few. Oh she'll give you her body, her children, even her life, but she'll always despise you. She has to, she's Chinese and we're *quai loh!*"

Ayeeyah, Gornt thought. That advice's proved itself time and time again. And saved me so much anguish. It'll be good to see the Old Man, he told himself. This year I'll give him a fine Christmas present: Struan's.

He was driving carefully down the left side of the winding road hugging the mountainside, the night good, the surface fine and the traffic light. Normally he would have been chauffeur-driven but tonight he wanted no witnesses to his meeting with Plumm.

No, he thought. Nor any witnesses when I meet Four Finger Wu. What the hell does that pirate want? Nothing good. Bound to be dangerous. Yes. But during the Korean War Wu did you a very large favor and perhaps now is the time he wants the favor repaid. There's always a reckoning sooner or later, and that's fair and that's Chinese law. You get a present, you give one back a little more valuable. You have a favor done . . .

In 1950 when the Chinese Communist armies in Korea were battering and bleeding their way south from the Yalu with monstrous losses, they were desperately short of all strategic supplies and very willing to pay mightily those who could slip through the blockade with the supplies they needed. At that time, Rothwell-Gornt was also in desperate straits because of their huge losses at Shanghai the previous year thanks to the conquest by Mao. So in December of 1950, he and his father had borrowed heavily and secretly bought a huge shipment of penicillin, morphine, sulfanilamides and other medical supplies in the Philippines, avoiding the obligatory export license. These they smuggled onto a hired ocean-going junk with one of their trusted crews and sent it to Wampoa, a bleak island in the Pearl River near Canton. Payment was to be in gold on delivery, but en route, in the secret backwaters of the Pearl River Estuary, their junk had been intercepted by river pirates favoring Chiang Kai-shek's Nationalists and a ransom demanded. They had no money to ransom the cargo, and if the Nationalists found out that Rothwell-Gornt was dealing with their hated Communist enemy, their own future in Asia was lost forever.

Through his compradore Gornt had arranged a meeting in Aberdeen Harbor with Four Finger Wu, supposedly one of the biggest smugglers in the Pearl River Estuary.

"Where ship now?" Four Finger Wu had asked in execrable pidgin English.

Gornt had told him as best he could, conversing in pidgin, not being able to speak Haklo, Wu's dialect.

"Perhaps, perhaps not!" Four Finger Wu smiled. "I phone three day. *Nee choh wah* password. Three day, *heya?*"

On the third day he phoned. "Bad, good, don' know. Meet two day Aberdeen. Begin Hour of Monkey." That hour was ten o'clock at night. Chinese split the day into twelve, two-hour segments, each with a name, always in the same sequence, beginning at 4:00 A.M. with the Cock, then at 6:00 A.M. with the Dog, and so on; Boar, Rat, Ox, Tiger, Rabbit, Dragon, Snake, Monkey, Horse and Sheep.

At the Hour of the Monkey on Wu's junk at Aberdeen two days later, he had been given the full payment for his shipment in gold *plus an extra 40 percent*. A staggering 500 percent profit.

Four Finger Wu had grinned. "Make better trade than *quai loh*, never mind. 28,000 taels of gold." A tael was a little more than an ounce. "Next time me ship. Yes?"

"Yes."

"You buy, me ship, me sell, 40 percent mine, sale price."

"Yes." Gornt had thankfully tried to press a much larger percentage on him this time but Wu had refused.

"40 percent only, sale price." But Gornt had understood that now he was in the smuggler's debt.

The gold was in five-tael smuggler bars. It was valued at the official rate of $35 U.S. an ounce. But on the black market, smuggled into Indonesia, India or back into China, it was worth two or three times as much . . . sometimes more. On this one shipment again with Wu's help, Rothwell-Gornt had made a million and a half U.S. and were on the road to recovery.

After that there had been three more shipments, immensely profitable to both sides. Then the war had ceased and so had their relationship.

Never a word since then, Gornt thought. Until the phone call this afternoon.

"Ah, old friend, can see? Tonight?" Four Finger Wu had said. "Can do? Anytime—I wait. Same place as old days. Yes?"

So now the favor's to be returned. Good.

Gornt switched on the radio. Chopin. He was driving the winding road automatically, his mind on the meetings ahead, the engine almost silent.

He slowed for an advancing truck, then swung out and accelerated on the short straight to overtake a slow-moving taxi. Going quite fast now he braked sharply in good time nearing the blind corner, then something seemed to snap in the innards of the engine, his foot sank to the floorboards, his stomach turned over and he went into the hairpin too fast.

In panic he jammed his foot on the brake again and again but nothing happened, his hands whirling the wheel around. He took the first corner badly, swerving drunkenly as he came out of it onto the wrong side of the road. Fortunately there was nothing coming at him but he overcorrected and lurched for the mountainside, his stomach twisting with nausea, overcorrected again, going very fast now and the next corner leapt at him. Here the grade was steeper, the road more winding and narrow. Again he cornered badly but once through he had a split second to grab the hand brake and this slowed him only a little, the new corner was on him, and he came out of it way out of his lane, oncoming headlights blinding him.

The taxi skittered in panic to the shoulder and almost went over the side, its horn blaring but he was passed by a fraction of an inch, lurching petrified for the correct side, and then went on down the hill out of control. A moment of straight road and he managed to jerk the gear lever into low as he hurtled into another blind corner, the engine howling now. The sudden slowing would have pitched him through the windshield but for his seat belt, his hands almost frozen to the wheel.

He got around this corner but again he was out too far and he missed the oncoming car by a millimeter, skidded back to his side once more, swerved, overcorrecting, slowing a little now but there was no letup in the grade or twisting road ahead. He was still going too fast into the new hairpin and coming out of the first part he was too far over. The heavily laden truck grinding up the hill was helpless.

Panic-stricken he tore the wheel left and just managed to get around the truck with a glancing blow. He tried to jerk the gear lever into reverse but it wouldn't go, the cogs shrieking in protest. Then, aghast, he saw slow traffic ahead in his lane, oncoming traffic in the other and the road vanish around the next bend. He was lost so he turned left into the mountainside, trying to ricochet and stop that way.

There was a howl of protesting metal, the back side window shattered and he bounced away. The oncoming car lurched for the far shoulder, its horn blaring. He closed his eyes and braced for the head-on collision but somehow it didn't happen and he was past and just had enough strength to jerk the wheel hard over again and went into the mountainside. He hit with a glancing blow. The front left fender ripped away. The car ploughed into the shrub and earth, then slammed into a rock outcrop, reared up throwing Gornt aside, but as the car fell back the near-side wheel went into the storm drain and held, and, just before smashing into the paralyzed little Mini ahead, it stopped.

Gornt weakly pulled himself up. The car was still half upright. Sweat was pouring off him and his heart was pounding. He found it hard to breathe or to think. Traffic both ways was stopped, snarled. He heard some horns hooting impatiently below and above, then hurried footsteps.

"You all right, old chap?" the stranger asked.

"Yes, yes I think so. My, my brakes went." Gornt wiped the sweat off his forehead, trying to get his brain to work. He felt his chest, then moved his feet and there was no pain. "I . . . the brakes went . . . I was turning a corner and . . . and then everything . . ."

"Brakes, eh? Not like a Rolls. I thought you were pretending to be Stirling Moss. You were very lucky. I thought you'd had it twenty times. If I were you I'd switch off the engine."

"What?" Then Gornt realized the engine was still gently purring and the radio playing so he turned the ignition off and, after a moment, pulled the keys out.

"Nice car," the stranger said, "but it's a right proper mess now. Always liked this model. '62, isn't it?"

"Yes. Yes it is."

"You want me to call the police?"

Gornt made the effort and thought a moment, his pulse still pounding in his ears. Weakly he unsnapped the seat belt. "No. There's a police station just back up the hill. If you'd give me a lift to there?"

"Delighted, old chap." The stranger was short and rotund. He looked around at the other cars and taxis and trucks that were stopped in both directions, their Chinese drivers and Chinese passengers gawking at them from their windows. "Bloody people," he muttered sourly. "You could be dying in the street and you'd be lucky if they stepped over you." He opened the door and helped Gornt out.

"Thanks." Gornt felt his knees shaking. For a moment he could not dominate his knees and he leaned against the car.

"You sure you're all right?"

"Oh yes. It's . . . that frightened me to death!" He looked at the damage, the nose buried into earth and shrub, a huge score down the right side, the car jammed well into the inside curve. "What a bloody mess!"

"Yes, but it hasn't telescoped a sausage! You were bloody lucky you were in a good car, old chap." The stranger let the door swing and it closed with a muted click. "Great workmanship. Well, you can leave it here. No one's likely to steal it." The stranger laughed, leading the way to his own car which was parked, its blinker lights on, just behind. "Hop in, won't take a jiffy."

It was then Gornt remembered the mocking half-smile on Dunross's face that he had taken for bravado as he left. His mind cleared. Would there have been time for Dunross to tamper . . . with his knowledge of engines . . . surely he wouldn't . . . ?

"Son of a bitch," he muttered, aghast.

"Not to worry, old chap," the stranger said, as he eased past the wreck, making the turn. "The police'll make all the arrangements for you."

Gornt's face closed. "Yes. Yes they will."

13

"Grand dinner, Ian, better than last year's," Sir Dunstan Barre said expansively from across the table.

"Thank you." Dunross raised his glass politely and took a sip of the fine cognac from the brandy snifter.

Barre gulped his port then refilled his glass, more florid than usual. "Ate too much, as usual, by God! Eh Phillip? Phillip!"

"Yes . . . oh yes . . . much better . . ." Phillip Chen muttered.

"Are you all right, old chap?"

"Oh yes . . . it's just . . . . oh yes."

Dunross frowned, then let his eyes rove the other tables, hardly listening to them.

There were just the three of them now at this round table that had seated twelve comfortably. At the other tables spread across the terraces and lawns, men were lounging over their cognac, port and cigars, or standing in clusters, all the ladies now inside the house. He saw Bartlett standing over near the buffet tables that an hour ago had been groaning under the weight of roast legs of lamb, salads, sides of rare beef, vast hot steak-and-kidney pies, roast potatoes and vegetables of various kinds, and the pastries and cakes and ice cream sculptures. A small army of servants was cleaning away the debris. Bartlett was in deep conversation with Chief Superintendent Roger Crosse and the American Ed Langan. In a little while I'll deal with him, he told himself grimly—but first Brian Kwok. He looked around. Brian Kwok was not at his table, the one that Adryon had hosted, or at any of the others, so he sat back patiently, sipped his cognac and let himself drift.

Secret files, MI-6, Special Intelligence, Bartlett, Casey, Gornt, no Tsu-yan and now Alan Medford Grant very dead. His phone call before dinner to Kiernan, Alan Medford Grant's assistant in London, had been a shocker. "It was sometime this morning, Mr. Dunross," Kiernan had said. "It was raining, very slippery and he was a motorcycle enthusiast as you know. He was coming up to town as usual. As far as we know now there were no witnesses. The fellow who found him on the country road near Esher and the A3 highway, just said he was driving along in the rain and then there in front of him was the bike on its side and a man sprawled in a heap on the edge of the road. He said as far as he could tell, AMG was dead when he reached him. He called the police and they've begun inquiries but . . . well, what can I say? He's a great loss to all of us."

"Yes. Did he have any family?"

"Not that I know of, sir. Of course I informed MI-6 at once."

"Oh?"

"Yes sir."

"Why?"

There was heavy static on the line. "He'd left instructions with me, sir. If anything happened to him I was to call two numbers at once and cable you, which I did. Neither number meant anything to me. The first turned out to be the private number of a high-up official in MI-6—he arrived within half an hour with some of his people and they went through AMG's desk and private papers. They took most of them when they left. When he saw the copy of the last report, the one we'd just sent you, he just about hit the roof, and when he asked for copies of all the others and I told him, following AMG's instructions, I always destroyed the office copy once we'd heard you had received yours, he just about had a hemorrhage. It seems AMG didn't really have Her Majesty's Government's permission to work for you."

"But I have Grant's assurance in writing he'd got clearance from HMG in advance."

"Yes sir. You've done nothing illegal but this MI-6 fellow just about went bonkers."

"Who was he? What was his name?"

"I was told, *told*, sir, not to mention any names. He was very pompous and mumbled something about the Official Secrets Act."

"You said two numbers?"

"Yes sir. The other was in Switzerland. A woman answered and after I'd told her, she just said, oh, so sorry, and hung up. She was foreign, sir. One interesting thing, in AMG's final instructions he had said not to tell either number about the other but, as this gentleman from MI-6 was, to put it lightly, incensed, I told him. He called at once but got a busy line and it was busy for a very long time and then the exchange said it had been temporarily disconnected. He was bloody furious, sir."

"Can you carry on AMG's reports?"

"No sir. I was just a feeder—I collated information that he got. I just wrote the reports for him, answered the phone when he was away, paid office bills. He spent a good part of the time on the Continent but he never said where he'd been, or volunteered anything. He was . . . well, he played his cards close to his nose. I don't know who gave him anything

—I don't even know his office number in Whitehall. As I said, he was very secretive. . . ."

Dunross sighed and sipped his brandy. Bloody shame, he thought. Was it an accident—or was he murdered? And when do MI-6 fall on my neck? The numbered account in Switzerland? That's not illegal either, and no one's business but mine and his.

What to do? There must be a substitute somewhere.

Was it an accident? Or was he killed?

"Sorry?" he asked, not catching what Barre had said.

"I was just saying it was bloody funny when Casey didn't want to go and you threw her out." The big man laughed. "You've got balls, old boy."

At the end of the dinner just before the port and cognac and cigars had arrived, Penelope had got up from her table where Linc Bartlett was deep in conversation with Havergill and the ladies had left with her, and then Adryon at her table, and then, all over the terraces, ladies had begun trickling away after her. Lady Joanna, who was sitting on Dunross's right, had said, "Come on girls, time to powder."

Obediently the other women got up with her and the men politely pretended not to be relieved with their exodus.

"Come along, dear," Joanna had said to Casey, who had remained seated.

"Oh I'm fine, thanks."

"I'm sure you are but, er, come along anyway."

Then Casey had seen everyone staring. "What's the matter?"

"Nothing, dear," Lady Joanna had said. "It's custom that the ladies leave the men alone for a while with the port and cigars. So come along."

Casey had stared at her blankly. "You mean we're sent off while the men discuss affairs of state and the price of tea in China?"

"It's just good manners, dear. When in Rome . . ." Lady Joanna had watched her, a slight, contemptuous smile on her lips, enjoying the embarrassed silence and the shocked looks of most of the men. All eyes went back to the American girl.

"You can't be serious. That custom went out before the Civil War," Casey said.

"In America I'm sure it did." Joanna smiled her twisted smile. "Here it's different, this is part of England. It's a matter of manners. Do come along, dear."

"I will—dear," Casey said as sweetly. "Later."

Joanna had sighed and shrugged and raised an eyebrow at Dunross and smiled crookedly and gone off with the other ladies. There was a stunned silence at the table.

"Tai-pan, you don't mind if I stay, do you?" Casey had said with a laugh.

"Yes, I'm sorry but I do," he had told her gently. "It's just a custom, nothing important. It's really so the ladies can get first crack at the loo and the pails of water."

Her smile faded and her chin began to jut. "And if I prefer not to go?"

"It's just our custom, Ciranoush. In America it's custom to call someone you've just met by his first name, it's not here. Even so . . ." Dunross stared back calmly, but just as inflexibly. "There's no loss of face in it."

"I think there is."

"Sorry about that—I can assure you there isn't."

The others had waited, watching him and watching her, enjoying the confrontation, at the same time appalled by her. Except Ed Langan who was totally embarrassed for her. "Hell, Casey," he said, trying to make a joke of it, "you can't fight City Hall."

"I've been trying all my life," she had said sharply—clearly furious. Then, abruptly, she had smiled gloriously. Her fingers drummed momentarily on the tablecloth and she got up. "If you gentlemen will excuse me . . ." she had said sweetly and sailed away, an astonished silence in her wake.

"I hardly threw her out," Dunross said.

"It was bloody funny, even so," Barre said. "I wonder what changed her mind? Eh Phillip?"

"What?" Phillip Chen asked absently.

"For a moment I thought she was going to belt poor old Ian, didn't you? But something she thought of changed her mind. What?"

Dunross smiled. "I'll bet it's no good. That one's as touchy as a pocketful of scorpions."

"Great knockers, though," Barre said.

They laughed. Phillip Chen didn't. Dunross's concern for him increased. He had tried to cheer him up all evening but nothing had drawn the curtain away. All through dinner Phillip had been dulled and monosyllabic. Barre got up with a belch. "Think I'll take a leak while there's space." He lurched off into the garden.

"Don't pee on the camellias," Ian called after him absently, then forced himself to concentrate. "Phillip, not to worry," he said, now that they were alone. "They'll find John soon."

"Yes, I'm sure they will," Phillip Chen said dully, his mind not so much swamped by the kidnapping as appalled by what he had discovered in his son's safety deposit box this afternoon. He had opened it with the key that he had taken from the shoebox.

"Go on, Phillip, take it, don't be a fool," his wife Dianne had hissed. "Take it—if we don't the tai-pan will!"

"Yes, yes I know." Thank all gods I did, he thought, still in shock, remembering what he had found when he'd rifled through the contents. Manila envelopes of various sizes, mostly itemized, a diary and phone book. In the envelope marked "debts" betting slips for 97,000 HK for current debts to illegal, off-course gamblers in Hong Kong. A note in favor of

Miser Sing, a notorious moneylender, for 30,000 HK at 3 percent per month interest; a long overdue sight demand note from the Ho-Pak Bank for $20,000 U.S. and a letter from Richard Kwang dated last week saying unless John Chen made some arrangements soon he would have to talk to his father. Then there were letters which documented a growing friendship between his son and an American gambler, Vincenzo Banastasio, who assured John Chen that his debts were not pressing: ". . . take your time, John, your credit's the best, anytime this year's fine . . ." and, attached, was the photocopy of a perfectly legal, notarized promissory note binding his son, his heirs or assignees, to pay Banastasio, on demand, $485,000 U.S., plus interest.

Stupid, stupid, he had raged, knowing his son had not more than a fifth of those assets, so he himself would have to pay the debt eventually.

Then a thick envelope marked "Par-Con" had caught his attention.

This contained a Par-Con employment contract signed by K. C. Tcholok, three months ago, hiring John Chen as a private consultant to Par-Con for ". . . $100,000 down ($50,000 of which is hereby acknowledged as already paid) and, once a satisfactory deal is signed between Par-Con and Struan's, Rothwell-Gornt or any other Hong Kong company of Par-Con's choosing, a further one million dollars spread over a five-year period in equal installments; and within thirty days of the signing of the above said contract, a debt to Mr. Vincenzo Banastasio of 85 Orchard Road, Las Vegas, Nevada, of $485,000 paid off, the first year's installment of $200,000, along with the balance of $50,000 . . ."

"In return for what," Phillip Chen had gasped helplessly in the bank vault.

But the long contract spelled out nothing further except that John Chen was to be a "private consultant in Asia." There were no notes or papers attached to it.

Hastily he had rechecked the envelope in case he had missed anything but it was empty. A quick leafing through the other envelopes produced nothing. Then he happened to notice a thin airmail envelope half stuck to another. It was marked "Par-Con II." It contained photocopies of handwritten notes from his son to Linc Bartlett.

The first was dated six months ago and confirmed that he, John Chen, would and could supply Par-Con with the most intimate knowledge of the innermost workings of the whole Struan complex of companies, ". . . of course this has to be kept totally secret, but for example, Mr. Bartlett, you can see from the enclosed Struan balance sheets for 1954 through 1961 (when Struan's went public) what I advise is perfectly feasible. If you look at the chart of Struan's corporate structure, and the list of some of the important stockholders of Struan's and their secret holdings, including my father's, you should have no trouble in any takeover bid Par-Con cares to mount. Add to these photocopies the other thing I told you about—I swear to God that you can believe me—I guarantee success. I'm putting my life on the line, that should be collateral enough, but if you'll advance me fifty of the first hundred now, I'll agree to let you have possession on arrival—on your undertaking to return it to me once your deal's set—or for use against Struan's. I guarantee to use it against Struan's. In the end Dunross has to do anything you want. Please reply to the usual post box and destroy this as we have agreed."

"Possession of what?" Phillip Chen had muttered, beside himself with anxiety. His hands were shaking now as he read the second letter. It was dated three weeks ago. "Dear Mr. Bartlett. This will confirm your arrival dates. Everything's prepared. I look forward to seeing you again and meeting Mr. K. C. Tcholok. Thanks for the fifty cash which arrived safely—all future monies are to go to a numbered account in Zurich—I'll give you the bank details when you arrive. Thank you also for agreeing to our unwritten understanding that if I can assist you in the way I've claimed I can, then I'm in for 3 percent of the action of the new Par-Con (Asia) Trading Company.

"I enclose a few more things of interest: note the date that Struan's demand notes (countersigned by my father) become due to pay Toda Shipping for their new super container ships—September 1, 11 and 15. There's not enough money in Struan's till to meet them.

"Next: to answer Mr. Tcholok's question about my father's position in any takeover or proxy fight. He can be neutralized. Enclosed photocopies are a sample of many that I have. These show a very close relationship with White Powder Lee and his cousin, Wu Sang Fang who's also known as Four Finger Wu, from the early fifties, and secret ownership with them —even today—of a property company, two shipping companies and Bangkok trading interests. Though outwardly, now, both pose as respectable businessmen, property developers and shipping millionaires, it's common knowledge they have been successful pirates and smugglers for years—and there's a very strong rumor in Chinese circles that they are the High Dragons of the opium trade. If my father's connection with them was made public it would take his face away forever, would sever the very close links he has with Struan's, and all the other *hongs* that exist today, and most important, would destroy forever his chance for a knighthood, the one thing he wants above all. Just the threat of doing this would be enough to neutralize him—even make him an ally. Of course I realize these papers and the others I have need further documentation to stick in a court of law but I have this already in abundance in a safe place. . . ."

Phillip Chen remembered how, panic-stricken, he had searched frantically for the further documentation, his mind shrieking that it was impossible for his son to have so much secret knowledge, impossible for him to have Struan's balance sheets of the prepublic days, impossible to know about Four Finger Wu and those secret things.

Oh gods that's almost everything I know—even Dianne doesn't know half of that! What else does John know—what else has he told the American?

Beside himself with anxiety he had searched every envelope but there was nothing more.

"He must have another box somewhere—or safe," he had muttered aloud, hardly able to think.

Furiously he had scooped everything into his briefcase, hoping that a more careful examination would answer his questions—and slammed the box shut and locked it. At a sudden thought, he had reopened it. He had pulled the slim tray out and turned it upside down. Taped to the underside were two keys. One was a safety deposit box key with the number carefully filed off. He stared at the other, paralyzed. He recognized it at once. It was the key to his own safe in his house on the crest. He would have bet his life that the only key in existence was the one that he always wore around his neck, that had never been out of his possession—ever since his father had given it to him on his deathbed sixteen years ago.

"Oh ko," he said aloud, once more consumed with rage.

Dunross said, "You all right? How about a brandy?"

"No, no thank you," Phillip Chen said shakily, back in the present now. With an effort he pulled his mind together and stared at the tai-pan, knowing he should tell him everything. But he dare not. He dare not until he knew the extent of the secrets stolen. Even then he dare not. Apart from many transactions the authorities could easily misconstrue, and others that could be highly embarrassing and lead to all sorts of court cases, civil if not criminal—stupid English law, he thought furiously, stupid to have one law for everyone, stupid not to have one law for the rich and another for the poor, why else work and slave and gamble and scheme to be rich—apart from all this he would still have had to admit to Dunross that he had been documenting Struan secrets for years, that his father had done so before him—balance sheets, stockholdings and other secret, very very private personal family things, smugglings and payoffs—and he knew it would be no good saying I did it just for protection, to protect the House, because the tai-pan would rightly say, yes but it was to protect the House of Chen and not the Noble House, and he would rightly turn on him, turn his full wrath on him and his brood, and in the holocaust of a fight against Struan's he was bound to lose—Dirk Struan's will had provided for that—and everything that almost a century and a half had built up would vanish.

Thank all gods that everything was not in the safe, he thought fervently. Thank all gods the other things are buried deep.

Then, suddenly, some words from his son's first letter ripped to the forefront of his mind, ". . . Add to these photocopies *the other thing* I told you about . . ."

He paled and staggered to his feet. "If you'll excuse me, tai-pan . . . I, er, I'll say good night. I'll just fetch Dianne and I . . . I'll . . . thank you, good night." He hurried off toward the house.

Dunross stared after him, shocked.

"Oh, Casey," Penelope was saying, "may I introduce Kathren Gavallan —Kathren's Ian's sister."

"Hi!" Casey smiled at her, liking her at once. They were in one of the antechambers on the ground floor among other ladies who were talking or fixing their makeup or standing in line, waiting their turn to visit the adjoining powder room. The room was large, comfortable and mirrored. "You both have the same eyes—I'd recognize the resemblance anywhere," she said. "He's quite a man, isn't he?"

"We think so," Kathren replied with a ready smile. She was thirty-eight, attractive, her Scots accent pleasing, her flowered silk dress long and cool. "This water shortage's a bore, isn't it?"

"Yes. Must be very difficult with children."

"No, chérie, the children, they just love it," Susanne deVille called out. She was in her late forties, chic, her French accent slight. "How can you insist they bathe every night?"

"My two are the same." Kathren smiled. "It bothers us parents, but it doesn't seem to bother them. It's a bore though, trying to run a house."

Penelope said, "God, I hate it! This summer's been ghastly. You're lucky tonight, usually we'd be dripping!" She was checking her makeup in the mirror. "I can't wait till next month. Kathren, did I tell you we're going home for a couple of weeks leave—at least I am. Ian's promised to come too but you never know with him."

"He needs a holiday," Kathren said and Casey noticed shadows in her eyes and care rings under her makeup. "Are you going to Ayr?"

"Yes, and London for a week."

"Lucky you. How long are you staying in Hong Kong, Casey?"

"I don't know. It all depends on what Par-Con does."

"Yes. Andrew said you had a meeting all day with them."

"I don't think they went much for having to talk business with a woman."

"That is the understatement," Susanne deVille said with a laugh, lifting her skirts to pull down her blouse. "Of course my Jacques is half French so he understands that women are in the business. But the English . . ." Her eyebrows soared.

"The tai-pan didn't seem to mind," Casey said, "but then I haven't had any real dealings with him yet."

"But you have with Quillan Gornt," Kathren said, and Casey, very much on guard even in the privacy of the ladies' room, heard the undercurrent in her voice.

"No," she replied. "I haven't—not before tonight—but my boss has."

Just before dinner she had had time to tell Bartlett the story of Gornt's father and Colin Dunross.

"Jesus! No wonder Adryon went cross-eyed!" Bartlett had said. "And in the billiard room too." He had thought a moment then he had shrugged. "But all that means is that this puts more pressure on Dunross."

"Maybe. But their enmity goes deeper than anything I've experienced, Linc. It could easily backfire."

"I don't see how—yet. Gornt was just opening up a flank like a good general should. If we hadn't had John Chen's advance information, what Gornt said could've been vital to us. Gornt's got no way of knowing we're ahead of him. So he's stepping up the tempo. We haven't even got our big guns out yet and they're both wooing us already."

"Have you decided yet which one to go with?"

"No. What's your hunch?"

"I haven't got one. Yet. They're both formidable. Linc, do you think John Chen was kidnapped because he was feeding us information?"

"I don't know. Why?"

"Before Gornt arrived I was intercepted by Superintendent Armstrong. He questioned me about what John Chen had said last night, what we'd talked about, exactly what was said. I told him everything I could remember—except I never mentioned I was to take delivery of 'it.' Since I still don't know what 'it' is."

"It's nothing illegal, Casey."

"I don't like not knowing. Not now. It's getting . . . I'm getting out of my depth, the guns, this brutal kidnapping and the police so insistent."

"It's nothing illegal. Leave it at that. Did Armstrong say there was a connection?"

"He volunteered nothing. He's a strong, silent English gentleman police officer and as smart and well trained as anything I've seen in the movies. I'm sure he was sure I was hiding something." She hesitated. "Linc, what's John Chen got that's so important to us?"

She remembered how he had studied her, his eyes deep and blue and quizzical and laughing.

"A coin," he had said calmly.

"What?" she had asked, astounded.

"Yes. Actually half a coin."

"But Linc, what's a coi—"

"That's all I'm telling you now, Casey, but you tell me does Armstrong figure there's some connection between Chen's kidnapping and the guns?"

"I don't know." She had shrugged. "I don't think so, Linc. I couldn't even give you odds. He's too cagey that one." Again she had hesitated. "Linc, have you made a deal, any deal with Gornt?"

"No. Nothing firm. Gornt just wants Struan out and wants to join with us to smash them. I said we'd discuss it Tuesday. Over dinner."

"What're you going to tell the tai-pan after dinner?"

"Depends on his questions. He'll know it's good strategy to probe enemy defenses."

Casey had begun to wonder who's the enemy, feeling very alien even here among all the other ladies. She had felt only hostility except from these two, Penelope and Kathren Gavallan—and a woman she had met earlier in the line for the toilet.

"Hello," the woman had said softly. "I hear you're a stranger here too."

"Yes, yes I am," Casey had said, awed by her beauty.

"I'm Fleur Marlowe. Peter Marlowe's my husband. He's a writer. I think you look super!"

"Thanks. So do you. Have you just arrived too?"

"No. We've been here for three months and two days but this is the first really English party we've been to," Fleur said, her English not as clipped as the others. "Most of the time we're with Chinese or by ourselves. We've a flat in the Old V and A annex. God," she added, looking at the toilet door ahead. "I wish she'd hurry up—my back teeth are floating."

"We're staying at the V and A too."

"Yes, I know. You two are rather famous." Fleur Marlowe laughed.

"Infamous! I didn't know they had apartments there."

"They're not, really. Just two tiny bedrooms and a sitting room. The kitchen's a cupboard. Still, it's home. We've got a bath, running water, and the loos flush." Fleur Marlowe had big gray eyes that tilted pleasingly and long fair hair and Casey thought she was about her age.

"Your husband's a journalist?"

"Author. Just one book. He mostly writes and directs films in Hollywood. That's what pays the rent."

"Why're you with Chinese?"

"Oh, Peter's interested in them." Fleur Marlowe had smiled and whispered conspiratorially, looking around at the rest of the women, "They're rather overpowering aren't they—more English than the English. The old school tie and all that balls."

Casey frowned. "But you're English too."

"Yes and no. I'm English but I come from Vancouver, B.C. We live in the States, Peter and I and the kids, in good old Hollywood, California. I really don't know what I am, half of one, half of the other."

"We live in L.A. too, Linc and I."

"I think he's smashing. You're lucky."

"How old are your kids?"

"Four and eight—thank God we're not water rationed yet."

"How do you like Hong Kong?"

"It's fascinating, Casey. Peter's researching a book here so it's marvelous for him. My God, if half the legends are true . . . the Struans and Dunrosses and all the others, and your Quillan Gornt."

"He's not mine. I just met him this evening."

"You created a minor earthquake by walking across the room with him." Fleur laughed. "If you're going to stay here, talk to Peter, he'll fill you in on all sorts of scandals." She nodded at Dianne Chen who was powdering her nose at one of the mirrors. "That's John Chen's step-mother, Phillip Chen's wife. She's wife number two—his first wife died. She's Eurasian and hated by almost everyone, but she's one of the kindest persons I've ever known."

"Why's she hated?"

"They're jealous, most of them. After all, she's wife of the compradore of the Noble House. We met her early on and she was terrific to me. It's . . . it's difficult living in Hong Kong for a woman, particularly an out-sider. Don't really know why but she treated me like family. She's been grand."

"She's Eurasian? She looks Chinese."

"Sometimes it's hard to tell. Her maiden name's T'Chung, so Peter says, her mother's Sung. The T'Chungs come from one of Dirk Struan's mistresses and the Sung line's equally illegitimate from the famous painter, Aristotle Quance. Have you heard of him?"

"Oh yes."

"Lots of, er, our best Hong Kong families are, well, old Aristotle spawned four branches . . ."

At that moment the toilet door opened and a woman came out and Fleur said, "Thank God!"

While Casey was waiting her turn she had listened to the conversations of the others with half an ear. It was always the same: clothes, the heat, the water shortages, complaints about *amahs* and other servants, how expensive everything was or the children or schools. Then it was her turn and afterward, when she came out, Fleur Marlowe had vanished and Penelope had come up to her. "Oh I just heard about your not wanting to leave. Don't pay any attention to Joanna," Penelope had said quietly. "She's a pill and always has been."

"It was my fault—I'm not used to your customs yet."

"It's all very silly but in the long run it's much easier to let the men have their way. Personally I'm glad to leave. I must say I find most of their conversation boring."

"Yes, it is, sometimes. But it's the principle. We should be treated as equals."

"We'll never be equal, dear. Not here. This is the Crown Colony of Hong Kong."

"That's what everyone tells me. How long are we expected to stay away?"

"Oh, half an hour or so. There's no set time. Have you known Quillan Gornt long?"

"Tonight was the first time I'd met him," Casey said.

"He's—he's not welcome in this house," Penelope said.

"Yes, I know. I was told about the Christmas party."

"What were you told?"

She related what she knew.

There was a sharp silence. Then Penelope said, "It's not good for strangers to be involved in family squabbles, is it?"

"No." Casey added, "But then all families squabble. We're here, Linc and I, to start a business—we're hoping to start a business with one of your big companies. We're outsiders here, we know that—that's why we're looking for a partner."

"Well, dear, I'm sure you'll make up your mind. Be patient and be cautious. Don't you agree, Kathren?" she asked her sister-in-law.

"Yes, Penelope. Yes I do." Kathren looked at Casey with the same level gaze that Dunross·had. "I hope you choose correctly, Casey. Everyone here's pretty vengeful."

"Why?"

"One reason's because we're such a closely knit society, very interrelated, and everyone knows everyone else—and almost all their secrets. Another's because hatreds here go back generations and have been nurtured for generations. When you hate you hate with all your heart. Another's because this is a piratical society with very few curbs so you can get away with all sorts of vengeances. Oh yes. Another's because here the stakes are high—if you make a pile of gold you can keep it legally even if it's made outside the law. Hong Kong's a place of transit—no one ever comes here to stay, even Chinese, just to make money and leave. It's the most different place on earth."

"But the Struans and Dunrosses and Gornts have been here for generations," Casey said.

"Yes, but individually they came here for one reason only: money. Money's our god here. And as soon as you have it, you vanish, European, American—and certainly the Chinese."

"You exaggerate, Kathy dear," Penelope said.

"Yes. It's still the truth. Another reason's that we live on the edge of catastrophe all the time: fire, flood, plague, landslide, riots. Half our population is Communist, half Nationalist, and they hate each other in a way no European can ever understand. And China—China can swallow us any moment. So you live for today and to hell with everything, grab what you can because tomorrow, who knows? Don't get in the way! People are rougher here because everything really is precarious, and nothing lasts in Hong Kong."

"Except the Peak," Penelope said. "And the Chinese."

"Even the Chinese want to get rich quickly to get out quickly—them more than most. You wait, Casey, you'll see. Hong Kong will work its magic on you—or evil, depending how you see it. For business it's the most exciting place on earth and soon you'll feel you're at the center of the earth. It's wild and exciting for a man, my God, it's marvelous for a man but for us it's awful and every woman, every wife, hates Hong Kong with a passion however much they pretend otherwise."

"Come on, Kathren," Penelope began, "again you exaggerate."

"No. No I don't. We're all threatened here, Penn, you know it! We women fight a losing battle . . ." Kathren stopped and forced a weary smile. "Sorry, I was getting quite worked up. Penn, I think I'll find Andrew and if he wants to stay I'll slip off if you don't mind."

"Are you feeling all right, Kathy?"

"Oh yes, just tired. The young one's a bit of a trial but next year he'll be off to boarding school."

"How was your checkup?"

"Fine." Kathy smiled wearily at Casey. "When you've the inclination give me a call. I'm in the book. Don't choose Gornt. That'd be fatal. 'Bye, darling," she added to Penelope and left.

"She's such a dear," Penelope said. "But she does work herself into a tizzy."

"Do you feel threatened?"

"I'm very content with my children and my husband."

"She asked whether you feel threatened, Penelope." Susanne deVille deftly powdered her nose and studied her reflection. "Do you?"

"No. I'm overwhelmed at times. But . . . but I'm not threatened any more than you are."

"Ah, *chérie,* but I am Parisienne, how can I be threatened? You've been to Paris, m'selle?"

"Yes," Casey said. "It's beautiful."

"It is the world," Susanne said with Gallic modesty. "Ugh, I look at least thirty-six."

"Nonsense, Susanne." Penelope glanced at her watch. "I think we can start going back now. Excuse me a second. . . ."

Susanne watched her go then turned her attention back to Casey. "Jacques and I came out to Hong Kong in 1946."

"You're family too?"

"Jacques's father married a Dunross in the First World War—an aunt of the tai-pan's." She leaned forward to the mirror and touched a fleck of powder away. "In Struan's it is important to be family."

Casey saw the shrewd Gallic eyes watching her in the mirror. "Of course, I agree with you that it is nonsense for the ladies to leave after dinner, for clearly, when we have gone, the heat she has left too, no?"

Casey smiled. "I think so. Why did Kathren say 'threatened'? Threatened by what?"

"By youth, of course by youth! Here there are tens of thousands of chic, sensible, lovely young *Chinoise* with long black hair and pretty, saucy *derrières* and golden skins who really understand men and treat sex for what it is: food, and often, barter. It is the gauche English puritan who has twisted the minds of their ladies, poor creatures. Thank God I was born French! Poor Kathy!"

"Oh," Casey said, understanding at once. "She's found out that Andrew's having an affair?"

Susanne smiled and did not answer, just stared at her reflection. Then she said, "My Jacques . . . of course he has affairs, of course all the men have affairs, and so do we if we're sensible. But we French, we understand that such transgressions should not interfere with a good marriage. We put correctly the amount of importance on to it, *non?*" Her dark brown eyes changed a little. *"Oui!"*

"That's tough, isn't it? Tough for a woman to live with?"

"Everything is tough for a woman, *chérie,* because men are such *cretins.*" Susanne deVille smoothed a crease away then touched perfume behind her ears and between her breasts. "You will fail here if you try to play the game according to masculine rules and not according to *feminine* rules. You have a rare chance here, mademoiselle, if you are woman enough. And if you remember that the Gornts are all poisonous. Watch your Linc Bartlett, Ciranoush, already there are ladies here who would like to possess him, and humble you."

14

Upstairs on the second floor the man came cautiously out of the shadows of the long balcony and slipped through the open French windows into the deeper darkness of Dunross's study. He hesitated, listening, his black clothes making him almost invisible. The distant sounds of the party drifted into the room making the silence and the waiting more heavy. He switched on a small flashlight.

The circle of light fell on the picture over the mantelpiece. He went closer. Dirk Struan seemed to be watching him, the slight smile taunting. Now the light moved to the edges of the frame. His hand reached out delicately and he tried it, first one side and then the other. Silently the picture moved away from the wall.

The man sighed.

He peered at the lock closely then took out a small bunch of skeleton keys. He selected one and tried it but it would not turn. Another. Another failure. Another and another, then there was a slight click and the key almost turned, almost but not quite. The rest of the keys failed too.

Irritably he tried the almost-key again but it would not work the lock.

Expertly his fingers traced the edges of the safe but he could find no secret catch or switch. Again he tried the almost-key, this way and that, gently or firmly, but it would not turn.

Again he hesitated. After a moment he pushed the painting carefully back into place, the eyes mocking him now, and went to the desk. There were two phones on it. He picked up the phone that he knew had no other extensions within the house and dialed.

The ringing tone went on monotonously, then stopped. "Yes?" a man's voice said in English.

"Mr. Lop-sing please," he said softly, beginning the code.

"There's no Lop-*ting* here. Sorry, you have a wrong number."

This code response was what he wanted to hear. He continued, "I want to leave a message."

"Sorry, you have a wrong number. Look in your phone book."

Again the correct response, the final one. "This is Lim," he whispered, using his cover name. "Arthur please. Urgent."

"Just a moment."

He heard the phone being passed and the dry cough he recognized at once. "Yes, Lim? Did you find the safe?"

"Yes," he said. "It's behind the painting over the fireplace but none of the keys fit. I'll need special equip—" He stopped suddenly. Voices were approaching. He hung up gently. A quick, nervous check that everything was in place and he switched off the flashlight and hurried for the balcony that ran the length of the north face. The moonlight illuminated him for an instant. It was Wine Waiter Feng. Then he vanished, his black waiter's clothes melding perfectly with the darkness.

The door opened. Dunross came in followed by Brian Kwok. He switched on the lights. At once the room became warm and friendly. "We won't be disturbed here," he said. "Make yourself at home."

"Thanks." This was the first time Brian Kwok had been invited upstairs.

Both men were carrying brandy snifters and they went over to the cool of the windows, the slight breeze moving the gossamer curtains, and sat in the high-backed easy chairs facing one another. Brian Kwok was looking at the painting, its own light perfectly placed. "Smashing portrait."

"Yes." Dunross glanced over and froze. The painting was imperceptibly out of place. No one else would have noticed it.

"Something's the matter, Ian?"

"No. No nothing," Dunross said, recovering his senses that had instinctively reached out, probing the room for an alien presence. Now he turned his full attention back to the Chinese superintendent, but he wondered deeply who had touched the painting and why. "What's on your mind?"

"Two things. First, your freighter, *Eastern Cloud*."

Dunross was startled. "Oh?" This was one of Struan's many coastal tramps that plied the trade routes of Asia. *Eastern Cloud* was a ten thousand tonner on the highly lucrative Hong Kong, Bangkok, Singapore, Calcutta, Madras, Bombay route, with a sometimes stop at Rangoon in Burma —all manner of Hong Kong manufactured goods outward bound, and all manner of Indian, Malayan, Thai and Burmese raw materials, silks, gems, teak, jute, foodstuffs, inbound. Six months ago she had been impounded by Indian authorities in Calcutta after a sudden customs search had discovered 36,000 taels of smugglers' gold in one of the bunkers. A little over one ton.

"The gold's one thing, your Excellency, that's nothing to do with us," Dunross had said to the consul general of India in Hong Kong, "but to impound our ship's something else!"

"Ah, very so sorry, Mr. Dunross sah. The law is the law and the smuggling of gold into India very serious indeed sah and the law says any ship with smuggled goods aboard may be impounded and sold."

"Yes, *may* be. Perhaps, Excellency, in this instance you could prevail on the authorities . . ." But all of his entreaties had been shuttled aside and attempted high-level intercessions over the months, here, in India, even in London, had not helped. Indian and Hong Kong police inquiries had produced no evidence against any member of his crew but, even so, *Eastern Cloud* was still tied up in Calcutta harbor.

"What about *Eastern Cloud?*" he asked.

"We think we can persuade the Indian authorities to let her go."

"In return for what?" Dunross asked suspiciously.

Brian Kwok laughed. "Nothing. We don't know who the smugglers are, but we know who did the informing."

"Who?"

"Seven odd months ago you changed your crewing policy. Up to that time Struan's had used exclusively Cantonese crew on their ships, then, for some reason you decided to employ Shanghainese. Right?"

"Yes." Dunross remembered that Tsu-yan, also Shanghainese, had suggested it, saying that it would do Struan's a lot of good to extend help to some of their northern refugees. "After all, tai-pan, they're just as good mariners," Tsu-yan had said, "and their wages are very competitive."

"So Struan's signed on a Shanghainese crew into *Eastern Cloud*—this was the first I believe—and the Cantonese crew that wasn't hired lost all face so they complained to their triad Red Rod leader wh—"

"Come off it for God's sake, our crews aren't triads!"

"I've said many times the Chinese are great joiners, Ian. All right, let's call the triad with Red Rod rank their union representative—though I know you don't have unions either—but this bugger said in no uncertain terms, *oh ko* we really have lost face because of those northern louts, I'll fix the bastards, and he tipped an Indian informer here who, for a large part of the reward, agreed of course in advance, and passed on the info to the Indian consulate."

"What?"

Brian Kwok beamed. "Yes. The reward was split twenty-eighty between the Indian and the Cantonese crew of the *Eastern Cloud* that should have been—Cantonese face was regained and the despised Shanghainese northern trash put into a stinking Indian pokey and their face lost instead."

"Oh Christ!"

"Yes."

"You have proof?"

"Oh yes! But let's just say that our Indian friend is helping us with future inquiries, in return for, er, services rendered, so we'd prefer not to name him. Your 'union shop steward'? Ah, one of his names was Big Mouth Tuk and he was a stoker on *Eastern Cloud* for three odd years. *Was* because, alas, we won't see him again. We caught him in full 14K regalia last week—in very senior Red Rod regalia—courtesy of a friendly Shanghainese informer, the brother of one of your crew that languished in said stinky Indian pokey."

"He's been deported?"

"Oh yes, quick as a wink. We really don't approve of triads. They are criminal gangs nowadays and into all sorts of vile occupations. He was off to Taiwan where I believe he won't be welcome at all—seeing as how the northern Shanghainese Green Pang triad society and the southern Cantonese 14K triad society are still fighting for control of Hong Kong. Big Mouth Tuk was a 426 all right—"

"What's a 426?"

"Oh, thought you might know. All officials of triads are known by numbers as well as symbolic titles—the numbers always divisible by the mystical number three. A leader's a 489, which also adds up to twenty-one, which adds up to three, and twenty-one's also a multiple of three, representing creation, times seven, death, signifying rebirth. A second rank's a White Fan, 438, a Red Rod's a 426. The lowest's a 49."

"That's not divisible by three, for God's sake!"

"Yes. But four times nine is thirty-six, the number of the secret blood oaths." Brian Kwok shrugged. "You know how potty we Chinese are over numbers and numerology. He was a Red Rod, a 426, Ian. We caught him. So triads exist, or existed, on one of your ships at least. Didn't they?"

"So it seems." Dunross was cursing himself for not prethinking that of course Shanghainese and Cantonese face would be involved so of course there'd be trouble. And now he knew he was in another trap. Now he had seven ships with Shanghainese crews against fifty-odd Cantonese.

"Christ, I can't fire the Shanghainese crews I've already hired and if I don't there'll be more of the same and loss of face on both sides. What's the solution to that one?" he asked.

"Assign certain routes exclusively to the Shanghainese, but only after consulting with their 426 Red Rod . . . sorry, with their shop stewards, and of course their Cantonese counterparts—*only* after consulting with a well-known soothsayer who suggested to you it would be fantastic joss to both sides to do this. How about Old Blind Tung?"

"Old Blind Tung?" Dunross laughed. "Perfect! Brian you're a genius! One good turn deserves another. For your ears only?"

"All right."

"Guaranteed?"

"Yes."

"Buy Struan's first thing tomorrow morning."

"How many shares?"

"As many as you can afford."

"How long do I hold them?"

"How are your *cojones*?"

Brian whistled tonelessly. "Thanks." He thought a moment, then forced his mind once more onto the matters in hand. "Back to *Eastern Cloud.* Now we come to one of the interesting bits, Ian. 36,000 taels of gold is legally worth $1,514,520 U.S. But melted down into the smugglers' five-tael bars and secretly delivered on shore in Calcutta, that shipment'd be worth two, perhaps three times that amount to private buyers—say 4.5 million U.S., right?"

"I don't know. Exactly."

"Oh, but I do. The lost profit's over 3 million—the lost investment about one and a half."

"So?"

"So we all know Shanghainese are as secretive and cliquey as Cantonese, or Chu Chow or Fukenese or any other tiny groupings of Chinese. So of course the Shanghainese crew were the smugglers—have to be, Ian, though we can't prove it, yet. So you can bet your bottom dollar that Shanghainese also smuggled the gold out of Macao to Hong Kong and onto *Eastern Cloud,* that Shanghainese money bought the gold originally in Macao, and that therefore certainly part of that money was Green Pang funds."

"That doesn't follow."

"Have you heard from Tsu-yan yet?"

Dunross watched him. "No. Have you?"

"Not yet but we're making inquiries." Brian watched him back. "My first point is that the Green Pang has been mauled and criminals loathe losing their hard-earned money, so Struan's can expect lots of trouble unless you nip the trouble in the bud as I've suggested."

"Not all Green Pang are criminals."

"That's a matter of opinion, Ian. Second point, for your ear only: We're sure Tsu-yan's in the gold-smuggling racket. My third and last point is that if a certain company doesn't want its ships impounded for smuggling gold, it could easily lessen the risk by reducing its gold imports into Macao."

"Come again?" Dunross said, pleasantly surprised to hear that he had managed to keep his voice sounding calm, wondering how much Special Intelligence knew and how much they were guessing.

Brian Kwok sighed and continued to lay out the information that Roger Crosse had given him. "Nelson Trading."

With a great effort, Dunross kept his face impassive. "Nelson Trading?"

"Yes. Nelson Trading Company Limited of London. As you know, Nelson Trading has the Hong Kong Government's exclusive license for the purchase of gold bullion on the international market for Hong Kong's jewelers, and, vastly more important, the equally exclusive monopoly for transshipment of gold bullion *in bond,* through Hong Kong to Macao—along with a minor second company, Saul Feinheimer Bullion Company, also of London. Nelson Trading and Feinheimer's have several things in common. Several directors for example, the same solicitors for example."

"Oh?"

"Yes. I believe you're also on the board."

"I'm on the board of almost seventy companies," Dunross said.

"True and not all of those are wholly or even partially owned by Struan's. Of course, some could be wholly owned through nominees, secretly, couldn't they?"

"Yes, of course."

"It's fortunate in Hong Kong we don't have to list directors—or holdings, isn't it?"

"What's your point, Brian?"

"Another coincidence: Nelson Trading's registered head offices in the city of London are in the same building as your British subsidiary, Struan London Limited."

"That's a big building, Brian, one of the best locations in the city. There must be a hundred companies there."

"Many thousands if you include all the companies registered with solicitors there—all the holding companies that hold other companies with nominee directors that hide all sorts of skeletons."

"So?" Dunross was thinking quite clearly now, pondering where Brian had got all this information, wondering too where in the hell all this was leading. Nelson Trading had been a secret, wholly owned subsidiary through nominees ever since it was formed in 1953 specifically for the Macao gold trade—Macao being the only country in Asia where gold importation was legal.

"By the way, Ian, have you met that Portuguese genius from Macao, Signore Lando Mata?"

"Yes. Yes I have. Charming man."

"Yes he is—and so well connected. The rumor is that some fifteen years ago he persuaded the Macao authorities to create a monopoly for the importation of gold, then to sell the monopoly to him, and a couple of friends, for a modest yearly tax: about one U.S. dollar an ounce. He's the same fellow, Ian, who first got the Macao authorities to legalize gambling . . . and curiously, to grant him and a couple of friends the same monopoly. All very cosy, what?"

Dunross did not answer, just stared back at the smile and at the eyes that did not smile.

"So everything went smoothly for a few years," Brian continued, "then in '54 he was approached by some Hong Kong gold enthusiasts—our Hong Kong gold law was changed in '54—who offered a now legal improvement on the scheme: their company buys the gold bullion legally in the world bullion markets on behalf of this Macao syndicate at the legal $35 an ounce and brings it to Hong Kong openly by plane or by ship. On arrival, our own Hong Kong customs fellows legally guard and supervise the transshipment from Kai Tak or the dock to the Macao ferry or the Catalina flying boat. When the ferry or flying boat arrives in Macao it's met by

Portuguese Customs officials and the bullion, all in regulation four-hundred-ounce bars, is transshipped under guard to cars, taxis actually, and taken to the bank. It's a grotty, ugly little building that does no ordinary banking, has no known customers—except the syndicate—never opens its door—except for the gold—and doesn't like visitors at all. Guess who owns it? Mr. Mata and his syndicate. Once inside their bank the gold vanishes!" Brian Kwok beamed like a magician doing his greatest trick. "Fifty-three tons this year so far. Forty-eight tons last year! Same the year before and the year before that and so on."

"That's a lot of gold," Dunross said helpfully.

"Yes it is. Very strangely the Macao authorities or the Hong Kong ones don't seem to care that what goes in never seems to come out. You with me still?"

"Yes."

"Of course, what really happens is that once inside the bank the gold's melted down from the regulation four-hundred-ounce bars into little pieces, into two, or the more usual five-tael bars which are much more easily carried, and smuggled. Now we come to the only illegal part of the whole marvelous chain: getting the gold out of Macao and smuggling it into Hong Kong. Of course, it's not illegal to remove it from Macao, only to smuggle it into Hong Kong. But you know and I know that it's relatively easy to smuggle anything into Hong Kong. And the incredible beauty of it all is that once in Hong Kong, *however the gold gets there*—it's perfectly legal for *anyone* to own it and no questions asked. Unlike say in the States or Britain where no citizen is ever allowed to own any gold bullion privately. Once legally owned, it can be legally exported."

"Where's all this leading to, Brian?" Dunross sipped his brandy.

Brian Kwok swilled the ancient, aromatic spirit in the huge glass and let the silence gather. At length he said, "We'd like some help."

"We? You mean Special Intelligence?" Dunross was startled.

"Yes."

"Who in SI? You?"

Brian Kwok hesitated. "Mr. Crosse himself."

"What help?"

"He'd like to read all your Alan Medford Grant reports."

"Come again?" Dunross said to give himself time to think, not expecting this at all.

Brian Kwok took out a photocopy of the first and last page of the intercepted report and offered it. "A copy of this has just come into our possession." Dunross glanced at the pages. Clearly they were genuine. "We'd like a quick look at all the others."

"I don't follow you."

"I didn't bring the whole report, just for convenience, but if you want it you can have it tomorrow," Brian said and his eyes didn't waver. "We'd appreciate it—Mr. Crosse said he'd appreciate the help."

The enormity of the implications of the request paralyzed Dunross for a moment.

"This report—and the others if they still exist—are private," he heard himself say carefully. "At least all the information in them is private to me personally, and to the Government. Surely you can get everything you want through your own intelligence channels."

"Yes. Meanwhile, Superintendent Crosse'd really appreciate it, Ian, if you'd let us have a quick look."

Dunross took a sip of his brandy, his mind in shock. He knew he could easily deny that the others existed and burn them or hide them or just leave them where they were, but he did not wish to avoid helping Special Intelligence. It was his duty to assist them. Special Intelligence was a vital part of Special Branch and the Colony's security and he was convinced that, without them, the Colony and their whole position in Asia would be untenable. And without a marvelous counterintelligence, if a twentieth of AMG's reports were true, all their days were numbered.

Christ Jesus, in the wrong hands . . .

His chest felt tight as he tried to reason out his dilemma. Part of that last report had leapt into his mind: about the traitor in the police. Then he remembered that Kiernan had told him that his back copies were the only ones in existence. How much was private to him and how much was known to British Intelligence? Why the secrecy? Why didn't Grant get permission? Christ, say I was wrong about some things being farfetched! In the wrong hands, in enemy hands, much of the information would be lethal.

With an effort he calmed his mind and concentrated. "I'll consider what you said and talk to you tomorrow. First thing."

"Sorry, Ian. I was told to in—to impress upon you the urgency."

"Were you going to say *insist?*"

"Yes. Sorry. We wish to ask for your assistance. This is a formal request for your cooperation."

"And *Eastern Cloud* and Nelson Trading are barter?"

"*Eastern Cloud*'s a gift. The information was also a gift. Nelson Trading is no concern of ours, except for passing interest. Everything said was confidential. To my knowledge, we have no records."

Dunross studied his friend, the high cheekbones and wide, heavy-lidded eyes, straight and unblinking, the face good-looking and well proportioned with thick black eyebrows.

"Did you read this report, Brian?"

"Yes."

"Then you'll understand my dilemma," he said, testing him.

"Ah, you mean the bit about a police traitor?"

"What was that?"

"You're right to be cautious. Yes, very correct. You're referring to the bit about a hostile being possibly at superintendent level?"

"Yes. Do you know who he is?"

"No. Not yet."

"Do you suspect anyone?"

"Yes. He's under surveillance now. There's no need to worry about that, Ian, the back copies'll just be seen by me and Mr. Crosse. They'll have top classification never mind."

"Just a moment, Brian—I haven't said they exist," Dunross told him, pretending irritation, and at once he noticed a flash in the eyes that could have been anger or could have been disappointment. The face had remained impassive. "Put yourself in my position, a layman," he said, his senses fine-honed, continuing the same line, "I'd be pretty bloody foolish to keep such info around, wouldn't I? Much wiser to destroy it—once the pertinent bits have been acted on. Wouldn't I?"

"Yes."

"Let's leave it at that for tonight. Until say ten in the morning."

Brian Kwok hesitated. Then his face hardened. "We're not playing parlor games, Ian. It's not for a few tons of gold, or some stock market shenanigans or a few gray area deals with the PRC however many millions're involved. This game's deadly and the millions involved are people and unborn generations and the Communist plague. Sevrin's bad news. The KGB's very bad news—and even our friends in the CIA and KMT can be equally vicious if need be. You'd better put a heavy guard on your files here tonight."

Dunross stared at his friend impassively. "Then your official position is that this report's accurate?"

"Crosse thinks it could be. Might be wise for us to have a man here just in case, don't you think?"

"Please yourself, Brian."

"Should we put a man out at Shek-O?"

"Please yourself, Brian."

"You're not being very cooperative, are you?"

"You're wrong, old chum. I'm taking your points very seriously," Dunross said sharply. "When did you get the copy and how?"

Brian Kwok hesitated. "I don't know, and if I knew I don't know if I should tell you."

Dunross got up. "Come on then, let's go and find Crosse."

"But why do the Gornts and the Rothwells hate the Struans and Dunrosses so much, Peter?" Casey asked. She and Bartlett were strolling the beautiful gardens in the cool of the evening with Peter Marlowe and his wife, Fleur.

"I don't know all the reasons yet," the Englishman said. He was a tall man of thirty-nine with fair hair, a patrician accent and a strange intensity behind his blue-gray eyes. "The rumor is that it goes back to the Brocks—

that there's some connection, some family connection between the Gornt family and the Brock family. Perhaps to old Tyler Brock himself. You've heard of him?"

"Sure," Bartlett said. "How did it start, the feud?"

"When Dirk Struan was a boy he'd been an apprentice seaman on one of Tyler Brock's armed merchantmen. Life at sea was pretty brutal then, life anywhere really, but my God in those days at sea . . . Anyway, Tyler Brock flogged young Struan unmercifully for an imagined slight, then left him for dead somewhere on the China coast. Dirk Struan was fourteen then, and he swore before God and the devil that when he was a man he'd smash the House of Brock and Sons and come after Tyler with a cat-o'-nine-tails. As far as I know he never did though there's a story he beat Tyler's eldest son to death with a Chinese fighting iron."

"What's that?" Casey asked uneasily.

"It's like a mace, Casey, three or four short links of iron with a spiked ball on one end and a handle on the other."

"He killed him for revenge on his father?" she said, shocked.

"That's another bit I don't know yet, but I'll bet he had a good reason." Peter Marlowe smiled strangely. "Dirk Struan, old Tyler and all the other men who made the British Empire, conquered India, opened up China. Christ, they were giants! Did I mention Tyler was one-eyed? One of his eyes was torn out by a whipping halyard in a storm in the 1830's when he was racing his three-masted clipper, the *White Witch*, after Struan with a full cargo of opium aboard. Struan was a day ahead in his clipper, *China Cloud*, in the race from the British opium fields of India to the markets of China. They say Tyler just poured brandy into the socket and cursed his sailors aloft to put on more canvas." Peter Marlowe hesitated, then he continued, "Dirk was killed in a typhoon in Happy Valley in 1841 and Tyler died penniless, bankrupt, in '63."

"Why penniless, Peter?" Casey asked.

"The legend is that Tess, his eldest daughter—Hag Struan to be—had plotted her father's downfall for years—you know she married Culum, Dirk's only son? Well, Hag Struan secretly plotted with the Victoria Bank, which Tyler had started in the 1840's and with Cooper-Tillman, Tyler's partners in the States. They trapped him and brought down the great House of Brock and Sons in one gigantic crash. He lost everything—his shipping line, opium hulks, property, warehouses, stocks, everything. He was wiped out."

"What happened to him?"

"I don't know, no one does for certain, but the story is that that same night, October thirty-first, 1863, old Tyler went to Aberdeen—that's a harbor on the other side of Hong Kong—with his grandson, Tom, who was then twenty-five, and six sailors, and they pirated an oceangoing lorcha—that's a ship with a Chinese hull but European rigged—and put out to sea. He was mad with rage, so they say, and he hauled up the Brock pennant to the masthead and he had pistols in his belt and a bloody cutlass in his hand—they'd killed four men to pirate the ship. At the neck of the harbor a cutter came after him and he blew it out of the water—in those days almost all boats were armed with cannon because of pirates—these seas have always been infected with pirates since time immemorial. So old Tyler put to sea, a good wind blowing from the east and a storm coming. At the mouth of Aberdeen he started bellowing out curses. He cursed Hag Struan and cursed the island, and cursed the Victoria Bank that had betrayed him, and the Coopers of Cooper-Tillman, but most of all he cursed the tai-pan who'd been dead more than twenty years. And old Tyler Brock swore revenge. They say he screamed out that he was going north to plunder and he was going to start again. He was going to build his House again and then, '. . . and then I be back by God . . . I be back and I be venged and then I be Noble House by God. . . . I be back. . . .'"

Bartlett and Casey felt a chill go down their backs as Peter Marlowe coarsened his voice. Then he continued, "Tyler went north and was never heard of again, no trace of him or the lorcha or his crew, ever. Even so, his presence is still here—like Dirk Struan's. You'd better remember, in any dealing with the Noble House you've got to deal with those two as well, or their ghosts. The night Ian Dunross took over as tai-pan, Struan's lost their freighter flagship, Lasting Cloud, in a typhoon. It was a gigantic financial disaster. She foundered off Formosa—Taiwan—and was lost with all hands except one seaman, a young English deckhand. He'd been on the bridge and he swore that they'd been lured onto the rocks by false lights and that he heard a maniac laughing as they went down."

Casey shivered involuntarily.

Bartlett noticed it and slipped his arm casually through hers and she smiled at him.

He said, "Peter, people here talk about people who've been dead a hundred years as though they're in the next room."

"Old Chinese habit," Peter Marlowe replied at once. "Chinese believe the past controls the future and explains the present. Of course Hong Kong's only a hundred and twenty years old so a man of eighty today'd . . . Take Phillip Chen, the present compradore, for example. He's sixty-five now—his grandfather was the famous Sir Gordon Chen, Dirk Struan's illegitimate son who died in 1907 at the age of eighty-six. So Phillip Chen would have been nine then. A sharp boy of nine'd remember all sorts of stories his revered grandfather would have told him about his father, the tai-pan, and May-may, his famous mistress. The story is that old Sir Gordon Chen was one hell of a character, truly an ancestor. He had two official wives, eight concubines of various ages, and left the sprawling Chen family rich, powerful and into everything. Ask Dunross to show you his portraits—I've only seen copies but, my, he was a handsome man. There're dozens of people alive here today who knew him—one of the original great founders. And my God, Hag Struan died only forty-six years ago. Look over there. . . ." He nodded at a wizened little man, thin as a bamboo and just as strong, talking volubly to a young woman. "That's Vincent McGore, tai-pan of the fifth great *hong*, International Asian Trading. He worked for Sir Gordon for years and then the Noble House." He grinned suddenly. "Legend says he was Hag Struan's lover when he was eighteen and just off the cattle boat from some Middle Eastern port—he's not really Scots at all."

"Come off it, Peter," Fleur said. "You just made that up!"

"Do you mind," he said, but his grin never left him. "She was only seventy-five at the time."

They all laughed.

"That's the truth?" Casey asked. "For real?"

"Who knows what's truth and what's fiction, Casey? That's what I was told."

"I don't believe it," Fleur said confidently. "Peter makes up stories."

"Where'd you find out all this, Peter?" Bartlett asked.

"I read some of it. There are copies of newspapers that go back to 1870 in the Law Court library. Then there's the *History of the Law Courts of Hong Kong*. It's as seamy a great book as you'll ever want if you're interested in Hong Kong. Christ, the things they used to get up to, so-called judges and colonial secretaries, governors and policemen, and the tai-pans, the highborn and the lowborn. Graft, murder, corruption, adultery, piracy, bribery . . . it's all there!

"And I asked questions. There are dozens of old China hands who love to reminisce about the old days and who know a huge amount about Asia and Shanghai. Then there are lots of people who hate, or are jealous and can't wait to pour a little poison on a good reputation or a bad one. Of course, you sift, you try to sift the true from the false and that's very hard, if not impossible."

For a moment Casey was lost in thought. Then she said, "Peter, what was Changi like? Really like?"

His face did not change but his eyes did. "Changi was genesis, the place of beginning again." His tone made them all chilled and she saw Fleur slip her hand into his and in a moment he came back. "I'm fine, darling," he said. Silently, somewhat embarrassed, they walked out of the path onto the lower terrace, Casey knowing she had intruded. "We should have a drink. Eh, Casey?" Peter Marlowe said kindly and made it all right again.

"Yes. Thank you, Peter."

"Linc," Peter Marlowe said, "there's a marvelous strain of violence that passes from generation to generation in these buccaneers—because that's what they are. This is a very special place—it breeds very special people." After a pause, he added thoughtfully, "I understand you may be going into business here. If I were you I'd be very, very careful."

15

Dunross, with Brian Kwok in tow, was heading for Roger Crosse, chief of Special Intelligence, who was on the terrace chatting amiably with Armstrong and the three Americans, Ed Langan, Commander John Mishauer the uniformed naval officer, and Stanley Rosemont, a tall man in his fifties. Dunross did not know that Langan was FBI, or that Mishauer was U.S. Naval Intelligence, only that they were at the consulate. But he did know that Rosemont was CIA though not his seniority. Ladies were still drifting back to their tables, or chattering away on the terraces and in the garden. Men were lounging over drinks, and the party was mellow like the night. Some couples were dancing in the ballroom to sweet and slow music. Adryon was among them, and he saw Penelope stoically coping with Havergill. He noticed Casey and Bartlett in deep conversation with Peter and Fleur Marlowe, and he would have dearly loved to be overhearing what was being said. That fellow Marlowe could easily become a bloody nuisance, he thought in passing. He knows too many secrets already and if he was to read our book . . . No way, he thought. Not till hell freezes! That's one book he'll never read. How Alastair could be so stupid!

Some years ago Alastair Struan had commissioned a well-known writer to write the history of Struan's to celebrate their 125 years of trading and had passed over old ledgers and trunks of old papers to him unread and unsifted. Within the year the writer had produced an inflammatory tapestry that documented many happenings and transactions that were thought to have been buried forever. In shock they had thanked the writer and paid him off with a handsome bonus and the book, the only two copies, put in the tai-pan's safe.

Dunross had considered destroying them. But then, he thought, life is life, joss is joss and providing only we read them, there's no harm.

"Hello, Roger," he said, grimly amused. "Can we join you?"

"Of course, tai-pan." Crosse greeted him warmly, as did the others. "Make yourself at home."

The Americans smiled politely at the joke. They chatted for a moment about inconsequential things and Saturday's races and then Langan, Rosemont and Commander Mishauer, sensing that the others wanted to converse privately, politely excused themselves. When they were alone, Brian Kwok summarized exactly what Dunross had told him.

"We will certainly appreciate your help, Ian," Crosse said, his pale eyes penetrating. "Brian's right about it possibly being quite dicey—if of course AMG's other reports exist. Even if they don't, some nasties might want to investigate."

"Just exactly how and when did you get the copy of my latest one?"

"Why?"

"Did you get it yourselves—or from a third party?"

"Why?"

Dunross's voice hardened. "Because it's important."

"Why?"

The tai-pan stared at him and the three men felt the power of his personality. But Crosse was equally willful.

"I can partially answer your question, Ian," he said coolly. "If I do, will you answer mine?"

"Yes."

"We acquired a copy of your report this morning. An intelligence agent —I presume in England—tipped a friendly amateur here that a courier was en route to you with something that'd interest us. This Hong Kong contact asked us if we'd be interested in having a look at it—for a fee of course." Crosse was so convincing that the other two policemen who remembered the real story were doubly impressed. "This morning, the photocopy was delivered to my home by a Chinese I'd never met before. He was paid—of course you understand in these things you don't ask for a name. Now, why?"

"When this morning?"

"At 6:04 if you want an exact time. But why is this important to you?"

"Because Alan Medford Gr—"

"Oh, Father, sorry to interrupt," Adryon said, rushing up breathlessly, a tall, good-looking young man in tow, his crumpled sacklike dinner jacket and twisted tie and scruffy brown-black shoes out of place in all this elegance. "Sorry to interrupt but can I do something about the music?"

Dunross was looking at the young man. He knew Martin Haply and his reputation. The English-trained Canadian journalist was twenty-five, and had been in the Colony for two years and was now the scourge of the business community. His biting sarcasm and penetrating exposés of personalities and of business practices that were legitimate in Hong Kong but nowhere else in the Western world were a constant irritation.

"The music, Father," Adryon repeated, running on, "it's ghastly. Mother said I had to ask you. Can I tell them to play something different, please?"

"All right, but don't turn my party into a happening."

She laughed and he turned his attention back to Martin Haply. "Evening."

"Evening, tai-pan," the young man said with a confident, challenging grin. "Adryon invited me. I hope it was all right to come after dinner?"

"Of course. Have fun," Dunross said, and he added dryly, "There are a lot of your friends here."

Haply laughed. "I missed dinner because I was on the scent of a dilly."

"Oh?"

"Yes. Seems that certain interests in conjunction with a certain great bank have been spreading nasty rumors about a certain Chinese bank's solvency."

"You mean the Ho-Pak?"

"It's all nonsense though. The rumors. Just more Hong Kong shenanigans."

"Oh?" All day Dunross had heard rumors about Richard Kwang's Ho-Pak Bank being overextended. "Are you sure?"

"Have a column on it in tomorrow's *Guardian.* Talking about the Ho-Pak though," Martin Haply added breezily, "did you hear that upwards of a hundred people took all their money out of the Aberdeen branch this afternoon? Could be the beginning of a run and—"

"Sorry, Father . . . come on Martin, can't you see Father's busy." She leaned up and kissed Dunross lightly and his hand automatically went around her and hugged her.

"Have fun, darling." He watched her rush off, Haply following. Cocky son of a bitch, Dunross thought absently, wanting tomorrow's column now, knowing Haply to be painstaking, unbribable and very good at his job. Could Richard be overextended?

"You were saying, Ian? Alan Medford Grant?" broke into his thoughts.

"Oh, sorry, yes." Dunross sat back at the table, compartmentalizing those problems. "AMG's dead," he said quietly.

The three policemen gaped at him. "What?"

"I got a cable at one minute to eight this evening, and talked to his assistant in London at 9:11." Dunross watched them. "I wanted to know your 'when' because it's obvious there'd be plenty of time for your KGB spy—if he exists—to have called London and had poor old AMG murdered. Wouldn't there?"

"Yes." Crosse's face was solemn. "What time did he die?"

Dunross told them the whole of his conversation with Kiernan but he withheld the part about the call to Switzerland. Some intuition warned him not to tell. "Now, the question is: was it accident, coincidence or murder?"

"I don't know," Crosse said. "But I don't believe in coincidences."

"Nor do I."

"Christ," Armstrong said through his teeth, "if AMG hadn't had clearance . . . Christ only knows what's in those reports, Christ and you, Ian. If you've got the only existing copies this makes them potentially more explosive than ever."

"If they exist," Dunross said.

"Do they?"

"I'll tell you tomorrow. At 10 o'clock." Dunross got up. "Will you excuse me, please," he said politely with his easy charm. "I must see to my other guests now. Oh, one last thing. What about *Eastern Cloud?*"

Roger Crosse said, "She'll be released tomorrow."

"One way or the other?"

Crosse appeared shocked. "Good Lord, tai-pan, we weren't bartering! Brian, didn't you say we were just trying to help out?"

"Yes sir."

"Friends should always help out friends, shouldn't they, tai-pan?"

"Yes. Absolutely. Thank you."

They watched him walk away until he was lost.

"Do they or don't they?" Brian Kwok muttered.

"Exist? I'd say yes," Armstrong said.

"Of course they exist," Crosse said irritably. "But where?" He thought a moment, then added more irritably and both men's hearts skipped a beat, "Brian, while you were with Ian, Wine Waiter Feng told me none of his keys would fit."

"Oh, that's bad, sir," Brian Kwok said cautiously.

"Yes. The safe here won't be easy."

Armstrong said, "Perhaps we should look at Shek-O, sir, just in case."

"Would you keep such documents there—if they exist?"

"I don't know, sir. Dunross's unpredictable. I'd say they were in his penthouse at Struan's, that'd be the safest place."

"Have you been there?"

"No sir."

"Brian?"

"No sir."

"Neither have I." Crosse shook his head. "Bloody nuisance!"

Brian Kwok said thoughtfully, "We'd only be able to send in a team at night, sir. There's a private lift to that floor but you need a special key. Also there's supposed to be another lift from the garage basement, nonstop."

"There's been one hell of a slipup in London," Crosse said. "I can't understand why those bloody fools weren't on the job. Nor why AMG didn't ask for clearance."

"Perhaps he didn't want insiders to know he was dealing with an outsider."

"If there was one outsider, there could have been others." Crosse sighed, and, lost in thought, lit a cigarette. Armstrong felt the smoke hunger pangs. He took a swallow of his brandy but that did not ease the ache.

"Did Langan pass on his copy, sir?"

"Yes, to Rosemont here and in the diplomatic bag to his FBI HQ in Washington."

"Christ," Brian Kwok said sourly, "then it'll be all over Hong Kong by morning."

"Rosemont assured me it would not." Crosse's smile was humorless. "However, we'd better be prepared."

"Perhaps Ian'd be more cooperative if he knew, sir."

"No, much better to keep that to ourselves. He's up to something though."

Armstrong said, "What about getting Superintendent Foxwell to talk to him, sir, they're old friends."

"If Brian couldn't persuade him, no one can."

"The governor, sir?"

Crosse shook his head. "No reason to involve him. Brian, you take care of Shek-O."

"Find and open his safe, sir?"

"No. Just take a team out there and make sure no one else moves in. Robert, go to HQ, get on to London. Call Pensely at MI-5 and Sinders at MI-6. Find out exact times on AMG, everything you can, check the tai-pan's story. Check everything—perhaps other copies exist. Next, send back a team of three agents here to watch this place tonight, particularly to guard Dunross, without his knowledge of course. I'll meet the senior man at the junction of Peak Road and Culum's Way in an hour, that'll give you enough time. Send another team to watch Struan's building. Put one man in the garage—just in case. Leave me your car, Robert. I'll see you in my office in an hour and a half. Off you both go."

The two men sought out their host and made their apologies and gave their thanks and went to Brian Kwok's car. Going down Peak Road in the old Porsche, Armstrong said what they both had been thinking ever since Dunross had told them. "If Crosse's the spy he'd have had plenty of time to phone London, or to pass the word to Sevrin, the KGB or who the hell ever."

"Yes."

"We left his office at 6:10—that'd be 11:00 A.M. London time—so it couldn't've been us, not enough time." Armstrong shifted to ease the ache in his back. "Shit, I'd like a cigarette."

"There's a packet in the glove compartment, old chum."

"Tomorrow—I'll smoke tomorrow. Just like AA, like a bloody addict!" Armstrong laughed but there was no humor in it. He glanced across at his friend. "Find out quietly who else's read the AMG file today—apart from Crosse—quick as you can."

"My thought too."

"If he's the only one who read it . . . well, it's another piece of evidence. It's not proof but we'd be getting there." He stifled a nervous yawn, feeling very tired. "If it's him we really are up shit's creek."

Brian was driving very fast and very well. "Did he say when he gave the copy to Langan?"

"Yes. At noon. They had lunch."

"The leak could be from them, from the consulate—that place's like a sieve."

"It's possible but my nose says no. Rosemont's all right, Brian—and Langan. They're professionals."

"I don't trust them."

"You don't trust anyone. They've both asked their HQs to check the Bartlett and Casey Moscow frankings."

"Good. I think I'll send a telex to a friend in Ottawa. They might have something on file on them also. That Casey's a bird amongst birds, isn't she though? Was she wearing anything underneath that sheath?"

"Ten dollars to a penny you never find out."

"Done."

As they turned a corner, Armstrong looked at the city below and the harbor, the American cruiser lit all over tied up at the dockyard, Hong Kong side. "In the old days we'd have had half a dozen warships here of our own," he said sadly. "Good old Royal Navy!" He had been in destroyers during the war, lieutenant R.N. Sunk twice, once at Dunkirk, the second time on D Day plus three, off Cherbourg.

"Yes. Pity about the Navy, but, well, time marches on."

"Not for the better, Brian. Pity the whole bloody Empire's up the spout! It was better when it wasn't. The whole bloody world was better off! Bloody war! Bloody Germans, bloody Japs . . ."

"Yes. Talking about Navy, how was Mishauer?"

"The U.S. Naval Intelligence fellow? He was okay," Armstrong said wearily. "He talked a lot of shop. He whispered to the Old Man that the U.S.'re going to double their Seventh Fleet. It's so supersecret he didn't even want to trust the phone. There's going to be a big land expansion in Vietnam."

"Bloody fools—they'll get chewed up like the French. Don't they read the papers, let alone intelligence reports?"

"Mishauer whispered also their nuclear carrier's coming in the day after tomorrow for an eight-day R and R visit. Another top secret. He asked us to double up on security—and wet-nurse all Yankees ashore."

"More bloody trouble."

"Yes." Armstrong added thinly, "Particularly as the Old Man mentioned a Soviet freighter 'limped in' for repairs on the evening tide."

"Oh Christ!" Brian corrected an involuntary swerve.

"That's what I thought. Mishauer almost had a coronary and Rosemont swore for two minutes flat. The Old Man assured them of course none of the Russian seamen'll be allowed ashore without special permission, as usual, and we'll tail them all, as usual, but a couple'll manage to need a doctor or whatever, suddenly, and mayhaps escape the net."

"Yes." After a pause Brian Kwok said, "I hope we get those AMG files, Robert. Sevrin is a knife in the guts of China."

"Yes."

They drove in silence awhile.

"We're losing our war, aren't we?" Armstrong said.

"Yes."

16

The Soviet freighter, *Sovetsky Ivanov*, was tied up alongside in the vast Wampoa Dockyard that was built on reclaimed land on the eastern side of Kowloon. Floodlights washed her. She was a twenty-thousand tonner that plied the Asian trade routes out of Vladivostok, far to the north. Atop her bridge were many aerials and modern radar equipment. Russian seamen lounged at the foot of the fore and the aft gangways. Nearby, a uniformed policeman, a youthful Chinese, in neat regulation khaki drills, short pants, high socks, black belt and shoes, was at each gangway. A shore-going seaman had his pass checked by his shipmates and then by the constable, and then, as he walked toward the dockyard gates, two Chinese in civilian clothes came out of the shadows and began to dog his footsteps—openly.

Another seaman went down the aft gangway. He was checked through and then, soon, more silent Chinese plainclothes police began to follow him.

Unnoticed, a rowing boat eased silently from the blind side of the ship's stern and ducked into the shadows of the wharf. It slid quietly along the high wall toward a flight of dank sea steps half a hundred yards away. There were two men in the boat and the rowlocks were muffled. At the foot of the sea steps the boat stopped. Both men began listening intently.

At the forward gangway a third seaman going ashore reeled raucously down the slippery steps. At the foot he was intercepted and his pass checked and an argument began. He was refused permission by the shore guard and he was clearly drunk, so, cursing loudly, he let fly at one of them, but this man sidestepped and gave him a haymaker which was returned in kind. Both policemen's attention zeroed on the one-sided brawl. The tousled, thickset man who sat in the aft of the rowing boat ran up the sea steps, across the floodlit wharf and railway tracks, and vanished into the alleyways of the dockyard without being seen. Leisurely the rowing boat began to return the way it had come, and in a moment, the brawl ceased. The helpless drunk was carried back aboard, not unkindly.

Deep in the dockyard's byways, the tousled man sauntered now. From time to time, casually and expertly, he glanced behind to ensure he was not being followed. He wore dark tropicals and neat rubber-soled shoes. His ship's papers documented him as Igor Voranski, seaman first class, Soviet Merchant Marine.

He avoided the dock gates and the policeman who watched them and followed the wall for a hundred yards or so to a side door. The door opened onto an alley in the Tai-wan Shan resettlement area—a maze of corrugated iron, plywood and cardboard hovels. His pace quickened. Soon he was out of the area and into brightly lighted streets of shops and stalls and crowds that eventually led him to Chatham Road. There he hailed a taxi.

"Mong Kok, quick as you can," he said in English. "Yaumati Ferry."

The driver stared at him insolently. "Eh?"

"*Ayeeyah!*" Voranski replied at once and added in harsh, perfect Cantonese, "Mong Kok! Are you deaf! Have you been sniffing the White Powder? Do you take me for a foreign devil tourist from the Golden Mountain—me who is clearly a Hong Kong person who has lived here twenty years? *Ayeeyah!* Yaumati Ferry on the other side of Kowloon. Do you need directions? Are you from Outer Mongolia? Are you a stranger, eh?"

The driver sullenly pulled the flag down and sped off, heading south and then west. The man in the back of the car watched the street behind. He could see no trailing car but he still did not relax.

They're too clever here, he thought. Be cautious!

At Yaumati Ferry station he paid off the taxi and gave the man barely the correct tip then went into the crowds and slid out of them and hailed another taxi. "Golden Ferry."

The driver nodded sleepily, yawned and headed south.

At the ferry terminal he paid off the driver almost before he had stopped and joined the crowds that were hurrying for the turnstiles of the Hong Kong ferries. But once through the turnstiles he did not go to the ferry gate but instead went to the men's room and then, out once more, he opened the door of a phone booth and went in. Very sure now that he had not been followed he was more relaxed.

He put in a coin and dialed.

"Yes?" a man's voice answered in English.

"Mr. Lop-sing please."

"I don't know that name. There's no Mr. Lop-*ting* here. You have a wrong number."

"I want to leave a message."

"Sorry you have a wrong number. Look in your phone book!"

Voranski relaxed, his heart slowing a little. "I want to speak to Arthur," he said, his English perfect.

"Sorry, he's not here yet."

"He was told to be there, to wait my call," he said curtly. "Why is there a change?"

"Who is this please?"

"Brown," he snapped, using his cover name.

He was somewhat mollified as he heard the other voice instantly take on just deference. "Ah, Mr. Brown, welcome back to Hong Kong. Arthur's phoned to tell me to expect your call. He asked me to welcome you and to say everything's prepared for the meeting tomorrow."

"When do you expect him?"

"Any moment, sir."

Voranski cursed silently for he was obliged to report back to the ship by phone within the hour. He did not like divergences in any plan.

"Very well," he said. "Tell him to call me at 32." This was the code name for their safe apartment in Sinclair Towers. "Has the American arrived yet?"

"Yes."

"Good. He was accompanied?"

"Yes."

"Good. And?"

"Arthur told me nothing more."

"Have you met her yet?"

"No."

"Has Arthur?"

"I don't know."

"Has contact been made yet with either of them?"

"Sorry, I don't know. Arthur didn't tell me."

"And the tai-pan? What about him?"

"Everything's arranged."

"Good. How long would it take you to get to 32, if necessary?"

"Ten to fifteen minutes. Did you want us to meet you there?"

"I'll decide that later."

"Oh Mr. Brown, Arthur thought you might like a little company after such a voyage. Her name's Koh, Maureen Koh."

"That was thoughtful of him—very thoughtful."

"Her phone number's beside the phone at 32. Just ring and she'll arrive within half an hour. Arthur wanted to know if your superior was with you tonight—if he'd need companionship also."

"No. He'll join us as planned tomorrow. But tomorrow evening he will expect hospitality. Good night." Voranski hung up arrogantly, conscious of his KGB seniority. At that instant the booth door swung open and the Chinese barged in and another blocked the outside. "What the—"

The words died as he did. The stiletto was long and thin. It came out easily. The Chinese let the body fall. He stared down at the inert heap for a moment then cleaned the knife on the corpse and slid it back into its sheath in his sleeve. He grinned at the heavyset Chinese who still blocked the glass windows in the upper part of the booth as though he was the next customer, then put a coin in and dialed.

On the third ring a polite voice said, "Tsim Sha Tsui Police Station, good evening."

The man smiled sardonically and said rudely in Shanghainese, "You speak Shanghainese?"

A hesitation, a click, and now another voice in Shanghainese said, "This is Divisional Sergeant Tang-po. What is it, caller?"

"A Soviet pig slipped through your mother-fornicating net tonight as easily as a bullock shits, but now he's joined his ancestors. Do we of the 14K have to do all your manure-infected work for you?"

"What Sovie—"

"Hold your mouth and listen! His turtle-dung corpse's in a phone booth at Golden Ferry, Kowloonside. Just tell your mother-fornicating superiors to keep their eyes on enemies of China and not up their fornicating stink holes!"

At once he hung up and eased out of the box. He turned back momentarily and spat on the body, then shut the door and he and his companion joined the streams of passengers heading for the Hong Kong ferry.

They did not notice the man trailing them. He was a short, tubby American dressed like all the other tourists with the inevitable camera around his neck. Now he was leaning against the starboard gunnel melding into the crowd perfectly, pointing his camera this way and that as the ferry skuttled toward Hong Kong Island. But unlike other tourists his film was very special, so was his lens, and his camera.

"Hello, friend," another tourist said with a beam, wandering up to him. "You having yourself a time?"

"Sure," the man said. "Hong Kong's a great place, huh?"

"You can say that again." He turned and looked at the view. "Beats the hell outta Minneapolis."

The first man turned also but kept his peripheral vision locked onto the two Chinese, then dropped his voice. "We got problems."

The other tourist blanched. "Did we lose him? He didn't double back, Tom, I'm certain. I covered both exits. I thought you had him pegged in the booth."

"You bet your ass he was pegged. Look back there, center row—the Chinese joker with the white shirt and the one next to him. Those two sons of bitches knocked him off."

"Jesus!" Marty Povitz, one of the team of CIA agents assigned to cover the *Sovetsky Ivanov*, carefully looked at the two Chinese. "Kuomintang? Nationalists? Or Commies?"

"Shit, I don't know. But the stiff's still in a phone booth back there. Where's Rosemont?"

"He's g—" Povitz stopped then raised his voice and became affable and tourist again as passengers began to crowd nearer the exit. "Lookit there," he said, pointing to the crest of the Peak. The apartment buildings were tall and well lit and so were the houses that dotted the slopes, one particularly, one very high, the highest private mansion in Hong Kong. It was floodlit and sparkled like a jewel. "Say, whoever lives there's just about on top of the world, huh?"

Tom Connochie, the senior of the two, sighed. "Gotta be a tai-pan's house." Thoughtfully he lit a cigarette and let the match spiral into the black waters. Then, openly chatting tourist-style, he took a shot of the house and casually finished the roll of film, taking several more of the two Chinese. He reloaded his camera and, unobserved, passed the roll of exposed film to his partner. Hardly using his lips, he said, "Call Rosemont up there, soon as we dock—tell him we got problems—then go get these processed tonight. I'll phone you when these two've bedded down."

"You crazy?" Povitz said. "You're not tailing them alone."

"Have to, Marty, the film might be important. We're not risking that."

"No."

"Goddamnit, Marty, I'm tai-pan of this operation."

"Orders says two g—"

"Screw orders!" Connochie hissed. "Just call Rosemont and don't foul up the film." Then he raised his voice and said breezily, "Great night for a sail, huh?"

"Sure."

He nodded at the sparkle of light on the crest of the Peak, then focused on it through his super-powered telescopic lens viewfinder. "You live up there, you got it made, huh?"

Dunross and Bartlett were facing each other in the Long Gallery at the head of the staircase. Alone.

"Have you made a deal with Gornt?" Dunross asked.

"No," Bartlett said. "Not yet." He was as crisp and tough as Dunross and his dinner jacket fitted as elegantly.

"Neither you nor Casey?" Dunross asked.

"No."

"But you have examined possibilities?"

"We're in business to make money, Ian—as are you!"

"Yes. But there're ethics involved."

"Hong Kong ethics?"

"May I ask how long you have been dealing with Gornt?"

"About six months. Are you agreeing to our proposal today?"

Dunross tried to put away his tiredness. He had not wanted to seek out Bartlett tonight but it had been necessary. He felt the eyes from all the portraits on the walls watching him. "You said Tuesday. I'll tell you Tuesday."

"Then until then, if I want to deal with Gornt or anyone else, that's my right. If you accept our offer now, it's a deal. I'm told you're the best, the Noble House, so I'd rather deal with you than him—providing I get top dollar with all the necessary safeguards. I'm cash heavy, you're not. You're Asian heavy, I'm not. So we should deal."

Yes, Bartlett told himself, covering his foreboding, though delighted that his diversion this morning with Gornt had produced the confrontation so quickly and brought his opponent to bay—at the moment, Ian, you're just that, an opponent, until we finalize, if we finalize.

Is now the time to blitzkrieg?

He had been studying Dunross all evening, fascinated by him and the undercurrents and everything about Hong Kong—so totally alien to anything he had ever experienced before. New jungle, new rules, new dangers. Sure, he thought grimly, with both Dunross and Gornt as dangerous as a swamp full of rattlers and no yardstick to judge them by. I've got to be cautious like never before.

He felt his tension strongly, conscious of the eyes that watched from the walls. How far dare I push you, Ian? How far do I gamble? The profit potential's huge, the prize huge, but one mistake and you'll eat us up, Casey and me. You're a man after my own heart but even so still an opponent and governed by ghosts. Oh yes, I think Peter Marlowe was right in that though not in everything.

Jesus! Ghosts and the extent of the hatreds! Dunross, Gornt, Penelope, young Struan, Adryon . . . Adryon so brave after her initial fright.

He looked back at the cold blue eyes watching him. What would I do now, Ian, if I were you, you with your wild-ass heritage standing there so outwardly confident?

I don't know. But I know me and I know what Sun Tzu said about battlefields: only bring your opponent to battle at a time and a place of your own choosing. Well it's chosen and it's here and now.

"Tell me, Ian, before we decide, how are you going to pay off your three September notes to Toda Shipping?"

Dunross was shocked. "I beg your pardon?"

"You haven't got a charterer yet and your bank won't pay without one, so it's up to you, isn't it?"

"The bank . . . there's no problem."

"But I understand you've already overextended your line of credit 20 percent. Doesn't that mean you'll have to find a new line of credit?"

"I'll have one if I need it," Dunross said, his voice edgy, and Bartlett knew he had gotten under his guard.

"12 million to Toda's a lot of cash when you add it to your other indebtedness."

"What other indebtedness?"

"The installment of $6,800,000 U.S. due September 8 on your Orlin International Banking loan of 30 million unsecured; you've 4.2 million in consolidated corporate losses so far this year against a written-up paper profit of seven and a half last year; and 12 million from the loss of *Eastern Cloud* and all those contraband engines."

The color was out of Dunross's face. "You seem to be particularly well informed."

"I am. Sun Tzu said that you've got to be well informed about your allies."

The small vein in Dunross's forehead was pulsating. "You mean enemies."

"Allies sometimes become enemies, Ian."

"Yes. Sun Tzu also hammered about spies. Your spy can only be one of seven men."

Bartlett replied as harshly, "Why should I have a spy? That information's available from banks—all you've got to do is dig a little. Toda's bank's the Yokohama National of Japan—and they're tied in with Orlin in a lot of deals—so're we, Stateside."

"Whoever your spy is, he's wrong. Orlin will extend. They always have."

"Don't bet on it this time. I know those bastards and if they smell a killing, they'll have your ass so fast you'll never know what happened."

"A killing of Struan's?" Dunross laughed sardonically. "There's no way Orlin or any god-cursed bank could—or would want us wrecked."

"Maybe Gornt's got a deal cooking with them."

"Christ Jesus. . . ." Dunross held on to his temper with an effort. "Has he or hasn't he?"

"Ask him."

"I will. Meanwhile if you know anything, tell me now!"

"You've got enemies every which way."

"So have you."

"Yes. Does that make us good or bad partners?" Bartlett stared back at Dunross. Then his eyes fell on a portrait at the far end of the gallery. Ian Dunross was staring down at him from the wall, the likeness marvelous, part of a three-masted clipper in the background.

"Is that . . . Jesus, that's gotta be Dirk, Dirk Struan!"

Dunross turned and looked at the painting. "Yes."

Bartlett walked over and studied it. Now that he looked closer he could see that the sea captain was not Dunross, but even so, there was a curious similarity. "Jacques was right," he said.

"No."

"He's right." He turned and studied Dunross as though the man was a picture, comparing them back and forth. At length he said, "It's the eyes and the line of the jaw. And the taunting look in the eyes which says, 'You'd better believe I can kick the shit out of you anytime I want to.'"

The mouth smiled at him. "Does it now?"

"Yes."

"There's no problem on a line of credit, new or old."

"I think there is."

"The Victoria's our bank—we're big stockholders."

"How big?"

"We've alternate sources of credit if need be. But we'll get everything we want from the Vic. They're cash heavy too."

"Your Richard Kwang doesn't think so."

Dunross looked back from the portrait sharply. "Why?"

"He didn't say, Ian. He didn't say anything, but Casey knows bankers and she read the bottom line and that's what she thinks he thinks. I don't think she's much taken by Havergill either."

After a pause, Dunross said, "What else does she think?"

"That maybe we should go with Gornt."

"Be my guest."

"I may. What about Taipei?" Bartlett asked, wanting to keep Dunross off balance.

"What about it?"

"I'm still invited?"

"Yes, yes of course. That reminds me, you're released into my custody by kind permission of the assistant commissioner of police. Armstrong will be so informed tomorrow. You'll have to sign a piece of paper that you guarantee you'll return when I do."

"Thanks for arranging it. Casey is still not invited?"

"I thought we settled that this morning."

"Just asking. What about my airplane?"

Dunross frowned, off balance. "I suppose it's still impounded. Did you want to use it for the Taipei trip?"

"It'd be convenient, wouldn't it, then we could leave to suit ourselves."

"I'll see what I can do." Dunross watched him. "And your offer's firm until Tuesday?"

"Firm, just as Casey said. Until close of business Tuesday."

"Midnight Tuesday," Dunross countered.

"Do you always barter whatever the hell someone says?"

"Don't you?"

"Okay, midnight Tuesday. Then one minute into Wednesday all debts and friendships are canceled." Bartlett needed to keep the pressure on Dunross, needed the counteroffer now and not Tuesday so he could use it with or against Gornt. "The guy from Blacs, the chairman, what was his name?"

"Compton Southerby."

"Yes, Southerby. I was talking to him after dinner. He said they were all the way in back of Gornt. He implied Gornt also has a lot of Eurodollars on call if he ever needed them." Again Bartlett saw the piece of information slam home. "So I still don't know how you're going to pay Toda Shipping," he said.

Dunross didn't answer at once. He was still trying to find a way out of the maze. Each time he came back to the beginning: the spy must be Gavallan, deVille, Linbar Struan, Phillip Chen, Alastair Struan, David MacStruan, or his father, Colin Dunross. Some of Bartlett's information the banks would know—but not their corporate losses this year. That figure had been too accurate. That was the shocker. And the ". . . written-up paper profit."

He was looking at the American, wondering how much more inside knowledge the man had, feeling the trap closing on him with no way to maneuver, yet knowing he could not concede too much or he would lose everything.

What to do?

He glanced at Dirk Struan on the wall and saw the twisted half-smile and the look that said to him, Gamble laddie, where are thy balls?

Very well.

"Don't worry about Struan's. If you decide to join us, I want a two-year deal—20 million next year too," he said, going for broke. "I'd like 7 on signing the contract."

Bartlett kept the joy off his face. "Okay on the two-year deal. As to the cash flow, Casey offered 2 million down and then one and a half per month on the first of each month. Gavallan said that would be acceptable."

"It's not. I'd like 7 down, the rest spread monthly."

"If I agree to that I want title to your new Toda ships as a guarantee this year."

"What the hell do you want guarantees for?" Dunross snapped. "The whole point of the deal is that we'd be partners, partners in an immense expansion into Asia."

"Yes. But our 7 million cash covers your September payments to Toda Shipping, takes you off the Orlin hook and we get nothing in return."

"Why should I give you any concession? I can discount your contract immediately and get an advance of 18 of the 20 million you provide with no trouble at all."

Yes, you can, Bartlett thought—once the contract's signed. But before that you've got nothing. "I'll agree to change the down payment, Ian. But in return for what?" Casually he glanced at a painting opposite him, but he did not see it for all of his senses were concentrating on Dunross, knowing they were getting down to the short strokes. Title to the huge Toda bulk-cargo ships would cover all of Par-Con's risk whatever Dunross did.

"Don't forget," he added, "your 21 percent of the Victoria Bank stock is already in hock, signed over as collateral against your indebtedness to them. If you fail on the Toda payment or the Orlin, your old pal Havergill'll jerk the floor out. I would."

Dunross knew he was beaten. If Bartlett knew the exact amount of their secret bank holdings, Chen's secret holdings, together with their open holdings, there was no telling what other power the American had over him. "All right," he said. "I'll give you title to my ships for three months, providing first, you guarantee to keep it secret between the two of us; second, that our contracts are signed within seven days from today; third, that you agree to the cash flow I've suggested. Last, you guarantee not to leak one word of this until I make the announcement."

"When do you want to do that?"

"Sometime between Friday and Monday."

"I'd want to know in advance," Bartlett said.

"Of course. Twenty-four hours."

"I want title to the ships for six months, contracts within ten days."

"No."

"Then no deal," Bartlett said.

"Very well," Dunross said immediately. "Then let's return to the party." He turned at once and calmly headed for the stairs.

Bartlett was startled with the abrupt ending of the negotiations. "Wait," he said, his heart skipping a beat.

Dunross stopped at the balustrade and faced him, one hand casually on the bannister.

Grimly Bartlett tried to gauge Dunross, his stomach twisting uneasily. He read finality in the eyes. "All right, title till January first, that's four months-odd, secret to you, me and Casey, contracts next Tuesday—that gives me time to get my tax people here—the cash flow as you laid it out subject to . . . when's our meeting tomorrow?"

"It was at ten. Can we make it eleven?"

"Sure. Then it's a deal, subject to confirmation tomorrow at eleven."

"No. You've no need for more time. I might have but you haven't." Again the thin smile. "Yes or no?"

Bartlett hesitated, all his instincts saying close now, stick out your hand and close, you've everything you wanted. Yes—but what about Casey? "This's Casey's deal. She can commit up to 20 million. You mind shaking with her?"

"A tai-pan deals with a tai-pan on a closing, it's an old Chinese custom. Is she tai-pan of Par-Con?"

"No," Bartlett said evenly. "I am."

"Good." Dunross came back and put out his hand, calling him, playing with him, reading his mind. "Then it's a deal?"

Bartlett looked at the hand then into the cold blue eyes, his heart pounding heavily. "It's a deal—but I want her to close it with you."

Dunross let his hand fall. "I repeat, who's tai-pan of Par-Con?"

Bartlett looked back levelly. "A promise is a promise, Ian. It's important to her, and I promised she had the ball up to 20 million."

He saw Dunross begin to turn away, so he said firmly, "Ian, if I have to choose between the deal and Casey, my promise to Casey, then that's no contest. None. I'd consider it a fav—" He stopped. Both their heads jerked around as there was a slight, involuntary noise from an eavesdropper in the shadows at the far end of the gallery where there was a group of high-backed settees and tall winged chairs. Instantly, Dunross spun on his heel and, catlike, hurtled silently to the attack. Bartlett's reactions were almost as fast. He, too, went quickly in support.

Dunross stopped at the green velvet settee. He sighed. It was no eaves-dropper but his thirteen-year-old daughter, Glenna, fast asleep, curled up, all legs and arms like a young filly, angelic in her crumpled party dress, his wife's thin rope of pearls around her neck.

Bartlett's heart slowed and he whispered, "Jesus, for a moment . . . Hey, she's as cute as a button!"

"Do you have any children?"

"Boy and two girls. Brett's sixteen, Jenny's fourteen and Mary is thir-teen. Unfortunately I don't see them very often." Bartlett, gaining his breath again, continued quietly, "They're on the East Coast now. Afraid I'm not very popular. Their mother . . . we, we were divorced seven years ago. She's remarried now but . . ." Bartlett shrugged, then looked down at the child. "She's a doll! You're lucky."

Dunross leaned over and gently picked up his child. She hardly stirred, just nestled closer to him, contentedly. He looked at the American thoughtfully. Then he said, "Bring Casey back here in ten minutes. I'll do what you ask—as much as I disapprove of it—because you wish to honor your promise." He walked away, surefooted, and disappeared into the east wing where Glenna's bedroom was.

After a pause, Bartlett glanced up at the portrait of Dirk Struan. The smile mocked him. "Go screw yourself," he muttered, feeling that Dunross had outsmarted him somehow. Then he grinned. "Eh, what the hell! Your boy's doing all right, Dirk old buddy!"

He went for the stairs. Then he noticed an unlit portrait in a half-hid-den alcove. He stopped. The oil painting was of an old gray-bearded sea captain with one eye, hook-nosed and arrogant, his face scarred, a cutlass on the table beside him.

Bartlett gasped as he saw that the canvas was slashed and coun-terslashed, with a short knife buried in the man's heart, impaling the painting to the wall.

Casey was staring at the knife. She tried to hide her shock. She was alone in the gallery, waiting uneasily. Dance music wafted up from below —rhythm and blues music. A short wind tugged the curtains and moved a strand of her hair. A mosquito droned.

"That's Tyler Brock."

Casey spun around, startled. Dunross was watching her. "Oh, I didn't hear you come back," she said.

"Sorry," he said. "I didn't mean to make you jump."

"Oh, that's all right."

She looked back at the painting. "Peter Marlowe was telling us about him."

"He knows a lot about Hong Kong, but not everything, and not all his information's accurate. Some of it's quite wrong."

After a moment she said, "It's . . . it's a bit melodramatic, isn't it, leaving the knife like that?"

"Hag Struan did it. She ordered it left that way."

"Why?"

"It pleased her. She was tai-pan."

"Seriously, why?"

"I was serious." Dunross shrugged. "She hated her father and wanted us all to be reminded about our heritage."

Casey frowned, then motioned at a portrait on the opposite wall. "That's her?"

"Yes. It was done just after she was married." The girl in the painting was slim, about seventeen, pale blue eyes, fair hair. She wore a low-cut ball gown—tiny waist, budding bosom—an ornate green necklace encircling her throat.

They stood there looking at the picture for a moment. There was no name on the little brass plaque on the bottom of the ornate gilt frame, just the years, 1825–1917. Casey said, "It's an ordinary face, pretty but ordinary, except for the lips. They're thin and tight and disapproving—and tough. The artist captured a lot of strength there. It's a Quance?"

"No. We don't know who painted it. It was supposed to be her favorite portrait. There's a Quance of her in the Struan penthouse, painted about the same time. It's quite different, yet very much the same."

"Did she ever have a portrait done in later life?"

"Three. She destroyed them all, the moment they were finished."

"Are there any photos of her?"

"Not to my knowledge. She hated cameras—wouldn't have one in the house." Dunross laughed and she saw the tiredness in him. "Once a reporter for the *China Guardian* took her picture, just before the Great War. Within an hour she sent an armed crew from one of our merchantmen into their offices with orders to burn the place if she didn't get the negative and all copies back, and if the editor didn't promise to 'cease and desist from harassing her.' He promised."

"Surely you can't do that and get away with it?"

"No, you can't—unless you're tai-pan of the Noble House. Besides, everyone knew that Hag Struan didn't want her picture taken and this cocky young bastard had broken the rule. She was like the Chinese. She believed every time your picture's taken you lose part of your soul."

Casey peered at the necklace. "Is that jade?" she asked.

"Emeralds."

She gasped. "That must have been worth a fortune."

"Dirk Struan willed the necklace to her—it was never to leave Asia—it was to belong to the wife of each tai-pan of the Noble House, an heirloom to be passed on from lady to lady." He smiled oddly. "Hag Struan kept the necklace all her life, and, when she died, she ordered it burned with her."

"Jesus! Was it?"

"Yes."

"What a waste!"

Dunross looked back at the portrait. "No," he said, his voice different. "She kept Struan's the Noble House of Asia for almost seventy-five years. She was *the* tai-pan, the real tai-pan, though others had the title. Hag Struan fought off enemies and catastrophes and kept faith with Dirk's legacy and smashed the Brocks and did whatever was necessary. So what's a pretty bauble that probably cost nothing in the first place? It was probably pirated from the treasury of some Mandarin who stole it from someone else, whose peasants paid for it with sweat."

Casey watched him staring at the face, almost past it into another dimension. "I only hope I can do as well," he muttered absently, and it seemed to Casey he was saying it to *her*, to the girl in the picture.

Her eyes strayed beyond Dunross to the portrait of Dirk Struan and she saw again the marvelous likeness. There was a strong family resemblance in all the ten large portraits—nine men and the girl—that hung on the walls amid landscapes of all sizes of Hong Kong and Shanghai and Tiensin and many seascapes of the elegant Struan clipper ships and some of their merchantmen. Below the portrait of each tai-pan was a small brass plaque with his name and the years of his life: "Dirk Dunross, 4th Tai-pan, 1852–1894, lost at sea in the India Ocean with all hands in *Sunset Cloud*" . . . "Sir Lochlin Struan, 3rd Tai-pan, 1841–1915" . . . "Alastair Struan, 9th Tai-pan, 1900–" . . . "Dirk Struan, 1798–1841" . . . "Ross Lechie Struan, 7th Tai-pan, 1887–1915, Captain Royal Scots Regiment, killed in action at Ypres" . . .

"So much history," she said, judging it time to break his thought pattern.

"Yes. Yes it is," he said, looking at her now.

"You're the 10th tai-pan?"

"Yes."

"Have you had your portrait done yet?"

"No."

"You'll have to, won't you?"

"Yes, yes in due course. There's no hurry."

"How do you become tai-pan, Ian?"

"You have to be chosen by the previous one. It's his decision."

"Have you chosen who'll follow you?"

"No," he said, but Casey thought that he had. Why should he tell me, she asked herself. And why are you asking him so many questions?

She looked away from him. A small portrait caught her attention. "Who's that?" she asked, disquieted. The man was misshapen, a hunchbacked dwarf, his eyes curious and his smile sardonic. "Was he a tai-pan too?"

"No. That's Stride Orlov, he was Dirk's chief captain. After *the tai-pan* was killed in the great typhoon and Culum took over, Stride Orlov became master of our clipper fleet. Legend has it he was a great seaman."

After a pause she said, "Sorry but there's something about him that gives me the creeps." There were pistols in Orlov's belt and a clipper ship in the background. "It's a frightening face," she said.

"He had that effect on everyone—except *the tai-pan* and Hag Struan—even Culum was supposed to have hated him." Dunross turned and studied her and she felt his probing. It made her feel warm and at the same time unsettled.

"Why did *she* like him?" she asked.

"The story is that right after the great typhoon when everyone in Hong Kong was picking up the pieces, Culum included, Devil Tyler started to take over the Noble House. He gave orders, assumed control, treated Culum and Tess like children . . . he sent Tess aboard his ship, the *White Witch*, and told Culum to be aboard by sunset or else. As far as Tyler was concerned the Noble House was now Brock-Struan and he was *the* tai-pan! Somehow or other—no one knows why or how Culum got the courage—my God, Culum was only twenty then and Tess barely sixteen—but Culum ordered Orlov to go aboard the *White Witch* and *fetch* his wife ashore. Orlov went alone, at once—Tyler was still ashore at the time. Orlov brought her back and in his wake left one man dead and another half a dozen with broken heads or limbs." Dunross was looking at her and she recognized the same half-mocking, half-violent, half-devilish smile that was on *the tai-pan*'s face. "Ever afterwards, Tess—Hag Struan to be—loved him, so they say. Orlov served our fleet well until he vanished. He was a fine man, and a great seaman, for all his ugliness."

"He vanished? He was lost at sea?"

"No. Hag Struan said he went ashore one day in Singapore and never returned. He was always threatening to leave and go home to Norway. So perhaps he went home. Perhaps he was knifed. Who knows, Asia's a violent place, though Hag Struan swore no man could kill Stride Orlov and that it must have been a woman. Perhaps Tyler ambushed him. Who knows?"

Inexorably her eyes went back to Tyler Brock. She was fascinated by the face and the implications of the knife. "Why did she do that to her father's image?"

"One day I'll tell you but not tonight, except to say that she hammered the knife into the wall with my grandfather's cricket bat and cursed before God and the devil anyone who took *her* knife out of *her* wall." He smiled at Casey and again she noticed an extraordinary tiredness in him and was glad because her own tiredness was creeping up on her and she did not want to make any mistakes now. He put out his hand. "We have to shake on a deal."

"No," Casey said calmly, glad to begin. "Sorry, I have to cancel out."

His smile evaporated. "What?"

"Yes. Linc told me the changes you want. It's a two-year deal—that ups our ante so I can't approve it."

"Oh?"

"No." She continued in the same flat but pleasant tone, "Sorry, 20 million's my limit so you'll have to close with Linc. He's waiting in the bar."

Understanding flashed over his face for an instant—and relief, she thought—and then he was calm again. "Is he now?" he said softly, watching her.

"Yes." She felt a wave of heat go through her, her cheeks began to burn and she wondered if the color showed.

"So we can't shake, you and I. It has to be Linc Bartlett?"

With an effort she kept her eyes unwavering. "A tai-pan should deal with a tai-pan."

"That's a basic rule, even in America?" His voice was soft and gentle. "Yes."

"Is this your idea or his?"

"Does it matter?"

"Very much."

"If I say it's Linc's, he loses face, and if I say it's mine, he still loses face, though in a different way."

Dunross shook his head slightly and smiled. The warmth of it increased her inner warmth. Although she was very much in charge of herself, she felt herself responding to his unadulterated masculinity.

"We're all bound by face, aren't we, in some way or another," he said.

She did not answer, just glanced away to give herself time. Her eyes saw the portrait of the girl. How could such a pretty girl become known as the *Hag*, she wondered. It must be hateful to become old in face and body when you're young at heart and still strong and tough—so unfair for a woman. Will I be known one day as Hag Tcholok? Or "that old dyke Tcholok" if I'm still alone, unmarried, in the business world, the man's world, still working for the same things they work for—identity, power and money—and hated for being as good or better than they are at it? I don't care so long as we win, Linc and I. So play the part you've chosen tonight, she told herself, and thank the French lady for her advice. "Remember, child," her father had drummed into her, "remember that advice, good advice, comes from unexpected places at unexpected times." Yes, Casey thought happily, but for Susanne's reminder about how a lady should operate in this man's world, Ian, perhaps I wouldn't have given you that face-saving formula. But don't be mistaken, Ian Struan Dunross. This is my deal, and in this I'm tai-pan of Par-Con.

Casey felt an untoward glow as another current went through her. Never before had she articulated her actual position in Par-Con to herself. Yes, she thought, very satisfied, that's what I am.

She looked at the girl in the portrait critically and she saw, now, how wrong she had been before and how very special the girl was. Wasn't she *the tai-pan*, in embryo, even then?

"You're very generous," Dunross said, breaking into her thoughts.

"No," she replied at once, prepared, and glanced back at him, and she was thinking, If you want the truth, tai-pan, I'm not generous at all. I'm merely being demure and sweet and gentle because it makes you feel more at home. But she said none of this to him, only dropped her eyes and murmured with the right amount of softness, "It's you who're generous."

He took her hand and bowed over it and kissed it with old-fashioned gallantry.

She was startled and tried to cover it. No one had ever done that to her before. In spite of her resolve she was moved.

"Ah Ciranoush," he said with mock gravity, "any time you need a champion, send for me." Then he grinned suddenly. "I'll probably make a bog of it but never mind."

She laughed, all tension gone now, liking him very much. "You've got yourself a deal."

Casually he put his arm around her waist and gently propelled her toward the stairs. The contact with him felt good—too good, she thought. This one's no child. Be cautious.

17

Phillip Chen's Rolls screeched to a halt in the driveway of his house. He got out of the backseat, flushed with rage, Dianne nervously in tow. The night was dark, the lights of the city and ships and high rises blazing far below. "Bolt the gates, then you come inside too," he snapped to his equally nervous chauffeur, then hurried for the front door.

"Hurry up, Dianne," he said, irritably shoving his key into the lock.

"Phillip, what on earth's the matter with you? Why can't you tell me? Wh—"

"Shut up!" he shouted, his temper snapping, and she jerked to a halt, shocked. "Just shut up and do what you're told!" He ripped the front door open. "Get the servants here!"

"But Phi—"

"*Ah Sun! Ah Tak!*"

The two tousled, sleepy *amahs* appeared hastily out of the kitchen and gaped at him, shocked at his untoward rage. "Yes Father? Yes Mother?" they chorused in Cantonese. "What in the name of all gods ha—"

"Hold your tongues!" Phillip Chen roared, his neck red and now his face more red. "Go into that room and stay there until I tell you all to come out!" He pulled the door open. It was their dining room and the windows faced the road north. "All of you stay there until I tell you to come out and if any of you moves or looks out of the windows before I come back I'll . . . I'll have some friends put weights on you and get you all thrown into the harbor!"

The two *amahs* began wailing but everyone hurriedly obeyed him and he slammed the door shut.

"Stop it both of you!" Dianne Chen screeched at the *amahs,* then reached over and pinched one sharply on the cheek. This stopped the old woman's wailing and she gasped, her eyes rolling, "What's got into everyone? What's got into Father? Oh oh oh, his rage's gone to Java . . . oh oh oh. . . ."

"Shut up, Ah Tak!" Dianne fanned herself, seething, beside herself with fury. What in the name of all gods *has* got into him? Doesn't he trust me—me, his only true wife and the love of his life? In all my life . . . And to rush off like that from the tai-pan's party when everything was going so fine—us the talk of Hong Kong and everyone admiring my darling Kevin, fawning on him, now surely the new heir of the House of Chen, for everyone agrees John Chen would certainly have died of shock when his ear was cut off. Anyone would! I certainly would.

She shivered, feeling her own ear being cut again and being kidnapped as in her dream this afternoon when she had awoken in a cold sweat from her nap.

"*Ayeeyah*," she muttered to no one in particular. "Has he gone mad?"

"Yes, Mother," her chauffeur said confidently, "I think he has. It's the result of the kidnapping. I've never seen Father like this in all my yea—"

"Who asked you?" Dianne shrieked. "It's all your fault anyway! If you'd brought my poor John home instead of leaving him to his mealy-mouthed whores this would never have happened!"

Again the two *amahs* began whimpering at her fury and she turned her spleen on them for a moment, adding, "And as to you two, while I think of it, the quality of service in this house's enough to give anyone loose bowels. Have you asked me if I need a physic or aspirins? Or tea? Or a cold towel?"

"Mother," one of them said placatingly, hopefully pointing at the lacquered sideboard, "I can't make tea but would you like some brandy?"

"*Wat?* Ah, very good. Yes, yes, Ah Tak."

At once the old woman bustled over to the sideboard and opened it, brought out some cognac that she knew her mistress liked, poured it into a glass. "Poor Mother, to have Father in such a rage! Terrible! What's possessed him and why doesn't he want us to look out of the window?"

Because he doesn't want you turtle-dung thieves to see him dig up his secret safe in the garden, Dianne was thinking. Or even me. She smiled grimly to herself, sipping the fine smooth liquor, calmer in the knowledge that she knew where the iron box was buried. It was only right that she should have protected him by secretly watching him bury it, in case, God forbid, the gods took him from this earth before he could tell her where the secret hiding place was. It had been her duty to break her promise not to watch him that night during the Japanese Occupation when he had wisely scooped up all their valuables and hidden them.

She did not know what was in the box now. She did not care. It had been opened and closed many times, all in secret, as far as he was concerned. She did not care so long as she knew where her husband was, where all his deposit boxes of various kinds were, their keys, just in case.

After all, she told herself confidently, if he dies, without me the House of Chen will crumble. "Stop sniveling, Ah Sun!" She got up and closed the long drapes. Outside the night was dark and she could see nothing of the garden, only the driveway, the tall iron gates and the road beyond.

"More drink, Mother?" the old *amah* asked.

"Thank you, little oily mouth," she replied affectionately, the warmth of the spirit soothing her anger away. "And then you can massage my neck. I've got a headache. You two sit down, hold your tongues and don't make a sound till Father gets back!"

Phillip Chen was hurrying down the garden path, a flashlight in one hand, a shovel in the other. The path curled downward through well-tended gardens that meandered into a grove of trees and shrubs. He stopped a moment, getting his bearings, then found the place he sought. He hesitated and glanced back, even though he knew he was well hidden from the house now. Reassured that he could not be watched he switched on the flashlight. The circle of light wandered over the undergrowth and stopped at the foot of a tree. The spot appeared to be untouched. Carefully he pushed aside the natural mulch. When he saw the earth below had been disturbed he cursed obscenely. "Oh the swine . . . my own son!" Collecting himself with difficulty he began to dig. The earth was soft.

Ever since he had left the party he had been trying to remember exactly when he had last dug up the box. Now he was sure it had been in the spring when he needed the deeds to a row of slum dwellings in Wanchai that he had sold for fifty times cost to Donald McBride for one of his great new developments.

"Where was John then?" he muttered. "Was he in the house?"

As he dug he tried to recall but he could not. He knew that he would never have dug up the box when it was dangerous or when there were strangers in the house and that he would always have been circumspect. But John? Never would I have thought . . . John must have followed me somehow.

The shovel struck the metal. Carefully he cleaned off the earth and pulled the protective cloth away from the box and heavy lock and opened it. The hinges of the lid were well greased. His fingers shaking, he held the flashlight over the open box. All his papers and deeds and private balance sheets seemed to be in order and undisturbed, but he knew they must all have been taken out and read—and copied or memorized. Some of the information in his son's safety deposit box could only have come from here.

All the jewel boxes, big and small, were there. Nervously he reached out for the one he sought and opened it. The half-coin had vanished and the document explaining about the coin had vanished.

Tears of rage seeped down his cheeks. He felt his heart pounding and

smelled the damp earth and knew if his son was there he would happily
have strangled him with his own hands.

"Oh my son my son . . . all gods curse you to hell!"

His knees were weak. Shakily he sat on a rock and tried to collect his
wits. He could hear his father on his deathbed cautioning him: "Never
lose the coin my son—it's our key to ultimate survival and power over the
Noble House."

That was in 1937 and the first time he had learned the innermost secrets of the House of Chen: that he who became compradore became the
ranking leader in Hong Kong of the Hung Mun—the great secret triad society of China that, under Sun Yat-sen had become the 14K, originally
formed to spearhead China's revolt against their hated Manchu overlords;
that the compradore was the main, legitimate link between the Chinese
hierarchy on the Island and the inheritors of the 14K on the Mainland;
that because of Chen-tse Jin Arn, known as Jin-qua, the legendary chief
merchant of the co-*hong* that had possessed the Emperor's monopoly on all
foreign trade, the House of Chen was perpetually interlinked with the
Noble House by ownership and by blood.

"Listen carefully, my son," the dying man had whispered. "The tai-pan,
Great-Grandfather Dirk Struan, was Jin-qua's creation, as was the Noble
House. Jin-qua nurtured it, formed it *and* Dirk Struan. The tai-pan had
two concubines. The first was Kai-sung, one of Jin-qua's daughters by a
fifth wife. Their son was Gordon Chen, my father, your grandfather. The
tai-pan's second concubine was T'Chung Jin May-may, his mistress for six
years whom he married in secret just before the great typhoon that killed
them both. She was twenty-three then, a brilliant, favored granddaughter
of Jin-qua, sold to the tai-pan when she was seventeen to teach him
civilized ways without his knowing he was being taught. From them came
Duncan and Kate who took the surname *T'Chung* and were brought up
in my father's house. Father married off Kate to a Shanghai China Trader
called Peter Gavallan—Andrew Gavallan is also a cousin though he
doesn't know it. . . . So many stories to tell and now so little time to tell
them. Never mind, all the family trees are in the safe. There are so many.
We're all related, the Wu, Kwang, Sung, Kau, Kwok, Ng—all the old
families. Use the knowledge carefully. Here's the key to the safe.

"Another secret, Phillip, my son. Our line comes from my father's second wife. Father married her when he was fifty-three and she sixteen. She
was the daughter of John Yuan, the illegitimate son of the great American
Trader Jeff Cooper, and a Eurasian lady, Isobel Yau. Isobel Yau was the
oh-so-secret Eurasian daughter of Robb Struan, the tai-pan's half-brother
and cofounder of the Noble House, so we have blood from both sides of
the Struans. Alastair Struan is a cousin and Colon Dunross is a cousin—
the MacStruans are not, their history's in Grandfather's diaries. My son,
the English and Scots barbarians came to China and they never married
those whom they adored and most times abandoned when they returned to

the gray island of mist and rain and overcast. My God how I hate the English weather and loathe the past!

"Yes, Phillip, we're Eurasian, not of one side or the other. I've never been able to come to terms with it. It is our curse and our cross but it is up to all of us to make it a blessing. I pass our House on to you rich and strong like Jin-qua wished—do so to your son and make sure he does it to his. Jin-qua birthed us, in a way, gave us wealth, secret knowledge, continuity and power—and he gave us one of the coins. Here, Phillip, read about the coin."

The calligraphy of the ancient scroll was exquisite: "On this eighth day of the sixth month of the year 1841 by barbarian count, I, Chen-tse Jin Arn of Canton, Chief Merchant of the co-*hong*, have this day loaned to Green-Eyed Devil the tai-pan of the Noble House, chief pirate of all foreign devils who have made war on the Heavenly Kingdom and have stolen our island Hong Kong, forty lacs of silver . . . one million sterling in their specie . . . and have, with this bullion, saved him from being swallowed by One-Eye, his archenemy and rival. In return, the tai-pan grants us special trade advantages for the next twenty years, promises that one of the House of Chen will forever be compradore to the Noble House, and swears that he or his descendents will honor all debts and the debt of the coins. There are four of them. The coins are broken into halves. I have given the tai-pan four halves. Whenever one of the other halves is presented to him, or to a following tai-pan, he has sworn whatever favor is asked will be granted . . . *whether within their law, or ours, or outside it.*

"One coin I keep; one I give to the warlord Wu Fang Choi, my cousin; one will be given to my grandson Gordon Chen; and the last recipient I keep secret. Remember, he who reads this in the future, do not use the coin lightly, for the tai-pan of the Noble House must grant anything—*but only once.* And remember that though the Green-Eyed Devil himself will honor his promise and so will his descendents, he is still a mad-dog barbarian, cunning as a filthy Manchu because of *our* training, and as dangerous always as a nest of vipers."

Phillip Chen shuddered involuntarily, remembering the violence that was always ready to explode in Ian Dunross. He's a descendent of Green-Eyed Devil all right, he thought. Yes, him and his father.

Goddamn John! What possessed him? What devilment has he planned with Linc Bartlett? Has Bartlett got the coin now? Or does John still have it with him and now perhaps the kidnappers have it.

While his tired brain swept over the possibilities, his fingers checked the jewel boxes, one by one. Nothing was missing. The big one he left till last. There was a tightness in his throat as he opened it but the necklace was still there. A great sigh of relief went through him. The beauty of the emeralds in the flashlight gave him enormous pleasure and took away some of his anxiety. How stupid of Hag Struan to order them to be burned with her body. What an arrogant, awful, unholy waste that would have been! How wise of Father to intercept the coffin before the fire and remove them.

Reluctantly he put the necklace away and began to close up the safe. What to do about the coin? I almost used it the time the tai-pan took away our bank stock—and most of our power. Yes. But I decided to give him time to prove himself and this is the third year and nothing is yet proved, and though the American deal seems grand it is not yet signed. And now the coin is gone.

He groaned aloud, distraught, his back aching like his head. Below was all the city, ships tied up at Glessing's Point and others in the roads. Kowloon was equally brilliant and he could see a jetliner taking off from Kai Tak, another turning to make a landing, another whining high overhead, its lights blinking.

What to do? he asked himself exhaustedly. Does Bartlett have the coin? Or John? Or the Werewolves?

In the wrong hands it could destroy us all.

TUESDAY

18

Gornt said, "Of course Dunross could have buggered my brakes, Jason!"

"Oh come on, for God's sake! Climbing under your car during a party with two hundred guests around? Ian's not that stupid."

They were in Jason Plumm's penthouse above Happy Valley, the midnight air good though the humidity had increased again. Plumm got up and threw his cigar butt away, took a fresh one and lit it. The tai-pan of Asian Properties, the third largest *hong*, was taller than Gornt, in his late fifties, thin-faced and elegant, his smoking jacket red velvet. "Even Ian bloody Dunross's not that much of a bloody berk."

"You're wrong. For all his Scots cunning, he's an animal of sudden action, unpremeditated action, that's his failing. I think he did it."

Plumm steepled his fingers thoughtfully. "What did the police say?"

"All I told them was that my brakes had failed. There was no need to involve those nosy buggers, at least not yet. But Rolls brakes just *don't* go wrong by themselves for God's sake. Well, never mind. Tomorrow I'll make sure Tom Nikklin gets me an answer, an absolute answer, if there is one. Time enough for the police then."

"I agree." Plumm smiled thinly. "We don't need police to wash our various linens however droll—do we?"

"No." Both men laughed.

"You were very lucky. The Peak's no road to lose your brakes on. Must have been very unpleasant."

"For a moment it was, Jason, but then it was no problem, once I was over the initial shock." Gornt stretched the truth and sipped his whiskey and soda. They had eaten an elegant dinner on the terrace overlooking Happy Valley, the racecourse and city and sea beyond, just the two of them—Plumm's wife was in England on vacation and their children grown up and no longer in Hong Kong. Now they were sitting over cigars in great easy chairs in Plumm's book-lined study, the room luxurious though subdued, in perfect taste like the rest of the ten-room penthouse.

"Tom Nikklin'll find out if my car was tampered with if anyone can," he said with finality.

"Yes." Plumm sipped a glass of iced Perrier water. "Are you going to wind up young Nikklin again about Macao?"

"Me? You must be joking!"

"No. I'm not, actually," Plumm said with his mocking well-bred chuckle. "Didn't Dunross's engine blow up during the race three years ago and he bloody nearly killed himself?"

"Racing cars are always going wrong."

"Yes, yes they do frequently, though they're not always helped by the opposition." Plumm smiled.

Gornt kept his smile but inside he was not smiling. "Meaning?"

"Nothing, dear boy. Just rumors." The older man leaned over and poured more whiskey for Gornt, then used the soda syphon. "Rumor has it that a certain Chinese mechanic, for a small fee, put . . . put, as we say, a small spanner in the works."

"I doubt if that'd be true."

"I doubt if it could be proved. One way or another. It's disgusting, but some people will do anything for quite a small amount of money."

"Yes. Fortunately we're in the big-money market."

"My whole point, dear boy. Now." Plumm tapped the ash off his cigar. "What's the scheme?"

"It's very simple: providing Bartlett does not actually sign a deal with Struan's in the next ten days we can pluck the Noble House like a dead duck."

"Lots of people have thought that before and Struan's is still the Noble House."

"Yes. But at the moment, they're vulnerable."

"How?"

"The Toda Shipping notes, and the Orlin installment."

"Not true. Struan's credit is excellent—oh, they're stretched, but no more than anyone else. They'll just increase their line of credit—or Ian will go to Richard Kwang—or Blacs."

"Say Blacs won't help—they won't—and say Richard Kwang's neutralized. That leaves only the Victoria."

"Then Dunross'll ask the bank for more credit and we'll have to give it to him. Paul Havergill will put it to a vote of the board. We all know we can't outvote the Struan's block so we'll go along with it and save face, pretending we're very happy to oblige, as usual."

"Yes. But this time I'm happy to say Richard Kwang will vote against Struan's. That will tie up the board, the credit request will be delayed—he won't be able to make his payments, so Dunross goes under."

"For God's sake, Richard Kwang's not even on the board! Have you gone bonkers?"

Gornt puffed his cigar. "No, you've forgotten my game plan. The one called Competition. It was started a couple of days ago."

"Against Richard?"

"Yes."

"Poor old Richard!"

"Yes. He'll be our deciding vote. And Dunross'll never expect an attack from there."

Plumm stared at him. "Richard and Dunross are great friends."

"But Richard's in trouble. The run's started on the Ho-Pak. He'll do anything to save himself."

"I see. How much Ho-Pak stock did you sell short?"

"Lots."

"Are you sure Richard hasn't got the resources to stave off the run—that he can't pull in extra funds?"

"If he does, we can always abort, you and I."

"Yes, yes we can." Jason Plumm watched his cigar smoke spiral. "But just because Dunross won't meet those payments doesn't mean he's finished."

"I agree. But after the Ho-Pak 'disaster,' the news that Struan's have defaulted will send his stock plummeting. The market'll be very nervous, there'll be all the signs of a crash looming which we fuel by selling short. There's no board meeting scheduled for a couple of weeks unless Paul Havergill calls a special meeting. And he won't. Why should he? He wants their chunk of stock back more than anything else in the world. So everything will be fixed beforehand. He'll set the ground rules for rescuing Richard Kwang, and voting as Paul decides will be one of them. So the board lets Ian stew for a few days, then offers to extend credit and restore confidence—in return for Struan's piece of the bank stock—it's pledged against the credit anyway."

"Dunross'll never agree—neither he nor Phillip Chen, nor Tsu-yan."

"It's that or Struan's goes under—providing you hold tight and you've voting control. Once the bank gets his block of stock away from him . . . if you control the board, and therefore the Victoria Bank, then he's finished."

"Yes. But say he gets a new line of credit?"

"Then he's only badly mauled, maybe permanently weakened, Jason, but we make a killing either way. It's all a matter of timing, you know that."

"And Bartlett?"

"Bartlett and Par-Con are mine. He'll never go with Struan's sinking ship. I'll see to that."

After a pause Plumm said, "It's possible. Yes, it's possible."

"Are you in then?"

"After Struan's, how are you going to gobble up Par-Con?"

"I'm not. But *we* could—possibly." Gornt stubbed out his cigar. "Par-

Con's a long-term effort and a whole different set of problems. First Struan's. Well?"

"If I get Struan's Hong Kong property division—35 percent of their landholdings in Thailand and Singapore and we're fifty-fifty on their Kai Tak operation?"

"Yes, everything except Kai Tak—I need that to round off All Asia Airways, I'm sure you'll understand, old boy. But you've a seat on the board of the new company, ten percent of the stock at par, seats on Struan's of course, and all their subsidiaries."

"15 percent. And chairmanship of Struan's, alternate years with you?"

"Agreed, but I'm first." Gornt lit a cigarette. Why not? he thought expansively. By this time next year Struan's will be dismembered so your chairmanship is really academic, Jason old boy. "So everything's agreed? We'll put it in a joint memo if you like, one copy for each of us."

Plumm shook his head and smiled. "Don't need a memo, perish the thought! Here." He held out his hand. "I agree!"

The two men shook hands firmly. "Down with the Noble House!" They both laughed, very content with the deal they had made. Acquisition of Struan's landholdings would make Asian Properties the largest land company in Hong Kong. Gornt would acquire almost a total monopoly of all Hong Kong's air cargo, sea freighting and factoring—and preeminence in Asia.

Good, Gornt thought. Now for Four Finger Wu. "If you'll call me a taxi I'll be off."

"Take my car, my chauffeur will—"

"Thanks but no, I'd rather take a taxi. Really, Jason, thanks anyway."

So Plumm phoned down to the concierge of the twenty-story apartment building which was owned and operated by his Asian Properties. While they waited, they toasted each other and the destruction of Struan's and the profits they were going to make. A phone rang in the adjoining room.

"Excuse me a moment, old chap." Plumm went through the door and half-closed it behind him. This was his private bedroom which he used sometimes when he was working late. It was a small, very neat room, soundproofed, fitted up like a ship's cabin with a built-in bunk, hi-fi speakers that piped in the music, a small self-contained hot plate and refrigerator. And, on one side, was a huge bank of elaborate, shortwave, ham radio transceiver equipment which had been Jason Plumm's abiding hobby since his childhood.

He picked up the phone. "Yes?"

"Mr. Lop-sing please?" the woman's voice said.

"There's no Mr. Lop-*ting* here," he said easily. "Sorry, you have a wrong number."

"I want to leave a message."

"You have a wrong number. Look in your phone book."

"An urgent message for Arthur: Center radioed that the meeting's postponed until the day after tomorrow. Stand by for urgent instructions at 0600." The line went dead. Again a dial tone.

Plumm frowned as he put the phone back on its cradle.

Four Finger Wu stood at the gunnel of his junk with Goodweather Poon watching Gornt get into the sampan that he had sent for him.

"He hasn't changed much in all this time, has he?" Wu said absently, his narrowed eyes glittering.

"Foreign devils all look alike to me, never mind. How many years is it? Ten?" Poon asked, scratching his piles.

"No, it's nearer twelve now. Good times then, *heya*," Wu said. "Lots of profit. Very good, slipping upstream toward Canton, evading the foreign devils and their lackeys, Chairman Mao's people welcoming us. Yes. Our own people in charge and not a foreign devil anywhere—nor a fat official wanting his hand touched with fragrant grease. You could visit all your family and friends then and no trouble, *heya*? Not like now, *heya*?"

"The Reds're getting tough, very clever and very tough—worse than the Mandarins."

Wu turned as his seventh son came on deck. Now the young man wore a neat white shirt and gray trousers and good shoes. "Be careful," he called out brusquely. "You're sure you know what to do?"

"Yes, Father."

"Good," Four Fingers said, hiding his pride. "I don't want any mistakes."

He watched him head awkwardly for the haphazard gangway of planks that joined this junk to the next and thence across other junks to a makeshift landing eight boats away.

"Does Seventh Son know anything yet?" Poon asked softly.

"No, no not yet," Wu said sourly. "Those dogmeat fools to be caught with my guns! Without the guns, all our work will be for nothing."

"Evening, Mr. Gornt. I'm Paul Choy—my uncle Wu sent me to show you the way," the young man said in perfect English, repeating the lie that was now almost the real truth to him.

Gornt stopped, startled, then continued up the rickety stairs, his sea legs better than the young man's. "Evening," he said. "You're American? Or did you just go to school there, Mr. Choy?"

"Both." Paul Choy smiled. "You know how it is. Watch your head on the ropes—and it's slippery as hell." He turned and began to lead the way back. His real name was Wu Fang Choi and he was his father's seventh son by his third wife, but, when he was born, his father Four Finger Wu had sought a Hong Kong birth certificate for him, an unusual act for a boat dweller, put his mother's maiden name on the birth certificate, added Paul and got one of his cousins to pose as the real father.

"Listen, my son," Four Finger Wu had said, as soon as Paul could understand, "when speaking Haklo aboard my ship, you can call me Father —but never in front of a foreign devil, even in Haklo. All other times I'm 'Uncle,' just one of many uncles. Understand?"

"Yes. But why, Father? Have I done something wrong? I'm sorry if I've offended you."

"You haven't. You're a good boy and you work hard. It's just better for the family for you to have another name."

"But why, Father?"

"When it's time you will be told." Then, when he was twelve and trained and had proved his value, his father had sent him to the States. "Now you're to learn the ways of the foreign devil. You must begin to speak like one, sleep like one, become one outwardly but never forget who you are, who your people are, or that all foreign devils are inferior, hardly human beings, and certainly not fornicating civilized."

Paul Choy laughed to himself. If Americans only knew—from tai-pan to meathead—and British, Iranians, Germans, Russians, every race and color, if they all really knew what even the lousiest coolie thought of them, they'd hemorrhage, he told himself for the millionth time. It's not that all the races of China despise foreigners, it's just that foreigners're just beneath any consideration. Of course we're wrong, he told himself. Foreigners are human and some are civilized—in their way—and far ahead of us technically. But we *are* better. . . .

"Why the smile?" Gornt asked, ducking under ropes, avoiding rubbish that scattered all the decks.

"Oh, I was just thinking how crazy life is. This time last month I was surfing at Malibu Colony, California. Boy, Aberdeen's something else, isn't it?"

"You mean the smell?"

"Sure."

"Yes it is."

"It's not much better at high tide. No one but me seems to smell the stench!"

"When were you last here?"

"Couple of years back—for ten days—after I graduated, B.A. in business, but I never seem to get used to it." Choy laughed. "New England it ain't!"

"Where did you go to school?"

"Seattle first. Then undergraduate school, University of Washington at Seattle. Then I got a master's at Harvard, Harvard Business School."

Gornt stopped. "Harvard?"

"Sure. I got an assist, a scholarship."

"That's very good. When did you graduate?"

"June last year. It was like getting out of prison! Boy, they really put your ass on the block if you don't keep up your grades. Two years of hell! After I got out I headed for California with a buddy, doing odd jobs here and there to make enough to keep surfing, having ourselves a time after sweating out so much school. Then . . ." Choy grinned. ". . . then a couple of months back Uncle Wu caught up with me and said it's time you went to work so here I am! After all, he paid for my education. My parents died years ago."

"Were you top of your class at Harvard?"

"Third."

"That's very good."

"Thank you. It's not far now, ours is the end junk."

They negotiated a precarious gangway, Gornt watched suspiciously by silent boat dwellers as they crossed from floating home to floating home, the families dozing or cooking or eating or playing mah-jong, some still repairing fishing nets, some children night fishing.

"This bit's slippery, Mr. Gornt." He jumped on to the tacky deck. "We made it! Home sweet home!" He tousled the hair of the sleepy little boy who was the lookout and said in Haklo, which he knew Gornt did not understand, "Keep awake, Little Brother, or the devils will get us."

"Yes, yes I will," the boy piped, his suspicious eyes on Gornt.

Paul Choy led the way below. The old junk smelled of tar and teak, rotting fish and sea salt and a thousand storms. Below decks the midship gangway opened on to the normal single large cabin for'ard that went the breadth of the ship and the length to the bow. An open charcoal fire burned in a careless brick fireplace with a sooty kettle singing over it. Smoke curled upward and found its way to the outside through a rough flue cut in the deck. A few old rattan chairs, tables and tiers of rough bunks lined one side.

Four Finger Wu was alone and he waved at one of the chairs and beamed. "Heya, good see," he said in halting, hardly understandable English. "Whiskey?"

"Thanks," Gornt said. "Good to see you too."

Paul Choy poured the good Scotch into two semiclean glasses.

"You want water, Mr. Gornt?" he asked.

"No, straight's fine. Not too much please."

"Sure."

Wu accepted his glass and toasted Gornt. "Good see you, heya?"

"Yes. Health!"

They watched Gornt sip his whiskey.

"Good," Gornt said. "Very good whiskey."

Wu beamed again and motioned at Paul. "Him sister son."

"Yes."

"Good school—Golden Country."

"Yes. Yes, he told me. You should be very proud."

"Wat?"

Paul Choy translated for the old man. "Ah thank, thank you. He talk good, *heya?*"

"Yes." Gornt smiled. "Very good."

"Ah, good never mind. Smoke?"

"Thank you." They watched Gornt take a cigarette. Then Wu took one and Paul Choy lit both of them. Another silence.

"Good with old frien'?"

"Yes. And you?"

"Good." Another silence. "Him sister son," the old seaman said again and saw Gornt nod and say nothing, waiting. It pleased him that Gornt just sat there, waiting patiently for him to come to the point as a civilized person should.

Some of these pink devils are learning at long last. Yes, but some have learned too fornicating well—*the* tai-pan for instance, him with those cold, ugly blue fish-eyes that most foreign devils have, that stare at you like a dead shark—the one who can even speak a little Haklo dialect. Yes, the tai-pan's too cunning and too civilized, but then he's had generations before him and his ancestors had the Evil Eye before him. Yes, but old Devil Green Eyes, the first of his line, who made a pact with my ancestor the great sea warlord, Wu Fang Choi and his son, Wu Kwok, and kept it, and saw that his sons kept it—and their sons. So this present tai-pan must be considered an old friend even though he's the most deadly of the line.

The old man suppressed a shudder and hawked and spat to scare away the evil spit god that lurked in all men's throats. He studied Gornt. Eeeee, he told himself, it must be vile to have to look at that pink face in every mirror—all that face hair like a monkey and a pallid white toad's belly skin elsewhere! Ugh!

He put a smile on his face to cover his embarrassment and tried to read Gornt's face, what was beneath it, but he could not. Never mind, he told himself gleefully, that's why all the time and money's been spent to prepare Number Seven Son—he'll know.

"Maybe ask favor?" he said tentatively.

The beams of the ship creaked pleasantly as she wallowed at her moorings.

"Yes. What favor, old friend?"

"Sister son—time go work—give job?" He saw astonishment on Gornt's face and this annoyed him but he hid it. "'Splain," he said in English then added to Paul Choy in guttural Haklo, "Explain to this Eater of Turtle Shit what I want. Just as I told you."

"My uncle apologizes that he can't speak directly to you so he's asked me to explain, Mr. Gornt," Paul Choy said politely. "He wants to ask if you'd give me a job—as a sort of trainee—in your airplane and shipping division."

Gornt sipped his whiskey. "Why those, Mr. Choy?"

"My uncle has substantial shipping interests, as you know, and he wants me to modernize his operation. I can give you chapter and verse on my background, if you'd consider me, sir—my second year at Harvard was directed to those areas—my major interest was transportation of all types. I'd been accepted in the International Division of the Bank of Ohio before my uncle jer—pulled me back." Paul Choy hesitated. "Anyway that's what he asks."

"What dialects do you speak, other than Haklo?"

"Mandarin."

"How many characters can you write?"

"About four thousand."

"Can you take shorthand?"

"Speedwriting only, sir. I can type about eighty words a minute but not clean."

"Wat?" Wu asked.

Gornt watched Paul Choy as the young man translated what had been said for his uncle, weighing him—and Four Finger Wu. Then he said, "What sort of trainee do you want to be?"

"He wants me to learn all there is to know about running shipping and airlines, the broking and freighting business also, the practical operation, and of course to be a profitable cog for you in your machine. Maybe my Yankee expertise, theoretical expertise, could help you somehow. I'm twenty-six. I've a master's. I'm into all the new computer theory. Of course I can program one. At Harvard I backgrounded in conglomerates, cash flows."

"And if you don't perform, or there's, how would you put it, a personality conflict?"

The young man said firmly, "There won't be, Mr. Gornt—leastways I'll work my can off to prevent that."

"Wat? What did he say? Exactly?" Four Fingers asked sharply in Haklo, noticing a change in inflection, his eyes and ears highly tuned.

His son explained, exactly.

"Good," Wu said, his voice a rasp. "Tell him exactly, if you don't do all your tasks to his satisfaction you'll be cast out of the family and my wrath will waste your days."

Paul Choy hesitated, hiding his shock, all his American training screaming to tell his father to go screw, that he was a Harvard graduate, that he was an American and had an American passport that *he'd* earned, whatever goddamn sampan or goddamn family he came from. But he kept his eyes averted and his anger off his face.

Don't be ungrateful, he ordered himself. You're not American, truly American. You're Chinese, and the head of your family has the right to rule. But for him you could be running a floating cathouse here in Aberdeen.

Paul Choy sighed. He knew that he was more fortunate than his eleven brothers. Four were junk captains here in Aberdeen, one lived in Bangkok and plied the Mekong River, one had a ferryboat in Singapore, another ran an import/export shipwright business in Indonesia, two had been lost at sea, one brother was in England—doing what he didn't know—and the last, the eldest, ruled the dozen feeder sampans in Aberdeen Harbor that were floating kitchens—and also three pleasure boats and eight ladies of the night.

After a pause Gornt asked, "What did he say? Exactly?"

Paul Choy hesitated, then decided to tell him, exactly.

"Thank you for being honest with me, Mr. Choy. That was wise. You're a very impressive young man," Gornt said. "I understand perfectly." Now for the first time since Wu had asked the original question he turned his eyes to the old seaman and smiled. "Of course. Glad to give nephew job."

Wu beamed and Paul Choy tried to keep the relief off his face.

"I won't let you down, Mr. Gornt."

"Yes, I know you won't."

Wu motioned at the bottle. "Whiskey?"

"No thank you. This is fine," Gornt said.

"When start job?"

Gornt looked at Paul Choy. "When would you like to start?"

"Tomorrow? Whenever's good for you, sir."

"Tomorrow. Wednesday."

"Gee, thanks. Eight o'clock?"

"Nine, eight thereafter. A six-day week of course. You'll have long hours and I'll push you. It'll be up to you how much you can learn and how fast I can increase your responsibilities."

"Thanks, Mr. Gornt." Happily Paul Choy translated for his father. Wu sipped his whiskey without hurrying. "What money?" he asked.

Gornt hesitated. He knew it had to be just the right sum, not too much, not too little, to give Paul Choy face and his uncle face. "1,000 HK a month for the first three months, then I'll review."

The young man kept his gloom off his face. That was hardly 200 U.S. but he translated it into Haklo.

"Maybe 2,000?" Wu said, hiding his pleasure. A thousand was the perfect figure but he was bargaining merely to give the foreign devil face and his son face.

"If he's to be trained, many valuable managers will have to take time away from their other duties," Gornt said politely. "It's expensive to train anyone."

"Much money Golden Mountain," Wu said firmly. "Two?"

"1,000 first month, 1,250 next two months?"

Wu frowned and added, "Month three, 1,500?"

"Very well. Months three and four at 1,500. And I'll review his salary after four months. And Paul Choy guarantees to work for Rothwell-Gornt for at least two years."

"Wat?"

Paul Choy translated again. Shit, he was thinking, how'm I going to vacation in the States on 50 bucks a week, even 60. Shit! And where the hell'm I gonna live? On a goddamn sampan? Then he heard Gornt say something and his brain twisted.

"Sir?"

"I said because you've been so honest with me, we'll give you free accommodation in one of our company houses—The Gables. That's where we put all our managerial trainees who come out from England. If you're going to be part of a foreign devil *hong* then you'd better mix with its future leaders."

"Yes sir!" Paul Choy could not stop the beam. "Yes sir, thank you sir."

Four Finger Wu asked something in Haklo.

"He wants to know where's the house, sir?"

"It's on the Peak. It's really very nice, Mr. Choy. I'm sure you'll be more than satisfied."

"You can bet your . . . yes sir."

"Tomorrow night be prepared to move in."

"Yes sir."

After Wu had understood what Gornt had said, he nodded his agreement. "All agree. Two year then see. Maybe more, *heya?*"

"Yes."

"Good. Thank old frien'." Then in Haklo, "Now ask him what you wanted to know . . . about the bank."

Gornt was getting up to go but Paul Choy said, "There's something else my uncle wanted to ask you, sir, if you can spare the time."

"Of course." Gornt settled back in his chair and Paul Choy noticed that the man seemed sharper now, more on guard.

"My uncle'd like to ask your opinion about the run on the Aberdeen branch of the Ho-Pak Bank today."

Gornt stared back at him, his eyes steady. "What about it?"

"There're all sorts of rumors," Paul Choy said. "My uncle's got a lot of money there, so've most of his friends. A run on that bank'd be real bad news."

"I think it would be a good idea to get his money out," Gornt said, delighted with the unexpected opportunity to feed the flames.

"Jesus," Paul Choy muttered, aghast. He had been gauging Gornt very carefully and he had noticed sudden tension and now equally sudden pleasure which surprised him. He pondered a moment, then decided to change tactics and probe. "He wanted to know if you were selling short."

Gornt said wryly, "He or you, Mr. Choy?"

"Both of us, sir. He's got quite a portfolio of stocks which he wants me to manage eventually," the young man said, which was a complete exaggeration. "I was explaining the mechanics of modern banking and the stock market to him—how it ticks and how Hong Kong's different from

Stateside. He gets the message very fast, sir." Another exaggeration. Paul Choy had found it impossible to break through his father's prejudices. "He asks if he should sell short?"

"Yes. I think he should. There have been lots of rumors that Ho-Pak's overextended—borrowing short and cheap, lending long and expensive, mostly on property, the classic way any bank would get into serious difficulties. For safety he should get all his money out and sell short."

"Next question, sir: Will Blacs, or the Victoria Bank do a bail-out?"

With an effort Gornt kept his face impassive. The old junk dipped slightly as waves from another chugging past lapped her sides. "Why should other banks do that?"

I'm trapped, Gornt was thinking, aghast. I can't tell the truth to them—there is no telling who else will get the information. At the same time, I daren't *not* tell the old bastard and his god-cursed whelp. He's asking for the return of *the* favor and I have to pay, that's a matter of face.

Paul Choy leaned forward in his chair, his excitement showing. "My theory's that if there's a real run on the Ho-Pak the others won't let it crash—not like the East India and Canton Bank disaster last year because it'd create shock waves that the market, the big operators in the market, wouldn't like. Everyone's waiting for a boom, and I bet the biggies here won't let a catastrophe wreck that chance. Since Blacs and the Victoria're the top bananas it figures they'd be the ones to do a bail-out."

"What's your point, Mr. Choy?"

"If someone knew in advance when Ho-Pak stock'd bottom out and either bank, or both, were launching a bail-out operation, that person could make a fortune."

Gornt was trying to decide what to do but he was tired now and not as sharp as he should be. That accident must have taken more out of me than I thought, he told himself. Was it Dunross? Was that bastard trying to even the score, repay me for *the* Christmas night or the Pacific Orient victory or fifty other victories—perhaps even the old Macao sore.

Gornt felt a sudden glow as he remembered the white hot thrill he had felt watching the road race, knowing that any moment the tai-pan's engine would seize up—watching the cars howl past lap after lap, and then Dunross, the leader, not coming in his turn—then waiting and hoping and then the news that he had spun out at Melco Hairpin in a metal screaming crash when his engine went. Waiting again, his stomach churning. Then the news that the whole racing car had exploded in a ball of fire but Dunross had scrambled out unscathed. He was both very sorry and very glad.

He didn't want Dunross dead. He wanted him alive and destroyed, alive to realize it.

He chuckled to himself. Oh it wasn't me who pressed the button that put that ploy into operation. Of course I did nudge young Donald Nikklin a little and suggest all sorts of ways and means that a little *h'eung yau* in the right hands . . .

His eyes saw Paul Choy and the old seaman waiting, watching him, and all of his good humor vanished. He pushed away his vagrant thoughts and concentrated.

"Yes, you're right of course, Mr. Choy. But your premise is wrong. Of course this is all theoretical, the Ho-Pak hasn't failed yet. Perhaps it won't. But there's no reason why any bank should do what you suggest, it never has in the past. Each bank stands or falls on its own merits, that's the joy of our free enterprise system. Such a scheme as you propose would set a dangerous precedent. It would certainly be impossible to prop up every bank that was mismanaged. Neither bank needs the Ho-Pak, Mr. Choy. Both have more than enough customers of their own. Neither has ever acquired other banking interests here and I doubt whether either would ever need to."

Horseshit, Paul Choy was thinking. A bank's committed to growth like any other business and Blacs and the Victoria are the most rapacious of all —except Struan's and Rothwell-Gornt. Shit, and Asian Properties and all the other *hongs*.

"I'm sure you're right, sir. But my uncle Wu'd appreciate it if you heard anything, one way or another."

He turned to his father and said in Haklo, "I'm finished now, Honored Uncle. This barbarian agrees the bank may be in trouble."

Wu's face lost color. "Eh? How bad?"

"I'll be the first in line tomorrow. You should take all your money out quickly."

"*Ayeeyah!* By all the gods!" Wu said, his voice raw, "I'll personally slit Banker Kwang's throat if I lose a single fornicating cash piece, even though he's my nephew!"

Paul Choy stared at him. "He is?"

"Banks are just fornicating inventions of foreign devils to steal honest people's wealth," Wu raged. "I'll get back every copper cash or his blood will flow! Tell me what he said about the bank!"

"Please be patient, Honored Uncle. It is polite, according to barbarian custom, not to keep this barbarian waiting."

Wu bottled his rage and said to Gornt in his execrable pidgin, "Bank bad, *heya?* Thank tell true. Bank bad custom, *heya?*"

"Sometimes," Gornt said cautiously.

Four Finger Wu unknotted his bony fists and forced calmness. "Thank for favor . . . yes . . . also want like sister son say *heya?*"

"Sorry, I don't understand. What does your uncle mean, Mr. Choy?"

After chatting with his father a moment for appearances, the young man said, "My uncle would consider it a real favor if he could hear privately, in advance, of any raid, takeover attempt or bail-out—of course it'd be kept completely confidential."

Wu nodded, only his mouth smiling now. "Yes. Favor." He put out his hand and shook with Gornt in friendly style, knowing that barbarians liked the custom though he found it uncivilized and distasteful, and contrary to correct manners from time immemorial. But he wanted his son trained quickly and it had to be with Second Great Company and he needed Gornt's information. He understood the importance of advance knowledge. Eeeee, he thought, without my friends in the Marine Police forces of Asia my fleets would be powerless.

"Go ashore with him, Nephew. See him into a taxi then wait for me. Fetch Two Hatchet Tok and wait for me, there, by the taxi stand."

He thanked Gornt again, then followed them to the deck and watched them go. His ferry sampan was waiting and he saw them get into it and head for the shore.

It was a good night and he tasted the wind. There was moisture on it. Rain? At once he studied the stars and the night sky, all his years of experience concentrating. Rain would come only with storm. Storm could mean typhoon. It was late in the season for summer rains but rains could come late and be sudden and very heavy and typhoon as late as November, as early as May, and if the gods willed, any season of the year.

We could use rain, he thought. But not typhoon.

He shuddered. Now we're almost into Ninth Month.

Ninth Month had bad memories for him. Over the years of his life, typhoon had savaged him nineteen times in that month, seven times since his father had died in 1937 and he had become Head of the House of the Seaborne Wu and Captain of the Fleets.

Of these seven times the first was that year. Winds of 115 knots tore out of the north/northwest and sank one whole fleet of a hundred junks in the Pearl River Estuary. Over a thousand drowned that time—his eldest son with all his family. In '49 when he had ordered all his Pearl River-based armada to flee the Communist Mainland and settle permanently into Hong Kong waters, he had been caught at sea and sunk along with ninety junks and three hundred sampans. He and his family were saved but he had lost 817 of his people. Those winds came out of the east. Twelve years ago from the east/northeast again and seventy junks lost. Ten years ago Typhoon Susan with her eighty-knot gales from the northeast, veering to east/southeast, had decimated his Taiwan-based fleet and cost another five hundred lives there, and another two hundred as far south as Singapore and another son with all his family. Typhoon Gloria in '57, one-hundred-knot gales, another multitude drowned. Last year Typhoon Wanda came and wrecked Aberdeen and most of the Haklo sea villages in the New Territories. Those winds came from the north/northwest and backed to northwest then veered south.

Wu knew the winds well and the number of the days well. September second, eighth, second again, eighteenth, twenty-second, tenth, and Typhoon Wanda first day. Yes, he thought, and those numbers add up to sixty-three, which is divisible by the magic number three, which then makes twenty-one which is three again. Will typhoon come on the third day of the Ninth Month this year? It never has before, never in all memory, but will it this year? Sixty-three is also nine. Will it come on the ninth day?

He tasted the wind again. There was more moisture in it. Rain was coming. The wind had freshened slightly. It came from north/northeast now.

The old seaman hawked and spat. Joss! If it's the third or ninth or second it's joss never mind. The only certain thing is that typhoon will come from some quarter or other and it will come in the Ninth Month—or this month which is equally bad.

He was watching the sampan now and he could see his son sitting amidships, alongside the barbarian, and he wondered how far he could trust him. The lad's smart and knows the foreign devil ways very well, he thought, filled with pride. Yes, but how far has he been converted to their evils? I'll soon find out never mind. Once the lad's part of the chain he'll be obedient. Or dead. In the past the House of Wu always traded in opium with or for the Noble House, and sometimes for ourselves. Once opium was honorable.

It still is for some. Me, Smuggler Mo, White Powder Lee, ah, what about them? Should we join into a Brotherhood, or not?

But the White Powders? Are they so different? Aren't they just stronger opium—like spirit is to beer?

What's the trading difference between the White Powders and salt? None. Except that now stupid foreign devil law says one's contraband and the other isn't! *Ayeeyah*, up to twenty-odd years ago when the barbarians lost their fornicating war to the fiends from the Eastern Sea, the government monopolized the trade here.

Wasn't Hong Kong trade with China built on opium, greased only by opium grown in barbarian India?

But now that they've destroyed their own producing fields, they're trying to pretend the trade never happened, that it's immoral and a terrible crime worth twenty years in prison!

Ayeeyah, how can a civilized person understand a barbarian?

Disgustedly he went below.

Eeeee, he thought wearily. This has been a difficult day. First John Chen vanishes. Then those two Cantonese dogmeat fornicators are caught at the airport and my shipment of guns is stolen by the fornicating police. Then this afternoon the tai-pan's letter arrived by hand: "Greetings Honored Old Friend. On reflection I suggest you put Number Seven Son with the enemy—better for him, better for us. Ask Black Beard to see you tonight. Telephone me afterwards." It was signed with the tai-pan's chop and "Old Friend."

"Old Friend" to a Chinese was a particular person or company who had done you an extreme favor in the past, or someone in business who had proved trustworthy and profitable over the years. Sometimes the years went over generations.

Yes, Wu thought, this tai-pan's an old friend. It was he who had suggested the birth certificate and the new name for his Seventh Son, who suggested sending him to the Golden Country and had smoothed the waters there and the waters into the great university, and had watched over him there without his knowledge—the subterfuge solving his dilemma of how to have one of his sons trained in America without the taint of the opium connection.

What fools barbarians are! Yes, but even so, this tai-pan is not. He's truly an old friend—and so is the Noble House.

Wu remembered all the profits he and his family had made secretly over the generations, with or without the help of the Noble House, in peace and war, trading where barbarian ships could not: contraband, gold, gasoline, opium, rubber, machinery, medical drugs, anything and everything in short supply. Even people, helping them escape from the Mainland or to the Mainland, their passage money considerable. With and without but mostly with the assistance of the Noble House, with this tai-pan and before him Old Hawk Nose, his old cousin, and before him, Mad Dog, his father, and before him the cousin's father, the Wu clan had prospered.

Now Four Finger Wu had 6 percent of the Noble House, purchased over the years and hidden with their help in a maze of nominees but still in his sole control, the largest share of their gold transmittal business, along with heavy investments here, in Macao, Singapore and Indonesia and in property, shipping, banking.

Banking, he thought grimly. I'll cut my nephew's throat after I've fed him his Secret Sack if I lose one copper cash!

He was below now and he went into the seamy, littered main cabin where he and his wife slept. She was in the big straw-filled bunk and she turned over in half-sleep. "Are you finished now? Are you coming to bed?"

"No. Go to sleep," he said kindly. "I've work to do."

Obediently she did as she was told. She was his *tai-tai,* his chief wife, and they had been married for forty-seven years.

He took off his clothes and changed. He put on a clean white shirt and clean socks and shoes, and the creases of his gray trousers were sharp. He closed the cabin door quietly behind him and came nimbly on deck feeling very uncomfortable and tied in by the clothes. "I'll be back before dawn, Fourth Grandson," he said.

"Yes, Grandfather."

"You stay awake now!"

"Yes, Grandfather."

He cuffed the boy gently then went across the gangways and stopped at the third junk.

"Goodweather Poon?" he called out.

"Yes . . . yes?" the sleepy voice said. The old man was curled up on old sacking, dozing.

"Assemble all the captains. I'll be back within two hours."

Poon was immediately alert. "We sail?" he asked.

"No. I'll be back in two hours. Assemble the captains!"

Wu continued on his way and was bowed into his personal ferry sampan. He peered at the shore. His son was standing beside his big black Rolls with the good luck number plate—the single number 8—that he had purchased for 150,000 HK in the government auction, his uniformed chauffeur and his bodyguard, Two Hatchet Tok, waiting deferentially beside him. As always he felt pleasure seeing his great machine and this overrode his growing concern. Of course, he was not the only dweller in the sea villages who owned a Rolls. But, by custom, his was always the largest and the newest. 8, *baat,* was the luckiest number because it rhymed with *faat* which meant "expanding prosperity."

He felt the wind shift a point and his anxiety increased. Eeeee, this has been a bad day but tomorrow will be worse.

Has that lump of dogmeat John Chen escaped to the Golden Country or is he truly kidnapped? Without that piece of dung I'm still the tai-pan's running dog. I'm tired of being a running dog. The 100,000 reward for John Chen is money well invested. I'd pay twelve times that for John Chen and his fornicating coin. Thank all gods I put spies in Noble House Chen's household.

He stabbed his hand shoreward. "Be quick, old man," he ordered the boatman, his face grim. "I've a lot to do before dawn!"

19

The day was hot and very humid, the sky sultry, clouds beginning a buildup. Since the opening this morning there had been no letup in the milling, noisy, sweating crowds inside and outside the small Aberdeen branch of the Ho-Pak Bank.

"I've no more money to pay out, Honorable Sung," the frightened teller whispered, sweat marking her neat *chong-sam*.

"How much do you need?"

"$7,457 for customer Tok-sing but there must be fifty more people waiting."

"Go back to your window," the equally nervous manager replied. "Delay. Pretend to check the account further—Head Office swore another consignment left their office an hour ago . . . perhaps the traffic . . . Go back to your window, Miss Pang." Hastily he shut the door of his office after her and, sweating, once more got on the phone. "The Honorable Richard Kwang please. Hurry. . . ."

Since the bank had opened promptly at ten o'clock, four or five hundred people had squirmed their way up to one of the three windows and demanded their money in full and their savings in full and then, blessing their joss, had shoved and pushed their way out into the world again.

Those with safety deposit boxes had demanded access. One by one, accompanied by an official, they had gone below to the vault, ecstatic or faint with relief. There the official had used his key and the client his key and then the official had left. Alone in the musty air the sweating client had blessed the gods that his joss had allowed him to be one of the lucky ones. Then his shaking hands had scooped the securities or cash or bullion or jewels and all the other secret things into a briefcase or suitcase or paper bag—or stuffed them into bulging pockets, already full with bank notes. Then, suddenly frightened to have so much wealth, so open and vulnerable, all the wealth of their individual world, their happiness had evaporated and they had slunk away to let another take their place, equally nervous, and, initially, equally ecstatic.

The line had started to form long before dawn. Four Finger Wu's people took the first thirty places. This news had rushed around the harbor, so others had joined instantly, then others, then everyone with any account whatsoever as the news spread, swelling the throng. By ten, the nervous, anxious gathering was of riot proportions. Now a few uniformed police were strolling among them, silent and watchful, their presence calming. More came as the day grew, their numbers quietly and carefully orchestrated by East Aberdeen police station. By noon a couple of Black Maria police vans were in one of the nearby alleys with a specially trained riot platoon in support. And European officers.

Most of the crowd were simple fisherfolk and locals, Haklos and Cantonese. Perhaps one in ten was born in Hong Kong. The rest were recent migrants from the People's Republic of China, the Middle Kingdom, as they called their land. They had poured into the Hong Kong sanctuary fleeing the Communists or fleeing the Nationalists, or famine, or just simple poverty as their forebears had done for more than a century. Ninety-eight of every hundred of Hong Kong's population were Chinese and this proportion had been the same ever since the Colony began.

Each person who came out of the bank told anyone who asked that they had been paid in full. Even so, the others who waited were sick with apprehension. All were remembering the crash of last year, and a lifetime in their home villages of other crashes and failures, frauds, rapacious money lenders, embezzlements and corruptions and how easy it was for a life's savings to evaporate through no fault of your own, whatever the government, Communist, Nationalist or warlord. For four thousand years it had always been the same.

And all loathed their dependence on banks—but they had to put their cash somewhere safe, life being what it was and robbers as plentiful as fleas. *Dew neh loh moh* on all banks, most were thinking, they're inventions of the devil—of the foreign devils! Yes. Before foreign devils came to the Middle Kingdom there was no paper money, just real money, silver or gold or copper—mostly silver and copper—that they could feel and hide, that would never evaporate. Not like filthy paper. Rats can eat paper, and men. Paper money's another invention of the foreign devil. Before they came to the Middle Kingdom life was good. Now? *Dew neh loh moh* on all foreign devils!

At eight o'clock this morning, the anxious bank manager had called Richard Kwang. "But Honored Lord, there must be five hundred people already and the queue goes from here all along the waterfront."

"Never mind, Honorable Sung! Pay those who want their cash. Don't worry! Just talk to them, they're mostly just superstitious fisherfolk. Talk them out of withdrawing. But those who insist—pay! The Ho-Pak's as strong as Blacs or the Victoria! It's a malicious lie that we're overstretched!

Pay! Check their savings books carefully and don't hurry with each client. Be methodical."

So the bank manager and the tellers had tried to persuade their clients that there was really no need for any anxiety, that false rumors were being spread by malicious people.

"Of course you can have your money, but don't you think . . ."

"*Ayeeyah*, give her the money," the next in line said irritably, "she wants her money, I want mine, and there's my wife's brother behind me who wants his and my auntie's somewhere outside. *Ayeeyah*, I haven't got all day! I've got to put to sea. With this wind there'll be a storm in a few days and I have to make a catch. . . ."

And the bank had begun to pay out. In full.

Like all banks, the Ho-Pak used its deposits to service loans to others— all sorts of loans. In Hong Kong there were few regulations and few laws. Some banks lent as much as 80 percent of their cash assets because they were sure their clients would never require back all their money at the same time.

Except today at Aberdeen. But, fortunately, this was only one of eighteen branches throughout the Colony. The Ho-Pak was not yet threatened.

Three times during the day the manager had had to call for extra cash from Head Office in Central. And twice for advice.

At one minute past ten this morning Four Finger Wu was grimly sitting beside the manager's desk with Paul Choy, and Two Hatchet Tok standing behind him.

"You want to close all your Ho-Pak accounts?" Mr. Sung gasped shakily.

"Yes. Now," Wu said and Paul Choy nodded.

The manager said weakly, "But we haven't en—"

Wu hissed, "I want all my money now. Cash or bullion. Now! Don't you understand?"

Mr. Sung winced. He dialed Richard Kwang and explained quickly. "Yes, yes, Lord." He offered the phone. "Honorable Kwang wants to speak to you, Honorable Wu."

But no amount of persuasion would sway the old seaman. "No. *Now*. My money, and the money of my people *now*. And also from those other accounts, the, er, those special ones wherever they are."

"But there isn't that amount of cash in that branch, Honored Uncle," Richard Kwang said soothingly. "I'd be glad to give you a cashier's check."

Wu exploded. "I don't want checks; I want money! Don't you understand? Money!" He did not understand what a cashier's check was so the frightened Mr. Sung began to explain. Paul Choy brightened. "That'll be all right, Honored Uncle," he said. "A cashier's check's . . ."

The old man roared, "How can a piece of paper be like cash money? I want money, my money now!"

"Please let me talk to the Honorable Kwang, Great Uncle," Paul Choy said placatingly, understanding the dilemma. "Perhaps I can help."

Wu nodded sourly. "All right, talk, but get my cash money."

Paul Choy introduced himself on the telephone and said, "Perhaps it'd be easier in English, sir." He talked a few moments then nodded, satisfied. "Just a moment, sir." Then in Haklo, "Great Uncle," he said, explaining, "the Honorable Kwang will give you payment in full in government securities, gold or silver at his Head Office, and a piece of paper which you can take to Blacs, or the Victoria for the remainder. But, if I may suggest, because you've no safe to put all that bullion in, perhaps you'll accept Honorable Kwang's cashier's check—with which I can open accounts at either bank for you. Immediately."

"*Banks!* Banks are foreign devil lobster-pot traps for civilized lobsters!"

It had taken Paul Choy half an hour to convince him. Then they had gone to the Ho-Pak's Head Office but Wu had left Two Hatchet Tok with the quaking Mr. Sung. "You stay here, Tok. If I don't get my money you will take it out of this branch!"

"Yes, Lord."

So they had gone to Central and by noon Four Finger Wu had new accounts, half at Blacs, half at the Victoria. Paul Choy had been staggered by the number of separate accounts that had had to be closed and opened afresh. And the amount of cash.

Twenty-odd million HK.

In spite of all his pleading and explaining the old seaman had refused to invest some of his money in selling Ho-Pak short, saying that that was a game for *quai loh* thieves. So Paul had slipped away and gone to every stockbroker he could find, trying to sell short on his own account. "But, my dear fellow, you've no credit. Of course, if you'll give me your uncle's chop, or assurance in writing, of course. . . ."

He discovered that stockbrokering firms were European, almost exclusively, the vast majority British. Not one was Chinese. All the seats on the stock exchange were European held, again the vast majority British. "That just doesn't seem right, Mr. Smith," Paul Choy said.

"Oh, I'm afraid our locals, Mr., Mr. . . . Mr. Chee was it?"

"Choy, Paul Choy."

"Ah yes. I'm afraid all our locals aren't really interested in complicated, modern practices like broking and stock markets—of course you know our locals are all immigrants? When we came here Hong Kong was just a barren rock."

"Yes. But I'm interested, Mr. Smith. In the States a stockbr—"

"Ah yes, America! I'm sure they do things differently in America, Mr. Chee. Now if you'll excuse me . . . good afternoon."

Seething, Paul Choy had gone from broker to broker but it was always the same. No one would back him without his father's chop.

Now he sat on a bench in Memorial Square near the Law Courts and the Struan's highrise and Rothwell-Gornt's, and looked out at the harbor, and thought. Then he went to the Law Court library and talked his way past the pedantic librarian. "I'm from Sims, Dawson and Dick," he said airily. "I'm their new attorney from the States. They want some quick information on stock markets and stockbroking."

"Government regulations, sir?" the elderly Eurasian asked helpfully.

"Yes."

"There aren't any, sir."

"Eh?"

"Well, practically none." The librarian went to the shelves. The requisite section was just a few paragraphs in a giant tome.

Paul Choy gaped at him. "This's all of it?"

"Yes sir."

Paul Choy's head reeled. "But then it's wide open, the market's wide open!"

The librarian was gently amused. "Yes, compared to London, or New York. As to stockbroking, well, anyone can set up as a broker, sir, providing someone wants them to sell shares and there's someone who wants them to buy and both are prepared to pay commission. The problem is that the, er, the existing firms control the market completely."

"How do you bust this monopoly?"

"Oh I wouldn't want to, sir. We're really for the status quo in Hong Kong."

"How do you break in then? Get a piece of the action?"

"I doubt if you could, sir. The, the British control everything very carefully," he said delicately.

"That doesn't seem right."

The elderly man shook his head and smiled gently. He steepled his fingers, liking the young Chinese he saw in front of him, envying him his purity—and his American education. "I presume you want to play the market on your own account?" he asked softly.

"Yeah . . ." Paul Choy tried to cover his mistake and stuttered, "At least . . . Dawson said for me—"

"Come now, Mr. Choy, you're not from Sims, Dawson and Dick," he said, chiding him politely. "If they'd hired an American—an unheard-of innovation—oh I would have heard of it along with a hundred others, long before you even arrived here. You must be Mr. Paul Choy, the great Wu Sang Fang's nephew, who has just come back from Harvard in America."

Paul Choy gaped at him. "How'd you know?"

"This is Hong Kong, Mr. Choy. It's a very tiny place. We have to know what's going on. That's how we survive. You do want to play the market?"

"Yes. Mr. . . . ?"

"Manuel Perriera. I'm Portuguese from Macao." The librarian took out a fountain pen and wrote in beautiful copybook writing an introduction on the back of one of his visiting cards. "Here. Ishwar Soorjani's an old friend. His place of business is just off the Nathan Road in Kowloon. He's a Parsee from India and deals in money and foreign exchange and buys and sells stocks from time to time. He might help you—but remember if he loans money, or credit, it will be expensive so you should not make any mistakes."

"Gee thanks, Mr. Perriera." Paul Choy stuck out his hand. Surprised, Perriera took it. Paul Choy shook warmly then began to rush off but stopped. "Say, Mr. Perriera . . . the stock market. Is there a long shot? Anything? Any way to get a piece of the action?"

Manuel Perriera had silver-gray hair and long, beautiful hands, and pronounced Chinese features. He considered the youth in front of him. Then he said softly, "There's nothing to prevent you from forming a company to set up your own stock market, a Chinese stock market. That's quite within Hong Kong law—or lack of it." The old eyes glittered. "All you need is money, contacts, knowledge and telephones. . . ."

"My money please," the old *amah* whispered hoarsely. "Here's my savings book." Her face was flushed from the heat within the Ho-Pak branch at Aberdeen. It was ten minutes to three now and she had been waiting since dawn. Sweat streaked her old white blouse and black pants. A long graying ratty queue hung down her back. "*Ayeeyah,* don't shove," she called out to those behind her. "You'll get your turn soon!"

Wearily the young teller took the book and glanced again at the clock. *Ayeeyah!* Thank all gods we close at three, she thought, and wondered anxiously through her grinding headache how they were going to close the doors with so many irritable people crammed in front of the grilles, pressed forward by those outside.

The amount in the savings book was 323.42 HK. Following Mr. Sung's instructions to take time and be accurate she went to the files trying to shut her ears to the stream of impatient, muttered obscenities that had gone on for hours. She made sure the amount was correct, then checked the clock again as she came back to her high stool and unlocked her cash drawer and opened it. There was not enough money in her till so she locked the drawer again and went to the manager's office. An undercurrent of rage went through the waiting people. She was a short clumsy woman. Eyes followed her, then went anxiously to the clock and back to her again.

She knocked on his door and closed it after her. "I can't pay Old Ah Tam," she said helplessly. "I've only 100 HK, I've delayed as much . . ."

Manager Sung wiped the sweat off his upper lip. "It's almost three so make her your last customer, Miss Cho." He took her through a side door to the vault. The safe door was ponderous. She gasped as she saw the empty shelves. At this time of the day usually the shelves were filled with neat stacks of notes and paper tubes of silver, the notes clipped together in their hundreds and thousands and tens of thousands. Sorting the money after closing was the job she liked best, that and touching the sensuous bundles of new, crisp, fresh bills.

"Oh this is terrible, Honorable Sung," she said near to tears. Her thick glasses were misted and her hair askew.

"It's just temporary, just temporary, Miss Cho. Remember what the Honorable Haply wrote in today's *Guardian!*" He cleared the last shelf, committing his final reserves, cursing the consignment that had not yet arrived. "Here." He gave her 15,000 for show, made her sign for it, and took 15 for each of the other two tellers. Now the vault was empty.

When he came into the main room there was a sudden electric, exciting hush at the apparently large amount of money, cash money.

He gave the money to the other two tellers, then vanished into his office again.

Miss Cho was stacking the money neatly in her drawer, all eyes watching her and the other tellers. One packet of 1,000 she left on the desk. She broke the seal and methodically counted out 320, and three ones and the change, recounted it and slid it across the counter. The old woman stuffed it into a paper bag, and the next in line irritably shoved forward and thrust his savings book into Miss Cho's face. "Here, by all the gods. I want seven thous—"

At that moment, the three o'clock bell went and Mr. Sung appeared instantly and said in a loud voice, "Sorry, we have to close now. All tellers close your—" The rest of his words were drowned by the angry roar.

"By all gods I've waited since dawn . . ."

"*Dew neh loh moh* but I've been here eight hours. . . ."

"*Ayeeyah,* just pay me, you've enough . . ."

"Oh please please please please . . ."

Normally the bank would just have shut its doors and served those within, but this time, obediently, the three frightened tellers locked their tills in the uproar, put up their CLOSED signs and backed away from the outstretched hands.

Suddenly the crowd within the bank became a mob.

Those in front were shoved against the counter as others fought to get into the bank. A girl shrieked as she was slammed against the counter. Hands reached out for the grilles that were more for decoration than protection. Everyone was enraged now. One old seaman who had been next in line reached over to try to jerk the till drawer open. The old *amah* was jammed in the seething mass of a hundred or more people and she fought to get to one side, her money clasped tightly in her scrawny hands. A young woman lost her footing and was trampled on. She tried to get up but the milling legs defied her so, in desperation, she bit into one leg and got enough respite to scramble up, stockings ripped, *chong-sam* torn and now in panic. Her panic whipped the mob further then someone shouted, "Kill the motherless whore's son . . ." and the shout was taken up, "Killllllll!"

There was a split second of hesitation, then, as one, they surged forward.

"*Stop!*"

The word blasted through the atmosphere in English and then in Haklo and then in Cantonese and then in English again.

The silence was sudden and vast.

The uniformed chief inspector stood before them, unarmed and calm, an electric megaphone in his hand. He had come through the back door into an inner office and now he was looking at them.

"It's three o'clock," he said softly in Haklo. "The law says banks close at three o'clock. This bank is now closed. Please turn around and go home! Quietly!"

Another silence, angrier this time, then the beginning of a violent swell and one man muttered sullenly, "What about my fornicating money . . ." and others almost took up the shout but the police officer moved fast, very fast, directly at the man, fearlessly lifted the countertop and went straight at him into the mob. The mob backed off.

"Tomorrow," the police officer said gently, towering over him. "You'll get all your money tomorrow." The man dropped his eyes, hating the cold blue fish-eyes and the nearness of a foreign devil. Sullenly he moved back a pace.

The policeman looked at the rest of them, into their eyes. "You at the back," he ordered, instantly selecting the man with unerring care, his voice commanding yet with the same quiet confidence, "Turn around and make way for the others."

Obediently the man did as he was ordered. The mob became a crowd again. A moment's hesitation then another turned and began to push for the door. "*Dew neh loh moh* I haven't got all day, hurry up," he said sourly.

They all began to leave, muttering, furious—but individually, not as a mob. Sung and the tellers wiped the sweat off their brows, then sat trembling behind the safety of the counter.

The chief inspector helped the old *amah* up. A fleck of blood was at the corner of her mouth. "Are you all right, Old Lady?" he asked in Haklo.

She stared at him without understanding. He repeated it in Cantonese.

"Ah, yes . . . yes," she said hoarsely, still clasping her paper bag tight against her chest. "Thank you, Honored Lord." She scuttled away into the crowd and vanished. The room emptied. The Englishman went out to the sidewalk after the last person and stood in the doorway, whistling tonelessly as he watched them stream away.

"Sergeant!"

"Yes sir."

"You can dismiss the men now. Have a detail here at nine tomorrow. Put up barriers and let the buggers into the bank just three at a time. Yourself and four men'll be more than enough."

"Yes sir." The sergeant saluted. The chief inspector turned back into the bank. He locked the front door and smiled at Manager Sung. "Rather humid this afternoon, isn't it?" he said in English to give Sung face—all educated Chinese in Hong Kong prided themselves in speaking the international language.

"Yes sir," Sung replied nervously. Normally he liked him and admired this chief inspector greatly. Yes, he thought. But this was the first time he had actually seen a *quai loh* with the Evil Eye, daring a mob, standing alone like a malevolent god in front of the mob, daring it to move, to give him the opportunity to spit fire and brimstone.

Sung shuddered again. "Thank you, Chief Inspector."

"Let's go into your office and I can take a statement."

"Yes, please." Sung puffed himself up in front of his staff, taking command again. "The rest of you make up your books and tidy up."

He led the way into his office and sat down and beamed. "Tea, Chief Inspector?"

"No thank you." Chief Inspector Donald C. C. Smyth was about five foot ten and well built, fair hair and blue eyes and a taut sunburned face. He pulled out a sheaf of papers and put them on the desk. "These are the accounts of my men. At nine tomorrow, you will close their accounts and pay them. They'll come to the back door."

"Yes of course. I would be honored. But I will lose face if so many valuable accounts leave me. The bank is as sound as it was yesterday, Chief Inspector."

"Of course. Meanwhile tomorrow at nine. In cash please." He handed him some more papers. And four savings books. "I'll take a cashier's check for all of these. Now."

"But Chief Inspector, today was extraordinary. There's no problem with the Ho-Pak. Surely you could . . ."

"Now." Smyth smiled sweetly. "Withdrawal slips are all signed and ready."

Sung glanced at them. All were Chinese names that he knew were nominees of nominees of this man whose nickname was the Snake. The accounts totaled nearly 850,000 HK. And that's just in this branch alone, he thought, very impressed with the Snake's acumen. What about the Victoria and Blacs and all the other branches in Aberdeen?

"Very well," he said wearily. "But I'll be very sorry to see so many accounts leave the bank."

Smyth smiled again. "The whole of the Ho-Pak's not broke yet, is it?"

"Oh no, Chief Inspector," Sung said, shocked. "We have published assets worth a billion HK and cash reserves of many tens of millions. It's just these simple people, a temporary problem of confidence. Did you see Mr. Haply's column in the *Guardian?*"

"Yes."

"Ah." Sung's face darkened. "Malicious rumors spread by jealous taipans and other banks! If Haply claims that, of course it's true."

"Of course! Meanwhile I am a little busy this afternoon."

"Yes. Of course. I'll do it at once. I, er, I see in the paper you've caught one of those evil Werewolves."

"We've a triad suspect, Mr. Sung, just a suspect."

Sung shuddered. "Devils! But you'll catch them all . . . devils, sending an ear! They must be foreigners. I'll wager they're foreigners never mind. Here, sir, I've made the checks . . ."

There was a knock on the door. A corporal came in and saluted. "Excuse me, sir, a bank truck's outside. They say they're from Ho-Pak's Head Office."

"*Ayeeyah*," Sung said, greatly relieved, "and about time. They promised the delivery at two. It's more money."

"How much?" Smyth asked.

"Half a million," the corporal volunteered at once, handing over the manifest. He was a short, bright man with dancing eyes.

"Good," Smyth said. "Well, Mr. Sung, that'll take the pressure off you, won't it."

"Yes. Yes it will." Sung saw the two men looking at him and he said at once, expansively, "If it wasn't for you, and your men . . . With your permission I'd like to call Mr. Richard Kwang now. I feel sure he would be honored, as I would be, to make a modest contribution to your police benevolent fund as a token of our thanks."

"That's very thoughtful, but it's not necessary, Mr. Sung."

"But I will lose terrible face if you won't accept, Chief Inspector."

"You're very kind," Smyth said, knowing truly that without his presence in the bank and that of his men outside, Sung and the tellers and many others would be dead. "Thank you but that's not necessary." He accepted the cashier's checks and left.

Mr. Sung pleaded with the corporal who, at length, sent for his superior. Divisional Sergeant Mok declined also. "Twenty thousand times," he said.

But Mr. Sung insisted. Wisely. And Richard Kwang was equally delighted and equally honored to approve the unsolicited gift. 20,000 HK. In immediate cash. "With the bank's great appreciation, Divisional Sergeant Mok."

"Thank you, Honorable Manager Sung," Mok said politely, pocketing it, pleased to be in the Snake's division and totally impressed that 20,000 was the exact fair market figure the Snake had considered their afternoon's work was worth. "I hope your great bank stays solvent and you weather this storm with your usual cleverness. Tomorrow will be orderly, of course. We will be here at nine A.M. promptly for our cash. . . ."

The old *amah* still sat on the bench on the harbor wall, catching her breath. Her ribs hurt but then they always hurt, she thought wearily. Joss.

Her name was Ah Tam and she began to get up but a youth sauntered up to her and said, "Sit down, Old Woman, I want to talk to you." He was short and squat and twenty-one, his face pitted with small pox scars. "What's in that bag?"

"What? What bag?"

"The paper bag you clutch to your stinking old rags."

"This? Nothing, Honored Lord. It's just my poor shopping that—"

He sat on the bench beside her and leaned closer and hissed, "Shut up, Old Hag! I saw you come out of the fornicating bank. How much have you got there?"

The old woman held on to the bag desperately, her eyes closed in terror and she gasped, "It's all my savings, Hon—"

He pulled the bag out of her grasp and opened it. "*Ayeeyah!*" The notes were old and he counted them. "$323!" he said scornfully. "Who are you *amah* to—a beggar? You haven't been very clever in this life."

"Oh yes, you're right, Lord!" she said, her little black eyes watching him now.

"My *h'eung yau's* 20 percent," he said and began to count the notes.

"But Honored Sir," she said, her voice whining now, "20 is too high, but I'd be honored if you'd accept 5 with a poor old woman's thanks."

"15."

"6!"

"10 and that's my final offer. I haven't got all day!"

"But sir, you are young and strong, clearly a 489. The strong must protect the old and weak."

"True, true." He thought a moment, wanting to be fair. "Very well, 7 percent."

"Oh how generous you are, sir. Thank you, thank you." Happily she watched him count 22 dollars, then reach into his jeans pocket and count out 61 cents. "Here." He gave her the change and the remainder of her money back.

She thanked him profusely, delighted with the bargain she had made. By all the gods, she thought ecstatically, 7 percent instead of, well, at least 15 would be fair. "Have you also money in the Ho-Pak, Honored Lord?" she asked politely.

"Of course," the youth said importantly as though it were true. "My Brotherhood's account has been there for years. We have . . ." He doubled the amount he first thought of. ". . . we have over 25,000 in this branch alone."

"Eeeee," the old woman crooned. "To be so rich! The moment I saw you I knew you were 14K . . . and surely an Honorable 489."

"I'm better than that," the youth said proudly at once, filled with bravado. "I'm . . ." But he stopped, remembering their leader's admonition to be cautious, and so did not say, I'm Kin Sop-ming, Smallpox Kin, and I'm one of the famous Werewolves and there are four of us. "Run along, old woman," he said, tiring of her. "I've more important things to do than talk with you."

She got up and bowed and then her old eyes spotted the man who had been in the line in front of her. The man was Cantonese, like her. He was a rotund shopkeeper she knew who had a poultry street stall in one of Aberdeen's teeming marketplaces. "Yes," she said hoarsely, "but if you want another customer I see an easy one. He was in the queue before me. Over $8,000 he withdrew."

"Oh, where? Where is he?" the youth asked at once.

"For a 15 percent share?"

"7—and that's final. 7!"

"All right. 7. Look, over there!" she whispered. "The fat man, plump as a Mandarin, in the white shirt—the one who's sweating like he's just enjoyed the Clouds and the Rain!"

"I see him." The youth got up and walked quickly away to intercept the man. He caught up with him at the corner. The man froze and bartered for a while, paid 16 percent and hurried off, blessing his own acumen. The youth sauntered back to her.

"Here, Old Woman," he said. "The fornicator had $8,162. 16 percent is . . ."

"$1305.92 and my 7 percent of that is $91.41," she said at once.

He paid her exactly and she agreed to come tomorrow to spot for him. "What's your name?" he asked.

"Ah Su, Lord," she said, giving a false name. "And yours?"

"Mo Wu-fang," he said, using a friend's name.

"Until tomorrow," she said happily. Thanking him again she waddled off, delighted with her day's profit.

His profit had been good too. Now he had over 3,000 in his pockets where this morning he had had only enough for the bus. And it was all windfall for he had come to Aberdeen from Glessing's Point to post another ransom note to Noble House Chen.

"It's for safety," his father, their leader, had said. "To put out a false scent for the fornicating police."

"But it will bring no money," he had said to him and to the others disgustedly. "How can we produce the fornicating son if he's dead and buried? Would you pay off without some proof that he was alive? Of course not! It was a mistake to hit him with the shovel."

"But the fellow was trying to escape!" his brother said.

"True, Younger Brother. But the first blow didn't kill him, only bent his head a little. You should have left it at that!"

"I would have but the evil spirits got into me so I hit him again. I only hit him four times! Eeeee, but these highborn fellows have soft skulls!"

"Yes, you're right," his father had said. He was short and balding with many gold teeth, his name Kin Min-ta, Baldhead Kin. "*Dew neh loh moh* but it's done so there's no point in remembering it. Joss. It was his own fault for trying to escape! Have you seen the early edition of *The Times*?"

"No—not yet, Father," he had replied.

"Here, let me read it to you: 'The Chief of all the Police said today that they have arrested a triad who they suspect is one of the Werewolves, the dangerous gang of criminals who kidnapped John Chen. The authorities expect to have the case solved any moment.'"

They all laughed, he, his younger brother, his father and the last member, his very good friend, Dog-eared Chen—Pun Po Chen—for they knew it was all lies. Not one of them was a triad or had triad connections, and none had ever been caught for any crime before, though they had formed their own Brotherhood and his father had, from time to time, run a small gambling syndicate in North Point. It was his father who had proposed the first kidnapping. Eeee, that was very clever, he thought, remembering. And when John Chen had, unfortunately, had himself killed because he stupidly tried to escape, his father had also suggested cutting off the ear and sending it. "We will turn his bad joss into our good. 'Kill one to terrify ten thousand!' Sending the ear will terrify all Hong Kong, make us famous and make us rich!"

Yes, he thought, sitting in the sun at Aberdeen. But we haven't made our riches yet. Didn't I tell father this morning: "I don't mind going all the way to post the letter, Father, that's sensible and what Humphrey Bogart would order. But I still don't think it will bring us any ransom."

"Never mind and listen! I've a new plan worthy of Al Capone himself. We wait a few days. Then we phone Noble House Chen. If we don't get immediate cash, then we snatch the compradore himself! Great Miser Chen himself!"

They had all stared at him in awe.

"Yes, and if you don't think he'll pay up quickly after seeing his son's ear—of course we'll tell him it was his son's ear . . . perhaps we'll even dig up the body and show him, *heya*?"

Smallpox Kin beamed, recalling how they had all chortled. Oh how they had chortled, holding their bellies, almost rolling on the floor of their tenement apartment.

"Now to business. Dog-eared Chen, we need your advice again."

Dog-eared Chen was a distant cousin of John Chen and worked for him as a manager of one of the multitudinous Chen companies. "Your information about the son was perfect. Perhaps you can supply us with the father's movements too?"

"Of course, Honored Leader, that's easy," Dog-eared Chen had said. "He's a man of habit—and easily frightened. So is his *tai-tai—ayeeyah*, that mealy-mouthed whore knows which side of the bed she sleeps in! She'll pay up very quickly to get him back. Yes, I'm sure he'll be very cooperative now. But we'll have to ask double what we would settle for because he's an accomplished negotiator. I've worked for the fornicating House of Chen all my working life so I know what a miser he is."

"Excellent. Now, by all the gods, how and when should we kidnap Noble House Chen himself?"

20

Sir Dunstan Barre was ushered into Richard Kwang's office with the deference he considered his due. The Ho-Pak Building was small and unpretentious, off Ice House Street in Central, and the office was like most Chinese offices, small, cluttered and drab, a place for working and not for show. Most times two or three people would share a single office, running two or three separate businesses there, using the same telephone and same secretary for all. And why not, a wise man would say? A third of the overhead means more profit for the same amount of labor.

But Richard Kwang did not share his office. He knew it did not please his *quai loh* customers—and the few that he had were important to his bank and to him for face and for the highly sought after peripheral benefits they could bring. Like the possible, oh so important election as a voting member to the super-exclusive Turf Club, or membership in the Hong Kong Golf Club or Cricket Club—or even *the* Club itself—or any of the other minor though equally exclusive clubs that were tightly controlled by the British tai-pans of great *hongs* where all the really big business was conducted.

"Hello, Dunstan," he said affably. "How are things going?"

"Fine. And you?"

"Very good. My horse had a great workout this morning."

"Yes. I was at the track myself."

"Oh, I didn't see you!"

"Just popped in for a minute or two. My gelding's got a temperature—we may have to scratch him on Saturday. But Butterscotch Lass was really flying this morning."

"She almost pipped the track record. She'll definitely be trying on Saturday."

Barre chuckled. "I'll check with you just before race time and you can tell me the inside story then! You can never trust trainers and jockeys, can you—yours or mine or anyone's!"

They chatted inconsequentially, then Barre came to the point.

Richard Kwang tried to cover his shock. "Close all your corporate accounts?"

"Yes, old boy. Today. Sorry and all that but my board thinks it wise for the moment, until you weath—"

"But surely you don't think we're in trouble?" Richard Kwang laughed. "Didn't you see Haply's article in the *Guardian*? '. . . malicious lies spread by certain tai-pans and a certain big bank. . . .'"

"Oh yes, I saw that. More of his poppycock, I'd say. Ridiculous! Spread rumors? Why should anyone do that? Huh, I talked to both Paul Havergill and Southerby this morning and they said Haply better watch out this time if he implies it's them or he'll get a libel suit. That young man deserves a horsewhipping! However . . . I'd like a cashier's check now— sorry, but you know how boards are."

"Yes, yes I do." Richard Kwang kept his smile on the surface of his face but he hated the big florid man even more than usual. He knew that the board was a rubber stamp for Barre's decisions. "We've no problems. We're a billion-dollar bank. As to the Aberdeen branch, they're just a lot of superstitious locals."

"Yes, I know." Barre watched him. "I heard you had a few problems at your Mong Kok branch this afternoon too, also at Tsim Sha Tsui . . . at Sha Tin in the New Territories, even, God help us, on Lan Tao." Lan Tao Island was half a dozen miles east of Hong Kong, the biggest island in the whole archipelago of almost three hundred islands that made up the Colony—but almost unpopulated because it was waterless.

"A few customers withdrew their savings," Richard Kwang said with a scoff. "There's no trouble."

But there was trouble. He knew it and he was afraid everyone knew it. At first it was just at Aberdeen. Then, during the day, his other managers had begun to call with ever increasing anxiety. He had eighteen branches throughout the Colony. At four of them, withdrawals were untoward and heavy. At Mong Kok, a bustling hive within the teaming city of Kowloon, a line had formed in early afternoon. Everyone had wanted all their money. It was nothing like the frightening proportions at Aberdeen, but enough to show a clear indication of failing confidence. Richard Kwang could understand that the sea villages would hear about Four Finger Wu's withdrawals quickly, and would rush to follow his lead—but what about Mong Kok? Why there? And why Lan Tao? Why at Tsim Sha Tsui, his most profitable branch, which was almost beside the busy Golden Ferry Terminal where 150,000 persons passed by daily, to and from Hong Kong?

It must be a plot!

Is my enemy and arch-rival Smiler Ching behind it? Is it those fornicators, those jealous fornicators at Blacs or the Victoria?

Is Thin Tube of Dung Havergill masterminding the attack? Or is it

Compton Southerby of Blacs—he's always hated me. These filthy *quai loh!* But why should they attack me? Of course I'm a much better banker than them and they're jealous but my business is with civilized people and hardly touches them. Why? Or has it leaked somehow that against my better judgment, over my objections, my partners who control the bank have been insisting that I borrow short and cheap and lend long and high on property deals, and now, through their stupidity, we are temporarily overextended and cannot sustain a run?

Richard Kwang wanted to shout and scream and tear his hair out. His secret partners were Lando Mata and Tightfist Tung, major shareholders of Macao's gambling and gold syndicate, along with Smuggler Mo, who had helped him form and finance the Ho-Pak ten years ago. "Did you see Old Blind Tung's predictions this morning?" he asked, the smile still on his face.

"No. What'd he say?"

Richard Kwang found the paper and passed it over. "All the portents show we're ready for boom. The lucky eight is everywhere in the heavens and we're in the eighth month, my birthday is the eighth of the eighth month. . . ."

Barre read the column. In spite of his disbelief in soothsayers, he had been too long in Asia to dismiss them totally. His heart quickened. Old Blind Tung had a vast reputation in Hong Kong. "If you believe him we're in for the biggest boom in the history of the world," he said.

"He's usually much more cautious. *Ayeeyah,* that would be good, *heya?*"

"Better than good. Meanwhile Richard old boy, let's finish our business, shall we?"

"Certainly. It's all a typhoon in an oyster shell, Dunstan. We're stronger than ever—our stock's hardly a point off." When the market had opened, there had been a mass of small offerings to sell, which, if not reacted to at once would have sent their stock plummeting. Richard Kwang had instantly ordered his brokers to buy and to keep buying. This had stabilized the stock. During the day, to maintain the position, he had had to buy almost five million shares, an unheard of number to be traded in one day. None of his experts could pinpoint who was selling big. There was no reason for a lack of confidence, other than Four Finger Wu's withdrawals. All gods curse that old devil and his fornicating, too smart Harvard-trained nephew! "Why not le—"

The phone rang. "'Scuse me," then curtly into the phone, "I said no interruptions!"

"It's Mr. Haply from the *Guardian,* he says it's important," his secretary, his niece, Mary Yok said. "And the tai-pan's secretary called. The Nelson Trading board meeting's brought forward to this afternoon at five o'clock. Mr. Mata called to say he would be there too."

Richard Kwang's heart skipped three beats. Why? he asked himself, aghast. *Dew neh loh moh* it was supposed to be postponed to next week. *Oh ko* why? Then quickly he put aside that question to consider Haply. He decided that to answer now in front of Barre was too dangerous. "I'll call him back in a few minutes." He smiled at the red-faced man in front of him. "Leave everything for a day or two, Dunstan, we've no problems."

"Can't, old boy. Sorry. There was a special meeting, have to settle it today. The board insisted."

"We've been generous in the past—you've forty million of our money unsecured now—we're joint venturing another seventy million with you on your new building program."

"Yes, indeed you are, Richard, and your profit will be substantial. But they're another matter and those loans were negotiated in good faith months ago and will be settled in good faith when they're due. We've never defaulted on a payment to the Ho-Pak or anyone else." Barre passed the newspaper back and with it, signed documents imprinted with his corporate seal. "The accounts are consolidated so one check will suffice."

The amount was a little over nine and a half million.

Richard Kwang signed the cashier's check and smiled Sir Dunstan Barre out, then, when it was safe, cursed everyone in sight and went back into his office, slamming the door behind him. He kicked his desk then picked up the phone and shouted at his niece to get Haply and almost broke the phone as he slammed it back onto its cradle.

"*Dew neh loh moh* on all filthy *quai loh*," he shrieked to the ceiling and felt much better. That lump of dogmeat! I wonder . . . oh, I wonder if I could prevail on the Snake to forbid any lines at all tomorrow? Perhaps he and his men could break a few arms.

Gloomily Richard Kwang let his mind drift. It had been a rotten day. It had begun badly at the track. He was sure his trainer—or jockey—was feeding Butterscotch Lass pep pills to make her run faster to shorten her odds—she'd be favorite now—then Saturday they'd stop the pills and back an outsider and clean up without him being in on the profit-making. Dirty dog bones, all of them! Liars! Do they think I own a racehorse to lose money?

The banker hawked and spat into the spittoon.

Maggot-mouthed Barre and dog bone Uncle Wu! Those withdrawals will take most of my cash. Never mind, with Lando Mata, Smuggler Mo, Tightfist Tung and the tai-pan I'm quite safe. Oh I'll have to shout and scream and curse and weep but nothing can really touch me or the Ho-Pak. I'm too important to them.

Yes, it had been a rotten day. The only bright spot had been his meeting this morning with Casey. He had enjoyed looking at her, enjoyed her clean-smelling, smart, crisp Americanness of the great outdoors. They had fenced pleasantly about financing and he felt sure he could get all or certainly part of their business. Clearly the pickings would be huge. She's so naive, he thought. Her knowledge of banking and finance's impressive but of the Asian world, nil! She's so naive to be so open with their plans. Thank all gods for Americans.

"I love America, Miss Casey. Yes. Twice a year I go there, to eat good steaks and go to Vegas—and to do business of course."

Eeeee, he thought happily, the whores of the Golden Country are the best and most available *quai loh* in the world, and *quai lohs*'re so cheap compared to Hong Kong girls! Oh oh oh! I get such a good feeling pillowing them, with their great deodorized armpits, their great tits and thighs and rears. But in Vegas it's the best. Remember the golden-haired beauty that towered over me but lying down she . . .

His private phone rang. He picked it up, irritated as always that he had had to install it. But he had had no option. When his previous secretary of many years had left to get married, his wife had planted her favorite niece firmly in her place, of course to spy on me, he thought sourly. Eeeee, what can a man do?

"Yes?" he asked, wondering what his wife wanted now.

"You didn't call me all day. . . . I've been waiting for hours!"

His heart leapt at the unexpected sound of the girl's voice. He dismissed the petulance, her Cantonese sweet like her Jade Gate. "Listen, Little Treasure," he said, his voice placating. "Your poor Father's been very busy today. I've—"

"You just don't want your poor Daughter anymore. I'll have to throw myself in the harbor or find another person to cherish me oh oh oh. . . ."

His blood pressure soared at the sound of her tears. "Listen, Little Oily Mouth, I'll see you this evening at ten. We'll have an eight-course feast at Wanchai at my fav—"

"Ten's too late and I don't want a feast I want a steak and I want to go to the penthouse at the V and A and drink champagne!"

His spirit groaned at the danger of being seen and reported secretly to his *tai-tai*. Oh oh oh! But, in front of his friends and his enemies and all Hong Kong he would gain enormous face to escort his new mistress there, the young exotic rising star in TV's firmament, Venus Poon.

"At ten I'll call f—"

"Ten's too late. Nine."

Rapidly he tried to sort out all his meetings tonight to see how he could accommodate her. "Listen, Little Treasure, I'll se—"

"Ten's too late. Nine. I think I will die now that you don't care anymore."

"Listen. Your Father has three meetings and I th—"

"Oh my head hurts to think you don't want me anymore oh oh oh. This abject person will have to slit her wrists, or. . . ." He heard the change in her voice and his stomach twisted at the threat, "Or answer the phone calls of others, lesser than her revered Father of course, but just as rich nonetheless and m—"

"All right, Little Treasure. At nine!"

"Oh you do *love* me don't you!" Though she was speaking Cantonese Venus Poon used the English word and his heart flipped. English was the language of love for modern Chinese, there were no romantic words in their own language. "Tell me!" she said imperiously. "Tell me you *love* me!"

He told her, abjectly, then hung up. The mealy-mouthed little whore, he thought irritably. But then, at nineteen she's a right to be demanding and petulant and difficult if you're almost sixty and she makes you feel twenty and the Imperial Yang blissful. Eeeee, but Venus Poon's the best I've ever had. Expensive but, eeee, she's got muscles in her Golden Gully that only the legendary Emperor Kung wrote about!

He felt his yang stir and scratched pleasantly. I'll give that little baggage what for tonight. I'll buy an extra specially large device, ah yes, a ring with bells on it. Oh oh oh! That'll make her wriggle!

Yes, but meanwhile think about tomorrow. How to prepare for tomorrow?

Call your High Dragon friend, Divisional Sergeant Tang-po at Tsim Sha Tsui and enlist his help to see that his branch and all branches in Kowloon are well policed. Phone Blacs and Cousin Tung of the huge Tung Po Bank and Cousin Smiler Ching and Havergill to arrange extra cash against the Ho-Pak's securities and holdings. Ah yes, phone your very good friend Joe Jacobson, VP of the Chicago Federal and International Merchant Bank—his bank's got assets of four billion and he owes you lots of favors. Lots. There're lots of *quai loh* who're deeply in your debt, and civilized people. Call them all!

Abruptly Richard Kwang came out of his reverie as he remembered the tai-pan's summons. His soul twisted. Nelson Trading's deposits in bullion and cash were huge. *Oh ko* if Nels—

The phone jangled irritably. "Uncle, Mr. Haply's on the line."

"Hello, Mr. Haply, how nice to talk to you. Sorry I was engaged before."

"That's all right, Mr. Kwang. I just wanted to check a couple of facts if I may. First, the riot at Aberdeen. The police w—"

"Hardly a riot, Mr. Haply. A few noisy, impatient people, that's all," he said, despising Haply's Canadian-American accent, and the need to be polite.

"I'm looking at some photos right now, Mr. Kwang, the ones that're in this afternoon's *Times*—it looks like a riot all right."

The banker squirmed in his chair and fought to keep his voice calm. "Oh—oh well I wasn't there so . . . I'll have to talk to Mr. Sung."

"I did, Mr. Kwang. At 3:30. Spent half an hour with him. He said if it hadn't been for the police they'd've torn the place apart." There was a hesitation. "You're right to play it down, but, say, I'm trying to help, and I can't without the facts, so if you'll level with me . . . How many folks wanted their money out at Lan Tao?"

Richard Kwang said, "18," halving the real figure.

"Our guy said 36. 82 at Sha Tin. How about Mong Kok?"

"A cupful."

"My guy said 48, and there was a good 100 left at closing. How about Tsim Sha Tsui?"

"I haven't got the figures yet, Mr. Haply," Richard Kwang said smoothly, consumed with anxiety, hating the staccato questioning.

"All the evening editions're heavy with the Ho-Pak run. Some're even using the word."

"*Oh ko. . . .*"

"Yeah. I'd say you'd better get ready for a real hot day tomorrow, Mr. Kwang. I'd say your opposition's very well organized. Everything's too pat to be a coincidence."

"I certainly appreciate your interest." Then Richard Kwang added delicately, "If there's anything I can do . . ."

Again the irritating laugh. "Have any of your big depositors pulled out today?"

Richard Kwang hesitated a fraction of a moment and he heard Haply jump into the breach. "Of course I know about Four Finger Wu. I meant the big British *hongs*."

"No, Mr. Haply, not yet."

"There's a strong rumor that Hong Kong and Lan Tao Farms's going to change banks."

Richard Kwang felt that barb in his Secret Sack. "Let's hope it's not true, Mr. Haply. Who're the tai-pans and what big bank or banks? Is it the Victoria or Blacs?"

"Perhaps it's Chinese. Sorry, I can't divulge a news source. But you'd better get organized—it sure as hell looks as though the big guys are after you."

21

"They don't sleep together, tai-pan," Claudia Chen said.

"Eh?" Dunross looked up absently from the stack of papers he was going through.

"No. At least they didn't last night."

"Who?"

"Bartlett and your Cirrannousshee."

Dunross stopped working. "Oh?"

"Yes. Separate rooms, separate beds, breakfast together in the main room—both neat and tidy and dressed in modest robes which is interesting because neither wears anything in bed."

"They don't?"

"No, at least they didn't last night."

Dunross grinned and she was glad that her news pleased him. It was his first real smile of the day. Since she had arrived at 8:00 A.M. he had been working like a man possessed, rushing out for meetings, hurrying back again: the police, Phillip Chen, the governor, twice to the bank, once to the penthouse to meet whom she did not know. No time for lunch and, so the doorman had told her, the tai-pan had arrived with the dawn.

She had seen the weight on his spirit today, the weight that sooner or later bowed all tai-pans—and sometimes broke them. She had seen Ian's father withered away by the enormous shipping losses of the war years, the catastrophic loss of Hong Kong, of his sons and nephews—bad joss piling on bad joss. It was the loss of Mainland China that had finally crushed him. She had seen how Suez had broken Alastair Struan, how that tai-pan had never recovered from that debacle and how bad joss had piled on bad joss for him until the Gornt-mounted run on their stock had shattered him.

It must be a terrible strain, she thought. All our people to worry about and our House, all our enemies, all the unexpected catastrophes of nature and of man that seem to be ever present—and all the sins and piracies and devil's work of the past that are waiting to burst forth from our own Pandora's box as they do from time to time. It's a pity the tai-pans aren't Chinese, she thought. Then the sins of the past would be so much gossamer.

"What makes you sure, Claudia?"

"No sleep things for either—pajamas or filmy things." She beamed.

"How do you know?"

"Please, tai-pan, I can't divulge my sources!"

"What else do you know?"

"Ah!" she said, then blandly changed the conversation. "The Nelson Trading board meeting's in half an hour. You wanted to be reminded. Can I have a few minutes beforehand?"

"Yes. In a quarter of an hour. Now," he said with a finality she knew too well. "What else do you know?"

She sighed, then importantly consulted her notepad. "She's never been married. Oh, lots of suitors but none have lasted, tai-pan. In fact, according to rumors, none have . . ."

Dunross's eyebrows shot up. "You mean she's a virgin?"

"Of that we're not sure—only that she has no reputation for staying out late, or overnight, with a gentleman. No. The only gentleman she goes out socially with is Mr. Bartlett and that's infrequently. Except on business trips. He, by the way, tai-pan, he's quite a gadabout—*swinger* was the term used. No one lady bu—"

"Used by whom?"

"Ah! Mr. Handsome Bartlett doesn't have one special girl friend, tai-pan. Nothing steady as they say. He was divorced in 1956, the same year that your Cirrrannnousshee joined his firm."

"She's not my Ciranoush," he said.

Claudia beamed more broadly. "She's twenty-six. She's Sagittarius."

"You got someone to snitch her passport—or got someone to take a peek?"

"Very good gracious no, tai-pan." Claudia pretended to be shocked. "I don't spy on people. I just ask questions. But 100 says she and Mr. Bartlett have been lovers at some time or another."

"That's no bet, I'd be astounded if they weren't. He's certainly in love with her—and she with him. You saw how they danced together. That's no bet at all."

The lines around her eyes crinkled. "Then what odds will you give me they've never been lovers?"

"Eh? What d'you know?" he asked suspiciously.

"Odds, tai-pan?"

He watched her. Then he said, "A thousand to . . . I'll give you ten to one."

"Done! A hundred. Thank you tai-pan. Now, about the Nels—"

"Where'd you get all this information? Eh?"

She extracted a telex from the papers she was carrying. The rest she put into his *in* tray. "You telexed our people in New York the night before last for information on her and to recheck Bartlett's dossier. This's just arrived."

He took it and scanned it. His reading was very fast and his memory almost photographic. The telex gave the information Claudia had related in bald terms without her embroidered interpretation and added that K. C. Tcholok had no known police record, $46,000 in a savings account at the San Fernando Savings and Loan, and $8,700 in her checking account at the Los Angeles and California Bank.

"It's shocking how easy it is in the States to find out how much you've got in the bank, isn't it, Claudia?"

"Shocking. I'd never use one, tai-pan."

He grinned. "Except to borrow from! Claudia, just give me the telex next time."

"Yes, tai-pan. But isn't my way of telling certain things more exciting?"

"Yes. But where's it say about the nakedness? You made that up!"

"Oh no, that's from my own source here. Third Toiletma—" Claudia stopped just too late to avoid falling into his trap.

His smile was seraphic. "So! A spy in the V and A! Third Toiletmaid! Who? Which one, Claudia?"

To give him face she pretended to be annoyed. *"Ayeeyah!* A spymaster may reveal nothing, *heya?"* Her smile was kindly. "Here's a list of your calls. I've put off as many as I can till tomorrow—I'll buzz you in good time for the meeting."

He nodded but she saw that his smile had vanished and now he was lost in thought again. She went out and he did not hear the door close. He was thinking about spymasters and AMG and his meeting with Brian Kwok and Roger Crosse this morning at ten, and the one coming at six o'clock.

The meeting this morning had been short, sharp and angry. "First, is there anything new on AMG?" he had asked.

Roger Crosse had replied at once, "It was, apparently, an accident. No suspicious marks on the body. No one was seen nearby, no car marks, impact marks or skid marks—other than the motorcycle. Now, the files, Ian—oh by the way we know now you've got the only copies existent."

"Sorry but I can't do what you asked."

"Why?" There had been a sour edge to the policeman's voice.

"I'm still not admitting one way or the other that they exist but y—"

"Oh for chrissake, Ian, don't be ridiculous! Of course the copies exist. Do you take us for bloody fools? If they didn't, you'd've come out with it last night and that would have been that. I strongly advise you to let us copy them."

"And I strongly advise you to have a tighter hold on your temper."

"If you think I've lost my temper, Ian, then you know very little about me. I formally ask you to produce those documents. If you refuse I'll invoke my powers under the Official Secrets Act at six o'clock this evening and tai-pan or not, of the Noble House or not, friend or not, by one minute past six, you'll be under arrest. You'll be held incommunicado and we'll go through all your papers, safes, deposit boxes until we've found them! Now kindly produce the files!"

Dunross remembered the taut face and the iced eyes staring at him, his real friend Brian Kwok in shock. "No."

Crosse had sighed. The threat in the sound had sent a tremor through him. "For the last time, why?"

"Because, in the wrong hands, I think they'd be damaging to Her Maj—"

"Good sweet Christ, I'm head of Special Intelligence!"

"I know."

"Then kindly do as I ask."

"Sorry. I spent most of the night trying to work out a safe way to giv—"

Roger Crosse had got up. "I'll be back at six o'clock for the files. Don't burn them, Ian. I'll know if you try and I'm afraid you'll be stopped. Six o'clock."

Last night while the house slept, Dunross had gone to his study and reread the files. Rereading them now with the new knowledge of AMG's death and possible murder, the involvement of MI-5 and -6, probably the KGB, and Crosse's astounding anxiety; and then the added thought that perhaps some of the material might not yet be available to the Secret Service, together with the possibility that many of the pieces he had dismissed as too farfetched were not—now all the reports took on new importance. Some of them blew his mind.

To hand them over was too risky. To keep them now, impossible.

In the quiet of the night Dunross had considered destroying them. Finally he concluded it was his duty not to. For a moment he had considered leaving them openly on his desk, the French windows wide to the terrace darkness, and going back to sleep. If Crosse was so concerned about the papers then he and his men would be watching now. To lock them in the safe was unsafe. The safe had been touched once. It would be touched again. No safe was proof against an absolute, concerted professional attack.

There in the darkness, his feet perched comfortably, he had felt the excitement welling, the beautiful, intoxicating lovely warmth of danger surrounding him, physical danger. Of enemies nearby. Of being perched on the knife edge between life and void. The only thing that detracted from his pleasure was the knowledge that Struan's was betrayed from within, the same question always grinding: Is the Sevrin spy the same as he who gave their secrets to Bartlett? One of seven? Alastair, Phillip, Andrew, Jacques, Linbar, David MacStruan in Toronto, or his father. All unthinkable.

His mind had examined each one. Clinically, without passion. All had
the opportunity, all the same motive: jealousy, and hatred, in varying degrees. But not one would sell the Noble House to an outsider. Not one.
Even so, one of them did.

Who?

The hours passed.

Who? Sevrin, what to do about the files, was AMG murdered, how
much of the files're true?

Who?

The night was cool now and the terrace had beckoned him. He stood
under the stars. The breeze and the night welcomed him. He had always
loved the night. Flying alone above the clouds at night, so much better
than the day, the stars so near, eyes always watching for the enemy
bomber or enemy night fighter, thumb ready on the trigger . . . ah, life
was so simple then, kill or be killed.

He stood there for a while, then, refreshed, he went back and locked
the files away and sat in his great chair facing the French windows, on
guard, working out his options, choosing one. Then, satisfied, he had
dozed an hour or so and awoke, as usual, just before dawn.

His dressing room was off his study which was next door to their master
bedroom. He had dressed casually and left silently. The road was clear.
Sixteen seconds were clipped from his record. In his penthouse he bathed
and shaved and changed into a tropical suit, then went to his office on the
floor below. It was very humid today with a curious look to the sky. A
tropical storm's coming, he had thought. Perhaps we'll be lucky and it
won't pass us by like all the others and it'll bring rain. He turned away
from his windows and concentrated on running the Noble House.

There was a pile of overnight telexes to deal with on all manner of negotiations and enterprises, problems and business opportunities throughout
the Colony and the great outside. From all points of the compass. As far
north as the Yukon where Struan's had an oil-prospecting joint venture
with the Canadian timber and mining giant, McLean-Woodley. Singapore
and Malaya and as far south as Tasmania for fruit and minerals to carry
to Japan. West to Britain, east to New York, the tentacles of the new international Noble House that Dunross dreamed about were beginning to
reach out, still weak, still tentative, and without the sustenance he knew
was vital to their growth.

Never mind. Soon they'll be strong. The Par-Con deal will make our
web like steel, with Hong Kong the center of the earth and us the nucleus
of the center. Thank God for the telex and telephones.

"Mr. Bartlett please."

"Hello?"

"Ian Dunross, good morning, sorry to disturb you so early, could we
postpone our meeting till 6:30?"

"Yes. Is there a problem?"

"No. Just business. I've a lot to catch up with."

"Anything on John Chen?"

"Not yet, no. Sorry. I'll keep you posted though. Give my regards to Casey."

"I will. Say, that was some party last night. Your daughter's a charmer!"

"Thanks. I'll come to the hotel at 6:30. Of course Casey's invited. See you then. 'Bye!"

Ah Casey! he thought.

Casey and Bartlett. Casey and Gornt. Gornt and Four Finger Wu.

Early this morning he had heard from Four Finger Wu about his meeting with Gornt. A pleasant current had swept through him on hearing that his enemy had almost died. The Peak Road's no place to lose your brakes, he thought.

Pity the bastard didn't die. That would have saved me lots of anguish. Then he dismissed Gornt and rethought Four Finger Wu.

Between the old seaman's pidgin and his Haklo they could converse quite well. Wu had told him everything he could. Gornt's comment on the Ho-Pak, advising Wu to withdraw his money, was surprising. And cause for concern. That and Haply's article.

Does that bugger Gornt know something I don't?

He had gone to the bank. "Paul, what's going on?"

"About what?"

"The Ho-Pak."

"Oh. The run? Very bad for our banking image, I must say. Poor Richard! We're fairly certain he's got all the reserves he needs to weather his storm but we don't know the extent of his commitments. Of course I called him the moment I read Haply's ridiculous article. I must tell you, Ian, I also called Christian Toxe and told him in no uncertain terms he should control his reporters and that he'd better cease and desist or else."

"I was told there was a queue at Tsim Sha Tsui."

"Oh? I hadn't heard that. I'll check. Even so, surely the Ching Prosperity and the Lo Fat banks will support him. My God, he's built up the Ho-Pak into a major banking institution. If he went broke God knows what'll happen. We even had some withdrawals at Aberdeen ourselves. No, Ian, let's hope it'll all blow over. Talking about that, do you think we'll get some rain? It feels dicey today, don't you think? The news said there might be a storm coming through. Do you think it'll rain?"

"I don't know. Let's hope so. But not on Saturday!"

"My God yes! If the races were rained out that would be terrible. We can't have that. Oh, by the way, Ian, it was a lovely party last night. I enjoyed meeting Bartlett and his girl friend. How're your negotiations with Bartlett proceeding?"

"First class! Listen, Paul . . ."

Dunross smiled to himself, remembering how he had dropped his voice even though in Havergill's office . . . Havergill's office which overlooked the whole of Central District was book-lined and very carefully sound-proofed. "I've closed my deal. It's two years initially. We sign the papers within seven days. They're putting up 20 million cash in each of the years, succeeding ones to be negotiated."

"Congratulations, my dear fellow. Heartiest congratulations! And the down payment?"

"Seven."

"That's marvelous! That covers everything nicely. It'll be marvelous to have the Toda specter away from the balance sheet—and with another million for Orlin, well, perhaps they'll give you more time, then at long last you can forget all the bad years and look forward to a very profitable future."

"Yes."

"Have you got your ships chartered yet?"

"No. But I'll have charterers in time to service our loan."

"I noticed your stock's jumped two points."

"It's on the way now. It's going to double, within thirty days."

"Oh? What makes you think so?"

"The boom."

"Eh?"

"All the signs point that way, Paul. Confidence's up. Our Par-Con deal will lead the boom. It's long overdue."

"That would be marvelous! When do you make the initial announcement about Par-Con?"

"Friday, after the market closes."

"Excellent. My thought entirely. By Monday everyone will be on the bandwagon!"

"But let's keep everything in the family until then."

"Of course. Oh, did you hear Quillan almost killed himself last night. It was just after your party. His brakes failed on the Peak Road."

"Yes I heard. He should have killed himself—that would have sent Second Great Company's stock skyrocketing with happiness!"

"Come now, Ian! A boom eh? You really think so?"

"Enough to want to buy heavily. How about a million credit—to buy Struan's?"

"Personal—or for the House?"

"Personal."

"We would hold the stock?"

"Of course."

"And if the stock goes down?"

"It won't."

"Say it does, Ian?"

"What do you suggest?"

"Well, it's all in the family so why don't we say if it goes two points below market at today's closing, we can sell and debit your account with the loss?"

"Three. Struan's is going to double."

"Yes. Meanwhile, let's say two until you sign the Par-Con deal. The House is rather a lot over on its revolving credit already. Let's say two, eh?"

"All right."

I'm safe at two, Dunross thought again, reassuring himself. I think.

Before he had left the bank he had gone by Johnjohn's office. Bruce Johnjohn, second deputy chief manager and heir apparent to Havergill, was a stocky, gentle man with a hummingbird's vitality. Dunross had given him the same news. Johnjohn had been equally pleased. But he had advised caution on projecting a boom and, contrary to Havergill, was greatly concerned with the Ho-Pak run.

"I don't like it at all, Ian. It's very smelly."

"Yes. What about Haply's article?"

"Oh, it's all nonsense. We don't go in for those sort of shenanigans. Blacs? Equally foolish. Why should we want to eliminate a major Chinese bank, even if we could. The Ching Bank might be the culprit. Perhaps. Perhaps old Smiler Ching would—he and Richard have been rivals for years. It could be a combination of half a dozen banks, Ching included. It might even be that Richard's depositors are really scared. I've heard all sorts of rumors for three months or so. They're in deep with dozens of dubious property schemes. Anyway, if he goes under it'll affect us all. Be bloody careful, Ian!"

"I'll be gald when you're upstairs, Bruce."

"Don't sell Paul short—he's very clever and he's been awfully good for Hong Kong and the bank. But we're in for some hairy times in Asia, Ian. I must say I think you're very wise to try to diversify into South America— it's a huge market and untapped by us. Have you considered South Africa?"

"What about it?"

"Let's have lunch next week. Wednesday? Good. I've an idea for you."

"Oh? What?"

"It'll wait, old chum. You heard about Gornt?"

"Yes."

"Very unusual for a Rolls, what?"

"Yes."

"He's very sure he can take Par-Con away from you."

"He won't."

"Have you seen Phillip today?"

"Phillip Chen? No, why?"

"Nothing."

"Why?"

"Bumped into him at the track. He seemed . . . well, he looked awful and very distraught. He's taking John's . . . he's taking the kidnapping very badly."

"Wouldn't you?"

"Yes. Yes I would. But I didn't think he and his Number One Son were that close."

Dunross thought about Adryon and Glenna and his son Duncan who was fifteen and on holiday on a friend's sheep station in Australia. What would I do if one of them were kidnapped? What would I do if a mutilated ear came through the mails at me like that?

I'd go mad.

I'd go mad with rage. I'd forget everything else and I'd hunt down the kidnappers and then, and then my vengeance would last a thousand years. I'd . . .

There was a knock on the door. "Yes? Oh hello, Kathy," he said, happy as always to see his younger sister.

"Sorry to interrupt, Ian dear," Kathy Gavallan said in a rush from the door to his office, "but Claudia said you had a few minutes before your next appointment. Is it all right?"

" 'Course it's all right," he said with a laugh, and put aside the memo he was working on.

"Oh good, thanks." She closed the door and sat in the high chair that was near the window.

He stretched to ease the ache in his back and grinned at her. "Hey, I like your hat." It was pale straw with a yellow band that matched her cool-looking silk dress. "What's up?"

"I've got multiple sclerosis."

He stared at her blankly. "What?"

"That's what the tests say. The doctor told me yesterday but yesterday I couldn't tell you or . . . Today he checked the tests with another specialist and there's no mistake." Her voice was calm and her face calm and she sat upright in the chair, looking prettier than he had ever seen her. "I had to tell someone. Sorry to say it so suddenly. I thought you could help me make a plan, not today, but when you've time, perhaps over the weekend. . . ." She saw his expression and she laughed nervously. "It's not as bad as that. I think."

Dunross sat back in his big leather chair and fought to get his shocked mind working. "Multiple . . . that's dicey, isn't it?"

"Yes. Yes it is. Apparently it's something that attacks your nervous system that they can't cure yet. They don't know what it is or where or how you . . . how you get it."

"We'll get other specialists. No, even better, you go to England with Penn. There'd be specialists there or in Europe. There's got to be some form of cure, Kathy, got to be!"

"There isn't, dear. But England is a good idea. I'm . . . Dr. Tooley said he'd like me to see a Harley Street specialist for treatment. I'd love to go with Penn. I'm not too advanced and there's nothing to be too concerned about, if I'm careful."

"Meaning?"

"Meaning that if I take care of myself, take their medication, nap in the afternoon to stop getting tired, I'll still be able to take care of Andrew and the house and the children and play a little tennis and golf occasionally, but only one round in the mornings. You see, they can arrest the disease but they can't repair the damage already done so far. He said if I don't take care of myself and rest—it's rest mostly he said—if I don't rest, it will start up again and then each time you go down a plateau. Yes. And then you can never get back up again. Do you see, dear?"

He stared at her, keeping his agony for her bottled. His heart was grinding in his chest and he had eight plans for her and he thought Oh Christ poor Kathy! "Yes. Well, thank God you can rest all you want," he said, keeping his voice calm like hers. "Do you mind if I talk to Tooley?"

"I think that would be all right. There's no need to be alarmed, Ian. He said I'd be all right if I took care of myself, and I told him I'd be ever so good so he needn't have any worries on that score." Kathy was surprised that her voice was calm and her hands and fingers rested in her lap so easily, betraying none of the horror she felt within. She could almost feel the disease bugs or microbes or viruses seeping through her system, feeding on her nerves, eating them away oh so slowly, second by second hour by hour until there would be more tingling and more numbness in her fingers and her toes, then her wrists and ankles and legs and and and and and oh Jesus Christ God almighty . . .

She took a little tissue out of her purse and gently dabbed beside her nose and forehead. "It's awfully humid today, isn't it?"

"Yes. Kathy, why is it so sudden?"

"Well it isn't dear, not really. They just couldn't diagnose it. That's what all the tests were for." It had begun as a slight dizziness and headaches about six months ago. She'd noticed it most when she was playing golf. She would be standing over her ball, steadying herself, but her eyes would go dizzy and she could not focus and the ball would split and become two and three and two again and they would never stay still. Andrew had laughed and told her to see an optician. But it wasn't glasses, and aspirins did not help, nor stronger pills. Then dear old Tooley, their family doctor forever, had sent her to Matilda Hospital on the Peak for tests and more tests and brain scans in case there was a tumor but they had shown nothing, nor had all the other tests. Only the awful spinal tap gave a clue. Other tests confirmed it. Yesterday. Oh sweet Jesus was it only yesterday they condemned me to the wheelchair, at length to become a helpless slobbering thing?

"You've told Andrew?"

"No dear," she said, pulled once more back from the brink. "I haven't told him yet. I couldn't, not yet. Poor dear Andrew does get into a tizzy so

easily. I'll tell him tonight. I couldn't tell him before I told you. I had to
tell you first. We always used to tell you everything first, didn't we?
Lechie, Scotty and I? You always used to know first. . . ." She was
remembering when they were all young, all the lovely happy times here in
Hong Kong and in Ayr at Castle Avisyard, at their lovely old rambling
house on the crest of the hill amid the heather, overlooking the sea—
Christmas and Easter and the long summer holidays, she and Ian—and
Lechie, the oldest, and Scott, her twin brother—such happy days when Father wasn't there, all of them terrified of their father except Ian who was
always their spokesman, always their protector, who always took the
punishments—no supper tonight, and write five hundred times I will not
argue anymore, a child's place is to be seen and not heard—who took all
the beatings and never complained. Oh poor Lechie and Scotty . . .

"Oh Ian," she said, her tears welling suddenly, "I'm so sorry." Then
she felt his arms wrap around her and she felt safe at last and the nightmare softened. But she knew it would never go away. Not now. Never.
Nor would her brothers come back, except in her dreams, nor would her
darling Johnny. "It's all right, Ian," she said through her tears. "It's not
for me, not me really. I was just thinking about Lechie and Scotty and
home at Ayr when we were small, and my Johnny, and I was oh ever so
sad for all of them. . . ."

Lechie was the first to die. Second Lieutenant, Highland Light Infantry. He was lost in 1940 in France. Nothing was ever found of him. One
moment he had been there beside the road, and then he was gone, the air
filled with acrid smoke from the barrage that the Nazi panzers had laid
down on the little stone bridge over the stream on the way to Dunkirk.
For all the war years they had all lived in the hope that Lechie was now a
POW in some good prison camp—not one of those terrible ones. And after
the war, the months of searching but never a sign, never a witness, not
even the littlest sign and then they, the family, and at length Father had
laid Lechie's ghost to rest.

Scott had been sixteen in '39 and he'd gone to Canada for safety, there
to finish schooling, and then, already a pilot, the day he was eighteen, in
spite of Father's howling protests, he had joined the Canadian Air Force,
wanting blood vengeance for Lechie. And he had got his wings at once
and joined a bomber squadron and had come over well in time for D Day.
Gleefully he had blown many a town to pieces and many a city to pieces
until February 14, 1945, now Squadron Leader, DFC and Bar, coming
home from the supreme holocaust of Dresden, his Lancaster had been
jumped by a Messerschmitt and though his copilot had brought the crippled plane to rest in England, Scotty was dead in the left seat.

Kathy had been at his funeral and Ian had been there—in uniform,
come home on leave from Chungking where he had been attached to
Chiang Kai-shek's air force after he was shot down and grounded. She
had wept on Ian's shoulder, wept for Lechie and wept for Scotty and wept

for her Johnny. She was a widow then. Flight Lieutenant John Selkirk, DFC, another happy god of war, inviolate, invincible, had been blown out of the sky, torched out of the sky, the debris burning on the way to earth.

Johnny had had no funeral. There was nothing to bury. Like Lechie. Just a telegram came. One for each of them.

Oh Johnny my darling my darling my darling . . .

"What an awful waste, Ian dear, all of them. And for what?"

"I don't know, little Kathy," he said, still holding her. "I don't know. And I don't know why I made it and why they didn't."

"Oh I'm ever so glad you did!" She gave him a little hug and gathered herself. Somehow she put away her sadness for all of them. Then she dried her tears, took out a small mirror and looked at herself. "God, I look a mess! Sorry." His private bathroom was concealed behind a bookcase and she went there and repaired her makeup.

When she came back he was still staring out of the window. "Andrew's out of the office at the moment but the moment he comes back I'll tell him," he said.

"Oh no dear, that's my job. I must do that. I must. That's only fair." She smiled up at him and touched him. "I love you, Ian."

"I love you, Kathy."

22

The cardboard box that the Werewolves had sent to Phillip Chen was on Roger Crosse's desk. Beside the box was the ransom note, key ring, driver's license, pen, even the crumpled pieces of torn newspaper that had been used for packing. The little plastic bag was there, and the mottled rag. Only its contents were missing.

Everything had been tagged.

Roger Crosse was alone in the room and he stared at the objects, fascinated. He picked up a piece of the newspaper. Each had been carefully smoothed out, most were tagged with a date and the name of the Chinese newspaper it had come from. He turned it over, seeking hidden information, a hidden clue, something that might have been missed. Finding nothing, he put it back neatly and leaned on his hands, lost in thought.

Alan Medford Grant's report was also on his desk, near the intercom. It was very quiet in the room. Small windows overlooked Wanchai and part of the harbor toward Glessing's Point.

His phone jangled. "Yes?"

"Mr. Rosemont, CIA, and Mr. Langan, FBI, sir."

"Good." Roger Crosse replaced his phone. He unlocked his top desk drawer and carefully put the AMG file on top of the decoded telex and relocked it. The middle drawer contained a high-quality tape recorder. He checked it and touched a hidden switch. Silently the reels began to turn. The intercom on his desk contained a powerful microphone. Satisfied, he relocked this drawer. Another hidden desk switch slid a bolt open on the door soundlessly. He got up and opened the door.

"Hello, you two, please come in," he said affably. He closed the door behind the two Americans and shook hands with them. Unnoticed, he slid the bolt home again. "Take a seat. Tea?"

"No thanks," the CIA man said.

"What can I do for you?"

Both men were carrying manila envelopes. Rosemont opened his and took out a sheaf of good-quality eight-by-ten photos, clipped into two sections. "Here," he said, passing over the top section.

They were various shots of Voranski running across the wharf, on the streets of Kowloon, getting into and out of taxis, phoning, and many more of his Chinese assassins. One photograph showed the two Chinese leaving the phone booth with a clear glimpse of the crumpled body in the background.

Only Crosse's superb discipline kept him from showing astonishment, then blinding rage. "Good, very good," he said gently, putting them on the desk, very conscious of the ones Rosemont had retained in his hand. "So?"

Rosemont and Ed Langan frowned. "You were tailing him too?"

"Of course," Crosse said, lying with his marvelous sincerity. "My dear fellow, this is Hong Kong. But I do wish you'd let us do our job and not interfere."

"Rog, we, er, we don't want to interfere, just want to backstop you."

"Perhaps we don't need backstopping." There was a sharpness to his voice now.

"Sure." Rosemont took out a cigarette and lit it. He was tall and thin with gray crew-cut hair and good features. His hands were strong, like all of him. "We know where the two killers're holed up. We think we know," he said. "One of our guys thinks he's pegged them."

"How many men have you got watching the ship?"

"Ten. Our guys didn't notice any of yours tailing this one. The diversion almost spooked us too."

"Very dicey," Crosse said agreeably, wondering what diversion.

"Our guys never got to go through his pockets—we know he made two calls from the booth. . . ." Rosemont noted Crosse's eyes narrow slightly. That's curious, he thought. Crosse didn't know that. If he doesn't know that, maybe his operators weren't tailing the target either. Maybe he's lying and the Commie was loose in Hong Kong until he was knifed. "We radioed a mug shot back home—we'll get a call back fast. Who was he?"

"His papers said, Igor Voranski, seaman first class, Soviet merchant marine."

"You have a file on him, Rog?"

"It's rather unusual for you two to call together, isn't it? I mean, in the movies, we're always led to believe the FBI and CIA are always at odds."

Ed Langan smiled. "Sure we are—like you and MI-5—like the KGB, GRU and fifty other Soviet operations. But sometimes our cases cross—we're internal U.S., Stan's external, but we're both out for the same thing: security. We thought . . . we're asking if we could all cooperate. This could be a big one, and we're . . . Stan and I're out of our depth."

"That's right," Rosemont said, not believing it.

"All right," Crosse said, needing their information. "But you first."

Rosemont sighed. "Okay, Rog. We've had a buzz for some time there's something hotting up in Hong Kong—we don't know what—but it sure as hell's got tie-ins to the States. I figure the AMG file's the link. Lookit: take Banastasio—he's Mafia. Big-time. Narcotics, the lot. Now take Bartlett and the guns. Guns—"

"Is Bartlett tied into Banastasio?"

"We're not sure. We're checking. We are sure the guns were put aboard in L.A.—Los Angeles—where the airplane's based. Guns! Guns, narcotics and our growing interest in Vietnam. Where do narcotics come from? The Golden Triangle. Vietnam, Laos and the Yunnan Province of China. Now we're into Vietnam and—"

"Yes, and you're ill-advised to be there, old chum—I've pointed that out fifty times."

"We don't make policy, Rog, any more than you do. Next: Our nuclear carrier's here and the goddamn *Sovetsky Ivanov* arrives last night. That's too convenient, maybe the leak came from here. Then Ed tips you off and we get AMG's wild-assed letters from London and now there's Sevrin! Turns out the KGB've plants all over Asia and you've a high-placed hostile somewheres."

"That's not yet proved."

"Right. But I know about AMG. He's nobody's fool. If he says Sevrin's in place and you've a mole, you've a mole. Sure we've got hostiles in the CIA too, so've the KGB. I'm sure Ed has in the FBI—"

"That's doubtful," Ed Langan interrupted sharply. "Our guys are hand-picked and trained. You get your firemen from all over."

"Sure," Rosemont said, then added to Crosse, "Back to narcotics. Red China's our big enemy and—"

"Again, you're wrong, Stanley. The PRC's not the big enemy anywhere. Russia is."

"China's Commie. Commies're the enemy. Now, it'd be real smart to flood the States with cheap narcotics and Red China . . . okay the People's Republic of China can open the dam gates."

"But they haven't. Our Narcotics Branch's the best in Asia—they've never come up with anything to support your misguided official theory that they're behind the trade. Nothing. The PRC are as anti-drug traffic as the rest of us."

"Have it your way," Rosemont said. "Rog, you got a file on this agent? He's KGB, isn't he?"

Crosse lit a cigarette. "Voranski was here last year. That time he went under the cover name of Sergei Kudryov, again seaman first class, again off the same ship—they're not very inventive, are they?" Neither of the two men smiled. "His real name's Major Yuri Bakyan, First Directorate, KGB, Department 6."

Rosemont sighed heavily.

The FBI man glanced at him. "Then you're right. It all ties in."

"Maybe." The tall man thought a moment. "Rog, what about his contacts from last year?"

"He acted like a tourist, staying at the Nine Dragons in Kowloon. . . ."

"That's in AMG's report, that hotel's mentioned," Langan said.

"Yes. We've been covering it for a year or so. We've found nothing. Bakyan—Voranski—did ordinary tourist activities. We had him on twenty-four-hour surveillance. He stayed a couple of weeks, then, just before the ship sailed, sneaked back aboard."

"Girl friend?"

"No. Not a regular one. He used to hang out at the Good Luck Dance Hall in Wanchai. Quite a cocksman, apparently, but he asked no questions and met no one out of the ordinary."

"He ever visit Sinclair Towers?"

"No."

"Pity," Langan said, "that'd've been dandy. Tsu-yan's got a place there. Tsu-yan knows Banastasio, John Chen knows Banastasio, and we're back to guns, narcotics, AMG and Sevrin."

"Yeah," Rosemont said, then added, "Have you caught up with Tsu-yan yet?"

"No. He got to Taipei safely, then vanished."

"You think he's holed up there?"

"I would imagine so," Crosse said. But inside he believed him dead, already eliminated by Nationalist, Communist, Mafia or triad. *I wonder if he could have been a double agent—or the supreme devil of all intelligence services, a triple agent?*

"You'll find him—or we will—or the Taiwan boys will."

"Roger, did Voranski lead you anywhere?" Langan asked.

"No. Nowhere, even though we've had tabs on him for years. He's been attached to the Soviet Trade Commission in Bangkok, he spent time in Hanoi, and Seoul, but no covert activities we know of. Once the cheeky bugger even applied for a British passport and almost got one. Luckily our fellows vet all applications and spotted flaws in his cover. I'm sorry he's dead—you know how hard it is to identify nasties. Waste of a lot of time and effort." Crosse paused and lit a cigarette. "His major's rank is quite senior which suggests something very smelly. Perhaps he was just another of their specials who was ordered to cruise Asia and get into deep cover for twenty or thirty years."

"Those bastards have had their game plan set for so long it stinks!" Rosemont sighed. "What're you going to do with the corpse?"

Crosse smiled. "I got one of my Russian-speaking fellows to call the captain of the ship—Gregor Suslev. He's a Party member, of course, but fairly harmless. Has a sporadic girl friend with a flat in Mong Kok—a bar girl who gets a modest allowance from him and entertains him when he's here. He goes to the races, theater, Macao gambling a couple of times, speaks good English. Suslev's under surveillance. I don't want any of your hotshots ponging on one of our known hostiles."

"So Suslev's regular here then?"

"Yes, he's been plying these waters for years, based out of Vladivostok—he's an ex-submarine commander by the way. He wanders around the fringe here, mostly under the weather."

"What do you mean?"

"Drunk, but not badly so. Cavorts with a few of our British pinkos like Sam and Molly Finn."

"The ones who're always writing letters to the papers?"

"Yes. They're more of a nuisance than a security risk. Anyway, under instructions, my Russian-speaking fellow told Captain Suslev we were frightfully sorry but it seemed that one of his seamen had had a heart attack in a phone booth at Golden Ferry Terminal. Suslev was suitably shocked and quite reasonable. In Voranski's pocket there 'happened' to be an accurate, verbatim report of the assassin's phone conversation. We put it in Russian as a further sign of our displeasure. They're all professionals aboard that ship, and sophisticated enough to know we don't remove their agents without very great cause and provocation. They know we just watch the ones we know about and, if we're really very irritated, we deport them." Crosse looked across at Rosemont, his eyes hard though his voice stayed matter-of-fact. "We find our methods more effective than the knife, garrotte, poison or bullet."

The CIA man nodded. "But who would want to kill him?"

Crosse glanced at the photos again. He did not recognize the two Chinese, but their faces were clear and the body in the background unbelievable evidence. "We'll find them. Whoever they are. The one who phoned our police station claimed they were 14K. But he only spoke Shanghainese with a Ningpo dialect, so that's unlikely. Probably he was a triad of some sort. He could be Green Pang. He was certainly a trained professional—the knife was used perfectly, with great precision—one moment alive, the next dead and no sound. Could be one of your CIA's trainees in Chiang Kai-shek's intelligence agency. Or perhaps the Korean CIA, more of your trainees—they're anti-Soviet too, aren't they? Possibly PRC agents, but that's improbable. Their agents don't usually go in for *quai loh* murder, and certainly not in Hong Kong."

Rosemont nodded and let the censure pass. He gave Crosse the remaining photos, wanting the Englishman's cooperation and needing it. "These're shots of the house they went into. And the street sign. Our guy couldn't read characters but it translates, 'Street of the First Season, Number 14.' It's a rotten little alley in back of the bus depot in North Point."

Crosse began to examine them with equal care. Rosemont glanced at his watch, then got up and went to the single window that faced part of the harbor. "Look!" he said proudly.

The other two went over to him. The great nuclear carrier was just rounding North Point heading for the navy yard, Hong Kong side. She was dressed overall, all her obligatory flags stiff in the breeze, crowds of white-clothed sailors on her vast deck, with neat lines of her vicious fighter jet airplanes. Almost 84,000 tons. No smokestack, just a vast, ominous bridge complex, with an eleven-hundred-foot angled runway that could retrieve and launch jets simultaneously. The first of a generation.

"That's some ship," Crosse said enviously. This was the first time the colossus had entered Hong Kong since her commissioning in 1960. "Pretty," he said, hating the fact she was American and not British. "What's her top speed?"

"I don't know—that's classified along with most everything else." Rosemont turned to watch him. "Can't you send that goddamn Soviet spy ship to hell out of port?"

"Yes, and we could blow it up, but that would be equally foolish. Stanley, relax, you have to be a little civilized about these things. Repairing their ships—and some of them really do need it—is a good source of revenue, and intelligence, and they pay their bills promptly. Our ways have been tried and tested over the years."

Yes, Rosemont was thinking without rancor, but your ways don't work anymore. The British Empire's no more, the British raj no more and we've a different enemy now, smarter rougher dedicated totalitarian fanatic, with no Queensberry rules and a worldwide plan that's lavishly funded by whatever it takes. You British've no dough now, no clout, no navy, no army, no air force, and your goddamn government's filled with socialist and enemy pus, and *we* think they sold you out. You've been screwed from within, your security's the pits from Klaus Fuchs and Philby on down. Jesus, we won both goddamn wars for you, paid for most of it and both times you've screwed up the peace. And if it wasn't for *our* Strategic Air Command, our missiles, our nuclear strike force, our navy, our army, our air force our taxpayers our dough, you'd all be dead or in goddamn Siberia. Meanwhile, like it or not I got to deal with you. We need Hong Kong as a window and right now your cops to guard the carrier.

"Rog, thanks for the extra men," he said. "We sure appreciate it."

"We wouldn't want any trouble while she's here either. Pretty ship. I envy you having her."

"Her captain'll have the ship and crew under tight wraps—the shore parties'll all be briefed, and warned, and we'll cooperate a hundred percent."

"I'll see you get a copy of the list of bars I've suggested your sailors stay out of—some're known Communist hangouts, and some are frequented by our lads off H.M.S. *Dart*." Crosse smiled. "There'll still be the odd brawl."

"Sure. Rog, this Voranski killing's too much of a coincidence. Can I send a Shanghai speaker to assist the interrogation?"

"I'll let you know if we need help."

"Can we have our copies of the tai-pan's other AMG reports now? Then we can get out of your hair."

Crosse stared back at him twisting uneasily, even though he was prepared for the question. "I'll have to get approval from Whitehall."

Rosemont was surprised. "Our top man in England's been on to your Great White Father and it's approved. You should have had it an hour ago."

"Oh?"

"Sure. Hell, we'd no idea AMG was on the tai-pan's payroll let alone passing classified stuff for chrissake! The wires've been red hot since Ed got the top copy of AMG's last will and testament. We got an all-points from Washington on getting copies of the other reports and we're trying to trace the call to Switzerland but—"

"Say again?"

"Kiernan's call. The second call he made."

"I don't follow you."

Rosemont explained.

Crosse frowned. "My people didn't tell me about that. Nor did Dunross. Now why should Dunross lie—or avoid telling me that?" He related to them exactly what Dunross had told him. "There was no reason for him to hide that, was there?"

"No. All right, Rog: Is the tai-pan kosher?"

Crosse laughed. "If you mean is he a one hundred percent British Royalist freebooter whose allegiance is to his House, himself and the Queen—not necessarily in that order—the answer's an emphatic yes."

"Then if we can have our copies now, Rog, we'll be on our way."

"When I've got Whitehall's approval."

"If you'll check your decoding room—it's a Priority 1-4a. It says to let us have copies on receipt."

1-4a's were very rare. They called for immediate clearance and immediate action.

Crosse hesitated, wanting to avoid the trap he was in. He dared not tell them he did not yet have possession of the AMG reports. He picked up the phone and dialed. "This is Mr. Crosse. Is there anything for me from Source? A 1-4a?"

"No sir. Other than the one we sent up an hour ago—that you signed for," the SI woman said.

"Thank you." Crosse put the phone down. "Nothing yet," he said.

"Shit," Rosemont muttered, then added, "They swore they'd already beamed it out and you'd have it before we got here. It's got to be here any second. If you don't mind we'll wait."

"I've an appointment in Central shortly. Perhaps later this evening?"

Both men shook their heads. Langan said, "We'll wait. We've been ordered to send 'em back instantly by hand with a twenty-four-hour guard.

An army transport's due now at Kai Tak to carry the courier—we can't even copy them here."

"Aren't you overreacting?"

"You could answer that. What's in them?"

Crosse toyed with his lighter. It had Cambridge University emblazoned on it. He had owned it since his undergraduate days. "Is it true what AMG said about the CIA and the Mafia?"

Rosemont stared back at him. "I don't know. You guys used all sort of crooks during World War Two. We learned from you to take advantage of what we've got—that was your first rule. Besides," Rosemont added with utter conviction, "this war's our war and whatever it takes we're going to win."

"Yes, yes we must," Langan echoed, equally sure. "Because if we lose this one, the whole world's gone and we'll never get another chance."

On the closed-in bridge of the *Sovetsky Ivanov* three men had binoculars trained on the nuclear carrier. One of the men was a civilian and he wore a throat mike that fed into a tape recorder. He was giving an expert, technical running commentary of what he saw. From time to time the other two would add a comment. Both wore light naval uniform. One was Captain Gregor Suslev, the other his first officer.

The carrier was coming up the roads nicely, tugs in attendance, but no tug ropes. Ferries and freighters tooted a jaunty welcome. A marine band played on her aft deck. White-clad sailors waved at passing ships. The day was very humid and the afternoon sun cast long shadows.

"The captain's expert," the first officer said.

"Yes. But with all that radar even a child could handle her," Captain Suslev replied. He was a heavy-shouldered, bearded man, his Slavic brown eyes deepset in a friendly face. "Those sweepers aloft look like the new GE's for very long-range radar. Are they, Vassili?"

The technical expert broke off his transmission momentarily. "Yes, Comrade Captain. But look aft! They've four F5 interceptors parked on the right flight deck."

Suslev whistled tonelessly. "They're not supposed to be in service till next year."

"No," the civilian said.

"Report that separately as soon as she docks. That news alone pays for our voyage."

"Yes."

Suslev fine-tuned his focus now as the ship turned slightly. He could see the airplanes' bomb racks. "How many more F5's does she carry in her guts, and how many atomic warheads for them?"

They all watched the carrier for a moment.

"Perhaps we'll get lucky this time, Comrade Captain," the first officer said.

"Let's hope so. Then Voranski's death won't be so expensive."

"The Americans are fools to bring her here—don't they know every agent in Asia'll be tempted by her?"

"It's lucky for us they are. It makes our job so much easier." Once more Suslev concentrated on the F5's that looked like soldier hornets among other hornets.

Around him the bridge was massed with advanced surveillance equipment. One radar was sweeping the harbor. A gray-haired impassive sailor watched the screen, the carrier a large clear blip among the myriad of blips.

Suslev's binoculars moved to the carrier's ominous bridge complex, then wandered the length of the ship. In spite of himself he shivered at her size and power. "They say she's never refueled—not since she was launched in 1960."

Behind him the door to the radio room that adjoined the bridge opened and a radio operator came up to him and saluted, offering the cable. "Urgent from Center, Comrade Captain."

Suslev took the cable and signed for it. It was a meaningless jumble of words. A last look at the carrier and he let the binoculars rest on his chest and strode off the bridge. His sea cabin was just aft on the same deck. The door was guarded, like both entrances to the bridge.

He relocked his cabin door behind him and opened the small, concealed safe. His cipher book was secreted in a false wall. He sat at his desk. Quickly he decoded the message. He read it carefully, then stared into space for a moment.

He read it a second time, then replaced the cipher book, closed the safe and burned the original of the cable in an ashtray. He picked up his phone. "Bridge? Send Comrade Metkin to my cabin!" While he waited he stood by the porthole lost in thought. His cabin was untidy. Photographs of a heavyset woman, smiling self-consciously, were on his desk in a frame. Another of a good-looking youth in naval uniform, and a girl in her teens. Books, a tennis racket and a newspaper on the half-made bunk.

A knock. He unlocked the door. The sailor who had been staring at the radar screen stood there.

"Come in, Dimitri." Suslev motioned at the decoded cable and relocked the door after him.

The sailor was short and squat, with graying hair and a good face. He was, officially, political commissar and therefore senior officer on the ship. He picked up the decoded message. It read: "Priority One. Gregor Suslev. You will assume Voranski's duties and responsibilities at once. London reports optimum CIA and MI-6 interest in information contained in blue-covered files leaked to Ian Dunross of Struan's by the British Intelligence coordinator, AMG. Order Arthur to obtain copies immediately. If Dunross has destroyed the copies, cable feasibility plan to detain him for chemical debriefing in depth." The sailor's face closed. He looked across at Captain Suslev. "AMG? Alan Medford Grant?"

"Yes."

"May that one burn in hell for a thousand years."

"He will, if there's any justice in this world or the next." Suslev smiled grimly. He went to a sideboard and took out a half-full vodka bottle and two glasses. "Listen, Dimitri, if I fail or don't return, you take command." He held up the key. "Unlock the safe. There're instructions about decoding and everything else."

"Let me go tonight in your place. You're more impor—"

"No. Thank you, old friend." Suslev clapped him warmly on the shoulders. "In case of an accident you assume command and carry out our mission. That's what we've been trained for." He touched glasses with him. "Don't worry. Everything will be fine," he said, glad he could do as he wished and very content with his job and his position in life. He was, secretly, deputy controller in Asia for the KGB's First Directorate, Department 6, that was responsible for all covert activities in China, North Korea and Vietnam; a senior lecturer in Vladivostok University's Department of Foreign Affairs, 2A–Counterintelligence; a colonel in the KGB; and, most important of all, a senior Party member in the Far East. "Center's given the order. You must guard our tails here. Eh?"

"Of course. You needn't worry about that, Gregor. I can do everything. But I worry about you," Metkin said. They had sailed together for several years and he respected Suslev very much though he did not know from where his overriding authority came. Sometimes he was tempted to try to find out. You're getting on, he told himself. You retire next year and you may need powerful friends and the only way to have the help of powerful friends is to know their skeletons. But Suslev or no Suslev your well-earned retirement will be honorable, quiet and at home in the Crimea. Metkin's heart beat faster at the thought of all that lovely countryside and grand climate on the Black Sea, dreaming the rest of his life away with his wife and sometimes seeing his son, an up-and-coming KGB officer presently in Washington, no longer at risk and in danger from within or without.

Oh God protect my son from betrayal or making a mistake, he prayed fervently, then at once felt a wave of nausea, as always, in case his superiors knew that he was a secret believer and that his parents, peasants, had brought him up in the Church. If they knew there would be no retirement in the Crimea, only some icy backwater and no real home ever again.

"Voranski," he said, as always cautiously hiding his hatred of the man. "He was a top operator, eh? Where did he slip?"

"He was betrayed, that was his problem," Suslev said darkly. "We will find his murderers and they will pay. If my name is on the next knife . . ." The big man shrugged, then poured more vodka with a sudden laugh. "So what, eh? It's in the name of the cause, the Party and Mother Russia!"

They touched glasses and drained them.

"When're you going ashore?"

Suslev bit on the raw liquor. Then, thankfully, he felt the great good warmth begin inside and his anxieties and terrors seemed less real. He motioned out of the porthole. "As soon as she's moored and safe," he said with his rolling laugh. "Ah, but she's a pretty ship, eh?"

"We've got nothing to touch that bastard, Captain, have we? Or those fighters. Nothing."

Suslev smiled as he poured again. "No, comrade. But if the enemy has no real will to resist they can have a hundred of those carriers and it doesn't matter."

"Yes, but Americans're erratic, one general can go off at half-cock, and they can smash us off the face of the earth."

"I agree, now they can, but they won't. They've no balls." Suslev drank again. "And soon? Just a little more time and we'll stick their noses up their asses!" He sighed. "It will be good when we begin."

"It'll be terrible."

"No, a short, almost bloodless war against America and then the rest'll collapse like the pus-infected corpse it is."

"Bloodless? What about their atom bombs? Hydrogen bombs?"

"They'll never use atomics or missiles against us, they're too scared, even now, of *ours!* Because they're *sure* we'll use them."

"Will we?"

"I don't know. Some commanders would. I don't know. We'll certainly use them back. But first? I don't know. The threat will always be enough. I'm sure we'll never need a fighting war." He lit a corner of the decoded message and put it in the ashtray. "Another twenty years of détente—ah what Russian genius invented that—we'll have a navy bigger and better than theirs, an air force bigger and better than theirs. We've got more tanks now and more soldiers, but without ships and airplanes we must wait. Twenty years is not long to wait for Mother Russia to rule the earth."

"And China? What about China?"

Suslev gulped the vodka and refilled both glasses again. The bottle was empty now and he tossed it onto his bunk. His eyes saw the burning paper in the ashtray twist and crackle, dying. "Perhaps China's the one place to use our atomics," he said matter-of-factly. "There's nothing there we need. Nothing. That'd solve our China problem once and for all. How many men of military age did they have at last estimate?"

"116 million between the ages of eighteen and twenty-five."

"Think of that! 116 million yellow devils sharing 5,000 miles of our frontiers . . . and then foreigners call us paranoiac about China!" He sipped the vodka, this time making it last. "Atomics'd solve our China problem once and for all. Quick, simple and permanent."

The other man nodded. "And this Dunross? The papers of AMG?"

"We'll get them from him. After all, Dimitri, one of our people is family, another one of his partners, another's in Special Intelligence, there's Arthur and Sevrin everywhere he turns, and then we've a dozen decadents to call on in his parliament, some in his government." They both began laughing.

"And if he's destroyed the papers?"

Suslev shrugged. "They say he's got a photographic memory."

"You'd do the interrogation here?"

"It'd be dangerous to do an in-depth chemic quickly. I've never done one. Have you?"

"No."

The captain frowned. "When you report tonight, get Center to ready an expert in case we need one—Koronski from Vladivostok if he's available."

Dimitri nodded, lost in thought. This morning's *Guardian*, lying half-crumpled on the captain's bunk, caught his eye. He went over and picked it up, his eyes alight. "Gregor—if we have to detain Dunross, why not blame them, then you've all the time you'll need?" The screaming headline read, SUSPECTS IN WEREWOLVES KIDNAP CASE. "If Dunross doesn't return . . . perhaps our man'd become tai-pan! Eh?"

Suslev began to chuckle. "Dimitri, you're a genius."

Rosemont glanced at his watch. He had waited long enough. "Rog, can I use your phone?"

"Certainly," Crosse said.

The CIA man stubbed out his cigarette and dialed the central CIA exchange in the consulate.

"This is Rosemont—give me 2022." That was the CIA communications center.

"2022. Chapman—who's this?"

"Rosemont. Hi, Phil, anything new?"

"No, excepting Marty Povitz reports a lot of activity on the bridge of the *Ivanov*, high-powered binoculars. Three guys, Stan. One's a civilian, others're the captain and the first officer. One of their short-range radar sweep's working overtime. You want us to notify the *Corregidor*'s captain?"

"Hell no, no need to make his tail wriggle more than needs be. Say, Phil, we get a confirm on our 40-41?"

"Sure Stan. It came in at . . . stand by one . . . it came in at 1603 local."

"Thanks, Phil, see you."

Rosemont lit another cigarette. Sourly Langan, a nonsmoker, watched him but said nothing as Crosse was smoking too.

"Rog, what are you pulling?" Rosemont asked harshly, to Langan's shock. "You got your Priority 1-4a at 1603, same time as we did. Why the stall?"

"I find it presently convenient," Crosse replied, his voice pleasant.

Rosemont flushed, so did Langan. "Well I don't and we've instructions, official instructions, to pick up our copies right now."

"So sorry, Stanley."

Rosemont's neck was now very red but he kept his temper. "You're not going to obey the 1-4a?"

"Not at the moment."

Rosemont got up and headed for the door. "Okay, Rog, but they'll throw the book at you." He ripped the bolt back, jerked the door open and left. Langan was on his feet, his face also set.

"What's the reason, Roger?" he asked.

Crosse stared back at him calmly. "Reason for what?"

Ed Langan began to get angry but stopped, suddenly appalled. "Jesus, Roger, you haven't got them yet? Is that it?"

"Come now, Ed," Crosse said easily, "you of all people should know we're efficient."

"That's no answer, Roger. Have you or haven't you?" The FBI man's level eyes stayed on Crosse, and did not phase Crosse at all. Then he walked out, closing the door after him. At once Crosse touched the hidden switch. The bolt slid home. Another hidden switch turned off his tape recorder. He picked up his phone and dialed. "Brian? Have you heard from Dunross?"

"No sir."

"Meet me downstairs at once. With Armstrong."

"Yes sir."

Crosse hung up. He took out the formal arrest document that was headed DETAINMENT ORDER UNDER THE OFFICIAL SECRETS ACT. Quickly he filled in "Ian Struan Dunross" and signed both copies. The top copy he kept, the other he locked in his drawer. His eyes roamed his office, checking it. Satisfied, he delicately positioned a sliver of paper in the crack of his drawer so that he alone would know if anyone had opened it or tampered with it. He walked out. Heavy security locks slid home after him.

23

Dunross was in the Struan boardroom with the other directors of Nelson Trading, looking at Richard Kwang. "No, Richard. Sorry, I can't wait till after closing tomorrow."

"It'll make no difference to you, tai-pan. It will to me." Richard Kwang was sweating. The others watched him—Phillip Chen, Lando Mata and Zeppelin Tung.

"I disagree, Richard," Lando Mata said sharply. "Madonna, you don't seem to realize the seriousness of the run!"

"Yes," Zeppelin Tung said, his face shaking with suppressed rage.

Dunross sighed. If it wasn't for his presence he knew they would all be raving and screaming at each other, the obscenities flying back and forth as they do at any formal negotiation between Chinese, let alone one as serious as this. But it was a Noble House law that all board meetings were to be conducted in English, and English inhibited Chinese swearing and also unsettled Chinese which was of course the whole idea. "The matter has to be dealt with now, Richard."

"I agree." Lando Mata was a handsome, sharp-featured Portuguese in his fifties, his mother's Chinese blood clear in his dark eyes and dark hair and golden complexion. His long fine fingers drummed continuously on the conference table and he knew Richard Kwang would never dare disclose that he, Tightfist Tung and Smuggler Mo controlled the bank. Our bank's one enterprise, he thought angrily, but our bullion's something else. "We can't have our bullion, or our cash, in jeopardy!"

"Never," Zeppelin Tung said nervously. "My father wanted me to make that clear too. He wants his gold!"

"*Madre de Dios*, we've almost fifty tons of gold in your vaults."

"Actually it's over fifty tons," Zeppelin Tung said, the sweat beading his forehead. "My old man gave me the figures—it's 1,792,668 ounces in 298,778 five-tael bars." The air in the large room was warm and humid, the windows open. Zeppelin Tung was a well-dressed, heavyset man of forty with small narrow eyes, the eldest son of Tightfist Tung, and his accent was upper-class British. His nickname came from a movie that Tightfist had seen the day of his birth. "Richard, isn't that right?"

Richard Kwang shifted the agenda paper in front of him which listed the quantity of gold and Nelson Trading's current balance. If he had to give up the bullion and cash tonight it would severely hurt the bank's liquidity and, when the news leaked, as of course it would, that would rock their whole edifice.

"What're you going to do, you dumbhead dog bone!" his wife had screamed at him just before he had left his office.

"Delay, delay and hope th—"

"No! Pretend to be sick! If you're sick you can't give them our money. You can't go to the meeting! Rush home and we'll pretend—"

"I can't, the tai-pan called personally. And so did that dog bone Mata! I daren't not go! Oh oh oh!"

"Then find out who's hounding us and pay him off! Where's your head? Who have you offended? You must have offended one of those dirty *quai lohs*. Find the man and pay him off or we'll lose the bank, lose our membership in the Turf Club, lose the horses, lose the Rolls and lose face forever! *Ayeeyah!* If the bank goes you'll never be Sir Richard Kwang, not that being Lady Kwang matters to me oh no! Do something! Find the . . ."

Richard Kwang felt the sweat running down his back but he kept his composure and tried to find a way out of the maze. "The gold's as safe as it could be and so's your cash. We've been Nelson Trading's bankers since the beginning, we've never had a sniff of trouble. We gambled heavily with you in the beginning—"

"Come now, Richard," Mata said, keeping his loathing hidden. "You don't gamble on gold. Certainly not on *our* gold." The gold belonged to the Great Good Luck Company of Macao which had also owned the gambling monopoly for almost thirty years. The present worth of the company was in excess of two billion U.S. Tightfist Tung owned 30 percent, personally, Lando Mata 40 percent personally—and the descendents of Smuggler Mo, who had died last year, the other 30 percent.

And between us, Mata was thinking, we own 50 percent of the Ho-Pak which you, you stupid lump of dog turd, have somehow put into jeopardy. "So sorry, Richard, but I vote Nelson Trading changes its bank—at least temporarily. Tightfist Tung is really very upset . . . and I have the Chin family's proxy."

"But Lando," Richard Kwang began, "there's nothing to worry about." His finger stabbed at the half-opened newspaper, the *China Guardian*, that lay on the table. "Haply's new article says again that we're sound— that it's all a storm in an oyster shell, all started by malicious ban—"

"That's possible. But Chinese believe rumors, and the run's a fact," Mata said sharply.

"My old man believes rumors," Zeppelin Tung said fervently. "He also believes Four Finger Wu. Four Fingers phoned him this afternoon telling him he'd taken out all his money and suggested he do the same, and within the hour we, Lando and I, we were in our Catalina and heading here and you know how I hate flying. Richard, you know jolly well if the old man wants something done *now,* it's done *now.*"

Yes, Richard Kwang thought disgustedly, that filthy old miser would climb out of his grave for fifty cents cash. "I suggest we wait a day or so . . ."

Dunross was letting them talk for face. He had already decided what to do. Nelson Trading was a wholly owned subsidiary of Struan's so the other directors really had little say. But even though Nelson Trading had the Hong Kong Government's exclusive gold-importing license, without the Great Good Luck Company's gold business—which meant without Tightfist Tung and Lando Mata's favor—Nelson Trading's profits would be almost zero.

Nelson Trading got a commission of one dollar an ounce on every ounce imported for the company, delivered to the jetty at Macao, a further one dollar an ounce on exports from Hong Kong. As a further consideration for suggesting the overall Hong Kong scheme to the company, Nelson Trading had been granted 10 percent of the real profit. This year the Japanese Government had arbitrarily fixed their official rate of gold at 55 dollars an ounce—a profit of 15 dollars an ounce. On the black market it would be more. In India it would be almost 98 dollars.

Dunross glanced at his watch. In a few minutes Crosse would arrive.

"We've assets over a billion, Lando," Richard Kwang repeated.

"Good," Dunross said crisply jumping in, finalizing the meeting. "Then, Richard, it really makes no difference one way or another. There's no point in waiting. I've made certain arrangements. Our transfer truck will be at your side door at eight o'clock precisely."

"But—"

"Why so late, tai-pan?" Mata asked. "It's not six o'clock yet."

"It'll be dark then, Lando. I wouldn't want to shift 50 tons of gold in daylight. There might be a few villains around. You never know. Eh?"

"My God, you think . . . triads?" Zeppelin Tung was shocked. "I'll phone my father. He'll have some extra guards."

"Yes," Mata said, "call at once."

"No need for that," Dunross told him. "The police suggested that we don't make too much of a show. They said they'll be there in depth."

Mata hesitated. "Well if you say so, tai-pan. You're responsible."

"Of course," Dunross said politely.

"How do we know the Victoria's safe?"

"If the Victoria fails we might as well not be in China." Dunross picked up the phone and dialed Johnjohn's private number at the bank. "Bruce? Ian. We'll need the vault—8:30 on the dot."

"Very well. Our security people will be there to assist. Use the side door
—the one on Dirk's Street."

"Yes."

"Have the police been informed?"

"Yes."

"Good. By the way, Ian, about . . . is Richard still with you?"

"Yes."

"Give me a call when you can—I'm at home this evening. I've been
checking and things don't look very good at all for him. My Chinese
banking friends are all very nervous—even the Mok-tung had a mini-run
out at Aberdeen, so did we. Of course we'll advance Richard all the
money he needs against his securities, bankable securities, but if I were
you I'd get any cash you control out. Get Blacs to deal with your check
first at clearing tonight." All bank clearing of checks and bank loans was
done in the basement of the Bank of London, Canton and Shanghai at
midnight, five days a week.

"Thanks, Bruce. See you later." Then to the others, "That's all taken
care of. Of course the transfer should be kept quiet. Richard, I'll need a
cashier's check for Nelson Trading balance."

"And I'll have one for my father's balance!" Zeppelin echoed.

Richard Kwang said, "I'll send the checks over first thing in the
morning."

"Tonight," Mata said, "then they can clear tonight." His eyes lidded
even more. "And, of course, another for my personal balance."

"There isn't enough cash to cover those three checks—no bank could
have that amount," Richard Kwang exploded. "Not even the Bank of
England."

"Of course. Please call whomever you wish to pledge some of your
securities. Or Havergill, or Southerby." Mata's fingers stopped drumming.
"They're expecting your call."

"What?"

"Yes. I talked to both of them this afternoon."

Richard Kwang said nothing. He had to find a way to avoid giving the
money over tonight. If not tonight, he would gain a day's interest and by
tomorrow perhaps it would not be necessary to pay. *Dew neh loh moh* on
all filthy *quai loh* and half *quai loh,* who're worse! His smile was as sweet
as Mata's. "Well, as you wish. If you'll both meet me at the bank in an
hour . . ."

"Even better," Dunross said. "Phillip will go with you now. You can
give him all the checks. Is that all right with you, Phillip?"

"Oh, oh yes, yes, tai-pan."

"Good, thank you. Then if you'll take them right over to Blacs, they'll
clear at midnight. Richard, that gives you plenty of time. Doesn't it?"

"Oh yes, tai-pan," Richard Kwang said, brightening. He had just thought of a brilliant answer. A pretended heart attack! I'll do it in the car going back to the bank and then . . .

Then he saw the coldness in Dunross's eyes and his stomach twisted and he changed his mind. Why should they have so much of my money? he thought as he got up. "You don't need me for anything more at the moment? Good, come along, Phillip." They walked out. There was a vast silence.

"Poor Phillip, he looks ghastly," Mata said.

"Yes. It's no wonder."

"Dirty triads," Zeppelin Tung said with a shudder. "The Werewolves must be foreigners to send his ear like that!" Another shudder. "I hope they don't come to Macao. There's a strong rumor Phillip's dealing with them already, negotiating with the Werewolves in Macao."

"There's no truth to that," Dunross said.

"He wouldn't tell you if he was, tai-pan. I'd keep that secret from everyone too." Zeppelin Tung stared gloomily at the phone. "*Dew neh loh moh* on all filthy kidnappers."

"Is the Ho-Pak finished?" Mata asked.

"Unless Richard Kwang can stay liquid, yes. This afternoon Dunstan closed all his accounts."

"Ah, so once again a rumor's correct!"

"Afraid so!" Dunross was sorry for Richard Kwang and the Ho-Pak but tomorrow he would sell short. "His stock's going to plummet."

"How will that affect the boom you've forecast?"

"Have I?"

"You're buying Struan's heavily, so I hear." Mata smiled thinly. "So has Phillip, and his *tai-tai*, and her family."

"Anyone's wise to buy our stock, Lando, at any time. It's very underpriced."

Zeppelin Tung was listening very carefully. His heart quickened. He too had heard rumors about the Noble House Chens buying today. "Did you see Old Blind Tung's column today? About the coming boom? He was very serious."

"Yes," Dunross said gravely. When he had read it this morning he had chortled, and his opinion of Dianne Chen's influence had soared. In spite of himself Dunross had reread it and had wondered briefly if the soothsayer had really been forecasting his own opinion.

"Is Old Blind Tung a relation, Zep?" he asked.

"No, tai-pan, no, not that I know of. *Dew neh loh moh* but it's hot today. I'll be glad to get back to Macao—the weather's much better in Macao. Are you in the motor race this year, tai-pan?"

"Yes, I hope so."

"Good! Damn the Ho-Pak! Richard will give us our checks, won't he? My old man will bust a blood vessel if one penny cash is missing."

"Yes," Dunross said, then noticed a strangeness in Mata's eyes. "What's up?"

"Nothing." Mata glanced at Zeppelin. "Zep, it's really important we have your father's approval quickly. Why don't you and Claudia track him down."

"Good idea." Obediently the Chinese got to his feet and walked out, closing the door. Dunross turned his attention to Mata. "And?"

Mata hesitated. Then he said quietly, "Ian, I'm considering taking all my funds out of Macao and Hong Kong and putting them in New York."

Dunross stared at him, perturbed. "If you did that you'd rattle our whole system. If you withdraw, Tightfist will too, and the Chins, Four Fingers . . . and all the others."

"Which is more important, tai-pan, the system or your own money?"

"I wouldn't want the system shaken like that."

"You've closed with Par-Con?"

Dunross watched him. "Verbally yes. Contracts in seven days. Withdrawing will hurt us all, Lando. Badly. What's bad for us will be very bad for you and very very bad for Macao."

"I'll consider what you say. So Par-Con's coming into Hong Kong. Very good—and if American Superfoods' takeover of the H. K. General Stores goes through, that'll add another boost to the market. Perhaps Old Blind Tung wasn't exaggerating again. Perhaps we'll be lucky. Has he ever been wrong before?"

"I don't know. Personally I don't think he has a private connection with the Almighty, though a lot of people do."

"A boom would be very good, very good indeed. Perfect timing. Yes," Mata added strangely, "we could add a little fuel to the greatest boom in our history. Eh?"

"Would you assist?"

"Ten million U.S., between myself and the Chins—Tightfist won't be interested, I know. You suggest where and when."

"Half a million into Struan's last thing Thursday, the rest spread over Rothwell-Gornt, Asian Properties, Hong Kong Wharf, Hong Kong Power, Golden Ferries, Kowloon Investments and H. K. General Stores."

"Why Thursday? Why not tomorrow?"

"The Ho-Pak will bring the market down. If we buy in quantity Thursday just before closing, we'll make a fortune."

"When do you announce the Par-Con deal?"

Dunross hesitated. Then he said, "Friday, after the market closes."

"Good. I'm with you, Ian. Fifteen million. Fifteen instead of ten. You'll sell the Ho-Pak short tomorrow?"

"Of course. Lando, do you know who's behind the run on the Ho-Pak?"

"No. But Richard is overextended, and he hasn't been too wise. People talk, Chinese always distrust any bank, and they react to rumors. I think the bank will crash."

"Christ!"

"Joss." Mata's fingers stopped drumming. "I want to triple our gold imports."

Dunross stared at him. "Why? You're up to capacity now. If you push them too fast they'll make mistakes and your seizure rate will go up. At the moment you've balanced everything perfectly."

"Yes, but Four Fingers and others assure us they can make some substantial bulk shipments safely."

"No need to push them—or your market. No need at all."

"Ian, listen to me a moment. There's trouble in Indonesia, trouble in China, India, Tibet, Malaya, Singapore, ferment in the Philippines and now the Americans are going into Southeast Asia which will be marvelous for us and dreadful for them. Inflation will soar and then, as usual, every sensible businessman in Asia, particularly Chinese businessmen, will want to get out of paper money and into gold. We should be ready to service that demand."

"What've you heard, Lando?"

"Lots of curious things, tai-pan. For example, that certain top U.S. generals want a full-scale confrontation with the Communists. Vietnam's chosen."

"But the Americans'll never win there. China can't let them, any more than they could in Korea. Any history book will tell them China *always* crosses her borders to protect her buffer zones when any invader approaches."

"Even so, the confrontation will take place."

Dunross studied Lando Mata whose enormous wealth and longtime involvement in the honorable profession of trading, as he described it, gave him vast entrée into the most secretive of places. "What else have you heard, Lando?"

"The CIA has had its budget doubled."

"That has to be classified. No one could know that."

"Yes. But I know. Their security's appalling. Ian, the CIA's into everything in Southeast Asia. I believe some of their misguided zealots are even trying to wheedle into the opium trade in the Golden Triangle for the benefit of their friendly Mekong hill tribes—to encourage them to fight the Viet Cong."

"Christ!"

"Yes. Our brethren in Taiwan are furious. And there's a growing abundance of U.S. Government money pouring into airfields, harbors, roads. In Okinawa, Taiwan and particularly in South Vietnam. Certain highly connected political families are helping to supply the cement and steel on very favorable terms."

"Who?"

"Who makes cement? Perhaps in . . . say in New England?"

"Good sweet Christ, are you sure?"

Mata smiled humorlessly. "I even heard that part of a very large government loan to South Vietnam was expended on a nonexistent airfield that's still impenetrable jungle. Oh yes, Ian, the pickings are already huge. So please order triple shipments from tomorrow. We institute our new hydrofoil services next month—that'll cut the time to Macao from three hours to seventy-five minutes."

"Wouldn't the Catalina still be safer?"

"No. I don't think so. The hydrofoils can carry much more gold and can outrun anything in these waters—we'll have constant radar communications, the best, so we can outrun any pirates."

After a pause, Dunross said, "So much gold could attract all sorts of villains. Perhaps even international crooks."

Mata smiled his thin smile. "Let them come. They'll never leave. We've long arms in Asia." His fingers began drumming again. "Ian, we're old friends, I would like some advice."

"Glad to—anything."

"Do you believe in change?"

"Business change?"

"Yes."

"It depends, Lando," Dunross answered at once. "The Noble House's changed little in almost a century and a half, in other ways it's changed vastly." He watched the older man, and he waited.

At length Mata said, "In a few weeks the Macao Government is obliged to put the gambling concession up for bids again. . . ." Instantly Dunross's attention zeroed. All big business in Macao was conducted on monopoly lines, the monopoly going to the person or company that offered the most taxes per year for the privilege. ". . . This's the fifth year. Every five years our department asks for closed bids. The auction's open to anyone but, in practice, we scrutinize very particularly those who are invited to bid." The silence hung a moment, then Mata continued, "My old associate, Smuggler Mo's already dead. His offspring're mostly profligate or more interested in the Western world, gambling in southern France or playing golf, than in the health and future of the syndicate. For the Mo it's the age-old destiny: one-in-ten-thousand coolie strikes gold, harbors money, invests in land, saves money, becomes rich, buys young concubines who use him up quickly. Second generation discontented, spend money, mortgage land to buy face and ladies' favors. Third generation sell land, go bankrupt for same favors. Fourth generation coolie." His voice was calm, even gentle. "My old friend's dead and I've no feeling for his sons, or their sons. They're rich, hugely rich because of me, and they'll find their own level, good, bad or very bad. As to Tightfist . . ." Again his fingers stopped. "Tightfist's dying."

Dunross was startled. "But I saw him only a week or so ago and he looked healthy, frail as always, but full of his usual piss and vinegar."

"He's dying, Ian. I know because I was his interpreter with the Portuguese specialists. He didn't want to trust any of his sons—that's what he told me. It took me months to get him to go to see them but both doctors were quite sure: cancer of the colon. His system's riddled with it. They gave him a month, two months . . . this was a week ago." Mata smiled. "Old Tightfist just swore at them, told them they were wrong and fools and that he'd never pay for a wrong diagnosis." The lithe Portuguese laughed without humor. "He's worth over 600 million U.S. but he'll never pay that doctor bill, or do anything but continue to drink foul-smelling, foul-tasting Chinese herbal brews and smoke his occasional opium pipe. He just won't accept a Western, a *quai loh* diagnosis—you know him. You know him very well, eh?"

"Yes." When Dunross was on his school holidays his father would send him to work for certain old friends. Tightfist Tung had been one of them and Dunross remembered the hideous summer he had spent sweating in the filthy basement of the syndicate bank in Macao, trying to please his mentor and not to weep with rage at the thought of what he had to endure while all his friends were out playing. But now he was glad for that summer. Tightfist had taught him much about money—the value of it, how to make it, hold on to it, about usury, greed and the normal Chinese lending rate, in good times, of 2 percent a month.

"Take twice as much collateral as you need but if he has none then look at the eyes of the borrower!" Tightfist would scream at him. "No collateral, then of course charge a bigger interest. Now think, can you trust him? Can he repay the money? Is he a worker or a drone? Look at him, fool, *he's* your collateral! How much of my hard-earned money does he want? Is he a hard worker? If he is, what's 2 percent a month to him—or 4? Nothing. But it's my money that'll make the fornicator rich if it's his joss to be rich. The man himself's all the collateral you ever need! Lend a rich man's son anything if he's borrowing against his heritage and you have the father's chop—it'll all be thrown away on singsong girls but never mind, it's his money not yours! How do you become rich? You save! You save money, buy land with one third, lend one third and keep one third in cash. Lend only to civilized persons and never trust a *quai loh* . . ." he would cackle.

Dunross remembered well the old man with his stony eyes, hardly any teeth—an illiterate who could read but three characters and could write but three characters, those of his name—who had a mind like a computer, who knew to the nearest copper cash who owed him what and when it was due. No one had ever defaulted on one of his loans. It wasn't worth the incessant hounding.

That summer he had been thirteen and Lando Mata had befriended him. Then, as now, Mata was almost a wraith, a mysterious presence who moved in and out of Macao's government spheres as he wished, always in the background, hardly seen, barely known, a strange Asian who came and went at whim, gathered what he liked, harvesting unbelievable riches as and when it pleased him. Even today there were but a handful of people who knew his name, let alone the man himself. Even Dunross had never been to his villa on the Street of the Broken Fountain, the low sprawling building hidden behind the iron gates and the huge stone encircling walls, or knew anything about him really—where he came from, who his parents were or how he had managed to acquire those two monopolies of limitless wealth.

"I'm sorry to hear about old Tightfist," Dunross said. "He was always a rough old bastard, but no rougher to me than to any of his own sons."

"Yes. He's dying. Joss. And I've no feeling for any of his heirs. Like the Chins, they'll be rich, all of them. Even Zeppelin," Lando Mata said with a sneer. "Even Zeppelin'll get 50 to 75 million U.S."

"Christ, when you think of all the money gambling makes . . ."

Mata's eyes lidded. "Should I make a change?"

"If you want to leave a monument, yes. At the moment the syndicate only allows Chinese gambling games: fan-tan, dominoes and dice. If the new group was modern, far-seeing, and they modernized . . . if they built a grand new casino, with tables for roulette, vingt-et-un, chemin de fer, even American craps you'd have all Asia flocking to Macao."

"What're the chances of Hong Kong legalizing gambling?"

"None—you know better than I do that without gambling and gold Macao'd drift into the sea and it's a cornerstone of British and Hong Kong business policy never to let that happen. We have our horse racing—you've the tables. But with modern ownership, new hotels, new games, new hydrofoils you'd have so much revenue you'd have to open your own bank."

Lando Mata took out a slip of paper, glanced at it, then handed it over. "Here are four groups of three names of people who might be allowed to bid. I'd like your opinion."

Dunross did not look at the list. "You'd like me to choose the group of three you've already decided on?"

Mata laughed. "Ah, Ian, you know too much about me! Yes, I've chosen the group that should be successful, if their bid is substantial enough."

"Do any of the groups know now that you might take them as partners?"

"No."

"What about Tightfist—and the Chins? They won't lose their monopoly lightly."

"If Tightfist dies before the auction, a new syndicate will come to pass. If not, the change will be made but differently."

Dunross glanced at the list. And gasped. All the names were well-known Hong Kong and Macao Chinese, all substantial people, some with curious pasts. "Well, they're certainly all famous, Lando."

"Yes. To earn such great wealth, to run a gambling empire needs men of vision."

Dunross smiled with him. "I agree. Then why is it I'm not on the list?"

"Resign from the Noble House within the month and you can form your own syndicate. I guarantee your bid will be successful. I take 40 percent."

"Sorry, that's not possible, Lando."

"You could have a personal fortune of 500 million to a billion dollars within ten years."

Dunross shrugged. "What's money?"

"Moh ching moh meng!" No money no life.

"Yes, but there's not enough money in the world to make me resign. Still, I'll make a deal with you. Struan's'll run the gambling for you, through nominees."

"Sorry, no. It has to be all or nothing."

"We could do it better and cheaper than anyone, with more flair."

"If you resign. All or none, tai-pan."

Dunross's head hurt at the thought of so much money, but he heard Lando Mata's finality. "Fair enough. Sorry, I'm not available," he said.

"I'm sure you'd, you personally, would be welcomed as a . . . as a consultant."

"If I choose the correct group?"

"Perhaps." The Portuguese smiled. "Well?"

Dunross was wondering whether or not he could risk such an association. To be part of the Macao gambling syndicate was not like being a steward of the Turf Club. "I'll think about that and let you know."

"Good, Ian. Give me your opinion within the next two days, eh?"

"All right. Will you tell me what the successful bid is—if you decide to change?"

"An associate or consultant should have that knowledge. Now a last item and I must go. I don't think you'll ever see your friend Tsu-yan again."

Dunross stared at him. "What?"

"He called me from Taipei, yesterday morning, in quite a state. He asked if I'd send the Catalina for him, to pick him up privately. It was urgent he said, he'd explain when he saw me. He'd come straight to my home, the moment he arrived." Mata shrugged and examined his perfectly manicured nails. "Tsu-yan's an old friend, I've accommodated old friends before, so I authorized the flight. He never appeared, Ian. Oh he came with the flying boat—my chauffeur was on the jetty to meet him." Mata looked up. "It's all rather unbelievable. Tsu-yan was dressed in filthy coolie rags with a straw hat. He mumbled something about seeing me later that night and jumped into the first taxi and took off as though all the devils from hell were at his heels. My driver was stunned."

"There's no mistake? You're sure it was he?"

"Oh yes, Tsu-yan's well known—fortunately my driver's Portuguese and can take some initiative. He charged in pursuit. He says Tsu-yan's taxi

headed north. Near the Barrier Gate the taxi stopped and then Tsu-yan
fled on foot, as fast as he could run, through the Barrier Gate into China.
My man watched him run all the way up to the soldiers on the PRC's side
and then he vanished into the guardhouse."

Dunross stared at Mata in disbelief. Tsu-yan was one of the best-known
capitalists and anti-Communists in Hong Kong and Taiwan. Before the
fall of the Mainland he had been almost a minor warlord in the Shanghai
area. "Tsu-yan'd never be welcome in the PRC," he said. "Never! He
must be top of their shit list."

Mata hesitated. "Unless he was working for them."

"It's just not possible."

"Anything's possible in China."

Twenty stories below, Roger Crosse and Brian Kwok were getting out
of the police car, followed by Robert Armstrong. A plainclothes SI man
met them. "Dunross's still in his office, sir."

"Good." Robert Armstrong stayed at the entrance and the other two
went for the elevator. On the twentieth floor they got out.

"Ah good evening, sir," Claudia said and smiled at Brian Kwok. Zeppelin Tung was waiting by the phone. He stared at the policemen in sudden
shock, obviously recognizing them.

Roger Crosse said, "Mr. Dunross's expecting me."

"Yes sir." She pressed the boardroom button and, in a moment, spoke
into her phone. "Mr. Crosse's here, tai-pan."

Dunross said, "Give me a minute, then show him in, Claudia." He replaced his phone and turned to Mata. "Crosse's here. If I miss you at the
bank tonight, I'll catch up with you tomorrow morning."

"Yes. I'm . . . please call me, Ian. Yes. I want a few minutes with you
privately. Tonight or tomorrow."

"At nine tonight," Dunross said at once. "Or anytime tomorrow."

"Call me at nine. Or tomorrow. Thank you." Mata walked across the
room and opened a hardly noticeable door that was camouflaged as part of
the bookshelves. This opened onto a private corridor which led to the floor
below. He closed the door behind him.

Dunross stared after him thoughtfully. I wonder what's on his mind?
He put the agenda papers in a drawer and locked it, then leaned back at
the head of the table trying to collect his wits, his eyes on the door, his
heart beating a little quicker. The phone rang and he jumped.

"Yes?"

"Father," Adryon said in her usual rush, "sorry to interrupt but Mother
wanted to know what time you'd be in for dinner."

"I'll be late. Ask her to go ahead. I'll get something on the run. What
time did you get in last night?" he asked, remembering that he had heard
her car return just before dawn.

"Early," she said, and he was going to give her both barrels but he heard unhappiness under her voice.

"What's up, pet?" he asked.

"Nothing."

"What's up?"

"Nothing really. I had a grand day, had lunch with your Linc Bartlett—we went shopping but that twit Martin stood me up."

"What?"

"Yes. I waited a bloody hour for him. We had a date to go to the V and A for tea but he never showed up. Rotten twit!"

Dunross beamed. "You just can't rely on some people, can you, Adryon? Fancy! Standing you up! What cheek!" he told her, suitably grave, delighted that Haply was going to get what for.

"He's a creep! A twenty-four-carat creep!"

The door opened. Crosse and Brian Kwok came in. He nodded to them, beckoned them. Claudia shut the door after them.

"Got to go, darling. Hey pet, love you! 'Bye!" He put the phone down. "Evening," he said, no longer perturbed.

"The files please, Ian."

"Certainly, but first we've got to see the governor."

"First I want those files." Crosse pulled out the warrant as Dunross picked up the phone and dialed. He waited only a moment. "Evening, sir. Superintendent Crosse's here . . . yes sir." He held out the phone. "For you."

Crosse hesitated, hard-faced, then took it. "Superintendent Crosse," he said into the phone. He listened a moment. "Yes sir. Very well, sir." He replaced the phone. "Now, what the hell shenanigans are you up to?"

"None. Just being careful."

Crosse held up the warrant. "If I don't get the files, I've clearance from London to serve this on you at six P.M. today, governor or no."

Dunross stared back at him, just as hard. "Please go ahead."

"You're served, Ian Struan Dunross! Sorry, but you're under arrest!"

Dunross's jaw jutted a little. "All right. But first by God we *will* see the governor!"

24

The tai-pan and Roger Crosse were walking across the white pebbles toward the front door of the Governor's Palace. Brian Kwok waited beside the police car. The front door opened and the young equerry in Royal Navy uniform greeted them politely, then ushered them into an exquisite antechamber.

His Excellency, Sir Geoffrey Allison, D.S.O., O.B.E., was a sandy-haired man in his late fifties, neat, soft-spoken and very tough. He sat at an antique desk and watched them. "Evening," he said easily and waved them to seats. His equerry closed the door, leaving them. "It seems we have a problem, Roger. Ian has some rather private property that he legally owns and is reluctant to give you—that you want."

"Legally want, sir. I've London's authority under the Official Secrets Act."

"Yes, I know that, Roger. I talked to the minister an hour ago. He said, and I agree, we can hardly arrest Ian and go through the Noble House like a dose of salts. That really wouldn't be very proper, or very sensible, however serious we are in obtaining the AMG files. And, equally, it wouldn't be very proper or sensible to acquire them with cloaks and daggers—that sort of thing. Would it?"

Crosse said, "With Ian's cooperation none of that would be necessary. I've pointed out to him that Her Majesty's Government was completely involved. He just doesn't seem to get the message, sir. He should cooperate."

"I quite agree. The minister said the same. Of course when Ian came here this morning he did explain his reasons for being so, so cautious . . . quite proper reasons if I may say so! The minister agrees too." The gray eyes became piercing. "Just exactly who is the deep-cover Communist agent in my police? Who are the Sevrin plants?"

There was a vast silence. "I don't know, sir."

"Then would you be kind enough to find out very quickly. Ian was kind enough to let me read the AMG report you rightly intercepted." The governor's face mottled, quoting from it, "'. . . this information should be leaked privately to the police commissioner or governor *should they be considered loyal . . .'* Bless my soul! What's going on in the world?"

"I don't know, sir."

"Well you're supposed to, Roger. Yes." The governor watched them. "Now. What about the mole? What sort of man would he be?"

"You, me, Dunross, Havergill, Armstrong—anyone," Crosse said at once. "But with one characteristic: I think this one's so deep that he's probably almost forgotten who he really is, or where his real political interest and loyalty lie. He'd be very special—like all of Sevrin." The thin-faced man stared at Dunross. "They must be special—SI's checks and balances are really very good, and the CIA's, but we've never had a whiff of Sevrin before, not a jot or a tittle."

Dunross said, "How're you going to catch him?"

"How're you going to catch your plant in Struan's?"

"I've no idea." Would the Sevrin spy be the same as the one who betrayed our secrets to Bartlett? Dunross was asking himself uneasily. "If he's top echelon, he's one of seven—all unthinkable."

"There you have it," Crosse said. "All unthinkable, but one's a spy. If we get one, we can probably break the others out of him if he knows them." Both the other men felt icy at the calm viciousness in his voice. "But to get the one, someone has to make a slip, or we have to get a little luck."

The governor thought a moment. Then he said, "Ian assures me there's nothing in the previous reports that names anyone—or gives any clues. So the other reports wouldn't help us immediately."

"They could, sir, in other areas, sir."

"I know." The words were quietly spoken but they said Shut up, sit down and wait till I've finished. Sir Geoffrey let the silence hang for a while. "So our problem seems to be simply a matter of asking Ian for his cooperation. I repeat, I agree that his caution is justified." His face tightened. "Philby, Burgess and Maclean taught us all a fine lesson. I must confess every time I make a call to London I wonder if I'm talking to another bloody traitor." He blew his nose in a handkerchief. "Well, enough of that. Ian, kindly tell Roger the circumstances under which you'll hand over the AMG copies."

"I'll hand them, personally, to the head or deputy head of MI-6 or MI-5, providing I have his Excellency's guarantee in writing that the man I give them to is who he purports to be."

"The minister agrees to this, sir?"

"If you agree, Roger." Again it was said politely but the undercurrent said You'd better agree, Roger.

"Very well, sir. Has Mr. Sinders agreed to the plan?"

"He will be here on Friday, BOAC willing."

"Yes sir." Roger Crosse glanced at Dunross. "I'd better keep the files then until then. You can give me a sealed pa—"

Dunross shook his head. "They're safe until I deliver them."

Crosse shook his head. "No. If we know, others'd know. The others're not so clean-handed as we are. We must know where they are—we'd better have a guard, around the clock."

Sir Geoffrey nodded. "That's fair enough, Ian?"

Dunross thought a moment. "Very well. I've put them in a vault at the Victoria Bank." Crosse's neck became pink as Dunross produced a key and laid it on the desk. The numbers were carefully defaced. "There're about a thousand safety deposit boxes. I alone know the number. This's the only key. If you'll keep it, Sir Geoffrey. Then . . . well, that's about the best I can do to avoid risks."

"Roger?"

"Yes sir. If you agree."

"They're certainly safe there. Certainly not possible to break open all of them. Good, then that's all settled. Ian, the warrant's canceled. You do promise, Ian, to deliver them to Sinders the moment he arrives?" Again the eyes became piercing. "I have really gone to a lot of trouble over this."

"Yes sir."

"Good. Then that's settled. Nothing yet on poor John Chen, Roger?"

"No sir, we're trying everything."

"Terrible business. Ian, what's all this about the Ho-Pak? Are they really in trouble?"

"Yes sir."

"Will they go under?"

"I don't know. The word seems to be they will."

"Damnable! I don't like that at all. Very bad for our image. And the Par-Con deal?"

"It looks good. I hope to have a favorable report for you next week, sir."

"Excellent. We could use some big American firms here." He smiled. "I understand the girl's a stunner! By the way, the Parliamentary Trade Delegation's due from Peking tomorrow. I'll entertain them Thursday—you'll come of course."

"Yes sir. Will the dinner be stag?"

"Yes, good idea."

"I'll invite them to the races Saturday—the overflow can go into the bank's box, sir."

"Good. Thank you, Ian. Roger, if you'll spare me a moment."

Dunross got up and shook hands and left. Though he had come with Crosse in the police car, his own Rolls was waiting for him. Brian Kwok intercepted him. "What's the poop, Ian?"

"I was asked to let your boss tell you," he said.

"Fair enough. Is he going to be long?"

"I don't know. Everything's all right, Brian. No need to worry. I think I dealt with the dilemma correctly."

"Hope so. Sorry—bloody business."

"Yes." Dunross got into the back of the Silver Cloud. "Golden Ferry," he said crisply.

Sir Geoffrey was pouring the fine sherry into two exquisite, eggshell porcelain cups. "This AMG business is quite frightening, Roger," he said. "I'm afraid I'm still not inured to treachery, betrayal and the rotten lengths the enemy will go to—even after all this time." Sir Geoffrey had been in the Diplomatic Corps all of his working life, except for the war years when he was a staff officer in the British Army. He spoke Russian, Mandarin, French and Italian. "Dreadful."

"Yes sir." Crosse watched him. "You're sure you can trust Ian?"

"On Friday you won't need London's clearance to proceed. You have an Order in Council. On Friday we take possession."

"Yes sir." Crosse accepted the porcelain cup, its fragility bothering him. "Thank you, sir."

"I suggest you have two men in the bank vaults at all times, one SI, one CID for safety, and a plainclothes guard on the tai-pan—quietly, of course."

"I'll arrange about the bank before I leave. I've already put him under blanket surveillance."

"You've already done it?"

"On him? Yes sir. I presumed he'd manipulate the situation to suit his purposes. Ian's a very tricky fellow. After all, the tai-pan of the Noble House is never a fool."

"No. Health!" They touched glasses delicately. The ring of the pottery was beautiful. "This tai-pan's the best I've dealt with."

"Did Ian mention if he'd reread all the files recently, sir? Last night, for instance?"

Sir Geoffrey frowned, rethinking their conversation this morning. "I don't think so. Wait a minute, he did say . . . exactly he said, 'When I first read the reports I thought some of AMG's ideas were too farfetched. But now—and now that he's dead, I've changed my mind . . .' That could imply he's reread them recently. Why?"

Crosse was examining the paper-thin porcelain cup against the light. "I've often heard he's got a remarkable memory. If the files in the vaults are untouchable . . . well, I wouldn't want the KGB tempted to snatch him."

"Good God, you don't think they'd be that stupid, do you? The tai-pan?"

"It depends what importance they put on the reports, sir," Crosse said dispassionately. "Perhaps our surveillance should be relatively open—that should scare them off if they happen to have that in mind. Would you mention it to him, sir?"

"Certainly." Sir Geoffrey made a note on his pad. "Good idea. Damnable business. Could the Werewolves . . . could there be a link between the smuggled guns and the John Chen kidnapping?"

"I don't know, sir. Yet. I've put Armstrong and Brian Kwok on to the case. If there's a connection they'll find it." He watched the dying sunlight on the pale, powder blue translucence of the porcelain that seemed to enhance the golden sheen of the dry La Ina sherry. "Interesting, the play of colors."

"Yes. They're T'ang Ying—named after the director of the Emperor's factory in 1736. Emperor Ch'en Leung actually." Sir Geoffrey looked up at Crosse. "A deep-cover spy in my police, in my Colonial Office, my Treasury Department, the naval base, the Victoria, telephone company, and even the Noble House. They could paralyze us and create untold mischief between us and the PRC."

"Yes sir." Crosse peered at the cup. "Seems impossible that it should be so thin. I've never seen such a cup before."

"You're a collector?"

"No sir. Afraid I don't know anything about them."

"These're my favorites, Roger, quite rare. They're called t'o t'ai—without body. They're so thin that the glazes, inside and out, seem to touch."

"I'm almost afraid to hold it."

"Oh, they're quite strong. Delicate of course but strong. Who could be Arthur?"

Crosse sighed. "There's no clue in this report. None. I've read it fifty times. There must be something in the others, whatever Dunross thinks."

"Possibly."

The delicate cup seemed to fascinate Crosse. "Porcelain's a clay, isn't it?"

"Yes. But this type is actually made from a mixture of two clays, Roger, kaolin—after the hilly district of Kingtehchen where it's found—and pan tun tse, the so-called little white blocks. Chinese call these the flesh and the bones of porcelain." Sir Geoffrey walked over to the ornate leather-topped table that served as a bar and brought back the decanter. It was about eight inches high and quite translucent, almost transparent. "The blue's remarkable too. When the body's quite dry, cobalt in powder form's blown onto the porcelain with a bamboo pipe. Actually the color's thousands of individual tiny specks of blue. Then it's glazed and fired—at about 1300 degrees." He put it back on the bar, the touch of the workmanship and the sight of it pleasing him.

"Remarkable."

"There was always an Imperial Edict against their export. We quai loh were only entitled to articles made out of hua shih, slippery stone, or tun ni—brick mud." He looked at his cup again, as a connoisseur. "The genius who made this probably earned 100 dollars a year."

"Perhaps he was overpaid," Crosse said and the two men smiled with one another.

"Perhaps."

"I'll find Arthur, sir, and the others. You can depend on it."

"I'm afraid I have to, Roger. Both the minister and I agree. He will have to inform the Prime Minister—and the Chiefs of Staff."

"Then the information has to go through all sorts of hands and tongues and the enemy'll be bound to find out that we may be on to them."

"Yes. So we'll have to work fast. I bought you four days' grace, Roger. The minister won't pass anything on for that time."

"Bought, sir?"

"Figuratively speaking. In life one acquires and gives IOUs—even in the Diplomatic Corps."

"Yes sir. Thank you."

"Nothing on Bartlett and Miss Casey?"

"No sir. Rosemont and Langan have asked for up-to-date dossiers. There seems to be some connection between Bartlett and Banastasio— we're not sure yet what it is. Both he and Miss Tcholok were in Moscow last month."

"Ah!" Sir Geoffrey replenished the cups. "What did you do about that poor fellow Voranski?"

"I sent the body back to his ship, sir." Crosse told him the gist of his meeting with Rosemont and Langan and about the photographs.

"That's a stroke of luck! Our cousins are getting quite smart," the governor said. "You'd better find those assassins before the KGB do—or the CIA, eh?"

"I have teams around the house now. As soon as they appear we'll grab them. We'll hold them incommunicado of course. I've tightened security all around the *Ivanov*. No one else'll slip through the net, I promise you. No one."

"Good. The police commissioner said he'd ordered CID to be more alert too." Sir Geoffrey thought a moment. "I'll send a minute to the secretary about your not complying with the 1-4a. American liaison in London's sure to be very upset, but under the circumstances, how could you obey?"

"If I might suggest, it might be better to ask him not to mention we haven't got the files yet, sir. That information might also get into the wrong hands. Leave well alone, as long as we can."

"Yes, I agree." The governor sipped his sherry. "There's lots of wisdom in laissez-faire, isn't there?"

"Yes sir."

Sir Geoffrey glanced at his watch. "I'll phone him in a few minutes, catch him before lunch. Good. But there's one problem I can't leave alone: the *Ivanov*. This morning I heard from our unofficial intermediary that Peking views that ship's presence here with the greatest concern." The quite unofficial spokesman for the PRC in Hong Kong and the ranking Communist appointment was believed to be, presently, one of the deputy chairmen of the Bank of China, China's central bank through which passed all foreign exchange and all the billion U.S. dollars earned by supplying consumer goods and almost all Hong Kong's food and water. Britain had always maintained, bluntly, that Hong Kong was British soil, a Crown Colony. In all of Hong Kong's history, since 1841, Britain had never allowed any *official* Chinese representative to reside in the Colony. None.

"He went out of his way to jiggle me about the *Ivanov*," Sir Geoffrey continued, "and he wanted to register Peking's extreme displeasure that a Soviet spy ship was here. He even suggested I might think it wise to expel it. . . . After all, he said, we hear one of the Soviet KGB spies posing as a seaman had actually got himself killed on our soil. I thanked him for his interest and told him I'd advise my superiors—in due course." Sir Geoffrey sipped some sherry. "Curiously, he didn't appear irritated that the nuclear carrier was here."

"That's strange!" Crosse was equally surprised.

"Does that indicate another policy shift—a distinct significant foreign-policy change, a desire for peace with the U.S.? I can't believe that. Everything indicates pathological hatred of the U.S.A."

The governor sighed and refilled the cups. "If it leaked that Sevrin's in existence, that we're undermined here . . . God almighty, they'd go into convulsions, and rightly so!"

"We'll find the traitors, sir, don't worry. We'll find them!"

"Will we? I wonder." Sir Geoffrey sat down at the window seat and stared out at the manicured lawns and English garden, shrubs, flower beds surrounded by the high white wall, the sunset good. His wife was cutting flowers, wandering among the beds at the far end of the gardens, followed by a sour-faced, disapproving Chinese gardener. Sir Geoffrey watched her a moment. They had been married thirty years and had three children, all married now, and they were content and at peace with each other. "Always traitors," he said sadly. "The Soviets are past masters in their use. So easy for the Sevrin traitors to agitate, to spread a little poison here and there, so easy to get China upset, poor China who's xenophobic anyway! Oh how easy it is to rock our boat here! Worst of all, who's *your* spy? The police spy? He must be at least a chief inspector to have access to that information."

"I've no idea. If I had, he'd've been neutralized long since."

"What are you going to do about General Jen and his Nationalist undercover agents?"

"I'm going to leave them alone—they've been pegged for months. Much better to leave known enemy agents in situ than to have to ferret out their replacements."

"I agree—they'd certainly all be replaced. Theirs, and ours. Sad, so sad! We do it and they do it. So sad and so stupid—this world's such a paradise, could be such a paradise."

A bee hummed in the bay windows then flew back to the garden again as Sir Geoffrey eased the curtain aside. "The minister asked me to make sure our visiting MPs—our trade delegation to China that returns tomorrow—to make sure their security was optimum, judicious, though totally discreet."

"Yes sir. I understand."

"It appears that one or two of them might be future cabinet ministers if the Labour Party get in. It'd be good for the Colony to create a fine impression on them."

"Do you think they've a chance next time? The Labour Party?"

"I don't comment on those sort of questions, Roger." The governor's voice was flat, and reproving. "I'm not concerned with party politics—I represent Her Majesty the Queen—but personally I really do wish some of their extremists would go away and leave us to our own devices for clearly much of their left wing socialist philosophy is alien to our English way of life." Sir Geoffrey hardened. "It's quite obvious some of them do assist the enemy, willingly—or as dupes. Since we're on the subject, are any of our guests security risks?"

"It depends what you mean, sir. Two are left-wing trades unionists backbenchers, fire-eaters—Robin Grey and Lochin Donald McLean. McLean openly flaunts his B.C.P.—British Communist Party—affiliations. He's fairly high on our S-list. All the other Socialists are moderates. The Conservative members are moderate, middle-class, all ex-service. One's rather imperialist, the Liberal Party representative, Hugh Guthrie."

"And the fire-eaters? They're ex-service?"

"McLean was a miner, at least his father was. Most of his Communist life's been as a shop steward and unionist in the Scottish coalfields. Robin Grey was army, a captain, infantry."

Sir Geoffrey looked up. "You don't usually associate ex-captains with being fire-eating trades unionists, do you?"

"No sir." Crosse sipped his sherry, appreciating it, savoring his knowledge more. "Nor with being related to a tai-pan."

"Eh?"

"Robin Grey's sister is Penelope Dunross."

"Good God!" Sir Geoffrey stared at him, astounded. "Are you sure?"

"Yes sir."

"But why hasn't, why hasn't Ian mentioned it before?"

"I don't know, sir. Perhaps he's ashamed of him. Mr. Grey is certainly the complete opposite of Mrs. Dunross."

"But . . . Bless my soul, you're sure?"

"Yes sir. Actually, it was Brian Kwok who spotted the connection. Just by chance. The MPs had to furnish the usual personal information to the PRC to get their visas, date of birth, profession, next of kin, etcetera. Brian was doing a routine check to make sure all the visas were in order to avoid any problem at the border. Brian happened to notice Mr. Grey had put 'sister, Penelope Grey' as his next of kin, with an address, Castle Avisyard in Ayr. Brian remembered that that was the Dunross family home address." Crosse pulled out his silver cigarette case. "Do you mind if I smoke, sir?"

"No, please go ahead."

"Thank you. That was a month or so ago. I thought it important enough for him to follow up the information. It took us relatively little time to establish that Mrs. Dunross really was his sister and next of kin. As far as we know now, Mrs. Dunross quarreled with her brother just after the war. Captain Grey was a POW in Changi, caught in Singapore in 1942. He got home in the later part of 1945—by the way their parents were killed in the London blitz in '43. At that time she was already married to Dunross—they'd married in 1943, sir, just after he was shot down—she was a WAAF. We know brother and sister met when Grey was released. As far as we can tell now, they've never met again. Of course it's none of our affair anyway, but the quarrel must have been—"

Crosse stopped as there was a discreet knock and Sir Geoffrey called out testily, "Yes?"

The door opened. "Excuse me, sir," his aide said politely, "Lady Allison asked me to tell you that the water's just gone on."

"Oh, marvelous! Thank you." The door closed. At once Crosse got up but the governor waved him back to his seat. "No, please finish, Roger. A few minutes won't matter, though I must confess I can hardly wait. Would you like to shower before you go?"

"Thank you, sir, but we've our own water tanks at police HQ."

"Oh yes. I forgot. Go on. You were saying—the quarrel?"

"The quarrel must have been pretty serious because it seems to have been final. A close friend of Grey told one of our people a few days ago that as far as he knew, Robin Grey had no living relatives. They really must hate each other."

Sir Geoffrey stared at his cup, not seeing it. Suddenly he was remembering his own rotten childhood and how he had hated his father, hated him so much that for thirty years he had never called him, or written to him, and, when he was dying last year, had not bothered to go to him, to make peace with the man who had given him life. "People are terrible to each other," he muttered sadly. "I know. Yes. Family quarrels are too easy. And then, when it's too late, you regret it, yes, you really regret it. People are terrible to each other . . ."

Crosse watched and waited, letting him ramble, letting him reveal himself, cautious not to make the slightest movement to distract him, wanting to know the man's secrets, and skeletons. Like Alan Medford Grant, Crosse collected secrets. Goddamn that bastard and his god-cursed files! God curse Dunross and his devilry! How in the name of Christ can I get those files before Sinders?

Sir Geoffrey was staring into space. Then the water gurgled delightedly in the pipes somewhere in the walls and he came back into himself. He saw Crosse watching him. "Hmmm, thinking aloud! Bad habit for a governor, eh?"

Crosse smiled and did not fall into the trap. "Sir?"

"Well. As you said, it's really none of our business." The governor finished his drink with finality and Crosse knew that he was dismissed. He got up. "Thank you, sir."

When he was alone the governor sighed. He thought a moment then picked up the special phone and gave the operator the minister's private number in London.

"This is Geoffrey Allison. Is he in please?"

"Hello, Geoffrey!"

"Hello, sir. I've just seen Roger. He assures me that the hiding place and Dunross will be completely guarded. Is Mr. Sinders en route?"

"He'll be there on Friday. I presume there have been no repercussions from that seaman's unfortunate accident?"

"No sir. Everything seems to be under control."

"The P.M. was most concerned."

"Yes sir." The governor added, "About the 1-4a . . . perhaps we shouldn't mention anything to our friends, yet."

"I've already heard from them. They were distressingly irritated. So were our fellows. All right, Geoffrey. Fortunately it's a long weekend this week so I'll inform them Monday and draft his reprimand then."

"Thank you, sir."

"Geoffrey, that American senator you have with you at the moment. I think he should be guided."

The governor frowned. *Guided* was a code word between them, meaning "watched very carefully." Senator Wilf Tillman, a presidential hopeful, was visiting Hong Kong en route to Saigon for a well-publicized fact-finding mission.

"I'll take care of it as soon as I'm off the phone. Was there anything else, sir?" he asked, impatient now to bathe.

"No, just give me a private minute on what the senator's program has been." *Program* was another code which meant to furnish the Colonial Office with detailed information. "When you've time."

"I'll have it on your desk Friday."

"Thank you, Geoffrey. We'll chat at the usual time tomorrow." The line went dead.

The governor replaced the phone thoughtfully. Their conversation would have been electronically scrambled and, at either end, unscrambled. Even so, they were guarded. They knew the enemy had the most advanced and sophisticated eavesdropping equipment in the world. For any really classified conversation or meeting he would go to the permanently guarded, concrete, cell-like room in the basement that was meticulously rechecked by security experts for possible electronic bugs every week.

Bloody nuisance, Sir Geoffrey thought. Bloody nuisance all this cloak-and-dagger stuff! Roger? Unthinkable, even so, once there was Philby.

25

6:20 P.M.:

Captain Gregor Suslev waved jauntily to the police at the dockyard gates in Kowloon, his two plainclothes detectives fifty yards in tow. He was dressed in well-cut civilians and he stood by the curb a moment watching the traffic, then hailed a passing taxi. The taxi took off and a small gray Jaguar with Sergeant Lee, CID, and another plainclothes CID man driving, followed smartly.

The taxi went along Chatham Road in the usual heavy traffic, southward, skirting the railway line, then turned west along Salisbury Road on the southmost tip of Kowloon, passing the railway terminus, near the Golden Ferry Terminal. There it stopped. Suslev paid it off and ran up the steps of the Victoria and Albert Hotel. Sergeant Lee followed him as the other detective parked the police Jag.

Suslev walked with an easy stride and he stood for a moment in the immense, crowded foyer with its high ceilings, lovely and ornate, and old-fashioned electric fans overhead, and looked for an empty table among the multitude of tables. The whole room was alive with the clink of ice in cocktail glasses and conversation. Mostly Europeans. A few Chinese couples. Suslev wandered through the people, found a table, loudly ordered a double vodka, sat and began to read his paper. Then the girl was standing near him.

"Hello," she said.

"Ginny, *doragaya!*" he said with a great beam and hugged her, lifting her off her little feet to the shocked disapproval of every woman in the place and the covert envy of every man. "It's been a long time, *golub-chik.*"

"*Ayeeyah,*" she said with a toss of her head, her short hair dancing, and sat down, conscious of the stares, enjoying them, hating them. "You late. Wat for you keep me wait? A lady no like wait in Victoria by her self, *heya?*"

"You're right, *golubchik!*" Suslev pulled out a slim package and gave it to her with another beam. "Here, all the way from Vladivostok!"

"Oh! How thank you?" Ginny Fu was twenty-eight and most nights she worked at the Happy Drinkers Bar in an alley off Mong Kok, half a mile or so to the north. Some nights she went to the Good Luck Ballroom. Most days she would pinch-hit for her friends behind the counter of tiny shops within shops when they were with a client. White teeth and jet eyes and jet hair and golden skin, her gaudy *chong-sam* slit high on her long, stockinged thighs. She looked at the present excitedly. "Oh thank, Gregor, thank very much!" She put it in her large purse and grinned at him. Then her eyes went to the waiter who was strolling up with Suslev's vodka, along with the smug, open contempt reserved by all Chinese for all young Chinese women who sat with *quai loh*. They must of course be third-class whores—who else would sit with a *quai loh* in a public place, particularly in the foyer of the Vic? He set down the drink with practiced insolence and stared back at her.

"*Dew neh loh moh* on all your pig-swill ancestors," she hissed in gutter Cantonese. "My husband here is a 489 in the police and if I say the word he'll have those insignificant peanuts you call your balls crushed off your loathsome body an hour after you leave work tonight!"

The waiter blanched. "Eh?"

"Hot tea! Bring me fornicating hot tea and if you spit in it I'll get my husband to put a knot in that straw you call your stalk!"

The waiter fled.

"What did you say to him?" Suslev asked, understanding only a few words of Cantonese, though his English was very good.

Ginny Fu smiled sweetly. "I just ask him bring tea." She knew the waiter would automatically spit in her tea now, or more probably, for safety, get a friend to do it for him, so she would not drink it and thus cause him to lose even more face. Dirty dog bone! "Next time no like meet here, lotsa nasty peoples," she said imperiously, looking around, then crinkled her nose at a group of middle-aged Englishwomen who were staring at her. "Too much body stinky," she added loudly, tossing her hair again, and chortled to herself seeing them flush and look away. "This gift, Gregy. Thank so very!"

"Nothing," Suslev said. He knew she would not open the gift now—or in front of him—which was very good, sensible Chinese manners. Then, if she did not like the gift or was disappointed or cursed aloud that what was given was the wrong size, or wrong color, or at the miserliness of the giver or bad taste or whatever, then he could not lose face and she could not lose face. "Very sensible!"

"Wat?"

"Nothing."

"You looks good."

"You too." It was three months since his last visit and though his mistress in Vladivostok was a Eurasian with a White Russian mother and Chinese father, he enjoyed Ginny Fu.

"Gregy," she said, then dropped her voice, her smile saucy. "Finish drink. We begin holiday! I got vodka . . . I got other things!"

He smiled back at her. "That you have, *golubchik!*"

"How many day you got?"

"At least three but . . ."

"Oh!" She tried to hide her disappointment.

". . . I'm back and forth to my ship. We've tonight, most of it, and tomorrow and all tomorrow night. And the stars will shine!"

"Three month long time, Gregy."

"I'll be back soon."

"Yes." Ginny Fu put away her disappointment and became pragmatic again. "Finish drink and we begin!" She saw the waiter hurrying with her tea. Her eyes ground into the man as he put it down. "Huh! Clearly it's cold and not fresh!" she said disgustedly. "Who am I! A dirty lump of foreign devil dogmeat? No, I'm a civilized person from the Four Provinces who, because her rich father gambled away all his money, was sold by him into concubinage to become Number Two Wife for this chief of police of the foreign devils! So go piss in your hat!" She got up.

The waiter backed off a foot.

"What's up?" Suslev asked.

"Don't pay for teas, Gregy. Not hot!" she said imperiously. "No give tip!"

Nonetheless Suslev paid and she took his arm and they walked out together, eyes following them. Her head was high, but inside she hated the looks from all the Chinese, even the young, starched bellboy who opened the door—the image of her youngest brother whose life and schooling she paid for.

Dunross was coming up the steps. He waited for them to pass by, an amused glint in his eyes, then he was bowed in politely by the beaming bellboy. He headed through the throng for the house phone. Many noticed him at once and eyes followed him. He walked around a group of tourists, camera bedecked, and noticed Jacques deVille and his wife Susanne at a corner table. Both were set-faced, staring at their drinks. He shook his head, wearily amused. Poor old Jacques has been caught again and she's twisting his infidelity in its well-worn wound. Joss! He could almost hear old Chen-chen laugh. "Man's life is to suffer, young Ian! Yes, it's the eternal yin warring on our oh so vulnerable yang. . . ."

Normally Dunross would have pretended not to notice them, leaving them to their privacy, but some instinct told him otherwise.

"Hello, Jacques—Susanne. How're things?"

"Oh hello, hello, tai-pan." Jacques deVille got up politely. "Would you care to join us?"

"No thanks, can't." Then he saw the depth of his friend's agony and he remembered the car accident in France. Jacques's daughter Avril and her husband! "What's happened? Exactly!" Dunross said it as a leader would say it, requiring an instant answer.

Jacques hesitated. Then he said, "Exactly, tai-pan: I heard from Avril. She phoned from Cannes just as I was leaving the office. She, she said, 'Daddy . . . Daddy, Borge's dead. . . . Can you hear me? I've been trying to reach you for two days . . . it was head-on, and the, the other man was . . . My Borge's dead . . . can you hear me. . . . '" Jacques's voice was flat. "Then the line went dead. We know she's in the hospital at Cannes. I thought it best for Susanne to go at once. Her, her flight's delayed so . . . so we're just waiting here. They're trying to get a call through to Cannes but I don't hope for much."

"Christ, I'm so sorry," Dunross said, trying to dismiss the twinge that had rushed through him as his mind had substituted Adryon for Avril. Avril was just twenty and Borge Escary a fine young man. They had been married just a year and a half and this was their first holiday after the birth of a son. "What time's the flight?"

"Eight o'clock now."

"Susanne, would you like us to look after the baby? Jacques, why not get on the flight—I'll take care of everything here."

"No," Jacques said. "Thanks but no. It's best that Susanne go. She'll bring Avril home."

"Yes," Susanne said, and Dunross noticed that she seemed to have sagged. "We have the *amahs* . . . it's best just me, tai-pan. *Merci*, but no, this way is best." A spill of tears went down her cheeks. "It's not fair is it? Borge was so nice a boy!"

"Yes. Susanne, I'll get Penn to go over daily so don't worry, we'll make sure the babe's fine and Jacques too." Dunross weighed them both. He was confident that Jacques was well in control. Good, he thought. Then he said as an order, "Jacques, when Susanne's safely on the flight go back to the office. Telex our man in Marseilles. Get him to arrange a suite at the Capitol, to meet her with a car and ten thousand dollars worth of francs. Tell him from me he's to be at her beck and call as long as she's there. He's to call me tomorrow with a complete report on Avril, the accident, who was driving and who the other driver was."

"Yes, tai-pan."

"You sure you're all right?"

Jacques forced a smile. "*Oui. Merci, mon ami.*"

"*Rien.* I'm so sorry, Susanne—call collect if we can do anything." He walked away. Our man in Marseilles is good, he thought. He'll take care of everything. And Jacques's a man of iron. Have I covered everything? Yes, I think so. It's dealt with for the moment.

God protect Adryon and Glenna and Duncan and Penn, he thought. And Kathy, and all the others. And me—until the Noble House is inviolate. He glanced at his watch. It was exactly 6:30. He picked up a house phone. "Mr. Bartlett, please." A moment, then he heard Casey's voice.

"Hello?"

"Ah, hello, Ciranoush," Dunross said. "Would you tell him I'm in the lobby."

"Oh hello, sure! Would you like to come up? We're—"

"Why don't you come down? I thought, if you're not too busy I'd take you on my next appointment—it might be interesting for you. We could eat afterwards, if you're free."

"I'd love that. Let me check."

He heard her repeat what he had said and he wondered, very much, about his bet with Claudia. Impossible that those two aren't lovers, he thought, or haven't been lovers, living so close together. Wouldn't be natural!

"We'll be right down, tai-pan!" He heard the smile in her voice as he hung up.

The Most High Headwaiter was hovering beside him now, waiting for the rare honor of seating the tai-pan. He had been summoned by the Second Headwaiter the moment the news had arrived that Dunross had been seen approaching the front door. His name was Afternoon Pok and he was gray-haired, majestic, and ruled this shift with a bamboo whip.

"Ah Honored Lord, this is a pleasure," the old man said in Cantonese with a deferential bow. "Have you eaten rice today?" This was the polite way of saying good-day or good evening or how are you in Chinese.

"Yes, thank you, Elder Brother," Dunross replied. He had known Afternoon Pok most of his life. As long as he could remember, Afternoon Pok had been the headwaiter in the foyer from noon till six, and many times when Dunross was young, sent on an errand here, sore from a whipping or cuffing, the old man would seat him in a corner table, slip him a pastry, tap him kindly on the head and never give him a bill. "You're looking prosperous!"

"Thank you, tai-pan. Oh, you are looking very healthy too! But you've still only one son! Don't you think it's time your revered Chief Wife found you a second wife?"

They smiled together. "Please follow me," the old man said importantly and led the way to the choice table that had miraculously appeared in a spacious, favored place acquired by four energetic waiters who had squeezed other guests and the tables out of the way. Now they stood, almost at attention, all beaming.

"Your usual, sir?" the wine waiter asked. "I've a bottle of the '52."

"Perfect," Dunross said, knowing this would be the La Doucette that he enjoyed so much. He would have preferred tea but it was a matter of face to accept the wine. The bottle was already there, in an ice bucket. "I'm expecting Mr. Bartlett and Miss Tcholok." Another waiter went at once to wait for them at the elevator.

"If there's anything you need, please call me." Afternoon Pok bowed and walked off, every waiter in the foyer nervously conscious of him. Dunross sat down and noticed Peter and Fleur Marlowe trying to control two pretty, boisterous girls of four and eight and he sighed and thanked God his daughters were past that age. As he sipped the wine approvingly, he saw old Willie Tusk look over at him and wave. He waved back.

When he was a boy he used to come over from Hong Kong three or four times a week with business orders for Tusk from old Sir Ross Struan, Alastair's father—or, more likely, they were orders from his own father who, for years, had run the foreign division of the Noble House. Occasionally Tusk would service the Noble House in areas of his expertise—anything to do with getting anything out of Thailand, Burma or Malaya and shipping it anywhere, with just a little *h'eung yau* and his standard trading fee of 7½ percent.

"What's the half percent for, Uncle Tusk?" he remembered asking one day, peering up at the man he now towered over.

"That's what I call my dollymoney, young Ian."

"What's dollymoney?"

"That's a little extra for your pocket to give away to dollies, to ladies of your choice."

"But why do you give money to ladies?"

"Well that's a long story, laddie."

Dunross smiled to himself. Yes, a very long story. That part of his education had had various teachers, some good, some very good and some bad. Old Uncle Chen-chen had arranged for his first mistress when he was fourteen.

"Oh do you really mean it, Uncle Chen-chen?"

"Yes, but you're not to tell anyone or your father will have my guts for garters! Huh," the lovely old man had continued, "your father should have arranged it, or asked me to arrange it but never mind. Now wh—"

"But when do I, when do I . . . oh are you sure? I mean how, how much do I pay and when, Uncle Chen-chen? When? I mean before or, or after or when? That's what I don't know."

"You don't know lots! You still don't know when to talk and when not to talk! How can I instruct you if you talk? Have I all day?"

"No sir."

"*Eeeee,*" old Chen-chen had said with that huge smile of his, "eeeee, but how lucky you are! Your first time in a Gorgeous Gorge! It will be the first time, won't it? Tell the truth!"

"Er . . . well er er well . . . er, yes."

"Good!"

It wasn't till years after that Dunross had discovered that some of the most famous houses in Hong Kong and Macao had secretly bid for the privilege of servicing the first pillow time of a future tai-pan and the great-great-grandson of Green-Eyed Devil himself. Apart from the face the house would gain for generations to be the one chosen by the compradore of the Noble House, it would also be enormous joss for the lady herself. First Time Essence of even the meanest personage was an elixir of marvelous value—just as, in Chinese lore, for the elderly man, the yin juices of the virgin were equally prized and sought after to rejuvenate the yang.

"Good sweet Christ, Uncle Chen-chen!" he had exploded. "It's true? You actually sold me? You mean to tell me you sold me to a bloody house! Me?"

"Of course." The old man had peered up at him, and chuckled and chuckled, bedridden now in the great house of the Chens on the ridge of Struan's Lookout, almost blind now and near death but sweetly unresisting and content. "Who told you, who, eh? Eh, young Ian?"

It was Tusk, a widower, a great frequenter of Kowloon's dance halls and bars and houses who had been told it as a legend by one of the mama-sans who had heard that it was a custom in the Noble House that the compradore had to arrange the first pillow time for the progeny of Green-Eyed Devil Struan. "Yes, old boy," Tusk had told him. "Dirk Struan said to Sir Gordon Chen, old Chen-chen's father, he'd put his Evil Eye on the House of Chen if they didn't choose correctly."

"Balls," Dunross had said to Tusk, who had continued, pained, that he was just passing on a legend which was now part of Hong Kong's folklore and, balls or not Ian old chum, your first bang-ditty-bang-bang was worth thousands Hong Kong to that old rake!

"I think that's pretty bloody awful, Uncle Chen-chen!"

"But why? It was a most profitable auction. It cost you nothing but gave you enormous pleasure. It cost me nothing but gave me 20,000 HK. The girl's house gained vast face and so did the girl. It cost her nothing but gave her years of a huge clientele who would want to share the specialness of your Number One choice!"

Elegant Jade had been the only name he knew her by. She had been twenty-two and very practiced, a professional since she had been sold to the house by her parents when she was twelve. Her house was called the House of a Thousand Pleasures. Elegant Jade was sweet and gentle—when it pleased her and a total dragon when it pleased her. He had been madly in love with her and their affair had lasted over two summer holidays from boarding school in England, which was the contract time that Chen-chen had arranged. The moment he had returned on the first day of the third summer he had hurried to the house, but she had vanished.

Even today Dunross could remember how distraught he had been, how he had tried to find her. But the girl had left no trace in her wake.

"What happened to her, Uncle Chen-chen? Really happened?"

The old man sighed, lying back in his huge bed, tired now. "It was time for her to go. It is always too easy for a young man to give too much to a girl, too much time, too much thought. It was time for her to go . . . after her you could choose for yourself and you needed to put your mind on the House and not on her. . . . Oh don't try to hide your desire, I understand, oh, how I understand! Don't worry, she was well paid, my son, you had no child by her . . ."

"Where is she now?"

"She went to Taiwan. I made sure she had enough money to begin her own house, she said that's what she wanted to do and . . . and part of my arrangement was that I bought her out of her contract. That cost me, was it 5 . . . or 10,000. . . . I can't remember. . . . Please excuse me, I'm tired now. I must sleep a little. Please come back tomorrow, my son. . . ."

Dunross sipped his wine, remembering. That was the only time that old Chen-chen ever called me my son, he thought. What a grand old man! If only I could be so wise, so kind and so wise, and worthy of him.

Chen-chen had died a week later. His funeral was the greatest Hong Kong had ever seen, with a thousand professional wailers and drums following the coffin to its burial place. The white-clad women had been paid to follow the coffin, wailing loudly to the Heavens, petitioning the gods to grease the way of this great man's spirit to the Void or rebirth or to whatever happens to the spirit of the dead. Chen-chen was a nominal Christian so he had had two services for safety, one Christian, the other Buddhist. . . .

"Hello, tai-pan!"

Casey was there with Linc Bartlett beside her. Both were smiling though both were looking a little tired.

He greeted them and Casey ordered a Scotch and soda and Linc a beer.

"How's your day been?" Casey asked.

"Up and down," he said after a pause. "How was yours?"

"Busy, but we're getting there," she said. "Your attorney, Dawson, canceled our date this morning—that's on again for tomorrow at noon. The rest of my day was on the phone and the telex to the States, getting things organized. Service is good here, this is a great hotel. We're all set to complete our side of the agreement."

"Good. I think I'll attend the meeting with Dawson," Dunross said. "That'll expedite matters. I'll get him to come over to our offices. I'll send a car for you at 11:10."

"No need for that, tai-pan. I know my way on the ferry," she said. "I went back and forth this afternoon. Best five cents American I've ever spent. How'd you keep the fares so low?"

"We carried forty-seven million passengers last year." Dunross glanced at Bartlett. "Will you be at the meeting tomorrow?"

"Not unless you want me for something special," he said easily. "Casey handles the legals initially. She knows what we want, and we've got Seymour Steigler III coming in on Pan Am's flight Thursday—he's our head counsel and tax attorney. He'll keep everything smooth with your attorneys so we can close in seven days, easy."

"Excellent." A smiling obsequious waiter brought their drinks and topped up Dunross's glass. When they were alone again Casey said quietly, "Tai-pan, your ships. You want them as a separate agreement? If the attorneys draw it up it won't be private. How do we keep it private?"

"I'll draw up the document and put our chop on it. That'll make it legal and binding. Then the agreement stays secret between the three of us, eh?"

"What's a chop, Ian?" Bartlett asked.

"It's the equivalent of a seal." Dunross took out a slim, oblong bamboo container, perhaps two inches long and half an inch square, and slid back the tight-fitting top. He took out the chop, which fitted the scarlet silk-lined box, and showed it to them. It was made of ivory. Some Chinese characters were carved in relief on the bottom. "This is my personal chop —it's hand-carved so almost impossible to forge. You stick this end in the ink . . ." The ink was red and almost solid, neatly in its compartment in one end of the box. ". . . and imprint the paper. Quite often in Hong Kong you don't sign papers, you just chop them. Most aren't legal without a chop. The company seal's the same as this, only a little bigger."

"What do the characters mean?" Casey asked.

"They're a pun on my name, and ancestor. Literally they mean 'illustrious, razor sharp, throughout the noble green seas.' The pun's on Green-Eyed Devil, as Dirk was called, the Noble House, and a dirk or knife." Dunross smiled and put it away. "It has other meanings—the surface one's 'tai-pan of the Noble House.' In Chinese . . ." He glanced around at the sound of a bicycle bell. The young bellhop was walking through the crowds carrying a small paging board aloft on a pole that bore the scrawled name of the person wanted. The page was not for them so he continued, "With Chinese writing, there are always various levels of meanings. That's what makes it complex, and interesting."

Casey was fanning herself with a menu. It was warm in the foyer though the ceiling fans were creating a gentle breeze. She took out a tissue and pressed it beside her nose. "Is it always this humid?" she asked.

Dunross smiled. "It's relatively dry today. Sometimes it's ninety degrees and ninety-five humidity for weeks on end. Autumn and spring are the best times to be here. July, August, September are hot and wet. Actually, though, they're forecasting rain. We might even get a typhoon. I heard on the wireless there's a tropical depression gathering southeast of us. Yes. If we're lucky it'll rain. There's no water rationing in the V and A yet, is there?"

"No," Bartlett said, "but after seeing the pails in your house last night, I don't think I'll ever take water for granted again."

"Nor me," Casey said. "It must be terribly hard."

"Oh, you get used to it. By the way my suggestion about the document is satisfactory?" Dunross asked Bartlett, wanting it settled and irritated with himself that he was trapped into having to ask. He was grimly amused to notice that Bartlett hesitated a fraction of a second and glanced imperceptibly at Casey before saying, "Sure."

"Ian," Bartlett continued, "I've got Forrester—the head of our foam division—coming in on the same flight. I thought we might as well get the show on the road. There's no reason to wait until we have papers, is there?"

"No." Dunross thought a moment and decided to test his theory. "How expert is he?"

"Expert."

Casey added, "Charlie Forrester knows everything there is to know about polyurethane foam—manufacturing, distribution and sales."

"Good." Dunross turned to Bartlett and said innocently, "Would you like to bring him to Taipei?" He saw a flash behind the American's eyes and knew that he had been correct. Squirm, you bastard, he thought, you haven't told her yet! I haven't forgotten the rough time you gave me last night, with all your secret information. Squirm out of this one with face! "While we're golfing or whatever, I'll put Forrester with my experts—he can check out possible sites and set that in motion."

"Good idea," Bartlett said, not squirming at all, and Dunross's opinion of him went up.

"Taipei? Taipei in Taiwan?" Casey asked excitedly. "We're going to Taipei? When?"

"Sunday afternoon," Bartlett said, his voice calm. "We're going for a couple of days, Ian an—"

"Perfect, Linc," she said with a smile. "While you're golfing, I can check things out with Charlie. Let me play next time around. What's your handicap, tai-pan?"

"Ten," Dunross answered, "and since Linc Bartlett knows I'm sure you do too."

She laughed. "I'd forgotten that vital statistic. Mine's fourteen on a very good day."

"Give or take a stroke or two?"

"Sure. Women cheat in golf as much as men."

"Oh?"

"Yes. But unlike men they cheat to lower their handicap. A handicap's a status symbol, right? The lower the score, the more the status! Women don't usually bet more than a few dollars so a low handicap's not that vital except for face. But men? I've seen them hit one deliberately into the rough to pick up two extra strokes if they were on a dynamite round that would drop their handicap a notch. Of course that was only if they weren't playing that particular round for money. What's the stake between your pairs?"

"500 HK."

She whistled. "A hole?"

"Hell, no," Bartlett said. "The game."

"Even so, I think I'd better kibitz this one."

Dunross said, "What's that mean?"

"To watch. If I'm not careful, Linc will put my end of Par-Con on the line." Her smile warmed both of them, and then, because Dunross had deliberately dropped Bartlett into the trap, he decided to extract him.

"That's a fine idea, Casey," he said, watching her carefully. "But on second thought, perhaps it would be better for you and Forrester to check out Hong Kong before Taipei—this will be our biggest market. And if your lawyer arrives Thursday you might wish to spend time with him here." He looked at Bartlett directly, the picture of innocence. "If you want to cancel our trip, that's all right too, you've plenty of time to go to Taipei. But I must go."

"No," Bartlett said. "Casey, you cover this end. Seymour will need all the help you can give him. I'll make a preliminary tour this time and we can do it together later."

She sipped her drink and kept her face clear. So I'm not invited, huh? she thought with a flash of irritation. "You're off Sunday?"

"Yes," Dunross said, sure that the finesse had worked, detecting no change in her. "Sunday afternoon I may be doing a hill climb in the morning, so that's the earliest I can make it."

"Hill climb? Mountain climbing, tai-pan?"

"Oh no. Just with a motorcar—in the New Territories. You're both welcome if you're interested." He added to Bartlett, "We could go directly to the airport. If I can clear your aircraft, I will. I'll ask about that tomorrow."

"Linc," Casey said, "what about Armstrong and the police? You're grounded here."

"I arranged that today," Dunross said, "he's parolled into my custody."

She laughed. "Fantastic! Just don't jump bail!"

"I won't."

"You're off Sunday, tai-pan? Back when?"

"Tuesday, in time for dinner."

"Tuesday's when we sign?"

"Yes."

"Linc, isn't that cutting it tight?"

"No. I'll be in constant touch. The deal's set. All we need is to put it on paper."

"Whatever you say, Linc. Everything will be ready for signature when you two get back. Tai-pan, I'm to deal with Andrew if there's any problem?"

"Yes. Or Jacques." Dunross glanced at the far corner. Now their table was occupied by others. Never mind, he told himself. Everything was done that could be done. "The phone service is good to Taipei so there's no need to worry. Now, are you free for dinner?"

"We certainly are," Bartlett said.

"What sort of food would you like?"

"How about Chinese?"

"Sorry, but you've got to be more specific," Dunross said. "That's like saying you want European cooking—which could run the gamut from Italian to boiled English."

"Linc, shouldn't we leave it to the tai-pan?" Casey said, and added, "Tai-pan, I have to confess, I like sweet and sour, egg rolls, chop suey and fried rice. I'm not much on anything far out."

"Nor am I," Bartlett agreed. "No snake, dog or anything exotic."

"Snake's very good in season," Dunross said. "Especially the bile—mixed with tea. It's very invigorating, a great pick-me-up! And little young chow dog stewed in oyster sauce is just perfect."

"You've tried it? You've tried dog?" She was shocked.

"I was told it was chicken. It tasted a lot like chicken. But never eat dog and drink whiskey at the same time, Casey. They say it turns the meat into lumps of iron that'll give you a very hard time indeed. . . ."

He was listening to himself make jokes and inconsequential small talk while he was watching Jacques and Susanne getting into a taxi. His heart went out to them and to Kathy and to all the others and he wanted to get on the plane himself, to rush there and bring Avril back safely—such a nice girl, part of his family. . . .

How in the name of Christ do you live as a man, rule the Noble House and stay sane? How do you help the family and make deals and live with all the rest of it?

"That's the joy and the hurt of being tai-pan," Dirk Struan had said to him in his dreams, many times.

Yes, but there's very little joy.

You're wrong and Dirk's right and you're being far too serious, he told himself. The only serious problems are Par-Con, the boom, Kathy, AMG's papers, Crosse, John Chen, Toda Shipping, and the fact that you turned down Lando Mata's offer, not necessarily in that order. So much money.

What is it I want out of life? Money? Power? Or all China?

He saw Casey and Bartlett watching him. Since these two've arrived, he thought, I've had nothing but trouble. He looked back at them. She was certainly worth looking at with her tight pants and clinging blouse. "Leave it to me," he said, deciding that tonight he would like some Cantonese food.

They heard the page bell and saw the paging board and the name was "Miss K. C. Shuluk." Dunross beckoned the youth. "He'll show you to the phone, Casey."

"Thanks." She got up. Eyes followed the long, elegant legs and her sensuous walk—the women jealous, hating her.

"You're a son of a bitch," Bartlett said calmly.

"Oh?"

"Yes." He grinned and that took the curse off everything. "20 to 1 says

Taipei was a probe—but I'm not calling you on it, Ian. No. I was rough last night—had to be, so maybe I deserved a roasting. But don't do that a second time with Casey or I'll hand you your head."

"Will you now?"

"Yes. She's off limits." Bartlett's eyes went back to Casey. He saw her pass the Marlowe table, stop a second and greet them and their children, then go on again. "She knows she wasn't invited."

Dunross was perturbed. "Are you sure? I thought . . . I didn't cover properly? The moment I realized you hadn't told her yet . . . Sorry, thought I'd covered."

"Hell, you were perfect! But five'll still get you ten she knows she wasn't invited." Bartlett smiled again, and, once more, Dunross wondered what was under the smile. I'll have to watch this bugger more closely, he thought. So Casey's off limits, is she? I wonder what he really meant by that?

Dunross had chosen the foyer deliberately, wanting to be seen with the now famous—or infamous Bartlett and his lady. He knew it would fuel rumors of their impending deal and that would further agitate the stock market and put the punters off balance. If the Ho-Pak crashed, provided it did not bring other banks down with it, the boom could still happen. If Bartlett and Casey would bend a little, he thought, and if I could really trust them, I could make a killing of killings. So many ifs. Too many. I'm out of control of this battle at the moment. Bartlett and Casey have all the momentum. How far will they cooperate?

Then something Superintendent Armstrong and Brian Kwok had said triggered a vagrant thought and his anxiety increased.

"What do you think of that fellow Banastasio?" he asked, keeping his voice matter-of-fact.

"Vincenzo?" Bartlett said at once. "Interesting guy. Why?"

"Just wondering," Dunross said, outwardly calm but inwardly shocked that he had been right. "Have you known him long?"

"Three or four years. Casey an' I have gone to the track with him a few times—to Del Mar. He's a big-time gambler there and in Vegas. He'll bet 50,000 on a race—so he told us. He and John Chen are quite friendly. Is he a friend of yours?"

"No. I've never met him but I heard John mention him once or twice," he said, "and Tsu-yan."

"How is Tsu-yan? He's another gambler. When I saw him in L.A., he couldn't wait to get to Vegas. He was at the track the last time we were there with John Chen. Nothing yet on John or the kidnappers?"

"No."

"Rotten luck."

Dunross was hardly listening. The dossier he had had prepared on Bartlett had given no indication of any Mafia connections—but Banastasio linked everything. The guns, John Chen, Tsu-yan and Bartlett.

Mafia meant dirty money and narcotics, with a constant search for legitimate fronts for the laundering of money. Tsu-yan used to deal heavily in medical supplies during Korea—and now, so the story went, he was heavily into gold smuggling in Taipei, Indonesia and Malaya with Four Finger Wu. Could Banastasio be shipping guns to . . . to whom? Had poor John Chen stumbled onto something and was he kidnapped for that reason?

Does that mean part of Par-Con's money is Mafia money—is Par-Con Mafia-dominated or controlled by Mafia?

"I seem to remember John saying Banastasio was one of your major stockholders," he said, stabbing into the dark again.

"Vincenzo's got a big chunk of stock. But he's not an officer or director. Why?"

Dunross saw that now Bartlett's blue eyes were concentrated and he could almost feel the mind waves reaching out, wondering about this line of questioning. So he ended it. "It's curious how small the world really is, isn't it?"

Casey picked up the phone, inwardly seething. "Operator, this is Miss Tcholok. You've a call for me?"

"Ah one moment plees."

So I'm not invited to Taipei, she was thinking furiously. Why didn't the tai-pan just come out and say it and not twist things around and why didn't Linc tell me about it too? Jesus, is he under the tai-pan's spell like I was last night? Why the secret? What else are they cooking?

Taipei, eh? Well I've heard it's a man's place so if all they're after's a dirty weekend it's fine with me. But not if it's business. Why didn't Linc say? What's there to hide?

Casey's fury began to grow, then she remembered what the Frenchwoman had said about beautiful *Chinoise* so readily available and her fury turned to an untoward anxiety for Linc.

Goddamn men!

Goddamn men and the world they've made exclusively to fit themselves. And it's worse here than anywhere I've ever been.

Goddamn the English! They're all so smooth and smart and their manners great and they say please and thank you and get up when you come in and hold your chair for you but, just under the surface, they're just as rotten as any others. They're worse. They're hypocrites, that's what they are! Well I'll get even. One day we'll play golf, Mr. Tai-pan Dunross and you'd better be good because I can play down to ten on a good day—I learned about golf in a man's world early—so I'll rub your nose in it. Yes. Or maybe a game of pool—or billiards. Sure, and I know what reverse English is too.

Casey thought of her father with a sudden shaft of joy, and how he had taught her the rudiments of both games. But it was Linc who taught her how to stab low on the left side with the cue to give the ball a twist to the right to swerve around the eight ball—showed her when, foolishly, she had challenged him to a game. He had slaughtered her before he gave her any lessons.

"Casey, you'd better make sure you know all a man's weak points before you battle with him. I wiped the board with you to prove a point. I don't play games for pleasure—just to win. I'm not playing games with you. I want you, nothing else matters. Let's forget the deal we made and get married and . . ."

That was just a few months after she had started working for Linc Bartlett. She was just twenty and already in love with him. But she still wanted revenge on the other man more, and independent wealth more and to find herself more, so she had said, "No, Linc, we agreed seven years. We agreed up front, as equals. I'll help you get rich and I'll get mine on the way to your millions, and neither of us owes the other anything. You can fire me anytime for any reason, and I can leave for any reason. We're equals. I won't deny that I love you with all my heart but I still won't change our deal. But if you're still willing to ask me to marry you when I reach my twenty-seventh birthday, then I will. I'll marry you, live with you, leave you—whatever you want. But not now. Yes I love you but if we become lovers now I'll . . . I'll never be able to . . . I just can't, Linc, not now. There's too much I have to find out about myself."

Casey sighed. What a twisted crazy deal it is. Has all the power and dealing and wheeling—and all the years and tears and loneliness been worth it?

I just don't know. I just don't know. And Par-Con? Can I ever reach my goal: Par-Con *and* Linc, or will I have to choose between them?

"Ciranoush?" came through the earpiece.

"Oh! Hello, Mr. Gornt!" She felt a surge of warmth. "This is a pleasant surprise," she added, collecting her wits.

"I hope I'm not disturbing you?"

"Not at all. What can I do for you?"

"I wondered if you are able to confirm this Sunday yet, if you and Mr. Bartlett are available? I want to plan my boat party and I'd like the two of you as my honored guests."

"I'm sorry, Mr. Gornt, but Linc can't make it. He's all tied up."

She heard the hesitation and then the covered pleasure in his voice. "Would you care to come without him? I was thinking of having a few business friends. I'm sure you'd find it interesting."

It might be very good for Par-Con if I went, she thought. Besides, if Linc and the tai-pan are going to Taipei without me, why can't I go boating without them? "I'd love to," she said, warmth in her voice, "if you're sure I won't be in the way."

"Of course not. We'll pick you up at the wharf, just opposite the hotel, near the Golden Ferry. Ten o'clock—casual. Do you swim?"

"Sure."

"Good—the water's refreshing. Water-ski?"

"Love it!"

"Very good!"

"Can I bring anything? Food or wine or anything?"

"No. I think we'll have everything aboard. We'll go to one of the outer islands and picnic, water-ski—be back just after sunset."

"Mr. Gornt, I'd like to keep this excursion to ourselves. I'm told Confucius said, 'A closed mouth catches no flies.'"

"Confucius said many things. He once likened a lady to a moonbeam."

She hesitated, the danger signals up. But then she heard herself say lightly, "Should I bring a chaperone?"

"Perhaps you should," he said and she heard his smile.

"How about Dunross?"

"He'd hardly be a chaperone—merely the destruction of what could perhaps be a perfect day."

"I look forward to Sunday, Mr. Gornt."

"Thank you." The phone clicked off instantly.

You arrogant bastard! she almost said aloud. How much are you taking for granted? Just thank you and click and no good-bye.

I'm Linc's and not up for grabs.

Then why did you play the coquette on the phone and at the party? she asked herself. And why did you want that bastard to keep your Sunday date quiet?

Women like secrets too, she told herself grimly. Women like a lot of things men like.

26

The coolie was in the dingy gold vaults of the Ho-Pak Bank. He was a small, old man who wore a tattered grimy undershirt and ragged shorts. As the two porters lifted the canvas sack onto his bent back, he adjusted the forehead halter and leaned against it, taking the strain with his neck muscles, his hands grasping the two worn straps. Now that he had the full weight, he felt his overtaxed heart pumping against the load, his joints shrieking for relief.

The sack weighed just over ninety pounds—almost more than his own weight. The tally clerks had just sealed it. It contained exactly 250 of the little gold smuggler bars, each of five taels—a little over six ounces—just one of which would have kept him and his family secure for months. But the old man had no thought of trying to steal even one of them. All of his being was concentrated on how to dominate the agony, how to keep his feet moving, how to do his share of the work, to get his pay at the end of his shift, and then to rest.

"Hurry up," the foreman said sourly, "we've still more than twenty fornicating tons to load. Next!"

The old man did not reply. To do so would take more of his precious energy. He had to guard his strength zealously tonight if he was to finish. With an effort he set his feet into motion, his calves knotted and varicosed and scarred from so many years of labor.

Another coolie took his place as he shuffled slowly out of the dank concrete room, the shelves ladened with a seemingly never-ending supply of meticulous stacks of little gold bars that waited under the watchful eyes of the two neat bank clerks—waited to be loaded into the next canvas sack, to be counted and recounted, then sealed with a flourish.

On the narrow stairway the old man faltered. He regained his balance with difficulty, then lifted a foot to climb another step—only twenty-eight more now—and then another and he had just made the landing when his calves gave out. He tottered against the wall, leaning against it to ease the weight, his heart grinding, both hands grasping the straps, knowing he could never resettle the load if he stepped out of the harness, terrified lest the foreman or a subforeman would pass by. Through the spectrum of pain he heard footsteps coming toward him and he fought the sack higher onto his back and into motion once more. He almost toppled over.

"Hey, Nine Carat Chu, are you all right?" the other coolie asked in Shantung dialect, steadying the sack for him.

"Yes . . . yes . . ." He gasped with relief, thankful it was his friend from his village far to the north and the leader of his gang of ten. "Fornicate all gods, I . . . I just slipped. . . ."

The other man peered at him in the coarse light from the single bare light overhead. He saw the tortured, rheumy old eyes and the stretched muscles. "I'll take this one, you rest a moment," he said. Skillfully he eased off the weight and swung the sack to the floorboards. "I'll tell that motherless foreigner who thinks he's got brains enough to be a foreman that you've gone to relieve yourself." He reached into his ragged, torn pants pocket and handed the old man one of his small, screwed-up pieces of cigarette foil. "Take it. I'll deduct it from your pay tonight."

The old man mumbled his thanks. He was all pain now, barely thinking. The other man swung the sack onto his back, grunting with the effort, leaned against the head band, then, his calves knotted, slowly went back up the stairs, pleased with the deal he had made.

The old man slunk off the landing into a dusty alcove and squatted down. His fingers trembled as he smoothed out the cigarette foil with its pinch of white powder. He lit a match and held it carefully under the foil to heat it. The powder began to blacken and smoke. Carefully he held the smoking powder under his nostrils and inhaled deeply, again and again, until every grain had vanished into the smoke that he pulled oh so gratefully into his lungs.

He leaned back against the wall. Soon the pain vanished and left euphoria. It was all-pervading. He felt young again and strong again and now he knew that he would finish his shift perfectly and this Saturday, when he went to the races, he would win the double quinella. Yes, this would be his lucky week and he would put most of his winnings down on a piece of property, yes, a small piece of property at first but with the boom my property will go up and up and up and then I'll sell that piece and make a fortune and buy more and more and then I'll be an ancestor, my grandchildren flocking around my knees . . .

He got up and stood tall then went back down the stairs again and stood in line, waiting his turn impatiently. "*Dew neh loh moh* hurry up," he said in his lilting Shantung dialect, "I haven't all night! I've another job at midnight."

The other job was on a construction site in Central, not far from the Ho-Pak and he knew he was blessed to have two bonus jobs in one night on top of his regular day job as a construction laborer. He knew, too, that it was the expensive white powder that had transformed him and taken his fatigue and pain away. Of course, he knew the white powder was dangerous. But he was sensible and cautious and only took it when he was at the limit of strength. That he took it most days now, twice a day most days now, did not worry him. Joss, he told himself with a shrug, taking the new canvas sack on his back.

Once he had been a farmer and the eldest son of landowning farmers in the northern province of Shantung, in the fertile, shifting delta of the Yellow River where, for centuries, they had grown fruit and grain and soybeans, peanuts, tobacco and all the vegetables they could eat.

Ah, our lovely fields, he thought happily, climbing the stairs now, oblivious of his pounding heart, our lovely fields rich with growing crops. So beautiful! Yes. But then the Bad Times began thirty years ago. The Devils from the Eastern Sea came with their guns and their tanks and raped our earth, and then, after warlord Mao Tse-tung and warlord Chiang Kai-shek beat them off, they fought among themselves and again the land was laid waste. So we fled the famine, me and my young wife and my two sons and came to this place, Fragrant Harbor, to live among strangers, southern barbarians and foreign devils. We walked all the way. We survived. I carried my sons most of the way and now my sons are sixteen and fourteen and we have two daughters and they all eat rice once a day and this year will be my lucky year. Yes. I'll win the quinella or the daily double and one day we'll go home to my village and I'll take our lands back and plant them again and Chairman Mao will welcome us home and let us take our lands back and we'll live so happily, so rich and so happy. . . .

He was out of the building now, in the night, standing beside the truck. Other hands lifted the sack and stacked it with all the other sacks of gold, more clerks checking and rechecking the numbers. There were two trucks in the side street. One was already filled and waiting under its guards. A single unarmed policeman was watching idly as the traffic passed. The night was warm.

The old man turned to go. Then he noticed the three Europeans, two men and a woman, approaching. They stopped near the far truck, watching him. His mouth dropped open.

"*Dew neh loh moh!* Look at that whore—the monster with the straw hair," he said to no one in particular.

"Unbelievable!" another replied.

"Yes," he said.

"It's revolting the way their whores dress in public, isn't it?" a wizened old loader said disgustedly. "Flaunting their loins with those tight trousers. You can see every fornicating wrinkle in her lower lips."

"I'll bet you could put your whole fist and whole arm in it and never reach bottom!" another said with a laugh.

"Who'd want to?" Nine Carat Chu asked and hawked loudly and spat and let his mind drift pleasantly to Saturday as he went below again.

"I wish they wouldn't spit like that. It's disgusting!" Casey said queasily.

"It's an old Chinese custom," Dunross said. "They believe there's an evil god-spirit in your throat which you've got to get rid of constantly or it will choke you. Of course spitting's against the law but that's meaningless to them."

"What'd that old man say?" Casey asked, watching him plod back into the side door of the bank, now over her anger and very glad to be going to dinner with them both.

"I don't know—I didn't understand his dialect."

"I'll bet it wasn't a compliment."

Dunross laughed. "You'd win that one, Casey. They don't think much of us at all."

"That old man must be eighty if he's a day and he's carried his load as though it was a feather. How'd they stay so fit?"

Dunross shrugged and said nothing. He knew.

Another coolie heaved his burden into the truck, stared at her, hawked, spat and plodded away again. "Up yours too," Casey muttered and then parodied an awful hawk and a twenty-foot spit and they laughed with her. The Chinese just stared.

"Ian, what's this all about? What're we here for?" Bartlett asked.

"I thought you might like to see fifty tons of gold."

Casey gasped. "Those sacks're filled with gold?"

"Yes. Come along." Dunross led the way down the dingy stairs into the gold vault. The bank officials greeted him politely and the unarmed guards and loaders stared. Both Americans felt disquieted under the stares. But their disquiet was swamped by the gold. Neat stacks of gold bars on the steel shelves that surrounded them—ten to a layer, each stack ten layers high.

"Can I pick one up?" Casey asked.

"Help yourself," Dunross told them, watching them, trying to test the extent of their greed. I'm gambling for high stakes, he thought again. I have to know the measure of these two.

Casey had never touched so much gold in her life. Nor had Bartlett. Their fingers trembled. She caressed one of the little bars, her eyes wide, before she lifted it. "It's so heavy for its size," she muttered.

"These're called smuggler bars because they're easy to hide and to transport," Dunross said, choosing his words deliberately. "Smugglers wear a sort of canvas waistcoat with little pockets in it that hold the bars snugly. They say a good courier can carry as much as eighty pounds a trip—that's almost 1,300 ounces. Of course they have to be fit and well trained."

Bartlett was hefting two in each hand, fascinated by them. "How many make up eighty pounds?"

"About two hundred, give or take a little."

Casey looked at him, her hazel eyes bigger than usual. "Are these yours, tai-pan?"

"Good God, no! They belong to a Macao company. They're shifting it from here to the Victoria Bank. Americans or English aren't allowed by law to own even one of these. But I thought you might be interested because it's not often you see fifty tons all in one place."

"I never realized what *real* money was like before," Casey said. "Now I can understand why my dad's and uncle's eyes used to light up when they talked about gold."

Dunross was watching her. He could see no greed in her. Just wonder.

"Do banks make many shipments like this?" Bartlett asked, his voice throaty.

"Yes, all the time," Dunross said and he wondered if Bartlett had taken the bait and was considering a Mafioso-style hijack with his friend Banastasio. "We've a very large shipment coming in in about three weeks," he said, increasing the lure.

"What's fifty tons worth?" Bartlett asked.

Dunross smiled to himself remembering Zeppelin Tung with his exactitude of figures. As if it mattered! "63 million dollars legally, give or take a few thousand."

"And you're moving it just with a bunch of old men, two trucks that're not even armored and no guards?"

"Of course. That's no problem in Hong Kong, which's one of the reasons our police are so sensitive about guns here. If they've the only guns in the Colony, well, what can the crooks and nasties do except curse?"

"But where're the police? I didn't see but one and he wasn't armed."

"Oh, they're around, I suppose," Dunross said, deliberately underplaying it.

Casey peered at the gold bar, enjoying the touch of the metal. "It feels so cool and so permanent. Tai-pan, if it's 63 million legal, what's it worth on the black market?"

Dunross noticed tiny beads of perspiration now on her upper lip. "However much someone's prepared to pay. At the moment, I hear the best market's India. They'd pay about $80 to $90 an ounce, U.S., delivered into India."

Bartlett smiled crookedly and reluctantly put his four bars back onto their pile. "That's a lot of profit."

They watched in silence as another canvas bag was sealed, the bars checked and rechecked by both clerks. Again the two loaders lifted the sack onto a bent back and the man plodded out.

"What're those?" Casey asked, pointing to some much bigger bars that were in another part of the vault.

"They're the regulation four-hundred-ounce bars," Dunross said. "They weigh around twenty-five pounds apiece." The bar was stamped with a hammer and sickle and 99,999. "This's Russian. It's 99.99 percent pure. South African gold is usually 99.98 percent pure so the Russian's sought after. Of course both're easy to buy in the London gold market." He let them look a while longer, then said, "Shall we go now?"

On the street there was still only one policeman and the sloppy, unarmed bank guards, the two truck drivers smoking in their cabins. Traffic eased past from time to time. A few pedestrians.

Dunross was glad to get out of the close confinement of the vault. He had hated cellars and dungeons ever since his father had locked him in a cupboard when he was very small, for a crime he could not now remember. But he remembered old Ah Tat, his *amah*, rescuing him and standing up for him—him staring up at his father, trying to hold back the terror tears that would not be held back.

"It's good to be out in the air again," Casey said. She used a tissue. Inexorably her eyes were dragged to the sacks in the nearly full truck. "That's real money," she muttered, almost to herself. A small shudder wracked her and Dunross knew at once that he had found her jugular.

"I could use a bottle of beer," Bartlett said. "So much money makes me thirsty."

"I could use a Scotch and soda!" she said, and the spell was broken.

"We'll stroll over to the Victoria and see the delivery begin, then we'll eat—" Dunross stopped. He saw the two men chatting near the trucks, partially in shadow. He stiffened slightly.

The two men saw him. Martin Haply of the *China Guardian* and Peter Marlowe.

"Oh, hello, tai-pan," young Martin Haply said, coming up to him with his confident grin. "I didn't expect to see you here. Evening, Miss Casey, Mr. Bartlett. Tai-pan, would you care to comment on the Ho-Pak matter?"

"What Ho-Pak matter?"

"The run on the bank, sir."

"I didn't know there was one."

"Did you happen to read my column about the various branches and the rumo—"

"My dear Haply," Dunross said with his easy charm, "you know I don't seek interviews or give them lightly . . . and never on street corners."

"Yes sir." Haply nodded at the sacks. "Transferring all this gold out's kinda rough for the Ho-Pak, isn't it? That'll put the kiss of death on the bank when all this leaks."

Dunross sighed. "Forget the Ho-Pak, Mr. Haply. Can I have a word in private?" He took the young man's elbow and guided him away with velvet firmness. When they were alone, half covered by one of the trucks, he let go of the arm. His voice dropped. Involuntarily, Haply flinched and moved back half a pace. "Since you are going out with my daughter, I just want you to know that I'm very fond of her and among gentlemen there are certain rules. I'm presuming you're a gentleman. If you're not,

God help you. You'll answer to me personally, immediately and without mercy." Dunross turned and went back to the others, full of sudden bonhomie. "Evening, Marlowe, how're things?"

"Fine, thank you, tai-pan." The tall man nodded at the trucks. "Astonishing, all this wealth!"

"Where did you hear about the transfer?"

"A journalist friend mentioned it about an hour ago. He said that some fifty tons of gold were being moved from here to the Victoria. I thought it'd be interesting to see how it was done. Hope it's not . . . hope I'm not treading on any corns."

"Not at all." Dunross turned to Casey and Bartlett. "There, you see, I told you Hong Kong was just like a village—you can never keep any secrets here for long. But all this"—he waved at the sacks—"this is all lead— fool's gold. The real shipment was completed an hour ago. It wasn't fifty tons, only a few thousand ounces. The majority of the Ho-Pak's bullion's still intact." He smiled at Haply who was not smiling but listening, his face set.

"This's all fake after all?" Casey gasped.

Peter Marlowe laughed. "I must confess I did think this whole operation was a bit haphazard!"

"Well, good night you two," Dunross said breezily to Marlowe and Martin Haply. He took Casey's arm momentarily. "Come on, it's time for dinner." They started down the street, Bartlett beside them.

"But tai-pan, the ones we saw," Casey said, "the one I picked up, that was fake? I'd've bet my life, wouldn't you have, Linc?"

"Yes," Bartlett agreed. "But the diversion was wise. That's what I'd've done."

They turned the corner, heading along toward the huge Victoria Bank building, the air warm and sticky.

Casey laughed nervously. "That golden metal was getting to me—and it was fake all the time!"

"Actually it was all real," Dunross said quietly and she stopped. "Sorry to confuse you, Casey. I only said that for Haply and Marlowe's benefit, to pour suspicion on their source. They could hardly prove it one way or another. I was asked to make the arrangements for the transfer little more than an hour ago—which I did, obviously, with great caution." His heart quickened. He wondered how many other people knew about the AMG papers and the vault and the box number in the vault.

Bartlett watched him. "I bought what you said, so I guess they did," he said, but he was thinking, Why did you bring us to see the gold? That's what I'd like to know.

"It's curious, tai-pan," Casey said with a little nervous laugh. "I knew, I just knew the gold was real to begin with. Then I believed you when you said it was fake, and now I believe you back again. Is it that easy to fake?"

"Yes and no. You only know for certain if you put acid on it—you've got to put it to the acid test. That's the only real test for gold. Isn't it?" he added to Bartlett and saw the half-smile and he wondered if the American understood.

"Guess that's right, Ian. For gold—or for people."

Dunross smiled back. Good, he thought grimly, we understand each other perfectly.

It was quite late now. Golden Ferries had stopped running and Casey and Linc Bartlett were in a small private hire-launch chugging across the harbor, the night grand, a good sea smell on the wind, the sea calm. They were sitting on one of the thwarts facing Hong Kong, arm in arm. Dinner had been the best they had ever eaten, the conversation filled with lots of laughter, Dunross charming. They'd ended with cognac atop the Hilton. Both were feeling marvelously at peace with the world and with themselves.

Casey felt the light pressure of his arm and she leaned against him slightly. "It's romantic, isn't it, Linc? Look at the Peak, and all the lights. Unbelievable. It's the most beautiful and exciting place I've ever been."

"Better than the south of France?"

"That was so different." They had had a holiday on the Côte d'Azur two years ago. It was the first time they had holidayed together. And the last. It had been too much of a strain on both of them to stay apart. "Ian's fantastic, isn't he?"

"Yes. And so are you."

"Thank you, kind sir, and so are you." They laughed, happy together.

At the wharf, Kowloon side, Linc paid the boat off and they strolled to the hotel, arm in arm. A few waiters were still on duty in the lobby.

"Evening, sir, evening, missee," the old elevator man said sibilantly, and, on their floor, Nighttime Chang scurried ahead of them to open the door of the suite. Automatically Linc gave him a dollar and they were bowed in. Nighttime Chang closed the door.

She bolted it.

"Drink?" he asked.

"No thanks. It'd spoil that brandy."

She saw him looking at her. They were standing in the center of the living room, the huge picture window displaying all of Hong Kong behind him, his bedroom to the right, hers to the left. She could feel the vein in her neck pulsing, her loins seemed liquid and he looked so handsome to her.

"Well, it's . . . thanks for a lovely evening, Linc. I'll . . . I'll see you tomorrow," she said. But she did not move.

"It's three months to your birthday, Casey."

"Thirteen weeks and six days."

"Why don't we finesse them and get married now. Tomorrow?"

"You've . . . you've been so wonderful to me, Linc, so good to be patient and put up with my . . . my craziness." She smiled at him. It was a tentative smile. "It's not long now. Let's do it as we agreed. Please?"

He stood there and watched her, wanting her. Then he said, "Sure." At his door he stopped. "Casey, you're right about this place. It is romantic and exciting. It's got to me too. Maybe, maybe you'd better get another room."

His door closed.

That night she cried herself to sleep.

WEDNESDAY

27

The two racehorses came out of the turn into the final stretch going very fast. It was false dawn, the sky still dark to the west, and the Happy Valley Racecourse was spotted with people at the morning workout.

Dunross was up on Buccaneer, the big bay gelding, and he was neck and neck with Noble Star, ridden by his chief jockey, Tom Leung. Noble Star was on the rails and both horses were going well with plenty in reserve. Then Dunross saw the winning post ahead and he had that sudden urge to jam in his heels and best the other horse. The other jockey sensed the challenge and looked across at him. But both riders knew they were there just to exercise and not to race, there to confuse the opposition, so Dunross bottled his almost blinding desire.

Both horses had their ears down now. Their flanks were wet with sweat. Both felt the bit in between their teeth. And now, well into the stretch, they pounded toward the winning post excitedly, the inner training sand track not as fast as the encircling grass, making them work harder. Both riders stood high in the stirrups, leaning forward, reins tight.

Noble Star was carrying less weight. She began to pull away. Dunross automatically used his heels and cursed Buccaneer. The pace quickened. The gap began to close. His exhilaration soared. This gallop was barely half a lap so he thought he would be safe. No opposing trainer could get an accurate timing on them so he kicked harder and the race was on. Both horses knew. Their strides lengthened. Noble Star had her nose ahead and then, feeling Buccaneer coming up fast, she took the bit, laid to and charged forward on her own account and drew away and beat Dunross by half a length.

Now the riders slackened speed and, standing easily, continued around the lovely course—a patch of green surrounded by massed buildings and tiers of high rises that dotted the mountainsides. When Dunross had cantered up the final stretch again, he broke off the exercising, reined in beside where the winner's circle would normally be and dismounted. He slapped the filly affectionately on the neck, threw the reins to a stable hand. The man swung into the saddle and continued her exercise.

Dunross eased his shoulders, his heart beating nicely, the taste of blood in his mouth. He felt very good, his stretched muscles aching pleasantly. He had ridden all of his life. Horse racing was still officially all amateur in Hong Kong. When he was young he had raced two seasons and he would have continued, but he had been warned off the course by his father, then tai-pan and chief steward, and again by Alastair Struan when he took over both jobs, and ordered to quit racing on pain of instant dismissal. So he had stopped racing though he continued to exercise the Struan stable at his whim. And he raced in the dawn when the mood was on him.

It was the getting up when most of the world slept, to gallop in half light—the exercise and excitement, the speed, and the danger that cleared his head.

Dunross spat the sweet sick taste of not winning out of his mouth. That's better, he thought. I could have taken Noble Star today, but I'd've done it in the turn, not in the stretch.

Other horses were exercising on the sand track, more joining the circuit or leaving it. Knots of owners and trainers and jockeys were conferring, *ma-foos*—stable hands—walking horses in their blankets. He saw Butterscotch Lass, Richard Kwang's great mare, canter past, a white star on her forehead, neat fetlocks, her jockey riding her tightly, looking very good. Over on the far side Pilot Fish, Gornt's prize stallion, broke into a controlled gallop, chasing another of the Struan string, Impatience, a new, young, untried filly, recently acquired in the first balloting of this season. Dunross watched her critically and thought she lacked stamina. Give her a season or two and then we'll see, he thought. Then Pilot Fish ripped past her and she skittered in momentary fright, then charged in pursuit until her jockey pulled her in, teaching her to gallop at his whim and not at hers.

"So, tai-pan!" his trainer said. He was a leather-faced, iron-hard Russian émigré in his late sixties with graying hair and this was his third season with Struan's.

"So, Alexi?"

"So the devil got into you and you gave him your heel and did you see Noble Star surge ahead?"

"She's a trier. Noble Star's a trier, everyone knows that," Dunross replied calmly.

"Yes, but I'd've preferred only you and I to be reminded of it today and not"—the small man jerked a calloused thumb at the onlookers and grinned—". . . and not every *viblyadok* in Asia."

Dunross grinned back. "You notice too much."

"I'm paid to notice too much."

Alexi Travkin could outride, outdrink, outwork and outstay a man half his age. He was a loner among the other trainers. Over the years he had told various stories about his past—like most of those who had been caught in the great turmoils of Russia and her revolutions, China and her revolutions, and now drifted the byways of Asia seeking a peace they could never find.

Alexi Ivanovitch Travkin had come out of Russia to Harbin in Manchuria in 1919, then worked his way south to the International Settlement of Shanghai. There he began to ride winners. Because he was very good and knew more about horses than most men know about themselves, he soon became a trainer. When the exodus happened again in '49 he fled south, this time to Hong Kong where he stayed a few years then drifted south again to Australia and the circuits there. But Asia beckoned him so he returned. Dunross was trainerless at that time and offered him the stable of the Noble House.

"I'll take it, tai-pan," he had said at once.

"We haven't discussed money," Dunross had said.

"You're a gentleman, so am I. You'll pay me the best for face—and because I'm the best."

"Are you?"

"Why else do you offer me the post? You don't like to lose either."

Last season had been good for both of them. The first not so good. Both knew this coming season would be the real test.

Noble Star was walking past, settling down nicely.

"What about Saturday?" Dunross asked.

"She'll be trying."

"And Butterscotch Lass?"

"She'll be trying. So will Pilot Fish. So will all the others—in all eight races. This's a very special meeting. We'll have to watch our entries very carefully."

Dunross nodded. He caught sight of Gornt talking with Sir Dunstan Barre by the winner's circle. "I'll be very peed off if I lose to Pilot Fish."

Alexi laughed. Then added wryly, "In that case perhaps you'd better ride Noble Star yourself, tai-pan. Then you can shove Pilot Fish into the rails in the turn if he looks like a threat, or put the whip across his jockey's eyes. Eh?" The old man looked up at him. "Isn't that what you'd've done with Noble Star today if it'd been a race?"

Dunross smiled back. "As it wasn't a race you'll never know—will you?"

A ma-foo came up and saluted Travkin, handing him a note. "Message, sir. Mr. Choi'd like you to look at Chardistan's bindings when you've a moment."

"I'll be there shortly. Tell him to put extra bran in Buccaneer's feed today and tomorrow." Travkin glanced back at Dunross, who was watching Noble Star closely. He frowned. "You're not considering riding Saturday?"

"Not at the moment."

"I wouldn't advise it."

Dunross laughed. "I know. See you tomorrow, Alexi. Tomorrow I'll work Impatience." He clapped him in friendly style and left.

Alexi Travkin stared after him; his eyes strayed to the horses that were in his charge, and their opposition that he could see. He knew this Saturday would be vicious and that Noble Star would have to be guarded. He smiled to himself, pleased to be in a game where the stakes were very high.

He opened the note that was in his hand. It was short and in Russian: "Greetings from Kurgan, Highness. I have news of Nestorova . . ." Alexi gasped. The color drained from his face. By the blood of Christ, he wanted to shout. No one in Asia knows my home was in Kurgan, in the flatlands on the banks of the River Tobol, nor that my father was Prince of Kurgan and Tobol, nor that my darling Nestorova, my child-wife of a thousand lifetimes ago, swallowed up in the revolution while I was with my regiment . . . I swear to God I've never mentioned her name to anyone, not even to myself. . . .

In shock he reread the note. Is this more of their devilment, the Soviets —the enemy of all the Russians? Or is it a friend? Oh Christ Jesus let it be a friend.

After "Nestorova" the note had ended, "Please meet me at the Green Dragon Restaurant, in the alley just off 189 Nathan Road, the back room at three this afternoon." There was no signature.

Across the paddock, near the winning post, Richard Kwang was walking toward his trainer when he saw his sixth cousin, Smiler Ching, chairman of the huge Ching Prosperity Bank, in the stands, his binoculars trained on Pilot Fish.

"Hello, Sixth Cousin," he said affably in Cantonese, "have you eaten rice today?"

The sly old man was instantly on guard. "You won't get any money out of me," he said coarsely, his lips sliding back from protruding teeth that gave him a perpetual smiling grimace.

"Why not?" Richard Kwang said equally rudely. "I've got 17 fornicating millions on loan to you an—"

"Yes but that's on ninety-day call and well invested. We've always paid the 40 percent interest," the old man snarled.

"You miserable old dog bone, I helped you when you needed money! Now it's time to repay!"

"Repay what? What?" Smiler Ching spat. "I've repaid you a fortune over the years. I've taken the risks and you've reaped the profit. This whole disaster couldn't happen at a worse time! I've every copper cash out —every one! I'm not like some bankers. My money's always put to good use."

The good use was narcotics, so legend went. Of course Richard Kwang had never asked, and no one knew for certain, but everyone believed that Smiler Ching's bank was secretly one of the main clearinghouses for the trade, the vast majority of which emanated from Bangkok. "Listen, Cousin, think of the family," Richard Kwang began. "It's only a temporary problem. The fornicating foreign devils are attacking us. When that happens civilized people have to stick together!"

"I agree. But you're the cause of the run on the Ho-Pak. You are. It's on you—not on my bank. You've offended the fornicators somehow! They're after you—don't you read the papers. Yes, and you've got all your cash out on some very bad deals so I hear. You, Cousin, you've put your own head into the cangue. Get money out of that evil son of a Malayan whore half-caste partner of yours. He's got billions—or out of Tightfist. . . ." The old man suddenly cackled. "I'll give you 10 for every 1 that old fornicator loans you!"

"If I go down the toilet the Ching Prosperity Bank won't be far behind."

"Don't threaten me!" the old man said angrily. His lips had a flick of saliva permanently in the corners and then they worked over his teeth once and fell apart again in his grimace. "If you go down it won't be my fault—why wish your rotten joss on family? I've done nothing to hurt you—why try and pass your bad joss on to me? If today . . . *ayeeyah*, if today your bad joss spills over and those dog bone depositors start a run on me I won't last the day!"

Richard Kwang momentarily felt better that the Ching empire was equally threatened. Good, very good. I could use all his business—particularly the Bangkok connection. Then he saw the big clock over the totalizator and groaned. It was just past six now and at ten, banks would open and the stock market would open and though arrangements had been made with Blacs, the Victoria and the Bombay and Eastern Bank of Kowloon to pledge securities that should cover everything and to spare, he was still nervous. And enraged. He had had to make some very tough deals that he had no wish to honor. "Come on, Cousin, just 50 million for ten days—I'll extend the 17 million for two years and add another 20 in thirty days."

"50 million for three days at 10 percent interest a day, your present loan to be collateral and I'll also take deed to your property in Central as further collateral!"

"Go fornicate in your mother's ear! That property's worth four times that."

Smiler Ching shrugged and turned his binoculars back on Pilot Fish. "Is the big black going to beat Butterscotch Lass too?"

Richard Kwang looked at Gornt's horse sourly. "Not unless my weevilmouthed trainer and jockey join together to pull her or dope her!"

"Filthy thieves! You can't trust one of them! My horse's never come in the money once. Never. Not even third. Disgusting!"

"50 million for one week—2 percent a day?"

"5. Plus the Central pro—"

"Never!"

"I'll take a 50 percent share of the property."

"6 percent," Richard Kwang said.

Smiler Ching estimated his risk. And his potential profit. The profit was huge if. If the Ho-Pak didn't fail. But even if it did, the loan would be well covered by the property. Yes, the profit would be huge, provided there wasn't a real run on himself. Perhaps I could gamble and pledge some future shipments and raise the 50 million.

"15 percent and that's final," he said knowing that he would withdraw or change by noon once he saw how the market was, and the run was— and he would continue to sell Ho-Pak short to great profit. "And also you can throw in Butterscotch Lass."

Richard Kwang swore obscenely and they bargained back and forth then agreed that the 50 million was on call at two o'clock. In cash. He would also pledge Smiler Ching 39 percent of the Central property as added collateral, and a quarter share in his mare. Butterscotch Lass was the clincher.

"What about Saturday?"

"Eh?" Richard Kwang said, loathing the grimace and buck teeth.

"Our horse's in the fifth race, *heya*? Listen, Sixth Cousin, perhaps we'd better make an accommodation with Pilot Fish's jockey. We pull our horse —she'll be favorite—and back Pilot Fish and Noble Star for safety!"

"Good idea. We'll decide Saturday morning."

"Better to eliminate Golden Lady too, eh?"

"John Chen's trainer suggested that."

"Eeeee, that fool, to get himself kidnapped. I'll expect you to give me the real information on who's going to win. I want the winner too!" Smiler hawked and spat.

"All gods defecate, don't we all! Those filthy trainers and jockeys! Disgusting the way they puppet us owners. Who pays their salaries, *heya*?"

"The Turf Club, the owners, but most the punters who aren't in the know. I hear you were at the Old Vic last night for foreign devil food."

Richard Kwang beamed. His dinner with Venus Poon had been an enormous success. She had worn the new knee-length Christian Dior he had bought for her, black clinging silk and gossamer underneath. When he had seen her get out of his Rolls and come up the steps of the Old Vic his heart had turned over and his Secret Sack had jiggled.

She had been all smiles at the effect her entrance had on the entire foyer, her chunky gold bracelets glittering, and had insisted on walking up the grand staircase instead of using the elevator. His chest had been tight with suppressed glee and terror. They had walked through the formal, well-groomed diners, European and Chinese, many in evening dress—husbands and wives, tourists and locals, men at business dinners, lovers and would-be lovers of all ages and nationalities. He was wearing a new, Savile Row dark suit of the most expensive lightweight cashmere wool. As they moved toward the choice table that had cost him a red—100 dollars—he had waved to many friends, and groaned inwardly four times as he saw four of his Chinese intimates with their wives, bouffant and overjeweled. The wives had stared at him glassily.

Richard Kwang shuddered. Wives really are dragons and all the same, he thought. Oh oh oh! And your lies sound false to them even before you've spoken them. He had not gone home yet to face Mai-ling who would have already been told by at least three very good friends about Venus Poon. He would let her rant and scream and weep and tear her hair for a while to release her devil wind and would say that enemies had filled her head with bile—how can she listen to such evil women?—and then he would meekly tell her about the full-length mink that he had ordered three weeks ago, that he was to collect today in time for her to wear to the races Saturday. Then there would be peace in the house—until the next time.

He chortled at his acumen in ordering the mink. That he had ordered it for Venus Poon and had, this morning, just an hour ago in the warmth of her embrace, promised it to her tonight so she would wear it to the races on Saturday did not bother him at all. It's much too good for the strumpet anyway, he was thinking. That coat cost 40,000 HK. I'll get her another one. Ah, perhaps I could find a secondhand one. . . .

He saw Smiler Ching leering at him. "What?"

"Venus Poon, *heya?*"

"I'm thinking of going into film production and making her a star," he said grandly, proud of the cover story he had invented as part of his excuse to his wife.

Smiler Ching was impressed. "Eeee, but that's a risky business, *heya?*"

"Yes, but there are ways to . . . to insure your risk." He winked knowingly.

"*Ayeeyah,* you mean a nudie film? Oh! Let me know when you set the production, I might take a point or two. Venus Poon naked! *Ayeeyah,* all Asia'd pay to see that! What's she like at the pillow?"

"Perfect! Now that I've educated her. She was a virgin when I fir—"

"What joss!" Smiler Ching said, then added, "How many times did you scale the Ramparts?"

"Last night? Three times—each time stronger than before!" Richard Kwang leaned forward. "Her Flower Heart's the best I've ever seen. Yes. And her triangle! Lovely silken hair and her inner lips pink and delicate. Eeeee, and her Jade Gate . . . her Jade Gate's really heart-shaped and her 'one square inch' is a perfect oval, pink, fragrant, and the Pearl on the Step also pink. . . ." Richard Kwang felt himself beginning to sweat as he remembered how she had spread herself on the sofa and handed him a big magnifying glass. "Here," she had said proudly. "Examine the goddess your baldheaded monk's about to worship." And he had. Meticulously.

"The best pillow partner I've ever had," Richard Kwang continued expansively, stretching the truth. "I was thinking about buying her a large diamond ring. Poor Little Mealy Mouth wept this morning when I left the apartment I've given her. She was swearing suicide because she's so *in love* with me." He used the English word.

"Eeeee, you're a lucky man!" Smiler Ching spoke no English except the words of love. He felt eyes on his back and he glanced around. In the next section of the stands, fifty yards away, slightly above him, was the foreign devil policeman Big Mountain of Dung, the hated chief of the CID Kowloon. The cold fish-eyes were staring at him, binoculars hanging from the man's neck. *Ayeeyah*, Ching muttered to himself, his mind darting over the various checks and traps and balances that guarded his main source of revenue.

"Eh? What? What's the matter with you, Smiler Ching?"

"Nothing. I want to piss, that's all. Send the papers over at two o'clock if you want my money." Sourly he turned away to go to the toilet, wondering if the police were aware of the imminent arrival of the foreign devil from the Golden Mountain, a High Tiger of the White Powders with the outlandish name of Vincenzo Banastasio.

He hawked and spat loudly. Joss if they do, joss if they don't. They can't touch me, I'm only a banker.

Robert Armstrong had noted that Smiler Ching was talking to Banker Kwang and knew surely that the pair of them were up to no good. The police were well aware of the whispers about Ching and his Prosperity Bank and the narcotics trade but so far had no real evidence implicating him or his bank, not even enough circumstantial evidence to merit SB detention, interrogation and summary deportation.

Well, he'll slip sometime, Robert Armstrong thought calmly, and turned his binoculars back on to Pilot Fish, then to Noble Star, then to Butterscotch Lass, and then to Golden Lady, John Chen's mare. Which one's got the form?

He yawned and stretched wearily. It had been another long night and he had not yet been to bed. Just as he was leaving Kowloon Police HQ last night there had been a flurry of excitement as another anonymous caller phoned to say that John Chen had been seen out in the New Territories, in the tiny fishing village of Sha Tau Kwok which bisected the eastern tip of the border.

He had rushed out there with a team and searched the village, hovel by hovel. His search had had to be done very cautiously for the whole border area was extremely sensitive, particularly at the village where there was one of the three border checkpoints. The villagers were a hardy, tough, uncompromising bellicose lot that wanted to be left alone. Particularly by foreign devil police. The search had proved to be just another false alarm though they had uncovered two illegal stills, a small heroin factory that converted raw opium into morphine and thence into heroin, and had broken up six illegal gambling dens.

When Armstrong had got back to Kowloon HQ there was another call about John Chen, this time Hong Kong side in Wanchai, down near Glessing's Point in the dock area. Apparently John Chen had been seen being bundled into a tenement house, a dirty bandage over his right ear. This time the caller had given his name and driver's license number so that he could claim the reward of 50,000 HK, offered by Struan's and Noble House Chen. Again Armstrong had brought units to surround the area and had led the meticulous search. It was already five o'clock in the morning by the time he called off the operation and dismissed his men.

"Brian, it's me for bed," he said. "Waste of another *fang-pi* night."

Brian Kwok yawned too. "Yes. But while we're this side, how about breakfast at the Para and then, then let's go and look at the morning workouts?"

At once most of Robert Armstrong's tiredness fell away. "Great idea!"

The Para Restaurant in Wanchai Road near Happy Valley Racecourse was always open. The food was excellent, cheap and it was a well-known meeting place for triads and their girls. When the two policemen strode into the large, noisy, bustling, plate-clattering room a sudden silence fell. The proprietor, One Foot Ko, limped over to them and beamed them to the best table in the place.

"*Dew neh loh moh* on you too, Old Friend," Armstrong said grimly and added some choice obscenities in gutter Cantonese, staring back pointedly at the nearest group of gaping young thugs who nervously turned away.

One Foot Ko laughed and showed his bad teeth. "Ah, Lords, you honor my poor establishment. *Dim sum?*"

"Why not?" *Dim sum*—small chow or small foods—were bite-sized dough envelopes packed with minced shrimps or vegetables or various meats then steamed or deep-fried and eaten with a touch of soya, or saucers of chicken and other meats in various sauces or pastries of all kinds.

"Your Worships are going to the track?"

Brian Kwok nodded, sipping his jasmine tea, his eyes roving the diners, making many of them very nervous. "Who's going to win the fifth?" he asked.

The restaurateur hesitated, knowing he'd better tell the truth. He said carefully in Cantonese, "They say that neither Golden Lady, Noble Star, Pilot Fish or Butterscotch Lass has . . . has yet been touted as having an edge." He saw the cold black-brown eyes come to rest on him and he tried not to shudder. "By all the gods, that's what they say."

"Good. I'll come here Saturday morning. Or I'll send my sergeant. Then you can whisper in his ear if some foul play's contemplated. Yes.

And if it turns out one of those are doped or cut and I don't know about it on Saturday morning . . . perhaps your soups will addle for fifty years."

One Foot smiled nervously. "Yes, Lord. Let me see to your food no—"

"Before you go, what's the latest gossip on John Chen?"

"None. Oh very none, Honored Lord," the man said, a little perspiration on his upper lip. "Fragrant Harbor's as clean of information on him as a virgin's treasure. Nothing, Lord. Not a dog's fart of a real rumor though everyone's looking. I hear there's an extra great reward."

"What? How much?"

"100,000 extra dollars if within three days."

Both policemen whistled. "Offered by whom?" Armstrong asked.

One Foot shrugged, his eyes hard. "No one knows, Sire. They say by one of the Dragons—or all the Dragons. 100,000 and promotion if within three days—if he's recovered alive. Please, now let me see about your food."

They watched him go. "Why did you lean on One Foot?" Armstrong asked.

"I'm tired of his mealy-mouthed hypocrisy—and all these rotten little thugs. The cat-o'-nine-tails'd solve our triad problems."

Armstrong called for a beer. "When I leaned on Sergeant Tang-po I didn't think I'd get such action so fast. 100,000's a lot of money! This can't be just a simple kidnapping. Jesus Christ that's a lot of reward! There's got to be something special about John."

"Yes. If it's true."

But they had arrived at no conclusions and when they came to the track, Brian Kwok had gone to check in with HQ and now Armstrong had his binoculars trained on the mare. Butterscotch Lass was leaving the track to walk back up the hill to the stables. She looks in great fettle, he thought. They all do. Shit, which one?

"Robert?"

"Oh hello, Peter."

Peter Marlowe smiled at him. "Are you up early or going to bed late?"

"Late."

"Did you notice the way Noble Star charged without her jockey doing a thing?"

"You've sharp eyes."

Peter Marlowe smiled and shook his head. He pointed at a group of men around one of the horses. "Donald McBride told me."

"Ah!" McBride was an immensely popular racing steward, a Eurasian property developer who had come to Hong Kong from Shanghai in '49. "Has he given you the winner? He'll know if anyone does."

"No, but he invited me to his box on Saturday. Are you racing?"

"Do you mind! I'll see you in the members' box—I don't cavort with the nobs!"

They both watched the horses for a while. "Golden Lady looks good."

"They all do."

"Nothing on John Chen yet?"

"Nothing." Armstrong caught sight of Dunross in his binoculars, talking to some stewards. Not far away was the SI guard that Crosse had assigned to him. Roll on Friday, the policeman thought. The sooner we see those AMG files the better. He felt slightly sick and he could not decide if it was apprehension about the papers, or Sevrin, or if it was just fatigue. He began to reach for a cigarette—stopped. You don't need a smoke, he ordered himself. "You should give up smoking, Peter. It's very bad for you."

"Yes. Yes I should. How's it going with you?"

"No trouble. Which reminds me, Peter, the Old Man approved your trip around the border road. Day after tomorrow, Friday, 6:00 A.M. on the dot at Kowloon HQ. That all right?"

Peter Marlowe's heart leaped. At long last he could look into Mainland China, into the unknown. In all the borderland of the New Territories there was only one accessible lookout that tourists could use to see into China, but the hill was so far away you could not see much at all. Even with binoculars. "How terrific!" he said, elated. At Armstrong's suggestion he had written to the commissioner and applied for this permission. The border road meandered from shore to shore. It was forbidden to all traffic and all persons—except locals in certain areas. It ran in a wide stretch of no-man's-land between the Colony and China. Once a day it was patrolled under very controlled circumstances. The Hong Kong Government had no wish to rock any PRC boats.

"One condition, Peter: You don't mention it or talk about it for a year or so."

"My word on it."

Armstrong suppressed another yawn. "You'll be the only Yank who's ever gone along it, perhaps ever will."

"Terrific! Thanks."

"Why did you become a citizen?"

After a pause Peter Marlowe said, "I'm a writer. All my income comes from there, almost all of it. Now people are beginning to read what I write. Perhaps I'd like the right to criticize."

"Have you ever been to any Iron Curtain countries?"

"Oh yes. I went to Moscow in July for the film festival. One of the films I wrote was the American entry. Why?"

"Nothing," Armstrong said, remembering Bartlett's and Casey's Moscow franks. He smiled. "No reason."

"One good turn deserves another. I heard a buzz about Bartlett's guns."

"Oh?" Armstrong was instantly attentive. Peter Marlowe was very rare in Hong Kong inasmuch as he crossed social strata and was accepted as a friend by many normally hostile groups.

"It's just talk probably but some friends have a theory—"

"Chinese friends?"

"Yes. They think the guns were a sample shipment, bound for one of our piratical Chinese citizens—at least, one with a history of smuggling— for shipment to one of the guerrilla bands operating in South Vietnam, called Viet Cong."

Armstrong grunted. "That's farfetched, Peter, Hong Kong's not the place to transit guns."

"Yes. But this shipment was special, the first, and it was asked for in a hurry and was to be delivered in a hurry. You've heard of Delta Force?"

"No," Armstrong said, staggered that Peter Marlowe had already heard of what Rosemont, CIA, had assured them in great secrecy was a very classified operation.

"I understand it's a group of specially trained U.S. combat soldiers, Robert, a special force who're operating in Vietnam in small units under the control of the American Technical Group, which's a cover name for the CIA. It seems they're succeeding so well that the Viet Cong need modern weapons fast and in great quantity and are prepared to pay handsomely. So these were rushed here on Bartlett's plane."

"Is he involved?"

"My friends doubt it," he said after a pause. "Anyway, the guns're U.S. Army issue, Robert, right? Well, once this shipment was approved, delivery in quantity was going to be easy."

"Oh, how?"

"The U.S. is going to supply the arms."

"What?"

"Sure." Peter Marlowe's face settled. "It's really very simple: Say these Viet Cong guerrillas were provided *in advance* with all exact U.S. shipment dates, exact destinations, quantities and types of arms—small arms to rockets—when they arrived in Vietnam?"

"Christ!"

"Yes. You know Asia. A little *h'eung yau* here and there and constant hijacking'd be simple."

"It'd be like them having their own stockpile!" Armstrong said, appalled. "How're the guns going to be paid for? A bank here?"

Peter Marlowe looked at him. "Bulk opium. Delivered here. One of our banks here supplies the financing."

The police officer sighed. The beauty of it fell into place. "Flawless," he said.

"Yes. Some rotten bastard traitor in the States just passes over schedules. That gives the enemy all the guns and ammunition they need to kill off our own soldiers. The enemy pays for the guns with a poison that costs them nothing—I imagine it's about the only salable commodity they've got in bulk and can easily acquire. The opium's delivered here by the Chinese smuggler and converted to heroin because this's where the expertise is. The traitors in the States make a deal with the Mafia who sell the heroin at enormous profit to more kids and so subvert and destroy the most important bloody asset we have: youth."

"As I said, flawless. What some buggers'll do for money!" Armstrong sighed again and eased his shoulders. He thought a moment. The theory tied in everything very neatly. "Does the name Banastasio mean anything?"

"Sounds Italian." Peter Marlowe kept his face guileless. His informants were two Portuguese Eurasian journalists who detested the police. When he had asked them if he could pass on the theory, da Vega had said, "Of course, but the police'll never believe it. Don't quote us and don't mention any names, not Four Finger Wu, Smuggler Pa, the Ching Prosperity, or Banastasio or anyone."

After a pause, Armstrong said, "What else have you heard?"

"Lots, but that's enough for today—it's my turn to get the kids up, cook breakfast and get them toddling off to school." Peter Marlowe lit a cigarette and again Armstrong achingly felt the smoke need in his own lungs. "Except one thing, Robert. I was asked by a friendly member of the press to tell you he'd heard there's to be a big narcotics meeting soon in Macao."

The blue eyes narrowed. "When?"

"I don't know."

"What sort of meeting?"

"Principals. 'Suppliers, importers, exporters, distributors' was the way he put it."

"Where in Macao?"

"He didn't say."

"Names?"

"None. He did add that the meeting'll include a visiting VIP from the States."

"Bartlett?"

"Christ, Robert, I don't know and he didn't say that. Linc Bartlett seems a jolly nice fellow, and straight as an arrow. I think it's all gossip and jealousy, trying to implicate him."

Armstrong smiled his jaundiced smile. "I'm just a suspicious copper. Villains exist in very high places, as well as in the boghole. Peter, old fellow, give your friendly journalist a message: If he wants to give me information, phone me direct."

"He's frightened of you. So am I!"

"In my hat you are." Armstrong smiled back at him, liking him, very glad for the information and that Peter Marlowe was a safe go-between who could keep his mouth shut. "Peter, ask him where in Macao and when and who and—" At a sudden thought, Armstrong said, stabbing into the unknown, "Peter, if you were to choose the best place in the Colony to smuggle in and out, where'd you pick?"

"Aberdeen or Mirs Bay. Any fool knows that—they're just the places that've always been used first, ever since there was a Hong Kong."

Armstrong sighed. "I agree." Aberdeen, he thought. What Aberdeen smuggler? Any one of two hundred. Four Finger Wu'd be first choice. Four Fingers with his big black Rolls and lucky 8 number plate, that bloody thug Two Hatchet Tok and that young nephew of his, the one with the Yankee passport, the one from Yale, was it Yale? Four Fingers would be first choice. Then Goodweather Poon, Smuggler Pa, Ta Sap-fok, Fisherman Pok . . . Christ, the list's endless, just of the ones we know about. In Mirs Bay, northeast beside the New Territories? The Pa Brothers, Big Mouth Fang and a thousand others . . .

"Well," he said, very very glad now for the information—something tweaking him about Four Finger Wu though there had never been any rumor that he was in the heroin trade. "One good turn deserves another: Tell your journalist friend our visiting members of Parliament, the trade delegation, come in today from Peking . . . What's up?"

"Nothing," Peter Marlowe said, trying to keep his face clear. "You were saying?"

Armstrong watched him keenly, then added, "The delegation arrives on the afternoon train from Canton. They'll be at the border, transferring trains at 4:32—we just heard of the change of plan last night so perhaps your friend could get an exclusive interview. Seems they've made very good progress."

"Thanks. On my friend's behalf. Yes thanks. I'll pass it on at once. Well, I must be off. . . ."

Brian Kwok came hurrying toward them. "Hello, Peter." He was breathing quite hard. "Robert, sorry but Crosse wants to see us right now."

"Bloody hell!" Armstrong said wearily. "I told you it'd be better to wait before checking in. That bugger never sleeps." He rubbed his face to clear his tiredness away, his eyes red-rimmed. "You get the car, Brian, and I'll meet you at the front entrance."

"Good." Brian Kwok hurried away. Perturbed, Armstrong watched him go.

Peter Marlowe said as a joke, "The Town Hall's on fire?"

"In our business the Town Hall's always on fire, lad, somewhere." The policeman studied Peter Marlowe. "Before I leave, Peter, I'd like to know what's so important about the trade delegation to you."

After a pause the man with the curious eyes said, "I used to know one of them during the war. Lieutenant Robin Grey. He was provost marshal of Changi for the last two years." His voice was flat now, more flat and more icy than Armstrong had imagined possible. "I hated him and he hated me. I hope I don't meet him, that's all."

Across the winner's circle Gornt had his binoculars trained on Armstrong as he walked after Brian Kwok. Then, thoughtfully, he turned them back on Peter Marlowe who was wandering toward a group of trainers and jockeys.

"Nosy bugger!" Gornt said.

"Eh? Who? Oh Marlowe?" Sir Dunstan Barre chuckled. "He's not nosy, just wants to know everything about Hong Kong. It's your murky past that fascinates him, old boy, yours and the tai-pan's."

"You've no skeletons, Dunstan?" Gornt asked softly. "You're saying you and your family're lily white?"

"God forbid!" Barre was hastily affable, wanting to turn Gornt's sudden venom into honey. "Good God no! Scratch an Englishman find a pirate. We're all suspect! That's life, what?"

Gornt said nothing. He despised Barre but needed him. "I'm having a bash on my yacht on Sunday, Dunstan. Would you care to come—you'll find it interesting."

"Oh? Who's the honored guest?"

"I thought of making it stag only—no wives, eh?"

"Ah! Count me in," Barre said at once, brightening. "I could bring a lady friend?"

"Bring two if you like, old chap, the more the merrier. It'll be a small, select, safe group. Plumm, he's a good sort and his girl friend's lots of fun." Gornt saw Marlowe change direction as he was called over to a group of stewards dominated by Donald McBride. Then, at a sudden thought, he added, "I think I'll invite Marlowe too."

"Why if you think he's nosy?"

"He might be interested in the real stories about the Struans, our founding pirates and the present-day ones." Gornt smiled with the front of his face and Barre wondered what devilment Gornt was planning.

The red-faced man mopped his brow. "Christ, I wish it would rain. Did you know Marlowe was in the Hurricanes—he got three of the bloody Boche in the Battle of Britain before he got sent out to Singapore and that bloody mess. I'll never forgive those bloody Japs for what they did to our lads there, here, or in China."

"Nor will I," Gornt agreed darkly. "Did you know my old man was in Nanking in '37, during the rape of Nanking?"

"No, Christ, how did he get out?"

"Some of our people hid him for a few days—we'd had associates there for generations. Then he pretended to the Japs that he was a friendly correspondent for the London *Times* and talked his way back to Shanghai. He still has nightmares about it."

"Talking about nightmares, old chap, were you trying to give Ian one last night by going to his party?"

"You think he got even by taking care of my car?"

"Eh?" Barre was appalled. "Good God! You mean your car was tampered with?"

"The master cylinder was ruptured by a blow of some kind. The mechanic said it could've been done by a rock thrown up against it."

Barre stared at him and shook his head. "Ian's not a fool. He's wild, yes, but he's no fool. That'd be attempted murder."

"It wouldn't be the first time."

"If I were you I'd not say that sort of thing publicly, old chap."

"You're not public, old chap. Are you?"

"No. Of cour—"

"Good." Gornt turned his dark eyes on him. "This is going to be a time when friends should stick together."

"Oh?" Barre was instantly on guard.

"Yes. The market's very nervous. This Ho-Pak mess could foul up a lot of all our plans."

"My Hong Kong and Lan Tao Farms's as solid as the Peak."

"You are, providing your Swiss bankers continue to grant you your new line of credit."

Barre's florid face whitened. "Eh?"

"Without their loan you can't take over Hong Kong Docks and Wharves, Royal Insurance of Hong Kong and Malaya, expand into Singapore or complete a lot of other tricky little deals you've on your agenda— you and your newfound friend, Mason Loft, the whiz kid of Threadneedle Street. Right?"

Barre watched him, cold sweat running down his back, shocked that Gornt was privy to his secrets. "Where'd you hear about those?"

Gornt laughed. "I've friends in high places, old chap. Don't worry, your Achilles' heel's safe with me."

"We're . . . we're in no danger."

"Of course not." Gornt turned his binoculars back on his horse. "Oh by the way, Dunstan, I might need your vote at the next meeting of the bank."

"On what?"

"I don't know yet." Gornt looked down at him. "I just need to know that I can count on you."

"Yes. Yes of course." Barre was wondering nervously what Gornt had in mind and where the leak was. "Always happy to oblige, old chap."

"Thank you. You're selling Ho-Pak short?"

"Of course. I got all my money out yesterday, thank God. Why?"

"I heard Dunross's Par-Con deal won't go through. I'm considering selling him short too."

"Oh? The deal's not on? Why?"

Gornt smiled sardonically. "Because, Dunstan—"

"Hello, Quillan, Dunstan, sorry to interrupt," Donald McBride said, bustling up to them, two men in tow. "May I introduce Mr. Charles Biltzmann, vice-president of American Superfoods. He'll be heading up the new General Stores–Superfoods merger and based in the Colony from now on. Mr. Gornt and Sir Dunstan Barre."

The tall, sandy-haired American wore a gray suit and tie and rimless glasses. He stuck out his hand affably. "Glad to meet you. This's a nice little track you've got here."

Gornt shook hands without enthusiasm. Next to Biltzmann was Richard Hamilton Pugmire, the present tai-pan of H.K. General Stores, a steward of the Turf Club, a short arrogant man in his late forties who carried his smallness as a constant challenge. "Hello, you two! Well, who's the winner of the fifth?"

Gornt towered over him. "I'll tell you after the race."

"Oh come on, Quillan, you know it'll be fixed before the horses even parade."

"If you can prove that I'm sure we'd all like to know. I certainly would, wouldn't you, Donald?"

"I'm sure Richard was just joking," Donald McBride replied. He was in his sixties, his Eurasian features pleasing, and the warmth of his smile pervaded him. He added to Biltzmann, "There're always these rumors about race fixing but we do what we can and when we catch anyone—off with his head! At least off the course he goes."

"Hell, races get fixed in the States too but I guess here where it's all amateur and wide open, it's got to be easier," Biltzmann said breezily. "That stallion you have, Quillan. He's Australian, partial pedigree, isn't he?"

"Yes," Gornt said abruptly, detesting his familiarity.

"Don here was explaining some of the rules of your racing. I'd sure like to be part of your racing fraternity—hope I can get to be a voting member too."

The Turf Club was very exclusive and very tightly controlled. There were two hundred voting members and four thousand nonvoting members. Only voting members could get into the members' box. Only voting members could own horses. Only voting members could propose two persons a year to be nonvoting members—the stewards' decision, approval or nonapproval being final, their voting secret. And only voting members could become a steward.

"Yes," Biltzmann repeated, "that'd be just great."

"I'm sure that could be arranged," McBride said with a smile. "The club's always looking for new blood—and new horses."

"Do you plan to stay in Hong Kong, Mr. Biltzmann?" Gornt asked.

"Call me Chuck. I'm here for the duration," the American replied. "I suppose I'm Superfoods of Asia's new tai-pan. Sounds great, doesn't it?"

"Marvelous!" Barre said, witheringly.

Biltzmann continued happily, not yet tuned to English sarcasm, "I'm the fall guy for our board in New York. As the man from Missouri said, the buck stops here." He smiled but no one smiled with him. "I'll be here at least a couple of years and I'm looking forward to every minute. We're getting ready to settle in right now. My bride arrives tomorrow an—"

"You're just married, Mr. Biltzmann?"

"Oh no, that's just a, an American expression. We've been married twenty years. Soon as our new place's fixed the way she wants it, we'd be happy for you to come to dinner. Maybe a barbecue? We got the steaks organized, all prime, T-bones and New Yorks, being flown over once a month. And Idaho potatoes," he added proudly.

"I'm glad about the potatoes," Gornt said and the others settled back, waiting, knowing that he despised American cooking—particularly charcoaled steaks and hamburgers and "gooped-up baked potatoes," as he called them. "When does the merger finalize?"

"End of the month. Our bid's accepted. Everything's agreed. I certainly hope our American know-how'll fit into this great little island."

"I presume you'll build a mansion?"

"No sir. Dickie here," Biltzmann continued, and everyone winced, "Dickie's got us the penthouse of the company's apartment building on Blore Street, so we're in fat city."

"That's convenient," Gornt said. The others bit back their laughter. The oldest and most famous of the Colony's Houses of Easy Virtue had always been on Blore Street at Number One. Number One, Blore Street, had been started by one of Mrs. Fotheringill's "young ladies," Nellie Blore, in the 1860's, with money reportedly given her by Culum Struan, and was still operating under its original rules—European or Australian ladies only and no foreign gentlemen or natives allowed.

"Very convenient," Gornt said again. "But I wonder if you'd qualify."

"Sir?"

"Nothing. I'm sure Blore Street is most apt."

"Great view, but the plumbing's no good," Biltzmann said. "My bride'll soon fix that."

"She's a plumber too?" Gornt asked.

The American laughed. "Hell no, but she's mighty handy around the house."

"If you'll excuse me I have to see my trainer." Gornt nodded to the others and turned away with, "Donald, have you a moment? It's about Saturday."

"Of course, see you in a moment, Mr. Biltzmann."

"Sure. But call me Chuck. Have a nice day."

McBride fell into step beside Gornt. When they were alone Gornt said, "You're surely not seriously suggesting he should be a voting member?"

"Well, yes." McBride looked uncomfortable. "It's the first time a big American company's made a bid to come into Hong Kong. He'd be quite important to us."

"That's no reason to let him in here, is it? Make him a nonvoting member. Then he can get into the stands. And if you want to invite him to your box, that's your affair. But a voting member? Good God, he'll probably have 'superfoods' as his racing colors!"

"He's just new and out of his depth, Quillan. I'm sure he'll learn. He's decent enough even though he does make a few gaffes. He's quite well off an—"

"Since when has money been an open sesame to the Turf Club? Good God, Donald, if that was the case, every upstart Chinese property gambler or stock market gambler who'd made a killing on our market'd swamp us. We wouldn't have room to fart."

"I don't agree. Perhaps the answer's to increase the voting membership."

"No. Absolutely not. Of course you stewards will do what you like. But I suggest you reconsider." Gornt was a voting member but not a steward. The two hundred voting members elected the twelve stewards annually by secret ballot. Each year Gornt's name was put on the open list of nominees for steward and each year he failed to get enough votes. Most stewards were reelected by the membership automatically until they retired, though from time to time there was lobbying.

"Very well," McBride said, "when his name's proposed I'll mention your opposition."

Gornt smiled thinly. "That'll be tantamount to getting him elected."

McBride chuckled. "I don't think so, Quillan, not this time. Pug asked me to introduce him around. I must admit he gets off on the wrong foot every time. I introduced him to Paul Havergill and Biltzmann immediately started comparing banking procedures here with those in the States, and not very pleasantly either. And with the tai-pan . . ." McBride's graying eyebrows soared. ". . . he said he was sure glad to meet him as he wanted to learn about Hag Struan and Dirk Struan and all the other pirates and opium smugglers in his past!" He sighed. "Ian and Paul'll certainly blackball him for you, so I don't think you've much to worry about. I really don't understand why Pug sold out to them anyway."

"Because he's not his father. Since old Sir Thomas died General Stores've been slipping. Still, Pug makes 6 million U.S. personally and has a five-year unbreakable contract—so he has all the pleasure and none of the headaches and the family's taken care of. He wants to retire to England, Ascot and all that."

"Ah! That's a very good deal for old Pug!" McBride became more serious. "Quillan, the fifth race—the interest's enormous. I'm worried there'll be interference. We're going to increase surveillance on all the horses. There're rumors th—"

"About doping?"

"Yes."

"There're always rumors and someone will always try. I think the stewards do a very good job."

"The stewards agreed last night that we'd institute a new rule: in future we'll have an obligatory chemical analysis before and after each race, as they do at the major tracks in England or America."

"In time for Saturday? How're you going to arrange that?"

"Dr. Meng, the police pathologist, has agreed to be responsible—until we have an expert arranged."

"Good idea," Gornt said.

McBride sighed. "Yes, but the Mighty Dragon's no match for the Local Serpent." He turned and left.

Gornt hesitated, then went to his trainer who stood beside Pilot Fish talking with the jockey, another Australian, Bluey White. Bluey White was ostensibly a manager of one of Gornt's shipping divisions—the title given to him to preserve his amateur status.

"G'day, Mr. Gornt," they said. The jockey touched his forelock.

"Morning." Gornt looked at them a moment and then he said quietly, "Bluey, if you win, you've a 5,000 bonus. If you finish behind Noble Star, you're fired."

The tough little man whitened. "Yes, guv!"

"You'd better get changed now," Gornt said, dismissing him.

"I'll win," Bluey White said as he left.

The trainer said uneasily, "Pilot Fish's in very good fettle, Mr. Gornt. He'll be try—"

"If Noble Star wins you're fired. If Noble Star finishes ahead of Pilot Fish you're fired."

"My oath, Mr. Gornt." The man wiped the sudden sweat off his mouth. "I don't fix who ge—"

"I'm not suggesting you do anything. I'm just telling you what's going to happen to you." Gornt nodded pleasantly and strode off. He went to the club restaurant, which overlooked the course, and ordered his favorite breakfast, eggs Benedict with his own special hollandaise that they kept for his exclusive use, and Javanese coffee that he also supplied.

On his third cup of coffee the waiter came over. "Excuse me, sir, you're wanted on the telephone."

He went to the phone. "Gornt."

"Hello, Mr. Gornt, this's Paul Choy . . . Mr. Wu's nephew. . . . I hope I'm not disturbing you."

Gornt covered his surprise. "You're calling rather early, Mr. Choy."

"Yes sir, but I wanted to be in early the first day," the young man said in a rush, "so I was the only one here a couple of minutes ago when the phone rang. It was Mr. Bartlett, Linc Bartlett, you know, the guy with the smuggled guns, the millionaire."

Gornt was startled. "Bartlett?"

"Yes sir. He said he wanted to get hold of you, implied it was kinda urgent, said he'd tried your home. I put two and two together and came up with you might be at the workout and I'd better get off my butt. I hope I'm not disturbing you?"

"No. What did he say?" Gornt asked.

"Just that he wanted to talk to you, and were you in town? I said I didn't know, but I'd check around and leave a message and give him a call back."

"Where was he calling from?"

"The Vic and Albert. Kowloon side 662233, extension 773—that's his office extension, not his suite."

Gornt was very impressed. "A closed mouth catches no flies, Mr. Choy."

"Jesus, Mr. Gornt, that's one thing you never need worry about," Paul Choy said fervently. "My old Uncle Wu wopped that into us all like there was no tomorrow."

"Good. Thanks, Mr. Choy. I'll see you shortly."

"Yes sir."

Gornt hung up, thought a moment, then dialed the hotel. "773 please."

"Linc Bartlett."

"Good morning Mr. Bartlett, this's Mr. Gornt. What can I do for you?"

"Hey, thanks for returning my call. I've had disturbing news which sort of ties in with what we were discussing."

"Oh?"

"Yes. Does Toda Shipping mean anything to you?"

Gornt's interest soared. "Toda Shipping's a huge Japanese conglomerate, shipyards, steel mills, heavy engineering. Struan's have a two-ship deal with them, bulk vessels I believe. Why?"

"It seems Toda have some notes due from Struan's, $6 million in three installments—on the first, eleventh, and fifteenth of next month—and another $6 million in 90 days. Then there's another 6.8 million due on the eighth to Orlin International Bank—you know them?"

With a great effort Gornt kept his voice matter-of-fact. "I've, I've heard of them," he said, astounded that the American would have such details of the debts. "So?" he asked.

"So I heard Struan's have only 1.3 million in cash, with no cash reserves and not enough cash flow to make payment. They're not expecting a significant block of income until they get 17 million as their share of one of Kowloon Investments' property deals, not due until November, and they're 20 percent overextended at the Victoria Bank."

"That's . . . that's very intimate knowledge," Gornt gasped, his heart thumping in his chest, his collar feeling tight. He knew about the 20 percent overdraft—Plumm had told him—all the directors of the bank would know. But not the details of their cash, or their cash flow.

"Why're you telling me this, Mr. Bartlett?"

"How liquid are you?"

"I've already told you, I'm twenty times stronger than Struan's," he said automatically, the lie coming easily, his mind churning the marvelous opportunities all this information unlocked. "Why?"

"If I go through with the Struan deal he'll be using my cash down payment to get off the Toda and Orlin hooks—if his bank doesn't extend his credit."

"Yes."

"Will the Vic support him?"

"They always have. Why?"

"If they don't, then he's in big trouble."

"Struan's are substantial stockholders. The bank is obliged to support them."

"But he's overdrawn there and Havergill hates him. Between Chen's stock, Struan's and their nominees, they've 21 percent. . . ."

Gornt almost dropped the phone. "Where the hell did you get that information? No outsider could possibly know that!"

"That's right," he heard the American say calmly, "but that's a fact. Could you muster the other 79 percent?"

"What?"

"If I had a partner who could put the bank against him just this once and he couldn't get credit elsewhere . . . bluntly: it's a matter of timing. Dunross's mortally overextended and that means he's vulnerable. If his bank won't give him credit, he's got to sell something—or get a new line of credit. In either case he's wide open for an attack and ripe for a takeover at a fire-sale price."

Gornt mopped his brow, his brain reeling. "Where the hell did you get all this information?"

"Later, not now."

"When?"

"When we're down to the short strokes."

"How . . . how sure are you your figures are correct?"

"Very. We've his balance sheets for the last seven years."

In spite of his resolve Gornt gasped. "That's impossible!"

"Want to bet?"

Gornt was really shaken now and he tried to get his mind working. Be cautious, he admonished himself. For chrissake control yourself. "If . . . if you've all that, if you know that and get one last thing . . . their interlocking corporate structure, if you knew that we could do anything we want with Struan's."

"We've got that too. You want in?"

Gornt heard himself say calmly, not feeling calm at all, "Of course. When could we meet? Lunch?"

"How about now? But not here, and not at your office. This has to be kept very quiet."

Gornt's heart hurt in his chest. There was a rotten taste in his mouth and he wondered very much how far he could trust Bartlett. "I'll . . . I'll send a car for you. We could chat in the car."

"Good idea, but why don't I meet you Hong Kong side. The Golden Ferry Terminal in an hour."

"Excellent. My car's a Jag—license's 8888. I'll be by the taxi rank."

He hung up and stared at the phone a moment, then went back to his table.

"Not bad news I hope, Mr. Gornt?"

"Er, no, no not at all. Thank you."

"Some more of your special coffee? It's freshly made."

"No, no thank you. I'd like a half bottle of the Taittinger Blanc de Blancs. The '55." He sat back feeling very strange. His enemy was almost in his grasp—if the American's facts were true and if the American was to be trusted and not in some devious plot with Dunross.

The wine came but he hardly tasted it. His whole being was concentrated, sifting, preparing.

Gornt saw the tall American come through the crowds and, for a moment, he envied him his lean, trim figure and the easy, careless dress—jeans, openneck shirt, sports coat—and his obvious confidence. He saw the elaborate camera, smiled sardonically, then looked for Casey. When it was obvious Bartlett was alone he was disappointed. But this disappointment did not touch the glorious anticipation that had possessed him ever since he had put the phone down.

Gornt leaned over and opened the side door. "Welcome Hong Kong side, Mr. Bartlett," he said with forced joviality, starting the engine. He drove off along Gloucester Road toward Glessing's Point and the Yacht Club. "Your inside information's astonishing."

"Without spies you can't operate, can you?"

"You can, but then that's amateur. How's Miss Casey? I thought she'd be with you."

"She's not in this. Not yet."

"Oh?"

"No. No, she's not in on the initial attack. She's more valuable if she knows nothing."

"She knows nothing of this? Not even your call to me?"

"No. Nothing at all."

After a pause he said, "I thought she was your executive VP . . . your right arm you called her."

"She is, but I'm boss of Par-Con, Mr. Gornt."

Gornt saw the level eyes and, for the first time, felt that that was true and that his original estimation was wrong. "I've never doubted it," he said, waiting, his senses honed, waiting him out.

Then Bartlett said, "Is there somewhere we can park—I've got something I want to show you."

"Certainly." Gornt was driving along the sea front on Gloucester Road in the usual heavy traffic. In a moment he found a parking place near

Causeway Bay typhoon shelter with its massed, floating islands of boats of all sizes.

"Here." Bartlett handed him a typed folder. It was a detailed copy of Struan's balance sheet for the year before the company went public. Gornt's eyes raced over the figures. "Christ," he muttered. "So *Lasting Cloud*'s cost them 12 million?"

"It almost broke them. Seems they had all sorts of wild-assed cargo aboard. Jet engines for China, uninsured."

"Of course they'd be uninsured—how the hell can you insure contraband?" Gornt was trying to take in all the complicated figures. His mind was dazed. "If I'd known half of this I'd've got them the last time. Can I keep it?"

"When we've made a deal I'll give you a copy." Bartlett took the folder back and gave him a paper. "Try this one on for size." It showed, graphically, Struan's stockholdings in Kowloon Investments and detailed how, through nominee companies, the tai-pan of Struan's exercised complete control over the huge insurance-property-wharfing company that was supposedly a completely separate company and quoted as such on the stock exchange.

"Marvelous," Gornt said with a sigh, awed by the beauty of it. "Struan's have only a tiny proportion of the stock publicly held but retain 100 percent control, and perpetual secrecy."

"In the States whoever figured this out'd be in jail."

"Thank God Hong Kong laws aren't the same, and that this's all perfectly legal, if a trifle devious." The two men laughed.

Bartlett pocketed the paper. "I've got similar details of the rest of their holdings."

"Bluntly, what have you in mind, Mr. Bartlett?"

"A joint attack on Struan's, starting today. A blitzkrieg. We go 50–50 on all spoils. You get the Great House on the Peak, the prestige, his yacht —and 100 percent of the box at the Turf Club including his stewardship."

Gornt glanced at him keenly. Bartlett smiled. "We know that's kind of special to you. But everything else right down the middle."

"Except their Kai Tak operations. I need that for my airline."

"All right. But then I want Kowloon Investments."

"No," Gornt said, immediately on guard. "We should split that 50–50, and everything 50–50."

"No. You need Kai Tak, I need Kowloon Investments. It'll be a great nucleus for Par-Con's jump into Asia."

"Why?"

"Because all great fortunes in Hong Kong are based on property. K. I. will give me a perfect base."

"For further raids?"

"Sure," Bartlett said easily. "Your friend Jason Plumm's next on the list. We could swallow his Asian Properties easy. 50–50. Right?"

Gornt said nothing for a long time. "And after him?"

"Hong Kong and Lan Tao Farms."

Again Gornt's heart leapt. He had always hated Dunstan Barre and that hatred was tripled last year when Barre had been given a knighthood in the Queen's Birthday Honors List—an honor maneuvered, Gornt was sure, with judicious contributions to the Conservative Party fund. "And how would you swallow him?"

"There's always a time when any army, any country, any company's vulnerable. Every general or company president has to take chances, sometime, to stay ahead. You've got to, to stay ahead. There's always some enemy snapping at your heels, wanting yours, wanting your place in the sun, wanting your territory. You've got to be careful when you're vulnerable."

"Are you vulnerable now?"

"No. I was two years ago but not now. Now I've the muscle I need—we need. If you're in."

A flock of seabirds were dipping and weaving and cawing overhead. "What do you want me to do?"

"You're the pathfinder, the spearhead. I defend the rear. Once you've punched a hole through his defense, I'll deliver the knockout. We sell Struan's short—I guess you've already taken a position on the Ho-Pak?"

"I've sold short, yes. Modestly." Gornt told the lie easily.

"Good. In the States you could get their own accountants to leak the cash flow facts to the right big mouth. That'd soon be all over town. Could the same ploy work here?"

"Probably. But you'd never get their accountants to do that."

"Not for the right fee?"

"No. But rumors could be started." Gornt smiled grimly. "It's very bad of Dunross to hide his inept position from his shareholders. Yes. That's possible. And then?"

"You sell Struan's short, as soon as the market opens. Big."

Gornt lit a cigarette. "I sell short, and what do you do?"

"Nothing openly. That's our ace in the hole."

"Perhaps it really is, and I'm being set up," Gornt said.

"What if I cover all losses? Would that be proof enough I'm with you?"

"What?"

"I pay all losses and take half the profit for today, tomorrow and Friday. If we haven't got him on the run by Friday afternoon you buy back in, just before closing, and we've failed. If it looks like we've got him, we sell heavily, to the limit, just before closing. That'll sweat him out over the weekend. Monday I jerk the rug and our blitzkrieg's on. It's infallible."

"Yes. If you're to be trusted."

"I'll put $2 million in any Swiss bank you name by ten o'clock today. That's 10 million HK which sure as hell's enough to cover any shorting losses you might have. $2 million with no strings, no paper, no promissory note, just your word it's to cover any losses, that if we win we split profits and the rest of the deal as it's been laid out—50–50 except Kowloon Investments for me, Struan's at Kai Tak Airport for you, and for Casey and me, voting membership at the Turf Club. We'll put it to paper Tuesday—after he's crashed."

'You'll put up 2 million U.S., and it's my decision as to when I buy to cover any losses?" Gornt was incredulous.

"Yes. 2 million's the extent of my gamble. So how can you get hurt? You can't. And because he knows how you feel about him, if you mount the attack he won't be suspicious, won't be prepared for a flanking blitz from me."

"This all depends on whether your figures are correct—the amounts and the dates."

"Check them out. There must be a way you can do that—enough to convince yourself."

"Why the sudden change, Mr. Bartlett? You said you'd wait till Tuesday—perhaps later."

"We've done some checking and I don't like the figures I've come up with. We owe Dunross nothing. We'd be crazy to go with him when he's so weak. As it is, what I'm offering you is a great gamble, great odds: the Noble House against 2 lousy million. If we win that'd be parlayed into hundreds of millions."

"And if we fail?"

Bartlett shrugged. "Maybe I'll go home. Maybe we'll work out a Rothwell-Gornt-Par-Con deal. You win sometimes and you lose a lot more times. But this raid's too good not to try it. Without you it'd never work. I've seen enough of Hong Kong to know it has its own special rules. I've no time to learn them. Why should I—when I've got you."

"Or Dunross?"

Bartlett laughed and Gornt read no guile in him. "You're not stretched, you're not vulnerable, he is—that's his bad luck. What d'you say? Is the raid on?"

"I'd say you're very persuasive. Who gave you the information—and the document?"

"Tuesday I'll tell you. When Struan's have crashed."

"Ah, there's a payoff to Mister X?"

"There's always a payoff. It'll come off the top, but no more than 5 percent—any more comes out of my share."

"Two o'clock Friday, Mr. Bartlett? That's when I decide to buy back in and perhaps lose your 2 million—or we confer and continue the surge?"

"Friday at two."

"If we continue over the weekend you'll cover any further risk with further funds?"

"No. You won't need any more. 2 million's tops. By Friday afternoon either his stock will be way down and we'll have him running scared, or

NOBLE HOUSE

not. This's no long-term, well-organized raid. It's a once, er, a onetime attempt to fool's mate an opponent." Bartlett grinned happily. "I risk 2 lousy million for a game that will go down in history books. In less than a week we knock off the Noble House of Asia!"

Gornt nodded, torn. How far can I trust you, Mr. Bloody Raider, you with the key to Devil Dunross? He glanced out of the window and watched a child skulling a boat among the junks, the sea as safe and familiar to her as dry land. "I'll think about what you said."

"How long?"

"Till eleven."

"Sorry, this's a raid, not a business deal. It's now—or not at all!"

"Why?"

"There's a lot to do, Mr. Gornt. I want this settled now or not at all."

Gornt glanced at his watch. There was plenty of time. A call to the right Chinese newspaper and whatever he told them would be on the stands in an hour. He smiled grimly to himself. His own ace in the hole was Havergill. Everything dovetailed perfectly.

A seabird cawed and flew inland, riding some thermals toward the Peak. He watched it. Then his eyes noticed the Great House on the crest, white against the green of the slopes.

"It's a deal," he said and stuck out his hand.

Bartlett shook. "Great. This is strictly between us?"

"Yes."

"Where d'you want the 2 million?"

"The Bank of Switzerland and Zurich, in Zurich, account number 181819." Gornt reached into his pocket, noticing his fingers were trembling. "I'll write it down for you."

"No need. The account's in your name?"

"Good God, no! Canberra Limited."

"Canberra Limited's 2 million richer! And in three days with any luck, you'll be tai-pan of the Noble House. How about that!" Bartlett opened the door and got out. "See you."

"Wait," Gornt said, startled, "I'll drop you wh—"

"No thanks. I've got to get to a phone. Then at 9:15 I've an interview with your friend Orlanda, Miss Ramos—thought there was no harm in it. After that maybe I'll take a few pictures." He waved cheerily and walked off.

Gornt wiped the sweat off his hands. Before leaving the club he had phoned Orlanda to phone Bartlett and make the date. That's very good, he thought, still in shock. She'll keep an eye on him once they're lovers, and they will be, Casey or not. Orlanda has too much to gain.

He watched Bartlett, envying him. In a few moments the American had vanished into the crowds of Wanchai.

Suddenly he was very tired. It's all too pat, too fine, too easy, he told himself. And yet . . . and yet! Shakily he lit a cigarette. Where did Bartlett get those papers?

Inexorably his eyes went back to the Great House on the Peak. He was possessed by it and by a hatred so vast that it swept his mind back to his ancestors, to Sir Morgan Brock whom the Struans broke, to Gorth Brock whom Dirk Struan murdered, to Tyler Brock whom his daughter betrayed. Without wishing it, he renewed the oath of vengeance that he had sworn to his father, that his father had sworn to his—back to Sir Morgan Brock who, penniless, destroyed by his sister, Hag Struan, paralyzed, a shell of a man, had begged for vengeance on behalf of all the Brock ghosts on the Noble House and all the descendents of the most evil man who had ever lived.

Oh gods give me strength, Quillan Gornt prayed. Let the American be telling the truth. I will have vengeance.

28

10:50 A.M.:

The sun bore down on Aberdeen through a slight overcast. The air was sultry, ninety-two degrees Fahrenheit with ninety percent humidity. It was low tide. The smell of rotting kelp and offal and exposed mudflats added to the oppressive weight of the day.

There were five hundred or more sullen impatient people jamming against one another, trying to surge through the bottleneck of barriers ahead that the police had erected outside this branch of Ho-Pak. The barriers allowed only one person through at a time. Men and women of all ages, some with infants, were constantly jostling each other, no one waiting a turn, everyone trying to inch forward to get to the head of the line.

"Look at the bloody fools," Chief Inspector Donald C.C. Smyth said. "If they'd stretch out and not crowd they'd all get through quicker, and we could leave one copper here to keep order and the rest of us could go to lunch instead of getting the riot squad ready. Do it!"

"Yes sir," Divisional Sergeant Mok said politely. *Ayeeyah*, he was thinking as he walked over to the squad car, the poor fool still doesn't understand that we Chinese are not stupid foreign devils—or devils from the Eastern Sea—who'll line up patiently for hours. Oh no, we civilized persons understand life and it's every man for himself. He clicked on the police transmitter. "Divisional Sergeant Mok! The chief inspector wants a riot squad here on the double. Park just behind the fish market but keep in contact!"

"Yes sir."

Mok sighed and lit a cigarette. More barriers had been erected across the street, outside Blacs and the Victoria Aberdeen branches, and more at the Ching Prosperity Bank around the corner. His khaki uniform was ironed sharp on the creases and there were big sweat rings under his arms. He was very concerned. This crowd was very dangerous and he did not want a repetition of yesterday. If the bank shut its doors before three he was sure the crowd would tear the place apart. He knew that if he still had any money in there, he would be the first to tear the door open to get *his* money. *Ayeeyah,* he thought, very thankful for the Snake's authority that had unlocked all their money this morning to the last penny.

"Piss on all banks!" Mok muttered to no one. "All gods, let the Ho-Pak pay all customers today! Let it fail tomorrow! Tomorrow's my day off so let it fail tomorrow." He stubbed out his cigarette.

"Sergeant Major?"

"Yes?"

"Look over there!" the eager young plainclothes detective said, hurrying up to him. He wore spectacles and was in his early twenties. "By the Victoria Bank. The old woman. The old *amah*."

"Where? Oh yes, I see her." Mok watched her for a while but detected nothing untoward. Then he saw her scuttle through the crowd and whisper to a young tough, wearing jeans, who was leaning against a railing. She pointed to an old man who had just come out of the bank. At once the young tough sauntered after him and the old *amah* squeezed and squirmed and cursed her way back to the head of the barrier where she could see those who entered and those who came out.

"That's the third time, sir," the young detective said. "The old *amah* points out someone who's just come out of the bank to the tough, then off he goes. In a few minutes he comes back again. That's the third time. I'm sure I saw him slip her something once. I think it was money."

"Good! Very good, Spectacles Wu. It's bound to be a triad shakedown. The old hag's probably his mother. You follow the young bastard and I'll intercept him the other way. Keep out of sight!"

Divisional Sergeant Mok slipped around the corner, down a busy alley lined with stalls and street hawkers and open shops, moving carefully through the crowds. He turned into another alley just in time to catch a glimpse of some money being passed over by the old man. He waited until Wu had blocked the other end of the alley, then he walked ponderously forward.

"What's going on here?"

"What? Eh? Nothing, nothing at all," the old man said nervously, sweat running down his face. "What's the matter? I've done nothing!"

"Why did you give this young man money, *heya*? I saw you give him money!" The young thug stared back at Mok insolently, unafraid, knowing he was Smallpox Kin, one of the Werewolves who had all Hong Kong petrified. "Is he accosting you? Trying to squeeze you? He looks like a triad!"

"Oh! I . . . I . . . I owed him 500 dollars. I've just got it out of the bank and I paid him." The old man was clearly terrified but he blustered on, "He's my cousin." A crowd began to collect. Someone hawked and spat.

"Why're you sweating so much?"

"All gods fornicate all pigs! It's hot! Everyone's sweating. Everyone!"

"That's fornicating right," someone called out.

Mok turned his attention on the youth who waited truculently. "What's your name?"

"Sixth Son Wong!"

"Liar! Turn out your pockets!"

"Me, I've done nothing! I know the law. You can't search people without a warran—"

Mok's iron fist snapped out and twisted the youth's arm and he squealed. The crowd laughed. They fell silent as Spectacles Wu came out of nowhere to search him. Mok held Smallpox Kin in a vise. Another uneasy undercurrent swept through the onlookers as they saw the rolls of money, and change. "Where'd you get all this?" Mok snarled.

"It's mine. I'm . . . I'm a moneylender and I'm collecting forn—"

"Where's your place of business?"

"It's . . . it's in Third Alley, off Aberdeen Road."

"Come on, we'll go and look."

Mok released the young man who, unafraid, still stared back angrily. "First give me my money!" He turned to the crowd and appealed to them. "You saw him take it! I'm an honest moneylender! These're servants of the foreign devils and you all know them! Foreign devil law forbids honest citizens being searched!"

"Give him back his fornicating money!" someone shouted.

"If he's a moneylender . . ."

The crowd began to argue back and forth and then Smallpox Kin saw a small opening in the crowd and he darted for it. The crowd let him pass and he fled up the alley, vanishing into the traffic, but when Spectacles Wu charged in pursuit they closed up and jostled him and became a little uglier. Mok called him back. In the momentary melee the old man had disappeared. Wearily Mok said, "Let the motherless turd go! He was just a triad—another triad turd who preys on law-abiding people."

"What're you going to do with his fornicating money?" someone called out from the back of the crowd.

"I'm going to give it to an old woman's rest home," Mok shouted back equally rudely. "Go defecate in your grandmother's ear!"

Someone laughed and the crowd began to break up and then they all went about their business. In a moment Mok and Spectacles Wu were standing like stones in a river, the passersby eddying around them. Once back on the main street, Mok wiped his brow. *"Dew neh loh moh!"*

"Yes. Why're they like that, Sergeant Major?" the young detective asked. "We're only trying to help them. Why didn't the old man just admit that triad bastard was squeezing him?"

"You don't learn about mobs of people in schoolbooks," Mok said kindly, knowing the anxiety of the youth to succeed. Spectacles Wu was new, one of the recent university graduates to join the force. He was not one of Mok's private unit. "Be patient. Neither of them wanted anything to do with us because we're police and they all still believe we'll never help them, only ourselves. It's been the same in China since the first policeman."

"But this is Hong Kong," the youth said proudly. "We're different. We're British police."

"Yes." Mok felt a sudden chill. He did not wish to disillusion the youth. I used to be loyal too, loyal to the Queen and to the *quai loh* flag. I learned differently. When I needed help and protection and security I got none. Never once. The British used to be rich and powerful but they lost the war to those Eastern Sea Devils. The war took all their face away and humbled them and put the great tai-pans into Stanley Prison like common thieves—even the tai-pans of the Noble House and Great Bank and even the great high governor himself—put them away like common criminals, into Stanley with all their women and all the children and treated them like turds!

And then after the war, even though they had humbled the Eastern Devils, they never regained their power, or their face.

Now in Hong Kong and in all Asia, now it's not the same and never will be as before. Now every year the British get poorer and poorer and less powerful and how can they protect me and my family from evildoers if they're not rich and powerful? They pay me nothing and treat me like dogmeat! Now my only protection is money, money in gold so that we can flee if need be—or money in land or houses if we do not need to flee. How can I educate my sons in England or America without money? Will the grateful Government pay? Not a fornicating brass cash, and yet I'm supposed to risk my life to keep the streets clean of fornicating triads and pickpockets and rioting lumps of leper turd!

Mok shivered. The only safety for my family is in my own hands as always. Oh how wise the teachings of our ancestors are! Was the police commissioner loyal to me when I needed money, even steerage money, for my son to go to school in America? No. But the Snake was. He loaned me 10,000 dollars at only 10 percent interest so my son went like a Mandarin by Pan American aircraft, with three years of school money, and now he's a qualified architect with a Green Card and next month he'll have an American passport and then he can come back and no one will be able to touch him. He can help protect my generation and will protect his own and his son's and his son's sons!

Yes, the Snake gave me the money, long since paid back with full interest out of money he helped me earn. I shall be loyal to the Snake—until he turns. One day he'll turn, all *quai loh* do, all snakes do, but now I'm a High Dragon and neither gods nor devils nor the Snake himself can hurt my family or my bank accounts in Switzerland and Canada.

"Come along, we'd better go back, young Spectacles Wu," he said kindly and when he got back to the barriers he told Chief Inspector Smyth what had happened.

"Put the money in our kitty, 'Major," Smyth said. "Order a grand banquet for our lads tonight."

"Yes sir."

"It was Detective Constable Wu? The one who wants to join SI?"

"Yes sir. Spectacles is very keen."

Smyth sent for Wu, commended him. "Now, where's that old *amah*?"

Wu pointed her out. They saw her looking at the corner the thug had gone around, waiting impatiently. After a minute she squirmed out of the swarm and hobbled away, muttering obscenities.

"Wu," Smyth ordered, "follow her. Don't let yourself be seen. She'll lead you to the rotten little bugger who fled. Be careful, and when she goes to ground, phone the 'major."

"Yes sir."

"Do *not* take any risks—perhaps we can catch the whole gang, there's bound to be a gang."

"Yes sir."

"Off you go." They watched him following her. "That lad's going to be good. But not for us, 'Major, eh?"

"No sir."

"I think I'll recommend him to SI. Perhaps—"

Suddenly there was an ominous silence, then shouts and an angry roar. The two policemen rushed back around the corner. In their absence the crowd had shoved aside parts of the barricade, overpowering the four policemen, and now were surging into the bank. Manager Sung and his assistant were vainly trying to close the doors against the shouting, cursing throng. The barricades began to buckle.

"Get the riot squad!"

Mok raced for the squad car. Fearlessly Smyth rushed to the head of the line with his bullhorn. The tumult drowned his order to stop fighting. More reinforcements came running from across the street. Quickly and efficiently they charged to Smyth's support, but the mob was gathering strength. Sung and his tellers slammed the door shut but it was forced open again. Then a brick came out of the crowd and smashed one of the plate-glass windows. There was a roar of approval. The people in front were trying to get out of the way and those at the back were trying to get to the door. More bricks were hurtled at the building, then pieces of wood grabbed from a building site nearby. Another stone went through the glass and it totally shattered. Roaring, the mob surged forward. A girl fell and was crushed.

"Come on," Smyth shouted, "give me a hand!" He grabbed one of the barriers and, with four other policemen, used it as a shield and shoved it against the front of the mob, forcing them back. Above the uproar he shouted for them to use their shoulders and they fought the frenzied crowd. Other policemen followed his lead. More bricks went into the bank and then the shout went up, "Kill the fornicating bank thieves, kill them, they've stolen our money . . ."

"Kill the fornicators . . ."

"I want my money . . ."

"Kill the foreign devils . . ."

Smyth saw the mood of those near him change and his heart stopped as they took up the shout and forgot the bank and their hands reached out for him. He had seen that look before and knew he was a dead man. That other time was during the riots of '56 when 200,000 Chinese suddenly went on a senseless rampage in Kowloon. He would have been killed then if he had not had a Sten gun. He had killed four men and blasted a path to safety. Now he had no gun and he was fighting for his life. His hat was ripped away, someone grabbed his Sam Browne belt and a fist went into his groin, another into his face and talons clawed at his eyes. Fearlessly, Mok and others charged into the milling mess to rescue him. Someone hacked at Mok with a brick, another with a piece of wood that tore a great gash in his cheek. Smyth was engulfed, his hands and arms desperately trying to protect his head. Then the riot squad's Black Maria, siren screaming, skidded around the corner. The ten-man team fell on the crowd roughly and pulled Smyth away. Blood seeped from his mouth, his left arm dangled uselessly.

"You all right, sir?"

"Yes, for chrissake get those sodding barriers up! Get those bastards away from the bank—fire hoses!"

But the fire hoses weren't necessary. At the first violent charge of the riot squad the front of the mob had wilted and now the rest had retreated to a safe distance and stood there watching sullenly, some of them still shouting obscenities. Smyth grabbed the bullhorn. In Cantonese he said, "If anyone comes within twenty yards, he'll be arrested and deported!" He tried to catch his breath. "If anyone wants to visit the Ho-Pak, line up a hundred yards away."

The scowling crowd hesitated, then as Mok and the riot squad came forward fast, they retreated hastily and began to move away, treading on each other.

"I think my bloody shoulder's dislocated," Smyth said and cursed obscenely.

"What do we do about those bastards, sir?" Mok asked, in great pain, breathing hard, his cheek raw and bleeding, his uniform ripped.

Smyth held his arm to take the growing pain away and looked across the street at the sullen, gawking crowd. "Keep the riot squad here. Get another from West Aberdeen, inform Central. Where's my bloody hat? If I catch the bas—"

"Sir!" one of his men called out. He was kneeling beside the girl who had been trampled on. She was a bar girl or a dance hall girl: she had that sad, sweet oh so hard, young-old look. Blood was dribbling from her mouth, her breathing coming in hacking gasps.

"Christ, get an ambulance!"

As Smyth watched helplessly, the girl choked in her own blood and died.

Christian Toxe, editor of the *Guardian,* was scribbling notes, the phone jammed against his ear. "What was her name, Dan?" he asked over the hubbub of the newsroom.

"I'm not sure. One savings book said Su Tzee-Ian," Dan Yap the reporter on the other end of the phone at Aberdeen told him. "There was $4,360 in it—the other was in the name . . . Hang on a second, the ambulance's just leaving now. Can you hear all right, Chris, the traffic's heavy here."

"Yes. Go on. The second savings book?"

"The second book was in the name of Tak H'eung fah. Exactly 3,000 in that one."

Tak H'eung fah seemed to touch a memory. "Do any of the names mean anything?" Toxe asked. He was a tall rumpled man in his untidy cubbyhole of an office.

"No. Except one means Wisteria Su and the other Fragrant Flower Tak. She was pretty, Chris. Might have been Eurasian. . . ."

Toxe felt a sudden ice shaft in his stomach as he remembered his own three daughters, six and seven and eight, and his lovely Chinese wife. He tried to push that perpetual cross back into the recess of his mind, the secret worry of was it right to mix East and West, and what does the future hold for them, my darlings, in this lousy rotten bigoted world?

With an effort he concentrated again. "That's quite a lot of money for a dance hall girl, isn't it?"

"Yes. I'd say she had a patron. One interesting bit: in her purse was a crumpled envelope dated a couple of weeks ago with a mushy love letter in it. It was addressed to . . . hang on . . . to Tak H'eung fah, apartment 14, Fifth Alley, Tsung-pan Street in Aberdeen. It was soppy, swearing eternal love. Educated writing though."

"English?" Toxe asked surprised, writing swiftly.

"No. Characters. There was something about the writing—could be a *quai loh.*"

"Did you get a copy?"

"The police wouldn't le—"

"Get a photocopy. Beg borrow or steal a photocopy in time for the afternoon edition. A week's bonus if you do it."

"Cash this afternoon?"

"All right."

"You have it."

"Any signature?"

"'Your only love.' The *love* was in English."

"Mr. Toxe! Mrs. Publisher's on line two!" The English secretary called out through the open door, her desk just outside the glass partition.

"Oh Christ, I'll . . . I'll call her back. Tell her I've got a big story breaking." Then into the phone again, "Dan, keep on this story—keep close to the police, go with them to the dead girl's flat—if it's her flat. Find out who owns it—who her people are, where they live. Call me back!" Toxe hung up and called out to his assistant editor, "Hey, Mac!"

The lean, dour, gray-haired man got up from his desk and wandered in. "Aye?"

"I think we should put out an extra. Headline . . ." He scrawled on a piece of paper, "Mob Kills Fragrant Flower!"

"How about 'Mob Murders Fragrant Flower'?"

"Or, 'First Death at Aberdeen'?"

"'Mob Murders' is better."

"That's it then. Martin!" Toxe called out. Martin Haply looked up from his desk and came over. Toxe ran his fingers through his hair as he told them both what Dan Yap had related. "Martin, do a follow-up: 'The beautiful young girl was crushed by the feet of the mob—but who were the real killers? Is it an incompetent government who refuses to regulate our outdated banking system? Are the killers those who started the rumors? Is the run on the Ho-Pak as simple as it sounds . . .' etcetera."

"Got it." Haply grinned and went back to his desk in the main office. He gulped a cold cup of coffee out of a plastic cup and started to type, his desk piled high with reference books, Chinese newspapers and stock market reports. Teletypes chattered in the background. A few silent copy boys and trainees delivered or picked up copy.

"Hey, Martin! What's the latest from the stock market?"

Martin Haply dialed a number without looking at the phone, then called back to the editor. "Ho-Pak's down to 24.60, four points from yesterday. Struan's are down a point though there's been some heavy buying. Hong Kong Lan Tao up three points—the story's just been confirmed. Dunstan Barre took their money out yesterday."

"They did? Then you were right again! Shit!"

"Victoria's off half a point—all banks are edgy and no buyers. There's a rumor a line's forming outside Blacs and the Victoria's head office in Central." Both men gasped.

"Send someone to check the Vic!" Mac hurried out. Jesus Christ, Toxe thought, his stomach churning, Jesus Christ if a run starts on the Vic the whole sodding island'll collapse and my sodding savings with it.

He leaned back in his old chair and put his feet on the desk, loving his job, loving the pressure and immediacy.

"Do you want me to call her?" his secretary asked. She was round and unflappable.

"Who? Oh shit, Peg, I'd forgotten. Yes—call the Dragon."

The Dragon was the wife of the publisher, Mong Pa-tok, the present head of the sprawling Mong family who owned this paper and three Chinese newspapers and five magazines, whose antecedents went back to the earliest days. The Mongs were supposed to have descended from the first editor-owner-publisher of the paper, Morley Skinner. The story was that Dirk Struan had given Skinner control of the paper in return for helping him against Tyler Brock and his son Gorth by hushing up the killing of Gorth in Macao. It was said Dirk Struan had provoked the duel. Both men had used fighting irons. Once, some years ago, Toxe had heard old Sarah Chen in her cups relate that when the Brocks came to collect Gorth's body they did not recognize him. The old woman had added that her father, Sir Gordon Chen, had had to mobilize most of Chinatown to prevent the Brocks from setting afire the Struan warehouses. Tyler Brock had set Tai-ping Shan alight instead. Only the great typhoon that came that night stopped the whole city from going up in flames—the same holocaust that had destroyed Dirk Struan's Great House and him and his secret Chinese wife, May-may.

"She's on line two."

"Eh? Oh! All right, Peg." Toxe sighed.

"Ah Mr. Toxe, I was waiting your call, *heya?*"

"What can I do for you, or Mr. Mong?"

"Your pieces on the Ho-Pak Bank, yesterday and today, that the adverse rumors about the Ho-Pak are untrue and started by tai-pans and another big bank. I see more today."

"Yes. Haply's quite sure."

"My husband and I hear this not true. No tai-pans or banks are putting out rumors or have put out rumors. Perhaps wise to drop this attack."

"It's not an attack, Mrs. Mong, just an attitude. You know how susceptible Chinese are to rumors. The Ho-Pak's as strong as any bank in the Colony. We feel sure the rumors were started by a bi—"

"Not by tai-pans and not big bank. My husband and I not like this attitude never mind. Please to change," she said and he heard the granite in her voice.

"That's editorial policy and I have control over editorial policy," he said grimly.

"*We* are publisher. It is *our* newspaper. *We* tell you to stop so you will stop."

"You're ordering me to stop?"

"Of course it is order."

"Very well. As you order it, it's stopped."

"Good!" The phone went dead. Christian Toxe snapped his pencil and threw it against the wall and began to curse. His secretary sighed and discreetly closed the door and when he was done Toxe opened the door. "Peg, how about some coffee? Mac! Martin!"

Toxe sat back at his desk. The chair creaked. He mopped the sweat off his cheeks and lit a cigarette and inhaled deeply.

"Yes, Chris?" Haply asked.

"Martin, cancel the piece I asked for and do another on Hong Kong banking and the need to have some form of banking insurance. . . ."

Both men gaped at him.

"Our publisher doesn't like the rumors approach."

Martin Haply flushed. "Well screw him! You heard the guys yourself at the tai-pan's party!"

"That proves nothing. You've no proof. We're stopping that approach. It's not proven so I can't take a stand."

"But, lo—"

Toxe's neck went purple. *"It's bloody well stopped,"* he roared. *"Understand?"*

Haply began to say something but changed his mind. Choked with rage he turned on his heel and left. He walked across the big room and jerked the front door open and slammed it behind him.

Christian Toxe exhaled. "He's got a lousy bloody temper that lad!"

He stubbed his cigarette out and lit another. "Christ, I'm smoking too much!" Still seething, his brown eyes watched the older man. "Someone must have called her, Mac. Now what would you like as a return favor if you were Mrs. Dragon Mong?"

Suddenly Mac beamed. "Na a voting membership of the Turf Club!"

"Go to the head of the class!"

Singh, the Indian reporter, came in with a foot of teletype. "You might need this for the extra, Chris."

It was a series of Reuters reports from the Middle East. "Teheran 0832 hours: High-level diplomatic sources in Iran report sudden extensive Soviet military maneuvers have begun close to their north border near the oil-rich border area of Azerbaijan where more rioting took place. Washington is reported to have asked permission to send observers to the area."

The next paragraph was: "Tel Aviv 0600 hours: The Knesset confirmed late last night that another huge irrigation project had been funded to further divert the waters of the River Jordan into the southern Negev Desert. There was immediate adverse and hostile reaction from Jordan, Egypt and Syria."

"Negev? Isn't Israel's brand spanking new atomic plant in the Negev?" Toxe asked.

"Aye. Now there's another splendid addition to the peace conference tables. Would the water be for that?"

"I don't know Mac, but this's certainly going to parch a few Jordanian and Palestinian throats. Water water everywhere but not a drop to shower in. I wish to Christ it would rain. Singh, tidy up these reports and we'll put them on the back page. They won't sell a single bloody paper. Do a follow-up piece on the Werewolves for the front page: 'The police have a vast dragnet out but the vicious kidnappers of Mr. John Chen continue to elude them. According to sources close to the family of his father, compradore of Struan's, no ransom note has yet been received but one is expected imminently. The *China Guardian* asks all its readers to assist in the capture of these fiends . . .' That sort of thing."

At Aberdeen Spectacles Wu saw the old woman come out of the tenement building, a shopping basket in her hand, and join the noisy crowds in the narrow alley. He followed cautiously feeling very pleased with himself. While he had waited for her to reappear he had struck up a conversation with a street hawker whose permanent place of business was a patch of broken pavement opposite. The hawker sold tea and small bowls of hot congee—rice gruel. Wu had ordered a bowl, and during his meal, the hawker had told him about the old woman, Ah Tam, who had been in the neighborhood since last year. She'd come to the Colony from a village near Canton with the huge waves of immigrants who had flooded over the border last summer. She didn't have any family of her own and the people she worked for had no sons around twenty, though he had seen her with a young man early this morning. "She says her village was Ning-tok. . . ."

It was then that Wu had felt a glow at this stroke of luck. Ning-tok was the same village his own parents had come from and he spoke that dialect.

Now he was twenty paces behind her and he watched her haggle brilliantly for vegetables, selecting only the very best onions and greens, all just a few hours fresh from the fields in the New Territories. She bought very little so he knew that the family she worked for was poor. Then she was standing in front of the poultry stall with its layers of barely alive, scrawny chickens crammed helplessly into cages, their legs tied. The rotund stall owner bartered with her, both sides enjoying the foul language, insults, choosing this bird, then that, then another, prodding them, discarding them, until the bargain was made. Because she was a good, salty trader, the man allowed his profit to be shaved. Then he strangled the bird deftly without thought, tossing the carcass to his five-year-old daughter, who squatted in a pile of feathers and offal, for plucking and cleaning.

"Hey, Mr. Poultryman," Wu called out, "I'd like a bird at the same price. That one!" He pointed at a good choice and paid no attention to the man's grumbling. "Elder Sister," he said to her politely, "clearly you have saved me a great deal of cash. Would you like to have a cup of tea while we wait for our birds to be cleaned?"

"Ah thank you, yes, these old bones are tired. We'll go there!" Her gnarled finger pointed to a stall opposite. "Then we can watch to make sure we get what we paid for." The poultry man muttered an obscenity and they laughed.

She shoved her way across the street, sat down on a bench, ordered tea and a cake and was soon telling Wu how she hated Hong Kong and living among strangers. It was easy for him to butter her up by using the odd word of Ning-tok patois; then pretending to be equally surprised when she switched to that dialect and told him she came from the same village and oh how wonderful it was to find a neighbor after all these months among foreigners! She told him that she had worked for the same family in Ning-tok ever since she was seven. But, sadly, three years ago her mistress—the child that she had brought up, now an old lady like herself—had died. "I stayed in the house but it had fallen on hard times. Then last year the famine was bad. Many in the village decided to come to this place. Chairman Mao's people didn't mind, in fact they encouraged us— 'Useless Mouths' as they called us. Somehow we got split up and I managed to get over the border and found my way to this place here, penniless, hungry, with no family, no friends, nowhere to turn. At length I got a job and now I work as a cook-*amah* for the family Ch'ung who're street cleaners. The dog bones pay me nothing but my keep and my food and chief wife Ch'ung's a maggot-mouthed hag but soon I'll be rid of all of them! You said your father came here with his family ten years ago?"

"Yes. We owned a field near the bamboo glade beside the river. His name was Wu Cho-tam an—"

"Ah, yes I think I remember the family. Yes, I think so. Yes, and I know the field. My family was Wu Ting-top and their family owned the pharmacy at the crossroads for more than a hundred years."

"Ah, Honorable Pharmacy Wu? Oh yes of course!" Spectacles Wu did remember the family well. Pharmacy Wu had always been a Maoist sympathizer. Once he had had to flee the Nationalists. In this village of a thousand souls he had been well liked and trusted and he had kept life in the village as calm and as protected from outsiders as he could.

"So, you're one of Wu Cho-tam's sons, Younger Brother!" Ah Tam was saying. "Eeeee, in the early days it was so wonderful in Ning-tok but for the last years . . . terrible."

"Yes. We were lucky. Our field was fertile and we tilled the soil like always but after a few years outsiders came and accused all the landowners —as if we were exploiters! We only tilled our own field. Even so, from time to time some landowners were taken away, some shot, so one night ten years ago my father fled with all of us. Now my father is dead but I live with my mother not far away."

"There were many fleeings and famines in the early days. I hear that now it is better. Did you hear too? Outsiders came, wasn't it? They would come and they would leave. The village is not so bad again, Younger Brother, oh no! Outsiders leave us alone. Yes, they left my mistress and us alone because Father was important and one of Chairman Mao's supporters from the beginning. My mistress's name was Fang-ling, she's dead now. There's no collective near us so life is like it's always been, though we all have to study Chairman Mao's Red Book. The village isn't so bad, all my friends are there. . . . Hong Kong is a foul place and my village is home. Life without family is nothing. But now . . ." Then the old woman dropped her voice and chortled, carried away with pleasure. "But now the gods have favored me. In a month or two I'm going home, home forever. I'll have enough money to retire on and I'll buy the small house at the end of my street and perhaps a little field and . . ."

"Retire?" Wu said, leading her on. "Who has that sort of money, Elder Sister? You said you were paid nothing th—"

"Ah," the old woman replied, puffed up. "I've an important friend."

"What sort of friend?"

"A very important business friend who needs my help! Because I've been so useful he's promised to give me a huge amount of money—"

"You're making this all up, Elder Sister," he scoffed. "Am I a foolish stranger wh—"

"I tell you my friend's so important he can hold the whole island in thrall!"

"There are no such persons!"

"Oh yes there are!" She dropped her voice and whispered hoarsely, "What about the Werewolves!"

Spectacles Wu gaped at her. "What?"

She chortled again, delighted with the impact of her confidence. "Yes."

The young man took hold of his blown mind and put the pieces quickly back together; if this were true he would get the reward and the promotion and maybe an invitation to join Special Intelligence. "You're making this up!"

"Would I lie to someone from my own village? My friend's one of them I tell you. He's also a 489 and his Brotherhood's going to be the richest in all Hong Kong."

"Eeeee, how lucky you are, Elder Sister! And when you see him again please ask if perhaps he can use someone like me. I'm a street fighter by trade though my triad's poor and the leader stupid and a stranger. Is he from Ning-tok?"

"No. He's . . . he's my nephew," she said, and the young man knew it was a lie. "I'm seeing him later. Yes, he's coming later. He owes me some money."

"Eeeee, that's good, but don't put it in a bank and certainly not in the Ho-Pak or y—"

"Ho-Pak?" she said suspiciously, her little eyes narrowing suddenly in the creases of her face. "Why do you mention the Ho-Pak? What has the Ho-Pak to do with me?"

"Nothing, Elder Sister," Wu said, cursing himself for the slip, knowing her guard was now up. "I saw the queues this morning, that's all."

She nodded, not convinced, then saw that her chicken was packaged and ready so she thanked him for the tea and cake and scuttled off, muttering to herself. Most carefully he followed her. From time to time she would look back but she did not see him. Reassured, she went home.

The CIA man got out of his car and walked quickly into police headquarters. The uniformed sergeant at the information desk greeted him. "Afternoon, Mr. Rosemont."

"I've an appointment with Mr. Crosse."

"Yes sir. He's expecting you."

Sourly Rosemont went to the elevator. This whole goddamn-piss-poor island makes me want to shit, and the goddamn British along with it.

"Hello, Stanley," Armstrong said. "What're you doing here?"

"Oh hi, Robert. Gotta meeting with your chief."

"I've already had that displeasure once today. At 7:01 precisely." The elevator opened. Rosemont went in and Armstrong followed.

"I hope you've got some good news for Crosse," Armstrong said with a yawn. "He's really in a foul mood."

"Oh? You in this meeting too?"

"Afraid so."

Rosemont flushed. "Shit, I asked for a private meeting."

"I'm private."

"You sure are, Robert. And Brian, and everyone else. But some bastard isn't."

Armstrong's humor vanished. "Oh?"

"No." Rosemont said nothing more. He knew he had hurt the Englishman but he didn't care. It's the truth, he thought bitterly. The sooner these goddamn limeys open their goddamn eyes the better.

The elevator stopped. They walked down the corridor and were ushered into Crosse's room by Brian Kwok. Rosemont felt the bolts slide home behind him and he thought how goddamn foolish and useless and unnecessary; the man's a knucklehead.

"I asked for a private meeting, Rog."

"It's private. Robert's very private, Brian is. What can I do for you, Stanley?" Crosse was politely cool.

"Okay, Rog, today I got a long list for you: first, you're personally 100 percent in the creek with me, my whole department, up to the director in Washington himself. I'm told to tell you—among other things—your mole's surpassed himself this time."

"Oh?"

Rosemont's voice was grating now. "For starters, we just heard from one of our sources in Canton that Fong-fong and all your lads were hit last night. Their cover's gone—they're blown." Armstrong and Brian Kwok looked shocked. Crosse was staring back at him and he read nothing in his face. "Got to be your mole, Rog. Got to be fingered from the tai-pan's AMG papers."

Crosse looked across at Brian Kwok. "Use the emergency wireless code. Check it!"

As Brian Kwok hurried out, Rosemont said again, "They're blown, the poor bastards."

"We'll check it anyway. Next?"

Rosemont smiled mirthlessly. "Next: Almost everything that was in the tai-pan's AMG papers's spread around the intelligence community in London—on the wrong side."

"God curse all traitors," Armstrong muttered.

"Yeah, that's what I thought, Robert. Next, another little gem—AMG was no accident."

"What?"

"No one knows the who, but we all know the why. The bike was hit by an auto. No make, no serial number, no witnesses, no nothing yet, but he was hit—and of course, fingered from here."

"Then why haven't I been informed by Source? Why's the information coming from you?" Crosse asked.

Rosemont's voice sharpened. "I just got off the phone to London. It's just past 5:00 A.M. there so maybe your people plan to let you know when they get to the office after a nice leisurely bacon and eggs and a goddamn cup of tea!"

Armstrong shot a quick glance at Crosse and winced at the look on his face.

"Your . . . your point's well taken, Stanley," Crosse said. "Next?"

"The photos we gave you of the guys who knocked off Voranski . . . what happened?"

"We had their place covered. The two men never reappeared, so I raided the place in the early hours. We went through that whole tenement, room by room, but found no one who looked anything like the photographs. We searched for a couple of hours and there were no secret doors or anything like that. They weren't there. Perhaps your fellow made a mistake. . . ."

"Not this time. Marty Povitz was sure. We had the place staked out soon as we deciphered the address but there was a time when it wasn't all covered, front and back. I think they were tipped, again by your mole." Rosemont took out a copy of a telex and passed it over. Crosse read it, reddened and passed it over to Armstrong.

> Decoded from Director, Washington, to Rosemont, Deputy Director Station Hong Kong: Sinders MI-6 brings orders from Source, London, that you are to go with him Friday to witness the handover of the papers and get an immediate photocopy.

"You'll get your copy in today's mail, Rog," the American said.

"I can keep this?" Crosse asked.

"Sure. By the way, we have a tail on Dunross too. W—"

Crosse said angrily, "Would you kindly not interfere in our jurisdiction!"

"I told you you were in Shitsville, Rog!" Tautly Rosemont placed another cable on the table.

> Rosemont, Hong Kong. You will hand this cable to Chief of SI personally. Until further orders Rosemont is authorized to proceed independently to assist in the uncovering of the hostile in any way he chooses. He is, however, required to stay within the law and keep you advised personally of what he is doing. Source 8–98/3.

Rosemont saw Crosse bite back an explosion. "What else've you authorized?" Crosse asked.

"Nothing. Yet. Next: We'll be at the bank on Fri—"

"You know where Dunross's put the files?"

"It's all over town—among the community. I told you your mole's been working overtime." Abruptly Rosemont flared, "Come on for chrissake, Rog, you know if you tell a hot item to someone in London, it's all over town! We've all got security problems but yours're worse!" With an effort the American simmered down. "You could've leveled with me about the Dunross screw-up—it would've saved us all a lot of heartache and a lotta face."

Crosse lit a cigarette. "Perhaps. Perhaps not. I was trying to maintain security."

"Remember me? I'm on our side!"

"Are you?"

"You bet your ass!" Rosemont said it very angrily. "And if it was up to me I'd have every safety deposit box open before sundown—and the hell with the consequences."

"Thank God you can't do that."

"For chrissake we're at war and God only knows what's in those other files. Maybe they'll finger your goddamn mole and then we can get the bastard and give him his!"

"Yes," Crosse said, his voice a whiplash, "or maybe there's nothing in the papers at all!"

"What do you mean?"

"Dunross agreed to hand the files over to Sinders on Friday. What if there's nothing in them? Or what if he burned the pages and gives us just the covers? What the hell do we do then?"

Rosemont gaped at him. "Jesus—is that a possibility?"

"Of course it's a possibility! Dunross's clever. Perhaps they're not there at all, or the vault ones are false or nonexistent. We don't know he put them there, he just says he put them there. Jesus Christ, there're fifty possibilities. You're so smart, you CIA fellows, you tell me which deposit box and I'll open it myself."

"Get the key from the governor. Give me and some of my boys private access for five hours an—"

"Out of the question!" Crosse snarled, suddenly red-faced, and Armstrong felt the violence strongly. Poor Stanley, you're the target today. He suppressed a shudder, remembering the times he had had to face Crosse. He had soon learned that it was easier to tell the man the truth, to tell everything at once. If Crosse ever really went after him in an interrogation, he knew beyond doubt he would be broken. Thank God he's never yet had reason to try, he thought thankfully, then turned his eyes on Rosemont who was flushed with rage. I wonder who Rosemont's informants are, and how he knows for certain that Fong-fong and his team have been obliterated.

"Out of the question," Crosse said again.

"Then what the hell do we do? Sit on our goddamn lard till Friday?"

"Yes. We wait. We've been ordered to wait. Even if Dunross has torn out pages, or sections, or disposed of whole files, we can't put him in prison—or force him to remember or tell us anything."

"If the director or Source decide he should be leaned on, there're ways. That's what the enemy'd do."

Crosse and Armstrong stared at Rosemont. At length Armstrong said coldly, "But that doesn't make it right."

"That doesn't make it wrong either. Next: For your ears only, Rog."

At once Armstrong got up but Crosse motioned him to stay. "Robert's my ears." Armstrong hid the laughter that permeated him at so ridiculous a statement.

"No. Sorry, Rog, orders—your brass and mine."

Armstrong saw Crosse hesitate perfectly. "Robert, wait outside. When I buzz come back in. Check on Brian."

"Yes sir." Armstrong went out and closed the door, sorry that he would not be present for the kill.

"Well?"

The American lit another cigarette. "Top secret. At 0400 today the whole Ninety-second Airborne dropped into Azerbaijan supported by large units of Delta Force and they've fanned out all along the Iran-Soviet border." Crosse's eyes widened. "This was at the direct request of the Shah, in response to massive Soviet military preparations just over the border and the usual Soviet-sponsored riots all over Iran. Jesus, Rog, can't you get some air conditioning in here?" Rosemont mopped his brow. "There's a security blanket all over Iran now. At 0600 support units landed at Teheran airport. Our Seventh Fleet's heading for the Gulf, the Sixth—that's the Mediterranean—is already at battle stations off Israel, the Second, Atlantic, is heading for the Baltic, NORAD's alerted, NATO's alerted, and all Poseidons are one step from Red."

"Jesus Christ, what the hell's going on?"

"Khrushchev is making another real play for Iran—always an optimum Soviet target right? He figures he has the advantage. It's right on his own border where his own lines of communication're short and ours huge. Yesterday the Shah's security people uncovered a 'democratic socialist' insurrection scheduled to explode in the next few days in Azerbaijan. So the Pentagon's reacting like mashed cats. If Iran goes so does the whole Persian Gulf, then Saudi Arabia and that wraps up Europe's oil and that wraps up Europe."

"The Shah's been in trouble before. Isn't this more of your overreacting?"

The American hardened. "Khrushchev backed down over Cuba—first goddamn time there's been a Soviet backoff—because JFK wasn't bluffing and the only thing Commies understand is force. *Big-massive-honest-to-goddamn force!* The Big K better back off this time too or we'll hand him his head."

"You'll risk blowing up the whole bloody world over some illiterate, rioting, fanatic nutheads who've probably got some right on their side anyway?"

"I'm not into politics, Rog, only into winning. Iran oil, Persian Gulf oil, Saudi oil're the West's jugular. We're not gonna let the enemy get it."

"If they want it they'll take it."

"Not this time, they won't. We're calling the operation Dry Run. The idea's to go in heavy, frighten 'em off and get out fast, quietly, so no one's the wiser except the enemy, and particularly no goddamn liberal fellow-traveler congressman or journalist. The Pentagon figures the Soviets don't believe we could possibly respond so fast, so massively from so far away, so they'll go into shock and run for cover and close everything down—until next time."

The silence thickened.

Crosse's fingers drummed. "What am I supposed to do? Why're you telling me this?"

"Because the brass ordered me to. They want all allied chief SIs to know because if the stuff hits the fan there'll be sympathy riots all over, as usual, well-coordinated rent-a-mob riots, and you'll have to be prepared. AMG's papers said that Sevrin had been activated here—maybe there's a tie-in. Besides, you here in Hong Kong are vital to us. You're the back door to China, the back door to Vladivostok and the whole of east Russia—and our best shortcut to their Pacific naval and atomic-sub bases." Rosemont took out another cigarette, his fingers shaking. "Listen, Rog," he said, controlling his grumbling anger, "let's forget all the interoffice shit, huh? Maybe we can help each other."

"What atomic subs?" Crosse said with a deliberate sneer, baiting him. "They haven't got atomic subs yet an—"

"Jesus Christ!" Rosemont flared. "You guys've got your heads up your asses and you won't listen. You spout détente and try to muzzle us and they're laughing their goddamn heads off. They got nuclear subs and missile sites and naval bases all over the Sea of Okhotsk!" Rosemont got up and went to the huge map of China and Asia that dominated one wall and stabbed the Kamchatka peninsula, north of Japan. ". . . Petropavlovsk, Vladivostok . . . they've giant operations all along this whole Siberian coast, here at Komsomolsk at the mouth of the Amur and on Sakhalin. But Petropavlovsk's the big one. In ten years, that'll be the greatest war-port in Asia with support airfields, atomic-protected subpens and atomic-safe fighter strips and missile silos. And from there they threaten all Asia—Japan, Korea, China, the Philippines—not forgetting Hawaii and our West Coast."

"U.S. forces are preponderant and always will be. You're overreacting again."

Rosemont's face closed. "People call me a hawk. I'm not. Just a realist. They're on a war footing. Our Midas III's have pinpointed all kinds of crap, our . . ." He stopped and almost kicked himself for letting his mouth run on. "Well, we know a lot of what they're doing right now, and they're not making goddamn ploughshares."

"I think you're wrong. They don't want war any more than we do."

"You want proof? You'll get it tomorrow, soon as I've clearance!" the American said, stung. "If it's proved, can we cooperate better?"

"I thought we were cooperating well now."

"Will you?"

"Whatever you want. Does Source want me to react in any specific way?"

"No, just to be prepared. I guess this'll all filter down through channels today."

"Yes." Crosse was suddenly gentle. "What's really bothering you, Stanley?"

Rosemont's hostility left him. "We lost one of our best setups in East Berlin, last night, a lot of good guys. A buddy of mine got hit crossing back to us, and we're sure it's tied into AMG."

"Oh, sorry about that. It wasn't Tom Owen, was it?"

"No. He left Berlin last month. It was Frank O'Connell."

"Don't think I ever met him. Sad."

"Listen, Rog, this mole thing's the shits." He got up and went to the map. He stared at it a long time. "You know about Iman?"

"Sorry?"

Rosemont's stubby finger stabbed a point on the map. The city was inland, 180 miles north of Vladivostok at a rail junction. "It's an industrial center, railways, lots of factories."

"So?" Crosse asked.

"You know about the airfield there?"

"What airfield?"

"It's underground, whole goddamn thing, just out of town, built into a gigantic maze of natural caves. It's got to be one of the wonders of the world. It's atomic capable, Rog. The whole base was constructed by Japanese and Nazi slave labor in '45, '6 and '7. A hundred thousand men they say. It's all underground, Rog, with space for 2500 airplanes, air crews and support personnel. It's bombproof—even atomic proof—with eighty runways that lead out onto a gigantic airstrip that circles eighteen low hills. It took one of our guys nine hours to drive around it. That was back in '46—so what's it like now?"

"Improved—if it exists."

"It's operational now. A few guys, intelligence, ours and yours, even a few of the better newspaper guys, knew about it even in '46. So why the silence now? That base alone's a massive threat to all of us and no one screams a shit. Even China, and she sure as hell's got to know about Iman."

"I can't answer that."

"I can. I think that info's being buried, deliberately, along with a lot of other things." The American got up and stretched. "Jesus, the whole world's falling apart and I got a backache. You know a good chiropractor?"

"Have you tried Doc Thomas on Pedder Street? I use him all the time."

"I can't stand him. He makes you wait in line—won't give you an appointment. Thank God for chiropractors! Trying to get my son to be one instead of an M.D."

The phone rang and Crosse answered it.

"Yes Brian?" Rosemont watched Crosse as he listened. "Just a minute, Brian. Stanley, are we through now?"

"Sure. Just a couple of open, routine things."

"Right. Brian, come in with Robert as soon as you come up." Crosse put the phone down. "We couldn't establish contact with Fong-fong. You're probably correct. They'll be MPD'd or MPC'd in forty-eight hours."

"I don't understand."

"Missing Presumed Dead or Missing Presumed Captured."

"Rough. Sorry to bring bad news."

"Joss."

"With Dry Run and AMG, how about pulling Dunross into protective custody?"

"Out of the question."

"You have the Official Secrets Act."

"Out of the question."

"I'm going to recommend it. By the way, Ed Langan's FBI boys tied Banastasio in with Bartlett. He's a big shareholder in Par-Con. They say he supplied the dough for the last merger that put Par-Con into the big time."

"Anything on the Moscow visas for Bartlett and Tcholok?"

"Best we can find is that they went as tourists. Maybe they did, maybe it was a cover."

"Anything on the guns?" This morning Armstrong had told Crosse of Peter Marlowe's theory and he had ordered an immediate watch on Four Finger Wu and offered a great reward for information.

"The FBI're sure they were put aboard in L.A. It'd be easy—Par-Con's hangar's got no security. They also checked on the serial numbers you gave us. They were all out of a batch that had gotten 'mislaid' en route from the factory to Camp Pendleton—that's the Marine depot in southern California. Could be we've stumbled onto a big arms-smuggling racket. Over seven hundred M14's have gotten mislaid in the last six months. Talking about that . . ." He stopped at the discreet knock. He saw Crosse touch the switch. The door opened and Brian Kwok and Armstrong came back in. Crosse motioned them to sit. "Talking about that, you remember the CARE case?"

"The suspected corruption here in Hong Kong?"

"That's the one. We might have a lead for you."

"Good. Robert, you were handling that at one time, weren't you?"

"Yes sir." Robert Armstrong sighed. Three months ago one of the vice-consuls at the U.S. Consulate had asked the CID to investigate the handling of the charity to see whether some light-fingered administrators were involved in a little take-away for personal profit. The digging and interviewing was still proceeding. "What've you got, Stanley?"

Rosemont searched in his pockets then pulled out a typed note. It contained three names and an address: Thomas K. K. Lim (Foreigner Lim), Mr. Tak Chou-lan (Big Hands Tak), Mr. Lo Tup-lin (Bucktooth Lo), Room 720, Princes Building, Central. "Thomas K. K. Lim is American, well heeled and well connected in Washington, Vietnam and South America. He's in business with the other two jokers at that address. We got a tip that he's mixed up in a couple of shady deals with AID and that Big Hands Tak is heavy in CARE. It's not in our bailiwick so it's over to you." Rosemont shrugged and stretched again. "Maybe it's something. The whole world's on fire but we still gotta deal with crooks! Crazy! I'll keep in touch. Sorry about Fong-fong and your people."

He left.

Crosse told Armstrong and Brian Kwok briefly what he had been told about Operation Dry Run.

Brian Kwok said sourly, "One day one of those Yankee madmen're going to make a mistake. It's stupid putting atomics into hair-trigger situations."

Crosse looked at them and their guards came up. "I want that mole. I want him before the CIA uncover him. If they get him first . . ." The thin-faced man was clearly very angry. "Brian, go and see Dunross. Tell him AMG was no accident and not to go out without our people nearby.

Under any circumstances. Say I would prefer him to give us the papers early, confidentially. Then he has nothing to fear."

"Yes sir." Brian Kwok knew that Dunross would do exactly as he wanted but he kept his mouth shut.

"Our normal riot planning will cover any by-product of the Iran problem and from Dry Run. However, you'd better alert CID an—" He stopped. Robert Armstrong was frowning at the piece of paper Rosemont had given him. "What is it, Robert?"

"Didn't Tsu-yan have an office at Princes Building?"

"Brian?"

"We've followed him there several times, sir. He visited a business acquaintance. . . ." Brian Kwok searched his memory. ". . . Shipping. Name of Ng, Vee Cee Ng, nicknamed Photographer Ng. Room 721. We checked him out but everything was above board. Vee Cee Ng runs Asian and China Shipping and about fifty other small allied businesses. Why?"

"This address's 720. Tsu-yan could tie in with John Chen, the guns, Banastasio, Bartlett—even the Werewolves," Armstrong said.

Crosse took the paper. After a pause he said, "Robert, take a team and check 720 and 721 right now."

"It's not in my area, sir."

"How right you are!" Crosse said at once, heavy with sarcasm. "Yes. I know. You're CID Kowloon, Robert, not Central. However, I authorize the raid. Go and do it. Now."

"Yes sir." Armstrong left, red-faced.

The silence gathered.

Brian Kwok waited, staring stoically at the desk top. Crosse selected a cigarette with care, lit it, then leaned back in his chair. "Brian. I think Robert's the mole."

29

1:38 P.M.:

Robert Armstrong and a uniformed police sergeant got out of the squad car and headed through the crowds into the vast maw of the Princes Arcade with its jewelry and curio shops, camera shops and radio shops stuffed with the latest electronic miracles, that was on the ground floor of the old-fashioned, high-rise office building in Central. They eased their way toward a bank of elevators, joining the swarm of waiting people. Eventually he and the sergeant squeezed into an elevator. The air was heavy and fetid and nervous. The Chinese passengers watched them obliquely and uncomfortably.

On the seventh floor Armstrong and the sergeant got out. The corridor was dingy and narrow with nondescript office doors on either side. He stood for a moment looking at the board. Room 720 was billed as "Pingsing Wah Developments," 721 as "Asian and China Shipping." He walked ponderously down the corridor, Sergeant Yat alongside.

As they turned the corner a middle-aged Chinese wearing a white shirt and dark trousers was coming out of room 720. He saw them, blanched, and ducked back in. When Armstrong got to the door he expected it to be locked but it wasn't and he jerked it open just in time to see the man in the white shirt disappearing out of the back door, another man almost jamming him in equal haste to flee. The back door slammed closed.

Armstrong sighed. There were two rumpled secretaries in the sleazy, untidy office suite of three cramped rooms, and they were gawking at him, one with her chopsticks poised in midair over a bowl of chicken and noodles. The noodles slid off her chopsticks and fell back into the soup.

"Afternoon," Armstrong said.

The two women gaped at him, then looked at the sergeant and back to him again.

"Where are Mr. Lim, Mr. Tak and Mr. Lo, please?"

One of the girls shrugged and the other, unconcerned, began to eat again. Noisily. The office suite was untidy and unkempt. There were two phones, papers strewn around, plastic cups, dirty plates and bowls and used chopsticks. A teapot and tea cups. Full garbage cans.

Armstrong took out the search warrant and showed it to them.

The girls stared at him.

Irritably Armstrong harshened his voice. "You speak English?"

Both girls jumped. "Yes sir," they chorused.

"Good. Give your names to the sergeant and answer his questions. Th—" At that moment the back door opened again and the two men were herded back into the room by two hard-faced uniformed policemen who had been waiting in ambush. "Ah, good. Well done. Thank you, Corporal. Now, where were you two going?"

At once the two men began protesting their innocence in voluble Cantonese.

"*Shut up!*" Armstrong snarled. They stopped. "Give me your names!" They stared at him. In Cantonese he said, "Give me your names and you'd better not lie or I will become very fornicating angry."

"He's Tak Chou-lan," the one with pronounced buck teeth said, pointing at the other.

"What's your name?"

"Er, Lo Tup-sop, Lord. But I haven't done anyt—"

"Lo Tup-sop? Not Lo Tup-lin?"

"Oh no, Lord Superintendent, that's my brother."

"Where is he?"

The buck-toothed man shrugged. "I don't know. Please what's go—"

"Where were you going in such a hurry, Bucktooth Lo?"

"I'd forgotten an appointment, Lord. Oh it was very important. It's urgent and I will lose a fortune, sir, if I don't go immediately. May I now please go, Honored Lo—"

"No! Here's my search warrant. We're going to search and take away any papers th—"

At once both men began to protest strenuously. Again Armstrong cut them short. "Do you want to be taken to the border right now?" Both men blanched and shook their heads. "Good. Now, where's Thomas K. K. Lim?" Neither answered so Armstrong stabbed his finger at the younger of the two men. "You, Mr. Bucktooth Lo! Where's Thomas K. K. Lim?"

"In South America, Lord," Lo said nervously.

"Where?"

"I don't know, sir, he just shares the office. That's his fornicating desk." Bucktooth Lo waved a nervous hand at the far corner. There was a messy desk and a filing cabinet and a phone there. "I've done nothing wrong, Lord. Foreigner Lim's a stranger from the Golden Mountain. Fourth Cousin Tak here just rents him space, Lord. Foreigner Lim just comes and goes as it pleases him and is nothing to do with me. Is he a foul criminal? If there's anything wrong I don't know anything about it!"

"Then what do you know about the thieving of funds from the CARE program?"

"Eh?" Both men gaped at him.

"Informers have given us proof you're all thieving charity money that belongs to starving women and children!"

At once both began protesting their innocence.

"Enough! The judge will decide! You will go to headquarters and give statements." Then he switched back into English once more. "Sergeant, take them back to headquarters. Corporal, let's st—"

"Honored sir," Bucktooth Lo began in halting, nervous English, "if I may to talk, in office, plees?" He pointed at the inner, equally untidy and cluttered office.

"All right."

Armstrong followed Lo, towering over him. The man closed the door nervously and began talking Cantonese quickly and very quietly. "I don't know anything about anything criminal, Lord. If something's amiss it's those other two fornicators, I'm just an honest businessman who wants to make money and send his children to university in America an—"

"Yes. Of course. What did you want to say to me privately before you go down to police headquarters?"

The man smiled nervously and went to the desk and began to unlock a drawer. "If anyone's guilty it's not me, Lord. I don't know anything about anything." He opened the drawer. It was filled with used, red, 100-dollar notes. They were clipped into thousands. "If you'll let me go, Lord . . ." He grinned up at him, fingering the notes.

Armstrong's foot lashed out and the drawer slammed and caught Lo's fingertips and he let out a howl of pain. He tore the drawer open with his good hand. "Oh oh oh my fornic—"

Armstrong shoved his face close to the petrified Chinese. "Listen, you dogmeat turd, it's against the law to try to bribe a policeman and if you claim your fingers're police brutality I'll personally grind your fornicating Secret Sack to mincemeat!"

He leaned back against the desk, his heart pounding, sickness in his throat, enraged at the temptation and sight of all that money. How easy it would be to take it and pay his debts and have more than enough over to gamble on the market and at the races, and then to leave Hong Kong before it was too late.

So easy. So much more easy to take than to resist—this time or all the other thousand times. There must be 30, 40,000 in that drawer alone. And if there's one drawer full there must be others and if I lean on this bastard he'll cough up ten times this amount.

Roughly he reached out and grabbed the man's hand. Again the man cried out. One fingertip was mashed and Armstrong thought Lo would lose a couple of fingernails and have plenty of pain but that was all. He was angry with himself that he had lost his temper but he was tired and knew it was not just tiredness. "What do you know about Tsu-yan?"

"Wat? Me? Nothing. Tsu-yan who?"

Armstrong grabbed him and shook him. "Tsu-yan! The gun-runner Tsu-yan!"

"Nothing, Lord!"

"Liar! The Tsu-yan who visits Mr. Ng next door!"

"Tsu-yan? Oh him? Gun-runner? I didn't know he's a gun-runner! I always thought he was a businessman. He's another Northerner like Photographer Ng—"

"Who?"

"Photographer Ng, Lord. Vee Cee Ng from next door. He and this Tsu-yan never come in here or talk to us. . . . Oh I need a doctor . . . oh my han—"

"Where's Tsu-yan now?"

"I don't know, Lord . . . oh my fornicating hand, oh oh oh. . . . I swear by all the gods I don't know him. . . . oh oh oh. . . ."

Irritably Armstrong shoved him in a chair and jerked open the door. The three policemen and two secretaries stared at him silently. "Sergeant, take this bugger to HQ and charge him with trying to bribe a policeman. Look at this. . . ." He beckoned him in and pointed at the drawer.

Sergeant Yat's eyes widened. *"Dew neh loh moh!"*

"Count it and get both men to sign the amount as correct and take it to HQ with them and turn it in."

"Yes sir."

"Corporal, you start going through the files. I'm going next door. I'll be back shortly."

"Yes sir."

Armstrong strode out. He knew that this money would be counted quickly, and any other money in the offices—if this drawer was full others would be—then the amount to be turned in would be quickly negotiated by the principals, Sergeant Yat and Lo and Tak, and the rest split among them. Lo and Tak would believe him to be in for a major share and his own men would consider him mad not to be. Never mind. He didn't care. The money was stolen, and Sergeant Yat and his men were all good policemen and their pay totally inadequate for their responsibilities. A little *h'eung yau* wouldn't do them any harm, it would be a godsend.

Won't it?

In China you have to be pragmatic, he told himself grimly as he knocked on the door of 721 and went in. A good-looking secretary looked up from her lunch—a bowl of pure white rice and slivers of roast pork and jet green broccoli steaming nicely.

"Afternoon." Armstrong flashed his ID card. "I'd like to see Mr. Vee Cee Ng, please."

"Sorry, sir," the girl said, her English good and her eyes blank. "He's out. Out for lunch."

"Where?"

"At his club, I think. He—he won't be back today until five."

"Which club?"

She told him. He had never heard of it but that meant nothing as there were hundreds of private Chinese lunching or dining or at mah-jong clubs.

"What's your name?"

"Virginia Tong. Sir," she added as an afterthought.

"Do you mind if I look around?" He saw her eyes flash nervously. "Here's my search warrant."

She took it and read it and he thought, full marks, young lady. "Do you think you could wait, wait till five o'clock?" she asked.

"I'll take a short look now."

She shrugged and got up and opened the inner office. It was small and empty but for untidy desks, phones, filing cabinets, shipping posters and sailing schedules. Two inner doors let off it and a back door. He opened one door on the 720 side but it was a dank, evil-smelling toilet and dirty washbasin. The back door was bolted. He slid the bolts back and went onto the dingy back-stairs landing that served as a makeshift fire escape and alternate means of exit. He rebolted it, watched all the time by Virginia Tong. The last door, on the far side, was locked.

"Would you open it please?"

"Mr. Vee Cee has the only key, sir."

Armstrong sighed. "I do have a search warrant, Miss Tong, and the right to kick the door in, if necessary."

She stared back at him so he shrugged and stood away from the door and readied to kick it in. Truly.

"Just . . . just a moment, sir," she stammered. "I . . . I'll see if there . . . if he left his key before he went out."

"Good. Thank you." Armstrong watched her open a desk drawer and pretend to search, then another drawer and another and then, sensing his impatience, she found a key under a money box. "Ah, here it is!" she said as though a miracle had happened. He noticed she was perspiring now. Good, he thought. She unlocked the door and stood back. This door opened directly onto another. Armstrong opened it and whistled involuntarily. The room beyond was large, luxurious, thick-carpeted with elegant suede leather sofas and rosewood furniture and fine paintings. He wandered in. Virginia Tong watched from the doorway. The fine antique rosewood, tooled leather desk was bare and clean and polished, a bowl of flowers on it, and some framed photographs, all of a beaming Chinese leading in a garlanded racehorse, and one of the same Chinese in dinner jacket shaking hands with the governor, Dunross nearby.

"That's Mr. Ng?"

"Yes sir."

Top-quality hi-fi and record player were to one side, and a tall cocktail cabinet. Another doorway let off this room. He pushed the half-opened door aside. An elegant, very feminine bedroom with a huge, unmade king-sized bed, mirror-lined ceiling and a decorator's bathroom off it, with perfumes, aftershave lotions, gleaming modern fittings and many buckets of water.

"Interesting," he said and looked at her.

She said nothing, just waited.

Armstrong saw that she had nylon-clad legs and was very trim with well-groomed nails and hair. I'll bet she's a dragon, and expensive. He turned away from her and looked around thoughtfully. Clearly this self-contained apartment had been made out of the adjoining suite. Well, he told himself with a touch of envy, if you're rich and you want a private, secret flat for an afternoon's nooky behind your office there's no law against that. None. And none against having an attractive secretary. Lucky bastard. I wouldn't mind having one of these places myself.

Absently he opened a desk drawer. It was empty. All the drawers were empty. Then he went through the bedroom drawers but found nothing of interest. One cupboard contained a fine camera and some portable lighting equipment and cleaning equipment but nothing suspicious.

He came back into the main room satisfied that he had missed nothing. She was still watching him, and though she tried to hide it, he could sense a nervousness.

That's understandable, he told himself. If I were her and my boss was out and some rotten *quai loh* came prying I'd be nervous too. No harm in having a private place like this. Lots of rich people have them in Hong Kong. His eye was caught by the rosewood cocktail cabinet. The key in the lock beckoned him. He opened it. Nothing out of the ordinary. Then his sharp, well-trained eyes noticed the untoward width of the doors. A moment's inspection and he opened the false doors. His mouth dropped open.

The side walls of the cabinet were covered with dozens of photographs of Jade Gates in all their glory. Each photograph was neatly framed and tagged with a typed name and a date. Involuntarily he let out a bellow of embarrassed laughter, then glanced around. Virginia Tong had vanished. Quickly he scanned the names. Hers was third from the last.

Another paroxysm of laughter was barely contained. The policeman shook his head helplessly. What some buggers'll do for fun—and I suppose some ladies for money! I thought I'd seen it all but this . . . Photographer Ng, eh? So that's where the nickname came from.

Now over his initial shock, he studied the photographs. Each of them had been taken with the same lens from the same distance.

Good God, he thought after a minute, astounded, there's really quite a lot of difference between . . . I mean if you can forget what you're looking at and just look, well, there's a fantastic amount of difference in the shape and size of the whole, the position and protuberance of the Pearl on the Step, the quality and quantity of pubicity and . . . *ayeeyah* there's one piece *bat jam gai*. He looked at the name. Mona Leung—now where have I heard that name before? That's curious—Chinese usually consider lack of pubicity unlucky. Now why . . . oh my God! He peered at the next name tag to make sure. There was no mistake. Venus Poon. *Ayeeyah*, he thought elatedly, so that's hers, that's what she really looks like, the darling of the telly who daily projects such sweet, virginal innocence so beautifully!

He concentrated on her, his senses bemused. I suppose if you compare hers with, say, say Virginia Tong's, well she does have a certain delicacy. Yes, but if you want my considered opinion I'd still rather have had the mystery and not seen these at all. None of them.

Idly his eyes went from name to name. "Bloody hell," he said, recognizing one: Elizabeth Mithy. She was once a secretary at Struan's, one of the band of wanderers from the small towns in Australia and New Zealand, girls who aimlessly found their way to Hong Kong for a few weeks, to stay for months, perhaps years, to fill minor jobs until they married or vanished forever. I'll be damned. Liz Mithy!

Armstrong was trying to be dispassionate but he could not help comparing Caucasian with Chinese and he found no difference. Thank God for that, he told himself, and chuckled. Even so he was glad the photographs were black and white and not in color.

"Well," he said out loud, still very embarrassed, "there's no law against taking photos that I know of, and sticking them in your own cabinet. The young ladies must've cooperated. . . ." He grunted, amused and at the same time disgusted. Damned if I'll ever understand the Chinese! "Liz Mithy, eh?" he muttered. He had known her slightly when she was in the Colony, knew that she was quite wild, but what could have possessed her to pose for Ng? If her old man knew, he'd hemorrhage. Thank God we don't have children, Mary and I.

Be honest, you bleed for sons and daughters but you can't have them, at least Mary can't, so the doctors say—so you can't.

With an effort Armstrong buried that everlasting curse again and relocked the cabinet and walked out, closing the doors after him.

In the outer office Virginia Tong was polishing her nails, clearly furious.

"Can you get Mr. Ng on the phone, please?"

"No, not until four," she said sullenly without looking at him.

"Then please call Mr. Tsu-yan instead," Armstrong told her, stabbing in the dark.

Without looking up the number, she dialed, waited impatiently, chatted gutturally for a moment in Cantonese and slammed the phone down. "He's away. He's out of town and his office doesn't know where he is."

"When did you last see him?"

"Three or four days ago." Irritably she opened her appointments calendar and checked it. "It was Friday."

"Can I look at that please?"

She hesitated, shrugged and passed it over, then went back to polishing her nails.

Quickly he scanned the weeks and the months. Lots of names he knew: Richard Kwang, Jason Plumm, Dunross—Dunross several times—Thomas K. K. Lim—the mysterious American Chinese from next door—Johnjohn from the Victoria Bank, Donald McBride, Mata several times. Now who's Mata? he asked himself, never having heard the name before. He was about to give the calendar back to her then he flipped forward. "Saturday 10:00 A.M.—V. Banastasio." His heart twisted. This coming Saturday.

He said nothing, just put the appointment calendar back on her desk, and leaned back against one of the files, lost in thought. She paid no attention to him. The door opened.

"Excuse me, sir, phone for you!" Sergeant Yat said. He was looking much happier so Armstrong knew the negotiation must have been fruitful. He would have liked to know how much, exactly, but then, face would be involved and he would have to take action, one way or another.

"All right, Sergeant, stay here till I get back," he said, wanting to make sure no secret phone calls were made. Virginia Tong did not look up as he left.

In the other office Bucktooth Lo was still moaning, nursing his hand, and the other man, Big Hands Tak, was pretending to be nonchalant, going through some papers, loudly berating his secretary for her inefficiency. As he came in both men started loudly protesting their continued innocence and Lo groaned with increasing vigor.

"Quiet! Why did you jam your fingers in the drawer?" Armstrong asked and added without waiting for a reply, "People who try to bribe honest policemen deserve to be deported at once." In the aghast silence he picked up the phone. "Armstrong."

"Hello, Robert, this is Don, Don Smyth at East Aberdeen . . ."

"Oh, hello!" Armstrong was startled, not expecting to hear from the Snake, but he kept his voice polite though he loathed him and loathed what he was suspected of doing within his jurisdiction. It was one thing for constables and the lower ranks of Chinese police to supplement their income from illicit gambling. It was another for a British officer to sell influence, and to squeeze like an old-fashioned Mandarin. But though almost everyone believed Smyth was on the make, there was no proof, he had never been caught, and had never been investigated. Rumor had it that he was protected by certain VIP individuals who were deeply involved with him as well as in their own graft. "What's up?" he asked.

"Had a bit of luck. I think. You're heading up the John Chen kidnapping, aren't you?"

"That's right." Armstrong's interest soared. Smyth's graft had nothing to do with the quality of his police work—East Aberdeen had the lowest crime rate in the Colony. "Yes. What've you got?"

Smyth told him about the old *amah* and what had happened with Sergeant Mok and Spectacles Wu, then added, "He's a bright young chap, that, Robert. I'd recommend him for SI if you want to pass it on. Wu followed the old bird back to her fairly filthy lair, then called us. He obeys orders too, which is rare these days. On a hunch I told him to wait around and if she came out, to follow her. What do you think?"

"A twenty-four-carat lead!"

"What's your pleasure? Wait, or pull her in for real questioning?"

"Wait. I'll bet the Werewolf never comes back but it's worth waiting until tomorrow. Keep the place under surveillance and keep me posted."

"Good. Oh very good!"

Armstrong heard Smyth chortle down the phone and he could not think why he was so happy. Then he remembered the huge reward that the High Dragons had offered. "How's your arm?"

"It's my shoulder. Bloody thing's dislocated and I lost my favorite sodding hat. Apart from that everything's fine. Sergeant Mok's going through all our mug shots now and I've got one of my lads doing an Identi-Kit on him—I think I even saw the sod myself. His face is quite pockmarked. If we've got him on file we'll have him nailed by sundown."

"Excellent. How's it going down there?"

"Everything under control but it's bad. The Ho-Pak's still paying out but too slowly—everyone knows they're stalling. I hear it's the same all over the Colony. They're finished, Robert. The queue'll go on till every last cent's out. There's another run on the Vic here and no letup in the crowds. . . ."

Armstrong gasped. "The Vic?"

"Yes, they're handing out cash by the bagful and taking nothing in. Triads are swarming . . . the pickings must be huge. We arrested eight pickpockets and busted up twenty-odd fights. I'd say it's very bad."

"Surely the Vic's okay?"

"Not in Aberdeen it isn't, old lad. Me, I'm liquid. I've closed all my accounts. I took every cent out. I'm all right. If I were you I'd do the same."

Armstrong felt queasy. His life's savings were in the Victoria. "The Vic's got to be all right. All the government funds're in it."

"Right you are. But nothing in their constitution says your money's protected too. Well, I've got to get back to work."

"Yes. Thanks for the info. Sorry about your shoulder."

"I thought I was going to have my bloody head bashed in. The sods'd just started the old 'kill the *quai loh*' bit. I thought I was a goner."

Armstrong shivered in spite of himself. Ever since the '56 riots it was a recurring nightmare of his that he was back in that insane, screaming mob again. It was in Kowloon. The mob had just overturned the car with the

Swiss consul and his wife in it and set it afire. He and other policemen had charged through the mob to rescue them. When they got to the car the man was already dead and the young wife afire. By the time they'd dragged her out, all her clothes had burned off her and her skin came away like a pelt. And all around, men, women and young people were raving, "*Kill the quai loh . . .*"

He shivered again, his nostrils still smelling burned flesh. "Christ, what a bastard!"

"Yes, but all in the day's work. I'll keep you posted. If that bloody Werewolf comes back to Aberdeen he'll be in a net tighter than a gnat's arsehole."

30

Phillip Chen stopped flipping through his mail, his face suddenly ashen. The envelope was marked, "Mr. Phillip Chen to open personally."

"What is it?" his wife asked.

"It's from them." Shakily he showed it to her. "The Werewolves."

"Oh!" They were at their lunch table that was set haphazardly in a corner of the living room of the house far up on the crest of Struan's Lookout. Nervously she put down her coffee cup. "Open it, Phillip. But, but better use your handkerchief in . . . in case of fingerprints," she added uneasily.

"Yes, yes of course, Dianne, how stupid of me!" Phillip Chen was looking very old. His coat was over his chair and his shirt damp. There was a slight breeze from the open window behind him but it was hot and humid and a brooding afternoon haze had settled over the Island. Carefully he used an ivory paper knife and unfolded the paper. "Yes, it's . . . it's from the Werewolves. It's . . . it's about the ransom."

"Read it out."

"All right: 'To Phillip Chen, comprador of the Noble House, greetings. I beg to inform you now how the ransom money is to be paid. 500,000 to you is as meaningless as a pig's scream in a slaughterhouse but to us poor farmers would be a heritage for our star—'"

"Liars!" Dianne hissed, her lovely gold and jade necklace glittering in a shaft of muted sunlight. "As if farmers would kidnap John or mutilate him like that. Dirty stinky foreign triads! Go on, Phillip."

"'. . . would be a heritage for our starving grandchildren. That you have already consulted the police is to us like pissing in the ocean. But now you will not consult. No. Now you will keep secret or the safety of your son will be endangered and he will not return and everything bad will be your own fault. Beware, our eyes are everywhere. If you try to betray us, the worst will happen and everything will be your own fault. Tonight at six o'clock I will phone you. Tell no one, not even your wife. Meanw—'"

"Dirty triads! Dirty whores' sons to try to spread trouble between husband and wife," Dianne said angrily.

"'. . . meanwhile prepare the ransom money in used 100-dollar notes. . . .'" Irritably Phillip Chen glanced at his watch. "I don't have much time to get to the bank. I'll have—"

"Finish the letter!"

"All right, be patient, my dear," he said placatingly, his overtaxed heart skipping a beat as he recognized the edge to her voice. "Where was I? Ah yes, '. . . notes. If you obey my instructions faithfully, you may have your son back tonight. . . .' Oh God I hope so," he said, breaking off momentarily, then continued, "'Do not consult the police or try to trap us. Our eyes are watching you even now. Written by the Werewolf.'" He took off his glasses. His eyes were red-rimmed and tired. Sweat was on his brow. "'Watching you even now?' Could one of the servants . . . or the chauffeur be in their pay?"

"No, no of course not. They've all been with us for years."

He wiped the sweat off, feeling dreadful, wanting John back, wanting him safe, wanting to strangle him. "That means nothing. I'd . . . I'd better call the police."

"Forget them! Forget them until we know what you have to do. Go to the bank. Get 200,000 only—you should be able to settle for that. If you get more you might be tempted to give it all to them if tonight . . . if they really mean what they say."

"Yes . . . very wise. If we could settle for that . . ." He hesitated. "What about the tai-pan? Do you think I should tell the tai-pan, Dianne? He, he might be able to help."

"Huh!" she said scornfully. "What help can he give us? We're dealing with dog-bone triads not foreign devil crooks. If we need help we have to stay with our own." Her eyes began boring into him. "And now you'd better tell me what's really the matter, why you were so angry the night before last and why you've been like a spiteful cat with a thorn in its rump ever since and not attending to business!"

"I've been attending to business," he said defensively.

"How many shares have you bought? Eh? Struan shares? Have you taken advantage of what the tai-pan told us about the coming boom? Do you remember what Old Blind Tung forecast?"

"Of course, of course I remember!" he stuttered. "I've, I've secretly doubled our holdings and have equally secret orders out with various brokers for half as much again."

Dianne Chen's abacus mind glowed at the thought of that vast profit, and all the private profit she would be making on all the shares she had bought on her own behalf, pledging her entire portfolio. But she kept her face cold and her voice icy. "And how much did you pay?"

"They averaged out at 28.90."

"Huh! According to today's paper Noble House opened at 28.80," she said with a disapproving sniff, furious that he had paid five cents less a share than she had. "You should have been at the market this morning instead of moping around here, sleeping your life away."

"I wasn't feeling very well, dear."

"It all goes back to the night before last. What sent you into that unbelievable rage? *Heya?*"

"It was nothing." He got up, hoping to flee. "Noth—"

"Sit down! *Nothing* that you shouted at me, me your faithful wife in front of the servants? *Nothing* that I was ordered into my own dining room like a common whore? *Heya?*" Her voice began rising and she let herself go, knowing instinctively that this was the perfect time, now that they were alone in the house, knowing that he was defenseless and she could press her advantage. "You think it's nothing that you abuse me, me who has given you the best years of her life, working and slaving and guarding you for twenty-three years? Me, Dianne Mai-wei T'Chung who has the blood of the great Dirk Struan in her veins, who came to you virgin, with property in Wanchai, North Point and even on Lan Tao, with stocks and shares and the best schooling in England? Me who never complains about your snoring and whoring or about the brat you sired out of that dance-hall girl you've sent to school in America!"

"*Eh?*"

"Oh I know all about you and her and all the others and all the other nasty things you do, and that you never loved me but just wanted my property and a perfect decoration to your drab life. . . ."

Phillip Chen was trying to close his ears but he could not. His heart was pounding. He hated rows and hated the shriek to her voice that, somehow, was perfectly tuned to set his teeth on edge, his brain oscillating and his bowels in turmoil. He tried to interrupt her but she overrode him, battering him, accusing him of all sorts of dalliances and mistakes and private matters that he was shocked she knew about.

". . . and what about your club?"

"Eh, what club?"

"The private Chinese lunch club with forty-three members called the 74 in a block off Pedder Street that contains a gourmet chef from Shanghai, teen-age hostesses and bedrooms and saunas and devices that dirty old men need to raise their Steamless Stalks? Eh?"

"It's nothing like that at all," Phillip Chen spluttered, aghast that she knew. "It's a pl—"

"Don't lie to me! You put up 87,000 good U.S. greenbacks as the down payment with Shitee T'Chung and those two mealy-mouthed friends of yours and even now pay 4,000 HK-a-month fees. Fees for what? You'd better . . . Where do you think you're going?"

Meekly he sat down again. "I—I was—I want to go to the bathroom."

"Huh! Whenever we have a discussion you want the bathroom! You're just ashamed of the way you treat me and guilty. . . ." Then, seeing him about to explode back at her, she switched abruptly, her voice crooningly gentle. "Poor Phillip! Poor boy! Why were you so angry? Who's hurt you?"

So he told her, and once he began the telling he felt better and his anguish and fear and fury started to melt away. Women are clever and cunning in these things, he told himself confidently, rushing on. He told her about opening John's safety deposit in the bank, about the letters to Linc Bartlett and about finding a duplicate key to his own safe in their bedroom. "I brought all the letters back," he said, almost in tears, "they're upstairs, you can read them for yourself. My own son! He's betrayed us!"

"My God, Phillip," she gasped, "if the tai-pan found out you and Father Chen-chen were keeping . . . if he knew he'd ruin us!"

"Yes, yes I know! That's why I've been so upset! By the rules of Dirk's legacy he has the right and the means. We'd be ruined. But, but that's not all. John knew where our secret safe was in the garden an—"

"Wat?"

"Yes, and he dug it up." He told her about the coin.

"Ayeeyah!" She stared at him in absolute shock, half her mind filled with terror, the other half with ecstasy, for now, whether John came back or not, he had destroyed himself. John would never inherit now! My Kevin's Number One Son now and future compradore to the Noble House! Then her fears drowned her excitement and she muttered, aghast, "If there's still a House of Chen."

"What? What did you say?"

"Nothing, never mind. Wait a moment, Phillip, let me think. Oh the rotten boy! How could John do this to us, we who have cherished him all his life! You . . . you'd better go to the bank. Get 300,000 out—in case you need to barter more. We must get John back at all costs. Would he keep the coin with him, on him, or would it be in his other safety deposit box?"

"It'd be in the box—or hidden at his flat in Sinclair Towers."

Her face closed. "How can we search that place with her in residence? That wife of his? That strumpet Barbara! If she suspects we're after something . . ." Her mind caught a vagrant thread. "Phillip, does it mean, whoever presents the coin gets whatever they want?"

"Yes."

"Eeeeee! What power!"

"Yes."

Now her mind was working cleanly. "Phillip," she said, in control again, everything else forgotten, "we need all the help we can get. Phone your cousin Four Fingers . . ." He looked at her, startled, then began to smile. ". . . arrange with him to have some of his street fighters follow you secretly to protect you when you pay over the ransom, then to follow the Werewolf to his lair and to rescue John whatever the cost. Whatever you do don't tell him about the coin—just that you want help to rescue poor John. That's it. We must get poor John back at all costs."

"Yes," he replied, much happier now. "Four Fingers is the perfect choice. He owes us a favor or two. I know where I can reach him this afternoon."

"Good. Off you go to the bank, but give me the key to the safe. I'll cancel my hairdressing appointment and I'll read John's papers at once."

"Very good." He got up immediately. "The key's upstairs," he said, lying, and hurried out, not wanting her prying into the safe. There were a number of things there he did not want her to know about. I'd better hide them somewhere else, he thought uneasily, just in case. His euphoria evaporated and his overwhelming anxiety returned. Oh my poor son, he told himself near tears. Whatever possessed you? I was a good father to you and you'll always be my heir and I've loved you like I loved your mother. Poor Jennifer, poor little thing, dying birthing my first-born son. O all gods: let me get my poor son back again, safe again, whatever he's done, let us extract ourselves from all this madness, and I'll endow a new temple for all of you equally!

The safe was behind the brass bedstead. He pulled it away from the wall, opened the safe and took out all of John's papers, then his very private deeds, letters and promissory notes which he stuffed into his coat pocket and went downstairs again.

"Here are John's letters," he said. "I thought I'd save you the trouble of moving the bed."

She noticed the bulge in his coat pocket but said nothing.

"I'll be back by 5:30 P.M. sharp."

"Good. Drive carefully," she said absently, her whole being concentrated on a single problem—how to get the coin for Kevin and herself. Secretly.

The phone rang. Phillip Chen stopped at the front door as she picked it up. "*Weyyyy?*" Her eyes glazed. "Oh hello, tai-pan, how're you today?" Phillip Chen blanched.

"Just fine thank you," Dunross said. "Is Phillip there?"

"Yes, yes just a minute." She could hear many voices behind Dunross's voice and she thought she heard an undercurrent of covered urgency which increased her dread. "Phillip, it's for you," she said, trying to keep the nervousness out of her voice. "The tai-pan!" She held up the phone, motioning him silently to keep the earpiece a little away from his ear so she could hear too.

"Yes, tai-pan?"

"Hello, Phillip. What're your plans this afternoon?"

"Nothing particular. I was just leaving to go to the bank, why?"

"Before you do that, drop by the exchange. The market's gone mad. The run on the Ho-Pak's Colony-wide now and the stock's teetering even though Richard's supporting it for all he's worth. Any moment it'll crash. The run's spilling over to lots of other banks, I hear—the Ching Prosperity, even the Vic . . ." Phillip Chen and his wife glanced at each other, perturbed. "I heard the Vic's got problems at Aberdeen and at Central. Everything's down, all our blue chips: the V and A, Kowloon Investments, Hong Kong Power, Rothwell-Gornt, Asian Properties, H.K.L.F., Zong Securities, Solomon Textiles, us . . . everyone."

"How many points are we off?"

"From this morning? Three points."

Phillip Chen gasped and almost dropped the phone. "What?"

"Yes," Dunross agreed pleasantly. "Someone's started rumors about us. It's all over the market that we're in trouble, that we can't pay Toda Shipping next week—nor the Orlin installment. I think now we're being sold short."

31

Gornt was sitting beside his stockbroker, Joseph Stern, in the exchange watching the big board delightedly. It was warm and very humid in the large room that was packed and noisy, phones ringing, sweating brokers, Chinese clerks and runners. Normally the exchange was calm and leisurely. Today it was not. Everyone was tense and concentrating. And uneasy. Many had their coats off.

Gornt's own stock was off a point but that did not bother him a bit. Struan's was down 3.50 now and Ho-Pak tottering. Time's running out for Struan's, he thought, everything's primed, everything's begun. Bartlett's money had been put into his Swiss bank within the hour, no strings —just 2 million transferred from an unknown account into his. Seven phone calls began the rumors. Another call to Japan confirmed the accuracy of the Struan payment dates. Yes, he thought, the attack's begun.

His attention went to the Ho-Pak listing on the board as some more sell offerings were written up by a broker. There were no immediate buyers.

Since he had secretly started selling Ho-Pak short on Monday just before the market closed at three o'clock—long before the run had started in earnest—he was millions ahead. On Monday the stock had sold at 28.60, and now, even with all the support Richard Kwang was giving it, it was down to 24.30—off more points than the stock had moved ever since the bank was formed eleven years ago.

4.30 times 500,000 makes 2,150,000, Gornt was thinking happily, all in honest-to-God HK currency if I wanted to buy back in right now which isn't bad for forty-eight hours of labor. But I won't buy back in yet, oh dear no. Not yet. I'm sure now that the stock will crash, if not today, tomorrow, Thursday. If not then, Friday—Monday at the latest, for no bank in the world can sustain such a run. Then, when the crash comes I'll buy back in at a few cents on the dollar and make twenty times half a million.

"Sell 200,000," he said, beginning to sell short openly now—the other shares hidden carefully among his secret nominees.

"Good God, Mr. Gornt," his stockbroker gasped. "The Ho-Pak'll have to put up almost 5 million to cover. That'll rock the whole market."

"Yes," he said jovially.

"We'll have a hell of a time borrowing the stock."

"Then do it."

Reluctantly his stockbroker began to leave but one of the phones rang. "Yes? Oh hello, Daytime Chang," he said in passable Cantonese. "What can I do for you?"

"I hope you can save all my money, Honorable Middleman. What is Noble House selling for?"

"25.30."

There was a screech of dismay. "Woe woe woe, there's barely half a dog-bone hour of trading left, woe woe woe! Please sell! Please sell all Noble House companies at once, Noble House, Good Luck Properties and Golden Ferry, also . . . what's Second Great Company selling at?"

"23.30."

"*Ayeeyah,* one point off from this morning? All gods bear witness to foul joss! Sell! Please to sell everything at once!"

"But Daytime Chang, the market's really quite sound an—"

"At once! Haven't you heard the rumors? Noble House will crash! Eeeee, sell, waste not a minute! Hold a moment, my associate Fung-tat wants to talk to you too."

"Yes, Third Toiletmaid Fung?"

"Just like Daytime Chang, Honorable Middleman! Sell! Before I'm lost! Sell and call us back with prices oh oh oh! Please hurry!"

He put the phone down. This was the fifth panic call he had had from old customers and he did not like it at all. Stupid to panic, he thought, checking his stock book. Between the two of them, Daytime Chang and Third Toiletmaid Fung had invested over 40,000 HK in various stocks. If he sold now they would be ahead, well ahead, but for the Struan losses today which would shave off most of their profit.

Joseph Stern was head of the firm of Stern and Jones that had been in Hong Kong for fifty years. They had become stockbrokers only since the war. Before that they were moneylenders, dealers in foreign exchange and ship's chandlers. He was a small, dark-haired man, mostly bald, in his sixties, and many people thought he had Chinese blood in him a few generations back.

He walked to the front of the board and stopped beside the column that listed Golden Ferry. He wrote down the combined Chang and Fung holdings in the sell column. It was a minor offering.

"I'll buy at 30 cents off listing," a broker said.

"There's no run on Golden Ferry," he said sharply.

"No, but it's a Struan company. Yes or no?"

"You know very well Golden Ferry's profits are up this quarter."

"Tough titty! Christ, isn't it bloody hot? Don't you think we could afford air conditioning in the exchange? Is it yes or no, old chap?"

Joseph Stern thought a moment. He did not want to fuel the nervousness. Only yesterday Golden Ferry had soared a dollar because all the business world knew their annual meeting was next week, it had been a good year and it was rumored there was going to be a stock split. But he knew the first rule of all exchanges: yesterday has nothing to do with today. The client had said, Sell.

"20 cents off market?" he asked.

"30. Last offer. What the hell do you care, you still get paid. Is it 30 off?"

"All right." Stern worked his way down the board, selling most of their stocks without trouble though each time he had to concede on price. With difficulty he borrowed the Ho-Pak stock. Now he stopped at the column listing the bank. There were many sell orders. Most of them were small figures. He wrote 200,000 at the bottom of the list in the sell column. A shock wave went through the room. He paid no attention, just looked at Forsythe, who was Richard Kwang's broker. Today he was the only buyer of Ho-Pak.

"Is Quillan trying to wreck the Ho-Pak?" a broker asked.

"It's already under siege. Do you want to buy the shares?"

"Not on your bloody life! Are you selling Struan short too?"

"No. No I'm not."

"Christ, I don't like this at all."

"Keep calm, Harry," someone else said. "The market's come alive for once, that's all that counts."

"Great day, what?" another broker said to him. "Is the crash on? I'm totally liquid myself, sold out this morning. Is it going to be a crash?"

"I don't know."

"Shocking about Struan's, isn't it?"

"Do you believe all the rumors?"

"No, of course not, but one word to the wise is sufficient they say, what?"

"I don't believe it."

"Struan's off 3½ points in one day, old boy, a lot of people believe it," another broker said. "I sold out my Struan's this morning. Will Richard sustain the run?"

"That's in the hands of . . ." Joseph Stern was going to say God but he knew that Richard Kwang's future was in the hands of his depositors and that they had already decided. "Joss," he said sadly.

"Yes. Thank God we get our commissions either way, feast or famine, jolly good, what?"

"Jolly good," Stern echoed, privately loathing the smug, self-satisfied upper-class English accent of the exclusive British public schools, schools that, because he was Jewish, he had never been able to attend. He saw

Forsythe put the phone down and look at the board. Once more he tapped his offering. Forsythe beckoned him. He walked through the throng, eyes watching him.

"Are you buying?" he asked.

"In due course, Joseph, old boy!" Forsythe added softly, "Between you and me, can't you get Quillan off our backs? I've reason to believe he's in cahoots with that berk Southerby."

"Is that a public accusation?"

"Oh come on, it's a private opinion, for chrissake! Haven't you read Haply's column? Tai-pans and a big bank spreading rumors? You know Richard's sound. Richard's as sound as . . . as the Rothschilds! You know Richard's got over a billion in res—"

"I saw the crash of '29, old chap. There were trillions in reserve then but even so everyone went broke. It's a matter of cash, credit and liquidity. And confidence. You'll buy our offering, yes or no?"

"Probably."

"How long can you keep this up?"

Forsythe looked at him. "Forever. I'm just a stockbroker. I just follow orders. Buy or sell I make a quarter of one percent."

"If the client pays."

"He has to. We have his stock, eh? We have rules. But while I think of it, go to hell."

Stern laughed. "I'm British, I'm going to heaven, didn't you know." Uneasily, he walked back to his desk. "I think he'll buy before the market closes."

It was a quarter to three. "Good," Gornt said. "Now I wa—" He stopped. They both looked back as there was an undercurrent. Dunross was escorting Casey and Linc Bartlett to the desk of Alan Holdbrook—Struan's in-house broker—on the other side of the hall.

"I thought he'd left for the day," Gornt said with a sneer.

"The tai-pan never runs away from trouble. It's not in his nature." Stern watched them thoughtfully. "They look pretty friendly. Perhaps the rumors are all wrong and Ian'll make the Par-Con deal and make the payments."

"He can't. That deal's going to fall through," Gornt said. "Bartlett's no fool. Bartlett'd be mad to throw in with that tottering empire."

. "I didn't even know until a few hours ago that Struan's were indebted to the Orlin Bank. Or that the Toda payments were due in a week or so. Or the even more nonsensical rumor that the Vic won't support the Noble House. Lot of nonsense. I called Havergill and that's what he said."

"What else would he say?"

After a pause, Stern said, "Curious that all that news surfaced today."

"Very. Sell 200,000 Struan's."

Stern's eyes widened and he plucked at his bushy eyebrows. "Mr. Gornt, don't you think th—"

"No. Please do as I ask."

"I think you're wrong this time. The tai-pan's too clever. He'll get all the support he needs. You'll get burned."

"Times change. People change. If Struan's have extended themselves and can't pay . . . Well, my dear fellow, this's Hong Kong and I hope the buggers go to the wall. Make it 300,000."

"Sell at what figure, Mr. Gornt?"

"At market."

"It'll take time to borrow the shares. I'll have to sell in much smaller lots. I'll hav—"

"Are you suggesting my credit's not good enough or you can't perform normal stockbroking functions?"

"No. No of course not," Stern replied, not wanting to offend his biggest customer.

"Good, then sell Struan's short. Now."

Gornt watched him walk away. His heart was beating nicely.

Stern went to Sir Luis Basilio of the old stockbroking firm of Basilio and Sons, who had a great block of Struan's personally, as well as many substantial clients with more. He borrowed the stock then walked to the board and wrote the huge offering in the sell column. The chalk scraped loudly. Gradually the room fell silent. Eyes switched to Dunross and Alan Holdbrook and the Americans, then to Gornt and back to Dunross again. Gornt saw Linc Bartlett and Casey watching him and he was glad she was there. Casey was wearing a yellow silk skirt and blouse, very Californian, a green scarf tying her golden hair back. Why is she so sexual, Gornt asked himself absently. A strange invitation seemed to surround her. Why? Is it because no man yet has ever satisfied her?

He smiled at her, nodding slightly. She half-smiled back and he thought he noticed a shadow there. His greeting to Bartlett was polite and returned equally politely. His eyes held Dunross and the two men stared at each other.

The silence mounted. Someone coughed nervously. Everyone was conscious of the immensity of the offering and the implications of it.

Stern tapped his offering again. Holdbrook leaned forward and consulted with Dunross who half shrugged and shook his head, then began talking quietly to Bartlett and Casey.

Joseph Stern waited. Then someone offered to buy a portion and they haggled back and forth. Soon 50,000 shares had changed hands and the new market price was 24.90. He changed the 300,000 to 250,000 and again waited. He sold a few more but the bulk remained. Then, as there were no takers, he came back to his seat. He was sweating.

"If that number stays there overnight it'll do Struan's no good at all."

"Yes." Gornt still watched Casey. She was listening intently to Dunross. He sat back and thought a moment. "Sell another 100,000 Ho-Pak—and 200,000 Struan's."

"Good God, Mr. Gornt, if Struan's gets brought down the whole market'll totter, even your own company'll lose."

"There'll be an adjustment, lots of adjustments, certainly."

"There'll be a bloodbath. If Struan's go, so will other companies, thousands of investors'll be wiped out an—"

"I really don't need a lecture on Hong Kong economics, Mr. Stern," Gornt said coldly. "If you don't want to follow instructions I'll take my business elsewhere."

Stern flushed. "I'll . . . I'll have to round up the shares first. That number . . . to get that sum . . ."

"Then I suggest you hurry up! I want that on the board today!" Gornt watched him go, enjoying the moment immensely. Cocky bastard, he was thinking. Stockbrokers are just parasites, every one of them. He felt quite safe. Bartlett's money was in his account. He could buy back Ho-Pak and Struan's even now and be millions ahead. Contentedly his eyes strayed back to Casey. She was watching him. He could read nothing in her expression.

Joseph Stern was weaving through the brokers. Again he stopped at the Basilio desk. Sir Luis Basilio looked away from the board and smiled up at him. "So, Joseph? You want to borrow more Noble House shares?"

"Yes, please."

"For Quillan?" Sir Luis asked. He was a fine old man, small, elegant, very thin, and in his seventies—this year's chairman of the committee that ran the exchange.

"Yes."

"Come, sit down, let's talk a moment, old friend. How many do you want now?"

"200,000."

Sir Luis frowned. "300,000 on the board—another 2? Is this an all-out attack?"

"He . . . he didn't say that but I think it is."

"It's a great pity those two can't make peace with one another."

"Yes."

The older man thought a moment, then said even more quietly, "I'm considering suspending dealing in Ho-Pak shares, and, since lunch, Noble House shares. I'm very worried. At this precise moment a Ho-Pak crash, coupled with a Noble House crash, could wreck the whole market. Madonna, it's unthinkable for the Noble House to crash, it would pull down hundreds of us, perhaps all Hong Kong, unthinkable!"

"Perhaps the Noble House needs overhauling. Can I borrow 200,000 shares?"

"First answer me this, yes or no, and if yes when: Should we suspend the Ho-Pak? Should we suspend Struan's? I've polled all the other members of the committee except you. They're divided almost equally."

"Neither have ever been suspended. It would be bad to suspend either.

This's a free society—in its best sense, I think. You should let it work itself out, let them sort themselves out, the Struans, and the Gornts and all the rest, let the best get to the top and the worst . . ." Stern shook his head wearily. "Ah but it's easy for me to say that, Luis, I'm not a big investor in either."

"Where's your money?"

"Diamonds. All Jews need small things, things you can carry and things you can hide, things you can convert easily."

"There's no need for you to be afraid here, Joseph. How many years has your family been here and prospered? Look at Solomon—surely he and his family are the richest in all Asia."

"For Jews fear is a way of life. And being hated."

Again the old man sighed. "Ah this world, this lovely world, how lovely it should be." A phone rang and he picked it up delicately, his hands tiny, his Portuguese sounding sweet and liquid to Stern though he understood none of it. He only caught "Señor Mata" said deferentially several times but the name meant nothing to him. In a moment Sir Luis replaced the receiver very thoughtfully. "The financial secretary called just after lunch, greatly perturbed. There's a deputation from Parliament here and a bank crash would look extremely bad for all of us," he said. He smiled a pixyish smile. "I suggested he introduce legislation for the governor's signature to govern banks like they had in England and the poor fellow almost had a fit. I really mustn't pull his leg so much." Stern smiled with him. "As if we need government interference here!" The eyes sharpened. "So Joseph, do you vote to let well alone—or suspend either or both of the stocks, if so when?"

Stern glanced at the clock. If he went to the board now he would have plenty of time to write up both sell offerings and still be able to challenge Forsythe. It was a good feeling to know that he held the fate of both houses in his hands, if only temporarily. "Perhaps it would be very good, perhaps bad. What's the voting so far?"

"I said, almost equal." There was another burst of excitement and both men looked up. Some more Struan shares were changing hands. The new market price dropped to 24.70. Now Phillip Chen was leaning over Hold-brook's desk.

"Poor Phillip, he doesn't look well at all," Sir Luis said compassionately.

"No. Pity about John. I liked him. What about the Werewolves? Do you think the papers are overplaying it?"

"No. No, I don't." The old eyes twinkled. "No more than you, Joseph."

"What?"

"You've decided to pass. You want to let today's time run out, don't you? That's what you want, isn't it?"

"What better solution could there be?"

"If I wasn't so old I'd agree with you. But being so old and not know-ing about tomorrow, or if I shall live to see tomorrow, I prefer my drama

today. Very well. I'll discount your vote this time and now the committee's
deadlocked so I will decide, as I'm allowed to do. You can borrow 200,000
Noble House shares until Friday, Friday at two. Then I may ask for them
back—I have to think of my own House, eh?" The sharp but kindly eyes
in the lined face urged Stern to his feet. "What are you going to do now,
my friend?"

Joseph Stern smiled sadly. "I'm a stockbroker."

He went to the board and wrote in the Ho-Pak sell column with a firm
hand. Then in the new silence he went to the Struan column and wrote
the figure clearly, conscious that he was on center stage now. He could
feel the hate and the envy. More than 500,000 Noble House shares were
now on offer, more than at any one time in the history of the exchange.
He waited, wanting the clock to run out. There was a flurry of interest as
Soorjani, the Parsee, bought some blocks of shares but it was well known
he was nominee for many of the Struan and Dunross family and supporters. And though he bought 150,000, it made little difference to the
enormity of Gornt's offering. The quiet was hurting. One minute to go
now.

"*We buy!*" The tai-pan's voice shattered the silence.

"All my shares?" Stern asked hoarsely, his heart racing.

"Yes. Yours and all the rest. At market!"

Gornt was on his feet. "With what?" he asked sardonically. "That's almost 9 million cash."

Dunross was on his feet too, a taunting half-smile on his face. "The
Noble House is good for that—and millions more. Has anyone ever
doubted it?"

"I doubt it—and I sell short tomorrow!"

At that moment the finish bell sounded shrilly, the tension broke and
there was a roar of approval.

"Christ what a day. . . ."

"Good old tai-pan. . . ."

"Couldn't stand much more of that . . ."

"Is Gornt going to beat him this time . . . ?"

"Maybe those rumors are all nonsense . . ."

"Christ I made a bloody fortune in commissions . . ."

"I think Ian's running scared. . . ."

"Don't forget he's got five days to pay for the shares . . ."

"He can't buy like that tomorrow . . ."

"Christ, tomorrow! What's going to happen tomorrow . . ."

Casey shifted in her seat, her heart thumping. She pried her eyes off
Gornt and Dunross and looked back at Bartlett, who sat staring at the
board, whistling tonelessly. She was awed—awed and a little frightened.

Just before coming here to meet Dunross, Linc Bartlett had told her his
plan, about his call to Gornt and all about the meeting with him. "Now
you know it all, Casey," he had said softly, grinning at her. "Now they're

both set up and we control the battlefield, all for 2 million. Both're at each other's throats, both going for the jugular, each ready to cannibalize the other. Now we wait. Monday's D Day. If Gornt wins, we win. If Dunross wins, we win. Either way we become the Noble House."

32

Alexi Travkin who trained the racehorses of the Noble House went up the busy alley off Nathan Road in Kowloon and into the Green Dragon Restaurant. He wore a small .38 under his left arm and his walk was light for a man of his age.

The restaurant was small, ordinary and drab, with no tablecloths on the dozen or so tables. At one of them, four Chinese were noisily eating soup and noodles, and, as he came in, a bored waiter by the cash register looked up from his racing form and began to get up with a menu. Travkin shook his head and walked through the archway that led to the back.

The little room contained four tables. It was empty but for one man.

"*Zdrastvuytye*," Suslev said lazily, his light clothes well cut.

"*Zdrastvuytye*," Travkin replied, his Slavic eyes narrowing even more. Then he continued in Russian, "Who're you?"

"A friend, Highness."

"Please don't call me that, I'm not a highness. Who're you?"

"Still a friend. Once you were a prince. Will you join me?" Suslev politely motioned to a chair. There was an opened bottle of vodka on his table and two glasses. "Your father Nicoli Petrovitch was a prince too, like his father and back for generations, Prince of Kurgan and even Tobol."

"You talk in ciphers, friend," Travkin said, outwardly calm, and sat opposite him. The feel of the .38 took away some of his apprehension. "From your accent you're Muscovite—and Georgian."

Suslev laughed. "Your ear is very good, Prince Kurgan. Yes I'm Muscovite but I was born in Georgia. My name's unimportant but I'm a friend wh—"

"Of me, Russia or the Soviets?"

"Of all three. Vodka?" Suslev asked, lifting the bottle.

"Why not?" Travkin watched the other man pour the two glasses, then without hesitation he picked up the wrong glass, the one farthest from him, and lifted it. "Health!"

Without hesitation Suslev picked up the other, touched glasses, drained it and poured again. "Health!"

"You're the man who wrote to me?"

"I have news of your wife."

"I have no wife. What do you want from me, *friend*?" The way Travkin used the word it was an insult. He saw the flash of anger as Suslev looked up from his glass and he readied.

"I excuse your rudeness this once, Alexi Ivanovitch," Suslev said with dignity. "You've no cause to be rude to me. None. Have I insulted you?"

"Who are you?"

"Your wife's name is Nestorova Mikail and her father was Prince Anotoli Zergeyev whose lands straddle Karaganda, which is not so far away from your own family lands east of the Urals. He was a Kazaki, wasn't he, a great prince of the Kazaki, whom some people call Cossacks?"

Travkin kept his gnarled hands still and his face impassive, but he could not keep the blood from draining from his face. He reached out and poured two more glasses, the bottle still half full. He sipped the spirit. "This's good vodka, not like the piss in Hong Kong. Where did you get it?"

"Vladivostok."

"Ah. Once I was there. It's a flat dirty town but the vodka's good. Now, what's your real name and what do you want?"

"You know Ian Dunross well?"

Travkin was startled. "I train his horses . . . I've . . . this is my third year, why?"

"Would you like to see the Princess Nestor—"

"Good sweet Christ Jesus whoever you are, I told you I have no wife. Now, for the last time, what do you want from me?"

Suslev filled his glass and his voice was even more kindly. "Alexi Ivanovitch Travkin, your wife the princess today is sixty-three. She lives in Yakutsk on th—"

"On the Lena? In Siberia?" Travkin felt his heart about to explode. "What *gulag* is that, you turd?"

Through the archway in the other room, which was empty now, the waiter looked up momentarily, then yawned and went on reading.

"It's not a *gulag*, why should it be a *gulag*?" Suslev said, his voice hardening. "The princess went there of her own accord. She's lived there since she left Kurgan. Her . . ." Suslev's hand went into his pocket and he brought out his wallet. "This is her *dacha* in Yakutsk," he said, putting down a photograph. "It belonged to her family, I believe." The cottage was snowbound, within a nice glade of trees, the fences well kept, and it was pretty with good smoke coming out of the chimney. A tiny bundled-up figure waved gaily at the camera—too far away for the face to be seen clearly.

"And that's my wife?" Travkin said, his voice raw.

"Yes."

"I don't believe you!"

Suslev put down a new snapshot. A portrait. The lady was white-haired and in her fifties or sixties and though the cares of a whole world marked her, her face was still elegant, still patrician. The warmth of her smile reached out and broke him.

"You . . . you KGB turd," he said hoarsely, sure that he recognized her. "You filthy rotten mother-eating . . ."

"To have found her?" Suslev said angrily. "To have seen that she was looked after and left in peace and not troubled and not sent to . . . to the correction places she and your whole class deserved?" Irritably he poured himself another drink. "I'm Russian and proud of it—you're émigré and you left. My father and his were *owned* by one of your class. My father died at the barricades in 1916, and my mother—and before they died they were starving. They . . ." With an effort he stopped. Then he said in a different voice, "I agree there's much to forgive and much to forget on both sides, and that's all past now but I tell you we Soviets, we're not all animals—not all of us. We're not all like Bloody Beria and the murdering archfiend Stalin. . . . Not everyone." He found his pack of cigarettes. "Do you smoke?"

"No. Are you KGB or GRU?" KGB stood for the Committee for State Security; GRU for the Chief Intelligence Directorate of the General Staff. This was not the first time Travkin had been approached by one of them. Before, he had always been able to slough them off with his drab, unimportant cover story. But now he was trapped. This one knew too much about him, too much truth. Who are you, bastard? And what do you really want? he thought as he watched Suslev light a cigarette.

"Your wife knows you're alive."

"Impossible. She's dead. She was murdered by mobs when our pal—when our house in Kurgan was sacked, put to the torch, torn apart—the prettiest, most unarmed mansion within a hundred miles."

"The masses had the right t—"

"Those weren't my people and they were led by imported Trotskyites who afterwards murdered my peasants by the thousands—until they themselves were all purged by more of their own vermin."

"Perhaps, perhaps not," Suslev said coldly. "Even so, Prince of Kurgan and Tobol, she escaped with one old servant and fled east thinking she could find you, could escape after you through Siberia to Manchuria. The servant came originally from Austria. Pavchen was her name."

The breath seemed to have vanished from Travkin's lungs. "More lies," he heard himself say, no longer believing it, his spirit ripped apart by her lovely smile. "My wife's dead. She'd never go so far north."

"Ah but she did. Her escape train was diverted northwards. It was autumn. Already the first snows had come so she decided to wait the winter out in Yakutsk. She had to. . . ." Suslev put down another snapshot.

". . . she was with child. This is your son and his family. It was taken last year." The man was good-looking, in his forties, wearing a Soviet major's air force uniform, self-consciously smiling at the camera, his arm around a fine woman in her thirties with three happy children, a babe, a beaming girl of six or seven missing front teeth, a boy of about ten trying to be serious. "Your wife called him Pietor Ivanovitch after your grandfather."

Travkin did not touch the photo. He just stared at it, his face chalky. Then he pried his eyes away and poured a drink for himself, and as an afterthought, one for Suslev. "It's . . . it's all a brilliant reconstruction," he said, trying to sound convincing. "Brilliant."

"The child's name is Victoria, the girl is Nichola after your grandmother. The boy is Alexi. Major Ivanovitch is a bomber pilot."

Travkin said nothing. His eyes went back to the portrait of the beautiful old lady and he was near tears but his voice was still controlled. "She knows I'm alive, eh?"

"Yes."

"For how long?"

"Three months. About three months ago. One of our people told her."

"Who're they?"

"Do you want to see her?"

"Why only three months—why not a year—three years?"

"It was only six months ago we discovered who you were."

"How did you do that?"

"Did you expect to remain anonymous forever?"

"If she knows I'm alive and one of your people told her then she'd've written. . . . Yes. They would have asked her to do that if . . ." Travkin's voice was strange. He felt out of himself, in a nightmare, as he tried to think clearly. "She would have written a letter."

"She has. I will give it to you within the next few days. Do you want to see her?"

Travkin forced his agony down. He motioned at the family portrait. "And . . . and he knows I'm alive too?"

"No. None of them do. That was not at our suggestion, Alexi Ivanovitch. It was your wife's idea. For safety—to protect him, she thought. As if we would wreak vengeance for the sins of the fathers on the sons! She waited out two winters in Yakutsk. By that time peace had come to Russia so she stayed. By that time she presumed you dead, though she hoped you were alive. The boy was brought up believing you dead, and knew nothing of you. He still doesn't. As you can see, he's a credit to you both. He was head of his local school, then went to university as all gifted children do nowadays. . . . Do you know, Alexi Ivanovitch, in my day I was the first of my whole province ever to get to a university, the very first, ever from a *peasant* family. We're fair in Russia today."

"How many corpses have you made to become what you are now?"

"A few," Suslev said darkly, "all of them criminals or enemies of Russia."

"Tell me about them."

"I will. One day."

"Did you fight the last war—or were you a commissar?"

"Sixteenth Tank Corps, Forty-fifth Army. I was at Sebastopol . . . and at Berlin. Tank commander. Do you want to see your wife?"

"More than my whole life is worth, if this really is my wife and if she's alive."

"She is. I can arrange it."

"Where?"

"Vladivostok."

"No, here in Hong Kong."

"Sorry, that's impossible."

"Of course." Travkin laughed without mirth. "Of course, *friend.* Drink?" He poured the last of the vodka, splitting it equally. "Health!"

Suslev stared at him. Then he looked down at the portrait and the snapshot of the air force major and his family and picked them up, lost in thought. The silence grew. He scratched his beard. Then he said decisively, "All right. Here in Hong Kong," and Travkin's heart leapt.

"In return for what?"

Suslev stubbed his cigarette out. "Information. And cooperation."

"What?"

"I want to know everything you know about the tai-pan of the Noble House, everything you did in China, who you know, who you met."

"And the cooperation?"

"I will tell you later."

"And in return you'll bring my wife to Hong Kong?"

"Yes."

"When?"

"By Christmas."

"How can I trust you?"

"You can't. But if you cooperate she will be here at Christmas." Travkin was watching the two photos Suslev toyed with in his fingers, then he saw the look in his eyes and his stomach twisted. "Either way, you must be honest with me. With or without your wife, Prince Kurgan, we always have your son and your grandchildren hostage."

Travkin sipped his drink, making it last. "Now I believe you are what you are. Where do you want to start?"

"The tai-pan. But first I want to piss." Suslev got up and asked the waiter where the toilet was and went out through the kitchen.

Now that Travkin was alone despair gripped him. He picked up the snapshot of the cottage that was still on the table and peered at it. Tears filled his eyes. He brushed them away and felt the gun that nestled beneath his shoulder but that did not help him now. With all his inner strength he resolved to be wise and not believe, but in his heart he knew he had seen her picture and that he would do anything, risk anything to see her.

For years he had tried to avoid these hunters, knowing that he was always pursued. He had been the leader of the Whites in his area across the Trans-Siberian Railroad and he had killed many Reds. At length he had wearied of the killing and in 1919 had left for Shanghai and a new home until the Japanese armies came, escaping them to join Chinese guerrillas, fighting his way south and west to Chungking, there to join other marauders, English, French, Australian, Chinese—anyone who would pay —until the Japanese unconditionally surrendered, and so back to Shanghai again, soon to flee once more. Always fleeing, he thought.

By the blood of Christ, my darling, I know you're dead. I know it. I was told by someone who saw the mob sack our palace, saw them swarm over you. . . .

But now?

Are you really alive?

Travkin looked at the kitchen door with hatred, knowing he would forever be haunted until he was certain about her. Who is that shit eater? he thought. How did they find me?

Grimly he waited and waited and then in sudden panic went to find him. The toilet was empty. He rushed into the street but it was filled with other people. The man had vanished.

There was a vile taste in Travkin's mouth now and he was sick with apprehension. In the name of God, what does he want with the tai-pan?

33

"Hello, Ian," Penelope said. "You're home early! How was your day?"

"Fine, fine," Dunross said absently. Apart from all the disasters, just before he left the office he had had a call from Brian Kwok saying, among other things, that AMG was probably murdered and warned him to take serious precautions.

"Oh, it was one of those, was it?" she said at once. "How about a drink? Yes. How about champagne?"

"Good idea." Then he noticed her smile and smiled back and felt much better. "Penn, you're a mind reader!" He tossed his briefcase onto a sideboard and followed her into one of the sitting rooms of the Great House. The champagne was already in an ice bucket, opened, with two glasses partially filled and another waiting for him in the ice.

"Kathy's upstairs. She's reading Glenna a bedtime story," Penelope said, pouring for him. "She . . . she's just told me about . . . about the, about the disease."

"Oh." He accepted the glass. "Thanks. How's Andrew taking it? He didn't mention anything today."

"She's going to tell him tonight. The champagne was to give her some courage." Penelope looked up at him, anguished. "She's going to be all right, isn't she, Ian?"

"I think so. I had a long talk with Doc Tooley. He was encouraging, gave me the names of the top three experts in England and another three in America. I've cabled for appointments with the three in England and Doc Ferguson's air-mailing them case histories—they'll be there when you arrive."

She sipped her wine. A light breeze made the sultry day much better. The French doors were open to the garden. It was near six o'clock. "Do you think we should go at once? Will a few days make any difference?"

"I don't think so."

"But we should go?"

"If it were you, Penn, we'd've been on the first plane the very first moment."

"Yes. If I'd told you."

"You would have told me."

"Yes. I suppose I would. I've made reservations for tomorrow. Kathy thought it a good idea too. The BOAC flight."

He was startled. "Claudia never mentioned it."

She smiled. "I made them myself. I'm really quite capable. I've reservations for Glenna, me and Kathy. We could take the case histories with us. I thought Kathy should go without any of her children. They'll be perfectly all right with the *amahs*."

"Yes, that's much the best. Doc Tooley was adamant about her taking it easy. That's the main thing he said, lots of rest." Dunross smiled at her. "Thanks, Penn."

She was staring at the beads of condensation on the outside of the bottle and the ice bucket. "Bloody awful, isn't it?"

"Worse, Penn. There's no cure. He thinks . . . he thinks the medication will arrest it." He finished his glass and poured for both of them. "Any messages?"

"Oh, sorry! Yes, they're on the sideboard. There was a long-distance call from Marseilles a moment ago."

"Susanne?"

"No. A Mr. Deland."

"He's our agent there."

"Rotten about young Borge."

"Yes." Dunross skimmed the messages. Johnjohn at the bank, Holdbrook, Phillip Chen, and the inevitable catchall "please call Claudia." He sighed. It was only half an hour since he left the office and he was going to call her anyway. No rest for the wicked, he thought, and smiled to himself.

He had enjoyed besting Gornt at the exchange. That he did not have the money at the moment to pay did not worry him. There's five days of grace, he thought. Everything's covered—with joss. Ah yes, joss!

Since his stockbroker had called him in panic at a few minutes past ten about the rumors sweeping the exchange and how their stock was shifting, he had been bolstering his defenses against the sudden, unexpected attack. With Phillip Chen, Holdbrook, Gavallan and deVille he had marshaled all the major stockholders they could reach and told them that the rumors Struan's couldn't meet their obligations were nonsense and suggested they refuse to lend Gornt any big blocks of Struan stock but to keep him dangling, letting him have a few shares here and there. He told the selected few in the strictest confidence that the Par-Con deal was signed, sealed and about to be chopped, and that this was a marvelous opportunity to smash Rothwell-Gornt once and for all.

"If Gornt sells short, let him. We pretend to be vulnerable but support the stock. Then Friday we announce, our stock'll soar and he'll lose his shirt, tie and trousers," he had told them all. "We get back our airline along with his, and with his ships and ours together, we'll dominate all air and surface inbound and outbound trade in Asia."

If we could really smash Gornt, he thought fervently, we'd be safe for generations. And we could, given joss, Par-Con and more joss. Christ, but it's going to be very dicey!

He had exuded confidence all day, not feeling confident at all. Many of his big stockholders had called nervously but he had quieted them. Both Tightfist Tung and Four Finger Wu owned major blocks of stock through devious nominees. He had phoned both this afternoon to get their agreement not to loan or sell their major holdings for the next week or so. Both had agreed but it had not been easy with either of them.

All in all, Dunross thought, I've fought off the initial onslaught. Tomorrow will tell the real story—or Friday: is Bartlett enemy, friend or Judas?

He felt his anger rising but he pushed it back. Be calm, he told himself, think calmly. I will but it's bloody curious that everything Bartlett said the night of the party—all those very secret things he had so readily and suddenly produced to shatter my defenses—miraculously went through the market today like a typhoon. Who's the spy? Who gave him the info? Is he the Sevrin spy too? Well, never mind for the moment, everything's covered. I think.

Dunross went to the phone and asked the operator to get Mr. Deland, person to person, and to call him back.

"Would Susanne be there yet?" Penelope asked.

"I think so. If her plane's on time. It's about eleven, Marseilles time, so it shouldn't be an emergency. Bloody shame about Borge! I liked him."

"What's Avril going to do?"

"She's going to be all right. Avril's going to come home to bring up the child and soon she'll meet a Prince Charming, a new one, and her son'll join Struan's and meanwhile she'll be protected and cherished."

"Do you believe that, Ian—about the Prince Charming?"

"Yes," he said firmly. "I believe everything will be all right. It's going to be all right, Penn, for her, for Kathy, for . . . for everyone."

"You can't carry everyone, Ian."

"I know. But no one, no one in the family will ever need for anything while I'm alive and that's going to be forever."

His wife looked at him and remembered the first time she had seen him, a godlike youth sitting in his shattered fighter that should have crashed but somehow miraculously hadn't. Ian, just sitting there, then getting out, holding the terror down, she seeing in his eyes for the first time what death was like but him dominating it and coming back and just accepting the cup of tea saying, "Oh, jolly good, thanks. You're new, aren't you?" in his lovely patrician accent that was so far from her own background.

Such a long time ago, a thousand years ago, another lifetime, she thought. Such wonderful ghastly terrible beautiful agonizing days: will he die today or come back today? Will I die today, in the morning bombing or in the evening one? Where's Dad and Mum and is the phone just bombed out of service as usual or has the rotten little terraced house in Streatham vanished along with all the other thousands like it?

One day it had and then she had no past. Just Ian and his arms and strength and confidence, and she terrified that he would go like all the others. That was the worst part, she told herself. The waiting and anticipating and knowing how mortal the Few were and we all are. My God how quickly we had to grow up!

"I hope it is forever, darling," she said in her cool, flat voice, wanting to hide the immensity of her love. "Yes. I want you to be immortal!"

He grinned at her, loving her. "I'm immortal, Penn, never mind. After I'm dead I'll still be watching over you and Glenna and Duncan and Adryon and all the rest."

She watched him. "Like Dirk Struan does?"

"No," he said serious now. "He's a presence I'll never match. He's perpetual—I'm temporary." His eyes were watching hers. "You're rather serious tonight, aren't you?"

"You're rather serious tonight, aren't you?"

They laughed.

She said, "I was just thinking how transient life is, how violent, unexpected, how cruel. First John Chen and now Borge, Kathy . . ." A little shiver went through her, ever petrified she would lose him. "Who's next?"

"Any one of us. Meanwhile be Chinese. Remember under heaven all crows are black. Life is good. Gods make mistakes and go to sleep so we do the best we can and never trust a *quai loh!*"

She laughed, at peace again. "There are times, Ian Struan Dunross, when I quite like you. Do you th—" The phone rang and she stopped and thought, God curse that bloody phone. If I was omnipotent I'd outlaw all phones after 6:00 P.M. but then poor Ian'd go mad, and the bloody Noble House'd crumble and that's poor Ian's life. I'm second, so are the children and that's as it should be. Isn't it?

"Oh hello, Lando," Dunross was saying, "what's new?"

"Hope I'm not disturbing you, tai-pan."

"Not at all," he replied, all his energy concentrated. "I've just got in. What can I do for you?"

"Sorry, but I'm withdrawing the 15 million support I promised for tomorrow. Temporarily. The market makes me nervous."

"Nothing to worry about," Dunross said, his stomach churning. "Gornt's up to his tricks. That's all."

"I'm really very worried. It's not just Gornt. It's the Ho-Pak and the way the whole market's reacting," Mata said. "With the bank run seeping over to the Ching Prosperity and even the Vic . . . all the signs are very bad so I want to wait and see."

"Tomorrow's the day, Lando. Tomorrow. I was counting on you."

"Have you tripled our next gold consignment as I asked?"

"Yes, I did that personally. I've Zurich's telexed confirms in the usual code."

"Excellent, excellent!"

"I'll need your letter of credit tomorrow."

"Of course. If you'll send a messenger to my home now I'll give you my check for the full amount."

"Personal check?" Dunross held on to his astonishment. "On which bank, Lando?"

"The Victoria."

"Christ, that's a lot of money to remove just now."

"I'm not removing it, I'm just paying for some gold. I'd rather have some of my funds in gold outside Hong Kong for the next week or so, and this's an ideal moment to do it. You can get them to telex it first thing tomorrow. First thing. Yes. I'm not withdrawing funds, Ian, just paying for gold. If I were you I'd try to get liquid too."

Again his stomach fell over. "What have you heard?" he asked, his voice controlled.

"You know me, I'm just more cautious than you, tai-pan. The cost of my money comes very high."

"No more than mine."

"Yes. We'll consult tomorrow, then we'll see. But don't count on our 15 million. Sorry."

"You've heard something. I know you too well. What is it? *Chi pao pu chu huo.*" Literally, Paper cannot wrap up a fire, meaning a secret cannot be kept forever.

There was a long pause, then Mata said in a lower voice, "Confidentially, Ian, old Tightfist's selling heavily. He's getting ready to unload *all* his holdings. That old devil may be dying but his nose is as sensitive to the loss of a brass cash as ever and I've never known him to be wrong."

"All his holdings?" Dunross asked sharply. "When did you talk to him?"

"We've been in contact all day. Why?"

"I reached him after lunch and he promised he wouldn't sell or loan any Struan's. Has he changed his mind?"

"No. I'm sure he hasn't. He can't. He hasn't any Struan stock."

"He has 400,000 shares!"

"He *did* have, tai-pan, though actually the number was nearer 600,000—Sir Luis had very few shares of his own, he's one of Tightfist's many nominees. He's unloaded all 600,000 shares. Today."

Dunross bit back an obscenity. "Oh?"

"Listen, my young friend, this is all in the strictest confidence but you should be prepared: Tightfist ordered Sir Luis to sell or loan all his Noble

House stock the moment the rumors started this morning. 100,000 was spread throughout the brokers and sold immediately, the remainder. . . . the half million shares you bought from Gornt were Tightfist's. The moment it was evident there was a major assault on the House and Gornt was selling short, Tightfist told Sir Luis to go ahead and loan it all, except for a token 1,000 shares, which he's kept. For face. Yours. When the exchange closed, Tightfist was very pleased. On the day he's almost 2 million ahead."

Dunross was standing rock still. He heard that his voice was matter-of-fact and level and controlled and that pleased him, but he was in shock. If Tightfist had sold, the Chins would sell and a dozen other friends would follow his lead and that meant chaos. "The old bugger!" he said, bearing him no grudge. It was his own fault, he had not reached Tightfist in time. "Lando, what about your 300,000 shares—plus?"

He heard the Portuguese hesitate and his stomach twisted again. "I've still got them. I bought at 16 when you first went public so I'm not worried yet. Perhaps Alastair Struan was right when he advised against going public—the Noble House's only vulnerable because of that."

"Our growth rate's five times Gornt's and without going public we could never have weathered the disasters I inherited. We're supported by the Victoria. We've still got our bank stock and a majority vote on the board so they have to support us. We're really very strong and once this temporary situation's over we'll be the biggest conglomerate in Asia."

"Perhaps. But perhaps you'd have been wiser to accept our proposal instead of leaving yourself constantly open to the risk of takeovers or market disasters."

"I couldn't then. I can't now. Nothing's changed." Dunross smiled grimly. Lando Mata, Tightfist Tung and Gambler Chin collectively had offered him 20 percent of their gold and gambling syndicate revenue for 50 percent of Struan's—if he kept it as a wholly private-owned company.

"Come, tai-pan, be sensible! Tightfist and I will give you 100 million cash today for 50 percent ownership. U.S. dollars. Your position as tai-pan will not be touched, you will head the new syndicate and manage our gold and gambling monopolies, secretly or openly—with 10 percent of all profit as a personal fee."

"Who appoints the next tai-pan?"

"You do—in consultation."

"There, you see! It's impossible. A 50 percent control gives you power over Struan's and that I'm not allowed to give. That would negate Dirk's legacy, make my oath invalid and give away absolute control. Sorry, it's not possible."

"Because of an oath to an unknown, unknowable god in which you don't believe—on behalf of a murdering pirate who's been dead over a hundred years?"

"For whatever reason the answer is, thank you, no."

"You could easily lose the whole company."

"No. Between the Struans and the Dunrosses we have 60 percent voting control and I alone vote all the stock. What I'd lose is everything material we own, and cease to be the Noble House, and that by the Lord God, is not going to happen either."

There was a long silence. Then Mata said, his voice friendly as always, "Our offer is good for two weeks. If joss is against you and you fail, the offer to head the new syndicate stands. I shall sell or lend my stock at 21."

"Below 20—not at 21."

"It will go that low?"

"No. Just a habit I have. 20 is better than 21."

"Yes. Good. Then let us see what tomorrow brings. I wish you good joss. Good night, tai-pan."

Dunross put down the phone and sipped the last of his champagne. He was up the creek without a paddle. That old bugger Tightfist, he thought again, admiring his cleverness—to agree so reluctantly not to sell or barter any Struan shares, knowing that only 1,000 remained, knowing the revenue from almost 600,000 was already safe—that old bastard's a great negotiator. It's so very clever of both Lando and Tightfist to make the new offer now. 100 million! Jesus Christ, that'd stop Gornt farting in church! I could use that to smash him to pieces, and in short order take over Asian Properties and put Dunstan into an early retirement. Then I could pass the House over to Jacques or Andrew in great shape and . . .

And then what? What would I do then? Retire to the moors and shoot grouse? Throw vast parties in London? Or go into Parliament and sleep in the Back Bench while the bloody Socialists give the country to the Communists? Christ, I'd be bored to bloody death! I'd . . .

"What?" He was startled. "Oh sorry, Penn, what did you say?"

"I just said that all sounded like bad news!"

"Yes. Yes it was." Then Dunross grinned and all his anxiety dropped away. "It's joss! I'm tai-pan," he said happily. "You've got to expect it." He picked up the bottle. It was empty. "I think we deserve another . . . No, pet, I'll get it." He went to the concealed refrigerator that was set into a vast old Chinese scarlet, lacquered sideboard.

"How do you cope, Ian?" she asked. "I mean, it always seems to be something bad, ever since you took over—and there's always some disaster, every phone call, you work all the time, never take a holiday . . . ever since we came back to Hong Kong. First your father and then Alastair and then . . . Isn't it ever going to stop pouring cats and dogs?"

"Of course not—that's the job."

"Is it worth it?"

He concentrated on the cork, knowing there was no future in this conversation. "Of course."

To you it is, Ian, she thought. But not to me. After a moment she said, "Then it's all right for me to go?"

"Yes, yes of course. I'll watch Adryon and don't worry about Duncan. You just have a great time and hurry back."

"Are you going to do the hill climb Sunday?"

"Yes. Then I'm going to Taipei, back Tuesday. I'm taking Bartlett."

She thought about Taipei and wondered if there was a girl there, a special girl, a Chinese girl, half her age, with lovely soft skin and warmth, not much warmer than herself or softer or trimmer but half her age, with a ready smile, without the years of survival bowing her—the rotten growing-up years, the good and terrible war years, and childbearing years and child-rearing years and the exhausting reality of marriage, even to a good man.

I wonder I wonder I wonder. If I was a man . . . there're so many beauties here, so anxious to please, so readily available. If you believe a tenth of what the others say.

She watched him pour the fine wine, the bubbles and froth good, his face strong and craggy and greatly pleasing, and she wondered, Does any woman possess any man for more than a few years?

"What?" he asked.

"Nothing," she said, loving him. She touched his glass. "Be careful on the hill climb."

"Of course."

"How do you cope with being tai-pan, Ian?"

"How do you cope with running a home, bringing up the kids, getting up at all hours, year after year, keeping the peace, and all the other things you've had to do? I couldn't do that. Never could. I'd've given up the ghost long ago. It's part training and part what you're born to do."

"A woman's place is in the home?"

"I don't know about others, Penn, but so long as you're in my home all's good in my world." He popped the cork neatly.

"Thank you, dear," she said and smiled. Then she frowned. "But I'm afraid I don't have much option and never had. Of course it's different now and the next generation's lucky, they're going to change things, turn things around and give men their comeuppance once and for all."

"Oh?" he said, most of his mind back on Lando Mata and tomorrow and how to get the 100 million without conceding control.

"Oh yes. The girls of the next generation aren't going to put up with the boring 'a woman's place is by the sink.' God how I hate housework, how every woman hates housework. Our daughters are going to change all that! Adryon for one. My God I'd hate to be her husband."

said, pouring. "This's great champagne. Remember how we did? Remember how we used to bitch, still do, about our parents' attitudes?"

"True. But our daughters have the pill and that's a whole new kettle of fish an—"

"Eh?" Dunross stared at her, shocked. "You mean Adryon's on the pill? Jesus Christ how long . . . do you mean sh—"

"Calm down, Ian, and listen. That little pill's unlocked womanhood from fear forever—men too, in a way. I think very few people realize what an enormous social revolution it's going to create. Now women can all make love without fear of having a child, they can use their bodies as men use their bodies, for gratification, for pleasure, and without shame." She looked at him keenly. "As to Adryon, she's had access to the pill since she was seventeen."

"What?"

"Of course. Would you prefer her to have a child?"

"Jesus Christ, Penn, of course not," Dunross spluttered, "but Jesus Christ who? You . . . you mean she's having an affair, had affairs or. . . ."

"I sent her to Dr. Tooley. I thought it best she should see him."

"You what?"

"Yes. When she was seventeen, she asked me what to do, said most of her friends were on the pill. As there are various types I wanted her to have expert advice. Dr. Too— What are you so red about, Ian? Adryon's nineteen now, twenty next month, it's all very ordinary."

"It isn't by God. It just isn't!"

"Och laddie but it is," she said, aping the broad Scots accent of Granny Dunross whom he had adored, "and my whole point is that the lassies of today know what they're aboot and dinna ye dare mention it to Adryon that I've told ye or I'll take my stick to your britches!"

He stared at her.

"Health!" Smugly she raised her glass. "Did you see the *Guardian* Extra this afternoon?"

"Don't change the subject, Penn. Don't you think I should talk to her?"

"Absolutely not. No. It's a . . . it's a very private matter. It's really her body and her life and whatever you say, Ian, she has the right to do with her life what she pleases and really nothing you say will make any difference. It'll all be very embarrassing for both of you. There's face involved," she added and was pleased with her cleverness. "Oh of course Adryon'll listen and take your views to heart but you really must be adult and modern for your own sake, as well as hers."

Suddenly an uncontrollable wave of heat went through his face.

"What is it?" she asked.

"I was thinking about . . . I was just thinking."

"About who was, is or could be her lover?"

"Yes."

Penelope Dunross sighed. "For your own sanity, Ian, don't! She's very sensible, over nineteen . . . well, quite sensible. Come to think of it I haven't seen her all day. The little rotter rushed out with my new scarf before I could catch her. You remember the blouse I lent her? I found it scrumpled up on her bathroom floor! I shall be very glad to see her off on her own and in her own apartment."

"She's too young for God's sake!"

"I don't agree, dear. As I was saying, there's really nothing you can do about progress, and the pill is a marvelous fantastic unbelievable leap forward. You really must be more sensible. Please?"

"It's . . . Christ, it's a bit sudden, that's all."

She laughed outright. "If we were talking about Glenna I could unders— Oh for God's sake, Ian, I'm only joking! It never really occurred to me that you wouldn't have presumed Adryon was a very healthy, well-adjusted though foul-tempered, infuriating, very frustrated young lady, most of whose frustrations spring from trying to please us with our old-fashioned ideas."

"You're right." He tried to sound convincing but he wasn't and he said sourly, "You're right even so . . . you're right."

"Laddie, dinna ye think ye'd better visit our Shrieking Tree?" she asked with a smile. It was an ancient clan custom in the old country that somewhere near the dwelling of the oldest woman of the laird's family would be the Shrieking Tree. When Ian was young, Granny Dunross was the oldest, and her cottage was in a glade in the hills behind Kilmarnock in Ayrshire where the Struan lands were. The tree was a great oak. It was the tree that you went out to when the deevil—as old Granny Dunross called it—when the deevil was with you, and alone, you shrieked whatever curses you liked. ". . . and then, lassie," the lovely old woman had told her the first night, ". . . and then, lassie, there would be peace in the home and never a body has need to really curse a husband or wife or lover or child. Aye, just a wee tree and the tree can bear all the curse words that the deevil himself invented. . . ."

Penelope was remembering how old Granny Dunross had taken her into her heart and into the clan from the first moment. That was just after she and Ian were married and visiting for the second time, Ian on sick leave, still on crutches, his legs badly burned but healing, the rest of him untouched in the flaming crash-landing but for his mad, all-consuming anger at being grounded forever, she so pleased secretly, thanking God for the reprieve.

"But whisht, lassie," Granny Dunross had added with a chuckle that night when the winter winds were whining off the moors, sleet outside, and they all warm and toasty in front of the great fire, safe from the bombing, well fed and never a care except that Ian should get well quickly, ". . . there was a time when this Dunross was six and, och aye, he had a terrible temper even then and his father Colin was off in those heathen foreign parts as always, so this Dunross would come to Ayr on holiday from boarding school. Aye, and sometimes he would come to see me and I'd tell him tales o' the clan and his grandfather and great-grand-father but this time nothing would take away the deevil that possessed him. It was a night like this and I sent him out, the poor wee bairn, aye I sent him out to the Shrieking Tree. . . ." The old woman had chuckled and chuckled and sipped whiskey and continued, "Aye and the young deevil went out, cock of the walk, the gale under his kilt, and he cursed the tree. Och aye, surely the wee beasties in the forest fled before his wrath and then he came back. 'Have you given it a good drubbing,' I asked him. 'Aye,' he said in his wee voice. 'Aye, Grandma, I gave it a good drubbing, the very best ever.'

" 'Good,' I said. 'And now you're at peace!'

" 'Well, not really, Grandmother, but I am tired.' And then, lassie, at that moment, there was an almighty crash and the whole house shook and I thought it was the end of the world but the wee little bairn ran out to see what had happened and a lightning bolt had blasted the Shrieking Tree to pieces. 'Och aye, Granny,' he said in his piping little voice when he came back, his eyes wide, 'that really was the very best I ever did. Can I do it again!' "

Ian had laughed. "That's all a story, I don't remember that at all. You're making it up, Granny!"

"Whisht on you! You were five or six and the next day we went into the glade and picked the new tree, the one you'll see tomorrow, lassie, and blessed it in the clan's name and I told young Ian to be a mite more careful next time!"

They had laughed together and then, later that night, she had woken up to find Ian gone and his crutches gone. She had watched and waited. When he came back he was soaked but tired and at peace. She pretended sleep until he was in bed again. Then she turned to him and gave him all the warmth she had.

"Remember, lassie," Granny Dunross had said to her privately the day they left, "if ye want to keep your marriage sweet, make sure this Dunross always has a Shrieking Tree nearby. Dinna be afeared. Pick one, always pick one wherever you go. This Dunross needs a Shrieking Tree close by though he'll never admit it and will never use it but rarely. He's like the Dirk. He's too strong. . . ."

So wherever they had gone they had had one. Penelope had insisted. Once, in Chungking, where Dunross had been sent to be an Allied liaison officer after he was well again, she had made a bamboo their Shrieking Tree. Here in Hong Kong it was a huge jacaranda that dominated the whole garden. "Don't you think you should pay her a wee visit?" The tree was always a her for him and a him for her. Everyone should have a Shrieking Tree, Penelope thought. Everyone.

"Thanks," he said. "I'm okay now."

"How did Granny Dunross have so much wisdom and stay so marvelous after so much tragedy in her life?"

"I don't know. Perhaps they built them stronger in those days."

"I miss her." Granny Dunross was eighty-five when she died. She was

Agnes Struan when she married her cousin Dirk Dunross—Dirk McCloud Dunross, whom his mother Winifred, Dirk Struan's only daughter, had named after her father in remembrance. Dirk Dunross had been fourth tai-pan and he had been lost at sea in *Sunset Cloud* driving her homeward. He was only forty-two when he was lost, she thirty-one. She never married again. They had had three sons and one daughter. Two of her sons were killed in World War I, the eldest at Gallipoli at twenty-one, the other gassed at Ypres in Flanders, nineteen. Her daughter Anne had married Gaston deVille, Jacques's father. Anne had died in the London bombing where all the deVilles had fled except Jacques who had stayed in France and fought the Nazis with the Maquis. Colin, the last of her sons, Ian's father, also had three sons and a daughter, Kathren. Two sons also were killed in World War II. Kathren's first husband, Ian's squadron leader, was killed in the Battle of Britain. "So many deaths, violent deaths," Penelope said sadly. "To see them all born and all die . . . terrible. Poor Granny! Yet when she died she seemed to go so peacefully with that lovely smile of hers."

"Perhaps it was joss. But the others, that was joss too. They only did what they had to, Penn. After all, our family history's ordinary in that. We're British. War's been a way of life for centuries. Look at your family —one of your uncles was lost at sea in the navy in the Great War, another in the last at El Alamein, your parents killed in the blitz . . . all very ordinary." His voice hardened. "It's not easy to explain to any outsider, is it?"

"No. We all had to grow up so quickly, didn't we, Ian?" He nodded and after a moment she said, "You'd better dress for dinner, dear, you'll be late."

"Come on, Penn, for God's sake, you take an hour longer than me. We'll put in a quick appearance and leave directly after chow. Wh—" The phone rang and he picked it up. "Yes? Oh hello, Mr. Deland."

"Good evening, tai-pan. I wish to report about Mme. deVille's daughter and son-in-law, M. Escary."

"Yes, please go ahead."

"I am sad to have the dishonor of bringing such bad tidings. The accident was a, how do you say, sideswipe on the upper Corniche just outside Eze. The driver of the other car was drunk. It was at two in the morning about, and when the police arrived, M. Escary was already dead and his wife, unconscious. The doctor says she will mend, very well, but he is afraid that her, her internal organs, her childbearing organs may have permanent hurt. She may require an operation. He—"

"Does she know this?"

"No, m'sieu, not yet, but Mme. deVille was told, the doctor told her. I met her as you ordered and have taken care of everything. I have asked for a specialist in these things from Paris to consult with the Nice Hospital and he arrives this afternoon."

"Is there any other damage?"

"Externally, *non*. A broken wrist, a few cuts, nothing. But . . . the poor lady is distraught. It was glad . . . I was glad that her mother came, that helped, has helped. She stays at the Métropole in a suite and I met her airplane. Of course I will be in the constant touch."

"Who was driving?"

"Mme. Escary."

"And the other driver?"

There was a hesitation. "His name is Charles Sessonne. He's a baker in Eze and he was coming home after cards and an evening with some friends. The police have . . . Mme. Escary swears his car was on the wrong side of the road. He cannot remember. Of course he is very sorry and the police have charged him with drunk driving an—"

"Is this the first time?"

"*Non. Non*, once before he was stopped and fined."

"What'll happen under French law?"

"There will be a court and then . . . I do not know, m'sieu. There were no other witnesses. Perhaps a fine, perhaps jail; I do not know. Perhaps he will remember he was on the right side, who knows? I'm sorry."

Dunross thought a moment. "Where does this man live?"

"Rue de Verte 14, Eze."

Dunross remembered the village well, not far from Monte Carlo, high above, and the whole of the Côte d'Azur below and you could see beyond Monte Carlo into Italy, and beyond Cap Ferrat to Nice. "Thank you, Mr. Deland. I've telexed you 10,000 U.S. for Mme. deVille's expenses and anything else. Whatever's necessary please do it. Call me at once if there's anything . . . yes and ask the specialist to call me immediately after he's examined Mme. Escary. Have you talked with Mr. Jacques deVille?"

"No, tai-pan. You did not instruct this. Should I phone?"

"No. I'll call him. Thank you again." Dunross hung up and told Penelope everything, except about the internal injuries.

"How awful! How . . . how senseless!"

Dunross was looking out at the sunset. It was at his suggestion the young couple had gone to Nice and Monte Carlo where he and Penelope had had so much fun, and marvelous food, marvelous wine and a little gambling. Joss, he thought, then added, Christ all bloody mighty!

He dialed Jacques deVille's house but he was not there. He left a message for him to return the call. "I'll see him at the dinner tonight," he said, the champagne now tasteless. "Well, we'd better get changed."

"I'm not going, dear."

"Oh but . . ."

"I've lots to do to get ready for tomorrow. You can make an excuse for me—of course you have to go. I'll be ever so busy. There's Glenna's school things—and Duncan gets back on Monday and his school things have to be sorted. You'll have to put him on the aircraft, make sure he has his passport . . . You can easily make an excuse for me tonight as I'm leaving."

He smiled faintly. "Of course, Penn, but what's the real reason?"

"It's going to be a big do. Robin's bound to be there."

"They're not back till tomorrow!"

"No, it was in the *Guardian's* Extra. They arrived this afternoon. The whole delegation. They're sure to be invited." The banquet was being given by a multimillionaire property developer, Sir Shi-teh T'Chung, partially to celebrate the knighthood he had received in the last Honors List, but mostly to launch his latest charity drive for the new wing of the new Elizabeth Hospital. "I've really no wish to go, and so long as you're there, everything'll be all right. I really want an early night too. Please."

"All right. I'll deal with these calls, then I'll be off. I'll see you though before I go." Dunross walked upstairs and went into his study. Lim was waiting there, on guard. He wore a white tunic and black pants and soft shoes. "Evening, Lim," Dunross said in Cantonese.

"Good evening, tai-pan." Quietly the old man motioned him to the window. Dunross could see two men, Chinese, loitering across the street outside the high wall that surrounded the Great House, near the tall, open iron gates. "They've been there some time, tai-pan."

Dunross watched them a moment, disquieted. His own guard had just been dismissed and Brian Kwok, who was also a guest at Sir Shi-teh's tonight, would come by shortly and go with him, acting as a substitute. "If they don't go away by dusk call Superintendent Crosse's office." He wrote the number down, then added in Cantonese, his voice abruptly hard, "While I think of it, Lim, if I want any foreign devil car interfered with, I will order it." He saw the old eyes staring back at him impassively. Lim Chu had been with the family since he was seven, like his father before him, and *his* father, the first of his line who, in the very old days, before Hong Kong had existed, had been Number One Boy and looked after the Struan mansion in Macao.

"I don't understand, tai-pan."

"You cannot wrap fire in paper. The police are clever and old Black Beard's a great supporter of police. Experts can examine brakes and deduce all sorts of information."

"I know nothing of police." The old man shrugged then beamed. "Tai-pan, I do not climb trees to find a fish. Nor do you. May I mention that in the night I could not sleep and I came here. There was a shadow on the veranda balcony. The moment I opened the study door the shadow slid down the drainpipe and vanished into the shrubs." The old man took out a torn piece of cloth. "This was on the drainpipe." The cloth was nondescript.

Dunross studied it, perturbed. He glanced at Dirk Struan's oil painting over the fireplace. It was perfectly in position. He moved it away and saw that the hair he had delicately balanced on a hinge of the safe was untouched. Satisfied, he replaced the picture, then checked the locks on the French windows. The two men were still loitering. For the first time Dunross was very glad that he had an SI guard.

34

It was hot and humid in Phillip Chen's study and he was sitting beside
the phone staring at it nervously. The door swung open and he jumped.
Dianne sailed in.

"There's no point in waiting anymore, Phillip," she said irritably.
"You'd better go and change. That devil Werewolf won't call tonight.
Something must have happened. Do come along!" She wore an evening
chong-sam in the latest, most expensive fashion, her hair bouffant, and she
was bejeweled like a Christmas tree. "Yes. Something must have happened. Perhaps the police . . . huh, it's too much to expect they caught
him. More likely that *fang pi* devil's playing with us. You'd better change
or we'll be late. If you hurr—"

"I really don't want to go," he snapped back at her. "Shitee T'Chung's
a bore and now that he's Sir Shitee he's a double one." Years ago Shi-teh
had adulterated down to become the nickname *Shitee* to his intimate
friends. "Anyway, it's hardly eight o'clock and dinner's not till 9:30 and
he's always late, his banquets are always at least an hour late. For God's
sake, you go!"

"*Ayeeyah* you've got to come. It's a matter of face," she replied, equally
ill-tempered. "My God, after today at the stock market . . . if we don't go
we'll lose terrible face and it's sure to push the stock down further! All
Hong Kong will laugh at us. They can't wait. They'll say we're so
ashamed the House can't pay its bills that we won't show our face in public. Huh! And as for Shitee's new wife, Constance, that mealy-mouthed
whore can't wait to see me humbled!" She was near screeching. Her losses
on the day exceeded 100,000 of her own secret private dollars. When Phillip had called her from the stock market just after three to relate what had
happened she had almost fainted. "*Oh ko* you have to come or we'll be
ruined!"

Miserably her husband nodded. He knew what gossips and rumor-
mongers would be at the banquet. All day he had been inundated with

questions, moans and panic. "I suppose you're right." He was down almost a million dollars on the day and if the run continued and Gornt won he knew he would be wiped out. Oh oh oh why did I trust Dunross and buy so heavily? he was thinking, so angry that he wanted to kick someone. He looked up at his wife. His heart sank as he recognized the signs of her awesome displeasure at the world in general, and him in particular. He quaked inside. "All right," he said meekly. "I won't be a moment."

When he got to the door the phone rang. Once more his heart twisted and he felt sick. There had been four calls since around six. Each had been a business call decrying the fate of the stock, and were the rumors true and *oh ko*, Phillip, I'd better sell—each time worse than the last. "*Weyyyy?*" he asked angrily.

There was a short pause, then an equally rude voice said in crude Cantonese, "You're in a foul temper whoever you are! Where are your fornicating manners?"

"Who's this? Eh, who's calling?" he asked in Cantonese.

"This is the Werewolf. The Chief Werewolf, by all the gods! Who're you?"

"Oh!" The blood drained from Phillip Chen's face. In panic he beckoned his wife. She rushed forward and bent to listen too, everything else forgotten except the safety of the House. "This . . . this is Honorable Chen," he said cautiously. "Please, what's . . . what's your name?"

"Are your ears filled with wax? I said I was the Werewolf. Am I so stupid to give you my name?"

"I'm . . . I'm sorry but how do I know you're . . . you're telling me the truth?"

"How do I know who you are? Perhaps you're a dung-eating policeman. Who are you?"

"I'm Noble House Chen. I swear it!"

"Good. Then I wrote you a letter saying I'd call about 6:00 P.M. today. Didn't you get the letter?"

"Yes, yes I got the letter," Phillip Chen said, trying to control a relief that was mixed with rage and frustration and terror. "Let me talk to my Number One Son, please."

"Every generation thinks they're going to change the world," Dunross

"That's not possible, no, not possible! Can a frog think of eating a swan? Your son's in another part of the Island . . . actually he's in the New Territories, not near a telephone but quite safe, Noble House Chen, oh yes, quite safe. He lacks for nothing. Do you have the ransom money?"

"Yes . . . at least I could only raise 100,000. Th—"

"All gods bear witness to my fornicating patience!" the man said angrily. "You know very well we asked for 500,000! 5 or 10 it's still like one hair on ten oxen to you!"

"Lies!" Phillip Chen shrieked. "That's all lies and rumors spread by my enemies! I'm not that rich. . . . Didn't you hear about the stock market today?" Phillip Chen groped for a chair, his heart pounding, and sat down still holding the phone so she could listen too.

"*Ayeeyah,* stock market! We poor farmers don't deal on the stock market! Do you want his other ear?"

Phillip Chen blanched. "No. But we must negotiate. Five is too much. One and a half I can manage."

"If I settle for one and a half I will be the laughingstock of all China! Are you accusing me of displaying a lamb's head but selling dogmeat? One and a half for the Number One Son of Noble House Chen? Impossible! It's face! Surely you can see that."

Phillip Chen hesitated. "Well," he said reasonably, "you have a point. First I want to know when I get my son back."

"As soon as the ransom's paid! I promise on the bones of my ancestors! Within a few hours of getting the money he'll be put on the main Sha Tin Road."

"Ah, he's in Sha Tin now?"

"*Ayeeyah,* you can't trap me, Noble House Chen. I smell dung in this conversation. Are the fornicating police listening? Is the dog acting fierce because his master's listening? Have you called the police?"

"No, I swear it. I haven't called the police and I'm not trying to trap you, but please, I need assurances, reasonable assurances." Phillip Chen was beaded with sweat. "You're quite safe, you have my oath, I haven't called the police. Why should I? If I call them how can we negotiate?"

There was another long hesitation, then the man said, somewhat mollified, "I agree. But we have your son so any trouble that happens is your fault and not ours. All right, I'll be reasonable too. I will accept 400,000, but it must be tonight!"

"That's impossible! You ask me to fish in the sea to catch a tiger! I didn't get your letter till after the banks were closed but I've got 100,000 cash, in small bills. . . ." Dianne nudged him and held up two fingers. "Listen, Honorable Werewolf, perhaps I can borrow more tonight. Perhaps . . . listen, I will give you two tonight. I'm sure I can raise that within the hour. 200,000!"

"May all gods smite me dead if I sell out for such a fornicating pittance. 350,000!"

"200,000 within the hour!"

"His other ear within two days or 300,000 tonight!"

Phillip Chen wailed and pleaded and flattered and cursed and they negotiated back and forth. Both men were adept. Soon both were caught up in the battle of wits, each using all his powers, the kidnapper using threats, Phillip Chen using guile, flattery and promises. At length, Phillip Chen said, "You are too good for me, too good a negotiator. I will pay 200,000 tonight and a further 100,000 within four months."

"Within one month!"

"Three!" Phillip Chen was aghast at the flow of obscenities that followed and he wondered if he had misjudged his adversary.

"Two!"

Dianne nudged him again, nodding agreement. "Very well," he said, "I agree. Another 100,000 in two months."

"Good!" The man sounded satisfied, then he added, "I will consider what you say and call you back."

"But wait a moment, Honorable Werewolf. When wil—"

"Within the hour."

"Bu—" The line went dead. Phillip Chen cursed, then mopped his brow again. "I thought I had him. God curse the motherless dog turd!"

"Yes." Dianne was elated. "You did very well, Phillip! Only two now and another hundred in two months! Perfect! Anything can happen in two months. Perhaps the dirty police will catch them and then we won't have to pay the hundred!" Happily she took out a tissue and blotted the perspiration off her upper lip. Then her smile faded. "What about Shitee T'Chung? We've got to go but you'll have to wait."

"Ah, I have it! Take Kevin, I'll come later. There'll be plenty of space for me whenever I get there. I'll . . . I'll wait for him to call back."

"Excellent! How clever you are! We've got to get our coin back. Oh very good! Perhaps our joss has changed and the boom will happen like Old Blind Tung forecast. Kevin's so concerned for you, Phillip. The poor boy's so upset that you have all these troubles. He's very concerned for your health." She hurried out, thanking the gods, knowing she would be back long before John Chen returned safely. Perfect, she was thinking, Kevin can wear his new white sharkskin dinner jacket. It's time he began to live up to his new position. "Kevinnnnn!"

The door closed. Phillip Chen sighed. When he had gathered his strength, he went to the sideboard and poured himself a brandy. After Dianne and Kevin had left, he poured himself another. At a quarter to nine the phone rang again.

"Noble House Chen?"

"Yes . . . yes, Honorable Werewolf?"

"We accept. But it has to be tonight!"

Phillip Chen sighed. "Very well. Now wh—"

"You can get all the money?"

"Yes."

"The notes will be hundreds as I asked?"

"Yes. I have 100,000 and can get another hundred from a friend . . ."

"You have rich friends," the man said suspiciously. "Mandarins."

"He's a bookmaker," Phillip Chen said quickly, cursing himself for his slip. "When you hung up I . . . I made the arrangements. Fortunately this happened to be one of his big nights."

"All right. Listen, take a taxi—"

"Oh but I have a car an—"

"I know you have a fornicating car and I know the license number," the man said rudely, "and we know all about you and if you try to betray us to the police you will never see your son again and you will be next on our list! Understand?"

"Yes . . . yes, of course, Honorable Werewolf," Phillip Chen said placatingly. "I'm to take a taxi—where to?"

"The triangle garden at Kowloon Tong. There's a road called Essex Road. There's a wall fence there and a hole in the wall. An arrow drawn on the pavement of the road has its arrowhead pointing at the hole. You put your hand in this hole and you'll get a letter. You read it then our street fighters will approach you and say 'Tin koon chi fook' and you hand the bag over."

"Oh! Isn't it possible I can hand it to the wrong man?"

"You won't. You understand the password and everything?"

"Yes . . . yes."

"How long will it take you to get there?"

"I can come at once. I'll . . . I can get the other money on the way, I can come at once."

"Then come immediately. Come alone, you cannot come with anyone else. You will be watched the moment you leave the door."

Phillip Chen mopped his brow. "And my son? When do I ge—"

"Obey instructions! Beware and come alone."

Again the phone went dead. His fingers were shaking as he picked up the glass and drained the brandy. He felt the warm afterglow but it took away none of his apprehension. When he had collected himself, he dialed a very private number. "I want to speak to Four Finger Wu," he said in Wu's dialect.

"One moment please." There were some muffled Haklo voices, and then, "Is this Mr. Chen, Mr. Phillip Chen?" the voice asked in American English.

"Oh!" he said, startled, then added cautiously, "Who's this?"

"This's Paul Choy, Mr. Chen. Mr. Wu's nephew. My uncle had to go out but he left instructions for me to wait until you called. He's made some arrangements for you. This is Mr. Chen?"

"Yes, yes, it is."

"Ah, great. Have you heard from the kidnappers?"

"Yes, yes I have." Phillip Chen was uneasy talking to a stranger but now he had no option. He told Paul Choy the instructions he had been given.

"Just a moment, sir."

He heard a hand being put over the phone and again muffled, indistinct talking in Haklo dialect for a moment. "Everything's set, sir. We'll send a cab to your house—you're phoning from Struan's Lookout?"

"Yes—yes, I'm home."

"The driver'll be one of our guys. There'll be more of my uncle's, er,

people scattered over Kowloon Tong so not to worry, you'll be covered
every foot of the way. Just hand over the money and, er, and they'll take
care of everything. My uncle's chief lieut—er, his aide, says not to worry,
they'll have the whole area swarming . . . Mr. Chen?"

"Yes, I'm still here. Thank you."

"The cab'll be there in twenty minutes."

Paul Choy put down the phone. "Noble House Chen says thank you,
Honorable Father," he told Four Finger Wu placatingly in their dialect,
quaking under the stony eyes. Sweat was beading his face. He tried unsuccessfully to hide his fear of the others. It was hot and stuffy in the
crowded main cabin of this ancient junk that was tied up in a permanent
berth to an equally ancient dock in one of Aberdeen's multitude of es-
tuaries. "Can I go with your fighters, too?"

"Do you send a rabbit against a dragon?" Four Finger Wu snarled.
"Are you trained as a street fighter? Am I a fool like you? Treacherous
like you?" He jerked a horny thumb at Goodweather Poon. "Lead the
fighters!" The man hurried out. The others followed.

Now the two of them were alone in the cabin.

The old man was sitting on an upturned keg. He lit another cigarette,
inhaled deeply, coughed and spat loudly on the deck floor. Paul Choy
watched him, the sweat running down his back, more from fear than from
the heat. Around them were some old desks, filing cabinets, rickety chairs
and two phones, and this was Four Fingers's office and communications
center. It was mostly from here that he sent messages to his fleets. Much
of his business was regular freighting but wherever the Silver Lotus flag
flew, his order to his captains was: Anything, shipped anywhere, at any
time—at the right price.

The tough old man coughed again and glared at him under shaggy eyebrows. "They teach you curious ways in the Golden Mountain, heya?"

Paul Choy held his tongue and waited, his heart thumping, and wished
he had never come back to Hong Kong, that he was still Stateside, or even
better in Honolulu surfing in the Great Waves or lying on the beach with
his girl friend. His spirit twisted at the thought of her.

"They teach you to bite the hand that feeds you, heya?"

"No, Honored Father, sorr—"

"They teach that my money is yours, my wealth yours and my chop
yours to use as you wish, heya?"

"No, Honored Lord. I'm sorry to displease you," Paul Choy muttered,
wilting under the weight of his fear.

This morning, early, when Gornt had jauntily come into the office from
the meeting with Bartlett, it was still before the secretaries were due so
Paul Choy had asked if he could help him. Gornt had told him to get several people on the phone. Others he had dialed himself on his private line.

Paul Choy had thought nothing of it at the time until he happened to overhear part of what was, obviously, inside information about Struan's being whispered confidentially over the phone. Remembering the Bartlett call earlier, deducing that Gornt and Bartlett had had a meeting—a successful one judging by Gornt's good humor—and realizing Gornt was relating the same confidences over and over, his curiosity peaked. Later, he happened to hear Gornt saying to his solicitor, ". . . selling short . . . No, don't worry, nothing's going to happen till I'm covered, not till about eleven. . . . Certainly. I'll send the order, chopped, as soon as . . ."

The next call he was asked to make was long distance to the manager of the Bank of Switzerland and Zurich that, discreetly, he listened to. ". . . I'm expecting a large draft of U.S. dollars this morning, before eleven. Phone me the instant, the very instant it's in my account . . ."

So, bemused, he had put the various pieces of the equation together and come up with a theory: If Bartlett has arranged a sudden secret partnership with Gornt, Struan's known enemy, to launch one of his raids, if Bartlett also takes part of the risk, or most of it—by secretly putting large sums in one of Gornt's numbered Swiss accounts to cover any sell-short losses—and lastly, if he's talked Gornt into being the front guy while he sits on the fence, the stuff is going to hit the fan in the exchange and Struan's stock has got to go down.

This precipitated an immediate business decision: Jump in quickly and sell Struan's short before the big guys and we'll make a bundle.

He remembered how he had almost groaned aloud because he had no money, no credit, no shares and no means to borrow any. Then he recalled what one of his instructors at Harvard Business School had kept drumming into them: A faint heart never laid a lovely lady. So he'd gone into a private office and phoned his newfound friend, Ishwar Soorjani, the moneylender and dealer in foreign exchange whom he had met through the old Eurasian at the library. "Say, Ishwar, your brother's head of Soorjani Stockbrokers, isn't he?"

"No, Young Master. Arjan is my very first cousin. Why?"

"If I wanted to sell a stock short would you back me?"

"Certainly, as I told you before, buying or selling I support you to the holster, if you have reasonable cash to cover any losses . . . or the equivalent. No cash or equivalent so sorry."

"Say I had some red-hot information?"

"The road to hell and debtor's prison is flooded to drowning with red-hot information, Young Master. I advise against red-hot informations."

"Boy," Paul Choy said unhappily, "I could make us a few 100,000 before three."

"Oh? Would you care to whisper the illustrious name of the stock?"

"Would you back me for . . . for 20,000 U.S.?"

"Ah, so sorry, Young Master, I'm a moneylender not a money giver. My ancestors forbid it!"

"20,000 HK?"

"Not even 10 dollars in your Rebel Dixie redbacks."

"Gee, Ishwar, you're not much help."

"Why not ask your illustrious uncle? His chop . . . and I would instantly go to half a million. HK."

Paul Choy knew that among his father's cash and assets transferred from the Ho-Pak to the Victoria had been many stock certificates and a list of securities held by various stockbrokers. One was for 150,000 Struan shares. Jesus, he thought, if I'm right the old man might get dumped. If Gornt presses the raid the old man could get caught.

"Good idea, Ishwar. I'll call you back!" At once he had phoned his father but he could not reach him. He left messages wherever he could and began to wait. His anxiety grew. Just before ten he heard Gornt's secretary answer the phone. "Yes? . . . Oh, one moment please. . . . Mr. Gornt? A person-to-person call from Zurich. . . . You're through."

Once more he had tried to reach his father, wanting to give him the urgent news. Then Gornt had sent for him. "Mr. Choy, would you please run this over to my solicitor at once." He handed over a sealed envelope. "Give it to him personally."

"Yes sir."

So he had left the office. At every phone he had stopped and tried to reach his father. Then he had delivered the note, personally, watching the solicitor's face carefully. He saw glee. "Is there a reply, sir?" he asked politely.

"Just say everything will be done as ordered." It was a few minutes past ten.

Outside the office door and going down in the elevator Paul Choy had weighed the pluses and the minuses. His stomach twisting uneasily, he stopped at the nearest phone. "Ishwar? Say, I've an urgent order from my uncle. He wants to sell his Struan stock. 150,000 shares."

"Ah, wise wise, there are terrible rumors speeding around."

"I suggested you and Soorjani's should do it for him. 150,000 shares. He asks can you do it instantly? Can you do that?"

"Like a bird on the wing. For the Esteemed Four Fingers we will go forth like Rothschilds! Where are the shares?"

"In the vault."

"I will need his chop at once."

"I'm going to get it now but he said to sell at once. He said to sell in small blocks so as not to shock the market. He wants the very best price. You'll sell at once?"

"Yes, never fear, at once. And we will get the best price!"

"Good. And most important, he said to keep this secret."

"Verily, Young Master, you may trust us implicitly. And the stock that you yourself wished to sell short?"

"Oh that . . . well that'll have to wait . . . until I've credit *heya*?"

"Wise very wise."

Paul Choy shivered. His heart was pounding now in the silence and he watched his father's cigarette, not the angry face, knowing those cold black eyes were boring into him, deciding his fate. He remembered how he had almost shouted with excitement when the stock had begun to fall almost immediately, monitoring it moment by moment, then ordering Soorjani to buy back in just before close and feeling light-headed and in euphoria. At once he had phoned his girl, spending nearly 30 of his valuable U.S. dollars telling her how fantastic his day had been and how much he missed her. She said how much she missed him too and when was he coming back to Honolulu? Her name was Mika Kasunari and she was *sansei*, third-generation American of Japanese descent. Her parents hated him because he was Chinese, as he knew his father would hate her because she was Japanese except they were both American, both of them, and they had met and fallen in love at school.

"Very soon, honey," he had promised her ecstatically, "guaranteed by Christmas! After today my uncle'll surely give me a bonus. . . ."

The work that Gornt gave him for the rest of the day he breezed through. Late in the afternoon Goodweather Poon had phoned to say his father would see him in Aberdeen at 7:30 P.M. Before he went there he had collected Soorjani's check made out to his father. 615,000 HK less brokerage.

Elated, he had come to Aberdeen and given him the check, and when he told him what he had done he was aghast at the extent of his father's rage. The tirade had been interrupted by Phillip Chen's phone call.

"I'm deeply sorry I've offended you, Hon—"

"So my chop is yours, my wealth is yours *heya?*" Four Finger Wu shouted suddenly.

"No, Honored Father," he gasped, "but the information was so good and I wanted to protect your stock as well as make money for you."

"But not for you *heya?*"

"No, Honored Father. It was for you. To make you money, and help repay all the money you invested in me . . . they were your shares and it's your money. I tried to ca—"

"That's no fornicating excuse! You come with me!"

Shakily Paul Choy got up and followed the old man onto the deck. Four Finger Wu cursed his bodyguard away and pointed a stubby finger at the befouled muddy waters in the harbor. "If you weren't my son," he hissed, "if you weren't my son you'd be feeding the fish there, your feet in a chain, this very moment."

"Yes, Father."

"If you ever again use my name, my chop, my anything without my approval you're a dead man."

"Yes, Father," Paul Choy muttered, petrified, realizing that his father had the means, the will and the authority to put that threat into effect without fear of retaliation. "Sorry, Father. I swear I'll never do that again."

"Good. If you'd lost one bronze cash you'd be there now. It's only because you fornicating won that you're alive now."

"Yes, Father."

Four Finger Wu glared at his son and continued to hide his delight at the huge windfall. 615,000 HK less a few dollars. Unbelievable! All with a few phone calls and inside knowledge, he was thinking. That's as miraculous as having ten tons of opium leap ashore over the heads of the Customs boat! The boy's paid for his education twenty times over and he's here hardly three weeks. How clever . . . but also how dangerous!

He shivered at the thought of other minions making decisions themselves. *Dew neh loh moh* then I would be in their power and surely in jail for their mistakes and not my own. And yet, he told himself helplessly, this is the way barbarians act in business. Number Seven Son is trained as a barbarian. All gods bear witness, I did not wish to create a viper!

He looked at his son, not understanding him, hating his direct way of speaking, the barbarian way and not in innuendo and obliquely like a civilized person.

And yet . . . and yet better than 600,000 HK in one day. If I had talked to him beforehand I would never have agreed and I would have lost all that profit! *Ayeeyah!* Yes, my stock would be down all that fortune in one day . . . oh oh oh!

He groped for a box and sat down, his heart thumping at that awful thought.

His eyes were watching his son. What to do about him? he asked himself. He could feel the weight of the check in his pocket. It seemed unbelievable that his son could make that amount of money for him in a few hours, without moving the stock from its hiding place.

"Explain to me why that black-faced foreign devil with the foul name owes me so much money!"

Paul Choy explained the mechanics patiently, desperate to please.

The old man thought about that. "Then tomorrow I should do the same and make the same?"

"No, Honored Father. You take your gains and keep them. Today was almost a certainty. It was a sudden attack, a raid. We do not know how the Noble House will react tomorrow, or if Gornt really intends to continue the raid. He can buy back in and be way ahead too. It would be dangerous to follow Gornt tomorrow, very dangerous."

Four Finger Wu threw his cigarette away. "Then what should I do tomorrow?"

"Wait. The foreign devil market's nervous and in the hands of foreign devils. I counsel you to wait and see what happens with the Ho-Pak and the Victoria. May I use your name to ask the foreign devil Gornt about the Ho-Pak?"

"What?"

Patiently Paul Choy refreshed his father's memory about the bank run and possible stock manipulation.

"Ah, yes, I understand," the old man said loftily. Paul Choy said nothing, knowing he did not. "Then we . . . then I just wait?"

"Yes, Honored Father."

Four Fingers pulled out the check distastefully. "And this fornicating piece of paper? What about this?"

"Convert it into gold, Honored Father. The price hardly varies at all. I could talk to Ishwar Soorjani, if you wish. He deals in foreign exchange."

"And where would I keep the gold?" It was one thing to smuggle other people's gold but quite another to have to worry about your own.

Paul Choy explained that physical possession of the gold was not necessary to own it.

"But I don't trust banks," the old man said angrily. "If it's my gold it's my gold and not a bank's!"

"Yes, Father. But this would be a Swiss bank, not in Hong Kong, and completely safe."

"You guarantee it with your life?"

"Yes, Father."

"Good." The old man took out a pen and signed his name on the back with instructions to Soorjani to convert it at once into gold. He gave it to his son. "On your head, my son. And we wait tomorrow? We don't make money tomorrow?"

"There might be an opportunity for further profit but I could not guarantee it. I might know around noon."

"Call me here at noon."

"Yes, Father. Of course if we had our own exchange we could manipulate a hundred stocks . . ." Paul Choy let the idea hang in the air.

"What?"

Carefully the young man began to explain how easy it would be for them to form their own exchange, a Chinese-dominated exchange, and the limitless opportunities for profit their own exchange would give. He talked for an hour, gaining confidence with the minutes, explaining as simply as he could.

"If it's so easy, my son, why hasn't Tightfist Tung done it—or Big Noise Sung—or Moneybags Ng—or that half-barbarian gold-smuggler from Macao—or Banker Kwang or dozens of others, *heya?*"

"Perhaps they've never had the idea, or courage. Perhaps they want to work within the foreign devil system—the Turf Club, Cricket Club, knighthoods, and all that English foolishness. Perhaps they are afraid to go against the tide or they haven't got the knowledge. We have the knowledge and expertise. Yes. And I've a friend in the Golden Mountain, a good friend, who was at school with me who co—"

"What friend?"

"He's Shanghainese and a dragon in stocks, a broker in New York now. Together, with the cash support, we could do it. I know we could."

"*Ayeeyah!* With a northern barbarian?" Four Finger Wu scoffed. "How could you trust him?"

"I think you could trust him, Honored Father—of course you'd set boundaries against weeds like a good market gardener does."

"But all business power in Hong Kong is in the hands of foreign devils. Civilized persons couldn't support an opposition exchange."

"You may be right, Honored Father," Paul Choy agreed cautiously, keeping his excitement off his face and out of his voice. "But all Chinese love to gamble. Yet at the moment there's not one civilized person stockbroker! Why do foreign devils keep us out? Because we'd outplay them. For us the stock market's the greatest profession in the world. Once our people in Hong Kong see our market is wide open to civilized persons and *their* companies, they'll flock to us. Foreign devils will be forced to open up their own exchange to us as well. We're better gamblers than they are. After all, Honorable Father"—he waved his hand at the shore, at the tall high rises and the boats and junks and floating restaurants—"this could be all yours! It's in stocks and shares and the stock market that the modern man *owns* the might of his world."

Four Fingers smoked leisurely. "How much would your stock market cost, Number Seven Son?"

"A year of time. An initial investment of . . . I don't know exactly." The young man's heart was grinding. He could sense his father's avarice. The implications of forming a Chinese stock exchange in this unregulated capitalistic society were so far-reaching to him that he felt faint. It would be so easy given time and . . . and how much? "I could give you an estimate within a week."

Four Fingers turned his shrewd old eyes on his son and he could read his son's excitement, and his greed. Is it for money, or for power? he asked himself.

It's for both, he decided. The young fool doesn't know that they're both the same. He thought about Phillip Chen's power and the power of the Noble House and the power of the half-coin that John Chen had stolen. Phillip Chen and his wife are fools too, he told himself. They should remember that there are always ears on the other side of walls and once a jealous mother knows a secret it is a secret no longer. Nor can secrets be kept in hotels, among foreign devils, who always presume servants cannot speak the barbarian tongue, nor have long ears and sharp eyes.

Ah sons, he mused. Sons are certainly the wealth of a father—but sometimes also cause the death of the father.

A man's a fool to trust a son. Completely. *Heya?*

"Very well, my son," he said easily. "Give me your plan, written down, and the amount. And I will decide."

* * *

Phillip Chen got out of the taxi at the grass triangle in Kowloon Tong, the attaché case clutched to his chest. The driver turned the meter off and looked at him. The meter read 17.80 HK. If it had been left up to Phillip he would not have taken the same taxi all the way from Struan's Lookout, which meant using the taxi ferry, the meter running all the time. No. He would have crossed the harbor by the Golden Ferry for 15 cents, and got another taxi in Kowloon and saved at least 8 dollars. Terrible waste of money, he thought.

Carefully he counted out 18 dollars. As an afterthought he added a thirty-cent tip, feeling generous. The man drove off and left him standing near the grassy triangle.

Kowloon Tong was just another suburb of Kowloon, a multitudinous nest of buildings, slums, alleys, people and traffic. He found Essex Road, that skirted the garden, and walked around the road. The attaché case seemed to be getting heavier and he felt sure everyone knew it contained 200,000 HK. His nervousness increased. In an area like this you could buy the death of a man for a few hundred if you knew whom to ask—and for this amount, you could hire an army. His eyes were on the broken pavement. When he had gone almost all the way around the triangle he saw the arrow on the pavement pointing at the wall. His heart was weighty in his chest, hurting him. It was quite dark here, with few streetlights. The hole was formed by some bricks that had fallen away. He could see what looked like a crumpled-up newspaper within the hole. He hastily took it out, made sure there was nothing else left, then went over to a seat under a lamp and sat down. When his heart had slowed and his breathing become more calm he opened the newspaper. In it was an envelope. The envelope was flat and some of his anxiety left him. He had been petrified that he was going to get the other ear.

The note said: "Walk to Waterloo Road. Go north toward the army camp, staying on the west side of the road. Beware, we are watching you now."

A shiver went through him and he looked around. No one seemed to be watching him. Neither friend nor foe. But he could feel eyes. His attaché case became even more leaden.

All gods protect me, he prayed fervently, trying to gather his courage to continue. Where the devil are Four Finger Wu's men?

Waterloo Road was nearby, a busy main thoroughfare. He paid the crowds no attention, just plodded north feeling naked, seeing no one in particular. The shops were all open, restaurants bustling, the alleyways more crowded. In the nearby embankment a goods train whistled mournfully, going north, mixing with the blaring horns that all traffic used indiscriminately. The night was bleak, the sky overcast and very humid.

Wearily he walked half a mile, crossing side streets and alleys. In a knot of people he stopped to let a truck pass, then went across the mouth of another narrow alleyway, moving this way and that as oncomers jostled him. Suddenly two young men were in front of him, barring his path, and one hissed, "*Tin koon chi fook!*"

"Eh?"

Both wore caps pulled down low, both wore dark glasses, their faces similar. "*Tin koon chi fook!*" Smallpox Kin repeated malevolently. "*Dew neh loh moh* give me the bag!"

"Oh!" Blankly Phillip Chen handed it to him. Smallpox Kin grabbed it. "Don't look around, and keep on walking north!"

"All right, but please keep your prom—" Phillip Chen stopped. The two youths were gone. It seemed that they had only been in front of him a split second. Still in shock he forced his feet into motion, trying to etch the little he had seen of their faces on his memory. Then an oncoming woman shoved him rudely and he swore, their faces fading. Then someone grabbed him roughly.

"Where's the fornicating bag?"

"What?" he gasped, staring down at the evil-looking thug who was Goodweather Poon.

"Your bag—where's it gone?"

"Two young men . . ." Helplessly he pointed backward. The man cursed and hurried past, weaving in and out of the crowd, put his fingers to his lips and whistled shrilly. Few people paid any attention to him. Other toughs began to converge, then Goodweather Poon caught sight of the two youths with the attaché case as they turned off the well-lit main road into an alley. He broke into a run, others following him.

Smallpox Kin and his younger brother went into the crowds without hurrying, the alley unlit except for the bare bulbs of the dingy stalls and stores. They grinned, one to another. Completely confident now, they took off their glasses and caps and stuffed them into their pockets. Both were very similar—almost twins—and now they melted even more into the raucous shoppers.

"*Dew neh loh moh* that old bastard looked frightened to death!" Smallpox Kin chortled. "In one step we have reached heaven!"

"Yes. And next week when we snatch him he'll pay up as easily as an old dog farts!"

They laughed and stopped a moment in the light of a stall and peeked into the bag. When they both saw the bundle of notes both sighed. "*Ayeeyah*, truly we've reached heaven with one step, Elder Brother. Pity the son is dead and buried."

Smallpox Kin shrugged as they went on, turning into a smaller alley, then another, surefooted in the darkening maze. "Honorable Father's right. We have turned ill luck into good. It wasn't your fault that bastard's head was soft! Not at all! When we dig him up and leave him on the Sha Tin Road with the note on his fornicating chest. . . ." He stopped a moment and they stepped aside in the bustling, jostling crowds to allow a laden, broken-down truck to squeeze past. As they waited he happened to glance back. At the far end of this alley he saw three men change direction, seeing him, then begin to hurry toward him.

"*Dew neh loh moh* we're betrayed," he gasped then shoved his way forward and took to his heels, his brother close behind.

The two youths were very fast. Terror lent cunning to their feet as they rushed through the cursing crowd, maneuvering around the inevitable potholes and small stalls, the darkness helping them. Smallpox Kin led the charge. He ducked between some stalls and fled down the narrow unlit passageway, the attaché case clutched tightly. "Go home a different way, Young Brother," he gasped.

At the next corner he rushed left and his brother went directly on. Their three pursuers split up as well, two following him. It was almost impossible to see now in the darkness and the alleys twisted and turned and never a dead end. His chest was heaving but he was well ahead of his pursuers. He fled into a shortcut and at once turned into a bedraggled store that, like all the rest, served as a dwelling. Careless of the family huddled around a screeching television he rushed through them and out the back door, then doubled back to the end of the alley. He peered around the corner with great caution. A few people watched him curiously but continued on their way without stopping, wanting no part of what clearly was trouble.

Then, hoping he was safe, he slid into the crowds and walked away quietly, his head down. His breath was still labored and his head was filled with obscenities and he swore vengeance on Phillip Chen for betraying them. All gods bear witness, he thought furiously, when we kidnap him next week, before we let him go I'll slice off his nose! How dare he betray us to the police! Hey, wait a moment, were those police?

He thought about that as he wandered along in the stream, cautiously doubling back from time to time, just in case. But now he was sure he was not followed. He let his mind consider the money and he beamed. Let's see, what will I do with my 50,000! I'll put 40 down on an apartment and rent it out at once. *Ayeeyah*, I'm a property owner! I'll buy a Rolex and a revolver and a new throwing knife. I'll give my wife a bracelet or two, and a couple to White Rose at the Thousand Pleasure Whorehouse. Tonight we'll have a feast. . . .

Happily he continued on his way. At a street stall he bought a small cheap suitcase and, in an alley, secretly transferred the money into it. Farther down the street in another side alley he sold Phillip Chen's good leather attaché case to a hawker for a handsome sum after haggling for five minutes. Now, very pleased with himself, he caught a bus for Kowloon City where his father had rented a small apartment in an assumed name as one of their havens, far away from their real home in Wanchai near Glessing's Point. He did not notice Goodweather Poon board the bus, nor the other two men, nor the taxi that followed the bus.

Kowloon City was a festering mess of slums and open drains and squalid dwellings. Smallpox Kin knew he was safe here. No police ever came, except in great strength. When China had leased the New Territories for ninety-nine years in 1898 it had maintained suzerainty over Kowloon City in perpetuity. In theory the ten square acres were Chinese territory. The British authorities left the area alone provided it remained quiet. It was a seething mass of opium dens, illegal gambling schools, triad headquarters, and a sanctuary for the criminal. From time to time the police would sweep through. The next day the Kowloon City would become as it had always been.

The stairs to the fifth-floor apartment in the tenement building were rickety and messy, the plaster cracked and mildewed. He was tired now. He knocked on the door, in their secret code. The door opened.

"Hello, Father, hello, Dog-eared Chen," he said happily. "Here's the cash!" Then he saw his younger brother. "Oh good, you escaped too?"

"Of course! Dung-eating police in civilian clothes! We ought to kill one or two for their impertinence." Kin Pak waved a .38. "We ought to have vengeance!"

"Perhaps you're right, now that we've got the first money," Father Kin said.

"I don't think we should kill any police, that would send them mad," Dog-eared Chen said shakily.

"*Dew neh loh moh* on all police!" young Kin Pak said and pocketed the gun.

Smallpox Kin shrugged. "We've got the cash th—"

At that moment the door burst open. Goodweather Poon and three of his men were in the room, knives out. Everyone froze. Abruptly Father Kin slid a knife out of his sleeve and ducked left but before he could throw it Goodweather Poon's knife was flailing through the air and it thwanged into his throat. He clawed at it as he fell backward. Neither Dog-eared Chen nor the brothers had moved. They watched him die. The body twitched, the muscles spasmed for a moment, then was still.

"Where's Number One Son Chen?" Goodweather Poon said, a second knife in his hand.

"We don't know any Num—"

Two of the men fell on Smallpox Kin, slammed his hands outstretched on the table and held them there. Goodweather Poon leaned forward and sliced off his index finger. Smallpox Kin went gray. The other two were paralyzed with fear.

"Where's Number One Son Chen?"

Smallpox Kin was staring blankly at his severed finger and the blood that was pulsing onto the table. He cried out as Goodweather Poon lunged again. "Don't don't," he begged, "he's dead . . . dead and we've buried him I swear it!"

"Where?"

"Near the Sha . . . the Sha Tin Road. Listen," he screeched desperately, "we'll split the money with you. We'll—" He froze as Goodweather Poon put the tip of his knife into his mouth.

"Just answer questions, you fornicating whore's turd, or I'll slit your tongue. Where's Number One Son's things? The things he had on him?"

"We, we sent everything to Noble House Chen, everything except the money he had. I swear it." He whimpered at the pain. Suddenly the two men put pressure on one of his elbows and he cried out, "All gods bear witness it's the truth!" He screamed as the joint went, and fainted. Across the room Dog-eared Chen groaned with fear. He started to cry out but one of the men smashed him in the face, his head crashed against the wall and he collapsed, unconscious.

Now all their eyes went to Kin Pak. "It's true," Kin Pak gasped in terror at the suddenness of everything. "Everything he told you. It's true!"

Goodweather Poon cursed him. Then he said, "Did you search Noble House Chen before you buried him?"

"Yes, Lord, at least I didn't, he . . ." Shakily he pointed at his father's body. "He did."

"You were there?"

The youth hesitated. Instantly Poon darted at him, moving with incredible speed for such an old man. His knife knicked Kin Pak's cheek a deliberate fraction below his eyes and stayed there. "Liar!"

"I was there," the youth choked out, "I was going to tell you, Lord, I was there. I won't lie to you I swear it!"

"The next time you lie it will be your left eye. You were there, *heya*?"

"Yes . . . yes, Lord!"

"Was he there?" he said pointing at Smallpox Kin.

"No, Lord."

"Him?"

"Yes. Dog-eared was there!"

"Did you search the body?"

"Yes, Lord, yes I helped our father."

"All his pockets, everything?"

"Yes yes everything."

"Any papers? Notebook, diary? Jewelry?"

The youth hesitated, frantic, trying to think, the knife never moving away from his face. "Nothing, Lord, that I remember. We sent all his things to Noble House Chen, except, except the money. We kept the money. And his watch—I'd forgotten his watch! It's, it's that one!" He pointed at the watch on his father's outstretched wrist.

Goodweather Poon swore again. Four Finger Wu had told him to recapture John Chen, to get any of his possessions the kidnappers still had, particularly any coins or parts of coins, and then, equally anonymously, to dispose of the kidnappers. I'd better phone him in a moment, he thought. I'd better get further instructions. I don't want to make a mistake.

"What did you do with the money?"

"We spent it, Lord. There were only a few hundred dollars and some change. It's gone."

One of the men said, "I think he's lying!"

"I'm not, Lord, I swear it!" Kin Pak almost burst into tears. "I'm not. Pl—"

"Shut up! Shall I cut this one's throat?" the man said genially, motioning at Smallpox Kin who was still unconscious, sprawled across the table, the pool of blood thickening.

"No, no, not yet. Hold him there." Goodweather Poon scratched his piles while he thought a moment. "We'll go and dig up Number One Son Chen. Yes that's what we'll do. Now, Little Turd, who killed him?"

At once Kin Pak pointed at his father's body. "He did. It was terrible. He's our father and he hit him with a shovel . . . he hit him with a shovel when he tried to escape the night . . . the night we got him." The youth shuddered, his face chalky, his fear of the knife under his eye consuming him. "It, it wasn't my fault, Lord."

"What's your name?"

"Soo Tak-gai, Lord," he said instantly, using their prearranged emergency names.

"Him?" The finger pointed at his brother.

"Soo Tak-tong."

"Him?"

"Wu-tip Sup."

"And him?"

The youth looked at his father's body. "He was Goldtooth Soo, Lord. He was very bad but we . . . we, we had to obey. We had to obey him, he was our, our father."

"Where did you take Number One Son Chen before you killed him?"

"To Sha Tin, Lord, but I didn't kill him. We snatched him Hong Kong side then put him in the back of a car we stole and went to Sha Tin. There's an old shack our father rented, just outside the village . . . he planned everything. We had to obey him."

Poon grunted and nodded at his men. "We'll search here first." At once they released Smallpox Kin, the unconscious youth who slumped to the floor, leaving a trail of blood. "You, bind up his finger!" Hastily Kin Pak grabbed an old dishcloth and, near vomiting, began to tie a rough tourniquet around the stump.

Poon sighed, not knowing what to do first. After a moment he opened the suitcase. All their eyes went to the mountain of notes. They all felt the greed. Poon shifted the knife into his other hand and closed the suitcase. He left it in the center of the table and started to search the dingy apartment. There was just a table, a few chairs and an old iron bedstead with a soiled mattress. Paper was peeling off the walls, the windows mostly boarded up and glassless. He turned the mattress over, then searched it but it concealed nothing. He went into the filthy, almost empty kitchen and switched on the light. Then into the foul-smelling toilet. Smallpox Kin whimpered, coming around.

In a drawer Goodweather Poon found some papers, ink and writing brushes. "What's this for?" he asked, holding up one of the papers. On it was written in bold characters: "This Number One Son Chen had the stupidity to try to escape us. No one can escape the Werewolves! Let all Hong Kong beware. Our eyes are everywhere!" "What's this for, *heya?*"

Kin Pak looked up from the floor, desperate to please. "We couldn't return him alive to Noble House Chen so our father ordered that . . . that tonight we were to dig Number One Son up and put that on his chest and put him beside the Sha Tin Road."

Goodweather Poon looked at him. "When you start to dig you'd better find him quickly, the first time," he said malevolently. "Yes. Or your eyes, Little Turd, won't be anywhere."

35

Orlanda Ramos came up the wide staircase of the vast *Floating Dragon* restaurant at Aberdeen and moved through the noisy, chattering guests at Sir Shi-teh T'Chung's banquet looking for Linc Bartlett—and Casey.

The two hours that she had spent with Linc this morning for the newspaper interview had been revealing, particularly about Casey. Her instincts had told her the sooner she brought the enemy to battle the better. It had been easy to have them both invited tonight—Shi-teh was an old associate of Gornt and an old friend. Gornt had been pleased with her idea.

They were on the top deck. There was a nice smell of the sea coming through the large windows, the night good though humid, overcast, and all around were the lights of the high rises and the township of Aberdeen. Out in the harbor, nearby, were the brooding islands of junks, partially lit, where 150,000 boat people lived their lives.

The room they were in, scarlet and gold and green, stretched half the length and the whole breadth of the boat, off the central staircase. Ornate wood and plaster gargoyles and unicorns and dragons were everywhere throughout the three soaring decks of the restaurant ablaze with lights and packed with diners. Below decks, the cramped kitchens held twenty-eight cooks, an army of helpers, a dozen huge cauldrons—steam, sweat and smoke. Eighty-two waiters serviced the *Floating Dragon.* There were seats for four hundred on each of the first two decks and two hundred on the third. Sir Shi-teh had taken over the whole top deck and now it was well filled with his guests, standing in impatient groups amid the round tables that seated twelve.

Orlanda felt fine tonight and very confident. She had again dressed meticulously for Bartlett. This morning when she had had the interview with him she had worn casual American clothes and little makeup, and the loose, silk blouse that she had selected so carefully did not flaunt her bralessness, merely suggested it. This daring new fashion pleased her greatly, making her even more aware of her femininity. Tonight she wore delicate white silk. She knew her figure was perfect, that she was envied for her open, unconscious sensuality.

That's what Quillan did for me, she thought, her lovely head high and the curious half-smile lighting her face—one of the many things. He made me understand sensuality.

Havergill and his wife were in front of her and she saw their eyes on her breasts. She laughed to herself, well aware that, even discreetly, she would be the only woman in the room who had dared to be so modern, to emulate the fashion that had begun the year before in Swinging London.

"Evening, Mr. Havergill, Mrs. Havergill," she said politely, moving around them in the crush. She knew him well. Many times he had been invited onto Gornt's yacht. Sometimes Gornt's yacht would steam out from the Yacht Club, Hong Kong side, with just her and Quillan and his men friends aboard and go over to Kowloon, to the sea-washed steps beside the Golden Ferry where the girls would be waiting, dressed in sun clothes or boating clothes.

In her early days with Quillan she too had had to wait Kowloon side, honoring the golden rule in the Colony that discretion was all important and when you live Hong Kong side you play Kowloon side, live Kowloon side, play Hong Kong side.

In the days when Quillan's wife was bedridden and Orlanda was openly, though still most discreetly, Quillan's mistress, Quillan would take her with him to Japan and Singapore and Taiwan but never Bangkok. In those days Paul Havergill was Paul or more likely, Horny—Horny Hav-a-girl, as he was known to most of his intimates. But even then, whenever she would meet him in public, like tonight, it would always be Mr. Havergill. He's not a bad man, she told herself, remembering that though most of his girls never liked him, they fawned on him for he was reasonably generous and could always arrange a sudden loan at low interest for a friend through one of his banking associates, but never at the Vic.

Wise, she thought, amused, and a matter of face. Ah, but I could write such a book about them all if I wanted to. I never will—I don't think I ever will. Why should I, there's no reason. Even after Macao I've always kept the secrets. That's another thing Quillan taught me—discretion.

Macao. What a waste! I can hardly remember what that young man looked like now, only that he was awful at the pillow and, because of him, my life was destroyed. The fool was only a sudden, passing fancy, the very first. It was only loneliness because Quillan was away a month and everyone away, and it was lust for youth—just the youth-filled body that had attracted me and proved to be so useless. Fool! What a fool I was!

Her heart began fluttering at the thought of all those nightmares: being caught, being sent to England, having to fight the youth off, desperate to please Quillan, then coming back and Quillan so cool and never pillowing with him again. And then the greater nightmare of adjusting to a life without him.

Terrifying days. That awful unquenchable desire. Being alone. Being excluded. All the tears and the misery then trying to begin again but cautiously, always hoping he would relent if I was patient. Never anyone in Hong Kong, always alone in Hong Kong, but when the urge was too much, going away and trying but never satisfied. Oh Quillan, what a lover you were!

Not long ago his wife had died and then, when the time was right, Orlanda had gone to see him. To seduce him back to her. That night she had thought that she had succeeded but he had only been toying with her. "Put your clothes on, Orlanda. I was just curious about your body, I wanted to see if it was still as exquisite as it was in *my* day. I'm delighted to tell you it is—you're still perfection. But, so sorry, I don't desire you." And all her frantic weepings and pleadings made no difference. He just listened and smoked a cigarette then stubbed it out. "Orlanda, please don't ever come here again uninvited," he had said so quietly. "You chose Macao."

And he was right, I did, I took his face away. Why does he still support me? she asked herself, her eyes wandering the guests, seeking Bartlett. Do you have to lose something before you find its true value? Is that what life is?

"Orlanda!"

She stopped, startled, as someone stepped in her way. Her eyes focused. It was Richard Hamilton Pugmire. He was slightly shorter than she was. "May I introduce Charles Biltzmann from America," he was saying with a leer, his nearness making her skin crawl. "Charles's going to be, the, er, the new tai-pan of General Stores. Chuck, this's Orlanda Ramos!"

"Pleased to meet you, ma'am!"

"How are you?" she said politely, instantly disliking him. "I'm sorry—"

"Call me Chuck. It's Orlanda? Say, that's a mighty pretty name, mighty pretty dress!" Biltzmann produced his visiting card with a flourish. "Old Chinese custom!"

She accepted it but did not reciprocate. "Thank you. Sorry, Mr. Biltzmann, would you excuse me? I have to join my friends an—" Before she could prevent it, Pugmire took her arm, led her aside a pace and whispered throatily, "How about dinner? You look fantas—"

She jerked her arm away trying not to be obvious. "Go away, Pug."

"Listen, Orlan—"

"I've told you politely fifty times to leave me alone! Now *dew neh loh moh* on you and all your line!" she said and Pugmire flushed. She had always detested him, even in the old days. He was always looking at her behind Quillan's back, leching, and when she had been discarded, Pugmire had pestered her and tried every way to get her into bed—still did. "If you ever call or talk to me again I'll tell all Hong Kong about you and your peculiar habits." She nodded politely to Biltzmann, let his card drop unnoticed and walked off. After a moment, Pugmire went back to the American.

"What a body!" Biltzmann said, his eyes still following her.

"She's—she's one of our well-known whores," Pugmire said with a sneer. "I wish to Christ they'd hurry up with the food. I'm starving."

"She's a tramp?" Biltzmann gaped at him.

"You can never tell here." Pugmire added, keeping his voice down, "I'm surprised Shitee T'Chung invited her. Still, I don't suppose he gives a shit now that his knighthood's dubbed and paid for. Years ago, Orlanda used to be a girlfriend of a friend but she was up to her old tricks of selling it on the side. He caught her at it and gave her the Big E."

"The Big E?"

"The Elbow—the shove."

Biltzmann could not take his eyes off her. "Jesus," he muttered, "I don't know about the Big E but I'd sure as hell like to give her the Big One."

"That's just a matter of money but I can assure you, old chap, she's not worth it. Orlanda's dreadful in the sack, I know, and nowadays you can never tell who's been there before, eh?" Pugmire laughed at the American's expression. "Never fancied her myself after the first time, but if you dip your wick there you'd better use precautions."

Dunross had just arrived and he was listening with half an ear to Richard Kwang who was talking grandly about the deals he had made to stave off the run, and how foul certain people were to spread such rumors.

"I quite agree, Richard," Dunross said, wanting to join the visiting MPs, who were at the far end of the room. "There really are a lot of bastards around. If you'll excuse me . . ."

"Of course, tai-pan." Richard Kwang dropped his voice but could not prevent some of his anxiety showing. "I might need a hand."

"Anything, of course, except money."

"You could talk to Johnjohn at the Vic for me. He'd—"

"He won't, you know that, Richard. Your only chance is one of your Chinese friends. What about Smiler Ching?"

"Huh, that old crook—wouldn't ask him for any of his dirty money!" Richard Kwang said with a sneer. Smiler Ching had reneged on their deal and had refused to lend him money—or credit. "That old crook deserves prison! There's a run on him too, but that's what he deserves! I think it's all started by the Communists, they're trying to ruin us all. The Bank of China! Did you hear about the queues at the Vic in Central? There're more at Blacs. Old Big Belly Tok's Bank of East Asia and Japan's gone under. They won't open their doors tomorrow."

"Christ, are you sure?"

"He called me tonight asking for 20 million. *Dew neh loh moh*, tai-pan, unless we all get help Hong Kong's going under. We've . . ." Then he saw Venus Poon in the doorway on the arm of Four Finger Wu and his heart skipped eight beats. This evening she had been furious when he did not arrive with the mink coat that he had promised her. She had wept and shouted and her *amah* had wailed and they would not accept his excuse that his furrier had let him down and they both had gone on and on until he promised without fail that before the races he would bring her the gift that he had promised.

"Are you taking me to Shi-teh's?"

"My wife changed her mind and now she's going, so I can't, but afterwards we'll go—"

"Afterwards I'll be tired! First no present and now I can't go to the party! Where's the aquamarine pendant you promised me last month? Where did my mink go? On your wife's back I'll bet! *Ayeeyah*, my hairdresser and her hairdresser are friends so I'll find out if it did. Oh woe woe woe you don't really love your Daughter anymore. I'll have to kill myself or accept Four Finger Wu's invitation."

"*Wat?*"

Richard Kwang remembered how he had almost had a hemorrhage then and there, and he had ranted and raved and screamed that her apartment cost him a fortune and her clothes cost thousands a week and she had ranted and raved and screamed back. "And what about the run on the bank? Are you solvent? What about my savings? Are they safe *heya?*"

"*Ayeeyah* you miserable whore, what savings? The savings I am going to put there for you? Huh! Of course they're safe, safe as the Bank of England!"

"Woe woe woe I'm penniless now. Your poor destitute Daughter! I'll have to sell myself or commit suicide. Yes, that's it! Poison . . . that's it! I think I'll take an overdose of . . . of aspirins. *Ah Pool Bring me an overdose of aspirins!*"

So he had begged and pleaded and eventually she had relented and allowed him to take away the aspirins and he had promised to rush back to the apartment the very moment the banquet was over and now his eyes were almost staring out of his head because there, at the doorway, was Venus Poon on the arm of Four Finger Wu, both resplendent, he puffed with pride, and she demure and innocent, wearing the dress he'd just paid for.

"What's up, Richard?" Dunross asked, concerned.

Richard Kwang tried to speak, couldn't, just tottered away toward his wife who tore her baleful eyes off Venus Poon and put them back on him.

"Hello, dear," he said, his backbone jelly.

"Hello, dear," Mai-ling Kwang replied sweetly. "Who's that whore?"

"Which one?"

"That one."

"Isn't that the . . . what's her name . . . the TV starlet?"

"Isn't her name Itch-in-her-drawers Poon, the VD starlet?"

He pretended to laugh with her but he wanted to tear all his hair out. The fact that his latest mistress had come with someone else would not be lost on all Hong Kong. Everyone would interpret it as an infallible sign that he was in absolute financial trouble and that she had, wisely, left the sinking junk for a safer haven. And coming with his uncle, Four Finger Wu, was even worse. That would confirm that all Wu's wealth had been removed from the Ho-Pak, and therefore most probably Lando Mata and the gold syndicate had done the same. All the civilized population that counted were sure that Wu was the syndicate's prime smuggler now that Smuggler Mo was dead. Woe woe woe! Troubles never come singly.

"Eh?" he asked wearily. "What did you say?"

"I said, is the tai-pan going to approach the Victoria for us?"

He switched into Cantonese as Europeans were nearby. "Regretfully that son of a whore's in trouble himself. No, he won't help us. We're in great trouble which is not our fault. The day has been terrible, except for one thing: we made a fine profit today. I sold all our Noble House stock."

"Excellent. At what price?"

"We made 2.70 a share. It's all in gold now in Zurich. I'm putting it all in our joint account," he added carefully, twisting the truth, all the while trying to figure out a ploy to get his wife out of the room so he could go over to Four Finger Wu and Venus Poon to pretend to everyone that everything was fine.

"Good. Very good. That's better." Mai-ling was toying with her huge aquamarine pendant. Suddenly Richard Kwang's testicles chilled. This was the pendant he had promised Venus Poon. Oh woe woe woe . . .

"Are you feeling all right?" Mai-ling asked.

"I, er, I must have eaten some bad fish. I think I need to go to the bathroom."

"You'd better go now. I suppose we'll eat soon. Shitee's always so late!" She noticed him take a nervous sidelong look at Venus Poon and Uncle Wu and her eyes turned baleful again. "That whore's really quite fascinating. I'm going to watch her until you get back."

"Why don't we go together?" He took her arm and guided her down the stairs to the door that led to the bathrooms, greeting friends here and there, trying to exude confidence. The moment she was launched into the ladies' room he rushed back up, walked over to Zeppelin Tung who was near them. He chatted a moment, then pretended to see Four Fingers. "Oh hello, Honored Uncle," he said expansively. "Thank you for bringing her here. Hello, little oily mouth."

"What?" the old man said suspiciously. "I brought her for me not for you."

"Yes, and don't you oily mouth me," Venus Poon hissed and deliberately took the old man's arm and Richard Kwang almost spat blood. "I talked to my hairdresser tonight! My mink on her back! And isn't that my aquamarine pendant too, the one she's wearing right now! To think I almost committed suicide tonight because I thought I'd displeased my Honored Father . . . and all the time it was lies lies lies. Oh I almost want to commit suicide again."

"Eh, don't do that yet, Little Mealy Mouth," Four Finger Wu whispered anxiously, having already negotiated a deal in excess of Smiler Ching's offer. "Go away, Nephew, you're giving her indigestion. She won't be able to perform!"

Richard Kwang forced a glazed smile, muttered a few pleasantries and went off shakily. He headed for the staircase to wait for his wife, and someone said, "I see a certain filly's left the paddock for more manured grass!"

"What nonsense!" he replied at once. "Of course I asked the old fool to bring her since my wife is here. Why else would she be with him? Is that old fool hung like a bullock? Or even a bantam cock? No. *Ayeeyah,* not even Venus Poon with all the technique I taught her can get up what has no thread! It's good for his face to pretend otherwise, *heya?* Of course, and she wanted to see her Old Father and to be seen too!"

"Eeeee, that's clever, Banker Kwang!" the man said, and turned away and whispered it to another, who said caustically, "Huh, you'd swallow a bucket of shit if someone said it was stewed beef with black bean sauce! Don't you know old Four Finger's Stalk's nurtured by the most expensive salves and ointments and ginseng that money can buy? Why only last month his Number Six Concubine gave birth to a son! Eeeee, don't worry about him. Before he's through tonight, Venus Poon's in for a drubbing that'll make her Golden Gully cry out for mercy in eight dialects. . . ."

"Are you staying for dinner, tai-pan?" Brian Kwok asked, intercepting him. "When and if it arrives."

"Yes. Why?"

"Sorry I've got to go back to work. But there'll be someone else to chaperone you home."

"For God's sake, Brian, aren't you overreacting?" Dunross said as quietly.

Brian Kwok kept his voice down. "I don't think so. I've just phoned Crosse to see what happened about those two loiterers outside your house. The moment our fellows arrived they took to their heels."

"Perhaps they were just thugs who don't like police."

Brian Kwok shook his head. "Crosse asked again that you give us the AMG papers right now."

"Friday."

"He told me to tell you there's a Soviet spy ship in port. There's already been one killing—one of their agents, knifed."

Dunross was shocked. "What's that got to do with me?"

"You know that better than we do. You know what's in those reports.

Must be quite serious or you wouldn't be so difficult—or careful—yourself. Crosse said . . . Never mind him! Ian, look, we're old friends. I'm really very worried." Brian Kwok switched to Cantonese. "Even the wise can fall into thorns—poisoned thorns."

"In two days the police Mandarin arrives. Two days is not long."

"True. But in two days the spy may hurt us very much. Why tempt the gods? It is my ask."

"No. Sorry."

Brian Kwok hardened. In English he said, "Our American friends have asked us to take you into protective custody."

"What nonsense!"

"Not such nonsense, Ian. It's very well known you've a photographic memory. The sooner you turn the papers over the better. Even afterwards you should be careful. Why not tell me where they are and we'll take care of everything?"

Dunross was equally set-faced. "Everything's taken care of now, Brian. Everything stays as planned."

The tall Chinese sighed. Then he shrugged. "Very well. Sorry, but don't say you weren't warned. Are Gavallan and Jacques staying for dinner too?"

"No, I don't think so. I asked them just to put in an appearance. Why?"

"They could've gone home with you. Please don't go anywhere alone for a while, don't try to lose your guard. For the time being, if you have any, er, private dates call me."

"Me, a private date? Here in Hong Kong? Really, what a suggestion!"

"Does the name Jen mean anything?"

Dunross's eyes became stony. "You buggers can be too nosy."

"And you don't seem to realize you're in a very dirty game without Queensberry rules."

"I've got that message, by God."

" 'Night, tai-pan."

" 'Night, Brian." Dunross went over to the MPs who were in a group in one corner talking with Jacques deVille. There were only four of them now, the rest were resting after their long journey. Jacques deVille introduced him. Sir Charles Pennyworth, Conservative; Hugh Guthrie, Liberal; Julian Broadhurst and Robin Grey, both Labour. "Hello, Robin," he said.

"Hello, Ian. It's been a long time."

"Yes."

"If you'll excuse me, I'll be off," deVille said, his face careworn. "My wife's away and we've a young grandchild staying with us."

"Did you talk to Susanne in France?" Dunross asked.

"Yes, tai-pan. She's . . . she'll be all right. Thank you for calling Deland. See you tomorrow. Good night, gentlemen." He walked off.

Dunross glanced back at Robin Grey. "You haven't changed at all."

"Nor have you," Grey said, then turned to Pennyworth. "Ian and I met in London some years ago, Sir Charles. It was just after the war. I'd just become a shop steward." He was a lean man with thin lips, thin graying hair and sharp features.

"Yes, it was some years ago," Dunross said politely, continuing the pattern that Penelope and her brother had agreed to so many years ago—that neither side was blood kin to the other. "So, Robin, are you staying long?"

"Just a few days," Grey said. His smile was as thin as his lips. "I've never been in this workers' paradise before so I want to visit a few unions, see how the other ninety-nine percent live."

Sir Charles Pennyworth, leader of the delegation, laughed. He was a florid, well-covered man, an ex-colonel of the London Scottish Regiment, D.S.O. and Bar. "Don't think they go much on unions here, Robin. Do they, tai-pan?"

"Our labor force does very well without them," Dunross said.

"Sweated labor, tai-pan," Grey said at once. "According to some of your own statistics, government statistics."

"Not our statistics, Robin, merely your statisticians," Dunross said. "Our people are the highest paid in Asia after the Japanese and this is a free society."

"Free? Come off it!" Grey jeered. "You mean free to exploit the workers. Well, never mind, when Labour gets in at the next election we'll change all that."

"Come now, Robin," Sir Charles said. "Labour hasn't a prayer at the next election."

Grey smiled. "Don't bet on it, Sir Charles. The people of England want change. We didn't all go to war to keep up the rotten old ways. Labour's for social change—and getting the workers a fair share of the profits they create."

Dunross said, "I've always thought it rather unfair that Socialists talk about the 'workers' as though they do all the work and we do none. We're workers too. We work as hard if not harder with longer hours an—"

"Ah, but you're a tai-pan and you live in a great big house that was handed down, along with your power. All that capital came from some poor fellow's sweat, and I won't even mention the opium trade that started it all. It's fair that capital should be spread around, fair that everyone should have the same start. The rich should be taxed more. There should be a capital tax. The sooner the great fortunes are broken up the better for all Englishmen, eh, Julian?"

Julian Broadhurst was a tall, distinguished man in his mid-forties, a strong supporter of the Fabian Society, which was the intellectual brain trust of the socialist movement. "Well, Robin," he said with his lazy, almost diffident voice, "I certainly don't advocate as you do that we take to the barricades but I do think, Mr. Dunross, that here in Hong Kong you could do with a Trades Union Council, a minimum wage scale, elected legislature, proper unions and safeguards, socialized medicine, workman's compensation and all the modern British innovations."

"Totally wrong, Mr. Broadhurst. China would never agree to a change in our colonial status, they would never allow any form of city-state on her border. As to the rest, who pays for them?" Dunross asked. "Our unfettered system here's outperforming Britain twenty times and—"

"You pay for it out of all your profits, Ian," Robin Grey said with a laugh. "You pay a fair tax, not 15 percent. You pay the same as we do in Britain and—"

"God forbid!" Dunross said, hard put to keep his temper. "You're taxing yourself out of business and out of c—"

"Profit?" the last MP, the Liberal, Hugh Guthrie interrupted caustically. "The last bloody Labour Government wiped out our profits years ago with bloody stupid profligate spending, ridiculous nationalization, giving the Empire away piecemeal with fatuous stupid abandon, disrupting the Commonwealth and shoving poor old England's face in the bloody mud. Bloody ridiculous! Attlee and all that shower!"

Robin Grey said placatingly, "Come on, Hugh, the Labour Government did what the people wanted, what the masses wanted."

"Nonsense! The enemy wanted it. The Communists! In barely eighteen years you gave away the greatest empire the world's ever seen, made us a second-class power and allowed the sodding Soviet enemy to eat up most of Europe. Bloody ridiculous!"

"I agree wholeheartedly that communism's dreadful. But as to 'giving away our empire, it was the wind of change, Hugh," Broadhurst said, calming him. "Colonialism had run its course. You really must take the long-term view."

"I do. I think we're up the creek without a paddle. Churchill's right, always was."

"The people didn't think so," Grey said grimly. "That's why he was voted out. The armed service vote did that, they'd had enough of him. As to the Empire, sorry Hugh old chap, but it was just an excuse to exploit natives who didn't know any better." Robin Grey saw their faces and read them. He was used to the hatred that surrounded him. He hated them more and always had. After the war he had wanted to stay in the Regular Army but he had been rejected—captains were two a penny then with decorations and great war service, while he spent the war a POW at Changi. So, filled with anger and resentment, he had joined Crawley's, a huge car manufacturer, as a mechanic. Quickly he had become a shop steward and union organizer, then into the lower ranks of the Trades Union General Council. Five years ago, he had become a Labour MP where he was now, a cutting, angry, hostile backbencher and protégé of the late left-wing Socialist Aneurin Bevan. "Yes, we got rid of Churchill and when we get in next year we'll sweep out a lot more of the old tired ways and upper-class infections back where they belong. We'll nationalize every industry an—"

"Really, Robin," Sir Charles said, "this is a banquet not a soapbox in Hyde Park. We all agreed to cut out politics while we were on the trip."

"You're right, Sir Charles. It was just that the tai-pan of the Noble House asked me." Grey turned to Dunross. "How is the Noble House?"

"Fine. Very fine."

"According to this afternoon's paper there's a run on your stock?"

"One of our competitors is playing silly buggers, that's all."

"And the bank runs? They're not serious either?"

"They're serious." Dunross was choosing his words carefully. He knew the anti–Hong Kong lobby in Parliament was strong and many members of all three parties were against its colonial status, against its nonvoting status and freewheeling nature—and most of all envious of its almost tax-free basis. Never mind, he thought. Since 1841 we've survived hostile Parliaments, fire, typhoon, pestilence, plague, embargo, depression, occupation and the periodic convulsions that China goes through, and somehow we always will.

"The run's on the Ho-Pak, one of our Chinese banks," Dunross said.

"It's the largest, isn't it?" Grey said.

"No. But it's large. We're all hoping it'll weather the problem."

"If it goes broke, what about all the depositors' money?"

"Unfortunately they lose it," Dunross said, backed into a corner.

"You need English banking laws."

"No, we've found our system operates very well. How did you find China?" Dunross asked.

Before Sir Charles could answer, Grey said, "Our majority view is that they're dangerous, hostile, should be locked up and the Hong Kong border sealed. They're openly committed to becoming a world irritant and their brand of communism is merely an excuse for dictatorship and exploitation of their masses."

Dunross and the other Hong Kong *yan* blanched as Sir Charles said sharply, "Come now, Robin, that's only your view and the Comm—the, er, and McLean's. I found just the opposite. I think China's very sincere in trying to deal with the problems of China, which are hideous, monumental and I think insoluble."

"Thank God there's going to be big trouble there," Grey said with a sneer. "Even the Russians knew it, why else would they get out?"

"Because they're enemies, they share a common five thousand miles of border," Dunross said trying to hold in his anger. "They've always distrusted each other. Because China's invader has always come out of the West, and Russia's always out of the East. Possession of China's always been Russia's obsession and preoccupation."

"Come now, Mr. Dunross," Broadhurst began. "You exaggerate, surely."

"It's to Russia's advantage to have China weak and divided, and Hong Kong disrupted. Russia *requires* China weak as a cornerstone of its foreign policy."

"At least Russia's civilized," Grey said. "Red China's fanatic, dangerous and heathen and should be cut off, particularly from here."

"Ridiculous!" Dunross said tightly. "China has the oldest civilization on earth. China desperately wants to be friends with the West. China's Chinese first and Communist second."

"Hong Kong and you 'traders' are keeping the Communists in power."

"Rubbish! Mao Tse-tung and Chou En-lai don't need us or the Soviets to stay in Peking!"

Hugh Guthrie said, "As far as I'm concerned Red China and Soviet Russia're equally dangerous."

"There's no comparison!" Grey said. "In Moscow they eat with knives and forks and understand food! In China we had nothing but rotten food, rotten hotels and lots of double-talk."

"I really don't understand you at all, old boy," Sir Charles said irritably. "You fought like hell to get on this committee, you're supposed to be interested in Asian affairs and you've done nothing but complain."

"Being critical's not complaining, Sir Charles. Bluntly, I'm for giving Red China no help at all. None. And when I get back I'm offering a motion to change Hong Kong's status entirely: to embargo everything from and to Communist China, to hold immediate and proper elections here, introduce proper taxes, proper unionism and proper British social justice!"

Dunross's chin jutted. "Then you'll destroy our position in Asia!"

"Of all the tai-pans, yes, the people no! Russia was right about China."

"I'm talking about the Free World! Christ almighty, it should be clear to everyone—Soviet Russia's committed to hegemony, to world domination and our destruction. China isn't," Dunross said.

"You're wrong, Ian. You can't see the wood for the trees," Grey said. "Listen! If Russia . . ."

Broadhurst interrupted smoothly. "Russia's just trying to solve her own problems, Mr. Dunross, one of them's the U.S. containment policy. They just want to be left alone and not surrounded by highly emotional Americans with their overfed hands on nuclear triggers."

"Balls! The Yanks're the only friends we've got," Hugh Guthrie said angrily. "As to the Soviets, what about the Cold War? Berlin? Hungary? Cuba, Egypt . . . they're swallowing us piecemeal."

Sir Charles Pennyworth sighed. "Life's strange and memories are so short. In '45, May second it was, in the evening, we joined up with the Russians at Wismar in northern Germany. I'd never been so proud or happy in my life, yes, proud. We sang and drank and cheered and toasted each other. Then my division and all of us in Europe, all the Allies had been held back for weeks to let the Russkies sweep into Germany all through the Balkans, Czechoslovakia and Poland and all the other places.

At the time I didn't think much about it, I was so thankful that the war was almost over at long last and so proud of our Russian allies, but you know, looking back, now I know we were betrayed, we soldiers were betrayed—Russian soldiers included. We got buggered. I don't really know how it happened, still don't, but I truly believe we were betrayed, Julian, by our own leaders, your bloody Socialists, along with Eisenhower, Roosevelt and his misguided advisors. I swear to God I still don't know how it happened but we lost the war, we won but we lost."

"Come now, Charles, you're quite wrong. We all won," Broadhurst said. "The people of the world won when Nazi Germany was sma—" He stopped, startled, as he saw the look on Grey's face. "What's the matter, Robin?"

Grey was staring at the other side of the room. "Ian! That man over there talking to the Chinese . . . do you know him? The tall bugger in the blazer."

Equally astonished, Dunross glanced at the other side of the room. "The sandy-haired fellow? You mean Marlowe, Pete—"

"Peter bloody Marlowe!" Grey muttered. "What's . . . what's he doing in Hong Kong?"

"He's just visiting. From the States. He's a writer. I believe he's writing or researching a book on Hong Kong."

"Writer, eh? Curious. Is he a friend of yours?"

"I met him a few days ago. Why?"

"That's his wife—the girl next to him?"

"Yes. That's Fleur Marlowe, why?"

Grey did not answer. There was a fleck of saliva at the corner of his lips.

"What's his connection with you, Robin?" Broadhurst asked, strangely perturbed.

With an effort Grey tore his eyes off Marlowe. "We were in Changi together, Julian, the Jap POW camp. I was provost marshal for the last couple of years, in charge of camp discipline." He wiped the sweat off his top lip. "Marlowe was one of the black marketeers there."

"Marlowe?" Dunross was astounded.

"Oh yes, Flight Lieutenant Marlowe, the great English gentleman," Grey said, his voice raw with bitterness. "Yes. He and his pal, an American called King, Corporal King, were the main ones. Then there was a fellow called Timsen, an Aussie. . . . But the American was the biggest, he was the King all right. A Texan. He had colonels on his payroll, English gentlemen all—colonels, majors, captains. Marlowe was his interpreter with the Jap and Korean guards . . . we mostly had Korean guards. They were the worst. . . ." Grey coughed. "Christ, it's such a short time ago. Marlowe and the King lived off the fat of the land—those two buggers ate at least one egg a day, while the rest of us starved. You can't imagine how . . ." Again Grey wiped the sweat off his lip without noticing it.

"How long were you a POW?" Sir Charles asked compassionately.

"Three and a half years."

"Terrible," Hugh Guthrie said. "My cousin bought it on the Burma railroad. Terrible!"

"It was all terrible," Grey said. "But it wasn't so terrible for those who sold out. On the Road or at Changi!" He looked at Sir Charles and his eyes were strange and bloodshot. "It's the Marlowes of the world who betrayed us, the ordinary people without privileges of birth." His voice became even more bitter. "No offense but now you're all getting your comeuppance and about time. Christ, I need a drink. Excuse me a moment." He stalked off, heading for the bar that was set up to one side.

"Extraordinary," Sir Charles said.

Guthrie said with a slight, nervous laugh, "For a moment I thought he was going for Marlowe."

They all watched him, then Broadhurst noticed Dunross frowning after Grey, his face set and cold. "Don't pay any attention to him, Mr. Dunross. I'm afraid Grey's very tiresome and a rather vulgar bore. He's . . . well he's not at all representative of the Labour echelon, thank God. You'd like our new leader, Harold Wilson, you'd approve of him. Next time you're in London I'd be glad to introduce you if you've time."

"Thank you. Actually I was thinking about Marlowe. It's hard to believe he 'sold out' or betrayed anyone."

"You never know about people, do you?"

Grey got a whiskey and soda and turned and went across the room. "Well, if it isn't Flight Lieutenant Marlowe!"

Peter Marlowe turned, startled. His smile vanished and the two men stared at one another. Fleur Marlowe froze.

"Hello, Grey," Marlowe said, his voice flat. "I heard you were in Hong Kong. In fact, I read your interview in the afternoon paper." He turned to his wife. "Darling, this is Robin Grey, MP." He introduced him to the Chinese, one of whom was Sir Shi-teh T'Chung.

"Ah, Mr. Grey, it's an honor to have you here," Shi-teh said with an Oxford English accent. He was tall, dark, good-looking, slightly Chinese and mostly European. "We hope your stay in Hong Kong will be good. If there's anything I can do, just say the word!"

"Ta," Grey said carelessly. They all noticed his rudeness. "So, Marlowe! You haven't changed much."

"Nor have you. You've done well for yourself." Marlowe added to the others, "We were in the war together. I haven't seen Grey since '45."

"We were POWs, Marlowe and I," Grey said, then added, "We're on opposite sides of the political blanket." He stopped and stepped out of the way to allow Orlanda Ramos to pass. She greeted Shi-teh with a smile and continued on. Grey watched her briefly, then turned back. "Marlowe old chap, are you still in trade?" It was a private English insult. "Trade" to someone like Marlowe who came from a long line of English officers meant everything common and lower class.

"I'm a writer," Marlowe said. His eyes went to his wife and his eyes smiled at her.

"I thought you'd still be in the RAF, regular officer like your illustrious forebears."

"I was invalided out, malaria and all that. Rather boring," Marlowe said, deliberately lengthening his patrician accent knowing that it would infuriate Grey. "And you're in Parliament? How very clever of you. You represent Streatham East? Wasn't that where you were born?"

Grey flushed. "Yes, yes it was . . ."

Shi-teh covered his embarrassment at the undercurrents between them. "I must, er, see about dinner." He hurried off. The other Chinese excused themselves and turned away.

Fleur Marlowe fanned herself. "Perhaps we should find our table, Peter," she said.

"A good idea, Mrs. Marlowe," Grey said. He was in as tight control as Peter Marlowe. "How's the King?"

"I don't know. I haven't seen him since Changi." Marlowe looked down on Grey.

"But you're in touch with him?"

"No. No, actually I'm not."

"You don't know where he is?"

"No."

"That's strange, seeing how close you two were." Grey ripped his eyes away and glanced at Fleur Marlowe and thought she was the prettiest woman he had ever seen. So pretty and fine and English and fair, just like his ex-wife Trina who went off with an American barely a month after he was reported missing in action. Barely a month. "Did you know we were enemies in Changi, Mrs. Marlowe?" he said with a gentleness that she found frightening.

"Peter's never discussed Changi with me, Mr. Grey. Or anyone that I know of."

"Curious. It was an awesome experience, Mrs. Marlowe. I've forgotten none of it. I . . . well, sorry to interrupt . . ." He glanced up at Marlowe. He began to say something but changed his mind and turned away.

"Oh, Peter, what an awful man!" Fleur said. "He gave me the creeps."

"Nothing to bother about, my darling."

"Why were you enemies?"

"Not now, my pet, later." Marlowe smiled at her, loving her. "Grey's nothing to us."

36

Linc Bartlett saw Orlanda before she saw him and she took his breath away. He couldn't help comparing her with Casey who was beside him talking to Andrew Gavallan. Orlanda was wearing white silk, floor-length, backless with a halter neck that, discreetly, somehow, seemed to offer her golden body. Casey wore her green that he had seen many times, her tawny hair cascading.

"Would you both like to come to Shi-teh's tonight?" Orlanda had asked him this morning. "It could be important for you and your Casey to be there."

"Why?"

"Because almost all business that counts in Hong Kong is done at this type of function, Mr. Bartlett. It could be very important for you to become involved with people like Shi-teh—and in the Turf Club, Cricket Club, even *the* Club itself, though that'd be impossible."

"Because I'm American?"

"Because someone has to die to create an opening—an English or Scotsman." She had laughed. "The waiting list's as long as Queen's Road! It's men only, very stuffy, old leather chairs, old men sleeping off their three-hour and ten-gin lunches, *The Times* and all that."

"Hell, that sounds exciting!"

She had laughed again. Her teeth were white and he could see no blemish in her. They had talked over breakfast and he had found her more than easy to talk to. And to be with. Her perfume was enticing. Casey rarely wore perfume—she said that she'd found it just another distraction to the businessmen she had to deal with. With Orlanda, breakfast had been coffee and toast and eggs and crisp bacon, American style, at a brand-new hotel she suggested, called the Mandarin. Casey didn't eat breakfast. Just coffee and toast sometimes, or croissants.

The interview had passed easily and the time too fast. He had never been in the company of a woman with such open and confident femininity. Casey was always so strong, efficient and cool and not feminine. By choice, her choice and my agreement, he reminded himself.

"That's Orlanda?" Casey was looking at him, one eyebrow arched.

"Yes," he replied, trying unsuccessfully to read her. "What do you think?"

"I think she's dynamite."

"Which way?"

Casey laughed. She turned to Gavallan who was trying to concentrate and be polite but whose mind was taken up with Kathy. After Kathy had told him this evening, he had not wanted to leave her but she had insisted, saying that it was important for him to be there. "Do you know her, Andrew?"

"Who?"

"The girl in white."

"Where? Oh! Oh yes, but only by reputation."

"Is it good or bad?"

"That, er, depends on your point of view, Casey. She's, she's Portuguese, Eurasian, of course. Orlanda was Gornt's friend for quite a few years."

"You mean his mistress?"

"Yes, I suppose that's the word," he told her politely, disliking Casey's directness intensely. "But it was all very discreet."

"Gornt's got taste. Did you know she was his steady, Linc?"

"She told me this morning. I met her at Gornt's a couple of days ago. He said they were still friends."

"Gornt's not to be trusted," Gavallan said.

Casey said, "He's got heavy backers, in and outside Hong Kong, I was told. Far as I know he's not stretched at the moment, as you are. You must have heard he wants us to deal with him, not you."

"We're not stretched," Gavallan said. He looked at Bartlett. "We do have a deal?"

"We sign Tuesday. If you're ready," Bartlett said.

"We're ready now."

"Ian wants us to keep it quiet till Saturday and that's fine with us," Casey said. "Isn't it, Linc?"

"Sure." Bartlett glanced back at Orlanda. Casey followed his eyes.

She had noticed her the first moment the girl had hesitated in the doorway. "Who's she talking to, Andrew?" The man was interesting-looking, lithe, elegant and in his fifties.

"That's Lando Mata. He's also Portuguese, from Macao." Gavallan wondered achingly if Dunross would manage to persuade Mata to come to their rescue with all his millions. What would I do if I was tai-pan? he asked himself wearily. Would I buy tomorrow, or make a deal with Mata and Tightfist tonight? With their money, the Noble House would be safe for generations, though out of our control. No point in worrying now.

Wait till you're tai-pan. Then he saw Mata smiling at Orlanda and then both of them looked over and began to thread their way toward them. His eyes watched her firm breasts, free under the silk. Taut nipples. Good God, he thought, awed, even Venus Poon wouldn't dare do that. When they came up he introduced them and stood back, odd man out, wanting to watch them.

"Hello," Orlanda said warmly to Casey. "Linc told me so much about you and how important you are to him."

"And I've heard about you too," Casey said as warmly. But not enough. You're much more lovely than Linc indicated, she thought. Very much more. So you're Orlanda Ramos. Beautiful and soft-spoken and feminine and a bitch piranha who has set her sights on my Linc. Jesus, what do I do now?

She heard herself making small talk but her mind was still thinking Orlanda Ramos through. On the one hand it would be good for Linc to have an affair, she thought. It would take the heat out of him. Last night was as lousy for him as it was for me. He was right about me moving out. But once this one's magic surrounds him could I extract him? Would she be just another girl like the others that were nothing to me and after a week or so, nothing to him either?

Not this one, Casey decided with finality. I've got two choices. I either stick to thirteen weeks and four days and do battle, or don't and do battle.

She smiled. "Orlanda, your dress is fantastic."

"Thanks. May I call you Casey?"

Both women knew the war had begun.

Bartlett was delighted that Casey obviously liked Orlanda. Gavallan watched, fascinated by the four of them. There was a strange warmth among them all. Particularly between Bartlett and Orlanda.

He turned his attention to Mata and Casey. Mata was suave, filled with old world charm, concentrating on Casey, playing her like a fish. I wonder how far he'll get with this one. Curious that Casey doesn't seem to mind Orlanda at all. Surely she's noticed that her boyfriend's smitten? Perhaps she hasn't. Or perhaps she couldn't care less and she and Bartlett are just business partners and nothing else. Perhaps she's a dyke after all. Or maybe she's just frigid like a lot of them. How sad!

"How do you like Hong Kong, Miss Casey?" Mata asked, wondering what she would be like in bed.

"Afraid I haven't seen much of it yet though I did go out to the New Territories on the hotel tour and peek into China."

"Would you like to go? I mean really go into China? Say to Canton? I could arrange for you to be invited."

She was shocked. "But we're forbidden to go into China . . . our passports aren't valid."

"Oh, you wouldn't have to use your passport. The PRC doesn't bother with passports. So few *quai loh* go into China there's no problem. They give you a written visa and they stamp that."

"But our State Department . . . I don't think I'd risk it right now."

Bartlett nodded. "We're not even supposed to go into the Communist store here. The department store."

"Yes, your government really is very strange," Mata said. "As if going into a store is subversive! Did you hear the rumor about the Hilton?"

"What about it?"

"The story is that they bought a marvelous collection of Chinese antiques for the new hotel, of course all locally." Mata smiled. "It seems that now the U.S. has decided they can't use any of it, even here in Hong Kong. It's all in storage. At least that's the story."

"It figures. If you can't make it in the States, you join the government," Bartlett said sourly.

"Casey, you should decide for yourself," Mata said. "Visit the store. It's called China Arts and Crafts on Queen's Road. The prices are very reasonable and the Communists really don't have horns and barbed tails."

"It's nothing like what I expected," Bartlett said. "Casey, you'd freak out at some of the things."

"You've been?" she asked, surprised.

"Sure."

"I took Mr. Bartlett this morning," Orlanda explained. "We happened to be passing. I'd be glad to go shopping with you if you wish."

"Thanks, I'd like that," Casey said as nicely, all her danger signals up. "But we were told in L.A. the CIA monitors Americans who go in and out because they're sure it's a Communist meeting place."

"It looked like an ordinary store to me, Casey," Bartlett said. "I didn't see anything except a few posters of Mao. You can't bargain though. All prices're written out. Some of the biggest bargains you ever did see. Pity we can't take them back home." There was a total embargo on all goods of Chinese origin into the States, even antiques that had been in Hong Kong a hundred years.

"That's no problem," Mata said at once, wondering how much he would make as a middleman. "If there's anything you want I'd be happy to purchase it."

"But we still can't get it into the States, Mr. Mata," Casey said.

"Oh that's easy too. I do it for American friends all the time. I just send their purchases to a company I have in Singapore or Manila. For a tiny fee they send it to you in the States with a certificate of origin, Malaya or the Philippines, whichever you'd prefer."

"But that'd be cheating. Smuggling."

Mata, Gavallan and Orlanda laughed outright and Gavallan said, "Trade's the grease of the world. Embargoed goods from the U.S. or Taiwan find their way to the PRC, PRC goods go to Taiwan and the U.S.—if they're sought after. Of course they do!"

"I know," Casey said, "but I don't think that's right."

"Soviet Russia's committed to your destruction but you still trade with her," Gavallan said to Bartlett.

"We don't ourselves," Casey said. "Not Par-Con, though we've been approached to sell computers. Much as we like profits they're a no-no. The government does, but only on very carefully controlled goods. Wheat, things like that."

"Wherever there's a willing buyer of anything, there'll always be a seller," Gavallan said, irritated by her. He glanced out of the windows and wished he was back in Shanghai. "Take Vietnam, your Algiers."

"Sir?" Casey said.

Gavallan glanced back at her. "I mean that Vietnam will bleed your economy to death as it did to France and as Algiers also did to France."

"We'll never go into Vietnam," Bartlett said confidently. "Why should we? Vietnam's nothing to do with us."

"I agree," Mata said, "but nevertheless the States is having a growing involvement there. In fact, Mr. Bartlett, I think you're being sucked into the abyss."

"In what way?" Casey asked.

"I think the Soviets have deliberately enticed you into Vietnam. You'll send in troops but they won't. You'll be fighting Viets and the jungle, and the Soviets will be the winners. Your CIA's already there in strength. They're running an airline. Even now airfields are being constructed with U.S. money, U.S. arms are pouring in. You've soldiers fighting there already."

"I don't believe it," Casey said.

"You can. They're called Special Forces, sometimes Delta Force. So sorry but Vietnam's going to be a big problem for your government unless it's very smart."

Bartlett said confidently, "Thank God it is. JFK handled Cuba. He'll handle Vietnam too. He made the Big K back off there and he can do it again. We won that time. The Soviets took their missiles out."

Gavallan was grimly amused. "You should talk to Ian about Cuba, old chap, that really gets him going. He says, and I agree, you lost. The Soviets sucked you into another trap. A fool's mate. He believes they built their sites almost openly—wanting you to detect them and you did and then there was a lot of saber-rattling, the whole world's frightened to death, and in exchange for the Soviet agreement to take the missiles out of Cuba your President tore up your Monroe Doctrine, the cornerstone of your whole security system."

"What?"

"Certainly. Didn't JFK give Khrushchev a written promise not to invade Cuba, not to permit an invasion from American territory—or from any other place in the Western Hemisphere? *Written*, by God! So now, a hostile European power, Soviet Russia, totally against your Monroe Doctrine, is openly established ninety miles off your coast, the borders of which are guaranteed in writing by your own President and ratified by your own Congress. The Big K pulled off a colossal coup never duplicated in your whole history. And all for nothing!" Gavallan's voice harshened. "Now Cuba's nicely safe, thank you very much, where it'll grow, expand and eventually infect all South America. Safe for Soviet subs, ships, aircraft. . . . Christ almighty that's certainly a marvelous victory!"

Casey looked at Bartlett, shocked. "But surely, Linc, surely that's not right."

Bartlett was as shocked. "I guess . . . if you think about it, Casey, I guess. . . . It sure as hell cost them nothing."

"Ian's convinced of it," Gavallan said. "Talk to him. As to Vietnam, no one here thinks President Kennedy can handle that either, much as we admire him personally. Asia's not like Europe, or the Americas. They think differently here, act differently and have different values."

There was a sudden silence. Bartlett broke it. "You think there'll be war then?"

Gavallan glanced at him. "Nothing for you to worry about. Par-Con should do very well. You've heavy industry, computers, polyurethane foam, government contracts into aerospace, petrochemicals, sonics, wireless equipment . . . With your goods and our expertise if there's a war, well, the sky's the limit."

"I don't think I'd like to profit that way," Casey said, irritated by him. "That's a lousy way to earn a buck."

Gavallan turned on her. "A lot of things on this earth are lousy, and wrong and unfair. . . ." He was going to give her both barrels, infuriated with the way she kept interrupting his conversation with Bartlett but he decided that now was not the time, nor the place, so he said pleasantly, "But of course you're right. No one wants to profit from death. If you'll excuse me I'll be going. . . . You know everyone has place cards? Dinner'll start any moment. Matter of face."

He walked off.

Casey said, "I don't think he likes me at all."

They laughed at the way she said it. "What you said was right, Casey," Orlanda told her. "You were right. War is terrible."

"You were here during it?" Casey asked innocently.

"Yes, but in Macao. I'm Portuguese. My mother told me it wasn't too bad there. The Japanese didn't trouble Macao because Portugal was neutral." Orlanda added sweetly, "Of course I'm only twenty-five now so I hardly remember any of it. I was not quite seven when the war ended. Macao's nice, Casey. So different from Hong Kong. You and Linc might like to go there. It's worth seeing. I'd love to be your guide."

I'll bet, Casey thought, feeling her twenty-six was old against Orlanda who had the skin of a seventeen-year-old. "That'd be great. But Lando, what's with Andrew? Why was he so teed off? Because I'm a woman VP and all that?"

"I doubt that. I'm sure you exaggerate," Mata said. "It's just that he's not very pro-American and it drives him mad that the British Empire's no more, that the U.S. is arbiter of the world's fate and making obvious mistakes, he thinks. Most British people agree with him, I'm afraid! It's part jealousy of course. But you must be patient with Andrew. After all, your government did give away Hong Kong in '45 to Chiang—only the British navy stopped that. America did side with Soviet Russia against them over Suez, did support the Jews against them in Palestine—there are dozens of examples. It's also true lots of us here think your present hostility to China's ill-advised."

"But they're as Communist as Russia. They went to war against us when we were only trying to protect freedom in South Korea. We weren't going to attack them."

"But historically, China's always crossed the Yalu when any foreign invader approached that border. *Always.* Your MacArthur was supposed to be a historian," Mata said patiently, wondering if she was as naive in bed, "he should have known. He—or your President—forced China into a path it did not want to take. I'm absolutely sure of that."

"But we weren't invaders. North Korea invaded the South. We just wanted to help a people be free. We'd nothing to gain from South Korea. We spend billions trying to help people stay free. Look what China did to Tibet—to India last year. Seems to me we're always the fall guy and all we want is to protect freedom." She stopped as a murmur of relief went through the room and people began heading for their tables. Waiters bearing silver-domed platters were trooping in. "Thank God! I'm starving!"

"Me too," Bartlett said.

"Shitee's early tonight," Mata said with a laugh. "Orlanda, you should have warned them it's an old custom always to have a snack before any of Shitee's banquets."

Orlanda just smiled her lovely smile and Casey said, "Orlanda warned Linc, who told me, but I figured I could last." She looked at her enemy who was almost half a head shorter, about five foot three. For the first time in her life she felt big and oafish. Be honest, she reminded herself, ever since you walked out of the hotel into the streets and saw all the Chinese girls and women with their tiny hands and feet and bodies and smallness, all dark-eyed and dark-haired, you've felt huge and alien. Yes. Now I can understand why they all gape at us so much. And as for the ordinary tourist, loud, overweight, waddling along . . .

Even so, Orlanda Ramos, as pretty as you are and as clever as you think you are, you're not the girl for Linc Bartlett. So you can blow it all out of your ass! "Next time, Orlanda," she said so nicely, "I'll remember to be very cautious about what you recommend."

"I recommend we eat, Casey. I'm hungry too."

Mata said, "I do believe we're all at the same table. I must confess I arranged it." Happily he led the way, more than ever excited by the challenge of getting Casey into bed. The moment he had seen her he had decided. Part of it was her beauty and tallness and beautiful breasts, such a welcome contrast to the smallness and sameness of the normal Asian girl. Part was because of the clues Orlanda had given him. But the biggest part had been his sudden thought that by breaking the Bartlett-Casey connection he might wreck Par-Con's probe into Asia. Far better to keep Americans and their hypocritical, impractical morality and meddling out of our area as long as we can, he had told himself. And if Dunross doesn't have the Par-Con deal, then he will have to sell me the control I want. Then, at long last, *I* become *the tai-pan* of the Noble House, all the Dunrosses and Struans notwithstanding.

Madonna, life is really very good. Curious that this woman could be the key to the best lock in Asia, he thought. Then he added contentedly, Clearly she can be bought. It's only a matter of how much.

37

Dinner was twelve courses. Braised abalone with green sprouts, chicken livers and sliced partridge sauce, shark's fin soup, barbecued chicken, Chinese greens and peapods and broccoli and fifty other vegetables with crabmeat, the skin of roast Peking duck with plum sauce and sliced spring onions and paper-thin pancakes, double-boiled mushrooms and fish maw, smoked pomfret fish with salad, rice Yangchow style, home sweet home noodles—then happiness dessert, sweetened lotus seeds and lily in rice gruel. And tea continuously.

Mata and Orlanda helped Casey and Bartlett. Fleur and Peter Marlowe were the only other Europeans at their table. The Chinese presented their visiting cards and received others in exchange. "Oh you can eat with chopsticks!" All the Chinese were openly astonished, then slid comfortably back into Cantonese, the bejeweled women clearly discussing Casey and Bartlett and the Marlowes. Their comments were slightly guarded only because of Lando Mata and Orlanda.

"What're they saying, Orlanda?" Bartlett asked quietly amid the noisy exuberance, particularly of the Chinese.

"They're just wondering about you and Miss Casey," she said as cautiously, not translating the lewd remarks about the size of Casey's chest, the wondering where her clothes came from, how much they cost, why she didn't wear any jewelry, and what it must be like to be so tall. They were saying little about Bartlett other than wondering out loud if he was really Mafia as one of the Chinese papers had suggested.

Orlanda was sure he wasn't. But she was sure also that she would have to be very circumspect in front of Casey, neither too forward nor too slow, and never to touch him. And to be sweet to her, to try to throw her off her stride.

Fresh plates for each course were laid with a clatter, the used ones whisked away. Waiters hurried to the dumbwaiters in the central section by the staircase to dispose of the old and grab steaming platters of the new.

The kitchens, three decks below, were an inferno with the huge four-feet-wide iron woks fired with gas that was piped aboard. Some woks for steaming, some for quick frying, some for deep frying, some for stewing, and many for the pure white rice. An open, wood-fired barbecue. An army of helpers for the twenty-eight cooks were preparing the meats and vegetables, plucking chickens, killing fresh fish and lobsters and crabs and cleaning them, doing the thousand tasks that Chinese food requires—as each dish is cooked freshly for each customer.

The restaurant opened at 10:00 A.M. and the kitchen closed at 10:45 P.M.—sometimes later when a special party was arranged. There could be dancing and a floor show if the host was rich enough. Tonight, though there was no late shift or floor show or dancing, they all knew that their share of the tip from Shitee T'Chung's banquet would be very good. Shitee T'Chung was an expansive host, though most of them believed that much of the charity money he collected went into his stomach or those of his guests or onto the backs of his lady friends. He also had the reputation of being ruthless to his detractors, a miser to his family, and vengeful to his enemies.

Never mind, the head chef thought. A man needs soft lips and hard teeth in this world and everyone knows which will last the longer. "Hurry up!" he shouted. "Can I wait all manure-infested night? Prawns! Bring the prawns!" A sweating helper in ragged pants and ancient, sweaty undershirt rushed up with a bamboo platter of the freshly caught and freshly peeled prawns. The chef cast them into the vast wok, added a handful of monosodium glutamate, whisked them twice and scooped them out, put a handful of steaming peapods on two platters and divided up the pink, glistening succulent prawns on top equally.

"All gods urinate on all prawns!" he said sourly, his stomach ulcer paining him, his feet and calves leaden from his ten-hour shift. "Send those upstairs before they spoil! *Dew neh loh moh* hurry . . . that's my last order. It's time to go home!"

Other cooks were shouting last orders and cursing as they cooked. They were all impatient to be gone. "Hurry it up!" Then one young helper carrying a pot of used fat stumbled and the fat sprayed onto one of the gas fires, caught with a whoosh and there was sudden pandemonium. A cook screamed as the fire surrounded him and he beat at it, his face and hair singed. Someone threw a bucket of water on the fire and spread it violently. Flames soared to the rafters, billowing smoke. Shouting, shoving cooks moving out of the fire were causing a bottleneck. The acrid, black, oil smoke began to fill the air.

The man nearest the single narrow staircase to the first deck grabbed one of the two fire extinguishers and slammed the plunger down and pointed the nozzle at the fire. Nothing happened. He did it again then someone else grabbed it from him with a curse, tried unsuccessfully to make it work, and cast it aside. The other extinguisher was also a dud. The staff had never bothered to test them.

"All gods defecate on these motherless foreign devil inventions!" a cook wailed and prepared to flee if the fire approached him. A frightened coolie choking on the smoke at the other end of the kitchen backed away from a shaft of flame into some jars and toppled them. Some contained thousand-year-old eggs and others sesame oil. The oil flooded the floor and caught fire. The coolie vanished in the sudden sheet of flame. Now the fire owned half the kitchen.

It was well past eleven o'clock and most diners had already left. The top deck of the *Floating Dragon* was still partially filled. Most of the Chinese, Four Finger Wu and Venus Poon among them, were walking out or had already left as the last course had already been served long since and it was polite Chinese custom to leave as soon as the last dish was finished, table by table. Only the Europeans were lingering over Cognac or port, and cigars.

Throughout the boat, tables of mah-jong were being set up by Chinese, and the clitter-clatter of the ivory tiles banging on the tables began to dominate.

"Do you play mah-jong, Mr. Bartlett?" Mata asked.

"No. Please call me Linc."

"You should learn—it's better than bridge. Do you play bridge, Casey?"

Linc Bartlett laughed. "She's a wiz, Lando. Don't play her for money."

"Perhaps we can have a game sometime. You play, don't you, Orlanda?" Mata said, remembering Gornt was an accomplished player.

"Yes, a little," Orlanda said softly and Casey thought grimly, I'll bet the bitch's a wiz too.

"I'd love a game," Casey said sweetly.

"Good," Mata said. "One day next week . . . oh, hello, tai-pan!"

Dunross greeted them all with his smile. "How did you enjoy the food?"

"It was fantastic!" Casey said, happy to see him and greatly aware of how handsome he looked in his tuxedo. "Would you like to join us?"

"Thanks bu—"

"Good night, tai-pan," Dianne Chen said, coming up to him, her son Kevin—a short, heavyset youth with dark curly hair and full lips—in tow.

Dunross introduced them. "Where's Phillip?"

"He was going to come but he phoned to say he was delayed. Well, good night . . ." Dianne smiled and so did Kevin and they headed for the door, Casey and Orlanda wide-eyed at Dianne's jewelry.

"Well, I must be off too," Dunross said.

"How was your table?"

"Rather trying," Dunross said with his infectious laugh. He had eaten with the MPs—with Gornt, Shi-teh and his wife at the Number One table

—and there had been sporadic angry outbursts above the clatter of plates. "Robin Grey's rather outspoken, and ill-informed, and some of us were having at him. For once Gornt and I were on the same side. I must confess our table got served first so poor old Shi-teh and his wife could flee. He took off like a dose of salts fifteen minutes ago."

They all laughed with him. Dunross was watching Marlowe. He wondered if Marlowe knew that Grey was his brother-in-law. "Grey seems to know you quite well, Mr. Marlowe."

"He has a good memory, tai-pan, though his manners are off."

"I don't know about that, but if he has his way in Parliament God help Hong Kong. Well, I just wanted to say hello to all of you." He smiled at Bartlett and Casey. "How about lunch tomorrow?"

"Fine," Casey said. "How about coming to the V and A?" She noticed Gornt get up to leave on the opposite side of the room and she wondered again who would win. "Just before dinner Andrew was say—"

Then, with all of them, she heard faint screams. There was a sudden hush, everyone listening.

"Fire!"

"Christ, look!" They all stared at the dumbwaiter. Smoke was pouring out. Then a small tongue of flame.

A split second of disbelief, then everyone jumped up. Those nearest the main staircase rushed for the doorway, crowding it, as others took up the shout. Bartlett leapt to his feet and dragged Casey with him. Mata and some of the guests began to run for the bottleneck.

"Hold it!" Dunross roared above the noise. Everyone stopped. "There's plenty of time. Don't hurry!" he ordered. "There's no need to run, take your time! There's no danger yet!" His admonition helped those who were overly frightened. They started easing out of the crammed doorway. But below, on the staircases, the shouts and hysteria had increased.

Not everyone had run at the first cry of danger. Gornt hadn't moved. He puffed his cigar, all his senses concentrated. Havergill and his wife had walked over to the windows to look out. Others joined them. They could see crowds milling around the main entrance two decks below. "I don't think we need to worry, my dear," Havergill said. "Once the main lot are out we can follow at leisure."

Lady Joanna, beside them, said, "Did you see Biltzmann rush off? What a berk!" She looked around and saw Bartlett and Casey across the room, waiting beside Dunross. "Oh, I'd've thought they'd've fled too."

Havergill said, "Oh come on, Joanna, not all Yankees are cowards!"

A sudden shaft of flame and thick black smoke poured out of the dumbwaiter. The shouting to hurry up began again.

On the far side of the room nearer the fire, Bartlett said hastily, "Ian, is there another exit?"

"I don't know," Dunross said. "Take a look outside. I'll hold the fort here." Bartlett took off quickly for the exit door to the half deck and

Dunross turned to the rest of them. "Nothing to worry about," he said, calming them and gauging them quickly. Fleur Marlowe was white but in control, Casey stared in shock at the people jamming the doorway, Orlanda petrified, near breaking. "Orlanda! It's all right," he said, "there's no danger . . ."

On the other side of the room Gornt got up and went nearer to the door. He could see the crush and knew that the stairs below would be jammed. Shrieks and some screams added to the fear here but Sir Charles Pennyworth was beside the doorway trying to get an orderly withdrawal down the stairs. More smoke billowed out and Gornt thought, Christ almighty, a bloody fire, half a hundred people and one exit. Then he noticed the unattended bar. He went to it and, outwardly calm, poured himself a whiskey and soda, but the sweat was running down his back.

Below on the crowded second-deck landing Lando Mata stumbled and brought a whole group down, Dianne Chen and Kevin with them, creating a blockage in this, the only escape route. Men and women shrieked impotently, crushed against the floor as others fell or stumbled over them in a headlong dash for safety. Above on the staircase, Pugmire held on to the banister and just managed to keep his feet, using his great strength to shove his back against the people and prevent more from falling. Julian Broadhurst was beside him, frightened too but equally controlled, using his height and weight with Pugmire. Together they held the breach momentarily, but gradually the weight of those behind overcame them. Pugmire felt his grip slipping. Ten steps below, Mata fought to his feet, trampled on a few people in his haste, then shoved on downstairs, his coat half torn from him. Dianne Chen clawed her way to her feet, dragging Kevin with her. In the shoving, milling mass of humanity she did not notice a woman grab her diamond pendant neatly and pocket it, then jostle away down the stairs. Smoke billowing up from the lower deck added to the horror. Pugmire's hold was broken. He was half-shoved into the wall by the human flood and Broadhurst missed his footing. Another small avalanche of people began. Now the stairs on both levels were clogged.

Four Finger Wu with Venus Poon had been on the first landing when the shout had gone up and he had darted down the last staircase and shoved his way out onto the drawbridge that led to the wharf, Venus Poon a few terrorized steps behind him. Safe on the wharf, he turned and looked back, his heart pounding, his breathing heavy. Men and women were stumbling out of the huge ornate doorway onto the jetty, some flames coming out of portholes near the waterline. A policeman who had been patrolling nearby ran up, watched aghast for a moment, then took to his heels for the nearest telephone. Wu was still trying to catch his breath when he saw Richard Kwang and his wife rush out pell-mell. He began to laugh and felt much better. Venus Poon thought the people looked very funny too. Onlookers were collecting in safety, no one doing anything to help, just gawking—which is only right, Wu thought in passing. One must never interfere with the decisions of the gods. The gods have their own rules and they decide a human's joss. It's my joss to escape and to enjoy this whore tonight. All gods help me to maintain my Imperial Iron until she screams for mercy.

"Come along, Little Mealy Mouth," Four Fingers said with a cackle, "we can safely leave them to their joss. Time's wasting."

"No, Father," she said quickly. "Any moment the TV cameras and press will arrive—we must think of our image, *heya?*"

"Image? It's the pillow and the Gorgeous G—"

"Later!" she said imperiously and he bit back the curse he was going to add. "Don't you want to be hailed as a hero?" she said sharply. "Perhaps even a knighthood like Shitee, *heya?*" Quickly she dirtied her hands and her face and carefully ripped one of the straps above her breast and went near to the gangway where she could see and be seen. Four Fingers watched her blankly. A *quai loh* honor like Shitee? he thought astounded. Eeeeee, why not! He followed her warily, taking great care not to get too close to any danger.

They saw a tongue of flame sweep out of the chimney on the top deck and frightened people looking down from the three decks of windows. People were collecting on the wharf. Others were stumbling out to safety in hysterics, many coughing from the smoke that was beginning to possess the whole restaurant. There was another shouting crush in the doorway, a few went down and some scuttled from under the milling feet, those behind shrieking at those in front to hurry, and again Four Fingers and other onlookers laughed.

On the top deck Bartlett leaned over the railings and looked down at the hull and the jetty below. He could see crowds on the wharf and milling, hysterical people fighting out of the entrance. There was no other staircase, ladder or escape possibility on either side. His heart was hammering but he was not afraid. There's no real danger, yet, he thought. We can jump into the water below. Easy. It's what, thirty, forty feet—no sweat if you don't belly flop. He ran back along the deck that used up half the length of the boat. Black smoke, sparks and a little flame surged out of the funnels.

He opened the top-deck door and closed it quickly in order not to create any added draft. The smoke was much worse and the flames coming out of the dumbwaiter were continuous now. The smoke smell on the air was acrid and carried the stench of burning meat. Almost everyone was crowded around the far doorway. Gornt was standing apart by himself watching them, sipping a drink. Bartlett thought, Jesus, there's one cold-blooded bastard! He skirted the dumbwaiter carefully, his eyes smarting from the smoke, and almost knocked over Christian Toxe who was hunched over the telephone shouting into it above the noise, ". . . I don't give a shit, get a photographer out here right now, and *then* phone the fire department!" Angrily Toxe slammed down the phone and muttering,

"Stupid bastards," went back to his wife, a matronly Chinese woman who stared at him blankly. Bartlett hurried toward Dunross. The tai-pan stood motionless beside Peter and Fleur Marlowe, Orlanda and Casey, whistling tonelessly.

"Nothing, Ian," he said quietly, noticing his voice sounded strange, "not a goddamn thing. No ladders, nothing. But we can jump, easy, if necessary."

"Yes. We're lucky being on this deck. The others may not be so lucky." Dunross watched the smoke and fire spurting from the dumbwaiter that was near the exit door. "We'll have to decide pretty soon which way to go," he said gently. "That fire could cut us off from the outside. If we go out we may never get back in and we'll have to jump. If we stay in, we can only use the stairs."

"Jesus," Casey muttered. She was trying to calm her racing heart and the feeling of claustrophobia that was welling up. Her skin felt clammy and her eyes were darting from the exit to the doorway and back again. Bartlett put an arm around her. "It's no sweat, we can jump anytime."

"Yes, sure, Linc." Casey was holding on grimly.

"You can swim, Casey?" Dunross asked.

"Yes. I . . . was caught in a fire once. Ever since then I've been frightened to death of them." It was a few years before when her little house in the Hollywood Hills of Los Angeles was in the path of one of the sudden summer conflagrations and she had been bottled in, the winding canyon road already burning below. She had turned on all the water sprinklers and begun to hose the roof. The clawing heat of the fire had reached out at her. Then the fire had crested, jumping from the top of one valley to the opposite side, to begin burning down both sides toward the valley floor, whipped by hundred-mile-an-hour gusts self-generated by the fire. The roaring flames obliterated trees and houses, came closer and there was no way out. In terror, she kept the hose on her roof. Cats and dogs from the homes above fled past her and one wild-eyed Alsatian cowered in the lee of her house. The heat and the smoke and the terror surrounded her and it went on and on but this part of the fire stopped fifty feet from her boundary. For no reason. Above, all the houses on her street had gone. Most of the canyon. A swath almost half a mile wide and two long burned for three days in the hills that bisected the city of Los Angeles.

"I'm all right, Linc," she said shakily. "I . . . I think I'd rather be outside than here. Let's get the hell out of here. A swim'd be great."

"I can't swim!" Orlanda was trembling. Then her control snapped and she got up to rush for the stairs.

Bartlett grabbed her. "Everything's going to be all right. Jesus, you'll never make it that way. Listen to the poor bastards down there, they're in real trouble. Stay put, huh? The stairs're no good." She hung on to him, petrified.

"You'll be all right," Casey said compassionately.

"Yes," Dunross said, his eyes on the fire and billowing smoke.

Marlowe said, "We, er, we're really in very good shape, tai-pan, aren't we? Yes. The fire's got to be from the kitchens. They'll get it under control. Fleur, pet, there'll be no need to go over the side."

"It's no sweat," Bartlett assured him. "There's plenty of sampans to pick us up!"

"Oh yes, but she can't swim either."

Fleur put her hand on her husband's arm. "You always said I should learn, Peter."

Dunross wasn't listening. He was consumed with fear and trying to dominate it. His nostrils were filled with the stench of burning meat that he knew oh so well and he was near vomiting. He was back in his burning Spitfire, shot out of the sky by a Messerschmitt 109 over the Channel, the cliffs of Dover too far away, and he knew the fire would consume him before he could tear the jammed and damaged cockpit canopy free and bail out, the horror-smell of scorching flesh, his own, surrounding him. In terror he smashed his fist impotently against the Perspex, his other beating at the flames around his feet and knees, choking from the acrid smoke in his lungs, half blinded. Then there was a sudden frantic roar as the cowl ripped away, an inferno of flames surged up and surrounded him and somehow he was out and falling away from the flames, not knowing if his face was gone, the skin of his hands and feet, his boots and flying overalls still smoking. Then the shuddering nauseating jerk as his chute opened, then the dark silhouette of the enemy plane hurtled toward him out of the sun and he saw the machine guns sparking and a tracer blew part of his calf away. He remembered none of the rest except the smell of burning flesh that was the same then as now.

"What do you think, tai-pan?"

"What?"

"Shall we stay or leave?" Marlowe repeated.

"We'll stay, for the moment," Dunross said and they all wondered how he could sound so calm and look so calm. "When the stairs clear we can walk out. No reason to get wet if we don't have to."

Casey smiled at him hesitantly. "These fires happen often?"

"Not here, but they do in Hong Kong, I'm afraid. Our Chinese friends don't care much about fire regulations . . ."

It was still only a few minutes since the first violent gust of fire had swirled up in the kitchen but now the fire had a full hold there and, through the access of the dumbwaiter, a strong hold on the central sections of the three decks above. The fire in the kitchen blocked half the room from the only staircase. Twenty terrified men were trapped on the wrong side. The rest of the staff had fled long since to join the heaving mass of people on the deck above. There were half a dozen portholes but these were small and rusted up. In panic one of the cooks rushed at the flaming barrier, screamed as the flames engulfed him, almost made it through but slipped and kept on screaming for a long while. A petrified moan burst from the others. There was no other escape possibility.

The head chef was trapped too. He was a portly man and he had been in many kitchen fires so he was not panicked. His mind ranged all the other fires, desperately seeking a clue. Then he remembered.

"Hurry," he shouted, "get bags of rice flour . . . rice . . . hurry!"

The others stared at him without moving, their terror numbing them, so he lashed out and smashed some of them into the storeroom, grabbed a fifty-pound sack himself and tore the top off. "Fornicate all fires hurry but wait till I tell you," he gasped, the smoke choking and almost blinding him. One of the portholes shattered and the sudden draft whooshed the flames at them. Terrified they grabbed a sack each, coughing as the smoke billowed.

"*Now!*" the head chef roared and hurled the sack at the flaming corridor between the stoves. The sack burst open and the clouds of flour doused some of the flames. Other sacks followed in the same area and more flames were swallowed. Another barrage of flour went over the flaming benches, snuffing them out. The passage was momentarily clear. At once the head chef led the charge through the remaining flames and they all followed him pell-mell, leaping over the two charred bodies, and gained the stairs at the far side before the flames gushed back and closed the path. The men fought their way up the narrow staircase and into the partial air of the landing, joining the milling mob that pushed and shoved and screamed and coughed their way through the black smoke into the open.

Tears streamed from most faces. The smoke was very heavy now in the lower levels. Then the wall behind the first landing where the shaft of the dumbwaiter was began to twist and blacken. Abruptly it burst open, scattering gargoyles, and flames gushed out. Those on the stairs below shoved forward in panic and those on the landing reeled back. Then, seeing they were so close to safety, the first ranks darted forward, skirting the inferno, jumping the stairs two at a time. Hugh Guthrie, one of the MPs, saw a woman fall. He held on to the banister and stopped to help her but those behind toppled him and he fell with others. He picked himself up, cursing, and fought a path clear for just enough time to drag the woman up before he was engulfed again and shoved down the last few stairs to gain the entrance safely.

Half the landing between the lower deck and the second deck was still free of flames though the fire had an unassailable hold and was fueling itself. The crowds were thinning now though more than a hundred still clogged the upper staircases and doorways. Those above were milling and cursing, not being able to see ahead.

"What's the holdup for chrissake. . . ."

"Are the stairs still clear . . . ?"

"For chrissake get on with it. . . ."

"It's getting bloody hot up here . . ."

"What a sodding carve-up. . . ."

Grey was one of those trapped on the second-deck staircase. He could see the flames gushing out of the wall ahead and knew the nearby wall would go any moment. He could not decide whether to retreat or to advance. Then he saw a child cowering against the steps under the banister. He managed to pull the little boy into his arms then pressed on, cursing those in front, darted around the fire, the way to safety below still jammed.

On the top deck Gornt and others were listening to the pandemonium below. There were only thirty or so people still here. He finished his drink, set the glass down and walked over to the group surrounding Dunross—Orlanda was still sitting, twisting her handkerchief in her hands, Fleur and Peter Marlowe still outwardly calm, and Dunross, as always, in control. Good, he thought, blessing his own heritage and training. It was part of British tradition that in danger, however petrified you are, you lose face by showing it. Then, too, he reminded himself, most of us have been bombed most of our lives, shot at, sunk, slammed into POW jails or been in the Services. Gornt's sister had been in the Women's Royal Naval Service—his mother an air raid warden, his father in the army, his uncle killed at Monte Cassino, and he himself had served with the Australians in New Guinea after escaping from Shanghai, and had fought his way into and through Burma to Singapore.

"Ian," he said, keeping his voice suitably nonchalant, "it sounds as though the fire's on the first landing now. I suggest a swim."

Dunross glanced back at the fire near the exit door. "Some of the ladies don't swim. Let's give it a couple of minutes."

"Very well. I think those who don't mind jumping should go on deck. That particular fire's really very boring."

Casey said, "I don't find it very boring at all."

They all laughed. "It's just an expression," Peter Marlowe explained.

An explosion below decks rocked the boat slightly. The momentary silence was eerie.

In the kitchen the fire had spread to the storage rooms and was surrounding the four remaining hundred-gallon drums of oil. The one that had blown up had torn a gaping hole in the floor and buckled the side of the boat. Burning embers and burning oil and some seawater poured into the scuppers. The force of the explosion had ruptured some of the great timbers of the flat-bottomed hull and water was seeping through the seams. Hordes of rats scrambled out of the way seeking an escape route.

Another of the thick metal drums blew up and ripped a vast hole in the side of the boat just below the waterline, scattering fire in all directions. The people on the wharf gasped and some reeled back though there was no danger. Others laughed nervously. Still another drum exploded and another shaft of flames sprayed everywhere. The ceiling supports and joists were seriously weakened and, oil soaked, began to burn. Above on the first deck, the feet of the frenzied escapees pounded dangerously.

Just above the first landing Grey still had the child in his arms. He held on to the banister with one hand, frightened, shoving people behind and in front of him. He waited his turn, then shielding the child as best he could, ducked around the flames on the landing and darted down the stairs, the way mostly clear. The carpet by the threshold was beginning to smoke and one heavyset man stumbled, the whole floor shaky.

"Come on," Grey shouted desperately to those behind. He made the threshold, others close behind and in front. Just as he reached the draw-bridge the last two drums exploded, the whole floor behind him disappeared and he and the child and others were hurled forward like so much chaff.

Hugh Guthrie rushed out of the onlookers and pulled them to safety. "You all right, old chap?" he gasped.

Grey was half stunned, gasping for breath, his clothes smoldering, and Guthrie helped beat them out. "Yes . . . yes I think so . . ." he said half out of himself.

Guthrie gently lifted the unconscious child and peered at him. "Poor little bastard!"

"Is he dead?"

"I don't think so. Here . . ." Guthrie gave the little Chinese boy to an onlooker and both men charged back to the gateway to help the others who were still numbed by the explosion and helpless. "Christ all bloody mighty," he gasped as he saw that now the whole entrance was impassable. Above the uproar, they heard the wail of approaching sirens.

The fire on the top deck near the exit was building nastily. Frightened, coughing people were streaming back into the room, forced back up the stairs by the fire that now owned the lower deck. Pandemonium and the stench of fear were heavy on the air.

"Ian, we'd better get the hell out of here," Bartlett said.

"Yes. Quillan, would you please lead the way and take charge of the deck," Dunross said. "I'll hold this end."

Gornt turned and roared, "Everyone this way! You'll be safe on deck . . . one at a time. . . ." He opened the door and positioned himself by it and tried to bring order to the hasty retreat—a few Chinese, the remainder mostly British. Once in the open everyone was much less frightened and grateful to be away from the smoke.

Bartlett, waiting in the room, felt excitement but still no fear for he knew he could smash any one of the windows and get Casey and himself out and into the sea. People stumbled past. Flames from the dumbwaiter increased and there was a dull explosion below.

"How you doing, Casey?"

"Okay."

"Out you go!"

"When you go."

"Sure." Bartlett grinned at her. The room was thinning. He helped Lady Joanna through the doorway, then Havergill, who was limping, and his wife.

Casey saw that Orlanda was still frozen to her chair. Poor girl, she thought compassionately, remembering her own absolute terror in her own fire. She went over to her. "Come on," she said gently and helped her up. The girl's knees were trembling. Casey kept her arm around her.

"I . . . I've lost . . . my purse," Orlanda muttered.

"No, here it is." Casey picked it up from the chair and kept her arm around her as she half-pushed her past the flames into the open. The deck was crowded but once outside Casey felt enormously better.

"Everything's fine," Casey said encouragingly. She guided her to the railing. Orlanda held on tightly. Casey turned back to look for Bartlett and saw both him and Gornt watching her from inside the room. Bartlett waved at her and she waved back, wishing he were outside with her.

Peter Marlowe herded his wife onto the deck and came up to her. "You all right, Casey?"

"Sure. How you doing, Fleur?"

"Fine. Fine. It's . . . it's rather pleasant outside, isn't it?" Fleur Marlowe said, feeling faint and awful, petrified at the idea of jumping from this great height. "Do you think it's going to rain?"

"The sooner the better." Casey looked over the side. In the murky waters, thirty feet below, sampans were beginning to collect. All boatmen knew that those on the top would have to jump soon. From their vantage they could see that the fire possessed most of the first and second decks. A few people were trapped there, then one man hurled a chair through one of the windows, broke the glass away, scrambled through and fell into the sea. A sampan darted forward and threw him a line. Others who were trapped followed. One woman never came up.

The night was dark though the flames lit everything nearby, casting eerie shadows. The crowds on the wharf parted as the screaming fire engines pulled up. Immediately Chinese firemen and British officers dragged out the hoses. Another detachment joined up to the nearby fire hydrant and the first jet of water played onto the fire and there was a cheer. In seconds six hoses were in operation and two masked firemen with asbestos clothing and breathing equipment strapped to their backs rushed the entrance and began to drag those who were lying unconscious out of danger. Another huge explosion sprayed them with burning embers. One of the firemen doused everyone with water then directed the hose back on the entrance again.

The top deck was empty now except for Bartlett, Dunross and Gornt. They felt the deck sway under them and almost lost their footing. "Jesus Christ," Bartlett gasped, "we going to sink?"

"Those explosions could've blown her bottom out," Gornt said urgently.
"Come on!" He went through the door quickly, Bartlett followed.

Now Dunross was alone. The smoke was very bad, the heat and stench
revolting him. He made a conscious effort not to flee, dominating his terror. At a sudden thought he ran back across the room to the doorway of
the main staircase to make sure there was no one there. Then he saw the
inert figure of a man on the staircase. Flames were everywhere. He felt his
own fear surging again but once more he held it down, darted forward
and began to drag the man back up the stairs. The Chinese was heavy
and he did not know if the man was alive or dead. The heat was scorching and again he smelt burning flesh and felt his bile rising. Then Bartlett
was beside him and together they half-dragged, half-carried the man across
the room out onto the deck.

"Thanks," Dunross gasped.

Quillan Gornt came over to them, bent down and turned the man over.
The face was partially burned. "You could have saved yourself the he-
roics. He's dead."

"Who is he?" Bartlett asked.

Gornt shrugged. "I don't know. Do you know him, Ian?"

Dunross was staring at the body. "Yes. It's Zep . . . Zeppelin Tung."

"Tightfist's son?" Gornt was surprised. "My God, he's put on weight.
I'd never have recognized him." He got to his feet. "We'd better get everyone ready to jump. This boat's a graveyard." He saw Casey standing by
the railing. "Are you all right?" he asked, going over to her.

"Yes, thanks. You?"

"Oh yes."

Orlanda was still beside her, staring blankly at the water below. People
were milling around the deck. "I'd better help get them organized," Gornt
said. "I'll be back in a second." He walked off.

Another explosion jarred the boat again. The list began to increase. Several people climbed over the side and jumped. Sampans went in to rescue
them.

Christian Toxe had his arm around his Chinese wife and he was staring
sourly overboard.

"You're going to have to jump, Christian," Dunross said.

"Into Aberdeen Harbor? You must be bloody joking old chap! If you
don't bounce off all the bloody effluvia you'll catch the bloody plague."

"It's that or a red-hot tail," someone called out with a laugh.

At the end of the deck Sir Charles Pennyworth was holding on to the
railing as he worked his way down the boat encouraging everyone. "Come
on, young lady," he said to Orlanda, "it's an easy jump."

She shook her head, petrified. "No . . . no not yet . . . I can't swim."

Fleur Marlowe put her arm around her. "Don't worry, I can't swim either. I'm staying too."

Bartlett said, "Peter, you can hold her hand, she'll be safe. All you have to do, Fleur, is hold your breath!"

"She's not going to jump," Marlowe said quietly. "At least, not till the last second."

"It's safe."

"Yes, but it's not safe for her. She's *enceinte*."

"What?"

"Fleur's with child. About three months."

"Oh Jesus."

Flames roared skyward out of one of the flues. Inside the top deck restaurant tables were afire and the great carved temple screens at the far end were burning merrily. There was a great gust of sparks as the inner central staircase collapsed. "Jesus, this whole boat's a firetrap. What about the folk below?" Casey asked.

"They're all out long ago," Dunross said, not believing it. Now that he was in the open he felt fine. His successful domination of his fear made him light-headed. "The view here is quite splendid, don't you think?"

Pennyworth called out jovially, "We're in luck! The ship's listing this way so when she goes down we'll be safe enough. Unless she capsizes. Just like old times," he added. "I was sunk three times in the Med."

"So was I," Marlowe said, "but it was in the Bangka Strait off Sumatra."

"I didn't know that, Peter," Fleur said.

"It was nothing."

"How deep's the water here?" Bartlett asked.

"It must be twenty feet or more," Dunross said.

"That'll be en—" There was a *whoopwhoopwhoop* of sirens as the police launch came bustling through the narrow byways between the islands of boats, its searchlight darting here and there. When it was almost alongside the *Floating Dragon,* the megaphone sounded loudly, first in Chinese, "All sampans clear the area, clear the area . . ." Then in English, "Those on the top deck prepare to abandon ship! The hull's holed, prepare to abandon ship!"

Christian Toxe muttered sourly to no one, "Buggered if I'm going to ruin my only dinner jacket."

His wife tugged at his arm. "You never liked it anyway, Chris."

"I like it now, old girl." He tried to smile. "You can't bloody swim either."

She shrugged. "I'll bet you fifty dollar you and me we swim like a one hundred percent eel."

"Mrs. Toxe, you have a bet. But it's only fitting we're the last to go. After all, I want an eyewitness account." He reached into his pocket and found his cigarettes, gave her one, trying to feel brave, frightened for her safety. He searched for a match, couldn't find one. She reached into her purse and rummaged around. Eventually she found her lighter. It lit on the third go. Both were oblivious of the flames that were ten feet behind them.

Dunross said, "You smoke too much, Christian."

The deck twisted sickeningly. The boat began to settle. Water was pouring through the great hole in her side. Firemen used their hoses with great bravery but they had little effect on the conflagration. A murmur went through the crowd as the whole boat shuddered. Two of the mooring guys snapped.

Pennyworth was leaning against the gunnel, helping others to jump clear. Quite a few were jumping now. Lady Joanna fell awkwardly. Paul Havergill helped his wife over the side. When he saw she had surfaced he leaped too. The police launch was still blaring in Cantonese to clear the area. Sailors threw life jackets over the side as others launched a cutter. Then, led by a young marine inspector, half a dozen sailors dived over the side to help those in trouble, men, women and a few children. A sampan darted in to help Lady Joanna, Havergill and his wife. Gratefully they clambered aboard the rickety craft. Others from the top deck plunged into the water.

The *Floating Dragon* was listing badly. Someone slipped on the top deck and knocked Pennyworth off balance. He half-jumped, half-fell backward before he could catch himself and fell like a stone. His head smashed into the stern of the sampan, snapping his neck, and he slithered into the water and sank. In the pandemonium no one noticed him.

Casey was hanging on to the railings with Bartlett, Dunross, Gornt, Orlanda and the Marlowes. Nearby, Toxe was puffing away, trying to summon his courage. His wife stubbed her cigarette out carefully. Flames were surging from the air vents, skylights and exit door, then the ship grounded heavily and lurched as another of her anchoring cables snapped. Gornt's hold was torn away and he crashed headfirst into the railing, stunning himself. Toxe and his wife lost their balance and went over the side, badly. Peter Marlowe held on to his wife and just managed to prevent her being smashed into a bulkhead as Bartlett and Casey half-tumbled, half-stumbled past and fell in a heap at the railing, Bartlett protecting her as best he could, her high heels dangerous.

Below, in the water, sailors were helping people to the rescue boat. One saw Toxe and his wife rise to the surface for an instant fifteen yards away, both gasping and spluttering, before they choked, and, flailing, went down again. At once he dived for them and after a seeming eternity, grabbed her clothing and shoved her, half-drowned, to the surface. The young lieutenant swam over to where he had seen Toxe and dived but missed him in the darkness. He came up for air and dived once more into the blackness, groping helplessly. When his lungs were bursting, his outstretched fingers touched some clothing and he grabbed and kicked for the surface. Toxe clung on in panic, retching and choking from all the seawater he had swallowed. The young man broke his hold, turned Toxe over and hauled him to the cutter.

Above them, the boat was tilted dangerously and Dunross picked himself up. He saw Gornt inert in a heap and he stumbled over to him. He tried to lift him, couldn't.

"I'm . . . I'm all right," Gornt gasped, coming around, then he shook his head like a dog. "Christ, thanks . . ." He looked up and saw it was Dunross. "Thanks," he said, smiled grimly as he got up shakily. "I'm still selling tomorrow and by next week you'll have had it."

Dunross laughed. "Jolly good luck! The idea of burning to death or drowning with you fills me with equal dismay."

Ten yards away, Bartlett was lifting Casey up. The angle of the deck was bad now, the fire worse. "This whole goddamn tub could capsize any second."

"What about them?" she asked quietly, nodding at Fleur and Orlanda. He thought a second, then said decisively, "You go first, wait below!"

"Got it!" At once she gave him her small purse. He stuffed it into a pocket and hurried away as she kicked off her shoes, unzipped her long dress and stepped out of it. At once she gathered up the light silk material into a rope, tied it around her waist, swung neatly over the railing and stood there poised on the edge a moment, gauged her impact point carefully, and leapt out into a perfect swan dive. Gornt and Dunross watched her go, their immediate danger forgotten.

Bartlett was beside Orlanda now. He saw Casey break the surface cleanly and before Orlanda could do anything he lifted her over the railing and said, "Hold your breath, honey," and dropped her carefully. They all watched her fall. She plummeted down feet first and went into the water a few yards from Casey who had already anticipated the spot and had swum down below the surface. She caught Orlanda easily, kicked for the surface, and Orlanda was breathing almost before she realized she was off the deck. Casey held her safely and swam strongly for the cutter, in perfect control.

Gornt and Dunross cheered lustily. The boat lurched again and they almost lost their footing as Bartlett stumbled over to the Marlowes.

"Peter, how's your swimming?" Bartlett asked.

"Average."

"Trust me with her? I was a lifeguard, beach bum, for years."

Before Marlowe could say no, Bartlett lifted Fleur into his arms and stepped over the railing onto the ledge and poised himself for a second. "Just hold your breath!" She put one arm around his neck and held her nose then he stepped into space, Fleur tightly and safely in his arms. He plunged into the sea cleanly, protecting her from the shock with his own legs and body, and kicked smoothly for the surface. Her head was hardly under a few seconds and she was not even spluttering though her heart was racing. In seconds she was at the cutter. She hung on to the side and they looked back.

When Peter Marlowe saw she was safe his heart began again. "Oh, jolly good," he muttered.

"Did you see Casey go?" Dunross asked. "Fantastic!"

"What? Oh, no, tai-pan."

"Just bra and pants with stockings attached and no ironworks and a dream dive. Christ, what a figure!"

"Oh those're pantyhose," Marlowe said absently, looking at the water below, gathering his courage. "They've just come out in the States, they're all the rage . . ."

Dunross was hardly listening. "Christ Agnes, what a figure." "Ah yes," Gornt echoed. "And what *cojones*."

The boat shrieked as the last of its mooring guys snapped. The deck toppled nauseatingly.

As one, the last three men went overboard. Dunross and Gornt dived, Peter Marlowe jumped. The dives were good but both men knew they were not as good as Casey's.

38

On the other side of the island the old taxi was grinding up the narrow street high above West Point in Mid Levels, Suslev sprawled drunkenly in the backseat. The night was dark and he was singing a sad Russian ballad to the sweating driver, his tie askew, coat off, his shirt streaked with sweat. The overcast had thickened and lowered, the humidity was worse, the air stifling.

"*Matyeryebyets!*" he muttered, cursing the heat, then smiled, the twisted obscenity pleasing him. He looked out the window. The city and harbor lights far below were misted by wisps of clouds, Kowloon mostly obscured. "It'll rain soon, comrade," he said to the driver, his English slurred, not caring if the man understood or not.

The ancient taxi was wheezing. The engine coughed suddenly and that reminded him of Arthur's cough and their coming meeting. His excitement quickened.

The taxi had picked him up at the Golden Ferry Terminal, then climbed to Mid Levels on the Peak, turned west, skirting Government House where the governor lived, and the Botanical Gardens. Passing the palace, Suslev had wondered absently when the Hammer and Sickle would fly atop the empty flagpole. Soon, he had thought contentedly. With Arthur's help and Sevrin's—very soon. Just a few more years.

He peered at his watch. He would be a little late but that did not worry him. Arthur was always late, never less than ten minutes, never more than twenty. Dangerous to be a man of habit in our profession, he thought. But dangerous or not, Arthur's an enormous asset and Sevrin, his creation, a brilliant, vital tool in our KGB armament, buried so deep, waiting so patiently, like all the other Sevrins throughout the world. Only ninety-odd thousands of us KGB officers and yet we almost rule the world. We've already changed it, changed it permanently, already we own half . . . and in such a short time, only since 1917.

So few of us, so many of *them*. But now our tentacles reach out into every corner. Our armies of assistants—informers, fools, parasites, traitors, the twisted self-deluders and misshapen, misbegotten believers we so deliberately recruit are in every land, feeding off one another like the vermin they all are, fueled by their own selfish wants and fears, all expendable sooner or later. And everywhere one of us, one of the elite, the KGB officers, in the center of each web, controlling guiding eliminating. Webs within webs up to the Presidium of all the Soviets and now so tightly woven into the fabric of Mother Russia as to be indestructible. We *are* modern Russia, he thought proudly. We're Lenin's spearhead. Without us and our techniques and our orchestrated use of terror there would be no Soviet Russia, no Soviet Empire, no driving force to keep the rulers of the Party all powerful—and nowhere on earth would there be a Communist state. Yes, we're the elite.

His smile deepened.

It was hot and sultry inside the taxi even though the windows were open as it curled upward through this residential area with its ribbons of great gardenless apartment blocks that sat on small pads chewed out of the mountainside. A bead of sweat trickled down his cheek and he wiped it off, his whole body feeling clammy.

I'd love a shower, he thought, letting his mind wander. A shower with cool sweet Georgian water, not this saline filth they put through Hong Kong's pipes. I'd love to be in the *dacha* near Tiflis, oh that would be grand! Yes, back in the *dacha* with Father and Mother and I'd swim in the stream running through our land and dry off in the sun, a great Georgian wine cooling in the stream and the mountains nearby. That's Eden if there ever was an Eden. Mountains and pastures, grapes and harvest and the air so clean.

He chuckled as he remembered the fabrication about his past he had told Travkin. That parasite! Just another fool, another tool to be used and, when blunt, discarded.

His father had been a Communist since the very early days—first in the Cheka, secretly, and then, since its inception in 1917, in the KGB. Now in his late seventies, still tall and upright and in honored retirement, he lived like an old-fashioned prince with servants and horses and bodyguards. Suslev was sure that he would inherit the same *dacha*, the same land, the same honor in due course. So would his son, a fledgling in the KGB, if his service continued to be excellent. His own work merited it, his record was impressive and he was only fifty-two.

Yes, he told himself confidently, in thirteen years I'm due for retirement. Thirteen great more years, helping the attack move forward, never easing up whatever the enemy does.

And who is the enemy, the real enemy?

All those who disobey us, all those who refuse our eminence—Russians most of all.

He laughed out loud.

The weary sour-faced young driver glanced up briefly at the rear mirror then went back to his driving, hoping his passenger was drunk enough to misread the meter and give him a great tip. He pulled up at the address he had been given.

Rose Court on Kotewall Road was a modern fourteen-story apartment block. Below were three floors of garage space and around it a small ribbon of concrete and below that, down a slight concrete embankment, was Sinclair Road and Sinclair Towers and more apartment blocks that nestled into the mountainside. This was a choice area to live. The view was grand, the apartments were below the clouds that frequently shrouded the upper reaches of the Peak where walls would sweat, linens would mildew and everything would seem to be perpetually damp.

The meter read 8.70 HK. Suslev peered at a bunch of notes, gave the driver 100 instead of a 10 and got out heavily. A Chinese woman was fanning herself impatiently. He lurched toward the apartment intercom. She told the driver to wait for her husband and looked after Suslev disgustedly.

His feet were unsteady. He found the button he sought and pressed it: Ernest Clinker, Esq., Manager.

"Yes?"

"Ernie, it's me, Gregor," he said thickly with a belch. "Are you in?"

The cockney voice laughed. "Not on your nelly! 'Course I'm in, mate! You're late! You sound as though you've been on a pub crawl! Beer's up, vodka's up, and me'n Mabel's here to greet you!"

Suslev headed for the elevator. He pressed the *down* button. On the lowest level he got out into the open garage and went to the far side. The apartment door was already open and a ruddy-faced, ugly little man in his sixties held out his hand. "Stone the bloody crows," Clinker said, a grin showing cheap false teeth, "you're a bit under the weather, ain'cher?" Suslev gave him a bear hug which was returned and they went inside.

The apartment was two tiny bedrooms, living room, kitchen, bathroom. The rooms were poorly furnished but pleasant, and the only real luxury a small tape deck that was playing opera loudly.

"Beer or vodka?"

Suslev beamed and belched. "First a piss, then vodka, then . . . then another and then . . . then bed." He belched hugely, lurching for the toilet.

"Right you are, Cap'n me old sport! Hey, Mabel, say hello to the Cap'n!" The sleepy old bulldog on her well-chewed mat opened one eye briefly, barked once and was almost instantly wheezily asleep again. Clinker beamed and went to the table and poured a stiff vodka and a glass of water. No ice. He drank some Guinness then called out, "How long you staying, Gregor?"

"Just tonight, *tovarich.* Perhaps tomorrow night. Tomorrow . . . tomorrow I've got to be back aboard. But tomorrow night . . . perhaps, eh?"

"What about Ginny? She throw you out again . . . ?"

In the nondescript van that was parked down the road, Roger Crosse, Brian Kwok and the police radio technician were listening to this conversation through a loudspeaker, the quality of the bug good with little static, the van packed with radio surveillance equipment. They heard Clinker chuckle and say again, "She threw you out, eh?"

"All evening we jig-jig and she . . . she says go stay with Ernie and leave me . . . leave me sleep!"

"You're a lucky bugger. She's a princess that one. Bring her over tomorrer."

"Yes . . . yes I . . . will. Yes she's the best."

They heard Suslev pour a bucket of water into the toilet and come back.

"Here, old chum!"

"Thank you." The sound of thirsty drinking. "I . . . I think . . . I think I want to lie down for . . . lie down. A few minutes . . ."

"A few hours more like! Don't you fret, I'll cook breakfast. Here, wanta 'nother drink. . . ."

The policemen in the van were listening carefully. Crosse had ordered the bug put into Clinker's apartment two years ago. Periodically it was monitored, always when Suslev was there. Suslev, always under loose surveillance, had met Clinker in a bar. Both men were submariners and they had struck up a friendship. Clinker had invited him to stay and from time to time Suslev did. At once Crosse had instituted a security check on Clinker but nothing untoward had been discovered. For twenty years Clinker had been a sailor with the Royal Navy. After the war he had drifted from job to job in the Merchant Marine, throughout Asia to Hong Kong, where he had settled when he retired. He was a quiet, easygoing man who lived alone and had been Rose Court's caretaker-janitor for five years now. Suslev and Clinker were a matched pair who drank a lot, caroused a lot and swapped stories. None of their hours of talk had produced anything considered valuable.

"He's had his usual tankful, Brian," Crosse said.

"Yes sir." Brian Kwok was bored and tried not to show it.

In the small living room Clinker gave Suslev his shoulder. "Come on, it's you for a kip." He stepped over the glass and helped Suslev into the small bedroom. Suslev lay down heavily and sighed.

Clinker closed the drapes then went over to another small tape deck and turned it on. In a moment heavy breathing and the beginnings of a snore came from the tape. Suslev got up soundlessly, his pretended drunkenness gone. Clinker was already on his hands and knees. He pulled away a mat and opened the trapdoor. Noiselessly, Suslev went down into it. Clinker grinned, slapped him on the back and closed the well-greased door after him. The trapdoor steps led to a rough tunnel that quickly joined the large, dry, subterranean culvert storm drain. Suslev picked his way carefully, using the flashlight that was in a bracket at the bottom of the steps. In a moment he heard a car grinding over Sinclair Road just above his head. A few more steps and he was below Sinclair Towers. Another trap-door led to a janitor's closet. This let out onto some disused back stairs. He began to climb.

Roger Crosse was still listening to the heavy breathing, mixed with opera. The van was cramped and close, their shirts sweaty. Crosse was smoking. "Sounds like he's bedded down for the night," he said. They could hear Clinker humming and his movements as he cleared up the broken glass. A red warning light on the radio panel started winking. The operator clicked on the sender. "Patrol car 1423, yes?"

"Headquarters for Superintendent Crosse. Urgent."

"This's Crosse."

"Duty Office, sir. A report's just come in that the *Floating Dragon* restaurant's on fire . . ." Brian Kwok gasped. ". . . Fire engines're already there, and the constable said that as many as twenty may be dead or drowned. It seems the boat caught fire from the kitchen, sir. There were several explosions. They blew out most of the hull and . . . Just a moment sir, there's another report coming in from Marine."

They waited. Brian Kwok broke the silence. "Dunross?"

"The party was on the top deck?" Crosse asked.

"Yes sir."

"He's much too smart to get burned to death—or drowned," Crosse said softly. "Was the fire an accident, or deliberate?"

Brian Kwok did not answer.

The HQ voice came in again. "Marine reports that the boat's capsized. They say it's a proper carve-up and it looks like a few got sucked under."

"Was our agent with our VIP?"

"No sir, he was waiting on the wharf near his car. There was no time to get to him."

"What about the people caught on the top deck?"

"Hang on a moment, I'll ask. . . ."

Again a silence. Brian Kwok wiped the sweat off.

". . . They say, twenty or thirty up there jumped, sir. Unfortunately most of them abandoned ship a bit late, just before the boat capsized. Marine doesn't know how many were swamped."

"Stand by." Crosse thought a moment. Then he spoke into the mike again. "I'm sending Superintendent Kwok there at once in this transport. Send a team of frogmen to meet him. Ask the navy to assist, Priority One. I'll be at home if I'm needed." He clicked off the mike. Then to Brian Kwok, "I'll walk from here. Call me the moment you know about Dunross. If he's dead we'll visit the bank vaults at once and to hell with the consequences. Fast as you can now!"

He got out. The van took off up the hill. Aberdeen was over the spine of mountains and due south. He glanced at Rose Court a moment, then down across the street below to Sinclair Towers. One of his teams was still watching the entrance, waiting patiently for Tsu-yan's return. Where is that bastard? he asked himself irritably.

Very concerned, he walked off down the hill. Rain began to splatter him. His footsteps quickened.

Suslev took an ice-cold beer from the modern refrigerator and opened it. He drank gratefully. 32 Sinclair Towers was spacious, rich, clean and well furnished, with three bedrooms and a large living room. It was on the eleventh floor. There were three apartments to each floor around two cramped elevators and exit steps. Mr. and Mrs. John Chen owned 31. 33 belonged to a Mr. K. V. Lee. Arthur had told Suslev that K. V. Lee was a cover name for Ian Dunross who, following the pattern of his predecessors, had sole access to three or four private apartments spread around the Colony. Suslev had never met either John Chen or Dunross though he had seen them at the races and elsewhere many times.

If we have to interview the tai-pan what could be more convenient? he thought grimly. And with Travkin as an alternate bait. . . .

A sudden squall whipped the curtains that were drawn over open windows and he heard the rain. He shut the windows carefully and looked out. Great drops were streaking the windows. Streets and rooftops were already wet. Lightning went across the sky. The rumble of thunder followed. Already the temperature had dropped a few degrees. This'll be a good storm, he told himself gratefully, pleased to be out of Ginny Fu's tiny, sleazy fifth-floor walkup in Mong Kok, and equally happy not to be at Clinker's.

Arthur had arranged everything: Clinker, Ginny Fu, this safe house, the tunnel, certainly as well as he himself could have done in Vladivostok. Clinker was a submariner and cockney and everything he was supposed to be except that he had always detested the officer class. Arthur had said it had been easy to subvert Clinker to the cause, using the man's built-in suspicions, hatreds and secretiveness. "Ugly Ernie knows only a little about you, Gregor—of course that you're Russian and captain of the Ivanov. As to the tunnel, I told him you're having an affair with a married woman in Sinclair Towers, the wife of one of the Establishment tai-pans. I told him the tape-recorded snores and secrecy are because the rotten Peelers are after you and they've sneaked in and bugged his flat."

"Peelers?"

"That's the cockney nickname for police. It came from Sir Robert Peel, Prime Minister of England, who founded the first police force. Cockneys've always hated Peelers and Ugly Ernie would delight in outwitting them. Just be pro-Royal Navy and he's your dog until death. . . ."

Suslev smiled. Clinker's not a bad man, he thought, just a bore.

He sipped his beer as he wandered back into the living room. The afternoon paper was there. It was the *Guardian* Extra, the headlines screaming, MOB MURDERS FRAGRANT FLOWER, and a good photograph of the riot. He sat in an armchair and read quickly.

Then his sharp ears heard the elevator stop. He went to the table beside the door and slid the loaded automatic with its silencer from under it. He pocketed the gun and peered through the spy hole.

The doorbell was muted. He opened it and smiled. "Come in, old friend." He embraced Jacques deVille warmly. "It's been a long time."

"Yes, yes it has, comrade," deVille said as warmly. The last time he had seen Suslev was in Singapore, five years before, at a secret meeting arranged by Arthur just after deVille had been induced to join Sevrin. He and Suslev had met just as secretly the first time in the great port of Lyons in France in June '41, just days before Nazi Germany invaded Soviet Russia when the two countries were outwardly still allies. At that time deVille was in the Maquis and Suslev second-in-command and secret political commissar of a Soviet submarine that was ostensibly in for a refit from patrol in the Atlantic. It was then that deVille was asked if he would like to carry on the *real war*, the war against the capitalist enemy as a secret agent after the fascists had been destroyed.

He had agreed with all his heart.

It had been easy for Suslev to subvert him. Because of deVille's potential after the war, the KGB had secretly had him betrayed to the Gestapo, then rescued from a Gestapo prison death by Communist guerrillas. The guerrillas had given him false proof that he had been betrayed by one of his own men for money. DeVille was thirty-two then and, like many, infatuated with socialism and with some of the teachings of Marx and Lenin. He had never joined the French Communist Party but now, because of Sevrin, he was an honorary captain in the KGB Soviet Security Force.

"You seem tired, Frederick," Suslev said, using deVille's cover name. "Tell me what's wrong."

"Just a family problem."

"Tell me."

Suslev listened intently to deVille's sad story about his son-in-law and daughter. Since their meeting in 1941 Suslev had been deVille's controller. In 1947 he had ordered him out to Hong Kong to join Struan's. Before the war deVille and his father had owned a highly successful import-export business with close ties to Struan's—as well as family ties—so the change had been easy and welcome. DeVille's secret assignment was to become a member of the Inner Court and, at length, tai-pan.

"Where's your daughter now?" he asked compassionately.

DeVille told him.

"And the driver of the other car?" Suslev committed the name and address to memory. "I'll see that he's dealt with."

"No," deVille said at once. "It . . . it was an accident. We cannot punish a man for an accident."

"He was drunk. There is no excuse for drunk driving. In any event you are important to us. We take care of our own. I will deal with him."

DeVille knew there was no point in arguing. A gust of rain battered the windows. "*Merde*, but the rain's good. The temperature must be down five degrees. Will it last?"

"The storm front's reported to be big."

DeVille watched globules running down the pane, wondering why he had been summoned. "How are things with you?"

"Very good. Drink?" Suslev went to the mirrored bar. "There's good vodka."

"Vodka's fine, please. But a short one."

"If Dunross retired are you the next tai-pan?"

"I would think it's between four of us: Gavallan, David MacStruan, myself and Linbar Struan."

"In that order?"

"I don't know. Except Linbar's probably last. Thanks." DeVille accepted his drink. They toasted each other. "I'd bet on Gavallan."

"Who's this MacStruan?"

"A distant cousin. He's done his five years as a China Trader. At the moment he's heading up our expansion into Canada—we're trying to diversify and get into wood fibers, copper, all the Canadian minerals, mostly out of British Columbia."

"How good is he?"

"Very good. Very tough. A very dirty fighter. Forty-one, ex-lieutenant, Paratroopers. His left hand was almost ripped off over Burma by a tangle in the shrouds of his parachute. He just tied a tourniquet around it and carried on fighting. That earned him a Military Cross. If I was tai-pan I'd choose him." DeVille shrugged. "By our company law only the tai-pan can appoint his successor. He can do it anytime, even in his will if he wants. Whatever way it's done it's binding on the Noble House."

Suslev watched him. "Has Dunross made a will?"

"Ian's very efficient."

A silence gathered.

"Another vodka?"

"*Non, merci*, I'll stay with this one. Is Arthur joining us?"

"Yes. How could we tip the scales for you?"

DeVille hesitated, then shrugged.

Suslev poured himself another drink. "It would be easy to discredit this MacStruan and the others. Yes. Easy to eliminate them." Suslev turned and looked at him. "Even Dunross."

"No. That's not the solution."

"Is there another one?"

"Being patient." DeVille smiled but his eyes were very tired and shadows lurked there. "I would not like to be the cause of . . . of his removal or that of the others."

Suslev laughed. "It's not necessary to kill to eliminate! Are we barbarians? Or course not." He was watching his protégé closely. DeVille needs toughening, he was thinking. "Tell me about the American, Bartlett, and the Struan–Par-Con deal."

DeVille told him all he knew. "Bartlett's money will give us everything we need."

"Can this Gornt effect a takeover?"

"Yes and no. And possibly. He's tough and he truly hates us. It's a long-term rival—"

"Yes, I know." Suslev was surprised deVille kept repeating information he already had been given. It's a bad sign, he thought, and glanced at his watch. "Our friend's twenty-five minutes late. That's unusual." Both men were too seasoned to worry. Meetings such as this could never be completely firm because no one could ever control the unexpected happening.

"Did you hear about the fire in Aberdeen?" deVille asked at the sudden thought.

"What fire?"

"There was a bulletin over the wireless just before I came up." DeVille and his wife had apartment 20 on the sixth floor. "The *Floating Dragon* restaurant at Aberdeen burned down. Perhaps Arthur was there."

"Did you see him?" Suslev was suddenly concerned.

"No. But I could easily have missed him. I left well before dinner."

Suslev sipped his vodka thoughtfully. "Has he told you yet who the others are in Sevrin?"

"No. I asked him, judiciously, as you ordered, but he nev—"

"Order? I don't order you, *tovarich*, I just suggest."

"Of course. All he said was, 'We'll all meet in due course.'"

"We'll both know soon. He's perfectly correct to be cautious." Suslev had wanted to test deVille and test Arthur. It was one of the most basic rules in the KGB that you can never be too cautious about your spies however important they are. He remembered his instructor hammering into them another direct quote from Sun Tzu's *The Art of War*, which was obligatory reading for all Soviet military: "There are five classes of spies—local spies, inward spies, converted spies, doomed spies and surviving spies. When all five categories are working in concert, the state will be secure and the army inviolate. Local spies are those who are local inhabitants. Inward spies are officials of the enemy. Converted spies are the enemies' spies you have converted. Doomed spies are those fed false information and reported to the enemy who will torture this false information from them and so be deceived. Surviving spies are those who bring back news from the enemy camp. Remember, in the whole army, none should more liberally be rewarded. But if a secret piece of news is divulged by a spy before the time is ripe, he or she must be put to death, together with the person to whom the secret is told."

If the other AMG reports are like the one already discovered, Suslev thought dispassionately, then Dunross is doomed.

He was watching deVille, measuring him, liking him, glad that again he had passed that test—and Arthur. The last paragraph of *The Art of War*—so important a book to the Soviet elite that many knew the slim volume by heart—sprang into his mind: "It is only the enlightened ruler and wise general who will use the highest intelligence of the army for the purposes of spying. Spies are the most important element in war because upon them depends an army's ability to move."

That's what the KGB does, he thought contentedly. We try for the best talent in all the Soviets. We *are* the elite. We *need* spies of all five categories. We need these men, Jacques and Arthur and all the others.

Yes, we need them very much.

"Arthur's never given any clue who the others are. Nothing," deVille was saying, "only that there are seven of us."

"We must be patient," Suslev said, relieved that Arthur was correctly cautious too, for part of the plan was that the seven should never know each other, should never know that Suslev was Sevrin's controller and Arthur's superior. Suslev knew the identities of all the Sevrin moles. With Arthur he had approved all of them over the years, continually testing them all, honing their loyalties, eliminating some, substituting others. You always test, and the moment a spy wavers that's the time to neutralize or eliminate him—before he neutralizes or eliminates you. Even Ginny Fu, he thought, though she's not a spy and knows nothing. You can never be sure of anyone except yourself—that's what our Soviet system teaches. Yes. It's time I took her on the trip I've always promised. A short voyage next week. To Vladivostok. Once she's there she can be cleansed and rehabilitated and made useful, never to return here.

He sipped his vodka, rolling the fiery liquid around his tongue. "We'll give Arthur half an hour. Please," he said, motioning to a chair.

DeVille moved the newspaper out of the way and sat in the armchair. "Did you read about the bank runs?"

Suslev beamed. "Yes, *tovarich*. Marvelous."

"Is it a KGB operation?"

"Not to my knowledge," Suslev said jovially. "If it is there's promotion for someone." It was a key Leninistic policy to pay particular attention to Western banks that were at the core of Western strength, to infiltrate them to the highest level, to encourage and assist others to foment disaster against Western currencies but at the same time to borrow capital from them to the utter maximum, whatever the interest, the longer the loan the better, making sure that no Soviet ever defaulted on any repayment, *whatsoever the cost*. "The crash of the Ho-Pak will certainly bring down others. The papers say there might even be a run on the Victoria, eh?"

DeVille shivered in spite of himself and Suslev noticed it. His concern deepened. "*Merde,* but that would wreck Hong Kong," deVille said. "Oh, I know the sooner the better but . . . but being buried so deep, sometimes you forget who you really are."

"That's nothing to worry about. It happens to all of us. You're in turmoil because of your daughter. What father wouldn't be? It will pass."

"When can we do something? I'm tired, so tired of waiting."

"Soon. Listen," Suslev said to encourage him. "In January I was at a top echelon meeting in Moscow. Banking was high on our list. At our last count we're indebted to the capitalists nearly 30 billions in loans—most of that to America."

DeVille gasped. "Madonna, I had no idea you'd been so successful."

Suslev's smile broadened. "That's just Soviet Russia! Our satellites are in for another 6.3 billions. East Germany's just got another 1.3 billion to purchase capitalist rolling mills, computer technology and a lot of things we need." He laughed, drained his glass and poured another, the liquor oiling his tongue. "I really don't understand them, the capitalists. They delude themselves. We're openly committed to consume them but they give us the means to do it. They're astonishing. If we have time, twenty years—at the most twenty—by that time our debt will be 60, 70 billions and as far as they're concerned we'll still be a triple-A risk, never having defaulted on a payment ever . . . in war, peace or depression." He let out a sudden burst of laughter. "What was it the Swiss banker said? 'Lend a little and you have a debtor—lend a lot and you have a partner!' 70 billions, Jacques old friend, and we own them. 70 and we can twist their policies to suit ourselves and then at any moment of our own choosing the final ploy: 'So sorry, Mr. Capitalist Zionist Banker, we regret we're broke! Oh very sorry but we can no longer repay the loans, not even the interest on the loans. Very sorry but from this moment all our present currency's valueless. Our new currency's a red ruble, one red ruble's worth a hundred of your capitalist dollars. . . .'"

Suslev laughed, feeling very happy. ". . . and however rich the banks are collectively they'll never be able to write off 70 billions. Never. 70 plus by that time with all the Eastern Bloc billions! And if the sudden announcement's timed to one of their inevitable capitalistic recessions as it will be . . . they'll be up to their Hebrew bankers' noses in their own panic shit, begging us to save their rotten skins." He added contemptuously, "The stupid bastards deserve to lose! Why should we fight them when their own greed and stupidity's destroying them. Eh?"

DeVille nodded uneasily. Suslev frightened him. I must be getting old, he thought. In the early days it was so easy to believe in the cause of the masses. The cries of the downtrodden were so loud and clear then. But now? Now they're not so clear. I'm still committed, deeply committed. I regret nothing. France will be better Communist.

Will it?

I don't know anymore, not for certain, not as I used to. It's a pity for all people that there must be some "ism" or other, he told himself, trying to cover his anguish. Better if there were no "isms," just my beloved Côte d'Azur basking in the sun.

"I tell you, old friend, Stalin and Beria were geniuses," Suslev was saying. "They're the greatest Russians that have ever been."

DeVille just managed to keep the shock off his face. He was remembering the horror of the German occupation, the humbling of France, all the villages and hamlets and vineyards, remembering that Hitler would never have dared attack Poland and start it all without Stalin's nonaggression pact to protect his back. Without Stalin there would have been no war, no holocaust and we would all be better off. "Twenty million Russians? Countless millions of others," he said.

"A modest cost." Suslev poured again, his zeal and the vodka taking him. "Because of Stalin and Beria we have all Eastern Europe from the Baltic to the Balkans—Estonia, Lithuania, Latvia, Czechoslovakia, Hungary, Rumania, Bulgaria, all Poland, Prussia, half of Germany, Outer Mongolia." Suslev belched happily. "North Korea, and footholds everywhere else. Their Operation Lion smashed the British Empire. Because of their support the United Nations was birthed to give us our greatest weapon in our arsenal of many weapons. And then there's Israel." He began to laugh. "My father was one of the controllers of that program."

DeVille felt the hackles of his neck rise. "What?"

"Israel was a Stalin-Beria coup of monumental proportions! Who helped it, overt and covert, come into being? Who gave it immediate recognition? *We did,* and why?" Suslev belched again, "To cement into the guts of Arabia a perpetual cancer that will suppurate and destroy both sides and, along with them, bring down the industrial might of the West. Jew against Mohammedan against Christian. Those fanatics'll never live at peace with one another even though they could, easily. They will never bury their differences even if it costs them their stupid lives." He laughed and stared at his glass blearily, swirling the liquid around. DeVille watched him, hating him, wanting to give him the lie back, afraid to, knowing himself totally in Suslev's power. Once, some years ago, he had balked over sending some routine Struan figures to a box number in Berlin. Within a day, a stranger had phoned him at home. Such a call had never happened before. It was friendly. But he knew.

DeVille suppressed a shudder and kept his face clear as Suslev glanced up at him.

"Don't you agree, *tovarich?*" the KGB man said, beaming. "I swear I'll never understand the capitalists. They make enemies of four hundred million Arabs who have all the world's real oil reserves one day they will need so desperately. And soon we'll have Iran and the Gulf and the Strait of Hormuz. Then we'll have a hand on the West's tap, then they're ours and no need for war—just execution." Suslev drained his vodka and poured another.

DeVille watched him, loathing him now, wondering frantically about his own role. Is it for this that I have been almost a perfect mole, for sixteen years keeping myself prepared and ready, with no suspicion against me? Even Susanne suspects nothing and everyone believes I'm anti-Communist, pro-Struan's which is the arch-capitalistic creation in all Asia. Dirk Struan's thoughts permeate us. Profit. Profit for the tai-pan and the Noble House and then Hong Kong in that order and the hell with everyone except the Crown, England and China. And even if I don't become tai-pan, I can still make Sevrin the wrecker of China that Suslev and Arthur want it to be. But do I want to now? Now that, for the first time, I've really seen into this . . . this monster and all their hypocrisy?

"Stalin," he said, almost wincing under Suslev's gaze. "Did . . . you ever meet him?"

"I was near him once. Ten feet away. He was tiny but you could feel his power. That was in 1953 at a party Beria gave for some senior KGB officers. My father was invited and I was allowed to go with him." Suslev took another vodka, hardly seeing him, swept by the past and by his family's involvement in the movement. "Stalin was there, Beria, Malenkov . . . Did you know Stalin's real name was Iosif Vissarionovich Dzhugashvili? He was the son of a shoemaker, in Tiflis, my home, destined for the priesthood but expelled from the seminary there. Strange strange strange!"

They touched glasses.

"No need for you to be so solemn, comrade," he said, misreading deVille. "Whatever your personal loss. You're part of the future, part of the march to victory!" Suslev drained his glass. "Stalin must have died a happy man. We should be so lucky, eh?"

"And Beria?"

"Beria tried to take power too late. He failed. We in the KGB are like Japanese in that we too agree the only sin is failure. But Stalin . . . There's a story my father tells that when at Yalta, for no concession, Roosevelt agreed to give Stalin Manchuria *and the Kuriles* which guaranteed us dominance over China and Japan and all Asian waters, Stalin had a hemorrhage choking back his laughter and almost died!"

After a pause, deVille said, "And Solzhenitsyn and the *gulags?*"

"We're at war, my friend, there are traitors within. Without terror how can the few rule the many? Stalin knew that. He was a truly great man. Even his death served us. It was brilliant of Khrushchev to use him to 'humanize' the USSR."

"That was just another ploy?" deVille asked, shaken.

"That would be a state secret." Suslev swallowed a belch. "It doesn't matter, Stalin will be returned to his glory soon. Now, what about Ottawa?"

"Oh. I've been in contact with Jean-Charles an—" The phone rang abruptly. A single ring. Their eyes went to it, their breathing almost stopped. After twenty-odd seconds there was a second single ring. Both men relaxed slightly. Another twenty-odd seconds and the third ring became continuous. One ring meant "Danger leave immediately"; two, that the meeting was canceled; three that whoever was calling would be there shortly; three becoming continuous, that it was safe to talk. Suslev picked up the phone. He heard breathing, then Arthur asked in his curious accent, "Is\Mr. Lop-sing there?"

"There's no Lop-*ting* here, you have a wrong number," Suslev said in a different voice, concentrating with an effort.

They went through the code carefully, Suslev further reassured by Arthur's slight, dry cough. Then Arthur said, "I cannot meet tonight. Would Friday at three be convenient?" Friday meant Thursday—tomorrow—Wednesday meant Tuesday, and so on. The three was a code for a meeting place: the Happy Valley Racecourse at the dawn workout.

Tomorrow at dawn!

"Yes."

The phone clicked off. Only the dial tone remained.

THURSDAY

39

About an hour before dawn in the pouring rain Goodweather Poon looked down at the half-naked body of John Chen and cursed. He had been through his clothes carefully and sifted through endless pounds of mud from the grave that the two youths, Kin Pak and Dog-eared Chen, had dug. But he had found nothing—no coins or parts of coins or jewelry, nothing. And Four Finger Wu had said earlier, "You find that half-coin, Goodweather Poon!" Then the old man had given him further instructions and Goodweather Poon was very pleased because that relieved him of any responsibility and he could then make no mistake.

He had ordered Dog-eared Chen and Kin Pak to carry the body downstairs and had threatened Smallpox Kin, who nursed his mutilated hand, that if the youth moaned once more he would slice out his tongue. They had left Father Kin's body in an alley. Then Goodweather Poon had sought out the King of the Beggars of Kowloon City who was a distant cousin of Four Finger Wu. All beggars were members of the Beggars' Guild and there was one king in Hong Kong, one in Kowloon and one in Kowloon City. In olden days begging was a lucrative profession, but now, due to stiff prison sentences and fines and plenty of well-paying jobs, it was not.

"You see, Honored Beggar King, this acquaintance of ours has just died," Goodweather Poon explained patiently to the distinguished old man. "He has no relations, so he's been put out in Flowersellers' Alley. My High Dragon would certainly appreciate a little help. Perhaps you could arrange a quiet burial?" He negotiated politely then paid the agreed price and went off to their taxi and car that waited outside the city limits, happy that now the body would vanish forever without a trace. Kin Pak was already in the taxi's front seat. He got in beside him. "Guide us to John Chen," he ordered. "And be quick!"

"Take the Sha Tin Road," Kin Pak said importantly to the driver. Dog-eared Chen was cowering in the backseat with more of Goodweather Poon's fighters. Smallpox Kin and the others followed in the car.

The two vehicles went northwest into the New Territories on the Sha Tin–Tai Po road that curled through villages and resettlement areas and shantytowns of squatters, through the mountain pass, skirting the railway that headed north for the border, past rich market gardens heavy with the smell of dung. Just before the fishing village of Sha Tin with the sea on their right, they turned left off the main road onto a side road, the surface broken and puddled. In a glade of trees they stopped and got out.

It was warm in the rain, the land sweet-smelling. Kin Pak took the shovel and led the way into the undergrowth. Goodweather Poon held the flashlight as Kin Pak, Dog-eared Chen and Smallpox Kin searched. It was difficult in the darkness for them to find the exact place. Twice they had begun to dig, before Kin Pak remembered their father had marked the spot with a crescent rock. Cursing and soaked, at length they found the rock and began to dig. The earth was parched under the surface. Soon they had unearthed the corpse which was wrapped in a blanket. The smell was heavy. Though Goodweather Poon had made them strip the body and had searched diligently, nothing was to be found.

"You sent everything else to Noble House Chen?" he asked again, rain on his face, his clothes soaking.

"Yes," the young Kin Pak said truculently. "How many fornicating times do I have to tell you?" He was very weary, his clothes sodden, and he was sure he was going to die.

"All of you take your manure-infested clothes off. Shoes socks everything. I want to go through your pockets."

They obeyed. Kin Pak wore a string around his neck with a cheap circle of jade on it. Almost everyone in China wore a piece of jade for good luck, because everyone knew if an evil god caused you to stumble, the spirit of jade would get between you and the evil and take the brunt of the fall from you and shatter, saving you from shattering. And if it didn't, then the Jade God was regretfully sleeping and that was your joss never mind.

Goodweather Poon found nothing in Kin Pak's pockets. He threw the clothes back at him. By now he was soaked too and very irritable. "You can dress, and dress the corpse again. And hurry it up!"

Dog-eared Chen had almost 400 HK and a jade bracelet of good quality. One of the men took the jade and Poon pocketed the money and turned on Smallpox Kin. All their eyes popped as they saw the big roll of notes he found in the youth's pants pocket.

Goodweather Poon shielded it carefully from the rain. "Where in the name of Heavenly Whore did you get all this?"

He told them about shaking down the lucky ones outside the Ho-Pak and they laughed and complimented him on his sagacity. "Very good, very clever," Poon said. "You're a good businessman. Put your clothes on. What was the old woman's name?"

"She called herself Ah Tam." Smallpox Kin wiped the rain out of his eyes, his toes twisting into the mud, his mutilated hand on fire now and aching very much. "I'll take you to her if you want."

"Hey, I need the fornicating light here!" Kin Pak called out. He was on his hands and knees, fighting John Chen's clothes into place. "Can't someone give me a hand?"

"Help him!"

Dog-eared Chen and Smallpox Kin hurried to help as Goodweather Poon directed the circle of light back on the corpse. The body was swollen and puffy, the rain washing the dirt away. The back of John Chen's head was blood-matted and crushed but his face was still recognizable.

"*Ayeeyah*," one of his men said, "let's get on with it. I feel evil spirits lurking hereabouts."

"Just his trousers and shirt'll do," Goodweather Poon said sourly. He waited until the body was partially dressed. Then he turned his eyes on them. "Now which one of you motherless whores helped the old man kill this poor fornicator?"

Kin Pak said, "I already t—" He stopped as he saw the other two point at him and say in unison, "He did," and back away from him.

"I suspected it all along!" Goodweather Poon was pleased that he had at last got to the bottom of the mystery. He pointed his stubby forefinger at Kin Pak. "Get in the trench and lie down."

"We have an easy plan how to kidnap Noble House Chen himself that'll bring us all twice, three times what this fornicator brought. I'll tell you how, *heya*?" Kin Pak said.

Goodweather Poon hesitated a moment at this new thought. Then he remembered Four Fingers's instructions. "Put your face in the dirt in the trench!"

Kin Pak looked at the inflexible eyes and knew he was dead. He shrugged. Joss. "I piss on all your generations," he said and got into the grave and lay down.

He put his head on his arms in the dirt and began to shut out the light of his life. From nothing into nothing, always part of the Kin family, of all its generations, living forever in its perpetual stream, from generation to generation, down through history into the everlasting future.

Goodweather Poon took up one of the shovels and because of the youth's courage he dispatched him instantly by putting the sharp edge of the blade between his vertebrae and shoving downward. Kin Pak died without knowing it.

"Fill up the grave!"

Dog-eared Chen was petrified but he rushed to obey. Goodweather Poon laughed and tripped him and gave him a savage kick for his cowardice. The man half-fell into the trench. At once the shovel in Poon's hands whirled in an arc and crunched into the back of Dog-eared Chen's head and he collapsed with a sigh on top of Kin Pak. The others laughed and one said, "Eeeee, you used that like a foreign devil cricket bat! Good. Is he dead?"

Goodweather Poon did not answer, just looked at the last Werewolf, Smallpox Kin. All their eyes went to him. He stood rigid in the rain. It was then that Goodweather Poon noticed the string tight around his neck. He took up the flashlight and went over to him and saw that the other end was dangling down his back. Weighing it down was a broken half-coin, a hole bored carefully into it. It was a copper cash and seemed ancient.

"All gods fart in Tsao Tsao's face! Where did you get this?" he asked, beginning to beam.

"My father gave it to me."

"Where did he get it, little turd?"

"He didn't tell me."

"Could he have got it from Number One Son Chen?"

Another shrug. "I don't know. I wasn't here when they killed him. I'm innocent on my mother's head!"

With a sudden movement Goodweather Poon ripped the necklace off. "Take him to the car," he said to two of his fighters. "Watch him very carefully. We'll take him back with us. Yes, we'll take him back. The rest of you fill up the grave and camouflage it carefully." Then he ordered the last two of his men to pick up the blanket containing John Chen and to follow him. They did so awkwardly in the darkness.

He trudged off toward the Sha Tin Road, skirting the puddles. Nearby was a broken-down bus shelter. When the road was clear he motioned to his men and they quickly unwrapped the blanket and propped the body in a corner. Then he took out the sign that the Werewolves had made previously and stuck it carefully on the body.

"Why're you doing that, Goodweather Poon, *heya?* Why're you do—"

"Because Four Fingers told me to! How do I know? Keep your fornicating mouth sh—"

Headlights from an approaching car rounding the bend washed them suddenly. They froze and turned their faces away, pretending to be waiting passengers. Once the car was safely past they took to their heels. Dawn was streaking the sky, the rain lessening.

The phone jangled and Armstrong came out of sleep heavily. In the half-darkness he groped for the receiver and picked it up. His wife stirred uneasily and awoke.

"Divisional Sergeant Major Tang-po, sir, sorry to wake you, sir, but we've found John Chen. The Were—"

Armstrong was instantly awake. "Alive?"

"*Dew neh loh moh* no sir, his body was found near Sha Tin at a bus stop, a bus shelter, sir, and those fornicating Werewolves've left a note on his chest, sir: 'This Number One Son Chen had the stupidity to try to escape us. No one can escape the Werewolves! Let all Hong Kong beware. Our eyes are everywhere!' He w—"

Armstrong listened, appalled, while the excited man told how police at Sha Tin had been summoned by an early-morning bus passenger. At once they had cordoned off the area and phoned CID Kowloon. "What should we do, sir?"

"Send a car for me at once."

Armstrong hung up and rubbed the tiredness out of his eyes. He wore a sarong and it looked well on his muscular body.

"Trouble?" Mary stifled a yawn and stretched. She was just forty, two years younger than he, brown-haired, taut, her face friendly though lined.

He told her, watching her.

"Oh." The color had left her face. "How terrible. Oh, how terrible. Poor John!"

"I'll make the tea," Armstrong said.

"No, no I'll do that." She got out of bed, her body firm. "Will you have time?"

"Just a cuppa. Listen to the rain . . . about bloody time!" Thoughtfully Armstrong went off to the bathroom and shaved and dressed quickly as only a policeman or doctor can. Two gulps of the hot sweet tea and just before the toast the doorbell rang. "I'll call you later. How about curry tonight? We can go to Singh's."

"Yes," she said. "Yes, if you'd like."

The door closed behind him.

Mary Armstrong stared at the door. Tomorrow is our fifteenth anniversary, she thought. I wonder if he'll remember. Probably not. In fourteen times, he's been out on a case eight, once I was in hospital and the rest . . . the rest were all right, I suppose.

She went to the window and pulled the curtains back. Torrents of rain streaked the windows in the half-light, but now it was cool and pleasant. The apartment had two bedrooms and it was their furniture though the apartment belonged to the government and went with the job.

Christ, what a job!

Rotten for a policeman's wife. You spend your life waiting for him to come home, waiting for some rotten villain to knife him, or shoot him or hurt him—most nights you sleep alone or you're being woken up at all rotten hours with some more rotten disasters and off he goes again. Overworked and underpaid. Or you go to the Police Club and sit around with other wives while the men get smashed and you swap lies with the wives and drink too many pink gins. At least they have children.

Children! Oh God . . . I wish we had children.

But then, most of the wives complain about how tired they are, how exhausting children are, and about *amahs* and school and the expense . . . and everything. What the hell does this life mean? What a rotten waste! What a perfectly rotten—

The phone rang. *"Shut up!"* she shrieked at it, then laughed nervously. "Mary Mary quite contrary where did your temper go?" she chided herself and picked the phone up. "Hello?"

"Mary, Brian Kwok, sorry to wake you but is Rob—"

"Oh hello, dear. No, sorry, he's just left. Something about the Were-wolves."

"Yes, I just heard, that's what I was calling about. He's gone to Sha Tin?"

"Yes. Are you going too?"

"No. I'm with the Old Man."

"Poor you." She heard him laugh. They chatted for a moment then he rang off.

She sighed and poured herself another cup of tea, added milk and sugar and thought about John Chen. Once upon a time she had been madly in love with him. They had been lovers for more than two years and he had been her first. This was in the Japanese Internment Camp in Stanley Prison on the south part of the island.

In 1940 she had passed the Civil Service exam in England with honors and after a few months had been sent out to Hong Kong, around the Cape. She had arrived late in '41, just nineteen, and just in time to be interned with all European civilians, there to stay until 1945.

I was twenty-two when I got out and the last two years, we were lovers, John and I. Poor John, nagged constantly by his rotten father, and his sick mother, with no way to escape them and almost no privacy in the camp, cooped up with families, children, babes, husbands, wives, hatred hunger envy and little laughter all those years. Loving him made the camp bearable. . . .

I don't want to think about those rotten times.

Or the rotten time after the camp when he married his father's choice, a rotten little harpy but someone with money and influence and Hong Kong family connections. I had none. I should have gone home but I didn't want home—what was there to go home to? So I stayed and worked in the Colonial Office and had a good time, good enough. And then I met Robert.

Ah, Robert. You were a good man and good to me and we had fun and I was a good wife to you, still try to be. But I can't have children and you . . . we both want children and one day a few years ago, you found out about John Chen. You never asked me about him but I know you know and ever since then you've hated him. It all happened long before I met you and you knew about the camp but not about my lover. Remember how before we got married I said, Do you want to know about the past, my darling? And you said, No, old girl.

You used to call me old girl all the time. Now you don't call me anything. Just Mary sometimes.

Poor Robert! How I must have disappointed you!

Poor John! How you disappointed me, once upon a time so fine, now so very dead.

I wish I was dead too.

She began to cry.

40

"It's going to continue to rain, Alexi," Dunross said, the track already sodden, heavy overcast and the day gloomy.

"I agree, tai-pan. If it rains even part of tomorrow too, the going will be foul on Saturday."

"Jacques? What do you think?"

"I agree," deVille said. "Thank God for the rain but *merde* it would be a pity if the races were canceled."

Dunross nodded.

They were standing on the grass near the winner's circle at the Happy Valley Racecourse, the three men dressed in raincoats and hats. There was a bad weal across Dunross's face, and bruises, but his eyes were steady and clear and he stood with his easy confidence, watching the cloud cover, the rain still falling but not as strongly as in the night, other trainers and owners and bystanders scattered about the paddock and stands, equally pensive. A few horses were exercising, among them Noble Star, Buccaneer with a stable jockey up and Gornt's Pilot Fish. All of the horses were being exercised gingerly with very tight reins: the track and the approach to the track were very slippery. But Pilot Fish was prancing, enjoying the rain.

"This morning's weather report said the storm was huge." Travkin's sloe eyes were red-rimmed with tiredness and he watched Dunross. "If the rain stops tomorrow, the going'll still be soft on Saturday."

"Does that help or hurt Noble Star's chances, Alexi?" Jacques asked.

"As God wills, Jacques. She's never run in the wet." It was hard for Travkin to concentrate. Last evening the phone had rung and it was the KGB stranger again and the man had rudely cut through his questions of why he had vanished so suddenly. "It's not your privilege to question, Prince Kurgan. Just tell me everything you know about Dunross. Now. Everything. His habits, rumors about him, everything."

Travkin had obeyed. He knew that he was in a vise, knew that the stranger who must be KGB would be taping what he said to check the truth of what he related, the slightest variation of the truth perhaps a death knell for his wife or son or his son's wife or son's children—if they truly existed.

Do they? he asked himself again, agonized.

"What's the matter, Alexi?"

"Nothing, tai-pan," Travkin replied, feeling unclean. "I was thinking of what you went through last night." The news of the fire at Aberdeen had flooded the airwaves, particularly Venus Poon's harrowing eyewitness account which had been the focus of the reports. "Terrible about the others, wasn't it?"

"Yes." So far the known death count was fifteen burned and drowned, including two children. "It'll take days to find out really how many were lost."

"Terrible," Jacques said. "When I heard about it . . . if Susanne had been here we would have been caught in it. She . . . Curious how life is sometimes."

"Bloody firetrap! Never occurred to me before," Dunross said. "We've all eaten there dozens of times—I'm going to talk to the governor this morning about all those floating restaurants."

"But you're all right, you yourself?" Travkin asked.

"Oh yes. No problem." Dunross smiled grimly. "Not unless we all get the croup from swimming in that cesspit."

When the *Floating Dragon* had suddenly capsized, Dunross, Gornt and Peter Marlowe had been in the water right below. The megaphone on the police launch had shouted a frantic warning and they had all kicked out desperately. Dunross was a strong swimmer and he and Gornt had just got clear though the surge of water sucked them backward. As his head went under he saw the half-full cutter pulled into the maelstrom and capsized and Marlowe in trouble. He let himself go with the boiling torrent as the ship settled onto her side and lunged for Marlowe. His fingers found his shirt and held on and they swirled together for a moment, drawn a few fathoms down, smashing against the deck. The blow almost stunned him but he held on to Marlowe and when the drag lessened he kicked for the surface. Their heads came out of the water together. Marlowe gasped his thanks and struck out for Fleur who was hanging on to the side of the overturned cutter with others. Around them was chaos, people gasping and drowning and being rescued by sailors and by the strong. Dunross saw Casey diving for someone. Gornt was nowhere to be seen. Bartlett came up with Christian Toxe and kicked for a life belt. He made sure that Toxe had hold of the life ring securely before he shouted to Dunross, "I think Gornt got sucked down and there was a woman . . ." and at once dived again.

Dunross looked around. The *Floating Dragon* was almost on her side now. He felt a slight underwater explosion and water boiled around him for a moment. Casey came up for air, filled her lungs and slid under the surface again. Dunross dived too. It was almost impossible to see but he groped his way down along the top deck that was now almost vertical in the water. He swam around the wreck, searching, and stayed below as long as he could, then surfaced carefully for there were many swimmers still thrashing around. Toxe was choking out seawater, precariously hanging on to the life ring. Dunross swam over and paddled him toward a sailor, knowing Toxe could not swim.

"Hang on, Christian . . . you're okay now."

Desperately Toxe tried to talk through his retching. "My . . . my wife's . . . she's down th . . . down there . . . down . . ."

The sailor swam over. "I've got him, sir, you all right?"

"Yes . . . yes . . . he says his wife was sucked down."

"Christ! I didn't see anyone . . . I'll get some help!" The sailor turned and shouted at the police launch for assistance. At once several sailors dived overboard and began the search. Dunross looked for Gornt and could not see him. Casey came up panting and held on to the upturned cutter to catch her breath.

"You all right?"

"Yes . . . yes . . . thank God you're okay . . ." she gasped, her chest heaving. "There's a woman down there, Chinese I think, I saw her sucked down."

"Have you seen Gornt?"

"No. . . . Maybe he's . . ." She motioned at the launch. People were clambering up the gangway, others huddling on the deck. Bartlett surfaced for an instant and dived again. Casey took another great breath and slid into the depths. Dunross went after her slightly to her right.

They searched, the three of them, until everyone else was safe on the launch or in sampans. They never found the woman.

When Dunross had got home Penelope was deep asleep. She awoke momentarily. "Ian?"

"Yes. Go back to sleep, darling."

"Did you have a nice time?" she asked, not really awake.

"Yes, go back to sleep."

This morning, an hour ago, he had not awakened her when he left the Great House.

"You heard that Gornt made it, Alexi?" he said.

"Yes, yes I did, tai-pan. As God wills."

"Meaning?"

"After yesterday's stock market it would have been very convenient if he hadn't made it."

Dunross grinned and eased an ache in his back. "Ah, but then I would have been very put out, very put out indeed, for I'd not have had the pleasure of smashing Rothwell-Gornt myself, eh?"

After a pause deVille said, "It's astonishing more didn't die." They watched Pilot Fish as the stallion cantered past looking very good. DeVille's eyes ranged the course.

"Is it true that Bartlett saved Peter Marlowe's wife?" Travkin asked.

"He jumped with her. Yes. Both Linc and Casey did a great job. Wonderful."

"Will you excuse me, tai-pan?" Jacques deVille nodded at the stands. "There's Jason Plumm—I'm supposed to be playing bridge with him tonight."

"See you at Prayers, Jacques." Dunross smiled at him and deVille walked off. He sighed, sad for his friend. "I'm off to the office, Alexi. Call me at six."

"Tai-pan . . ."

"What?"

Travkin hesitated. Then he said simply, "I just want you to know I . . . I admire you greatly."

Dunross was nonplussed at the suddenness and at the open, curious melancholy that emanated from the other man. "Thanks," he said warmly and clapped him on the shoulder. He had never touched him as a friend before. "You're not so bad yourself."

Travkin watched him walk off, his chest hurting him, tears of shame adding to the rain. He wiped his face with the back of his hand and went back to watching Noble Star, trying to concentrate.

In the periphery of his vision he saw someone and he turned, startled. The KGB man was in a corner of the stands, another man joining him now. The man was old and gnarled and well known as a punter in Hong Kong. Travkin searched his mind for the name. Clinker. That's it! Clinker!

He watched them blankly for a moment. Jason Plumm was in the stands just behind the KGB man and he saw Plumm get up to return Jacques deVille's wave and walk down the steps to meet him. Just then the KGB man glanced in his direction and he turned carefully, trying not to be sudden again. The KGB man had lifted binoculars to his eyes and Travkin did not know if he had been noticed or not. His skin crawled at the thought of those high-powered binoculars focused on him. Perhaps the man can lip-read, he thought, aghast. Christ Jesus and Mother of God, thank God I didn't blurt out the truth to the tai-pan.

His heart was grinding nastily and he felt sick. A flicker of lightning went across the eastern sky. Rain was puddling the concrete and the open, lower section of the stands. He tried to calm himself and looked around helplessly not knowing what to do, wanting very much to find out who the KGB man was. Absently he noticed Pilot Fish was finishing his workout in fine form. Beyond him Richard Kwang was talking intently to a group of other Chinese he did not know. Linbar Struan and Andrew Gavallan were leaning on the rails with the American Rosemont and others from the consulate he knew by sight. They were watching the horses, oblivious of the rain. Near the changing rooms, under cover, Donald McBride was talking to other stewards, Sir Shi-teh T'Chung, Pugmire and Roger Crosse among them. He saw McBride glance over to Dunross, wave and beckon him to join them. Brian Kwok was waiting for Roger Crosse on the outskirts of the stewards. Travkin knew both of them but not that they were in SI.

Involuntarily his feet began to move toward them. The foul taste of bile rose into his mouth. He dominated his urge to rush up to them and blurt out the truth. Instead he called over his chief *ma-foo*. "Send our string home. All of them. Make sure they're dry before they're fed."

"Yes sir."

Unhappily Travkin trudged for the changing rooms. From the corner of his eye he saw that the KGB man had his binoculars trained on him. Rain trickled down his neck and mixed with the fear-sweat.

"Ah, Ian, we were thinking that if it rains tomorrow, we'd better cancel the meet. Say at 6:00 P.M. tomorrow," McBride said. "Don't you agree?"

"No, actually I don't. I suggest we make a final decision at ten Saturday morning."

"Isn't that a little late, old boy?" Pugmire asked.

"Not if the stewards alert the wireless and television fellows. It'll add to the excitement. Particularly if you release that news today."

"Good idea," Crosse said.

"Then that's settled," Dunross said. "Was there anything else?"

"Don't you think . . . it's a matter of the turf," McBride said. "We don't want to ruin it."

"I quite agree, Donald. We'll make a final decision Saturday at ten. All in favor?" There were no dissenters. "Good! Nothing else? Sorry, but I've got a meeting in half an hour."

Shi-teh said uncomfortably, "Oh, tai-pan, I was terribly sorry about last night . . . terrible."

"Yes. Shitee, when we meet the governor in Council at noon we should suggest he implants new, very severe fire regulations on Aberdeen."

"Agreed," Crosse said. "It's a miracle more weren't lost."

"You mean close the restaurants down, old boy?" Pugmire was shocked. His company had an interest in two of them. "That'll hurt the tourist business badly. You can't put in more exits. . . . You'd have to start from scratch!"

Dunross glanced back at Shi-teh. "Why don't you suggest to the governor that he order all kitchens at once be put on barges that can be moored alongside their mother ship? He could order that fire trucks be kept nearby until the changes have been made. The cost'd be modest, it would be easy to operate and the fire hazard would be solved once and for all."

They all stared at him. Shi-teh beamed. "Ian, you're a genius!"

"No. I'm only sorry we didn't think of it before. Never occurred to me. Rotten about Zep . . . and Christian's wife, isn't it? Have they found her body yet?"

"I don't think so."

"God knows how many others went. Did the MPs get out, Pug?"

"Yes, old chap. Except Sir Charles Pennyworth. Poor sod got his head bashed in on a sampan when he fell."

Dunross was shocked. "I liked him! What bloody bad joss!"

"There were a couple of the others near me at one stage. That bloody radical bastard, what's his name? Grey, ah yes, Grey that's it. And the other one, the other bloody Socialist berk, Broadhurst. Both behaved rather well I thought."

"I hear your Superfoods got out too, Pug. Wasn't our 'Call me Chuck' first ashore?"

Pugmire shrugged uneasily. "I really don't know." Then he beamed. "I . . . er . . . I hear Casey and Bartlett did a very good job, what? Perhaps they should have a medal."

"Why don't you suggest it?" Dunross said, anxious to leave. "If there's nothing else . . ."

Crosse said, "Ian, if I were you I'd get a shot. There must be bugs in that bay that haven't been invented yet."

They all laughed with him.

"Actually I've done better than that. After we got out of the water I grabbed Linc Bartlett and Casey and we fled to Doc Tooley." Dunross smiled faintly. "When we told him we'd been swimming in Aberdeen Harbor he almost had a hemorrhage. He said, 'Drink this,' and like bloody berks we did and before we knew what was happening we were retching our hearts out. If I'd had any strength I'd've belted him but we were all on our hands and knees fighting for the loo not knowing which end was first. Then Casey started laughing between heaves and then we were rolling on the bloody floor!" He added with pretended sadness, "Then, before we knew what was happening, Old Sawbones was shoving pills down our throats by the barrel and Bartlett said, 'For chrissake, Doc, how about a suppository and then you've a hole in one!'" They laughed again.

"Is it true about Casey? That she stripped and dived like an Olympic star?" Pugmire asked.

"Better! Stark bollock naked, old boy," Dunross exaggerated airily. "Like Venus de Milo! Probably the best . . . everything . . . I've ever seen."

"Oh?" Their eyes popped.

"Yes."

"My God, but swimming in Aberdeen Harbor! That sewer!" McBride said, eyebrows soaring. "If you all live it'll be a miracle!"

"Doc Tooley said the very least'll be gastroenteritis, dysentery or the plague." Dunross rolled his eyes. "Well, here today gone tomorrow. Anything else?"

"Tai-pan," Shi-teh said, "I . . . hope you don't mind but I've . . . I'd like to start a fund for the victims' families."

"Good idea! The Turf Club should contribute too. Donald, would you canvass the other stewards today and get their approval? How about 100,000?"

"That's a bit generous, isn't it?" Pugmire said.

Dunross's chin jutted. "No. Then let's make it 150,000 instead. The Noble House will contribute the same." Pugmire flushed. No one said anything. "Meeting adjourned? Good. Morning." Dunross raised his hat politely and walked off.

"Excuse me a moment." Crosse motioned Brian Kwok to follow him. "Ian!"

"Yes, Roger?"

When Crosse came up to Dunross he said quietly, "Ian, we've a report that Sinders is confirmed on the BOAC flight tomorrow. We'll go straight to the bank from the airport if that's convenient."

"The governor will be there too?"

"I'll ask him. We should be there about six."

"If the plane's on time." Dunross smiled.

"Did you get *Eastern Cloud*'s formal release yet?"

"Yes, thanks. It was telexed yesterday from Delhi. I ordered her back here at once and she sailed on the tide. Brian, you remember the bet you wanted—the one about Casey. About her knockers—fifty dollars to a copper cash they're the best in Hong Kong?"

Brian Kwok reddened, conscious of Crosse's bleak stare. "Er, yes, why?"

"I don't know about the best, but like the judgment of Paris, you'd have one helluva problem if it—they—were put to the test!"

"Then it's true, she was starkers?"

"She was Lady Godiva to the rescue." Dunross nodded to both of them pleasantly and walked off with, "See you tomorrow."

They watched him go. At the exit an SI agent was waiting to follow him.

Crosse said, "He's got something cooking."

"I agree, sir."

Crosse tore his eyes off Dunross and looked at Brian Kwok. "Do you usually bet on a lady's mammary glands?"

"No sir, sorry sir."

"Good. Fortunately women aren't the only source of beauty, are they?"

"No sir."

"There're hounds, paintings, music, even a killing. Eh?"

"Yes sir."

"Wait here please." Crosse went back to the other stewards.

Brian Kwok sighed. He was bored and tired. The team of frogmen had met him at Aberdeen and though he had found out almost at once that Dunross was safe and had already gone home, he had had to wait most of the night helping to organize the search for bodies. It had been a ghoulish task. Then when he was about to go home Crosse had called him to be at Happy Valley at dawn so there had been no point in going to bed. Instead he had gone to the Para Restaurant and glowered at the triads and One Foot Ko.

Now he was watching Dunross. What's that bugger got in the reaches of his mind? he asked himself, a twinge of envy soaring through him. What couldn't I do with his power and his money!

He saw Dunross change direction for the nearby stand, then noticed Adryon sitting beside Martin Haply, both staring at the horses, oblivious of Dunross. *Dew neh loh moh,* he thought, surprised. Curious that they'd be together. Christ, what a beauty! Thank God I'm not father to that one. I'd go out of my mind.

Crosse and the others had also noticed Adryon and Martin Haply with astonishment. "What's that bastard doing with the tai-pan's daughter?" Pugmire asked, his voice sour.

"No good, that's certain," someone said.

"Blasted fellow creates nothing but trouble!" Pugmire muttered and the others nodded agreement. "Can't understand why Toxe keeps him on!"

"Bloody man's a Socialist that's why! He should be blackballed too."

"Oh come off it, Pug. Toxe's all right—so're some Socialists," Shi-teh said. "But he should fire Haply, and we'd all be better off!" They had all been subject to Haply's attacks. A few weeks ago he had written a series of scathing exposés of some of Shi-teh's trading deals within his huge conglomeration of companies and implied that all sorts of dubious contributions were being made to various VIPs in the Hong Kong Government for favors.

"I agree," Pugmire said, hating him too. Haply, with his accuracy, had reported the private details of Pugmire's forthcoming merger with Superfoods and had made it abundantly clear Pugmire benefited far more than his shareholders in General Stores who were barely consulted on the terms of the merger. "Rotten bastard! I'd certainly like to know where he gets his information."

"Curious Haply should be with her," Crosse said, watching their lips, waiting for them to speak. "The only major company he hasn't gone after yet is Struan's."

"You think it's Struan's turn and Haply's pumping Adryon?" one of the others asked. "Wouldn't that be smashing!"

Excitedly they watched Dunross go into the stands, the two young people still not having noticed him.

"Maybe he'll whip him like he did the other bastard," Pugmire said gleefully.

"Eh?" Shi-teh said. "Who? What was that?"

"Oh, I thought you knew. About two years ago one of the Vic's junior execs straight out from England started pursuing Adryon. She was sixteen, perhaps seventeen—he was twenty-two, as big as a house, bigger than Ian, his name was Byron. He thought he was Lord Byron on the rampage and he mounted a campaign. The poor girl was bowled over. Ian warned him a last time. The creep kept calling, so Ian invited him out to his gym at Shek-O, put on gloves—he knew the bugger fancied himself as a boxer—and proceeded to pulp him." The others laughed. "Within the week the bank had sent him packing."

"Did you see it?" Shi-teh asked.

"Of course not. They were alone for God's sake, but the bloody fool was really in a bad way. I wouldn't like to go against the tai-pan—not when his temper's up."

Shi-teh looked back at Dunross. "Perhaps he'll do the same to that little rotter," he said happily.

They watched. Hopefully. Crosse wandered off with Brian Kwok, going closer.

Dunross was running up the steps in the stands now with his easy strength and he stopped beside them. "Hello, darling, you're up early," he said.

"Oh hello, Dad," Adryon said, startled. "I didn't se— What happened to your face?"

"I ran into the back end of a bus. Morning, Haply."

"Morning, sir." Haply half got up and sat down again.

"A bus?" she said, then suddenly, "Did you prang the Jag? Oh, did you get a ticket?" she asked hopefully, having had three this year herself.

"No. You're up early aren't you?" he said, sitting beside her.

"Actually we're late. We've been up all night."

"Oh?" He held on to forty-eight immediate questions and said instead, "You must be tired."

"No. No, actually I'm not."

"What's this all about, a celebration?"

"No. Actually it's poor Martin." She put a gentle hand on the youth's shoulder. With an effort Dunross kept his smile as gentle as her hand. He turned his attention to the young Canadian. "What's the problem?"

Haply hesitated, then told him what had happened at the paper when the publisher had called and Christian Toxe, his editor, had canceled his rumor series. "That bastard's sold us out. He's allowed the publisher to censor us. I know I'm right. I know I'm right."

"How?" Dunross asked, thinking, What a callous little bastard you are!

"Sorry, I can't reveal my source."

"He really can't, Dad, that's an infringement of freedom of the press," Adryon said defensively.

Haply was bunching his fists, then absently he put his hand on

Adryon's knee. She covered it with one of her own. "The Ho-Pak's being shoved into the ground for nothing."

"Why?"

"I don't know. But Gor—but tai-pans are behind the raid and it doesn't make sense."

"Gornt's behind it?" Dunross frowned at this new thought.

"I didn't say Gornt, sir. No I didn't say that."

"He didn't, Father," Adryon said. "What should Martin do? Should he resign or just swallow his pride an—"

"I just can't, Adryon," Martin Haply said.

"Let Father talk, he'll know."

Dunross saw her turn her lovely eyes back on him and he felt a glow at her confident innocence that he had never felt before. "Two things: First you go back at once. Christian will need all the help he can get. Second, y—"

"Help?"

"Haven't you heard about his wife?"

"What about her?"

"Don't you know she's dead?"

They stared at him blankly.

Quickly he told them about Aberdeen. Both of them were shocked and Haply stuttered, "Jesus, we . . . we didn't listen to a radio or anything . . . we were just dancing and talking. . . ." He jumped up and started to leave then came back. "I . . . I'd better go at once. Jesus!"

Adryon was on her feet. "I'll drop you."

Dunross said, "Haply, would you ask Christian to emphasize in bold type that anyone who got dunked or went swimming should see their doctors right smartly—very important."

"Got it!"

Adryon said anxiously, "Father, did you see Doc Too—"

"Oh yes," Dunross said. "Cleansed inside and out. Off you go!"

"What was the second thing, tai-pan?" Haply asked.

"Second was that you should remember it's the publisher's money, therefore his newspaper and he can do what he likes. But publishers can be persuaded. I wonder, for instance, who got to him or her and why he and she agreed to call Christian. . . . if you're so sure your story's true."

Haply beamed suddenly. "Come on, honey," he said and shouted thanks. They ran off hand-in-hand.

Dunross stayed sitting in the stands for the moment. He sighed deeply, then got up and went away.

Roger Crosse was with Brian Kwok under cover near the jockeys' changing rooms and he had been lip-reading the tai-pan's conversation. He watched him leave, the SI guard following him. "No need to waste any more time here, Brian. Come along." He headed for the far exit. "I wonder if Robert found anything at Sha Tin."

"Those bloody Werewolves are going to have a field day. All Hong Kong'll be frightened to death. I'll bet we . . ." Brian Kwok stopped suddenly. "Sir! Look!" He nodded at the stands, noticing Suslev and Clinker among the scattered groups who watched out of the rain. "I wouldn't've thought he'd be up yet!"

Crosse's eyes narrowed. "Yes. That's curious. Yes." He hesitated, then changed direction, watching their lips carefully. "Since he's honored us we might as well have a little chat. Ah . . . they've seen us. Clinker really doesn't like us at all." Leisurely he led the way into the stands.

The big Russian put a smile on his face and slid out a thin flask and took a sip. He offered it to Clinker.

"No thanks, mate, I just drink beer." Clinker's cold eyes were on the approaching policemen. "Proper niffy around here, ain't it?" he said loudly.

"Morning, Clinker," Crosse said, equally coldly. Then he smiled at Suslev. "Morning, Captain. Filthy day, what?"

"We're alive, *tovarich*, alive, so how can a day be filthy, eh?" Suslev was filled with outward bonhomie, continuing his cover as a hail-fellow-well-met. "Will there be racing Saturday, Superintendent?"

"Probably. The final decision'll be made Saturday morning. How long will you be in port?"

"Not long, Superintendent. The repairs to the rudder go slowly."

"Not too slowly I hope. We all get very nervous if our VIP harbor guests don't get very rapid service." Crosse's voice was crisp. "I'll talk to the harbor master."

"Thank you, that's . . . that's very thoughtful of you. And it was thoughtful of your department . . ." Suslev hesitated, then turned to Clinker. "Old friend, do you mind?"

"Not on your nelly," Clinker said. "Narks make me nervous." Brian Kwok looked at him. Clinker looked back unafraid. "I'll be in me car." He wandered off.

Suslev's voice hardened. "It was thoughtful of your department to send back the body of our poor comrade Voranski. Have you found the murderers?"

"Unfortunately no. They could be hired assassins—from any point of the compass. Of course if he hadn't slipped ashore mysteriously he'd still be a useful operative of the . . . of whatever department he served."

"He was just a seaman and a good man. I thought Hong Kong was safe."

"Did you pass on the assassins' photographs and information about their phone call to your KGB superiors?"

"I'm not KGB, piss on KGB! Yes, the information was passed on . . . by my superior," Suslev said irritably. "You know how it is, Superintendent, for God's sake. But Voranski was a good man and his murderers must be caught."

"We'll find them soon enough," Crosse said easily. "Did you know Voranski was in reality Major Yuri Bakyan, First Directorate, Department 6, KGB?"

They saw shock on Suslev's face. "He was . . . he was just a friend to me and he came with us from time to time."

"Who arranges that, Captain?" Crosse said.

Suslev looked at Brian Kwok who stared back at him with unconcealed distaste. "Why're you so angry? What have I done to you?"

"Why's the Russian empire so greedy, particularly when it comes to Chinese soil?"

"Politics!" Suslev said sourly then added to Crosse, "I don't interfere in politics."

"You buggers interfere all the time! What's your KGB rank?"

"I don't have one."

Crosse said, "A little cooperation could go a long way. Who arranges your crews, Captain Suslev?"

Suslev glanced at him. Then he said, "A word in private, eh?"

"Certainly," Crosse said. "Wait here, Brian."

Suslev turned his back on Brian Kwok and led the way down the exit stairs onto the grass. Crosse followed. "What do you think of Noble Star's chances?" Suslev asked genially.

"Good. But she's never raced in the wet."

"Pilot Fish?"

"Look at him—you can see for yourself. He loves the wet. He'll be the favorite. You plan to be here Saturday?"

Suslev leaned on the railings. And smiled. "Why not?"

Crosse laughed softly. "Why not indeed?" He was sure they were quite alone now. "You're a good actor, Gregor, very good."

"So're you, comrade."

"You're taking a hell of a risk, aren't you?" Crosse said, his lips hardly moving now as he talked.

"Yes, but then all life's a risk. Center told me to take over until Voranski's replacement arrives—there are too many important contacts and decisions to be made on this trip. Not the least, Sevrin. And anyway, as you know, Arthur wanted it this way."

"Sometimes I wonder if he's wise."

"He's wise." The lines around Suslev's eyes crinkled with his smile. "Oh yes. Very wise. I'm pleased to see you. Center's very very pleased with your year's work. I've much to tell you."

"Who's the bastard who leaked Sevrin to AMG?"

"I don't know. It was a defector. As soon as we know, he's a dead man."

"Someone's betrayed a group of my people to the PRC. The leak had to come from the AMG file. You read my copy. Who else on your ship did? Someone's infiltrated your operation here!"

Suslev blanched. "I'll activate a security check immediately. It could have come from London, or Washington."

"I doubt it. Not in time. I think it came from here. And then there's Voranski. You're infiltrated."

"If the PRC . . . yes, it will be done. But who? I'd bet my life there's no spy aboard."

Crosse was equally grim. "There's always someone who can be subverted."

"You have an escape plan?"

"Several."

"I'm ordered to assist in any way. Do you want a berth on the *Ivanov?*"

Crosse hesitated. "I'll wait until I've read the AMG files. It would be a pity after such a long time . . ."

"I agree."

"It's easy for you to agree. If you're caught you just get deported and asked politely, please don't come back. Me? I wouldn't want to be caught alive."

"Of course." Suslev lit a cigarette. "You won't get caught, Roger. You're much too clever. You have something for me?"

"Look down there, along the rails. The tall man."

Casually Suslev put his binoculars to his eyes. He took his time about centering the man indicated, then looked away.

"That's Stanley Rosemont, CIA. You know they're tailing you?"

"Oh yes. I can lose them if I wish to."

"The man next to him's Ed Langan, FBI. The bearded fellow's Mishauer, American Naval Intelligence."

"Mishauer? That sounds familiar. Do you have files on them?"

"Not yet but there's a deviate in the consulate who's having a jolly affair with the son of one of our prominent Chinese solicitors. By the time you're back on your next trip he'll be happy to oblige your slightest wish."

Suslev smiled grimly. "Good." Again, casually, he glanced at Rosemont and the others, cementing their faces into his memory. "What's his job?"

"Deputy chief of station. CIA for fifteen years. OSS and all that. They've a dozen more cover businesses here and safe houses everywhere. I've sent a list in microdots to 32."

"Good. Center wants increased surveillance of all CIA movements."

"No problem. They're careless but their funding's big and growing."

"Vietnam?"

"Of course Vietnam."

Suslev chuckled. "Those poor fools don't know what they've been sucked into. They still think they can fight a jungle war with Korean or World War Two tactics."

"They're not all fools," Crosse said. "Rosemont's good, very good. By the way, they know about the Iman Air Base."

Suslev cursed softly and leaned on one hand, casually keeping it near his mouth to prevent any lip-reading.

". . . Iman and almost all about Petropavlovsk, the new sub base at Korsakov on Sakhalin. . . ."

Suslev cursed again. "How do they do it?"

"Traitors." Crosse smiled thinly.

"Why are you a double agent, Roger?"

"Why do you ask me that every time we meet?"

Suslev sighed. He had specific orders not to probe Crosse and to help him every way he could. And although he was KGB controller of all Far Eastern espionage activities, it was only last year that even he had been allowed into the secret of Crosse's identity. Crosse, in KGB files, had the highest secret classification, an importance on the level of a Philby. But even Philby didn't know that Crosse had been working for the KGB for the last seven years.

"I ask because I'm curious," he said.

"Aren't your orders not to be curious, comrade?"

Suslev laughed. "Neither of us obeys orders all the time, no? Center enjoyed your last report so much I've been told to tell you your Swiss account will be credited with an extra bonus of $50,000 on the fifteenth of next month."

"Good. Thank you. But it's not a bonus, it's payment for value received."

"What does SI know about the visiting delegation of Parliament?"

Crosse told him what he had told the governor. "Why the question?"

"Routine check. Three are potentially very influential—Guthrie, Broadhurst, and Grey." Suslev offered a cigarette. "We're maneuvering Grey and Broadhurst into our World Peace Council. Their anti-Chinese sentiments help us. Roger, would you please put a tail on Guthrie. Perhaps he has some bad habits. If he was compromised, perhaps photographed with a Wanchai girl, it might be useful later, eh?"

Crosse nodded. "I'll see what can be done."

"Can you find the scum who murdered poor Voranski?"

"Eventually." Crosse watched him. "He must have been marked for some time. And that's ominous for all of us."

"Were they Kuomintang? Or Mao's bandits?"

"I don't know." Crosse smiled sardonically. "Russia isn't very popular with any Chinese."

"Their leaders are traitors to communism. We should smash them before they get too strong."

"Is that policy?"

"Since Genghis Khan." Suslev laughed. "But now . . . now we have to be a little patient. You needn't be." He jerked a thumb backward at Brian Kwok. "Why not discredit that *matyeryebyets*? I don't like him at all."

"Young Brian's very good. I need good people. Inform Center that

Sinders, of MI-6, arrives tomorrow from London to take delivery of the AMG papers. Both MI-6 and the CIA suspect AMG was murdered. Was he?"

"I don't know. He should have been, years ago. How will you get a copy?"

"I don't know. I'm fairly certain Sinders'll let me read them before he goes back."

"And if he doesn't?"

Crosse shrugged. "We'll get to look at them one way or another."

"Dunross?"

"Only as a last resort. He's too valuable where he is and I'd rather have him where I can see him. What about Travkin?"

"Your information was invaluable. Everything checked." Suslev told him the substance of their meeting, adding, "Now he'll be our dog forever. He'll do anything we want. Anything. I think he'd kill Dunross if necessary."

"Good. How much of what you told him was true?"

Suslev smiled. "Not much."

"Is his wife alive?"

"Oh yes, *tovarich,* she's alive."

"But not in her own *dacha?*"

"Now she is."

"And before?"

Suslev shrugged. "I told him what I was told to tell him."

Crosse lit a cigarette. "What do you know about Iran?"

Again Suslev looked at him sharply. "Quite a lot. It's one of our eight remaining great targets and there's a big operation going on right now."

"The Ninety-second U.S. Airborne's on the Soviet-Iranian border right now!"

Suslev gaped at him. "What?"

Crosse related all that Rosemont had told him about Dry Run and when he came to the part about the U.S. forces having nuclear arms Suslev whitened palpably. "Mother of God! Those god-cursed Americans'll make a mistake one day and then we'll never be able to extricate ourselves! They're fools to deploy such weapons."

"Can you combat them?"

"Of course not, not yet," Suslev said irritably. "The core of our strategy's never to have a direct clash until America's totally isolated and there's no doubt about final victory. A direct clash would be suicide now. I'll get on to Center at once."

"Impress on them the Americans consider it just a dry run. Get Center to take your forces away and cool everything. Do it at once or there will be trouble. Don't give the U.S. forces any provocation. In a few days the Americans will go away. Don't leak the invasion to your inward spies in Washington. Let it come first from your people in the CIA."

"The Ninety-second's really there? That seems impossible."

"You'd better get your armies more airborne, more mobile with more firepower."

Suslev grunted. "The energies and resources of three hundred million Russians are channeled to solve that problem, *tovarich*. If we have twenty years . . . just twenty more years."

"Then?"

"In the eighties we rule the world."

"I'll be dead long since."

"Not you. You'll rule whatever province or country you want. England?"

"Sorry, the weather there's dreadful. Except for one or two days a year, most years, when it's the most beautiful place on earth."

"Ah, you should see my home in Georgia and the country around Tiflis." Suslev's eyes were sparkling. "That's Eden."

Crosse was watching everywhere as they talked. He knew they could not be overheard. Brian Kwok was sitting in the stand waiting, half-asleep. Rosemont and the others were studying him covertly. Down by the winner's circle Jacques deVille was strolling casually with Jason Plumm.

"Have you talked to Jason yet?"

"Of course, while we were in the stands."

"Good."

"What did he say about deVille?"

"That he doubted, too, if Jacques'd ever be chosen as tai-pan. After my meeting last night I agree—he's obviously too weak, or his resolve's softened." Suslev added, "It often happens with deep-cover assets who have nothing active to do but wait. That's the hardest of all jobs."

"Yes."

"He's a good man but I'm afraid he won't achieve his assignment."

"What do you plan for him?"

"I haven't decided."

"Convert him from an inward spy to a doomed spy?"

"Only if you or the others of Sevrin are threatened." For the benefit of any watchers Suslev tipped the flask to his lips and offered it to Crosse who shook his head. Both knew the flask contained only water. Suslev dropped his voice. "I have an idea. We're increasing our effort in Canada. Clearly the French Separatist Movement is a tremendous opportunity for us. If Quebec was to split from Canada it would send the whole North American continent reeling into a completely new power structure. I was thinking that it would be perfect if deVille took over Struan's in Canada. Eh?"

Crosse smiled. "Very good. Very very good. I like Jacques too. It would be a pity to waste him. Yes, that would be very clever."

"It's even better than that, Roger. He has some very important French-Canadian friends from his Paris days just after the war, all openly separatist, all left-wing inclined. A few of them are becoming a prominent national political force in Canada."

"You'd get him to drop his deep cover?"

"No. Jacques could give the separatist issue a push without jeopardizing himself. As head of an important branch of Struan's . . . and if one of his special friends became foreign minister or prime minister, eh?"

"Is that possible?"

"It's possible."

Crosse whistled. "If Canada swung away from the U.S. that would be a coup of coups."

"Yes."

After a pause, Crosse said, "Once upon a time a Chinese sage was asked by a friend to bless his newly born son. His benediction was, 'Let's pray he lives in interesting times.' Well, Gregor Petrovitch Suslev whose real name is Petr Oleg Mzytryk, we certainly live in interesting times. Don't we?"

Suslev was staring at him in shock. "Who told you my name?"

"Your superiors." Crosse watched him, his eyes suddenly pitiless. "You know me, I know you. That's fair, isn't it?"

"Of . . . of course. I . . ." The man's laugh was forced. "I haven't used that name for so long I'd . . . I'd almost forgotten it." He looked back at the eyes, fighting for control. "What's the matter? Why are you so edgy, eh?"

"AMG. I think we should close this meeting for now. Our cover's that I tried to subvert you but you refused. Let's meet tomorrow at seven." Seven was the code number for the apartment next to Ginny Fu's in Mong Kok. "Late. Eleven o'clock."

"Ten is better."

Crosse motioned carefully toward Rosemont and the others. "Before you go I need something for them."

"All right. Tomorrow I'll ha—"

"It must be now." Crosse hardened. "Something special—in case I can't get a look at Sinders's copy, I'll have to barter with them!"

"You divulge to no one the source. No one."

"All right."

"Never?"

"Never."

Suslev thought a moment, weighing possibilities. "Tonight one of our agents takes delivery of some top-secret material from the carrier. Eh?"

The Englishman's face lit up. "Perfect! Is that why you came?"

"One reason."

"When and where's the drop?"

Suslev told him, then added, "But I still want copies of everything."

"Of course. Good, that'll do just fine. Rosemont will be really in my debt. How long's your asset been aboard?"

"Two years, at least that's when he was first subverted."

"Does he give you good stuff?"

"Anything off that whore's valuable."

"What's his fee?"

"For this? $2,000. He's not expensive, none of our assets are, except you."

Crosse smiled equally mirthlessly. "Ah, but I'm the best you have in Asia and I've proved my quality fifty times. Up to now I've been doing it practically for love, old chap."

"Your costs, old chap, are the highest we have! We buy the entire NATO battle plan, codes, everything, yearly for less than $8,000."

"Those amateur bastards are ruining our business. It is a business, isn't it?"

"Not to us."

"Balls! You KGB folk are more than well rewarded. *Dachas,* places in Tiflis, special stores to shop in. Mistresses. But I have to tell you, squeezing money out of your company gets worse yearly. I'll expect a rather large increase for Dry Run and for the AMG matter when it's concluded."

"Talk to them direct. I've no jurisdiction over money."

"Liar."

Suslev laughed. "It's good—and safe—dealing with a professional. *Prosit!*" He raised his flask and drained it.

Crosse said abruptly, "Please leave angrily. I can feel binoculars!"

At once Suslev began cursing him in Russian, softly but vehemently, then shook a fist in the policeman's face and walked off.

Crosse stared after him.

On the Sha Tin Road Robert Armstrong was looking down at the corpse of John Chen as raincoated police rewrapped it in its blanket, then carried it through the gawking crowds to the waiting ambulance. Fingerprint experts and others were all around, searching for clues. The rain was falling more heavily now and there was a great deal of mud everywhere.

"Everything's messed up, sir," Sergeant Lee said sourly. "There're footprints but they could be anyone's."

Armstrong nodded and used a handkerchief to dry his face. Many onlookers were behind the crude barriers that had been erected around the area. Passing traffic on the narrow road was slowed and almost jammed, everyone honking irritably. "Keep the men sweeping within a hundred-yard area. Get someone out to the nearest village, someone might have seen something." He left Lee and went over to the police car. He got in, closing the door, and picked up the communicator. "This is Armstrong. Give me Chief Inspector Donald Smyth at East Aberdeen, please." He began to wait, feeling dreadful.

The driver was young and smart and still dry. "The rain's wonderful, isn't it, sir?"

Armstrong looked across sourly. The young man blanched. "Do you smoke?"

"Yes sir." The young man took out his pack and offered it. Armstrong took the pack. "Why don't you join the others? They need a nice smart fellow like yourself to help. Find some clues. Eh?"

"Yes sir." The young man fled into the rain.

Carefully Armstrong took out a cigarette. He contemplated it. Grimly he put it back and the pack into a side pocket. Hunching down into his seat, he muttered, "Sod all cigarettes, sod the rain, sod that smart arse and most of all sod the sodding Werewolves!"

In time the intercom came on crackling, "Chief Inspector Donald Smyth."

"Morning. I'm out at Sha Tin," Armstrong began, and told him what had happened and about finding the body. "We're covering the area but in this rain I don't expect to find anything. When the papers hear about the corpse and the message we'll be swamped. I think we'd better pick up the old *amah* right now. She's the only lead we have. Do your fellows still have her under surveillance?"

"Oh yes."

"Good. Wait for me, then we'll move in. I want to search her place. Have a team stand by."

"How long will you be?"

Armstrong said, "It'll take me a couple of hours to get there. Traffic's sodded up from here all the way back to the ferry."

"It is here too. All over Aberdeen. But it's not just the rain, old lad. There's about a thousand ghouls gawking at the wreck, then there're more bloody mobs already at the Ho-Pak, the Victoria . . . in fact every bloody bank in the vicinity, and I hear there's already about five hundred collecting outside the Vic in Central."

"Christ! My whole miserable bloody life savings're there."

"I told you yesterday to get liquid, old boy!" Armstrong heard the Snake's laugh. "And by the way, if you've any spare cash, sell Struan's short—I hear the Noble House is going to crash."

The New
Walt Whitman
Handbook

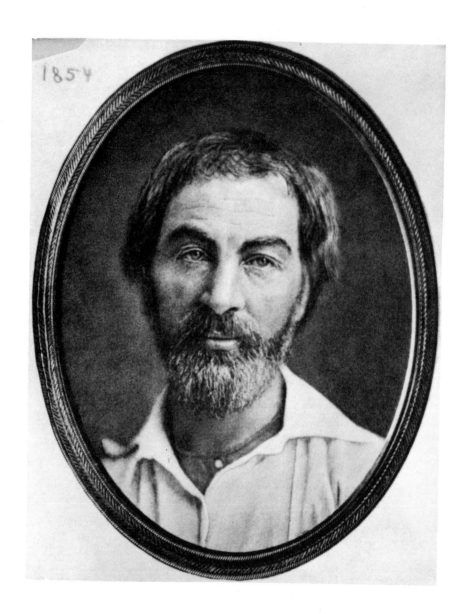

1854

The New
Walt Whitman
Handbook

Gay Wilson Allen

New York: New York University Press
1975

To
Arthur Golden
II Kings 2.13

Preface

When I proposed a "Handbook" for Walt Whitman to a major textbook publisher in 1944, I was told that such works for major British authors were needed, but not yet for an American poet. However, when I suggested the idea to Professor Walter Hendricks, who had recently started the venturesome Packard and Company in Chicago (later Hendricks House in New York), he offered me a contract without hesitation. Except for his faith and foresight, the *Walt Whitman Handbook* might not have been written; but his confidence was justified, for the time had indeed arrived for such a reference and critical guide to Whitman. To my great surprise, the book was favorably reviewed in the *New York Times Book Review, Saturday Review of Literature*, and the *New York Herald Tribune Book Review*. Of course I expected reviews in scholarly journals, but they were better than I had dared hope. And the book sold well enough to justify two reprintings—unfortunately without corrections or revisions.

It is now possible, nearly a generation later, to publish a complete and thorough revision. Every page of this edition has received at least minor emendations, and every chapter except IV (formerly V) has been greatly augmented or entirely rewritten. Chapter I has been brought up to date and extended. Major biographies were published in the 1950s, and important biographical interpretations since then, such as Edwin H. Miller's *Whitman's Poetry: A Psychological Journey*. Chapter II needed considerable rewriting because important texts have been edited in recent years. Scholars also now count *six* editions of *Leaves of Grass* instead of nine or ten as formerly.

I have discarded former chapters III and IV and combined the subject matter in a new approach. The social and political ideas of former Chapter III have been used to introduce the new Chapter III on Whitman's intellectual world; and in the new Chapter I eliminated the pedantic definitions and discussions of the "Great Chain of Being" and "Pantheism." Though "Chain of Being" concepts are certainly in Whitman's poems, the poet never used the term and may have been unaware of the concept. As for "Pantheism," that term is too handy and familiar in Whitman criticism to be avoided altogether, but I have tried to approach his cosmic and theistic assumptions and metaphors through the contemporary science he knew (Joseph Beaver's *Walt Whitman, Poet of Science* should be better known), through his familiarity with French rationalistic theism, and concepts of cosmic evolution (partly original) for which there seem to be illuminating parallels in the writings of the late Pierre Teilhard de Chardin. Hindu scholars have also discovered Vedantic parallels in *Leaves of Grass*, and I have made some use of these, though I personally find Whitman's "mysticism" more like Teilhard's cosmotheism.

The chapter on Whitman's literary techniques (now Chapter IV) I have let stand. Recently in a dissertation at the University of California (at Davis) Charles T. Kollerer used modern linguistic analysis and musical notation in a new approach to Whitman's prosody. He very kindly loaned me his unpublished manuscript, and I admit that his method may lead to subtler ways of analyzing and explaining Whitman's poetic techniques. But the basic Hebraic "thought-rhythm" will, I believe, remain, though Dr. Kollerer, or others, may supplement it. Until these new approaches are published my old chapter may still be useful, key portions of which have been reprinted in anthologies of poetic theory and Whitman criticism and are widely used.

But for Chapter V (former Chapter VI) there was no question of the new information needed. Whitman was already a major world poet in 1946, and since then there have been many new translations in almost every country in the world (except the new nations), and important criticism in several languages. Some of this information was given in 1955 in my edition of *Walt Whitman Abroad*, but the celebration of the Centennial of *Leaves of Grass* that very year outdated parts of that book. Chapter V will be found to be greatly enlarged and, I hope, enriched. To a considerable extent the state of the world is reflected in foreign criticism of Whitman—cf. Pablo Neruda's.

Of course all bibliographies have been updated, and the notes extended. To eliminate some notes I have placed page numbers in square brackets [thus] for consecutive analysis of a single title.

In addition to the many friends and scholars who made the first edition possible, I am indebted to many new ones for this revised edition, including my colleague Edwin H. Miller; all editors of the new *Collected Writings of Walt Whitman* (Thomas L. Brasher, Floyd Stovall, Harold W. Blodgett, Sculley Bradley, Edwin Miller, Edward Grier, Herbert Bergman, and William White); Arthur Golden, editor of the *Blue Book*; Fredson Bowers, editor of *Whitman's Manuscripts* (*1860*); Malcolm Cowley, for provocative and stimulating criticism; Charles S. Grippi, for his dissertation on Whitman in Italy; Roger Asselineau, for all his excellent Whitman publications, including his recent edition of *Walt Whitman in Europe Today* (and to the contributors); Sholom Kahn in Jerusalem for his critical ideas and invaluable information about Whitman in Hebrew; the late Kornei Chukovsky in Russia; Juliusz Zuławski in Poland; Ladislas Orszagh in Hungary; Om Prakesh Sharme, T. R. Rajasekharaiah in India; in Japan William Moore, Shigetaka Naganuma, Iwao Matsuhara, Norihiro Nabeshima, and Shigenobu Sadoya; Fernando Alegría at Stanford; V. K. Chari in Canada (formerly India); Peter Mitilineos, translator of Jannaccone; Stephen Stepanchev for information about Whitman in Slavic countries; and Charles E. Feinberg, the perennial friend of Whitman scholars. My wife, Evie Allison Allen, has translated, given bibliographical assistance, and read proof. The Managing Editor of the New York University Press, Robert Bull, and his able associate Editor, Despina Papazoglore, have aided the project at all stages, with patience, kindness, and technical skill. I am particularly grateful to Arthur Golden for sharing his bibliographical expertise and his assistance in reading proof.

For permission to quote several lines from Pessoa's "Saudação a Walt Whitman" I am indebted to Edwin Honig, the translator, and the Swallow Press. My gratitude for the "Carybé" drawing reproduced on the jacket and a second pen-sketch goes to the Brazilian painter Hector Júlio Páride Bernabó, and to Simona and Frederic Tuten for locating this famous artist in Bahïa, Brazil, and securing his written consent for me.

G. W. A.
ORADELL, N. J.
February 1975

Chronological Table

1819   Born May 31 at West Hills, Huntington Township, Long Island. (Now 246 Walt Whitman Rd., Huntington Station, N.Y. 11746.)

1823   Family moved to Brooklyn.

1825   Lafayette visited Brooklyn, July 4—one of the poet's most cherished memories.

1825-30 Attended public school in Brooklyn. Family frequently shifted residence in city.

1830-31 Office boy in lawyer's office, then doctor's; probably quit school at this time.

1831-32 Worked in printing offices, began to learn the trade. Printer's apprentice on *Long Island Patriot*.

1832   Summer. Worked at Worthington's printing establishment.

1832   Fall—to May 12, 1835. Worked as compositor on *Long Island Star*.

1833   The Whitman family moved back to the country.

1835   May 12th—till May, 1836. Worked in printing offices in New York City.

1836-38   Taught in various schools on Long Island. Participated in debating societies.

1838   Spring—Spring, 1839. Edited *Long-Islander* in Huntington.

1839-41   Returned to teaching on Long Island.

1840   Fall. Campaigned for Van Buren.

1841   May. Went to New York and worked as compositor for *The New World*.

1842   Edited for a few months *The Aurora* and *The Tattler*.

1843   Spring. Edited *The Statesman*.

1844   Summer. Edited *The New York Democrat*.

1844   October. Worked on *The New York Mirror*.

1841-48   Contributed to several prominent New York journals: *Democratic Review, Broadway Journal, American Review, New York Sun, Columbian Magazine*.

1846-47   Edited the Brooklyn *Daily Eagle*.

1848   Quit (or was discharged from) editorship of *Eagle* in January. February 11 left, with brother Jeff, for New Orleans to take up editorial position on the *Crescent*. First number of *Crescent*, published March 5, contained Whitman's poem "Sailing the Mississippi at Midnight." May 24 resigned position, sailed to St. Louis May 27. Arrived home June 15. Back in Brooklyn, became editor of the *Brooklyn Freeman*, first number issued Sept. 9, 1848, office burned that night.

1849   In spring the *Freeman* became a daily. In April Whitman
        was also conducting a printing office and bookstore on
        Myrtle Avenue—still listed in the *Brooklyn Directory* for
        1851.
        Resigned editorship Sept. 11, Free-Soilers having joined
        regular party.

1851-54 Built houses in Brooklyn.
        Addressed Brooklyn Art Museum, March 31, 1851.

1855   First edition of *Leaves of Grass* published by the author,
        on or near July 4; Father died July 11. Fowler and Wells
        were agents for the book. Conway first to visit the poet.
        Emerson wrote his "greetings" July 21.

1856   Second edition of *Leaves of Grass*, published sometime
        between Aug. 16 and Sept. 12, Fowler and Wells unac-
        knowledged publisher. In November Alcott and Thoreau
        visited the poet—Emerson the following year.

1857-59 Edited Brooklyn *Times*; unemployed by summer of 1859.
        Frequented Pfaff's Restaurant, a Bohemian gathering
        place.

1860   Third edition of *Leaves of Grass* published in Boston by
        Thayer and Eldridge; rejected Emerson's advice to omit
        "Children of Adam" poems.

1861   Thayer and Eldridge failed and the plates for the third
        edition were secured by a dishonest publisher, who printed
        and sold pirated copies for a number of years. Soon after
        the bombardment of Fort Sumter, April 18, Whitman
        recorded in his diary a moral and physical dedication.
        About this time deserted Pfaff's and Bohemian friends.

1862   Dec. 14 read brother George's name in list of wounded and
        went immediately to the war front in Virginia to find him.
        In Washington began daily visits to soldiers in hospitals.

1863-64 Worked in field and army hospitals. Beginning of friend-

ship with O'Connor and Burroughs.
Health broke down in mid-summer of '64 and he returned
to his mother's home in Brooklyn for six months.

1865–66 In January 1865 appointed clerk in Indian Bureau of the
Department of the Interior, discharged by James Harlan on
June 30, but in July became clerk in Attorney General's
office. *Drum-Taps* issued in 1865; *Drum-Taps* with annex
called *Sequel to Drum-Taps* published in fall, containing
"When Lilacs Last in the Dooryard Bloom'd and Other
Pieces." After Whitman's discharge from clerkship,
O'Connor began writing his "vindication," published in
1866 as *The Good Gray Poet.*

1867 Fourth edition of *Leaves of Grass.* Reviewed by William
Rossetti. Burroughs published first biography, *Notes on
Walt Whitman as Poet and Person.*

1868 Rossetti edited selections from *Leaves of Grass*; well received in England. O'Connor published *The Carpenter,*
presenting in thin disguise Whitman as a modern Christ.

1869 Mrs. Anne Gilchrist became acquainted with Whitman's
poetry.

1870 Mrs. Gilchrist published "An English-woman's Estimate of
Walt Whitman" in the Boston *Radical Review.* First edition of *Democratic Vistas*, incorporating essays published
in the *Galaxy* during 1867–68.

1871 Fifth edition of *Leaves of Grass.* First edition of *Demo-
cratic Vistas*, incorporating essays published in the *Galaxy*
during 1867–68; *Passage to India* pamphlet.
Delivered "After All, Not to Create Only" ["Song of the
Exposition"] at opening of the American Institute of New
York.
Swinburne greeted Whitman in *Songs Before Sunrise;*
Tennyson wrote fraternal letters; Rudolf Schmidt trans-
lated *Democratic Vistas* into Danish.
Mrs. Gilchrist wrote a proposal of marriage and Whitman
diplomatically declined in letter of November 3.

1872   Delivered "As a Strong Bird on Pinions Free" ["Thou Mother with thy Equal Brood" in 1881 ed.] at Dartmouth College commencement. Thérèse Bentzon (Mme. Blanc) published critical article in *Revue des Deux Mondes*, June 1.
        Quarrel with O'Connor over Negro suffrage, and perhaps personal matters.

1873   Paralysis in February after preliminary spells of dizziness for over a year. Began living with brother George in Camden, New Jersey. Mother died May 23.

1874   "The Song of the Universal" read at Tufts College commencement by proxy.
        Discharged during midsummer from position in Washington, which had been filled by a substitute since Feb. 1873. In "Prayer of Columbus" the poet identified himself with the "battered, wrecked old man."

1876   Wrangle in United States over Whitman's neglect started by article published in Jan. 26 *West Jersey Press*, which Robert Buchanan quoted in London *Daily News*, March 13.
        Spring to autumn spent at Timber Creek.
        Celebrates 1876 Centennial with publication of poems and prose in two volumes: *Leaves of Grass* (I), *Two Rivulets* (II), with "Passage to India" annex. Rossetti and Mrs. Gilchrist sold many copies in England; the money and recognition aided poet's recovery.
        In September Mrs. Gilchrist arrived in Philadelphia and rented a house, which Whitman visited frequently.

1877   January, spoke in Philadelphia on Tom Paine's anniversary. February, New York friends gave a reception and lionized the poet. Visited Burroughs on the Hudson. In May, Edward Carpenter arrived from England. Dr. R. M. Bucke, recently appointed head of asylum at London, Ontario, visited Whitman and became close friend.
        Burroughs published "The Flight of the Eagle" in *Birds and Poets*.

1878   Health better. Repeated excursion up Hudson.

1879   April 14 gave Lincoln lecture in New York (given each year for thirteen years).
        Sept. 10 started trip West—visited St. Louis (where favorite brother, Jeff, lived), Topeka, Rockies, Denver.

1880   Returned from western trip in January.
        April, delivered the Lincoln Memorial Address in Boston. June, went to Canada to visit Dr. Bucke. Took boat trip up St. Lawrence.

1881   Sixth edition of *Leaves of Grass*, published in Boston by Osgood (title-page bears 1881–82).

1882   February, the Society for the Suppression of Vice claimed the Osgood edition immoral. May 17 Osgood ceased publication, gave plates to Whitman. After his own "Author's Edition" in Camden, Whitman found a new publisher in Rees Welsh and Company, Philadelphia (soon succeeded by David McKay). Edition of 3,000 copies sold in one day. *Leaves of Grass* now practically complete, subsequent editions being reprints with annexes.
        Pearsall Smith, wealthy Philadephia glass merchant and prominent Quaker, became friend.
        Specimen Days and Collect published in autumn.

1883   Dr. Bucke published his biography with Whitman's collaboration.

1884   Sale of the Philadelphia issue enabled Whitman to buy a house in Mickle Street, Camden, New Jersey; March 26 moved in, remained until his death.
        June, Edward Carpenter made a second visit.
        New friends: Traubel, Harned, Talcott Williams, Donaldson, Ingersoll, others.

1885   Sun stroke in July. Walking became difficult and many friends, headed by Donaldson, bought a horse and phaeton for Whitman.

1886   Royalties from 1881 edition dwindled. *Pall Mall Gazette* promoted fund which resulted in a New Year's present of eighty pounds. Boston friends made up a purse of $800 for a cottage on Timber Creek (never built).

1887	The Lincoln lecture at Madison Square Theatre attended by many notables—took in $600. Poet sculptured by Sidney Morse and painted by Herbert Gilchrist and Thomas Eakins.
1888	Another paralytic stroke, early in June. Managed to finish *November Boughs*.
1889	"House-tied."
1891	Last birthday dinner in Mickle Street home. Dec. 17, chilled, took pneumonia.
1892	Managed to publish "authorized" issue of *Leaves of Grass*, which the literary executors (Traubel, Harned, Bucke) were commanded to perpetuate. Died March 26, buried in prepared tomb in Harleigh Cemetery, Camden, N.J.

Contents

Illustrations*

*Notes on illustrations, p. 376

Chapter I

The Growth of Walt Whitman Biography

When I read the book, the biography famous,
And is this then (said I) what the author calls a man's life?
And so will some one when I am dead and gone write my life?
—"When I Read the Book"

INTRODUCTION

Leaves of Grass is one of the most personal, and in many ways the most naively frank, collections of poetry ever written. From 1855 to 1892, Walt Whitman himself did everything in his power to foster the literary illusion that the poet and the book were identical.

I celebrate myself, and sing myself,

he announced in his song of himself, adding later in "So Long,"

Camerado, this is no book,
Who touches this touches a man.

It is hardly an exaggeration to say that after the 1855 edition, Whitman's every act, gesture, manner of dress, and creative expression was calculated to achieve this literary purpose. The poetic theory which he enunciated in the '55 Preface was his own personal ambition. The bard who was "to be commensurate with a people," to "incarnate" its geography and life, and to span his country from east to west, was of course himself. The poet who believed that "All beauty comes from beautiful blood and a beautiful brain" was confessing a personal ambition—even a dedication of himself to an ideal—to live and to record a beautiful life.

1

So devoutly did Walt Whitman desire to live the ideal life envisioned in *Leaves of Grass*—and so sincerely did he believe in his success—that in the first biographies, which he helped to write, the illusion of the complete identity between the man and his book was further strengthened and developed (we might say the thesis documented), thus postponing, almost thwarting, a critical biography for many years. It was inevitable, therefore, that most biographers would search for the details of the poet's life in the confessions of his poems—and this is the secret of his perennial fascination. But *Leaves of Grass*, however autobiographical it may be, is also a work of art, which is to say the product of a creative imagination, and to search for biographical fact in its pages is to write literary criticism rather than the history of a man's life. Yet, it is not possible, even less so than with most poets, to separate the criticism of his work from the biography of his life.

Walt Whitman biography has grown, therefore, not by the simple accumulation of newly discovered and more exact information concerning his daily goings and comings, but by new and fresh insight into his motives, wider knowledge of the intellectual world in which he lived and moved, clearer understanding of the meanings which his poetry and prose have had for himself and for the many critics who have interpreted him. Moreover, his biography is no longer simply the story of Walt Whitman, or of a remarkable book which he wrote. He has become a legend, a national symbol, even a pivotal figure in an international literary movement. To tell the story of his biographical growth is also to tell much of the story of the growth of modern literature and thought. For this reason, what critics and biographers have thought of Walt Whitman and the theories on which they have based their interpretations of him, is fully as important as the literal facts of his life. After discovering when and why the various interpretations arose, however, the student of Whitman should be better able to sift fact from legend. Furthermore, if definite trends are discovered in the evolution of these biographies, perhaps future stages of Whitman scholarship may be anticipated—even aided and hastened.

THE TESTIMONY OF FRIENDS:
O'CONNOR, BURROUGHS, BUCKE

The circumstances under which Walt Whitman's friends began to write about his life profoundly affected the course and development of his biography. On June 30, 1865, he was dismissed from his government clerkship by the Secretary of the Interior, Mr. James Harlan, who had discovered that his employee was the author of *Leaves of Grass*, a book which Mr. Harlan thought to be "full of indecent passages," meaning of course the sex poems ("Enfans d'Adam" and "Calamus" in the 1860 edition). One of the poet's devoted friends, William Douglas O'Connor, a government clerk, several months later published a bitter denunciation of Harlan and "a vindiction" of Whitman which he called *The Good Gray Poet.* [1]

Though hardly to be called a biography, this pamphlet laid the foundation for the first legends in Whitman biography and influenced many succeeding interpretations in Europe as well as America. The personality described by O'Connor sprang from the poet's avowed purposes in *Leaves of Grass* fully as much as from O'Connor's personal love and admiration. This personality, familiar to "thousands of people in New York, in Brooklyn, in Boston, in New Orleans, and latterly in Washington [is] . . . a man of striking masculine beauty—a poet—powerful and venerable in appearance; large, calm, superbly formed; oftenest clad in the careless, rough, and always picturesque costume of the common people." [3] There is something almost mythical in the description of the "head, majestic, large, Homeric, and set upon his strong shoulders with the grandeur of ancient sculpture." Reverently O'Connor continues:

I marked the countenance, serene, proud, cheerful, florid, grave; the brow seamed with noble wrinkles; the features, massive and handsome, with firm blue eyes; the eyebrows and eyelids especially showing that fulness of arch seldom seen save in the antique busts; the flowing hair and fleecy beard, both very gray, and tempering with a look of age the youthful aspect of one who is but forty-five; the simplicity and purity of his dress, cheap and plain, but spotless, from snowy falling collar to burnished boot, and exhaling faint fragrance; the whole form surrounded with manliness, as with a nimbus, and breathing, in its perfect health and vigor, the august charm of the strong. [4]

Almost everyone who knew Walt Whitman intimately was conquered by his magnetic presence, and there is no reason whatever to doubt the sincerity of O'Connor's enthusiatic description; nevertheless, we have here the first of the superman legends. "We who have looked upon this figure, or listened to that clear, cheerful, vibrating voice, might thrill to think, could we but transcend our age, that we had been thus near to one of the greatest of the sons of men."

O'Connor is also the first source for some of the typical anecdotes. "I hold it the surest proof of Thoreau's insight, that after a conversation, seeing how he incarnated the immense and new spirit of the age, and was the compend of America, he came away to speak the electric sentence, 'He is Democracy!' " The names of Whitman and Lincoln are linked by the story of the President's seeing the poet walk by the White House, inquiring who he was, and remarking thoughtfully, "Well, *he* looks like a MAN!" The anecdote of Lafayette's passing through Brooklyn and by chance holding the future poet in his arms sounds like an omen of his future destiny. And at the time he wrote the essay, O'Connor could say of Whitman, as of a Modern Christ:

He has been a visitor of prisons; a protector of fugitive slaves; a constant voluntary nurse, night and day, at the hospitals, from the beginning of the war to the present time; a brother and friend through life to the neglected and the forgotten, the poor, the degraded, the criminal, the outcast; turning away from no man for his guilt, nor woman for her vileness.[7]

On the theory that Whitman's poems grew out of the "great goodness, the great chastity of spiritual strength and sanity" of this saintly life, no vileness can possibly be found even in the frankest of them, though O'Connor admits that in all some eighty lines in the entire book might be objectionable to the ultra-prudish and squeamish. But he maintains that if these were expurgated, far greater portions of the Bible, the *Iliad* and the *Odyssey*, Shakespeare, Dante, and other masterpieces in world literature would also have to be rejected.

On the one hand *Leaves of Grass* is elevated to an eminent position in the greatest literature of all time, and on the other hand it is praised as "a work purely and entirely American, autochthonic, sprung from our own soil; no savor of Europe nor of the past, nor of any other literature in it."[26] Such of course was the poet's own ideal, and we have here the first glorified confirmation of Walt Whitman's literary fame on his own grounds.

John Burroughs, a friend of the same period, no less ardent but with more reserved emotions and intellect, published his first book on Whitman two years later, 1867. *Notes on Walt Whitman as Poet and Person* was a collaboration, for parts of it were actually written by Whitman himself and he freely edited the whole manuscript.[2] Both Burroughs and Whitman have been severely blamed by some commentators for this fact, but John Burroughs was then a young man taking his first steps in writing, more or less under Whitman's tutelage, and he doubtless thought that the poet's help made the book more accurate and authoritative. Nevertheless, Burroughs's *Notes* presented interpretations which must have been thoroughly congenial to Whitman himself and should be considered, like Burroughs's later studies and Bucke's more systematic account, as semi-autobiography.

The *Notes* is divided into two parts: the first a study and interpretation of *Leaves of Grass*, including a defense of the author's theory and expression of Beauty and Personality; and the second, a personal biographical sketch, followed by a criticism of *Drum-Taps*. The book is, therefore, mainly an exegesis, more or less "official," although the manner in which the author exploits his own country origin gives it an informal, personal tone which sounds completely original. But considering the origin of the *Notes*, it is significant that Burroughs confesses: "I am not able, nor is it necessary, to give the particulars of the poet's youthful life."[79] In fact, he is convinced that the "long foreground" mentioned in Emerson's famous "greeting" letter of 1855, "that vast previous, ante-dating requirement of physical, moral, and emotional experiences, will forever remain untold."[83] However, the Lafayette episode is given, and we are also told that "From the immediate mother of the poet come, I think, his chief traits."[79] Here is the basis, but not yet the elaboration, of the theory soon to be developed by Bucke and Whitman himself that the poet's genius was a product of his ancestry and environment.

The mythical account given of his travels may have been due either to Whitman's vagueness concerning his New Orleans period or to Burroughs's drawing erroneous factual conclusions from the literary theory that the poet must first absorb his country, sounding every experience, before expressing it in verse. At any rate, the reader is told that in 1849 Whitman began traveling, and is given the impression that he spent one year in New Orleans (actually only a little over two months) and another wandering around in the West. "He saw Western and Northwestern nature and character in all their phases, and probably took there and then the decided inspiration of his future poetry. After some two years, returning to Brooklyn. ..."[82] It is an ironical commentary that when Whitman actually did visit the West in 1879—exactly thirty years later!—he re-announced in *Specimen Days:* "I have found the law of my own poems." Already in Burroughs's *Notes* biographical fact and poetic imagination have become almost inseparably intergrown, perhaps for the very reason that the poet, "Like Egypt's lord he builds against his form's annihilation. . . . Strange immortality! For in this book Walt Whitman, even in his habit as he lived, and ever gathering hearts of young and old, is to surely walk, untouched by death, down through the long succession of all the future ages of America."[73]

The *Notes* contains also the theory on which all the early friends of *Leaves of Grass* were to justify and explain the style which most of the first readers found obscure: "The poet, like Nature, seems best pleased when his meaning is well folded up, put away, and sur-rounded by a curious array of diverting attributes and objects."[43]

The first complete life of the author of *Leaves of Grass* was Dr. Richard Maurice Bucke's *Walt Whitman*, 1883. Whitman told Edward Carpenter that he himself "wrote the account of my birthplace and antecedents which occupies the first twenty-four pages of the book."[3] So highly did he think of this collaborated biography that in 1888 he asked Bucke not to revise it but to *"let it stand just as it is,"*[4] and on his seventy-second birthday he defended this work as the final word on his life: "I thoroughly accept Dr. Bucke's book."[311]

The poet who had announced at thirty-seven:

My tongue, every atom of my blood, form'd from this soil, this air,
Born here of parents born here from parents the same, and their
    parents the same.["Song of Myself," Sec. 1]

and who prided himself that,

Before I was born out of my mother generations guided me,
My embryo has never been torpid, nothing could overlay it.[Sec. 44]

has now had time to investigate his genealogy and to draw definite conclusions regarding his ancestry. With the aid of Savage's *Genealogical Dictionary* he thought he could trace his lineage back to Abijah Whitman in seventeenth-century England, whose son, the Rev. Zechariah Whitman, came to America on the *True-Love* in 1640, or "soon after."[5]

Though the ancestry is presented as sound on both sides, the Whitmans as "a solid, tall, strong-framed, long-lived race of men" and the Van Velsors as "a warm-hearted and sympathetic" people, we read that

There is no doubt that both Walt Whitman's personality and writings are to be credited very largely to their Holland origin through his mother's side. A faithful and subtle investigation (and a very curious one it would be) might trace far back many of the elements of *Leaves of Grass*, long before their author was born. From his mother also he derived his extraordinary affective nature, spirituality and human sympathy. From his father chiefly must have come his passion for freedom, and the firmness of character which has enabled him to persevere for a lifetime in what he has called "carrying out his own ideal."[17]

But to Louisa Van Velsor is given chief credit: "Walt Whitman could say with perhaps a better right than almost any man for such a boast, that he was 'Well-begotten and rais'd by a perfect mother.' "[18]

The environment, however, is found to be no less perfect: "Perhaps, indeed, there are few regions on the face of the earth better fitted for the concrete background of such a book as *Leaves of Grass*."[18] The poems have achieved the purpose announced in the '55 Preface, for it is now said that, "In their amplitude, richness, unflagging movement and gay color, *Leaves of Grass* . . . are but the putting in poetic statements of the Manhattan Island and Brooklyn of those years [poet's youth], and of today."[20]

The mythical travels encountered in Burroughs's *Notes* are continued:

The fifteen years from 1840 to 1855 were the gestation or formative periods of *Leaves of Grass*, not only in Brooklyn and New

York, but from several extensive jaunts through the States. . . . Large parts of the poems, and several of them wholly, were incarnated on those jaunts or amid these scenes. Out of such experiences came the physiology of *Leaves of Grass*, in my opinion the main part. The psychology of the book is a deeper problem; it is doubtful whether the latter element can be traced. It is, perhaps, only to be studied out in the poems themselves, and is a hard study there.[136]

These "extensive jaunts through the States" are puzzling not only because later biographers have found no record of them, but also because in *Specimen Days*, published one year before Bucke's biography, Whitman gives an accurate, though general, account of his New Orleans trip. In a newspaper article, reprinted in *Specimen Days*, he does make a statement which, for lack of punctuation, could have been misunderstood by Bucke: "I enjoy'd my journey and Louisiana life much. Returning to Brooklyn [,] a year or two afterward I started the 'Freeman'. . . ."[6] But surely in his close cooperation—or collaboration—with Dr. Bucke on the biography Whitman would have corrected the mistaken belief that he returned to Brooklyn *a year or two after* the New Orleans trip. One must conclude that the poet had no objection to such imaginative interpretations of the origin of his poems.

The point is that Dr. Bucke accepted in the most literal sense Whitman's literary claim that his poems were the expression of the life which he had absorbed. On such grounds the admirer of *Leaves of Grass* feels himself compelled to idealize the poet's whole life and background. Thus his education in printing offices, contact with people, and private study were not only adequate but "the most comprehensive equipment ever attained by a human being."[19] One wonders whether Taine's theory of "race, surroundings, epoch"[7] could have influenced both the poet and the biographer in their belief that the creator of literature must be the product of perfect ancestry, perfect environment, and perfect training or experience. On the romantic doctrine of "absorbing" and "expressing" the life of a nation, they thought the poet's meager formal education was more than compensated by his contact with "things" and "humanity"; hence that "reading did not go for so very much" in his education.[21]

Bucke's *Walt Whitman* does not attempt to solve one of the greatest problems in the biography of the poet, the almost miraculous contrast between Whitman's writings before and after 1855. But it was the personal contact with Whitman and the study of his writings that later led Dr. Bucke, the alienist, to study the phenomenon of mysticism, which the doctor called "cosmic consciousness."[8] The double nature of the poet, a profound spirituality mingled with an exuberant animality, remains a paradox in the biography—though it is not treated as such. But Dr. Bucke's later book helps to explain this puzzle, for it is a familiar paradox among mystics. In defense of the animal side of Whitman's disposition, Bucke claims in his biography that the "Children of Adam" poems have established "the purity, holiness and perfect sanity of the sexual relation,"[166] while "Calamus" presents "an exalted friendship, a love into which sex does not enter as an element." Not the slightest taint of abnormality is seen in either of these groups. And as for Whitman's illness in the summer of 1864 and his paralysis in 1873, these are attributed simply to the contraction of "hospital malaria" and overwork as a war-nurse.

O'Connor's interpretation of Whitman as a modern prophet is strongly confirmed by Bucke: *Leaves of Grass* belongs to a religious era not yet reached, of which it is the revealer and herald. . . . What the Vedas were to Brahmanism, the Law and the Prophets to Judaism . . . the Gospels and Pauline writings to Christianity . . . will *Leaves of Grass* be to the future of American civilization." It is "the bible of Democracy."[183–85]

The great value of Dr. Bucke's biography is that it conveys the remarkable personality of Walt Whitman. And others have confirmed the testimony which he gave after the poet's death: "To the last [his face] had no lines of care or worry—he lived in an upper spiritual stratum—above all mean thoughts, sordid feelings, earthly harassments."[9] Such observations led this devoted friend to study the lives of other mystics and to write a forerunner of William James's analysis of the psychology of mysticism in *The Varieties of Religious Experience*.

FIRST BRITISH INTERPRETATIONS:
ROSSETTI TO SYMONDS

Before continuing the story of Whitman biography in America, we need to observe his reception and growing reputation abroad— especially in England—for what the foreign critics said about him had, sooner or later, considerable influence on American evaluations. Professor Harold Blodgett has already ably told the story of Walt Whitman in England[10] and it need not be repeated here in detail, but it is important to know that the first edition of *Leaves of Grass* reached the British several months after its appearance in America, and that by the 1860s Whitman had many prominent admirers there, including William Michael Rossetti, John A. Symonds, Moncure Conway, Mrs. Anne Gilchrist, Swinburne (who later renounced Whitman), and others.

In 1866 Conway published an account[11]—later denounced by Whitman as fanciful[12]—of a visit to the poet in which he found him lying on his back on the parched earth in a blazing sun of nearly 100°, "one of his favorite places and attitudes for composing 'poems.' "[13] The following year William Michael Rossetti published a sane and discriminating article on Whitman in the London *Chronicle*.[14] This led, Rossetti says, to an opportunity to edit the poems, and the edition was published in 1868.

This edition, called *Poems by Walt Whitman*,[15] was both a selection and an expurgation, for the only reason for not reprinting the complete fourth edition of *Leaves of Grass* was the desire of Rossetti and the publisher to eliminate the "objectionable" poems, and Whitman would not agree to outright expurgation of the complete collection.[16] Rossetti's "Prefatory Notice"—mainly the *Chronicle* article—is reserved and admits the poet's faults (as Rossetti saw them) as freely as his virtues. The faults: "he speaks on occasion of gross things in gross, crude, and plain terms"; he uses "absurd or ill-constructed" words; his style is sometimes "obscure, fragmentary, and agglomerative"; and "his self-assertion is boundless"[17]—though partly forgivable as being vicarious. But these are balanced by the poet's great distinctions, "his absolute and entire originality," and his comprehension and intensity in both subject matter and expression, which Rossetti thinks great enough to enlarge the canon of poetic art. The volume contains about half the poems of the 1867 edition of the *Leaves* and the original preface. The selections are well chosen and proved a fortunate introduction of Walt Whitman to England. But it is significant to observe that the British were spared the poems which had so shocked America and that even Whitman's friendly editor found objectionable crudities in the style of *Leaves of Grass*, as have most British critics since then.

As a result of Rossetti's edition, one of the most remarkable episodes in Whitman's life and literary influence took place. Mrs. Anne Gilchrist, the brilliant widow of the great biographer of Blake, read Rossetti's *Selections*, then the complete *Leaves of Grass*, and came to feel that the American poet's message was a personal plea for love which she could answer. The strange story of this one-sided and pathetic courtship is well known and has been sympathetically told by Holloway.[18] Whitman fully appreciated her tender feeling for his poems but was unable to return a personal emotion, even after she had come to America and he had been hospitably received in her Philadelphia home. Of special interest to the growth of his reputation, however, is the essay, "An Englishwoman's Estimate of Walt Whitman," published in the Boston *Radical Review*, May, 1870.[19] Here for the first time a woman, and one widely known in artistic and literary circles, defended in print the sanity and purity of the infamous sex poems. The article was doubly reassuring to Whitman after Rossetti's reserved critical introduction.

After Rossetti and Mrs. Gilchrist's championship of Whitman came Edward Dowden. In his essay on "The Poetry of Democracy: Walt Whitman"[20] he shows considerably more enthusiasm than Rossetti. Like Burroughs and Bucke he interprets Whitman as the product and representative of American environment and life. He thinks that the American poet is "not shaped out of old-world clay ... and [is] hard to name by any old-world name." As the spokesman for "a great democratic world, as yet but half-fashioned"[473] he is not terrified by the fear of vulgarity, and selection seems forbidden to him; all words are eligible for his poetry, and he does not have to sacrifice directness and vividness to propriety. Here we have a new twist to Whitman's own theory, an application not possible for his American biographers, and yet given with admiring approval, just as the sex poems are declared to the product of "a robust, vigorous, clean man, enamored of living, unashamed of body as he is unashamed of soul, absolutely free from pruriency of imagination, absolutely inexperienced in the artifical excitements and enchancements of jaded lusts."[505]

In 1886 Ernest Rhys edited a new selection of *Leaves of Grass*.[21] The complete work was still too strong for British tastes, despite the fact that the book was far more widely appreciated in England than in America. Rhys's introduction adds nothing new to Whitman's biography or criticism, merely echoing the poet's old-age conclusion that his function is initiative, rather than a consummation in poetry and that his "poetic vision [is] fearlessly equal to the far range of later science,"[xi] a claim later amplified by an Australian scientist, William Gay.[22]

One of the keenest and most competent students of Whitman's life and art in the nineteenth century was the brilliant classical scholar, John Addington Symonds. Admitting that at the age of twenty-five *Leaves of Grass* was a revelation to him, influencing him more than any other book except possibly the Bible, and that, "It is impossible for me to speak critically of what has so deeply entered into the fibre and marrow of my being,"[23] he nevertheless was actually the first critic to raise certain embarrassing questions which have agitated biographers ever since.

In the strictly biographical part of his book Symonds agrees with Bucke and Burroughs that, "Walt inherited on both sides a sound constitution, untainted blood, comeliness of person, well-balanced emotions, and excellent moral principles,"[11–12] and gives a sketch of the biographical facts which differs from the previous accounts only in the more restrained and discriminating language. But in the "Study" of *Leaves of Grass* we encounter the first attack on O'Connor's "modern Christ" interpretation: "the ways [Whitman] chose for pushing his gospel and advertising his philosophy, put a severe strain on patience. Were Buddha, Socrates, Christ, so interested in the dust stirred up around them by second-rate persons, in third-rate cities, and in more than fifth-rate literature?"[38]

As a student of "Greek friendship" and Renaissance homosexuality among artists, Symonds recognized in the "Calamus" poems symptoms of emotional abnormality in the poet. Finally he wrote Whitman a frank letter asking for information. The reply, dated August 19, 1890, has become famous:

My life, young manhood, mid-age, times South, &c., have been jolly bodily, and doubtless open to criticism. Though unmarried I have had six children—two are dead—one living Southern grandchild, fine boy, writes to me occasionally—circumstances (connected with their fortune and benefit) have separated me from intimate relations.[24]

Symonds did not publish this letter, and it was not made public until Edward Carpenter quoted it in 1906, but it had an important influence on Symonds's own thinking. In fact, he seems to have been so convinced by it that he was reassured about "Calamus." He decided that what the poet called "the 'adhesiveness' of comradeship is meant to have no interblending with the 'amativeness' of sexual love ... it is undeniable that·Whitman possessed a specially keen sense of the fine restraint and continence, the cleanliness and chastity, that are inseparable from the perfectly virile and physically complete nature of healthy manhood."[25] And yet he must admit that "those unenviable mortals who are the inheritors of sexual anomalies, will recognize their own emotion in Whitman's 'superb friendship ... latent in all men.' " Symonds is still "not certain whether [Whitman's] own feelings upon this delicate topic may not have altered since the time when 'Calamus' was first composed."

Like all the English critics, Symonds is bothered by Whitman's "form," or rather lack of conventional form. "Speaking about him," he says, "is like speaking about the universe ... Not merely because he is large and comprehensive, but because he is intangible, elusive, at first sight self-contradictory, and in some sense formless, does Whitman resemble the universe and defy critical analysis." Such a justification would, of course, have pleased the poet who declared,

I am large, I contain multitudes.

Despite all his misgivings and reservations, however, Symonds renders homage to the man who helped him to strip his own soul of social prejudices, and he gratefully recommends *Leaves of Grass* to others.

THE AMERICAN APOTHEOSIS: TRAUBEL, KENNEDY, DONALDSON, BURROUGHS

Whitman's death in 1892 stimulated his personal friends in America to renewed activity in spreading his fame, an activity which long ago had become a "cause," an almost religious as well as a literary crusade. One of the first acts of his literary executors, Horace L. Traubel, Dr. R. M. Bucke, and Thomas B. Harned, was to publish a memorial volume called *In Re Walt Whitman*.[26] In addition to the tributes of friends and admirers, this book contains translations of the most important criticisms which had appeared in France, Germany, and Denmark. Here we find abundant proof that the American poet had already attained considerable international reputation and influence (a subject to be treated later in this *Handbook*).[27]

In Re is also the first of the Boswellian publications of the inner circle. Traubel, especially, had long been recording indiscriminately the poet's old-age garrulity and had now begun to question his family and acquaintances. His record of conversations with Walt's brother George [33–40], however, opens up new biographical possibilities. Here we get a glimpse of the Whitman family. It is revealing to see their literary ignorance, their indifference and even antagonism to the young poet's ambitions because he showed so little desire for making money; we are not surprised that Walt was never known to fall in love, in fact, seemed completely indifferent to girls, and they to him. Whether or not Walt was as "clean in his habits" as George thought he was, we nevertheless get in these notes a convincing picture of uneventful, commonplace, though not uncongenial family background. Walt Whitman's family did not lack affection for him, but it was as unaware of his genius as were his literary enemies. George's testimony helps to explain the loneliness, discouragement and despair so evident in the third edition of *Leaves of Grass*.

Another contributor to the *In Re* volume was William Sloane Kennedy, a devoted friend of the poet in his Camden period, who in two essays discussed the "Dutch" and the "Quaker Traits of Walt Whitman."[195–99; 213–14] These interpretations Kennedy amplified in his *Reminiscences of Walt Whitman*, published in 1896. There was nothing new in emphasizing these traits in which the poet himself took considerable pride, but Kennedy contributed to the subject a richer fund of information and a more vigorous gusto than previous biographers had displayed. Kennedy himself could be Quixotic as any of the "hot little prophets," to use Bliss Perry's phrase, but he brought to his Whitman idolatry an alert and cultivated mind. Reporting a conversation with the poet in 1880, Kennedy remarks, "I can't tell how it was, but the large personality of the man so vivified the few words he spoke that all the majesty of Greece—especially her sculpturesque art-idea—seemed to loom up before me as never before in my life, although the study of Greek literature had been a specialty of my collegiate and post-collegiate years."[1]

Reminiscences includes a good deal of biographical material, "Memories, Letters, Etc.," and some valuable sympathetic criticism of *Leaves of Grass*. The second part of the book, "Drift and Cumulus," is still useful to a Whitman student for its analyses of the meaning of individual poems; and the third part, "The Styles of Leaves of Grass," contains the first adequate explanation of the "organic principle" which Whitman had borrowed or inherited indirectly from German romanticism. The poet himself had insisted that the analogy of his rhythm was to be found in Nature, but Kennedy made the first real start in rationalizing his prosodic theory and practice. His *Fight of a Book for the World*, 1926, which might be called the first Whitman handbook, continues the interpretations of Kennedy's earlier publication and is of considerable value to the Whitman bibliographer.

The year 1896 also saw the publication of a second book by one of Walt Whitman's personal friends, Thomas Donaldson.[28] His *Walt Whitman, the Man* was based on first-hand knowledge of the poet during two periods, Washington from 1862–73 and Camden 1873–1892, but it contains meager biographical details. "No man tells the public the whole story of his life," says Mr. Donaldson. "Mr. Whitman never told the public the story of his life. . . . I do not now propose to tell it for him."[17] Perhaps this is negative evidence that Whitman told his friends little about his early life. But Donaldson's book made one positive contribution which was later to be extensively amplified. He indicated plainly that Whitman's poems celebrating "love of comrades" were written not out of actual experience but as a compensation for his own loneliness. He put into his poems the "passionate love of comrades" for which he found no human recipient. If Donaldson had developed this interpretation he would have been the first psychological biographer of Whitman. The book remains best known, however, for its testimony to the way the poet affected his intimate associates. "I never met a man of such standing who possessed as little personal egotism, or rather who made it less manifest in contact with him."[77]

The third friend to publish a book in 1896 was John Burroughs, who called his new biography *Walt Whitman, A Study*. He pled guilty to the same sort of "one-sided enthusiasm" found in all the publications of the personal friends: Bucke, Kennedy, Traubel, and Donaldson. When Burroughs met Whitman in the fall of 1863 "he was so sound and sweet and gentle and attractive as a man, and withal so wise and tolerant" that Burroughs soon trusted the book as he trusted the man, for he "saw that the work and the man were one, and that the former must be good as the latter was good."[29] If Whitman could have had the same hand in this book that he had had in the *Notes*, the work could not have been more favorable.

Although John Burroughs knew Whitman over a longer period

than most of the friends who wrote about him, the theory which he held—following the author's own clues—of the origin of *Leaves of Grass* was not likely to lead him to question, examine, or discover new biographical information. "What apprenticeship he served, or with whom he served it, we get no hint,"[72] he is content to say. Of course the apprenticeship and the days of doubt and uncertainty were nearly or entirely over by the time Burroughs made Whitman's acquaintance in Washington; hence he can truthfully testify: "We never see him doubtful or hesitating; we never see him battling for his territory, and uncertain whether or not he is upon his own ground." All these interpretations are based on the theory that Whitman himself cultivated: " 'Leaves of Grass' is an utterance out of the depths of primordial, aboriginal human nature. It embodies and exploits a character not rendered anaemic by civilization, but preserving a sweet and sane savagery, indebted to culture only as a means to escape culture, reaching back always, through books, art, civilization, to fresh, unsophisticated nature, and drawing his strength from thence."[76] This theory would not encourage Burroughs to undertake biographical research.

He made another interpretation, however, which might have— and in recent years has—led to literary investigation. "We must look for the origins of Whitman," he says, " . . . in the deep world-currents that have been shaping the destinies of the race for the past hundred years or more; in the universal loosening, freeing, and removing obstructions; in the emancipation of the people . . .; in the triumph of democracy and of science: . . . the sentiment of realism and positivism, the religious hunger that flees the churches . . . etc."[231]

Although Burroughs finally became impatient with Whitman's senile pleasure in the fawning of the Camden and Philadelphia claque, he never modified the conviction which he expressed in "The Flight of the Eagle," published in *Birds and Poets*, 1877: "to tell me that Whitman is not a large, fine, fresh, magnetic personality, making you love him, and want always to be with him, were to tell me that my whole past life is a deception, and all the impression of my perceptives a fraud."[30] Clara Barrus's valuable book, *Whitman and Burroughs, Comrades,* was later (1931) to document this friendship with the publication of many interesting letters, which reveal Burroughs as a more intelligent partisan than most of the inner circle, but one who, until the end of his life, was unwavering in his loyalty and devotion to Whitman. This record of one of the most important friendships in the poet's life is itself a distinguished contribution to scholarship, containing much new material on Whitman's reputation at home and abroad, and sound, intelligent critical judgments. The publication of the ten-volume deluxe edition of Whitman's works in 1902[31] may be taken as a convenient termination of the first stage of his biography. Two intimate admirers (Trowbridge and Edward Carpenter—to be discussed presently) were to publish important testimony after this date, but the first cycle had practically run its course. The biographical "Introduction" to the Camden Edition, written by the literary executors Bucke, Harned, and Traubel, adds only a few meager details. But since this Introduction is based on the publications of Burroughs, Bucke, Donaldson, Kennedy and the favorable criticism of friends and admirers in Europe, a précis of the essay will serve to emphasize the state of Whitman biography in 1902.

The sketch begins by stressing the antiquity and typical Americanism of the poet's ancestry. These "working people, possessed of little or no formal culture, and with no marked artistic tastes in any direction," had large families, were long-lived, and passed on to Walt their virile moral and physical energy. "There was no positive trace of degeneracy anywhere in the breed."[I, xviii] Little seems to be known about Walter Whitman, Senior; the brothers are vaguely described as of "solid, strong frame, fond of animals, and addicted to the wholesome labors and pleasures of the open air";[xxi] but the simple, almost illiterate, mother is represented as sweet, spiritual, ideal, and the poet's most important ancestor.[xxi]

Whitman's "long foreground" is interpreted as mainly his boyhood environment, the outdoor scenes and activities on Long Island and his contact with all sorts of people, especially unlettered folk. This "study of life" is said to have provided a better education for the future poet than the schools could possibly have done. Although his reading of Shakespeare, Homer, and the Bible is emphasized, these biographers agree that books were less important in his "apprenticeship" than outdoor experiences, urban life, and such amusements as the opera, concerts, theatrical performances, and fairs and museums.[xxvi–xxviii]

The New Orleans trip is thought to have been significant in the poet's development, but "There was an atmosphere of mysteriousness unconsciously thrown about the episode."[xxxv] The only known reason for Whitman's leaving was Jeff's poor health. No precise information is given for his inability to hold any job more than a few weeks or months.

In the publication of the first edition of *Leaves of Grass* the "hidden purpose of his life was suddenly revealed."[xxxvii] The gestation, experimentation—in short, the sources—of this work are unknown to these biographers. Since they believe that the book is "cosmic and baffles all adequate account," they are not predisposed to exert much effort to find the "hidden purpose." From this time on they make the story of the book the story of Walt Whitman. Everything is grist for the mill; any effort to spread the "new gospel" is laudable, even writing anonymous reviews and self-advertizing; the poet's life and personality are observed to grow more Christ-like each day. The sex poems express the divine order of paternal and fraternal love; the poet sacrificed his health in his overly-zealous hospital ministrations; all persecutors and depreciators of the man or his book are properly condemned. But through all suffering, disappointments, and misunderstanding Walt Whitman grows daily more serene, lovable, and triumphant over the world and the flesh. Such was the apotheosis of Walt Whitman in 1902, ten years after his calm death in Camden.

FIRST STEPS IN A RE-EVALUATION: TROWBRIDGE, EDWARD CARPENTER

The process of re-evaluation had already begun in 1903. Although John Townsend Trowbridge was one of Walt Whitman's Boston friends, his autobiography, *My Own Story: with Recollections of Noted Persons*, shows plainly the new epoch dawning in Whitman's biographical and critical interpretation. Ever since O'Connor's partisan defence of the "Good Gray Poet," Whitman's indebtedness to Emerson had become a problem in criticism and biography. After addressing Emerson as "Master" in the impulsive open-letter of the second edition of *Leaves of Grass*, Whitman finally in a letter to Kennedy in 1887 denied flatly that he had read the master before beginning his own book.[32] Burroughs, whose youthful enthusiasm for Emerson first led him to read Whitman, was always divided on the question. The Camden circle tried to deny any influence whatever. Of considerable value, therefore, is Trowbridge's testimony that when the poet visited Boston in 1860 to see his ill-fated third edition through the press he confessed to having read Emer-

son's *Essays* in 1854. "He freely admitted that he could never have
written his poems if he had not first 'come to himself,' and that
Emerson helped him to 'find himself' . . . 'I was simmering, simmering, simmering; Emerson brought me to a boil.' "[33]

Traubel, Harned, and Bucke, were always inclined to accept
every utterance of the poet as gospel truth, but Trowbridge expresses
the opinion that Whitman's long invalidism affected his memory.[34]
For example, it is obviously not true that without the Civil War years
"and the experience they gave, *Leaves of Grass* would not now be
existing,"[398] for the third edition was published in 1860. Furthermore, Trowbridge is convinced that "in matters of taste and judgment he was extremely fallible, and capable of doing unwise and
wayward things for the sake of a theory or a caprice."[397] He can
foresee the time when "some future tilter at windmills will attempt
to prove that the man we know as Walt Whitman was an uncultured
impostor," but Trowbridge sensibly concludes that "after all deduc-
tions it remains to be unequivocally affirmed that Whitman stands as
a great original force in our literature."[400]

At this point we might note the corroborating evidence and
opinion of the British disciple, Edward Carpenter—though at the
moment we are violating strict chronology, for *Days with Walt
Whitman* appeared in 1906, after important books by Binns, Perry,
and Bertz. Edward Carpenter was a young, impressionable English
poet who visited Whitman for the first time in 1877 and thereafter
joined the band of followers, even to the extent of trying to adopt
the thought and style of *Leaves of Grass* in his own poetry. But when
he came to write his book, Carpenter perceived clearly that the inner
circle of American friends was "more concerned to present an ideal
personality than a real portrait."[52] Without in the least minimizing his admiration or personal indebtedness, Carpenter tried to
give a "real portrait," and thereby succeeded in making a valuable
contribution to the growth of Whitman biography.

Carpenter's most sensational revelation is Whitman's letter to
Symonds in 1890 regarding the illegitimate children.[142-43] As we
have already seen, this letter seems to have allayed Symonds's worst
suspicions about the origin of the "Calamus" emotions, but Carpenter can see that there is more to the subject than has yet been
revealed. Remembering Doyle's testimony that he had never known
"a case of Walt's being bothered up by a woman,"[35] George's word
that Walt had always been indifferent to girls,[36] and Burroughs's

statement that the poet's "intimacies with men were much more numerous and close than with women,"[37] Carpenter concluded that there must have been "a great tragic element in his nature"[47] which prevented happiness in love affairs. And yet he knows that love ruled Whitman's life, "that he gave his life for love." The implications are plain that the poems are a sublimation of this love.

Walt Whitman's "double nature" had been hinted before, but Carpenter offers fresh evidence of this paradoxical disposition. He records his impression of the poet's "contradictory, self-willed, tenacious, obstinate character, strong and even extreme moods, united with infinite tenderness, wistful love, and studied tolerance ..."[38] Carpenter reports a most revealing confession that Whitman made to him: "There is something in my nature *furtive* like an old hen! ... That is how I felt in writing 'Leaves of Grass.' Sloane Kennedy calls me 'artful'—which about hits the mark."[43] And then Whitman added a sentence which deserves to be italicized: *"I think there are truths which it is necessary to envelop or wrap up."* Carpenter left for later biographers the pastime of guessing what these "truths" were, but he fully appreciated the importance of the confessed "furtive" sensation which the poet experienced in writing *Leaves of Grass* (meaning how many editions?). In the summer of 1886 Whitman demonstrated his own understanding of the psychological significance of these revelations in a self-analysis for Carpenter: "The *Democratic Review* essays and tales came from the surface of the mind, and had no connection with what lay below—a great deal of which indeed was below consciousness. At last came the time when the concealed growth had to come to light ..."[73]

Carpenter no less than Bucke thought Whitman's cosmic consciousness his strongest faculty. For this reason both believed he was a new type of man. But Carpenter did not see him with the distorted perspective of the "hot little prophets" who would like to worship at the shrine of a new Messiah: "while [Whitman] does not claim to deliver a new Gospel, he seems to claim to take his place in the line of those who have handed down a world-old treasure of redemption for mankind."[75] In "To Him that was Crucified" we have not a successor of Christ but a continuer of a world-wide and age-long tradition.[76] In an appendix called "Whitman as Prophet" Carpenter cites parallels to *Leaves of Grass* from the Upanishads. This emphasis on religious tradition and literary analogies for *Leaves of Grass* links Edward Carpenter with the first of the critical biographers, though his first-hand information and his literary discipleship classify him as one of the apostles—even if at times a doubting Thomas.

CRITICAL BIOGRAPHY: BINNS, BERTZ

We have already seen how arbitrary classifications of the biographers can be. Although on the whole Burroughs wrote as much under the spell of Whitman's personal influence as anyone, at times he could be acutely objective and critical. And both Symonds and Edward Carpenter, who eagerly confessed their profound indebtedness to the American poet, did much to bring about a complete re-evaluation of Walt Whitman in biography; while Henry Bryan Binns, an Englishman whose *Life of Walt Whitman* (1905) is the first complete, factual, and exhaustive biography, was as tenderly sympathetic with the poet as his most intimate friends had been.

Binns did his job so thoroughly that his book is still, seventy years later, one of the most reliable accounts of Walt Whitman's life. Not content with reading all available Whitman literature, Mr. Binns came to the United States and observed the scenes which had exerted the greatest influence on the life of his subject. For example, when Sculley Bradley visited Timber Creek and made an exhaustive study of the place where Whitman one summer regained the use of his limbs after a spell of invalidism, he found that only Binns had given an accurate description of the place.[38] Such accuracy was certainly new in Whitman biography, though in his Preface Binns disclaims any intention of writing a "critical" or "definitive" life.

Nevertheless, after a factual account of Whitman's youth and early manhood, Binns originates the most colorful of all the conjectures about the poet's mysterious New Orleans period. In the attempt to account for the marked change which seems to have come over Whitman after this trip, he creates a New Orleans romance.

It seems that about this time Walt formed an intimate relationship with some woman of higher social rank than his own—a lady of the South where social rank is of the first consideration—that she became the mother of his child, perhaps, in after years, of his children; and that he was prevented by some obstacle, presumably of family prejudice, from marriage or the acknowledgment of his paternity.[39]

As evidence for this conjecture Binns cites the letter to Symonds, Whitman's old-age remarks to Traubel, and the emotional awakening and poetic power which is evident in *Leaves of Grass* a few years after this trip. The awakening and the power are acknowledged by all the biographers, but Binns was the first to create so bold a theory: "Who emancipated him? May we not suppose it was a passionate and noble woman who opened the gates for him and showed him himself in the divine mirror of her love?"[52] Future biographers were slow to relinquish so romantic a picture as the warm-blooded, dark-skinned Southern lady of high-born Creole caste.

This theory works best for the "Children of Adam" poems. The "Calamus" group is explained by Binns as not the product of experience but of frustrated love: "he who knew and loved so many men and women, seems to have carried forward with him no equal friendship from the years of his youth. ... He longed for Great Companions, but he did not meet them at this time upon the open road of daily intercourse."[163]

Despite Binns's avowed purpose not to indulge in critical interpretations, he was the first biographer or critic to attempt a close reading of the subjective meaning of Whitman's poems as they developed through the many editions. For example, *Drum-Taps* "is a Song of the Broad-Axe, not a scream of the war-eagle."[209] The poet who had formerly expressed his awakened sensibility and his frustrated longing for human companionship learned, through the War and the hospital, social solidarity and a "sense of citizenship."

Binns also uses effectively the comparative method to clarify Whitman's relations to his age and to other writers. Like Triggs,[40] he finds revealing parallels in the thought of Whitman and Browning. Tolstoi, with his "Oriental tendency toward pessimism and asceticism,"[295] serves mainly as a contrast. Whitman's mysticism is thought to be indirectly indebted to George Fox, and his individualism directly influenced by Mill's *Principles of Economy*.[298, 308] A very interesting parallel is Proudhon, "the peasant, who . . . looked forward to voluntarism as the final form of society."[309]

In a calm, reasonable manner Binns accepts Whitman as a modern prophet. "To be an American prophet-poet, to make the American people a book which should be like the Bible in spiritual appeal and moral fervour, but a book of the New World and of the new spirit—such seems to have been the first and the last of Whitman's daydreams."[55] But whereas, "Other men have given themselves out to be a Christ, or a John the Baptist, or an Elijah; Whitman, without their fanaticism, but with a profound knowledge of himself, recognized in a peasant-born son of Manhattan, an average American artisan, the incarnation of America herself."[335]

The story of the rise and growth of the Whitman cult in Germany belongs to the history of *Leaves of Grass* in world literature more than to the growth of biography, and will therefore be treated in Chapter V. But the publicaton of Eduard Bertz's *Der Yankee-Heiland* in 1905 marks an important turn in Whitman biography because this was the first outright attempt to destroy completely the "Yankee-Saint" legend. Whitman's works were discussed in Germany as early as 1868 by Ferdinand Freiligrath. And soon after Knortz-Rolleston's translation in 1889 the American poet was practically worshiped in the Rhineland,[41] much as Shakespeare had been in the eighteenth century. But most German critics merely elaborated the "official" portrait created by Whitman and his acolytes, though more fanatically than even the most ardent American friends. Especially is this true in the writings of Johannes Schlaf.[42]

Bertz first read *Leaves of Grass* in 1882 while he was living in his "woodland retreat" in Tennessee. After returning to Germany he sent Whitman in 1889 an appreciative article which he had published in the *Deutsche Press* to celebrate the poet's seventieth birthday. In response Whitman showered Bertz with favorable reviews and self-advertizing, and the German admirer could not reconcile this action with his idealization of the saintly prophet. Bertz, still and always, regarded Whitman as one of the major lyric poets of the world,[43] but from this time on he became suspicious and critical of Whitman's life and character.

These suspicions led to a study of Walt Whitman's sex pathology, published as "Walt Whitman, ein Charakterbild" in the *Jahrbuch für sexuelle Zwischenstufen*, 1906. Here Bertz argued that Whitman belonged to the "intermediate sex", to use Edward Carpenter's term, or "Uranians".[44] This psychopathic interpretation dominates Bertz's attempt to unmask the poet in *Der Yankee-Heiland*.

The feminine and even hysterical *Grundton* of his being is obvious to any observant reader, in the emotional, impassioned character of his world-outlook. No one familiar with modern psychology and sex-pathology is in the slightest doubt that the erotic friendship, which is found in the poetry and life of our wonderful prophet, is to be explained in any other way than by his constitutional deviation from the masculine norm.[228-29]

This interpretation casts a new light on many phases of Whitman's life. His love for the young soldiers suffering in the hospitals was "fundamentally sexual,"[205] though sublimated and ennobled. His "abundant joy" was another myth; actually "his life was filled with the intense agony of a confused soul. His love was unrequited; it was a renunciation and so he placed it beyond the grave."[212] Even his "supposedly universal sympathy . . . [was] rooted not so much in his heart as in his phantasy" and turns out to be only a "formal, artistic theory."[203] In the same manner, Whitman's paralysis is thought to have been the result of some hereditary taint; the breakdown due to the hospital strain was a myth, like the similar myth about Nietzsche's hospital work.[30]

Bertz's attempt to destroy the "prophet myth" results also in an attack upon Whitman's pretensions as a thinker and a philosopher. Though he claimed to be the poet of science and progress, he was "at heart opposed to Darwinism but afraid to say so openly."[127] His "new religion" actually came far more from the Hebrew prophets than from scientific thought, though he fooled himself into thinking that he had reconciled the two through some sort of Hegelian sophistry. His chiliasm and theodicy[45] were intuitive and romantic and irreconcilable with empirical rationalism.

. . . if he had wished to be nothing except a lyricist his poetic greatness would certainly be uncontested. But unfortunately he wanted above all to be a prophet and . . . the founder of a tenable scientific religion with a definitely philosophic world outlook, and this point of view conflicted with his spiritual nature; his purely lyrical talent was not sufficient for that. [100]

SCHOLARLY BIOGRAPHY IN AMERICA:
PERRY AND GEORGE RICE CARPENTER

The beginnings of Whitman scholarship—the attempt to discover and tell the whole truth—might be dated from Binns. But before Bliss Perry's *Whitman* in 1906 at least no one in America had even attempted to tell the poet's life completely and impartially. Perry did not have access to many of the private notebooks and unpublished manuscripts which have since been collected and edited by Holloway and Furness, but he made the most of the sources available.

In his biography Perry traces down the known facts of Whitman's ancestry, which he finds to be undistinguished but respectable. The events of his youth and early manhood are recited calmly and without bias. Not even the New Orleans trip provokes any fanciful guesses or romantic interpretations. Where the facts are inadequate or missing altogether, Perry freely admits the lacunae. He rejects the pathological interpretations of the "Calamus" poems, though agreeing with Burroughs that there was a good deal of the woman as well as the man in Walt Whitman. He agrees also with Burroughs that there is "abundant evidence that from 1862 onward his life was stainless so far as sexual relations were concerned,"[46] yet frankly admits that the evidence for earlier years is scanty. The first *Leaves of Grass* was "a child of passion" and "sexual emotion" helped to generate it. "Its roots are deep down in a young man's body and soul," but it is "a clean, sensuous body and a soul untroubled as yet by the darker mysteries."[47] In the poems of joy Perry finds "the spirit of blissful vagrancy which dominated his early manhood."[21] Perry travels a road separate from that of the later psychological biographers.

Without denying or minimizing Walt Whitman's affectations of dress and manner, a sympathetic interpretation is placed on them by the observation that "the flannel shirt and slouch hat are as clearly symbolical as George Fox's leathern breeches, or the peasant dress of Count Tolstoi."[74] Whitman's letters to his mother and friends give the reader a clear, eye-witness account of the War and the hospital experiences. With kindly detachment Perry chronicles the poet's dismissal from his clerkship in Washington and O'Connor's feud not only with the puritanical Harlan but also with all British literature and European influences. Even the Camden period—with "its *vates sacer*, ... the band of disciples, the travel-stained pilgrims and ultimately the famous tomb"[214]—is neither satirized nor sentimentalized.

But probably Perry's greatest service for Whitman biography and criticism, and for American literature, was his interpretation of *Leaves of Grass* in terms of international literary and artistic developments. "A generation trained to the enjoyment of Monet's landscapes, Rodin's sculptures, and the music of Richard Strauss will not be repelled from Whitman merely because he wrote in an unfamiliar form."[282-83] Perry also helped to lessen the shock for readers by calling attention to the parallels between *Leaves of Grass* and Oriental poetry (so much admired by the American Transcendentalists) and the familiar English version of the poetry of the Bible.[276]

Whitman's faults and literary lapses are also freely admitted. In a left-handed manner the "physiological passages" are defended as usually bearing "the mark, not so much of his imaginative energy as of his automatic describing-machine."[289] Perry finds absent in Whitman love of man for woman and a sense of family, home, and social cooperation. "Beyond the unit he knows nothing more definite than his vague 'divine average' until he comes to 'these States' and finds himself on sure ground again."[293] But most objectionable to the Camden disciples was such a criticism as this: "Monist as he was in philosophy, he was polytheist in practice: he dropped on his knees anywhere, before stick or stone, flesh or spirit, and swore that each in turn was divine."[294] Nevertheless, Walt Whitman, "in spite of the alloy which lessens the purely poetic quality and hence the permanence of his verse, is sure . . . to be somewhere among the immortals."[307]

The condition in which Perry left Whitman biography after the publication of his book may be summed up in his own conclusion:

No Whitman myth, favorable or unfavorable, can forever withstand the accumulated evidence as to Whitman's actual character. . . . The 'wild buffalo strength' myth, which he himself loved to cultivate, has gone; the Sir Galahad myth, so touchingly cherished by O'Connor, has gone, too; and Dr. Bucke's 'Superman' myth is fast going. We have in their place something very much better; a man earthy, incoherent, arrogant, but elemental and alive.[291]

It is not in the least surprising that Perry's biography should have, as Kennedy put it, "excited . . . much protest from Whitmanites."[46] And he, himself, was no exception. The Whitmanites could not bear any qualification of their hero and were quick to attribute any reservations either to prudery or the stultifying influence of "culture." Kennedy thought the book was "written with an eye on Mrs. Grundy," by an author who lived in the stuffy air of libraries and the class-room. "He is a spokesman of the genteel, conforming, half-baked middle-class. . . ."[94]

A work more to the taste of the "Whitmanites" was Horace Traubel's *With Walt Whitman in Camden*, the first volume of which appeared in 1906. Three more volumes were published, the fifth in 1964.[47] From March 28, 1888, Traubel kept daily notes of his conversations with Whitman, and in these books he reports them with a fullness that puts Boswell to shame—though unfortunately Traubel had Boswell's industry without his genius. Because the books do provide many minute details of the poet's last years that would not otherwise have survived, they have some value for the student of his ideas; but they also do Whitman a disservice by embalming his trivial, garrulous, and often foggy thoughts in the final years of pain, failing memory, and perhaps at times of outright delusion.[48] Only limitless veneration and uncritical judgment could have enabled anyone to accumulate such a mass of commonplace manuscript—though Traubel did preserve valuable letters.

The new epoch of scholarly biographies in America was continued, however, with George Rice Carpenter's *Walt Whitman*, published in the "English Men of Letters" series in 1909. This book, like others in the series, is not particularly original or distinguished, though it summarizes the facts accurately and coherently. It might be described as a concise version of Bucke (for facts) and Perry (for interpretation). Bucke's account of Whitman's sound ancestry is retained in chastened rhetoric, Binns's New Orleans romance is passed over in silence, and the story of the illegitimate children is unquestioningly accepted. "We know (and wish to know) nothing more than that he had at times been lured by the pleasures of the flesh, like many a poet before him, and that he had known the deep and abiding love of woman."[49] (Later biographers were to lack such well-bred reticence.) In the next to the last paragraph of the biography Carpenter mentions literary relationships but quickly asserts that these are "not of great importance in Whitman's case. He was little influenced by books,"[171] and apparently was thought not to have influenced others—as of course he had not in America before 1906, though he had in Europe.

FRENCH AND BRITISH CRITICS: BAZALGETTE, DE SELINCOURT, LAWRENCE, BULLETT

In 1908 Léon Bazalgette, in his *Walt Whitman: L'Homme et son Oeuvre*—still known in the United States mainly in a bowdlerized translation[50] —revived the idealized interpretations of Burroughs and Bucke with a critical enthusiasm and lack of reserve possible only to a master of the French language. Like the earliest biographers, he believes that the man cannot be separated from the book, and therefore frequently "evoke[s] the work to explain the man."[5] As a matter of fact, he deliberately carries on the work of the Bucke school, for he announces in the preface the intention of building, "to the measure of my strength, a French dwelling for the American bard."[xvii] And his sources are Whitman's personal friends, rather than later biographies: "I efface myself as much as possible, in the humility of a compiler, behind those who were in personal contact with him and caught him on the spot."[4]

Once more the poet's ancestry shines in resplendent glory. From the Whitmans, "the most vigorous British element in one section" of the isle, and the Van Velsors, "typical representatives of the old Americanized Dutch," Walt Whitman inherited, from the one, "firmness of character verging almost upon hardness," and from the other, "abundant vitality and joviality."[12, 13] Little Walt "found in his cradle the enormous strength and health accumulated by his family, nowise diminished like the family fortune, but increased each generation."[23] The "centuries of silent labour close to the earth and to the sea, centuries of robustness and open air"[94] had prepared the way for him.

Bazalgette idealizes Whitman's youth and apprenticeship years with a more vivid imagination than either Burroughs or Bucke possessed. "The memory of this happy period remained dear as ever to the poet, past the period of his virility . . . What animal strength and what largeness these intervals of life, wild, exultant, diffusive of unconscious joy, near the sea and on it, were preparing for the individual!"[35] And then when he comes to the young man's sexual awakening, which again is believed to have been the New Orleans period, Bazalgette displays an exuberance which evidently shocked the American translator, for she thought it necessary to leave whole paragraphs unrevealed in sober English.

It is not easy in a few words to explain Bazalgette's exact interpretations of the New Orleans period, for it is both subtle and sophisticated. He is quite aware that Walt Whitman did not conduct himself like a typical Anglo-Saxon young man in love. But Bazalgette is sure that he was not abnormal. Whitman merely appeared to be cold because he did not abandon himself to flirtations and pretty speeches. And he may not have been sexually aroused until his brief sojourn in the South:

Il est possible, toutefois, que, jusqu'à son séjour à La Nouvelle-Orléans, l'amour n'ait été pour lui qu'une expérience concrète parmi mille autres expériences et qu'il n'ait pas eu encore la révélation totale de la femme, âme et corps, la sensation despotique et toute-puissante de son être entier, aimant et aimé.[51]

But the hypothetical romance first created by Binns, "dans son livre si nourri, si pieux, si chaleureux,"[52] seems to Bazalgette to exaggerate the importance of this education in love. The future poet tore himself away and returned to his home in the North because "he could not endure that a woman should hold a place in his life which might fatally lessen the domain of his liberty."[84] Still, "Walt had plunged into the heart of the continent and, undoubtedly, into the heart of woman."[86]

Although other biographers admit the scarcity of exact information concerning Whitman's life between the New Orleans trip and the first edition of *Leaves of Grass*, Bazalgette asserts confidently that at thirty "the perfect concordance between the interior Walt and his physical appearance is a genuine subject of astonishment." In fact, "however magnificent, however eternal may be for us his book, Walt, the man in the flesh who is about to put it forth, is at least its peer at ths moment."[91] Perhaps such enthusiastic statements were intended to be understood in a symbolical manner, for Bazalgette goes on to say that Walt Whitman "was more a Whitman man than his father or his brother George, more a Van Velsor than his mother or his brother Jeff. . . ."[97] When so little is known about either family, this superinheritance must be mystical rather than biological. And the same is true in Bazalgette's treatment of the "Calamus" motif in *Leaves of Grass*. He admits the "impassioned character" of some of Whitman's "attachments of man to man,"[220] but thinks Schlaf[53] has successfully replied to the psychopaths who had seen in these friendships "a sexual anomaly":

In any case, it is not the searchers for anomalies who will ever find the key. Perhaps he who shall describe the exact nature of the attachment which united the Apostle of Galilee [*sic*] to his diciple John will be able to clear the mystery of love which is concealed in the tender comradeships of the Good Gray Poet.[220-221]

After this point, to summarize the rest of Bazalgette's book would be an anticlimax in this account of the growth of Whitman biography, not because the French biographer falters or weakens, but because from here on the point of view is thoroughly familiar to us. With gusto Bazalgette dilates on "Walt Whitman, a Cosmos," with vicarious pleasure he exults in O'Connor's avenging the Harlan "insult," shares the pride of the intimate friends over the poet's victories in the British Isles, and finally with loving tenderness describes the calm death "while the rain gently fell," and the "pagan funeral" which intrusted the last remains to the elements. No biographer has written Walt Whitman's life with more genuine emotion.

Basil De Selincourt's English biography shares a good deal in spirit and point of view with the French biography of Bazalgette and was no doubt influenced by it. Both are, strictly speaking, critics rather than biographers, for they are interested less in discovering facts and establishing new evidences for their interpretations than in reading the text sympathetically; and at times their reading is so sympathetic that they too become mythmakers.

De Selincourt does, however, give a new twist to the New Orleans hypothesis started by Binns: "There can be no doubt that his trip South was taken with conscious intention, that his new job attracted him because of the new contexts it would afford to his daily dreams and meditations."[54] Not even Burroughs and Bucke assumed that the poet thus consciously planned and controlled his destiny. Accepting Binn's theory completely that Whitman first experienced love in the romantic South, De Selincourt discovers a pregnant symbolism: "This visit to the South, always associated in his mind with the ecstatic and desolating history of his loves, became typical to him of the fusion of the Northern and Southern States into a nation, and seemed to give him the right to speak as representative of the whole."[18-19]

Although he insists that Whitman "was not the type to sow wild oats," De Selincourt nevertheless accepts completely the story of the six illegitimate children and the romance with the New Orleans lady of "gentle birth," but

his six children were not all the offspring of one mother, their father convincing himself, under the influence partly of his feelings, partly of confused theory, that, as an exceptional man, loved now by this woman and now by that, he could find and give an adequate conjugal love in more than one relationship . . . pledged already to transcendental union with his country, [he] may have felt that the serene confiding joys of domesticity and its complete personal surrender must not be his.[20-22]

Such promiscuity on principle certainly reaches a new high, or a new low, of some sort in Whitman biography! De Selincourt asserts that "Out of the Cradle Endlessly Rocking," which he conveniently dates back to "one of the all but earliest *Leaves*," is "the song virtually of a husband mourning for the death of one who was in all but name his wife,"[23-24] *i.e.*, the New Orleans woman of gentle birth, while "Once I Pass'd through a Populous City" may refer to a "humble woman."

De Selincourt admits an inconsistency in Whitman's pretending to despise culture yet trying to write poetry. "He was without the discipline of education and underrated or ignored its value."[31] And another paradox is found in the war poems: although Whitman "regarded himself and we regard him as peculiarly the poet of the war; yet . . . the bulk of his most characteristic expression preceded it,"[42-43] for much of *Drum-Taps* had already been completed when Walt went to Virginia to look for George. But in Whitman's letters to his mother and to Peter Doyle, De Selincourt thinks that we observe for the first time "his actual personality by the side of the assumed personality of the hero of *Leaves of Grass*, and find to our astonishment that the man is greater than the book and different from it; in fact, that he is its complement."[45]

Bucke and Whitman himself would have approved this interpretation of the poet's spontaneous unconventionality:

His own wild music, ravishing, unseizable, like the song of a bird, came to him, as by his own principles it should have come, when he was not searching for it. And his greatness as a poet, when we regard his poetry on its formal side, is that conventional echoes damaged him so little, that in spite of unavoidable elements of wilfulness and reaction in his poetry, he was able to achieve so real an independence.[73]

Perhaps only a European critic could have declared finally that Walt Whitman "epitomised his people so perfectly that he could make no impression upon them."[241]

Four years later, in 1918, a French critic, Valéry Larbaud,

voiced a revolt from the Bazalgette interpretation which was to be heard in ever-increasing volume in the next two decades. He rejected three Whitman legends, those of the prophet, the laborer, and the philosopher, and we might add a fourth, that of the American:

Oui, il est Américan; mais c'est parce que nous flairons dans la partie vivante de son oeuvre une certaine odeur (indéfinissable) que nous trouvons aussi dans Hawthorne, Thoreau, un roman de H. K. Viélé et trois nouvelles de G.W. Cable. Mais il n'est pas Américain parce qu'il s'est proclamé le poète de l'Amérique. Encore le démenti immédiat: il a été aussi méconnu aux Etats-Unis que Stendhal à Grenoble ou Cézanne à Aix. Sa doctrine est allemande, et ses maîtres sont anglais; par toute sa vie purement intellectuelle il fut un Européen habitant l'Amérique. Mais, surtout la plupart de "the happy few" vivent en Europe. C'est donc en Europe seulement qu'il pouvait être reconnu et qu'il l'a été.[55]

In his chapter on Whitman in *Studies in Classic American Literature* (1918) D.H. Lawrence attacked savagely a mystical doctrine and a personal characteristic of the poet in a manner wholly new in biography and criticism of him. When Whitman looks at the slave, says Lawrence, he *merges* with him, vicariously shares his wounds—"is it not myself who am also bleeding with wounds?" But, "This was not *sympathy*. It was merging and self-sacrifice."[56] The merging theme is morbid and disintegrating. Whitman starts out boldly on the open road—explorer, adventurer, pioneer—but then he wants to merge with everything, all people, nature, the womb, finally with Death. He confounds sympathy (which would help the slave to free himself or the prostitute to secure medical and economic aid) with sentimental Christianity.

But the prophet and carpenter legend died hard. As late as 1921 Will Hayes, one of the last fundamentalists, published in London a book called *Walt Whitman: the Prophet of the New Era*, with chapters on "The Christ of Our Age," "The Carpenter of Brooklyn," and "A Sermon on the Mount." The book is too trivial to mention except as an example that the old faith still lingered on.

The extent to which Rossetti's attitudes toward Whitman had survived in Great Britain is evidenced in Gerald Bullett's *Walt Whitman: A Study and a Selection,* 1924. "If we regard a poet as an infallible seer," says Bullett, "we are at once saved the trouble of reading his work intelligently, with critical faculty alert," and this, he thinks, is exactly what some of Whitman's countrymen have done, they "who regard every word that he wrote, every comma that he omitted, as so infinitely precious that they reprint even his juvenile metrical verse, his temperance novel, and his newspaper reports."[57]

"Apart from the defect in taste that blemished his literary expression, he possessed personal idiosyncrasies that were due largely to an excess of qualities admirable in themselves. His occasional mawkishess, the endearments and kisses bestowed on the men who were his dearest friends: this, I feel, was but the odious superflux of a generous affection."[30] Like most of the British critics, Bullett censures Whitman for blabbing about intimate details of life that should be kept secret and accuses him of utter lack of artistic sense and taste. "Why make bones about it that Whitman at thirty-five was a satyr, and some of the first *Leaves of Grass* the natural expression of a satyr?"[3] He knew nothing of selection. But he was not lacking in poetic power. He was best when he was cosmic. And when by "sheer strength of thought or depth of passion" his work escapes from graphic journalism it rises to the realm of great literature.[45]

John Bailey's *Walt Whitman* (1926) stands in about the same relation to the English biographies as G. R. Carpenter's book to the American biographies. It is reliable, complete, and always reasonable and conservative in interpretations, without adding anything new or especially significant. Bailey has great respect for those men fortunate enough to have known the poet personally and yet is always suspicious of their unrestrained enthusiasm. "In a man's lifetime lucky or unlucky personal characteristics often lead to his receiving more praise, or less, than his achievement deserved. But the function of later criticism is to take the book, or other work, and judge it as it is, apart from all prejudices of personal liking or disliking."[58] These words adequately summarize the state of Whitman biography and criticism in 1926. The influence of the "hot little prophets" had almost faded out completely and sober criticism both of the man's life and his work were becoming well established. As the living personality of Walt Whitman faded from the memory of men, the scholar and the critic began to turn a concentrated light upon the poetry itself and to read it with increasing depth of understanding and appreciation. After all, the man and the book were not exactly one and the same, even in a mystical sense, for the man had passed on but the book remained.

RESEARCH AND TEXTUAL STUDY:
HOLLOWAY, CATEL, SCHYBERG

Emory Holloway laid the foundation for a new era in Whitman studies when he published in 1921 the *Uncollected Poetry and Prose of Walt Whitman,* containing the poet's private notebooks, early journalistic writings, and other juvenilia in poetry and prose.[59] Later Professor Holloway and his assistants continued to salvage and edit practically every journalistic scrap that can be assigned to Whitman, along with some that can be credited to him only hypothetically. Consequently, when Holloway was ready to publish his biography, *Whitman, An Interpretation in Narrative* (1926), he was undoubtedly familiar with more of the poet's total life output of writing than anyone else. His greatest achievement, therefore, was the first full account of Walt Whitman's life as journalist and editor. And on the natural assumption that the child is father to the man, he attempted to explain the mature poet in terms of his early life and intellectual development.

Holloway's book begins, therefore, not with the poet's ancestors—about which, after all, little can ever be known except names, dates, places of residence, and occupations—but with the journalistic years in Brooklyn, a subject on which the author had already become a recognized authority. Perhaps, as Holloway remarks, Whitman could hardly have become the poet of Democracy without his training and experience in the newspaper office. But the astonishing thing is that the more we learn of the mediocre mind and expression of Walt Whitman the journalist, the greater seems the miracle of his becoming, in the short space of four or five years, a genuine poet. Some of the relaxed, undisciplined habits of thought and expression were carried over into *Leaves of Grass,* but in his more inspired moments he does seem literally a new man.

No one has ever been more aware of this miracle than Professor Holloway himself. In fact, so conscious is he of it, and so inadequately do the journalistic writings provide any satisfactory clues, that once more the biographer must fall back upon two of the earlier hypotheses, *viz.,* Dr. Bucke's mysticism and Binns's New Orleans romance. Practically all the biographers are unanimous on Whitman's mystical experiences, but Holloway's acceptance of the New Orleans conjecture shows the ironical dilemma he is in, for he himself had convincingly demolished the whole "romance"-school in an earlier article.[60] One of the supposed bits of evidence nearly always cited to support the New Orleans theory is the poem, "Once I Pass'd through a Populous City," but Professor Holloway discovered that in the manuscript the poem was addressed to a man rather than a woman and belonged, therefore, to the "Calamus" group. Perhaps one poem does not prove or disprove the theory, but so great is Holloway's dilemma that he now cites the same poem once more to substantiate the love-affair which he had once rejected on the basis of this poem. "I am convinced," he explains, "by many years of study and investigation that the gossip which linked the young journalist with the peculiar *demi monde* of New Orleans was substantially true."[61] No new and conclusive evidence, however, is brought forth.

The reader has the feeling that the biographer knows more than he dares to tell. Commenting on the first edition of *Leaves of Grass*, Holloway says, "Indeed, had [Whitman] known as much about psychology as we do to-day, he might not have had the temerity to publish such a book."[123] In discussing the "Calamus" poems Holloway says of Whitman, "he did not carefully distinguish between . . . the sort of affection which most men have for particular women and that which they experience toward members of their own sex." [169] And he adds that these poems were born of "an unhealthy mood."[173]

Perhaps the basis for these paradoxes is the fact that, as Holloway accurately points out, *Leaves of Grass* contains several kinds of sex poems: (1) the "sentimental lyrics born of an ideal romance" (*i.e.*, hetero-sexual love), (2) celebrations of procreation (philosophical), (3) "emotions which accompany the initial act of paternity," (physiological); and to these the biographer at least implies a fourth type, the poems celebrating what the poet called "manly attachment."[169-70] Which of these types represents Whitman's real nature? Or is it possible for one man to experience all of these different sexual emotions? These questions are not answered, though perhaps Holloway inclines to a belief in the poet's sexual versatility, for he regards as pathetic and almost tragic the craving for manly affection in the third edition. "The emotion here venting itself was so great as to carry with it, for a time, Walt's every ambition. The book was published when his craving for affection was at its height." [172] Later he succeeded in spiritualizing the passion. On the strength of Mrs. O'Connor's testimony Holloway accepts the story of Whitman's being in love with a married woman in Washington, apparently believing that soon after the third edition he recovered from his "unhealthy mood."

Perhaps in line with this interpretation, Holloway finds a great change in Whitman after 1870. He now "makes rendezvous, not with the Great Companions, but with the Comrade perfect."[245] He who declared in 1856, "Divine am I inside and out," now has ideals for his gods. "He sings, not the 'average man,' but the 'Ideal Man' ..." The meaning of the poems written in former periods now takes on a new significance for the poet himself. Concerning the "Children of Adam" poems, for example. "It was characteristic of his type of mind that he should himself have read into these poems, not merely the youthful impulses out of which they were born, but the religious aspirations which succeeded."[260]

In making these illuminating interpretations, Holloway went considerably beyond any previous biographer and opened the way for further searches for the poet's psyche in his unconscious betrayals in *Leaves of Grass*.

And Whitman biography did not have long to wait. In Jean Catel's *Walt Whitman: La Naissance du Poète* the soul of the poet was exhumed for a psychoanalytical autopsy. With clinical thoroughness this critic searches, like Holloway, through every fragment of juvenilia, through diaries, letters, and finally *Leaves of Grass* for the key to Whitman's genius, and there in the first edition he believes he finds the answer.

In *Leaves of Grass* we discover what escapes us in his real life and emotion. And of *Leaves of Grass*, it is the first edition which retains in its music the secret that Whitman consecrated his life to disguise. If it is not there, it is nowhere. It is not in his public life, nor his journalistic articles, nor in his relations with a group of friends as ardent as they were blind. It is not in the biographical notes which he wrote himself, nor in those which he asked Horace Traubel to transmit to posterity. So much concern on his part lest he be misunderstood must arouse our suspicion.[11]

Thus for what he hid Whitman substituted the soul of a poet ready to receive the habiliments of glory. To his real self he preferred a legend. He forgot only one thing—for one can not remember everything—: that first edition, all aquiver in a revolt which maturity and old age were to repudiate. After that edition is pruned, recast, and diluted into the later editions of *Leaves of Grass*, it lacks the air of reality of that first long, revealing cry."[11]

Once more biography has returned to the identification of the poet and his work, but a vast gulf of psychology separates Catel from Bucke. Dr. Bucke believed that the poet was able to tap the sources of intellectual power of a "cosmic consciousness" but he scarcely thought of searching in the subconscious for the hidden motives of daily action.

The first illusion which Catel attempts to dispel is Walt Whitman's sound ancestry. He finds it impossible "to agree with the optimism of Mr. Bazalgette . . . [that] 'The union of the two races [English and Dutch] was the extraordinary promise of a completer human type, one profiting by all the power of a new soil.' On the contrary, everything tended to create a type of mediocre humanity, harassed by anxiety."[22, n.2] In short, the marriage of the discontented and austere Walter Whitman with the loving, sunny Louisa Van Velsor was an unfortunate union. "Some would say that it was a fortunate mis-mating, since it produced a poet. Undoubtedly true, but this poet was not the product of a perfect equilibrium of physical and moral forces, as he and his devoted friends thought and said."[22]

Believing from the study of other writers, such as Dickens and Chateaubriand, that the adolescent impressions registered on the memory are the ones that reappear in the images and imaginative scenes of the creative mind of an author, Catel searches Whitman's writings for clues to his youth. What he discovers is a boy who felt himself from all sides "pushed out of doors, for at the time when the home is the most solid reality to the average child, it did not exist for him. At fifteen he felt himself to have no part in the house which his father had built and was living in temporarily."[38] Therefore, "young Whitman, having only the loosest home ties, roamed the streets of Brooklyn and they received him with affection; they were like a home to him."[39] Thus does Catel account for the vividness with which the mature poet describes moving crowds, trips on the ferry, and the pleasure of merging his own ego with the mass of humanity.

Catel's thorough examination of Whitman's journalistic writings before he began *Leaves of Grass* reveals a maladjusted young man, unsuccessful in the economic world, unsure of himself, unable to make social adjustments. In New Orleans, far from having "found himself" as some biographers believed, he was faced by the same necessities as in Brooklyn and New York, and once again failed miserably to meet them, having to return home after a row with his employer. But by this time one of the chief causes of his difficulties becomes apparent. There is some peculiarity in his sexual nature. Catel finds strong indications that Whitman had had experiences with "professional love" in New York or Brooklyn,[62] but this sauntering, dreaming, introspective young man did not find satisfaction in these relationships, for he was naturally "auto-erotic."[435] And it is this peculiarity which accounts for his maladjustment to life.[63]

After returning to Brooklyn, and unsuccessfully trying journalism again, he abandoned so far as possible the physical struggle for adjustment to the world of reality and began to create a compensating inner world of fantasy and imagination, which found expression through his poems. Thus does Catel explain Whitman's almost miraculous acquisition of literary power without recourse either to mysticism or a sexual awakening in the romantic city of the South. Furthermore, the explanation gives a revealing significance to the style, the egoism, and the motifs of *Leaves of Grass*.

The myself that Whitman 'celebrates' on each page . . . is the projection of the unconscious. If in reading Whitman's work, the reader will replace mentally the *I* or the *myself* by 'my unconscious', while giving to this word the dynamic sense which we have indicated, then he will understand better: first, the origin, the profound reason for the first edition of *Leaves of Grass*; second, the end, what certain critics have called the messianic in Whitman.[400-01]

His conscious mind agitated by a sense of failure, frustration, and loneliness. Whitman's poetic imagination returns to an idealized childhood of peace, innocence, and purity, and it is then that he feels in his soul that he is the equal of God.

Books became a powerful force in Whitman's attempt to find happiness through artistic creation. The subjective philosophy of the post-Kantians in America, and of Emerson especially, provided both a framework and a rationalization for the psychological adjustments which his inner nature compelled him to make. Perhaps he was only dimly aware of his great debt to Emerson, but Transcendentalism, like a religion, opened up a new life to Walt Whitman. Like many a man who has experienced a religious conversion, from this time forth Whitman's whole life, outer as well as inner, became harmonized and tranquilized. He had found a pattern and a purpose.

As the years passed and the adjustment became more settled and habitual, perhaps the poet himself forgot, or may never fully have understood, the emotions which he first conquered in *Leaves of Grass*. Certainly he was inclined more and more to interpret those first naïve confessions with a disingenuousness that has baffled many a biographer. A study of the successive editions reveals the life-long effort which he gave to revising, deleting, and disguising those first outpourings of his subconscious in his attempt to spiritualize and sublimate the record of his inner life. But there in the 1855 edition is the secret of the whole life and the completed book—the key to Whitman's poetic stimulus, his literary expression, his symbolism, and his unceasing efforts to perpetuate an "official portrait" of himself.

The prodigious researches of Holloway and the Freudian interpretations of Catel culminated in 1933 in the most extensive study of the editions and of Walt Whitman's place in world literature so far accomplished, Frederik Schyberg's *Walt Whitman*.[64] Although Schyberg's language predetermined a small audience for his book, his nationality and geographical location gave him advantages not possessed by American or English biographers. Like most Danish scholars, possessing a knowledge of several languages, including English, and being thoroughly familiar with the history of European literature, Schyberg was able to interpret and judge Whitman in terms of the international currents of thought and poetic theory to which he was unconsciously indebted.

Schyberg's first chapter, an attempt to orient Whitman with respect to the national history and the culture of the poet's land, is superficial and has little value for the American student. His second chapter, a strictly biographical sketch, is of interest mainly because it indicates the author's sources and attitudes. Here we see that Schyberg is fully aware of his debt to Catel, though he does not accept Catel's whole thesis and eventually goes far beyond him. He calls the publication of the journalistic writings "negative research"; they contributed to destroy the myths, but offered nothing to fill the gap. We can see Schyberg's indebtedness to Catel in his belief that the myths which Whitman invented to conceal the uneventful periods in his life—or to shield some innate weakness of character—, he thought concerned himself and himself alone.[6] Thus, the Danish biographer believes with Catel that there were truths and secrets which the poet concealed, either consciously or unconsciously, but he makes less use of Freud than the French biographer did. He is equally sure, however, that the New Orleans romance never existed except in the brain of Bazalgette and his followers, but he disagrees with Catel on the auto-eroticism; he thinks that Whitman was simply abnormally slow in his biological development, and that he always retained some feminine characteristics (as even John Burroughs had observed.)[65]

On one fundamental point Schyberg agrees with Bertz: "At one time Whitman's followers wanted to make him more than a poet; they wanted to make him a philosopher and a prophet. Both rôles were impossible . . . Whitman was a lyricist, not a logician; he was a mystic, not a philosopher."[8] Schyberg acknowledges that he was a religious prophet in the same sense and degree that Nietzsche and Carlyle were, but no more. In his lyric forms and his treatment of sex Walt Whitman created a new epoch and became a major figure in world literature, and these were superlative achievements, but Schyberg sweeps aside all other claims for the American poet.

Although the earliest biographers often quoted the poet's ideal-ization of himself, his ancestry, and his conception of his own mission in *Leaves of Grass*, no one before Schyberg had examined all the editions to discover Whitman's biography in the *changes* and *growth* of the editions.

Schyberg's long and intricate analysis of the first edition belongs rather to the subject of textual criticism than biographical interpre-tation, but significant here is the fact that he also finds "the joy, confidence, and optimism" of the first volume a literary rather than a biographical reality.[44, 83] And in the comparison of the wording and the feeling of Whitman's cosmic visions and pantheistic senti-ments with the works of many European romanticists, we see that they were not unique and that they need not, therefore, have been the product of distinctly abnormal psychology.

The second edition of *Leaves of Grass*, coming only one year after the first, was similar to the '55 version. It was the third edition, in Schyberg's opinion, not the first, that recorded the poet's psycho-logical crisis. If Whitman did experience a tragic romance, it must have been between 1855 and '60, for in this 1860 edition traces of some sort of defeat are plainly visible. Since some of the private notebooks for this period are missing (possibly destroyed by the poet himself), Schyberg wonders whether he might not have led a dis-graceful and dissolute saloon life[143] until the war broke out in 1861, when he recorded his dedication of himself to inaugurating a new regime which would give him "a purged, cleansed, spiritualized, invigorated body."[66] Soon he walked out of Pfaff's restaurant and turned his back on the New York Bohemians. But whatever the secret of this period may be, Whitman guarded it well—except for the emotional tone of that third edition. The key poems express personal grief and discouragement.

"The unspoken word, 'the word' which Whitman sought so zealously and so arrogantly in Section 50 of 'Song of Myself,' and of which he said:

It is not chaos or death—it is form, union, plan—
it is eternal life—it is happiness.

that word Whitman found in the years between 1856–1860, and it was both death and chaos—but primarily death."[147] What loved one had died we do not know, but the real theme of "Out of the Cradle" is "Two together," and the fact that in later revisions the poet generalized and partly disguised the extremely personal tone of the first version lends credence to the suspicion that the original poem gave expression to some deep and genuine experience between the second and third editions. Schyberg notes also a sense of frustration and despair in "As I Ebb'd with the Ocean of Life."[149] The "ship-wreck motif" is prominent in this edition. And it is highly significant that *Leaves of Grass* has become "a few dead leaves." Certainly, "The arrogant pantheism of the earlier editions had become a hopeless pantheism."[150]

The only clue to the morbidity of the 1860 *Leaves* is probably the "Calamus" poems of that edition. In future revisions the poet gradually blurred the original impulses, even eliminating some poems altogether (despite his refusal to expurgate a single line for Thayer and Eldridge). On the basis of the later versions, Binns and Bazalgette tried to interpret these poems as a social program, but Schyberg thinks they are just as unmistakably love poems as Sappho's are, and the only love poems that Whitman ever wrote[159]—for the "Children of Adam" group is philosophical rather than personal. "In Paths Untrodden," which gives the "program" of this group, suggests that there is something different and rather daring in this love. And it is significant that two of the most revealing poems were later deleted: "Long I Thought that Knowledge Alone Would Suffice" expresses the poet's willingness to give up his songs because his lover is jealous, and in "Hours Continuing Long,

Sore and Heavy-Hearted" we find him in utter dejection because he has lost his lover: "Hours sleepless . . . discouraged, distracted . . . Hours when I am forgotten . . ."

> Sullen and suffering hours! (I am ashamed—but it is useless—
> I am what I am;)
> Hours of my torment—I wonder if other men ever have the like,
> out of the like feelings?

Schyberg thinks that this poem, and the experience it reveals, rather than a tragic New Orleans romance, gives the real origin of "Out of the Cradle Endlessly Rocking." However, he adds that, "Whitman probably wrote these verses quite innocently and published them without considering how he exposed himself—because they spring from unrequited love . . . ."[160] D. H. Lawrence and Whitman released their erotic impulses in their work, not in their lives.[67] Furthermore, the puberal and effeminate character of Whitman's erotic mentality[162] is paralleled in the writings of other mystics, such as the medieval Heinrich Suso and the Persian Rumi. It is not an isolated phenomenon in *Leaves of Grass* but is common in the history of religious and poetic mystics. Furthermore, after the first impulse of the poems had passed, "Calamus" became for Whitman a "city of friends," and in *Democratic Vistas* (1871) he was able to give it a genuine social interpretation.

The 1860 edition contains not only the record of the great spiritual crisis of Whitman's life—in which he seems to have contemplated suicide—but it also reveals the means by which he saved himself. This is a discovery of vast importance both to Whitman biography and the critical interpretation of *Leaves of Grass*. Though torn and racked by conflicts within, he was struggling for both a personal and a literary unity. (The "Poem of Many in One"—later "By Blue Ontario's Shore"—is characteristic.) Conflicts within himself would be conquered because they were found collected in one body as the many poems were collected in one book.[154] And by a kind of unconscious ironical symbolism, the nation was becoming divided as Walt Whitman had been. Thus he proclaimed the Union when the states were on the verge of a break; he hailed adhesiveness, though he had not found it. In "To a President," "To the States," and other poems we find "spontaneous confession of the real situation." Thus it was not entirely accidental that, "For Whitman the great democratic fiasco of these years came to correspond to the fateful character of his love in the 'Calamus' poems, and thus confirmed the duality of the book's proclamation of 'evil as well as good!' "[172] But presently he turned his attention to America's future greatness, and thus regained his faith and confidence. "On the Beach at Night" in the 1871 edition answers the despairing question of "As I Ebb'd with the Ocean of Life" in the 1860 edition. By this time Whitman's spiritual crisis was completely over.

What saved him, above all else, was the unifying effect of the Civil War—not only through his own patriotic and devoted services in the army hospitals, but also because the war gave Whitman and the nation Abraham Lincoln.

Lincoln and Whitman complemented each other. Lincoln saved the union and he probably saved Whitman spiritually and practically, and it is also interesting that he appreciated *Leaves of Grass*. In Lincoln Whitman found his great Camerado, and the funeral hymn speaks of him as "my departing comrade." At any rate, at that time a revolution took place in Whitman's inner life, a recovery from "the 1860 psychosis."[181] Because the "Wound-Dresser" became a man who personally did what he had celebrated as an ideal, Schyberg finds *Drum-Taps* (1865) "an important and remarkable advance" in Whitman's art. The poet's sex emotions have become completely sublimated in his hospital work and in his poetry. "The Washington period was a peak in Whitman's life, a great strain, but also a great release and relief."[186] After *Drum-Taps* Whitman's works really became a unity, though gradually, step by step.

Discouragements returned to the poet after the Washington period, as in his "Prayer of Columbus" (written 1874), in which the mood of the "batter'd, wreck'd old man" is that of the paralyzed and dependent poet himself;[232] but the progress toward personal and literary unity continued until, in "A Backward Glance" (*November Boughs*, 1888), he could relax the struggle and look back upon his work as an evolution, a growth.[246] The links in the stages of development, however, had been obscured by the earlier efforts for unity, and the 1892 edition remained a record of the life Whitman wanted remembered, not entirely the one he had actually lived.

In his final chapter Schyberg says:

To discuss Whitman in world literature is to discuss those he resembled and those who resemble him. If we limit the problem to include only his imitators and followers in modern literature, we rob it of the greater share of its interest. In the relationships of literary history the influence of one author on another is only half the story, and often the least interesting; on the other hand, the problem of types, of parallel intellectual development of authors who may never have heard of each other, is a genuine and truly interesting one.[248]

Since Whitman's place in world literature is the subject of the final chapter in this *Handbook* it is sufficient here to point out that Schyberg's study has an important bearing on Whitman biography, for it reveals the American poet as less of a unique phenomenon and an anomaly than his friends and most of the biographers have thought. His temperament, conduct, and characteristic expression link him with the lives and writings of the great mystics of all ages and all lands. And in his typical thought and poetic form he was preceded and followed by similar poets in the current of European romanticism. This interpretation not only makes Walt Whitman personally less abnormal but it also helps to explain his astounding world-fame and influence.

MASTERS AND SHEPHARD TO
FURNESS AND CANBY

Edgar Lee Masters' poorly-organized *Whitman* (1937), the first full-length life in the United States after Catel's and Schyberg's books in France and Denmark, made no significant contribution to Walt Whitman scholarship or biography, but it did plainly indicate changing attitudes toward the life of the American poet. Here we find a frank discussion of Whitman as one of those "sports" in nature which sex pathologists call "Uranians." Masters applies to Whitman de Joux's definition: "They are enthusiastic for poetry and music, are often eminently skilful in the fine arts, and are overcome with emotion and sympathy at the least sad occurrence. Their sensitiveness, their endless tenderness for children, their love of flowers, their great pity for beggers and crippled folk are truly womanly."[68] The same authority on the conduct of this type of man: "As nature and social law are so cruel as to impose a severe celibacy on him his whole being is consequently of astonishing freshness and superb purity, and his manners of life as modest as those of a saint."[143] Thus on the basis of modern psychology Whitman's character is now defended with a new tolerance and veneration.

The poet of Spoon River thinks Whitman's "poems of nakedness" not a "survival of youthful exhibitionism," but the result of
"his free and barbaric innocent days in the country, by the sea . . .
and of his own wonderful health and vitality."[44] And of "Calamus": "Whitman took America for his love and his wife, in somewhat the same way as Vachel Lindsay did later."[45] Masters admits
that there was unusual warmth in the poet's affection for Doyle but
does not think there was anything shameful about it. "Foreigners
have remarked that men in America are not really friends, and that
love is not so passionate, so tender, among Americans as among the
Latin races, or the Germans."[132]

In the opinion of Masters, Whitman's greatest achievements were
his literary pioneering and his breaking the bonds of narrow conventionalism. "He was a great influence in inaugurating this better
respect for the body which we know today. He stood for sanity in
matters of sex and for the outspoken championship of sexual delight
as one of the blessings of human life."[323] As poet "he felled to
some extent the encumbering forest and let later eyes see in part
what the lay of the land was . . ."[327]

In the following year (1938) the bitterest attack on Whitman
since Bertz's *Yankee-Heiland* was published in the United States by
Esther Shephard as *Walt Whitman's Pose.* Mrs. Shephard would deny
that it was an attack, but so disillusioned was she by her "discoveries" that she branded Whitman's whole literary career as a "pose"
and a calculated attempt to deceive the public. She found such
striking parallels between *Leaves of Grass* and the epilogue of George
Sand's *Countess of Rudolstadt* that she concluded the American poet
got the first conception of his literary rôle from George Sand's "vagabond poet, dressed in laborer's garb, who goes into a trance and
composes what is described as 'the most magnificent poem that can
be conceived.' "[69] Likewise Sand's *Journeyman Joiner* which Whitman reviewed in 1847, gave him ideas for this pose:

It is a story of a beautiful, Christ-like young carpenter, a proletary
philosopher, who dresses in a mechanic's costume but is scrupulously
clean and neat. He works at carpentering with his father but patiently takes time off whenever he wants to in order to read, or give
advice on art, or share a friend's affection. In short, he is very much
the kind of carpenter that Walt Whitman became in the time of the
long foreground . . . [201]

There can be no doubt that Whitman read George Sand before writing the first edition of *Leaves of Grass*, and he was also certainly influenced by the French novelist. Mrs. Shephard admits that, "If *Leaves of Grass* is a great book, it does not matter that Walt Whitman was a sly person and a poseur."[237] But in her whole discussion she makes him sound like a fraud and seems to cast suspicion not only on his honesty but also on the value of his literary creation.[70] Undoubtedly her discovery did have some influence on later Whitman biography, for she had at least proven that books had had a great deal more importance in his life than most of the biographers had yet realized. But there were other writers aside from George Sand whom he could—and certainly did draw upon too.[71] Nearly every critic who reviewed Mrs. Shephard's book agreed that she had exaggerated the importance of this one source. And anyway, like the "Happy Hypocrite" of Max Beerbohm's delightful little allegory, Whitman wore his mask with such sincere intention that underneath he too became, no less than Beerbohm's reformed rake, an exact and genuine facsimile of the former disguise. At the beginning of his career as the poet of *Leaves of Grass*, Walt Whitman may have assumed a pose in his life and his book, but all eye-witnesses of his conduct and personality confirm the belief of most biographers that to a remarkable degree he actually became the person and poet he wished to be.

By a lucky coincidence, Haniel Long's *Walt Whitman and the Springs of Courage* (1938) answered the skepticism of Mrs. Shephard's "pose theory," though unfortunately the book was published by an obscure press[72] and is not yet well known. "Wars and pestilence and pestilential literary fashions come and go," says Long, "but literature remains the picture of man adapting himself to the new-old necessities of intimacy with the universe and himself."[142-43] This book is not, properly speaking, a biography but it is a critical interpretation which reveals Whitmans's biography in a new light. As the author says, "To examine Whitman's life with an eye to observing what his springs of courage were, is simply to respond to our need of outwitting and defying those forces in society today which would rob us of the last shred of self-confidence."[3] Or to put it a little differently:

Now I will begin writing what I can discern of the things that gave Whitman trouble, and the things that gave him no trouble; and how, in spite of troubles which were his fault, or the fault of others, or merely the result in any age of being born, he was able to grow into a tremendous oak, root himself well in the soil, and extend wide branches for any who for centuries to come might be needing shade.[7]

Since this book is not, as stated above, a conventional biography, Whitman's faults and troubles are not treated specifically, but anyone familiar with the story of his life knows in general what they were. Starting then, with a recognition that Walt Whitman's life was haunted by doubts, uncertainties, and human frailty, what was the secret of the healing courage which he attained and all men desire? "First of all is the diverting fact that Whitman, like Rilke's Fraülein Brahe, lived in wonderland—though his sojourn there was brief."[9] This wonderland was phrenology. Every student of Whitman's life knows that at one time he took stock in this pseudo-science and cherished for years the flattering interpretation that had been made of his own cranial bumps. One scholar, Edward Hungerford, even reached the conclusion that the phrenologist's extremely favorable reading of Whitman's "chart of bumps" first gave him the serious ambition of trying to be a poet[73]—a theory perhaps as oversimplified as Mrs. Shephard's. Long does not know whether "phrenology told Whitman correctly where he was strong and where he was weak," but, "We need to be praised, we need also to be alarmed, about ourselves,"[14] and phrenology temporarily served this purpose.

That pseudo-science furnished Whitman a picture of a balanced harmonious life, from which if one were sensible nothing human need be excluded: which makes it an important factor in his growth. Its terminology has not stuck, its names seem fantastic. Yet it achieved an enviable simplification, and above all it heartened one with its moral blessings and warnings. American life was neither balanced nor harmonious, nor was Whitman's own life. By including all aspects of his being, and by indicating certain aspects of himself he might well guard against, phrenology left him with a vigorous hope for himself, and for his native land. It was part and parcel of the gospel of the 'healthy-mindedness,' and Whitman became its poet.[15]

Thus phrenology met the pragmatic test for Walt Whitman, as

religion and all sorts of rag-tags of philosophy do for other men.

The second spring of courage for Whitman was Emerson.[16ff] First of all his essays, his poems, and his transcendentalism; and second, that generous, impulsive greeting of the 1855 *Leaves of Grass*. The letter went to Whitman's head for a while and made him do some silly things, but it gave him courage at a time when he most needed it and ultimately strengthened his self-reliance until he had less need for Emerson. The arrogant tone of the first two editions is misleading; actually, "Whitman exceeded the rest of the brotherhood of writers in his anxiety to make sure of bouquets."[26] He needed more, not less, than most men to find "springs of courage."

This need was intensified by the hostile opposition which he encountered on almost every side: prudish conventionalism, the Bostonians' belief that American culture should "stay close to the mother culture of England,"[40] and ignorant blindness of readers unconditioned to a new poetic art. Much of Long's book is taken up with the courage the poet derived from his contact with common people, personal friends, Mrs. Gilchrist, Peter Doyle, and from the philosophy and religion which he painfully worked out for himself. This book might be called *an intellectual biography*. It attempts to lay bare the organic pattern of ideas and faiths, and the expression of them which integrated one man's life and gave it the strength of an oak tree with shade for future generations of men.

Newton Arvin's *Whitman* is even less biography than Long's book, for it is mainly a study of Whitman's social thinking, but it deserves to be mentioned among the memorable publications of 1938 which future biographers must take into consideration in their re-evaluation of *Leaves of Grass* and its author. Arvin finds two powerful and opposing intellectual currents in the life and thought of Whitman. "He was so powerfully worked upon by the romantic mood of his generation that it has largely been forgotten or ignored how much he had been affected, in boyhood and earliest youth, by an older and tougher way of thought . . . he was the grandchild of the Age of Reason."[74] Arvin makes out Whitman's father to have been a sort of intellectual rebel himself, a subscriber to the "free-thought" journal edited by Frances Wright and Robert Dale Owen, a follower of the unorthodox Hicksite Quakers, and a democrat of the Jefferson and Paine tradition. No other critic or biographer had given Walter Whitman credit for so much intellectual curiosity and vitality.

Although he raises in the mind of the reader the possibility of an intellectual antithesis in the Whitman home, the father leaning toward eighteenth-century rationalism and the mother toward romantic mysticism, Arvin is careful to point out that this contradiction was actually characteristic of the age in which the poet grew up. Even the leading scientists, "almost to a man . . . succeeded in 'reconciling' their inherited Calvinism or Arminianism with their Newtonian or their Darwinian knowledge."[170-71]

Nevertheless, the Quaker influence which Whitman derived in part at least through his family was unfortunate because the "inner light" doctrine encouraged him "in a flaccid irrationalism,"[174] and "For the poet whose book was allegedly to be pervaded by the conclusions of the great scientists, this was hardly the wisest habit to form." Arvin thinks that Whitman's anti-intellectualism and obscurantism grew with age. In the first edition he found the earth sufficient, but as he became older he found it less and less sufficient and he sought assurance in "world-weary and compensatory mysticisms."[229]

On the vexing question of Whitman's sex "anomaly," Arvin is unequivocal. "There was a core of abnormality in Whitman's emotional life," but it was not the whole of his nature; "he remained to the end, in almost every real and visible sense, a sweet and sane human being . . . who had proved himself capable of easy and genial friendship with hundreds of ordinary people."[277] Arvin expresses the opinion that "it would not be incredible if even the most personal poems in 'Calamus' should come to be cherished, as Shakespeare's sonnets have been, by thousands of normal men and women,"[278] and adds the information that André Malraux and Thomas Mann have accepted Whitman's "virile fraternity" and "a patriotism of humanity" as social and political slogans.[282]

The duality which Arvin finds in Whitman's age and in the poet's own life and conduct gives this critic himself a divided attitude toward his subject. Though he bitterly denounces Whitman's refusal to take an active part in the Abolitionist movement—believing to the last that the Civil War was only a struggle to preserve the Union[75] — and deplores his indifference to socialism and trade unionism, Arvin nevertheless concluded that *Leaves of Grass* is a full and brave "anticipatory statement of a democratic and fraternal humanism."[290]

Whether or not Long's and Arvin's books would occupy a permanent place in Whitman scholarship, they did at least contribute

intelligent discussions of fundamental critical and biographical problems. But the old schools were not dead. In 1941 Frances Winwar
published *American Giant: Walt Whitman and His Times*, an inaccurate, sentimental and journalistic rehash of the worst features of
nearly all the previous biographies, though it was audaciously advertised as a "definitive life." Here we find the dust brushed from the
hoary New Orleans romance, even the Washington romance revived
from Holloway, and the most dogmatic denial of any taint of homosexual psychology in the "Calamus" poems. Despite her fanciful
idealization of her hero, she perpetuates the inaccurate story of the
"thousands of dollars" which the supposedly indigent poet spent in
the building of his tomb. The whole Whitman family is sentimentalized, but especially is this true of "Mother Whitman," who is made
into an ideal mother and housekeeper and a sort of moral saint.

Clifton Furness, the editor of the *Workshop*,[76] corrected the
worst of Winwar's errors in a long review in *American Literature*.[77]
From unpublished manuscripts he quoted passages to show the real
emotions back of one of the poems which she used to support her
belief in a normal love-affair in New Orleans, and he quoted from
Mother Whitman's illiterate letters to show the confusion, squalor,
bickering, and complaining in her household.

Meanwhile, Mrs. Katharine Molinoff had already published a
monograph, *Some Notes on Whitman's Family* (1941)[78] which
revealed sufficient reason for Mother Whitman's dejection and her
whining letters. Her daughter Mary was capricious and headstrong.[79]
Her youngest son, Edward, was a life-long cripple and imbecile, a
constant care and worry to Walt and his mother. The oldest son,
Jesse, died in the lunatic asylum. Andrew, an habitual drunkard,
married a disreputable woman, who after her husband's death of
tuberculosis of the throat, "became a social outcast and set her children to beg on the streets." Hannah married a mean, improvident
artist who starved and beat her—not without "ample cause"—until
she became psychopathic.

The whole picture is almost incredibly sordid, and yet there are
only the vaguest hints in the biographies before 1941 of these conditions. Furness and Mrs. Molinoff, in these brief and pathetic
glimpses into Walt Whitman's family relationships, gave a better
understanding of "that baffling reluctance to mention any member
of his family which is so puzzling to biographers."[5] Furthermore,
Walt's letters to his mother, his constant financial help for her and

Eddie, and his worrying and planning for them, reveal his devotion, unselfishness, and gentleness as no biographer has done. In these relationships he is truly and incontrovertably heroic.

Furness's review of Winwar and Mrs. Molinoff's sordid revelations increased the Whitman scholar's dissatisfaction with all the published biographies. Furness had let it be known that he was working on a life of Whitman based on all existing sources, especially unpublished letters and manuscripts, and his biography was impatiently awaited. In 1942 Hugh I'Anson Fausset published *Walt Whitman: Poet of Democracy,* but it was not the kind of book Furness had promised, and even the title was misleading, for the author was less concerned with the poet's democratic ideas than Arvin had been— and more superficial in his treatment. He presented "the poet of democracy" in the manner of Rossetti and Dowden, and more or less Symonds and Bailey, *i.e.,* as the true representative of a raw, undeveloped, undiscriminating American culture.

The thesis of Fausset's book is that Whitman was a split personality, never able to achieve poise, serenity, and unity in either art or life. This thesis leads Fausset into a dilemma familiar to the reader of Whitman biography. The man he reveals is mentally indolent, uncritical, almost sloven; as a personality, by turns affectionate and secretive, egotistical and shrinking; as a poet, undisciplined, unsure of his technique, a "true poet" only on rare and lucky occasions. Yet Fausset wrote the book because he was convinced of the importance of Walt Whitman as a poet, a man whose heart was in the right place but head always undependable. The biographer, in short, finds himself unable to explain the literary power and world-wide fame of the man he attempts to analyze.

A year later (1943) one of the major literary editors and critics of the period, Henry Seidel Canby, almost produced the biography so eagerly awaited. His *Walt Whitman: An American* epitomizes the best of recent Whitman scholarship, resolves many of the biographical cruxes with plausible and sensible conclusions, and leaves the reader with the conviction that Walt Whitman, both as man and poet, deserves the reputation and influence which he has attained throughout the modern world.

Canby has not presumed to write a "final book on Whitman," or to assemble, "for the benefit of scholars, . . . all known information about his friends, his family, and his daily doings"—information "much needed, and . . . soon to be made readily accessible in a book by my friend, Mr. Furness"[v] ; his book is frankly an interpretation, an attempt to "make intelligible Whitman himself and his 'Leaves'."[vi] Canby's success is due in part to his basic assumption that, "Walt Whitman's America was not a real America, though the real America was his background and a source of his inspiration. It was a symbolic America, existing in his own mind, and always pointed toward a future of which he was prophetic." He agrees with Catel and confirms Schyberg (whose book had been translated orally to him) that "a satisfactory biography of Whitman must be essentially a biography of an inner life and the mysterious creative processes of poetry."[2] But he does not psychoanalyze or draw sensational contrasts between fiction and reality:

This biographer and that, using hints or boastings, or the dubious evidence of poems, has endeavored to spice this daily life with hypothetical journeys, unverified quadroon lovers, illegitimate children, and dark suggestions of vice and degeneracy. Yet even if all these stories about Whitman's hidden activities were true, they would not account for a passionate fervor that has deeper and more burning sources.[3]

For despite the fact that he was "a poseur sometimes, and often a careless carpenter of words," Whitman "made articulate and gave an enduring life in the imagination to the American dream of a continent where the people should escape from the injustices of the past and establish a new and better life in which everyone would share."

Most biographers have attempted to explain the mystery of this ordinary youth who suddenly revealed himself as a poetic genius. Some thought he was aroused by a "dark lady," others by psychological frustration, but most were inclined to believe that a mystical experience "made him a prophet and a poet." Canby finds no mystery at all—except in so far as poetic genius is always something of a miracle. During Whitman's childhood in Brooklyn and his youthful contact with the country and village people of Long Island, he was storing up experiences and impressions which enabled him to become a "representative" poet of nineteenth-century America. Small towns, printing offices, country schools, political newspapers, all these were important during the formative years when the future poet's "imagination was like a battery charging."[29] Canby thus makes little of Whitman's boasted heredity, much of his environment.

This approach enables Canby to avoid some of the pitfalls of other biographers, for he is content to describe Whitman's social and intellectual milieu instead of attempting to create or reconstruct his inner life before he became articulate. "He was a happy familiar of streets and market-places, and a spokesman for society [through his editorials], before he began to be egoist, rebel, and prophet."[72] After 1847, when Whitman began to record in his notebooks his poetic ambitions and his intimate thoughts, subjective biography is possible, and with these as the primary source this critic-biographer began the "inner life" of his subject.

When the young journalist turns poet and mystic, the biographer meets his first real test. To Whitman's contemporaries, and even to many later critics, "This self-assumed apostleship, this mantle of a prophet put on at the age of twenty-eight, seems a little strong."[92] Canby shows that, "This new Walt Whitman proposes to inspire because he is inspired. Greatness is growth, he says, and his soul has become great because in mystical, imaginative experiences it has grown until it identifies itself with the power of the universe." He was neither his own ego nor the editorial "we," "but 'my soul,' by which he meant an identification of himself with the power for greatness which he felt intuitively to be entering his own spirit." The poet thus began the long career of dramatizing this "soul," pre- senting "a 'Walt Whitman' who was symbolic, yet in his knowledge of men and cities and scenes and emotions of the common man was also representative of the merely human Walt who had been ab- sorbing the life of America so passionately for many years."[93] No previous biographer had so convincingly reconciled the "symbolic" Whitman with the objective Whitman.

This reconciliation, however, does not eliminate the "problems" which have harassed the biographers for half a century; nor does it necessarily "solve" them, but what it does do above all else is to undermine their former importance. No doubt in some cases, too, it is too facile. For example, Canby, like Schyberg, recognizes in the 1860 edition the evidences of spiritual "crisis", and he readily admits that during the later 1850s the poet was troubled by "deep pertur- bations of sexual passion,"[162] but Canby's thesis leads him to attribute Whitman's crisis to national rather than personal causes— "this was a decade of rising hate," and hate was the antithesis of the poet's dream of an "ideal democracy."

Canby does not, however, attempt to deny or disguise the sex problem in Whitman's life and writing; he refuses to conjecture or theorize where there is no evidence. "There may of course have been, as his later biographers think, other journeys, other residences in the South before 1860—perhaps lovers, perhaps a mother of his alleged children. We do not know, and there is no real evidence."[168] Discussing "Children of Adam," Canby says, "This man's greatness is in some respects a function of his excessive sexuality. Whole sections of the 'Leaves' are either sheer rhetorical fantasy or the articulation and sublimation of experience." But, he adds, "Of that experience we know actually very little . . . [186] Unfortunately, much has to be omitted because we simply have no facts and in all probability never will have."[187]

Like Catel, Schyberg, and Masters, Canby recognizes in Whitman a kind of extraordinary sexual versatility which is at least in part responsible for his universal love and cosmic imagination. Canby calls this characteristic "auto-eroticism," but thinks it was psychological rather than physical:

He could feel like a woman. He could feel like a man. He could love a woman—though one suspects that it was difficult for him to love women physically, unless they were simple and primitive types. He could love a man with a kind of father-mother love, mingled, as such love often is, with obscure sexuality. Because all reference was back to his own body, he seemed to himself to be a microcosm of humanity. There are, I think no truly objective love poems in the 'Leaves of Grass.'[204-05]

Schyberg thought that Whitman's "turmoils" were calmed by his active participation in the war through his hospital work, and Canby added more weight to the argument, extending the influence from the personal to the intellectual realm. The poet "becomes less interested in himself as a religion incarnate, less rhetorical about democracy, more certain of his confidence that democracy has firm ground in human nature."[230] Fully aware of the "corruption, degeneracy, pettiness, both physical and spiritual,"[263] in his postwar America, Whitman attempted to counteract these evils by preaching respect for the individual personality and the dangers of selfishness. No other biographer or critic has succeeded so well in combatting the superficial belief that Whitman's democratic teachings were impractically visionary and optimistic. "His vision of democracy as the guardian of personality, the nurse of individual growth, seems overconfident until one discovers how much more he knew of the danger and diseases of democracy than even the ablest of his critics."[268] Not only, therefore, does Canby regard Walt Whitman as a true prophet of American democracy, who is "intelligible and dynamic" for this generation, but he succeeds in unifying the poet's personality, his literary creations, and his message into a new symbolical expression of the ideals which Americans profess— and may some day apply: "it is impossible today to escape his voice." Therefore, "Intent upon a task not yet amenable to fact and reason, he was like the Hebrew prophets who had no private life that mattered."[354] With all its admirable insights, Canby's book is unsatisfactory because he concludes, finally, that intimate details of Whitman's physical life are far less important than his life of imagination and artistic creation. But by mid-century biographers were becoming more acutely aware that the psychic and physical life feed on each other—a doctrine, in fact, which Walt Whitman himself emphasized in the first edition of *Leaves of Grass*:

> I have said that the soul is not more than the body,
> And I have said that the body is not more than the soul, . . .
> "Song of Myself," sec. 48.

ASSELINEAU, ALLEN, AND CHASE

The first biographer following Canby to attempt a deeper exploration of Whitman's psyche and the source of his art was Roger Asselineau in France. After two years of intensive research in the United States, he wrote a doctoral dissertation for the Sorbonne entitled *L'Evolution de Walt Whitman après la Première Edition des Fueilles d'Herbe,* which received the highest mark of approval by the Université de Paris and was published by Didier in 1954. Asselineau began his study with the first edition because Catel had already traced Whitman's development from his childhood through 1855— though Asselineau did draw upon details of the poet's early life when they were needed in his interpretation. Since this book was originally a thesis, it conformed to the French academic tradition of "L'Homme et l'Oeuvre."

In his translation, which the Harvard University Press published in 1960 and 1962 in two volumes, Asselineau called the first volume *The Evolution of Walt Whitman: The Creation of a Personality* and the second . . . *The Creation of a Book.* The division had both advantages and disadvantages, but Asselineau handled it with such skill and grace that one easily forgives the artificiality of the dichotomy, and it does emphasize the two great ambitions of Walt Whitman: to achieve his own idea of a perfect personality and to express it in a poetic masterpiece.

Whitman himself said that his childhood was unhappy, and Asselineau traces his vain searchings, continuing into early manhood, in a series of frustrated attempts to find friends and "lovers" to satisfy his emotional hungers. He was by nature homosexual, and he did not know how to come to terms with society or himself. He longed to be an example of joyous, healthy, masculinity, but he knew where he was "most weak," and as a consequence was lonely even in the midst of crowds. He sought compensation, therefore, in the creation of a lyrical "I" corresponding to his dreams of love, power, and happiness. Like Schyberg, Asselineau thinks that if Whitman had found relief in sexual relations, he would not have become a poet—or at least not the kind he did become. His poems were not only a substitute for physical satisfactions, but also a therapy, and the marvel is how nearly he succeeded in healing himself. In his final years he appeared to be the wise, serene, heroic personality he had longed to become when he began that first edition of *Leaves of Grass*.

In *The Creation of a Book* Asselineau, like Schyberg, gives adequate attention to the poet's stages of evolution through the various editions of *Leaves of Grass*, but his method is less historical and bibliographical than philosophical. In separate chapters he defines and illustrates Whitman's "physical mysticism," his "implicit metaphysics," his ethics, his aesthetics, his sex life, his egocentrism and patriotism, social thought, etc.; and in Part Two Whitman's style, language, prosody. At the heart of Asselineau's interpretation is the inter-relationship of the poet's sensations and philosophical-artistic intuitions. Whitman started always with his body, but "his sensuality, instead of remaining exclusively carnal, opens out and is sublimated."[4] He broke the strongest social taboos of his time by transposing "the center of sensibility" from the heart to the genitals: "On this point he prefigures Freud."[p.5] This was not a completely new observation, but no one had ever before seen its importance so clearly in Whitman biography and criticism, or made such effective use of it. For example, Whitman's spiritual solution to evil: "the soul is always good and beautiful, but the flesh is sometimes rotten; in other words, matter is the obstacle which provisionally prevents the soul from blossoming out . . . there are no wicked, but only sick people (he prefigures the psychoanalysts in this respect). . . ."[54]

In his conclusions Asselineau extends the insight of all previous psychological biographers of Whitman:

Poetry was for him a means of purification which, if it did not make him normal, at least permitted him to retain his balance in spite of his anomaly. In this sense, . . . his *Leaves of Grass* are "fleurs du mal". . . . His poetry is not the song of a demigod or a superman, as some of his admirers would have it, but the sad chant of a sick soul seeking passionately to understand and to save itself. . . . His anomaly, which in all likelihood was what drove him to write *Leaves of Grass*, also explains certain of his limitations, and notably his inability to renew himself as he grew older—unlike Goethe. He lived too much alone, too much wrapped up in himself. . . . he is, despite appearances, the poet of anguish. . . .

Whitman had thus, at the very core of himself, a sense of defeat and frustation. He had had the ambition to create two masterpieces: a book of immortal poems and a life, the nobility and greatness of which would become legendary. He succeeded in one respect only, but his failure was, perhaps, the condition of that success.[II, 259-60]

My own biography, *The Solitary Singer: A Critical Biography of Walt Whitman*, was published a year later than Asselineau's *L'Evolution de Walt Whitman*, but was written almost simultaneously with it.[80] M. Asselineau and I had exchanged views in conversations and correspondence and found that we agreed on major questions. Furthermore, we were both influenced by the interpretations of Catel and Schyberg. Consequently, the reader will find that our biographies differ less in basic answers than in methods of presenting them. We agree that Whitman was more erotically aroused by men than women, but that clear evidence of his homosexual life is lacking. For this reason I label his sexual emotions as *homoerotic*, whereas Asselineau uses the unequivocal term *homosexual*, which is commonly interpreted to imply pederasty or other aberrant sexual practices. Perhaps today these distinctions are less important than they seemed in the decade of the 1950s.

Celebrated poets now flaunt their homosexuality and identify with Whitman as a man of their own kind. But whether or not homosexuality is *abnormal*, as most people thought in the 1950s, including psychiatrists, the evidence is overwhelming that a century earlier Whitman's erotic impulses made him feel alienated, and this caused him to rebel against the sexual taboos of his society, though he openly fought for sexual freedom in general, not for the preferences of a minority, and opposed all censorship in literature. But he did not stop with condemning prudery: he fantasized solutions to his personal problems; hence his cult of "Calamus" (or "manly love"), which he sublimated into universal brotherhood, and his rôle as "the poet of democracy." Either by coincidence or logical choice, both Asselineau and I made thematic use of Whitman's characterization of himself as "the solitary singer."

I had not intended to attempt a biography of Whitman until Clifton Furness died without having produced the book Canby had confidently predicted.[81] It then seemed to me that someone should make use of the new information about the poet's family which Furness and Molinoff had begun to reveal, and to extend the search for such material for the whole of Whitman's life. In addition to finding letters and unpublished manuscripts containing personal information hitherto not known, or suppressed by the poet and his biographers, I also examined intensively Whitman's whole social and intellectual background, not only for "sources" and "influences," but also for the purpose of orienting his life and writings in his contemporary world. Asselineau's French view of the American setting enabled him to make some refreshing observations, but his scheme did not permit him the space to treat this background in depth. However, the reader of *The Solitary Singer* will find familiar resemblances to Asselineau's portrait in my narrative, perhaps especially of the pain-wracked old man in Camden, courageously cultivating resignation, charming his many foreign visitors by his rambling garrulities. For its thoroughness some critics called my book the "definitive" biography, but it is doubtful that there ever can be a completely definitive biography of so complicated and paradoxical a man as Walt Whitman.

Instead of tracing the poet's chronological growth and decline in massive detail, Asselineau was more interested in an overview of Whitman's psychology, philosophy, and aesthetics, which he presented in highly successful critical essays in his second volume. I gave considerable attention to the influence of space on Whitman, both geographical and astronomical, but Asselineau showed how both psychologically and aesthetically the dimensions of space shrank with the poet's decline of physical vigor. In "Song of Myself" he inventoried ecstatically the sights of the earth and the worlds beyond.

He needed no less than the whole earth at the beginning of his career; in his old age, he was satisfied with a flower, a bird, a street, a printer's case—and a few lines. And yet, these humble vignettes still imply and suggest the rest of the world in the manner of the Japanese hokkus of the best period. "The first dandelion" reminds us of the everlastingness of life, the canary in its cage celebrates the "joie de vivre" in its own way; all mankind walks up and down Broadway and the "font of type" contains in latent form all the passions of men. His imagination has lost its former vigor, but his glance has remained as piercing as ever and his sight still carries to the utmost confines of the universe.[II, 101]

As Oscar Wilde said to Whistler, "I wish I had said that," and now by endorsement I do. It is exactly right, written by one poet of another.

In 1955, the first centennial of *Leaves of Grass*, Richard Chase published another biographical study entitled *Walt Whitman Reconsidered*. The first chapter, called "Beginnings," is superficial and inaccurate in a considerable number of minor facts carelessly summarized from other biographies. But Chase's book should not be dismissed as unimportant. He agreed with Schyberg (whose Danish book was now available in English)[82] and Asselineau that Whitman was not the happy extrovert of robust health and heroic personality the poet created for himself, but a troubled man torn by discordant elements in his mind and character. Yet this discord enabled him to write his masterpiece, "Song of Myself," which Chase calls "the profound and lovely comic drama of the self . . ."[48]

No one had ever before called "Song of Myself" a *comic* poem, and Chase's so labeling it gave a new direction both to biography and criticism of Whitman. Since the poet himself tried to play the role of moral leader in his poem, calling it "comic" implies that he failed on his own—or Emersonian—terms. Here Chase agrees with D. H. Lawrence, who called this Whitmanian role "tricksy-tricksy." And "as in all true, or high, comedy, the sententious, the too overtly insisted-on morality (if any) plays a losing game with ironical realism."[59] Whitman says he resists anything better than his own diversity, yet his subject is the diversity of the self celebrated in his poem. Chase thinks that Whitman himself saw the comic aspects of his incongruous diversity and deliberately assumed the tone of American humor—a point Constance Rourke had made in her *American Humor*.[83]

There is also a striking similarity, Chase says, between the "self" in "Song of Myself" and Christopher Newman in Henry James's *The American*, whom James describes as having the "look of being committed to nothing in particular, of standing in an attitude of general hospitality to the chances of life." To James, Newman was the archetypical American, whom Chase calls "the fluid, unformed personality exulting alternately in its provisional attempts to define itself and in its sense that it has no definition."[60] Chase cannot take seriously "the imagined world" of Whitman's poem, "a fantastic world in which it is presumed that the self can become identical with all other selves in the universe, regardless of time and space," as in Hindu poetry.[63] Nevertheless, this "idiosyncratic and illusory . . . relation of the self to the rest of the universe is a successful aesthetic or compositional device,"[64] enabling the poet to make of his paradoxes a comic "drama of identity." Later he lost the sense of paradox, forgetting "that self and en-masse are in dialectic opposition," and then he wrote such mechanical and vaguely abstract poems as "Passage to India."[65] This tendency finally ruined Whitman as a poet.

To the extent that Chase finds Whitman's literary successes and failures the consequence of character and personality, he is in agreement with Catel, Schyberg, and Asselineau, but as a critic he stands alone—with the possible exception of D. H. Lawrence[84] and Leslie Fiedler.[85] Malcolm Cowley also shares with him a preference for Whitman's concrete and realistic imagery and diction, but at the same time admires "Song of Myself" as an American kind of Hindu poem.[86]

Chase does not say that all of Whitman's poems after "Song of Myself" were failures, but only those, in whole or in part, in which he became vague and mechanical. The "saving grace" of "Crossing Brooklyn Ferry" is the confessional voice of "weakness and uncertainty."[108] Whitman became a great poet "under the pressure of his extraordinary capacity to imagine his own destruction."[125] He had a remarkable "sensibility of annihilation." In "Out of the Cradle" this sensibility gives meaning to "chaos and death," and " 'As I Ebb'd with the Ocean of Life' expresses the final helplessness of man before the mystery of the universe."[124] In these poems

Whitman's healthy irony saves him from self-pity, and makes him a great elegiac poet.

Whitman's strongest "personal impulses" were away from reality, reinforced by "Quaker mysticism and transcendental idealism."[134] But the excitement of the Civil War overwhelmed his introspective tendencies and enabled him to achieve a "new realism" in his *Drum-taps*. However, his "war experiences did not find a satisfactory expression in his poetry, although some of them did in *Specimen Days*. ... The truth is that Whitman's career of hospital visiting became a substitute for poetry and not the inspiration of it."[136] In *Drum-Taps* it is obvious that his "visionary grasp of things is weakening," and he never recovered it. Some of his later poems have "valuable qualities," but most of them reveal "a mind in which productive tensions have been relaxed, conflicts dissipated, particulars generalized, inequities equalized." Dionysius had become "not Apollonian but positively Hellenistic—prematurely old, nerveless, sooth-saying, spiritually universalized."[148]

The "Hellenistic" Whitman was the Whitman Dr. Bucke knew. The poet told his first biographer (if we except Burroughs's *Notes* as a biography) that, "the character you give me is not the true one in the main—I am by no means the benevolent, equable, good happy creature you portray."[87] [174] Chase thinks he told the truth, and that he resembled the Carlyle he described in his memorial essay,[88] a person torn between "two conflicting agonistic elements."[175] Whitman called Carlyle a man whose heart was "often at odds with his scornful brain," the heart demanding reform and the brain denouncing it because his mind was haunted by "the spectre of world-destruction." To Chase the "agonistic Whitman" was the true Whitman, though it was obscured by "the bland, emasculate, pseudo-messianic ideal imposed upon him by his admirers and on the whole acquiesced in by himself."[89] [175]

SUMMARY AND CONCLUSION

Walt Whitman biography began with the hagiography of William D. O'Connor, John Burroughs, and Dr. R. M. Bucke, who adored Whitman personally and wanted to do something to overcome what they regarded as public misunderstanding and neglect of a great poet. Whitman appreciated their efforts and encouraged them. Aware that his first edition of *Leaves of Grass* was an affront to the leading poets and literary critics of mid-nineteenth-century America, Whitman himself began as early as 1855 to "promote" himself by writing anonymous reviews of his poems and cultivating the sympathy of friendly editors. Other poets have been guilty of such breaches of decorum and good taste, but few so impulsively as Walt Whitman. Even though his true greatness was not generally recognized until long after his death in 1892, he did receive some favorable reviews even for his first edition (as well as that flattering "greeting" from Emerson), and successive editions increased his audience. Whether the hagiography did any good at all is questionable. Certainly the idolatry and sentimentalism of O'Connor and Bucke (Burroughs was somewhat more discriminating) offended many possible friends, and may have delayed rather than hastened his winning the fame he deserved.

But there was at least one notable exception. At Cambridge University in England a young man from South Africa named Jan Christian Smuts (future Prime Minister of his country) read these hagiographies and decided three years after Whitman's death that his life showed "that rarest flowering of humanity—a true personality, strong, original . . . a whole and sound piece of manhood such as appears but seldom, even in the course of centuries."[90] Whitman seemed to Smuts to represent the ideal personality for an "organic" philosophy which was evolving in his mind. Of course Smuts also believed that the most perfect expression of this personality was *Leaves of Grass*, the poet's cherished conviction, too, but it is significant that the *man* was more interesting to Smuts than the poems themselves, though he presumed the "I" in the poems to be Walt Whitman. He had not heard of Yeats's *persona*, later developed in psychology by Jung, which distinguishes the *person* (the author) from his creative image (or *persona*). In fact, knowledge of the relations between the author's personal self and his *persona* would have to wait for the development of the "depth psychology" of Freud, Jung, and other psychoanalysts. Not only for Smuts, but for all of Whitman's early biographers, he literally celebrated and sang himself: ". . . this is no book,/ Who touches this touches a man."

Gradually Whitman biographies became more critical, though they were still, for the most part, by intimate friends and admirers who valued *Leaves of Grass* because the man they adored wrote it. John T. Trowbridge, however, thought that Whitman's long invalidism affected his memory, causing him to delude some of his biographers by making erroneous statements. To Edward Carpenter, the young English socialist, discovering *Leaves of Grass* had been a revelation, almost a religious experience, but in visiting Whitman in Camden he found the poet in person to be a bundle of contradictions, willful, obstinate, furtive, yet also tender and loving. Although himself homoerotic, Carpenter was puzzled by Whitman's letter in 1890 to Symonds angrily denying the interpretation of the "Calamus" poems as homosexual.[91] Carpenter decided that there was "a great tragic element in his nature"—thus anticipating Schyberg a generation later. The previous year (1905) Eduard Bertz had attacked the official "Yankee Saint" portrait of Whitman and detailed his charges of homosexuality. This was now a problem not easily ignored, but Carpenter concealed his doubts and insisted that he could believe the love in "Calamus" to be fraternal and democratic.

Another English admirer of Whitman, Henry Bryan Binns, came to the United States to gather material for the first fully detailed life of Whitman (1905), but he hypothicated a "romance" in New Orleans with a "southern lady," resulting in the birth of at least one child. This "romance" would haunt Whitman biography for decades, but otherwise Binns did write a reliable and informative life of the American poet.

The following year Bliss Perry made an even greater effort to dispel the myths and present the true Whitman, a man more human, "elemental and alive." Perry was not happy with the nakedness of Whitman's sex themes and motifs, but he regarded them more as literary subjects than autobiography. This was both a retreat and an advance in comprehension. A quarter century later Emory Holloway came no nearer than Perry in reaching a compromise between myth and truth (he still clung to the "New Orleans romance"), but he had done a vast amount of documentary research, especially for Whitman's years in journalism, and gave the fullest account until Rubin in 1973[92] of Whitman's activities to 1855. Scholarly biography had now replaced the glorified, sentimental accounts of Whitman's personal friends. In fact, meanwhile fashions in English biography had changed, and the goal in biography now most respected was *truth*. This new type of biography continued with Canby (1943), Asselineau (1954), and Allen (1955), who made the fullest use of new information about the poet's sordid family background, his relations with the Civil War soldiers, and his invalidism.

Before mid-century, however, literary criticism based on twentieth-century psychology had caught up with Walt Whitman. The first to use it was Jean Catel, who found the poet's most carefully-guarded secrets revealed in the first edition of *Leaves of Grass*—his unappeased erotic hungers, his latent homosexuality, and his fantasy compensations. Schyberg in 1933 extended this search through all editions of *Leaves of Grass*, paying special attention to the poet's revisions and editorial suppressions for clues to his psychic tensions and crises. The pursuit of biographical truth through close textual study was a new road for biographers of Whitman to take. Asselineau also traveled this route to still further discoveries of Whitman's psychological problems and resolution of them. He was particularly successful in showing the effects of the poet's state of health on his imagination and artistic grasp—another application of the "wound and the bow" myth of Philoctetes.

I also picked up some useful information and *aperçus* on the borders of these psychological paths, as in Whitman's annotations in the margins of his large collection of magazine clippings, his revisions of the "program" poem "Starting from Paumanok" (in one version Whitman expressed the desire to give up his role as poet for the nation and become the exclusive poet of his male lover), his correspondence with soldiers (in which erotic emotions mingled with sublimated paternity), and in the alteration of his literary plans at different periods of his life.

All of Whitman's recent biographers agree that in his poems he sought compensations for his physical, sexual, and social failures, and found, usually, beneficial therapy both for himself and his readers. In examining the contradictions in the drama of Whitman's identity of the self, Chase also joined the procession of these psychological biographers: ". . . Whitman achieved the remarkable feat of being an eccentric by taking more literally and mythicizing more simply and directly than anyone else the expressed intentions and ideals of democracy."[81] His "comic vision" became "a great releasing and regenerative force" for himself and American literature.

It is possible that some future biographer may yet find a letter or a diary giving evidence of some disgrace or moral perversion in Whitman's life, though the search has been so intensive during the past half century that it is unlikely. But the biographers and critics have found so much strength growing out of this poet's overcoming his weaknesses and misfortunes that scarcely anything could now be found to endanger his secure reputation. It also appears at the present time that factual biography has gone about as far as it can, though critical interpretation of the facts and the literary texts may flourish indefinitely. One of the latest examples is Edwin Miller's *Walt Whitman's Poetry: A Psychological Journey* (1968). Rejecting Whitman both as a "prophet" and a "philosopher," he finds that "when he orders his feelings in his great poems, our response is visceral. For as the lonely poet of monologue, of the inner frontier, of love and death—of our anxieties—he refreshes our spirits, and our lives at least for a moment do not seem fractured and chaotic."[223] Thus have Whitman's critics, sharing the knowledge of the biographers, found, like Sampson, honey in the carcass of the lion.

10

The wild gander leads his flock through the cool night,
Ya-honk! he says, and sounds it down to me like an invitation;
The pert suppose it meaningless, but I listen closer,
I find its place and aim up there toward the November sky,

The sharp-hoofed moose of the north, the cat on the housesill, the chickadee, the prairie-dog,
The litter of the grunting sow as they tug at her teats,
The brood of the turkey-hen, and she with her half-spread wings,
I see in them and myself the same old law.

The press of my foot to the earth springs a hundred affections,
They scorn the best I can do to relate them —

MANUSCRIPT FRAGMENT OF "SONG OF MYSELF"

This is an early version, canceled by the poet (notice the strike through the whole stanza). The manuscript for the 1855 edition was destroyed. This sheet is owned by Charles E. Feinberg and is reproduced by his kind permission.

Chapter II

The Growth of Leaves of Grass and the Prose Works

I myself make the only growth by which I can be appreciated,
I reject none, accept all, then reproduce all in my own forms.
—"By Blue Ontario's Shore"

"ORGANIC GROWTH" OF *LEAVES OF GRASS*

Every reader acquainted with *Leaves of Grass* and the circumstances under which it was written knows that the title designates not a single work, a book, like the *Faerie Queene* or one of Shakespeare's plays, but the whole *corpus* of Walt Whitman's verse published between 1855 and 1892. During these years not one but nine books bore the title *Leaves of Grass*, six of these quite different in organization and even content, though each edition after the first contained most of the poems of its predecessor in revised form, and often under new titles.[1]

If the final edition were simply an unabridged accumulation of the poems of all former publications, the earlier editions would be of interest only to scholars or readers curious about the genesis of the poet's style or his artistic growth, and a scholarly edition of *Leaves of Grass* similar to the *Variorum Spenser* would be sufficient for these final purposes. But the 1892 *Leaves* is more than an accumulation. The metaphor "growth" has often been applied to the work,[2] and is perhaps the best descriptive term to use, but even assuming that many branches have died, atrophied, been pruned away, and new ones grafted on, the metaphor is still not entirely accurate—unless we think of a magical tree that bears different fruit in different seasons, now oranges, now lemons, occasionally a fragrant pomegranate. Not only by indefatigable revising, deleting, expanding, but also by constant re-sorting and rearranging the poems through six editions did Whitman indicate his shifting poetic intentions. Thus each of the editions and issues has its own distinctive form, aroma, import, though nourished by the same sap.

Why does the critic fall so easily into these biological metaphors in discussing the "growth" of the editions of Leaves of Grass? The nature of the work, the manner of its publication, and the theory by which the poet composed and interpreted his poems indicate the answer. In the first place, the seminal conception of the first edition was a new sort of allegory—we might even say an attempt, extending over nearly half a century, to make a life into a poetic allegory. In a novel and daringly literal application of the "organic" theory of literary composition, Walt Whitman began his first edition with the attempt to "incarnate"[3] in his own person the whole range of life, geography, and national consciousness of nineteenth-century America.

Simultaneously the poet of Leaves of Grass tries to express: (1) his own ego, (2) the spirit of his age and country, (3) the spiritual unity of all human experience, (4) and all of these in a justification of the ways of God to man.[4] Thus he can call the United States themselves "essentially the greatest poem" and without inconsistency attempt to span his country from coast to coast, while "On him rise solid growths that offset [i.e., tally or symbolize] the growths of pine and cedar and hemlock and liveoak," etc.[5] Also he can transcend time and space, for "The prescient poet projects himself centuries ahead and judges performer or performance after the changes of time."[6]

The symbolical nature of these poetic ambitions explains why Walt Whitman did not plan, write, and finish one book but continued for the remainder of his life to labor away at the same book. He was writing not an autobiography in the ordinary sense, nor a creative history of an age like Dos Passos's U.S.A.—tasks which can be definitely completed—but was attempting to express the inexpressible. Writing intuitively, he could give only "hints," "indirections," symbols. Hence, so long as the afflatus moved him, he could not finish his life-work or feel satisfied with the tangible words, pages, bound volumes. On his birthday in 1861, and again in 1870, Whitman declared of his book, "The paths to the house are made—but where is the house? . . . I have not done the work and cannot do it. But you [the reader] must do the work and make what is within the following song [*i.e., Leaves of Grass*]."[7] And not long before the end of his life he could still refer to his decades of effort as, "Those toils and struggles of baffled impeded articulation."[8] None of these statements, however, were published. Although Whitman always insisted that the real poem was what the reader made out of the printed words themselves, he nevertheless found it expedient in his prefaces and public utterances about *Leaves of Grass* to make the most of what unity he could find in the work.

Furthermore, the "organic" theory helped not only to explain the poet's fundamental intentions but also rationalized the form at any given stage. After the fifth edition he believed with Burroughs that the whole volume was best understood when viewed "as 'a series of growths, or strata, rising or starting out from a settled foundation or centre and expanding in successive accumulations,' "[9] and a similar statement is found in Dr. Bucke's biography, which Whitman co-authored.[10] Of the 1881–82 edition, Bucke declared: "Now it appears before us, perfected, like some grand cathedral that through many years or intervals has grown and grown until the original conception and full design of the architect stand forth."[155] The influence of this self-inspired explanation is interestingly echoed by the poet's friend. E. C. Stedman, in a letter to Burroughs, in which he declared after Whitman's death: "Before he died ... he rose to synthesis, and his final arrangement of his life-book is as beauteously logical and interrelated as a cathedral."[11] This authorized interpretation was officially repeated and emphasized by Dr. Oscar L. Triggs in 1902 in the essay, "The Growth of 'Leaves of Grass,' " published in the *Complete Writings*.[12] Though ostensibly the first critical study of the editions, this essay is of value mainly for its bibliographical information, with some comments on textual changes. The initial assumption on which it was based prevented genuine critical analysis:

Leaves of Grass has a marked tectonic quality. The author, like an architect, drew his plans, and the poem, like a cathedral long in building, slowly advanced to fulfillment. Each poem was designed and written with reference to its place in an ideal edifice.[101]

The accuracy and truth of this "organic" defense of the unity of *Leaves of Grass* can only be determined by examining all the editions, but the important point here is that for many years the biological and architectural metaphors prevented readers and critics from going back of the final, "authorized," edition of *Leaves of Grass*. Both the rejected passages of the manuscript of "A Backward Glance"[13] and the published preface (1888) show plainly that the poet was still conscious of the imperfect realization of his original intentions; but having in 1881 achieved the most satisfying unity so far accomplished, and being conscious of his waning physical strength and poetic energy, Whitman began to say with increasing conviction that he had accomplished his purpose. He continued to add poems until the year of his death, but attempted no major revision or rearrangement after 1881.

Finally convinced that he had done his best to express and "put on record" his life and his age, he authorized his literary executors to publish only the 1892 issue (with the inclusion of the posthumous "Old Age Echoes") and practically anathematized anyone who might dare to disturb the bones of the earlier versions of his work.[14] So sympathetically has this wish been obeyed that to this day no other text for a complete edition of *Leaves of Grass* has ever been published.[15] In fact, not until De Selincourt, did any biographer or scholarly critic question the full truth of the claim that the final *Leaves of Grass* is a perfect organism or logical structure. Concerning the organizaton of the book, De Selincourt declared in 1914: ". . . being a poor critic of his own writings, [Whitman] finally arranged them without regard for their poetic value, considering merely in what order the thought of each would be most effective in its contribution to the thought of all."[16] And of the additions after 1881: "The whole of the latter part of *Leaves of Grass* . . . exists only as a sketch."[180]

This admirable beginning, however, was not immediately followed by other investigations of the editions. The next contribution was William Sloane Kennedy's chapter, "The Growth of 'Leaves of Grass' as a Work of Art (Excisions, Additions, Verbal Changes)," in *The Fight of a Book for the World*; but this, like Dr. Triggs's essay, is superficial, being concerned mainly with a few verbal improvements in the text. The first biographer to become skeptical of the cathedral analogy was Jean Catel, who found the 1855 edition interesting for its unconscious psychological revelations,[17] and he deserves credit for stimulating research on the growth of the final text.

A few years after the publication of Catel's biography Floyd Stovall made a study of Whitman's emotional and intellectual growth as revealed in the key-poems of the various editions, which he called

"Main Drifts in Whitman's Poetry."[18] This was the first really significant critical contribution to the subject. It was followed two years later by Killis Campbell's "The Evolution of Whitman as Artist,"[19] based on a more extensive examination of verbal changes than Kennedy's study, but agreeing in the main with the conclusions of Triggs and Kennedy that Whitman's revisions improved the style and thought of his poems.

Meanwhile Frederik Schyberg in Denmark had made the most extensive of all attempts to unravel the difficult pattern, to present *Leaves of Grass* in its gradual evolution through the six editions from 1855 to the final edition[20] in 1881,[21] but his book was known to few Whitman scholars in America until Evie Allison Allen's translation in 1951—so little, in fact, that in 1941 Irving C. Story could declare, "no detailed comparative study that considers the several editions as units, and as successive stages in an evolution toward a final product has yet been made."[22] Story was the first scholar in the United States to attempt "a complete picture of the relations of the successive editions"[23] and to point out the necessity of a variorum edition of *Leaves of Grass* for a complete understanding of Whitman's message and artistic achievement.

The need for a variorum edition was further emphasized in 1941 by Sculley Bradley in a paper read at the English Institute,[24] in which he discussed the problems that must be solved in preparing such an edition. He concluded that the text must be based on the last edition, because Whitman's purposes are apparent only in his final grouping of the poems. Here, as in Schyberg's study, we see that one of the major problems for the critic is understanding the poet's intentions as indicated by the continued experiments in grouping his poems. "The Structural Pattern of *Leaves of Grass*"[25] further corroborated this conclusion. It is significant that three scholars, widely separated and working independently, reached virtually the same judgment.

In 1958 Sculley Bradley, with the collaboration of Harold W. Blodgett, undertook the preparation of a *Variorum Leaves of Grass* as a major unit in the *Collected Writings of Walt Whitman* to be published by the New York University Press. One of their first decisions was to publish the text of *Leaves of Grass* in two editions, one using the 1892 "authorized" text purged of errors, and the other, using the same text but with the poems arranged in the order of their book publication. The first, called *Comprehensive Reader's Edition*

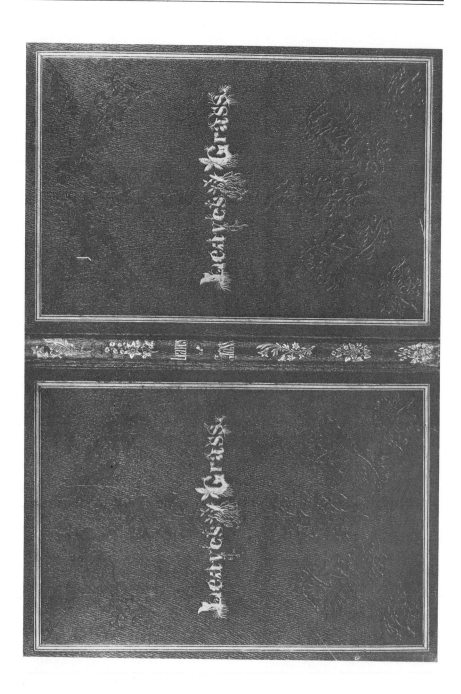

of Leaves of Grass (see note 1 above) has been published, and the *Variorum* is in process of publicaton. This will provide a workshop for the study of the growth of *Leaves of Grass* from any angle, textual, esthetic, structural, ideational, or other.

FIRST EDITION, 1855

Although Walt Whitman published a number of poems in various journals during the 1840s and early '50s, his poetic début took place with the publication of the 1855 *Leaves of Grass*, printed for him by the Rome Brothers in Brooklyn. It was a thin quarto of ninety-five pages bound in green cloth stamped with an elaborate rococo design of flowers and foliage. The title, printed in gold, sprouted roots, leaves, and branches from all sides, perhaps intended to symbolize the "organic" theory on which the poems were written. Especially symbolical is the portrait inside facing the title page and taking the place of the author's name, which is found only in the copyright notice and on page 29 of the poem later called "Song of Myself," "Walt Whitman, an American, one of the roughs, a kosmos . . ." The portrait shows the poet in the characteristic rôle of this poem, in shirt sleeves, the top of his colored undershirt showing, standing in a slouch posture, wearing a large black hat and a scraggly beard—"one of the roughs."

The book contains a prefatory essay in prose (though parts were later arranged as verse in "By Blue Ontario's Shore") and twelve poems, none of which have separate titles. Though the Preface is well known, the importance of the first edition cannot be accurately indicated without a summary. Whitman's first avowed purpose is to give expression to his own national life and age. America, he realizes, is still in the formative state—"the slough still sticks to opinions and manners and literature while the life which served its requirements has passed into the new life of the new forms." This national self-reliance leads to the theory that the poet must "incarnate" his country, since "The United States themselves are essentially the greatest poem." And the expression must be "transcendent and new."

Accepting Emerson's doctrine that "the poet is representative" and "stands among partial men for the complete man,"[26] Whitman defines his poet as a "seer" and an individual who "is complete in himself . . . the others are as good as he, only he sees it, and they do not." He is a "kosmos," a leader and an encourager of other poets. He will show men and women "the path between reality and their souls."

Whitman anticipates "Pragmatism" and much of the realistic literary theory of the twentieth century in his belief that the poet shall be enamored of *facts* and *things*; that with "perfect candor" and sound health he shall represent nature, the human form, and life accurately—empirically. Hence he will strive for art without artificial ornamentation. But this must not be at the expense of spirituality. "The largeness of nature or the nation were monstrous without a corresponding largeness and generosity of the spirit of the citizen." He "does not moralize or make application of morals; . . . he knows the soul."

In a similar duality, the poet shall flood himself "with the immediate age as with vast oceanic tides" and at the same time he shall be universal: to him shall be "opened the eternity which gives similitude to all periods and locations and processes and animate and inanimate forms." Like Shelley and Emerson, Whitman thinks "There will soon be no more priests"; a new breed of poet-prophets shall take their place, and "every man shall be his own priest." But the final "proof of the poet is that his country absorbs him as affectionately as he has absorbed it."

Nearly half of the volume is taken up with the first poem, here untitled, later called "Walt Whitman," and finally in 1881 "Song of Myself." It is undoubtedly, as the title indicates, his most personal poem, and it appropriately dominates the first edition, which is certainly the most personal of all the editions, the most naïve and rudimentary. Without a guiding title, without section numbers, and covering forty-three quarto pages—no wonder the first readers could make little sense out of it. In fact, Carl F. Strauch was the first critic ever to print a defense of its logic.[27] His outline of the structure deserves to be quoted:

1. Paragraphs 1-18, the Self; mystical interpenetration of the Self with all life and experience

2. Paragraphs 19-25, definition of the Self; identification with the degraded, and transfiguration of it; final merit of Self withheld; silence; end of the first half

3. Paragraphs 26-38, life flowing in upon Self, then evolutionary interpenetration of life

4. Paragraphs 39-41, the Superman

5. Paragraphs 42-52, larger questions of life—religion, faith, God, death; immortality and happiness mystically affirmed.[599]

Since Strauch's outline, various critics have attempted other summaries—including the present author in the first edition of this *Handbook*, Malcolm Cowley in his Introduction to an edition of the 1855 *Leaves of Grass*,[28] and James E. Miller in *A Critical Guide to Leaves of Grass*.[29] They all agree in principle, but offer different interpretations of the order, the message, and the "mystical experience."

Cowley finds nine *sequences* [xvii–xx]. He calls the sections (unnumbered in 1855) "chants," and groups them as follows:

Chants 1-4: "the poet or hero introduced to his audience."
Chant 5: "the ecstasy."
Chants 6-19: "the grass."
Chants 20-25: "the poet in person."
Chants 26-29: "ecstasy through the senses."
Chants 30-38: "the power of identification."
Chants 39-41: "the superman."
Chants 42-50: "the sermon."
Chants 51-52: "the poet's farewell."

James E. Miller calls "Song of Myself" an "Inverted Mystical Experience," by which he means that it is "not necessarily a transcript of an actual mystical experience," as described, for example, by Evelyn Underhill,[30] but a work of art "conceived in the imagination" and presented dramatically with "the author assuming the main role." Thus in sections 1 and 5 the "I" of the poem enters "into the mystical state"; the self awakes in 6-16; is purified in 17-32; experiences "Illumination and the dark night of the soul," in 33-37; "union (faith and love)" in 38-43; "union (perception)" in 44-49; and "Emerges from the mystical state" in 50-52.

V. K. Chari[31] agrees with Miller that "Song of Myself" is a "dramatic representation of a mystical experience,"[122] but he thinks that Miller's dividing the poem into seven phases forces the poem into an arbitrary mould. There is, says Chari, no "clear progression" from entry to emergence from the "mystical state," nor is the poem "arranged in the narrative order of a 'moment of ecstasy' followed by a 'sequel,' as has been suggested by Cowley."[123] To Chari "the underlying principle of organization" in "Song of Myself" is the "paradox of identity,"[121] though he uses the phrase in a different sense from Chase, who meant the poet's attempt to achieve unity out of the deep-seated diversity of his own personal identity (see Chap. I); whereas Chari means the paradox of the simultaneous centrifugal and centripetal movements of the "I" of the poem, or the relating of the subjective "self" to the world of experience. This *relating* gives the order of the poem, which the poet draws from his stream of consciousness.

Cowley speaks of a "wave-like flow"[xvi] and Allen and Davis of "a spatial" rather than a logical form.[32] Chari also stresses the "static situation," his "paradox of identity,"[33] and agrees with Roy Harvey Pearce that, "There is a movement here, but not a form."[34] The movement "derives from the motion of the protagonist's sensibility . . ."[73] Some critics have compared this semblance of "motion" to stream-of-consciousness or association of ideas, but Pearce calls it "hypnagogic meditation, controlled not by rules or method but by the intensely personal pulsations and periodicities of the meditative act."[77]

Students of Whitman may have as much difficulty in understanding the subtleties of some of these terms as the poem itself, but there is general critical agreement that, (1) "Song of Myself" has a structure and an order of development, but the order is not logical or temporal; rather (2) it is the order of perception of the nature of the self (the "I" of the poem) and its relations to the world, as experienced in the mind of the poet as he composed the poem. He also developed it thematically in the musical sense (like "movements" in a symphony), with the "grass" serving both as major theme and symbol.

From the grass, "sprouting alike in broad zones and narrow zones," the protagonist miraculously soars across the continent, observing and participating vicariously in the multiple phases of its life, returning as in a trance to the first, faint beginnings of life and finding "tokens" of himself at every stage of the evolutionary journey (secs. 31-32, and 43, lines 1149-1168). In this life of "perpetual transfers and promotions" (sec. 49), sex (fecundity) is the divine, propelling energy, and the motion is circular, from birth to death to rebirth. As the protagonist flies "the flight of the swallowing soul," he transcends time and space—a theme illustrated by the esthetic structure and order of the contents of the poem, which dispenses with Aristotelian time and space. Time in the poem is an all-embracing present.

Critics like Chase who look for autobiography in "Song of Myself" find a poet (or man) searching for unity in his own divided—or even fragmented—identity. Those who read it as a literary performance, as Chari does, find intuitive revelations of the nature of *the self*, and an appreciation of its dynamic possibilities: "It is an epic of the self set in the framework of heroic and cosmic concepts, comparable in its expansive quality to *Paradise Lost*, or better yet, the heroic Song of Krishna in the Bhagavad-Gita."[127]

Which is it, then? Psychological autobiography (it is certainly not literally autobiographical) or cosmic truth? The poem can be read either way. And they need not be mutually exclusive. But this very fact—and it does seem to be a fact—also means that no two critics, or readers, are ever likely to end with complete agreement. Whether accidental or intentional, the omission of the final period appropriately indicates the open-endedness of the poem, as the poet's last words do also:

> Failing to fetch me at first keep encouraged,
> Missing me one place search another,
> I stop some where waiting for you

Critics now agree that "Song of Myself" is an extremely subtle poem, and they no longer regard it as the "barbaric yawp" of a literary barbarian. Not the least remarkable feature of the poem is its capacity for yielding surprises after many rereadings. It is now generally acknowledged to be Walt Whitman's masterpiece, especially in the version of the first edition, and one of the most provocative and stimulating poems in world literature.

The second poem in the first edition ["A Song for Occupations"], is a further development of the occupations-theme in sec. 15 of "Song of Myself." It is like a sermon continued from the first poem on the "drift" of the message—the impulse to preach dominated Whitman in 1855. The poem has poor unity and coherence, even in the final version. The extremely intimate appeal to his readers in the first seven lines—"Come closer to me,/ Push close my lovers and take the best I possess"—was dropped in later editions, drastically changing the motivation. Here it is a forerunner of the search for companions and anticipates the "Calamus" group—though after it was revised and shifted to a position in the midst of the later "Songs," the reader could scarcely guess its origin.

The third poem, ["To Think of Time"], is also a further treatment of a major theme in "Song of Myself," an animistic interpretation of death. There is no death. Everything has a soul: in cosmic processes are "promotion" and "transformation" but no death: "there is nothing but immortality! . . . all preparation is for it . . . and identity is for it . . . and life and death are for it."

This poem is most remarkable, however, for personalizing the subject of death: what it is like to *think* of one's ceasing to exist in the physical world:

> To think that the rivers will come to flow, and the snow fall,
>   and fruits ripen . . . and act upon others as upon us now
>   . . . . yet not act upon us; . . .

It is difficult to say whether this is pathos or irony, but it is both in sec. 4, which realistically images the burial of an omnibus driver in December, under "A gray discouraged sky" with "half-frozen mud in the streets." The bleak but hurried decency of the funeral is effectively pathetic, but the presence of the corpse in the midst of the living drivers in whom he (or it) takes "no interest" is subtly ironic—so physically close yet so infinitely remote.

The fourth poem, ["The Sleepers"], is the most successfully motivated, and the most interesting psychologically, of any in the first edition. Though again taking his theme from the universal sympathy motif of "Song of Myself," Whitman achieves both poetic and mystic unity by projecting himself like a spirit among the sleepers of all lands, visiting, healing, and soothing each in turn. Dr. Bucke made one of his most acute observations when he called this poem "a representation of the mind during sleep," made of "connected, half-connected, and disconnected thoughts and feelings as they occur in dreams, some commonplace, some weird, some voluptuous, and all given with the true and strange emotional accompaniments that belong to them."[35] Malcolm Cowley calls the poem more concisely "that fantasia of the unconscious."[x]

All modern critics agree that "The Sleepers" intimately reveals the poet's sex psychology. Schyberg sees in it his "adolescent . . . eroticism," and Edwin H. Miller "a re-enactment of ancient puberty rites."[36] But Miller thinks "the drama of Whitman's poem, of necessity, is played out in the protagonist's consciousness, and that the conclusion is sublimation."

As in "Song of Myself," the symbols can be interpreted in various ways, as is the nature of literary symbols. "Night," the time of dreams, also symbolizes death. "Mother" is nature, the origin of life, the unconscious to which the protagonist wishes to return (to Freud "the womb"), or in the Emersonian-Hindu sense, the "Over-Soul" or *At-man*. Thus, in the latter sense, the emergence, return, and rebirth of the soul is a process of *migration*, but unlike the Hindu doctrine, there is no transmigration. In this interpretation, *day* is the life of the body and *night* is death, which, like sleep, reinvigorates the soul and prepares it for a new *dawn*. Actually, both the psychology of eroticism in the subconscious and the philosophy of the "Over-Soul" seem to be implicit in both the imagery and the symbolism of the poem, which also succeeds esthetically.

The next poem ["I Sing the Body Electric"] also gains in meaning when read after "The Sleepers." In the "Children of Adam" group it seems generic rather than personal. Here, minus the somewhat mechanical descriptions of the parts of the body added in 1856 (and thereafter retained as sec. 9), the doctrine that the body and soul are inseparable seems to have intimate connotations for the poet.

The sixth poem ["Faces"] gives vivid expression to a variety of transmigration first encountered in "Song of Myself." As the poet looks at faces, especially those of the wicked, the deformed, the diseased, he is consoled by the thought that this is but a temporary abode for the soul; he will "look again in a score or two of ages" and will "meet the real landlord perfect and unharmed."

> Off the word I have spoken I except not one . . . . red white
>   or black, all are deific,
> In each house is the ovum . . . . it comes forth after a
>   thousand years.
>
> Spots or cracks at the windows do not disturb me,
>
>   .   .   .   .   .
>
> I read the promise and patiently wait.

Since the biographical revelations of Molinoff and Furness, this doctrine has acquired a new pathos and yields greater insight into the poetic mind of Walt Whitman. The poem underwent few changes and was finally placed near the end of the *Leaves* in a group called "From Noon to Starry Night."

One poem, the eighth ["Europe"] had been published before as "Resurgemus" in the New York *Daily Tribune*, June 21, 1850, the only poem in the volume not appearing for the first time. The thought is undistinguished—that the spirits of men murdered by tyrants will live on to fight for Liberty, but Schyberg has found the poem important for a psychological reason:

It describes defeat, but the mood is optimistic and full of faith. It thus lays a foundation for all Whitman's lyricism. Just as his love poems grew out of the conflict between what he dreamed and what he actually attained, so his political lyric emerged out of the discrepancy between the America he saw and the America he wished for. That is the background of Whitman's whole paradoxical political position throughout all the editions of *Leaves of Grass* . . . Optimism of defiance—that is the formula of Whitman's lyricism.[37]

The ninth poem ["A Boston Ballad"] was probably written in 1854, for the subject is the seizure of a fugitive slave, Anthony Burns, in Boston and his return by the Court to his Virginia owner in June, 1854. It is therefore chronologically close to the other poems in the 1855 edition, but in manner it is unlike anything else in *Leaves of Grass*, for it is a satire, and Whitman did not later find this sarcastic tone congenial. In a jig tune the poet declares that King George's coffin should be exhumed and the king shipped back to Boston. Since it was Whitman's intention to use no explanatory notes in *Leaves of Grass*, he later intended to delete this poem, but Trowbridge persuaded him to let it stand.

The tenth poem ["There Was a Child Went Forth"] was much edited in later editions. The subject is the influence of natural objects on the life of a child (a Wordsworthian theme, but probably autobiographical here). The loving portrait of the mother and the description of the father as "mean, angered, unjust" give further evidence of the personal nature of this first edition, for nearly all biographers accept this poem as self-revealing in spite of Whitman's later denials. Of minor interest is the fact that the months are conventionally named, not yet called "Fourth-month" and "Fifth-month" after the Quaker custom.

The last two poems ["Who Learns My Lesson Complete" and "Great are the Myths"] are probably the weakest in the volume. The former merely asserts again that immortality is wonderful and miraculous. It was probably written hastily and carelessly. The ideas were to be much better expressed later in "Salut au Monde!," "Song of the Rolling Earth," and elsewhere. The final poem, eventually rejected, exclaims, even less effectively, that everything is great. Possibly it does serve as a general summary of the themes in the edition, though in no systematic manner, and it contains nothing to suggest new interpretations. Worst of all, it is anticlimactic.

Long regarded as more of a bibliographical curiosity and a collectors' item than a literary masterpiece, the first edition of *Leaves of Grass* has gained in reputation in recent years. In 1959 Malcolm Cowley called it "the buried masterpiece of American writing" (buried because of its small circulation), "a unified work, unlike any other edition, . . . [giving] us a different picture of Whitman's achievement. . . ." He pronounced the 1855 text of "Song of Myself" the "purest text . . . since many of the later corrections were also corruptions of the style and concealments of the original meaning."[38] This opinion has become widely accepted by other Whitman critics, and the '55 text of "Song of Myself" is now the text most often printed in anthologies. This is not true of "The Sleepers," but the first text of this poem is equally superior to it also; and the same might be said for the other ten poems of the 1855 edition.

SECOND EDITION, 1856

Fowler & Wells, the phrenological firm, were agents for the first edition of *Leaves of Grass*, and they were the secret publishers of the second edition in 1856. Presumably they were too apprehensive of the poet's reputation, after the critical buffeting he had received for his "immoral" first edition, to give the book their official imprint.[39]

The new book was a small volume, 16 mo, of 384 pages, with a green cloth binding stamped with floral designs not quite so ornate as those of the first edition. On the backstrip, in gold letters, appeared "I Greet You at the/ Beginning of A/ Great Career/ R. W. Emerson," which Whitman had quoted from Emerson's spontaneous letter without bothering to ask permission. So great was the influence of this letter upon the second edition of *Leaves of Grass*, and probably upon Whitman's whole subsequent career as a poet, that it deserves to be quoted in full. In thanks for his complimentary copy of the first edition Emerson wrote:

Concord 21 July
Massts.   1855

Dear Sir,

I am not blind to the worth of the wonderful gift of "Leaves of Grass." I find it the most extraordinary piece of wit & wisdom that America has yet contributed. I am very happy in reading it, as great power makes us happy. It meets the demand I am always making of what seemed the sterile & stingy nature, as if too much handiwork or too much lymph in the temperament were making our western wits fat & mean.

I give you joy of your free & brave thought. I have great joy in it. I find incomparable things said incomparably well, as they must be. I find the courage of *treatment*, which so delights us, & which large perception only can inspire.

I greet you at the beginning of a great career, which yet must have had a long foreground somewhere, for such a start. I rubbed my eyes a little to see if this sunbeam were no illusion; but the solid sense of the book is a sober certainty. It has the best merits, namely, of fortifying & encouraging.

I did not know until I, last night, saw the book advertised in a newspaper, that I could trust the name as real & available for a post-office. I wish to see my benefactor, & have felt much like striking my tasks, & visiting New York to pay you my respects.

R. W. EMERSON[40]

Mr Walter Whitman

The controversy stirred up by the publication of this letter without asking Emerson's permission has scarcely died down even yet; but whether or not Whitman was justified in using it as he did, its importance in the preparation of the second edition of his poems can scarcely be overestimated. Whitman's friends report that he was tremendously "set up" by it, and during the summer of 1855 he carried the letter around with him in his pocket. It may even have encouraged him to go on writing and printing his poems despite his recent fiasco. Certainly the exuberant confidence of the second edition is remarkable.

Not content with printing the letter in an appendix to the new volume, Whitman wrote a boastful and garrulous reply in which he addressed Emerson as "Master." The reply begins, "Here are thirty-two Poems, which I send you, dear Friend and Master, not having found how I could satisfy myself with sending any usual acknowledgment of your letter."[346] Then without regard to the true circumstances, he claims that the thousand-copy edition of the first volume readily sold and that he is printing several thousand copies of the second. He expects in a few years a sale of ten or twenty thousand copies. Then he launches into a theoretical discussion which is especially revealing and shows plainly that Whitman himself was not unaware of the paradox mentioned by Schyberg, the incongruity between his dream and reality. In the spirit of the literary nationalism of his day, he complains that the genius of America is still unexpressed in art. His evaluation of American life and character is almost as heroic as Paul Bunyan folklore, but the magnificence is *latent*, not actual. "Up to the present ... the people, like a lot of large boys, have no determined tastes, are quite unaware of the grandeur of themselves, and of their destiny, and of their immense strides..."[352] At present America is only "a divine true sketch."[354]

In addition to helping complete the "sketch," Whitman recognizes another responsibility in the development and recording of American culture: it is the honest, truthful expression of sex:

the body of a man or woman ... is so far quite unexpressed in poems ... Of bards for These States, if it come to a question, it is whether they shall celebrate in poems the eternal decency of the amativeness of Nature, the motherhood of all, or whether they shall be the bards of the fashionable delusion of the inherent nastiness of sex, and of the feeble and querulous modesty of deprivation.[356]

Much sex imagery is to be found in the first edition, especially in "Song of Myself" and "The Sleepers," but beginning with the second edition it is now to be a program, a "cause," a campaign against both asceticism and puritanism.

In the twenty new poems which Whitman added in the second edition to the twelve of the former collection, his faith in himself, his sanguinary hopes, and the crystallization of his "program" are clearly discernible. The poems now have titles and their arrangement is the poet's first experiment in working out a dramatic-allegorical

sequence. Omitting the '55 Preface, which was gradually being transferred to new compositions in verse, he begins the volume with the
poem which in all editions will continue to be a good theme-catalog,
here called "Poem of Walt Whitman, an American" (finally in 1881
"Song of Myself"), and progresses through the gamut of personal
identity, sex, friendship, evolution, cosmic sympathy, to eternity and
immortality. Neither here nor later do the poems treat the perpetual
journey of the soul from the germ to the grave in a narrative or
logical manner, but already they are falling into a kind of abstract
allegory resembling Carlyle's "out of eternity, into eternity."

In 1856 Whitman's "sex program" was still so intimately a part
of his whole inspiration that the new sex poems are scattered
throughout the whole book. Following "Song of Myself" comes
"Poem of Women" (later "Unfolded out of the Folds"). The theme
is both maternity and self-reliance: "First the man is shaped in the
woman, he can then be shaped in himself." The treatment is abstract,
ethical, and ideal; only physically and morally strong women can
produce a strong race. It is one aspect of Whitman's dream of the
future glory of America.

The next sex poem is No. 7, now called "Poem of the Body" ("I
Sing the Body Electric"), taken over from the first edition but considerably revised. Number 13, "Poem of Procreation" ("A Woman
Waits for Me"), further extends the theme that "sex contains all."
Number 28, "Bunch Poem" ("Spontaneous Me"), is the least abstract and most bizarre of the group. The "bunch" is a seminal
figure, like "herbage" in "Scented Herbage of My Breast" (1860),
which, however, is a "Calamus" poem, and hence not procreative.
"Bunch Poem" is definitely auto-erotic, for the poet is conscious of
his own body rather than the body of his lover. It celebrates the life
impulse latent in him, but it is not in imagery, feeling, or thought a
love poem, and may be indicative of ambiguous emotions in
Whitman himself at this period.

The "Poem of the Propositions of Nakedness" is not, as the title
might indicate, a sex poem, except indirectly. It is composed of a
long list of satirical paradoxes for those who distrust nakedness, sex,
truth, democracy, love, nature, themselves—note the relation of sex
to the whole "program." After his ironical mood had passed (Cf.
"Boston Ballad" in the first edition), Whitman apparently did not
know exactly what to do with this poem. It was included in "Chants
Democratic" (1860) as poem No. 5, later called "Respondez" and

finally in 1881 rejected except for the six lines of "Reversals" and three of "Transpositions."

Though the second edition contained no poem equal in power to "Song of Myself" in 1855, it did include four or five of his most successful compositions. The first of these (No. 3) is "Poem of Salu-tation" ("Salut au Monde!"), in which the national "incarnation" ambition of the '55 Preface has expanded into a lyric embrace of the whole world:

My spirit has passed in compassion and determination around the whole earth,
I have looked for brothers, sisters, lovers, and found them ready for me in all lands.

This poem contradicts the theory of many critics that after failing to gain acceptance in his own country, Whitman developed an inter-national sentiment as a compensation. And as within him "latitude widens, longitude lengthens," Walt Whitman gains tremendously in poetic power. World sentiment invigorated and stimulated his lyric growth and came in the flush of his inspiration, not afterwards.

"Broad-Axe Poem" ("Song of the Broad-Axe") contains a good deal of Whitman's earlier nationalism, perhaps imperialism, but this is due in part to the spirit of "arrogant, masculine, naïve, rowdyish" perfect health in which the broad-axe symbolizes the human activity of all lands. "Muscle and pluck forever! What invigorates life, invigor-ates death." The prophecy of one hundred Free States, "begetting another hundred north and south," is less imperialistic in its context than out of it, for the vision of "the shapes of fullsized men" and of vigorous women to be their equals includes all lands and peoples, "Shapes bracing the whole earth, and braced with the whole earth."

"Sun-Down Poem" (1860: "Crossing Brooklyn Ferry") is usually regarded as the best of the new poems in the second edition. In it Whitman attained a more subtle use of symbols and an allegori-cal structure which marked a new departure in his art.[41] As Chari observes, the basic symbolism is the paradox of "fixity in motion."[42] The protagonist commands time to stand still that he may prolong his moment of enjoyment, but only the poem, the work of art, achieves stasis—the motif of Keats's "Ode on a Grecian Urn." How-ever, Edwin H. Miller suggests a better comparison in Wallace Stevens's "Sunday Morning," in which the lady "welcomes flux, for

'Death is the mother of beauty.' " Like Stevens's poem, Whitman's is also "a hedonistic statement of faith."[43] Although Chase is more interested in the "confession of weakness and uncertainty" (the "dark patches" in sec. 6) in this poem, he also says that here Whitman "brings a new lyric austerity and control to his capacity for pathos and musing reflection."[44]

In the carefree, light-hearted "Poem of the Road" ("Song of the Open Road"), the poetic vision expands over the whole world—and finally the universe: "Afoot and lighthearted I take to the open road! Healthy, free, the world before me! . . . The earth expanding . . . I will scatter myself among men and women as I go." The themes of travel, physical joy, and companionship are happily blended. Phrenological "adhesiveness,"[45] which was building for the poet a "city of friends" where "manly affection" would reign, is defined by the question: "Do you know what it is as you pass to be loved by strangers?" The poet travels always toward the "great companions." His poem is a new *Pilgrim's Progress*:

To know the universe itself as a road—as many roads—as roads for
    traveling souls! . . .
All parts away for the progress of souls,
All religion, all solid things, arts, governments—all that was or is
    apparent upon this globe or any globe, falls into niches and
    corners before the processions of souls along the grand roads of
    the universe, . . .

He probably knew little about Hegelianism at this time, but he could declare,

Now understand me well—it is provided in the essence of things, that
    from any fruition of success, no matter what, shall come forth
    something to make a greater struggle necessary.

My call is the call of battle—I nourish active rebellion,

thus preparing the way for his justification of evil in "Chanting the Squre Deific" a decade later.

Even the religious concept of individualism, first formulated in the '55 Preface, takes on new depth and breadth when whole passages of the Preface are transferred to "Poem of Many in One" (later "By Blue Ontario's Shore")[46] and are motivated with cosmic significance. In addition to singing a new nation, which is to build on the past and henceforth lead the world, the poet has taken on a philosophical search for the meaning of the universe.

I match my spirit against yours, you orbs, growths, mountains, brutes,
I will learn why the earth is gross, tantalizing, wicked,
I take you to be mine, you beautiful, terrible, rude forms.

This search for the meaning of life and existence also has considerable bearing on the poet's theory of language. In the Preface he had declared that "The English language befriends the grand American expression . . . it is brawny enough and limber and full enough," and concluded that, "It is the medium that shall well night express the inexpressible." The more mystic his poems become, the more Whitman strives to "express the inexpressible," and this leads to a fuller development of his theory of words. As a consequence of the esthetic doctrine in the Preface that "All beauty comes from beautiful blood and a beautiful brain," Whitman explains in "Poem of Many in One" that to use the language the poet must "prepare himself, body and mind." Linguistic expression is thus the product of character. In "Poem of the Sayers of the Words of the Earth" ("Song of the Rolling Earth"), Whitman gives this idea an Emersonian interpretation; in fact, he is probably indebted to the Transcendentalist belief that "Words are signs of natural facts."[47] *Words* are not sounds or marks on paper, says Whitman, but reality; the words of the poem are "the words of the eloquent dumb great mother."

I swear I begin to see little or nothing in audible words!
I swear I think all merges toward the presentation of the unspoken meanings of the earth!
Toward him who sings the songs of the body, and of the truths of the earth,
Toward him who makes the dictionaries of the words that print cannot touch.

Hence the need for symbols, for "indirections"—"This is a poem for the sayers of the earth—these are hints of meanings," which echo the tones and phrases of souls.

Perhaps the greatest importance of the second edition is the testimony it bears to the courage and fortitude of Walt Whitman in the face of literary failure. Nearly every new poem in the book radiates his faith in himself, in his ideas, and in his newly-invented technique. And despite the brashness and bad taste of the open-letter to Emerson, this edition shows unmistakable growth in lyric power, especially when the cosmic emotion or universal sympathy carries his Muse on a vicarious journey into all lands and ages, as in "Salut au Monde!," "Crossing Brooklyn Ferry," or "Song of the Rolling Earth." Even in his most personal sex lyrics, which seem to reflect some inner struggle or irrepressible urge, he is already striving to sublimate the emotion. He has, in short, not yet attained the poise and tranquility which grew upon him after his service in the army hospitals; but as the first edition reveals his lyrical power, so does the second map out the paths which he is to follow through succeeding editions of *Leaves of Grass*.

THIRD EDITION, 1860

Soon after Fowler & Wells printed the second edition of *Leaves of Grass* (possibly even before[48]), Whitman began planning a third edition. At first his plan was to add 68 new poems to the 32 of the 1856 edition, to make a round hundred. In his notes he referred to the augmented collection as "the New Bible," meaning, apparently, a "Bible" for American Democracy, and in June 1857 he predicted, "It ought to be ready in 1859."[49]

In 1858 or early '59 the Rome Brothers, who had printed the first *Leaves of Grass*, began setting up the new poems, mainly for the purpose of giving Whitman printed versions to correct—he liked to revise in proof. Whitman may also have intended to have the Romes print the new edition, for on June 20, 1857,[50] he planned to recover the plates from Fowler & Wells and re-use them in printing a new edition. These simple details show that Whitman was planning a third edition similar to his second, with new poems simply added on to the old ones: technically, a new *issue* instead of a new edition because the 32 poems would not be reset.

The manuscripts set up by the Rome Brothers have been edited by Fredson Bowers,[51] and they are of more than bibliographical interest. For one thing, Whitman was planning a "Proem" to explain his poetic program. He first called it "Premonition," and then "Proto-Leaf" (finally "Starting from Paumanok"). The second title suggests its introductory function, which would not have been appropriate for a poem appended to the 1856 collection, and this fact shows that Whitman was considering organizing his third edition on a thematic plan, to be introduced by a program poem.

More important, the manuscript versions of "Proto-Leaf" reveal more clearly than the final version the crises and vacillations of the poet during the gestation of the third edition. Whitman's first ambition was to tally and vocalize his native land: "Solitary, singing in the west, I strike up for a new world."[52]

> Take my leaves, America!
> Make welcome for them everywhere, for
>   they are your own offspring; . . .[7]

This motif leads easily to the theme of "companionship, . . . what alone can compact The States, . . ."[12] But later in the manuscript the companions are reduced to a single "comrade," a young man "kissing me so long with his daily kiss . . ."[18] After more experimental songs to his native land, the poet seeks a "rendezvous at last" with his comrade, "us two only!"[34]

That some personal experience motivated this switching from the role of national bard to personal lover is indicated further by a group of poems which Whitman at first called "Live Oak with Moss," which could be called the "proto-leaf" of the 1860 "Calamus" cluster.[53] This group consisted of twelve numbered poems, in theme and form resembling an Elizabethan sonnet-sequence, probably Whitman's literary model. The poet is so emotionally attached to this male lover that he becomes indifferent to his songs celebrating "the grandeur of The States, and the examples of heroes." Now "It is to be enough for each of us that we are together. . . ."[54] One of the most lyrical of these (free-verse) sonnets describes the poet's happiness in the anticipation and arrival of his lover.[55] Other poems, however, are concerned with loneliness, pensive longing, and a sense of guilt: "it is useless—I am what I am."[56]

These embryonic "Calamus" poems, which "tell the secret of my night and days,"[57] seem at times to describe a very real love-relationship, but more often the poet seeks compensation in a fantasy "City of Friends,"[58] and in this dream-world the themes of national bard and lover combine. The poet is consoled by the thought that "a century hence"[59] his readers will love and understand him. In an 1876 preface Whitman confessed that he had "sent out *Leaves of Grass* to arouse and set flowing in men's and women's hearts, young and old, (my present and future readers,) endless streams of living, pulsating love and friendship, directly from them to myself, now and ever."[60] This "terrible, irrepressible yearning" deep in his soul was never more intense than in the year or so preceding the publication of his 1860 edition, when he was writing the early versions of the "Calamus" poems.

The manuscripts which the Rome Brothers set up also contain five of the "Enfans d'Adam" cluster in the 1860 edition, but they do not go very far toward carrying out the intention Whitman recorded in his notes, to write "A string of Poems, (short etc.) embodying the amative love of woman—the same as *Live Oak Leaves* do the passion of friendship for man,"[61] and in a later note, after he had changed "Live Oak" to "Calamus": "Theory of a Cluster of Poems the same *to the passion of Woman-Love* as the *Calamus-Leaves* are to adhesiveness, manly love. Full of animal-fire, tender, burning. . . ."[62] Thus in addition to forecasting the conflicting motifs of national bard and "tender lover" of one person (eventually sublimated into "you" the reader), and the literary strategy of balancing homosexual and heterosexual love in two "clusters" of poems, these preliminary drafts also show the poet in the process of reorganizing and rearticulating the sequence of his poems in his next edition.

A major cluster in the third edition, "Chants Democratic," is also well represented in the Bowers edition (forty-five pages), but the unifying theme of "A nation announcing itself, (many in one,)" ("Chant" No. 1 in the 1860 edition) is still elusive, and the miscellaneous fragments are still incoherent (not individually but as an embryonic cluster). However, some of the motifs of the group appear, such as the national pride in "America always! . . . Always our own feuillage!"[63] And "How can I but invite you for yourself to collect bouquets of the incomparable feuillage of These States?"[64] Also the theme of the poet as "time-binder":

O strain musical, flowing through ages and continents—now reaching me and America!
I take your strong chords—I intersperse them, and cheerfully pass them forward.[65]

Realizing that the democratic nation he celebrates is still more dream than reality, and that he himself has not yet fulfilled his bardic announcements, the poet becomes prophetic, and addresses

Poets to come!
Not to-day is to justify me, and Democracy, and what we are for,
But you, a new brood, native, athletic, continental, greater than
    before known,
You must justify me.[66]

In the manuscript cluster for "Leaves of Grass" (a very ambiguous group-title) the poet seems to feel a compulsion to confess and to "give fair warning," calling himself "culpable" and a "traitor."[67]

Inside these breast-bones I lie smutch'd and choked,
Beneath this face that appears so impassive, hell's tides continually
    run,
Lusts and wickedness are acceptable to me,
I walk with delinquents with passionate love,
I feel I am of them—I belong to those convicts and prostitutes
    myself,
And henceforth I will not deny them—for how can I deny myself?

Whether this identification with the wicked is Christ-like compassion or a crushing sense of personal guilt, the psychological effect is clear in the versions of the next cluster to be called "Messenger Leaves" in the 1860 edition: the poet has derived positive benefit from his impassioned confession. Now, in fact, he assumes a priestly rôle for himself. In "To One Shortly to Die"

I absolve you from all except yourself, spiritual, bodily—
    that is eternal,
(The corpse you will leave will be but excrementitous.)

    .   .   .   .   .

I do not commiserate you—I congratulate you.[68]

In several short poems "To You" (the reader) the poet continues to solicit confessions: "Tell me the whole story—Tell me what you would not tell your brother, wife, husband, or physician."[69] Then as if purged of his own guilt, he writes seventeen pages (in the Bowers edition) of experimental verses for a "Poem of Joys." Among the many joys is "the beautiful touch of Death, . . . discharging my excrementitous body, . . . My voided body, nothing more to me, returning to the purifications, further offices, eternal uses of the earth."[70]

The exact date of composition of these lines has not been determined, though they were written between 1857 and 1859. The mood suggests the latter year, during which Whitman wrote two poems in the same state of mind. One was "Bardic Symbols" (title used for the version published in the *Atlantic Monthly*, April, 1860—later "As I Ebb'd with the Ocean of Life"), in which the poet, walking the shores of Paumanok, identified with the debris cast up by the waves. He felt "balked,/ Bent to the very earth," mocked for his "insolent poems," without "the least idea who or what I am. . . ."[71]

In this poem Whitman used two major symbols which he would develop in subsequent poems: the *shore*, physical reality (also addressed as "father"); and the *ocean*, "the measureless float" (he had used "float" once before in "Sun-Down Poem"), the source and the dissolver of life (also "mother"). The poet envisioned his drowning in two lines which James Russell Lowell, the editor of the *Atlantic Monthly*, found too realistic and deleted (Whitman restored them in his 1860 edition):

(See! from my dead lips the ooze exuding at last!
See—the prismatic colors, glistening and rolling!)

Whitman wrote this poem during an ebb-tide of his life. One of his personal discouragements may have been the loss of the "lover" in the early versions of the "Calamus" poems, and he was doubtless also disappointed in not having been able to find a means of publishing his planned third edition of *Leaves of Grass*. But more important, here is the dramatic rôle of the sea, the "fierce old mother" who endlessly cries for her "castaways," singing "that dirge of Nature."

Another poem written at this time (probably the autumn of 1859) is linked to "Bardic Symbols" by theme, symbols, and the pathos of death; or, more specifically, the poem treats the relations of love, death, and poetry. This poem is "A Child's Reminiscence" (retitled "A Word Out of the Sea" in 1860 and "Out of the Cradle Endlessly Rocking" in 1871), published on December 24, 1859, in the New York *Saturday Press*. It tells a story which the poet presents as an experience rememberd from his childhood on the shore of Paumanok, the story of a male mockingbird calling melodiously, from early spring to autumn, for his lost mate. (How the boy knew the singing bird was male is not part of the poem, but the assumption is another subjective aspect of the poem.) Hearing the song at night, in the moonlight, the waves hissing on the sand, the boy felt that the bird sang to him of love and death.

> The dusky demon aroused—the fire, the sweet hell within,
> The unknown want—the destiny of me.

In remembering these "thousand warbling echoes" the boy became a man—and a poet—whose fate also was to be "a solitary singer," singing of lost love and searching for the meaning of the loss.

A passage in this poem omitted after 1860 (except for the first two lines) shows its intimate connection with the poet's despair in "Bardic Symbols":

> O give me some clew!
> O if I am to have so much, let me have more!
> O a word! O what is my destination?
> O I fear it is henceforth chaos!
> O how joys, dreads, convolutions, human shapes, and all shapes,
>   spring as from graves around me!
> O phantoms! you cover all the land, and all the sea!
> O I cannot see in the dimness whether you smile or frown upon me!
> O vapor, a look, a word! O well-beloved![72]
> O you dear women's and men's phantoms!

In "Bardic Symbols" the only answer the sea, "the old mother," gave the poet was that "the flow will return," but in "A Child's Reminiscence" it is the "delicious word Death," the key to these poems on love and death.

About six weeks after the publication of "A Child's Reminiscence" Whitman received a letter which unexpectedly made possible a third edition of *Leaves of Grass*. On February 10, 1860, Thayer & Eldridge, a young but reputable firm in Boston, wrote him: "We want to be the publishers of Walt Whitman's Poems—Leaves of Grass."[73] They offered to buy the stereotype plates of the second edition, but also inquired whether he had new poems to add to the book. When they learned that he had over one hundred unpublished poems and a plan for a greatly expanded book, they offered him a free hand in designing and supervising the printing of a new edition of *Leaves of Grass*, on a standard ten percent royalty basis.

In March, 1860, Whitman went to Boston and stayed until the book was finished in mid-May,[74] with a first printing of one thousand copies, which was sold out in July[75] and reprinted (probably another thousand copies). The book was a fat volume, 8vo, bound in heavy cloth, blind stamped,[76] with 456 pages. It was well printed in ten-point type on heavy white paper, with extensive decorative devices on the binding and throughout the book as head- and tail-pieces. Three of the tail-pieces (line drawings) seem to be symbolic: a butterfly poised on forefinger[77] (also blind-stamped on the spine over the poet's name), a globe in space revealing the western hemisphere (stamped on the front cover between *Leaves* and *Grass*), and a sunset [78] at sea (likewise stamped on the back cover between *Leaves* and *Grass*). Perhaps these emblems signified the poet's global and cosmic inspiration and his intimacy with all living creatures.[79] But they give no intimation of the personal pathos in some sections of this intricately organized book.

Printer's copy for the 1860 *Leaves of Grass* has not survived, but it could not have been the proofs of the poems set up by the Rome Brothers because of the wide differences between the published versions and the manuscripts edited by Bowers. Probably Whitman took a set of these proof sheets (now lost) with him to Boston, which he had already substantially emended and amplified. The 1860 *Leaves* contains 146 poems new to the collection, extensive revisions of the old poems, and many new titles, some of them final. The order of the poems is Whitman's first attempt at a thematic pattern, only partly successful. The following table will show how he attempted to integrate the new and old poems:

"Proto-Leaf"
"Walt Whitman" [first untitled poem in 1855 edition; "Song of Myself," 1881]
"CHANTS DEMOCRATIC and Native American" [poems numbered from 1 to 21, without titles; some new, some old] [80]
"Leaves of Grass" [numbered from 1 to 24, without title, some new, some old]
"Salut au Monde" ["Poem of Salutation," 1856]
"Poem of Joys"
"A Word Out of the Sea" ["A Child's Reminiscence," 1859]
"A Leaf of Faces" [sixth untitled poem in 1855; "Poem of Faces," 1856]

"Europe the 72d and 73d Years of These States" [untitled in 1855; "Poem of the Dead Young Men of Europe," 1856]

"ENFANS D'ADAM" [poems numbered from 1 to 15, without title]

"Poem of the Road" [1856; "Song of the Open Road," 1881]

"To the Sayers of Words" ["Poem of Sayers of The Words of The Earth," 1856]

"A Boston Ballad, the 78th Year of These States" [untitled in 1855; "Poem of Apparitions in Boston, the 78th Year of These States," 1856]

"CALAMUS" [45 numbered poems, without title]

"Crossing Brooklyn Ferry"

"Longings for Home"

"MESSENGER LEAVES" [fifteen short poems with titles "To . . ." various persons, including three to the reader]

"Mannahatta"

"France, the 18th Year of These States"

"THOUGHTS" [without title, numbered 1 to 7—epigrammatic]

"Unnamed Lands"

"Kosmos"

"A Hand-Mirror"

"Beginners"

"Tests"

"Savantism"

"Perfections"

"SAYS" [strophes numbered from 1 to 8 as if short poems, but six begin "I say," and they seem to be parts of one poem]

"Debris" [epigrams, without separate titles]

"Sleep-Chasings" [fourth untitled poem in 1855; "Night Poem," 1856; "The Sleepers," 1871]

"Burial" [third untitled poem in 1855; "Burial Poem," 1856; "To Think of Time," 1871]

"To My Soul"

"So long!"

It would take too much space to give either a bibliographical description of the revised poems or a detailed analysis of the contents of all the 146 new poems, but a few observations can be made on the *schema*. It was apparent even in the manuscript versions of "Proto-Leaf" that it was to be a "program" poem. In 1860 it still shows the poet trying to ride two horses—spokesman for democracy and the pathos of "two together" (love and death), but Whitman has made some progress in resolving the contradictions. The poem ends with the poet triumphantly joining hands with his reader, hastening toward the companionship which shall compact These States. But "Proto-Leaf" suffers from its juxtaposition to "Walt Whitman" ("Song of Myself"). The new title fits in with the 1860 "program," but it lacks the overwhelming lyric power of "Song of Myself," which with less contrivance introduced the first edition (not counting the Preface in prose).

"Chants Democratic," the cluster most copiously represented in the manuscripts set up by the Rome Brothers, discussed above, is a collection of twenty-one numbered poems without titles, sixteen of which were new.[81] The group is introduced by the exclamatory poem, "Apostroph" (not in the Rome proof sheets and perhaps composed in Boston during the typesetting of the third edition). It enumerates, often in phrases later repeated in this group of poems, the various themes and intentions of the "Chants." "Apostroph" was rejected in all subsequent editions, probably not only because of its hysterical style but also because when this group was broken up in the next edition and the contents redistributed, its purpose vanished. It is interesting here only because it shows Whitman's growing tendency to use prologue poems to introduce his "clusters."

The first numbered poem in the "Chants Democratic" group is the 1856 version of the 1855 Preface, called in 1856 "Poem of Many in One" and finally in 1881 "By Blue Ontario's Shore." It proclaims Whitman's theory of the "nation announcing itself," and appropriately precedes the 1856 "Song of the Broad-Axe" and the 1855 (later title) "Song for Occupations." As Schyberg has remarked, it is ironical that just before the outbreak of the Civil War Whitman should sing the unity of The States, which he declares in poem No. 4 (later called "Our Old Feuillage") to be as united in "one identity" as the parts of his own body.[82] But it is a theoretical identity, transcending political borders, uniting the poet and his countrymen with the "antecedents" of all lands (cf. No. 7, later called "With Antecedents"), and prophesying "the ideal man, the American of the future" (No. 10, "To a Historian"). These "Chants" are less a celebration of national achievement than a search for the foundations of an ethical Democracy, which the poet finds at last (No. 19) not in history, nor in fables or legends, but in a culmination of the existence in the average life of the day, in things, inventions, customs, people. Therefore he proclaims as the most solid of all realities, Liberty, Freedom, and the "divine average" (No. 21),

> And our visions, the visions of poets . . .
> Democracy rests finally upon us . . .
> And our visions sweep through eternity.

If "Leaves of Grass," the next cluster, has a central theme it is, perhaps, the poet's own crisis of identity. L. G. No. 1 (untitled) is the *Atlantic Monthly* poem "Bardic Symbols" ("As I Ebb'd with . . ."), discussed above. But the poems of this cluster do not follow autobiographical chronology, or even a logical sequence of vicarious experiences. No. 2 returns to the 1855 confidence in the greatness of myth, truth, law, man, earth, etc. [twelfth 1855 poem, later "Great are the Myths"]. And No. 3 is the 1856 "Faith Poem."

As if recording a resolution, No. 10 begins, "It is ended—I dally no more," and proclaims that henceforth the poet will endure hardships of every kind, but he ends by asserting his independence of all restraints and charges his followers to "leave all free, as I left all free." The moods of the remaining poems in the group are so various that they seem to be a miscellany, though some are memorable, such as No. 17, in which the poet looks out upon "all the sorrows of the world" while he remains silent and inert. No. 24 is one of Whitman's cherished "farewell" poems, which partly characterize the third edition, as if he suspected it might be his last. The poet fancies that whoever is holding his book is affectionately embracing him, and to that unknown person he gives a parting kiss—a preliminary sketch of his epilogue poem, "So long!"

After the "Leaves of Grass" section in the third edition, and the miscellaneous poems which have already been discussed, we find the notorious "Enfans d'Adam" (called "Children of Adam" in 1867 and thereafter). Although twelve of these fifteen poems are new, the theme had been announced in sec. 40 of "Song of Myself":

> On women fit for conception I start bigger and nimbler
>   babes,
> This day I am jetting the stuff of far more arrogant
>   republics.

Indeed, these poems may have been a conscious attempt to develop this earlier theme. Thoreau believed that in the group Whitman "does not celebrate love at all. It is as if the beasts spoke."[83] D. H. Lawrence's comment was: ". . . what is Woman to Walt Whitman? Not much. She is a great function—no more."[84] The "Calamus" poems sound like genuine love poems; but the expression of "Children of Adam" is theoretical and philosophical. In No. 1 ("To the Garden the World") *love* is presented as the means of pantheistic transmigration: ". . . here behold my resurrection, after slumber,/ The revolving cycles, in their wide sweep, having brought me again . . ." Even in the second poem, which later had such a suggestive title as "From Pent-up Aching Rivers," the poet sings "something yet unfound, though I have diligently sought it, ten thousand years." He later changed this line to "sought it many a year," thus eliminating the connotation of transmigration. It is interesting that he attempted to make these poems more rather than less personal, as in his usual revisions, such as we have noticed in "Out of the Cradle." But it is perhaps still more remarkable that in this poem on the theme of birth and procreation he also sings "the song of prostitutes." This sexual attraction he declares to be "the true song of the Soul."

No. 3 in this group is less polemical and more lyrical, showing an artist's delight in the contours of the human form, especially of the body in motion. But in No. 4 we find one of the first crude attempts to give this sex program a social meaning: "I shall demand perfect men and women out of my love-spendings . . ." No. 5 ("Spontaneous Me") was first published in the second edition. Despite the careful descriptions of both male and female erotic sensations, it is vividly personal in the sense of touch, but it is autoerotic. It contains the fantastic figure "bunch" for seminal seed, which suggests the botanical imagery characteristic of the "Calamus" poems.

The central procreative theme is by no means uniformly or consistently maintained in the "Children of Adam" group. In No. 6 ("One Hour to Madness and Joy") the emotion is promiscuous, "O to be yielded to you, whoever you are," and the free love doctrine blends into the literary program of reckless abandon to impulse. In No. 7 ("We Two How Long We Were Fool'd") the "two" were apparently fooled by abstinence, by artificial repression; and there is a suggestion again of transmigration in, "We have circled and circled till we have arrived home again—we two have . . ." No. 8 ("Native Moments") is a paean of "libidinous joys only."

I am for those who believe in loose delights—I share
the midnight orgies of young men, . . .

and No. 9 ("Once I Pass'd through a Populous City") was originally,
as Holloway discovered,[85] a "Calamus" poem. No. 10 ("Facing West
from California's Shores") is connected with the procreation theme
only in a vague pantheistic manner, being an anticipation of the
"Passage to India" motif: "I, a child, very old, over waves, toward the
house of maternity, the land of migrations, look afar . . ." No. 15
("As Adam Early in the Morning") serves as an epilogue for the
group and returns to the Garden of Eden allegory, closing the section
with lyric praise of the human body, especially the sense of touch.
Thus the "Children of Adam" poems contain several mingled themes
and motifs carried over from the first two editions and overlap the
purposes of several other poems in the third edition. The central
thought is a pantheistic interpretation of procreation, but some of
the poems are personal in the revolt against conventional attitudes
toward sex and in the author's abnormally acute sensitivity to touch.
They are in no sense love poems. The ones which are not abstract
and philosophical are autoerotic or hedonistic. The poet reveals a
love only for his own sensibility, and accepts indiscriminately all
stimuli. Although his reverence for the origins of humanity is almost
religious, he gives scarcely a hint of any social control of the sexual
emotions.

"Calamus" is the most unified group in the third edition. All
forty-five poems are new, and though the "great companions" motif
had appeared in "Proto-Leaf" and was a part of Whitman's earliest
poetic program, the tender feeling and shy expression in "Calamus"
was entirely absent in "Children of Adam" and was never again
duplicated in Leaves of Grass. In short, "Calamus" contains Whitman's love poems. As Schyberg puts it: "Whitman first celebrated
the emotion of love in all its nuances in 'Calamus.' In 'Children of
Adam' he was self-confident and supercilious, in 'Calamus,' shy,
hesitant, wistfully stuttering."[86]

The kind of love which these poems reveal will perhaps always
be debated among Anglo-Saxon critics, who cannot enjoy the lyrics
of Sappho without first assessing her morality. It is like the controversy over the "Book of Canticles," whether it is erotic or a veiled
allegory of church history. Let those who wish interpret "Calamus"

as an allegory of democratic brotherhood.[87] The fact remains that the expression is the poetry of love, and sometimes almost as tender and beautiful as the expression of affection and friendship in Shakespeare's sonnets, which these poems parallel in a number of ways, except for being in free verse.

The first poem in the group gives the setting: a secluded spot beside a pond "in paths untrodden." The theme is "manly attachment"; the mood is shy, secretive, utterly unlike the boastful, erotic display in "Children of Adam." In this damp retreat, the "Scented Herbage of my Breast" imagery in the second poem becomes morbidly symbolical:

> Scented herbage of my breast,
> Leaves from you I yield, I write, to be perused best afterwards,
> Tomb-leaves, body-leaves, growing up above me, above death.

In "Song of Myself" and "This Compost" *leaves* grow out of death and corruption but symbolize resurrection and the eternal cycles of life. Here they seem to be a private confession of some hidden secret, and remembering the "bunch" metaphor of "Spontaneous Me," we guess that the leaves also have a sexual symbolism. But they and the fragrant calamus root likewise suggest Death:

> Yet you are very beautiful to me, you faint-tinged roots—you make me think of Death,
> Death is beautiful from you—(what indeed is beautiful, except Death and Love?)

What is the connection between this association of Death and Love and the tragic tone of "Out of the Cradle" and "As I Ebb'd with the Ocean of Life"? This association is the outstanding characteristic of the third edition of *Leaves of Grass*. The poet who doted on himself in 1855 and declared in "Song of Myself" (sec. 24), "The scent of these arm-pits is aroma finer than prayer," now writes like this:

> Do not fold yourselves so in your pink-tinged roots, timid leaves!
> Do not remain down there so ashamed, herbage of my breast!

Come, I am determined to unbare this broad breast of mine—I have
    long enough stifled and choked . . .

Something of the psychological origin of these poems is indicated in No. 3 (addressed to "Whoever You Are"): the poet writes to
solicit love, and like a lover he is jealous and all-demanding; furthermore, he gives "fair warning" that he is "not what you supposed . . .
The way is suspicious" (Cf. also No. 12). In No. 4 ("These I Singing
in Spring") he gives tokens to all, but the calamus root "only to
them that love, as I myself am capable of loving." These select lovers
are obviously a minority; they seem to be in some way different
from the mass. However, in No. 5 ("For you O Democracy") the
poet makes an attempt to evolve from these calamus roots and leaves
a general democratic symbolism. His kind of "new friendship" shall
compact the States.

Affection shall solve every one of the problems of
    freedom,
Those who love each other shall be invincible . . .

As in Shakespeare's sonnets, however, it is difficult to trace a
consecutive story of an experience in these poems. They are not
arranged either in the chronology of the experience or in the order of
a psychological drama. The social application of the love emotion in
No. 5 may be the culmination of the "Calamus" experience, but in
the group it is followed by several poems which reveal a crisis that
must surely have preceded the solution and the catharsis. No. 7, for
example, presents "The Terrible Doubt of Appearances." For a while
all existence seems a dream and a delusion, but then all doubts "are
curiously answered by my lovers, my dear friends." Whether these
were real friends or vicarious lovers created by poetic fancy, the
poem does not reveal.
    More revealing is No. 8 ("Long I Thought that Knowledge Alone
would Suffice"), and one wonders why it was never again printed.
Had the sentiment passed or was it too personal? Whitman must have
known himself that it was a good poem, and several admirers protested its rejection. John Addington Symonds confessed it was this
poem which first aroused his interest in Leaves of Grass and was one
of the great experiences of his life. [88] The story that the poem tells is
the following: the poet believed at one time that knowledge alone

would suffice, and he aspired to be the orator of his country; then, "to enclose all, it came to me to strike up the songs of the New World," but now the lands must find another singer:

For I can be your singer of songs no longer—One who loves me is jealous of me, and withdraws me from all but love,
With the rest I dispense—I sever from what I thought would suffice me, for it does not—it is now empty and tasteless to me,
I heed knowledge, and the grandeur of The States, and the example of heroes, no more,
I am indifferent to my own songs—I will go with him I love,
It is to be enough for us that we are together—We never separate again.

The very next poem, No. 9 ("Hours Continuing Long, Sore and Heavy-Hearted") was also published only once. It is the most painful of the group, and one of the most deeply moving in *Leaves of Grass*. The poet feels himself to be so tormented and lonely that he wonders if he is not an anomaly.

Hours sleepless . . . discouraged, distracted . . . when I am forgotten . . .
Hours of my torment—I wonder if other men ever have the like, out of the like feelings?
Is there even one other like me—distracted—his friend, his lover, lost to him?

No. 16 ("Who is Now Reading This") was likewise rejected in 1867, possibly because it was also too personal, too revealing. The poet confesses that he is puzzled at himself:

As if I were not puzzled at myself!
Or as if I never deride myself! (O conscience-struck! O self-convicted!)
Or as if I do not secretly love strangers! (O tenderly, a long time, and never avow it;)
Or as if I did not see, perfectly well, interior in myself, the stuff of wrong-doing,
Or as if it could cease transpiring from me until it must cease.

The mood of loneliness and discouragement returns again (or

perhaps was the same occasion as in No. 9) in No. 20, "I Saw in Louisiana a Live-Oak Growing."

... I wondered how it could utter joyous leaves, standing alone there, without its friend, its lover near—for I knew I could not ...

Here we have also another, though similar, clue to the "leaves" symbolism. The word "utter" especially suggests that Whitman's *leaves* were his poems, and between the jealousy of the lover who will permit no rival distraction and the dejection of the poet when he feels his love to be unreturned, the *Leaves of Grass* experiment seems near an end.

Paradoxically, however, both of these frustrations drive the poet to a vicarious release in verse. In fact, he now has a new poetic ambition (No. 10); he wants to be known not so much for his poems as for the "measureless oceans of love within him,"

Nor speak of me that I prophesied of The States, and led them the way of their glories; . . . [but]
Publish my name and hang up my picture as that of the tenderest lover . . .

This poem is followed by the most ecstatic in the group (No. 11), and perhaps the most beautiful. It would be difficult to find in the whole literature of love a more tender and convincing description of the joyous day when the lover returns. Also tender, but a great deal more obscure, is No. 17, the poet's dream of his lover's death. Curiously the dream seems to reconcile the poet to death, which he henceforth finds everywhere. This experience is obviously connected in some way with the theme of "Out of the Cradle" and Whitman's philosophy of death.

Poem No. 23 shows that the "Calamus" emotions underlie Whitman's universal sympathy and his international sentiments. The poet's yearning for love leads him to think of men of other lands who might also be yearning and he decides that they could all "be brethren and lovers" together. In the next poem he would establish "The institution of the dear love of comrades." In No. 26, however, he returns to the theme of "two together." This poem, like "Song of the Open Road," probably describes an ideal rather than an actuality. Two boys roam the lands, enjoying all activities, "One the other never leaving." But the general application of the "Calamus" emotion revives again in No. 34, which describes how the poet "dreamed in a dream" of a "new City of Friends," and in No. 35 he believes that the germ of exalted friendship is "latent in all men."

In the brief, three-line poem numbered 39, the steps of the process of sublimation are clearly indicated:

Sometimes with one I love, I fill myself with rage, for fear I effuse unreturned love;
But now I think there is no unreturned love—the pay is certain, one way or another,
Doubtless I could not have perceived the universe, or written one of my poems, if I had not freely given myself to comrades, to love.

And this explanation is amplified in poems No. 41 and 42, in which we can plainly see Whitman's rôle as prophet and teacher, seeking followers and pupils, originating in the emotions of "Calamus."

This interpretation is still further strengthened by No. 44, which repeats and emphasizes the confessional introductory poems. "Here," says the poet, are "the frailest leaves of me, and yet my strongest lasting." In these "leaves" he hides his thoughts, and "yet they expose me more than all my other poems." Could anything say more plainly that the *secret* of Walt Whitman's poetic inspiration is recorded in the "Calamus" poems? Out of these emotions grew his Christ-like love for humanity, his St. Francis-like sympathy for all living things, and the psychic turmoil for which he could find expression and release only in his life-book. In these poems we can understand Walt Whitman better than in any other section of *Leaves of Grass*. Their relationship to the whole book is appropriately indicated by Whitman himself in the final poem of this group, No. 45, in which he speaks to his readers of a century or more hence, and invites the reader of the future to be his lover. In the 1860 edition this poem provided a transition to "Crossing Brooklyn Ferry," which immediately followed the "Calamus" group. This sequence is so fortunate and meaningful that it is difficult to understand why Whitman used it only in this one edition—though it is not the only example that the 1860 edition *Leaves of Grass* is the most personal of all editions.

A poem in the third edition which some biographers have used to support their theories of a New Orleans romance[89] is "Longing for Home" (later "O Magnet South"). Such lines as

> O Magnet-South! O glistening, perfumed South!
> My South!
> O quick mettle, rich blood, impulse, and love!
> Good and evil! O all dear to me!

lend themselves to these romantic speculations, but as a whole the diction is trite and sentimental, in the "Carry me back to Old Virginny" tradition. The poet sings of the "trees where I was born" and the rivers in Florida, Georgia, and Carolina—which he never saw, so far as we know—and ends like a popular song-writer with, "O I will go back to old Tennessee, and never wander more!"

The remainder of the third edition is fragmentary, though it contains one more large group, "Messenger Leaves," and several smaller and even less-developed groups, such as "Thoughts" and "Says." "Messenger Leaves" has no well-defined theme, though the Messiah-rôle is prominent in several poems, such as "To Him That was Crucified," "To One Shortly to Die," "To a Common Prostitute," and "To Rich Givers."

The final poems in the book show that Whitman was working toward an arrangement to suggest an allegory of his life as a poet. Near the end we find "To Think of Time" (1855), now renamed "Burial," and this is followed by "To My Soul" (in the 1871 edition renamed "As the Time Draws Nigh" and used to introduce a new section called "Songs of Parting"). In this poem a premonition of death seems to be tremendously strong, thus emphasizing the themes of both the sea-side and "Calamus" poems of 1860. The final poem, "So long!," which was hereafter to remain the valedictory of all editions through the final arrangement in 1881, has a double farewell meaning, serving both as an *au revoir* and an *adieu*. The poet concludes his message, anticipates the end of his life, and prophesies his influence on the "plentiful athletic bards" and the "superb persons" which *Leaves of Grass* is intended to generate. With a parting kiss and a "so long!" he writes his final lines:

> Remember my words—I love you—I depart from
>   materials,
> I am as one disembodied, triumphant, dead.

The first edition of this *Handbook* stated in 1946: "Of all editions of *Leaves of Grass* before the final arrangement of the poems in 1881, the third gives us the clearest insight into Walt Whitman's growth as a poet." In making this statement, the author was influenced by Frederik Schyberg, who was the first to discover (1933) the importance of the third edition. Since then Schyberg's view has been confirmed in American scholarship, aided considerably by the edition of the transitional manuscripts by Bowers, and by a facsimile of the third edition by Roy Harvey Pearce.[90] In his Introduction Pearce says that "the 1860 *Leaves of Grass* is an articulated whole, with an argument. The argument is that of the poet's life as it furnishes a beginning, middle, and end to an account of his vocation." [xxv-xxvi]

The bulk of the new poems shows that this volume is the product of Whitman's most creative period, which included "Out of the Cradle Endlessly Rocking," admired by most critics, but not all.[91] Stephen E. Whicher, one of the admirers, says it shows that "the outsetting bard of love will be the bard of unsatisfied love because there is no other kind [for him]."[92] Pearce regards it as "a turning point" in Whitman's development as a poet; moreover "the earlier version, set in its earlier context [the third edition], is even greater than the later [1871]."[93]

The two most prominent themes of the third edition, love and death, appeared in the first and second editions, but in the third they take on such overwhelmingly tragic significance that we perceive Walt Whitman, in his tormented struggle to reconcile them, becoming a major poet—Pearce says inventing "modern poetry," discovering "the poet's vocation in the modern world."[94]

Yet at times in the third edition Whitman seems almost ready to give up the struggle and renounce his ambition to be the poet of his age and country. In his final invocation in "So long!" he has a premonition either that death is near or that this may be the last act of his poetic drama. This mood of tragic foreboding gives to the 1860 edition an intensity, a sincerity, and a tenderness lacking in the 1855 and 1856 editions. Indeed, in spite of the evidence that Whitman was growing in creative imagination and lyric skill, this might have been the last publication of his poems had not the national crisis in 1861 rescued him from his morbid obsession with his own inner problems. He was destined, like Faust in Goethe's fable, to find happiness in service to his country—in extroverted, but compassionate, activity.

ABORTED EDITIONS

In the summer of 1860 Whitman's publishing prospects seemed the brightest they had ever been. Thayer & Eldridge wrote him highly enthusiastic letters. Edwin Miller says, "On July 29, the partners conjectured that the second edition [meaning the second printing] would be exhausted within a month, and proposed a cheaper ($1) edition for the next printing as well as a slightly more expensive volume."[95] With this encouragement, Whitman began preparation of another volume of poems, and Thayer & Eldridge announced it in an advertisement in the abolitionist newspaper the *Liberator* early in November.[96] The title was to be *Banner at Day-Break*, and would contain, besides the title poem, "Washington's First Battle," "Errand Bearers," "Pictures," "Quadrel" ("Chanting the Square Deific"), "The Ox-Tamer," "Poemet," "Mannahatta," "Sonnets," and enough poems to make a book of about one hundred and fifty pages.

This book was never published because Thayer & Eldridge began to fail in the autumn of 1860, and went bankrupt in December. Apparently the new issue of *Leaves of Grass* (paperback and deluxe) was aborted also. Several of the announced poems were later published in *Drum-Taps*,[97] which would be annexed to the 1867 edition of *Leaves of Grass*. But only two of these poems are of significance. "The Errand-Bearers" was published in the New York *Times* on June 27, 1860, in commemoration of a parade on Broadway June 16, in honor of the Japanese ambassadors who had come to the United States to negotiate a treaty. Though not one of Whitman's best poems, it envisions a cultural marriage of Orient and Occident, and anticipates the 1871 "Passage to India." "Quadrel" became "Chanting the Square Deific" in *Drum-Taps*, though it was written (or begun) in 1860, and had no connection with the Civil War (see discussion below under *Drum-Taps*).

In preparation for a new edition of *Leaves of Grass* Whitman wrote rough drafts of a prose introduction and began revising the 1860 edition. One introduction, dated May 31, 1861, his forty-second birthday (he liked to reassess and rededicate his life as a poet on his anniversaries), declared: "So far, so well, but the most and the best of the Poem [*Leave of Grass*] I perceive remains unwritten, and is the work of my life yet to be done."[98] Going even further, he confessed, "The paths to the house are made—but where is the house itself?" This was partly a plea to the reader to help him finish his task, and partly the acceptance of a theory which was growing on him that all a poem could do, anyway, was to suggest—an anticipation of the later movement call "Symbolism."[99]

Dear friend! not here for you, melodious narratives, no pictures here, for you to con at leisure, as bright creations all outside yourself. But of SUGGESTIVENESS, with new centripetal reference out of the miracles of every day, this is the song—naught made complete by me for you, but only hinted to be made by you by robust exercise. I have not done the work and cannot do it. But you must do the work and make what is within the following song.[100]

In another introduction he claims to have "felt every thing from an American point of view," but insists that "America to me, includes humanity and is the universal."[101] He is trying, apparently, to generalize and universalize his book, "giving up all my private interior musings, yearnings, extasies and contradictory moods . . . "[102] He now sees his basic themes as "sacredness of the individual," Love fusing and combining "the whole," and the "idea" of "Religion." In another manuscript in this packet Whitman attempted an "Inscription/ To the Reader/ at the Entrance of Leaves of Grass" in prose,[103] a preliminary and prolix version of the poem "Inscription" eventually used to introduce the 1867 edition. By the time Whitman was finally able to get out a fourth edition, he wisely abandoned all these didactic and confusing introductions, except for the "Inscription" in verse form. Their literary value is low, but their biographical value is considerable, for they show Whitman unaware of his great achievement in his 1860 edition and now trying to impersonalize and universalize it. The poems are to depict an archetypal *great person*, "a large, sane, perfect Human Being or character for an American man and for woman."[104] Even in the third edition, as in "Proto-Leaf" and the "Calamus" poems, the lyric poet began to wage a losing battle with the didactic poet, but in 1860, as Pearce has observed, Whitman definitely "moved away from the mode of archetypal autobiography toward that of prophecy."[105] Fortunately for Whitman (as a poet) the Civil War diverted him for a few years from the plans glimpsed in these manuscript introductions.

During the Civil War period, however, Whitman did not forget his ambition to publish a revised and enlarged *Leaves of Grass*. In a copy of the 1860 edition, which he called his "Blue Book" because he had bound it in a blue wrapper, he studiously made emendations, outlines, and plans for his next edition.[106] It has now been definitively edited by Arthur Golden in two volumes, one a facsimile (so faithful that even the paste-ins have been reproduced and inserted exactly where Whitman attached them), and another volume of textual analysis, with an informative Introduction.[107]

Only a few of Whitman's revisions in the Blue Book are dated, and these are labeled 1864, 1865, and one 1866. It is known, however, that he began these revisions before he went to Washington in late 1862, leaving the Blue Book and other manuscripts (including his earliest *Drum-Taps* poems) with his mother in Brooklyn. In November he recovered these items on a visit to Brooklyn. In December 1864 and the following January he went through the poems again, marking some for deletion and others to be retained in revised form. For example, for "Chant Democratic" No. 3, after having previously written "? take this out and alter it and verify for future volume," he decided on Dec. 7, 1864, "This is satisfactory as it now is." He had changed the title to "Song of Occupatons" (retained in subsequent editions). In January 1865 (no day of month given) he also found "A Word Out of the Sea" satisfactory, except for changing "A" to "The," which he changed back to "A" in 1867. He had made extensive revisions in the text, but had not yet discovered the symbolic rhythm of his first line simply by changing it from "Out of the rocked cradle," to "Out of the cradle endlessly rocking . . ."

The Blue Book has special significance in Whitman's biography because this was the copy of *Leaves of Grass* which Secretary James Harlan surreptitiously examined and decided that its disreputable author should be discharged from his clerkship in the Department of the Interior. This sequence of events caused some biographers to deduce that Whitman's "toning down" some of his grosser sex references had called Harlan's attention to them. However, the present author decided in *The Solitary Singer* that Whitman was not eliminating such passages, but simply attempting literary improvements, which sometimes resulted in stronger emphasis on sex rather than less, and Arthur Golden has authoritatively confirmed this observation. [108] One example of this kind (though not exclusively sexual) is "Calamus" No. 18, which began innocuously in 1860, "City of my walks and joys!" Whitman revised the line to read, "City of orgies . . .!"

What Whitman did de-emphasize in his Blue Book revisions was the personal despair in some of his 1860 poems. He cancelled, or marked "Out for revision," the "Calamus" poems numbered 8, 9, 12, 16, and 44, though retaining No. 7, "Of the Terrible Doubt of Appearances." Nos. 8 and 9, "Long I Thought that Knowledge Alone Would Suffice" and "Hours Continuing Long . . ." would be dropped in 1867, but No. 12, a warning to the new person drawn to him ("Are You . . ."), which Whitman marked in the Blue Book "Out without fail" would actually be retained in '67. The relation of the Blue Book to the 1867 edition is similar, therefore, to the relation of the manuscripts edited by Bowers to the 1860 edition.

Most of Whitman's Blue Book revisions were improvements in diction, rhythm, and the elimination of repetition. "Apostroph," which introduced the 1860 "Chants Democratic," was eliminated completely, and finally. The inept first line of "Chants Democratic" No. 20, "American mouth-songs" became the melodious "I hear America singing, the varied songs I hear, . . ." The imagery and rhythm of this line-title would cause this poem to be set to music by several composers in the twentieth century, be sung often in concerts, and recorded on discs and tapes.

But not all of Whitman's brilliant improvements would be used in 1867. A curious example is "Elemental Drifts" (No. 1 in the 1860 "Leaves of Grass" cluster), in which in the Blue Book he cancelled the first line and started with "As I walked where the sea-ripples wash you, Paumanok," and shifted his best line, "As I ebb'd with the ocean of life" to follow his third verse. Not until 1881 would Whitman discover his lucky first line and title in "As I ebb'd . . ." "Sleep Chasings" would also have to wait until 1871 to become "The Sleepers."

In revising the Blue Book at the time of his emotional experiences during the war, Whitman inserted references to them, even in the 1855 "Song of Myself" (still called "Walt Whitman"). In stanza 19 (1860 text) after "The sickness of one of my folks, or of myself, or ill-doing, or loss of money, or depressions or exaltations," he interpolated "Battles, the horrors of fratricidal war, the fever of doubtful news, the fitful events, . . ." As Golden has observed, the addition was inappropriate, but another three-line insertion added to stanza 341, depicting "a variety of closely personal experiences,"[109] does harmonize with the tone of the passage:

The soldier camp'd, or in battle, on the march is mine;

On the night ere the pending battle many seek me, & I do not fail
  them
On that solemn night, (it may be the last,) those that know me seek
  me. . . .

Thus the Blue Book gives insights into both the emotional life of
Walt Whitman during his composition of *Drum-Taps* and the preparation of the fourth edition of *Leaves of Grass*. In his Introduction
Golden points out the progression from Whitman's extreme nationalism during the war years to his more characteristic tolerance in the
later editions of *Leaves of Grass*.

DRUM-TAPS, 1865

In "A Backward Glance O'er Travel'd Roads," the preface to
November Boughs (1888), Walt Whitman estimated the influence of
the Civil War on his life and works:

I went down to the war fields in Virginia (end of 1862), lived thence-
forward in camp—saw great battles and the days and nights
afterward—partook of all the fluctuations, gloom, despair, hopes
again arous'd, courage evoked—death readily risk'd—*the cause*, too—
along and filling those agonistic and lurid following years, 1863-'64-
'65—the real parturition years (more than 1776-'83) of this henceforth homogeneous Union. Without those three or four years and the
experiences they gave, "Leaves of Grass" would not now be
existing.[14]

Precisely what Whitman meant by the last sentence it is difficult
to say, though if he referred to *Leaves of Grass* in the 1881 or 1888
editions, he was no doubt speaking accurately. As we have already
noticed, he closed the 1860 edition as if he expected it to be his last,
and the tone of the poems of that period supports this conclusion.
Furthermore, all biographers agree that Whitman's war experiences
were of great importance. Charles I. Glicksberg states that, "The
influence of the Civil War on his work can . . . hardly be exaggerated.
It was for Whitman a national crisis, a living epic, a creative
force."[110] Schyberg adds that the poet who declared in 1855,

Behold I do not give lectures or a little charity,
What I give I give out of myself.

was through his wound-dressing services successful in actually realizing his ideal.[111]

After the war finally ended, and the Union had been preserved, Whitman published in New York in 1865 a seventy-two page pamphlet of a collection of poems entitled *Drum-Taps*, to which he presently added a *Sequel: When Lilacs Last in the Door-Yard Bloom'd and Other Poems*, Washington, 1865-6, of twenty-four more pages. These two publications, usually known as *Drum-Taps* and *Sequel to Drum-Taps*, were added to the 1867 edition of *Leaves of Grass* as annexes, but in 1871-2 were incorporated into the main body of the *Leaves*.

Drum-Taps contains 53 poems, all new.[112] The emotions generated by the out-break of the war, the horrifying shock of the Confederate victory at Bull Run, and later Whitman's first-hand observations at the front in Virginia and in the war hospitals of Washington—all these experiences found expression in these poems, and gave them a greater unity and coherence than is to be found in his works of any other period. Not all of *Drum-Taps*, however, was written in the same place or near the same time. A large number seem to have been composed in Brooklyn between the attack on Fort Sumter in April 1861 and Whitman's leaving home in December 1862 to search for his wounded brother in Virginia. Walt left the manuscript with his mother and he mentions it in his letters to her, cautioning her to take good care of it.[113]

We have no way of knowing precisely which were the poems in this manuscript, but a number of the poems obviously reflect the "shock electric" felt in the metropolis at the first war news and the surge of patriotic fervor which followed. In the initial poem, untitled but beginning, "First, O songs, for a prelude!" we feel this nervous enthusiasm: "It's O for a manly life in the camp!" "Beat! Beat! Drums!" and "City of Ships" catch the excitement of parades and marching feet. The poem called "1861" states that the poet for the "arm'd year . . . of struggle" must be "a strong man, erect, clothed in blue clothes, advancing, carrying a rifle on your shoulder." Perhaps Whitman is thinking of enlisting. At any rate, the war is still adventurous—and remote.

Then there are other poems which, whether or not they were written after Whitman's visit to the front, at least show a sympathetic understanding of the life of camp and battle field. Among these are "By the Bivouac's Fitful Flame"—solemn, thoughtful, a little homesick—,"Vigil Strange I Kept on the Field One Night," "A Sight in Camp in the Day-Break Dim and Grey," and "A March in the Ranks Hard-Prest, and the Road Unknown." They sound authentic. They do not glorify war or the cause. In fact, they are forerunners of realism and give us the impression that the poet is not writing from theory or standing aloof from the conflict.

Not all poems in *Drum-Taps* are directly about the war, though even when Whitman treats other themes we can see the impact of the national crisis upon his thinking and feeling. For example, "Shut Not Your Doors to Me Proud Libraries" is an obvious war poem in *Drum-Taps* but later Whitman revised and transferred it to "Inscriptions," where it is a general plea for acceptance of *Leaves of Grass*; but in the 1867 version of the poem the poet thinks he has a patriotic service to render through his songs. In "From Paumanok Starting I Fly Like a Bird" we have an interesting example of the patriotic application of an idea from the program-poem "Proto-Leaf" ("Starting From Paumanok"); the preservation of the Union fits easily into Whitman's whole poetic program since 1855.

Apparently this grave period left its imprint upon every subject that Whitman attempted to handle during this time. In 1861 he was engaged in writing a series of antiquarian articles about Brooklyn. But as he wrote about the past, he kept finding reminders of the present emergency. For example, Washington Park in Brooklyn inspires "The Centenarian's Story." And his pleasant rambles on Long Island must be given up for "the duration." In "Give Me the Splendid Silent Sun" he renounces the sun, the woods, and Nature for people who are aroused by the passions of war. Similarly, in "Rise O Days from Your Fathomless Deeps" he has "lived to behold man burst forth, and warlike America Rise:"

Hence I will seek no more the food of the northern
  solitary wilds,
No more on the mountains roam, or sail the stormy sea.

In subject-matter and imagery "Pioneers! O Pioneers!" seems remote enough from the fratricidal war of the 60s. The theme is somewhat patriotic, since it celebrates "pioneers," and of course the word suggests the great American migration; but Whitman uses it especially for the marching army of civilization—a theme that always fascinated him. What specifically distinguishes this composition as originally a *Drum-Taps* poem (it was later shifted to "Birds of Passage") is the trochaic meter and almost conventional stanza pattern. It is a marching poem. Under the strong emotional stress of a country engaged in deadly combat, Whitman's rhythms become more regular. That is true of nearly all the poems in this collection. The fact that they are less philosophical and introspective, more concerned with some definite experience or exact spot, and with the simple emotions of courage, loyalty, or pity may account to some extent for their being briefer, more unified, and nearer conventional patterns. Perhaps they were written more hastily, "on the spot," than the earlier poems. Some critics have thought them artistically inferior to the earlier work, and no doubt the greater regularity of form is inconsistent with Whitman's literary theory; but it is also interesting to find him so absorbed in external events, and so dedicating himself to a worthy cause that for the time he can forget himself and his theory.

One of the most puzzling poems in the original *Drum-Taps* is "Out of the Rolling Ocean, the Crowd," which seems to be a perfect description of Whitman's meeting his English adorer, Mrs. Gilchrist— but the poem was published several years before he even knew of her existence, and long before her visit to America.[114] At any rate, except for the date of composition the poem does not belong in *Drum-Taps* (unless some unknown love affair in the poet's life took place during the war, and there is no other evidence in *Drum-Taps*); in the next edition it was shifted to "Children of Adam"—though the sentiment and imagery are nearer "Calamus."

Death is no less prominent in *Drum-Taps* than in the third edition of *Leaves of Grass* but the treatment is neither morbid nor romantic, as in the Novalis-like blend in "Out of the Cradle." "Come up from the Fields, Father" cannot be autobiographical, but it accurately conveys the meaning of a soldier's death to his family back home. And toward the end of the collection we get a close-up view of death, as Whitman himself finally observed it, in "Camps of Green" (later shifted to "Songs of Parting"), "As Toilsome I Wander'd Virginia's Woods," "Hymn of Dead Soldiers," and others.

Though no poet could be more deeply moved by the sight of a fallen comrade or the grave of an unknown soldier than Walt Whitman, these experiences did not embitter or disillusion him but aroused his great motherly compassion, which embraced the stricken of both armies and found a prophetic reconciliation in his poems. His

"Calamus" love found an outlet in his activities as a "wound-dresser" (Cf. "The Dresser," later renamed "The Wound-Dresser").

The hurt and the wounded I pacify with soothing hand,
I sit by the restless all the dark night—some are so young;
Some suffer so much—I recall the experience sweet and sad;
(Many a soldier's loving arms about this neck have cross'd and rested,
Many a soldier's kiss dwells on these bearded lips.)

In 1881 Whitman added three lines to this poem which significantly interpret the *Drum-Taps* collection:

(Arous'd and angry, I'd thought to beat the alarum, and urge relent-
less war,
But soon my fingers fail'd me, my face droop'd and I resign'd myself,
To sit by the wounded and soothe them, or silently watch the dead;) . . .

This all-embracing sympathy enabled Whitman to affirm in "Over the Carnage Rose Prophetic a Voice" that "Affection shall solve the problems of Freedom yet." This is a new and sublimated "Calamus" poem. In "Years of the Unperform'd" ("Years of the Modern") he envisions, in the spirit of his earliest poems, "the solidarity of races," and in "Weave in, Weave in, My Hardy Life" (later shifted to "From Noon to Starry Night") he uses the imagery of war to describe "the campaigns of peace." But the complete catharsis for the war-tragedy is Nature's dirge, "Pensive on Her Dead Gazing, I Heard the Mother of All."

Pensive, on her dead gazing, I heard the Mother of All,
Desperate, on the torn bodies, on the forms covering the battle-fields gazing;
As she call'd to her earth with mournful voice while she stalk'd;
Absorb them well, O my earth, she cried—I charge you, lose not my sons! lose not an atom;

.   .   .   .   .

Exhale me them centuries hence—breathe me their breath—let not an atom be lost;
O years and graves! O air and soil! O my dead, an aroma sweet!
Exhale them perennial, sweet death, years, centuries hence.

The poet has now covered the whole gamut of his own and his country's war emotions, from beating the drums for the first volunteers to burying the dead, and he ends with an epilogue in which he states his final claim for these poems ("Not Youth Pertains to Me"):

I have nourish'd the wounded, and sooth'd many a
    dying soldier;
And at intervals I have strung together a few songs,
Fit for war, and the life of the camp.

Although *Drum-Taps* was issued as a separate publication, the *Sequel* may be thought of as part of the same work. In the first place, it was soon combined in a second issue of *Drum-Taps*. Wells and Goldsmith state in their *Concise Bibliography of Walt Whitman* that, "A few copies were issued containing 'Drum Taps' only. On the death of Lincoln, Whitman held up the edition and added 'When Lilacs Last in the Dooryard Bloom'd,' with separate title-page and pagination."[115] Moreover, the *Sequel* is a continuation of *Drum-Taps* in other and more intrinsic ways. For one thing, many poems were shifted from the *Sequel* to the final (1881) text of *Drum-Taps*, such as "Spirit Whose Work is Done," "As I Lay with my Head in Your Lap, Camerado," "Dirge for Two Veterans," "Lo! Victress on the Peaks!," and "Reconciliation." The first of these is an invocation to the spirit of war to inspire the poet's martial songs; the second is a remotivated "Calamus" sentiment, though not a love poem; and the last continues the theme of reconciliation begun in *Drum-Taps*—". . . my enemy is dead, a man divine as myself is dead."

If "Chanting the Square Deific" has any special significance in this collection, it is difficult to perceive. As an epitome of Whitman's eclectic religion, clearly announced in "Song of Myself" and "Proto-Leaf" and alluded to elsewhere, it is a poem of considerable importance; but in tone it has much of the arrogance of the second edition, and as Sixbey has shown,[116] the ideas had been crystalizing for ten years. Possibly, as Sixbey has also mentioned, Whitman's deification of the spirit of rebelliousness may have been influenced by the rebellion against the Union.[117] At any rate, Whitman's earlier indignation had now given way to conciliating sympathy and forgiveness. Possibly also this spirit may have influenced the expression of the side of the "Consolator most mild," especially the following one line deleted in 1881:

(Conquerer yet—for before me all the armies and soldiers of the earth
  shall yet bow—and all the weapons of war become impotent:)
  . . .

But the main poems in the *Sequel*, for which Whitman stopped
the press, were the Lincoln elegies, later grouped as "Memories of
President Lincoln." The first of these, "When Lilacs Last in the
Dooryard Bloom'd," is widely admitted to be a masterpiece. In
structure it resembles the other great poem on death, "Out of the
Cradle Endlessly Rocking," especially in the use of the bird song. But
his use of symbols, the "Lilac blooming perennial and the drooping
star in the west," and the song of the thrush, are handled with a skill
found nowhere else in *Leaves of Grass*. The lilac with the "heart-
shaped leaves" of love, the hermit thrush singing his "song of the
bleeding heart," the resurrection of the "yellow-spear'd wheat" in
the spring, the coffin journeying night and day through the Union
that Lincoln had preseved—these are interwoven in a mighty symphony of imagery and sound, each theme briefly advanced, then
developed in turn, finally summarized in a climax (first part of sec.
16) and then repeated gently once more in a coda as the "sweetest,
wisest soul of all my days and lands" comes to rest,

> There in the fragrant pines, and the cedars dusk and
> dim.

Not since the third edition, in which love and death were so
inseparably intertwined, had Whitman used sea imagery in any striking manner. Perhaps this may have been because he had, as he said,
renounced his pleasant contacts with nature for the duration of the
war, or it may have been because in Washington he had little time for
the seashore. A better explanation, however, is that *Drum-Taps* is less
subjective and introspective than "Calamus" or "Out of the Cradle"
and "As I Ebb'd with the Ocean of Life." Whatever spiritual and
emotional crisis Whitman had passed through, the wound-dressing
preoccupations had been psychologically beneficial. Now once more,
when he is stirred to the depths of his being by the tragic death of
Lincoln, sea imagery comes back to him, and the word that the
ocean whispers is the same: "lovely and soothing Death" undulating
"round the world." But the "Dark Mother, always gliding near, with
soft feet," brings redemption and delivery, not chaos and despair.

Approach, encompassing death—strong Deliveress!
When it is so—when thou hast taken them, I joyously sing the dead,
Lost in the loving, floating ocean of thee,
Laved in the flood of thy bliss, O Death.[sec. 14]

In this great elegy Walt Whitman attained a spiritual poise and emotional tranquility that was never again wholly to leave him—except possibly for one brief period (see "Prayer of Columbus," 1874).

After the lilac poem, the other verses in the *Sequel to Drum-Taps* are an anti-climax. "O Captain! My Captain!," in syncopated iambic metre and regular stanzaic pattern, is similar to the beating of the drums in *Drum-Taps*. The music is more like Poe than Whitman, and Whitman himself later became sick of it. True, it has been his most popular poem, but it is almost impossible to appreciate it soon after reading the lilac symphony.

The original *Sequel* ends with a prophecy in "To the Leaven'd Soil They Trod," which remained largely unfulfilled,

The Northern ice and rain, that began me, nourish me to the end;
But the hot sun of the South is to ripen my songs.

The poet felt deeply this wish to reconcile the North and the South through his songs, and it is an appropriate application of his earliest poetic program, but except in a remote symbolical sense the wish was never realized. Walt Whitman was, however, soon to become a more truly *national* poet.

FOURTH EDITION, 1867

The 1867 *Leaves of Grass* might be called "The Workshop Edition," for the revisions indicate great critical activity, although in organization it is the most chaotic of all the editions. Exclusive of the annexes (two of which have been discussed above under *Drum-Taps*), this edition contains only six new poems,[118] all short and of minor significance. What makes it important is Whitman's great exertion to rework the book by deletion, emendation, and rearrangement of the poems. The confused state of the published work, therefore, bears testimony to the poet's literary and spiritual life during the War.

The manner of publication is no less confused than the contents.

The book was printed for Whitman (whose name appears only in the copyright date, 1866),[119] by a New York printer, William E. Chapin, and was bound and distributed during the year in at least four different forms: (1) *Leaves of Grass* 338 pp.; (2) *Leaves of Grass* with *Drum-Taps* (72 pp.) and *Sequel to Drum-Taps* (24 pp.); (3) *Leaves of Grass* with *Drum-Taps, Sequel to Drum-Taps*, and *Songs Before Parting* (36 pp.). Wells and Goldsmith say: "This edition was crude and poorly put together. [The copies] were probably bound up in small lots as sold. This may account for the many variations."[120]

The first poem in this edition, one of the new compositions, is "Inscription" ("One's-Self I Sing"), which was henceforth to stand as the opening poem in all subsequent editions. "Inscription" outlines the main subjects of the collection of the *Leaves* and gives a suggestion of their order. These subjects are: (1) "one's-self," or individualism; (2) "Man's physiology complete from top to toe"; (3) "the word of the modern . . . En-Masse";[121] (4) "My days I sing, and the Lands—with interstice I knew of hapless war"; (5) finally a personal appeal to the reader to journey with the poet. These subjects correspond roughly to (1) the personal poems, "Starting from Paumanok" and "Walt Whitman" ("Song of Myself"); (2) the physiological "Children of Adam" poems, which now follow "Walt Whitman"; (3) the consciousness of social-solidarity and world-citizenship of all humanity found both in "Calamus" and the succeeding major poems, such as "Salut au Monde!" and "Song of the Broad-Axe"; (4) the war-experiences in the annex *Drum-Taps*; and (5) the final appeal to the reader in "So long!," which now stands at the end of the last annex, "Songs Before Parting," where it would remain. So well did Whitman like the scheme outlined in this prologue that he finally expanded it to twenty-four "Inscriptions"—though few of the poems were written specifically for this purpose, most of them having been used first in various other groups. But in the 1867 "Inscription" we have a skeleton plan of the final *Leaves of Grass*, a revelation of the emerging purposes and the congealing form.

The extent to which Whitman revised his work for the fourth edition is obvious in the first poem after the "Inscription," which is now called "Starting from Paumanok"—originally "Proto-Leaf" in the third edition, where it also served as an introduction. Nearly every section contains some revisions, but the first illustrates the nature, general purpose, and extent of the changes. "Proto-Leaf" began:

Free, fresh, savage,
Fluent, luxuriant, self-content, fond of persons and
    places,
Fond of fish-shape Paumanok, where I was born,
Fond of the sea—lusty-begotten and various,
Boy of the Mannahatta, the city of ships, my city,
Or raised inland, or of the south savannas,
Or full-breath'd on Californian air, or Texan or Cuban air,
Tallying, vocalizing all—resounding Niagara—resounding Missouri,
Or rude in my home in Kanuck woods,
Or wandering and hunting, my drink water, my diet
    meat,

            .   .   .   .   .

Aware of the mocking-bird of the wilds at daybreak,
Solitary, singing in the west, I strike up for a new
    world.

This becomes:

Starting from fish-shape Paumanok, where I was born,
Well-begotten, and rais'd by a perfect mother;
After roaming many lands—lover of populous pavements;
Dweller in Mannahatta, city of ships, my city—or on southern
    savannas;
Or a soldier camp'd, or carrying my knapsack and gun—or a miner in
    California;
Or rude in my home in Dakotah's woods, my diet meat, my drink
    from the spring;

            .   .   .   .   .

Having studied the mocking-bird's tones, and the mountain hawk's,
And heard at dusk the unrival'd one, the hermit thrush from the
    swamp-cedars,
Solitary, singing in the West, I strike up for a New World.

Aside from the improvements in diction and rhythm, and the
beginning of the mannerism of writing past participles with 'd, in the
new version the poet attempts to give the impression that he has now
experienced what he expressed as poetic theory in 1860. The "Boy
of Mannahatta . . . raised inland, or of the south savannas . . ., Tallying, vocalizing all" on the basis of the '55 program, now extends his

rôle to "roaming many lands . . . Or a soldier camp'd . . . Or rude in my home in Dakotah's woods . . ." It is not a new rôle, rather the application of the "incarnating" doctrine of the first Preface, incorporating the poet's *Drum-Taps* experiences, his contact with frontiersmen (*i.e.*, soldiers from Dakota and other remote places), and his wider knowledge of America. The 1867 edition is thus an attempt to bring the poetic record up to date.

In this interim of revision Whitman tears apart most of the groups which he had started in 1860 but he has not yet had sufficient time to construct new groups. He demolishes "Chants Democratic," one of the major groups in the third edition, and redistributes the poems. The group previously called "Leaves of Grass" with twenty-four numbered poems, disappears as a unit, although five miscellaneous clusters (including one in the annex, *Songs Before Parting*) are given this ambiguous title. The only two clusters to remain more or less intact are "Children of Adam" (formerly called "Enfans d'Adam") and "Calamus." Of these two, the former has been changed least, though it is shifted from the center of the book toward the front—in accordance with the plan of the "Inscription."

"Calamus," however, needed considerable revision to bring it into line with Whitman's newest intentions. Perhaps the most disturbing reminder which he found of his 1860 mood was the three poems which he felt compelled to delete entirely, "Long I Thought that Knowledge Alone Would Suffice" (No. 8), "Hours Continuing Long, Sore, and Heavy-Hearted" (No. 9), and "Who is Now Reading This?" (No. 16). In 1867, having watched and even participated in the tragedies of the national struggle and found healing catharsis in the *Drum-Taps* experiences, Whitman blotted from the record these morbid confessions of the third edition.

"Calamus" poem No. 5 of 1860 provides another interesting example of the effect of Whitman's war experiences on his original "Calamus" program. In 1860 he had already socialized this program:

States!
Were you looking to be held together by the lawyers?
By an agreement on a paper? Or by arms?

Away!
I arrive, bringing these, beyond all the forces of courts and arms,
These! to hold you together as firmly as the earth itself is held
    together.

But he brashly wished to make his "manly affection" an evangelism associated with his own name:

There shall from me be a new friendship—It shall be called after my
    name,

    .   .   .   .   .

Affection shall solve every one of the problems of freedom,
Those who love each other shall be invincible,
They shall finally make America completely victorious, in my name.

Whitman never ceased believing that affection could solve all problems, but his personal desire for recognition became sublimated in his enlarged patriotism. In the 1867 edition a large part of this poem is rejected and the remainder is divided into two compositions, the first being one of the most musical of the new "Calamus" group, called "A Song," ("For You O Democracy"), with a stanzaic pattern and a repetend, and the second being a *Drum-Taps* poem, "Over the Carnage Rose Prophetic A Voice." Thus without renouncing his earlier doctrines of comradeship, Whitman now blends them with his new nationalism.

It would be a mistake, however, to conclude that the revised "Calamus" group is depersonalized. No. 10, called in '67 "Recorders Ages Hence," is a good illustration. In 1860 it began:

You bards of ages hence! when you refer to me, mind not so much
    my poems,
Nor speak of me that I prophesied of The States, and led them the
    way of their glories;
But come, I will take you down underneath this impassive exterior—I
    will tell you what to say of me:
Publish my name and hang up my picture as that of the tenderest
    lover, . . .

This becomes:

Recorders ages hence!
Come, I will take you down underneath this impassive exterior—I
    will tell you what to say of me;
Publish my name and hang up my picture as that of the tenderest
    lover, . . .

The poet believes in his Calamus-program as strongly as ever, but he is acutely aware that his prophecies of The States have not "led them the way of their glories."

Some of the revised "Calamus" poems are considerably more personal than the earlier versions, like No. 39, "Sometimes with One I Love," which originally ended:

Doubtless I could not have perceived the universe, or written one of
    my poems, if I had not freely given myself to comrades, to love.

This becomes:

(I loved a certain person ardently, and my love was not return'd;
Yet out of that, I have written these songs.)

The chief difference, therefore, between these two versions of "Calamus" is not a change in motive or conviction, but in tone and emphasis. The poet has carefully erased most of the record of morbidity and discouragement of 1860, along with the temporary whim to abandon his poet-prophet rôle for the rôle of tender lover.

Perhaps the only safe conclusion to draw from the five groups (counting the third annex) called "Leaves of Grass" in the fourth edition is that Whitman had evidently not decided yet what to do with these poems. Most of the poems appeared in the 1855, 1856, and 1860 editions and have merely been reshuffled. They are drawn from several previous groups and were later placed in various other groups. It is of some importance, however, that No. 20 ("So Far and So Far, and on Toward the End") of the third edition was dropped permanently in '67. In 1860 Whitman confessed in this poem that his poetic powers had "not yet fully risen," and that

Whether I shall attain my own height, to justify these [songs], yet
    unfinished,
Whether I shall make THE POEM OF THE NEW WORLD, trans-
    cending all others—depends, rich persons, upon you,

            .   .   .   .   .

And you, contemporary America.

In 1867 Whitman was almost as unrecognized by "contemporary

America" as in the depth of his discouragement seven years previous; but the poet of *Drum-Taps* and the *Sequel* had inner resources of courage and strength which he had not had before the War.

Some of the revised "Leaves" also reveal the poet's growth, both in art and mental poise. One of these is "On the Beach at Night Alone" ("Clef Poem" in 1856; "Leaves of Grass," No. 12, in 1860). The fifteen verses of the '67 version have a far greater unity than the thirty-four of 1856-60, and this is sufficient justification for the revision. But in the original version the emphasis is on the poet's personal and physical satisfaction with this life:

> This night I am happy;
>
> .   .   .   .   .   .
>
> What can the future bring me more than I have?

whereas in the 1867 text the central theme is the mystic intuition which comes to the poet "On the beach at night alone," that "A vast similitude interlocks all." The "similitude" section was also in the original composition, but it was preceded by seven stanzas of personal conviction that nothing in eternity can improve upon the goodness and completeness of the poet's present existence. This is not a doctrine which Whitman ever rejected, but in various periods he expressed it with different emphasis.

Since we have already discussed two of the annexes to this volume, *Drum-Taps* and the *Sequel*, which were attached to the fourth edition without revision, they need not be mentioned further here. But the third annex, *Songs Before Parting*, is a major attempt in reorientation and is, therefore, one of the most important sections of the book.

In this annex we have the beginning of a new and permanent group, *Songs of Parting*. But none of the poems were new in 1867, two of them being from 1856, "As I Sat Alone by Blue Ontario's Shore" and "Assurances," and eleven from 1860, of which five were from "Leaves of Grass" (Nos. 18, 19, 21, 22, and 23). In the fifth edition this group became the final section of *Leaves of Grass* where it remained (exclusive of annexes) throughout all future editions. But in 1871 the number of poems was pared to eight, of which only three were retained from 1867, and in the final version the number was increased to seventeen, including only four of the original group.

Thus about all that finally remained of *Songs Before Parting* was the symbolical name and the use of *So long!* as a half-personal, half-prophetic benediction.

The introductory and concluding poems in *Songs Before Parting* were extensively revised for this annex, and these changes probably reveal not only Walt Whitman's intentions in 1867 for the group but his broader purposes also. "As I Sat Alone by Blue Ontario's Shore" appeared first in the 1856 edition as "Poem of Many in One," in 1860 as No. 1 of "Chants Democratic" (the longest and perhaps the most ambitious group of the third edition), and was finally called "By Blue Ontario's Shore" in the last (1881) arrangement of the *Leaves*, where it is still one of the major poems.

The 1856-60 version of this poem is merely a poetic arrangement of the 1855 Preface, even retaining many of the same phrases and clauses. It begins with the motif of "A nation announcing itself," but the central theme is that of "the bard [who] walks in advance, the leader of leaders," teaching "the idea of perfect and free individuals, the idea of These States." In the 1867 version the whole composition has been greatly improved both in coherence and dramatic effect by the addition of an introduction, with the present shore motif, and a conclusion, changing the "Many in One" motif to the expanded vision of "the free Soul of poets," and of the "Bards" capable of singing "the great Idea" of Democracy, "the wondrous inventions . . . the marching armies," the times, the land, and the life of The States.

In 1867 Whitman developed one of the subordinated ideas of the 1856-60 poem,

Others take finish, but the Republic is ever constructive, and ever keeps vista, [sec. 8]

as the major theme—the throes of Democracy—now symbolized by the apostrophes to the "Mother" figure. To show how Whitman has amplified the call for "Bards" in "Poem of Many in One" into the new theme of Democracy in travail, the whole first section (all new) needs to be quoted:

As I sat alone, by blue Ontario's shore,
As I mused of these mighty days, and of peace return'd, and the dead that return no more,

A Phantom, gigantic, superb, with stern visage, accost'd me;
Chant me a poem, it said, of the range of the high Soul of Poets,
And chant of the welcome bards that breathe but my native air—
    invoke those bards;
And chant me, before you go, the Song of the throes of Democracy.

(Democracy—the destined conqueror—yet treacherous lip-smiles
    everywhere,
And Death and infidelity at every step.)

These parenthetical interpolations run like a contrapuntal theme
throughout the poem, exposing the danger to Mother-Democracy
and the Sister-States—as later in Democratic Vistas—, but also
indicating the hope and the means of political salvation:

    (O mother! O Sisters dear!
If we are lost, no victor else has destroy'd us;
It is by ourselves we go down to eternal night.)[sec. 2]

    .   .   .   .   .

    (Soul of love, and tongue of fire!
Eye to pierce the deepest deeps, and sweep the world!
—Ah, mother! prolific and full in all besides—yet how long barren,
    barren?)[sec. 9]

    .   .   .   .   .

(Mother! with subtle sense—with the naked sword in your hand,
I saw you at last refuse to treat but directly with individuals.)[sec.
    15]

    .   .   .   .   .

    (Mother! bend down, bend close to me your face!
I know not what these plots and deferments are for;
I know not fruition's success—but I know that through war and
    peace your work goes on, and must yet go on.) [sec. 20;18 in
    1881]

    The tragic war has been fought and the honor of the national
flag preserved ("Angry cloth I saw there leaping!"),[sec. 11] but it is
not to celebrate the past that the poet invokes the Muse:

O my rapt song, my charm—mock me not!

Not for the bards of the past—not to invoke them have I launch'd
   you forth, . . .
But, O strong soul of Poets,
Bards for my own land, ere I go, I invoke.[sec. 22]

   One of the unconscious ironies of this poem is that Whitman's
new call for native bards leads him into an excessive nationalism—
which he dropped when he revised the composition again for the
1881 edition. For example, the characteristic robust-health motif of
1856,

How dare a sick man, or an obedient man, write poems?
Which is the theory or book that is not diseased?

became in 1867:

America isolated I sing;
I say that works made here in the spirit of other lands, are so much
   poison to These States.

How dare these insects assume to write poems for America?
For our armies, and the offspring following the armies.[122] [sec.4]

If the "great Idea" was still largely unachieved in These States, why
would "works made . . . in the spirit of other lands" be worse poison
than the sinister forces already working here against Democracy?
Furthermore, these "isolationist" sentiments are oddly at variance
with the universal sympathy and cosmic themes of the poet's earlier
works, as he himself no doubt later realized. Possibly this inconsistency arose from the fact that in "As I Sat Alone by Blue Ontario's
Shore" Whitman was still groping his way toward the theory of
Democratic Vistas.
   In the final poem of "Songs Before Parting," the revised "So
long!" of the third edition, we find eliminated the tentative, discouraged tone of 1860, when the poet evidently despaired of
accomplishing his ambitious program of 1855. For example, in 1860
strophe 2 read:

I remember I said to myself at the winter-close, before my leaves
   sprang at all, that I would become a candid and unloosed
   summer-poet.

I said I would raise my voice jocund and strong, with reference to
consummations.

In 1867 this reads:

I remember I said, before my leaves sprang at all,
I would raise my voice jocund and strong, with reference to
consummations.

A number of lines have been dropped in which Whitman had claimed
to be not the Messiah but a John the Baptist preparing the way:

Yet not me, after all—let none be content with me,
I myself seek a man better than I am, or a woman better than I am,
I invite defiance, and to make myself superseded,
All I have done, I would cheerfully give to be trod under foot, if it
    might only be the soil of superior poems.[1860, sec. 4]
I have established nothing for good,
I have but established these things, till things farther onward shall be
    prepared to be established,
And I am myself the preparer of things farther onward.[1860, sec.
    5.]

In 1867 Walt Whitman no longer regards his poems either as failures
or as tentative experiments for which he must apologize. Through the
Drum-Taps years he had gained tremendously in poise and self-
confidence (real confidence instead of the bravado of 1855–1856),
and he now begins in earnest to prepare his book for posterity.

DEMOCRATIC VISTAS, 1871

Although in his youthful and journalistic days Walt Whitman
published a great deal more prose than poetry, it was not until 1871,
with the publication of *Democratic Vistas*,[123] that he made a serious
contribution to prose literature. Financially the book was no more
successful than the editions of *Leaves of Grass* had been, and even to
the present day Whitman has gained only a few admirers for his
prose, which always remained extremely loose, mannered, and improvised; but nothing else he ever wrote so clarifies and rounds out
both his literary and democratic theory as this essay.

Many of the ideas in *Democratic Vistas* were first expressed in the 1855 Preface, and touched upon in many poems, such as "Song of Myself," "Salut au Monde!," "Song for Occupations," and "Starting from Paumanok"—as indicated in the discussion of the fourth edition of *Leaves of Grass*—; but the immediate starting point of the essay seems to have been some short papers which Whitman published in *The Galaxy* in 1867 and 1868. The first of these, entitled "Democracy," was an attempt to answer Carlyle's attack on democracy in *Shooting Niagara*. But the more Whitman studied the problem, the more he came to agree with Carlyle's charges, though not with his whole condemnation. The second forerunner of *Democratic Vistas* was an essay on "Personalism," the central doctrine in the book, and a philosophical term which the American poet seems to have introduced into America. In writing these papers Whitman's thinking for the past fifteen or twenty years apparently came to a head and he felt the necessity of publishing a more complete treatment. It is interesting also that in doing so he was returning to a purpose which he had once dreamed of achieving through oratory, *i.e.*, leading his country through the eloquence of words.

This purpose is partly indicated by the word *Vistas*: "Far, far, indeed, stretch, in distance, our Vistas!"[124] He is writing more of the future of democracy than of its achievements to date, and makes a powerful homiletic appeal to his countrymen to turn their professed democratic ideals into reality.

Sole among nationalities, these States have assumed the task to put in forms of lasting power and practicality, on areas of amplitude rivaling the operations of the physical kosmos, the moral political speculations of ages, long, long deferr'd, the democratic republican principle, and the theory of development and perfection by voluntary standards, and self-reliance. [362]

But no one is more aware than Walt Whitman that these "moral [and] political speculations of ages" have not yet been honestly tried in America:

... society, in these States, is canker'd, crude, superstitious, and rotten ... Never was there, perhaps, more hollowness at heart than at present ... here in the United States ... The depravity of the business classes of our country is not less than has been supposed,

but infinitely greater . . . Our New World democracy . . . [despite] –
materialistic development . . . is, so far, an almost complete failure in
its social aspects . . . [369]

What kind of people make up the American nation? Looking
around him, Whitman observes almost everywhere low morals, poor
health, and bad manners. Here his dilemma is most acute, but he
attempts to solve it by an analysis of the mass vs. the individual. He
agrees that "man, viewed in the lump, displeases, and is a constant
puzzle and affront" to what he calls "the merely educated
classes."[376] Despite the fact, however, that the masses lack taste,
intelligence, and culture, the "cosmical, artist-mind" sees their
"measureless wealth of latent power." The war justified Whitman's
faith in the common man, for the "unnamed, unknown rank and
file" were responsible for the heroic courage, sacrifice, and "labor of
death," and these were "to all essential purposes, volunteer'd," even
in the face of "hopelessness, mismanagement, [and] defeat."[377]
     Whitman thinks that the function of government in a democracy
is often misunderstood. It is not merely "to repress disorder, &c. but
to develop, to open up to cultivation."[379] Democracy is not so
much a political system as a "grand experiment"[380] in the development of individuals. He is not concerned either with the romantic
theory of the innate goodness of the masses or with the political
theory of the sovereignty of the people, but with Democracy as a
moral and ethical ideal–in fact, a religion: "For I say at the core of
democracy, finally, is the religious element. All the religions, old and
new, are there."[381] He admits that he has had his doubts, especially "before the war" (around 1860?), and that "I have everywhere found, primarily thieves and scallawags arranging the
nominations to offices, and sometimes filling the offices themselves";
yet he still believes that, "Political democracy, as it exists and practically works in America, with all its threatening evils, supplies a
training-school for making first-class men."
     At this point Whitman reiterates, in a more specific context and
as the cornerstone of his democratic idealism, the literary theory
which he had advanced in the 1855 Preface, and continued to reword
in the versions of "By Blue Ontario's Shore." Although the American
people have, he still believes, a great potential capacity for democracy, their genius (or potentiality) is still unexpressed. There is as yet
no Democratic Literature to guide them; hence America's greatest

need is a new school of artists and writers. This call for native authors is subject to misunderstanding, and at times Whitman's own enthusiasm misleads him into an excessive patriotism; but in the larger implications, it is clear that his nationalism is a consequence and not the original motive of his plea for indigenous art. The function of literature is to unite the people with common social and ethical ideals and to establish a moral pattern for its citizens. Thus Whitman's nationalistic poets would combat the greatest enemy of These States, their own moral and, therefore, political corruption. Current literature and "culture" are rejected because they do not provide sufficient moral guidance for a democratic people.

Personalism[125] is the term which Whitman uses to cover his whole program, an all-round development of the self and the individual, including health, eugenics, education, cultivation of moral and social conscience, etc. He rejects institutionalized religion, but a genuine, personal religious life is of paramount importance. Personalism fuses all these developments, including participation in politics and removing the inequality of women. Since the future American democracy depends upon the development of great persons (or personalities) such as the world has never known before, literature and art must not be imitative or derivative of other times or nations, for none of them possessed or attempted to achieve the great American dream of a transcendent democracy.

Here Whitman's Calamus sentiments become completely socialized and emotionally reinforce his democratic idealism:

Many will say it is a dream, and will not follow my inferences: but I confidently expect a time when there will be seen, running like a half-hid warp through all the myriad audible and visible worldly interests of America, threads of manly friendship, fond and loving, pure and sweet, strong and life-long, carried to degrees hitherto unknown—not only giving tone to individual character, and making it unprecedentedly emotional, muscular, heroic, and refined, but having the deepest relations to general politics.[414]

This new democratic literature needs also the help of empiricism and modern science, even necessitating a "New World metaphysics."[417] True, science and materialism have further endangered American democracy by intensifying the greed for things and by "turning out . . . generations of humanity like uniform iron castings."[424] But by believing, like all romanticists, in the goodness and friendliness of Nature to man, Whitman thinks that further knowledge of the processes of cosmic melioration will aid mankind in conceiving and establishing a society of perfect equality and human development. Thus Whitman's democracy is finally idealistic and cosmic, and he believes that his social and literary ideals are predestined by the laws of the universe to triumph eventually.

FIFTH EDITION, 1871-72

As with the fourth edition of *Leaves of Grass*, the fifth is difficult to define satisfactorily. The first issue appeared in 1871, and contained 384 pages, but a second issue included "Passage to India" and 74 other poems, 24 of them new, adding 120 extra pages, numbered separately. In 1872 this edition was reissued, from Washington, D.C., dated 1872 on the title page but copyrighted 1870. All the latter copies contain "Passage to India," still with separate pagination, and a later issue includes as supplement "After All Not to Create Only," with 14 extra pages. One of the '72 issues may have been an English pirated edition.[126]

In the following discussion the fifth edition will be regarded as the 1871-72 *Leaves of Grass* (practically identical in all issues), plus the annex, *Passage to India*.[127]

At first glance this does not appear to be an especially important edition, for aside from the annexes it contains only thirteen new poems, all fairly short and individually of no great distinction. But this hasty impression is entirely misleading, for in the revisions and the new poems (including the *Passage to India* supplement) *Leaves of Grass* comes to a great climax, and probably what Walt Whitman intended to be the end of this book and the beginning of a new one, as the prefaces of 1872 and 1876 plainly indicate.

To begin at the first poem of the fifth edition, we notice that the "Inscription" of the fourth edition has now been increased to a whole section containing nine poems, though only two of them are new. Whitman is still trying to clarify the purposes and themes of the book by these prologue poems. "One's-Self I Sing" has become the permanent summary of the themes of *Leaves of Grass*, but the other inscriptions also indicate the nature of the 1871 version.

In 1867 the themes were the great national tragic conflict and the ensuing reconciliation. The war scenes and experiences were naturally still the poet's most vivid memories, though he had come through the tragedy spiritually purged and ennobled. Now the war years have retreated into the background, and both the poet and the nation are busy with reconstruction. In "As I Ponder'd in Silence" a phantom arises and tells the poet that all bards who have achieved a lasting reputation have sung of war. He replies that he too sings of war, the greatest of all, the eternal struggle of life and death. And as we shall see, in his new poems Whitman channels his war emotions and energies into new outlets.

The third "Inscription" (second new poem), "In Cabin'd Ships at Sea," is prophetic not only of the thought of the fifth edition but is also a radical departure from Whitman's former sea imagery. Heretofore, and especially in the great emotional poems of 1860, his imagination always returned to the seashore, where the fierce old mother incessantly moaned, whenever he was deeply moved by an experience or a memory. "Sea-Shore Memories" is an accurate title for the group of poems in the *Passage to India* supplement, which contains "Out of the Cradle" and "Elemental Drifts" ("As I Ebb'd, &c."). In 1871, however, we find the poet venturing beyond the shore, even embarking on ships and vicariously sailing the oceans. Why Walt Whitman was no longer shore-bound we can best decide after further examination of this edition.

But first let us complete the tour of the 1871 *Leaves*. The order of the main part of the book has now become settled, almost as in the final arrangement. After "Inscriptions" come the unclassified "Starting from Paumanok" and "Walt Whitman" (soon to become "Song of Myself"). These are followed by "Children of Adam" and "Calamus." The addition to the latter group of "The Base of All Metaphysics" makes further progress toward the sublimation and reinterpretation of the original personal confessions.

Yet underneath Socrates clearly see—and underneath Christ the
    divine I see,
The dear love of man for his comrade—the attraction of friend to
    friend, . . .

The "Calamus" sentiment is now so generalized that it is to be the foundation, as in *Democratic Vistas*, of a New World "metaphysics."

Drum-Taps, now in *Leaves of Grass* for the first time, has been considerably revised and many of the poems redistributed in sections called "Marches Now the War is Over" and "Bathed in War's Perfume." The title of "Songs of Insurrection" may possibly have been suggested by the war, but the contents are such early poems as "To a Foil'd European Revolutionaire" and "France, the 18th Year of

These States." The new grouping is merely an attempt to give these poems a context in the aftermath of the national struggle.[128]

The fact that in this edition Whitman feels the necessity of giving his poems a topical connotation is of considerable importance, for it offers further testimony that the war enabled him to enter more fully into the life of the nation and think less about himself than he did while writing and editing the 1860 edition. In fact, he is even becoming an "occasional" poet. For example, "Brother of All with Generous Hand" is a memorial to George Peabody, the philanthropist. "The Singer in Prison" records the concert of Parepa Rosa in Sing Sing Prison. Most of the remaining war poems are occasional in a general sense, like "A Carol of Harvest, for 1876" ("Return of the Heroes"), which is a memorial to the Civil War dead on the occasion of a harvest of peace and returning prosperity. (The most *occasional* of all, "Songs of the Exposition" and "Passage to India," will be considered later.)

The 1871 *Leaves of Grass*, exclusive of annexes, ends with the cluster called "Songs of Parting." On the surface there is nothing remarkable in this fact, for the poems are not new, and since 1860 Whitman has been ending his book with "So Long!" However, it rounds out *Leaves of Grass* in such a manner that we wonder if the poet is not planning to make this the last of all the editions. That this is his intention becomes clear during the next six years.

The best of all indications that Whitman was planning a major change in strategy is that nearly a third of his collected poems, including much of his best work, has been removed from *Leaves of Grass* proper and rearranged in *Passage to India*. It is significant that in planning a new collection Whitman did not start out with writing a new book, but began by writing an introductory poem and pulling out of his completed and published work enough pieces to fill out a 120-page pamphlet, which he would presently tack onto the *Leaves* as a supplement. This would be characteristic of his method through the remainder of his life.

The title poem in the supplement, "Passage to India," was occasioned by three events of the greatest international importance: the completion of the Suez Canal, connecting Europe and Asia by water; the finishing of the Union Pacific Railroad, spanning the North American continent; and the laying of the cable across the Atlantic Ocean, thus joining by canal, rail, and cable Europe, North America, and Asia. In celebrating these great scientific and material achievements, Whitman was at last fulfilling one of the announced intentions of his 1855 program: he was now giving expression to the times in which he lived. Thus "Passage to India" is the most important occasional poem in the 1871 edition.

But "Passage to India" is a great deal more than a poetic celebration of nineteenth-century engineering feats, though no other poet of the age seems to have so fully appreciated these materialistic achievements. Having always been fascinated by the history of the human race and its long upward journey through the cycles of evolution, Whitman now sees these events as symbols and spiritual prophecies.

> Lo, soul! seest thou not God's purpose from the first?
> The earth to be spann'd, connected by net-work,
> The people to become brothers and sisters,
> The races, neighbors, to marry and be given in marriage,
> The oceans to be cross'd, the distant brought near,
> The lands to be welded together.[sec. 3]

Once more, as in *Salut au Monde!*, the poet's cosmic vision returns to him:

> O, vast Rondure, swimming in space!
> Cover'd all over with visible power and beauty!

And with the lyric inspiration of his pre-war poems he sketches the history of the race,[sec. 6] saluting the restless soul of man, which has explored the continents and founded the civilizations. Returning to his old poetic conviction, Whitman announces once more that after the engineers, inventors, and scientists

> Finally shall come the Poet, worthy that name;
> The true Son of God shall come, singing his songs.[sec. 6]

All this is repetition in a new context of the poet's great dream of 1855–56, but here both the expression and the application of the theory take on the imagery and meaning of the fifth edition.

> We too take ship, O soul!
> Joyous, we too launch out on trackless seas! [sec. 11; 8 in 1881]

No longer does the poet search for the meaning of life and death in the sibilant waves that wash the shore of Paumanok. Fearlessly he and his soul set out on a voyage, singing their songs of God. Both the theme and mood have changed, for instead of questioning, now the poet affirms. And instead of addressing himself vaguely to "whoever you are up there," he now prays,

Bathe me, O God, in thee—mounting to thee,
I and my soul to range in range of thee.

O Thou transcendant!
Nameless—the fibre and the breath!
Light of the light—shedding forth universes—thou centre of them!
  [sec. 8]

Then comes the final development and culmination of the "Calamus" motif: "Waitest not haply for us, somewhere there, Comrade perfect?" First the love poems of 1860 developed into a search for lovers among the readers, then came the creation of an ideal "city of friends," which gradually became a social and patriotic program. Now the poet in his old age looks to God for perfect comradeship.

This is not to say, however, that in "Passage to India" Whitman's religion has become orthodox. Though his language and imagery have profoundly altered, his conception of death and immortality is as pantheistic as in 1855.

Swiftly I shrivel at the thought of God,
At Nature and its wonders, Time and Space and Death,
But that I, turning, call to thee O soul, thou actual Me,
And lo! thou gently masterest the orbs,
Thou matest Time, smilest content at Death,
And fillest, swellest full, the vastness of Space.[sec. 8]

His "soul" is "greater than stars or suns." He and his soul take "passage to more than India"; sounding "below the Sanscrit and the Vedas," they voyage to the shores of the "aged fierce enigmas," plunge to the "secret of the earth and sky," through "seas of God." In 1855-56 Death was a philosophical problem, in 1860 it was chaos and frustration, but now the concept and expectation have become joyous, personal liberation—though still pantheistic in intellectual context.

"Whispers of Heavenly Death," the title poem of a new cluster by this name, comes nearest to returning to the older imagery,

Labial gossip of night—sibilant chorals, . . .
Ripples of unseen rivers—tides of a current, flowing, forever flowing; . . .

But even this poem ends with calling death a "parturition" and an "immortal birth,"

Some Soul is passing over.

"Some Soul is passing over"—soaring, sailing, bidding the shore good-bye (cf. "Now Finale to the Shore"), such are the emotions of the *Passage to India* collection, which ends with "Joy, Shipmate, Joy!" The old poems here grouped as "Sea-Shore Memories" merely emphasize the contrast.

In the other great poem in this collection, "Proud Music of the Storm," we also find the same spiritual exaltation and emotional catharsis. It is not one of Whitman's most famous works, but no-where else did he use his characteristic symphonic structure with greater unity of effect or with richer symbolism. It is his only poem which is literally a symphony of sound, like Lanier's deliberate musical experiments.

The orchestration of the storm ranges through the elemental sounds of all creation and the music of humanity,

Blending, with Nature's rhythmus, all the tongues of nations, . . .

raising allegories with every blast, which it would be tedious to analyze here. It is a private performance, anyway, for the poet's own "Soul":

Come forward, O my Soul, and let the rest retire;
Listen—lose not—it is toward thee they tend;
Parting the midnight, entering my slumber-chamber,
For thee they sing and dance, O Soul. [sec. 2]

First comes a "festival song" of marriage, followed by the beating of war drums and the "shouts of a conquering army," but this gives way to "airs antique and medieval," and then by contrast "the great organ sounds,"

Bathing, supporting, merging all the rest—maternity of all the rest;
And with it every instrument in multitudes,
The players playing—all the world's musicians, . . .[sec. 5]

It is a symphony in which man, who has strayed from Nature like Adam from Paradise, returns,

The journey done, the Journeyman come home,
And Man and Art with Nature fused again.

Section 7 revives the theme of the 1855 "There was a Child Went Forth":

Ah, from a little child,
Thou knowest, Soul, how to me all sounds became music; . . .

But equally sweet to the poet are "All songs of current lands," and the vocalists whom he heard as a young man, best of all the "lustrous orb—Venus contralto," Alboni herself. In section 9 he lists his favorite operas, then passes on (10) to "the dance-music of all nations," Egypt, China, Hindu (11), and (12) Europe.

Finally the poet wakes from his trance, and tells his Soul that he has found the clue he sought so long. What the Soul has heard was not the music of nature or of other lands and times, but

. . . a new rhythmus fitted for thee,
Poems, bridging the way from Life to Death, vaguely wafted in night
     air, uncaught, unwritten,
Which, let us go forth in the bold day, and write.[sec. 15]

Here we have the significance of the supplement to the 1871 *Leaves of Grass*. At this time Walt Whitman plans to close his first life-book, his poems of "physiology from top to toe" and his songs of "Modern Man," described in the first "Inscription," and begin a new collection of "Poems bridging the way from Life to Death." "Proud Music of the Storm" announces the new intention and "Passage to India" was evidently planned to launch this new poetic voyage.

THE 1872 PREFACE

The poems in Whitman's two pamphlet publications of 1871 and '72, "After All, Not to Create Only" ("Song of the Exposition") and "As a Strong Bird on Pinions Free" ("Thou Mother with Thy Equal Brood"), are of distinctly minor importance. The fact that they were both written by invitation, the one for the 40th Annual Exhibition in New York City and the other to be read at the Dartmouth College commencement in 1872—and may therefore have been composed under forced inspiration—might explain their perfunctory tone. Both are poetic restatement of the nationalistic ideas in *Democratic Vistas*.

However, the Preface[129] which Whitman wrote for the latter pamphlet, *As a Strong Bird on Pinions Free*, is highly important in the history and growth of *Leaves of Grass* because in it the poet states unequivocally that he has brought the *Leaves* to an end and is starting a new book. He says, in words that need to be italicized, that his *"New World songs, and an epic of Democracy, having already had their published expression, as well as I can expect to give it, in LEAVES OF GRASS, the present and any future pieces from me are really but the surplusage forming after that Volume, or the wake eddying behind it."* The suspicion that the *Passage to India* supplement was intended to start a new book is here confirmed. In the same paragraph Whitman makes a further confession, no less revealing. He is not sure of his new literary intentions, and he is at least vaguely aware (perhaps subconsciously) that he has written himself out. Now in retrospect he feels sure that in *Leaves of Grass* he "fulfilled . . . an imperious conviction, and the commands of my nature as total and irresistible as those which make the sea flow, or the globe revolve." To what extent the "organic" metaphor may have influenced the exaggerated finality of this pronouncement, we cannot say; but never before had Whitman spoken with such finality of *Leaves of Grass*. As for the new project:

But of this Supplementary Volume, I confess I am not so certain. Having from early manhood abandoned the business pursuits and applications usual in my time and country, and obediently yielded my self up ever since to the impetus mentioned, and to the work of expressing those ideas, it may be that mere habit has got dominion of me, when there is no real need of saying anything further . . .

No doubt Whitman intended this comment to apply to the supposedly finished book, but the seven poems of this pamphlet, like the 1871 "Song of the Exposition," lack the fervor and conviction of the 1860's. They are the work of a poet who is tired, written out, and on the brink of physical collapse, for it was only a few months before he would be stricken down by paralysis, never entirely to recover.

Even the remainder of this Preface is simply a repetition of the nationalistic ideal which he had already expressed in *Democratic Vistas*:

Our America to-day I consider in many respects as but indeed a vast seething mass of *materials*, ampler, better, (worse also,) than previously known—eligible to be used to carry toward its crowning stage, and build for good the great Ideal Nationality of the future, the Nation of the Body and the Soul . . .

The finished book and the projected book are to be differentiated in this way:

LEAVES OF GRASS, already published, [*note!*] is, in its intentions, the song of a great composite *Democratic Individual*, male or female. And following on and amplifying the same purpose, I suppose I have in my mind to run through the chants of this Volume, (if ever completed,) the thread-voice, more or less audible, of an aggregated, inseparable, unprecedented, vast, composite, electric *Democratic Nationality*.

Notice the uncertainty: "I *suppose* I have in my mind"—and "if ever completed."

Only two of the seven new poems in the 1872 pamphlet are of sufficient importance to be mentioned, and of these two, "As a Strong Bird on Pinions Free" ("Thou Mother with Thy Equal Brood") merely repeats earlier ideas and moods. Once again the poet declares his function to be the initiator of democratic nationalism, making "paths to the house."

The motif of the "strong bird on pinions free" is also reminiscent of Shelley's "Skylark," even though Whitman asserts that "The conceits of the poets of other lands I'd bring thee not." But more important: the poem is merely a restatement of the nationalistic literary program of the '55 Preface, "By Blue Ontario's Shore," and other early works.

More significant is "The Mystic Trumpeter," but it is also a summing up rather than a new achievement in thought or lyric expression. Professor Werner has advanced the interesting theory that the poem is an autobiographical record of moods parallel to Whitman's own life: his early fondness for Scott's feudalism; his celebration of love in the early *Leaves*; the Civil War; his post-war despair at the evils of humanity; and his final optimism and ecstasy. Thus interpreted, the poem seems no longer utterly formless, nor an assembly of the chief poetic themes, but a chronological summary of Whitman's poetic life.[130]

"AUTHOR'S EDITION," 1876

Near the end of his first year in Washington, D.C., during the Civil War Whitman hoped to publish a book to be called *Memoranda of a Year (1863)*, and on October 21, 1863, he proposed this title to James Redpath, a Boston publisher who had befriended him during the printing of the 1860 *Leaves of Grass*. The book would contain extracts from Whitman's war diaries and hospital notebooks. Redpath was interested and sympathetic, but found that it would be more expensive to publish than he could afford.[131]

At the end of the war this book was still unpublished, but in 1875, while recuperating in Camden, N. J., from his paralytic stroke in 1873, Whitman employed the print shop of the *New Republic*, a Camden newspaper, to set up and print a small book of 68 pages (ten consisting of notes) entitled *Memoranda During the War*, labeled "Author's Publication." It is estimated that not over a hundred copies were printed.[132] It was indeed a private edition, and Whitman tried in various ways to personalize it, such as printing a page headed "Remembrance Copy," with space for the name of the recipient and giver, and a "Personal Note" (brief autobiography). He also inserted two photographs of himself—though some copies had only one. The main value of this book is bibliographical (and it is a rare collector's item), for the notebooks and diaries were absorbed into *Specimen Days* seven years later.

At this period Whitman's creative energy was at low ebb, but he was restless and frustrated and greatly desired to commemorate the Centennial of the nation (nearby Philadelphia was having an Exhibition) with a new edition of his works. Without any prospects of a publisher, he again employed the *New Republic* printing office. For *Leaves of Grass* he simply reprinted the 1871 edition from the uncorrected electrotyped plates—this making a *new issue* and not a new edition. But on a new title-page he printed a poem from the Christmas 1874 number of the New York *Graphic*:

> Come, said my Soul,
> Such verses for my Body let us write, (for we are one,)
> That should I after death invisibly return,
> Or, long, long hence, in other spheres,
> There to some group of mates the chants resuming,
> (Tallying Earth's soil, trees, winds, tumultuous waves,)
> Ever with pleased smile I may keep on,
> Ever and ever yet the verses owning—as, first, I here and now,
> Signing for Soul and Body, set to them my name,
>   [signature]

After the signature: "AUTHOR'S EDITION/ *with portraits from life./* CAMDEN, NEW JERSEY./ 1876." The copyright date was also 1876. Another issue was labeled "Centennial Edition."

The companion volume, *Two Rivulets*, was a hodgepodge of poetry and prose—and of printing methods also. The *New Republic* shop set up a new Preface and fourteen poems collected for the first time—three for the last time.[133] To carry out the motif of the title poem, "Two rivulets side by side," Whitman printed poems on the top half of the page and prose "Thoughts for the Centennial" on the second half: observations on Democracy, nationalism, Darwinism, manners, and other pertinent topics.

About mid-way in the volume Whitman printed a second group of four poems called "Centennial Songs—1876." The first, "Song of the Exposition," was the 1871 American Institute poem, "After All, Not to Create Only," simply retitled. The other three poems were: "Song of the Redwood-Tree," "Song of the Universal," and "Song for All Seas," the first reprinted from *Harper's Magazine* (1874) and the other two from the New York *Daily Graphic*. A new typesetting was required for this group.

For the remainder of the book, Whitman simply used the original plates, without change in pagination, for the pamphlets *Democratic Vistas, As a Strong Bird on Pinions Free, Memoranda During the War*, and *Passage to India*. Thus the 1876 *Leaves of Grass* was entirely a reprint, and *Two Rivulets* mostly reprints in a contrived assemblage.

However, the Preface to *Two Rivulets* has interesting information about Whitman's future plans for editions of his poems. In a footnote Whitman says the Preface "is not only for the present collection, but, in a sort, for all my writings, both Volumes [*Leaves of Grass* and *Two Rivulets*]."[134] He also states that *Passage to India*, which he refers to as "chants of Death and Immortality," was intended "to stamp the coloring-finish of all, present and past. For terminus and temperer to all, they were originally written; and that shall be their office to the last." Having had to give up the plan of making *Passage to India* the nucleus of a new collection of songs, he now plans to regard it as a sort of epilogue of all his poems, but by reprinting it in *Two Rivulets* he postponed the time when it would become a part of *Leaves of Grass*. It is thus still unassimilated, though regarded as an epitome of the *Leaves*. In a long footnote Whitman also says that "*Passage to India*, and its cluster, are but freer vent and fuller expression to what, from the first, and so on throughout, more or less lurks in my writings, underneath every page, every line, everywhere." This is a good example of the way the poet would continue to improvise and compromise in his plans during the remaining editions of *Leaves of Grass*.

In this same footnote he confesses that he has had to relinquish his plan to write a second collection of poems:

It was originally my intention, after chanting in LEAVES OF GRASS the songs of the Body and Existence, to then compose a further, equally needed Volume, based on those convictions of perpetuity and conservation which, enveloping all precedents, make the unseen Soul govern absolutely at last. . . . But the full construction of such a work (even if I lay the foundation, or give impetus to it) is beyond my powers, and must remain for some bard in the future.[135]

Characteristically, however, he does not entirely give up his earlier scheme: "Meanwhile, not entirely to give the go-by to my original plan, and far more to avoid a mark'd hiatus in it, than to entirely fulfill it, I end my books with thoughts, or radiations from thoughts, on Death, Immortality, and a free entrance into the Spiritual world." This intention can be plainly seen in the constant resorting and rearranging of the poems up until the year of Whitman's death.

A note in this Preface, dated May 31, 1875, reveals the second spiritual crisis in Whitman's life (the first being visible in the third edition): "O how different the moral atmosphere amid which I now revise this Volume, from the jocund influences surrounding the growth and advent of LEAVES OF GRASS."[136] As he indicates presently, the "moral atmosphere" to which he refers is his extreme mental depression following his mother's death, a shock from which he seems never to have recovered, and his "tedious attack of paralysis." This depression is also partly responsible for Whitman's interpretation of the first volume (i.e., *Leaves of Grass*) as radiating "Physiology alone," whereas "the present One, though of the like origin in the main, more palpably doubtless shows the Pathology which was pretty sure to come in time from the others." Although the later poems do lack the "vehemence of pride and audacity" to be found in the earlier editions—"composed in the flush of my health and strength—,"[137] it is not strictly true that the first six editions of *Leaves of Grass* dealt exclusively with "Birth and Life."[138] For Death and Immortality are prominent themes in every edition, including the first, though the treatment does vary somewhat from period to period. But in his sickness and old age Whitman was inclined to idealize the physiological vigor and joy of his healthier and happier days.

In another reminiscence, however, he makes one of his most revealing confessions about the psychological origins of much of the earlier *Leaves*:

Something more may be added—for, while I am about it, I would make a full confession. I also sent out LEAVES OF GRASS to arouse and set flowing in men's and women's hearts, young and old, (my present and future readers,) endless streams of living, pulsating love and friendship, directly from them to myself, now and ever. To this terrible, irrepressible yearning, (surely more or less down underneath in most human souls,)—this never-satisfied appetite for sympathy, and this boundless offering of sympathy—this universal democratic comradeship—this old, eternal, yet ever-new interchange of adhesiveness, so fitly emblematic of America—I have given in that book, undisguisedly, declaredly, the openest expression.[139]

Aside from the phrenological term "adhesiveness," which Whitman uses to indicate the "Calamus" emotion, no clearer statement can be found of the fact that the impulse of Whitman's songs came not from the desire to express love experiences but to compensate for the absence of experience. In 1876 Whitman still needs sympathy, but the "terrible, irrepressible yearning" came to a climax in the third edition, was appeased through the activities of the "wound-dresser," and is now almost entirely sublimated in the democratic idealism of such poetry and prose as *Democratic Vistas*, "Thoughts for the Centennial," the centennial songs, and other pieces in *Two Rivulets*, including the Preface, which summarizes Whitman's social and literary theory.

The dominant mood of Whitman during the first years of his invalidism is poignantly mirrored in the chief poems of *Two Rivulets*, the "Prayer of Columbus" and the "Song of the Redwood-Tree." The poet was obviously thinking of himself when he described Columbus in his late years as, "A batter'd, wreck'd old man." Almost with the grief of Job, Columbus reminds God that not once has he "lost nor faith nor ecstasy in Thee." He is resigned to "The end I know not, it is all in Thee." In a climax of pathos he feels mocked and perplexed, but then

> As if some miracle, some hand divine unseal'd my eyes,
> Shadowy, vast shapes, smile through the air and sky,
> And on the distant waves sail countless ships,
> And anthems in new tongues I hear saluting me.

No doubt a similar dream of future reward and recognition in "new tongues" sustained Walt Whitman in the hour of his deepest suffering and discouragement.

We might say that in "Prayer of Columbus" the poet's solution is some variety of religious faith, whereas in "Song of the Redwood-Tree" it is a philosophical consolation, perhaps derived indirectly from Hegel. The subject of this poem is the death-chant of a "mighty dying tree." It too has "consciousness, identity," as "all the rocks and mountains have, and all the earth." In typical Whitmanesque fashion the spirit of the tree is projected into the future—the poet's

"Vistas"—, "Then to a loftier strain" the chant turns to the "occult deep volitions" which are shaping the "hidden national will,"

Clearing the ground for broad Humanity, the true America, heir of
    the past so grand,
To build a grander future.[sec. 6]

The philosophical thought and the imagery of this poem are perhaps more clearly explained in "Eidólons," which in 1881 was shifted to the "Inscriptions" group, thus indicating that Whitman regarded it as one of the keys to Leaves of Grass. It is an abstract treatment of Whitman's subjective and idealistic philosophy. Each object, as well as rivers, worlds, and universes, has a spirit, soul, or "eidólon," and the seer tells the poet to celebrate these instead of physical things. This "eidólon" is the poet's "real I myself," and his soul is a part of the great Nature-soul of all creations, so that the only genuine and ultimate reality is eidólons.

The "Song of the Universal" is another Hegelian expression of the Democratic Vistas faith in the ultimate triumph of the poet's ideals:

In this broad Earth of ours,
Amid the measureless grossness and the slag,
Enclosed and safe within its central heart,
Nestles the seed Perfection.

"Nature's amelioration" is constantly evolving the universal "good" out of the "bad majority."

In "Song of Myself" this doctrine was a belief in cosmic evolution, and was then expressed with a plenitude in harmony with the poet's exuberant vigor and audacious ambitions. It is still essentially the same doctrine, but it has now been modified by Whitman's discovery of Hegel and by the calming influence of sickness and old age. In 1855 Whitman gave lyric utterance to philosophical ideas; in 1876 the lyric power has largely evaporated and even the language has become abstract. This is the great change that had taken place over the years. In the 1876 issue of Leaves of Grass and Two Rivulets, Walt Whitman's poetic fire has notably cooled; but as his inspiration slackens and his vigor ebbs away, he turns more resolutely than ever to critical commentary and editorial revision of his life's work.

SIXTH EDITION, 1881-82

Whitman's bad luck with Boston publishers held until the end, for soon after James R. Osgood and Company brought out the 1881-82 edition of *Leaves of Grass* the District Attorney of Boston threatened prosecution if the book were not withdrawn from the mails or expurgated. When Whitman refused permission to delete any lines whatever, Osgood abandoned publication and turned the plates over to the author, who soon secured a new publisher in Rees Welsh and Company, Philadelphia, and the book was reissued in 1882. Later the same year David McKay took over this edition and remained Whitman's loyal friend and publisher for the rest of his life. McKay imprints of the sixth edition are also dated 1883, 1884, and 1888, but they are from the same plates—though some copies are on larger paper, and in 1888 a small batch was printed with "Sands at Seventy" as an annex.[140]

Whether in 1881-82 Whitman intended this to be the last version of *Leaves of Grass*, we do not know; nevertheless, in this edition the poems received their final revisions of text, their last titles, and their permanent positions. Whitman continued to write poems almost up to his death in 1892, but two installments of these he attached in 1888-89 and 1892 as annexes and he left instructions that his posthumous verse be placed in a third annex, thus leaving the 1881 *Leaves* intact and unaltered. The 1881 edition, therefore, is essentially the final, definitive *Leaves of Grass*, though all modern "inclusive" editions contain also the three annexes, and Blodgett's and Bradley's Comprehensive Reader's Edition includes, besides all the annexes, the poems Whitman dropped from *Leaves of Grass* and his uncollected and unpublished poems.[141]

The sixth edition contains twenty new poems, placed in various groups. All of these new compositions, however, are comparatively short and none is of major importance. Several reflect the old-age activities of the poet, such as his reading Hegel ("Roaming in Thought"), his trip to the West ("The Prairie States," "From Far Dakota's Cañons," "Spirit that Form'd this Scene"), and his anticipations of the end of his life ("As at Thy Portals also Death"). A short poem called "My Picture Gallery" is highly indicative of Whitman's old-age editorial methods. It is actually, as Professor Holloway discovered,[142] a fragment of a very early poem, one of the ur-*Leaves*, parts of the original manuscript having been used in various places. The printing of this unused fragment in 1881 as a new poem indicates that Whitman was salvaging, re-sorting, and editing his old manuscripts—perhaps scraping the bottom of the barrel. The two new bird poems in this edition are also significant. "To the Man-of-War-Bird" is actually a translation from Michelet,[143] and John Burroughs has testified that "The Dalliance of the Eagles" was written from an account which he gave Whitman.[144] As he grew older, Whitman made greater use of borrowed observations, journalistic articles, and events in the day's news.

In 1860 Whitman began groping toward the organization of *Leaves of Grass* which he finally adopted and made permanent in 1881. The nine "Inscriptions" of 1871 have now been increased to 24, though only one, a final two-line dedication to "Thou Reader," is new. Half of these, however, were first published in 1860, before Whitman had started this group, and the final section is thus an improvised prologue rather than a carefully planned unit. At first glance it seems to be a poetic index, or "program," for the contents of *Leaves of Grass*, but on close examination the program-symbolism is vague, unsystematic, incomplete, though some of the intentions and motifs are suggested. The first "Inscription" announces the theme of "One's Self," the third the ship motif (like Shelley's West Wind, the ship carries Whitman's poems to all lands). In "Poets to Come" the "main things" are expected from future bards, and the group ends with a solicitation of friendship and personal intimacy from the reader. Considering the fact that nearly all these poems were first published in other clusters, such as "Chants Democratic," "Drum-Taps," "Calamus," "Two Rivulets," etc., and were transferred to this cluster over a period of ten years, it is surprising that they serve as well as they do to introduce *Leaves of Grass*. And it is characteristic of Whitman that instead of deliberately planning and writing an introductory poem, or series, he selected, like an anthologist, poems already completed under various circumstances and impulses.

The "Inscriptions" also characterize the arrangement of the whole book in a manner that is not obvious to the reader who has not studied the poems chronologically. Since Whitman's avowed purpose was to put on record his own life, which he regarded as typical and representative, we would expect the poems of his life-record to be arranged either in chronology of their composition (which is to say, the chronology of his poetic and emotional development) or classified so that their subject-matter at least suggests a natural biographical sequence. Although the prologue poems are followed by the most ostensibly autobiographical works in the book, "Starting from Paumanok" and "Song of Myself" (new title in 1881), and the collection ends with groups symbolizing old age and approaching death, the life-allegory arrangement is still quite general and unsystematic, and there is little visible attempt at chronology inside the groups.

This observation will become clarified and illustrated as we survey the remaining groups in this final arrangement. The two especially autobiographical and doctrinaire poems are followed by "Children of Adam" and "Calamus," groups which do, of course, typify Whitman's psychology and sentiments from about 1855 to '60, but both groups have since then been considerably revised and edited—and "Calamus," as we have seen, has even been remotivated.

Then come the great songs in an unnamed group. The earliest of these are "Song of the Answerer" and "A Song for Occupations" (1855) and the latest is "Song of the Redwood-Tree" (1874). The group begins with "Salut au Monde!" and contains "A Song of the Rolling Earth," both cosmic in theme and imagery, and they help give unity to these poems in which the poet's universal sympathy and his cosmic lyric inspiration were at white-heat intensity (about 1856, the date of five of these poems). Thus chronologically these poems should precede "Children of Adam" and "Calamus," but they were probably placed after these groups in order that the physiological and sex motifs might precede the cosmic ones—a logical arrangement in terms of Whitman's general philosophy.

The first of the new groups is "Birds of Passage," a title which seems to compare life to the migrations of the bird kingdom. The poems come from various periods, but the general theme of the collection is the evolution and migration of the human race through Time and Space, as in "Song of the Universal," "Pioneers! O Pioneers!," and "With Antecedents." The group has very little personal significance or relation to the life-allegory motif of the whole book. There is, however, a certain appropriateness in placing the "pioneer" motif after the great cosmic songs.

The next group has been renamed "Sea-Drift" (called "Sea-Shore Memories" in 1871). It contains the two major sea poems, "Out of the Cradle Endlessly Rocking" (1859) and "As I Ebb'd with the Ocean of Life" (1860), but also represents different moods from various periods, as in "Tears" (1867), "On the Beach at Night Alone" (1856) and "On the Beach at Night" (1871). In chronological sequence Whitman's seashore poems reveal the major crises of his poetic career and form a psychological drama, but this grouping suggests only that the sea provided much of the poet's inspiration. The group is unified by a common subject and locale, and is not without its own logic, but the student must search through other groups to complete the experiences vaguely hinted here.

Another new group is "By the Roadside," in miscellaneous collection of short poems on many topics and extending from "Europe" (1850) and "Boston Ballad" (1854) to "Roaming in Thought" (1881). They are merely samples of experiences and poetic inspirations along Whitman's highway of life.

Drum-Taps has been considerably revised and enlarged since 1865, and the introductory poem of 1871–76 has been discarded. "Virginia—The West" is a good example of the way Whitman shifted poems around. It first appeared in *As a Strong Bird on Pinions Free* (1872), then in *Two Rivulets* ('76), and now comes to rest in *Drum-Taps*. Also the poem which introduced this group in '71 and '76 is now a part of section 1 of "The Wound-Dresser"—"Arous'd and angry, I'd thought to beat the alarum," etc. Several poems first published in *Sequel to Drum-Taps* have finally been placed in this group, thus making it a record not only of the war but of the aftermath too, except for the memorial poems for President Lincoln, which are now called "Memories of President Lincoln."

The latter group is followed by perhaps the most revised composition in *Leaves of Grass*, now called for the first time, after the sixth change in title, "By Blue Ontario's Shore." In 1856 Whitman incorporated parts of his "55 Preface in this poem, and with each succeeding edition until 1881 made extensive revisions. Perhaps his difficulty in making up his mind what to do with the composition was due in part to his having meanwhile expressed and exemplified his poetic theory in many ways. At any rate, in subject-matter this poem is akin to "Starting from Paumanok" and "Song of Myself," but it now appears after the war and Lincoln poems because in 1867 Whitman had remotivated it as a "Chant . . . from the soul of America," singing the "throes of Democracy" and victory (a transition from *Drum-Taps* to *Democratic Vistas*).

"Autumn Rivulets," another new cluster title, does not signify poems associated with the autumn of the poet's life, although in the introductory "As Consequent, etc." he compares these songs to "wayward rivulets" flowing after the "store of summer rains." He also thinks of his life and the experiences which he has recorded in his poems as "waifs from the deep, cast high and dry" onto the shore. Instead of Emerson's Over-Soul metaphor, Whitman uses "the sea of Time," from whence his own identity has come and toward which it is ever flowing, there to blend finally with "the old streams of death." Thus in the imagery of his group-title Whitman re-expresses his philosophy of life and death through this new poem.

But this symbolism is found only in the lead poem. In the other poems of the group, from the 1855 "There was a Child Went Forth" to the 1881 "Italian Music in Dakota" neither these images nor "Autumn Rivulets" motifs reappear. Furthermore, the majority of the poems date back to 1856 and 1860 and reflect the moods and sentiments of those periods: "This Compost" ('56), "To a Common Prostitute" ('60), "O Star of France" ('71), etc. "My Picture-Gallery" was evidently rescued from the barrel of old manuscripts.

Throughout the remainder of *Leaves of Grass* the poems are in general arranged to emphasize the "spiritual" purposes which Whitman professedly began with "Passage to India." Even here, however, he often places an earlier poem, like "The Sleepers" ('55) or "To Think of Time" ('55), both of which come between "Passage to India" and the 1871 cluster—still retained—, "Whispers of Heavenly Death." Then, after a brief interval, comes the new section called "From Noon to Starry Night," a title which happily permits the poet to follow his usual procedure of selecting typical poems from various periods of his career. The group is introduced by a new poem, "Thou Orb Aloft Full-Dazzling," a prayer to the sun, with which the poet feels a special affinity and a reminder of his own prime:

As for thy throes, thy perturbations, sudden breaks and shafts of
    flame gigantic,
I understand them, I know those flames, those perturbations well.

He adores the sun also because it "impartially infoldest all" and liberally gives of itself. He invokes the sun to prepare his "starry nights." The section ends patly with a short epilogue-poem, "A Clear Midnight," on the images of "Night, sleep, death and the stars."

The final cluster, also with a new title, is the inevitable "Songs of Parting," which of course ends with the 1860 "So Long!" The theme is death in its many connotations: personal anticipation, memory of the poet's mother, the death of soldiers in the war, the assassination of President Garfield, and the triumphant journey of the soul into the realms of eternity. But the anticipated end of the poet's life did not come for eleven years and he was spared to write many more postscripts and epitaphs.

As editor of his own work, Whitman is ingenious. His final group titles are appropriate for this anthology of his life-work, and there is a certain kind of poetic logic in his arrangement of the poems inside the various groups. But the student who has closely examined the growth of the editions will also find serious objections to Whitman's belief that the 1881 *Leaves of Grass* is as unified as a cathedral or as inevitable in structure as an organism in nature. In chronological order his poems do tell the inner story of the poet's long struggle to put on record his own life and the literary ambitions which he was trying to achieve, but in this final arrangement the story is inconsecutive and often obscured by the deletions and emendations which Whitman had made throughout the years as his concept of his own poetic rôle fluctuated. Perhaps he had deliberately obscured it. His arrangement of the poems by subject-matter seems to indicate that this is true. An inconsistency, however, remains. Such cluster titles as "Autumn Rivulets," "From Noon to Starry Night," and "Songs of Parting" suggest a chronology of life-experiences, but the contents of these groups reveal ideational rather than biological sequences. Furthermore, often the symbolism of these titles scarcely carries beyond the introductory poem and possibly an epilogue.

Perhaps critics will never agree upon the poet's success in this final arrangement, for everything depends upon what one wants in an edition of *Leaves of Grass*. The very fact that this was so indisputably Walt Whitman's final choice, and that he was still satisfied with it a decade later, leaves no doubt that this edition does show his intentions—especially his intention to suggest (*indirectly*, as he might have said) that this "is no book" but a man's life, though he reserved the right to erase and emend any parts of the record that violated his later ideals, and to arrange the parts so that they would not suggest the realism of biography. After all, this is a *poetic record*, not objective history or prosaic autobiography. Thus the reader of Whitman will no doubt always cherish the poet's own final edition. But for the student who is interested in the growth of Whitman's thought or the development of his prosodic techniques and artistry, or the solution of psychological mysteries, a chronological text is well-nigh indispensable.

SPECIMEN DAYS, 1882

About one-third of the material in *Specimen Days* had been published in 1875 in *War Memoranda*, but in 1882 Whitman collected this and other prose pieces, including *Democratic Vistas*, into what was historically the second edition of the *Complete Works* in two volumes (volume one being a reprint of the 1881 *Leaves*) but what was now essentially the *Complete Prose*.

Whitman himself called *Specimen Days* a "way-ward book," and it is certainly improvised, much of it having been copied from notebooks, diaries, and scraps of manuscript, evidently with little revision—though these notes are perhaps more authentic "specimens" for not having been rewritten. The book covers three main subjects, the first being a brief autobiography which Whitman says he wrote for a friend in 1882; the second being war memoranda, taken from "verbatim copies of those lurid and blood-smutch'd little notebooks" written in Washington and Virginia from the end of 1862 through 1865; and the third being diary and nature-notes for 1876–81 and miscellaneous short essays and articles.

The autobiography throws some light on the growth of Whitman as a poet because we can see in the glorification of his ancestry and the importance he attaches to his environment some of the processes by which he transmuted the commonplace into the idealism of his verse. In the war memoranda, however, we get a side of Whitman which is almost entirely lacking in his poems and which therefore supplements the poetry. In his graphic descriptions of the camp of the wounded, with the amputated arms and legs lying under the trees, he anticipates later American realism. And the exact account of many individual cases of the wounded documents the record. Atrocities are told with great anguish of spirit but without partisanship. Without preaching Whitman reveals the bestiality of war. He concludes that, "the real war will never get in the books," and adds that it was so horrible that perhaps it should not. But he comes nearer telling it than anyone else in America was to do for half a century to come, and he tells it all without sentimentality or propaganda for pacifism which followed World War I.

The third part of *Specimen Days* reveals still another side of Whitman's life. Before the war he had been a great nature lover, and nature plays a prominent part in all his poems, but the record of his Timber Creek experiences reads almost like a summer idyl. More amateurish than Thoreau in his botanical and ornithological observations, even priding himself on deficiency in exact information, Whitman's enjoyment of nature is as intimate and personal as one can find in romantic prose. But it is probably not accidental that he now expresses himself in loose, informal language, for he seems to have been living in the most satisfying repose of his life. The great seashore poems were not written in such a mood of quiet resignation. Even in the accounts of his travels of 1889, which he seems to have enjoyed as thoroughly as his youthful trip across the Alleghanies on his way to St. Louis, we find this same repose, this Indian summer atmosphere, which *Specimen Days* more clearly reflects than the old-age poems.

NOVEMBER BOUGHS, 1888

Specimen Days marks the transition to Whitman's final attitude toward life and his art as expressed in *November Boughs*, a large 8 vo book, bound in maroon or green cloth, published in Philadelphia by David McKay. Its 140 pages contain a long Preface, "A Backward Glance O'er Travel'd Roads," twenty essays on literary subjects and personal experiences, and sixty-four new poems grouped in two clusters, "Sands at Seventy" and "Fancies at Navesink." In 1892 these two clusters will become the "First Annex" to *Leaves of Grass* (i.e., annexed to the 1881 text), but the essays will remain outside Whitman's *Prose Works* because he will not live long enough to edit an expanded edition. However, he did append the contents of *November Boughs* to his 900-page quarto, *Complete Poems and Prose of Walt Whitman, 1855–1888*.

The poems in *November Boughs* are mainly the product of old-age reflection, November reminiscences. After completing his poems he is "curious to review them in the light of their own (at the time unconscious, or mostly unconscious) intentions, with certain unfoldings of the thirty years they seek to embody."[145] Gone are the ambitious boastings, the grandiose claims to fame. With tranquil confidence and utmost frankness Whitman now admits in his Preface, "I have not gain'd the acceptance of my own time, but have fallen back on fond dreams of the future." Yet despite the fact that *Leaves of Grass* has always been a financial failure, "I have had my say entirely in my own way, and put it unerringly on record—the value thereof to be decided by time."[146] The work was always an experiment, "as, in the deepest sense, I consider our American Republic itself to be, with its theory." He is content that he has "positively gain'd a hearing."

Once more Whitman reiterates his original purpose: "to exploit [his own] Personality, identified with place and date, in a far more candid and comprehensive sense than any hitherto poem or book." With this part of his original program he is still satisfied, but he is not so sure about another intention:

Modern science and democracy seem'd to be throwing out their challenge to poetry to put them in its statements in contra-distinction to the songs and myths of the past. As I see it now (perhaps too late,) I have unwittingly taken up that challenge and made an attempt at such statements—which I certainly would not assume to do now, knowing more clearly what it means.[147]

It is interesting and a little pathetic that Whitman's failure to gain wide acceptance in his own time and country have convinced him that "in verbal melody and all the conventional technique of poetry, not only the divine works that to-day stand ahead in the world's reading, but dozens more, transcend (some of them immeasurably transcend) all I have done, or could do," though he still believes that "there must imperatively come a readjustment of the whole theory and nature of Poetry. . . ."[148] Today, after such a readjustment has taken place, it is difficult for us to understand the nineteenth-century intolerance in poetic technique.

For the most part, the remainder of this Preface merely reaffirms Whitman's familiar doctrines: that the function of a poem is to fill a person "with vigorous and clean manliness,"[149] that American democratic individuality is yet unformed, and that the great poet will express the goodness of all creation.

The poems in this book scarcely need discussion. They seem to be mainly fragments from unpublished manuscripts (i.e., uncollected in *Leaves of Grass*; some were published in newspapers to earn a few dollars), or stray thoughts and echoes from earlier compositions. Some are ruminations long after the passing of the emotions and experiences which first gave rise to lyric utterance. Whitman himself is fully conscious of his true condition. In "Memories" he refers to the "sweet . . . silent backward tracings," and in "As I Sit Writing Here" he fears that the old-age vexations of the flesh "May filter in my daily songs." With conscious effort he tries to make his last days happiest of all, "The brooding and blissful halcyon days" ("Halcyon Days").

In his last years the poet also feels close to the sea once more, and at times both the sight of the ocean and his reflections almost fan to life the old lyric sparks, as in the group "Fancies at Navesink," or "A sudden memory-flash comes back" in "The Pilot in the Midst." The ocean revives the emotional symbolism of his greatest poems in "With Husky-Haughty Lips, O Sea":

> The tale of cosmic elemental passion,
> Thou tellest to a kindred soul.

But these are merely echoes too, like "Old Salt Kossabone," based on the family tradition about the sailor on his mother's side which he had already used in section 35 of "Song of Myself," and "Going Somewhere" revives the theme of two 1867 poems, "Small the Theme of My Chant" and the first "Inscription." As in "After Supper and Talk" the old poet is "loth to depart" and "garrulous to the very last."

GOOD-BYE MY FANCY, 1891

In 1891 David McKay published *Good-Bye My Fancy*, a slender volume of sixty-six pages, uniform in size and style with *November Boughs*. It was subtitled "2d Annex to Leaves of Grass," but the book contained both prose and poems, and of course only the thirty-two poems of the new cluster "Good-Bye My Fancy" constituted the annex. Gravely ill, Whitman knew that his career as a poet was unmistakably drawing near, and he opened with "Sail Out for Good, Eidólon Yacht!" In a footnote to the first of his two poems with the title "God-Bye My Fancy" he asked:

Why do folks dwell so fondly on the last words, advice, appearance, of the departing? Those last words are not samples of the best, which involve vitality at its full, and balance, and perfect control and scope. But they are valuable beyond measure to confirm and endorse the varied train, facts, theories and faith of the whole preceding life.

These new poems are permeated with old-age apparitions, twilight, departing ships, funeral wreaths, sunset, the chill of winter, but also "unseen buds" waiting "under the snow and ice" to burst into new life. In the final "Good-Bye" the poet has a kind of agnostic optimism:

Good-bye my Fancy!
Farewell dear mate, dear love!
I'm going away, I know not where,
Or to what fortune, or whether I may ever see you again,
So Good-bye my Fancy.

. . . . .

Long indeed have we lived, slept, filter'd, become really blended into one;
Then if we die we die together, (yes, we'll remain one,)
If we go anywhere we'll go together to meet what happens,

. . . . .

Good-bye—and hail! my Fancy.

In his "Preface Note to 2d Annex,/ concluding L. of G.—1891," Whitman himself wonders, "Had I not better withhold (in this old age and paralysis of me) such little tags and fringe-dots (maybe specks, stains,) as follow a long dusty journey, and witness it afterward?" He is "not at all clear" himself that this new batch of verse and prose "is worth printing," but he begs indulgence because doing so enables him to "while away the hours of my 72d year." Besides, he hopes these "last droplets of and after spontaneous rain" will "filter" to the heart and brain of America. Furthermore, his prose reminiscences of the war years may help "this vast rich Union" to realize and appreciate the cost of its preservation. About half of these prose pieces are autobiographical sketches similar to passages in *Specimen Days*, being, admittedly, items saved from "a vast batch left to oblivion." Yet his final thought is not that he has written himself out, "But how much—how many topics, of the greatest point and cogency, I am leaving untouch'd!"

AUTHORIZED *LEAVES OF GRASS*, 1891-92

The 1891-92 issue of *Leaves of Grass* is widely known as the "death-bed edition" but it is not, as defined at the beginning of this chapter (see note 1), a new *edition*, and the book which his intimate friends called the "death-bed edition" was a book hastily assembled in December, 1891, from unbound sheets of the 1889 reprint so that Whitman might hold the promised "new edition" in his hands before he died. A few copies were bound for the poet's friends, but it was, in a sense, a fake, and certainly not the projected final and definitive 1892 *Leaves of Grass*.

Several months later David McKay did publish the promised volume, dated on the title-page 1891-92, and a uniform volume of the *Complete Prose Works* (reprinted from the 1882 plates of *Specimen Days and Collect*, which in turn had been reprinted with wide margins and bound quarto size as *Complete Poems and Prose of Walt Whitman, 1855-1888*).

The 1891-1892 issue was actually, through page 382, a reprint of the 1881 edition from the James R. Osgood plates, which the Boston publisher had turned over to Whitman after a district attorney threatened prosecution for publishing an obscene book. To the 1881 text Whitman annexed, first, the cluster "Sands at Seventy" from *November Boughs* (using the *November Boughs* plates), and then a second cluster, "Good-Bye My Fancy" from *Good-Bye My Fancy* (using the *Good-Bye . . .* plates), designated as the "2d Annex." In 1889 McKay had printed an issue containing the first Annex, but not the second. The 1891-1892 issue also published for the first time the injunction Whitman placed on all future editors and publishers of *Leaves of Grass* (using the untechnical term "editions"):

As there are now several editions of L. of G., different texts and dates, I wish to say that I prefer and recommend this present one, complete, for future printing, if there should be any; a copy and fac-simile, indeed, of the text of these 438 pages. The subsequent adjusting interval which is so important to form'd and launch'd work, books especially, has pass'd; and waiting till fully after that, I have given (pages 423-438) my concluding words.

W. W.

The "concluding words" were those of the *November Boughs* (1888)

Preface, "A Backward Glance O'er Travel'd Roads." This "author-ized" text (except for the 1888 Preface) has been honored by nearly all editors of Whitman's poems down to the present time, including Harold W. Blodgett and Sculley Bradley in their "Comprehensive Reader's Edition" (1965).

In 1897 Small, Maynard and Co., in Boston, published an issue with "posthumous additions" called "Old Age Echoes," a title chosen by Whitman himself—held "in reserve," he told Horace Traubel, one of his three literary executors. This cluster of thirteen short poems included some uncollected fragments of earlier years, but most of the poems were Whitman's last compositions. On March 16, 1892, ten days before his death, he handed Traubel some slips of paper on which he had written "A Thought of Columbus."[150] It was appro-priate that his very last poem should have been a combined saluta-tion and prayer to the martyred explorer with whom he had felt a kindred identity since writing his "Prayer of Columbus" during one of the darkest years of his life (1874).[151]

With the 1897 issue, the official canon of *Leaves of Grass* was now complete: consisting of the 1881 text (sixth edition), plus the cluster "Sands at Seventy" from *November Boughs*, the cluster "Good-Bye My Fancy," from the book of the same title, and the posthumous cluster "Old Age Echoes."

Chapter III

The Realm of Whitman's Ideas

*All these separations and gaps shall be taken up and hook'd
and link'd together,
The whole earth, this cold impassive, voiceless earth, shall
be completely justified.—*
"Passage to India"

SOCIETY

Just as the whaling ship was Herman Melville's "Yale and Harvard," so was the newspaper office Walt Whitman's university. In fact, the printing office might also be called his elementary school, for there he learned to spell, punctuate, and compose sentences, rather than in the mediocre public school which he attended until his twelfth year. Later as a reporter and editor of several newspapers he received a practical education in sociology and politics. His moral and intellectual development in printing shop and newspaper office has been traced by several scholars,[1] but fullest and most authoritatively by Joseph Jay Rubin in *The Historic Whitman* (1973). Rubin calls this period of Whitman's life "his Antaen earth,"[2] and certainly it was then that he learned the realities of life in Brooklyn and New York City, and became acutely aware of the larger issues which were already dividing the nation.

Before the Civil War nearly all American newspapers were supported and controlled by political parties. Whitman learned typesetting from Samuel E. Clements, editor of the Long Island *Patriot*, which was Democratic and loyal to the "bosses" of New York City's Tammany Hall. The "Pat" solicited the support of the mechanics and artisans in Brooklyn, who included Walt Whitman's father, a carpenter, and ardent follower of working-men's causes.

Walter Whitman, Sr., was a personal friend of Tom Paine, and a

161

great admirer of the notorious socialist and reformer, Frances Wright, whose lectures Walt attended with his father.[3] At home the boy read Paine's *Age of Reason*, Count Volney's Ruins (a treatise on the ideas which brought about the French Revolution), and Frances Wright's *A Few Days in Athens* (imaginary conversations on the philosophy of Epicurus).[4] At this stage young Whitman's political orientation was passionately proletarian and egalitarian, and in religion Deistic. His political heroes were General Lafayette, whose visit to Brooklyn he witnessed at the age of six,[5] and Andrew Jackson, who made a triumphant tour of the city eight years later.[6] He would always remain a Jacksonian Democrat.

Whitman's Deism, however, was considerably modified by the influence of the radical Long Island Quaker, Elias Hicks, another personal friend of the Whitman family. What might seem like anti-clericalism derived from Paine and Volney was more likely a sympathetic sharing of Hicks's attitude toward all religious institutions as the source of moral authority. As Whitman later recalled, Hicks "believ'd little in a church as organiz'd—even his own—with houses, ministers, or with salaries, creeds, Sundays, saints, Bibles, holy festivals, &c. But he believ'd always in the universal church, in the soul of man, invisibly rapt, ever-waiting, ever-responding to universal truth."[7]

In his childhood Walt Whitman accompanied his parents to hear Hicks preach, and his interest in this unusual Quaker continued into his old age, when he published a long essay on him in *November Boughs* (1888). There he says, "Elias taught throughout [his life], as George Fox began it, or rather reiterated and verified it, the Platonic doctrine that the ideals of character, of justice, of religious action, whenever the highest is at stake, are to be conform'd to no outside doctrine of creeds, Bibles, legislative enactments, conventionalities, or even decorums, but are to follow the inward Deity-planted law of the emotional soul."[8]

All Quakers believed in the moral guidance of the "inner light," but Hicks went further than most of them in sweeping away everything else as nonessential. He had been suspected of holding heretical views on the Divinity of Christ and the Atonement, but he finally created an outright schism in the Society of Friends when he declared at a meeting in Philadelphia in 1829: "The blood of Christ—the blood of Christ—why, my friends, the actual blood of Christ in itself was no more effectual than the blood of bulls and goats. . . ."[9]

Though Walt Whitman never joined a Quaker sect of any kind, and always regarded "churches, sects, pulpits" as lacking "any solid convictions," existing "by a sort of tacit, supercilious, scornful sufferance,"[10] no one believed more devoutly than he in the "inward Deity-planted law of the emotional soul." (By "emotional" he meant *feeling*; one knew what was right by inward, emotional conviction.)

When Whitman first became a political journalist, he supported the candidates and doctrines of the Democratic party in New York State, but he never sold his Quaker conscience to any party or faction, and eventually this brought him into conflict with the party bosses. For a history of Whitman's journalistic career, the reader should consult Rubin's *Historic Whitman*. For the present purpose we need to notice only the major social and political ideas expressed in his editorials in the Brooklyn *Eagle*, which he edited in 1846 and 1847, and later in the *Brooklyn Times* in 1857–59.[11]

Whitman assumed the editorship of the Brooklyn *Eagle* in March 1846 during one of the most momentous periods in American history. Since 1844 the United States had been in a heated dispute with Great Britain over the Northwest boundary line. That year the Democrats had won the Presidential election on the slogan "Fifty-four forty or fight," and fighting was still a real possibility until Britain agreed in June 1846 on what is still the boundary line between the United States and Canada. The line was far short of 54°40′, which would have included British Columbia, but it did extend the territory of the United States clear to the Pacific Ocean, opening up vast possibilities for future economic and demographic growth.

In the spring of 1846 President Polk also ordered the American army to invade Mexico, which had refused to cede California and other Southwest territory (including present New Mexico, Utah, Arizona, Nevada, and parts of Wyoming and Colorado) to the United States. Annexation of Texas the previous December by American citizens living there illegally had precipitated the war with Mexico, but United States imperialists were only too glad of the opportunity to increase the territory of the nation, some calling it the country's "manifest destiny," a phrase coined by the editor of *The United States Magazine and Democratic Review*, John L. O'Sullivan.

Walt Whitman, editor of a prominent Democratic newspaper, might have been expected to support the war with Mexico—which the Whigs called "Jimmy Polk's war"—and to exult over the favorable settlement of the Oregon question. Uncritically, and almost mindlessly, he accepted the "manifest destiny" doctrine with naive idealism. On June 23, 1846, he declared in an editorial that expansion of the United States was natural and inevitable, "and for our part, we look on that increase of territory and power . . . with the faith which the Christian has in God's mystery.—Over the rest of the world, the swelling impulse of freedom struggles, too; though *we* are ages ahead of them."[12] Whitman's imperialist euphoria continued into 1847. On February 8 he shouted that the United States "may one day put the Canadas and Russian America [Alaska] in its fob pocket!" He maintained, however, that his nation "will tenderly regard human life, property and rights" and "*never* be guilty of furnishing duplicates to the Chinese war, the 'operations of the British in India,' or the 'extinguishment of Poland.' "[13]

Partisanship had temporarily blinded Whitman to the fact that Southern slave owners wanted Texas in order to extend slavery, and would strive with all their might to carry slaves into the other territories acquired in the Oregon settlement. He was opposed to slavery as an institution and had published editorials denouncing the slave trade in words that must have pleased the Abolitionists, but he was slow to realize that the war with Mexico strengthened the slave-owner's interests. This was partly because he still believed that slavery could be abolished by peaceful means and he disliked the violent language of the Abolitionists, the chief critics of the Mexican War.

Above all else, Whitman feared that confrontations over abolition might break up the Union, which he regarded as the greatest "political blessing on earth"[14]—exactly the stand Abraham Lincoln would take a decade later. However, Senator Calhoun opened his eyes to the intentions of the Southern Democrats when he proclaimed in the spring of 1847 that "a large majority of both parties in the non-slave-holding States, have come to a fixed determination to appropriate all the territories of the United States now possessed, or hereafter acquired, to themselves, *to the entire exclusion of the slaveholding States*."[15] Whitman pounced on these italicized phrases, pointing out that with the possible exception of South Carolina, the majority of freemen in the South did not own slaves. "The only persons who will be excluded will be the *aristocracy* of the South— the men who work only with other men's hands."

Whitman, son of a carpenter and friend of the working men, saw the extension of slavery into the new territories as an ominous threat to free labor, especially in the industrial North. "The voice of the North proclaims that *labor must not be degraded*. The young men of the free States must not be shut out from the new domain (where slavery does not now exist) by the *introduction* of an institution which will render their honorable industry no longer respectable."[16]

However, Whitman did not see in the immigration of the poor of Europe a threat to American labor, as the Whig "Nativists" or "Know-Nothing" party did. In actual fact most of the immigrants were ignorant and unskilled and they did flood the labor market with cheap manpower. But here Whitman took an idealistic stand. After describing their wretchedness in the Old World, he asked: "How, then, can any man with a heart in his breast, begrudge the coming of Europe's needy ones, to the plentiful storehouse of the New World?"[17] He advocated raising funds to speed these destitute people to the unsettled West, predicting that the time would come when they would be able to achieve in this country "something of that destiny which we may suppose God intends eligible for mankind. And this problem is to be worked out through the people, territory, and government of the United States."[18] This, of course, was true prophecy, but Whitman did not forsee the Armageddon which would precede the fulfillment.

In advocating "free trade" Whitman was also opposing Whig "protectionism," but again he looked upon this issue from the point of view of the working man. High tariff, he said, would raise prices and restrict trade, thereby depressing wages, contrary to Whig arguments. In one editorial he declared:

When we hear of the immense purchases [bribes], donations, or "movements" of our manufacturing capitalists of the North, we bethink ourselves how reasonable it is that they should want "protection"—and how nice a game they play in asking a high tariff "for the benefits of the working men." What lots of cents have gone out of poor folks' pockets, to swell the dollars in the possession of owners of great steam mills! Molière, speaking of a wealthy physician, says: "He must have killed a great many people to be so rich!" Our American capitalists of the manufacturing order, would *poor* a great many people to be rich![19]

Whitman never wavered on these issues in which his opinions coincided with the liberal principles of the Democratic Party, but on the issue of "free soil" the Democrats of New York State split, and Whitman found himself in the minority faction. This came about as a result of the Wilmot Proviso, a bill introduced by Congressman David Wilmot to prohibit slavery in the new territories. Of course the Southern Democrats were solidly opposed to the Proviso, and in the attempt to preserve Party unity both in the New York Legislature and the Democratic convention at Syracuse in 1847 the New York Democrats refused to take a definite stand on the question. In the November election the Democrats were solidly defeated in New York, and Whitman thought it was because the Party had not been "sufficiently bold, open and radical [liberal], in its avowals of sentiment."[20] Specifically, he blamed it for not having taken a firm and honest stand on the Wilmot Proviso, and he editorialized this warning:

We must plant ourselves firmly on the side of freedom and openly espouse it. The late election is a terrific warning of the folly of all half-way policy in such matters—of all compromises that neither receive or reject a great idea to which the people are once fully awakened.[21]

The owner of the Brooklyn *Eagle* was Isaac Van Anden, one of the conservative leaders of the New York Democrats. When his editor continued to support the "radicals," now called in derision the "Barn-burners" (they would burn the barn to destroy the rats), a rupture was inevitable, though it did not actually take place until about January 4, 1848. General Lewis Cass had written an open letter opposing the Wilmot Proviso. Whitman refused to print it, though he attacked Cass's arguments on January 3. On January 5 the letter was published in full and the *Eagle* was under new editorial management.

A few days after leaving the Brooklyn *Eagle* Whitman was offered an editorial position on a fledgling newspaper in New Orleans, where he spent the spring of 1848. But in the summer he returned to Brooklyn and the free soil Democrats encouraged him to start a weekly newspaper to support their cause. He called his paper the *Freeman* and published the first issue on September 9. That night a fire destroyed the building in which the *Freeman* was edited and printed—arson was strongly suspected. Undaunted, Whitman recouped his resources, bought new type, and continued to publish his paper after a short delay, and was even able to make it a daily in the spring. But by September the New York free soil Democratic politicians had made peace with the conservative faction and Whitman lost his financial support for the *Freeman*. On September 11 he gave up the attempt to keep it going. Had he been willing to compromise his honest conviction, he could no doubt have found another editorial position, but he was a man of principle.

The Whigs, of course, had no use for Walt Whitman either. As a Jeffersonian-Jacksonian Democrat by conviction, he opposed their whole political philosophy. He thought they exaggerated the intricacy of government:

The error lies in the desire after *management*, the great curse of our Legislation: every thing is to be regulated and made straight by force of statute. And all this while, evils are accumulating, in very consequence of excessive management. The true office of government is simply to preserve the rights of each citizen from spoilation: when it attempts to go beyond this, it is intrusive and does more harm than good.[22]

With nowhere to go in journalism, Walt Whitman turned to building houses (mainly as a contractor) in Brooklyn. He felt not only that the politicians in his Party had betrayed him but also the great cause of freedom itself in surrendering to the slave-owning Democrats of the South. In June he published a satirical poem on the Biblical text "I was wounded in the house of my friends" (Zechariah xiii. 6): "If thou art balked, O Freedom,/ The Victory is not to thy manlier foes;/ From the house of friends comes the death stab." He exhorted the "young North" to "arise," because "Our elder blood flows in the veins of cowards."[23]

In Europe, too, reactionaries were again in control after the abortive revolutions of 1848. In the summer of 1850 Whitman expressed his disappointment—and hope—in a poem called "Resurgemus"[24] (resurgence):

Suddenly, out of its state and drowsy air, the air of slaves,
[1855 corrected to read: stale . . . lair . . . lair]

God, 'twas delicious!
That brief, tight, glorious grip
Upon the throats of kings.

But the sweetness of mercy brewed bitter destruction,
And frightened rulers come back:

[Yet] Those corpses of young men,

. . . . .

Cold and motionless as they seem,
Live elsewhere with undying vitality;
They live in other young men, O, kings,

. . . . .

Not a grave of those slaughtered ones,
But is growing its seed of freedom,
In its turn to bear seed,
Which the winds shall carry afar and resow,
And the rains nourish.

Whitman's bitterness of 1848 had now been softened by faith in the ultimate workings of Providence.

Building houses, operating a small printing shop part-time, occasionally contributing verse and articles to New York and Brooklyn newspapers, had enabled him to rise above the political strife and think of ultimate outcomes. He found time to read, attend the opera, visit the studios of Brooklyn artists, and, above all, to think. As a consequence this became the most creative period of his life, during which he conceived and wrote the poems and preface for his remarkable first edition of *Leaves of Grass*, so far superior to anything he had published before that it seemed like the work of a different person—as, psychologically, it was. However, in his passion for political and social equality and justice, the development of character without institutional restraints, and the use of natural resources for the good of every citizen of the nation, Whitman was the same man who wrote editorials welcoming territorial expansion, defended the Wilmot Proviso, and denounced economic exploitation of working men.

Whitman's 1855 Preface inaugurates his revolutionary esthetic program, but it is also social and political, aiming, above all else, to cultivate in every citizen a magnanimity and generosity of spirit to match the territorial expanse and abundance of natural resources of the nation. His ideal "greatest poet" hardly knows pettiness or triviality. "If he breathes into any thing that was before thought small it dilates with the grandeur and life of the universe."[25] This is his impossible goal—no less. He calls the United States themselves a great poem, and he wants every person to make his own life a "poem," that is, a thing of beauty and perfection. He even suggests what might be called a "creed" to attain this self-perfection:

Love the earth and sun and the animals, despise riches, give alms to every one that asks, stand up for the stupid and crazy, devote your income and labor to others, hate tyrants, argue not concerning God, have patience and indulgence toward the people, take off your hat to nothing known or unknown or to any man or number of men, go freely with powerful uneducated persons and with the young and with the mothers of families, read these leaves [*Leaves of Grass*] in the open air every season of every year of your life, re-examine all you have been told at school or church or in any book, dismiss whatever insults your own soul, and your very flesh shall be a great poem and have the richest fluency not only in its words but in the silent lines of its lips and face and between the lashes of your eyes and in every motion and joint of your body.[26]

Here the "beatitudes" of Christ, Quaker customs and the radical teachings of Elias Hicks, American patriotic arrogance and humility, and the romantic pieties of Walt Whitman mingle in an eclectic creed Whitman intended for his "New Religion." He predicts that "There will soon be no more priests," at least in the church sense:

A new order shall arise and they shall be the priests of man, and every man shall be his own priest. The churches built under their umbrage shall be the churches of men and women. Through the divinity of themselves shall the kosmos[27] and the new breed of poets be interpreters of men and women and of all events and things. They shall find their inspiration in real objects today, symptoms of the past and future.[28]

Whitman's final and ultimate ideal is that "An individual is as superb as a nation when he has the qualities which make a great nation." His own ambition was to achieve this in his own life, or at least in his poetry as a literary archetype, and he ended his Preface with the declaration that, "The proof of a poet is that his country absorbs him as affectionately as he has absorbed it."[29] By this test he would fail during his lifetime, and especially with his 1855 edition,

Ralph Waldo Emerson being one of the few readers to see merit in it.[30] Emerson's praise, however, encouraged him to put out a second edition the following year, which was an even greater failure than the first.

By this time Whitman had also become active in journalism again, but as a free-lance writing special articles for a magazine called *Life Illustrated*. One of his most important contributions, entitled simply "The Slave Trade," was an exposé of the fitting out of ships in the New York harbor to engage secretly in transporting slaves from Africa. He gave explicit details of exactly how the operations were carried out, how much they cost, what the profits were (about 900%), and how the Federal Court in New York permitted the culprits to escape with very light penalties or none at all. Two slavers had left New York for Africa in the past few days (late July, 1856), "and all along they have been slipping off at the rate of a dozen or twenty for every one caught."[31]

Though not a declared Abolitionist, Whitman was nevertheless deeply concerned in the summer of 1856 with events growing out of slavery. His indignation with the political parties became almost frenetic when the Democrats nominated James Buchanan and the Native Americans (Know-Nothing—and late Whigs) Millard Fillmore for the Presidency. Buchanan represented the faction which had betrayed Whitman and the free soil Democrats in 1847-48; and Fillmore, an unsuccessful Whig candidate in 1852, who had succeeded to the Presidency after the death of Zachary Taylor, had signed the Fugitive Slave Law. Whitman knew that neither man would be able to stop the guerilla warfare in Kansas between the free soil settlers and the invading slave owners. The new Republican Party nominated John Charles Frémont, western explorer, adventurer, maverick politician, and no friend of the slave interests. It is possible that Whitman had some hopes for him, though he never gave an open endorsement, and he may have feared that Frémont's election would split the Union, as the election of Republican Abraham Lincoln four years later actually did.

Feeling that someone should speak for the six million "mechanics, farmers, sailors, &c.," Whitman wrote a political tract called "The Eighteenth Presidency!,"[32] which he set up in type and apparently distributed in proof to some "editors of the independent press," hoping that they or "any rich person, anywhere" might "circulate and reprint this Voice of mine for the workingmen's sake."[33] There is no evidence whatever that Whitman was trying to start a new party to represent labor, and if he hoped to aid any of the candidates for President, it would have had to be Frémont, but this was a very ambiguous way to accomplish that. Not surprisingly, his call for reform was ignored; no editor printed his tract, so far as is known, and it was not published until long after Whitman's death. Yet despite his abortive effort, the tract is invaluable as evidence of Whitman's understanding of the political situation in the years immediately preceding the Civil War, and history has corroborated many of his insights.

The main thesis of "The Eighteenth Presidency!" is that under the corrupt party system in the United States of that time government has ceased to be representative, and the ideals of the founding fathers have been betrayed:

At present, the personnel of the government of these thirty millions, in executives and elsewhere, is drawn from limber-tongued lawyers, very fluent but empty, feeble old men, professional politicians . . . rarely drawn from the solid body of the people . . .

I expect to see the day when the like of the present personnel of the governments, federal, state, municipal, military and naval, will be looked upon with derision, and when qualified mechanics and young men will reach Congress and other official stations, sent in their working costumes, fresh from their benches and tools, and returning to them again with dignity.[34]

Whitman, of course, over-simplified the education and skill needed for public office, though four years hence Abraham Lincoln, the "Rail-Splitter," did fulfill part of this expectation—however, he had studied and practiced law. Yet conditions during the campaign for the "eighteenth-Presidency" were not far different from Whitman's description:

To-day, of all the persons in public office in These States, not one in a thousand has been chosen by any spontaneous movement of the people, nor is attending to the interests of the people; all have been nominated and put through by great or small caucuses of the politicians [state primary elections were not general until about 1917], or appointed as rewards for electioneering; and all consign themselves to personal and party interests . . . The berths, the Presidency included, are bought, sold, electioneered for, prostituted, and filled with prostitutes.[35]

One part of the country was no better than the other. In the North were "office-vermin" and "kept-editors"; in the South braggarts who would dissolve the Union. "Are lawyers, dough-faces, and the three hundred and fifty thousand owners of slaves, to sponge the mastership of thirty millions?"[36] This, of course, was the real crux. Even today the democratic majority may be fooled and misled by political trickery, but the immediate cause of the conditions Whitman condemned was that a small band of Southern slave-owning Democrats managed to control the national Party for their own interests. In fact, to preserve party and national unity both the Whigs and the Democrats had yielded to chicanery, subterfuge, expediency, and cowardly compromise on the extension of slavery into the territories throughout the sixteenth and seventeenth Presidencies. And now once more the politicians had nominated "men both patterned to follow and match the seventeenth term," men sworn to "the theories that balk and reverse the main purposes of the founders of These States." One party flaunted "Americanism," using the "great word . . . without yet feeling the first aspiration of it"; while the other [he seemed to ignore the Republican] distorted the meaning of "democracy," whereas "What the so-called democracy are now sworn to perform would eat the faces off the succeeding generations of common people worse than the most horrible disease."[37]

Whitman had lost confidence in any party, and thought America had "outgrown parties; hence forth it is too large, and they too small":

I place no reliance upon any old party, nor upon any new party. Suppose one to be formed under the noblest auspices, and getting into power with the noblest intentions, how long would it remain so? . . . As soon as it becomes successful, and there are offices to be bestowed, the politicians leave the unsuccessful parties and rush toward it, and it ripens and rots with the rest.[38]

This cynicism explains, perhaps, why Whitman had no enthusiasm for the Republican candidate. And, "Platforms are of no account" either. "The right man is everything." He had not lost faith in all men, or in the "organic compact of These States," which was sufficient platform for any party. He even regarded the Constitution as a sacred and prophetic document, but it could be misused, as it had been in enforcing the Fugitive Slave Act. What was most needed was a great leader with integrity and courage. "Whenever the day comes for him to appear, the man who shall be the Redeemer President of The States, is to be the one that fullest realizes the rights of individuals signified by the impregnable rights of The States, the substratum of this Union."[39] It was not until after Lincoln's election in 1860 that Whitman recognized in him the "Redeemer President," but he did come to that realization and almost worshipped him thereafter.

In spite of Whitman's bitter disappointment with party politics during the Fillmore-Buchanan campaign, he still had faith in the future of democracy because he believed the whole course of world history was against the anti-democratic conduct of the American politicians. "Freedom against slavery is not issuing here alone," he declared, "but is issuing everywhere." He saw in modern inventions and engineering such as the steamship, locomotive, telegraph, mass production of books and newspapers, the means of "interlinking the inhabitants of the earth ... as groups of one family." All signs pointed to "unparalleled reforms" in society:

On all sides tyrants tremble, crowns are unsteady, the human race restive, on the watch for some better era, some divine war. No man knows what will happen next, but all know that some such things are to happen as mark the greatest moral convulsions of the earth. Who shall play the hand for America in these tremendous games?[40]

When the war came, Whitman soon discovered that it was not "divine," but it was certainly a great moral convulsion which changed the course of American history. During the political and economic corruption following the war, he would find that "democracy" was still more an ideal than a reality in the United States; so he had to make another attempt to analyze the problem and find grounds for continued hope. That he would attempt in *Democratic Vistas*.

NATURE

One can only speak of Walt Whitman's "philosophy" in a loose and colloquial sense, for, like Emerson, he was not a systematic thinker, and his conceptions of the world he lived in and man's place in it came from various sources, some of them contradictory. But by the time he had written what was to be the first edition of *Leaves of Grass* he had found a blend of concepts and abstractions which satisfied his own needs both as a person and a poet. Since they were eclectic, they carried over some connotations from their sources, with consequent ambiguity. Moreover, Whitman used these concepts and terms both as expressions of faith in the things he held sacred and as metaphors for his cosmic visions, but they meshed sufficiently to form the semblance of an intelligible *Weltanschauung*. If he was not a philosopher, he was at least concerned with answers to the most profound questions regarding the destiny of man:

> To be in any form, what is that?
>
> .   .   .   .   .   .
>
> What is a man anyhow? what am I? what are you?[41]

And in his 1855 Preface he declared: "The poets of the kosmos [he may have meant cosmic poets] advance through all interpositions and coverings and turmoils and stratagems to first principles."[42] What these "first principles" were the poet revealed not in a single preface, an ontological poem like Lucretius's *De rerum natura*, or a prose treatise, but piecemeal through the progressive versions of *Leaves of Grass.*

First of all, Whitman was heir to the Cartesian dualism which separated *mind* and *body*, a dualism which no theory has ever satisfactorily explained. Whitman himself often used the word *soul*, in a variety of contexts (some of which will be examined later), always with the conviction that it was "immortal." But exactly what Whitman meant by immortality of the soul is not easy to determine— possibly not survival of personal identity as most Christians believed. When he used the word *heaven* (usually plural) he almost invariably designated the region of the stars and planets. He never referred to a Day of Judgment, or to the Christian *Atonement*, for he did not believe in "original sin," or that men needed to atone for anything except acts of greed and selfishness. We have seen above in his personal social creed striking resemblances to the "Beatitudes" of Jesus. Yet he did not look to a future life for rewards or punishments in any orthodox Christian sense—though in an evolutionary sense he did, as we shall see below. The idea of *resurrection* also occurs frequently in Whitman's poems, but on the analogy of the life cycles of plants and animals: that is, the sequence of seed, germination, growth, organic death, and rebirth from another seed. This favorite theme is prominent in all Whitman's writings and is one of the best clues to his philosophy of man and nature.

What most shocked Whitman's contemporaries was his emphasis on the physicality of life, in which sex was as prominent and necessary as birth and death. Throughout most of its history the Christian Church had tolerated sexual intercourse as a necessity for procreation, but regarded it as shameful, degrading, and sinful if indulged in for pleasure. The Catholic Church had always held chastity to be one of the highest virtues, and in nineteenth-century America several Protestant sects, most conspicuously the Shakers, had founded celibate communities. In practically all Christian denomintions sex was associated with the forbidden fruit in the Garden of Eden.

When Christianity assimilated Neo-Platonism, it exalted mind over body, and gave Nature an inferior position. According to the Platonic myth the soul domiciled in a human body is a homesick exile, longing always to return to its spiritual home, which it might be able to do if not too much defiled by its association with the body and the world of material things. To return, of course, the body must die, but some Neo-Platonists such as Plotinus believed that in a state of mystical ecstasy the soul could catch glimpses of the world of pure spirit. These fleeting experiences were the highest and most desirable possible for the human mind.

Doctrines of the supremacy of the soul over the body had come down to Whitman by too many channels of religious instruction and literary tradition not to have strong impacts on his thinking, but they were rivaled by other, more materialistic, concepts. The most influential of these was eighteenth-century rationalism and early nineteenth-century science. In Tom Paine's *Age of Reason*, which Whitman read in his youth,[43] he was taught that God's true revelation was in Nature, not in the Bible or other religious documents. From science he learned that the world was not six thousand years old, as both the Jewish and Christian churches had taught for centuries, but millions of years old, as the geologists had proven from the strata of rocks and paleontologists from fossils of plants and animals embedded in the ancient rocks. Moreover, the fossils seemed to reveal strong resemblances and gradations of form and structure between the widely distributed specimens of plants and animals of the different geological ages. These resemblances and gradations suggested kinships and systematic variations which led to the idea of "evolution" long before Darwin published his *Origin of Species* in 1859.

In addition to the *Age of Reason*, the discoveries of geologists about the age of the earth, and of prehistoric life by paleontologists, Whitman found in Count Volney's *Ruins* (one of the books he said he had been "raised" on[44]) a complete philosophy of "Natural Religion" and a rationalistic account of the various religions of the world. The title of this book means the "ruins" of great nations,[45] which had fallen because of the greed of their rulers and the ignorance of their peoples. Volney was not a disciple of Rousseau, who believed in the innate goodness of human nature and blamed man's corrupt condition on society. Like Thomas Hobbes, Volney thought that man in a "savage state" was "A brutal, ignorant animal, a wicked and ferocious beast, like bears and Ourang-outangs.[sic]"[46] The strong ruled the weak, and the weak were too ignorant to find means of protecting themselves. Even after the beginning of an organized society, the strong deified themselves and demanded worship and obedience from the ignorant masses. Religion began with men's worship of the stars, and especially of the sun, whose life-giving effects they could see and feel, but tyrannical rulers exploited the natural religious sentiment as a means of gaining power over their subjects.

Aside from the perverse history of religions, Volney pointed out that they all claimed divine origin and presented their doctrines as the only truth. Obviously, with their different gods and theologies, they could not all be right; how then could an honest man choose the *true* religion? Volney said this was easy, that the God who created the universe had revealed his divine truths through his creation. Therefore, to understand God's plan for man, study Nature. The laws of nature were discernible to man's senses, and did not depend upon hearsay traditions or texts which had several times been translated and probably garbled. The laws of nature could be observed and tested. The only authority a man needed was the evidence of his own senses and experiences:

To establish therefore an uniformity of opinion, it is necessary first to establish the certainty, completely verified, that the portraits which the mind forms are perfectly like the originals: that it reflects the objects correctly as they exist. . . . we must trace a line of distinction between those that are capable of verification, and those that are not, and separate by an inviolable barrier, the world of fantastical beings, from the world of realities . . .[47]

Of course Volney's sensational epistemology had its own naive assumptions, as John Locke's critics of his similar theory of knowledge pointed out, but it appealed to men's "common sense." Volney granted that men could be deceived by their senses, but only when they were swayed by ignorance (superstitition) or passion, both of which could be avoided by rational study of the physical world.[48] By "law of nature" Volney meant:

. . . the constant and regular order of facts, by which God governs the universe; an order which his wisdom presents to the senses and to the reason of men, as an equal and common rule for their actions, to guide them, without distinction of country or of sect, towards perfection and happiness.[49]

Like Bishop Paley and the other "Natural Religion" theologians, Volney argued that no intelligent person could examine "the astonishing spectacle of the universe" without believing in "a supreme agent, an universal and identic mover, designated by the appellation of God. . . ." Men whose ideas of God were formed on the "law of nature" would entertain "stronger and nobler ideas of the Divinity than most other men," for they would "not sully him with the foul ingredients of all the weaknesses and passion entailed on humanity."[50] (One example Volney probably had in mind was the jealous and vindictive God of Calvinism.) In deriving a whole code of ethics and morality from the impartial, undeviating, and inexorable "Law of Nature," as Volney did in twelve chapters under this heading, he had to make more assumptions than he realized; and the virtues derived from them resembled those of the Judeo-Christian religion— except for holding pleasure, self-love, and egotism to be positively good so long as they did no harm to anyone.

It was not from Volney, however, that Whitman got his idea of "evolution." Volney believed that societies, or nations, had progressed from barbarism to civilization in various places at various times, but they had also just as frequently regressed. A decadent nation became the easy prey of a stronger nation or of revolt by its oppressed masses, resulting either in social chaos or rejuvenation. Although these cycles could be said to resemble the growth and decay of plants and animals, and thus to obey some law of nature, Volney did not make this connection, perhaps because he regarded the death of a nation as unnatural, man-made, and thus avoidable.

Walt Whitman actually got his ideas of evolution not directly from biologists, but indirectly from lectures and books on geology and astronomy—discussed below. To judge from the nature of his ideas on this subject, they came indirectly from Jean Baptiste Lamarck (1744–1829), who was the most influential evolutionist during the half-century preceding Darwin. Lamarck believed that all plants and animals had continuously evolved throughout the periods of geological time, each species making gradual alterations in structure and form to adapt to its environment.

The most controversial part of Lamarck's theory was that acquired characteristics could be transmitted to the offspring. Moreover, the hypothesis implied purpose, that somewhere in the process of change intelligence was at work making choices. Of course this confirmation of cosmic teleology appealed to religious leaders, who saw in it a means of preserving faith in a benevolent Creator. But before the end of the century most scientists had accepted Darwin's theory of fortuitous mutations, accidental changes in structure which happened to give an individual plant or animal an advantage in the struggle for survival, thereby enabling it to live long enough to produce offspring. This was the Darwinian "law" of "natural selection." Meanwhile Gregory Mendel was discovering the mathematical laws of hybridization, but his work did not become generally known until about 1900.

Although we know today that Darwin never ceased wondering whether some intelligent direction of energy might be aiding the mutations—what came to be called "Vitalism"—he never found any proof that this was actually true, though his *Movement and Habits of Climbing Plants* (1876) has been thought to leave room for the operation of psychic energy.[51] At any rate, by the end of the century the vitalists had lost credibility and Darwinian mechanical chance had won the field. However, in recent years something like Vitalism has been creeping back into speculations on the origin and development of living organisms.[52] A few scientists now suspect that even plants have some sort of mind or psychic energy, and that they, as well as animals, may have survived not because they were lucky but clever. Or as Emerson says, "Nature's dice are always loaded."[53]

Walt Whitman himself would have doubtless approved this speculation on the minds of plants, or Pierre Teilhard de Chardin's theory that every cell and molecule has some kind of innate intelligence, which multiplies and gains in strength with each increase in the combining of cells into more complex organisms, and the process is always toward greater complexity—the true evolutionary trend of the cosmos.[54] The great mystery is how the life of each cell in an organized complex obeys the command of some mysterious center of control. Teilhard speculated that mind is that controlling force, and that cosmic evolution is the order of the universe. Eventually the whole "biosphere" will become a "Noosphere" (realm of mind).[55]

Walt Whitman actually seems to have anticipated Teilhard in some ways—and here no specific source for Whitman is known. In his preparatory notes written between 1847 and the printing of his first edition of *Leaves of Grass* he declared:

The soul or spirit transmits itself into all matter—into rocks, and can live the life of a rock—into the sea, and can feel itself the sea—into the oak, or other tree—into an animal, and feel itself a horse, a fish, or bird—into the earth—into the motions of the suns and stars—[56]

Whitman cautions himself: "Never speak of the soul as any thing but intrinsically great.—The adjective affixed to it must always testify greatness and immortality and purity.—" What he means by "intrinsic" greatness is elaborated in a theory strongly tinged with Neo-Platonism:

The effusion or corporation of the soul is always under the beautiful laws of physiology—I guess the soul itself can never be anything but great and pure and immortal; but it makes itself visible only through matter—a perfect head, and bowels and bones to match is the easy gate through which it comes from its embowered garden, and pleasantly appears to the sight of the world.—[57]

This is a plain statement of the Platonic idea of the "preexistence of the soul" (expressed by Wordsworth in his "Ode: Intimations of Immortality"), but Whitman's physiological application has the stamp of his own mind and character: "A twisted skull, and blood watery or rotten by ancestry or gluttony, or rum or bad disorders [in Whitman's editorials bad disorders meant venereal disease],—they are the darkness toward which the plant will not grow, although its seed lie waiting for ages.—"[58] Similar to this thought, he says, "Wickedness is most likely the absence of freedom and health in the soul." But if the soul is "pure" (inviolable?) and "immortal," how can matter have any influence on it? We might conclude that a degraded human body has no soul—or at least is not able to expand in it: "the darkness toward which the plant will not grow. . . ." But then in another note Whitman adds: "The universal and fluid soul impounds within itself not only all good characters, and hero[e]s, but the distorted characters, murderers, thieves[.] "[59]

Perhaps these contradictory statements cannot be logically reconciled, and maybe they were only *trial thoughts* anyway. But they reveal attitudes toward mind and matter, and the miraculous nature of both, which carried over into Whitman's poetry and sustained his childlike wonder at existence, "being in any form . . .":

My life is a miracle and my body which lives is a miracle; but of what I can nibble at the edges of the limitless and delicious wonder I know that I cannot separate them, and call one superior and the other inferior, any more than I can say my sight is greater than my eyes.—[60]

In short, these are mysteries which the poet himself does not understand, but he *feels* their existence, and simply accepts them as facts in his experience—an attitude resembling the Buddhist's non-intellectual acceptance of the existence of the unseen God. This faith was also accompanied by an over-belief in what Whitman called "dilation," which he conceived to be a cosmic evolutionary process:

I think the soul will never stop, or attain to any growth beyond which it shall not go.—When I walked at night by the sea shore and looked up at the countless stars, I asked of my soul whether it would be filled and satisfied when it should become god enfolding all these, and open to the life and delight and knowledge of everything in them or of them; and the answer was plain to me at the breaking water on the sands at my feet; and the answer was, No, when I reach there, I shall want to go further still.—[61]

Here are more enormous ambiguities. How will the "soul . . . become god enfolding" the innumerable stars of stellar space? Certainly this is no vision of a Christian heaven or of eternal happiness, for it is the nature of Whitman's "soul" never to be satisfied, or to cease growing. This concept has led many critics and scholars to find parallels to Vedanta and other religious-philosophical concepts of India. While still others are content simply to label Whitman a "mystic." Certainly the far-traveling soul is *migrating* if not trans-migrating. But some definite clues both to the source of these huge soul-concepts and to Whitman's future literary use of them are given in some of the poet's trial lines for "Song of Myself":

I am the poet of reality
I say the earth is not an echo
Nor man an apparition;
But that all things seen are real,

The witness and albic dawn of things equally real.

I have split the earth and the hard coal and rocks and the solid bed of
    the sea
And went down to reconnoitre there a long time,
And bring back a report,
And I understand that those are positive and dense every one
And that what they seem to the child they are.

   .   .   .   .   .   .

Afar in the sky was a nest,
And my soul flew thither and squat, and looked out
And saw the journeywork of suns and systems of suns,
And that a leaf of grass is not less than they
And that the pismire is equally perfect, and all grains of sand, and
    every egg of the wren,
And the tree-toad is a chef d'oeuvre for the highest,
And the running blackberry would adorn the parlors of Heaven
And the cow crunching with depressed neck surpasses every
    statue, . . .[62]

SCIENCE

In writing his experimental lines for his 1855 poems Whitman's creative imagination was drawing upon two paradoxical concepts, one animistic in the most primitive sense (everything has a soul), and the other materialistic and naively "common sense": "all things seen are real . . . what they seem to the child they are."[63] And yet they are more than any child could understand, for things are not only "equal," "perfect," and "beautiful," but the whole universe is con-

structed of the same stuff, which is both material and immaterial—
mind and matter—joined in a timeless journey, or as Whitman
expressed the thought (or faith) in an old-age poem: "The world, the
race, the soul—in space and time the universes,/ . . . all surely going
somewhere."[64]

Some light may be thrown on the nature of this journey and its
destination by examining how Whitman got his interstellar observations of "the journeywork of suns and systems of suns. . . ." Until
Joseph Beaver published his *Walt Whitman—Poet of Science* (1951)
most biographers and critics of Whitman had taken too seriously his
occasional impatience with the minutiae of exact science and his
demanding a "free margin" for his imagination. Most misleading of
all was his poem "When I Heard the Learned Astronomer," which
describes how the "charts and diagrams" and mathematical demon-
strations wearied and sickened him until he left the lecture room and
found relief in simply looking up "in perfect silence at the stars."
More often, however, he was not bored by the "learned astronomer,"
who, in fact, as Beaver has shown, gave him a general education in
the nineteenth-century scientific view of the universe.

Several astronomers lectured in New York in the 1840s, but the
one who particularly attracted Whitman's attention was Ormsby
MacKnight Mitchell,[65] who lectured in the Broadway Tabernacle in
December, 1848, and published *A Course of Six Lectures on Astronomy* the following year. Whether Whitman attended all six lectures
or not, he certainly read the book, drawing upon it many times for
imagery and allusions in his poems. He also got his idea of a "nest" in
the sky as an observation post from Mitchell's lectures, for the
astronomer liked to invite his audience to take imaginary trips with
him through interstellar space. In numerous poems Whitman looks
down upon the "rolling," "bowling," or "sidelong" revolving earth
("sidelong" referring to the inclined axis). For example, in "Salut au
Monde!" he sees "a great round wonder rolling through space," and
in "Pioneers! O Pioneers!":

Lo, the darting bowling orb!
Lo, the brother orbs around, all the clustering suns and plants, . . .

Beaver found a more specific test of Mitchell's influence in a
passage from "On the Beach at Night":

On the beach at night,
Stands a child with her father,
Watching the east, the autumn sky.

Up through the darkness,
While ravening clouds, the burial clouds, in black masses spreading,
Lower sullen and fast athwart and down the sky,
Amid a transparent clear belt of ether yet left in the east,
Ascends large and calm the lord-star Jupiter,
And nigh at hand, only a very little above,
Swim the delicate sisters the Pleiades.

Beaver comments:

Jupiter, in the course of its apparent movement around the zodiac, passes the Pleiades only once every twelve years. This happened in late April and early May, 1870, but Jupiter's slowly changing position made it [the Pleiades] still "only a little above" Jupiter in the early autumn months of the same year. Actually, in September and October, 1870, Jupiter was about 30° from the Pleiades, a fairly large angle. But in 1867, 1868, and 1869, Jupiter would have been *above* the Pleiades, not below them, as that cluster rose in the eastern sky. . . . Whitman, then, first wrote "On the Beach at Night" in the fall of 1870 . . . [Whitman's editors and biographers agree on this date.] Whitman's "only a very little above" seems, in view of the 30° arc which actually separated Jupiter and the Pleiades, to place the bodies closer together than they really were, but it must be remembered that a slight shift in the direction of his vision would have comprehended both. Jupiter was very close to the Pleiades in April and May, 1870, but the Pleiades (and, consequently, Jupiter—in that year) are not visible in the late spring and summer months.[66]

In dozens of passages in his poetry and prose Whitman referred to the position of a planet or constellation. Beaver verified these references with the aid of the *Nautical Almanack* without finding a single error, and he concluded that "Whitman's knowledge of astronomy, though perhaps not technical, was more detailed than has been suspected, and his observations far more accurate than has been admitted or known," and that even his "apparently lush descriptions of celestial objects—of planets in particular—frequently have a basis in natural fact. . . ."[67]

Another example of Whitman's drawing upon Mitchell's lectures is his reference to Saturn in "Song of Myself," sec. 33:

Speeding through space, speeding through heaven and the stars,
Speeding amid the seven satellites and the broad ring, and the
    diameter of eighty thousand miles, . . .

Though Whitman might have learned of the seven satellites from
other books on astronomy, Mitchell's 79,000 miles diameter was
closest to the poet's round 80,000.[68] (Today the diameter of Saturn
is estimated at 75,100 miles, and the number of satellites at twelve
or, possibly, thirteen.)

Whitman also shared Mitchell's enthusiasm for comets. In one
lecture Mitchell said:

There are other mysterious bodies, which seem not to obey the laws
that govern these movements. While the planets are circular in their
orbits and the satellites nearly the same, we find dim, mysterious
bodies, wandering through the uttermost regions of Space,—we see
them coming closer and closer, and as they approach our system,
they fling out their mighty banners, wing their lightning flight
around the Sun and speed away to the remotest limits of vacuity.[69]

The passage from "Song of Myself" quoted above continues:

Speeding with tail'd meteors, throwing fire-balls like the rest,
Carrying the crescent child that carries its own full mother in its
    belly, [answer to the riddle: moon in first quarter]
Storming, enjoying, planning, loving, cautioning,
Backing and filling, appearing and disappearing,
I tread day and night such roads.

Still exploiting the comet metaphor, Whitman continues:

I visit the orchards of spheres and look at the product,
And look at quintillions ripen'd and look at quintillions green.

As interesting as the comet metaphor-vehicle is the "orchard"
metaphor, which in the 1855 version was "orchards of God," thus
anthropomorphizing the astronomical theory of planetary evolution:
some spheres are still in a "green" or early gaseous state of development, while others are more condensed or "ripened." In sec. 44 of
"Song of Myself" Whitman says "the nebula cohered to [i.e., into, or

became] an orb." He was evidently familiar with the "nebular hypothesis."

But it was the comet that most fascinated Whitman, for it seemed to defy all the laws of astronomy, with an orbit of its own so vast that it periodically disappeared into outer space and then returned to swing around our sun and disappear again. The poet liked to think of himself as a comet:

I but advance a moment only to wheel and hurry back in the
darkness. ("Poets to Come")

Mitchell said that as comets "approach our system, they fling out their mighty banners,"[70] meaning of course the streamers of gases which expand in the heat of the sun. It was also believed that in this process the comet partly consumed itself, an idea which Whitman incorporated in his comet-departure near the end of "Song of Myself":

I depart as air, I shake my white locks at the runaway sun,
I effuse my flesh in eddies, and drift it in lacy jags.

The moon also appealed to Whitman's imagination, but in a less exciting manner. He accepted the astronomer's opinion that it was a dead body, without atmosphere, whose "shine" was only light reflected from the sun. Unlike the romantic poets, he did not usually call the moonlight "yellow," or use it to symbolize beauty and love. In "Song of Myself" (sec. 21) he refers to "the vitreous pour [strained through glass] of the full moon just tinged with blue!," which is an accurate description. In sec. 49 "the ghastly glimmer is noonday sunbeams reflected." The dead satellite is a fit symbol for death and decay, and that is the way Whitman used it in sec. 49, and in "Out of the Cradle. . . " where the light is "brown yellow." In the *Drum-Taps* poem "Look Down Fair Moon" he does call the moon "fair" and "sacred," but he implores it to pour down softly on the purple faces of the soldiers' corpses. Thus his connotations are consistently tinged with factual reality.

For all his celebration of the eternal precision and perfect balance of the stars and planets circling in the fields of gravitation, "wheels within wheels," he knows that "the immortal stars" are immortal only as his body is, and that they too obey nature's laws of birth and decay:

(The stars, the terrible perturbations of the suns,
Swelling, collapsing, ending, serving their longer, shorter use, . . .)
—"Eidólons"

It is surprising to find Whitman aware of a *Nova*, or exploding star, but still more curious that he should write in "Song of Myself" (sec. 16):

The bright suns I see and the dark suns I cannot see, are in their place,
The palpable is in its place and the impalpable is in its place.

Possibly he meant suns too far away to be seen even with the telescope, but astronomers today believe there are collapsed stars so dense that they cannot reflect light and are therefore "black holes" in space. Perhaps here by accident Whitman was prophetic, but at least the concept shows how attentive he had been to the lectures (and books) on astronomy, and the awe with which he vicariously took his position in the observatory in "Song of Myself," sec. 45:

I open my scuttle at night and see the far-sprinkled systems,
And all I see multiplied as high as I can cipher edge but the rim of the farther systems.

To summarize the influence of astronomy on Whitman's thinking, he learned, above all else, that physical laws are the basis of all meaningful theories of man's place and function in nature. In Whitman's own words in "Song of the Rolling Earth":

There can be no theory of any account unless it corroborate the theory of the earth. (sec. 3)

In these laws he saw "the ensemble of the world, and the compact truth of the world"—"Laws for Creation." In "Solid, Ironical, Rolling, Orb" he called these *compact truths* the test of his "ideal dreams."

In specific laws Whitman found also analogies for his subjective life. Thus gravitation in the *Children of Adam* poem "I Am He That Aches with Love": "Does the earth gravitate? does not all matter, aching, attract all matter?/ So the body of me to all I meet or know." Gravitation and magnetism, which seemed somehow akin to gravitation (the relation is still not entirely known to science) always fascinated Whitman, and he saw in both some Divine energy operating "Through Space and Time . . . and the flowing eternal identity" ("As They Draw to a Close").

Of course contemporary pseudo-scientific theories on "animal magnetism" (mesmerism, hypnotism, etc.) mingled in Whitman's mind with the solider aspects of physics, but he was not the only intelligent person of the time to be confused. The confusion was no more serious than his finding analogies between his amorous urges and the attraction of matter for other matter. Thus in "Song of Myself" (sec. 27) the electric "charge" and "conductors":

Mine is no callous shell,
I have instant conductors all over me whether I pass or stop,
They seize every object and lead it harmlessly through me.
I merely stir, press, feel with my fingers, and am happy,
To touch my person to some one else's is about as much as I can
    stand.

Whitman took pride in his own strong "animal magnetism,"[71] as he did also for a few years in his phrenological chart,[72] but often natural phenomena merely provided him with metaphors for poetizing human experiences, such as the inseminating "touch" in sexual intercourse in "Song of Myself" (sec. 29):

Blind loving wrestling touch . . .
Parting track'd by arriving, perpetual payment of perpetual
    loan,
Rich showering rain, and recompense richer afterward.

Sprouts take and accumulate, stand by the curb prolific and
    vital,
Landscapes projected masculine, full-sized and golden.

But it was not entirely from astronomy and physics (then called "natural philosophy") that Whitman derived his deepest insights into the mysteries of nature. In fact, his main concept of evolution came from earth science, as presented by Samuel G. Goodrich in *A Glance at the Physical Sciences* (1844), and a few years later (after the first edition of *Leaves of Grass*) by Richard Owen in *Key to the Geology of the Globe* (1857). From such books as these he learned about "vestiges of creation" (the phrase was popularized by Robert Chambers[73] in *The Vestiges of the Natural History of Creation*, 1844), which had "stucco'd [him] with quadrupeds and birds all over" ("Song of Myself," sec. 31), and made him wonder of the animals "where they got those tokens,/ Did I pass that way huge times ago and negligently drop them?" Though this may seem like evolution in reverse, the poet leaves no doubt in sec. 44 that he is aware of the ages of preparation nature has made for his arrival (or of any human being) on earth:

Immense have been the preparations for me,
Faithful and friendly the arms that have help'd me.

Cycles ferried my cradle, rowing and rowing like cheerful boatmen,
For room to me stars kept aside in their own rings,
They sent influences to look after what was to hold me.

Before I was born out of my mother generations guided me,
My embryo has never been torpid, nothing could overlay it.

For it the nebula cohered to an orb,
The long slow strata piled to rest it on,
Vast vegetables gave it sustenance,
Monstrous sauroids transported it in their mouths and deposited it
    with care.

All forces have been steadily employ'd to complete and delight me,
Now on this spot I stand with my robust soul.

SOUL

At all times Walt Whitman was as much concerned with the health of his soul as the health of his body, and the latter was almost an obsession with him. But what did he mean by "soul" (capitalized or lower case)? In the English language the word has many meanings, and it is not surprising that Whitman used it in various senses and connotations: as a synonym of mind, consciousness, imagination, psychic energy, the self, *élan vital* or "spark of life," or even *God*. Sometimes in "Song of Myself" the "I" is any of these synonyms for *soul*, and the lyrical pronoun might be said (often if not always) to be the poet's faculty of articulation. But these considerations do not help the reader in defining the term. Perhaps the best method by which to do that is to approach the problem inductively.

Unlike Emerson and most poets of the nineteenth century, Whitman always insisted on the equality of the body and soul. In "Starting from Paumanok" (sec. 13) he asks and replies:

Was somebody asking to see the soul?
See, your own shape and countenance, persons, substances, beasts,
    the trees, the running rivers, the rocks and sands.

All hold spiritual joys and afterwards loosen them;
How can the real body ever die and be buried?

Of your real body and any man's or woman's real body,
Item for item it will elude the hands of the corpse-cleaners and pass
    to fitting spheres,
Carrying what has accrued to it from the moment of birth to the
    moment of death.

.   .   .   .   .

Behold, the body includes and is the meaning, the main concern, and
    includes and is the soul;
Whoever you are, how superb and how divine is your body, or any
    part of it!

Though the poet does say in one verse that "the body . . . is the soul," he has previously qualified this statement by "real body." What survives, then, is something less—or more—than the physiological body, which could "elude . . . the corpse-cleaners" only in a conservation-of-energy sense, its chemicals passing into other living organisms. At the end of "Song of Myself" the "I" does say "look for me under your boot-soles," but the "I . . . somewhere waiting for you" is a *self*, or *soul*, or spiritual-identity of some sort.

Emerson has often been thought to have been the main source of Whitman's "transcendental" ideas, but there are marked differences between his doctrines of matter and spirit (or soul) and Whitman's. The "certain poet" in *Nature* (1836) who speaks Emersonian ideas says: "The foundations of man are not in matter, but in spirit. But the element of spirit is eternity [in Plato's sense].... In the cycle of the universal man [Platonic archetype], from whom the known individuals proceed, centuries are points, and all history is but the epoch of one degradation." Thus, "A man is a god in ruins." And "Man is a dwarf of himself."[74]

In "The Poet" Emerson says, "The soul makes the body," and "The universe is the externisation of the soul." Possibly this doctrine could be dialectically reconciled with Whitman's concept of the immortality of the "real body," but the emphasis of the two poets is totally different. Emerson continues: "Our science is sensual and therefore superficial. The earth, and the heavenly bodies, physics, and chemistry, we sensually treat, as if they were self-existent; but these are the retinue of that Being we have."[75]

In "Song of Myself" (sec. 3) Whitman chants:

Clear and sweet is my soul, and clear and sweet is all that is not my soul.

Lacks one lacks both, and the unseen is proved by the seen,
Till that becomes unseen and receives proof in its turn.

This statement may be taken as a clue to the relationship of the body and soul, the "seen" and the "unseen." In the lines quoted above from "Starting from Paumanok" Whitman said if you would see the soul, look at the body, and he frequently asserts (as in sec. 48 of "Song of Myself") that "the soul is not more than the body" and "the body is not more than the soul." But he usually mentions them as if they were two, somehow joined in one transitory identity. In fact, "identity" of the self is apparently made possible by this union. That the "soul" is immortal is a belief found in most religions, but few, if any, believe with Whitman "in the flesh and the appetites"—at least not to the extent of declaring ("Song of Myself," sec. 24):

Divine am I inside and out, and I make holy whatever I touch or am touch'd from;
The scent of these arm-pits is aroma finer than prayer,
This head is more than churches or bibles or creeds.

Yet he admits (sec. 49) that the body becomes "good manure," though this does not offend his nostrils because this is only a necessary process in the "perpetual transfers and promotions" of the undying self, the "I" of "Song of Myself." This *self* corresponds to the more conventional concepts of the *soul*.

But there is another Neo-Platonic aspect of Whitman's soul-doctrine. In the 1855 poem "To Think of Time" Whitman says (sec. 7):

It is not to diffuse you that you were born of your mother and
    father—it is to identify you,
It is not that you should be undecided, but that you should be
    decided;
Something long preparing and formless is arrived and formed in you,
You are thenceforth secure, whatever comes or goes.

Here identity seems to be more than simply knowing who or what one is—one's place in society and (possibly) history. Several lines later:

The guest that was coming. . . . he waited long for reasons. . . . he is
    now housed,
He is one of those who are beautiful and happy. . . . he is one of
    those that to look upon and be with is enough.

In this context "guest" seems to be the "soul," and *house* the body. But the antecedent of the first "he" is "guest," while the "he" of the second verse seems to be a person: a person who is a proper house for the long-arriving soul. This interpretation is strengthened by the poet's further insistence that "The law of promotion and transformation cannot be eluded. . . ."

Further light is thrown on this Neo-Platonic doctrine in other poems. In "The Sleepers" (sec. 7) the "myth of heaven" indicates the rôle of the soul:

The soul is always beautiful. . . . it appears more or it appears less. . . .
    it comes or lags behind,
It comes from its embowered garden and looks pleasantly on itself
    and encloses the world;

    .   .   .   .   .

The soul is always beautiful,
The universe is duly in order. . . . every thing is in its place,
What is arrived is in its place, and what waits is in its place; . . .

This does not mean that some bodies do not have a soul—that the soul skips around and chooses its abode. It "advances" regardless of the circumstances of the body it is to inhabit. In another 1855 poem, "Faces" (sec. 4):

The Lord advances and yet advances:
Always the shadow in front. . . . always the reached hand bringing up
    the laggards.

"Faces" dramatizes the poet's doctrine of souls. Some faces are hideous from disease, congenital deformities, or self-abuse, but the beauty of the enclosed soul is only temporarily clouded:

In each house is the ovum. . . . it comes forth after a thousand years.

Spots or cracks at the windows do not disturb me,
Tall and sufficient stand behind and make signs to me;
I read the promise and patiently wait.

All persons, "red white or black . . . are deific," but they may not attain the full potentiality of their divine heritage. This is Whitman's message: let (or aid) your soul attain its "promise." In fact, whether one regards this teaching as trite or profound, it is Whitman's spiritual teaching in *Leaves of G..ss*, which he always maintained was a religious book, a "New Theology" (1872 Preface), a "more splendid Theology" of the "Real . . . behind the Real" (1876 Preface), "poetry suitable to the human soul" (1888 Preface to *November B..ghs*). He had announced this purpose in his 1855 Preface when he said of his ideal poet that readers had a right to expect him "to indicate more than the beauty and dignity which always attach to dumb real objects . . . they expect him to indicate the path between reality and their souls."[76] Whatever the soul was, Whitman's most serious ambition was to show the "path" to it.

MYSTICISM

✓ Many critics have called Whitman a mystic,[77] and extensive comparisons have been made between his utterances and those of the most renowned mystics. Some have seen in the mating of the poet's body and soul in section 5 of "Song of Myself" the origin of his poetic genius, his visionary power:

I mind how we lay in June, such a transparent summer morning;
You settled your head athwart my hips and gently turned over upon
    me,
And parted the shirt from my bosom-bone, and plunged your tongue
    to my barestript heart,
And reached till you felt my beard, and reached till you held my
    feet.

Swiftly arose and spread around me the peace and joy and knowl-
    edge that pass all the art and argument of the earth;
And I know that the hand of God is the elderhand of my own,
And I know that the spirit of God is the eldest brother of my own,
And that all the men ever born are also my brothers. . . . and the
    women my sisters and lovers,
And that a kelson of the creation is love;
And limitless are leaves stiff or drooping in the fields,
And brown ants in the little wells beneath them,
And mossy scabs of the wormfence, and heaped stones, and elder
    and mullen and pokeweed. [1855 text]

It was this experience, some maintain, which transformed Walt
Whitman from a mediocre literary hack into the most original poet
of his generation. The passage does, indeed, vividly describe the kind
of psychological experience which William James has labeled "mystical states of consciousness,"[78] during which the subject believes himself to be in direct communication with the supernatural, or the
recipient of some miraculous energy from a nonmaterial source.
James calls this kind of mysticism "sporadic,"[79] and, indeed, Whitman's writings contain only this one example. It fits James's definition almost perfectly: it takes place while the poet's will (or the "I"
of the poem) is passive (loafing, lying on the June grass); it is transient ("Mystical states cannot be sustained for long"[80]); it can be
described only in symbolical language (James's "ineffability"); and it
has "noetic quality" ("states of insight into depths of truth un-
plumbed by the discursive intellect"). Such states of consciousness
are also called "illuminations" and "epiphanies."

Because the epiphany described in "Song of Myself" was so
rare—or even unique—with Whitman, James assumed that he was not
a sporadic mystic: "Whitman in another place expresses in a quieter
way what was probably with him a chronic mystical perception"[81]:

There is, apart from mere intellect, in the make-up of every superior human identity, (in its moral completeness, considered as *ensemble*, not for that moral alone, but for the whole being, including physique,) a wondrous something that realizes without argument, frequently without what is .called education, (though I think it the goal and apex of all education deserving the name)—an intuition of the absolute balance, in time and space, of the whole of this multifarious, mad chaos of fraud, frivolity, hoggishness—this revel of fools, and incredible make-believe and general unsettledness, we call *the world*; a soul-sight of that divine clue and unseen thread which holds the whole congeries of things, all history and time, and all events, however trivial, however momentous, like a leash'd dog in the hand of the hunter. Such soul-sight and root-centre for the mind—mere optimism explains only the surface or fringe of it. . . .[82]

Whitman's friend, Dr. R. M. Bucke, called this "soul-sight" by another name, "cosmic consciousness": "The prime characteristic of cosmic consciousness is as its name implies a consciousness of the cosmos, that is, of the life and order of the universe."[83] Dr. Bucke himself had experienced such an "intellectual enlightenment," and he thought that Walt Whitman lived in an almost constant state of this kind of consciousness. Bucke described his own experience as a "sense of exultation, of immense joyousness accompanied or immediately followed by an intellectual illumination, impossible to describe." This sounds more like James's "sporadic" mysticism than Whitman's more "chronic" type.

But whether Whitman experienced "cosmic consciousness," either sporadically or chronically, it was mainly before the Civil War that strong feelings of "elevation, elation, and joyousness" influenced his poetry. Later in old age he fondly recalled those precious times:

In that condition of health, (old style) the whole body is elevated to a state by others unknown—inwardly and outwardly illuminated, purified, made solid, strong, yet buoyant. A singualr charm, more than beauty, flickers out of, and over, the face—a curious transparency beams in the eyes, both in the iris and the white—the temper partakes also. Nothing that happens—no event, recontre, weather, etc.—but it is confronted—nothing but is subdued into sustenance—such is the marvelous transformation from the old timorousness and the old process of causes and effects. Sorrows and disappointments cease—there is no more borrowing trouble in advance. A man realizes the venerable myth—he is a god walking the earth, he sees new eligibilities, powers and beauties everywhere; he himself has a new eye-sight and hearing. The play of the body in motion takes a previously unknown grace. Merely *to move* is then a happiness, a pleasure—to breathe, to see, iⁿ also. All the beforehand gratifications, drink, spirits, coffee, grease, stimulants, mixtures, late hours, luxuries, deeds of the night, seem as vexatious dreams, and now the awaken-ing;—many fall into their natural places, wholesome, conveying diviner joys.[84]

Roger Asslineau calls Whitman's mysticism of this period his "poetry of the body," and makes a point of the greatest significance in understanding his ecstatic poetry, that though it begins in sensual delight, it leads to spiritual insight:

[Whitman's] sensuality, instead of remaining exclusively carnal, opens out and is sublimated. The spirit, in order to be manifest, cannot do without matter and, of course, all mysticism depends on and is accompanied by emotions of the flesh. But what is original with Whitman, at least in 1855–56, is that, contrary to Wordsworth, Shelley, or Emerson, for instance, he always has the sharp conscious-ness of the purely sensual source of his mystical intuitions. Instead of proceeding at once to a spiritualization, like the English romantics or the American transcendentalists, he never forgets that his body is the theatre and the point of origin for his mystical states. . . .[85]

Another characteristic of Whitman's mysticism is that he (or the *persona* of his poems) never loses his consciousness of his own unique individuality in contemplation of the Godhead or the realm of spirit. In fact, he is not curious about God, and understands Him "not in the least," yet he hears and beholds God "in every object." In "Song of Myself" (sec. 48) he asks:

Why should I wish to see God better than this day?
I see something of God each hour of the twenty-four, and each
    moment then,
In the faces of men and women I see God, and in my own face in the
    glass?
I find letters from God dropped in the street, and every one is signed
    by God's name,
And I leave them where they are, for I know that others will
    punctually come forever and ever.

In the 1946 edition of this *Walt Whitman Handbook* Whitman's finding God in His creation was called *pantheism*, and to a certain extent the term seems to apply (and had frequently been applied by earlier Whitman scholars), but there is a subtle distinction between God *in* nature, and God's revealing His power and Beauty *through* matter. As Sister Flavia Maria has observed in comparing Whitman's ideas with those of Pierre Teilhard de Chardin, "Song of Myself" seems almost to presage Teilhard's cosmic theology.[86] She quotes this significant passage from *The Divine Milieu*:

God penetrates the world as a ray of light does a crystal; and, with the help of the great layers of creation, he is universally perceptible and active—very near and very distant at one and the same time.

God truly waits for us in things, unless indeed he advances to meet us. The manifestation of his sublime presence in no way disturbs the harmony of our human attitude, but, on the contrary, brings it its true form and perfection. Our lives . . . and the whole of our world are full of God.[87]

Like Whitman, Teilhard refuses to separate God from the material universe. We have seen above in the discussion of science and Whitman how strongly contemporary astronomy, geology, and paleontology stirred the poet's imagination and gave him notions of man's place in cosmic evolution. Teilhard, a reputable geologist and anthropologist, with considerable knowledge of the other physical and biological sciences, articulated the "New Theology" which Whitman called for, and in some ways vividly anticipated. Compare, for example, his vision of the "apices of the stairs" up which the human soul and body have traveled ("Song of Myself," sec. 44) with Teilhard's prophecy of the "New Earth":

We live at the centre of the network of cosmic influences as we live at the heart of the human crowd or among the myriads of stars, without, alas, being aware of their immensity. We should be astonished at the extent and the intimacy of our relationship with the universe.

The roots of our being plunge back and down into the unfathomable past. However autonomous our soul, it is indebted to an inheritance worked upon from all sides—before ever it came into being—by the totality of the energies of the earth.

The human soul is inseparable, in its birth and in its growth, from the universe into which it is born. In each soul, God loves and partly saves the whole world which that soul sums up in an incommunicable and particular way.

Beneath our efforts to put spiritual form into our own lives, the world slowly accumulates, starting with the whole of matter, that which will make of it the . . . New Earth.[88]

Whitman seems to have anticipated Teilhard's theory of "cosmic influence" in two ways. In the 1860 poem, "With Antecedents," he says, "We touch all laws and tally all antecedents,/. . . We stand amid time beginningless and endless . . ."

All swings around us—there is as much darkness as light,
The very sun swings itself and its system of planets around us,
Its sun, and its again, all swing around us.

Later (1874) in "Song of the Universal," Whitman says that for the soul "the entire star-myriads roll through the sky, /In Spiral routes by long detours. . . ," but always "the real to the ideal tends." Although Whitman would still not dally "with the mystery," his soul in "Passage to India" acknowledges God as the "pulse" and "motive of the stars, suns, systems," the "fibre and breath" creating and animating the universes. Finally in "A Thought of Columbus" (1891) a "breath of Deity" unfolds "the bulging universe" and the "farthest evolutions of the world and man."

The other way in which Whitman anticipated Teilhard—an extension of his "breath of Deity" doctrine—was that the soul itself grows or "dilates" with insatiable ambition (more resembling Milton's Satan or Goethe's Faust than a Christian "soul"). In 1855 "Song of Myself" (sec. 45) all creation is on an evolutionary journey:

There is no stoppage, and never can be stoppage;
If I and you and the worlds and all beneath or upon their surfaces,
    and all the palpable life, were this moment reduced back to a
    pallid float, it would not avail in the long run,
We should surely bring up again where we now stand,
And as surely go as much farther, and then farther and farther.

And again in sec. 46:

This day before dawn I ascended a hill and looked at the crowded heaven,

And I said to my spirit, When we become the enfolders of those orbs and the pleasure and knowledge of every thing in them, shall we be filled and satisfied then?
And my spirit said No, we level that lift to pass and continue beyond.

Does this mean that the poet expected after the death of his body that his soul would pass to other planets? This would be a fairly literal and simple interpretation of his words, and Kant's theory of eternal cycles of cosmic evolution and devolution (universes endlessly winding and unwinding themselves, mentioned in some of the astronomy lectures Whitman had heard) encouraged the idea that souls might migrate from one cosmic system to another to continue their evolutionary growth in the "orchards of God." Of course by mating with Time and smiling at death Whitman could have meant only to convey the idea of the immortality of the soul. But the other verse—"fillest, swellest full the vastness of space"—does seem to mean something more than merely immortality, or a soul free of time and space.

However, before attempting further to determine the kind of "immortality" Whitman attributed to the soul, we should notice that he often used the idea to symbolize his literary "life" after his death. In such passages he might use "I," "Me," or "Myself" instead of his "soul," but all of these words were but synonyms for his deeper self, the "real Me," or as in "So Long!" (1860) the "best of me." Here he invisions his poems dropping "seed ethereal" into the ground of posterity, to spread when he is "no longer visible":

I feel like one who has done work for the day to retire awhile,
I receive now again of my many translations, from my avataras ascending, while others doubtless await me,
An unknown sphere more real than I dream'd, more direct, darts awakening rays about me, So long!
Remember my words, I may again return,
I love you, I depart from materials,
I am as one disembodied, triumphant, dead. [1881 version]

Phrases like "return awhile," "my many translations," "avataras ascending" (or descending?), and "I may return again" carry connotations of Hindu "incarnation." But all the time the poet is thinking of the perennial life of his book, and enjoying vicariously his expected perpetuity in the minds of his readers.

The second caution is that some of Whitman's boldest assertions of the soul's immortality are incantations resembling "sympathetic magic"—like praying for faith in times of doubt. In "Darest Thou Now O Soul" (1868), for example, the poet (or "I") asks his soul if it is ready to venture into "the unknown region," without "map" or "guide":

> I know it not O soul,
> Nor dost thou, all is a blank before us,
> All waits undream'd of in that region, that inaccessible land.

Yet without further assurances even of the existence of "that inaccessible land," the poet says that when his ties to the earth loosen,

> Then we burst forth, we float,
> In Time and Space O soul, prepared for them,
> Equipt, equipt at last . . .

The real intent of the cluster of poems called "Whispers of Heavenly Death" is perhaps most clearly indicated in "A Noiseless Patient Spider," in which the poet, with a tone of deep pathos and almost desperation, implores his soul to continue throwing out lifelines, like the spider in vacant space,

> . . . throwing, seeking the spheres to connect them,
> Till the bridge you will need be form'd, till the ductile anchor hold,
> Till the gossamer thread you fling catch somewhere, O my soul.

Thus it was not out of confidence in the immortality of his soul (in the sense of a personal identity) that Walt Whitman wrote his invocations to liberating death, but in a desperate attempt to build a "bridge" to belief in the life of the soul in other "spheres" (and note the ambiguity of spheres, ranging from planets to immaterial realms of spiritual existence). In a poem called "The Last Invocation" he begs his soul "to ope the doors" softly:

> Tenderly—be not impatient,
> (Strong is your hold O mortal flesh,
> Strong is your hold O Love.)

To construct a mythology of the "spheres" to which Whitman expects his soul to migrate is to interpret his metaphors too literally and simple-mindedly. He had *hope* of some kind of spiritual life after his mortal end, but his imagination was unequal to visualize it with the vitality of a Blake or a Swedenborg. However, in a less personal, more universal sense, he did have a prophetic vision of the cosmic destiny of the "soul" of the human race, a destiny in which the generic soul of the poet (meaning all true poets) had a special rôle to perform.

In "Passage to India" Whitman calls the poet "the true son of God," by which he means that the poet he himself has tried so hard to be will be the interpreter of the purpose of cosmic creation, as Christ was the intermediary between God and his children. (That Whitman was aware of competing with Milton's Christian epic is also indicated by his repeating *justify*: Milton's "justify the ways of God to men.")

> O vast Rondure, swimming in space,
> Cover'd all over with visible power and beauty,
> Alternate light and day and the teeming spiritual darkness,
> Unspeakable high processions of sun and moon and countless
>   stars above,
> Below, the manifold grass and waters, animals, mountains, trees,
> With inscrutable purpose, some hidden prophetic intention,
> Now first it seems my thought begins to span thee.

The thought which *spans* cosmology and life on the earth is that the "unsatisfied soul" of God's "feverish children" was responding all along to a divine compulsion. The explorers, scientists, and engineers were predestined to develop the resources of the earth to their utmost possibility, but God's cosmic plan also calls for a humanizing and spiritualizing of these achievements. After the seas are all crossed, the poet's soul (representative, as in "Song of Myself" of all human souls) will "front" God. Then "fill'd with friendship, love complete, the Elder Brother found,/The Younger melts in fondness in his arms." This prophetic wish doubtless does apply to Walt Whitman's own personal hope for his own soul, but the whole context of the poem implies a universal extension. And here again Teilhard seems the best commentator on Whitman's idea. The "religion" defined by Teilhard in *Building the Earth* is strikingly parallel to

Whitman's cosmic theology (the "new religion"[89] he mentions many times in his notes and prefaces):

Religion is not an option or a strictly individual intuition, but represents the long unfolding, the collective experience of all mankind, of the existence of God—God reflecting himself personally on the organized sum of thinking beings, to guarantee a sure result of creation, and to lay down exact laws for man's hesitant activities.[90]

.   .   .   .   .

A substantial part of this tide of available energy will immediately be absorbed in the expansion of man in matter. But another part, and that the most precious, will inevitably flow back to the levels of spiritualized energy.

Spiritualized Energy is the flower of Cosmic Energy.[91]

.   .   .   .   .

To be super spiritualized in God, must not mankind first be born and grow in conformity with the whole system of what we call evolution?

The sense of earth opening and flowering upwards in the sense of God, and the sense of God rooted and nourished from below in the sense of earth. The transcendent personal God and the universe in evolution, no longer forming two antagonistic poles of attraction, but entering into a hierarchic conjunction to uplift the human mass in a single tide.[92]

VISTAS

Whitman predicted as early as his 1855 Preface, as we have seen, that the poet would take the place of the priest and that literature must supply a "new religion" more capable than the old of ministering to the social and moral needs of mankind in a scientific age, and in each succeeding preface he repeated this opinion and stated his own program to meet the need. Although he had no specific social or political program, his literary program was in the broadest and deepest sense both social and political. Finally in *Democratic Vistas* he attempted an extended treatise on his idea of democracy and the means of converting the ideal into reality.

Democratic Vistas is wordy, turgid, and syntactically distracting (partly the result, perhaps, of combining three essays—or condensing three into two),[93] but some distinguished critics have found in it an important contribution to the theory of political democracy. Admitting that "our New World democracy . . . is, so far, an almost complete failure in its social aspects, and in really grand religious, moral, literary, and aesthetic results," Whitman nevertheless points out:

Sole among nationalities, these States have assumed the task to put in forms of lasting power and practicality, on areas of amplitude rivaling the operations of the physical kosmos, the moral political speculations of ages, long, long deferr'd, the democratic republican principle, and the theory of development and perfection by voluntary standards, and self-reliance.[94]

Whitman began *Democratic Vistas* as a reply to Carlyle's attack in *Shooting Niagara* on American democracy,[95] which the Scotchman saw as a degradation of society and an infectious threat to other nations. But as Whitman worked on his reply he became almost as severe as Carlyle on the present reality, with its political hypocrisy, "depravity of the business classes," corruption in government, and general cynicism of "respectable" citizens.[96] Yet it was not, Whitman believed, that democracy had failed; it had, like Christianity, not been tried. That was the problem. How, then, could it be solved? First of all, Whitman argued, democracy must be understood for what it was: not so much a form of government as a method for men to live together in equality and mutual respect—which must rest on respect for themselves:

Political democracy, as it exists and practically works in America, with all its threatening evils, supplies a training-school for making first-class men. It is life's gymnasium, not of good only, but of all. We try often, though we fall back often. A brave delight, fit for freedom's athletes, fills these arenas, and fully satisfies, out of the action in them, irrespective of success. Whatever we do not attain, we at any rate attain the experiences of the fight, the hardening of the strong campaign, and throb with currents of attempt at least. . . .[97]

Whitman's experiences in the Civil War had convinced him that ordinary people were capable of governing themselves democratically. The trouble was the corruption at the top. The average soldier, from the "unknown rank and file," had shown courage, loyalty, and

incredible patience and endurance in spite of the hopeless mismanagement of their officers, and often in the face of defeat and
imminent death. In the same way, it was not the average citizen but
the professional politician who thwarted political democracy. For
this reason Whitman distrusted all parties (as he had in "The Eighteenth Presidency!"). Everyone should enter politics and vote, he
advised, but "Disengage yourself from parties."[98] By remaining independent the voter could elect the best man to office. He hoped also
that in the future women could participate, for "The day is coming
when the deep questions of woman's entrance amid the arenas of
practical life, politics, the suffrage, etc., will not only be argued all
around us, but may be put to decision, and real experiment." Whitman had always stood for equal rights for women, and he thought
their entrance into politics might help the American "experiment" in
self-government to work better.

Above all else, however, Whitman looked to literature to aid the
production of men and women with sufficient character (sure of
their "identity" and with well-developed individualism) to create a
viable democratic society. It must be a new literature because that of
the past had been tainted by feudalism, caste, and privilege: "Literature, strictly considered [i.e., as literature], has never recognized the
People, and, whatever may be said, does not today." Democracy has
"a fit scientific estimate and reverent appreciation of the People—of
their measureless wealth of latent power and capacity. . . ."[99]

The new literature will be religious in the sense of religion in
"Passage to India," which recognizes the importance of both matter
and spirit in the development of each individual soul on its cosmic
journey. And here again Teilhard's evolutionary process of the "earth
opening and flowering upward" (quoted above) both parallels and
illustrates Whitman's theory of the future development of democracy—its vistas. In The Future of Man Teilhard says there are
three stages:

The first phase was the formation of proteins up to the stage of the
cell. In the second phase individual cellular complexes were formed,
up to and including Man. We are now at the beginning of a third
phase, the formation of an organico-social super-complex, which, as
may easily be demonstrated, can only occur in the case of reflective,
personalized elements. First the vitalization of matter, associated
with the grouping of molecules; then the hominisation of Life, associated with a super-grouping of cells; and finally the planetisation of

Mankind, associated with a closed grouping of people: Mankind, born on this planet and spread over its entire surface, coming gradually to form around its earthly matrix a single, hyper-complex, hyper-centrated, hyper-conscious arch-molecule, coexistensive with the heavenly body on which it was born. Is not this what is happening at the present time—the closing of this spherical, thinking circuit?[100]

In "Passage to India" Whitman says that after the earth is spanned by man's science and engineering, his thought will return to its spiritual origins, symbolized by India; then he will take passage to "more than India," or "the seas of God." In *Democratic Vistas* (written about the same time) he also has three stages, or subdivisions of Teilhard's "planetisation of Mankind." But Whitman gives more attention than Teilhard to the political process:

For the New World, indeed, after two grand stages of preparation-strata, I perceive that now a third stage, being ready for, (and without which the other two were useless,) with unmistakable signs appears. The First stage was the planning and putting on record the political foundation rights of immense masses of people—indeed all people—in the organization of republican National, State, and municipal governments, all constructd with reference to each, and each to all. This is the American programme, not for classes, but for universal man, and is embodied in the compacts of the Declaration of Independence . . . the Federal Constitution—and in the State governments. . . . The Second stage relates to material prosperity. . . . The Third stage, rising out of the previous ones, to make them and all illustrious, I, now, for one, promulge, announcing a native expression-spirit, getting into form, adult, and through mentality, for these States . . . and by a sublime and serious Religious Democracy sternly taking command, dissolving the old, sloughing off surfaces, and from its own interior and vital principles, reconstructing, democratizing society.[101]

Ray Benoit thinks that Teilhard's stages of evolution point "to just that third stage Whitman envisioned in *Democratic Vistas*"[102] and which he had poetized in "Passage to India":

The linkage "Tying the Eastern to the Western Sea,/ The road between Europe and Asia" heralds the first glimmer of what Teilhard termed the Noosphere, a layer of mind as the zenith of evolution when physical complexity and sheer plurality are such that psychic unity will be complete and earth will arrive at its Omega Point—"the gradual incorporation of the World in the Word Incarnate." So, in the poem, "The true son of God shall come singing his songs" and

All these separations and gaps shall be taken up and hook'd and
    link'd together,
The whole earth, this cold, impassive, voiceless earth, shall be
    completely justified.

Once again that Miltonic word *justified*, meaning basically that the physical world has fulfilled its divinely-intended purpose. Not believing in man's sinful nature, Whitman could hardly mean justify in the Puritan theological sense of forgiveness and purification of man's soul, though it does have its Whitmanian sublime connotation. In "Song of Myself" he had declared (sec. 24):

Through me many long dumb voices,

        .   .   .   .   .

Voices of cycles of preparation and accretion,
And of the threads that connect the stars—and of wombs, and the
    fatherstuff, . . .

For nearly two decades Whitman had been articulating these "dumb voices," attempting both in the imagery of his poems and the theory of a spiritual democracy in *Democratic Vistas* to weave the "threads" connecting the co-equal and co-related worlds of matter and spirit.

? *Apostroph Democratic* ~~tr to grim tufs~~

take this piece out altogether

tr to Drum *tafs*

~~CHANTS~~

~~DEMOCRATIC~~

to Drum *tafs*

~~NATIVE AMERICAN.~~

O brood Continental!
(apostroph.)

~~Apostroph.~~

~~O mater! O fils!~~
O brood continental ! *~~naturally the posture~~* !
~~O flowers of the prairies !~~
~~O space boundless ! O hum of mighty products !~~
O you teeming cities ! ~~Of~~ so invincible, turbulent,
     proud !
~~O race of the future ! O women !~~
~~O fathers !~~ O ~~you~~ men of passion and the storm !
~~O native power only !~~ ~~O beauty !~~
~~O yourself ! O God ! O divine average !~~ *yours*
~~O you bearded roughs ! O bards !~~ O all those slum-
     berers !
Arouse ! ~~A~~rouse ! the dawn-bird's throat sounds shrill ! *yours* ~~Do~~
~~you not hear the cock crowing ?~~ *exultant*
Arouse ! ~~A~~s I walk'd the beach, I heard the mournful notes
     foreboding a tempest — ~~the~~ the low, oft-repeated
     shriek of the diver, the long-lived loon ; *I heard*
(105)

Chapter IV

Literary Technique in
Leaves of Grass

The words of my book nothing, the drift of it everything,
A book separate, not link'd with the rest nor felt by the intellect,
But you ye untold latencies will thrill to every page.
                                    —"Shut Not Your Doors, Proud Libraries."

THE ANALOGOUS FORM

If it were possible to separate thought from form, we might say that the style of *Leaves of Grass* has puzzled the critics, from 1855 until recent times, even more than the ideas.[1] Certainly many of the most serious efforts of the Whitman scholars and critics have been directed toward the interpretation and rationalization of this poet's art. They have often failed, however, because they did not understand Whitman's ideas and his intentions (though it is by no means certain that he always understood them himself). But some of the ambiguity of both thought and form was implicit in his intentions— either intended or unavoidable. He was right when he claimed in 1876: "My form has strictly grown from my purports and facts, and is the analogy of them."[2] Both his successes and failures as a poet were closely analogous to his theories and literary ambitions.

When Whitman chose to mention style, or someone nudged him into committing himself, he was likely to be disingenuous. To Traubel's questions he replied:

I have never given any study merely to expression: it has never appealed to me as a thing valuable or significant in itself: I have been deliberate, careful, even laborious: but I have never looked for finish—never fooled with technique more than enough to provide for simply getting through: after that I would not give a twist of my chair for all the rest.[3]

On another occasion he claimed that "What I am after is the content not the music of words. Perhaps the music happens—it does no harm."[4]

It is possible that Whitman's form was intuitive. De Selincourt may have been right when he declared romantically that, "His own wild music, ravishing, unseizable, like the song of a bird, came to him, as by his own principles it should have come, when he was not searching for it"[5]—though anyone who has studied Whitman's tortured manuscripts must doubt that this miracle ever happened when the poet "was not searching for it"; he chose the path even if he did not always know the way.

We can never know exactly what went on in Whitman's head either while he composed or while he indefatigably revised and re-edited his manuscripts year after year. As Furness says, "He was imbued more thoroughly perhaps with the 'daemonic' theory of inspiration and execution than any other poet of the nineteenth century."[6] But however unconscious he may have been of technique, he was so concerned with his theory of expression that it became his favorite theme in his various prefaces. The theory has been misunderstood because it was Whitman's avowed purpose in 1855 to achieve a style which would be not only "transcendent and new" but also "indirect and not direct or descriptive or epic,"[7] and "the medium that shall well nigh express the inexpressible."[728] Certainly this is no ordinary demand to make of literary technique. Whitman had no stories to tell, no descriptions of humble life, no melody to sing like Longfellow, Whittier, or Poe. *Poetry* to him was neither words nor beautiful sounds but something within, intangible—"poetic quality ... is in the soul,"[714] and he called "The United States themselves ... essentially the greatest poem."[709]

Whitman's inability or unwillingness to discuss his technique in terms of craftsmanship was imbedded in his fundamental assumptions about his literary intentions. Not only must his form be capable of expressing his mystical ideas, but to admit conscious planning and molding of the expression would have meant casting doubt on its authenticity and his own sincerity. To what extent his literary strategy was conscious, it is difficult to say: nevertheless, his very ambiguity was, for his purposes, clever strategy, as he was not entirely unaware himself:

Without effort and without exposing in the least how it is done the greatest poet brings the spirit of any or all events and passions and scenes and persons some more and some less to bear on your individual character as you hear or read. [716]

What he is attempting, therefore, is not so much the complete "expression" or communication of a thought or an experience as exerting an influence on the reader so that he himself, by willing cooperation with the poet, may have an esthetic-religious experience of his own. It is literally true that Whitman attempts less to create a "poem," as the term is usually understood, than to present the materials of a poem for the reader to use in creating his own work of art. No doubt in a sense, as Croce has argued, this is the manner in which all esthetic experience takes place; but Whitman aims to do nothing more than "indicate," though this is on a grand, mystical scale:

The land and sea, the animals fishes and birds, the sky of heaven and the orbs, the forests mountains and rivers, are not small themes . . .[8] but folks expect of the poet to indicate more than the beauty and dignity which always attach to dumb real objects . . . they expect him to indicate the path between reality and their souls. [714]

There we have the poet's most fundamental literary intention: *to indicate the path between reality and the soul.* And this is why both the theory and the expression must always remain vague and ambiguous. It is also why Whitman attaches so much importance to gestures and "indirections." His ideal poet "is most wonderful in his last half-hidden smile or frown . . . by that flash of the moment of parting the one that sees it shall be encouraged or terrified afterwards for many years." [716] Or again in 1888, after *Leaves of Grass* had been virtually completed:

I round and finish little, if anything; and could not, consistently with my scheme. The reader will always have his or her part to do, just as much as I have had mine. I seek less to state or display any theme or thought, and more to bring you, reader, into the atmosphere of the theme or thought—there to pursue your own flight.[9]

Believing that his function was to hint rather than state, to initiate rather than complete, Whitman adopted and developed for his own purposes the "organic" theory of poetic expression. Poetry should imitate not things but the spirit of things, not God or creation but His creativity. Hence fluency, logical structure, finish, were looked upon as artificial and useless ornamentation: "Who troubles himself about his ornaments or fluency is lost."

The poetic quality is not marshalled in rhyme or uniformity or abstract addresses to things nor in melancholy complaints or good precepts, but is the life of these and much else and is in the soul. The profit of rhyme is that it drops seeds of a sweeter and more luxuriant rhyme, and of uniformity that it conveys itself into its own roots in the ground out of sight. The rhyme and uniformity of perfect poems show the free growth of metrical laws and bud from them as unerringly and loosely as lilacs or roses on a bush, and take shapes as compact as the shapes of chestnuts and oranges and melons and pears, and shed the perfume impalpable to form. The fluency and ornaments of the finest poems or music or orations or recitations are not independent but dependent.[10]

Kennedy was echoing Whitman when in defending the style of *Leaves of Grass* he declared: "it is a truism that Nature, in all her forms, avoids base mechanical regularity."[11] Perhaps Whitman began his prosody with this negative principle: to represent Nature, or the order of creation, he must avoid conventional regularity—which meant of course rime and meter as they were known in the 1850s.

One of the most curious paradoxes in Whitman's literary doctrine is his insistence upon the "simplicity" of this "organic" theory or analogy: "The art of art, the glory of expression and the sunshine of the light of letters is simplicity. Nothing is better than simplicity." This, however, is his idea of stylistic simplicity: "But to speak in literature with the perfect rectitude and insousiance [*sic*] of the movements of animals and the unimpeachableness of the sentiment of trees in the woods and grass by the roadside is the flawless triumph of art."[12] Equally paradoxical is the added statement that, "The greatest poet has less a marked style and is more the channel of thoughts and things without increase or diminution, and is the free channel of himself."

This conception of the poet as a passive agent, through whom the currents of the universe flow without hindrance or his conscious direction, did not of course, in practical terms, result in a literary form either simple or unmannered. But the theory did determine what the form was not—and perhaps eventually what it was. In the first place, it was not to be restrained, disciplined.

> . . . . I permit to speak at every hazard,
> Nature without check with original energy.[13]

From this doctrine and the resulting uninhibited flow of confessions bubbling up from the poet's inner life came his own apparent belief that he could solve the problem of form by rejecting all conventional techniques. But if he actually did believe this, it was the greatest of all his illusions, for without conventions of some sort there can be no communication whatever. Understanding depends upon the ability of the hearer or reader to recognize some form of order in the linguistic symbols of the speaker or writer.

Of course Whitman did not evolve brand-new techniques. But he did reject and modify or readapt enough conventions to short-circuit communication for many readers for many years, and is not always intelligible even today. He is, however, more easily understood in our day than in his own because critical interpreters have sufficiently clarified his intentions for the reasonably literate reader to know at least what the poet was attempting. For no other American poet has criticism rendered so great a service, or been so necessary.

Before attempting to discover in detail what kind of form and technique Whitman created and adapted for his purposes, we might ask ourselves, by way of summary, what he wanted the "new" style to do. It must, as we have seen, express an inner rather than an outer harmony. He is not so much concerned with things and appearances as with the "spirit" of their relationships. And these are to be suggested or implied rather than explicitly stated. The form must be "organic," though he aims not at describing or imitating external nature but at conveying the creativity of Nature, with her fecundity and variety. It must, therefore, be a democratic-animistic style. Never before, he thought, had "poetry with cosmic and dynamic features of magnitude and limitlessness suitable to the human soul"[14] been possible.

THE EXPANDING EGO

All critics who have seriously tried to understand Whitman have observed that the "I" of his poems is generic: he celebrates himself as a representative man. His "soul" is but a fragment of the World-Soul, and is mystically and animistically related to all the souls of the universe. In asserting his own uniqueness he merely gives expression— at least philosophically and intentionally—to the creative power of the innate soul "identified" through his own personality.

This much is obvious to anyone who is familiar with Whitman's ideas and avowed poetic purposes. The almost inevitable result on his literary technique is that his poetic form is analogous to his "purports and facts." His point of view (except in a few of the shorter and more truly personal lyrics) will not be finite and stationary but ubiquitous and soaring—a migrating soul transcending time and space. It is not in the least unusual for a lyric poet to identify himself with some one object or place, like Shelley in "The Cloud" or "Ode to the West Wind," but Whitman's ego is in constant motion, flitting like a humming bird from object to object and place to place with miraculous speed.

> My ties and ballasts leave me, my elbows rest in sea-gaps,
> I skirt sierras, my palms cover continents,
> I am afoot with my vision.[15]

This is his point of view not only in his spectacular cosmic visions but in nearly all his poems. Even when he is less mystical, not obviously trying to hover over the earth watching the "great round wonder rolling through space,"[16] the imagery is panoramic, unending, flowing, expanding. Whitman's description of the manner in which he "abstracts" himself from the book and stretches his mind (or poetic imagination) in all directions probably gives the best clue to the method by which he developed his style and technique. In the 1855 Preface the "bard" is not only "commensurate with a people" and attempts to "incarnate" flora, fauna, and topography, but he also "spans . . . from east to west and reflects what is between them."[17] The point of view of the first section of "Salut au Monde!" is therefore typical of Whitman's art in general:

> O take my hand Walt Whitman!
> Such gliding wonders! such sights and sounds!
> Such join'd unended links, each hook'd to the next,
> Each answering all, each sharing the earth with all.

Although this method results in the long catalogs, in the piling up of image on top of image with meager enumeration of attributes, the poet is not content with merely photographing from an airplane. However unselected the mass of images may seem to some readers, he intended them to symbolize a spiritual unity in himself and all creation.

What widens within you Walt Whitman?

.   .   .   .   .

Within me latitude widens, longitude lengthens, . . .

The externals, the catalog of concrete details, are transcendental symbols of what he might call "spiritual truths." Thus we have the curious paradox in Whitman's style of snapshot imagery joined to ambiguity. Even in his most vivid realism he is still allegorical and subjective.

The effect of this style has not been unobserved by critics. Paul Elmer More, the late "New Humanist," wrote:

This sense of indiscriminate motion is . . . the impression left finally by Whitman's work as a whole . . . Now the observer seems to be moving through clustered objects beheld vividly for a second of time and then lost in the mass, and, again, the observer himself is stationary while the visions throng past him in almost dizzy rapidity; but in either case we come away with the feeling of having been merged in unbroken processions, whose beginning and end are below the distant horizon, and whose meaning we but faintly surmise.[18]

Reed has called this attempt to present cosmic unity in flux "The Heraclitan Obsession of Walt Whitman."[19] He finds it logically contradictory, however, because the "progressive integration" of form is not "opposed by a contrary disunity of some sort." How can he blend body and soul without a dualism?

But this logical impasse does not appear to have bothered Whitman, and criticism of his thinking need not detain us here. What is of interest . . . is the psychological effect as it is imprinted on the poems. With unification as an ideal, Whitman, one would expect, would show a fine sure insight into the oneness of the phenomenal world. Yet the reader of his poems gains no awareness of such unity. The feeling is rather of disintegration and extreme multiplicity.

This criticism calls attention to the fundamental problem in Whitman's use of the expanding ego. Perhaps the effect depends largely upon the reader's own philosophy. To the Absolutist the effect is no doubt confusion, to the Relativist probably not. Perhaps this is saying that the unity is not in the poem but in the mind of the reader, as it was no doubt in the mind (or intention) of the poet—to whom these "gliding wonders" were "join'd unended links, each hook'd to the next."

This interpretation suggests Whitman's anticipation of both the modern "stream of consciousness" literary technique and the movement known in the 1920s as "Expressionism."[20] Dahlström's characterization of this doctrine in Germany might almost be a summary of Whitman's theory and practice and indicates the need for a study of the American poet's possible influence on the movement:

Foremost among the elements [of Expressionism] is the concept of the *Ausstrahlungen des Ichs*—the radiation, expansion, and unfolding of the ego. This is partly explained by the phrase 'stream of consciousness' which is current in our English terminology. Yet 'stream of consciousness' offers too frequently the possibility of itemization of the elements of consciousness, lingers too close to the realm of psychology. For the expressionist, consciousness is no manifoldly died punch press turning out countless items of similar or dissimilar pattern. It is rather a unifying instrument that moulds oneness of the countless items poured into it. The ego is the predominant element in our universe; it is, indeed, the very heart of the world's reality. For the artist, the ego is a magic crystal in which the absolute is in constant play. It is the subject that registers the everlasting *state of becoming* that qualifies our world; and this subject has an anti-pole *object* which is functional only in giving meaning to the subject. Conversely, the subject must give meaning to the object. It is this ego, this subject, this magic crystal that actually gathers reality in its ultimate character.[49-50]

The "magic crystal" accurately characterizes Whitman's technique of dynamic, creative, enumeration of the kind of spiritual reality in which he believed, and it was his fundamental purpose to register through the eyes of his expanding ego "the everlasting state of becoming that qualifies our world." For the expression of such basic ideas as his cosmic evolution, his animism, and his adaptation of the "temporalized Chain of Being" concept this technique was astonishingly appropriate.

THE SEARCH FOR A "DEMOCRATIC" STRUCTURE

In so far as the expanding ego psychology results in an enumerative style, the cataloging of a representative and symbolical succession of images, conveying the sensation of subjective unity and endless becoming, it is itself a literary technique. But though this psychology may be called the background or basic method of Whitman's poetic technique, the catalog itself was not chronologically the first stylistic device which he adopted. It emerged only after he had found a verse structure appropriate for expressing his cosmic inspiration and democratic sentiment. Nowhere in the universe does he recognize caste or subordination. Everything is equally perfect and equally divine. He admits no supremes, or rather insists that "There can be any number of supremes."[21]

The expression of such doctrines demands a form in which units are co-ordinate, distinctions eliminated, all flowing together in a synonymous or "democratic" structure. He needed a grammatical and rhetorical structure which would be cumulative in effect rather than logical or progressive.

Possibly, as many critics have believed, he found such a structure in the primitive rhythms of the King James Bible, though some of the resemblances may be accidental. The structure of Hebraic poetry, even in English translation, is almost lacking in subordination. The original language of the Old Testament was extremely deficient in connectives, as the numerous "ands" of the King James translation bear witness.[22] It was a language for direct assertion and the expression of emotion rather than abstract thought or intellectual subtleties. Tied to such a language, the Hebraic poet developed a rhythm of thought, repeating and balancing ideas and sentences (or independent clauses) instead of syllables or accents. He may have had other prosodic conventions also, no longer understood or easily discernible; but at least in the English translation this rhythm of thought or parallelism characterizes Biblical versification.[23]

That Walt Whitman fully understood the nature of these Biblical rhythms is doubtful, and certainly his own language did not tie him down to such a verse system. Despite the fact that he was thoroughly familiar with the Bible and was undoubtedly influenced by the scriptures in many ways, it may, therefore, have been a coincidence that in searching for a medium to express his animism he naturally (we might almost say atavistically) stumbled upon parallelism as his basic structure. Furthermore, parallelism is found in primitive poetry other than the Biblical; in fact, it seems to be typically primitive,[24] and it is perhaps not surprising that in the attempt to get rid of conventional techniques Whitman should have rediscovered a primitive one.

But whatever the sources of Whitman's verse techniques, the style of the King James Version is generally agreed to provide convenient analogies for the prosodic analysis of *Leaves of Grass*.[25]

"The principles which governed Hebrew verse," says Gardiner, "can be recovered only in part, but fortunately the one principle which really affects the form of the English has been clearly made out, the principle of parallel structure: in the Hebrew poetry the line was the unit, and the second line balanced the first, completing or supplementing its meaning."[26]

Even the scholars of the Middle ages were aware of the parallelism of Biblical verse (*Verdoppelten Ausdruck* or "double expression,"[27] they called it) but it was first fully explained by Bishop Lowth in a Latin speech given at Oxford in 1753. Since his scheme demonstrates the single line as the unit, let us examine it.

1. *Synonymous* parallelism: This is the most frequent kind of thought rhythm in Biblical poetry. "The second line enforces the thought of the first by repeating, and, as it were, *echoing* it in a varied form, producing an effect at once grateful to the ear and satisfying to the mind."[28]

> How shall I curse, whom God hath not cursed?
> Or how shall I defy, whom the Lord hath not defied?
>   —*Nu*. 23:8.

The second line, however, does not have to be identical in thought with the first. It may be merely similar or parallel to it.

> Sun, stand thou still upon Gibeon;
> And thou, Moon, in the valley of Ajalon.
>   —*Josh*. 10:12.

2. *Antithetic* parallelism: The second line denies or contrasts the first:

> A wise son maketh a glad father,
> But a foolish son is the heaviness of his mother.
>   —*Prov*. 10:1.

For the Lord knoweth the way of the righteous;
But the way of the ungodly shall perish.

—Ps. 1:6.

3. *Synthetic* or *constructive* parallelism: Here the second line (sometimes several consecutive lines) supplements or completes the first. (Although all Biblical poetry tends more toward the "end-stopped" than the "run-on" line, it will be noticed that synthetic parallelism does often have a certain degree of *enjambement*.)

Better is a dinner of herbs where love is,
Than a stalled ox and hatred therewith.

—Pr. 15:17.

Answer not a fool according to his folly,
Lest thou also be like unto him.

—Pr. 26:4.

As a bird that wandereth from her nest,
So is a man that wandereth from his place.

—Pr. 27:8.

"A comparison, a reason, a consequence, a motive, often constitutes one of the lines in a synthetic parallelism."

4. To Lowth's three kinds of parallelism Driver adds a fourth, which for convenience we may include here. It is called *climactic* parallelism—or sometimes "ascending rhythm." "Here the first line is itself incomplete, and the second line takes up words from it and completes them."

Give unto the Lord, O ye sons of the mighty,
Give unto the Lord *glory and strength.*

—Ps. 29:1.

The voice of the Lord shaketh the wilderness;
The Lord shaketh the wilderness *of Kadesh.*

—Ps. 29:8.

Till thy people pass over, O Lord,
Till the people pass over *which thou hast purchased.*

—Ex. 15:16.

It will be noticed in these examples that parallelism is sometimes a repetition of grammatical constructions and often of words, but the main principle is the balancing of thoughts alongside or against each other. And this produces not only a rhythmical thought-pattern, but also, and consequently, a speech rhythm which we will consider later. This brief summary presents only the most elementary aspects of Biblical rhythm, but it is sufficient to establish the fact that in parallelism, or in the "rhythm of thought," *the single line must by necessity be the stylistic unit.* Before taking up other aspects of parallelism let us see if this fundamental principle is found in Whitman's poetry.

Many critics have recognized parallelism as a rhythmical principle in *Leaves of Grass*. Perry even suggested that *The Lily and the Bee*, by Samuel Warren, published in England in 1851 and promptly reprinted in America by Harpers, may have given Whitman the model for his versification;[29] though Carpenter has pointed out that Whitman's new style had already been formed by 1851.[30] Perry's conjecture is important, however, because parallelism is unquestionably the stylistic principle of *The Lily and the Bee*, and in making the conjecture he is rightly calling attention to this principle of Whitman's style.

But if parallelism is the foundation of the rhythmical style of *Leaves of Grass*, then, as we have already seen in the summary of the Lowth system, the verse must be the unit. Any reader can observe that this is true in *Leaves of Grass*, and many critics have pointed it out. De Selincourt says:

The constitution of a line in *Leaves of Grass* is such that, taken in its context, the poetic idea to be conveyed by the words is only perfectly derivable from them when they are related to the line as a unit; and the equivalence of the lines is their equivalent appeal to our attention as contributors to the developing expression of the poetic idea of the whole.[31]

And Ross adds, more concretely:

Whitman's verse—with the exception that it is not metered—is farther removed from prose than is traditional verse itself, for the reason that the traditional verse is, like prose, composed in sentences, whereas Whitman's verse is composed in lines ... A run-on line is rare in Whitman—so rare that it may be considered a "slip." The law of his structure is that *the unit of sense is the measure of the line.* The lines, in sense, are end-stopped. Whitman employed everywhere a system of punctuation to indicate his structure. Look down any page of *Leaves of Grass*, and you will find almost every line ending in a comma; you will find a period at the end of a group of lines or a whole poem. Syntactically, there may be many sentences in the groups of the whole poem, there may be two or three sentences in one line. But Whitman was composing by lines, not by sentences, and he punctuated accordingly.[32]

WHITMAN'S PARALLELISM

It was only after several years of experimentation that Whitman definitely adopted parallelism as his basic verse structure. In a poem of 1850, "Blood-Money,"[33] he was already fumbling for this technique, but here he was paraphrasing both the thought and the prose rhythm of the New Testament (*Matthew* 26-27):

Of olden time, when it came to pass
That the beautiful god, Jesus, should finish his work
    on earth,
Then went Judas, and sold the divine youth,
And took pay for his body.

The run-on lines show how far the poet still is from the characteristic style of *Leaves of Grass*. He is experimenting with phrasal or clausal units; not yet "thought rhythm." But his arrangement of the verse is a step in that direction.

In "Europe," another poem of 1850, we also see the new form slowly evolving. It begins with long lines that at first glance look like the typical verse of the later poems, but on closer observation we see that they are not.

Suddenly, out of its stale and drowsy lair, the lair of slaves,
Like lightning Europe le'pt forth . . . . half startled at itself,
Its feet upon the ashes and the rags . . . . Its hands tight to the throat
    of kings.[1855 Ed.]

The disregard for grammatical structure suggests the poet's mature style—the antecedent of *it* is merely implied and the predicate is entirely lacking—, but the lines are only vaguely synonymous.

We see the next stage of this evolving style in the 1855 Preface, which, significantly, is arranged as prose, but the thought-units are often separated by periods, indicating that the author is striving for a rhythmical effect which conventional prose punctuation can not achieve.

He sees eternity less like a play with a prologue and a denouement
. . . he sees eternity in men and women . . . he does not see men and
women as dreams or dots. Faith is the antiseptic of the soul . . . it
pervades the common people and preserves them . . . they never give
up believing and expecting and trusting.[713]

The greatest poet forms the consistence of what is to be from what
has been and is. He drags the dead out of their coffins and stands
them again on their feet . . . he says to the past, Rise and walk before
me that I may realize you. He learns the lesson . . . he places himself
where the future becomes present. The greatest poet does not only
dazzle his rays over character and scenes and passions . . . he finally
ascends and finishes all . . . he exhibits the pinnacles that no man can
tell what they are for or what is beyond . . . He glows a moment on
the extremest verge. He is most wonderful in his last half-hidden
smile or frown. . . .[34]

Notice that the parallelism asserts without qualifications. The
poet is chanting convictions about which there is to be no argument,
no discussion. He develops or elaborates the theme by enumeration,
eliminating so far as possible transitional and connective words. The
form is rhapsodic, the tone that of inspired utterance.

In this Preface the third person is used, but the rhetorical form is
that of the expanding ego, as clearly revealed in this catalog:

On him rise solid growths that offset the growths of pine and cedar
and hemlock and liveoak and locust and chestnut and cypress and
hickory and limetree and cottonwood and tuliptree and cactus and
wildvine and tamarind and persimmon . . . and tangles as tangled as
any canebreak or swamp . . . and forests coated with transparent ice
and icicles hanging from the boughs and crackling in the wind . . .
and sides and peaks of mountains. . . .[711]

The "ands" are evidently an attempt to convey the effect of endless
continuity in an eternal present—the cosmic unity which the poet
incarnates as he sweeps over the continent. Here in this rhapsodic
Preface, both in the ideas and the manner in which they are expressed, we see the kind of literary form and style which Whitman
has adopted as analogous to his "purports and facts."

And in ten of the twelve poems of the 1855 edition of *Leaves of
Grass* parallelism is the structural device, chiefly the *synonymous*

variety, though the others are found also, especially the *cumulative* and *climactic*. As a matter of fact, it is often difficult to separate these three, for as Whitman asserts or repeats the same idea in different ways—like a musician playing variations on a theme—he tends to build up to an emotional, if not logical, climax. The opening lines of "Song of Myself" are obviously cumulative in effect:

> I celebrate myself, [and sing myself],
> And what I assume you shall assume,
> For every atom belonging to me as good belongs to you.

The following lines are synonymous in thought, though there is a cumulation and building up of the emotion:

> I loafe and invite my soul,
> I lean and loafe at my ease . . . . observing a spear of
>   summer grass.

(No doubt much of this effect is due to the pronounced caesura—which we will consider later.)

In this poem, as in the following ones, the parallelism has three functions. First of all it provides the basic structure for the lines. Each line makes an independent statement, either a complete or an elliptical sentence. In the second place, this repetition of thought (with variations) produces a loose rhythmical chanting or rhapsodic style. And, finally, the parallelism binds the lines together, forming a unit something like a stanza in conventional versification.

> This grass is very dark to be from the white heads of old mothers,
> Darker than the colorless beards of old men,
> Dark to come from under the faint red roofs of mouths.

> O I perceive after all so many uttering tongues!
> And I perceive they do not come from the roofs of mouths for
>   nothing.

> I wish I could translate the hints about the dead young men and
>   women,
> And the hints about old men and mothers, and the offspring taken
>   soon out of their laps.

> What do you think has become of the young and old men?

And what do you think has become of the women and children?

They are alive and well somewhere;
The smallest sprout shows there is really no death,
And if ever there was it led forward life, and does not wait at the end
    'to arrest it,
And ceased the moment life appeared.

All goes onward and outward . . . . and nothing collapses,
And to die is different from what any one supposed, and luckier.[36]

Here Whitman's characteristic structure and rhythm is completely developed and he handles it with ease and assurance. But that
he does not yet completely trust it is perhaps indicated by the occasional use of a semicolon (as in next to the last stanza or strophe
above) and four periods to emphasize a caesura. In his later verse
(including revisions of this poem) he depended upon commas in both
places.

In the above extract from "Song of Myself" the similarity of the
parallelism to that of Biblical poetry is probably closer than in more
typical passages of Whitman's longer poems, for the couplet, triplet,
and quatrain are found more often in the Bible than in Leaves of
Grass; and the Bible does not have either long passages of synonymous parallelism or extended catalogs. The Biblical poets were
not, like Whitman, attempting to inventory the universe in order to
symbolize its fluxional unity. They found unity in their monotheism,
not (or seldom) in a pantheism. But when Whitman's poetic vision
sweeps over the occupations of the land, as in section 15 of "Song of
Myself," he enumerates dozens of examples in more or less synonymous parallelistic form. And he repeats the performance in section
33 in a kind of omnipresent world-panorama of scenes, activities, and
pictures of life, in a strophe (or sentence) of 82 lines.

Another poem in the first edition, later known as "There Was a
Child Went Forth," further amplifies both the psychology of the
poet's identification of his consciousness with all forms of being and
his expression of it through enumeration and parallelism:

There was a child went forth every day,
And the first object he looked upon and received with wonder or
    pity or love or dread, that object he became,

And that object became part of him for the day or a certain part of the day . . . . or for many years of stretching cycles of years.

Then comes the list—early lilacs, grass, morning glories, March-born lambs, persons, streets, oceans, etc.—a veritable photomontage. The catalog and parallelism techniques arise from the same psychological impulse and achieve the same general effects of poetic identification.

The catalog, however, is most typical of the 1855-56 poems, when Whitman's cosmic inspiration found its most spontaneous and unrestrained expression. But even here we find a number of strophes arranged or organized as "envelopes" of parallelism, a device which the poet found especially useful in the shorter and more orderly poems of "Calamus," *Drum-Taps*, and the old-age lyrics. It is essentially a stanzaic form, something like the quatrain of the Italian sonnet. The first line advances a thought or image, succeeding lines amplify or illustrate it by synonymous parallelism, and the final line completes the whole by reiterating the original line or concluding the thought. For example, in section 21 of "Song of Myself":

Smile O voluptuous coolbreathed earth!
Earth of the slumbering and liquid trees!
Earth of departed sunset! Earth of the mountains misty-topt!
Earth of the vitreous pour of the full moon just tinged with blue!
Earth of shine and dark mottling the tide of the river!
Earth of the limpid gray of clouds brighter and clearer for my sake!
Far-swooping elbowed earth! Rich apple-blossomed earth!
Smile, for your lover comes!

Far more common, however, is the incomplete envelope, the conclusion being omitted, as in the 1860 "Song at Sunset":

Good in all,
In the satisfaction and aplomb of animals,
In the annual return of the seasons,
In the hilarity of youth,
In the strength and flush of manhood,
In the grandeur and exquisiteness of old age,
In the superb vistas of death.

But of course an "incomplete envelope" is not an envelope at all. Without a conclusion it is not a container. And it is characteristic of

Whitman, especially in 1855–56, that he more often preferred not to finish his comparisons, analogies, representative examples of reality, but let them trail off into infinity. In his later poems, however, the envelope often provides a structure and unity for the whole composition, as in "Joy, Shipmate, Joy!":

Joy, shipmate, joy!
(Pleas'd to my soul at death I cry,)
Our life is closed, our life begins,
The long, long anchorage we leave,
The ship is clear at last, she leaps!
She swiftly courses from the shore,
Joy, shipmate, joy!

OTHER REITERATIVE DEVICES

In the above discussion parallelism was referred to as both a *structure* and a *rhythm* in Whitman's verse technique. Since rhythm means orderly or schematic repetition, a poem can have several kinds of rhythms, sometimes so coördinated in the total effect that it is difficult to isolate and evaluate the separate function of each. Thus Whitman's parallelism can give esthetic pleasure as a recognizable pattern of thought, which is to say that it is the basis of the structure of the composition. This does not necessarily result in a repetition or rhythm of sounds, cadences, music, etc. But since thoughts are expressed by means of spoken sounds (or symbols that represent spoken sounds), it is possible for the *thought rhythm* to produce, or to be accompanied by, *phonic rhythm*. The latter need not be a rhythm of accents or stressed syllables (though it often is in *Leaves of Grass* as will be demonstrated later). Rime, or repetition of similar sounds according to a definite pattern, is another kind of phonic rhythm, and may serve several purposes, such as pleasing the ear (which has been conditioned to anticipate certain sounds at regular intervals) or grouping the lines and thereby (in many subtle ways) emphasizing the thought.

Whitman's parallelism, or thought rhythm, is so often accompanied and reinforced by parallel wording and sounds that the two techniques are often almost identical. An easy way to collect examples of his "thought rhythm" is to glance down the left-hand margin and notice the lines beginning with the same word, and usually the same grammatical construction: "I will ... I will ... I will . . ." or "Where . . . Where . . . Where . . ." or "When . . . When . . . When," etc.[37]

These repetitions of words or phrases are often found in modern conventional meters. Tennyson, for example,[38] repeats consecutively the same word or phrase throughout many passages; and the refrain and repetend in Poe's versification is the same device in a somewhat different manner. In conventional meters these reiterations may even set up a rhythm of their own, either syncopating or completely distorting the regular metrical pattern. But there is this very important difference between reiteration in rime and meter and reiteration in *Leaves of Grass*: in the former the poem has a set pattern of accents (iambic, trochaic, anapestic, etc.), whereas in Whitman's verse the pattern of sounds and musical effects is entirely dependent upon the thought and structure of the separate lines.

In every emotionally and intellectually pleasing poem in *Leaves of Grass* these reiterations do set up a recognizable pattern of sounds.[39] Since the line is not bound by a specific number of syllables, or terminated by conventional rime, the sound patterns may seem to the untrained reader entirely free and lawless. It was part of Whitman's "organic" style to make his rhythms freer than those of classical and conventional versification, but they are no freer than those of the best musical compositions of opera and symphony. They can, of course, be too free to recognize, in which case Whitman failed as a poet—and like almost all major poets, he has many failures to his name. But in the best poems of *Leaves of Grass*—such as "Out of the Cradle Endlessly Rocking," "When Lilacs Last in the Dooryard Bloom'd," or "Passage to India,"—the combined thought and sound patterns are as definite and organized as in "Lycidas" or "Samson Agonistes."

Several names have been given Whitman's reiterative devices in addition to the ones used here (phonic reiteration, etc.). Miss Autrey Nell Wiley, who has made the most thorough study of this subject, uses the rhetorical terms *epanaphora* and *epanalepsis*.[40] The nineteenth-century Italian scholar, Jannaccone,[41] calls these reiterations *rima psichica iniziale e terminale* (initial and terminal psychic rime) and *rima psichica media e terminale*. "Psychic rime" is a suggestive term, but it probably overemphasizes the analogy with conventional rime—though it is important to notice the initial, medial, and terminal positions of Whitman's reiterations. The initial is most common, as in the "Cradle" poem:

Out of the cradle endlessly rocking,
Out of the mocking-bird's throat, the musical shuttle,
Out of the Ninth-month midnight.

Although this reiteration might be regarded as "psychic rime," its most significant function is the setting up of a cadence to dominate the whole line, as the "Give me" reiteration does in "Give Me the Splendid Silent Sun," or the "What," "I hear," "I see," etc. in "Salut au Monde!," though scarcely any poem in *Leaves of Grass* is without the combined use of parallelism and reiteration. Often a short poem is a single "envelope" of parallelism with initial reiteration, as in "I Sit and Look Out":

I sit and look out upon all the sorrows of the world, and upon all oppression and shame,
I hear secret convulsive sobs from young men at anguish with themselves, remorseful after deeds done,
I see in low life the mother misused by her children, dying, neglected, gaunt, desperate,
I see the wife misused by her husband, I see the treacherous seducer of young women,
I mark the ranklings of jealousy and unrequited love attempted to be hid, I see these sights on the earth,
I see the workings of battle, pestilence, tyranny, I see martyrs and prisoners,
I observe a famine at sea, I observe the sailors casting lots who shall be kill'd to preserve the lives of the rest,
I observe the slights and degradations cast by arrogant persons upon laborers, the poor, and upon negroes, and the like;
All these—all the meanness and agony without end I sitting look out upon,
See, hear, and am silent.

Initial reiteration, as in the above passage, occurs oftener in *Leaves of Grass* than either medial or final. Miss Wiley has estimated that 41 percent of the more than 10,500 lines in the *Leaves* contains epanaphora, or initial reiteration.[42] But words and phrases are frequently repeated in other positions. "When Lilacs Last in the Dooryard Bloom'd" contains an effective example of a word from the first line repeated and interwoven throughout succeeding lines:

Over the breast of the spring, the land, *amid* cities,
Amid lanes and through old woods, where lately the violets peep'd
     from the ground, spotting the gray debris,
Amid the grass in the fields each side of the lanes, *passing* the endless
     grass,
Passing the yellow-spear'd wheat, every grain from its shroud in the
     dark-brown fields uprisen,
Passing the apple-tree blows of white and pink in the orchards,
Carrying a corpse to where it shall rest in the grave,
Night and day journeys a coffin.

Here the reiterations have little to do with cadences but aid greatly in
the effect of ceaseless motion—and even of *enjambement*, so rare in
Leaves of Grass—as the body of the assassinated president is carried
"night and day" from Washington to the plains of Illinois.

Final reiteration is found, though Whitman used it sparingly,
perhaps because it too closely resembles refrains and repetends in
conventional versification, and also because he had little use for the
kind of melody and singing lyricism which these devices produce.
When he does use final reiteration, it is more for rhetorical emphasis
than music, as in sec. 24 of "Song of Myself":

Root of wash'd sweet-flag! timorous pond-snipe! nest of guarded
     duplicate eggs! *it shall be you!*
Mix'd tussled hay of head, beard, brawn, *it shall be you!*
Trickling sap of maple, fibre of manly wheat, *it shall be you!*
Sun so generous *it shall be you!*

and so on throughout sixteen lines.

Sometimes Whitman uses reiteration through the entire line, as
in "By Blue Ontario's Shore":

I will know if I am to be less than they,
I will see if I am not as majestic as they,
I will see if I am not as subtle and real as they,
I will see if I am to be less generous than they, . . .[Sec. 18]

C. Alphonso Smith in his study of repetitions in English and
American poetry (he does not mention Whitman, however) has
defined the difference between reiterations in prose and poetry:

In prose, a word or group of words is repeated for emphasis; whereas in verse, repetition is chiefly employed not for emphasis (compare the use of the refrain), but for melody of rhythm, for continuousness or sonorousness of effect, for unity of impression, for banding lines or stanzas, and for the more indefinable though not less important purposes of suggestiveness.[43]

Of course, Smith is thinking of conventional versification, but continuousness of effect, unity of impression, joining of lines and stanzas, and suggestiveness all apply to Whitman's use of reiteration.

   Although Whitman's reiteration is not musical in the sense that Poe's is (*i.e.*, for melody and harmony), it is musical in a larger sense. Many critics have developed the analogy of music in Whitman's technique, but De Selincourt's comments are especially pertinent here. "The progress of Whitman's verse," he says, "has much in common with that of a musical composition. For we are carrying the sense of past effects along with us more closely and depending more intimately upon them than is possible in normal verse." And he observes that:

repetition, which the artist in language scrupulously avoids, is the foundation and substance of musical expression. Now Whitman . . . uses words and phrases more as if they were notes of music than any other writer . . . it was to him part of the virtue and essence of life that its forms and processes were endlessly reduplicated; and poetry, which was delight in life, must somehow, he thought, mirror this elemental abundance.[44]

   Of course Whitman's repetition concerns not only words and phrases (Jannaccone's "psychic rime") but thought patterns as well. In fact, his favorite method of organizing a long poem like "The Sleepers," "Proud Music of the Storm," "Mystic Trumpeter," or even "Song of the Redwood-Tree" is, as remarked elsewhere, symphonic. He likes to advance a theme, develop it by enumeration and representative symbols, advance other themes and develop them in similar manners, then repeat, summarize, and emphasize. Thus Whitman's repetition of thought, of words, of cadences,—playing variations on each out of exuberance and unrestrained joy both in the thought and form—, all combine to give him the satisfaction and conviction that he has "expressed" himself, not logically or even coherently, but by suggestion and by sharing his own emotions with the reader.

Another kind of reiteration which Whitman uses both for the thought and the musical effect is what Jannaccone calls "grammatical" and "logical rime"[45]—though *grammatical rhythm* might be a more convenient and appropriate term. Instead of repeating the same identical word or phrase, he repeats a part of speech or grammatical construction at certain places in the line. This has nearly the same effect on the rhythm and cadence as the reiteration of the same word or phrase, especially when "grammatical rime" is initial. For example, parallel verbs:

Flow on, river! *flow* with the flood-tide, and *ebb* with the ebb-tide!
Frolic on, crested and scallop-edg'd waves!
Gorgeous clouds of the sunset! *drench* with your splendor me or the
    men and women generations after me!
Cross from shore to shore, countless crowds of passengers!
Stand up, tall masts of Mannahatta! . . .
                —"Crossing Brooklyn Ferry," sec. 9.

The following Jannaccone calls "logical rime":[46]

Long and long has the *grass* been *growing*,
Long and long has the *rain* been *falling*,
Long has the *globe* been rolling *round*.
                —"Song of the Exposition," sec. 1.

Not only are *growing, falling,* and *rolling* grammatically parallel, but they are also the natural (and logical) things for the *grass,* the *rain,* and the *globe* to be doing.

Sometimes Whitman reiterates cognates:

The *song* is to the *singer,* and comes back most to him,
The *teaching* is to the *teacher,* and comes back most to him,
The *murder* is to the *murderer,* and comes back most to him, . . .
                —"Song of the Rolling Earth," sec. 2.

In all these examples the various kinds of reiterations produce also a pattern of accents which can be scanned like conventional verse.

Long and long has the grass been growing, . . .

Parallelism gives these lines a *thought* rhythm, but this is reinforced by the phonic recurrences, giving additional rhythm which depends upon *sounds* for its effect. Of course these examples are unusually regular (or simple), whereas the same principles in other passages give a much greater variety and complexity of phonic stress. But the combined reiterations always (at least when successful) produce a composite musical pattern—a pattern more plastic than any to be found in conventional versification, but one which the ear can be trained to appreciate no less than patterns of rime and meter.

"ORGANIC" RHYTHM

As we have repeatedly emphasized, Whitman's parallelism and his phonic reiterations do not exclude accentual patterns. Anyone who examines with care the versification of *Leaves of Grass* will discover many lines that can be scanned with ease, but most critics have regarded such passages as sporadic and uncharacteristic. Several, in fact, have thought the style of *Drum-Taps* inferior to other periods of Whitman's poetry, and a contradiction of his professed theory, because they are much nearer to conventional patterns of verse than his earlier poems.

Sculley Bradley, however, claims accentual patterns as the "Fundamental Metric Principle" of *Leaves of Grass*.[47] He does not challenge the widely accepted interpretations of Whitman's basic parallelism and reiteration, but regards these as obvious—though somewhat incidental. He thinks that many lines in which these devices are not used are also rhythmical and esthetically pleasing. In other words, there must be some other—still more *fundamental*—principle in Whitman's prosody.

Such a principle would have to be an exemplification of the poet's "organic" theory, his belief that form must spring from within, that a poetic experience will find its own natural rhythm in the act of expression. Certainly this was Whitman's most fundamental literary theory, as his various analogies—and those of numerous critics—indicate. Thus he compares his rhythms to the "recurrence of lesser and larger waves on the seashore, rolling in without intermission, and fitfully rising and falling."[48]

Bradley points out the similarity of Whitman's "organic" theory to Coleridge's distinction between "mechanic" and "organic" form, as expressed in his lecture on "Shakespeare, a Poet Generally":

The form is mechanic, when on any given material we impress a pre-determined form, not necessarily arising out of the properties of the material;—as when to a mass of wet clay we give whatever shape we wish it to retain when hardened. The organic form, on the other hand, is innate; it shapes, as it develops, itself from within, and the fullness of its development is one and the same with the perfection of its outward form. Such as the life is, such is the form. Nature, the prime genial artist, inexhaustible in diverse powers, is equally inexhaustible in forms;—each exterior is the physiognomy of the being within,—its true image reflected and thrown out from the concave mirror;—and even such is the appropriate excellence of her chosen poet. . . .[49]

It was on such a theory as this that Whitman's friend, Kennedy, defended the art of *Leaves of Grass* as conforming to the variety and multiplicity of Nature instead of the "base mechanical regularity" of conventional poetry. De Selincourt would agree with this general interpretation, but he also insists that: "The identity of the lines in metrical poetry is an identity of pattern. The identity of the lines in *Leaves of Grass* is an identity of substance."[50] To this statement Bradley objects:

For in the majority of the lines of Whitman, which are not brought into equivalence by repetition of substance and phrases, there is still the equivalence of a rhythm regulated by a periodicity of stress so uniformly measured as to constitute a true "meter." It is a device capable of infinite subtlety, and we must understand it fully in order to appreciate the extent of the poet's craftsmanship.[51]

One of the principal means by which Bradley establishes his "periodicity of stress" is in the use of "hovering accent" in his scansion: "It becomes apparent to the attentive reader of Whitman, especially when reading aloud, that in a great many cases the stress does not fall sharply on a single vowel, but is distributed along the word, or a pair of words, or even a short phrase."[444] As an example:

Which of the young men does she like the best?

Ah the homeliest of them is beautiful to her.

This is, of course, as Bradley himself would agree, a subjective interpretation, but it is undoubtedly a dramatic and effective reading of
the lines. As he himself says, without the glide or hovering accent,
the second line "becomes jocose instead of pathetic."[445]
     As an extended example of both organic rhythm and a "unified
organic whole," Bradley scans the poem "Tears" in this manner:[449]

3   Tears! tears! tears!

3   In the night, in solitude, tears,

5   On the white shore dripping, dripping, suck'd in by the sand,

5   Tears, not a star shining, all dark and desolate,[52]

3   Moist tears from the eyes of a muffled head;

5   O who is that ghost? that form in the dark, with tears?

6   What shapeless lump is that, bent, crouch'd there on the sand?

5   Streaming tears, sobbing tears, throes, choked with wild cries;

6   O storm, embodied, rising, careering with swift steps and along
        the beach!

6   O wild and dismal night storm, with wind—O belching and
        desperate!

8   O shade so sedate and decorous by day, with calm countenance
        and regulated pace,

7   But away at night as you fly, none looking—O then the
        unloosen'd ocean,

3   Of tears! tears! tears!

     Here Bradley makes a valuable contribution to the understand-
ing and appreciation of Whitman's art by calling attention to the
symmetry of the form. His scansion divides the poem into three
free-verse stanzas, each with its own definite accentual pattern, and
the whole with a pyramidal structure which suggests "a large wave or
breaker with three crests."[449] And he cites several interesting
examples to demonstrate that such structure, especially the pyramidal form, is characteristic of Whitman's more successful versification.

Without in the least denying or detracting from the value of this interpretation, we should also observe, however, that even here Whitman uses repetitions as an integral part of his organic structure. The parallelism and phonic reiteration are less obvious than in "Song of Myself" and the earlier and longer poems, but they are present in this characteristic composition of the 1860s. The word *tears* is "psychic rime" and a kind of refrain, weaving in and out and influencing both the pathos and cadences. There is also a subtle repetition of thought throughout, with the epithets for tears, the references to the "ghost" and the "storm." Furthermore, the parallelism does not entirely divide according to Bradley's stanzaic scheme, but laps over from the second to the third divisions:

(a) O storm, embodied, rising, careering with swift steps along the beach!
(a) O wild and dismal night storm, with wind—O belching and desperate!

The thought structure of the whole is, of course, the envelope, which was mentioned in the section on "Parallelism."

But the fact that Whitman so successfully combines thought, rhetoric, syllabic accent, and stanzaic form in an "organic" whole is sufficient evidence of expert craftsmanship and his ability to adapt technique to his literary purposes. Bradley's reading of the lines with hovering stresses also indicates that Whitman had a keener ear for sound and cadence than has been commonly supposed. Sometimes, indeed, the "subtle patterns are embroidered upon each other in a manner comparable to that of great symphonic music. . . ."[455]

A careful study of Whitman's punctuation will also reveal that it was not erratic or eccentric, as many readers have thought, but that it was an accurate index to the organic rhythm, the musical effects which the poet hoped to have brought out in the reading. We have already noticed that the comma at the end of nearly every line except the last is an indication not of the usual sense-pause but of the end of a prosodic unit—usually ending in a *cadence* or falling of the voice. Perhaps it might be called a final caesura—a slight pause before the voice continues with the recitative. In the first edition Whitman frequently used semicolons at the end of lines which were grammatically complete (either complete predications or elliptical sentences), but later he adopted commas. Inside the line he was still forced to punctuate somewhat according to thought, but his internal commas and dashes are also often caesural pauses.

Whitman has a great variety of caesuras, and an exhaustive study of them would reveal much about his word-music that is still little known. Only a few examples can be given here. We might begin with one of the most rudimentary effects, which may be called a catalog-caesura:

The blab of the pave,/ tires of carts,/ sluff of boot-soles,/ talk of the
    promenaders,/
The heavy omnibus,/ the driver with his interrogating thumb,/ the
    clank of the shod horses on the granite floor,/ . . .[53]

Notice the cumulative effect of the cadences, aided by the slight caesural pauses:

The blab of the pave, tires of carts, sluff of boot-soles,

the omitted unaccented syllable before "tires" and "sluff" breaking the monotony of the pattern and emphasizing the beat, presently giving way to longer sweeps in the following line,

    . . . the driver with his interrogating thumb,
the clank of the shod horses on the granite floor . . . .

A similar caesura, but with many subtle variations:

I hear bravuras of birds,/ bustle of growing wheat,/ gossip of flames,/
    clack of sticks cooking my meals,//
I hear the sound I love,/ the sound of the human voice,//
I hear all sounds running together,/ combined, fused or following,/
Sounds of the city and sounds out of the city,/ sounds of the day
    and night, . . .[57]

Notice how much the shortening or lengthening of the pause can contribute to both the rhythm and the thought. The first line is cumulative in effect, the second balanced, the third suggestive or illustrative, the fourth is emphatic.

Sometimes the caesura divides the parallelism and is equivalent to the line-end pause:

There is that in me—/ /I do not know what it is—but I know it is in
    me.

Wrench'd and sweaty—/ calm and cool/ then my body becomes,/
I sleep—// I sleep long.//

I do not know it—// it is without name—// it is a word unsaid,//
It is not in any dictionary,/ utterance,/ symbol.[55]

Another caesural effect Jannaccone calls "thesis" and "arsis"[56]
because the second half line echoes the thought of the first and
receives a weaker stress and perhaps a lower pitch:

Great are the myths—// I too delight in them,
Great are Adam and Eve—// I too look back and accept them. . . [57]

This is of course also another example of Whitman's parallelism, and
another indication of why he used parallelism so extensively. The
employment of connectives or subordination would destroy the ring
of inspired authority which he wished to give to his prophetic
utterances.

Whitman's use of the parenthesis in this verse structure throws
further light on his organic rhythms. Although the parenthesis in
Leaves of Grass has been frequently regarded as merely a manerism
without special significance so far as the versification is concerned,
two critics have advanced interesting explanations. De Selincourt
says:

The use of parenthesis is a recurring feature of Whitman's technique,
and no explanation of his form can be adequate which does not
relate this peculiarity to the constructive principles of the whole. He
frequently begins a paragraph or ends one with a bracketed sentence
. . . sometimes even begins or ends a poem parenthetically . . . This
persistent bracketing falls well into the scheme we have laid down of
independent units that serve an accumulating effect. The bracket,
one need not remark, secures a peculiar detachment for its contents;
it also, by placing them outside the current and main flow of the
sense, relates them to it in a peculiar way. And although for the time
being the flow is broken, it by no means follows . . . that our sense of
the flow is broken; on the contrary, it is probably enhanced. We look
down upon the stream from a point of vantage and gauge its speed
and direction. More precisely, the bracket opening a poem or paragraph gives us, of course, the idea which that whole poem or paragraph presupposes, while the closing bracket gives the idea by which

what precedes is to be qualified and tempered. We have thus as it were a poem within a poem; or sometimes, when a series of brackets is used, we have a double stream of poetry, as in "By Blue Ontario's Shore". . . .[58]

Catel argues, as one proof of his thesis that Whitman's art is that of the orator, that the parentheses indicate a change of voice or gesture. Sometimes, he points out, the parenthetical matter is "un aveu murmuré, comme un aparté, un à-côté personnel,"[59] as in:

The young fellow drives the express-wagon, (I love him, though I do
    not know him;) . . . .
The canal boy trots . . . .
The conductor beats time . . . .
The child is baptized . . . .
The regatta is spread . . . . (how the white sails sparkle!)[60]

Often, as Catel says, the parenthesis is not necessary for the thought, and unless it indicates a change in tone, pitch, or emphasis there is no explanation for its use.

I do not trouble my spirit to vindicate itself or be understood,
I see that the elementary laws never apologize,
(I reckon I behave no prouder than the level I plant my house by,
    after all.)[61]

Or in the following:

All truths wait in all things,
They neither hasten their own delivery nor resist it, ...
The insignificant is as big to me as any,
(What is less or more than a touch?)[62]
I hear all sounds running together . . . .
The steam-whistle . . . .
The slow march play'd at the head of the association marching two
    and two,
(They go to guard some corpse, the flag-tops are draped with black
    muslin.)[63]

As both a summary and supplement to these interpretations, we can say that almost invariably Whitman's parentheses indicate a break or change in the organic rhythm. Often, as in the first example above, the general rhythmical pattern for the passage seems to be suspended momentarily by the bracketed comment: "The young fellow drives . . . . (I love him though I do not know him) . . . . The canal boy trots . . . . The conductor beats time . . . . The child is baptized . . . . The regatta is spread . . . . (how the white sails sparkle!)," etc.

But in some passages Catel's theory of a change of voice or gesture applies only as a thin analogy. In the following example the bracketed passage seems fully as emphatic as the preceding and succeeding lines, although it does not have quite the same cadence as the "to the" reiterations and also presents a specific image in a passage of panoramic and symbolical details:

To the leaven'd soil they trod calling I sing for the last,
(Forth from my tent emerging for good, loosing, untying the tent-
    ropes,)
In the freshness the forenoon air, in the far-stretching circuits and
    vistas again to peace restored,
In the fiery fields emanative and the endless vistas beyond, to the
    South and the North,
To the leaven'd soil of the general Western world to attest my songs,
To the Alleghanian hills and the tireless Mississippi, . . .
To the plains . . .

Such uses of the parenthesis add further proof that Whitman's rhythm is in actuality as well as in theory formed from within, and also controlled and shaped to harmonize with both his thought and emotion. The very fact that so many analogies occur to the critics is evidence both of an "organic form" and at the same time of Whitman's success in subordinating his technique to his "purports and facts." Thus De Selincourt thinks of the punctuation as indicating the ebb and flow of musical composition and Catel as stage directions for an orator. In attempting to explain Whitman's form, Matthiessen uses three analogies—oratory, opera, and the ocean.[65] No poet ever tried more conscientiously to wed sound and sense. As Matthiessen says:

When he spoke of his "liquid-flowing syllables," he was hoping for the same effect in his work as when he jotted down as the possible genesis for a poem: "Sound of walking barefoot ankle deep in the edge of the water by the sea." He tried again and again to describe what he wanted from this primal force, and put it most briefly when he said that if he had the choice of equalling the greatest poets in theme or in metre or in perfect rhyme,

These, these, O sea, all these I'd gladly barter,
Would you the undulation of one wave, its trick to me
    transfer,
Or breathe one breath of yours upon my verse,
And leave its odor there.[66]

This ambition, however, should not lead the reader to expect pronounced onomatopoeia in Whitman's verse. Not even in "When Lilacs Last in the Dooryard Bloom'd" does the vicarious bird-singing sound convincingly like the notes of the "gray-brown bird." What the poet does is to convey the spirit, the lyric feeling, of the time and place of his allegory. What he makes is music of the soul, not a literal mimicry of lapping waves or bird-chirping.

The song, the wondrous chant of the gray-brown bird,
And the tallying chant, the echo arous'd in my soul,

    .   .   .   .   .

For the sweetest, wisest soul of all my days and lands—and this for
    his dear sake,
Lilac and star and bird twined with the chant of my soul,
There in the fragrant pines and the cedars dusk and dim.

Here the esthetic problem is quite similar to that of "program" *vs.* abstract music—except for the fact that music depends entirely upon sound, whereas in poetry the *words* convey ideas and images in addition to rhythms and tones. Many imaginative listeners think they hear in the marvelous symphonies of Sibelius the pine-tree whisperings of Finlandia, but it is doubtful that Sibelius has attempted any literal imitation of these sounds. And seldom is there any indication that Whitman's object is the phonographic reproduction of rustling or splashing water. What he wants in his verse is the "breath" and the "odor" of the sea (abstractions), and "the echo arous'd in my soul." Freneau might capture the rhythms of the "katy-did" or Emerson of the "humble-bee," but Walt Whitman's "organic" rhythms are those of the spirit of Nature "twined with the chant of my soul." This is why he anticipated Expressionism in modern art and was adopted by the French Symbolists as one of their own, though he was neither Expressionist nor Symbolist, but Walt Whitman, poet of a "spiritual democracy."

CONVENTIONAL TECHNIQUES IN *LEAVES OF GRASS*

Although Whitman's "organic" theory of poetic style is commonly assumed to be completely antithetical to conventional techniques, there is no logical reason why the poet might not occasionally have an experience or an emotion which would find natural expression in rime and meter. According to the organic principle, the form must be shaped from within, not from external conventions. But who can say that the inner experience can never find a conventional outlet? At any rate, it is true, as Miss Ware has said, that Whitman "exemplified at some point or other virtually all of the conventions that he professed to eschew, and that he employed some of these conventions on a large scale."[67]

The most obvious conventions against which Whitman was supposedly revolting were rime and meter. Yet we find him using rime in several of his mature poems, all written after the adoption of his "organic" style. The earliest of these is in the first section (or strophe) of "Song of the Broad Axe," which was apparently written in 1856. The rhythm is "organic" in the sense that it varies from line to line, and the lines themselves are often of different lengths, but the accents are surprisingly metrical and the final syllables are so nearly rimed that the pattern is trochaic tetrameter couplets:[68]

Weapon shapely, naked, wan,
Head from the mother's bowels drawn,
Wooded flesh and metal bone, limb only one and lip only one,
Gray-blue leaf by red-heat grown, helve produced from a little seed sown,
Resting the grass amid and upon,
To be lean'd and to lean on.

Curiously enough, this effective trochaic movement survives from an early manuscript, in which the poet was apparently trying to imitate the sound of rain drops:

The irregular tapping of rain off my house-eaves at night after the storm has lulled, [probably the subject, not a line for a poem],

Gray-blue sprout so hardened grown
Head from the mother's bowels drawn
Body shapely naked and wan
Fibre produced from a little seed sown.[69]

In this case it would seem, then, that the rhythm was salvaged from a manuscript poem having nothing to do with the subject-matter of the "Broad-Axe"; it did not grow from within but was adapted—not however, inappropriately.

The first section of "By Blue Ontario's Shore" also rimes in almost the same manner, being *aabbcb*. The main part of this poem was also published in 1856, but the version including these rimes was not added until 1867. The conventionality of "O Captain! My Captain!," 1865, has probably been observed by all students of Whitman. The stanza is composed of four long lines and four short ones, the latter being used as a refrain. The meter is iambic and the stanzaic pattern is approximately as follows: $a_5 a_7 b_7 b_7 c_3 d_8 e_4 d_3$. But one of the most conventional of all poems in *Leaves of Grass* is the prisoner's song in "The Singer in Prison," 1869. The first stanza is almost completely regular:

A soul confined by bars and bands,
Cries, help! O help! and wrings her hands,
Blinded her eyes, bleeding her breast,
Nor pardon finds, nor balm of rest, . . .

Still another poem with a definite rime-scheme is "Ethiopia Saluting the Colors," 1871. The scheme is approximately $(a)a_6 bb_7$ (the first being an internal rime).

In addition to the above poems in more or less conventional stanzas, Whitman also used stanza forms in the following poems: "A Noiseless Patient Spider," 1862–63, a five-line stanza in irregular meter but recognizably metrical; "For You O Democracy," 1860, in a five-line and four-line stanza with a refrain, ending with a free-verse couplet (of parallelism); "Pioneers! O Pioneers!," 1865, in four-line trochaic stanzas, the first line being mainly three-stress and the fourth line being the refrain of the title; "Dirge for Two Veterans," 1865–66, in four-line stanzas, the scheme being mainly *3-4-3-6*; "Old War Dreams," 1865–56, in a four-line stanza, the fourth being a refrain; "Gods," 1870, in short unrimed strophes (mainly triplets) with refrain; "In Cabin'd Ships at Sea," 1871, in iambic eight-line stanzas, each first and last line being shorter than the others; and "Eidólons," 1876, in four-line stanzas, the first and fourth lines being dimeters and trimeters and the second and third being longer, of indefinite length.

Nearly half of these poems are, as indicated, in conventional meters. Especially interesting is the anapestic-iambic "Beat! Beat! Drums!"

Beat! beat! drums—blow! bugles! blow!

Over the traffic of cities—over the rumble of wheels in the streets;

Are beds prepared for sleepers at night in the houses? no sleepers

    must sleep in those beds,

No bargainers' bargains by day—no brokers or speculators—would

    they continue?

One of the most metrical poems in *Leaves of Grass* is the trochaic "Pioneers! O Pioneers!," 1865. The number of stresses in the second and third lines varies from seven to ten, and occasionally an iamb is substituted for a trochee, but the pattern is almost as regular as in conventional verse.

    For we cannot tarry here,

We must march my darlings, we must bear the brunt of danger,

We the youthful sinewy races, all the rest on us depend,

    Pioneers! O Pioneers!

Most of Whitman's poems contain occasional lines that scan easily as iamblic, trochaic, anapestic, or—very rarely—dactyllic. The poems mentioned above are nearly all that adhere closely to a definite conventional metrical pattern—though most of the *Leaves* can be scanned by Bradley's method.

But it will be observed that most of these examples were first published in the 1860s. Both *Drum-Taps* and *Sequel to Drum-Taps* are a great deal more conventional in form and style than earlier poems in the *Leaves*. Apparently the poet found more conventional metrics either convenient or necessary for the expression of his experiences and emotions connected with the war. Even "Pioneers! O

Pioneers!" is a marching poem. But what is more natural than that the poet's heartbeat would throb to the rhythms of marching feet—especially a poet who aspired to give organic expression to his own age and country?

Throughout most of his poems, of all periods, Whitman made extensive use of other conventional devices, such as alliteration, both vowel and consonantal, and assonance, but these are rather embellishments (perhaps often unconscious) than fundamental techniques. They are interesting in view of Whitman's determination in the 1855 Preface not to use any ornamentation in his verse, but they have so long been taken for granted in English poetry that they can hardly be called a contradiction of the poet's doctrines. In a poem like "Tears" they are almost inevitable, and it is not surprising to find them in the more onomatopoetic description of seashore experiences and memories. Although Miss Ware probably attaches too much importance to these particular conventions, her conclusion is no doubt sound:

A comparison of the results found by a study of *Leaves of Grass* and the *Uncollected Poetry and Prose of Walt Whitman* would seem to indicate that when Whitman discarded the more obvious poetic devices—like regular stanza forms, meter, and rhyme,—he unconsciously adopted the less obvious conventions, such as alliteration, assonance, repetition, refrain, parallelism, and end-stopped lines.[70]

Whether these survive in Whitman's versification unconsciously or not, it is difficult to say, but it is quite certain that he could not very well write intelligible poetry without retaining some conventions—and adapting or creating some basic prosodic techniques not altogether "transcendent and new." But they were sufficiently new to puzzle his own generation, and as the many critics have demonstrated, need to be explained and interpreted even today.

THE ORGANIC THEORY OF WORDS

Since the publication of the first edition of *Leaves of Grass*, critics have been interested in Whitman's bold use of words and have tried to discover the secret of his large but indiscriminate vocabulary. Wordsworth's poetic reform, as set forth in the Preface to *Lyrical Ballads*, was mainly concerned with diction, with the rejection of artificial "poetic diction" of neo-classicism and the adoption of living speech of ordinary people (though pruned of the grossest crudities).

Many critics have assumed that Whitman was completing the reform begun by Wordsworth. Catel says, "Whitman a retrouvé, par un instinct très sûr de poète, la source vive du langage qui est le style oral, ce qu'il a appelé lui-même 'a vocal style.' "[71]

Whitman himself anticipated modern linguistic theory by declaring in his *American Primer* that "Pronunciation is the stamina of language,—it is language,"[72] and there is no doubt that he tried to make extensive use of the vernacular in his poems. Perhaps it would not have been inconsistent with his other literary theories for him to have cultivated almost exclusively a vernacular vocabulary. But it is a notorious fact that he did not do so. True, he greets the earth as "top-knot"[73] and he likes to close his poems with a "so long"[74] to the reader, but he practically ransacks the dictionaries for literary words like "chyle," "recusant," and "circumambient."[75] And he is almost childishly fond of foreign words, especially French[76] and Spanish ones, which he sometimes uses with a reckless disregard for correct spelling or meaning.[77] English biographers and critics, especially,[78] still cringe at the democratic "mélange" which often resulted from Whitman's indiscriminate mixture of all levels of linguistic usage. No one with literary taste can deny that this self-styled poet of democracy often brewed a linguistic concoction as strange as the barbaric rituals of Melville's Quequeg. Possibly, too, many of his philological indiscretions were due to ignorance or primitive delight in verbal displays; but his theory of language was more fully developed than some critics have realized, and it harmonizes surprisingly well with his "organic" conception of poetic form.

And nowhere do we find evidence of Whitman's indebtedness to Emerson and Transcendentalism more than in his theory of words. In "The Poet" Emerson says that,

Things admit of being used as symbols, because nature is a symbol, in the whole, and in every part. Every line we can draw in the sand, has expression; and there is no body without its spirit or genius. All form is an effect of character; all condition, of the quality of the life; all harmony, of health; (and, for this reason, a perception of beauty should be sympathetic, or proper only to the good).

From this Swedenborgian point of view, "the world is a temple, whose walls are covered with emblems, pictures and commandments of the Deity," and it is also interesting to see that here, as in Whitman's cosmic equalitarianism, "the distinctions which we make in events, and in affairs, of low and high, honest and base, disappear when nature is used as a symbol."

The poet is the man, above all others, who has the power to use symbols, and thus to indicate men's relationships to nature, God, and the universe they inhabit. "We are symbols and inhabit symbols; workmen, work, and tools, words and things, birth and death, all are emblems. . . ." But the poet gives to words and things "a power which makes their old use forgotten, and put eyes, and a tongue, into every dumb and inanimate object." Thus to Emerson, words are symbols of symbols. Above all they are images with spiritual significance. Even more to him than to the philologist, "Every word was once a poem," and language itself "is fossil poetry."

On the basis of this theory Emerson declares that:

The vocabulary of an omniscient man would embrace words and images excluded from polite conversation. What would be base, or even obscene, to the obscene, becomes illustrious, spoken in a new connection of thought. The piety of the Hebrew prophets purges their grossness. The circumcision is an example of the power of poetry to raise the low and offensive. Small and mean things serve as well as great symbols. The meaner the type by which a law is expressed, the more pungent it is, and the more lasting in the memories of men . . . Bare lists of words are found suggestive to an imaginative and excited mind . . .

There we have Whitman's complete theory and attitude toward words. He added little if anything to it, but it was he, not Emerson, who made the broadest application of the theory. Here we find the foundation of Whitman's doctrine in the 1855 Preface that words reveal the character and the inner harmony of the speaker, and that "All beauty comes from beautiful blood and a beautiful brain. If the greatnesses are in conjunction in a man or woman it is enough."[79] Or as he later expressed it in *An American Primer*, "Words follow character."[80] And thus in his great faith in the future of the Democratic Republic he envisions a nation of people who will be "the most fluent and melodious voiced people in the world . . . the most perfect users of words." Some critics have thought Whitman an atavistic savage who believed in the magic of words. Actually, however, he worships neither words nor images, but the mystic powers and relationships which they feebly signify. If the meaning is not in the user of words, it cannot be in the verbal symbols which he employs. As Matthiessen comments, "Whitman's excitement [in naming things] carries weight because he realized that a man cannot use words so [as Whitman did] unless he has experienced the facts that they express, unless he has grasped them with his senses."[81]

Whitman's propensity for inventorying the universe is, therefore, evidence of his desire to know life—*being*—in all its details, the small and the mean as well as the great and the good. Locked in the words is the vicarious experience of the poet, to whom even bare lists are suggestive and exciting.

A perfect writer would make words sing, dance, kiss, do the male and female act, bear children, weep, bleed, rage, stab, steal, fire cannon, steer ships, sack cities, charge with cavalry or infantry, or do anything, that man or woman or the natural powers can do.

Latent, in a great user of words, must actually be all passions, crimes, trades, animals, stars, God, sex, the past, might, space, metals, and the like—because these are the words, and he who is not these, plays with a foreign tongue, turning helplessly to dictionaries and authorities.—How can I tell you?—I put many things on record that you will not understand at first—perhaps not in a year—but they must be (are to be) understood.—The earth, I see, writes with prodigal clear hands all summer, forever, and all winter also, content, and certain to be understood in time—as, doubtless, only the greatest user of words himself fully enjoys and understands himself.[82]

Although Whitman's poetic form and technique throughout *Leaves of Grass* exemplify both his theory and attitude toward words, he treated the problem specifically in the 1856 "Poem of the Sayers of the Words of the Earth."[83]

Earth, round, rolling, compact—suns, moons, animals—all these are words,
Watery, vegetable, sauroid advances—beings, premonitions, lispings of the future, these are vast words.

Were you thinking that those were the words—those upright lines? those curves, angles, dots?
No, those are not the words—the substantial words are in the ground and sea,
They are in the air—they are in you.[84]

Though this doctrine is mystical and transcendental, it is also *semantic*. What Whitman is trying to get at is "meaning," and meaning, he says, is in cosmic processes (evolution: "sauroid advances" and "lispings of the future"), in things, and "in you." Language is conduct and words are merely gestures:

A healthy presence, a friendly or commanding gesture, are words, sayings, meanings,
The charms that go with the mere looks of some men and women are sayings and meanings also.[85]

But though the meaning of words is subjective, it must tally with objective fact. Whitman anticipated modern semantic doctrine in his insistence on this harmony between the inner and outer meaning:

I swear the earth shall surely be complete to him or her who shall be complete!
I swear the earth remains broken and jagged only to him or her who remains broken and jagged!

I swear there is no greatness or power that does not emulate those of the earth!
I swear there can be no theory of any account, unless it corroborate the theory of the earth![86]

Far from worshipping words or mistaking them for reality, Whitman sees their inadequacy and searches for the meaning behind words:

I swear I begin to see little or nothing in audible words!
I swear I think all merges toward the presentation of the unspoken meanings of the earth!
Toward him who sings the songs of the body, and of the truths of the earth,
Toward him who makes the dictionaries of the words that print cannot touch.

As a poet Whitman must make carols of words, but he knows that these are only "hints of meanings" which "echo the tones of Souls, and the phrases of Souls." This attitude toward words and the form of his poems he never renounced, but continued to regard his poems as mere hints and "indirections," and, as Hermann Bahr says, to present and arrange the materials of poems instead of finished products.[87] In 1855 he liked to think of the poet (or himself as a poet) as a "kosmos,"[88] or a kind of microcosm symbolizing the macrocosm. But it is just as accurate to say that he thought of a poem itself as a mirror-like monad (to use Leibniz's term) which reflected in itself the form, structure, and spiritual laws of the universe.

In a manuscript dating from around 1850 Holloway has discovered[89] a great deal about the nature of Whitman's inspiration and the manner in which he composed his poetry. The poem, only a fragment of which was included in Leaves of Grass, was called "Pictures." Bucke printed four lines in Notes and Fragments:

O Walt Whitman, show us some pictures;
America always Pictorial! And you Walt Whitman to name them
Yes, in a little house I keep suspended many pictures—it is not a
    fixed house.
It is round—Behold! it has room for America, north and south,
    seaboard and inland, persons . . .[90]

This crude picture-gallery allegory was not published as a single poem because the various images and catalogs which it contained were expanded into a number of separate poems—in fact, might be thought of as the genesis of the first editions of Leaves of Grass. In an outline for the original "Pictures," we glimpse the poet's method:

Poem of Pictures. Each verse presenting a picture of some characteristic scene, event, group or personage—old or new, other countries or our own country. Picture of one of the Greek games—wrestling, or the chariot race, or running. Spanish bull fight.[91]

Of the finished "Pictures" Holloway says:

Each is a microcosm of the whole "Leaves of Grass," which the author looked upon less as a book than as a picture of himself in all his cosmopolitan diversity. And the more we learn of the facts of Whitman's comprehensive life, whether experience, reading, or meditation, the more we realize that before each thumb-nail picture was set down on paper it had really been hung, as a personal possession, on the walls of his "Picture-Gallery."[92]

Thus in his desire to explore life, personality, and the inner meaning of Being, Whitman turned to Emerson's theory of symbols for guidance in the development of a literary technique. By imaginative identification of his own ego with the creative processes of nature, and by the vicarious exploration of all forms of existence, he evolved the technique of panoramic imagery, "organically" echoing a subjective harmony and rhythm of his own "Soul," and revealing by "hints" and "indirections" the spiritual truths of the universe. Both in form and content *Leaves of Grass* is primarily cosmic, animistic, and democratic, and Walt Whitman's literary technique is admirably adapted for his "purports and facts and is the analogy of them."

Chapter V

Walt Whitman and World Literature

My spirit has pass'd in compassion and determination around the whole earth,
I have look'd for equals and lovers and found them ready for me in all lands . . .
—"Salut au Monde!"

WORLD POET

Walt Whitman was the first American poet to gain world recognition, and he is still one of the best-known of American authors in nearly every country of the globe, with complete translations of his *Leaves of Grass* in France, Germany, Spain (and Latin America), Italy, Greece, and Japan, and selections of his poems in nearly all other languages, but especially in the Soviet Union, where editions of his writings sell far better than they do in the United States. Professor Harold Blodgett, who has taught in Holland, India, and Iran, says "one cannot travel anywhere in the world without coming upon distinguished and sensitive people to whom Whitman is the greatest American poet."[1]

In the Preface to his first edition of *Leaves of Grass* Whitman declared that the "bard" of the United States should be "commensurate" with his nation, his spirit responding to "his country's spirit," and that he should incarnate "its geography and natural life."[2] Such a poet would be nationalistic in every sense of the term, and Whitman left no doubt that this was his ambition. In fact, he ended his 1855 Preface with the confident assertion that, "The proof of a poet is that his country absorbs him as affectionately as he has absorbed it."[3] But he failed by his own test. His country did not "absorb" him during his lifetime—not to any great extent, in fact, until about 1955,[4] when his country celebrated the first centennial

249

of the 1855 edition, as did admirers in Moscow, Tokyo, New Delhi, and elsewhere.

In his old-age preface to *November Boughs* ("A Backward Glance O'er Travel'd Roads") Whitman admitted candidly, "I have not gain'd the acceptance of my own time, but have fallen back on fond dreams of the future."[5] Because of this realization the aged poet was pathetically grateful to the British authors, under the leadership of William Rossetti and Mrs. Alexander Gilchrist, who came to his financial rescue in 1876 during a period of illness and extreme discouragement.[6]

Discussions of Whitman in Great Britain actually resulted in his first extensive literary reputation, with helpful "feedback" results in the United States. It was about this time also that he began to receive encouragement from several foreign countries. While in exile in Great Britain, Ferdinand Freiligrath became acquainted with Whitman's poems, and after his return to Germany he published an appreciative newspaper article in 1868.[7] Four years later Rudolf Schmidt in Denmark began writing articles on Whitman, which he mailed to the ailing poet in Camden, N. J. In 1876 he published a Danish translation of *Democratic Vistas*.[8]

This did not mean that Whitman had fulfilled his "Salut au Monde!" prophecy (see epigraph at the head of this chapter), but he began to have hopes, especially in 1881 when an Irishman, Dr. John Fitzgerald Lee, wrote him from Dresden asking for permission to do a translation of *Leaves of Grass* into Russian.[9] What qualification Dr. Lee had for this difficult undertaking is not known, but Whitman assumed that he was Russian (the name should have told him that the man was Irish), and he replied enthusiastically with his blessing and greetings to the Russian people. In this letter Whitman confessed:

As my dearest dream is for an internationality of poems and poets binding the lands of the earth closer than all treaties and diplomacy—as the purpose beneath the rest in my book is such hearty comradeship, for individuals to begin with, and for all the Nations of the earth as a result—how happy I should be to get the hearing and emotional contact of the great Russian peoples.[10]

Dr. Lee had become acquainted with Whitman's poems through his Dublin friend Thomas W. Rolleston, who also wanted to make a translation of selected poems into German. On April 5, 1884, Rolleston wrote Whitman that his translation was nearly finished, and received this reply:

...I had more than my own native land in view when I was composing Leaves of Grass. I wished to take the first step toward calling into existence a cycle of international poems. The chief reason for being of the United States of America is to bring about the common good will of all mankind, the solidarity of the world. What is still lacking in this respect can perhaps be accomplished by the art of poetry, through songs radiating from all the lands of the globe. I had also in mind, as one of my objects, to send a hearty greeting to these lands in America's name. And glad, very glad, should I be to gain entrance and audience among the Germanic people.[11]

Just when in composing *Leaves of Grass* Whitman began to have more than his own land in view is not easily determined, but by the 1870s the words and acts of friends abroad did make him feel that his 1856 prophecy that he would find "equals and lovers . . . in all lands" was coming true.

Today the abundance of foreign criticism of Whitman, the number of translations of his poetry and prose, and his influence on poets in other lands make his importance in world literature so vast a subject that only the highlights can be presented in a single chapter. It is a field for a richly-detailed book, or several books. The chapter on "Walt Whitman and World Literature" in the 1946 edition of this *Handbook* was the first systematic attempt to cover the subject. W. S. Kennedy's *Fight of a Book for the World* (1926)[12] contained a good deal of scattered information, but it was so poorly organized and amateurishly presented that it did not give a coherent account. Frederik Schyberg's *Walt Whitman* (1933) had a highly valuable chapter on "Whitman in World Literature,"[13] but he was particularly interested in "those he resembled and those who resembled him"—a comparative literature approach. Much valuable information was obtained from Schyberg for the chapter in the *Walt Whitman Handbook*. In fact, it was through Schyberg's influence that the chapter was undertaken at all. Praise of his work led to the translation and publication of his book in this country,[14] where it is still admired and used.

In 1955 *Walt Whitman Abroad*[15] made available in English some of the best critical essays on Whitman in nine languages. This anthology also contained surveys (introductions to the selections) by competent scholars of Whitman's reputation and influence in Germany, France, Denmark, Norway, Sweden, Russia, Italy, Spain and Latin America, Israel, and India, with some inadequate notes on Japan, for Whitman had had a far greater reception in Japan than the editor knew at the time. These introductory essays still remain the fullest survey of Whitman in the countries covered, but they need to be updated, for in every major country there has been great activity during the past twenty years in translating and interpreting Whitman.

In 1954 Fernando Alegría published a model study in his *Walt Whitman en Hispanoamerica*,[16] but this, too, needs updating. Charles Grippi's exhaustive dissertation, *The Literary Reputation of Walt Whitman in Italy* (1971) remains unpublished—though available on microfilm. Obviously much remains to be done, and it is hoped that this revised—but necessarily inadequate—survey of "Walt Whitman and World Literature" will serve as a guide to what has been done and indicate where more scholarly work still needs to be done.

AMERICAN TRANSCENDENTALISM

One reason both for the many striking parallels to Whitman's thought and expression in World Literature and for his dynamic influence on later writers is that his own major literary sources were international in origin. The first and most important of these was ostensibly American, being the "transcendentalism" of Emerson, Thoreau, Alcott, Margaret Fuller, Channing, Hedge, etc., that group of congenial minds which came together informally in the 1830s and 40s and generated not a school but a fermentation of ideas and attitudes which became the major stimulation of literary activity in the United States during the "American Renaissance."[17] This group followed no single master, creed, or even philosophy, but all members were profoundly interested in speculative thinking and in the great minds of the past. Most of them read and translated writings from Plato to Goethe and George Sand. They were especially interested in German Idealism, which came to them directly from the study and discussion of the Kantian school and indirectly through Coleridge and Carlyle, who were also reading and interpreting the poetry and philosophy of the German Romantic School.

To complete the international cycle, the Germans were, in turn, influenced by the mysticism both of Neo-Platonism and of the Orient. In fact, many of the leaders of the Romantic School in

Germany, like the Schlegels, were philologists and Orientalists. The American Transcendentalists, however, became sufficiently interested in the literature and religion of Asia, especially of the Hindus, to make some explorations of their own. Sanskrit was taught at Harvard, and India was frequently discussed in newspapers and popular magazines—to judge by the large number of clippings which Whitman amassed in his own scrapbooks.[18] American Transcendentalism was not a creed, a "school," or a systematic philosophy, but its basic assumptions came simultaneously from East and West, modified, of course, by American experience and Yankee character.[19]

One of the first Transcendentalist assumptions was the Rousseauistic belief in the innate goodness of human nature. The Emersonian absolute moral and intellectual self-reliance might also be regarded as the ultimate in Protestantism, the last phase of the Reformation, and a reaction against Calvinism. The greatest single philosophical influence on this group of American thinkers was probably the "transcendentalism" of Immanuel Kant, or at least the interpretations which they (partly following Coleridge and Carlyle) made of the *Critique of Pure Reason* (1781). In this work Kant, attempting to establish the limits of human reason, concluded that the finite mind could deal reliably only with phenomena. He did not deny the possible reality or existence of *something* behind appearances or phenomena, but insisted that it was unknowable. Kant admitted, however, the human need for belief in such supra-rational ideas as God, Immortality, Freedom, etc., and the result was that, especially in Great Britain and the United States, speculative minds were stimulated to explore the realm of the unknowable, the hypothetical "world-beyond-phenomena." W. F. Taylor has summarized the result in this manner:

The transcendentalists, then, were mystics. They hoped to "transcend" the realm of phenomena, and receive their inspirations toward truth at first hand from the Deity, unsullied by any contact with matter. Spiritual verities alone were of great importance to the transcendentalists; and, like the "divine and supernatural light" of Jonathan Edwards, these were immediately imparted to the soul from God. Yet God, the Over-Soul, was revealed also in nature, which was a beautiful web of appearances veiling the spirituality of the universe, a living garment, half concealing, half revealing, the Deity within.[20]

Some of the close parallels between Whitman's thought and the ideas of the Transcendentalists may be due to the fact that he also wrote as a mystic; but it would have been impossible for him to escape some direct influence from such members of the group as Channing, Hedge, Parker, Margaret Fuller, Thoreau, and Emerson, who wrote for the very magazines and newspapers which Whitman read and to which he also contributed during the 1840s. In fact, nearly all scholars now agree that Emerson himself was the one single greatest influence on Whitman during the years when he was planning and writing the first two or three editions of *Leaves of Grass*. Arvin was probably right when he declared that Emerson was for Whitman what Epicurus was for Lucretius or Spinoza for Goethe.[21] Another critic, who made a special investigation of the relationship, decided that, "Whitman was more indebted to Emerson than to any other for fundamental ideas in even his earliest *Leaves of Grass*."[22] Despite the fact that "on certain occasions [he] endeavored to minimize his debt to Emerson . . . Whitman ultimately arrived at an open, almost undeviating, allegiance both to Emerson as a person and to Emersonian ideas in general."[23]

A later critic, however, has pointed out what he regards as a significant difference between the thought of Emerson and Whitman. This difference, as presented by Leon Howard,[24] is parallel to the contrast which we have already mentioned between true Kantian transcendentalism and Coleridge and Carlyle's interpretation of Kant. It is the old question of the *reality* of phenomena, "appearances," matter, etc. Howard regards transcendentalism as monist, the true *reality* being spirit or Soul: "Running through Whitman's poetry is the constantly iterated idea of equalitarianism, one aspect of which is the avowal of equality between body and soul."[25] From this point of view the famous argument which Emerson gave Whitman on the Boston Common against the inclusion of the sex poems in the third edition was a struggle "between militant materialism combined with idealism and idealism in its transcendental purity."[26] However, it is still a moot question whether Emerson was a monist, a pure idealist, or a dualist. The humanistic critics argue that Emerson placed neither mind nor matter over the other. This argument merely indicates the close parallels between Emerson and Whitman's mystical pantheism. As F. I. Carpenter says, Emerson always "expressed his mystical belief in 'the eternal ONE.' By religion, rather than by philosophy, he was a monist, as 'The Over-Soul' and 'Brahma' bear witness."[27]

We see these tendencies further in two more of Emerson's theories which are also parallel to Whitman's ideas. One is the Plotinian theory of *emanation*, and the other is cosmic evolution:

Emanation may be described as an idealistic monism; evolution as a materialistic monism. The first readily adapted itself to the theory (then merely a suggestion, but now well established), of the identity of energy and matter—energy continually "emanating" from God, and condensing itself, as it were, in the forms of the material world. The second, describing the gradual evolution of life from inanimate to animate matter, and from lower to higher forms until it issues at last in the intelligence of man, also seemed to furnish such a satisfactory monistic theory, and recommended itself especially to Emerson as confirming his idea of progress, or melioration.[28]

WHITMAN, CARLYLE, AND GERMAN IDEALISM

In the case of Carlyle, however, it is easier to differentiate. Whitman's interest in Carlyle was perhaps second only to his interest in Emerson, but he usually found himself combatting Carlyle's ideas, though he finally came around to a grudging admiration of the dour Scotsman who was so critical of American democracy. In fact, almost all Whitman knew about German philosophy he got either from American popularizations or from Carlyle. Thus Carlyle was one of Whitman's main sources. But the following differences should be clearly borne in mind: (1) For Whitman *things* are real (even though they may be symbolized by pantheistic metaphors); for Carlyle nature is illusory and dream-like. (2) To Whitman, the poet of democracy, every man is a hero; whereas to Carlyle the average are merely "hodmen," whom the "heroes" have the divine right to rule. (3) Though Whitman believes that all symbols are in a sense religious, he does not, like Carlyle, think that the highest symbol is the Church. (4) There is in Whitman, unlike Carlyle, no renunciation, no hatred of evil, no need for expiation for sins.[29]

Yet despite these contrasts, Whitman undoubtedly owed a great debt to Carlyle—especially, as remarked above, for arousing his curiosity in German philosophy. It is difficult to assess this debt, for Carlyle was only one of Whitman's sources of information about German Idealism, others being Gostwick's popular handbook, *German Literature*, Hedge's *Prose Writers of Germany*, and of course Emerson. But Whitman's manuscript notes on Kant, Fichte, Schlegel,

Hegel, etc., show considerable knowledge of Carlyle's discussion of these men.[30]

John Burroughs declared (undoubtedly with Whitman's approval) that *Leaves of Grass* "tallies . . . the development of the Great System of Idealistic Philosophy in Germany,"[31] and in 1884 Whitman called himself "the greatest *poetical* representative of German philosophy."[32] Although these pretentious claims may amuse the scholars, there is no reason to doubt the poet's sincerity, and there is even some truth in the claim. Arvin remarks that,

At some indeterminate period—though the chances are that it was after two editions of *Leaves of Grass* had appeared and perhaps mainly during the sixties—Whitman began looking more closely and more curiously into the significance of certain stupendous names that had recurred invitingly in so much that he had heard and read, in Coleridge, in Carlyle, in Emerson too; and these were the names of the great German metaphysicians of idealism, Leibniz, Kant, Fichte, Schelling, Hegel. . . .[33]

Probably he actually read little of the "Critiques," "Systems," and "Encyclopaedias"; however, though Whitman "was certainly neither a professional nor a formal thinker, [he] was responsive enough to these activities of the ideologues to go into the subject at his own leisure and in his own way."[34]

What the poet got primarily from Leibniz, Kant, and Hegel seems to have been, in his own words, "the religious tone, . . . the recognition of the future, of the unknown, of Diety over and under all, and of the divine purpose, [which] are never absent, but indirectly give tone to all."[35] Though this "tone" may be vague, it is important because it indicates not only Whitman's assumptions and attitudes but also the scope and application of his ideas. However general his borrowings, the German names and theories gave him confidence in the ideas which he had already adapted for his "message." As Riethmuller puts it, "His comprehensive mind affectionately absorbed the great literary ideas of the Germanic countries and rejected or moulded them to fit his compass of a national American literature."[36] The route by which Whitman derived these ideas cannot be clearly traced, and is perhaps best indicated by the figurative language of Woodbridge Riley: "The migrations of the Germanic mysticism form a strange story. It began with what has been called the pantheism of the Rhine region; it ended, if it has ever ended, with the poetic pantheism of Walt Whitman, for in this modern American may be found traces of a remote past, and echoes of a distant land."[37]

As for specific authors, Hegel has often been cited as both source and parallel for Whitman's ideas. Boatright made the first extensive investigation of the subject, and he came to the conclusion that Hegel at least "strengthened Whitman's convictions"[38] — especially in his cosmic evolution, his pantheistic "unity," and his synthesis of Good with which the antithesis, Evil, merges and disappears. But he thought that the poet's knowledge of Hegelianism came more from Gostwick than Hegel's own writings, a deduction which Fulghum has since then amplified and further demonstrated.[39] Falk has also studied the relationship and decided that:

In the case of Hegel, Whitman certainly buttressed, and possibly largely derived, his evolutionary conception of a universe, exhibiting conflict and struggle, yet tending toward a vague divine culmination in the return of the individual souls to the Absolute. But most of all, he saw in the Hegelian metaphysic a logical rationalization of the New World Democracy which he aimed to glorify.[40]

A later investigator of this subject, however, Miss Parsons, believes that "many of the likenesses [between Whitman and Hegel] cited from time to time are misleading, if not fallacious, or are too general to be of significance."[41] Her argument is based mainly on Whitman's failure, or perhaps inability, to understand the Hegelian dialectic. In this contention she is probably quite correct, but this admission does not contradict the popularized Hegelianism which the American poet derived indirectly, through Gostwick and others. At any rate, Whitman's relations to Hegel seem closer than those with other philosophers of the Rhineland. Falk says,

In the case of the other German metaphysicians, we can ascribe no certain influence; yet, it is true that Whitman reveals parallels in thought and even phrase with most of the transcendental philosphers from Kant on down. In all of them Whitman sees lessons for American Democracy.[42]

Alfred H. Marks thinks that the test of Whitman's Hegelianism should be his use of Hegel's Dialectic, indicated by his frequently employing terms of "fusing," "blending," "uniting," "joining," suggestive of the "dialectical 'synthesis.' " Whitman frequently "calls up paired contradictories or 'thesis' and 'antithesis' and handles them as if there were no opposition between them."[43] As an example: "Do I contradict myself?/ Very well then I contradict myself,/ (I am large, I contain multitudes.)" If critics would pay attention to Whitman's dialectical "synthesis" they would find fewer contradictions than they imagine. Furthermore, Marks finds this process of two contradictory images (or ideas) resolved in a third employed throughout *Leaves of Grass*. Though one may wonder whether Whitman actually learned this way of thinking from Hegel, Marks does succeed in showing a basic Hegelian "dialectic" in Whitman's poems, giving the poet the right to call Hegel *his philosopher*.

WHITMAN AND INDIA

Whitman's indebtedness to Oriental literature and Hindu mysticism is even more difficult to trace than his relations with German philosophy; and yet almost from the first edition students of Oriental thought have recognized in *Leaves of Grass* such striking parallels to the *Bhagavad Gita* and other Indian poems that they have speculated on Whitman's use of translations as primary sources for his poems. In 1856 Thoreau, an amateur but ardent Orientalist, called *Leaves of Grass* "wonderfully like the Orientals . . . considering that when I asked [Whitman] if he had read them, he answered, 'No: Tell me about them.' "[44] Later, on numerous occasions, Whitman evinced some knowledge of Hindu and other Oriental translations. In *A Backward Glance*, for example, he claims to have read "the ancient Hindoo poems"[45] in preparation for *Leaves of Grass*— *i.e.*, apparently before publishing the first edition. Whether in his reply to Thoreau's question he was trying to conceal this source, or whether Thoreau's question directed his attention to this field and stimulated his curiosity to explore it, we can at present only guess. But as with the German influence, this Orientalism was very much in the American intellectual atmosphere of the 1840s and 50s,[46] and it would have been impossible for Whitman to escape at least some indirect influence. Indeed, American Transcendentalism, as we have seen, received it from two directions: German Idealism and Romanticism were strongly indebted to Oriental mysticism,[47] and American Transcendentalism might be called the offspring of a German father and a Hindu mother.

In 1866 Viscount Strangford, an Oriental scholar, observed the similarity of Whitman's rhythms to those of Persian poets,[48] and in the same year Moncure D. Conway found Asia the key to both Whitman and the Transcendentalists.[49] In 1889 Gabriel Sarrazin declared that "Walt Whitman in his confident and lofty piety, is the direct inheritor of the great Oriental mystics, Brahma, Proclus, Abou Saïd."[50] In 1906 Edward Carpenter cited interesting parallels (which he did not claim as sources) between the Upanishads and *Leaves of Grass*.[51]

The first extensive investigation of the similarities between the *Bhagavad Gita* and *Leaves of Grass* was made by Dorothy Frederica Mercer in a doctoral dissertation at the University of California (Berkeley) in 1933, parts of which she later published in *Vedanta and the West*.[52] Labeled a "Comparative Study," this thesis did not claim the *Bhagavad Gita* as an actual source, though the author quoted an Indian scholar who believed Whitman "must have studied the *Bhagavad Gita*, for in his *Leaves of Grass* one finds the teaching of Vedanta; the Song of Myself is but an echo of the sayings of Krishna."[53]

The first striking parallel between Whitman's ideas and the Vedantic teaching is the doctrine of the *self*. "Whitman's soul, like the self of the *Bhagavad Gita*, is the unifying energy."[54] The self is not material, but spiritual; "it is the passive spectator; it is Brahma incarnate in the body; and it is permanent, indestructible, eternal, all-pervading, unmanifest." In the same way Whitman's "Me, Myself" is immortal, and through his cosmic "I" he merges with all creation, feeling himself to be at one with the spirit of the universe.

Other Vedanta doctrines Dr. Mercer found paralleled in *Leaves of Grass* were reincarnation, intuition in place of learning, and knowledge through love.[55] The most important parallel was on God and the self. It may be objected, however, that all of these terms and ideas are sufficiently ambiguous as to be capable of various interpretations. The importance of Dr. Mercer's study was that she interpreted Whitman as various Indian minds had seen him; there was—and is—something in Whitman's poems to provoke these responses.

In 1959 the major American critic, Malcolm Cowley, decided after reading Heinrich Zimmer's *The Philosophies of India* (1951): "Most of Whitman's doctrines, though by no means all of them, belong to the mainstream of Indian philosophy."[56] Unlike the Indian sages, he was not a consistent idealist; he did not despise the body, and he did not wish union with the Over-Soul by "subjugating the senses, as advised by yogis and Buddhists alike. . . ." Yet at times he seems to be a Mahayana Buddhist "promising nirvana for all after countless reincarnations, and also sharing the belief of some Mahayana sects that the sexual act can serve as one of the sacraments."[57] At other times he proclaims "joyous affirmation" like an apostle of Tantric Brahmanism. In *The Gospel of Sri Ramakrishna* Cowley found "this priest of Kali, the Mother Goddess . . . delivering some of Whitman's messages in—what is more surprising—the same tone of voice."[58] To Cowley the importance of these resemblances was that they help the modern reader to understand Whitman. For example, his idea of God:

✓ In "Song of Myself" as originally written, God is neither a person nor, in the strict sense, even a being; God is an abstract principle of energy that is manifested in every living creature, as well as in "the grass that grows wherever the land is and the water is." In some ways this God of the first edition resembles Emerson's Over-soul, but he seems much closer to the Brahman of the *Upanishads*, the absolute, unchanging, all-enfolding Consciousness, the Divine Ground from which all things emanate and to which all living things may hope to return. And this Divine Ground is by no means the only conception that Whitman shared with Indian philosophers, in the days when he was writing "Song of Myself."[59]

In 1964 V. K. Chari, a graduate of Benares Hindu University and a superbly-trained scholar in Vedanta, published a closely and subtly reasoned study of *Whitman in the Light of Vedantic Mysticism*.[60] Like Cowley, Chari was less interested in possible sources than in useful interpretation. "The theme of self, of relating the self to the world of experience, is central to the comprehensive intent of Whitman's poems. . . ."[61] The subject matter of Whitman's poetry is no other than the nature of experience itself, . . . the fact of human consciousness." The way to read "Whitman's poetry is . . . as a direct dramatization of the act of consciousness." Whitman's "intuitional sense enables man to realize the oneness of the universe." This sense is what Dr. Bucke called "cosmic consciousness," which Chari defines as "the consciousness of the self that is the cosmos."[62] This view places in a new light Whitman's calling himself "kosmos"[63] — because the self and *Atman* are one—and his statement in the 1855

Preface that, "The poets of the cosmos advance through all inter-positions and coverings and turmoils and strategems to first principles."[64]

In Vedantic mysticism there is no duality of subject and object, and Whitman's imaginative identification with everything and every-one is based on this principle. His conception of the self is not that of the post-Kantian idealists, because "for all these philosophers dialectic is the vehicle of their thought," and for them the self is also dialectical: "The self is a dialectical and antithetical being to which dualism and opposition become a necessary condition of exis-tence."[65] For Hegel, "The self subsists by subduing the opposition of the non-self."

Whitman's essentially mystical thinking would be opposed to any doctrine that accords to the individual but a dependent and inferior status. Whitman asserts, "And nothing, not God, is greater to one than one's self is." A true doctrine of self is that which holds that the individual is coeval and coeternal with the absolute and accords to every particle of the universe the status of the supreme.[66]

Chari opposes all those critics who derive both Emerson's and Whitman's thought from German philosophy. Whether one agrees with him or not, it must be conceded that Chari's interpreta-tion is consistent, penetrating, and more illuminating than the dialectical approaches. He is especially good on Whitman's democratic philosophy:

Whitman's democratic faith is born out of his conception of the mystical self. Since the central problem of democracy is the resolu-tion of the inherent conflict between the individual and the universe, Whitman resolves it at the level of the transpersonal self, where the individual being himself is also the self of all. . . . The faith that there is a central identity of self running through all life is the foundation of democracy and freedom. Each individual is unique, and yet he is identical with the all. It is this conviction of the uniqueness and intrinsic worth of every human being that accounts for Whitman's individualism and his espousal of democracy as the surest guarantee of individual values.[67]

In 1966 another Hindu, Professor O. K. Nambiar, of Mysore University, published a study called *Walt Whitman and Yoga*.[68] Nam-biar did not claim that Whitman knew or practiced Yogic discipline.

"Patanjali, the greatest authority on Yoga Sastra mentions . . . those rare geniuses born with the Yogic gift—the natural Yogis—who rise to cosmic consciousness or *Brahma Chit* without religious striving."[69] Whitman did that, Nambiar contends, in section 5 of "Song of Myself."[70] There he describes attaining Kundalini, "a psycho-physical energy present in every individual," but usually attained only by those who employ Yogic techniques of meditation and breath control. One who attains the Kundalini level of consciousness, as described in "Song of Myself," experiences the "unitive life based on Love."[71]

Nambiar says that he does not regard his book as cultist, though he does think that Whitman is a good example of the religious life possible for everyone, and greatly needed by all people. He would use *Leaves of Grass* as a text which the Western world could understand, with such aid as his book provides. In view of Whitman's ambition to write a "New Bible" for Democracy, this view is interesting, and gives Whitman credit for more than most Western critics have seen in his poems—that is, since the "hot little prophets" of the poet's Camden era.[72]

However, another Indian, T. R. Rajasekharaiah, has tried in *The Roots of Whitman's Grass* (1970)[73] to settle the question of Whitman's actual indebtedness to Indian sources—with results quite different from those of Chari and Nambiar. He began by making a list of the books and articles in English on Eastern literature, philosophy, and religion available to Whitman in the years immediately preceding 1855. He found that the Astor Library, which Whitman used, had over 500 items on this subject. Rajasekharaiah then went through each of these looking for parallels to passages in Whitman's poems. He found many, some of which he thought were so close that he decided, like Esther Shepherd,[74] he had discovered Walt Whitman's closely-guarded "secret." Whitman had borrowed his ideas, much of his imagery, and his fake "mysticism" from translations and popularizations of Oriental literature, especially Hindu. Though, again like Shepherd, this author insists that he is not attacking Whitman's position as a great poet, his accusations do question not only the poet's honesty but also his talent, if his power rested on plagiarism.

Some of Rajasekharaiah's examples are striking and may, indeed, indicate the possibility of actual source material, but many of them seem far-fetched and doubtful. Some, too, could be coincidence, such as Whitman's symbolical "leaves" of grass and the sacred Kusa grass of a Hindu sect. As a source study *The Roots of Whitman's Grass* is a failure, yet it still has value because of the parallels cited. It is unfortunate that the author did not use his material for a comparative study—but that did not fit his strong conviction. If read for comparisons, this book does have value and may contribute to further understanding of Whitman in relation to the literature of India.

During the 1950s and 60s there was so much interest in Whitman in India that the Sahitya Akademi (National Academy) began publishing translations of Whitman, with the assistance of UNESCO, into the eighteen languages of the country. So far only two have been published, 101 poems into Kannada by M. Gopalakrishna Adiga in 1966;[75] and 114 poems into Punjabi by Gurbakhsh Singh in 1968[76]—both with an Introduction by Gay Wilson Allen.[77] Since nearly all educated Indians read English, Whitman's reception in that nation is not limited to his availability in the native languages; nevertheless, the translations should create more interest in the American poet.

THE FRENCH BACKGROUND

These American, English, German, and Indian parallels—and possible origins—provide clues and analogues for Whitman's "mysticism" and philosophical idealism. But there was also another side of his thought and expression, which Arvin refers to as "a kind of Transcendental atheism."[78] This is the Whitman of French rationalism, skepticism, and "free thought," who declares in the 1855 Preface that, "There will soon be no more priests. Their work is done. . . . A new order shall arise and they shall be the priests of man, and every man shall be his own priest."[79] This is partly Emersonian "self-reliance" and the ultimate result of the Reformation, but it is also the offspring of the French Revolution, and of Thomas Jefferson and Tom Paine in America.

As the heir of this tradition Whitman wrote such early poems as "Europe," "Boston Ballad," and "To a Foil'd European Revolutionaire," and felt great sympathy for the defeated revolutionists of France (and other European countries) of 1848. He too shouts "Equality!" and "Liberty!" At this time the "headsman" is a symbol to him of reactionary Europe, where the oppressors of mankind are "hangman, priest, tax-gatherer." Whitman's realization that the ideals of the American and French Revolutions had been thwarted in Europe intensified his own nationalism and increased his conviction that, politically, the United States was the only hope of the world for freedom and equality.

Even his Christ-rôle, his vicarious sympathy, was to some extent the product of these times and influences.

> Through me many long dumb voices,
> Voices of the interminable generations of slaves,
> Voices of prostitutes, and of deformed persons . . .[80]

The above interpretation is strengthened by the fact that he was more exercised over abstract political slavery than the concrete example of racial slavery in his own nation.

Whitman's interest in comparative religion and his attempt to construct a theology which would fuse and extract the best of all religions probably also came to a considerable degree from French deism and rationalism, both directly and indirectly (see Chap. III, "Nature").

> Magnifying and applying come I,
> Outbidding at the start the old cautious hucksters,
>   [i.e., priests of historical religions].[81]

He will accept only "the rough deific sketches to fill out better in myself." Bibles and religions "have all grown out of you . . . It is not they who give the life . . . . it is you who give the life."[82] Institutionalized religion is dead and ought to be buried:

Allons! From all formulas!
From your formulas, O bat-eyed and materialistic priests!
The stale cadaver blocks up the passage—the burial waits no longer.[83]

And the only guide is each person's own conscience:

I only am he who places over you no master, owner, better, God,
   beyond what waits intrinsically in yourself.[84]

Of course there are many possible sources for Whitman's "free thought" and "natural religion." In Chapter III the influence of Thomas Paine's *Age of Reason*, Frances Wright's *A Few Days in*

Athens, and Volney's *Ruins* on Whitman in his youth were pointed out. Certainly these were important in the formative stage of Whitman's mind, though a source for only one aspect of his thought, a distinctly limited aspect which does not entirely harmonize with all his ideas. But when we come to the romantic as distinguished from the rationlistic French authors, it is still more difficult to separate source from parallel. Bliss Perry regarded Whitman as an heir of Rousseau,[85] but what romantic poet in Europe or America was not? No one can deny the influence of the doctrines of innate goodness of .human nature and "primitivism" on *Leaves of Grass*. Of course Whitman was well acquainted with Rousseauism, but it is not an influence which can be weighed objectively.

Of the French Romantic School, George Sand has been claimed not only as a major but even as Whitman's main source. Professor Esther Shephard[86] thought that in the wandering carpenter poet of the *Countess of Rudolstadt* Whitman found the literary rôle (she called it a "pose") which he was thereafter to adopt as his own through all the editions of *Leaves of Grass*. That he read and admired this and other novels by George Sand, there can be no doubt. It is even possible that George Sand's carpenter poet aroused in Walt Whitman the literary ambitions which he sought to achieve in *Leaves of Grass*, but Professor Shephard's claims for this source lose much of their strength when we discover equally striking parallels in the works of other French romanticists.

One of these is Victor Hugo—though Whitman seems not to have admired him as much as he admired George Sand.[87] However, they had much in common, as Kennedy has pointed out:

Walt Whitman continually suggests another great humanitarian poet,—Victor Hugo. That which chiefly affines them is sympathy, compassion. To redeem our erring brothers by love, and not inflexible savage justice, is the message of each. Who is worthy to be placed beside these two as promulgators of the distinctive democratic ideas of these times,—the thirst for individual growth, space for the expansion of one's own soul, and equal rights before the law? . . . They have the same love of the sea and the immensities, and the same ingrained love of freedom.[88]

More specifically, one might compare Hugo's assertion that everything has a soul with Whitman's animism, or his including the ugly as a necessary part of his esthetic with Whitman's complete equalitarianism, or his belief that the spirit is always advancing toward something better[90] with Whitman's cosmic meliorism. Although these parallels indicate not so much sources or direct influences as a general literary movement to which both belonged, the very fact that the American poet shared these fundamental resemblances with one of the major poets of nineteenth-century France indicates that the ground was already partly prepared for Whitman's later reception in France.

Another French writer of the period whose thought and expression parallel Whitman's to an astonishing degree is the historian, Jules Michelet. In 1847 Whitman reviewed his *History of France*[91] and in 1876 he paraphrased (one might almost say plagiarized) a passage from Michelet's *The Bird* in his poem, "To the Man-of-War Bird." Before he published the first edition of *Leaves of Grass* Whitman probably also read Michelet's *The People*,[92] but there is no conclusive evidence. Nevertheless, the literary theory on which Michelet wrote this book is completely analogous to Whitman's poetic program. In his preface Michelet says, "This book is more than a book; it is myself, therefore it belongs to you . . . Receive, then, this book of *The People*, because it is you, because it is I . . ."[93] Compare:

> Camerado, this is no book,
> Who touches this touches a man, . . .[94]

"Son of the people," says Michelet, "I have lived with them, I know them, they are myself . . . I unite them all in my own person."[95] Whitman:

> In all people I see myself, none more and not one a barley-corn less,
> And the good or bad I say of myself I say of them.[96]

Through Michelet's historian and Whitman's poet "the people" find their voice:

The people, in the highest sense of the word, is seldom to be found in the people . . . it exists in its truth, and at its highest power in the man of genius; in him resides the great soul . . . the whole world [vibrates] at the least word he utters . . . That voice is the voice of the people; mute of itself, it speaks in this man, and God in him.[97]

This "genius" is Whitman's ideal poet, who "is to be commensurate with a people . . . He is a seer . . . he is individual . . . he is complete in himself . . . the others are as good as he, only he sees it and they do not."[98] Throughout the 1855 Preface Whitman insists that only the poet, who is the true man of genius, can express the heart of the people; only through the poet can the people become articulate.

Michelet also anticipates Whitman in the cult of the barbarian:

The rise of the people, the progress, is often nowadays compared to the invasion of the *Barbarians*! yes! that is to say, full of sap, fresh, vigorous, and for ever springing up . . . travellers toward the Rome of the future.[99]

As one of the barbarians, he glories in their crude, untutored, natural strength of expression,

striving to give everything at once—leaves, fruit, and flowers—till it breaks or distorts the branches. But those who start up thus with the sap of the people in them, do not the less introduce into art a new burst of life and principle of youth; or at least leave on it the impress of a great result.[100]

We could easily imagine that these are Whitman's words, he who sounds his "barbaric yawp over the roofs of the world,"[101] and would have his verse break forth loosely like lilacs on a bush.[102] Even more than Michelet he strives "to give everything at once . . . till it breaks or distorts the branches."

There is another curious parallel between Michelet's sentimental story in *L'Oiseau* of a nightingale during a storm near Nantes and Whitman's mocking-bird on Long Island.[103] If a translation[104] of *L'Oiseau* had been available to Whitman in 1859, this story might be regarded as a possible source for the bird motif in "Out of the Cradle . . ." Nevertheless, the parallels do show that the two authors shared a common intellectual world in which birds and animals could speak the language of "Art and the Infinite,"[105] to use Michelet's term. This is less important, however, than the fact that Whitman attempted in his rôle of poet of Democracy to embody Michelet's ideal of the literary genius of the people who would be the articulate voice of the masses—in which Michelet succeeded better than the American poet.

WHITMAN IN ENGLAND:
RECEPTION AND INFLUENCE

In beginning a survey of Whitman's reception, reputation, and influence in foreign countries, we inevitably start with the British Isles, where he was first appreciated and first recognized as a major poet.[106] The story need not be told in complete detail, however, for it is familiar to most students of American literature, and much of it has already been covered in this book in the account of the biographies. Furthermore, it is largely the story of Whitman's reputation in Great Britain (and the poet's reflected fame at home), for even to the present time he has had less actual literary influence in England than in France or Germany.

The introduction of *Leaves of Grass* to the British Isles began more or less by accident. Several months after the almost complete failure of the first edition to gain sales or recognition in America, Thomas Dixon, a cork cutter of Sunderland, bought a copy from a peddler, James Grinrod, a veteran of the American Civil War. Dixon sent this copy to his friend William Bell Scott, a minor poet and sculptor. Scott gave a copy to William Rossetti for a Christmas present in 1856, and Rossetti was so pleased with the work that he immediately began telling his friends about it.[107] In the same year Emerson sent a copy, with an apologetic note, to Carlyle, but until his death Carlyle remained either indifferent or merely irritated by Whitman's poems.[108]

English criticism of Whitman did not get under way, however, until about 1866. Lord Strangford published a critical essay in *The Pall Mall Gazette*, February 16, 1866,[109] in which he recognized the American poet's Oriental style without approving his use of it. Whitman, he says, "has managed to acquire or imbue himself with not only the spirit, but with the veriest mannerism, the most absolute trick and accent of Persian poetry."[110] Instead of wasting his gifts on *Leaves of Grass*, he should have translated Rumi. This observation might have started interesting and fruitful discoveries in comparative literature, but no one at the time, not even Lord Strangford, pursued the comparison any further. In October of the same year, Moncure

Conway, who had visited Whitman in America, wrote a personal sketch of the poet for the October *Fortnightly Review*.

Over ten years after his introduction to *Leaves of Grass*, Rossetti published his first article on Whitman in the *Chronicle*, July 6, 1867. He attempted to enlarge the theory of poetry by declaring that, "Only a very restricted and literal use of the word, rhythm, could deny the claim of these writings to being both poetic and rhythmical." He called *Leaves of Grass* "incomparably the largest poetic work of our period."[111] But in the introduction to his edition of *Selections*[112] published the next year, he was cautious and judicious, perhaps the best strategy for increasing Whitman's reputation in England. Also the fact that his poems were edited in England at this time by Rossetti, a man known and respected by the literary profession, who carefully eliminated the most daring sex poems, accounts to a considerable extent for Whitman's greater fame in Britain than at home.

It was this edition of selected poems which Mrs. Anne Gilchrist read in 1869, having borrowed a copy from Madox Brown. She was not satisfied, however, with a censored edition and borrowed the complete *Leaves* from Rossetti himself. So profoundly affected was she that she wrote the famous "An Englishwoman's Estimate of Walt Whitman," published in the *Boston Radical*, May, 1870. To her, *Leaves of Grass* was not only sacred literature but also a personal plea for love. It is doubtful that anywhere else in the whole range of Whitman criticism any other person ever responded to the poet's message with such absolute sympathy and understanding—such sympathy, in fact, that she fell in love with the man through the book, and after this one article the story belongs to biography rather than to criticism.[113]

Ironically, one of Whitman's most ardent and impetuous friends and critics in England at this time was that eccentric enemy of the Rossetti-Swinburne circle, Robert Buchanan. This son of socialist and "infidel" parents was the first in Great Britain to accept Whitman unreservedly as a prophet and a modern Socrates. Blodgett calls his first criticism, published in *The Broadway Magazine* (1868) and reprinted in the same year in the book *David Gray*, "the most exhilarating that had yet appeared on Whitman in England."[114] But Buchanan worked himself into an embarrassing position in 1871 in an attack on the sensuality of Swinburne, Dante Gabriel Rossetti, Baudelaire, and others, which he called "The Fleshly School of

Poetry."[115] When Swinburne inquired why Buchanan "despised so much the Fleshly School of Poetry in England and admired so much the poetry which is widely considered unclean and animal in America,"[116] he was hard pressed for a defense of "Children of Adam," and even admitted that *Leaves of Grass* contained about "fifty lines of a thoroughly indecent kind."[117] But the controversy only intensified his loyalty to Whitman, whose cause he did at least two good services. In the first place, he was one of the earliest foreign critics to recognize the literary quality of Whitman's "wonderful poetic prose, or prose-poetry,"[118] and in the second place, in 1876 he started a storm of controversy over Whitman's neglect which stimulated the sale of his books and raised a substantial sum of money for him. Hearing that the poet, "old, poor, and paralyzed,"[119] was shamefully neglected in America, Buchanan wrote a letter to *The London Daily News* hotly denouncing the poet's unappreciative countrymen. Naturally many Americans resented the charge and Whitman's cause thereby became entangled with Anglo-American antagonisms which lingered on for years. After visiting the United States in 1885, Buchanan poured more oil on the fire with a satirical poem against the Bostonians for their indifference to Whitman, and in 1887 he added that in his native land Whitman was "simply *outlawed*":

In a land of millionaires, in a land of which he will one day be known as the chief literary glory, he is almost utterly neglected. Let there be no question about this; all denial of it is disingenuous and dishonest. The literary class fights shy of him.[120]

Swinburne's criticism of Whitman illustrates anew the fortuitous and erratic reception of *Leaves of Grass* in Great Britain. A copy of the 1855 edition found its way into the hands of George Howard, the ninth Earl of Carlyle, who passed it on to Swinburne.[121] It interested Swinburne so much that he ordered a copy for himself, and then later procured a copy of the 1860 edition. In the latter volume he greatly admired "Out of the Cradle Endlessly Rocking" (then called "A Word Out of the Sea").[122] In his biography of Blake (1868) he compared the Universal Republic and the spiritual democracy of the two poets. Their writings seemed to him like "fragments . . . of the Pantheistic poetry of the East."[123] After *Drum-Taps* was published, Swinburne declared the threnody on Lincoln to be "the most sweet and sonorous nocturne ever chanted in the church of the world." The height of his admiration for Whitman was reached in 1871 when in *Songs Before Sunrise*, dedicated to Mazzini, he addressed a poem "To Walt Whitman in America." Whitman and his friends took the poem as a personal greeting, but as Blodgett points out, Swinburne's "interest in political freedom, never realistic, took the form of a passtionately expressed idealism in which Walt Whitman appeared as the prophet of liberty, the 'strong-winged soul with prophetic lips hot with the blood-beats of song.' " Whitman and his country were "apostrophized as symbols of the freedom which with Swinburne was a seductive abstraction. . . ."[124]

The following year (1872), in *Under the Microscope*, Swinburne's admiration for Whitman's poetry became more restrained and judicious. While still accepting the American poet's democracy, he began to find fault with his style and his lapses from good taste. *Under the Microscope* was directed especially at Buchanan, and it is understandable that Swinburne would begin to have his doubts about the poet so noisily praised by the enemy of Swinburne's circle.

Edmund Gosse thought Watts-Dunton was responsible for the cooling of Swinburne's enthusiasm for the American poet,[125] but later investigators found nothing either remarkable or treacherous in his increasing impatience with Whitman as formalist and thinker, the two special deficiencies mentioned in *Under the Microscope*. Even the notorious "Whitmania," published first in *The Fortnightly Review*, August, 1887, and reprinted in *Studies in Poetry and Prose* (1894), is, as Cairns says, "directed primarily against those enthusiasts who give Whitman a place 'a little beneath Shakespeare, a little above Dante, or cheek by jowl with Homer.' "[126] It was no outright "recantation," for Swinburne still admired Whitman's "genuine passion of patriotic and imaginative sympathy" and his "earnest faith in freedom,"[127] but he objected to the weakness of thought, the unpoetic style, and the manner of treating sex. It is not surprising that a poet of Swinburne's temperament and culture would eventually find the self-appointed poet of American Democracy uncongenial, and his objections are essentially those of the later British biographers, such as John Bailey and Hugh I'Anson Fausset.[128]

The biographical and critical contributions of John Addington Symonds to Whitman literature in England have been treated in a previous chapter,[129] but we may note here that he became acquainted with Whitman's writings in 1865 at Trinity College, Cambridge, through his friend Frederic Myers. Young university men in

Great Britain seem to have been especially attracted by Whitman at this time. Other bookish men drawn to him were Lionel Johnson, Robert Louis Stevenson, and Edward Dowden.

Edward Dowden, Professor of English Literature and Oratory at Trinity College, Dublin, was one of the most gifted and remarkable critic-admirers of Whitman in the British Isles. What especially attracted him to *Leaves of Grass* were the spiritual values. In his first book on Shakespeare (1879) he ranked Whitman with the "spiritual teachers": Wordsworth, Coleridge, Shelley, Carlyle, Browning, and others.[130] Whitman's form, however, was a challenge to his powers of analysis and he attempted to rationalize it.

Dowden's essay, "The Poetry of Democracy: Walt Whitman," was rejected in 1869, as too dangerous to print, by *Macmillan's Magazine* and *The Contemporary Review* but was finally published by *The Westminster Review* in July, 1871 (reprinted in *Studies in Literature*, London, 1878). In this essay Dowden accepted the view that America lacked native literature before Whitman and regarded *Leaves of Grass* as democratic art, which must reject aristocratic form and make its own rules and techniques. However, he valued Whitman as a poet despite his unconventional form, not because of it. Though he admitted guardedly that Whitman might not have been sufficiently reserved in the treatment of sex, he did not think that the poet exalted the body over the soul. On the whole, Dowden accepted Whitman on his own terms, but brought to his interpretations a literary skill and critical background which greatly advanced the American poet's reputation abroad—and even influenced the course of his reception at home. The distinguished Dublin professor found himself embarrassed and repulsed by Whitman's American disciples, but this did not affect his critical opinions or published support. He reviewed *Specimen Days* in *The Academy*, November 18, 1882, and arranged for an English edition of Dr. Bucke's biography, for which he collected and arranged an appendix, "English Critics on Walt Whitman."

Despite Dowden's championship of Whitman, however, *Leaves of Grass* was removed from the Trinity College library after Boston banned the 1881–82 edition. But meanwhile other Irish scholars were also active in spreading Whitman's fame in the British Isles. Standish O'Grady ("Arthur Clive") published "Walt Whitman: the Poet of Joy" in the December, 1875, *Gentleman's Magazine*. With Irish exuberance he elaborated in the vein of O'Connor and

Bucke: "Often we think one of the elements of nature has found a voice, and thunders great syllables in our ears."[131] O'Grady's friend, Thomas W. Rolleston, discovered Whitman in 1877. After four years in Germany, he published at Dresden a study called *Über Wordsworth und Walt Whitman* (1883). Rolleston was one of the first critics to perceive Whitman's connection with German philosophy and to interpret him not as a "primitive" but in terms of comparative literature—an important step toward the recognition of Whitman as a "world poet." However, like the American disciples, he thought that criticizing Whitman was like criticizing Nature. Rolleston also translated a book of "selections" from *Leaves of Grass* into German (1884), but it was not published until Dr. Karl Knortz, a German-American scholar, revised it and finally got J. Schabelitz, of Zürich, to bring it out in Switzerland in 1889.

Scotland was slow in accepting Whitman. John Nichol, Professor of English Literature at the University of Glasgow, discussed him in an article on "American Literature" in the ninth edition of the *Encyclopaedia Britannica* (1875) in the following tone:

... although this author on various occasions displays an uncouth power, his success is in the main owing to the love of novelty, wildness, and even of absurdity, which has infected a considerable class of critics and readers on both sides of the Atlantic. ... he discards not only rhyme, but all ordinary rhythm. ... "The Leaves of Grass" is redeemed by a few grand descriptive passages from absolute barbarism both of manner and matter. It is a glorification of nature in her most unabashed forms, an audacious protest against all that civilization has done to raise men above the savage state.

These views were amplified in Nichol's book, *American Literature* (1882), in which he decided that "If Shakespeare, Keats, and Goethe are poets, Whitman is not."[132] He regretted Swinburne's favorable comparisons of Blake and Whitman. The Earl of Lytton and Sir Leslie Stephen also, as Blodgett says, "felt the need of British austerity toward American literary bumptiousness,"[133] and many Scottishmen seem to have shared their attitudes. One of these was Peter Bayne, a prominent editor of the day, who in the December, 1875, *Contemporary Review* "pounced upon Whitman like a Sunday school superintendent upon a bad boy, and he plainly intimates, in doing so, that he is exposing the hoax that Dowden, Rossetti, and Buchanan had been playing off on the British public." Blodgett also rightly calls this "A very plausible Tory attack," stating "the formidable case that all respectable persons have against *Leaves of Grass.*"[134] But another Scotsman, John Robertson, published a kind and sympathetic though undistinguished pamphlet, *Walt Whitman: Poet and Democrat*, at Edinburgh in 1884.

Despite the Tory opposition, Whitman made steady progress in England, partly, as Blodgett suggests, because, "In the seventies or eighties a young critic or journalist, trying to get a foothold in the London literary world, would be quite likely to seize upon Whitman for 'material.' "[135] Among these young critics were H. Buxton Forman, Ernest Rhys, and Edmund Gosse. Forman observed similarities between Whitman and Shelley and tried, without much success, to interest Whitman in Shelley. At the age of twenty-five Rhys turned from mining engineering to literature in order to advance the cause of labor, and he thought he saw in Whitman the enemy of "the stronghold of caste and aristocracy and all selfishness between rich and poor."[136] Consequently Rhys gave popular lectures on Whitman and edited, with a good critical introduction, a pocket edition of selected poems. It was Rhys's intention to make Whitman known to the common people, the very kind of audience which the poet had originally attempted to address in his own country. Gosse, like Swinburne, passed from ardent admiration to cool objectivity in his criticism of Whitman and was regarded with increasing hostility by the Camden circle. But he was one of the most competent critics that Whitman had in Great Britain.

There were, however, other distinguished critics. One was George Saintsbury, who reviewed *Leaves of Grass* in *The Academy*, October 10, 1874. He admired Whitman as poet and artist, though demurring somewhat at his idealization of the animal. He found Whitman's rhythm "singularly fresh, light, and vigorous," and praised his technique in the great *History of Prosody* (1910). Another critic, George C. Macaulay, gave a more philosophical analysis in *The Nineteenth Century*, December, 1882, describing Whitman's religion as pantheistic, his ethics as Greek, and his sympathy as universal. Still earlier William Kingdon Clifford, Professor of Mathematics at the University College, London, had made one of the first contributions to the understanding of Whitman's mysticism by citing him as an illustration of "Cosmic Emotion" in *The Nineteenth Century*, October, 1877. In 1886 even the staid *Quarterly Review* (in a review of Stedman's *Poets of America*, published in the October number) called Whitman "a lyric genius of the highest order," praising especially his cosmic qualities.

Though Walt Whitman was befriended by such famous men in England as William Rossetti, John Addington Symonds, and Lord Tennyson (who remained a steadfast friend and correspondent though not a public critic), and had what might be called a strong personal following, his actual literary influence in the British Isles was negligible. In fact, it included only one well-known writer and a small group of left-wing socialists and reformers in Lancashire. The one writer was Edward Carpenter, a young poet, socialist, and idealistic reformer who, in Blodgett's words, "felt himself dedicated, heart and soul, to the life work of interpreting and expanding Whitman's dream of democratic brotherhood."[137] *Toward Democracy* is such an expansion, and *My Days and Dreams* outlines in detail a social program inspired by *Leaves of Grass*, though it probably goes far beyond anything Whitman ever dreamed.

The one group of ordinary folk who organized a club to study and apply Whitman's doctrines was known as "Bolton College," a satirical name adopted by the members, middle-class Lancashire business men, professional men, and artisans. Two of the members visited Whitman and wrote books about the meeting.[138] The group had no great influence on the course of Whitman criticism, but, as Blodgett remarks, "it is strangely interesting that the story of Whitman's English following should begin with the effort of Thomas Dixon, corkcutter, to call attention to him, and end with the homage of a middle-class coterie in the cotton-manufacturing town of Bolton."[139]

What pleased and encouraged Walt Whitman most about his reception in Great Britain was the friendly praise and the personal comradeship of both the professional writers and the disciples. This recognition sustained him during the dark hours of his neglect in America. But it can not be said that many of these critics made permanent contributions to Whitman criticism, except for some psychological interpretations which the poet could never appreciate.

It was the British who first tried to penetrate the mystery of the "Calamus" emotions, first Symonds, then Carpenter, and finally Havelock Ellis. Carpenter, like Symonds, seems to have felt in himself something of the same emotion and he never gave up the attempt to understand both himself and Whitman, and to discover the social value of "manly love." He did not shrink from the analysis of "sexual inversion,"[140] but he also thought that "The Comradeship on which Whitman founds a large portion of his message may in course of time become a general enthusiasm. . . ."[141] It was Ellis, however, who came nearest getting to the bottom of this question and who analyzed Whitman's psychology with the most penetrating insight. But he also warned that:

It is as [a prophet-poet] that Whitman should be approached, and I would desire to protest against the tendency, now marked in many quarters, to treat him merely as an invert, and to vilify him or glorify him accordingly. However important inversion may be as a psychological key to Whitman's personality, it plays but a small part in Whitman's work, and for many who care for that work a negligible part.[142]

Out of Whitman's emotional sensitivity came a more sane and wholesome attitude toward the physical basis of life: "Whitman represents, for the first time since Christianity swept over the world, the re-integration, in a sane and whole-hearted form, of the instincts of the entire man, and therefore he has a significance which we can scarcely over-estimate."[143] Here we have the foundation for the later growth of reputation and understanding of the message of Walt Whitman in both Europe and America.

The question of "inversion" may also have been involved in the reaction of Gerard Manley Hopkins when his friend Robert Bridges accused him in 1882 of having been influenced by Whitman. Hopkins replied that he knew Whitman only from two or three articles in the *Athenaeum* and *Academy*. One of these was a review by George Saintsbury with short extracts from *Leaves of Grass*. These few lines were hardly enough to influence his style, but he admitted that Whitman attracted him, for:

. . . I always knew in my heart Walt Whitman's mind to be more like my own than any other man's living. As he is a very great scoundrel this is not a pleasant confession. And this also makes me the more desirous to read him and the more determined that I will not.[144]

In spite of denying that Whitman's savage style had influenced his own "sprung rhythm," Hopkins admitted resemblances, especially in his and Whitman's fondness for the alexandrine. But the important point is that Hopkins respected Whitman as a poet, felt attracted to him personally, and admitted, "His 'savage' style has advantages. . . ."

In 1910, in his monumental *History of English Prosody*, Saints-bury also defended Whitman's right to compose poems in his own original manner. He thought that if Whitman had chosen, "he could have written beautiful verse proper [i.e., according to convention]. Yet it is clear also, that in passages, and many of them, the marriage of matter and form justifies itself as a true marriage."[145]

Edith Sitwell agreed with Saintsbury, and *A Poet's Notebook* (1943) contains a considerable number of quotations from Whit-man's prefaces and notebooks on "The Nature of Poetry," "Techni-cal Matters," "The Natural World and Inspiration," etc. Miss Sitwell includes him with Dunbar and Dryden as one of the "giants of our poetry." In her Preface to the anthology *The American Genius* she calls Blake and Whitman "Pentecostal Poets." Both "were born at the time when their characteristics were most needed"; Blake when eighteenth-century materialism "was freezing poetry," and Whitman "after a time of vague misty abstractions, to lead poetry back to the '*divine, original concrete*.'"[146] But in one respect they were dif-ferent: "Blake could not forgive the Fool, or believe that he could enter Heaven." Whitman tolerated even the fool, "and believed it to be the mission of the great poet to lead men back from the delusion of Hell."

One poet could scarcely admire another to this extent without being influenced, but Whitman's literary influence on Edith Sitwell is not obvious or easily traced. All that can be said truthfully is that this gifted and eccentric member of the Sitwell family aided in sustaining Whitman's reputation in Great Britain during the first half of the twentieth century. William Butler Yeats made a similar contri-bution, and was perhaps influenced even less, but a recent observer quotes from Yeats's letters to prove a "sustained interest" in the American poet during most of Yeats's adult life.[147]

One British writer who was unmistakably influenced by Whit-man was D. H. Lawrence.[148] His satire on Whitman's *merging* was quoted in Chapter I on "Whitman in Biography." But he was also as strongly attracted as repelled. Edwin H. Miller correctly calls Law-rence's interpretation of Whitman in *Studies in Classic American Literature* "brilliantly insightful but also brilliantly wrongheaded," and adds, in Lawrence's criticism "the author of *Leaves of Grass* becomes the author of *Women in Love*, an extraordinary novel which the poet of 'Calamus' could not have written."[149]

James E. Miller, Jr., with his colleagues Karl Shapiro and Bernice Slote, in *Start with the Sun*, see both Lawrence and Whitman as two of the great "Cosmic Poets" of modern literature. By this term they mean poets of "pagan joy and wonder in the natural world, the living cosmos."[150] They are the poets of the carnal self and the unconscious. Lawrence called Whitman "the first heroic seer to seize the soul by the scruff of her neck and plant her down among the potsherds."[151] He agreed with Whitman that the soul and body are one, and that "the root of poetry" is "phallic consciousness," not "cerebral sex-consciousness."[152] Lawrence called the Freudian unconscious "the cellar in which the mind keeps its own bastard spawn."[153] In *Start with the Sun* the "Laurentian unconscious" is described as "the unconscious *pristine*, primitive, elemental, unsullied by mind: this unconscious, asserts Lawrence, *is* the soul."[154] This was Whitman's concept also, though he did not use the term "unconscious" for it. He did, however, in his 1855 Preface seem to anticipate Jung's "collective unconscious" or "racial memory," when, after enumerating the traits of character needed by a great poet, he declared, "these are called up of the float of the brain of the world to be parts of the greatest poet from his birth out of his mother's womb and from her birth out of her mother's."[155]

The authors of *Start with the Sun* also claim Dylan Thomas as not only a "cosmic poet," but also as one strongly, and admittedly, influenced by Whitman. The tradition to which both belong is "affirmative, physical, intuitive, incantatory."[156] As a Welshman Thomas inherited the "bardic" tradition, but it was reinforced by Whitman's "body poetry," emphasizing "birth and procreation." Thus Thomas's metaphors, rhythms, and themes were the offspring of Welsh paganism and the "neo-paganism" of Walt Whitman.

In the opinion of some critics the great literary innovator, James Joyce, also made use of Whitman. About 1926 Sylvia Beach, the American expatriate and first publisher of Joyce's *Ulysses*, staged an exhibition of Whitman in her Paris bookshop. " 'The Crowd' [American writers]," she reports in *Shakespeare and Company*, "couldn't put up with him, especially after T.S. Eliot aired *his* views about Walt. Only Joyce and the French and I were still old-fashioned enough to get along with Whitman. I could see with half an eye Whitman's influence on Joyce's work."[157] Richard Chase found strong evidence of that influence in *Finnegans Wake*. For example, Joyce alludes to "old Whiteman self," and has him say: "I foredreamed for thee and more than full-maked: I prevened for thee in the haunts that joybelled frail light-a-leaves for sturdy traemen.

... ."[158] In this passage Joyce parodies Whitman's tolerance for prostitutes, rowdies, "prater brothers," his comradeship with everyone, and his "evangel of good tidings."

This may not sound very friendly to "old Whiteman," but Chase thinks the " 'panromain' which 'Watllwewhistlen sang' may easily have suggested to Joyce how a work of literature might picture 'the soul of everyelsebody rolled into olesoleself.' "[159] Joyce's protagonist Earwicker "has the same capacity as the 'I' of 'Song of Myself' to merge ('at no spatial time') with and become anyone and anything in the universe." The reincarnation motif in "Song of Myself," sec. 27-31, parallels Joyce's revolving cycles. "In a very real sense, then, *Finnegans Wake* is the ultimate development of a literary method 'foredreamed' in 'Song of Myself.' " Moreover, "The references to Whitman in *Finnegans Wake* (brief as they are) are fresher and more moving to the modern reader than are those, for example, in Hart Crane's *The Bridge*, where Whitman is understood only as the aspirational prophet."[160]

At this point it becomes unprofitable to consider Whitman's reputation and influence in England and the United States separately. In Hart Crane the influence of Whitman, Eliot, and the French Symbolists (some of whom were Whitman's greatest admirers in France) mingle inextricably. Allen Tate did not think Whitman's influence on Crane altogether fortunate,[161] and Yvor Winters blamed Whitman for Crane's suicide.[162] Then, to increase the tangle, Eliot, who strongly disliked Whitman's "ideas" but grudgingly admitted some pleasure in his imagery and music,[163] was in turn thought by a New Zealand scholar, S. Musgrove,[164] to have been influenced by Whitman, an opinion in which Pearce concurs.

Then there is Pound, the American poet with the international and tragic career, who found difficulty in acknowledging his debt to his "pig-headed father,"[165] but nevertheless did. As early as 1909 he confessed that, "Mentally I am a Walt Whitman who has learned to wear a collar and a dress shirt. . . ."[166] And in his famous "truce" (later changed to "pact") he declared, "We have one sap and one root—/ Let there be commerce between us." In 1934 in his *ABC of Reading* he called Whitman's faults "superficial," and said he had written the *historie morale* of nineteenth-century America.[167] As for direct influence, Roy Harvey Pearce finds evidence in some of the *Cantos*, especially 82, 85, and 93, and in the "gross structure" of the *Cantos*, as difficult to define as the structure of "Song of Myself," with which they have definite analogues.[168] Thus throughout the English speaking world Walt Whitman's fame and influence continued to grow through the twentieth century—and still continues.

WHITMAN IN FRANCE: RECEPTION
AND INFLUENCE

The first critics of Walt Whitman in France used him as a horrible example of the cultural chaos to be expected of rampant "democracy" and "republicanism" in a semi-civilized country like the United States of America. This was the opinion, during the reign of Emperor Napoleon III, of Louis Etienne in his "Walt Whitman, poète, philosophe et 'rowdy,' " *Revue européenne*, November, 1861, adding, however, "mais gardons-nous de confondre la nation de Washington et de Franklin avec les héros de ce nouveau Tyrtée."

In 1872, soon after the founding of the Third Republic, Mme. Blanc (Thèrése Bentzon) still held essentially the same view:

Soi-même et en masse, l'égoïsme et la démocratie, voilà les sujets favoris des chants de Whitman; à ce titre, ils sont essentiellement modernes. Certes aucun érivain européen, poète ni prosateur, n'est tombé dans les excès d'énergique mauvais goût que voudraient inaugurer sur les ruines de l'idéal Walt Whitman et ses sectaires; mais enfin il existe malheureusement chez nous, depuis quelque années, une tendance marquée vers ce réalisme qui est le contraire du naturel et de la vérité, une disposition à confondre les musclès avec le génie.[169]

But despite the fact that she associated Whitman's "muscle and pluck" with the school of realism, Bentzon was fully aware of Whitman's mystic identification of himself with the universe—though she regarded this as a "pretension":

Une des prétentions de Walt Whitman est non-seulement de représenter un citoyen de l'univers, comme il nous le fait entendre en déclarant qu'il est un vrai Parisien, un habitant de Vienne, de Pétersbourg, de Londres (tant de villes sont énumérées dans son hymne *Salut au monde* qu'on croirait lire une lecon de géographie ancienne et moderne), mais encore de contenir en lui-même l'univers tout entier.[170]

In such comments as these Bentzon did not misunderstand or misrepresent Whitman; she was merely unsympathetic and afraid of the "tendencies" which he represented in literature. Immediately Émile Blémont, a Parnassian poet, replied to Bentzon in a series of articles on "La Poésie en Angleterre et aux États-Unis," published in *Renaissance littéraire et artistique*. He understood and approved Whitman's new "ensemble" of body and soul and the significance of his *one's-self* and *en-masse*, accurately summarizing the thought in this concise manner:

Il est biblique, mais comme Hegel, il admet le principe de l'identité dans les contraires. Il est réaliste et optimiste, il est spiritualiste aussi; pour lui le mal n'existe pas, ou s'il existe, il est utile. Il a les vigoureuses conceptions d'une forte santé, chaste et sobre. Il est le champion sans honte de la sainteté de la chair, et des instincts charnels.[171]

Following the poet's own clues, Blémont idealized him as a man of the people, a prophet, and an original genius. This of course prevented the critic from a full comprehension of Whitman's literary antecedents and his relations to other writers. It is significant, though, that Blémont did understand fairly well the "organic style," for it was Whitman's form perhaps more than anything else that for many years prevented most French critics from appreciating *Leaves of Grass*.

Five years later Henri Cochin, in "Un poète américain, Walt Whitman," *Le Correspondant*, November 25, 1877, still thought that Whitman's democracy and friendship degraded society and threatened the safety of all nations. He saw in *Leaves of Grass* "democracy run wild, a form of insanity and megalomania."[172] Whitman, he thought, had no moral code at all, advocating chaos and license; and his form was equally contradictory and incoherent. But even in the attacks of Etienne, Bentzon, and Cochin on Whitman as a materialist, vulgarian, and political menace, "they recognized," as Pucciani says, "his growing stature in world literature, and that he was at all events a figure to be coped with."[173]

By 1884 Whitman was no longer feared in France. The violent opposition had spent itself, but his form was still a major difficulty. Léo Quesnel thought that Whitman fooled himself in believing that poetic sentiments intuitively generated artistic form: "N'est-ce pas une naïveté que de croire que parce qu'un poète aura le coeur plein de beaux sentiments, l'esprit rempli de hautes pensées, la rime et la césure viendront d'elle-mêmes se ranger sous sa plume?"[174] Quesnel predicted that Whitman would be slow in winning the recognition in France that he had already received in Great Britain. In the first place, his "langue riche et libre" is difficult to translate; in fact, "Whitman traduit n'est plus Whitman." And in the second place, the French are still children of Greece, from whence they have inherited a sense of delicacy and elegance in language. He regards Whitman as a great poet for Americans (who are not "children of Greece"!), but not for Frenchmen.

    Still, discussions such as Quesnel's brought Whitman to the attention of French men of letters and prepared the way for appreciation of him. This appreciation came during the period of Symbolism, during the 80s and 90s. It was the Symbolists "who brought Whitman to France, who espoused him, translated him, and to some extent recognized in him a literary parent,"[175] and he is still associated with the "decadents," as Rockwell Kent's illustrations bear witness.[176] Catel thinks Whitman a forerunner of Symbolism, but Pucciani points out, for example, Whitman's dissimilarities to Mallarmé.[177] It seems, in fact, to have been mainly the "decadent" aspect of Whitman which the Symbolists adopted. In the broader aspects he and they were quite different, for Whitman's symbols were universal, theirs specialized and often so subjective that they had little meaning for anyone except the author.

    Although the early critics translated fragments of *Leaves of Grass* in their articles, it was the Symbolist poet, Jules Laforgue, who in 1886 published three numbers of translations in *La Vogue* and thus stimulated interest in Whitman among the young poets of France. The following year the American expatriate, Francis Vielé-Griffin, translated the entire "Song of the Broad-Axe" for *La Revue indépendante*. It was through Laforgue, however, that Whitman most strongly influenced the *vers-librists*.[178]

    In 1888 a comprehensive, scholarly critique of Whitman was published by Gabriel Sarrazin, first in the *Nouvelle revue*, May 1, 1888, and a year later in his book, *La Renaissance de la poésie anglaise*. Especially valuable for the assimilation of Whitman in France was Sarrazin's comprehension of the poet's pantheism, which revealed an inheritance from the mysticism of the East and linked him in modern times to German Idealism, especially Hegel. Unlike most of Whitman's contemporary admirers in America, this learned

French critic did not regard him as an untutored "original genius" but as a man who knew his way around Parnassus. "Non seulement il n'était point un illettré, mais il avait lu tout ce que nous avons lu nous-mêmes. Il avait vu aussi beaucoup plus que nous, et bien plus distinctement. . . ."[179] Pucciani thinks Sarrazin's special virtue the fact that he sees Whitman as "an event in world literature that has already been operative for some time."[180]

The Symbolists, themselves influenced by the free verse of the Bible, were the first critics fully to appreciate the Biblical style of *Leaves of Grass*. Rémy de Gourmont mentions it in 1890: "en Whitman, le grand poète américain, se régénère l'esprit ancien de simplicité, l'esprit biblique. . . ."[181] This "Biblical spirit" has a curious international relationship to the Symbolists because they were also influenced, especially through Gustave Kahn, the editor of *La Vogue*, by the style of the German Bible, as Rémy de Gourmont has pointed out in *Le Problème du style* (1902)[182] and *Promenades littéraires* (1904).

Walt Whitman was sufficiently known in France in 1892 for news of his death to arouse a new flurry of critical activity. We are thus enabled to see that Sarrazin's effort had been only partly successful. For example, Paul Desjardins, in "Walt Whitman," *Journal des débats*, April 4, 1892, still regards the American poet as "a kind of beautiful primitive,"[183] to use Pucciani's phrase, lacking in restraint and self-control—and this amoral interpretation was also repeated by Théodor de Wyzewa[184] and B. H. Gausseron,[185] the latter thinking that Whitman had rejected all laws and all traditions. But Desjardins admires Whitman's patriotism, understands his doctrine of good and evil, and thinks the poet a *précurseur* of future popular literature.

At this time Henri Bérenger, who had quoted Whitman as early as 1873 in his novel *L'Effort*, and had shown an interest in his themes—though not his forms—in *L'Ame moderne* (1890), translated Havelock Ellis's essay on Whitman (*L'Ermitage*, June, 1892). Thus the course of French criticism was influenced by this English sexologist, whose brilliant and sensible interpretation has seldom been equalled in Whitman scholarship. Ellis understood even better than Sarrazin Whitman's mysticism, his cosmic philosophy, his doctrine of the equality of matter and spirit, and the immortality of the Ego. It is safe to say that no previous critic had been so well prepared to appreciate the sanity of the poet's attitude toward sex. He saw also the similarity between Whitman and Millet. On the subject of Whitman's reading he struck a happy medium, somewhere near the real truth. Without being either a blind admirer or a skeptical detractor, Ellis fully appreciated Whitman's personality. This essay did a great deal for the American poet's reputation on the continent.

It was also in *L'Ermitage* (December, 1902) that Henri Davray undertook to present Whitman to French readers through faithful, accurate translations, with little or no interpretation. Before Whitman could be widely known in France, such translations as these were needed, and they prepared the way for others.

During the next two decades Walt Whitman became almost a major force in French literature. But he continued to be identified with special groups and movements, each finding some special doctrines, attitudes, or tricks of style to admire or to confirm its own theories. Whitman's importance in World Literature is in great measure due to his astonishing adaptability. Just as the Symbolists found much in him to support their own program, so also did two of the three movements of reaction against Symbolism: *naturisme* and *unanimisme*. The *romanisme* of Moréas and Maurras, with its attempt to restore classicism, had of course no use for Whitman. But the whole generation of *naturisme* poets and critics adopted the pantheism, the glorification of physical joy and health, and the anti-art-for-art's-sake attitude of the American poet. The Unanimist school, led by Jules Romains, was interested especially in Whitman's mystic and cosmic *ensemble*. The influence is particularly evident in the section of Romains' *La Vie unanime* which he entitled, significantly, "L'Individu."[186] Baldensperger is authority for the statement that, "The movement known as *l'unanimisme*, aiming at a sort of pantheistic and pan-social vision where the poor individual is more or less absorbed, claimed [Whitman] as a master."[187]

The Unanimist who did most for Whitman in France was Léon Bazalgette,[188] whose first biography, *Walt Whitman: l'homme et son oeuvre*, appeared in 1908, followed in 1909 by his complete translation, *Feuilles d'herbe*. Both the biography and the translation highly idealized Whitman and his language, but they influenced a whole generation of young writers, among them the Abbaye group, which included Georges Duhamel, a later Whitmanesque poet. During this period, however, it is difficult to separate influence from parallels, for as Pierre de Lanux has emphasized,[189] Whitman's point of view exactly suited the new twentieth century, especially his mysticism, his humanism, his belief in the present, and his functional style without ornamentation.

On June 1, 1912 a critic in *Nouvelle revue française* mentioned *le Whitmanisme* as a real force in French poetry. About the same time Henri Ghéon declared, "Il a nourri notre jeunesse."[190] Jean-Richard Bloch, in *L'Anthologie de l'Effort* (1912) praised Whitman as "the prophet from whom Vildrac and Duhamel, André Spire and Jules Romains, have learned most."[191] Duhamel himself said in *Les Poètes et la poésie* (1914), "J'ai dit que Walt Whitman fut et demeure un grand introducteur à la vie poétique."[192]

In 1914 Valéry Larbaud traced the history of Whitman criticism in France, giving a factual and sensible account up to that date. In 1918 this essay was used as the preface to a book of translations called *Walt Whitman: Oeuvres choisies*, composed of poetry and prose rendered into French by Jules Laforgue, Louis Fabulet, André Gide, and Francis Vielé-Griffin. André Gide himself had been highly displeased by Bazalgette's "prettified" version and had spent much time during the first World War on a translation of his own, which finally appeared in 1918 in the "Important World Literature" series of *Nouvelle revue française*. In 1918 Eugène Figuière also gave a series of lectures on Whitman, accompanied by recitations by various people, at the Odéon Theatre in Paris; and the following year, June 10, 1919, John Erskine lectured on him at Dijon. There was no longer any doubt in France about Whitman's being a poet. An interesting side-light on his reputation was provided in January, 1919, by Jean Guehenno in an article in *Revue de Paris* entitled "Whitman, Wilson et l'esprit moderne," in which the author accused President Wilson of having borrowed his "Fourteen Points" from Walt Whitman—a charge repeated in Germany several months later.[193]

The culmination of outright Whitman worship in France was reached in 1921 when Bazalgette published the last of his studies, *Le Poème-Évangile de Walt Whitman*. Although the attitude had been anticipated in Bazalgette's earlier biography, it is difficult to imagine how any one could go further in deifying the poet-prophet and his evangel-poem. As Schyberg remarks, this latest "idealization of the Whitman figure was too much even for the prophets in America."[194] Both this new interpretation and the re-publication of Bazalgette's translation of *Leaves of Grass* in 1922 raised a fresh protest from Gide and his friends.

Throughout these years the name of the American poet was

frequently mentioned in Baldensperger's *Revue de littérature comparée*, and in 1929 Baldensperger's former student, Jean Catel, published his great study, *Walt Whitman: La Naissance du poète* (discussed in Chap. I),[195] followed in 1930 by a penetrating analysis of style, *Rythme et langage dans la première édition des "Leaves of Grass."* Both are interesting contributions to Whitman scholarship—and testify anew to the fact that this scholarship has become truly international.

In his critical biography Catel attempted to discover the reality hidden beneath Whitman's imagery, or poetic symbols. His basic theory is that here we have a poet isolated from humanity by his genius. *Leaves of Grass* is a plea for love, an attempt to solve the personal problem. Failing to identify himself with humanity or nature, the poet tried *identité* exclusively (i.e., attempted to pierce to the soul of things, to understand the phenomenon of being). Whether or not later critics would accept this psychological interpretation, they could hardly ignore it. In subtlety and suggestiveness the French criticism of Whitman had thus surpassed the English or American—but after Catel it is uninspired until Asselineau.

In the above rapid survey of Whitman's reception in France several references have been made to his influence on French literature. Some idea of its extent and importance may be gained by a brief discussion of a few key examples.

The Unanimist lyric socialism closely parallels Whitman's "adhesiveness" and "comradeship," and was at least in part inspired by "Calamus." Schyberg refers to Jules Romains' novel of brotherly love, *Les Copains* (1913) as "the half glorification of the 'manly friendship' which is at once Calamus-sentimentality and devil-may-care swaggering"; but Romains' lyric poetry shows a greater Whitman influence, "with its wholly religious worship of life and its entirety and democratic multiplicity."[196] The four prophets and masters of the Unanimists were Hugo, Whitman, Verhaeren, and Claudel, "and usually all the Unanimist lyricism can be traced to the influence of one of these four." Bazalgette was mainly responsible for the group's admiration for Whitman. Other Unanimists who used Whitman themes were Georges Duhamel, Pierre Jean Jouve, and Charles Vildrac. Duhamel's *Vie des martyrs* (1917), written from his experiences as a doctor in the first World War, is reminiscent of Whitman's *Drum-Taps* and Civil War diaries. Both Jouve and Vildrac adopted the loose verse-form of *Leaves of Grass*, as Vildrac plainly indicated in *Verslibrism* (1902) and *La Technique poétique* (1910). Closely related to the Unanimists was another group of writers who were united through their internationalist sympathy and Gide's *Nouvelle revue francaise*, the organ of a number of French intellectuals during World War I. Two of these who were especially affected by Whitman's influence were Panaït Istrati and Valéry Larbaud.[197] Istrati, who wrote romances of an Oriental nature—cf. *Dyra Kyralina* and *Mikail*—used the vagabond friendship motifs in the Whitman manner, even to the length of phrase and cadence. Larbaud, whose preface has already been mentioned, was one of the revolutionary leaders of his literary generation, a champion in France of D. H. Lawrence and James Joyce in addition to Walt Whitman.

Most revealingly Whitmanesque is Larbaud's *Les Poésies de A. O. Barnabooth* (definitive edition, 1923). The irony and satire in the character of Barnabooth is un-Whitmanesque—or perhaps rather like a parody of Whitman—but the vicarious desire to cover continents, to share every human experience, to embrace all knowledge, and to live in his verses after his death are extremely close in theme and spirit to many poems in *Leaves of Grass*. Schyberg calls "Europe" a "reworked Whitman poem" in which the poet greets in turn the great cities, the seas, and the rivers of Europe, all of which he wished to embrace simultaneously in one grand panoramic vision. "This is 'Salut au Monde' in a modern French version. A fastidious artist has fallen so deeply in love with Whitman's poetry that he has copied it not only in content but also in form, with catalogues, participles, shouts, hails, parentheses, everything."[198]

For this brief period of post-war internationalism in France, Larbaud's Whitmanism appealed to a small coterie of intellectuals. But for a more deep and sustained influence we turn back to André Gide, who first became interested in the American poet in 1893 through Marcel Schwob, a distinguished Symbolist critic, poet, and romancer, who had discovered consolation in Whitman after deep personal bereavement. Like Symonds in England, these men found *Leaves of Grass* a spiritual tonic. According to Rhodes, who has made a close study of the influence of Whitman on André Gide,[199] in 1893 Gide was struggling to emancipate himself from two great handicaps, puritanism and the sort of physical *anomalie* which Whitman expressed in "Pent-up Aching Rivers" and other poems in "Calamus" and "Children of Adam." These poems "gave Gide the assurance he needed that 'la perversion de [son] instinct était naturelle. . .' Morally as well as spiritually, he felt he had been saved; he felt he was a new man, reborn to life as well as to art."[200]

This experience turned Gide from Symbolism, his nihilistic cynicism, and his earlier "Christian concept of the duality of human passion." In *Les Nourritures terrestres* (1897),

He turned away from reading and dreaming to desiring and living. His emotions blossomed out; he felt every sensation with the fervor of a religious experience. He hungered for a fresh awareness of the world about him to be apprehended not only by his reason but also by his senses. "Il ne me suffit pas de *lire* que les sables des plages sont doux; je veux que mes pieds nus les sentent." To be alive, merely to be, had become a voluptuous and intense satisfaction to him.[201]

In addition to the emancipation of his senses, Gide also found in Whitman "an attachment similar to that he was finding in Dostoievsky 'for the precious image of Christ before us,' who 'worked His first miracle to help men's gladness. . . .' "[202] Thus he could share the religious joy of life and love of all things of Whitman's "Song of Joys" or "Song of the Rolling Earth." "Je n'ai jamais rien vue de doucement beau dans ce monde, sans désirer aussitôt que toute ma tendresse le touche. Amoureuse beauté de la terre, l'effloraison de ta surface est merveilleuse. O paysage où mon désir s'est enfoncé!"[203] Also Whitman's doctrine of the inseparability of good and evil healed Gide's divided spirit and convinced him of the goodness and unity of all creation. Freed from "the metaphysics of symbolist ideologies 'en dehors du temps et des contingences,' uttering the shadows of words instead of their substance," Gide "took up and lived the life of *Les Nourritures terrestres*, and sang it subsequently."[204]

Whitman was of course not solely responsible for Gide's spiritual and literary growth:

He had started moving in the same direction from the beginning. His moral and social preoccupations have become not less but more intense with the passing of time . . . The ideal both he and Whitman have pursued has been the same: the salvation of the individual soul in the modern world. The course Gide has followed describes thus a spiritual curve that runs somewhat parallel to that of Whitman. Having discovered him at the start of his career, and felt his influence, he meets him again at its close.[205]

Here we have not only the clue to the growth of Whitman's reputation in France from Etienne to Gide, but also a clue to his importance in the modern world. The American poet was in the strong currents of a world stream of social and artistic change. Like André Gide, the twentieth century mind and spirit might have arrived at the same conclusions without Whitman, but he quickened the human sympathy and strengthened the social conscience of democratic writers in all countries—and in none more than France.[206]

In the great socialistic Belgian poet, Émile Verhaeren, we find a literary artist so like Whitman in temperament, in lyric inspiration, and in oratorical style (with its catalogues, parallelisms, and reiterations), that it is hard to believe he was not an adoring disciple; yet he apparently had no direct knowledge of the American poet, and in the words of his biographer, "independently and unconsciously arrived at the same goal from the same starting point."[207] But as Schyberg remarks, "the influence of Jules Laforgue on him, as on all 'La Jeune Belgique,' was important in helping him to revolt against all traditional forms, to find his 'free form,' 'this free verse so satisfying to the contemporary soul' . . ."[208]

Verhaeren's first poems, written under the inspiration of Symbolism, were not Whitmanesque, being protests against modern life, against industrialism and the city. But he soon threw off the shackles of Symbolism, or at least its "décadence," and in *Les Visages de la vie* (1899), *Les Forces tumulteuses* (1902), *La Multiple splendeur* (1906), and *Les Poèmes ardents* (1913) he celebrated the joy of existence in the modern world. Schyberg says:

The poet wants to feel the whole rhythm of life in his verse, the wind, the forest, the water, and "the thunder's loud roar," the entire world unfolding from North to South, from East to West, from the cities of India and China to the "gleaming cities" along the shores of America and Africa. He wants to share the life of each individual person, whether priest, scientist, soldier, moneychanger, swindler, or sailor.

Il faut admirer tout pour s'exalter soi-même,[209]

and

Je ne distingue plus le monde de moi-même,

he writes in *La Multiple splendeur*.

In this collection he writes hymns to work and to words, to the wind, which, full of love, roams over the earth, to the grass, into which he throws himself in an excess of happiness, to the enthusiasm which inspires the poets of his day and produces "the new forms for the new time," to the joy in which he, in Whitmanesque phrases, celebrates all parts of his body . . .[210]

Professor P. M. Jones summarizes the Belgian poet's major points of view in three of his most important works:

In *Les Forces tumulteuses* he has sung the mysterious union which pervades all forms of reality; in *La Multiple splendeur* the ethical role of admiration; while *Les Rythmes souverains* gives the world its most august ideal of the struggle of man to reach divinity and free himself from the sway of chance and the supernatural.[211]

Jones finally decides, however, that Verhaeren went far beyond Whitman, though in a way that fulfilled and developed Whitman's program:

Broadly speaking, Whitman theorizes, Verhaeren achieves. In spite of all the former has said on the subject of science and industry, he has written no poems like "La Science" or "Les Usines." Many themes which have received full treatment from Verhaeren exist as hints or indications in Whitman's works. And although Emile Verhaeren is considered one of the most original of living [*i.e.*, in 1914] Continental poets, his work so often appears to realize the ideals of the American prophet-poet that he seems, all unconsciously, to be the first to have answered Whitman's appeal to the "poets to come."

I myself but write one or two indicative words for the future[212]

Another Belgian poet who also reflects the reputation and influence of Whitman is Charles van Lerbherge (1861–1907). His *Chanson d'Eve* (1904) has the themes and sentiments of *Children of Adam* and a verse form that reminds one of *Leaves of Grass*. This is especially apparent in "Eve's discovery of the beautiful earth, her pantheistic feeling about God, and her yearning for death as a release, the sound, a note in the whistle and roar of the universe."[213] It is, however, Whitman's "decadent" aspects which suggest the comparison. As Schyberg says, "There is a consistent parallel between

Whitman and the *fin de siècle* poets that is astonishing."[214] But it is not the whole of Whitman, and to an English reader *Leaves of Grass* is more unlike than like Symbolist and "decadent" poetry. The most remarkable thing about Walt Whitman's influence abroad, however, is his adaptability. He could provide inspiration for Symbolists, *fin de siècle* poets, Unanimists, and democratic humanitarians like Verhaeren and Gide (in their "redeemed" phases). Each group found something to admire or adopt from the American poet, thus testifying to his fertility and his perennially dynamic vision of life and its meaning.

Those French writers still living who admired Whitman so much earlier in this century are still loyal to his memory. In 1972 Roger Asselineau, the present leading French authority on Whitman, invited several to contribute to a symposium, called *Walt Whitman in Europe Today*.[215] Jules Romains, now a member of the *L'Académie Française*, remembered how he and his friends "discovered" Whitman in Bazalgette's translation. "Our enthusiasm was aroused by the fact that the American poet renewed the relationship between poetry and man. . . ." Jean Guehenno, also a member of the *L'Académie* and a former co-editor with Bazalgette of *Europe*, "loved" Whitman for the same reason he loved Montaigne, who also wrote one of "the most intimate, the most carnal of books." Furthermore, Whitman "perceived men as more similar than different and all ruled by the same fate." Jean Marie Le Clezio first read *Leaves of Grass* at fifteen, and "it struck me as a miracle. . . . What Whitman has told us we still do not know completely, but he has shown the way, as Rimbaud did with the same words: the straight, unutterable beauty of the modern world. . . ."

If one can judge from these examples, it is Whitman's personality and his serving as a symbol of democracy which remains most alive in France today. In 1948 Paul Jamati[216] in a spirited but inaccurate introduction to a mediocre translation of major selections of *Leaves of Grass* revived Bazalgette's glorified saintly prophet, and condemned all studies of Whitman's psychological aberrations, exclaiming, "*O psychoanalyse, que de ravages!*" The "Calamus" poems are simple celebrations of comradeship and brotherly love. All attempts to find pathology in this kind of affection Jamati called a "*contre-légende*" perpetrated by antidemocratic critics to discredit Whitman. This was the conviction—or strategy—of most Communist champions of Whitman in the 1940s and 50s.

However, objective Whitman scholarship continued in France. In 1956 Roger Asselineau followed his excellent biographical-critical study with the best translation France had yet had.[217] Asselineau knew Whitman as well as any contemporary scholar anywhere, and he had also mastered not only the English language but even the American idiom. His *Feuilles d'herbe* does not contain all of *Leaves of Grass*, but all of "Song of Myself" and the major poems, with well-chosen selections from the shorter poems. As he has explained, French is more prolix than English, and Whitman is very difficult to translate into French. In German and other cognate languages of English it is easier to reproduce the sound and rhythm of Whitman's verse. Nevertheless, Asselineau has succeeded in conveying the spirit and core meaning of *Leaves of Grass*. His translation provides a sound foundation for further French criticism and understanding of Whitman. Yet, aside from Asselineau, there are no outstanding critics of Whitman in France today. However, translation continues. In 1959 Alain Bosquet,[218] a poet of considerable distinction, published a volume of selected translations in an excellent literary style, faithful to the tone of Whitman's verse, but not as strictly accurate as Asselineau's. To introduce Whitman to the French-speaking African nations (République du Congo, Guinée, Mali, Maroc, Tunesie) Asselineau made a special selection from his translation in 1966, with the title *Chants de la terre qui tourne*.[219] In his Introduction he stresses the Whitman of "Salut au Monde!":

O toi, Africain à l'âme divine, aux origines obscures, grand, noir, à la tête et aux formes nobles, promis à un destin superbe à égalité avec moi!

Thus, through France, Whitman now moves to Africa, where perhaps a chapter in his reception is beginning. The President of the Republic of Senegal, Léopold Sédar Senghor, known in France for his poetry, says that "with Whitman it is truly primeval man and *natura naturans* which get expressed to the rhythm of days and nights, of ebb and flow, a rhythm which, for all its freedom, is strongly stressed." This, he thinks, is "why Whitman's poetry immediately gripped me."[220]

In French-speaking Canada the well-known Franco-American poet Rosaire Dion-Lévesque (winner of several decorations and prizes from both the French Academy and the Royal Society of Canada) published his first translation, *Walt Whitman: ses meilleures pages*, in 1933 in Montreal, and a revised edition in Quebec in 1965.[221] His translation has been praised in France by Vielé-Griffin, Valéry Larbaud, F. Delattre, and Auguste Viatte.

WHITMAN IN GERMANY: RECEPTION
AND INFLUENCE

In no other country in the world has Walt Whitman been so extravagantly admired and even worshipped as in Germany. But from England came the initial impetus, for while a political exile in Great Britain Ferdinand Freiligrath read the Rossetti edition of Whitman's poems and felt moved, as one critic has expressed it, "to contribute toward the realization of Goethe's ideal of 'Welt-Literatur' "[222] by publishing an appreciative account in a German newspaper, April 24, 1868.[223] This enthusiastic essay aroused little interest, but it is significant that in the "ego" of *Leaves of Grass* Freiligrath found a "part of America, a part of the earth, of humanity, of the universe."[224] The structure of the poems reminded him of the "Northern Magus," of Hamann, of Carlyle, and, above all, of the Bible, and he thought they might, like Wagner's music, shatter "all our canons and theories." It was thus as a world poet that Walt Whitman gained his first, though obscure, recognition in Germany. Freiligrath followed up this article with some undistinguished and inaccurate translations from the Rossetti edition, which seems to have been the only one he knew; and when he returned to Germany in 1869 he encouraged his friend, Adolf Strodtmann, who had also been exiled and had spent 1852–56 in the United States, to undertake other translations from *Leaves of Grass*.[225] These translations, however, attracted almost no attention.

For two decades after this unpromising beginning, Whitman was almost completely ignored in Germany—perhaps not surprising when one considers the period, which was a time of intense nationalism, of scientific interest, and of social agitation. Meanwhile in 1882 a German-American, Karl Knortz, published an essay on the American poet in a German language newspaper in New York, later reprinted as a monograph, *Walt Whitman, der Dichter der Demokratie*.[226] His biographical interpretation was based on Bucke and O'Connor, and he himself wrote like a member of the "inner circle." Thus Knortz helped to lay the foundation for the Whitman cult in Germany. But he, too, did not stop with criticism. After T. W. Rolleston was unable to get his translations of *Leaves of Grass* published in Germany,[227] Knortz revised the manuscript and found a publisher in Switzerland in 1889. Knortz's contribution to this book seems to have been mainly editorial, but he added some translations of his own to a third edition of his *Walt Whitman, der Dichter der Demokratie* (1889). Not only were these versions superior to Freiligrath's, though still literal and crude, but German readers also got for the first time such long, characteristic, poems as "Song of Myself," "Starting from Paumanok," and "Out of the Cradle."

As early as 1883 Rolleston had tried to call attention to Whitman's embodiment of democratic ideals, but the time was not yet ripe for the appreciation in Germany of a "democratic" poet. By the time the Rolleston-Knortz edition appeared, however, the ground had been prepared. Especially among the young socialists and revolutionaries there was a great desire to break with the traditions of the past and to find new forms and expression for art and society. Both the ideas and the style of *Leaves of Grass* quickly became vitalizing symbols for many of the young writers. Eduard Bertz felt that the high point of his visit to the United States was making the acquaintance of Whitman's poetry, which he considered naturally religious, with a gnarled originality and strength. J. V. Widmann[228] declared in the same tone: "Walt Whitman is to be understood as a Jacob Boehme, an Angelus Silesius. In him the basic principle of his ideas and creations is always an overwhelmingly strong feeling of the sacredness and innate nobility of all existence."[229] This complete acceptance of Whitman as a prophet of a new natural religion, or ontological monism, was the central faith of the Whitman cult in Germany—and "cult" is not too strong a term.[230]

The most ardent disciple of this cult was Johannes Schlaf, who, much like Carpenter in England—though more uncritical—was to make the promotion of Whitman the great work of his life. The American poet's doctrine of the unity of all creation, of man and nature, of spirit and matter, strongly influenced Schlaf's volume of poems, *Der Frühling* (1896). Among his many publications on Whitman, the best known are his monograph, *Walt Whitman*, first published in 1896 and reissued in 1904,[231] and his translation, *Grashalme, in Auswahl* [selection], 1907, 1919. He also adapted or improvised upon O'Connor's work in his essay, *Vom Guten Grauen Dichter*, 1904, and made an attempt to translate the English biography of Binns. But unfortunately Schlaf knew English so imperfectly that he botched all his translations, both prose and poetry, and drew down upon his head scathing denunciations, especially from

Eduard Bertz, who attempted to expose Schlaf's ignorance and pretence.[232] But this infatuated disciple was undaunted by such attacks and was still "promoting" Whitman as late as 1933.[233]

There would have been a "Whitman movement" in Germany without Schlaf's efforts, though it might not have been so fanatical. In 1904 Karl Federn published a collection of selected poems in translation,[234] using as Introduction an essay which he had written five years before.[235] He called the poems "simple and crude" like the Psalms or the Eddas. Goethe and Whitman were said to be alike in that "the man and his work are inseparably united." Here we find also an observation which explains not only Whitman's appeal to these German admirers but also his astonishing world-wide reception: he "possessed one secret, which is the profoundest secret of the real poet, namely that of calling forth in the reader his own mood."

Federn's translations are more poetic than those of Knortz and vastly superior to Schlaf's, though Law-Robertson has pointed out serious inaccuracies.[236] Especially noteworthy is the fact that Federn arranges the poems chronologically. His text is based on the 1881 edition. The same year (1904) Wilhelm Schölermann published still another translation, but in his attempt to make his version poetic he resorted to rhyme and omitted some of the repetitions from "Song of Myself." Needless to say, the result was not characteristic of the original. But in his introductory essay Schölermann provided an interesting illustration of the German deification of Whitman during this period:

Whitman belongs to a class of individuals who are more than life size, who spring into existence in a moment of lavish exuberance on the part of procreative nature . . . Beethoven and Bismarck are men of similar calibre; Whitman also betrays a number of traits in common with that awe-inspiring man-of-men (*Ganzmenschen*) Jesus of Nazareth, for example, his exalted, tender kindness, his heroic love . . . The healing power of this kindness and goodness, that ancient miracle-performing gift which causes the blind to see and the lame to walk, that gift Whitman also possessed.[237]

Less exalted but no less ardent was the declaration in 1905 of O. E. Lessing, who had spent a year on the faculty at the University of Illinois, that Whitman "is the center, summit, and fountain-head of a first great epoch in the intellectual life of the new world."[238] He called Whitman "the greatest poet since Goethe . . . He is the embodiment, the representative, and the illuminator of American Literature in the same sense that Dante is of the Italian, Shakespeare of the English, and Goethe of the German." Several years later in his retraction Lessing could truthfully say that he had "made Whitman *only* a superman instead of a God as my predecessors had done."[239] But in 1905 his prose translations, in the main accurate and competent, were a great boon to the Whitman movement in Germany. In his sound introduction he quoted from Whitman's notebooks, especially, as Law-Robertson remarks, "those which show his cosmic world outlook as well as his personal opinions about personal and human relationships."[240]

From about 1895 to 1905 or 1907, Whitman's name was a convenient literary and social symbol for many of the more revolutionary German writers, but aside from Schlaf, his actual influence is difficult to assess. Schlaf eagerly adopted Whitman's religious and cosmic ideas and attempted to re-express them in his own lyrics. *Frühling* was written under the direct inspiration of Schlaf's secondhand knowledge of *Leaves of Grass. Sommerlied* (1903), though more conventional in form, showed strong influence of "Children of Adam," while *Das Gottlied* (1922), an attempt to treat the theme of the origin of the world, was consciously Whitmanesque in manner. Like Whitman, Schlaf expected a new poetic language to emerge from the age of science and materialism, a view which he shared with his friend Arno Holz, who deliberately tried to establish a modern theory and technique in his *Revolution der Lyrik* (1899). Because Holz was friendly both to Schlaf and Whitman at the time he was experimenting with free (Whitman's "organic") rhythms, he has often been accused of indebtedness to the American poet. But Holz admired Whitman as a personality and ethical leader, not as a poet. In a letter he explained:

Quite a different man from Goethe or Heine was Whitman. I shall never write the name without taking off my hat to this American. He is one of the names dearest to me in the literature of the world. He wanted the change which has now taken place. But although he broke the old forms, he did not give us new ones.[241]

Amelia von Ende, in the best article on the subject in English, says of Whitman:

His aim was to give us new values of life, not new forms of art. This he has accomplished; he has given us a view of life, which it will take generations to accept, to assimilate and to put into practice. Whitman is a man among men, a poet for mankind. Holz is a poet among poets, a poet for poets.[242]

To the present writer, the chief link between Whitman and Holz seems to be their cosmic mysticism and evolutionary transmigration. Holz projects himself backward and forward in time, identifying himself with various objects in Whitman's manner, but decidedly not in his poetic form.[243]

Law-Robertson thinks that in the impressionistic school, which regarded Schlaf's *Frühling* as something of a "program," Whitman did influence the form of certain German lyricists.[244] He mentions especially Alfons Paquet's *Auf Erden* (1904–05). "Paquet's impressionistic sketches are compressed into compact pictures and therefore lack the strong exuberance of the cosmic breadth of Whitman's verse. Otherwise he uses the same stylistic methods—repetitions, enumerations, participle constructions."[245] In a letter to Law-Robertson, Paquet acknowledged his indebtedness to Whitman, whom he regarded as the "Great American poet, the great prototype ... and as often as I read his poetry, there always streams out something of the infinite space, of the simplicity and brave goodness of humanity, such as I felt in a few unforgettable happy days [in the United States], especially in the wilderness of Colorado."[246] But other impressionists, like Karl Röttger, found the basis for their "free rhythms" in older German literature, and some members of the group broke with conventional rules without knowing Whitman.[247]

The reaction against Whitman began as early as 1900 when Knut Hamsun's savage attack in a Danish paper was translated into German,[248] though the editor felt compelled to insert a footnote saying, "We who love Whitman prefer to learn about him from Johannes Schlaf."[249] Hamsun's argument was simply that of the literary conservatives of all countries, not least of Whitman's own contemporary Americans: he is not a poet, but an uncouth fraud. He is modern only in his brutality. In short, Hamsun attempted with heavy irony to demolish every one of the poet's literary pretentions.

Eduard Bertz was first an admirer but later a disillusioned critic of Whitman. In 1881–83 he lived in Tennessee (in one of the numerous American social experiments similar to Brook Farm) and later settled in London. He was thus better prepared than most of the German critics for genuine understanding of Whitman. In 1889 he wrote: "As the greatest benefit which I derived from my sojourn in America, nay as one of the happiest events of my life, I regard the acquaintance with the writings of the most original and deepest of all American poets."[250] Bertz sent this article to Whitman, who responded so eagerly—bombarding the author with material for future articles—that Bertz was shocked and wrote a reserved account of the poet for Spemann's *Goldenes Buch der Weltliteratur* (1900). Now suspicious, he re-examined Whitman's claims—and the claims made in his name by his over-zealous disciples—to being the founder of a new religion. In 1905 he attempted to reveal what he now regarded as Whitman's sex pathology,[251] agreeing with Edward Carpenter in the verdict. In *Der Yankee-Heiland* Bertz attempted further to destroy the "prophet myth," though he still regarded Whitman as a great lyric poet.[252] Schlaf replied to these attacks upon his "saint," and it was as a result of this quarrel that Bertz so mercilessly exposed Schlaf's pretentions as a translator and scholar.

O. E. Lessing was likewise drawn into the controversy, against Schlaf. In 1910 he confessed "to the guilt of a serious attack of Whitman"—as previously mentioned.[253] Many critics had tried to couple Whitman's name with Nietzsche's, partly, no doubt, because Nietzsche was a great name to conjure with in the late nineteenth and early twentieth century, but also because these Germans could think of no one else who had created a literary form so daring and impressive. Lessing, however, now used this comparison to "debunk" Whitman:

As artists [Nietzsche and Whitman] have fallen below many a less famous poet. Neither *Zarathustra* nor *Leaves of Grass* are, strictly speaking, poetical compositions. They contain a wealth of esthetic material. . . . Accepting Sainte-Beuve's view[254] that a work of art should rather suggest emotions than give definite form to an esthetic experience, Whitman, in true romantic fashion, meets the critic's objection to the hazy vagueness of the majority of his poems.[255]

But Whitman's poetry in "its final effect is enervating rather than invigorating. In this Whitman resembles a vastly superior artist: Richard Wagner, whom Nietzsche justly calls the great sorcerer."[256] Both "possessed . . . an indomitable sensuality, the magnetism of which, vibrating through all their compositions, causes an ecstatic intoxication invariably followed by utter exhaustion."[257]

Although the first great wave of Whitman enthusiasm in Germany had ebbed by 1910, he was not forgotten. In 1906 the Alsatian, Friedrich Lienhardt, considered the American poet the successor of Goethe.[258] A year later the proletarian poet of Austria, M. R. von Stern, hailed him as an Hegelian conditioned by a "strong autochthonic democratic instinct. There is no other poet who is so consistently permeated by democratic ideas."[259] In 1911 Knortz entered the controversy over Whitman's abnormality by publishing *Walt Whitman und seine Nachahmer, Ein Beitrag zur Literatur der Edelurninge*. He agreed in the main with Carpenter and Bertz on the subject, which he said he deliberately ignored in his *Dichter der Demokratie* in order to secure a favorable response to Whitman in Germany. This admission was an indication of the passing of the "cult."

In only a few years, however, the second Whitman movement in Germany began when the labor press discovered him at the beginning of the first World War. He was hailed by the people as he had never been in America. As Jacobson remarks, *Drum-Taps* and "Whispers of Heavenly Death" "struck upon the ear and heart of an era that experienced a similar disaster."[260] These writers were interested not so much in the poet as in the "wound-dresser" and social prophet. He became, in fact, a kind of official spokesman for the Social Democrats. Franz Diedrich thought the poet of *Drum-Taps* could be "consoler, physician, pathfinder" to the enslaved and oppressed,[261] and Max Hayek praised him in the same way in the *Sozialistische Monatsheft*, in which he frequently published translations from *Leaves of Grass* between 1914–1931. In emphasizing this aspect of Whitman, the Social Democrats were also strongly influenced by Schlaf—thus to some extent reviving the "cult."

Of the World War I poets who were influenced by Whitman, one of the most interesting was Gerrit Engelke, a young German poet who read Whitman in the trenches and was killed in battle. His posthumous book, *Rhythmus des neuen Europa* (1923), shows us, as Jacobson remarks, "how Whitman's message became his gospel,"[262] though "his racing through all continents is not a mere imitation of Whitman, but an inevitable outcome of his inner feeling." Karl Otten's song "An die Besiegten" is also reminiscent of *Drum-Taps*. And though the poems of Heinrich Lersch are more conventional in form than Whitman's, we find in them many of the themes and sentiments of *Leaves of Grass*, especially significant being the eternal now, embracing past, present, and future.

When the war ended, Whitman became in Germany the poet of peace, and also more than ever the symbol of Democracy. Hugo Wolf, reviewing Hayek's translation, "Ich Singe das Leben," in *Der Friede*, July, 1919, declared that President Wilson's "fourteen points" had been plagiarized from Whitman.[263] Many celebrations were held in honor of the poet's centenary. Schlaf hailed him again as the perfect social and religious leader.[264] The Socialists of the November Revolution considered him as a comrade, and the Communist poet, Johannes Becher, wrote a poem to "Bruder Whitman." Max Hayek called *Leaves of Grass* "in fact the Bible of Democracy. . . . Walt Whitman's time has only now arrived. He is the poet of the modern day . . . of the year that now unfolds [1919]."[265] Whitman not only wrote of Democracy, but he lived it himself; therefore, he is a perfect example for "Social Democracy" in Germany. The working men were summoned to study Whitman.[266] But in Austria and Hungary, translations of Whitman's works were suppressed[267]—the proletariat had found in him the power of the masses. *Freie Jugend*, a very radical paper, published a translation of Whitman's "To a Foil'd European Revolutionaire." "Here," as Jacobson says, "Whitman is celebrated as the enemy of the state because of his love for order among men, as the enemy of the church because of his religion and conscience."[268]

This new cult led to Whitman evenings, "with slides and recitations, as for instance, in Vienna, where an actor makes out of Whitman's 'Mystic Trumpeter' a symphony of drama and lyricism, or in Munich, in Frankfort, and in Berlin, where Hans Reisiger and a great Reinhardt actress try to introduce Whitman into larger circles, the actress even over the radio."[269] Meanwhile the "expressionists" had also taken up Whitman,[270] and René Schickele included three of his poems (in Landauer's translation)[271] in *Menschliche Gedichte im Kriege* (1918). In fact, during the turbulent years in Germany from about 1918 to 1922 the American poet of Democracy seems to have been all things to all men.

Despite the great critical excitement over Whitman, however, no really good translations of his poems existed in Germany until the gifted Munich poet, Hans Reisiger, undertook the task. His first small volume of selections appeared in 1919, and was followed in 1922 with a greatly expanded translation in two volumes, with an eloquent

Introduction.[272] This work is now regarded as a classic. Herman
Stehr declared: "it is as if the great American had written not in
English, but in German."[273] And Law-Robertson, who has pointed
out serious faults in all previous attempts to turn Whitman's poems
into German, is almost lyrical in praise of this one. In his now-
famous Introduction Reisiger idealized Whitman almost as much as
Schlaf had done, but he wrote from full knowledge of the poet and
his work and his eloquence is due not to subjective fictionizing but
to his deep, intelligent conviction of Walt Whitman's importance. In
his psychological approach he also anticipated Catel, Schyberg, and
Canby: "Walt Whitman was one of the fortunate people who, even in
ripe old age, remained wrapped in a strong and warm mother-
world. . . ."[274] At the heart of Walt Whitman's being was the fact that
he had never lost the miraculous twilight gleam of childhood, the
gleam of the first delightful surprise in mere existence."[275] Like
many of his contemporaries in Germany, Reisiger appreciated more
deeply than most Americans what the Civil War had meant to the
author of *Leaves of Grass*, and he thought that *Democratic Vistas*
had a special meaning for the post-war generation in Germany.

Had political history in this nation followed a different road
from the one the people were already unconsciously choosing even in
1922, Reisiger's great work might have been the beginning of a long
and fruitful Whitman epoch in Germany rather than the crest of the
interest which would soon recede. With unconscious irony Reisiger
declared at this time:

The quick success of my first selected translation in 1919 and the
fact that I can now bring out this larger work are proofs of the
ever-growing interest taken by the German speaking intellectuals of
Europe in this man who is being recognized with increasing certainty
as the most powerful, purest, and most virile embodiment of a truly
cosmo-democrat.

In the developing democracy of Germany—I use the word
democracy in its political as well as its social sense—Walt Whitman
will be more and more regarded as *the* poet of a new community of
mankind, who has, by his truly magnetic personality, succeeded in
blending most completely the contrast between individuality and the
mass; who, fully conscious of the wonder of his existence in the
midst of the universe, the wonder of Now and Here, expresses it with
the highest power of love, and, dwelling thus in his Self, embraces
All; whose work is nothing less than the natural, wild, and sweet

language of an exalted type of future humanity, totally liberated in himself, lovingly housed in the Seen and Unseen; in a word, a Columbus of the Soul, who truly leads on God's seas to a New World.[276]

The irony of these optimistic hopes first appears in the use which the renowned novelist, Thomas Mann, made of the American poet in 1922. Mann seems to have discovered Whitman in the early 1920s at a time when he despaired of his own negative inheritance from Schopenhauer, Nietzsche, and Wagner. In thanking Reisiger for a copy of his two-volume translation Mann called it a "holy gift" and declared it to be of special benefit "to us Germans who are old and unripe at one and the same time, to whom contact with this powerful member of humanity, the humanity of the future, can prove a very blessing if we are able to receive his message."[277] But could Germany receive the message? No one was more fearful than Mann himself, for in the same year he saw the tragic necessity of beginning a personal fight to prolong the life of the young Republic. In his historic speech, *Von Deutscher Republik*,[278] delivered in 1922 to strengthen popular approval of the new democratic experiment in Germany, he hailed the identity of American Democracy with German Humanity, and cited Whitman and Novalis as the archetypes of each, as in his letter to Reisiger he had cited Whitman and Goethe. Mann also tried to contribute to this *rapprochement* by extoling Whitman's "athletic" Democracy, an appeal which even a National Socialist might understand; but from this time on Whitman's influence in Germany rapidly faded. The American poet was still loved by Stefan Sweig,[279] Franz Werfel,[280] and the Mann family[281] —but they were soon writing in exile, like the first German critic and translator three-quarters of a century before, Ferdinand Freiligrath.

World War II was not followed by another surge of interest in Whitman, though *Leaves of Grass* continued to be translated, read, and quietly studied. Of course Whitman was included in the various American Studies programs which have flourished in German universities during the past two decades. Georg Goyert, the famous translator of James Joyce, published a well-received volume of selections of *Grashalme* in 1948,[282] and he also translated Henry Seidel Canby's biography of Whitman the same year.[283] Herbert Pfeiffer in *Der Tages Spiegel* (April 21, 1948) thought Canby's book lacked objectivity, but he envied a country in which an individual could still be a hero in biography. In 1961 Rowohlt published in its Monographien series a translation by Kurt Kusenberg of Gay Wilson Allen's brief biography *Walt Whitman*.[284] But Professor Hans-Joachim Lang, of the University of Erlangen-Nuremberg, in his contribution to *Walt Whitman in Europe Today* (1972) can not point to any important recent publications on Whitman. He ends his essay with this rhetorical question: "Is it an academic illusion to believe that more people in Germany today have a surer grip on the original text of Whitman and a better personal acquaintance with American life . . . than 50 years ago?"[285] —when so many German writers were deifying "the Poet of Democracy."

WHITMAN IN SCANDINAVIA

Denmark, as Schyberg has pointed out with some pride,[286] discovered Whitman almost as soon as England and Germany, and contemporaneously with France. In 1872 Rudolf Schmidt began writing articles on him in Copenhagen and two years later he published a translation of *Democratic Vistas*. His "Walt Whitman, the Poet of American Democracy" is a sympathetic but fair summary and analysis of the poet's ideas and art, well worth reading today.[287] In 1888 Niels Møller translated *Autumn Rivulets*, but Schyberg says that because of its "remarkably complicated rhythmic diction," it did not contribute to the future understanding of Whitman's poetic art.[288] However, the fact that Whitman had no influence on Danish writers of the late nineteenth century is probably attributable to the complete indifference to him of Georg Brandes,[289] the critical dictator of the period; and Knut Hamsun, of Norway, was openly hostile.[290] Johannes V. Jensen counteracted this indifference and hostility when he published his novel, *Hjulet (The Wheel)*, in 1905. This is a very unusual contribution to Whitman criticism, for both the hero and the villain represent the American poet's doctrines on two planes, that of a social idealist and of a charlatan "prophet." The book contains long translated passages from *Leaves of Grass*, which Jensen and Otto Gelsted edited in an enlarged edition in 1918, with a critical Introduction by Gelsted. This collection is said to have had considerable influence on the generation of World War I lyricists in Denmark.[291]

In 1929 Børge Houmann translated "Song of Myself" and some other poems, with a highly romantic Introduction. And in 1933 Frederik Schyberg published his biographical and critical study, which has been mentioned so frequently in this *Handbook* that little more need be said about it. In the same year he also published another book of translations.[292] There were at this time, according to this competent witness, several Whitmanesque Danish poets, notably Harald Bergstedt, "a kindred spirit of Whitman's—not only in his great democratic declamations" but also in his lyric style. Bergstedt denies the influence, though he admits that he has known Whitman since he began writing.[293]

J∮rgen Erik Nielsen, in the latest summary and evaluation of Whitman in Denmark, reports Torben Brostr∮m's assertion in *Dansk Litteraturhistorie* (IV, 1966) that "the 'modernism' in Danish literature in the 1930s was inspired by Whitman rather than Baudelaire."[294] Although there is still no complete translation of *Leaves of Grass* into Danish, translation of his poetry and prose continues: a selection of *Specimen Days* (*Fuldkomme Dage*) by P. E. Seeberg in 1950; in 1965 Poul S∮rensen's 64 pages devoted to Whitman translations and critical comment in his *Moderne amerikansk lyrik: Fra Whitman til Sandburg*; and Emma Cortes's volume of selections, *Til Graesset ved S∮ens Bred Er Jeg Flygtet* ("I Have Fled to the Grass by the Edge of the Water") in 1970. Professor Neilsen's evaluation is that this translation has some merit, but shows insufficient familiarity with the Danish language. As for the other translations, Houmann's is faithful but prosaic; Schyberg's "runs smoothly and pleasantly" but is not always accurate, "and the reader is forced to consult the original." Jensen's and Gelsted's rank somewhere between these two. "Poul S∮rensen's translations have a modern ring; they are reliable and contain some extremely beautiful renderings." Since the study of English in Denmark begins in grammar school, the "original" offers most Danes little difficulty, and this may explain the lack of a complete translation of *Leaves of Grass*.

Rudolf Schmidt's Danish translation of *Democratic Vistas* in 1872 was the means of Whitman's first introduction to Norway (the literary languages of the two countries were then essentially the same). Schmidt's *Demokratiske Fremblik* aroused the enthusiasm of Bj∮rnstjerne Bj∮rnson,[295] and also influenced Kristofer Janson to visit America.[296] After his return Janson praised the American poet in *Amerikanske Forhold* (American Culture), published in Copenhagen in 1881. However, Knut Hamsun, whose trip to the United States disillusioned him, made a speech in the Copenhagen Student Union in 1889 in which he satirized Whitman's claims to being a poet, calling *Leaves of Grass* "not poetry at all; no more than the multiplication tables are poetry."[297] Hamsun called Whitman "a savage" and "a voice of nature in an uncultivated land." Apparently Hamsun and Georg Brandes stifled any further interest in Norway until he twentieth century.

Schyberg's 1933 translation and his biographical-critical study called Whitman again to the attention of Norway. One result was the translation of the complete "Song of Myself" into Landsmaal (or Nynorsk), the more colloquial of the two official Norwegian languages, by Per Arneberg in 1947.[298] This is still probably the most successful of all Scandinavian versions of Whitman, perhaps partly because of the compatibility of Landsmaal with Whitman's language, but more to the skill of the poet-translator.[299] Kjell Krogvig immediately recognized the similarities between Whitman and Norway's great early nineteenth century poet, Henrik Wergeland (1808–1845), especially in Wergeland's long epic-drama (1830) *Skabelsen, Mennesket og Messias* (*Creation, Mankind, and Messiah*). Krogvig recommended that Norwegians approach Whitman through Wergeland, who offered parallels in ideas, imagery, and even rhythms; and "if one did not know it to be impossible, one might be tempted to speak of direct influences."[300] But how many Norwegian readers followed his advice is not known. Whitman is also, as in Germany, taught in the country's university American Studies programs.

Frederic Fleisher says that probably the first mention of Walt Whitman in Sweden was "in 1895 in a poem by Gustaf Uddgren, a minor author and journalist."[301] Culturally Sweden has long been closer to Finland than to Denmark or Norway, and it was through a group of modern Finnish authors that Whitman began to arouse some interest in Sweden in the twentieth century. "The influence of Whitman on Edith Sölergran, perhaps the outstanding Finnish-Swedish poet of this century, is quite marked." The Swedish author Arthur Lundkvist, novelist, poet, and critic, though not a champion of Whitman, helped to make him known to the literary world. Schyberg's Danish translation stimulated Roland Fridholm to publish an essay in 1934 called "Pindarus från Paumanok" ("Pindar from Paumanok"),[302] and the following year K. A. Svensson published a selected translation, *Strån av gräs*.[303] Fleisher says it was not very good and received little attention. In 1937 Erik Blomberg, poet, art historian, and critic, published a "far superior" translation. He was a well-known socialist, and was interested in Whitman for ideological reasons, as were many other European socialists in the 1930s. The first Finnish translation of selected poems was made by Viljo Laitinen in 1954, but Fleisher does not mention it. "During the past three decades," he says, "Whitman's name has been mentioned on numerous occasions, but he has not gained much attention. He has assumed the role of a classic who is respected but [is] no longer a major source of inspiration."

It is different, however, in Iceland. There, "where grass is prized as the ultimate in vegetation and every third intellectual is a poet," writes Leedice Kissane, a visiting professor in the University of Iceland, writers have "responded understandably to *Leaves of Grass*."[304] Editions of Whitman's poems in English reached the National Library in the 1880s, and later in complete editions of his works. Many single poems have been translated at various times into Icelandic, and around mid-twentieth century Whitman became a strong influence on several of the *Atomskald* poets, "a name coined by Nobel Prize winner Halldor Laxness to designate their modern obscurity and flouting of poetic conventions." Among these, Einar Bragi Sigurdsson recently translated "What Think You I Take My Pen in Hand," which describes the emotional parting of two men on a pier.

One Icelandic poet who makes no secret of Whitman's influence on him is Matthias Johannessen, who is also editor of Reykjavik's leading newspaper, *Morgunblade*. Kassane writes:

He recalls reading *Leaves of Grass* voraciously in his youth and points to the initial poem in his first book, *Borgin Hlo* (*The City Laughs*), as clearly echoing Whitman's "Song of Myself." This poem begins in the manner of Whitman—"I sing of you, City"—and continues with descriptions of Reykjavik, its harbor, streets, buildings, and sea gulls, thus recalling the American poet's many tributes to his own harbor cities of Brooklyn and Manhattan. . . . Though he attributes to Whitman's influence the freedom won in breaking the strictures of rhyme and alliteration, he respects the spareness and integrity of the Saga tradition, and his later poetry may be said to revert to that tradition in a sort of "revolution within a revolution."[305]

WHITMAN IN RUSSIA

In the summer of 1955 the first centennial of *Leaves of Grass* was celebrated in various parts of the world: in the United States by the publicaton of biographies and interpretations of Whitman by television programs, exhibitions, and lectures; in Russia by a mass meeting in the Academy of the Soviet Union. Before an enlarged fifty-foot portrait of the poet addresses were given by the Secretary of the Union of Soviet Writers and the two leading Russian authorities on Whitman, M. Mendelssohn and Kornei Chukovsky. The Soviet Embassy in Washington supplied the Library of Congress with published accounts of this meeting, and after studying them Mary McGrory wrote in the Washington *Star*:

> The Russians, one gathers from a study of such papers as *Pravda,* *Izvesta* and the *Literary Gazette* of the Union of Soviet writers, discovered Whitman much earlier than his fellow Americans. Turgenev in the 1870's was translating "this remarkable and striking poet" and Tolstoy, who particularly admired Whitman's "Leaves of Grass" recommended translation of all his works.[306]

The tone of this American report reflected the tension of the "Cold War" years, as perhaps the Russian speeches did also. In fact, the Voice of America radio station in New York countered some of the Russian claims by a broadcast given by the author of this *Handbook* on Whitman's concept of individual freedom, which the Russians had overlooked. Thus Whitman was used for propaganda purposes on both sides of the Iron Curtain. But the Russians had a right to celebrate "their" Whitman, for he did enter Russian literature early and may have been a vital influence in Soviet culture before he was in his own. What Russians value in Whitman is not exactly what Americans find in him, but this has been true of his reception in every country, as we have seen.

Whitman was mentioned in Russian journals as early as 1861,[307] but the first Russian critical notice occurred as a result of a lecture by Whitman's friend John Swinton in 1882, which was translated in *Zagranichnyi Vestnik (Foreign Herald)*.[308] This caused N. Popov to publish an article on "Uolt Guitman" in the *Herald* in March, 1883, in which the critic asked and attempted to answer: "Who is this Walt Whitman? He is the spirit of revolt and pride, Milton's Satan. He is Goethe's Faust, but a happier one. . . . he has solved the riddle of life; he is drunk with life, such as it is; he extols birth equally with death because he sees, knows, senses, immortality."[309] In his first response to the question Popov hit the keynote of Whitman's appeal in pre-revolutionary Russia: "He is the spirit of revolt." In tsarist Russia this statement might have been enough to get the critic into trouble, but he added something else that the censor pounced upon. In "This Compost" Whitman had wondered how the earth can grow "such sweet things out of such corruptions"—diseased corpses and decaying matter. Popov paraphrased: "Every life is composed of thousands of corpses," without indicating the redeeming transformation Whitman found in Nature. Consequently, Popov's essay was classified as "decadent," the author thrown into prison, and the magazine suspended. For many years thereafter it was dangerous to praise or translate Whitman in Russia. Perhaps this hazard made him more tempting to young writers.

Yet for all Whitman's admiration of American men and women in the mass, and his ambition to be a representative common man, the hero of his epic cycle of poems, there were enormous differences between his experiences and those of the Russian revolutionary writers (i.e., both those who preceded the abortive revolt in 1905 and the great revolution of 1917). In the United States Black people were enslaved until Lincoln's Emancipation Proclamation in 1863 (effective date), though it did not bring economic freedom. But slavery was a Southern institution, and Brooklyn-reared Whitman had no firsthand experience with slavery—with the exception of two months observation in New Orleans. As editor of the Brooklyn *Eagle* he did fight to prevent the extension of slavery to the new territories (see Chapter III), thereby causing his journalistic career to come to an end, or very nearly so.

It was during this time that Whitman wrote his impassioned poem "To a Foil'd European Revolutionaire."[310] This poem established his credentials in radical Russian circles in the last quarter of the nineteenth century. But most of his poems were not of this kind. He did not write abolitionist poems like Whittier. His revolution was mainly of the heart and mind; it was religious, philosophical, and esthetic rather than directly political. This the Russians could appreciate also, but they needed a more militant activist—or a poet who could be so used—and they partly recreated Whitman.

Like Nikolai Nekrasov, Whitman was also a poet-democrat and a poet-patriot, but the United States did not have an enslaved peasantry similar to Russia's. Negro slavery was certainly as reprehensible, and Whitman opposed it, at least in principle, but it was not the main substance of his experience or the subject-matter of his poems. As Chukovsky says, the hero of Nekrasov's great poem *Who Lives Happily in Russia?* is "the whole Russian people."[311] Whitman attempted to make his persona the symbolical voice of the American people, but most critics agree that *Leaves of Grass* is personal, lyrical, and for the most part joyous, and only occasionally the anguished voice of protest over unbearable social conditions, as Nekrasov's voice was. In America Whitman was condemned. Once an edition of *Leaves* was suppressed because of his free treatment of sex, but he was never officially persecuted, as Nekrasov was, for his literary attacks on political autocracy. Thus from the very beginning, the Russians selected what they most wanted or needed from Whitman, and magnified his rôle as "poet of the people." As has often been observed, Whitman's fondest wish was to be that kind of poet, but he never succeeded because he was more literary than he knew. Nor could he have reached the Russian people even if Fitzgerald Lee[312] had been able to make his proposed translation. Aside from likely censorship, the Russian masses were illiterate.

But a few of Russia's intellectuals did begin to discover Whitman fairly early. One of these was Turgenev. In 1872, in Paris, where Turgenev was living in exile, Whitman's poems were called to his attention, and he was so deeply moved by them that he offered to make some translations for *Nedeli* (*The Week*), but soon found his linguistic skills unequal to the task. The manuscript of his attempt to translate "Beat! Beat! Drums!" still exists in the National Library in Paris.[313] Turgenev is said to have told Henry James that Whitman's poems contained much chaff but also some sound grain.[314]

Tolstoy's first reaction to Whitman was unfavorable, but later found pleasure in the "Calamus" poems—interpreting them, of course, as all Russians have, as poems of comradeship. However, Tolstoy still thought Whitman lacked a coherent philosophy of life.[315]

The news of Whitman's death in 1892 was widely reported in Russian newspapers, and Russian émigrés in Switzerland learned about the poet in their Russian-language newspaper. The Russian Symbolists, like the French, were attracted by Whitman. Russia had Symbolists too, and in 1905 Konstantin Balmont published the first book of selected Whitman poems in translation.[316] It was immediately denounced by Kornei Chukovsky as weak, inaccurate, and in a style wholly unsuitable. Chukovsky himself then began translating Whitman, and soon established himself as the poet's major Russian translator, publishing edition after edition for the rest of his life, ending with a thoroughly revised posthumous edition in 1970 (he died in 1969). Three years earlier he had published *My Walt Whitman*, containing a personal account of his long experience in reading, translating, and interpreting Whitman, with a selection of his favorite poems, and a critical bibliography of books he had used.

In *My Walt Whitman* Chukovsky says, "Walt Whitman was the idol of my youth."[317] In 1901 he bought a copy of Whitman's poems from a sailor in Odessa for 25 copecks. He was "shaken to the core by the novelty of [Whitman's] perception of life," and responded "fervently to his call for ecstatic friendship, his paeans to equality, labour and democracy, his joyful intoxication with life, and his daring words glorifying the emancipation of the flesh, which had terrified the hypocrites of that time."

Chukovsky's first translation was published in 1907 in a St. Petersburg University student magazine, *Circle of Youth*.[318] Later he realized how poor his versions were, but he continued to learn and improve, until he had published ten editions by 1944, to which he added others in 1953, 1955, and 1970. "I continued to preach the gospel of Whitman everywhere, and there was no publication, it seemed, in which I did not print an article about him or translations of *Leaves of Grass*."[319] Meanwhile, Chukovsky became not only Whitman's leading translator in Russia, but also the leading translator of Shakespeare, Defoe, Mark Twain, Kipling, and other British and American authors. He was also the most popular author of children's books, read in every school and most homes of the land. In 1967 Oxford University awarded him an honorary degree of Doctor of Literature.[320]

In spite of his great admiration for Whitman, Chukovsky strove to present both the man and his work with the greatest fidelity possible. He depended mainly upon the "mythmakers," Bucke, Burroughs, O'Connor, and Horace Traubel, for his facts until he read Asselineau's *L'Evolution de Walt Whitman* and Allen's *The Solitary Singer*. In a letter addressed to *Walt Whitman in Europe Today* he says that with these books "the Whitman chronicle was finally purged of the myths and legends with which it had been cluttered."[321] By this time he had also used the newly edited volumes in the New York University edition of Whitman's *Collected Writings*; and he expressed his gratitude to the editor of the *Correspondence*, Edwin H. Miller, as well as to Floyd Stovall, editor of the

Prose Works 1892. Thus it appears that Russian Whitman scholarship is profiting from the American.

Chukovsky had all along welcomed intelligent criticism of Whitman. In 1935 he printed D. S. Mirsky's essay, "Walt Whitman: Poet of American Democracy," as an Introduction to his current translation. And Mirsky did not see Whitman as the prophet of a new society, but as "the last great poet of the bourgeoise era of humanity, the last in the line that begins with Dante."[322] He "is the poet of American democracy of the Fifties and Sixties, in all its organic strength. . . . He accepted it as something already existent in the nature of the American people and needed only to be brought to light. . . . Later on, in the Seventies, he had to confess that America of the present was yet far from the ideal. . . ,"[323] though he continued to hope for the future.

Whitman, of course, believed that democracy would be saved—or attained—by the character of individual Americans. But the Marxists believed that society must be remade before the individual could improve. This was the great chasm between Whitman and the Marxists. Mirsky found Whitman's importance not in his thought but his artistry: "It is not as to a prophet with a system that we should come to Whitman, but as to an artist. . . . those concrete forms to which he brought all the depth and strength of his emotion, all that he as an artist had learned from the American scene."[324] This Whitman "occupies an honorable place with the great poets of the past, who have afforded us . . . a vision of that full man who in reality is only able to exist as at once the builder and the creator of constructive socialism."[325]

In the same year Leonard Spier, writing in the English-language magazine published in Moscow, *International Literature*, gave a similar interpretation: "Whitman was a great critic of his nation who essayed to probe its future and influence it. His major deficiency, however, lay in his recourse to a false or pseudo dialectic."[326] This condemnation of Whitman's Hegelian mysticism had been voiced earlier in Germany by Bertz, and Arvin repeated it in the United States in 1938. But Spier concluded that "the best in Whitman belongs to the future and 'the future rests in the hands of the radicals' . . . what gold there is in this mountain is ours."

Whitman's greatest influence on Soviet poetry, according to Chukovsky, was in the 1920s and 30s, especially in the work of Mayakovsky and Khlebnikov.[327] He does not mention Yevtushenko and the poets of his generation.

POLAND, HUNGARY, CZECHOSLOVAKIA, YUGOSLAVIA AND RUMANIA

In other Communist countries of Eastern Europe there has been sporadic interest in Whitman, with numerous translations of single short poems or fragments of longer poems. In Poland Whitman was discussed as early as 1887, and after World War I a group of poets called "Skamander" espoused the American poet and experimented with his free rhythms.[328] Stanislaw de Vincenz published *Trzy Poematy* (*Three Poems*) in 1921, and S. Napieralski *75 Poematów* (*75 Poems*) in 1934. Two recent editions have appeared, *Walt Whitman, Poezje Wybrane* (*Selected Poems*) by several hands, edited by Hieronim Michalski, 1973, and *Żdźbla Trawey, Wybrane (Leaves of Grass, Selected Poems)*, edited with Introduction by Juliusz Zutawski, 1965. Zulawaki has also published a biographical study, of nearly four hundred pages, *Wielka Podróz Walta Whitmana*, 1971, based on the latest American scholarship. He stresses the contribution of Poles in American history in order to arouse the interest of his fellow countrymen in America's most representative poet.[329]

Of all Eastern European countries Hungary is perhaps best supplied with modern translations. Keszthelyi Zoltán published a small volume in Budapest in 1947.[330] Kardos László and Szenczi Miklós edited a greatly augmented edition, over 400 pages, by various translators, in 1955,[331] and Országh László a still larger edition of nearly 800 pages in 1964.[332]

Czechoslovakia has the problem of two languages. Professor Ján Boor reports that "Czech literature is quite rich indeed in Whitman translations."

The great national poet Jaroslav Vrchlický was the first translator of the great American poet as early as in 1895. Later he made a representative selection of Whitman's poetry, published separately in 1906. Another Czech poet, Emanuel z Leshradu, translated poems of Whitman at the same time as Vrchlicky. Among other translators Arnost Vanecek and Pavel Eisner must be mentioned. Their modern translations—especially that of Pavel Eisner in 1945—made Whitman widely known throughout Czechoslovakia. Finally, the biggest choice of both poetry and prose of Whitman was given by two Czech translators, Jiri Kolár and Zdenek Urbánek, in 1955 and reprinted several times since then.[333]

The Slovak language has only one translation, *Pozdrav svetu*

("Salut au Monde!"), published in 1956; it contains fifty poems and all of *Democratic Vistas*. In 1969 a Whitman jubilee was held in Bratislava, for which the American (now living in Japan) William Moore wrote a drama, produced on Czechoslovakian television. Professor Boor says that a revival of interest in Whitman is taking place among the younger Czechoslovakian poets.

In Yugoslavia the language problem is still more complicated, but there have been translations of selections from Whitman's poems in Croatian (in 1900, 1909, and 1919); a lecture on Whitman in Serbian (1919); and, according to Sonja Bašić, "a series of remarkable translations by the great Croatian Bohemian poet and translator Augustin Ujević," was published in Zagreb in 1951, "retaining the powerful rhetorical flow of Whitman's poetry and his unconventional, rich vocabulary."[334]

Janez Stanonik has been translating and writing about Whitman in Slovenian since the first World War, and his latest translation appeared in 1962. There have also been translations of some poems into Macedonian and Serbian. Several Yugoslav poets are thought to have been influenced by Whitman but the subject has not been closely studied.

The most versatile volume of translations of Whitman in Eastern Europe is Rumania's *Opera Alese* (*Selected Work*) translated and edited by Mihnea Gheorghiu (Bucharest, 1956).[335] It contains a long historical and critical introduction, 234 pages of poems, 224 pages of prose (including early prose, autobiography, prefaces, and literary essays), two critical studies of Whitman (comparing him with Tolstoy and Mayakovsky), some letters, and poems to Whitman by García Lorca, Pablo Neruda, and Geo Bogza of the Rumanian Academy.

WHITMAN IN ITALY

Italy has also been hospitable to Walt Whitman, as Charles S. Grippi shows in his *The Literary Reception of Walt Whitman in Italy*, (1971).[336] Whitman has been translated, subjected to extensive critical analysis, and used as a symbol in the ideological conflicts. The bibliography of Whitman in Italy is so voluminous that a short sketch can do little more than name the major translators and critics.

There are two complete translations of *Leaves of Grass* in Italian, the first by Luigi Gamberale, *Foglie di erba*, in 1907 and 1923 editions;[337] the second by Enzo Giachino, *Foglie d'erba e prose*, 1950.[338] In 1972 Mariolina Meliadò Freeth wrote of the latter: "This beautiful translation, which also had the merit of bringing to the public's notice a selection from the prose, completely superseded Gamberale's old version and did much to stimulate criticism on Whitman."[339] Mrs. Freeth herself has translated the entire *Specimen Days*[340] (the only complete edition of this work in a foreign language), which Professor Roger Asselineau calls "a brilliant translation."[341]

As early as 1872 Enrico Nencioni discovered Whitman by way of French criticism, and interested his friends in the strange new American poet. In 1879 Nencioni published his first article on Whitman, in which he warned his readers that the poet was rude, shocking, and violated good taste, but had primitive strength and magnetism.[342] These traits, of which Whitman boasted himself, were the main attractions for his first Italian readers. Giovanni Papini, the leader of an Italian school of Pragmatism, declared that in discovering Whitman in his youth he had discovered poetry. He thought Italian poetry had become over-refined and effete, and, "If we would find again the poetry we have lost, we must go back a little toward barbarism—even toward savagery."[343]

When Giosuè Carducci read Nencioni's article he also responded with enthusiasm, declaring that "Italy has need to heal itself," and Whitman sounded like good medicine.[344] "The healing reference," says Grippi, "was a reaction to 'consumptive Leopardianism' and 'dropsical Manzonianism' of the ugly aspects of romantic sentimentalism that he saw in contemporary Italian literature."[345] Actually, Whitman seemed to answer several needs: recovery from sickly romanticism, from cultural insecurity, and from moribund literary conventions. It is curious, and doubtless significant, that most of the early Whitman enthusiasts in Italy were classical scholars, several of them teachers, like Carducci, who first thought of trying to translate Whitman's poems into Homeric hexameters.[346] Perhaps the long lines and Whitman's rhythms suggested this form, but the comparison also showed a desire to find Homeric qualities in this New World poet.

Carducci, D'Annunzio, and Giovanni Pascoli, the dominant triad of Italian poetry at the end of the nineteenth century, found Greek characteristics in Whitman to counteract their own exhausted Latinity. This attitude also made them more receptive to Whitman's open-ended prosody and new esthetics. They saw that his art was not lawless, but simply innovative in the use of old forms. Pascoli said the rhythms of *Leaves of Grass* resembled those of the Bible.[347]

But it remained for a young precocious scholar, Pasquale Jannaccone (who later became an economist and a statesman, not a poet) to observe parallels between Whitman's rhythms and those of primitive Greek hymns.[348] He was so taken by this discovery, and resemblances to other primitive poetry, that he proceeded to analyze the principles of Whitman's prosody—at a time when nearly everyone thought.he had no prosody, though some of his friends in America had defended his verse-forms as "organic," operating on their own internal laws.[349] Jannaccone's *La Poesia di Walt Whitman e l'Evoluzione delle Forme Ritmiche* has been discussed in Chapter IV. Some of the poets disagreed with Jannaccone's methodical analysis, though they were apparently influenced by the very patterns of sounds and rhythms he dissected. One of these poets was Pascoli, especially in his "Il fanciullim," which Mariolina Meliadò has shown to resemble Whitman's "Out of the Cradle Endlessly Rocking."[350] This critic, in fact, sees in Giovanni Pascoli's poetry the "subterranean influence" of Whitman which provided the transition to modern Italian poetry.

The three major twentieth-century critics of Whitman in Italy have been Cesare Pavese (1908–50), Carlo Bo, and Glauco Cambon. Pavese discovered Whitman in his youth, wrote a university dissertation on him, and continued until his suicide in 1950 to write about Whitman. He challenged the usual sentimental image of Whitman—the old man with a white beard holding a butterfly on his index finger—and anticipated American critics by several decades in his opinion that Whitman's best poetry was in his earliest editions, and that with declining health his poetry degenerated. Pavese also rejected Whitman's claims to having put his own country and the nineteenth century "on record" in his book:

Walt Whitman lived out the idea of this mission so intensely that, though not avoiding the fatal failure of such a design, he yet avoided through it the failure of his work. He did not write the primitive poem of which he dreamed, but the poem of that dream. He did not succeed in his absurd attempt to create a poetry adapted to the democratic and republican world and to the character of the newly discovered land—because poetry is one—but as he spent his life repeating this design in various forms, he made poetry out of this very design, the poetry of the discovery of a world new in history and of the singing of it. To put the apparent paradox in a nutshell, he wrote poetry out of poetry-writing.[351]

This was a very acute observation, but critics of Pavese accused him of being highly subjective and of writing more about himself than Whitman. Carlo Bo, however, went even further in subjectivity by insisting on a "hermetic" or private reading of *Leaves of Grass*, a theory heavily indebted to French Symbolism and Surrealism. He took seriously Whitman's ambition to create poetry which would indicate "the paths between reality and the soul," or as he declared in his 1855 Preface: "The poets of the kosmos advance through all interpositions and coverings and turmoils and stratagems to first principles."[352] Bo's "hermetic" criticism linked Whitman to Symbolism in an entirely new way, one which no American critic attempted until Charles Feidelson wrote his *Symbolism and American Literature* (1953).[353]

In *Walt Whitman Abroad* the present author remarked apropos Giachino's translation that "Evidently Whitman still has a future in Italy."[354] Cambon retorted, "We can agree with Allen that Whitman has an open account with us for the future because he has already had an excellent past, both distant and recent."[355] Cambon himself studied the American idiom and literature in the United States and in a series of articles attempted to interpret Whitman's language and to explicate key poems. He also traced "Whitman's fortune in Italy," as Mrs. Freeth expresses it.[356] She herself praises Cambon for having called attention to the "literary worth" of Whitman's prose in "La parola come emanazione" (1959). Italian critics have been especially interested in Whitman's language. S. Perosa's study, Mrs. Freeth says, "shows Matthiessen's influence in establishing Whitman as a classic in Italy," and it is natural that they would have been affected by Matthiessen's theories about *Leaves of Grass* as "a language experiment."[357]

Not all Italian criticism, however, has been favorable. Mario Praz, of the University of Rome, had little use for Whitman, classifying him with Proust as "men-women, or better, human beings who have remained infantile in an essential part of their psyche."[358] Mario Alicata, like Paul Jamati in France,[359] branded all such interpretations of Whitman as the attempts of political reactionaries to discredit Whitman's "humanism and democracy."[360] Thus in Italy, as in other countries, Whitman criticism has been affected by the conflict of social and political ideologies.

WHITMAN IN SPAIN, PORTUGAL,
LATIN AMERICA AND GREECE

The cultural interchange between Spain and the Spanish-speaking South American countries, as well as Portugal and Brazil, makes the Spanish and Portuguese reception of Whitman the most extensive geographically of any languages. Both Spain and Ecuador have complete translations of *Leaves of Grass*, by Concha Zardoya in Madrid, 1946, and Francisco Alexander, Quito, 1953.[361] There are also numerous selections in Spanish, ranging from the Catalan version of Cebría Montoliu, Barcelona, 1909, reprinted in Buenos Aires in 1943, to Armando Vasseur's in Valencia, 1912, reprinted in Montevideo in 1939, and numerous others.[362] *Democratic Vistas* has been translated in Spain by Concha Zardoya (1946) and in Argentina by Luis Azua (1944).[363]

Both Spain and Latin America first became interested in the mythical Whitman of Bazalgette, and Cameron Rogers's fictionized *The Magnificent Idler*, as the biographical introductions of the various translations reveal. Even the Prologue by John Van Horne in Concha Zardoya's translation—and her own Introduction too—show the glorified Whitman against which Pavese in Italy protested;[364] however, the more realistic biographies of Asselineau and Allen had not yet been published—and there was also the usual cultural lag. Whitman, in fact, as a person was not very real to his Latin hosts. While making his study of Whitman in Latin America, Fernando Alegría wrote:

To study Whitman in Spanish American poetry is to trace the wanderings of a ghost that is felt everywhere and seen in no place. His verses are quoted with doubtful accuracy by all kinds of critics; poets of practically all tendencies have been inspired by his message and have either written sonnets celebrating his genius or repeated his very words with a somewhat candid self-denial.[365]

In Spain, at least, one major poet has been definitely influenced by Whitman. Miguel de Unamuno began translating and writing about him as early as 1906. In his own poems he adopted some of Whitman's mannerisms, echoed him in his "credo poético," and, as Concha Zardoya testifies, "In writing his great poem *El Cristo de*

Velázquez, he had very much in mind—as is known—Whitman's rhythmic liberties."[366] In "El canto adámico" ("Adam's Song") he wrote the most eloquent and imaginative defense of Whitman's "catalogs" ever published.[367]

Usually the Spanish poets most interested in Whitman had visited the United States. While studying at Cornell University, León Felipe Camino was attracted by Whitman. Later he translated, or paraphrased, "Song of Myself" with such freedom that he did not know himself whether his versions of sections 44 and 45 "are from the Bible, from Whitman or are mine."[368] In "Resumen" he declared, "I am Walt Whitman. In my blood there is an American romantic. . . ."[369] His own poems have enumerations, repetitions, epic lyricism, and "prosaism" which Zordoya says came from Whitman.

Federico García Lorca also became acquainted with Whitman's poems in New York, and wrote "Oda a Walt Whitman,"[370] which is generally agreed to be one of the greatest poems ever addressed to this American poet. Yet Lorca's own poems show no influence of Whitman in his themes or style. His ode is merely the heart-felt tribute of one poet to another.

In Jorge Guillén's Castilian *Cántico* (Madrid, 1926, 1928) there are resemblances to Whitman's cosmic pantheistic lyricism, though it is not known whether he was acquainted with Whitman before he wrote this book. Guillén came to the United States in 1940, and may have read Whitman then. His collection of all his poems in one volume, *Aire nuestro* (1968), reminds Concha Zardoya of Whitman's final *Leaves*.[371]

The realism and social consciousness of Rafael Alberti also "recalls Walt Whitman. In 'Siervos,' for example: 'I send you a greeting/ and I call you comrades.' " Since the Spanish Civil War poetry has become more social and humanistic. "Gabriel Celaya is, perhaps, the most representative poet of this tendency, not only for his subject matter but for his use of enumeration (occupations, things, places.")[372]

In Latin America three literary movements of modern times have, according to Alegría, responded in different ways to Whitman.[373] First the Modernista period: in 1887 José Martí, the Cuban poet and journalist, wrote an article on Whitman after hearing him read his Lincoln address in New York. The Nicaraguan poet, Rubén Darío addressed a sonnet to Whitman in his book, *Azul* (1888), and

Armando Vasseur translated the bulk of *Leaves of Grass* in 1912. But most of these writers knew Whitman very superficially, even Darío. Alegria says, "Whitman's voice is present throughout the modernist movement, but not his spirit."[374] The Chilean poet, Pablo de Rokha, comes nearest, in Alegría's opinion, of matching the genius and expression of Whitman. Today Alegría would probably agree that another poet of his country, the Nobel Prize winner, Pablo Neruda, has profited even more from Whitman's nourishing influence—though he is no imitator. Neruda himself gladly acknowledges the "internal debt," which began when he was barely fifteen. Whitman not only helped him become a poet, he "has helped me to exist." Then this remarkable tribute from one of the greatest poets of the twentieth century:

There are many kinds of greatness, but let me say (though I be a poet of the Spanish tongue) that Walt Whitman has taught me more than Spain's Cervantes: in Walt Whitman's work one never finds the ignorant being humbled, nor is the human condition ever found offended.[375]

In these words Neruda pays tribute to Whitman not so much as a poet but as a moral force (which of course Whitman exerted through his poems), and that is the kind of tribute the American poet would have valued. Neruda defined his own poetry as "impure," meaning his esthetics was "confused [with the] impurity of the human condition."[376] Doubtless he hoped his poetry would help to sanitize and humanize that condition, but he pessimistically anticipated the "predators gnawing within"[377] who overthrew the Allende regime a few days before Neruda's own death from natural causes. Allende was his friend, whom he had served as Ambassador to France until illness forced his resignation. In his prophetic poem, "Fin de mundo" ("World's End") he had sorrowfully admitted, "Walt Whitman doesn't belong to us. . . ."[378] The point is that Whitman belongs to a free world—though at times men in bondage have turned to him for help in gaining freedom, as they did in Russia before and after the Revolution, in Italy under Fascism, in Spain during and since the Civil War. It is significant that *Democratic Vistas* is admired both in Spain and Latin America. *O Camarada Whitman*, by the great Brazilian sociologist, Gilberto Freyre, is ostensibly about the "good gray Whitman," but its main subject is his *Democratic Vistas*, in which Freyre finds a faith for both North and South America.[379]

To turn back to Europe briefly for Whitman's reception in another Latin country, an ardent but eccentric admirer of Whitman flourished in Portugal both before and during its political dictatorships. He was Fernando Pessoa (1888–1935), born in South Africa of Portuguese parents, but returned to Portugal for his career. Some of his poetry expresses social protest, and possibly all of it in subtle ways, but Pessoa was not an "activist." Whitman influenced him only in finding his own poetic form and idiom. Pessoa created several heteronyms under which he could express his private emotions without inhibitions, for which he was perhaps more indebted to Valéry Larbaud's A. O. Barnabooth than to Walt Whitman, but Whitman meant a great deal to him.

Pessoa's "Salutation to Walt Whitman"[380] is a clever parody, but without rancor, and can easily be taken for homage. From Portugal, with "all the ages" in his brain, Pessoa salutes his "brother in the universe," who, he is sure, knows him, "clasping hands, with the universe doing a dance in our soul." (Not two souls joined, but the one soul they share in common.) The following stanza is a fair sample of the poem:

O singer of concrete absolutes, always modern and eternal,
Fiery concubine of the scattered world,
Great pederast brushing up against the diversity of things,
Sexualized by rocks, by trees, by people, by their trades,
Rutting on the move, with casual encounters, with mere observations,
My enthusiast for the contents of everything,
My great hero going to meet death by leaps and bounds,
Roaring, screaming, bellowing greetings to God.[381]

The poet tells Walt he is not his disciple, not his friend, or his singer:

You know that I am You, and you are happy about it!

[Reprinted from *Selected Poems by Fernando Pessoa*, trans. Edwin Honig, with permission of The Swallow Press. © 1971 by Edwin Honig.]

He regrets not having Whitman's "self-transcending calm," and that is why he is crying out—saluting the "Great Liberator." The poem ends:

Goodbye, bless you, live forever, O Great Bastard of Apollo,
Impotent and ardent lover of the nine muses and the graces,
Cable-car from Olympus to us and from us to Olympus.[382]

[Reprinted from *Selected Poems by Fernando Pessoa*, trans. Edwin
Honig, with permission of The Swallow Press. © 1971 by Edwin
Honig.]

No one who could write like this could be called a disciple of
Whitman, and though Pessoa was liberated by him from certain literary conventions, and echoed him in some poems, such as "Triumphal
Ode," he hated the machine age which Whitman innocently welcomed. As Octavio Paz says in a Preface to Pessoa's poems, "*Triumphal Ode* is neither romantic nor Epicurean [like the poems of
Larbaud and Whitman] nor triumphant; it is a song of hate and
defeat. And this is the basis of its originality."[383] Here also we have
the vast distance between Whitman and Pessoa, in spite of the
American poet's influence.

In another southern European country, Greece (not Latin but
the mother of Latin tongues), *Leaves of Grass* has been admired sufficiently to be translated by the poet Nick Proestopoulos and published in an edition of selections and in a complete version.[384] The
language used is demotic Greek, perhaps because the translator
thought it to be equivalent to Whitman's language. But whether
appropriate or not, the two volumes show that Whitman has aroused
some interest in Greece, even during the great turmoils since World
War II.

WHITMAN IN OTHER COUNTRIES:
JAPAN, ISRAEL, CHINA

Several Japanese scholars have written articles on the reception
and influence of Walt Whitman in Japan.[385] They give abundant
titles, dates, and names of translators—a surprising number—and
critics. Evidently Whitman has attracted wide attention in Japan, at
least in academic circles. But beneath the smoke, how brightly does
the fire burn? For one who does not read Japanese, it is a guessing
game. Translating poetry into any language is, as Roger Asselineau
says, "an impossible task."[386] If that is true of translating Whitman
into French, how much more difficult it must be in a language using
idiographs instead of an alphabet.

In Japan, however, most of the scholars interested in American literature—and there have been many since World War II—can read English, so that they are not entirely dependent upon Whitman in Japanese. Perhaps it is for this reason that interest in Whitman seems to be largely, though not entirely, in the academic world. In Professor Shigenobu Sadoya's bibliography[387] the first article on Whitman appeared in 1892 in the University of Tokyo *Journal of Philosophy*.[388] By 1914 ten more articles had been published in magazines of limited circulation. After World War I the pace increased, and then rapidly multiplied after World War II, explained in part by the introduction of American literature in university studies during the years of reconstruction.

The major translator of *Leaves of Grass* has been Shigetaka Naganuma, though he was not the first. He became interested in Horace Traubel's work in 1917, and visited him in 1919 to secure his blessing for a translation of his poems, but Traubel persuaded him to translate Whitman instead.[389] After several editions of selections, Naganuma was able to publish a complete *Leaves of Grass* in Japanese in 1950, and a revised edition in 1954.[390] In 1958 he finished a translation of Walt Whitman's letters to his mother during the Civil War.[391]

As early as 1898 a literary critic, Rinjiro Takayama, at Waseda University, "passionately admired Whitman," especially his doctrine that "there is no soul apart from the body."[392] A Christian professor in Tokyo, Kanzo Uchimura, thought Whitman "must be a true Christian or prophet, not a poet." He concluded that "no racial discrimination nor expansion of armaments will be raised in America when Americans have attained to the height of Whitman's ideal."[393] Takeo Arishima, who became a novelist of note before his early suicide, published literary interpretations of Whitman and some translations. Arishima belonged to the Shirakaba (White Birch) literary circle, which opposed the dominant Naturalism of the early twentieth century (influenced by Flaubert, Dostoevsky, and Zola).[394] This group also associated Whitman with Blake and briefly published a magazine devoted to the two poets.

Since World War II Whitman has, of course, been treated in the various Japanese surveys of American Literature and included in anthologies of English and American poetry. In 1953 Masaru Shiga's translation of *Democratic Vistas* was published, and the following year Kinichi Ishikawa's translation of Van Wyck Brooks's *The Times of Melville and Whitman.*[395] During the 1950s visiting American scholars lectured on Whitman in universities and American Cultural Centers.[396]

Also since World War II a very enthusiastic American Whitmanian, Professor William Moore, has given many lectures on his favorite poet at the International Christian University in Tokyo and elsewhere. In 1967 Professor Moore made what will probably be a lasting contribution to the study of Whitman in Japan by publishing (in English) Whitman's complete *Leaves of Grass*, with "Prose Essences and Annotations."[397] The subject-matter of Whitman's poems is often so alien to a Japanese student that he has difficulty in understanding "what the poem says." Here, out of his long experience both in studying and in teaching Whitman to youthful readers in Japan, Professor Moore is uniquely qualified to aid, encourage, and stimulate. He deserves a special note in the history of Walt Whitman in Japan.

In Israel, too, university professors have made the most significant contributions to the reception of Whitman. One is Professor Simon Halkin, well-known poet, novelist, critic, and teacher in the Hebrew University of Jerusalem, who published a translation of *Leaves of Grass* (not complete but full) in 1952.[398] There have been numerous other translations of single poems or brief selections, but Halkin's version remains the fullest and most respected. Then in critical interpretation there are the studies of Professor Sholom Kahn, also of the Hebrew University, who studied at Columbia University under Mark Van Doren before becoming an Israeli citizen.[399]

Among the other poets who have been translating Whitman is S. Sholom. In 1950 he explained his fondness for Whitman in an interview for the New York *Herald Book Review*: "Whitman's pioneering is very close to us, and so are his Biblical rhythms. To translate him into Hebrew is like translating a writer back into his own language."[400]

Some of Israel's leading poets, such as Uri Zvi Grinberg, were writing about Whitman before Israel became a nation. In 1964 Benjamin Krushovski, author of an authoritative study of free verse in modern poetry, published a long essay called "Theory and Practice in U. Z. Grinberg's Expressionist Poetry." A summary in English states:

Grinberg's two-level rhythm is compared to the rhythm of Mayakovsky and Whitman. In Mayakovsky's poetry there is uniformity on
the upper level and freedom on the lower one, while in Grinberg's
Expressionist poetry it is vice versa. Whitman's long lines are free to
an extent on both levels, but this freedom is limited.[401]

Several years ago Professor Kahn wrote that he had been finding
reminders of Whitman in the collected poems of Moshe Bassok
(1907–66), a Lithuanian with Hassidic ancestry who joined a collective farm in Israel in 1936.[402] Kahn is not sure that Bassok had
read Whitman, but the Hassidic background reminds one that Frederik Schyberg in 1933 compared Whitman to the Hassidic poets.[403]
And recently E. Fred Carlisle has based a book-length study on
similarities between Whitman's "drama of the soul" and Martin
Buber's Hassidic philosophy, in *The Uncertain Self: Whitman's
Drama of Identity* (1973).

In a survey of Whitman in Israel in 1961 Kahn found his shadow
in many places, but he wondered about the presence of the real man.
Eight years later he wrote: "I find much more to report: presence,
spirit, scholarship—on all levels, Whitman seems very much alive in
Israel today."[404] This is an opinion which he still holds in 1974.[405]

It is perhaps appropriate to end this chapter on Whitman and
World Literature with a note on the People's Republic of China.
Little is known about Chinese interest in Whitman, but a translation
of selections from Whitman's *Leaves of Grass* (324 pages) published
in 1955 lifts the bamboo curtain slightly.[406] In his preface the translator, T'u-nan Ch'u, says he began translating Whitman's poems
thirty years ago (1925), sending out "the rendered pieces, a few at a
time, to the periodicals that would accept them. Later they were
collected and published in book form." (Does this mean before
1955?) The bibliographical details are missing. But the earlier translations have obviously been revised, for the reviewer of this interesting volume, Angela Chih-Ying Jung Palandri, says that the
simplified written characters have been used, which of course were
introduced by Mao Tse-tung. Also in a few places Whitman's words
have been slightly slanted to favor Chinese Communist politics—or
what was the country's politics in 1955—though on the whole the
reviewer finds the translation accurate. Furthermore, the preface
ends with these sentences:

Whitman is indeed the most distinguished poet of realism and democracy. His poetry serves not only as a warning flare to ward off the American ruling reactionary groups in their military expansion, racial prejudice, and abuse of human rights, but it also serves as a shining banner guiding all the peoples, including the American people, who strive for real democracy that leads to world peace and progress.[407]

In view of the thaw in Chinese-American relations, it will be interesting to see what Walt Whitman's future will be in the People's Republic of China.

NOTES

NOTES FOR CHAPTER I

1. *The Good Gray Poet: A Vindication* was first published for O'Connor in pamphlet form by Bunce and Huntington, New York, 1866, but was reprinted in Richard Maurice Bucke's *Walt Whitman* (Philadelphia: David McKay, 1883), pp. 99-130. References in this chapter are made to the original pamphlet.

2. John Burroughs, *Notes on Walt Whitman as Poet and Person* (New York: American News Co., 1867). A second revised and enlarged edition was published in New York by J. S. Redfield, 1871, but references in this chapter are given to the 1867 edition. For argument that Whitman wrote earlier chapters of this book see F. P. Hier, Jr., "End of a Literary Mystery," *American Mercury*, I, 471-78 (April, 1924).

3. Edward Carpenter, *Days with Walt Whitman* (London: George Allen, 1906), 37.

4. Horace Traubel, *In Re Walt Whitman* (Philadelphia: David McKay, 1893), v.

5. See *Specimen Days*, in *Prose Works 1892*, ed. Floyd Stovall (New York University Press, 1963), I, 5. Dr. Bucke says 1635 [p. 13], but there is no evidence for this date. Bliss Perry discovered that the Rev. Zechariah Whitman had no children, *Walt Whitman: His Life and Works* (Boston: Houghton Mifflin, 1906), p. 2, note 2.

6. *Prose Works 1892* (ed. Stovall), I, 288.

7. Hippolyte Adolphe Taine expressed this doctrine in his famous intro- ·duction to his *L'Histoire de la littérature anglaise* (1864), translated into English by H. Van Laun in 1873.

8. Richard Maurice Bucke, *Cosmic Consciousness: A Study in the Evolu-

tion of the Human Mind (Philadelphia: Innes and Sons, 1901). Fourth ed., New York: E. P. Dutton, 1923.

9. Charles N. Elliot, *Walt Whitman as Man, Poet and Friend* (Boston: Richard G. Badger, 1915), 50.

10. Harold Blodgett, *Walt Whitman in England* (Ithaca: Cornell University Press, 1934).

11. Moncure D. Conway, "Walt Whitman," *The Fortnightly Review*, VI, 538-48 (Oct. 15, 1866).

12. See William Sloane Kennedy, *Reminiscences of Walt Whitman* (London: Alexander Gardner, 1896), 51-74.

13. Conway (see note 11 above) omitted this implausible statement in his *Autobiography* (Boston: Houghton, Mifflin and Co., 1905), I, 218.

14. "Walt Whitman's Poems," *The London Chronicle*, July 6, 1867.

15. *Poems by Walt Whitman* (London: John Camden Hotten, 1868).

16. See Blodgett, 25-30.

17. *Poems* (ed. Rossetti), 3-4.

18. Emory Holloway, *Walt Whitman* (New York: Alfred A. Knopf, 1926), 257-64.

19. *In Re Walt Whitman*, 41-55.

20. *The Westminster Review*, XCVI, 33-68 (July, 1871); reprinted in *Studies in Literature* (London, 1878).

21. Published in the Canterbury Poets Series (London: Walter Scott, 1886).

22. William Gay, *Walt Whitman: His Relation to Science and Philosophy* (Melbourne: Firth and M'Cutcheon, 1895).

23. John Addington Symonds, *Walt Whitman: A Study* (London: George Routledge, New York: E. P. Dutton, 1893), 41.

24. Quoted by Edward Carpenter, 142-43.

25. J. A. Symonds, 92-93.

26. See note 19 above.

27. Chap. V.

28. Thomas Donaldson, *Walt Whitman, the Man* (New York: Harper, 1896).

29. John Burroughs, *Walt Whitman, A Study* [not to be confused with *Notes*, see note 2 above] (Boston: Houghton Mifflin, 1896), 4.

30. *Birds and Poets* (Boston: Houghton Mifflin, 1877, 1895), 188.

31. *The Complete Writings of Walt Whitman*, issued under the editorial supervision of his literary executors, Richard Maurice Bucke, Thomas B. Harned, and Horace L. Traubel; with additional bibliographical and critical material by Oscar Lovell Triggs (New York and London: G. P. Putnam's Sons, 1902).

32. Kennedy, 76.

33. John Townsend Trowbridge, *My Own Story: With Recollections of Noted Persons* (Boston: Houghton Mifflin, 1903), 366-67.

34. Cf. testimony of Whitman's friends on his "unconscious fabrications" regarding the mysterious "children"—Clara Barrus, *Whitman and Burroughs: Comrades* (Boston: Houghton Mifflin, 1931), 336-38.

35. See Introduction to *Calamus* [Whitman's letters to Peter Doyle], ed. R. M. Bucke (Boston: Laurens Maynard, 1897), 25. Also *Complete Writings*, VIII, 7.

36. *In Re Walt Whitman*, 34.

37. Quoted by Edward Carpenter, 150.

38. Sculley Bradley, "Walt Whitman on Timber Creek," *American Literature*, V, 235-46 (Nov., 1933).

39. Henry Bryan Binns, *A Life of Walt Whitman* (London: Methuen, 1905), 51.

40. Oscar L. Triggs, *Browning and Whitman: A Study in Democracy* (Chicago: University of Chicago, 1893).

41. Cf. Chap. V, 295.

42. Schlaf's best known work is his monograph *Walt Whitman*, 1904, published as Vol. XVIII of *Die Dichtung*.

43. Eduard Bertz, *Der Yankee-Heiland: Ein Beitrag zur Modernen Religionsgeschichte* (Dresden: Verlag von Carl Reissner, 1906), 100.

44. W. C. Rivers in *Walt Whitman's Anomaly* (London, 1913) makes a similar classification: "If Walt Whitman was homosexual, then, to what variety of male inversion did he belong? Essentially the *passive* kind, as one might expect from his pronounced feminine nature," p. 64. Edward Carpenter in *Some Friends of Walt Whitman: A Study in Sex-psychology* (London, 1924), accuses Rivers of having accentuated "the petty or pathological marks," p. 14. Carpenter thinks that Nature may be evolving a new form of humanity, "inclusive of male and female."

45. Bertz finds striking parallels between Novalis and Whitman's doctrine that "there is really no evil in the world," 146-47.

46. William Sloane Kennedy, *The Fight of A Book for the World* (West Yarmouth, Mass.: Stonecroft Press, 1926), 93.

47. *With Walt Whitman in Camden: January 21—April 7, 1889* (Carbondale: Southern Illinois University Press, 1959). (Counted as Vol. IV in ser.)

48. See note 34 above.

49. George Rice Carpenter, *Walt Whitman* (New York: Macmillan, 1909), 64 (note).

50. *Walt Whitman: the Man and His Work*, translated from the French by Ellen FitzGerald (Garden City: Doubleday, Page and Co., 1920). The translator states: ". . . I have felt justified in abridging M. Balzagette's treatment of the New Orleans episode, not that it may not be true but that it is a mystery which neither H. B. Binns nor he can clear by elaborate guess work; I have also as much as is consistent with the unity of the book lightened his emphasis on the *Leaves of Grass* conflict," viii. The warm description of Whitman's supposed first sexual ecstasies are freely deleted.

51. Léon Bazalgette, *Walt Whitman: L'Homme et son oeuvre* (Paris: Mercure de France, 1908), 92. Quotations from these passages which Miss Fitzgerald so discreetly omitted are kept in the original in order to avoid any confusion between the French and American versions of Bazalgette's biography.

52. Cf. note 42 above. Johannes Schlaf also wrote *Walt Whitman Homosexueller*, Kritische Revision einer Whitman-Abhandlung von Dr. Eduard Bertz (Minden: Bruns' Verlag, 1906).

53. FitzGerald trans. of Bazalgette, 220-21.

54. Basil De Selincourt, *Walt Whitman: A Critical Study* (London: Martin Secker, 1914), 18.

55. *Walt Whitman: Oeuvres choisies, poémes et proses*, traduits par Jules Laforgue [et autres], précédes d'une étude par Valéry Larbaud (Paris: Gallimard, 1930–6 éd.), 43.

56. D. H. Lawrence, "Whitman," *Studies in Classic American Literature* (New York: Albert Boni, 1923), 260; Doubleday Anchor Book, 188. The earlier, "Uncollected Versions," of this book has been edited by Armin Arnold, with a Preface by Harry T. Moore, *The Symbolic Meaning* (London: Centaur Press, 1962); Whitman, 253-64.

57. Gerald Bullett, *Walt Whitman: A Study and a Selection* (London: Grant Richards, 1924), 27. Bullett has in mind Cleveland Rodgers and John Black's *The Gathering of the Forces* [editorials from Brooklyn *Eagle*] (New York: G. P. Putnam's Sons, 1920), 2 vols.; and Emory Holloway's *Uncollected Poetry and Prose of Walt Whitman* (New York: Doubleday, 1921), 2 vols.

58. John Bailey, *Walt Whitman* (New York: Macmillan, 1926), 197.

59. See note 57 above.

60. Emory Holloway, "Walt Whitman's Love Affairs," *The Dial*, LXIX, 473-83 (Nov., 1920). In this article Holloway also discusses the evidence for an affair with a married woman in Washington.

61. Emory Holloway, *Whitman* (Biog.), 66.

62. Jean Catel, *Walt Whitman: La Naissance du Poète* (Paris: Les Éditions Rieder, 1929), 41. (Trans. by G. W. A.)

63. "Il est certain, d'un côté, que Walt n'entretenait pas avec les jeunes filles de ces relations sentimentales (à la Byron) dont il s'est moqué et que, d'un autre côté, Walt Whitman fréquentait les heux de plaisir, il ne pouvait étranger aux joies sexuelles . . . Il est probable que le jeune Walt connut de plaisir des sens et que, sans doute, New-York lui offirit les facilités de l'amour professionel . . .", 254.

64. Frederik Schyberg, *Walt Whitman* (København: Gyldendalske Boghandel, 1933). Translated by Evie Allison Allen, with Introduction by Gay Wilson Allen (New York: Columbia University Press, 1951). All references are to the translation.

65. See Schyberg, 53 and 75; Clara Barrus, 339.

66. Notebook entry for April 16, 1861, first quoted by Binns, 181.

67. Schyberg, 342, note 77.

68. Edgar Lee Masters, *Whitman* (New York: Charles Scribner's Sons, 1937), 142. The authorities used by Masters are: Edward Carpenter, *The Intermediate Sex*; De Joux, *Die Enterbten des Liebes-glückes*; and Havelock Ellis, *Psychology of Sex*.

69. Esther Shephard, *Walt Whitman's Pose* (New York: Harcourt, Brace, 1938), 141. Mrs. Shephard was not the first, however, to exploit the "pose" theory. That doubtful honor goes to Harvey O'Higgins for his attack on the poet in "Alias Walt Whitman," *Harper's Magazine*, CLVIII, 698-707 (May, 1929), later published (same title) in New York: W. W. Stone, 1929, 49 pp.; limited edition, 1930. For a good critique of both Shephard and O'Higgins see F. I. Carpenter, "Walt Whitman's 'Eidólon'," *College English*, III, 534-45 (March, 1942).

70. Whitman "never possessed a great poet's imagination" nor "mastery over his materials," and "he revised and rejected not as an artist but rather as the poseur that he was, fame-greedy and fearful lest his secret be betrayed," —Shephard, 242.

71. Cf. Gay Wilson Allen, "Walt Whitman and Jules Michelet," *Études anglaises*, I, 230-37 (May, 1937); and "The Foreground" in *A Reader's Guide to Walt Whitman* (New York: Farrar, Straus, and Giroux, Noonday ser., 1970), 17–44.

72. Haniel Long, *Walt Whitman and the Springs of Courage* (Santa Fe: Writers Editions, 1938).

73. Edward Hungerford, "Walt Whitman and His Chart of Bumps," *American Literature*, II, 350-84 (Jan., 1931). See also Arthur Wrobel, "Whitman and the Phrenologists: the Divine Body and the Sensuous Soul," *PMLA*, LXXXIX, 17-23 (Jan., 1974).

74. Newton Arvin, *Whitman* (New York: Macmillan, 1938), 161.

75. *Ibid.*, 33: "We shall find no other dose so acrid or so hard to swallow . . . [as] his rather inglorious record in the days of the Abolitionists."

76. Clifton J. Furness, *Walt Whitman's Workshop: A Collection of Unpublished Manuscripts* (Cambridge: Harvard University Press, 1928).

77. *American Literature*, XIII, 423-32 (January 1942).

78. Privately printed for the author.

79. The description of the "capricious and headstrong—but tender and very affectionate—sister Mary" in Whitman's juvenile story, "The Half Breed," is evidently his own sister. See Molinoff, 4 ff.

80. Published by Macmillan in 1955; reprinted by Grove Press in 1959; revised edition, New York Universtiy Press, 1967, 1972.

81. Furness did indeed complete a manuscript, but over a dozen publishers found it unworthy of publication. After Furness's death I acquired his manuscript and notebooks into which he had transcribed unpublished holographs. These copies were useful in locating manuscript material (and for

some not located), but the biography was useless—a pathetic failure, perhaps partly the result of Furness's rapid decline in health. I have deposited this unpublished biography in the Fales Collection of the Bobst Library, New York University, where anyone who is interested may examine it.—G.W.A.

82. See note 64 above.

83. Constance Rourke, *American Humor: A Study in National Character* (New York: Harcourt, Brace, 1931), esp. Chap. VI, "I Hear America Singing."

84. D. H. Lawrence, Chap. 12. See note 56 above.

85. The "I" in "Song of Myself is "half-heroic, half-ironic," Leslie Fiedler, Introduction to *Whitman*, Laurel Poetry Series (New York: Dell Publishing Co., 1959), 16.

86. Introduction to *Walt Whitman's Leaves of Grass: The First (1855) Edition* (New York: Viking, 1959), esp. x-xiv.

87. Letter dated February 7, 1882, in *The Correspondence of Walt Whitman*, ed. Edwin H. Miller (New York University Press, 1964), III, 266. (Whitman wrote "pourtray.")

88. "Death of Thomas Carlyle," *Prose Works 1892* (ed. Stovall), I, 248-62.

89. Chase quotes only part of the sentence in Whitman's letter to Bucke (see note 87 above); it ends: ". . . but let that pass—I have left it [the biography] as you wrote it." It is now known, however, that Whitman did write and emend a considerable part of the book—see *Walt Whitman's Autograph Revision of the Analysis of Leaves of Grass* (For Dr. R. M. Bucke's *Walt Whitman*), New York: New York University Press, 1974. This edition reproduces the second part of Bucke's *Walt Whitman*, the analysis of *Leaves of Grass* and the quotations in the Appendix supplied by Whitman. Quentin Anderson has written a long Introduction for this edition, which is based only on the manuscript owned by Daniel Maggin; other manuscript versions are in the Duke University Library and the Charles E. Feinberg Collection in the Library of Congress.

90. Jan Christian Smuts, *Walt Whitman: A Study in the Evolution of Personality*, ed. Alan L. McLeod (Detroit: Wayne State University Press, 1973), 26. In 1895 Smuts submitted the manuscript of this book to two British publishers, both of whom rejected it. The manuscript remained unpublished until this posthumous edition.

91. See above pp. 277-278.

92. Joseph Jay Rubin, *The Historic Whitman* (University Park: The Pennsylvania State University Press, 1973).

NOTES FOR CHAPTER II

1. For many years Whitman scholars have counted *nine* editions of

Leaves of Grass, but William White, who is preparing the definitive bibliography for *The Collected Writings of Walt Whitman* (New York University Press) says only *six* fit the strict definition of bibliographical authorities. See "Editions of *Leaves of Grass*: How Many?", *Walt Whitman Review*, XIX, 111 (September 1973). Ronald B. McKerrow in *Introduction to Bibliography for Literary Students* (Oxford, 1927) defines an edition as "the whole number of copies of a book printed at any time or times from one setting-up of type (including copies printed from the stereotype or electrotype plates made from the setting-up of type)...," 175. By this definition the true editions of *Leaves of Grass* were printed in 1855, 1856, 1860, 1867, 1871, and 1881. All other so-called editions are reprints or "issues," using a former setting of type (or unbound sheets from a former printing) to which some new (or revised) poems were added in a new setting of type. More bibliographical details will be given below in descriptions of the "issues" of 1876, 1892, and 1897. The Comprehensive Reader's Edition of *Leaves of Grass*, edited by Harold W. Blodgett and Sculley Bradley (New York University Press, 1965), contains all the poems ever included in an edition or issue of *Leaves of Grass*, plus the posthumous "Old Age Echoes" and other unpublished or uncollected poems. This is the most complete and scholary of all editions of *Leaves of Grass*.

2. For example: "['Leaves of Grass' must be] considered as a growth and as related to the author's own life process. . . . Succeeding editions have the character of expansive growths, like the rings of a tree. . . ." Oscar Triggs, "The Growth of 'Leaves of Grass,' " *The Complete Writings of Walt Whitman* (New York and London: G. P. Putnam's Sons, 1902), X, 102. But Frederik Schyberg declares that: "Bogen er nok et levende Hele, men dens Historie fremgaar ikke af Ringene i den som de nu er lagt," 17. (The book is a living unit but in its present state [i.e., final text] its history is *not* shown by annual rings of growth.)

3. Reader's Ed. of *L. G.* (see note 1 above), 713.

4. In "Passage to India" Whitman uses "justify" in the Miltonic sense several times.

5. Reader's Ed. of *L. G.* 713.

6. *Ibid.*, 728.

7. From a manuscript draft of an unpublished preface first dated May 31, 1861, then redated May 31, 1870. Printed in Clifton J. Furness, *Walt Whitman's Workshop* (Harvard University Press, 1928), 135-37.

8. Found in a rejected passage for "A Backward Glance," printed in "Notes and Fragments," ed. Dr. R. M. Bucke, in *Complete Writings* (see note 2 above), IX, 17.

9. Furness, *Workshop*, 9-10.

10. R. M. Bucke, *Walt Whitman* (Philadelphia: David McKay, 1883), 147.

11. Quoted by Clara Barrus, *Whitman and Burroughs, Comrades* (Boston:

Houghton Mifflin, 1931), 318: letter dated Feb. 12, 1896.

12. See note 2 above.

13. See note 8.

14. Reader's Ed. of *L. G.*, 560, note.

15. Stuart P. Sherman's chronological edition of *Leaves of Grass* (New York: Charles Scribner's, 1922), contains none of the poems published after 1881. The revised *Viking Portable Whitman* (New York: Viking Press, 1974) reprints texts of some 1855, 1856, and 1860 poems, but it is a selected anthology. Blodgett and Bradley in their Reader's Ed. include the rejected and unpublished poems, but they base their text on the one "authorized" by the poet in 1892.

16. Basil De Selincourt, *Walt Whitman: A Study* (London: Martin Secker, 1914), 164.

17. Jean Catel, *Walt Whitman: La Naissance du Poète* (Paris: Éditions Rieder, 1929).

18. Floyd Stovall, "Main Drifts in Whitman's Poetry," *American Literature*, IV, 3-21 (March 1932).

19. Killis Campbell, "The Evolution of Whitman as Artist," American Literature, VI, 254-63 (November 1934).

20. See note 1 above.

21. Schyberg (trans.), 12.

22. Irving C. Story, "The Growth of *Leaves of Grass*: A Proposal for a Variorum Edition," *Pacific University Bulletin*, XXXVII, 1-11 (February 1941).

23. *Ibid.*, 4.

24. "The Problem of a Variorum Edition of Whitman's *Leaves of Grass*," *English Institute Annual, 1941* (New York: Columbia University Press, 1942), 128-37.

25. *Pacific University Bulletin*, XXXVIII, No. 3, pp. 1-12 (Jan., 1942).

26. "The Poet," second paragraph.

27. Carl F. Strauch, "The Structure of Walt Whitman's Song of Myself," *English Journal* (College Ed.), XXVII, 597-607 (September 1938).

28. *Leaves of Grass: The First (1855) Edition* (New York: Viking, 1959).

29. James E. Miller, *A Critical Guide to Leaves of Grass* (Chicago: University of Chicago, 1957), 6-35.

30. Evelyn Underhill, *Mysticism: A Study in the Nature and Development of Man's Spiritual Consciousness* (London: Methuen, 11th ed., 1926).

31. V. K. Chari, *Walt Whitman in the Light of Vedantic Mysticism* (Lincoln: University of Nebraska Press, 1965).

32. *Walt Whitman's Poems*, eds. Gay Wilson Allen and Charles T. Davis (New York University Press, 1955), 9.

33. Chari, 124.

34. Roy Harvey Pearce, *The Continuity of American Poetry* (Princeton: Princeton University Press, 1961), 73.

35. Schyberg (trans.), 124.

36. Edwin H. Miller, *Walt Whitman's Poetry* (New York University Press, 1968), 72.

37. Schyberg (trans.), 59.

38. Cowley, x.

39. See letter to Mrs. Sarah Tyndale quoted by G. W. Allen in *The Solitary Singer* (New York: Macmillan, 1955), 217. *Correspondence*, I, 42.

40. This version is printed from the holograph letter now in the Charles E. Feinberg Collection at the Library of Congress. Whitman printed it in his 1856 *Leaves of Grass* (345-46) with slight alterations in punctuation.

41. See "Mutations in Whitman's Art," *Walt Whitman as Man, Poet, and Legend* (Carbondale: Southern Illinois University Press, 1961), 46-62; reprinted in *Walt Whitman: A Collection of Criticism*, ed. Arthur Golden (New York: McGraw-Hill, 1974).

42. Chari, 41.

43. Edwin H. Miller, 200.

44. Richard Chase, *Walt Whitman Reconsidered* (New York: William Sloane, 1955), 107.

45. For interpretation of Whitman's phrenological vocabulary, see Edward Hungerford, "Walt Whitman and His Chart of Bumps," *American Literature*, II, 350-84 (January 1931).

46. See Willie T. Weathers, "Whitman's Poetic Translations of His 1855 Preface," *American Literature*, XIX, 21-40 (March 1947).

47. *Nature* (1836), "Language."

48. See Fredson Bowers, *Whitman's Manuscripts: Leaves of Grass (1860): A Parallel Test* (Chicago: University of Chicago Press, 1955), xxxv.

49. *Complete Writings*, IX, 6.

50. Sarah Tyndale letter, *Correspondence*, I, 42 (Miller points out that Whitman's date of "July 20" was a mistake for June 20.

51. See note 48 above.

52. Bowers, 3.

53. *Ibid.*, xxxvi, 100. Whitman numbered these twelve poems with Roman numbers, but Bowers found them scattered throughout the "Calamus" MSS.

54. No. VIII, Bowers, 82.

55. *Ibid.*, 88-89; quoted in *Solitary Singer*, 223.

56. Nos. IV and VIII; *Solitary Singer*, 223-24.

57. Bowers, 69.

58. *Ibid.*, 115.

59. *Ibid.*, 122.

60. Reader's Ed. *L. G.*, 751, 160n.

61. *Complete Writings*, X, 18.
62. *Ibid.*,IX, 150.
63. *Ibid.*, 125.
64. *Ibid.*, 134.
65. *Ibid.*, 145; in "Chants Democratic," No. 8, changed to "Song at Sunset" in 1867, and thereafter, 1. 39.
66. Bowers, 161.
67. *Ibid.*, 173.
68. *Ibid.*, 85-86.
69. *Ibid.*, 192.
70. *Ibid.*, 211.
71. "Bardic Symbols" was not in the manuscripts Bowers edited, an indication that it was written after Whitman had the Rome Brothers set up poems he hoped to use in a third edition, and he did not revise the *Atlantic Monthly* text before printing it in his third edition about the same time it appeared in the magazine.
72. Schyberg (Allen translation) comments on the significance of this passage, 147-48; also on the conclusion, which read in 1859 and '60: "Which I do not forget,/ But fuse the song of two together," changed later to "song of my dusky demon and brother, . . ."
73. Quoted by Bowers, xxxii; G. W. Allen, *The Solitary Singer*, 236-37.
74. See *The Solitary Singer*, 237; *Correspondence*, I, 49.
75. *Correspondence*, I, 48, n. 7: Thayer and Eldridge to W. W., June 14: "The first edition is nearly all gone, and the second is all printed and ready for binding. . . ."
76. The first binding was probably yellow; a later, green; and another, plum-colored. As many as twelve different bindings have survived, according to Carolyn Wells and Alfred F. Goldsmith in *A Concise Bibliography* (Boston: Houghton Mifflin Co., 1922), 8. After the bankruptcy of Thayer & Eldridge the plates came into the possession of a piratical printer in New York, Richard Worthington, who printed many copies without the poet's permission. On the verso of the title-page the Thayer & Eldridge edition bears these words: "Electrotyped at the Boston Stereotype Foundry. Printed by George C. Rand and Avery." Spurious copies lack these words.
77. Esther Shephard, *Walt Whitman's Pose* (New York: Harcourt, Brace & Co., 1938), discovered that the butterfly was a photographer's prop, p. 250-52.
78. The drawing could be of either a sunrise or sunset, but the latter was probably intended because of the sunset in "Crossing Brooklyn Ferry."
79. Whitman also used a butterfly on the backstrip of his 1881 edition of *Leaves of Grass*, and a famous photograph taken of him in 1883 shows him posing with the same cardboard butterfly on his forefinger: See *The Artistic Legacy of Walt Whitman*, edited by Edwin H. Miller (New York University Press, 1970), figure 18 and p. 134.

80. The old poems are: No. 1, adaptations from 1855 preface; "Poem of Many in One," 1856; "As I Sat Alone by Blue Ontario's Shore," 1867; "By Blue Ontario's Shore," 1881. No. 2, "Broad-Axe Poem," 1856; "Song of the Broad-Axe," 1867. No. 3, second poem in 1855; "Poem of The Daily Work of The Workmen and Workwomen of These States," 1856; finally "A Song for Occupations," 1881. No. 5, "Poem of the Proposition of Nakedness," 1856; "Respondez," 1867; dropped 1881—parts transferred. No. 6, "Poem of Remembrance for a Girl or Boy of These States," 1856. No. 15, "Poem of The Heart of The Son of Manhattan," 1856; "Excelsior," 1867.

81. New poems, to use later titles, were: "Apostroph" (never reprinted); "Our Old Feuillage"; "With Antecedents"; "Song at Sunset"; "Thoughts," sec. 1; "To a Historian"; "Thoughts," sec. 2; "Vocalism," sec. 1; "Laws for Creation"; "Poets to Come"; "Mediums"; "On Journeys through the States"; "Me Imperturbe"; "I Was Looking a Long While"; "I Hear America Singing"; "As I Walk these Broad Majestic Days."

82. Schyberg (translation), 171.

83. In a letter to Harrison Blake, Dec. 7, [1856], *The Correspondence of Henry David Thoreau*, eds. Walter Harding and Carl Bode (New York University Press, 1958), 444.

84. "Appreciation of Walt Whitman," *The Nation* (London), XXIX, 617 (July 23, 1921).

85. Emory Holloway, "Walt Whitman's Love Affairs," *The Dial*, LXIX, 473-83 (Nov., 1920). Holloway discusses, among other hypotheses, a love affair with a married woman in Washington, D. C.

86. Schyberg (trans.), 158.

87. The great Brazilian sociologist Gilberto Freyre says Whitman's "fraternalistic sense of life" was "so vibrant as to seem at times homosexualism gone mad whereas it was probably only bisexualism sublimated into fraternalism," in *O Camarada Whitman*, translated in *Walt Whitman Abroad*, ed. Gay Wilson Allen (Syracuse University Press, 1955), 229.

88. John Addington Symonds, *Walt Whitman: A Study* (London: George Routledge & Sons, 1893), 158.

89. Emory Holloway, *Whitman: An Interpretation in Narrative* (New York: Knopf, 1926), 81.

90. *Leaves of Grass By Walt Whitman: Facsimile Edition of the 1860 Text*, ed. with Introduction by Roy Harvey Pearce (Ithaca: Cornell University Press, 1961).

91. Quentin Anderson in his Introduction to *Walt Whitman's Revision of the Analysis of Leaves of Grass (For Dr. R. M. Bucke's Walt Whitman)*, (New York University Press, 1974), says "this sentimental poem . . . has proved a trap for critics," 35.

92. "Whitman's Awakening to Death," in *The Presence of Walt Whitman: Selected Papers from the English Institute*, ed. with a Foreword by R. W. B. Lewis (New York: Columbia University Press, 1962), 22.

93. Facsimile 1860 Ed., xxxiii.

94. *Presence of Walt Whitman*, 80.

95. *Correspondence*, I, 48, note 7.

96. Arthur Golden, editor, *Walt Whitman's Blue Book: the 1860-61 Leaves of Grass Containing His Manuscript Additions and Revisions* (New York Public Library, 1968), xxxiv.

97. "Banner at Day-Break," retitled "Song of the Banner at Day-Break"; "Washington's First Battle" became "The Centenarian's Story, Volunteer of 1861 (At Washington Park, Brooklyn, assisting the Centenarian)"; "Pictures," not published by Whitman but edited by Emory Holloway (New York, 1927); "Quadrel," probably "Chanting the Square Deific"—also "Quadriune" or "Deus Quadriune," written over CONTENTS (p. iii) in Blue Book; "Sonnets," probably some of the "Calamus" poems. See note 53 above.

98. These manuscripts, now in the Oscar Lion Collection of the New York Public Library, have been edited by Furness (see note 7 above), 117-37; 167-74—"paths to the house," 135.

99. See Gay Wilson Allen and Charles T. Davis, eds., *Walt Whitman's Poems* (New York University Press, 1955), 16-21.

100. Furness, *Workshop*, 137.

101. *Workshop*, 127.

102. *Workshop*, 130.

103. *Workshop*, 131.

104. *Workshop*, 136.

105. Pearce, *Facsimile Edition of the 1860 Text*, xlvii.

106. The copy is now in the Lion Collection of the NYPL. See note 104 above.

107. Vol. I contains the facsimile; Vol. II, Golden's Introduction and Textual Analysis.

108. Golden, *Blue Book*, II, lvi ff.

109. Golden, *Blue Book*, II, lii.

110. Charles I. Glicksberg, *Walt Whitman and the Civil War* (Philadelphia: University of Pennsylvania Press, 1933), 8.

111. Schyberg (trans.), 181.

112. The "Drum-Taps" of the final edition of *Leaves of Grass* contains only about half of the original collection; thirty-three poems were shifted to other sections and six were added to the group after 1865.

113. Letter dated March 31, 1863, *Correspondence*, I, 85-86.

114. However, Clara Barrus in *Life and Letters of John Burroughs* (Boston: Houghton Mifflin, 1925) says that Miss Juliette H. Beach was "The friend to whom Whitman wrote 'Out of the rolling ocean.' She wrote many beautiful letters to Walt which J. B. tried in vain to get her consent to publish. She died many years ago." I, 120, note.

115. Wells and Goldsmith, 11.

116. G. L. Sixbey, "Chanting the Square Deific—A Study in Whitman's Religion," *American Literature*, IX, 174 (May, 1937).

117. *Ibid.*, 72.

118. They are: "Inscription (One's Self I Sing)," "The Runner," "Tears! Tears! Tears!," "Aboard at a Ship's Helm," "When I Read the Book," "The City Dead-House."

119. With its separate title-page and pagination this annex appears to be an independent publication, though it has no copyright notice.

120. Wells and Goldsmith, 14.

121. In his final revision (1871) of this poem Whitman reversed the order of 1 and 2 as summarized here.

122. The context indicates that "offspring" means national results, not biological—as in the American war in Viet Nam.

123. An 84-page pamphlet, with green cover, printed by J. S. Redfield, New York. Title page: *Democratic/ Vistas./* Washington, D. C./ 1871.

124. Quotations from "Democratic Vistas" in *Prose Works 1892* (Stovall), II, 389. Bracketed numbers in subsequent quotations refer to this edition.

125. Whitman never defined "personalism," but he used it to include his whole program of all-round development of the self and the individual, including health, eugenics, education, moral and social conscience.

126. Pamphlet of 24 pages, published by Roberts Brothers, Boston, 1871. See Wells and Goldsmith, 18.

127. A 120-page pamphlet, with green cover, printed by J. S. Redfield, New York. Title page: *Passage/ to/ India./* Washington, D.C./ 1871.

128. Lines 4, 5, 6 of "The Wound Dresser" (1881) were used in 1871 and 1876 as epigraph for the "Drum-Taps" cluster: "(Arous'd and angry . . . watch the dead;)."

129. *Prose Works 1892* (Stovall), II, 458-64.

130. W. L. Werner, "Whitman's 'The Mystic Trumpeter' as Auto-biography," *American Literature*, VII, 455-58 (January 1936).

131. Redpath letter, dated October 28, 1863, quoted by Roy Basler in Introduction to his facsimile edition of *Walt Whitman's Memoranda [&] Death of Abraham Lincoln* (Indiana University Press, 1962), 11-12, *Correspondence*, I, 170n, 171-72.

132. Wells and Goldsmith, 19.

133. The three poems which Whitman did not include in any later collections: "Two Rivulets," "From My Last Years," "In Former Songs." Another poem, "Or from That Sea of Time," was incorporated into "As Consequent, Etc." (1881), with omissions. The other poems in this group of *TR*: "Eidolons," "Spain, 1873–'74," "Prayer of Columbus," "Out from Behind This Mask," "To a Locomotive in Winter," "The Ox-Tamer," "Wandering at Morn," "An Old Man's Thoughts at School," "With All Thy Gifts," "After the Sea-Ships."

134. Reader's Ed. *L. G.*, 744-54.

135. *Ibid.*, 746.

136. *Ibid.*, 747.

137. *Ibid.*

138. "In Former Songs" (1876, *Two Rivulets*, p. 31) stresses this division in Whitman's poems, but it was dropped after 1876, probably because the poet had given up dividing his poems into two books.

139. Reader's Ed. *L. G.*, 751.

140. This issue contains 404 instead of 382 pages. See Wells and Goldsmith, 27.

141. See note 1 above.

142. See Emory Holloway, "Whitman's Embryonic Verse," *Southwest Review*, X, 28-40 (July 1925); also Introduction to *Pictures: An Unpublished Poem by Walt Whitman* (London: Faber and Gwyer, 1928).

143. See Adeline Knapp, "Walt Whitman and Jules Michelet, Identical Passages," *Critic*, XLIV, 467-68 (1907); also Gay W. Allen, "Walt Whitman and Jules Michelet," *Études Anglaises*, I, 230-37 (May 1937).

144. Barrus, xxiv.

145. Reader's Ed. *L. G.*, 712.

146. *Ibid.*, 562.

147. *Ibid.*, 564.

148. *Ibid.*, 566.

149. *Ibid.*, 570.

150. *Ibid.*, 581, note.

151. *Solitary Singer*, 459.

NOTES FOR CHAPTER III

1. By most biographers, but especially by Emory Holloway in Introduction to *The Uncollected Poetry and Prose of Walt Whitman* (New York: Doubleday, Doran, 1921).

2. Joseph Jay Rubin, *The Historic Whitman* (Pennsylvania State University Press, 1973), xii.

3. Horace Traubel, *With Walt Whitman in Camden* (New York: Appleton, 1908), II, 205.

4. For influence, G. W. Allen, *A Reader's Guide to Walt Whitman* (Farrar, Straus & Giroux, 1970), 21-22.

5. *Prose Works 1892* (Stovall, ed.), I, 13.

6. *Ibid.* 17.

7. *Solitary Singer*, 13.

8. *Prose Works 1892*, II, 639.

9. *Ibid.*, 645.

10. *Ibid.*, 647.

11. *Solitary Singer*, 208.

12. *Gathering of the Forces*, edited by Cleveland Rodgers and John Black (New York: G. P. Putnam's Sons, 1920), I, 23.

13. *Ibid.*, I, 33.

14. *Ibid.*, 229; cf. also 234-39.

15. *Ibid.*, 203.

16. *Ibid.*, 205-06.

17. *Ibid.*, 18.

18. *Ibid.*, 28.

19. *Ibid.*, II, 70-71.

20. *Ibid.*, I, 218.

21. *Ibid.*, 222.

22. *Ibid.*, 54.

23. "The House of Friends," New York *Tribune*, June 14, 1850; collected by Thomas L. Brasher in *The Early Poems and the Fiction of Walt Whitman* (New York University Press, 1963), 36-37.

24. *Ibid.*, 38-40.

25. Reader's Edition of *LG*, 713.

26. *Ibid.*, 714-15.

27. In "Song of Myself" Whitman called himself a "kosmos," perhaps meaning that his "greatest poet" in the 1855 Preface is an all-inclusive system, independent of outside forces. His preference for the Greek spelling, Κόδμος, which came from Sanskrit *cad*, "to distinguish one's self," indicates emphasis on independent order and harmony as an attribute of his own "divinity."

28. Reader's Edition of *LG*, 727.

29. *Ibid.*, 729.

30. *Ibid.*, 729-30.

31. Reprinted in *New York Dissected*, edited by Emory Holloway and Ralph Adimari (New York: Rufus Rockwell Wilson, 1936), 108.

32. *The Eighteenth Presidency!* A Critical Text [with an Introduction] edited by Edward F. Grier (University of Kansas Press, 1956).

33. *Ibid.*, 42.

34. *Ibid.*, 19-20.

35. *Ibid.*, 22.

36. *Ibid.*, 23.

37. *Ibid.*, 30.

38. *Ibid.*, 33.

39. *Ibid.*, 39.

40. *Ibid.*, 44.

41. "Song of Myself," sec. 27 and sec. 20.

42. Reader's Edition of *LG*, 721.

43. Traubel, II, 205. See also David Goodale, "Some of Walt Whitman's Borrowings," *American Literature*, X, 202-13 (May 1938).

344 WALT WHITMAN HANDBOOK

44. Traubel, II, 445.

45. Full title: *The Ruins; or Meditation on the Revolution of Empires*, by Count C. F. Volney, Count and Peer of France. . . . To Which is Added *The Law of Nature*. . . . (New York: Calvin Blanchard, n.d.) The French edition was published in 1791; the American translation after Volney's visit to Philadelphia in 1797—probably around 1800.

46. *Ruins*, 184.

47. *Ibid.*, 173.

48. *Ibid.*, 182.

49. *Ibid.*, 175.

50. *Ibid.*, 179.

51. See Peter Tompkins and Christopher Bird, *The Secret Life of Plants* (New York: Harper & Row, 1972), 125-26.

52. In addition to Tompkins and Bird (note 51, above), see also Arthur Koestler's discussion of "Evolution" (Chaps. XI and XII) in *The Ghost in the Machine* (New York: Macmillan, 1967), 151-71.

53. *Nature* (1836), part V. In *The Collected Works of Ralph Waldo Emerson*, edited by Robert E. Spiller and Alfred R. Ferguson (Harvard University Press, 1971), I, 25.

54. This is the argument of Pierre Teilhard de Chardin in *Man's Place in Nature: The Human Zoological Group*, translated by René Hague (New York: Harper & Row, 1966); and *The Phenomenon of Man*, translated by Bernard Wall (New York: Harper & Row, 1961).

55. *Man's Place in Nature*, 79-121.

56. *Uncollected Poetry and Prose of Walt Whitman*, II, 64.

57. *Ibid.*, 65.

58. *Ibid.*

59. *Ibid.*, 65-66.

60. *Ibid.*, 66.

61. *Ibid.*

62. *Ibid.*, 69-70.

63. *Ibid.*, 70. Floyd Stovall thinks that these trial lines of verse may have been written as late as 1854: See "Dating Whitman's Early Notebooks," *Studies in Bibliography* (University of Virginia), XXIV, 197-204 (1971).

64. "Going Somewhere" (1887).

65. Joseph Beaver, *Walt Whitman—Poet of Science* (New York: King's Crown Press, 1951; Octagon Press, 1974), 44.

66. *Ibid.*, 37-38.

67. *Ibid.*, 38.

68. *Ibid.*, 58.

69. Quoted by Beaver, 59-60.

70. *Ibid.*, 60.

71. See Edmund Reiss, "Whitman's Debt to Animal Magnetism," *PMLA*, LXXVIII, 80-88 (March 1963).

72. See Edward Hungerford, "Walt Whitman and His Chart of Bumps," (*American Literature*, II, 350-84) and Haniel Long, *Walt Whitman and the Springs of Courage* (Santa Fe, N. M.: Writers Editions, 1938). Also Arthur Wrobel, "Whitman and the Phrenologists: The Divine Body and the Sensuous Soul," *PMLA*, LXXXIX, 17-23 (January 1974).

73. *Vestiges* was published anonymously and Robert Chambers's authorship was not established until 1884. *New Century Cyclopedia of Names* (New York: Appleton-Century-Crofts, 1954). The book was so popular that the idea of "vestiges of creation" was known to many people who had not read the book.

74. *Nature* (1836), part viii; *Collected Works* (1971), I, 42.

75. "The Poet," first essay in second series (1844) of *Essays*, 15.

76. Reader's Edition of *LG*, 714.

77. Two recent examples: James E. Miller, " 'Song of Myself' as Inverted Mystical Experience," *A Critical Guide to* Leaves of Grass (University of Chicago Press, 1957), 6-35; and Malcolm Cowley, Introduction to *Walt Whitman's* Leaves of Grass: *The First (1855) Edition* (New York: Viking Press, 1959), esp. p. xii ff.

78. William James, *The Varieties of Religious Experience* (New York: Longmans, Green, and Co., 1902), 379.

79. *Ibid.*, 395.

80. *Ibid.*, 381.

81. *Ibid.*, 396, n.1.

82. *Prose Works 1892* (Stovall, ed.), I, 257-58.

83. Richard Maurice Bucke, *Cosmic Consciousness: A Study in the Evolution of the Human Mind* (New York: E. P. Dutton, 1901), 3.

84. *Prose Works 1892* (Stovall, ed.), II, 678.

85. Roger Asselineau, *The Evolution of Walt Whitman: The Creation of a Book* (Harvard University Press, 1962), 4.

86. Sister Flavia Maria, C. S. J., " 'Song of Myself': A Presage of Modern Teilhardian Paleontology," *Walt Whitman Review*, XV, 43-49 (March 1969).

87. Pierre Teilhard de Chardin, *The Divine Milieu* (New York: Harper & Row, 1960), 47. (Quoted by Sister Flavia Maria, 44.)

88. See Ray Benoit, "The Mind's Return: Whitman, Teilhard, and Jung," *Walt Whitman Review*, XIII, 21-28 (March 1968). However, Benoit does not mention *Building the Earth*, quoted below, and Benoit's parallels in Jung are omitted here.

89. Cf. Bucke, *Notes and Fragments*, 57; note No. 14.

90. Pierre Teilhard de Chardin, *Building the Earth* (Wilkes-Barre, Pa.: Dimensions Books, 1965), 63. (In this special edition, designed and illustrated by Sister Rose Ellen, Teilhard's sentences are printed as poetry; here they are quoted as prose.)

91. *Ibid.*, 71.

92. *Ibid.*, 117.

93. *The Galaxy* published "Democracy" in December, 1867, and "Personalism" in May 1868. Whitman intended to publish a third essay to be called "Literature," but it was not published, and possibly was not finished, though Whitman added his thoughts on literature to his book, *Democratic Vistas*, privately printed in Washington, D. C., in 1871. It was added to his *Prose Works* in 1882. See bibliographical note by Stovall in *Prose Works*, II, 361-62.

94. *Prose Works 1892* (Stovall, ed.), II, 362.

95. See Whitman's note, *Prose Works*, II, 375.

96. *Prose Works 1892*, II, 386.

97. *Ibid.*, 385.

98. *Ibid.*, 399.

100. Pierre Teilhard de Chardin, *The Future of Man* (New York: Harper & Row, 1964), 100.

101. *Prose Works* (Stovall, ed.), II, 409-10.

102. Quoted by Benoit, *WWR* XIII, 22, from *The Future of Man*, 35.

NOTES FOR CHAPTER IV

1. Hermann Bahr, in his Introduction to Max Hayek's translation, *Ich Singe Das Leben* (Leipzig, Wien, Zürich: E. P. Tall & Co., 1921), 7, says: "[*Grashalme*] ist kunstlos, es bringt eigentlich nur das Material für ein Kunstwerk, diesen Eindruck hat man immer wieder."

2. *Prose Works 1892*, ed. Floyd Stovall (New York University Press, 1964), II, 473.

3. Horace Traubel, *With Walt Whitman in Camden* (New York: Mitchell Kennerley, 1914), III, 84.

4. *Ibid.*, I, 163.

5. Basil De Selincourt, *Walt Whitman: A Critical Study* (London: Martin Secker, 1914), 73.

6. Clifton Joseph Furness, *Walt Whitman's Workshop* (Cambridge: Harvard University Press, 1928), 30.

7. Reader's Ed. *L. G.*, 712.

8. The three periods do not indicate editorial omission but Whitman's punctuation to indicate a caesura in the 1855 edition; sometimes four periods—the number was inconsistent.

9. Reader's Ed. *L. G.*, 570.

10. Preface to 1855 edition. Reader's Ed. *L. G.*, 714.

11. W. S. Kennedy, *Reminiscences of Walt Whitman* (London: Alexander Gardner, 1896), 151.

12. Reader's Ed. *L. G.*, 717.

13. "Song of Myself," 1. 13.

14. "A Backward Glance," Reader's Ed. *L. G.*, 566.

15. "Song of Myself," sec. 33.
16. "Salut au Monde!," sec. 4.
17. Reader's Ed. *L. G.*, 711.
18. Paul Elmer More, *Shelburne Essays*, 4th ser. (Boston: Houghton Mifflin, 1922), 203.
19. Harry B. Reed, "The Heraclitan Obsession of Walt Whitman," *The Personalist*, XV, 125-38 (April 1934).
20. For definition and history of the term, see Carl Enoch William Leonard Dahlström's Introduction to *Strindberg's Dramatic Expressionism* (Ann Arbor: University of Michigan, 1930), 3-10; 35-38; 221-26.
21. "By Blue Ontario's Shore," sec. 3.
22. See A. S. Cook, "The 'Authorized Version' and Its Influence," *Cambridge History of English Literature* (New York and London: G. P. Putnam's Sons, 1910), IV, 29-58.
23. See S. R. Driver, *Introduction to the Literature of the Old Testament* (New York: Charles Scribner's Sons, 1910), 361 ff. Also see E. Kautsch, *Die Poesie und die poetischen Bücher des Alten Testaments* (Tübingen und Leipzig, 1902), 2. Bishop Lowth first pointed out the prosodic principles of parallelism in the Bible in *De sacra poesi Hebraeorum praelectiones academiae Oxoni habitae*, 1753. See Driver, 362. In the main the Lowth system is the basis for R. G. Moulton's arrangement of Biblical poetry in his *Modern Reader's Bible* (New York: Macmillan, 1922). See also note 25 below.
24. For example, in American Indian rhythms. Cf. Mary Austin's *The American Rhythm* (New York: Harcourt, Brace, 1913).
25. Observed by many critics, but first elaborated by Gay Wilson Allen, "Biblical Analogies for Walt Whitman's Prosody," *Revue Anglo-Americaine*, X, 490-507 (Aug., 1933). Basis for same author's chapter on Whitman in *American Prosody* (New York: American Book Co., 1935), 217-43.
26. J. H. Gardiner, *The Bible as English Literature* (New York: Charles Scribner's Sons, 1906), 107.
27. Kautsch, 2.
28. Driver, 340.
29. Bliss Perry, *Walt Whitman* (Boston: Houghton Mifflin, 1906), 92.
30. George Rice Carpenter, *Walt Whitman* (New York: Macmillan, 1924), 42.
31. De Selincourt, 103-4.
32. E. C. Ross, "Whitman's Verse," *Modern Language Notes*, XLV, 363-64 (June 1930). Autrey Nell Wiley demonstrates this view in "Reiterative Devices in 'Leaves of Grass,'" *American Literature*, I, 161-70 (May 1929). She says: "In more than 10,500 lines in *Leaves of Grass*, there are, by my count, only twenty run-on lines," 161.
33. Whitman himself misdated this poem 1843. It was published in The New York *Tribune*, Supplement, March 22, 1850, and the occasion of the

WALT WHITMAN HANDBOOK

satire was Webster's speech on March 7, 1850, regarding the Fugitive Slave Law.

34. Reader's Ed. *L. G.*, 716.

35. Reader's Ed. *L. G.*, 711.

36. "Song of Myself," sec. 6.

37. Cf. "Song of Myself," sec. 33, and "Salut au Monde!"

38. Cf. Emile Lauvriere, *Repetition and Parallelism in Tennyson* (London: Oxford University Press, 1901).

39. Here again Emerson's theory preceded Whitman's practice. In the section on "Melody, Rhyme, and Form," in his essay "Poetry and Imagination" Emerson wrote: "Another form of rhyme is iteration of phrases. . . ."

40. See note 32 above.

41. P. Jannaccone, *La Poesia di Walt Whitman e L'Evoluzione delle Forme Ritmiche* (Torino, 1898), 64 ff. Translated by Peter Mitilineos. *Walt Whitman's Poetry and the Evolution of Rhythmic Forms* (Washington, D. C.: Microcard Editions, 1973).

42. Wiley, 161-62.

43. C. Alphonso Smith, *Repetition and Parallelism in English Verse* (New York, 1894), 9.

44. De Selincourt, 104-9.

45. Jannaccone (trans.), 70.

46. *Ibid.*, 74.

47. Sculley Bradley, "The Fundamental Metrical Principle in Whitman's Poetry," *American Literature*, X, 437-59 (January 1939).

48. Quoted by Perry from unpublished preface, 207; cf. Traubel, I, 414.

49. Samuel Taylor Coleridge, *Essays and Lectures on Shakespeare and Some Other Old Poets and Dramatists* (London: Everyman Library, n.d.), 46-47.

50. De Selincourt, 96-97.

51. Bradley, 447.

52. Would it not increase the pathos to read "all dark" and "desolate" with hovering accent? But this scansion would not affect Bradley's accent count.

53. "Song of Myself," sec. 8.

54. "Song of Myself," sec. 26. Compare the similar idea (and "I hear . . ." reiteration) in "Salut au Monde!," sec. 3, with caesural effect.

55. "Song of Myself," sec. 50.

56. Jannaccone (trans.), 93.

57. "Great are the Myths," sec. 1.

58. De Selincourt, 106-08.

59. Jean Catel, *Rythme et langage dans la 1re édition des "Leaves of Grass," 1855* (Paris: Rieder, 1930), 126.

60. "Song of Myself," sec. 15.

61. *Ibid.*, sec. 20.

62. *Ibid.*, sec. 30.

63. *Ibid.*, sec. 26.

64. "To the Leaven'd Soil They Trod."

65. F. O. Matthiessen, *American Renaissance* (New York: Oxford University Press, 1941), 549-77.

66. *Ibid.*, 565: poem quoted, "Had I the Choice."

67. Ware, 47.

68. Since "bone—one" and "grown—sown" are approximate rimes, the third and fourth lines are also tetrameter couplets.

69. *Complete Writings*, III, 161.

70. Ware, 53.

71. Catel, 84.

72. *An American Primer*, ed. Horace Traubel (Boston: Small, Maynard and Co., 1904), 12. Ed. William White, *Walt Whitman's Day-Books and Other Diaries* (New York University Press, 1975).

73. "Song of Myself," sec. 40 (1. 990).

74. Closing poem in third edition.

75. See Matthiessen, 517-32. In the first edition of *Leaves of Grass* Whitman was especially fond of such rare or obsolete words as *exurge* (p. 60), *caoutchouc* (p. 83), and *albescent* (p. 84).

76. See Louise Pound, "Walt Whitman and the French Language," *American Speech*, I, 421-30 (May 1926). Also Asselineau, II, 225-38.

77. Cf. Louise Pound, "Walt Whitman's Neologisms," *American Mercury*, IV, 199-201 (Feb. 1925). Louis Untermeyer, "Whitman and the American Language," New York *Evening Post*, May 31, 1919, calls Whitman "the father of the American language."

78. Cf. John Bailey, *Walt Whitman* (New York: Macmillan, 1926), 87 ff. Hugh l'Anson Fausset, *Walt Whitman: Poet of Democracy* (New Haven: Yale University Press, 1942) shares Bailey's lack of sympathy and understanding of the principles on which Whitman chose his diction and form. He simply regards the poet as ignorant and careless.

79. Reader's Ed. *L. G.*, 714. Cf. Jean Gorely, "Emerson's Theory of Poetry," *Poetry Review*, XXII, 263-73 (Aug. 1931), and Emerson Grant Sutcliffe, "Emerson's Theory of Literary Expression," *University of Illinois Studies in Language and Literature*, VIII, 9-143 (1923).

80. *American Primer*, 2.

81. Matthiessen, 518.

82. *American Primer*, 16-17.

83. Renamed in 1881 "Song of the Rolling Earth."

84. Version of 1856 edition; first three lines in this passage were dropped in 1881. See also "Song of Myself," sec. 25.

85. "Poem of the Sayers of the Words of the Earth" (1856); "Song of the Rolling Earth," sec. 1.

86. *Ibid.*, sec. 3.

87. See note 1, above.

88. See Reader's Ed. *L. G.*, 718; also "Song of Myself," sec. 12.

89. First published in "Whitman's Embryonic Verse," *Southwest Review*, X, 28-40 (July 1925), later in *Pictures: an Unpublished Poem by Walt Whitman*, Introduction and Notes by Emory Holloway (London: Faber and Gwyer, 1927); reprinted in Reader's Ed. *L. G.*, 642-49.

90. Richard Maurice Bucke, *Notes and Fragments* (London; Ontario, printed for the editor, 1899), 27.

91. *Ibid.*, 179.

92. Holloway, *Pictures*, 10-11. See also Allen and Davis, *Whitman's Poems*, 5-8.

NOTES FOR CHAPTER V

1. Harold W. Blodgett, "Whitman in 1960," *Walt Whitman Review*, VI, 23 (June 1960).

2. Reader's Ed. of *L. G.*, 711.

3. *Ibid.*, 729.

4. As early as 1900 Whitman was accepted as a major poet. See, for example, Barrett Wendell's *A Literary History of the United States* (New York: Charles Scribner's Sons, 1901), 465-79. But Randall Jarrell's defense of Whitman in "Walt Whitman: He Had His Nerve," *Kenyon Review*, XIV (Winter 1952), 63-71, marked a turning point in Whitman's reputation with leading poets and critics.

5. Reader's Ed. of *L. G.*, 562.

6. See *The Solitary Singer*, 472.

7. *Allgemeinen Zeitung*, Augsburg, April 24, 1868; reprinted in *Gesammelte Dichtung* (Stuttgart: Goschen'sche, 1877), IV, 86-87.

8. See Frederik Schyberg, *Walt Whitman*, trans. by Evie Allison Allen (New York: Columbia University Press, 1951), 220-24.

9. *Correspondence*, III, 259.

10. *Ibid.* Quoted by Kornei Chukovsky in "Walt Whitman's Greeting to the Russian People," *Sputnik*, June, 1967, pp. 88-93; reprinted in *Walt Whitman in Europe Today*, edited by Roger Asselineau and William White (Detroit: Wayne State University Press, 1972), 35-40. Whitman's letter, dated "Dec. 20, '81," quoted by Horst Frenz, editor, *Whitman and Rolleston: A Correspondence* (Indiana University Press, 1951), 49.

11. *Ibid.*, 89.

12. William Sloane Kennedy, *The Fight of a Book for the World: A Companion Volume to Leaves of Grass* (New York: privately printed, 1926); Part I, "Story of the Reception of 'Leaves of Grass' by the World."

13. Frederik Schyberg, *Walt Whitman* (Copenhagen: Gyldendalske Boghandel, 1933); "Whitman i Verdenlitteraturen."

14. See note 8, above. Professor Lionel Trilling read the praise of Schy-

berg in the *Walt Whitman Handbook* and recommended that the Columbia University Press publish a translation; Mrs. Allen was invited to do a translation.

15. Gay Wilson Allen, editor, *Walt Whitman Abroad: Critical Essays from Germany, France, Scandinavia, Russia, Italy, Spain and Latin America, Israel, Japan and India* (Syracuse University Press, 1955).

16. Fernando Alegría *Walt Whitman en Hispanoamerica* (Mexico: Ediciones Studium, 1954).

17. The phrase is used by F. O. Matthiessen in one of the best interpretations of the period, *The American Renaissance: Art and Expression in the Age of Emerson and Whitman* (New York: Oxford University Press, 1941).

18. See *Notes and Fragments*, Part V, 193-534—especially items no. 210-36, 332-39, and 395.

19. This is essentially Arthur Christy's attitude toward the Orientalism of Emerson and Thoreau in *The Orient in American Transcendentalism* (New York: Columbia University Press, 1932).

20. Walter F. Taylor, *A History of American Letters* (New York: American Book Co., 1936), 145-46.

21. Newton Arvin, *Whitman* (New York: Macmillan and Co., 1938), 190.

22. John B. Moore, "The Master of Whitman," *Studies in Philology*, XXIII, 77 (January 1926). See also Clarence Gohdes, "Whitman and Emerson," *Sewanee Review*, XXXVII, 79-93 (January 1929).

23. Moore, 77.

24. Leon Howard, "For a Critique of Whitman's Transcendentalism," *Modern Language Notes*, XLVII, 79-85 (February 1952).

25. *Ibid.*, 83.

26. *Ibid.*, 85.

27. F. I. Carpenter, *Emerson: Representative Selections* (New York: American Book Co., 1934), xxxiii.

28. *Ibid.* However, as pointed out in Chap. III (see p. 190), whereas Emerson's evolution starts from spirit or soul, Whitman's starts from matter impregnated by spirit—always co-equal.

29. For a good summary of Carlyle's ideas, see Charles Frederick Harrold, *Carlyle and German Thought* (New Haven: Yale University Press, 1934), esp. Chap. IV, "Carlyle's Universe."

30. See *Notes and Fragments*, 132-41. In his notes on Goethe and Schiller (105-06) Whitman mentions Carlyle several times, as if he were taking notes from Carlyle's books.

31. Richard Maurice Bucke, *Walt Whitman* (Philadelphia: David McKay, 1883), 211. Bucke attributes the quotation to Burroughs.

32. Clifton Joseph Furness, *Walt Whitman's Workshop* (Cambridge: Harvard University Press, 1928), 236, note 138.

33. Arvin, 191.

34. *Ibid.*

35. *Prose Works 1892* (Stovall, ed.), II, 418, note.

36. Richard Riethmuller, "Walt Whitman and the Germans," *German American Annals*, New Ser., IV (1906), 126.

37. Woodbridge Riley, *The Meaning of Mysticism* (New York: Richard R. Smith, 1936), 64.

38. Mody C. Boatright, "Whitman and Hegel," *Studies in English*, No. 9, University of Texas Bulletin, July 8, 1929, p. 150.

39. W. B. Fulghum, Jr., "Whitman's Debt to Joseph Gostwick," *American Literature*, XII, 491-96 (January 1941).

40. Robert P. Falk, "Walt Whitman and German Thought," *Journal of English and Germanic Philology*, XL, 329 (July 1941).

41. Olive W. Parsons, "Whitman the Non-Hegelian,"*PMLA*, LVIII, 1073 (December 1943).

42. Falk, 330.

43. Alfred H. Marks, "Whitman's Triadic Imagery," *American Literature*, XXIII, 99 (March 1951).

44. Henry Thoreau, *Familiar Letters* (Boston: Houghton Mifflin Co., 1894), 347. Quoted by Bliss Perry, *Walt Whitman* (Boston: Houghton Mifflin Co., 1906), 121-22.

45. *Prose Works 1892* (Stovall, ed.), II, 722.

46. See Christy, note 19, above. Also F. I. Carpenter, *Emerson and Asia* (Cambridge: Harvard University Press, 1930); O. B. Frothingham, *Transcendentalism in New England* (New York: Putnam's Sons, 1876), Chaps. I-III; H. C. Goddard, *Studies in New England Transcendentalism* (New York: Columbia University Press, 1908).

47. Cf. Friedrich von Schlegel, "The Indian Language, Literature, and Philosophy," reprinted in *Aesthetic and Miscellaneous Works* (London: George Bell and Sons, 1900), 425-526. Edwyn C. Vaughn says, in *The Romantic Revolt* (New York: Charles Scribner's and Sons, 1907), that this work "forms nothing short of an epoch in the history of European learning, and even of letters and philosophy." See also Arthur F. J. Remy, *The Influence of India and Persia in the Poetry of Germany* (New York: Columbia University Press, 1910).

48. Lord Strangford, "Walt Whitman," *The Pall Mall Gazette*, February 16, 1866; reprinted in *A Selection from the Writings of Viscount Strangford* (London, 1869), II, 297 ff. See Harold Blodgett, *Walt Whitman in England* (Ithaca: Cornell University Press, 1934), 198.

49. Moncure D. Conway, "Walt Whitman," *The Fortnightly Review*, VI, 538-48 (October 15, 1866).

50. Gabriel Sarrazin, translated by Harrison B. Morris from *La Renaissance de la Poèsie Anglaise, 1798–1889*, in *In Re Walt Whitman* (Philadelphia: David McKay, 1893), 161 ff. French text reprinted in *The*

Universal Review (London), No. 22, February 15, 1890, pp. 247-69.

51. Edward Carpenter, *Days with Walt Whitman* (London: George Allen, 1906), 94-102.

52. Dorothy Frederica Mercer, "Walt Whitman on Reincarnation," *Vedanta and the West*, IX, 180-85 (November-December 1946); "Walt Whitman on Learning and Wisdom," X, 57-58 (March-April, 1947); "Walt Whitman on God and the Self," X, 80-87 (May-June 1947); "Walt Whitman on Love," X, 107-13 (July-August 1947).

53. Mercer (thesis), 51.

54. *Ibid.*, 110.

55. See note 52, above.

56. Malcolm Cowley (editor), Introduction to *Walt Whitman's* Leaves of Grass: *The First (1855) Edition* (New York: Viking Press, 1959), xxii.

57. *Ibid.*

58. *Ibid.*

59. *Ibid.*, xiv.

60. V. K. Chari, *Whitman in the Light of Vedantic Mysticism: An Interpretation*, With an Introduction by Gay Wilson Allen (Lincoln: University of Nebraska Press, 1964).

61. *Ibid.*, 18.

62. *Ibid.*, 34.

63. *Ibid.* "Walt Whitman, a kosmos," "Song of Myself," sec. 24, 1. 1.

64. Reader's Ed. of *L. G.*, 721.

65. Chari, 54.

66. *Ibid.*

67. *Ibid.*, 127.

68. O. K. Nambiar, *Walt Whitman and Yoga* (Bangalore: Jevan Publications, 1966).

69. *Ibid.*, vii.

70. *Ibid.*, viii.

71. *Ibid.*,

72. See Chap. I of this *Handbook*, p. 27.

73. T. R. Rajasekharaiah, *The Roots of Whitman's Grass* (Madison, N. J.: Fairleigh Dickinson University Press, 1970).

74. See Chap. I of this *Handbook*, p. 45.

75. *Hullina Dalagalu* [101 selected poems from *Leaves of Grass*], translated by M. Gopalakrishna Adiga [New Delhi]: Sahitya Akademi, 1966), 222 pp.

76. *Ghah Diyan Pattiyan*: Punjabi translation by Gurbakhsh Singh; Selected Poems from Whitman's *Leaves of Grass* ([New Delhi]: Sahitya Akademi, 1968), 260 pp.

77. "Walt Whitman: Passage to India," *Indian Literature*, II, 38-44 (April-September 1959). Half-yearly Journal of Sahitya Akademi, New Delhi.

78. Arvin, 201.

79. Reader's Ed. of *L. G.*, 727.

80. "Song of Myself," sec. 24 (1855 edition).

81. *Ibid.*, sec. 41.

82. "Song of Occupations," sec. 3 (1855 edition).

83. "Poem of the Road" (1856 edition); "Song of the Open Road."

84. "Poem of You" (1856); 1881 title, "To You."

85. Perry, 277-80.

86. Esther Shephard, *Walt Whitman's Pose* (New York: Harcourt, Brace and Co., 1936).

87. *Uncollected Poetry and Prose*, II, 53.

88. W. S. Kennedy, *Reminiscences of Walt Whitman* (London: Alexander Gardner, 1896), 106.

89. Cf. Hugo's Preface to *Cromwell*.

90. See Schyberg (trans.), 268-70.

91. See *Uncollected Poetry and Prose*, I, 134.

92. Gay Wilson Allen, "Walt Whitman and Jules Michelet," *Études Anglaises*, I, 230-37 (May 1937). Whitman's paraphrase of Michelet's poem on the Man-of-War bird was first pointed out by Adeline Knapp, "Walt Whitman and Jules Michelet, Identical Passages," *Critic*, XLIV, 467-68 (1907).

93. Jules Michelet's *The People*, translated by G. H. Smith (New York: Appleton, 1846), 6.

94. "So Long!," ll. 53-54.

95. *The People*, 25.

96. "Song of Myself," sec. 20.

97. *The People*, 135.

98. Reader's Ed. of *L. G.*, 713-16.

99. *The People*, 24.

100. *Ibid.*

101. "Song of Myself," sec. 52.

102. Reader's Ed. of *L. G.*, 714.

103. Discussed by Gay Wilson Allen in "Whitman and Michelet—Continued," *American Literature*, XLV, 428-32 (November 1973). The "Continued" refers to an article by Arthur Geffen, "Walt Whitman and Jules Michelet—One More Time," *American Literature*, XLV, 107-13 (March 1973). "One More Time" refers to Allen's article listed in note 92, above.

104. *L'Oiseau* was published in France in 1857, and T. Nelson and Sons published a translation in 1869. Scholars agree that Whitman could not read French. "Out of the Cradle Endlessly Rocking" (final title) was composed and published in 1859.

105. Michelet's two chapters in *The Bird* on the nightingale are entitled "Art and the Infinite."

106. Blodgett. See note 48, above.

107. *Ibid.*, 14 ff.

108. *Ibid.*, 163-66.

109. Reprinted in *A Selection from the Writings of Viscount Strangford* (London, 1869), II, 297 ff. Blodgett, 198.

110. *Ibid.*

111. Quoted from *Chronicle* article by Blodgett, 22.

112. See Chap. I, pp. 10-11.

113. *Ibid.*, p. 48.

114. Blodgett, 78.

115. Published in *The Contemporary Review*, October 1871, and reissued in an expanded pamphlet, London, 1872.

116. Quoted by Blodgett, 79.

117. *Ibid.*

118. *The Fleshly School of Poetry* (London: Strahan, 1872), 97.

119. Article in *The Athenaeum*, March 11, 1876, partly reprinted from *The West Jersey Press* (Camden), January 26, 1876. The original article on the American neglect of Whitman may have been written by the poet himself. See Furness, *Workshop*, 245.

120. Robert Buchanan, "The American Socrates," *A Look Round Literature* (London: Ward and Downey, 1887), 344.

121. Blodgett, 105.

122. Swinburne used the 1867 title.

123. Algernon Charles Swinburne, *William Blake* (London: Hotten, 1868), 335.

124. Blodgett, 108.

125. See especially W. B. Cairns, "Swinburne's Opinion of Whitman," *American Literature*, III, 125-35 (May 1931). Also W. S. Monroe, "Swinburne's Recantation of Walt Whitman," *Revue Anglo-Américaine*, IX, 347-51 (March 1931).

126. Cairns, 131.

127. Quoted by Cairns, 131-32, from *Fortnightly Review.*

128. See Chap. I, p. 51.

129. See pp. 33 and 51.

130. Edward Dowden, *Shakespeare: A Critical Study of His Mind and Art* (London: C. Kegan Paul and Co., 1879), 40. Mentioned by Blodgett, 43.

131. Reprinted in part by Traubel *et al, In Re*, 284.

132. Quoted by Blodgett, 185.

133. *Ibid.*, 186.

134. *Ibid.*, 199.

135. *Ibid.*, 190.

136. *Ibid.*, 193.

137. *Ibid.*, 201.

138. John Johnston and J. W. Wallace, *Visits to Walt Whitman in 1890-1891 by Two Lancashire Friends* (London: Allen & Unwin, 1917).

139. Blodgett, 215.

140. Cf. *Homogenic Love* (1894), *Love's Coming of Age* (1896), *An Unknown People* (1897), *Some Friends of Walt Whitman* (1904), *The Intermediate Sex* (1912).

141. *The Intermediate Sex* (New York: Mitchell Kennerley, 1912), 117.

142. Havelock Ellis, *Sexual Inversion* (Philadelphia: David McKay, 1915, 3rd ed.), 51.

143. Havelock Ellis, *The New Spirit* (New York: Modern Library, 1921), 31.

144. *The Letters of Gerard Manley Hopkins to Robert Bridges*, ed. Claude C. Abbott (London: Oxford University Press, 1935), 155. Reprinted by Edwin H. Miller (ed.), *A Century of Whitman Criticism* (Bloomington: Indiana University Press, 1969), 77-80.

145. George Saintsbury, *A History of English Prosody* (London: Macmillan, 1910), III, 492. Reprinted by Edwin H. Miller, 56 f.

146. *The American Genius: An Anthology of Poetry and Some Prose.* Selected with a Preface by Edith Sitwell (London: John Lehmann, 1952), x-xi.

147. James E. Quinn, "Yeats and Whitman: 1887-1925," *Walt Whitman Review*, XV, 106-08 (September 1974).

148. See Schyberg (Allen translation), 321-26; D. H. Lawrence, *Studies in Classic American Literature* (New York: Doubleday—Anchor Books, 1953), Chap. 12.

149. Edwin H. Miller (see note 144, above), xxxiv.

150. James E. Miller, Jr., Karl Shapiro, and Bernice Slote, *Start with the Sun* (Lincoln: University of Nebraska Press, 1960), 4.

151. *Studies in Classic American Literature*, 184.

152. Quoted by Miller, Shapiro, Slote, 80, from letter to Harriet Monroe, March 15, 1928.

153. Miller, Shapiro, Slote, 106.

154. *Ibid.*, 47.

155. Reader's Ed. *L. G.*, 723.

156. Miller, Shapiro, Slote, 170.

157. Sylvia Beach, *Shakespeare and Company* (New York: Harcourt, Brace, 1959), 128.

158. *Finnegans Wake* (New York: Viking Press, 1959), 263. Reprinted by Edwin H. Miller, *A Century &c*, 171.

159. *Finnegans Wake*, 551. Reprinted, *Ibid.*

160. Richard Chase, *Whitman* (New York: Sloane Associates, 1955). In a note on p. 89 Chase explains Joyce's *panromain*: "Presumably—pan-Roman (i.e., "universal") and pan-romaine (i.e., a vegetable: 'Leaves of Grass') and pan-*roman* (the universal novel).

161. Cf. Brom Weber, *Hart Crane* (New York: Bodley Press, 1948), 303.

162. Yvor Winters, *In Defense of Reason* (New York: Swallow Press & William Morrow, 1947), 590.

163. T. S. Eliot, "Whitman and Tennyson," *The Nation and Athenaeum*, XL, 426 (Dec. 18, 1926). Reprinted Edwin H. Miller, 162-63.

164. S. Musgrove, *T. S. Eliot and Walt Whitman* (Wellington: University of New Zealand Press, 1952).

165. "A Pact," poem written in 1913.

166. Herbert Bergman, "Ezra Pound and Walt Whitman," *American Literature*, XXVII, 56-61 (March, 1955). An unpublished 1909 essay.

167. Quoted by Roy Harvey Pearce, *The Continuity of American Poetry* (Princeton: Princeton University Press, 1961), 84.

168. *Ibid*.

169. "Un poète américain, Walt Whitman: 'Muscle and Pluck Forever,' " *Revue Deux Mondes*, XLII, 566-67 (June 1, 1872).

170. *Ibid*.

171. Quoted by O. F. Pucciani, "French Criticism of Walt Whitman" (Harvard University doctoral dissertation, 1943—unpublished), 70-71, from Émile Blémont, "La Poésie en Angleterre et aux États-Unis," III: "Walt Whitman," *Renaissance littéraire et artistique*, 1872. The article ran in three numbers: June 8, July 6, July 13, 1872.

172. Quoted by F. Baldensperger, "Walt Whitman and France," *Columbia University Quarterly*, Oct., 1919, p. 302.

173. Pucciani, 58.

174. Léo Quesnel, "Poètes américains: Walt Whitman," *Revue politique et littéraire*, Feb. 16, 1884, p. 215.

175. Pucciani, 94.

176. *Leaves of Grass*, with one hundred drawings by Rockwell Kent (New York: Heritage Press, 1936).

177. Pucciani, 141.

178. Édouard Dujardin, in "Les premièrs poètes du vers libre," *Mercure de France*, March 15, 1921 (vol. 146, pp. 577-621), denies that Whitman had any influence on "free verse" in France, pointing out: "Exactement parlant, le vers de Walt Whitman, du moins celui des *Brins d'Herbe*, n'est pas le vers libre, mais le verset . . . Nous avons vu que le vers libre et le verset sont de la même famille, et qu'on pouvait considérer le verset comme un vers libre élargi, le plus-souvent composé lui-même de plusieurs vers libres étroitement associés," 606. It would seem significant, however, that Laforgue was experimenting with the new form at the same time that he was translating Whitman (see *La Vogue*, II, No. 7; III, Nos. 1, 3, 8, 1886); and the following year Gustave Kahn, editor of *La Vogue*, published "La Belle au château rêvenant" in *Revue indépendante*, Sept., 1887. And even Dujardin admits that "le vers libre et le verset sont de la même famille." It seems likely, therefore, that Whitman's form had some effect on the French experiments. See also P. M. Jones, "Influence of Walt Whitman on the 'Vers Libre,' " *Modern Language Review*, XI, 186-194 (April, 1916). "Perhaps it would be safest to say that in the days when the first *vers libres* were being written, the poets who knew Whitman—and they were few, though important—were attracted mainly

through the appeal made by his brusque originality to their pronounced taste for literary novelties."194.

179. Gabriel Sarrazin, *La Renaissance de la poésie anglaise, 1778-1889*, (Paris: Perrin, 1889), 236-37. Translation in *In Re Walt Whitman*, 160.

180. Pucciani, 103.

181. In a review of Havelock Ellis's *New Spirit* in *Mercure de France*, June 1890, tome 1, p. 220.

182. "Le vers libre, tel que le comprend ce dernier poète [Francis Vielé-Griffin], vient en partie de Whitman; mais Whitman était lui-même un fils de la Bible et ainsi le vers libre, ce n'est peut-être, au fond, que le verset hébraïque des prophètes; c'est bien également de la Bible, mais de la Bible allemande, cette fois, que semble nous venir une autre nuance du vers libre, celle qui a valu sa réputation à M. Gustave Kahn," *Le Problème du style* (Paris: Mercure de France, 1924 [first ed. 1902], p. 159.

183. Pucciani, 118.

184. Théodor de Wyzewa, "Walt Whitman," *Revue politique et littéraire*, XLIX, 513-19 (April 1892).

185. B. H. Gausseron, "Walt Whitman," *Revue encyclopédique*, May 15, 1892, pp. 721-26.

186. Jules Romains, *La Vie unanime* (Paris: "L'Abbaye," 1908), 121-236.

187. Baldensperger, 307.

188. See Dominique Braga, "Walt Whitman," *Europe nouvelle*, anné 5, N. 35 (August 19, 1922), 1042.

189. Pierre de Lanux, *Young France and New America* (New York: Macmillan, 1917).

190. Baldensperger, 307.

191. *Ibid*.

192. Georges Duhamel, *Les Poètes et la poésie, 1912-1914* (Paris: Mercure de France, 1914), 141.

193. See p. 287.

194. Schyberg (trans.), 355, note 70.

195. See Chap. I, p. 36.

196. Schyberg (trans.), 300-1.

197. *Ibid*., 302.

198. *Ibid*., 304.

199. S. A. Rhodes, "The Influence of Walt Whitman on André Gide," *Romanic Review*, XXXI, 156-71 (April 1940). See also Huberta F. Randall, "Whitman and Verhaeren—Priests of Human Brotherhood," *French Review*, XVI, 36-43 (1942).

200. Rhodes, 159.

201. *Ibid*., 161.

202. *Ibid*., 162.

203. *Ibid*., 163.

204. *Ibid.*, 170.

205. *Ibid.*, 170-71.

206. This conclusion is supported by Klaus Mann, *André Gide and the Modern Spirit* (New York: Creative Age Press, 1944).

207. Stefan Zweig, *Emile Verhaeren* (Boston: Houghton Mifflin Co., 1914), 108.

208. Schyberg (trans.), 297.

209. *La Multiple Splendeur.*

210. Schyberg (trans.), 298.

211. P. M. Jones, "Whitman and Verhaeren," *Aberystwyth Studies* (University College of Wales), II, 82-83 (1914).

212. *Ibid.*, 106.

213. Schyberg (trans.), 297.

214. *Ibid.*, 300.

215. *Walt Whitman in Europe Today*, eds. Roger Asselineau and William White (Detroit: Wayne State University Press, 1972).

216. *Walt Whitman, Une étude, un choix de poèmes* par Paul Jamati (Paris: Pierre Seghers, 1948). 229 pp.

217. *Walt Whitman: Feuilles d'herbe* (Choix), Introduction et traduction de Roger Asselineau (Paris: Societé d'Édition "Les Belles Lettres," 1956). 358 pp. A bilingual edition with introduction by Roger Asselineau, Paris: Aubier-Flammarion, 1972. 511 pp.

218. *Whitman*, by Alain Bosquet [long introduction on the man and his work, with translation of selected poems and prose] (Paris: Gallimard, 1959). 270 pp.

219. Walt Whitman: *Chants de la terre qui tourne*, Préface et Traduction de Roger Asselineau (Paris: Nouveaux Horizons, 1966). 303 pp.

220. *Walt Whitman in Europe Today*, 33.

221. *Walt Whitman, ses meilleures pages traduites de l'anglais par* Rosaire Dion-Lévesque (Montreal: Les Elzévirs, 1933). 240 pp. Same title (Québec: Les Presses de l'Université Laval, 1965). 240 pp.

222. O. E. Lessing, "Walt Whitman and His German Critics prior to 1910," *American Collector*, III, 7 (October 1926).

223. First published in *Allgemeinen Zeitung*, Augsburg, April 24, 1868; reprinted in *Gesammelte Dichtung*, Stuttgart, 1877.

224. Lessing, 7.

225. These were published in 1870 in *Amerikanische Antologie*; see Harry Law-Robertson, *Walt Whitman in Deutschland* (Giessen, 1935), 13-14.

226. The paper was *New Yorker Staatszeitung*. The essay was translated for *In Re Walt Whitman* (Philadelphia: David McKay, 1893), 215-30. *Walt Whitman, der Dichter der Demokratie* appeared in several German editions, 1882, 1886, 1889, and 1899.

227. On September 9, 1884, Rolleston wrote Whitman that he had not been able to find a German publisher for his translation and had been told

"there would probably be difficulties with the police, who in Germany exercise a most despotic power."—*Whitman and Rolleston: A Correspondence*, ed. Horst Frenz (Bloomington: Indiana University Press, 1951), 94. See also Horace Traubel, *With Walt Whitman in Camden* (Boston: Small, Maynard, 1906), I, 18. Earlier, Rolleston had discussed Whitman's democratic ideas in *Über Wordsworth und Walt Whitman* (Dresden, 1883), written in collaboration with C. W. Cotterill.

228. Quoted by Law-Robertson, 39, from *Deutsche Presse*, Jg. II, No. 23, 1889.

229. Quoted by Law-Robertson, 39, from *Magazin für Literatur des In- und Auslandes*, No. 37, p. 584 (1889).

230. "Most of the references to Whitman [1889-1909] are characterized by a supreme admiration which, in some instances, rises in intensity even to the point of fanaticism or deification. It is this extravagant admiration for the poet which justifies the term cult as a name for the agitation as a whole." Edward Thorstenberg, "The Walt Whitman Cult in Germany," *Sewanee Review*, XIX, 77 (January 1911).

231. Lessing, 10, says, "This little book is an unparalleled example of high-handed arrogance, cowardly imposition, and utter ignorance." Lessing claims (following Bertz, see note 232 below) that Schlaf had read no more than 15 percent of Whitman's writings, and those in German translations.

232. In *Jahrbuch für sexuelle Zwischenstufen*, IX, 551-64 (Jg. 1908). Law-Robertson, 51, discusses the controversy.

233. See Law-Robertson, 85.

234. *Grashalme, Eine Auswahl*, Leipzig, 1904.

235. Written for *Aus Amerikanischen Kriegszeiten*. See Lessing, 10.

236. Law-Robertson, 20.

237. Translated by Thorstenberg, 79, from Schölermann's *Grashalme*, xiv.

238. *Walt Whitman: Prosaschriften*, Auswahl übersetz (Munich and Leipzig: R. Piper & Co., 1905), xxvi.

239. Lessing, 11.

240. Law-Robertson, 21.

241. Quoted by Amelia von Ende, "Walt Whitman and Arno Holz," *Poet Lore*, XVI, 63 (Summer 1905).

242. *Ibid.*

243. For example, one of the poems quoted by Amelia von Ende (from *Phantasus*), 65:

> Seven billions of years before my birth
> I was an iris.
> My roots
> Were imbedded
> In a star.
> Upon its dark waters floated
> My large blue blossom.

244. Law-Robertson, 65-66.

245. *Ibid.*, 65.

246. *Ibid.*, 66-67.

247. Cf. *Ibid.*, 68.

248. "Walt Whitman," translated by Rudolf Komadina, for *Die Gesellschaft Halbmonatschrift für Litteratur, Kunst, und Sozialpolitik*, XVI, Bd. I, pp. 24-35 (Jg. 1900).

249. *Ibid.*, 24.

250. "Walt Whitman zu seinem siebzigsten Geburtstag," *Deutsche Presse*, II, No. 23. Quoted by Lessing, 8.

251. See note 232, above.

252. See Chap. I, p. 63.

253. See note 239, above.

254. *Prose Works 1892* (Stovall, ed.), II, 482.

255. Lessing, 14. Lessing first published his essay "Walt Whitman and the German Critics" in the *Journal of English and Germanic Philology*, IX, 85-98 (1910), but to avoid confusion references are given here only to the *American Collector* version.

256. Lessing, 14-15.

257. *Ibid.*, 15.

258. Quoted by Law-Robertson, 69, from *Wege nach Weimar*, Bd. I, S. 279 (1906).

259. *Ibid.*

260. Anna Jacobson, "Walt Whitman in Germany since 1914," *Germanic Review*, I, 133 (April 1926).

261. Quoted *Ibid.*, from "Ein Beispiel Kriegsdichtung," *Die Neue Zeit.* Dez. 1914, pp. 373-82.

262. Jacobson, 136.

263. The same charge had previously been made in France. See note 193, above.

264. Law-Robertson, 71.

265. "Whitman der Dichter der Demokratische, zu seinem 100. Geburtstag, 31 Mai 1919," *Der Kampf, Sozialdemokratische Wochenschrift*, May 31, 1919, pp. 342-44.

266. According to Associated Press dispatches in the *New York Times*, Jan. 1 and March 11, 1922.

267. Jacobson, 134.

268. *Ibid.*

269. *Ibid.*

270. "Drei Lieder Whitmans," übertragen von Gustav Landauer, *Menschliche Gedichte im Kriege*, Herausgegeben von René Schickele (Zürich, 1918).

271. Gustav Landauer. See Law-Robertson, 78.

272. *Walt Whitmans Werk*, Ausgewählt, übertragen und eingeleitet von Hans Reisiger (Berlin: S. Fischer, 1922), 2 vols.

273. Quoted by Law-Robertson, 30, from *Vossische Zeitung*, Nov. 17, 1919 (review of first edition in one volume).

274. Reisiger, I, xiii.

275. *Ibid.*, xix.

276. Quoted by Theodore Stanton, in a review of Reisiger's work, "Walt Whitman in Germany," *The Literary Review*, formerly the Literary Supplement of the *New York Evening Post*, September 30, 1922, p. 68. Most of this article is devoted to printing valuable letters from Reisiger and Thomas Mann.

277. Quoted *Ibid.* Same letter also quoted by Law-Robertson, 73-74, from *Frankfurter Zeitung*, V, April 16, 1922.

278. Republished in *Bemühungen, Neue Folge Gesammelten Abhandlungen und kleinen Aufsätze* (Berlin: Fischer, 1925), 141-90.

279. Stefan Zweig himself, in his biography, *Emile Verhaeren* (Boston: Houghton Mifflin, 1914), is often Whitmanesque in style.

280. Cf. Law-Robertson, 78. Actual influence of Whitman on Werfel is debatable. See also Detlev W. Schumann, "Enumerative Style and Its Significance in Whitman, Rilke, Werfel," *Modern Language Quarterly*, III, 171-204 (June 1942).

281. See especially the article by Thomas Mann's son, Klaus Mann, "The Present Greatness of Whitman," *Decision*, I, 14-30 (April 1941). Klaus Mann's *André Gide and the Modern Spirit* (New York: Creative Age Press, 1944) shows great admiration for Whitman.

282. *Grashalme*, Auswahl von Georg Goyert ins Deutsche übertragen (Berlin: Lothar Blansvalet Verlag, 1948). 106 pp.

283. *Walt Whitman, Ein Amerikaner* (Berlin: Lothar Blansvalet Verlag, 1948).

284. *Walt Whitman in Selbstzeugnissen und Bilddokumenten*, Darstellt von Gay Wilson Allen, Herausgegeben von Kurt Kusenberg ([Hamburg]: Rowohlt, 1961).

285. *Walt Whitman in Europe Today* (see note 215, above), 15.

286. Schyberg (trans.), 220.

287. "Walt Whitman, det Amerikanske Democratis Digter," *Ide og Virkelighed*, I, 152-216 (1872); "Walt Whitman," *Buster og Masker*, 1882, pp. 123-92.

288. Schyberg (trans.), 308.

289. *Ibid.*

290. A translation of Hamsun's satirical speech, "The Primitive Poet, Walt Whitman," by Evie Allison Allen is in *Walt Whitman Abroad*, ed. Gay Wilson Allen (Syracuse: Syracuse University Press, 1955), 112-23.

291. Schyberg (trans.), 312. Whitman's influence on Jensen himself is found mainly in his series of novels called (in translation) *The Long Journey*. See G. W. Allen, "Walt Whitman's 'Long Journey' Motif," *Journal of English and Germanic Philology*, XXXVIII, 76-95 (January 1939); reprinted in *Walt*

Whitman as Man, Poet, and Legend, ed. G. W. Allen (Carbondale: Southern Illinois University Press, 1961), 62-82.

292. *Walt Whitman, Digte* (Copenhagen: Gyldendal, 1933). 126 pp.

293. Schyberg (trans.), 311.

294. *Walt Whitman in Europe Today*, 28.

295. Gay Wilson Allen, "Walt Whitman's Reception in Scandinavia," *Papers of the Bibliographical Society of America*, XL, 259-75, Fourth Quarter 1946. The visit of an American university professor to Bjørnson is quoted from R. B. Anderson, *Life Story* (Madison, Wisconsin: privately printed, 1915. See also Arne Kildal, *Amerikas Stemme* (Voice of America) (Oslo: Steenske, 1939), "Walt Whitman," 69-86.

296. Kristofer Janson, *Amerikanske Forhold: fem foredrag* (Copenhagen: Gyldendal, 1881). "The most original poetic mind America has at present is undeniably Walt Whitman," p. 63.

297. *Walt Whitman Abroad* (see note 291, above), 112.

298. *Walt Whitman: Sangen om Meg Selv av Leaves of Grass*, Oversettelse og Innledning ved Per Arneberg, Tegninger [illustrations] av Kai Fjell (Oslo: H Aschehoug & Co., 1947). 123 pp.

299. See Gay Wilson Allen, "The Problem of Metaphor in Translating Walt Whitman's "Leaves of Grass," *English Studies Today* (Bern, Switzerland: Francke Verlag, 1961), 269-80.

300. Kjell Krogvig, "Til Whitman Gjennem Wergeland," *Samtiden*, 57 Aarg., Heft 3, 196-202 (1948). Translated by Sigrid Moe, *Walt Whitman Abroad*, 137-43.

301. *Walt Whitman in Europe Today*, 29.

302. Translation by Evie Allison Allen in *Walt Whitman Abroad*, 127-36.

303. *Strån av Gräss* av Walt Whitman, Ett Urval Översättning och med Inledning av K. A. Svensson (Stockholm: A. B. Seelig & Co., 1935). 207 pp.

304. *Walt Whitman in Europe Today*, 30.

305. *Ibid.*, 31-32.

306. *The Sunday Star*, Washington, D. C., January 1, 1956.

307. Stephen Stepanchev, in *Walt Whitman Abroad*, 144.

308. *Ibid.*, 145.

309. *Ibid.*

310. First published in 1856 *Leaves of Grass* as "Liberty Poem for Asia, Africa, Europe, America, Australia, Cuba, and The Archipelagoes of the Sea." The same edition contained "Poem of the Dead Young Men of Europe...," first published as "Resurgemus" in the New York *Daily Tribune*, June 21, 1850.

311. Kornei Chukovsky, "A Poet of Wrath and Sorrow [Nikolai Nekrasov]," *Soviet Life*, Dec. 1971, pp. 46-47.

312. See p. 252, above.

313. I. Chistova, "Turgenev and Whitman," *Russkay Literatura*, No. 2, 1966, pp. 196-99. Kornei Chukovsky, "Turgenev and Whitman" [in Russian], *Literaturnaya Rossiya*, July 28, 1967.

314. *Walt Whitman Abroad*, 145.

315. *Ibid.*, 146.

316. *Ibid.*, 147.

317. From Chukovsky's own translation of an extract from *Moi Uitmen*, "My Whitman," *Sputnik*, June, 1967, p. 86.

318. *Ibid.*

319. *Walt Whitman Abroad*, 149.

320. *Sputnik* [editor's introductory note], June 1967, pp. 84-85.

321. *Walt Whitman in Europe*, 35.

322. D. Mirsky, "Poet of American Democracy," translated by Samuel Putnam, *Walt Whitman Abroad*, 169.

323. *Ibid.*, 170, 172.

324. *Ibid.*, 185.

325. *Walt Whitman Abroad*, 185.

326. Leonard Spier, "Walt Whitman," *International Literature*, No. 9, September 1935, p. 89.

327. *Walt Whitman in Europe Today*, 34.

328. *Walt Whitman Abroad*, 156; also Juliusz Zuławski's introduction, "Słowo Wstepne," to his edition of *Źdźbła Trawy* (Warszawa: Institut Wydawniczy, 1966), 5-17.

329. Juliusz Zuławski, *Wielka Podróz Walta Whitmana* (Warszwa: Państowy Instytut Wydawniczy, 1971). 375 pp.

330. *Walt Whitman: Költeményei*, Keszthelyi Zoltán Fordításában (Budapest: Magyar-Amerikai Társaság Kiadása, 1947). 93 pp.

331. *Walt Whitman: Füszálak* (Budapest: Új Magyar Könyvkiadó 1955). 419 pp.

332. *Walt Whitman: Füszálak*, Osszes Költemények (Budapest: Magyar Helikon, 1964). 772 pp.

333. *Walt Whitman in Europe Today*, 23-24.

334. Sonja Basić, "Walt Whitman in Yugoslavia," *Walt Whitman in Europe Today*, 24-26.

335. *Walt Whitman: Opere Alese*, Traducere si prezentare de Mihnea Gheorghiu (Bucuresti: Editura de Stat Pentru Literatura si Arta, 1956). 590 pp.

336. Ph. D. dissertation at New York University, unpublished.

337. *Foglie di erba*, translated by Luigi Camberale (Palermo: Remo Sandron, 1907; rev. 1923). 2 vols.

338. *Foglie d'erba e Prose di Walt Whitman*, traduzione di Enzo Giachino Einaudi, 1950). 958 pp.

339. Mariolina Meliadò Freeth, "Walt Whitman in Italy," *Walt Whitman in Europe Today*, 20.

340. *Walt Whitman, Giorni rappresentativi e altre prose*, ed. Mariolina Meliadò Freeth (Vicenza: Neri Pozza, 1968).

341. *Walt Whitman in Europe Today*, 22, n. 11.

342. "Walt Whitman," *Fanfulla della domencia*, Dec. 7, 1879, p. 1.

343. "Walt Whitman," *Ritratti straniere: 1908-1921*, Firenze, 1932. Trans. by Roger Asselineau, *Walt Whitman Abroad*, 189.

344. Grippi, 61.

345. *Ibid.*, 62. Giacomo Leopardi (1798-1837), Alessandro Manzoni (1785-1873).

346. Letter to Nencioni, August 26, 1881, in Carducci, *Lettere* (Bologna, 1951), XIII, 172-73. (Quoted by Grippi, 63.)

347. Quoted by Grippi, 99.

348. Pasquale Jannaccone, *La Poesia di Walt Whitman e l'Evoluzione delle Forme Ritmiche* (Torino: Roux, 1898). Translated by Peter Mitilineos, *Walt Whitman's Poetry and the Evolution of Rhythmic Forms* (Washington, D. C.: Microcard Edition, 1973), esp. pp. 104, 137-38.

349. Cf. W. S. Kennedy, *Reminiscences of Walt Whitman* (London: Alexander Gardener, 1896), 151.

350. Grippi, 137. Meliadò, *Walt Whitman nella cultura italiani, 1872-1903* (unpublished thesis, University of Rome, 1961).

351. "Whitman—Poetry of Poetry Writing," trans. by Roger Asselineau, *Walt Whitman Abroad*, 193; from *La Letteratura Americana e Altri Saggi* (Turin: Einaudi, 1951).

352. Reader's Ed. *L. G.*, 721; "reality and the soul," 714.

353. "Whitman" in "Four American Symbolists," 16-26, *Symbolism and American Literature* (University of Chicago Press, 1953).

354. *Walt Whitman Abroad*, 188.

355. Cambon, "Walt Whitman in Italy," *Aut-Aut*, n. 39 (July 1957), 244. Quoted, Grippi, 258.

356. *Walt Whitman in Europe Today*, 21.

357. Whitman used the phrase in *American Primer*, and F. O. Matthiessen, in *American Renaissance: Art and Expression in the Age of Emerson and Whitman* (New York: Oxford University Press, 1941), uses this as a text for analysing the language of *Leaves of Grass*.

358. Mario Praz, "Whitman e Proust," *Mondo*, (March 24, 1951), p. 8. Quoted by Grippi, 276.

359. See p. 293, above.

360. Mario Alicata, "Note su Whitman," *Rinascita* [Communist monthly], anno V, no. 8 (1943), 310. Quoted by Grippi, 268.

361. *Walt Whitman: Obras Escogidas*: Ensayo, Biográficocrítico, Versión, Notas y Bibliografía de Concha Zardoya (Madrid: M. Aguilar, 1946); *Hojas de Hierba*, Version Directa e Integra, Conforme al Texto de la Edicion Definitiva de 1891-2, por Francisco Alexander (Quito, Ecuador: Casa de la Cultura Ecuatoriana, 1953).

362. See *Walt Whitman Abroad*, 279; and Concha Zardoya, "Walt Whitman in Spain," *Walt Whitman in Europe Today*, 9-12.

363. Zardoya, *Obras Escogidas*, 703-811; *Perspectivas Democráticas*, estudio preliminar por Dardo Cuneo, traducción de Luis Azua (Buenos Aires: Ed. Americalee, 1944).

364. See p. 317, above.

365. From unpublished manuscript supplied the author while writing the first edition of this *Handbook* (see p. 334, 1946 ed.).

366. Zardoya, *Walt Whitman in Europe Today*, 10.

367. Translation in *Walt Whitman Abroad*, 220-23.

368. Zardoya, *Walt Whitman in Europe Today*, 11; quoted from *Obras completas* (Buenos Aires: Losada, 1944), 197.

369. Zardoya, 11; *Obras completas*, 225.

370. Translated by Edwin Honig in *García Lorca* (Norfolk, Conn.: New Directions, 1944), 90.

371. *Walt Whitman in Europe Today*, 11.

372. *Ibid.*, 12.

373. Fernando Alegría, *Walt Whitman en Hispanoamerica* (Mexico: Ediciones Studium, 1954).

374. See note 365, above.

375. Pablo Neruda, "We Live in a Whitmanesque Age," *New York Times*, April 14, 1972; reprinted in *Walt Whitman in Europe Today*, 41-42.

376. "Toward an Impure Poetry," *Pablo Neruda: Five Decades: Poems 1925–1970*, a bilingual edition edited and translated from the Spanish by Ben Belitt (New York: Grove Press, 1974), xxi-ii.

377. Quoted by Belitt, xvii, from "El siglo muere."

378. *Five Decades*, 389.

379. *Walt Whitman Abroad*, 232.

380. *Selected Poems by Fernando Pessoa*, translated by Edwin Honig (Chicago: Swallow Press, 1971), 56-71.

381. *Ibid.*, 59.

382. *Ibid.*, 71.

383. *Ibid.*, 12.

384. Complete version unseen; selections: *Phylla Chloes (Leaves of Grass)*, Greek rendition by Nick Proestopoulos (Athens: M. Pechlibanides [1936]. Reviewed by Peter Mitilineos *The Long-Islander*, Huntington, L. I., September 27, 1972 (annual Walt Whitman page, Section One, p. 11).

385. Iwao Matsuhara, "Walt Whitman in Japan," *Thought Currents in English Literature* (Tokyo), XXIX (Jan. 1957); reprinted in *Norton Critical Edition of* Leaves of Grass (New York: Norton, 1973), 912-18. Shigenobu Sadoya, *Walt Whitman in Japan* (Fukuoka: Bulletin No. 9, Research Institute, Seinan Gakuin University, 1969). Abstract in English, pp. 1-7; Bibliography, 9-20.

386. *Walt Whitman in Europe Today*, 38.

387. See note 385, above.

388. Kinnosuke (Sōseki) Natsume, "On Walt Whitman's Poetry—a Democratic Poet in the Literary World," *Tetsugaku Zasshi* (The Journal of Philosophy), Oct. 1892.

389. Letter from Naganuma in the *Long-Islander* (annual Whitman page [See note 384 above], May 29, 1969, p. 2, Whitman Section.

390. *Complete: Leaves of Grass*, vol. I, II, Trans. completely by Shigetaka Naganuma (Tokyo: Mikasa-shobō, 1950; revised edition, 1954.

391. Mentioned in Naganuma's letter. See note 389, above.

392. Sadoya, 2.

393. *Ibid.*

394. *Ibid.*, 4.

395. *Ibid.*, 6.

396. Matsuhara, 917, names: Leon Howard, 1954; Robert A. Jelliffe, 1955; Gay Wilson Allen, 1955.

397. Tokyo: Taibundo, 1966.

398. *Alei Esev (Leaves of Grass) by Walt Whitman*, being a selection and translation into Hebrew (with notes and an essay on the poet's life and work) by Simon Halkin (Merhavia: Sifriat Poalim [Workers' Book Guild], 1952).

399. Sholom Kahn contributed "Whitman's Sense of Evil: Criticisms," to *Walt Whitman Abroad*, 236-53.

400. *New York Herald Tribune Book Review*, March 26, 1950.

401. *Hasifrut*: Quarterly for the Study of Literature, Tel-Aviv University, Vol. I, No. 1 (Spring, 1968), 176-205. Summary in English, xiv.

402. "Whitman in Israel, 1969," *The Long-Islander*, May 29, 1969. See note 389 above.

403. Schyberg (trans.), 251.

404. See note 402, above.

405. Letter to author [G. W. A.].

406. *Selections from Whitman's "Leaves of Grass,"* Translated and Selected by T'u-nan Ch'u (Peking: People's Literary Publishing Society, 1955). 324 pp. Review by Angela Chih-ying Jung Palandri in *Walt Whitman Review*, IV, 94-97 [should be pp. 110-13] (Sept., 1958).

407. Quoted from Palandri's translation in her review. See note 406 above.

SELECTED BIBLIOGRAPHY
Chapter I: Growth of Biography

BOOKS

ALLEN, GAY WILSON. *The Solitary Singer: A Critical Biography of Walt Whitman*. New York: Macmillan. 1955. 616 pp. Grove Press, 1959. Rev. ed.: New York University Press. 1967.
(The Fullest biography.)

ARVIN, NEWTON. *Whitman*. New York: The Macmillan Co. 1938. 320 pp.
[Whitman as social thinker.]

ASSELINEAU, ROGER. *L'Evolution de Walt Whitman: Après la première édition des Feuilles d'herbe*. Paris: Didier. 1954. 567 pp. *The Evolution of Walt Whitman: The Creation of a Poet*. Harvard University Press. 1960. 376 pp. *The Evolution of Walt Whitman: The Creation of a Book*. Harvard University Press. 1962. 392 pp.
[A major biography and critical interpretation.]

BAILEY, JOHN. *Walt Whitman*. London and New York: The Macmillan Co. 1926. 220 pp.
[Unoriginal life in the English Men of Letters Series.]

BARRUS, CLARA. *Whitman and Burroughs: Comrades*. Boston: Houghton Mifflin and Co. 1931. 392 pp.
[Contains valuable correspondence of Burroughs, Whitman and their friends—also reliable criticism.]

BAZALGETTE, LÉON. *Walt Whitman, L'Homme et son oeuvre*. Paris: Mercure de France. 1908. 2 vols.
[A romantic biography.]

369

———. *Walt Whitman, the Man and His Work*. Translated by Ellen FitzGerald. Garden City: Doubleday. 1920. xviii, 355 pp.
[The translation is expurgated and slightly edited.]
BERTZ, EDUARD. *Der Yankee-Heiland*. Dresden: Carl Reissner. 1906. 253 pp.
[An attack on Whitman's claim as a prophet and thinker; analysis of sex pathology.]
BINNS, HENRY BRYAN. *A Life of Walt Whitman*. London: Methuen and Co. 1905. 369 pp.
[First exhaustive life—very sympathetic. Binns started the theory of the New Orleans romance.]
BLODGETT, HAROLD. *Walt Whitman in England*. Ithaca, N.Y.: Cornell University Press, 1934. 244 pp.
[Not a biography but discusses the English biographies.]
BORN, HELENA. *Whitman's Ideal Democracy*. Boston: Everett Press, 1902. 88 pp.
[Impassioned defense of Whitman by a devoted socialist friend.]
BUCKE, RICHARD MAURICE, M.D. *Walt Whitman*. Philadelphia: David McKay. 1883. 236 pp.
[An "official portrait," edited and partly written by Whitman himself. Contains also: "Appendix: *The Good Gray Poet* reprinted from the pamphlet of 1866, with an Introductory Letter (1883), written for this volume by William D. O'Connor."]
BUCKE, RICHARD MAURICE; HARNED, THOMAS B.; and TRAUBEL, HORACE L. "Introduction" [biographical] to *The Complete Writings of Walt Whitman*. New York: G. P. Putnam's Sons. 1902. Vol. I, pp. xiii-xcvi.
[Last official biography by Whitman's literary executors.]
BULLETT, GERALD. *Walt Whitman, a Study and a Selection*. London: Grant Richards. 1924. Philadelphia: J. B. Lippincott. 1925. 166 pp.
[Discriminating biographical essay, pp. 3-24.]
BURROUGHS, JOHN. *Notes on Walt Whitman as Poet and Person*. New York: American News Co. 1867. 108 pp. Sec. Ed., New York: J. S. Redfield. 1871.
[Whitman wrote some of this first book on his life.]
———. "The Flight of the Eagle." *Birds and Poets*. Boston: Houghton Mifflin and Co. 1877, 1895. Pp. 185-235.
———. *Whitman, A Study*. Boston: Houghton Mifflin and Co. 1896. 268 pp.
[Mainly critical rather than biographical.]

CANBY, HENRY SEIDEL. *Walt Whitman, An American*. Boston: Houghton Mifflin and Co. 1943. 381 pp.
[Reassertion of Whitman's importance as national poet and critic of democracy. A valuable contribution to Whitman interpretation rather than of biographical fact.]

CARPENTER, EDWARD. *Days with Walt Whitman: with Some Notes on His Life and Works*. London: George Allen; New York: The Macmillan Co. 1906. 187 pp.
[Friendly but critical—first publication of Whitman's letter to Symonds claiming the paternity of six children. An important book in the growth of Whitman biography.]

CATEL, JEAN. *Walt Whitman: la Naissance du Poète*. Paris: Les Éditions Rieder. 1929. 483 pp.
[Psychological study of the origin of *Leaves of Grass*. Oversimplifies the problem, but illuminating.]

CHASE, RICHARD. *Walt Whitman Reconsidered*. New York: Sloane Associates. 1955. 191 pp.
[Whitman's "sensibility of annihilation" enabled him to give meaning to "chaos and death" in his best poems; "Song of Myself" is a comic "drama of identity."]

CLARKE, WILLIAM. *Walt Whitman*. London: Swan Sonnenschein and Co.; New York: Macmillan and Co. 1892. 132 pp.
[Of little value to the modern student; good at time of publication.]

DE SELINCOURT, BASIL. *Walt Whitman: A Critical Study*. London: Martin Secker. 1914. 250 pp.
[Another romantic life, like Bazalgette's, though more critical. New Orleans romance still flourishes.]

DEUTSCH, BABETTE. *Walt Whitman, Builder for America*. New York: Messner. 1941. 278 pp.
[A competent biography for juveniles.]

DONALDSON, THOMAS. *Walt Whitman, the Man*. New York: Francis P. Harper. 1896. 278 pp.
[By an intimate friend of the Camden period; adds little to Bucke and Burroughs, but somewhat more critical.]

DOWDEN, EDWARD. "The Poetry of Democracy: Walt Whitman." *Studies in Literature: 1789-1877*. London: C. Kegan Paul and Co. 1878. Pp. 468-523.
[Interprets Whitman as product and representative of American environment, life, and unstabilized culture.]

ELLIOT, CHARLES N. *Walt Whitman, as Man, Poet and Friend*.

Boston: Badger. 1915. 257 pp.

[Autograph tributes of friends and admirers; a curiosity, but of little biographical value.]

FAUSSETT, HUGH I'ANSON. *Walt Whitman: Poet of Democracy.* New Haven: Yale University Press. 1942. 320 pp.

[Presents Whitman as a divided personality.]

GLICKSBERG, CHARLES I. *Walt Whitman and the Civil War: A Collection of Original Articles and Manuscripts.* Philadelphia: University of Pennsylvania Press. 1933. 201 pp.

[New source of material for the Civil War period.]

HAYES, WILL. *Walt Whitman: the Prophet of the New Era.* London: C. W. Daniel. n.d. [1921]. 194 pp.

[Continuation of the literal interpretation of Whitman's prophetic rôle.]

HOLLOWAY, EMORY. *Whitman: an Interpretation in Narrative.* New York: Knopf. 1926. 330 pp.

[Still one of the major biographies.]

———. *Free and Lonesome Heart: The Secret of Walt Whitman.* New York: Vantage Press. 1960. 232 pp.

[The "secret" is Whitman's illegitimate children; Holloway identified a John Whitman Wilder said to be Walt Whitman's son.]

KELLER, ELIZABETH LEAVITT. *Walt Whitman in Mickle Street.* New York: Mitchell Kennerley. 1921. 227 pp.

[Details of Whitman's domestic life in Camden, N. J.]

KENNEDY, WILLIAM SLOANE. *Reminiscences of Walt Whitman,* with extracts from his letters and remarks on his writings. London: Alexander Gardner. 1896. 190 pp.

[First-hand account by a friend of the Camden period—very sympathetic. Excellent discussion of the poet's "organic" theory of style.]

LAWRENCE, D. H. "Whitman." *Studies in Classic American Literature.* New York: Albert Boni. 1923. Pp. 241-264.

[A condemnation of Whitman's sentimental Christianity.]

LONG, HANIEL. *Walt Whitman and the Springs of Courage.* Santa Fe: Writers Editions, Inc. 1938. 144 pp.

[On the origins of the poet's self-confidence and intellectual history.]

LOVING, JEROME (Editor). *Civil War Letters of George Washington Whitman.* Introduction by Gay Wilson Allen. Durham: Duke University Press. 1975. 173 pp.

MASTERS, EDGAR LEE. *Whitman.* New York: Charles Scribner's Sons. 1937. 342 pp.
[A mediocre biography, but frank treatment of the "Calamus" problem.]

MILLER, EDWIN H. *Walt Whitman's Poetry: A Psychological Journey.* Boston: Houghton Mifflin Co. 1968. 245 pp. Reprinted by New York University Press. 1969.
[This critical study of Whitman's poetry includes considerable psychoanalytical interpretation of his life.]

MOLINOFF, KATHERINE. *Some Notes on Whitman's Family:* Mary Elizabeth Whitman, Edward Whitman, Andrew and Jesse Whitman, Hannah Louisa Whitman. Introduction by Oscar Cargill. Brooklyn: privately printed by the author. 1941. 43 pp.
[New and important information.]

MORRIS, HARRISON S. *Walt Whitman, a Brief Biography with Reminiscences.* Cambridge, Mass.: Harvard University Press. 1929. 122 pp.
[Interesting for the reminiscences; otherwise of slight value.]

O'CONNOR, WILLIAM DOUGLAS. *The Good Gray Poet, A Vindication.* New York: Bunce and Huntington. 1866. Pamphlet.
[Reprinted in Bucke's *Walt Whitman*, 1883, q.v.]
[A defense of Whitman's life and character after his dismissal by Harlan. The first biography and the beginning of the "Modern Christ" legend.]

PERRY, BLISS. *Walt Whitman, His Life and Work.* London: Archibald Constable and Co.; Boston: Houghton Mifflin and Co. 1906. 318 pp.
[The first scholarly biography.]

REISIGER, HANS. *Walt Whitman* [in German]. Berlin: Suhrkamp Verlag. 1946. 104 pp.
[A brief biography by one of Whitman's friendly critics and translators in Germany.]

RIVERS, W. C. *Walt Whitman's Anomaly.* London: George Allen. 1913. 70 pp.
[Study in sex pathology—circulation limited to the medical profession.]

ROGERS, CAMERON. *The Magnificent Idler: The Story of Walt Whitman.* Garden City: Doubleday, Page and Co. 1926. 312 pp.
[Fictionized and romanticized, but faintly anticipates Catel and Schyberg.]

RUBIN, JOSEPH JAY. *The Historic Whitman.* University Park: The

Pennsylvania State University Press. 1973. 406 pp.
[Excellent history of Whitman as journalist to 1855.]

SCHYBERG, FREDERIK. *Walt Whitman*. Kφbenhavn: Gyldendalske
Boghandel. 1933. 349 pp.
[Continues the interpretation of Catel by searching through all
the editions of *Leaves of Grass* for autobiographical revelations.]
——. *Walt Whitman*. Translated by Evie Allison Allen. New York:
Columbia University Press. 1951. 387 pp.

SHEPHARD, ESTHER. *Walt Whitman's Pose*. New York: Harcourt,
Brace and Co. 1938. 453 pp.
[A source study affecting biographical interpretation.]

SMITH, LOGAN P. "Walt Whitman." *Unforgotten Years*. Boston:
Little, Brown and Co. 1939. Pp. 79-108.
[Charming reminiscences of the poet's visits in the Smith
home.]

SMUTS, JAN CHRISTIAN. *Walt Whitman: A Study of the Evolution
of a Personality*. Edited by Alan L. McLeod. Detroit: Wayne
State University Press. 1973. 205 pp.
[Written in 1895, and out of date as biography, but valuable as
criticism and history of Whitman's reputation.]

STOUTENBURG, ADRIEN, and BAKER, LAURA NELSON. *Listen
America: A Life of Walt Whitman*. New York: Charles Scribner's
and Sons. 1968. 182 pp.
[A biography for young readers.]

SYMONDS, JOHN ADDINGTON. *Walt Whitman, A Study*. London:
George Routledge; New York: E. P. Dutton. 1893. 160 pp.
[Critical study by a friend and admirer—still valuable.]

THOMSON, JAMES. *Walt Whitman, the Man and the Poet*. With an
introduction by Bertram Dobell. London: Bertram Dobell.
1910. 106 pp.
[Biographical details mainly from Burroughs and Bucke, but
some critical comments give the work value.]

TRAUBEL, HORACE. *With Walt Whitman in Camden, March
28–July 14, 1888*. Boston: Small Maynard and Co. 1906. Second Volume, *July 16–October 31, 1888*. New York: D. Appleton and Co. 1908. Third Volume, *November 1, 1888–January
20, 1889*. New York: Mitchell Kennerly, 1914. Fourth Volume,
January 21–April 7, 1889. Carbondale: Southern Illinois University Press. 1959.
[This record of daily conversations with Whitman, though often

tedious and trivial, is nevertheless a source-book for the poet's later years.]

TRAUBEL, HORACE; BUCKE, RICHARD MAURICE; and HARNED, THOMAS B. *In Re Walt Whitman.* Edited by his Literary Executors. Philadelphia: David McKay, 1893. 452 pp.

[Along with much worthless praise by the "disciples," some valuable new testimony from Doyle, George Whitman, etc., and translations of critical essays from French, German, and Danish.]

TRIMBLE, W. H. *Walt Whitman and Leaves of Grass, an Introduction.* London: Watts and Co. 1905. 100 pp.

[Of slight biographical importance but interesting because compiled from lectures given in Dunedin, New Zealand, 1904.]

TROWBRIDGE, JOHN TOWNSEND. *My Own Story: with Recollections of Noted Persons.* Boston: Houghton Mifflin and Co., 1903. Pp. 360-401.

[Valuable for poet's own testimony to Trowbridge of Emerson's influence.]

WINWAR, FRANCES. *American Giant: Walt Whitman and His Times.* New York: Harper and Brothers. 1941. 341 pp.

[Journalistic and sentimental narrative—unreliable.]

ARTICLES OF BIOGRAPHICAL VALUE

BRADLEY, SCULLEY. "Walt Whitman on Timber Creek." *American Literature*, V, 235-246 (November, 1933).

[Based on visits to the place.]

BYCHOWSKI, GUSTAV. "Walt Whitman—A Study in Sublimation," *Psychoanalysis and the Social Sciences*, III (1950), 223-61.

CARPENTER, F. I. "Walt Whitman's Eidólon." *College English*, III, 534-545 (March, 1942).

[Refutation of O'Higgins and Shephard; Whitman achieved his ideal in his poetry if not in his own life—anticipation of Canby's "Symbolical Whitman."]

CHUPACK, HENRY. "Walt Whitman and the Camden Circle," *Proceedings of the New Jersey Historical Society*, LXXII (1955), 274-99.

FURNESS, CLIFTON JOSEPH. Review of Winwar's *American Giant: Walt Whitman and His Times. American Literature*, XIII,

423-432 (January, 1942).
[Although ostensibly a book review, this essay contains new and startling information about Whitman's family and the motives of some of his poems.]

HOLLOWAY, EMORY. "Walt Whitman's Love Affairs." *The Dial*, LXIX, 473-483 (November, 1920).
[The discovery that in the original manuscript "Once I Pass'd Through a Populous City" was a "Calamus" poem led Holloway to reject the New Orleans romance.]

O'HIGGINS, HARVEY. "Alias Walt Whitman." *Harper's Magazine*, CLVIII, 698-707 (May, 1929).
[Anticipates Esther Shephard's interpretation of Whitman's "pose"; a relentless attempt to expose the poet as a fraud.]

NOTE: See also "Anthologies of Criticism," pp. 399-400.

NOTES ON ILLUSTRATIONS

The dauguerrotype, taken in Brooklyn in 1854, is reproduced from a negative presented to the author by the late Oscar Lion. The original daguerrotype is now in the Lion Collection of the New York Public Library.***The drawing by "Carybé" is reproduced from *Poemas*, Versión de Armando Vasseur (Buenos Aires, 1943?) with the permission of the artist in Brazil, Hector Júlio Páride Bernabó. ***Whitman meeting Lafayette is from a page of a comic book in color distributed to the Armed Forces by the U. S. Government during World War II.***The photograph of the 1855 *Leaves of Grass* is from the collection of the late Clifton Furness, though the author also owns this volume.***"I am ashamed. . . ," from a woodcut by Franz Masereel, in *Calamus: Poèmes*, vérsion nouvelle de Léon Bazalgette, Geneva, 1919.***Editions in Russian, French, Oriya, Spanish, photographed by R. J. Mason, Westwood, N. J. ***Russian exhibition, courtesy of Library of Congress, from photographs supplied by Russian Embassy.

SELECTED BIBLIOGRAPHY
Chapter II: Growth of Leaves of Grass

BIBLIOGRAPHY

[There is no definitive bibliography for Whitman.]

ALLEN, EVIE ALLISON. "A Checklist of Whitman Publications 1945-1960." In *Walt Whitman as Man, Poet, and Legend*. By Gay Wilson Allen. Carbondale: Southern Illinois University Press. 1961. Pp. 179-260.

[See Allen, Gay Wilson, below, and Tanner, below.]

ALLEN, GAY W. *Twenty-Five Years of Walt Whitman Bibliography: 1918-1942*. Boston: The F. W. Faxon Co., 1943. 57 pp.

[Supplements Holloway and Saunders. See below.]

HOLLOWAY, EMORY, and SAUNDERS, HENRY S. "[Bibliography of Walt] Whitman." *Cambridge History of American Literature*. New York: G. P. Putnam's Sons. 1918. Vol. II, pp. 551-581.

[Best up to 1918.]

LIBRARY OF CONGRESS. *Walt Whitman, a Catalog Based Upon the Collections of the Library of Congress With Notes*. Washington, D. C.: Government Printing Office. 1955. 147 pp.

SHAY, FRANK. *The Bibliography of Walt Whitman*. New York: Friedmans'. 1920. 46 pp.

[Editions.]

TANNER, JAMES T. *Walt Whitman, a Supplementary Bibliography 1961-67*. Kent State University Press. 1968. 59 pp.

[Supplements Allen, E. A., and G. W., above.]

TRIGGS, OSCAR LOVELL. "Bibliography of Walt Whitman." *Complete Writings of Walt Whitman*. New York and London: G. P. Putnam's Sons. 1902. Vol. X, pp. 139-233.
[Useful description of editions with extended list of biographical and critical material before 1902.]

WELLS, CAROYLN, and GOLDSMITH, ALFRED F. *A Concise Bibliography of the Works of Walt Whitman*. Boston: Houghton Mifflin and Co. 1922. 107 pp.
[A descriptive checklist of editions with a selection of fifty books about Whitman.]

WHITE, WILLIAM. "Walt Whitman's Journalism: A Bibliography." *Walt Whitman Review*, Vol. 14, No. 3 (Sept., 1968), 67-141.
[Whitman's journalistic writings are also discussed in considerable detail by Thomas L. Brasher in *Whitman as Editor of the Brooklyn Daily Eagle* (Detroit: Wayne State University, 1970), 264 pp.; and Joseph Jay Rubin in *The Historic Whitman* (The Pennsylvania State University Press, 1973), xv, 406 pp.]

EDITIONS AND ISSUES

Note: The first publication of all of Whitman's books and pamphlets, 1855-1892, is listed here, but not all reprints or special issues of the major editions.

Leaves of Grass. Brooklyn: [Printed by Rome Brothers]. 1855. (xii, 95 pp. 29cm.)
[First edition. About 1000 copies printed, bound in batches at different times, with slight variations in binding, which was blind-stamped green cloth with gilt letters. Frontispiece steel engraving by Samuel Hollyer from daguerrotype by Gabriel Harrison. Author's name only in copyright notice and in poem ("Song of Myself") on p. 29.]

———. Facsimile of 1855 edition. With an Introduction by Clifton Joseph Furness. Facsimile Text Society, Publication No. 47. New York: Columbia University Press. 1939 [Out of print.]

———. A Facsimile of the First Edition 1855 As Issued by Whitman and Received by Emerson. New York: The Eakins Press. 1966.
[Original cover reproduced with high fidelity; deluxe.]

——. A Facsimile of the First Edition. With an Introduction, a note on the text, and a bibliography prepared by Richard Bridgman. San Francisco: Chandler Publishing Company. 1968. [Inexpensive paperback, fair print, good Introduction.]

Walt Whitman's Leaves of Grass: The First (1855) Edition. Edited, with an Introduction, by Malcolm Cowley. New York: The Viking Press. 1959. [Not a true facsimile, but accurate text in new typesetting, with valuable Introduction.]

Leaves of Grass. Brooklyn: [Fowler & Wells]. 1856. (iv, 384 pp. 16cm.) [Second edition. Frontispiece same as first edition. Bound in green cloth; stamped on backstrip in gold: "I greet You at the/ Beginning of a Great Career/ R. W. Emerson." An Appendix called "Leaves-Droppings" contains Emerson's "Greeting" letter, dated July 21, 1855, and Whitman's open-letter reply to his "Master." Appendix also contains reviews of the first edition. The 1855 preface omitted; poems numbered and titled, the original twelve now being, after much revision, Nos. 1, 4, 32, 26, 7, 27, 19, 16, 22, 25, 29, and 6.]

Leaves of Grass. Boston: Thayer and Eldridge. Year 85 of the States, 1860-61. (iv, 456 pp. front. port. 19½cm.)
[Third edition. Two printings (possibly a third) of 1000 copies each, several color bindings, first orange cloth, second green, third plum. Frontispiece portrait from painting by Charles Hine. 146 new poems; total of 152 grouped in "clusters." Later many pirated copies were printed from these plates, which lack this inscription on copyright page: Electrotyped at the Boston Stereotype Foundry. Printed by George C. Rand & Avery.]

——. Facsimile Edition of the 1860 Text. With an Introduction by Roy Harvey Pearce. Ithaca: Cornell University Press. 1961. [Paper cover, good print, valuable Introduction.]

Walt Whitman's Drum-Taps. New York: [Printed by Peter Eckler]. 1865. (iv, 72 pp. 19 cm.)
[After President Lincoln's death Whitman withdrew this edition until he could add his elegy—in all three elegies, but the "great hymn" was "When Lilacs Last in the Dooryard Bloom'd," which he published in the autumn of 1865 in a *Sequel to Drum-Taps.*]

Walt Whitman's Drum-Taps. New York: [Printed by Peter Eckler]. 1865. (72, 24 pp. 19 cm.)
[Second issue of *Drum-Taps* with *Sequel* appended, pp. 1-24. Title-page: *Sequel to Drum-Taps*/ (Since the Preceding Came

From the Press.)/ WHEN LILACS LAST IN THE DOOR-YARD
BLOOM'D./ And Other Pieces./ Washington./ 1865-6. Seventeen
poems besides "Lilacs," including "O Captain! My Captain!"]

Leaves of Grass. New York: [Printed by William E. Chapin]. 1867.
(338, 72, 24, 36 pp. 20 cm.)
[Fourth edition. Separate title page and pagination for *Drum-
Taps* (72 pp.), *Sequel . . .* (24 pp.), and *Songs Before Parting* (36
pp.)]

After All, Not to Create Only. Recited by Walt Whitman on Invitation
of Managers of the American Institute on Opening their 40th
Annual Exhibition, New York, noon, September 7th, 1871.
Boston: Roberts Brothers. 1871. (24 [4] pp. 20 cm.)

Democratic Vistas. Washington, D. C. 1871. [New York: J. S. Redfield, publisher.] (84 pp. 21 cm.) [Light green paper cover.]

Leaves of Grass. Washington, D. C. [J. S. Redfield] 1871. (384 pp.
21 cm.)
[Fifth edition. Second issue in 1872 includes *Passage to India*,
with 120 added pages. Thirteen new poems exclusive of the
annexes in the later printings. In the fifth edition the groupings
and revisions approach the final arrangement.]

Memoranda During the War. Camden, N. J.: Author's Publication.
1875-76 [c. 1875] ([2] 68 [3] pp. 20½ cm.)
[On cover: "Walt Whitman's Memoranda of the War written on
the spot 1863-1865."]

Leaves of Grass. Camden, N. J.: Author's edition, with portraits from
life. 1876. (384[3] pp. 2 ports. 20½ cm.)
[Reprinted from 1871-72 plates. Backstrip: Centennial edition.
Bound in half-leather, marble boards, uniform with *Two Rivulets*,
the two volumes to constitute *Whitman's Complete Works.*]

*Two Rivulets, Including Democratic Vistas, Centennial Songs, and
Passage to India.* Camden, N.J.: Author's edition. 1876. (32, 84,
18, x, 16, 68, 120 pp. 20 cm.)
[Centennial edition. Poetry and prose. New setting of type for
Two Rivulets; other parts reprinted from plates on hand. Sold as
Vol. II of Author's Edition of the *Complete Works.*]

Leaves of Grass. Boston: James R. Osgood & Co. 1881-82 [c 1881].
(382 pp. 21 cm.)
[Sixth edition (formerly called seventh). Poems arranged in final
order, later additions made in annexes without disturbing the

1881 text. Reprinted in Philadelphia by Rees Welsh and Co. in 1882 (also later issues) and by David McKay in 1888.]

Specimen Days and Collect. Philadelphia: Rees Welsh & Co. 1882–83. (374 pp. port. 20 cm.)

[Reprinted by David McKay, 1882–83.]

November Boughs. Philadelphia: David McKay. 1888. (140 pp. 23½ cm.)

[Prose includes "A Backward Glance O'er Travel'd Roads" and miscellaneous notes which were reprinted in the 1892 *Prose Works*, pp. 375-476. Poems in cluster "Sands at Seventy," which became the First Annex to the 1892 *Leaves of Grass.*]

Complete Poems and Prose of Walt Whitman 1855 ... 1888. Authenticated & Personal Book (Handled by W. W.) Portraits from Life ... Autograph. Philadelphia: [Printed by Ferguson Brothers & Co.]. 1888. (900 pp. 27 cm.)

[Reprint of 1882 *Leaves of Grass and Specimen Days*, with poems from *November Boughs* and "A Backward Glance ..." annexed.]

Good-Bye My Fancy: 2d Annex to Leaves of Grass. Philadelphia: David McKay. 1891. (66 pp. 23½ cm.)

[Uniform with *November Boughs*; prose and poems.]

Leaves of Grass. Philadelphia: David McKay. 1891–92. (438 pp. 21½ cm.)

[Often called the "ninth edition" but actually a reprint of the sixth (1881–82) edition, with poems from *November Boughs* added as First Annex and poems from *Good-Bye My Fancy* as Second Annex. Whitman "authorized" this text for all future reprints.]

Leaves of Grass. Boston: Small, Maynard and Co. 1897. (455 pp. 21½ cm.)

[This has been called the "tenth edition" because it contains the posthumous cluster, "Old Age Echoes"; however, except for the posthumous poems it is a reprint of the 1891–92 issue.]

Complete Prose Works. Philadelphia: David McKay. 1892. (522 pp. 21½ cm.)

[Contains all the prose of *Specimen Days and Collect, November Boughs*, and *Good-Bye My Fancy*. This was also sold as Vol. II of *Complete Works*.]

The Complete Writings of Walt Whitman. Issued under the editorial Supervision of the Literary Executors, Richard Maurice Bucke,

Thomas B. Harned, and Horace L. Traubel, with additional bibliographical and critical material by Oscar Lowell Triggs, Ph.D. New York and London: Putnam's Sons. 1902. 10 vols. [Although this became the standard edition of Whitman for half a century, it was not "complete," as claimed, and it was edited by amateurs. It is now being superseded by *The Collected Writings of Walt Whitman* published by the New York University Press under the general editorship of Gay Wilson Allen and Sculley Bradley. The Putnam edition was sold in a variety of issues, with different paper and bindings. It contained all the poetry and prose which up to 1902 had been collected, with a biographical essay by the literary executors, letters of the poet to his mother, *Notes and Fragments* previously edited by Dr. Bucke, and other miscellanies.]

The Collected Writings of Walt Whitman. General Editors Gay Wilson Allen and Sculley Bradley. New York University Press. Volumes published 1963–75:

> *Prose Works 1892.* Edited by Floyd Stovall. Volume I, *Specimen Days.* 1963. (xx[2], 358 pp.) Volume II, *Collect and Other Prose.* 1964. (xvi, 359-803[2]pp.) New York: New York University Press.

> *The Early Poems and the Fiction.* Edited by Thomas L. Brasher. 1963. (xx, 352 pp.)

> *Leaves of Grass.* Reader's Edition, Including the Annexes, The Prefaces, "A Backward Glance O'er Travel'd Roads," "Old Age Echoes," the Excluded Poems and Fragments, and the Uncollected Poems and Fragments. Edited by Harold W. Blodgett and Sculley Bradley. 1965. (lviii[2], 768 pp.)

> *The Correspondence.* Edited by Edwin Haviland Miller. Volume I: 1842-1867. 1961. (x[1], 394 pp.) Volume II: 1868-1875. (viii[1], 387 pp. 1961. Volume III: 1876-1885. (ix[1], 473 pp.) 1964. Volume IV: 1886-1889. (viii[1], 458 pp.) 1969. Volume V: 1890-1892. (ix[1], 365 pp.) 1969.

> *Day-Books and Other Diaries.* Edited by William White. [Scheduled for publication in 1975.]

UNCOLLECTED WRITINGS

(In order of publication)

Calamus: A Series of Letters Written during the Years 1868–1880. By Walt Whitman to a Young Friend (Peter Doyle). Edited with an Introduction by Richard Maurice Bucke, M.D. Boston: Laurens Maynard. 1897. (viii, 172 pp.)

The Wound-Dresser: A Series of Letters Written from the Hospitals in Washington during the War of Rebellion By Walt Whitman. Edited by Richard Maurice Bucke, M.D. Boston: Small, Maynard and Co. 1898. viii, 201 pp.

Notes and Fragments. Edited by Dr. Richard Maurice Bucke. (Printed for Private Distribution Only.) London, Ontario, Canada. 1899. 211 pp.
[Manuscript fragments of both poetry and prose, including some early notebooks and a list of magazine and newspaper clippings kept by the poet (now in the Trent Collection, Duke University Library). *Notes and Fragments* also included in *The Complete Writings of Walt Whitman*, Vol. IX. Most of this material is being re-edited by Edward F. Grier for the new edition of *Collected Writings* . . .]

Letters Written by Walt Whitman to His Mother from 1866 *To* 1872. Together with Certain Papers Prepared from Material now First Utilized. Edited by Thomas B. Harned. New York and London: G. P. Putnam's Sons. 1902.
[Excerpted from *Complete Writings*, Vol. VIII, 169-243. Reprinted by Alfred F. Goldsmith, with an Introductory Note by Rollo G. Silver. New York. 1936. 71 pp. Now included in Edwin H. Miller's *Correspondence*.]

Walt Whitman's Diary in Canada. With Extracts from other of his Diaries and Literary Note-Books. Edited by William Sloane Kennedy. Boston: Small, Maynard and Co. 1904. 73 pp.
[*Diary in Canada* is included in William White's edition of *Walt Whitman's Day-Books and Other Diaries* in *Collected Writings*.]

An American Primer. With Facsimiles of the Original Manuscript. Edited by Horace Traubel. Boston: Small, Maynard and Co. 1904. 35 pp.
[Also included by White in *Day-Books and Other Diaries*. See above.]

The Letters of Anne Gilchrist and Walt Whitman. Edited by Thomas B. Harned. New York: Doubleday, Doran and Co. 1918. 241 pp.

The Gathering of the Forces. Editorials, Essays, Literary and Dramatic Reviews and other Material Written by Walt Whitman as

Editor of the Brooklyn *Daily Eagle* in 1846 and 1847. Edited by Cleveland Rodgers and John Black. With a foreword and a sketch of Whitman's Life and Work During Two Unknown Years. New York and London: G. P. Putnam's Sons. 1920. 2 Vols.

The Uncollected Poetry and Prose of Walt Whitman. Much of Which Has Been But Recently Discovered with Various Early Manuscripts Now First Published. Collected and Edited by Emory Holloway. New York: Doubleday, Doran and Co. 1921. 2 Vols. Reprinted by Peter Smith, New York, 1932.
[These manuscripts are being re-edited by Edwin F. Grier and the fiction has been edited by Thomas L. Brasher. See *Collected Writings*, New York University Press.]

Pictures. An Unpublished Poem by Walt Whitman. With an Introduction and Notes by Emory Holloway. New York: The June House. 1927. London: Faber and Gwyer. 1927. 37 pp.
[Included by Blodgett and Bradley in Comprehensive Reader's Edition of *Leaves of Grass*, 642-49.]

The Half-Breed and Other Stories. Edited by Thomas Ollive Mabbott. New York: Columbia University Press. 1927. 129 p.

Walt Whitman's Workshop. Edited by Clifton Joseph Furness. Cambridge: Harvard University Press. 1928. x, 265 pp.
[Speeches and unpublished prefaces; these are being included in the *Collected Writings*, New York University Press, but Furness's notes (181-265) still have useful information.]

I Sit and Look Out. Editorials from the Brooklyn *Daily Times*. Selected and Edited by Emory Holloway and Vernolian Schwarz. New York: Columbia University Press. 1932. xii, 248 pp.

New York Dissected. A Sheaf of Recently Discovered Newspaper Articles by the author of *Leaves of Grass*. Introduction and Notes by Emory Holloway and Ralph Adimari. New York: Rufus Rockwell Wilson. 1936. 257 pp.

Whitman's Manuscripts: Leaves of Grass (1860): A Parallel Text. Edited with Notes and Introduction by Fredson Bowers. Chicago: University of Chicago Press. 1955. lxxiv, 264 pp.

The Eighteenth Presidency! A Critical Text Edited by Edward F. Grier. Lawrence: University of Kansas Press. 1956. 47 pp.

An 1855–56 Notebook Toward the Second Edition of Leaves of

Grass. Introduction and Notes by Harold W. Blodgett. With a Foreword by Charles E. Feinberg. Additional Notes by William White. Carbondale: Southern Illinois University Press. 1959. x, 41[1] pp.

Walt Whitman's Blue Book: The 1860-61 *Leaves of Grass* Containing His Manuscript Additions and Revisions. Vol. I: Facsimile of the unique copy in the Oscar Lion Collection of the New York Public Library. Vol. II: Textual analysis by Arthur Golden. New York: The New York Public Library. 1968. Vol. I, 456 pp. (third edition of *LG*); Vol. II, lxv, 428 pp.

Walt Whitman's Autograph Revision of the Analysis of Leaves of Grass (For Dr. R. M. Bucke's Walt Whitman). Introductory Essay by Quentin Anderson. Text Notes by Stephen Railton. With thirty-five facsimile pages of the manuscript. New York: New York University Press. 1974. 191 pp.

SPECIAL EDITIONS

Walt Whitman's Poems: Selections with Critical Notes. Edited by Gay Wilson Allen and Charles T. Davis. New York: New York University Press. 1955. (x, 280 pp.) Paper cover, 1968, 1972.

Walt Whitman: Complete Poetry and Selected Prose. Edited by James E. Miller, Jr. Boston: Houghton Mifflin Co. (Riverside Editions.) 1959. (liii, 516 pp.)

Leaves of Grass: A Norton Critical Edition. Edited by Sculley Bradley and Harold W. Blodgett. New York: W. W. Norton & Co. 1973. (lx, 1008 pp.)
[Reprint of the contents of The Reader's Edition of *Leaves of Grass*, plus "Whitman on His Art" and essays by thirty critics. Inexpensive paper cover edition.]

The Portable Walt Whitman. Revised and enlarged edition. Edited by Mark Van Doren [revised by Malcolm Cowley]. Introduction by Mark Van Doren. "A Note on the New Edition" by Malcolm Cowley. Chronology and Bibliographical Check List by Gay Wilson Allen. New York: The Viking Press. 1974. (xxxi, 648 pp.)
[Seven poems and the 1855 Preface reprinted from the 1855 edition; other poems from the 1891-92 text; complete text of *Specimen Days*.]

TEXTUAL STUDIES
(*Alphabetical order*)

ALLEN, GAY WILSON. *The Solitary Singer: A Critical Biography of Walt Whitman.* New York: The Macmillan Company. 1955. New York University Press. 1968. (xii, 616 pp.) [Discussion oi first edition, 149-176; second, 177-190; third, 221-259.]

ASSELINEAU, ROGER. *The Evolution of Walt Whitman*: The Creation of a Book. Cambridge: Harvard University Press. 1962. (392 pp.)

BLODGETT, HAROLD W., and BRADLEY, SCULLEY, editors. "Introduction: The Growth of 'Leaves of Grass,' " *Leaves of Grass*: Comprehensive Reader's Edition. New York: New York Universtiy Press. 1965. (Pp. [xxvi]-liii.)

BOWERS, FREDSON. "The Walt Whitman Manuscripts of 'Leaves of Grass' (1860)." *Textual and Literary Criticism.* Cambridge: Cambridge University Press. 1959. (Pp. 35-65.)
[See also Bowers' edition of these MSS, above, "Uncollected Writings."]

CAMPBELL, KILLIS. "The Evolution of Whitman as Artist." *American Literature*, VI, 254-263 (November, 1934).
[Traces the poet's growth by means of his textual improvements.]

CATEL, JEAN. *Walt Whitman: La Naissance due Poète.* Paris: Les Editions Rieder. 1929. (483 pp.)
[Whitman's "naissance" in 1855.]

COWLEY, MALCOLM. "Editor's Introduction." *Walt Whitman's Leaves of Grass: The First (1855) Edition.* New York: The Viking Press. 1959. (Pp. [vii]-xxxvii.)

CRAWLEY, THOMAS EDWARD. *The Structure of* Leaves of Grass. Austin & London: University of Texas Press. 1970. (xii, 256 pp.)
[More on themes than bibliography.]

DE SELINCOURT, BASIL. *Walt Whitman: A Study.* New York: Mitchell Kennerley. 1914. London: Martin Secker. 1914. (Chap. VI, "Plan," traces the "skeleton design" of *Leaves of Grass*.)

GOLDEN, ARTHUR. See Vol. II of *Walt Whitman's Blue Book*, above, "Uncollected Writings."

KENNEDY, WILLIAM SLOANE. "The Growth of 'Leaves of Grass' as a Work of Art (Excisions, Additions, Verbal Changes)." *The Fight of a Book for the World.* West Yarmouth, Mass.: Stone-

croft Press. 1926. (304 pp.)
[Much valuable information but erratic criticism.]

SCHYBERG, FREDERIK. *Walt Whitman.* Translated from the Danish by Evie Allison Allen. Introduction by Gay Wilson Allen. New York: Columbia University Press. 1951. (xv, 387 pp.) [Schyberg's biographical interpretations are based on textual studies of the editions of *Leaves of Grass.*]

STOVALL, FLOYD. "Main Drifts in Whitman's Poetry." *American Literature*, IV, 3-21 (March 1932).

STRAUCH, CARL F. "The Structure of Walt Whitman's 'Song of Myself,'" *English Journal* (College Edition), XXVII, 597-607 (September 1938).

WEATHERS, WILLIE T. "Whitman's Poetic Translations of His 1855 Preface," *American Literature*, XIX, 21-40 (March 1947).

SELECTED BIBLIOGRAPHY
Chapter III: Whitman's Ideas

BACKGROUND

CARGILL, OSCAR. *Intellectual America: Ideas on the March*. New York: Macmillan. 1941.
[Discussion of fecundity especially pertinent, 538 ff.]

CARPENTER, FREDERIC I. *Emerson and Asia*. Cambridge: Harvard University Press 1930.

CHRISTY, ARTHUR. *The Orient in American Transcendentalism*. New York: Columbia University Press. 1932.

EMERSON, RALPH WALDO. *Nature* (1836), *Collected Works*, I, 7-45. Edited by Robert E. Spiller and Alfred R. Ferguson. Cambridge: Harvard University Press. 1971.

HARROLD, CHARLES F. *Carlyle and German Thought, 1819–1834*. New Haven: Yale University Press. 1934.

JAMES, WILLIAM. "Mysticism," *Varieties of Religious Experience*, pp. 379-420. London: Longmans, Green. 1902. Facsimile reprint: New Hyde Park: University Books. 1963.

KNUDSON, ALBERT C. *The Philosophy of Personalism*. New York: Abingdon Press. 1927.

KOESTLER, ARTHUR. *The Ghost in the Machine*. New York: Macmillan. 1967.

OTTO, RUDOLF. *Mysticism East and West: A Comparative Analysis of the Nature of Mysticism*. New York: Macmillan. 1932.

RILEY, WOODBRIDGE. *The Meaning of Mysticism*. New York: Harper and Brothers. 1930.

[Compares "the pantheism of the Rhine region . . . with the poetic pantheism of Walt Whitman . . ."]

RUSSELL, BERTRAND. *Mysticism and Logic and Other Essays*. London: Longmans, Green. 1921.

TEILHARD DE CHARDIN, PIERRE. *Man's Place in Nature: The Human Zoological Group*. Translated by René Hague. New York: Harper & Row. 1966. *The Phenomenon of Man*. Translated by Bernard Wall. New York: Harper & Row. 1961. *The Divine Milieu*. New York: Harper & Row. 1960. *Building the Earth*. Translated by Noël Lindsay. Wilkes-Barre, Pa.: Dimensions Books 1965.

TOMPKINS, PETER, and BIRD, CHRISTOPHER. *The Secret Life of Plants*. New York: Harper & Row. 1972.

UNDERHILL, EVELYN. Mysticism: *A Study in the Nature and Development of Man's Spiritual Consciousness*. New York: E. P. Dutton. 11th Ed. 1926.

VOLNEY, COUNT C. F. *The Ruins; or Meditation on the Revolution of Empires* . . . To Which is Added *The Law of Nature*. New York: Calvin Blanchard, n. d. [*c*.1800.]

WALZEL, OSKAR. *German Romanticism*. Translated by Alma Elise Lussky, from *Deutsche Romantik* (Berlin, 1923). New York: Putnam. 1932.

CRITICAL STUDIES

ALLEN, GAY WILSON. "Walt Whitman's 'Long Journey' Motif," *Journal of English and Germanic Philology*. XXXVIII, 76-95 (January 1939).

[The "Long Journey" is the evolution of the human race.]

ARVIN, NEWTON. *Whitman*. New York: Macmillan. 1938.

[Discusses social and political ideas, and relations of Whitman's ideas to French rationalism and German romanticism.]

BEAVER, JOSEPH. *Walt Whitman, Poet of Science*. New York: King's Crown Press. 1951.

[Strongest on astronomy—demonstrates Whitman's knowledge.]

BECK, MAXIMILIAN. "Walt Whitman's Intuition of Reality." *Ethics*, LIII, 14-24 (October 1942).

BENOIT, RAY. "The Mind's Return: Whitman, Teilhard, and Jung," *Walt Whitman Review*, XIII, 31-28 (March 1958).

BERTZ, EDUARD. *Der Yankee-Heiland*. Dresden: Reissner. 1906.
[Debunks Whitman as a thinker; compares him unfavorably with
Novalis and Nietzsche.]

BOATRIGHT, MODY C. "Whitman and Hegel." *Studies in English
(The University of Texas Bulletin)*, IX, 134-50 (July 8, 1929).

BUCKE, RICHARD MAURICE. *Cosmic Consciousness*. New York:
E. P. Dutton. 1923.
[Gives examples of Whitman's mystical experiences.]

CARPENTER, EDWARD. *Days with Walt Whitman*. London:
George Allen. 1906.
[In chapter on "Whitman as Prophet" cites parallels between
Upanishads and *Leaves of Grass*; also Emerson and Whitman.]

CARPENTER, FREDERIC I. "Walt Whitman's Eidólon." *College
English*, III, 534-45 (March 1942).
[On Whitman's "idealism."]

COLUM, MARY M. "The Ideas that Have Made Modern Literature,"
From These Roots, pp. 260-311. New York: Charles Scribner &
Sons. 1937.

COOKE, ALICE LOVELACE. "Whitman's Background in the Industrial Movements of His Time." *Studies in English (The University of Texas Bulletin:*, XV, 89-115 (July 8, 1935).

COWLEY, MALCOLM. Introduction to *Walt Whitman's Leaves of
Grass: His Original (1855) Edition*. New York: Viking Press.
1959.

FALK, ROBERT P. "Walt Whitman and German Thought." *Journal
of English and Germanic Philology*, XL, 315-30 (July 1941).

FULGHUM, W. B., JR. "Whitman's Debt to Joseph Gostwick."
American Literature, XII, 491-96 (January 1941).

GIRGUS, SAM B. "Culture and Post-Culture in Walt Whitman." *The
Centennial Review*, XVIII, 392-410 (Fall 1974).

GODHES, CLARENCE. "Whitman and Emerson." *Sewanee Review*,
XXXVII, 79-93 (January 1929).

GOODALE, DAVID. "Some of Walt Whitman's Borrowings." *American Literature*, X, 202-13 (May 1938).
[Borrowings from Volney, Frances Wright, and others.]

HOWARD, LEON. "For a Critique of Whitman's Transcendentalism."
Modern Language Notes, XLVII, 79-85 (February 1932).

HUNGERFORD, EDWARD. "Walt Whitman and His Chart of
Bumps." *American Literature*, II, 350-84 (January 1931).
[Phrenology as an important source.]

JENSEN, MILLIE. "Whitman and Hegel: The Curious Triplicate Process." *Walt Whitman Review*, X, 27-34 (June 1964).

LONG, HANIEL. *Walt Whitman and the Springs of Courage*. Santa Fe, N. M.: Writers' Editions. 1938.

MATTHIESSEN, F. O. "Whitman," *American Renaissance*: Art and Expression in the Age of Emerson and Whitman, pp. 517-625. New York: Oxford University Press. 1941.

MAXWELL, WILLIAM. "Some Personalist Elements in the Poetry of Whitman." *Personalist*, XII, 190-99 (July 1931).

MOORE, JOHN B. "The Master of Whitman." *Studies in Philology*, XXIII, 77-89 (January 1926).

MYERS, HENRY ALONZO. "Whitman's Conception of the Spiritual Democracy, 1855–56." *American Literature*, VI, 239-53 (November 1934).
[Whitman's basic metaphysical assumptions.]

——. "Whitman's Consistency." *American Literature*, VIII, 243-57 (November 1936).
[Consistency of his "idealism."]

PAINE, GREGORY. "The Literary Relations of Whitman and Carlyle with Especial Reference to their Contrasting views of Democracy." *Studies in Philology*, XXXVI, 550-63 (July 1939).

PARSONS, OLIVE W. "Whitman the Non-Hegelian." *PMLA*, 1073-93 (December 1943).

REED, H. B. "The Heraclitan Obsession of Whitman." *Personalist*, XV, 125-38 (Spring 1934).

REISS, EDMUND. "Whitman's Debt to Animal Magnetism." *PMLA*, LXXVIII, 80-88 (March 1963).

SARRAZIN, GABRIEL. "Walt Whitman," translated by Harrison S. Morris, *In Re Walt Whitman*, pp. 159-94. Philadelphia: David McKay. 1893.
[First critical interpretation of Whitman's "pantheism."]

SHIPLEY, M. "Democracy as a Religion: The Religion of Walt Whitman." *Open Court*, XXXIII, 385-93 (July 1919).
[Study of Whitman's ideas for a "new religion."]

SMITH, FRED M. "Whitman's Debt to *Sartor Resartus*." *Modern Language Quarterly*, III, 51-65 (March 1942).

——. "Whitman's Poet-Prophet and Carlyle's Hero." *PMLA*, LV, 1146-64 (December 1940).
[Important study of Carlyle's influence on Whitman.]

STOVALL, FLOYD. "Main Drifts in Whitman's Poetry." *American*

Literature, IV, 3-21 (March 1932).

[Shift in attitudes and thought as Whitman matured.]

———. *The Foreground of Leaves of Grass*. Charlottesville: University of Virginia Press. 1974.

[Exhaustive study of sources.]

SYMONDS, JOHN ADDINGTON. *Walt Whitman: A Study*. London: George Routledge. 1893.

TANNER, JAMES. "The Lamarckian Theory of Progress in 'Leaves of Grass.'" *Walt Whitman Review*, IX, 3-11 (March 1963).

WROBEL, ARTHUR. "Whitman and the Phrenologists: The Divine Body and the Sensuous Soul." *PMLA*, LXXXIX, 17-23 (January 1974).

SELECTED BIBLIOGRAPHY
Chapter IV: Literary Technique

BACKGROUND—STYLE AND STRUCTURE

COOK, A. S. "The 'Authorized Version' and Its Influence." *Cambridge History of English Literature*, IV, 29-58. New York and London: G. P. Putnam's Sons. 1910.

DAHLSTROM, C. W. W. L. *Strindberg's Dramatic Expressionism*, pp. 3-82. Ann Arbor: University of Michigan. 1930.
[Definitions and history of "Expressionism."]

DRIVER, S. R. *Introduction to the Literature of the Old Testament*. New York: Charles Scribner & Sons. 1910.

GARDINER, J. H. *The Bible as English Literature*. New York: Charles Scribner & Sons. 1906.

GROSS, HARVEY. *Sound and Form in Modern Poetry: A Study of Prosody from Thomas Hardy to Robert Lowell*. Ann Arbor: University of Michigan Press. 1964. (See index for Whitman.)

HRUSHOVSKI, BENJAMIN. "The Theory and Practice of Rhythm in the Expressionist Poetry of U. Z. Grinberg." *Hasifrut*: Quarterly for the Study of Literature, Tel-Aviv University, I, 176-205 (Spring, 1968).
[Compares rhythms of Mayakovsky and Whitman in relation to Grinberg's two levels of rhythm. Written in Hebrew.]

KAUTZSCH, EMIL FRIEDRICH. *Die Poesie und die Poetischen Bücher der Alten Testaments*. Tübingen: Mohr. 1902.

[Based   on Bishop Lowth's discovery of parallelism as the prosodic principle of Biblical verse: *De sacra poesi Hebraeorum
praelectiones academiae oxonii habitae*, 1753.]

MOULTON, R. G. *The Literary Study of the Bible*. Boston: D. C.
Heath. 1895.
[Parallelism. *Moulton's Modern Reader's Bible* (New York: Macmillan, 1922) arranges the Biblical poetry in accordance with the
principles of "thought-rhythm."]

SMITH, C. ALPHONSO. *Repetition and Parallelism in English Verse*.
New York: University Publishing Co. 1894.

SUTCLIFFE, EMERSON GRANT. "Emerson's Theories of Literary
Expression." *University of Illinois Studies in Language and
Literature*, VIII, 9-143 (1943).
[Background for influence of Transcendentalism on Whitman's
theory and practice.]

WAGGONER, HYATT, H. *American Poets: From the Puritans to the
Present*. Boston: Houghton Mifflin Co. 1968.
[Argues that Emerson's influence on Whitman has not been
sufficiently appreciated.]

TEXTS OF SPECIAL IMPORTANCE

AN AMERICAN PRIMER. Edited by Horace Traubel. Boston:
Small, Maynard and Co. 1904. Re-edited by William White in
Walt Whitman's Day-Books and Other Diaries. New York: New
York University Press. (Scheduled for publication 1975.)

NOTES AND FRAGMENTS. Edited by Richard Maurice Bucke.
London, Ontario: printed for the editor. 1899. Reprinted:
Folcroft, Pa.: Folcroft Library Editions. 1972.

PICTURES. Edited by Emory Holloway, from unpublished manu-
script. London: Faber and Gwyer. 1927. Reprinted: *Leaves of
Grass: Comprehensive Reader's Edition*, pp. 642-649. Edited by
Harold W. Blodgett and Sculley Bradley. New York: New York
University Press. 1965.

PREFACES. Reprinted in *Reader's Edition*; see above.

CRITICAL STUDIES

ALLEN, GAY WILSON. "Biblical Analogies for Walt Whitman's Prosody." *Revue Anglo-Américaine*, X, 490-507 (August 1933).

——. "Walt Whitman," *American Prosody*, pp. 217-42. New York: American Book Co. 1935.

[Parallelism as Whitman's basic rhythmical principle.]

——. "Form and Structure," *A Reader's Guide to Walt Whitman*, pp. 156-212. New York: Farrar, Straus & Giroux. 1970.

[Adds "expressive form" to previous analyses of Whitman's prosody.]

ASSELINEAU, ROGER. *The Evolution of Walt Whitman: The Creation of a Book*. Cambridge: Harvard University Press. 1962.

[Part Two discusses Style, Language, and Prosody.]

BAHR, HERMANN. Introduction to Max Hayek's translation, *Ich Singe das Leben*. Leipzig, Wien, Zürich: E. P. Tall and Co. 1921.

BRADLEY, SCULLEY. "The Fundamental Metrical Principles in Whitman's Poetry." *American Literature*, X, 437-59 (January 1939).

[Tries to prove that Whitman's "organic rhythms" are fundamentally metrical.]

CATEL, JEAN. *Rythme et langage dans la 1er édition des "Leaves of Grass," 1855*. Paris: Les Editions Rieder. [1930]

[Stresses oratory as great influence in formation of Whitman's poetic style.]

CHRISTADLER, MARTIN. "Walt Whitman: Sprachtheorie und Dichtung," *Jahrbuch für Amerikanstudien*, 13 (1968), 84-97.

COFFMAN, STANLEY K. " 'Crossing Brooklyn Ferry': A Note on the Catalogue Technique in Whitman's Poetry." *Modern Philology*, LI, 225-32 (May 1954).

CORY, ROBERT E. "The Prosody of Walt Whitman." *North Dakota Quarterly*, XXVIII (1960), 74-79.

COY, REBECCA. "A Study of Whitman's Diction." *University of Texas Studies in English*, XVI, 115-124 (July 1936).

DE SELINCOURT, BASIL. *Walt Whitman: A Critical Study*. London: Martin Secker. 1914.

[Especially good on analogies with music.]

ERSKINE, JOHN. "A note on Whitman's Prosody." *Studies in Philology*, XX, 336-44 (July 1923).

FANER, ROBERT D. *Walt Whitman & Opera*. Philadelphia: University of Pennsylvania Press. 1951.

[Weak on actual influence of opera on Whitman's versification, but provides information for such a study.]

FEIDELSON, CHARLES, JR. *Symbolism and American Literature*.

Chicago: University of Chicago Press. 1953.

[On Symbolist esthetics.]

FURNESS, CLIFTON JOSEPH. *Walt Whitman's Workshop*. Cambridge: Harvard University Press. 1928.

[Notes contain many observations on style and technique.]

GRIFFIN, ROBERT J. "Notes on Structural Devices in Whitman's Poetry." *Tennessee Studies in Literature*, VI (1961), 15-24.

HINDUS, MILTON. "Notes Toward the Definition of a Typical Poetic Line in Whitman." *Walt Whitman Review*, IX (1963), 75-81.

HOLLIS, C. CARROLL. "Whitman and the American Idiom." *Quarterly Journal of Speech*, LXIII (1957), 408-20.

HOPKINS, GERARD MANLEY. *Letters of Gerard Manley Hopkins*, 154-58. Edited by Claude Colleer Abbott. (London, 1935). Reprinted by Edwin H. Miller in *A Century of Whitman Criticism* (Bloomington: Indiana University Press. 1969), pp. 77-80. [Letter to Robert Bridges regarding Whitman's influence on Hopkins's "sprung rhythm"—which Hopkins denies.]

HOSBAUM, PHILIP. "Eliot, Whitman and the American Tradition." *Journal of American Studies*, III, 239-64 (1969).

JANNACCONE, P. *La Poesia di Walt Whitman e l'Evoluzione delle Forme Ritmiche*. Torino. 1898. Translated by Peter Mitilineos. Washington, D. C.: Microcard Editions. 1973.

[Demonstrates Whitman's primitive techniques but also discovers metrical patterns in his rhythms.]

KALLSEN, T. J. " 'Song of Myself': Logical Unity through Analogy." *West Virginia University Bulletin*, IX (1953), 33-40.

KENNEDY, W. S. "The Style of Leaves of Grass." *Reminiscences of Walt Whitman*, pp. 149-90. London: Alexander Gardner. 1896. [Defends the "organic" style.]

McELDERRY, BRUCE, JR. "Personae in Whitman (1855–1860)." *American Transcendental Quarterly*, No. 12 (Fall 1971), 26-28. (1971), 26-28.

MATTHIESSEN, F. O. "Only a Language Experiment." *American Renaissance*, pp. 517-625. New York: Oxford University Press. 1941.

[A major critical contribution.]

MITCHELL, ROGER. "A Prosody for Whitman?" *PMLA*, LXXXIV (1969), 1606-12.

MORE, PAUL ELMER. "Walt Whitman." *Shelburne Essays*, 4th Ed., New Ser., pp. 180-211. Boston: Houghton Mifflin. 1922.

PEARCE, ROY HARVEY. *The Continuity of American Poetry*, Chap. IV. Princeton: Princeton University Press. 1961.

POLLAK, GEORGIANA. "The Relationship of Music to 'Leaves of Grass,' " *College English*, XV, 384-94 (April 1954).

REED, HARRY B. "The Heraclitan Obsession of Walt Whitman." *The Personalist*, XV, 125-38 (April 1934).
[On flux and progression in Whitman's literary style.]

ROBBINS, J. ALBERT. "The Narrative Form of 'Song of Myself,' " *American Transcendental Quarterly*, No. 12 (Fall 1971), 17-20.

ROSS, E. C. "Whitman's Verse." *Modern Language Notes*, XLV, 363-364 (June 1930).
[Importance of punctuation and end-stopped lines.]

SCHUMANN, DETLEV W. "Enumerative Style and Its Significance in Whitman, Rilke, Werfel." *Modern Language Quarterly*, III, 171-204 (June 1942).

SCHYBERG, FREDERIK. *Walt Whitman*. Translated by Evie Allison Allen. New York: Columbia University Press. 1951.

SCOTT, FRED NEWTON. "A Note on Whitman's Prosody." *Journal of English and Germanic Philology*, VII, 134-53 (1908).

TANNENBAUM, KARL. "Pattern in Whitman's 'Song of Myself.' " *CLA Journal*, VI, 44-49 (September 1962).

TEMPLEMAN, W. D. "Hopkins and Whitman: Evidence of Influence and Echoes." *Philological Quarterly*, XXXIII, 48-65 (1954).

WARE, LOIS. "Poetic Conventions in Leaves of Grass." *Studies in Philology*, XXVI, 47-57 (January 1929).

WASKOW, HOWARD. *Whitman: Exploration in Form*. Chicago: University of Chicago Press. 1966.

WEATHERS, WILLIE T. "Whitman's Poetic Translations of His 1855 Preface." *American Literature*, XIX, 21-40 (March 1947).

WEEKS, RUTH M. "Phrasal Prosody" [with special reference to Whitman]. *English Journal*, X 11-19 (January 1921).

WILEY, AUTREY NELL. "Reiterative Devices in 'Leaves of Grass.' " *American Literature*, I, 161-70 (May 1929).
[Rhetorical devices of epanaphora and epanalepsis.]

WILLIAMS, WILLIAM CARLOS. "An Essay on *Leaves of Grass*," pp. 22-31. *Leaves of Grass One Hundred Years After*. Edited by Milton Hindus. Palo Alto: Stanford University Press. 1955.

ANTHOLOGIES OF CRITICISM

Leaves of Grass: One Hundred Years After. Edited with Introduction by Milton Hindus. Stanford: Stanford University Press. 1955.

Whitman: A Collection of Critical Essays. Edited by Roy Harvey Pearce. Englewood Cliffs, N.J.: Prentice-Hall Inc. 1962.

A Century of Whitman Criticism. Edited by Edwin H. Miller. Bloomington: University of Indiana Press. 1969.

Walt Whitman: The Critical Heritage. Edited by Milton Hindus. London: Routledge & Kegan Paul. (Critical Heritage series.) 1971.

Studies in Leaves of Grass. Compiled by Gay Wilson Allen. Columbus, Ohio: Charles E. Merrill Publishing Co. 1972.

Walt Whitman in Europe Today. Edited by Roger Asselineau and William White. Detroit: Wayne State University Press. 1972.

Walt Whitman: A Collection of Criticism. Edited by Arthur Golden. New York: McGraw-Hill, Inc. 1974.

The Walt Whitman Review, edited by William White and Charles E. Feinberg, published by Wayne State University Press, prints criticism, scholarly articles, book reviews and current bibliography of Whitman publications.

SELECTED BIBLIOGRAPHY
Chapter V: World Literature

GENERAL

Walt Whitman Abroad: Critical Essays from Germany, France, Scandinavia, Russia, Italy, Spain and Latin America, Israel, Japan, and India. Edited by Gay Wilson Allen. Syracuse University Press. 1955.
Contents: *Germany*: Introduction by editor; translations of Freiligrath, Hans Reisiger, Thomas Mann, Hermann Pongs. *France*: Introduction by editor; translations of Valéry Larbaud, Jean Catel, Roger Asselineau. *Scandinavia*: Introduction by editor; translations of Knut Hamsun, Johannes V. Jensen, Roland Fridholm, Kjell Krogvig; *Russia and other Slavic Countries*: Introductions by Stephen Stepanchev; translations of Anon. reviewer of Chukovsky, D. Mirsky. *Italy*: Introduction by editor; translations from Giovanni Papini, Cesare Pavese. *Spain and Latin America*: Introduction by editor; translations of José Martí, Cebria Montoliu, Miguel de Unamuno, Gilberto Freyre. *Israel*: Introduction by editor; essay by Sholom Kahn. *Japan*: Introduction by editor. *India*: Introduction by editor; essay by V. K. Chari. *Note*: below, this work will be abbreviated WWA.
Walt Whitman in Europe Today: A Collection of Essays. Edited by Roger Asselineau and William White. Detroit: Wayne State University Press. 1972.

Contents: Walt Whitman in *Spain*, by Concha Zardoya; *Germany*, Hans-Joachim Lang; *Belgium*, Guillaume Toebosch; *France*, Marcel Martinet, Jules Romains, Jean Guehenno, Jean Marie Le Clezio; *Italy*, Mariolina Meliadò Freeth; *Czechoslovakia*, Ján Boor; *Jugoslavia*, Sonja Basić; *Denmark*, Jørgen Erik Nielsen; *Sweden*, Frederic Fleisher; *Iceland*, Leedice Kissane; contributions by Jorge Guillén (*Spain*), Léopold Sédar Senghor (*Senegal*), Chukovsky (*Russia*), Asselineau (*France*), and Pablo Neruda (*Chile*). *Note*: below, this work will be abbreviated WWET.

ENGLAND AND AMERICAN TRANSCENDENTALISM

BLODGETT, HAROLD W. *Walt Whitman in England*, Ithaca: Cornell University Press. 1934.

FROTHINGHAM, O. B. *Transcendentalism in New England*. New York: G. P. Putnam's Sons. 1876.

GODDARD, H. C. *Studies in New England Transcendentalism*. New York: Columbia University Press. 1908.

MUSGROVE, S. *T. S. Eliot and Whitman*. Wellington: New Zealand University Press. 1952.

INDIA

CARPENTER, EDWARD. [The Upanishads and *Leaves of Grass*] *Days With Walt Whitman*, pp. 94-102. London: George Allen. 1906.

CARPENTER, F. I. *Emerson and Asia*. Cambridge: Harvard University Press. 1930.

CHARI, V. K. *Whitman in the Light of Vedantic Mysticism: An Interpretation*. Lincoln: University of Nebraska Press. 1965.

CHRISTY, ARTHUR. *The Orient in American Transcendentalism*. New York: Columbia University Press. 1932.

GUTHRIE, WILLIAM N. *Walt Whitman, Camden Sage*. Cincinnati: Robert Clarke Co. 1897.

MERCER, DOROTHY FREDERICA. *Leaves of Grass* and *the Bhagavad Gita*. Doctoral Dissertation, unpublished. 1933 (See note 52 to Chap. V.)

RAJASEKHARAIAH, T. R. *The Roots of Leaves of Grass: Eastern Sources of Walt Whitman's Poetry*. Rutherford, N. J.: Fairleigh Dickinson University Press. 1970.

GERMANY

CLARK, GRACE DELANO. "Walt Whitman in Germany." *Texas Review*, VI, 123-37 (Jan., 1921).

FALK, ROBERT P. "Walt Whitman and German Thought." *Journal of English and Germanic Philology*, XL, 315-30 (July 1941).

JACOBSON, ANNA. "Walt Whitman in Germany since 1914."*Germanic Review*, I, 132-41 (April 1926).

LAW-ROBERTSON, HARRY. *Walt Whitman in Deutschland.* Giessen: Münchowsche Universitäts. 1935.

LANG, HANS-JOACHIM. See WWET.

LESSING, OTTO EDUARD. "Walt Whitman and His German Critics prior to 1910." *American Collector*, III, 7-15 (October 1926).

POCHMANN, HENRY. "Walt Whitman," *German Culture in America: 1600–1900*, pp. 416-70. Madison: University of Wisconsin Press. 1957.

RIETHMUELLER, RICHARD. "Walt Whitman and the Germans." *The German American Annals*, n. s. IV, nos. 1-3 (January-March, 1906).

THORNSTENBERG, EDWARD. "The Walt Whitman Cult in Germany." *Sewanee Review*, XIX, 71-86 (January 1911).

VON ENDE, AMELIA. "Walt Whitman and Arno Holtz." *Poet Lore*, XVI, 61-65 (Summer 1905).

ZAREK, OTTO. "Walt Whitman and German Poetry." *Living Age*, CCXVI (Vol. XXIX in 8th ser.), 334-37 (February 10, 1923).

FRANCE

BALDENSPERGER, F. "Walt Whitman in France." *Columbia University Quarterly*, XXI, 298-309 (October 1919).

JONES, P. M. "On the Track of an Influence in 1913." *Comparative Literature Studies*, VI-VII, 20-21 (1942).
[Notes on Whitman's influence in France before World War I.]

——. "Whitman and Verhaeren." *Aberystwyth Studies* (University College, Wales), II, 71-106 (1914).
[A very important comparative study.]

LANUX, PIERRE DE. *Young France and New America.* New York: Macmillan. 1917.
[Whitman frequently mentioned.]

PUCCIANI, O. F. *French Criticism of Walt Whitman.* (Doctoral dissertation Harvard University, unpublished, 1943.)

SARRAZIN, GABRIEL. *La Renaissance de la Poésie Anglasie, 1798-1889.* Paris: Perrin, 1889. (Translation, *In Re Walt Whitman*, 159-94).

SCANDINAVIA

ALLEN, GAY WILSON. "Walt Whitman's Reception in Scandinavia." *Papers of the Bibliographical Society of America*, XL, 259-75 (Fourth Quarter 1946).
FLEISHER See WWET.
KISSANE See WWET.
NEILSEN See WWET.
SCHYBERG, FREDERIK. *Walt Whitman.* Translated by Evie Allison Allen. New York: Columbia University Press. 1951.

RUSSIA

CHUKOVSKY See WWET.
MIRSKY See WWA.
STEPANCHEV See WWA, for Russia and Other Slavic Countries.

ITALY

FREETH See WWET.
GRIPPI, CHARLES S. *The Literary Reputation of Walt Whitman in Italy.* (Doctoral dissertation, unpublished, New York University, 1971.
McCAIN, REA. "Walt Whitman in Italy." *Italica*, XX, 4-16 (March 1943).

SPAIN AND LATIN AMERICA

ALEGRÍA, FERNANDO. *Walt Whitman en Hispanoamerica.* Mexico: Ediciones Studium. 1954.
DE MOSHINSKI, ELENA AIZÉN. *Walt Whitman y La America Latina.* Mexico City: Universidad Nacional Autonoma de Mexico. 1950.
DONOSO, ARMANDO. "The Free Spirit of Walt Whitman." *Inter-America*, III, 340-46 (August 1920).
ZARDOYA See WWET.

JAPAN

MATSUHARA, IWAO. "W. Whitman in Japan." *Thought Currents in English Literature* (Aoyama Gakuin University). 1957. (Reprinted in *Norton Critical Edition of* Leaves of Grass, ed. Harold Blodgett and Sculley Bradley, New York: W. W. Norton, 1973, pp. 912-18.)

SADOYA, SHIGENOBU. *Walt Whitman in Japan: His Influence in Modern Japan.* Fukuoka: Bulletin No. 9, Reserach Institute, Seinan Gakuin University. 1969.

[Mostly in Japanese, but in English: "Walt Whitman in Japan (Abstract)," 1-7; Bibliography: Selected Literary Essays and Studies, 9-16; Translations, 16-20 [translations listed.]

TRANSLATIONS

(Selected)

CHINESE

Selections from Whitman's "Leaves of Grass" [title in Chinese]. Translated and Selected by T'u-nan Ch'u. Peking: People's Literary Publishing Society, 1955. 324 pp.

Song of the Open Road and Other Poems [title in Chinese]. Translated by Kao Han. Shanghai: Tu-shu cheu-pan she, 1947. 273 pp.

Whitman: Selections [title in Chinese]. Translated by Chow Tao-Naa. Peking: People's Literary Publishing Society, 1957. 324 pp.

CZECH

Walt Whitman: Demokracie, Zeno Ma! [Democracy, Ma Femme!]. Translated and edited by Pavel Eisner. Prague: Jaroslav Podrouzek, 1945. 181 pp.

Walt Whitman: Pozdrav Svety [Selected Poetry—poetry, prose, and letters]. Translated by Ján Boor. Bratislava: SVKL, 1956, 224 pp.

Pozdrav Svety: Výber z diela. [*Leaves of Grass*, selections, translated by Ján Boor, *Democratic Vistas* by Magda Seppová.] Bratislava: Slovenské Vydavatel'stvo, Krásnej Literatúry. 1956. 224 pp.

DANISH

Walt Whitman: Digte [Poetry—selected]. Translated by Frederik Schyberg. Kφbenhavn: Gyldendal, 1949 (2nd rev. ed.). 133 pp.
Walt Whitman: Fuldkomne Dage [Specimen Days—selections]. Translated by P. E. Seeberg. Kφbenhavn: Steen Hasselbachs Forlag (Hasselbachs Kultur-Bibliotek, Bind XCV), 1950. 55 pp.

DUTCH

Grashalmen [*Leaves of Grass*]. Translated by Maurits Wagenvoort. Amsterdam: Wereld-Biblioteek, 1956 (3rd ed.).

FINNISH

Walt Whitman: Ruohonlehtiá [Selections.]. Translated by Viljo Laitinet. Turku: Suomentajan Kustantama, 1954. 114 pp.

FRENCH

Walt Whitman: Choix de Poèmes. Traduction et préface de Pierre Messiaen. Paris: Aubier [1951]. 354 pp.
Walt Whitman: Feuilles d'herbe (Choix). Introduction et traduction de Roger Asselineau, Paris: Société d'Édition "Les Belles Lettres," 1956. 358 pp.
"Walt Whitman: Fragments politiques inédits en français" [extracts from "The Eighteenth Presidency!", *Democratic Vistas*, and a letter to a would-be Russian translator], *La Nouvelle critique*, VII (juil-août 1955), 239-56.
"Walt Whitman, Perspectives Democratiques" [selections from *Democratic Vistas*] in *L'Énigme du Nouveau-Monde.* [Introductory note and translation by] Ch. Neveu. Paris: Flammarion [1946], pp. 41-72.
Walt Whitman: Une Étude, un choix de poèmes. Par Paul Jamati. Paris: Pierre Seghers, 1948. 238 pp.
Whitman [biographical-critical study with translation of selected poetry and prose]. Par Alain Bosquet. Paris: Gallimard (La Bibliotheque Ideale), 1959. 270 pp.

GERMAN

Tagebuch: 1862–1864, 1876–1882 [selections from *Specimen Days*]. Deutsch von Hans Reisiger. Berlin: Suhrkamp Verlag, 1946. 84 pp.

Grashalme [*Leaves of Grass*]. Auswahl von Georg Goyert ins Deutsche übertragen. Berlin: Lothar Blanvalet Verlag, 1948. 106 pp.

Grashalme. In Auswahl neu übertragen von Elisabeth Serelman-Küchler und Walther Küchler. Stuttgart: Dipax Verlag, 1947. 331 pp.

Walt Whitmans Werk [complete *Leaves of Grass*]. Übertragen und eingeleitet von Hans Reisiger. Hamburg: Rowohlt Verlag, 1956. 502 pp.

GREEK

Ἐκλογή ἀπό τά Φύλλα Χλόης. Ἑλληνική Ἀπόδοση Νίκου Προεστόπουλου. "Ἐκλεκτά,,. Βιβλία τῆς Τσέπης ᾿Αθῆναι. [n.d.β 1936?] 153 pp.
[Selections from *Leaves of Grass* translated by Nick Proestopoulos]

Φύλλα Χλόης. Ἑλληνική Ἀπόδοση Νίκου Προεστόπουλου. Προλογικό Σημείωμα ᾿Αγγέλου Σικελιανοῦ. Βιβλιοπωλεῖον τῆς " Ἑστίας,,. [Athens, n.d.]
[Complete *Leaves of Grass*, translated by Nick Proestopoulos, Home Bookshop, Athens, undated.]

HEBREW

Aleyesev . . . [*Leaves of Grass being a selection and translation into Hebrew with notes and an essay on the poet's life and work*]. By Simon Halkin. Jerusalem: Workers Book Guild, *1952. 550 pp.*

HUNGARIAN

Fuszálak, Osszes Koltemények. . [Translations by 21 people, edited by Országh László.] [Budapest:] Magyar Helikon. 1964.

INDIAN

Durbadala. [*Leaves of Grass* in the Oriya language.] Orissa, India: Prafulla Chandra Das. 1957. 74 pp.

Hullina Dalagalu. [101 selections from *Leaves of Grass.*] Translated into Kannada by M. Gopalakrishna Adiga. [New Delhi:] Sahitya Akademi. 1966. 222 pp.

Ghah Diyan Pattiyan: Selections from Whitman's *Leaves of Grass.* Translation into Punjabi by Gurbakhsh Singh. [New Delhi:] Sahitya Akademi. 1968. 260 pp.

ITALIAN

Walt Whitman: Foglie d'erba e Prose [*Leaves of Grass* and (selected) Prose]. Traduzione di Enzo Giachino. Torino: Giulio Einaudi, 1950. 958 pp.

Giorni Rappresentativi e Altre Prose [selected prose]. Traduzione di Mariolina Meliadò Freeth. Vicenza: Neri Pozza. 1968.

JAPANESE

Kusa no Ha [*Leaves of Grass*]. Translation and introduction by Shigetaka Naganuma. Tokyo: (vol. I) Nippon Dokusho Kumiai, 1946; (vol. II) Mikasa Shobo, 1950. 354 and 345 pp. (Complete *Leaves of Grass* in 2 vols., based on 1892 text.)

Kusa no Ha. Translated by Saika Tomita. Tokyo: Asahi Shimbun-sha, 1950. 502 pp.

Wago Kuso yo Saraba [*Good Bye My Fancy*]. Translated by Izumi Yanagida. Tokyo: Nippon Dokusho Kumiai, 1947. 295 pp.

[*Whitman's Letters to His Mother and to Jeff*]. Translated by Shigetaka Naganuma. Tokyo: Arechi Shuppan-sha, 1958. 270 pp.

Whitman Shisen [Selected Poems of Whitman]. Translated by Kōju Kiguchi and Masao Yahisa. Tokyo: Azuma-shobo, 1949. 279 pp.

Whitman Shishū [Poems—selected]. Translated by Makoto Asano. Tokyo: Sojin-sha. 1953. 294 pp.

Whitman Shishū. Translated by Akira Asano. Tokyo: Kanto-sha (229 pp.) and Sojin-sha (294 pp.), 1950.

Whitman Shishū. Translated by Shogo Shiratori. Nara: Yotoku-sha, Tambashi-machi, 1947, 128 pp.; Tokyo: Oizumi Shoten, 1949, 285 pp.; Tokyo: Shincho-sha (Bunko Series), 1954, 171 pp.

JUGOSLAVIAN (*Serbo-Croatian*)

Vlati Trave [*Leaves of Grass*—selections]. Translated by Tin Ujević; Preface by Gustave Krklec. Zagreb: Zora, 1951. 140 pp.

NORWEGIAN

Walt Whitman: Sangen om Meg Selv ["Song of Myself"] *av Leaves of Grass*. Oversettelse og Innledning ved Per Arneberg. Tegninger [illustrations] av Kai Fjell. Oslo: Forlagt av H. Aschehoug & Co., 1947. 123 pp.

POLISH

Źdźbla Trawy, Poezje Wybrane [*Leaves of Grass*, Selections] Słowe wstepne wybór i opracowanie Juliusz Zuławski. Warsawa: Panstwowy Instytut Wydawniczy. 1966. 212 pp.

Walt Whitman, Poezje Wybrane [selected poetry]. Wyboro dokanali wstepem opatrzył Hieronim Michalski. Warsawa: Ludowa Społdzielnia Wydawnicza. 1970. 183 pp.

PORTUGUESE

Cançao da Estrada Larga. Traducao de Luis Cardim. Lisbon: Cadernos da "Seara Nova" Secção de Textos Literários, 1947. 26 pp.

Cantos de Walt Whitman. Traducão de Oswaldino Marques; introducão de Anibal Machado. Rio de Janeiro: Editora José Olympio, 1946. 88 pp.

Videntes e Sonâmbulos: Coletâneo de Poemas Norte-Americanos [Collection of North American Poems]. [Edited and translated by] Oswaldino Marques. Dio de Janeiro: Ministério do Educacio e Cultura, 1955. Whitman, pp. 36-79.

RUMANIAN

Poeme, Talmaciri. Commenta si Vignete de Margareta Sterian. Bucuresti: Pro Pace, 1945. 38 pp.

Walt Whitman: Opere Alese [Selections]. Traducere si presentare de Mihnea Gheorghiu. Bucureşti: Editură de Stăt Pentru Literatură si Artă, 1956. 592 pp.

RUSSIAN

Uolt Uitmen: List'ya Travy [Walt Whitman: *Leaves of Grass*—selected]. (Introductions by Kornei Chukovsky and M. Mendelssohn; several translators, including Chukovsky.) Mosco: OGIZ [Government Publishing Office for Belles Lettres], 1955. 355 pp.

SPANISH

Hojas de Hierba [*Leaves of Grass*]. Version directa e integra conforme al texto de la edicion definitiva de 1891–2. Por Francisco Alexander. Quito [Ecuador]: Casa de la Cultura Ecuatoriana, 1953. 603 pp. (Complete *Leaves of Grass.*)

La ultima vez que florecieron las lilas en el patio ["When Lilacs Last in the Dooryard Bloom'd"]. Traducción de Arturo Torres-Rioseco. Mexico City: Coleccion Literaria de la Revista Iberioamericana, 1946. 13 pp.

Saludo al Mundo ["Salut au Monde!"]. Traducción de Gregorio Gasman. Santiago, Chile: Libreria Negra, 1949. 44 pp.

Walt Whitman, Cantor de la Democracia: Ensayo biográfico y breve antologia [Walt Whitman, Poet of Democracy: Biographical Essay and brief Anthology]. Por Miguel R. Mendoza. Mexico City: Secretaría de Educación Pública, 1946. 76 pp.

Walt Whitman: Obras Escogidas: Ensayo Biográficocrítico [selections with a biographical-critical essay]. Versión, notas, y bibliografía de Concha Zardoya; prólogo de John Van Horne. Madrid: M. Aguilar, 1946. 851 pp.

Whitman y Otras Cronicas [Whitman and Other Chronicles]. Selección prólogo y notas de Emilio Abreu Gomez. Washington, D. C.: Unión Panamericana, 1950. "Yo Canto al cuerpo eléctrico de Walt Whitman" ["I Sing the Body Electric"], introducción, traducción y notas por Fernando Alegría, *ARS*, No. 1 (October-December 1951), pp. 47-54.

SWEDISH

Strån av Gräss [*Leaves of Grass*]. Ett urval i översätting och med inledning av K. A. Svensson. Stockholm: A. -B. Seelig & C:o. 1935. 207 pp.

INDEX

411